THE WORKS OF ALEXANDRE DUMAS

THE WORKS OF ALEXANDRE DUMAS

The Three Musketeers

Twenty Years After

LONGMEADOW PRESS

This 1993 edition is published by Longmeadow Press,
201 High Ridge Road, Stamford, Connecticut 06904
by special arrangement with W.S. Konecky associates.

ISBN 0-681-45512-8

10 9 8 7 6 5 4 3 2 1

Manufactured in the U.S.A.

The case of this book is
made of bonded leather—fibers.

TABLE
OF
CONTENTS

The Three Musketeers

CONTENTS.

CONTENTS.

CONTENTS.

PREFACE.

In which it is proved that, notwithstanding their Names in *Os* and *Is*, the Heroes of the History which we are about to have the honour to relate to our Readers have nothing Mythological about them.

A SHORT time ago, whilst making researches in the " Bibliothèque Royal," for my History of Louis XIV., I stumbled by chance upon the " Memoirs of Monsieur d'Artagnan," printed—as were most of the works of that period, in which authors could not tell the truth without the risk of a residence, long or short, in the Bastille,—at Amsterdam, by Pierre Rouge. The title struck me : I took them home with me, not without the permission of the *conservateur* though, and devoured them.

It is not my intention here to enter into an analysis of this curious work ; I shall satisfy myself with referring such of my readers as appreciate the pictures of the period to its pages. They will therein find portraits pencilled by the hand of a master ; and, although these sketches may be, for the most part, traced upon the doors of barracks and the walls of cabarets, they will not find the likenesses of Louis XIII., Anne of Austria, Richelieu, Mazarin, and the courtiers of the period, less faithful than in the history of M. Anquetil.

But, as it is well known, that which strikes the capricious mind of the poet is not always that which affects the mass of his readers. Now, whilst admiring, as others doubtless will admire, the curious details we have to relate, the thing which attracted our attention most strongly is a thing to which no one before ourselves had given a thought.

D'Artagnan relates, that on his first visit to M. de Tréville, captain of the king's musketeers, he met in his antechamber three young men, serving in the illustrious corps into which he was soliciting the honour of being received, bearing the names of Athos, Porthos, and Aramis.

We must confess these three foreign names appeared strange, and it immediately occurred to us that they were but pseudo-names under which D'Artagnan had disguised names, probably illustrious, or else that the bearers of these borrowed names had themselves chosen them on the day in which, from caprice, discontent, or want of fortune, they had donned the simple musketeer's uniform.

From that moment we had no rest till we had searched all the contemporary works within our reach for some trace of these extraordinary names, which had so strongly awakened our curiosity.

The catalogue alone of the books we read with this object would fill a whole chapter, which, although it might be very instructive, would certainly afford our readers but little amusement. It will suffice, then, to tell them, that at the moment at which, discouraged by so many fruitless investigations, we were about to abandon our search, we at length found, guided by the counsels of our illustrious friend Paulin Pâris, a manuscript in folio, endorsed 4,772 or 4,773, we don't recollect which, having for title, " Memoir of M. le Comte de la Fère, touching some Events which passed in France towards the End of the Reign of King Louis XIII. and the Commencement of the Reign of King Louis XIV."

It may be easily imagined how great our joy was, when, in turning over this manuscript, absolutely our last hope, we found at the twentieth page the name of Athos, at the twenty-seventh the name of Porthos, and at the thirty-first the name of Aramis.

The discovery of a completely unknown manuscript at a period in which historical science is carried to such a high degree, appeared almost miraculous. We hastened, therefore, to obtain permission to print it, with the view of presenting ourselves some day with the *pack* of others at the doors of the Académie des Inscriptions et Belles Lettres, if we should not succeed—a very probable thing, by-the-by— in gaining admission to the Académie Française with our own proper *pack*. This permission, we feel bound to say, was graciously granted ; which compels us here to give a public contradiction to the slanderers who pretend that we live under a government but moderately indulgent to men of letters.

Now, this is the first part of this precious manuscript which we offer to our readers, restoring to it the title which belongs to it, and entering into an engagement, that if, of which we entertain no doubt, this first part should obtain the success it merits, to publish the second incontinently.

In the meanwhile, as the godfather is a second father, we beg the reader to lay to our account, and not to that of the Count de la Fère, the pleasure or the *ennui* he may experience.

This being understood, let us proceed with our history.

THE THREE MUSKETEERS.

———◦———

CHAPTER I.

THE THREE PRESENTS OF M. D'ARTAGNAN THE ELDER.

ON the first Monday of the month of April, 1625, the bourg of Meung,
in which the author of the "Romance of the Rose" was born, appeared
to be in as perfect a state of revolution as if the Huguenots had just
made a second Rochelle of it. Many citizens, seeing the women flying
towards the High Street, leaving their children crying at the open
doors, hastened to don the cuirass, and, supporting their somewhat uncertain courage with a musket or a partizan, directed their steps towards
the hostelry of the Franc-Meunier, before which was gathered, increasing
every minute, a compact group, vociferous and full of curiosity.

In those times panics were common, and few days passed without
some city or other enregistering in its archives an event of this kind.
There were nobles who made war against each other; there was the
king, who made war against the cardinal; there was Spain, which made
war against the king. Then, in addition to these, concealed or public,
secret or patent wars, there were, moreover, robbers, mendicants,
Huguenots, wolves, and scoundrels who made war upon everybody.
The citizens always took up arms readily against thieves, wolves, or
scoundrels—often against nobles or Huguenots—sometimes against the
king—but never against the cardinal or Spain. It resulted, then, from
this habit, that on the said first Monday of the month of April, 1625,
the citizens, on hearing the clamour, and seeing neither the red and
yellow standard, nor the livery of the Duke de Richelieu, rushed towards the hostel of the Franc-Meunier.

When arrived there, the cause of this hubbub was apparent to all.

A young man—we can sketch his portrait at a dash—imagine to
yourself a Don Quixote of eighteen; a Don Quixote without his corse-
let, without his coat of mail, without his cuistres; a Don Quixote
clothed in a woollen doublet, the blue colour of which had faded into a
nameless shade between lees of wine and a heavenly azure; face long
and brown; high cheek-bones, a sign of astucity; the maxillary muscles
enormously developed, an infallible sign by which a Gascon may always
be detected, even without his barret-cap—and our young man wore a
barret-cap, set off with a sort of feather; the eye open and intelligent;
the nose hooked, but finely chiselled. Too big for a youth, too small
for a grown man, an experienced eye might have taken him for a

farmer's son upon a journey, had it not been for the long sword, which, dangling from a leathern baldrick, hit against the calves of its owner as he walked, and against the rough side of his steed when he was on horseback.

For our young man had a steed, which was the observed of all observers. It was a Béarn pony, from twelve to fourteen years old, yellow in his hide, without a hair in his tail, but not without wind-galls on his legs, which, though going with his head lower than his knees, rendering a martingale quite unnecessary, contrived, nevertheless, to perform his eight leagues a day. Unfortunately, the qualities of this horse were so well concealed under his strange-coloured hide and his unaccountable gait, that at a time when everybody was a connoisseur in horseflesh, the appearance of the said pony at Meung, which place he had entered about a quarter of an hour before, by the gate of Beaugency, produced an unfavourable feeling, which extended to his master.

And this feeling had been the more painfully perceived by young D'Artagnan—for so was the Don Quixote of this second Rosinante named—from his not being able to conceal from himself the ridiculous appearance that such a steed gave him, good horseman as he was. He had sighed deeply, therefore, when accepting the gift of the pony from M. d'Artagnan the elder. He was not ignorant that such a beast was worth at least twenty livres ; and the words which accompanied the present were above all price.

"My son," said the old Gascon gentleman, in that pure Béarn *patois* of which Henry IV. could never get rid—"my son, this horse was born in the house of your father, about thirteen years ago, and has remained in it ever since, which ought to make you love it. Never sell it—allow it to die tranquilly and honourably of old age ; and if you make a campaign with it, take as much care of it as you would of an old servant. At court, provided you have ever the honour to go there," continued M. d'Artagnan the elder, "an honour to which, remember, your ancient nobility gives you right, sustain worthily your name of *gentleman*, which has been worthily borne by your ancestors during five hundred years, both for your own sake and that of those that belong to you. By these I mean your relations and friends. Endure nothing from any one but M. le Cardinal and the king. It is by his courage, please to observe, by his courage alone, that a gentleman can make his way nowadays. Whoever trembles for a second perhaps allows the bait to escape, which, during that exact second, fortune held out to him. You are young ; you ought to be brave for two reasons—the first is that you are a Gascon, and the second is that you are my son. Never fear quarrels, but seek hazardous adventures. I have taught you how to handle a sword ; you have thews of iron, a wrist of steel : fight on all occasions ; fight the more for duels being forbidden, since, consequently, there is twice as much courage in fighting. I have nothing to give you, my son, but fifteen crowns, my horse, and the counsels you have just heard. Your mother will add to them a receipt for a certain balsam, which she had from a Bohemian, and which has the miraculous virtue of curing all wounds that do not reach the heart. Take advantage of all, and live happily and long. I have but one word to add, and that is to propose an example to you—not mine, for I myself have never appeared at court, and have only taken part in religious wars as a volunteer ; I speak of M. de Tréville, who was formerly my neighbour, and who had the honour to be as a child the playfellow of our king, Louis XIII., whom God preserve ! Sometimes their play degenerated into battles, and in these battles the king was not always the stronger. The blows which he received from him gave him a great esteem and friendship for M. de Tréville. Afterwards, M. de Tréville fought with others : in his first journey to Paris, five times ; from the death of the late king to the majority of the young one, without reckoning wars and sieges, seven times ; and from that majority up to the present day, a hundred times perhaps ! So that in spite of edicts, ordinances, and decrees, there he is captain of the musketeers—that is to say, leader of a legion of Cæsars, whom the king holds in great esteem, and whom the cardinal dreads—he who dreads nothing, as it is said. Still further, M. de Tréville gains ten thousand crowns a year ; he is, therefore, a great noble. He began as you begin ; go to him with this letter, and make him your model, in order that you may do as he has done."

Upon which M. d'Artagnan the elder girded his own sword round his son, kissed him tenderly on both cheeks, and gave him his benediction.

On leaving the paternal chamber, the young man found his mother, who was waiting for him with the famous recipe, of which the counsels we have just repeated would necessitate the so frequent employment. The adieux were on this side longer and more tender than they had been on the other ; not that M. d'Artagnan did not love his son, who was his only offspring, but M. d'Artagnan was a man, and he would have considered it unworthy of a man to give way to his feelings ; whereas Madame d'Artagnan was a woman, and, still more, a mother. She wept abundantly, and, let us speak it to the praise of M. d'Artagnan the younger, notwithstanding the efforts he made to be as firm as a future musketeer ought to be, nature prevailed, and he shed many tears, of which he succeeded with great difficulty in concealing the half.

The same day the young man set forward on his journey, furnished with the three paternal presents, which consisted, as we have said, of fifteen crowns, the horse, and the letter for M. de Tréville, the counsels being thrown into the bargain.

With such a *vade mecum* D'Artagnan was, morally and physically, an exact copy of the hero of Cervantes, to whom we so happily compared him, when our duty of an historian placed us under the necessity of sketching his portrait. Don Quixote took windmills for giants, and sheep for armies ; D'Artagnan took every smile for an insult, and every look as a provocation ; whence it resulted that from Tarbes to Meung his fist was constantly doubled, or his hand on the hilt of his sword ;

and yet the fist did not descend upon any jaw, nor did the sword issue from its scabbard. It was not that the sight of the wretched pony did not excite numerous smiles on the countenances of passers-by ; but as against the side of this pony rattled a sword of respectable length, and as over this sword gleamed an eye rather ferocious than haughty, these said passers-by repressed their hilarity, or, if hilarity prevailed over prudence, they endeavoured to laugh only on one side, like the masks of the ancients. D'Artagnan, then, remained majestic and intact in his susceptibility till he came to this unlucky city of Meung.

But there, as he was alighting from his horse at the gate of the Franc-Meunier, without any one, host, waiter, or ostler, coming to hold his stirrup or take his horse, D'Artagnan spied, through an open window on the ground-floor, a gentleman well made and of good carriage, although of rather a stern countenance, talking with two persons who appeared to listen to him with respect. D'Artagnan fancied quite naturally, according to his custom, that he must be the object of their conversation, and listened. This time D'Artagnan was only in part mistaken : he himself was not in question, but his horse was. The gentleman appeared to be enumerating all his qualities to his auditors, and, as I have said, the auditors seeming to have great deference for the narrator, they every moment burst into fits of laughter. Now, as a half smile was sufficient to awaken the irascibility of the young man, the effect produced upon him by this vociferous mirth may be easily imagined.

Nevertheless, D'Artagnan was desirous of examining the appearance of this impertinent personage who was laughing at him. He fixed his haughty eye upon the stranger, and perceived a man of from forty to forty-five years of age, with black and piercing eyes, a pale complexion, a strongly-marked nose, and a black and well-shaped moustache. He was dressed in a doublet and hose of a violet colour, with aiguillettes of the same, without any other ornaments than the customary slashes through which the shirt appeared. This doublet and hose, though new, looked creased like travelling clothes for a long time packed up in a portmanteau. D'Artagnan made all these remarks with the rapidity of a most minute observer, and, doubtless, from an instinctive feeling that this unknown was destined to have a great influence over his future life.

Now, as at the moment in which D'Artagnan fixed his eyes upon the gentleman in the violet doublet, the gentleman made one of his most knowing and profound remarks respecting the Béarnese pony, his two auditors laughed even louder than before, and he himself, though contrary to his custom, allowed a pale smile (if I may be allowed to use such an expression) to stray over his countenance. This time there could be no doubt, D'Artagnan was really insulted. Full, then, of this conviction, he pulled his cap down over his eyes, and, endeavouring to copy some of the court airs he had picked up in Gascony among young travelling nobles, he advanced, with one hand on the hilt of his sword and the other leaning on his hip. Unfortunately, as he advanced, his anger increased at every step, and, instead of the proper and lofty speech he had prepared as a prelude to his challenge, he found nothing at the tip of his tongue but a gross personality, which he accompanied with a furious gesture.

"I say, sir, you, sir, who are hiding yourself behind that shutter !— yes, you, sir, tell me what you are laughing at, and we will laugh together."

The gentleman withdrew his eyes slowly from the nag to his master, as if he required some time to ascertain whether it could be to him that such strange reproaches were addressed ; then, when he could not possibly entertain any doubt of the matter, his eyebrows slightly bent, and, with an accent of irony and insolence impossible to be described, replied to D'Artagnan :

"I was not speaking to you, sir !"

"But I am speaking to you !" replied the young man, additionally exasperated with this mixture of insolence and good manners, of politeness and scorn.

The unknown looked at him again with a slight smile, and, retiring from the window, came out of the hostelry with a slow step, and placed himself before the horse within two paces of D'Artagnan. His quiet manner and the ironical expression of his countenance redoubled the mirth of the persons with whom he had been talking, and who still remained at the window.

D'Artagnan, seeing him approach, drew his sword a foot out of the scabbard.

"This horse is decidedly, or rather has been in his youth, a *bouton d'or*" (buttercup), resumed the unknown, continuing the remarks he had begun, and addressing himself to his auditors at the window, without paying the least attention to the exasperation of D'Artagnan, who, however, placed himself between him and them. "It is a colour very well known in botany, but till the present time very rare among horses."

"There are people who laugh at a horse that would not dare to laugh at the master of it," cried the young emulator of the furious Tréville.

"I do not often laugh, sir," replied the unknown, "as you may perceive by the air of my countenance ; but, nevertheless, I retain the privilege of laughing when I please."

"And I," cried D'Artagnan, "will allow no man to laugh when it displeases me !"

"Indeed, sir," continued the unknown, more calm than ever,— "Well ! that is perfectly right !" and, turning on his heel, was about to re-enter the hostelry by the front gate, under which D'Artagnan, on arriving, had observed a saddled horse.

But D'Artagnan was not of a character to allow a man to escape him thus, who had had the insolence to laugh at him. He drew his sword entirely from the scabbard, and followed him, crying :

"Turn, turn, Master Joker, lest I strike you behind !"

"Strike me !" said the other, turning sharply round and surveying the young man with as much astonishment as contempt. "Why, my good fellow, you must be mad!" Then, in a suppressed tone, as if speaking to himself:—"This is annoying," continued he. "What a God-send this would be for his Majesty, who is seeking everywhere for brave fellows to recruit his musketeers!"

He had scarcely finished, when D'Artagnan made such a furious lunge at him, that if he had not sprung nimbly backward, he would have jested for the last time. The unknown then, perceiving that the matter was beyond a joke, drew his sword, saluted his adversary, and placed himself on his guard. But at the same moment his two auditors, accompanied by the host, fell upon D'Artagnan with sticks, shovels, and tongs. This caused so rapid and complete a diversion to the attack, that D'Artagnan's adversary, whilst the latter turned round to face this shower of blows, sheathed his sword with the same precision, and from an actor, which he had nearly been, became a spectator of the fight, a part in which he acquitted himself with his usual impassibility, muttering, nevertheless :

"A plague upon these Gascons! Put him on his orange horse again, and let him begone!"

"Not before I have killed you, poltroon!" cried D'Artagnan, making the best face possible, and never giving back one step before his three assailants, who continued to shower their blows upon him.

"Another gasconade!" murmured the gentleman. "By my honour, these Gascons are incorrigible! Keep up the dance, then, since he will have it so. When he is tired, he will, perhaps, tell us that he has enough of it."

But the unknown was not acquainted with the headstrong personage he had to do with ; D'Artagnan was not the man ever to cry for quarter. The fight was, therefore, prolonged for some seconds ; but at length D'Artagnan's sword was struck from his hand by the blow of a stick, and broken in two pieces. Another blow full upon his forehead, at the same moment, brought him to the ground, covered with blood and almost fainting.

It was at this period that people came flocking to the scene of action from all parts. The host, fearful of consequences, with the help of his servants, carried the wounded man into the kitchen, where some trifling attention was bestowed upon him.

As to the gentleman, he resumed his place at the window, and surveyed the crowd with a certain air of impatience, evidently annoyed by their remaining undispersed.

"Well, how is it with this madman?" exclaimed he, turning round as the opening door announced the entrance of the host, who came to inquire if he was unhurt.

"Your excellency is safe and sound?" asked the host.

"Oh, yes! perfectly safe and sound, my good host, and wish to know what is become of our young man."

"He is better," said the host ; "he fainted quite away."

"Indeed!" said the gentleman.

"But before he fainted, he collected all his strength to challenge you, and to defy you whilst challenging you."

"Why, this fellow must be the devil in person !" cried the unknown.

"Oh, no, your excellency !" replied the host with a grin of contempt ; " he is not the devil, for during his fainting we rummaged his valise, and found nothing but a clean shirt and twelve crowns, which, however, did not prevent his saying, as he was fainting, that if such a thing had happened in Paris you should have instantly repented of it, whilst here you would only have cause to repent of it at a later period."

"Then," said the unknown, coldly, " he must be some prince in disguise."

"I have told you this, good sir," resumed the host, "in order that you may be on your guard."

"Did he name no one in his passion ?"

"Yes ! he struck his pocket and said :—' We shall see what M. de Tréville will think of this insult offered to his *protégé.*'"

"M. de Tréville ?" said the unknown, becoming attentive : "he put his hand upon his pocket whilst pronouncing the name of M. de Tréville ? Now, my dear host ! whilst your young man was insensible, you did not fail, I am quite sure, to ascertain what that pocket contained. What was there in it ?"

"A letter addressed to M. de Tréville, captain of the musketeers."

"Indeed !"

"Exactly as I have the honour to tell your excellency."

The host, who was not endowed with great perspicacity, did not observe the expression which his words had given to the physiognomy of the unknown. The latter rose from the front of the window, upon the sill of which he had leaned with his elbow, and knitted his brows like a man suddenly rendered uneasy.

"The devil !" murmured he, between his teeth. "Can Tréville have set this Gascon upon me ? He is very young ; but a sword-thrust is a sword-thrust, whatever be the age of him who gives it, and a youth is less to be suspected than an older man ; a weak obstacle is sometimes sufficient to overthrow a great design."

And the unknown fell into a reverie which lasted some minutes.

"Host," said he, "could you not contrive to get rid of this frantic boy for me ? In conscience, I cannot kill him ; and yet," added he, with a coldly menacing expression, "and yet he annoys me. Where is he ?"

"In my wife's chamber, where they are dressing his hurts, on the first floor."

"His things and his bag are with him ? Has he taken off his doublet ?"

"On the contrary, everything is in the kitchen. But if he annoys you, this young crazy fool——"

"To be sure he does. He causes a disturbance in your hostelry, which respectable people cannot put up with. Go, make out my bill, and call my servant."

"What, sir ! do you mean to leave us already ?"

"You know I was going, as I ordered you to get my horse saddled. Has not my desire been complied with ?"

"Yes, sir ; and as your excellency may have observed, your horse is in the great gateway, ready saddled for your departure."

"That is well ; do as I have directed you then."

"What the devil !" said the host to himself, "can he be afraid of this boy?" But an imperious glance from the unknown stopped him short, he bowed humbly, and retired.

"Milady* must see nothing of this fellow," continued the stranger. "She will soon pass—she is already late. I had better get on horseback, and go and meet her. I should like, however, to know what this letter addressed to Tréville contains !"

And the unknown, muttering to himself, directed his steps towards the kitchen.

In the meantime, the host, who entertained no doubt that it was the presence of the young man that drove the unknown from his hostelry, reascended to his wife's chamber, and found D'Artagnan just recovering his senses. Giving him to understand that the police would deal with him pretty severely for having sought a quarrel with a great lord, for, in the opinion of the host, the unknown could be nothing less than a great lord, he insisted that, notwithstanding his weakness, he should get up and depart as quickly as possible. D'Artagnan, half stupefied, without his doublet, and with his head bound up in a linen cloth, arose then, and, urged forward by the host, began to descend the stairs ; but on arriving at the kitchen, the first thing he saw was his antagonist, talking calmly, at the step of a heavy carriage, drawn by two large Norman horses.

His interlocutor, whose head appeared through the carriage window, was a woman of from twenty to two-and-twenty years of age. We have already observed with what rapidity D'Artagnan seized the expression of a countenance : he perceived then, at a glance, that this woman was young and beautiful ; and her style of beauty struck him the more forcibly, from its being totally different from that of the southern countries in which D'Artagnan had hitherto resided. She was pale and fair, with long curls falling in profusion over her shoulders ; had large blue, languishing eyes, rosy lips, and hands of alabaster. She was talking with great animation with the unknown.

"His eminence, then, orders me——" said the lady.

"To return instantly to England, and to inform him immediately the duke leaves London."

"And my other instructions ?" asked the fair traveller.

"They are contained in this box, which you will not open until you are on the other side of the Channel."

"Very well ; and you, what are you going to do ?"

* We are well aware that this term "milady" is only properly used when followed by a family name. But we find it thus in the manuscript, and we do not choose to take upon ourselves to alter it.

"I, oh ! I shall return to Paris."

"What, without chastising this insolent boy ?" asked the lady.

The unknown was about to reply, but at the moment he opened his mouth, D'Artagnan, who had heard all, rushed forward through the open door.

"This insolent boy chastises others," cried he, "and I have good hope that he whom he means to chastise will not escape him as he did before."

"Will not escape him ?" replied the unknown, knitting his brow.

"No, before a woman, you would not dare to fly, I presume ?"

"Remember," said milady, seeing the unknown lay his hand on his sword, "remember that the least delay may ruin everything."

"True," cried the gentleman ; "begone then, on your part, and I will depart as quickly on mine." And bowing to the lady, he sprang into his saddle, her coachman at the same time applying his whip vigorously to his horses. The two interlocutors thus separated, taking opposite directions, at full gallop.

"Your reckoning ! your reckoning !" vociferated the host, whose respect for the traveller was changed into profound contempt, on seeing him depart without settling his bill.

"Pay him, booby !" cried the unknown to his servant, without checking the speed of his horse ; and the man, after throwing two or three pieces of silver at the foot of mine host, galloped after his master.

"Base coward ! false gentleman !" cried D'Artagnan, springing forward, in his turn, after the servant. But his wound had rendered him too weak to support such an exertion. Scarcely had he gone ten steps when his ears began to tingle, a faintness seized him, a cloud of blood passed over his eyes, and he fell in the middle of the street, crying still :

"Coward ! coward ! coward !"

"He is a coward indeed," grumbled the host, drawing near to D'Artagnan, and endeavouring by this little flattery to make up matters with the young man, as the heron of the fable did with the snail he had despised the evening before.

"Yes, a base coward," murmured D'Artagnan, "but she, she was very beautiful."

"What she ?" demanded the host.

"Milady," faltered D'Artagnan, and fainted a second time.

"Ah ! it's all one," said the host ; "I have lost two customers, but this one remains, of whom I am pretty certain for some days to come ; and that will be eleven crowns gained, at all events."

We must remember that eleven crowns was just the amount that was left in D'Artagnan's purse.

The host had reckoned upon eleven days of confinement at a crown a day, but he had reckoned without his guest. On the following morning, at five o'clock, D'Artagnan arose, and descending to the kitchen, without help, asked, among other ingredients the list of which has not come down to us, for some oil, some wine, and some rosemary, and with his mother's receipt in his hand, composed a balsam, with which he anointed his numerous wounds, replacing his bandages himself, and positively refusing the assistance of any doctor. Thanks, no doubt, to the efficacy of the Bohemian balsam ; and perhaps also, thanks to the absence of any doctor, D'Artagnan walked about that same evening, and was almost cured by the morrow.

But when the time came to pay for this rosemary, this oil, and the wine, the only expense the master had incurred, as he had preserved a strict abstinence ; whilst, on the contrary, the yellow horse, by the account of the hostler, at least, had eaten three times as much as a horse of his size could reasonably be supposed to have done, D'Artagnan found nothing in his pocket but his little old velvet purse with the eleven crowns it contained : as to the letter addressed to M. de Tréville, it had disappeared.

The young man commenced his search for the letter with the greatest patience, turning out his pockets of all kinds over and over again, rummaging and re-rummaging in his valise, and opening and re-opening his purse ; but when he had come to the conviction that the letter was not to be found, he flew, for the third time, into such a rage as was near costing him a fresh consumption of wine, oil, and rosemary ; for upon seeing this hot-headed youth become exasperated and threaten to destroy every thing in the establishment if his letter were not found, the host seized a spit, his wife a broom-handle, and the servants the same sticks they had used the day before.

"My letter of recommendation !" cried D'Artagnan, "my letter of recommendation ! or, by God's blood, I will spit you all like so many ortolans !"

Unfortunately there was one circumstance which created a powerful obstacle to the accomplishment of this threat ; which was, as we have related, that his sword had been in his first conflict broken in two, and which he had perfectly forgotten. Hence it resulted, that when D'Artagnan proceeded to draw his sword in earnest, he found himself purely and simply armed with a stump of a sword of about eight or ten inches in length, which the host had carefully placed in the scabbard. As to the rest of the blade, the master had slily put that on one side to make himself a larding pin.

But this deception would probably not have stopped our fiery young man if the host had not reflected that the reclamation which his guest made was perfectly just.

"But after all," said he, lowering the point of his spit, "where is this letter ?"

"Yes, where is this letter ?" cried D'Artagnan. "In the first place, I warn you that that letter is for M. de Tréville, and it must be found ; if it be not quickly found, he will know how to cause it to be found, I'll answer for it !"

This threat completed the intimidation of the host. After the king and the cardinal, M. de Tréville was the man whose name was perhaps most frequently repeated by the military, and even by citizens. There was, to be sure, Father Joseph, but his name was never pronounced but with a subdued voice, such was the terror inspired by his Gray Eminence, as the cardinal's familiar was called.

Throwing down his spit then, and ordering his wife to do the same with her broom-handle, and the servants with their sticks, he set the first example of commencing an earnest search for the lost letter.

"Does the letter contain anything valuable?" demanded the host, after a few minutes of useless investigation.

"Zounds! I think it does, indeed," cried the Gascon, who reckoned upon this letter for making his way at court; "it contained my fortune!"

"Bills upon Spain?" asked the disturbed host.

"Bills upon his majesty's private treasury," answered D'Artagnan, who, reckoning upon entering into the king's service in consequence of this recommendation, thought he could make this somewhat hazardous reply without telling a falsehood.

"The devil!" cried the host, at his wit's end.

"But it's of no importance," continued D'Artagnan, with national assurance; "it's of no importance, the money is nothing,—that letter was everything; I would rather have lost a thousand pistoles than have lost it."—He would not have risked more if he had said twenty thousand; but a certain juvenile modesty restrained him.

A ray of light all at once broke upon the mind of the host, as he was giving himself to the devil upon finding nothing.

"That letter is not lost!" cried he.

"What!" said D'Artagnan.

"No; it has been stolen from you."

"Stolen! by whom?"

"By the gentleman who was here yesterday. He came down into the kitchen, where your doublet was. He remained there some time alone. I would lay a wager he has stolen it."

"Do you think so?" answered D'Artagnan, but little convinced, as he knew better than any one else how entirely personal the value of this letter was, and saw nothing in it likely to tempt the cupidity of any one. The fact was that none of the servants, none of the travellers present, could have gained anything by being possessed of this paper.

"Do you say!" resumed D'Artagnan, "that you suspect that impertinent gentleman?"

"I tell you I am sure of it," continued the host; "when I informed him that your lordship was the *protégé* of M. de Tréville, and that you even had a letter for that illustrious gentleman, he appeared to be very much disturbed, and asked me where that letter was, and immediately came down into the kitchen, where he knew your doublet was."

"Then that's the man that has robbed me," replied D'Artagnan: "I will complain to M. de Tréville, and M. de Tréville will complain to the king." He then drew two crowns majestically from his purse, gave them to the host, who accompanied him cap in hand to the gate, remounted his yellow horse, which bore him without any further accident to the gate of St. Antoine at Paris, where his owner sold him for three crowns, which was a very good price, considering that D'Artagnan had ridden him hard from Meung. Thus the dealer to whom D'Artagnan sold him for the said nine livres did not conceal from the young man, that he only gave that enormous sum for him on account of the originality of his colour.

Thus D'Artagnan entered Paris on foot, carrying his little packet under his arm, and walked about till he found an apartment to be let on terms suited to the scantiness of his means. This chamber was a sort of garret, situated in the Rue des Fossoyeurs, near the Luxembourg.

As soon as the earnest-penny was paid, D'Artagnan took possession of his lodging, and passed the remainder of the day in sewing on to his doublet and hose some ornamental braiding which his mother had taken off from an almost new doublet of M. d'Artagnan's the elder, and which she had given to him secretly ; next he went to the Quai de Ferraille, to have a new blade put to his sword, and then returned towards the Louvre, inquiring of the first musketeer he met with for the situation of the hotel of M. de Tréville, which proved to be in the Rue du Vieux-Colombier, in the immediate vicinity of the chamber hired by D'Artagnan ; a circumstance which appeared to furnish a happy augury for the success of his journey.

After which, satisfied with the way in which he had conducted himself at Meung, without remorse for the past, confident in the present, and full of hope for the future, he retired to bed, and slept the sleep of the brave.

This sleep, provincial as it was, brought him to nine o'clock in the morning, at which hour he rose in order to repair to the residence of M. de Tréville, the third personage in the kingdom in paternal estimation.

CHAPTER II.

THE ANTECHAMBER OF M. DE TRÉVILLE.

M. DE TROISVILLE, as his family was still called in Gascony, or M. de Tréville, as he has ended by styling himself in Paris, had really commenced life as D'Artagnan now did, that is to say, without a sou in his pocket, but with a fund of courage, shrewdness, and intelligence, that makes the poorest Gascon gentleman often derive more in his hope from the paternal inheritance than the richest Pengordian or Berrichan gentleman derives in reality from his. His insolent bravery, his still more insolent success at a time when blows poured down like hail, had borne him to the top of that ladder called court favour, which he had climbed four steps at a time.

He was the friend of the king, who honoured highly, as every one knows, the memory of his father, Henry IV. The father of M. de Tréville had served him so faithfully in his wars against the League, that for want of money—a thing to which the Béarnais was accustomed all his life, and who constantly paid his debts with that of which he never stood in need of borrowing, that is to say, with ready wit,—for want of money, we repeat, he authorised him, after the reduction of Paris, to assume for his arms a golden lion passant upon gules, with the device of : *Fidelis et fortis.* This was a great matter in the way of honour, but very little in the way of wealth ; so that when the illustrious companion of the great Henry died, the only inheritance he was able to leave his son was his sword and his device. Thanks to this double gift and the spotless name that accompanied them, M. de Tréville was admitted into the household of the young prince, where he made such good use of his sword, and was so faithful to his device, that Louis XIII., one of the good blades of his kingdom, was accustomed to say that, if he had a friend who was about to fight, he would advise him to choose as a second, himself first, and Tréville next, or even, perhaps before him.

Thus Louis XIII. had a real liking for Tréville, a royal liking, a selfish liking, it is true, but which was still a liking. At that unhappy period it was an important consideration to be surrounded by such men as De Tréville. Many might take for their device the epithet of *strong*, which formed the second part of his motto, but very few gentlemen could lay claim to the *faithful*, which constituted the first. Tréville was one of these latter ; his was one of those rare organisations, endowed with an obedient intelligence like that of the dog, with a blind valour, a quick eye, and a prompt hand, to whom sight appeared only to be given to see if the king were dissatisfied with any one, and with the hand to strike this displeasing any one, whether a Besme, a Maurevers, a Poltiot de Méré, or a Vitry. In short, up to this period, nothing had been wanting to De Tréville but opportunity ; but he was ever on the watch for it, and he promised himself that he would never fail to seize it by its three hairs whenever it came within reach of his hand. Louis XIII. then made De Tréville the captain of his Musketeers, who were to Louis XIII., in devotedness, or rather in fanaticism, what his Ordinaries had been to Henry III., and his Scotch Guard to Louis XI.

On his part, and in this respect, the cardinal was not behind-hand with the king. When he saw the formidable and chosen body by which Louis XIII. surrounded himself, this second, or rather this first king of France, became desirous that he too should have his guard. He had his musketeers then, as Louis XIII. had his, and these two powerful rivals vied with each other in procuring the most celebrated swordsmen, not only from all the provinces of France, but even from all foreign states. It was not uncommon for Richelieu and Louis XIII. to dispute over their evening game of chess, upon the merits of their servants. Each boasted the bearing and the courage of his own people, and whilst exclaiming loudly against duels and broils, they excited them secretly to quarrel, deriving an immoderate satisfaction or a true regret at the success or defeat of their own combatants. We learn this from the memoirs of a man who was concerned in some few of these defeats and in many of these victories.

Tréville had seized on the weak side of his master, and it was to this address that he owed the long and constant favour of a king who has not left the reputation behind him of having been very faithful in his friendships. He paraded his musketeers before the cardinal Armand Duplessis with an insolent air, which made the grey moustache of his eminence curl with ire. Tréville was a master of the war of that period, in which he who did not live at the expense of the enemy, lived at the expense of his compatriots : his soldiers formed a legion of devil-may-care fellows, perfectly undisciplined as regarded every one but himself.

Loose, half-drunk, imposing, the king's musketeers, or rather M. de Tréville's, spread themselves about in the cabarets, in the public walks, and the public sports, shouting, twisting their moustaches, clanking their swords, and taking great pleasure in annoying the guards of M. le Cardinal whenever they could fall in with them ; then drawing in the open streets, as if it were the best of all possible sports ; sometimes killed, but sure in that case to be both wept and avenged ; often killing others, but then certain of not rotting in prison, M. de Tréville being there to claim them. Thus M. de Tréville was praised to the highest note by these men, who absolutely adored him, and who, ruffians as they were, trembled before him like scholars before their master, obedient to his least word, and ready to sacrifice themselves to wash out the smallest insult.

M. de Tréville employed this powerful machine for the king in the first place, and the friends of the king—and then for himself and his own friends. For the rest, in none of the memoirs of this period, which has left so many memoirs, is this worthy gentleman accused even by his enemies, and he had many such among men of the pen, as well as among men of the sword ; in no instance, we are told, was this worthy gentleman accused of deriving personal advantage from the co-operation of his minions. Endowed with a rare genius for intrigue, which rendered him the equal of the ablest intriguers, he remained an honest man. Still further, in spite of sword-thrusts which weaken, and painful exercises which fatigue, he had become one of the most gallant frequenters of revels, one of the most insinuating squires of dames, one of the softest whisperers of interesting nothings of his day ; the *bonnes fortunes* of De Tréville were talked of as those of M. de Bassompierre had been talked of twenty years before, and that was not saying a little. The captain of the musketeers then, was admired, feared, and loved, which constitutes the apogee of human fortunes.

Louis XIV. absorbed all the smaller stars of his court in his own vast radiance ; but his father, a sun *pluribus impar*, left his personal splendour to each of his favourites, his individual value to each of his courtiers. In addition to the *lever* of the king and that of the cardinal, there might be reckoned in Paris at that time more than two hundred smaller *levers*, each, in its degree, attended. Among these two hundred *levers*, that of De Tréville was one of the most thronged.

The court of his hotel, situated in the Rue du Vieux-Colombier, resembled a camp, and that by six o'clock in the morning in summer and eight o'clock in winter. From fifty to sixty musketeers, who appeared to relieve each other in order always to present an imposing number, paraded constantly about, armed to the teeth and ready for anything. On one of those immense staircases upon whose space modern civilisation would build a whole house, ascended and descended the solicitors of Paris, who were in search of favours of any kind : gentlemen from the provinces anxious to be enrolled, and servants in all sorts of liveries, bringing and carrying messages between their masters and M. de Tréville. In the antechamber, upon long circular benches, reposed the elect, that is to say, those who were called. In this apartment a continued buzzing prevailed from morning till night, whilst M. de Tréville, in his closet contiguous to this antechamber, received visits, listened to complaints, gave his orders, and, like the king in his balcony at the Louvre, had only to place himself at the window to review both men and arms.

The day on which D'Artagnan presented himself, the assemblage was imposing, particularly for a provincial just arriving from his province : it is true that this provincial was a Gascon, and that particularly at this period, the compatriots of D'Artagnan had the reputation of not being easily intimidated. When he had once passed the massive door, covered with long square-headed nails, he fell into the midst of a troop of men of the sword, who crossed each other in their passage, calling out, quarrelling, and playing tricks one among another. To make way through these turbulent and conflicting waves, it required to be an officer, a great noble, or a pretty woman.

It was, then, into the midst of this tumult and disorder that our young man advanced with a beating heart, ranging his long rapier up his lanky leg, and keeping one hand on the edge of his cap, with that provincial half-smile which affects confidence. When he had passed one group he began to breathe more freely ; but he could not help observing that they turned round to look at him, and, for the first time in his life, D'Artagnan, who had till that day entertained a very good opinion of himself, felt that he was the object of ridicule.

When arrived at the staircase it was still worse ; there were four musketeers on the bottom steps amusing themselves with the following exercise, whilst ten or twelve of their comrades waited upon the landing-place their turns to take their places in the sport.

One of them, placed upon the top stair, naked sword in hand, prevented, or at least endeavoured to prevent, the three others from going up.

These three others fenced against him with their agile swords, which D'Artagnan at first took for foils, and believed to be buttoned ; but he soon perceived, by certain scratches, that every weapon was pointed and sharpened, and that at each of these scratches, not only the spectators, but even the actors themselves, laughed like so many madmen.

He who at the moment occupied the upper step, kept his adversaries in check admirably. A circle was formed around them ; the conditions required that at every hit, the person hit should quit the game, losing his turn of audience to the advantage of the person who had hit him. In five minutes three were slightly wounded, one on the hand, another on the chin, and the third on the ear, by the defender of the stair, who himself remained intact : a piece of skill which was worth to him, according to agreement, three turns of favour.

However difficult it might be,, or rather as he pretended it was, to astonish our young traveller, this pastime really astonished him ; he had seen in his province—that land in which heads become so easily heated —a few of the preliminaries of duels, but the gasconades of these four fencers appeared to him the strongest he had ever heard, even in Gascony. He believed himself transported into that famous country of giants into which Gulliver since went and was so frightened ; and yet he had not gained the goal, for there were still the landing-place and the antechamber.

On the landing they were no longer fighting, but amused themselves with stories about women, and in the antechamber with stories about the court. On the landing, D'Artagnan blushed ; in the antechamber, he trembled. His warm and fickle imagination, which in Gascony had rendered him formidable to young chambermaids, and even sometimes to their mistresses, had never dreamt, even in moments of delirium, of half the amorous wonders, or a quarter of the feats of gallantry, which were here set forth, accompanied by names the best known, and with details the least delicate. But if his morals were shocked on the landing, his respect for the cardinal was scandalised in the antechamber. There, to his great astonishment, D'Artagnan heard the policy which made all Europe tremble, criticised aloud and openly, as well as the private life of the cardinal, which had brought about the punishment of so many great nobles for having dared to pry into : that great man, who was so revered by D'Artagnan the elder, served as an object of ridicule to the musketeers, who cracked their jokes upon his bandy legs and his hump-back ; some sang ballads upon Madame d'Aiguillon, his mistress, and Madame Cambalet, his niece ; whilst others formed parties and plans to annoy the pages and guards of the cardinal duke,—all things which appeared to D'Artagnan monstrous impossibilities.

Nevertheless, when the name of the king was now and then uttered unthinkingly amidst all these cardinal jokes, a sort of gag seemed to close for a moment all these jeering mouths ; they looked hesitatingly around them, and appeared to doubt the thickness of the partition between them and the closet of M. de Tréville ; but a fresh allusion soon brought back the conversation to his eminence, and then the laughter recovered its loudness, and no colouring was spared to any of his actions.

"Certes, these fellows will all be either embastilled or hung," thought the terrified D'Artagnan, "and I, no doubt, with them ; for from the moment I have either listened to or heard them, I shall be held to be an accomplice. What would my good father say, who so strongly pointed out to me the respect due to the cardinal, if he knew I was in the society of such pagans ?"

We have no need, therefore, to say that D'Artagnan did not venture to join in the conversation ; only he looked with all his eyes and listened with all his ears, stretching his five senses so as to lose nothing; and, in spite of his confidence in the paternal monitions, he felt himself carried by his tastes and led by his instincts to praise rather than to blame the unheard of things which were passing before him.

D'Artagnan being, however, a perfect stranger in the crowd of M. de Tréville's courtiers, and this his first appearance in that place, he was at length noticed, and a person came to him and asked him his business there. At this demand, D'Artagnan gave his name very modestly, laid a stress upon the title of compatriot, and begged the servant who had put the question to him to request a moment's audience of M. de Tréville—a request which the other, with an air of protection, promised to convey in time and season.

D'Artagnan, a little recovered from his first surprise, had now leisure to study costumes and countenances.

The centre of the most animated group was a musketeer of great height, of a haughty countenance, and dressed in a costume so peculiar as to attract general attention. He did not wear the uniform cloak—which, indeed, at that time, less of liberty than of still greater independence, was not obligatory—but a cerulean blue doublet, a little faded and worn, and over this a magnificent baldrick worked in gold, which shone like water-ripples in the sun. A long cloak of crimson velvet fell in graceful folds from his shoulders, disclosing in front the splendid baldrick, from which was suspended a gigantic rapier.

This musketeer had just come off guard, complained of having a cold, and coughed from time to time affectedly. It was for this reason, he said to those around him, he had put on his cloak, and whilst he spoke with a lofty air, and twisted his moustache, all admired his embroidered baldrick, and D'Artagnan more than any one.

"What do you make a wonder about?" said the musketeer; "the fashion is coming in ; it is a folly, I admit, but still it is the fashion. Besides, one must lay out one's inheritance somehow."

"Ah, Porthos !" cried one of his companions, "don't think to palm upon us that you obtained that baldrick by paternal generosity : it was given to you by that veiled lady I met you with the other Sunday, near the gate Saint-Honoré."

"No, 'pon honour ; by the faith of a gentleman, I bought it with the contents of my own purse," answered he whom they designated under the name of Porthos.

"Yes, about in the same manner," said another musketeer, "as I bought this new purse with the money my mistress put into the old one."

"It's true, though," said Porthos ; "and the proof is, that I paid twelve pistoles for it."

The wonder was increased, though the doubt continued to exist.

"Is it not true, Aramis ?" said Porthos, turning towards another musketeer.

This other musketeer formed a perfect contrast with his interrogator, who had just designated him by the name of Aramis : he was a stout man, of about two or three and twenty, with an open, ingenuous countenance, a black, mild eye, and cheeks rosy and downy as an autumn peach ; his delicate moustache marked a perfectly straight line upon his upper lip : he appeared to dread to lower his hands lest their veins should swell, and he pinched the tips of his ears from time to time to preserve their delicate pink transparency. Habitually he spoke little and slowly, bowed frequently, laughed without noise, showing his teeth, which were fine, and of which, as of the rest of his person, he appeared to take great care. He answered the appeal of his friend by an affirmative nod of the head.

This affirmation appeared to dispel all doubts with regard to the baldrick ; they continued to admire it, but said no more about it ; and, with one of the rapid changes of thought, the conversation passed suddenly to another subject.

"What do you think of the story Chalais' esquire relates ?" asked another musketeer, without addressing any one in particular.

"And what does he say?" asked Porthos, in a self-sufficient tone.

"He relates that he met at Brussels Rochefort, the *âme damnée* of the cardinal, disguised as a capuchin ; and that this cursed Rochefort, thanks to his disguise, had tricked M. de Laigues, like a simpleton as he is."

"A simpleton, indeed !" said Porthos ; "but is the matter certain ?"

"I had it from Aramis," replied the musketeer.

"Indeed !"

"Why, you know it is, Porthos," said Aramis ; "I told you of it yesterday—say nothing more about it."

"Say nothing more about it—that's your opinion !" replied Porthos. "Say nothing more about it ! *Peste !* you come to your conclusions quickly. What ! the cardinal sets a spy upon a gentleman, has his letters stolen from him by means of a traitor, a brigand, a rascal—has, with the help of this spy, and thanks to this correspondence, Chalais' throat cut, under the stupid pretext that he wanted to kill the king and marry monsieur to the queen ! Nobody knew a word of this enigma. You unravelled it yesterday, to the great satisfaction of all ; and whilst we are still gaping with wonder at the news, you come and tell us to-day—'Let us say no more about it.'"

"Well, then, let us speak about it, since you desire it," replied Aramis, patiently.

"This Rochefort," cried Porthos, "if I were poor Chalais' esquire, should pass a minute or two very uncomfortably with me."

"And you—you would pass rather a sad half-hour with the Red Duke," replied Aramis.

"Oh ! oh ! the Red Duke ! bravo ! bravo ! the Red Duke !" cried Porthos, clapping his hands and nodding his head. "The Red Duke is capital. I'll circulate that saying, be assured, my dear fellow. Who says this Aramis is not a wit ? What a misfortune it is you did not follow your first vocation—what a delightful abbé you would have made !"

"Oh, it's only a temporary postponement," replied Aramis ; "I shall be one, some day.   You very well know, Porthos, that I continue to study theology for that purpose."

"He will be one, as he says," cried Porthos ; "he will be one, sooner or later."

"Soon," said Aramis.

"He only waits for one thing to determine him to resume his cassock, which hangs behind his uniform," said another musketeer.

"What is he waiting for ?" asked another.

"Only till the queen has given an heir to the crown of France."

"No jokes upon that subject, gentlemen," said Porthos ; "thank God, the queen is still of an age to give one."

"They say that M. de Buckingham is in France," replied Aramis, with a significant smile, which gave to this sentence, apparently so simple, a tolerably scandalous meaning.

"Aramis, my good friend, this time you are wrong," interrupted Porthos, "your wit is always leading you astray ; if M. de Tréville heard you, you would repent of speaking thus."

"Are you going to teach me better, Porthos," cried Aramis, from whose usually mild eye a flash passed like lightning.

"My dear fellow, be a musketeer or an abbé.   Be one or the other, but not both," replied Porthos.   "You know what Athos told you the other day : you eat at everybody's mess.   Ah ! don't be angry, I beg of you, that would be useless ; you know what is agreed upon between you, Athos, and me.   You go to Madame d'Aiguillon's, and you pay your court to her ; you go to Madame de Bois-Tracy's, the cousin of Madame de Chevreuse, and you pass for being far advanced in the good graces of that lady.   Oh, good Lord ! don't trouble yourself to reveal your good fortunes ; no one asks for your secret—all the world knows your discretion.   But since you possess that virtue, why the devil don't you make use of it with respect to her Majesty ?   Let whoever likes talk of the king and the cardinal, and how he likes ; but the queen is sacred, and if any one speaks of her, let it be well."

"Porthos, you are as vain as Narcissus, I plainly tell you so," replied Aramis ; "you know I hate moralising, except when it is done by Athos.   As to you, good sir, you wear too magnificent a baldrick to be strong on that head.   I will be an abbé if it suits me ; in the meanwhile I am a musketeer : in that quality I say what I please, and at this moment it pleases me to say that you annoy me."

"Aramis !"

"Porthos !"

"Gentlemen ! gentlemen !" cried the surrounding group.

"Monsieur de Tréville awaits M. d'Artagnan," cried a servant, throwing open the door of the cabinet.

At this announcement, during which the door remained open, every one became mute, and amidst the general silence the young man crossed the antechamber in a part of its length, and entered the apartment of the captain of the musketeers, congratulating himself with all his heart at having so narrowly escaped the end of this strange quarrel.

CHAPTER III.

THE AUDIENCE.

M. DE TRÉVILLE was at the moment in rather an ill-humour; nevertheless, he saluted the young man politely, who bowed to the very ground, and he smiled on receiving his compliment, the Béarnese accent of which recalled to him at the same time his youth and his country, a double remembrance, which makes a man smile at all ages. But stepping towards the antechamber, and making a sign to d'Artagnan with his hand, as if to ask his permission to finish with others before he began with him, he called three times, with a louder voice at each time, so that he went through all the tones between the imperative accent and the angry accent.

"Athos! Porthos! Aramis!"

The two musketeers, with whom we have already made acquaintance, and who answered to the last two of these three names, immediately quitted the group of which they formed a part, and advanced towards the cabinet, the door of which closed after them as soon as they had entered. Their appearance, although it was not quite at ease, excited by its carelessness, at once full of dignity and submission, the admiration of D'Artagnan, who beheld in these two men demi-gods, and in their leader an Olympian Jupiter, armed with all his thunders.

When the two musketeers had entered, when the door was closed behind them, when the buzzing murmur of the antechamber, to which the summons which had been made had doubtless furnished fresh aliment, had recommenced; when M. de Tréville had three or four times paced in silence, and with a frowning brow, the whole length of his cabinet, passing each time before Porthos and Aramis, who were as upright and silent as if on parade, he stopped all at once full in front of them, and, covering them from head to foot with an angry look—

"Do you know what the king said to me," cried he, "and that no longer ago than yesterday evening—do you know, gentlemen?"

"No," replied the two musketeers, after a moment's silence—"no, sir, we do not."

"But I hope that you will do us the honour to tell us," added Aramis, in his politest tone, and with the most graceful bow.

"He told me that he should henceforth recruit his musketeers from among the guards of Monsieur the Cardinal."

"The guards of M. the Cardinal! and why so?" asked Porthos, warmly.

"Because he plainly perceives that his piquette* stands in need of being enlivened by a mixture of good wine."

* A liquor squeezed out of grapes, when they have been pressed, and water poured upon them.

The two musketeers coloured up to the eyes. D'Artagnan did not know where he was, and would have wished to be a hundred feet under ground.

"Yes, yes," continued M. de Tréville, growing warmer as he spoke, "and his Majesty was right, for, upon my honour, it is true that the musketeers make but a miserable figure at court. M. le Cardinal related yesterday, whilst playing with the king, with an air of condolence not very pleasing to me, that the day before yesterday those damned musketeers, those dare-devils—he dwelt upon those words with an ironical tone still more unpleasing to me—those braggarts, added he, glancing at me with his tiger-cat's eye, had made a riot in the Rue Ferou, in a cabaret, and that a party of his guards (I thought he was going to laugh in my face) had been forced to arrest the rioters. Morbleu! you must know something about it! Arrest musketeers! You were among them—you were! Don't deny it; you were recognised, and the cardinal named you. But it's all my fault! yes, it's all my fault, because it is myself who select my men. You, now, Aramis, why the devil did you ask me for a uniform, when you would have been so much better in a cassock? And you, Porthos, do you only wear such a fine golden baldrick to suspend a sword of straw from it? And Athos—I don't see Athos! Where is he?"

"Sir," replied Aramis, in a sorrowful tone, "he is ill, very ill!"

"Ill—very ill, say you? And what is his malady?"

"It is feared that it is the small-pox, sir," replied Porthos, desirous of getting a word in the conversation; "and, what is worst, that it will certainly spoil his face."

"The small-pox! That's a pretty glorious story to tell me, Porthos! Sick of the small-pox at his age! No, no; but wounded, without doubt—perhaps killed. Ah, if I knew! *Sang Dieu!* Messieurs musketeers, I will not have this haunting of bad places, this quarrelling in the streets, this sword-play in cross-ways; and, above all, I will not have occasion given for the cardinal's guards, who are brave, quiet, skilful men, who never put themselves in a position to be arrested, and who, besides, never allow themselves to be arrested, to laugh at you! I am sure of it—they would prefer dying on the spot to being arrested, or to giving back a step. To save yourselves, to scamper away, to fly! a pretty thing to be said of the king's musketeers!"

Porthos and Aramis trembled with rage; they could willingly have strangled M. de Tréville, if, at the bottom of all this, they had not felt it was the great love he bore them which made him speak thus. They stamped upon the carpet with their feet, they bit their lips till the blood sprang, and grasped the hilts of their swords with all their strength. Without, all had heard, as we have said, Athos, Porthos, and Aramis called, and had guessed from M. de Tréville's tone of voice that he was very angry about something. Ten curious heads were glued to the tapestry, and became pale with fury; for their ears, closely applied to the door, did not lose a syllable of what he said, whilst their mouths repeated, as he went on, the insulting expressions of the captain to the whole population of the antechamber. In an instant, from the door of the cabinet to the street-gate, the whole hotel was in a state of commotion.

"Ah ! the king's musketeers are arrested by the guards of M. the Cardinal, are they !" continued M. de Tréville, as furious within as his soldiers ; but emphasising his words, and plunging them, one by one, so to say, like so many blows of a stiletto, into the bosoms of his auditors. "What ! six of his eminence's guards arrest six of his majesty's musketeers ! *Morbleu !* my part is taken ! I will go straight to the Louvre; I will give in my resignation as captain of the king's musketeers, to take a lieutenancy in the cardinal's guards ; and if he refuses me, *morbleu !* I will turn abbé."

At these words, the murmur without became an explosion ; nothing was to be heard but oaths and blasphemies. The *morbleus !* the *sang Dieus !* the *morts de touts les diables !* crossed each other in the air. D'Artagnan looked round for some tapestry behind which he might hide himself, and felt an immense inclination to crawl under the table.

"Well, mon capitaine," said Porthos, quite beside himself, "the truth is, that we were six against six ; but we were not captured by fair means ; and before we had time to draw our swords two of our party were dead ; and Athos, grievously wounded, was very little better. For you know Athos. Well, captain, he endeavoured twice to get up, and fell again twice. And we did not surrender—no ! they dragged us away by force. On the way we escaped. As for Athos, they believed him to be dead, and left him very quietly on the field of battle, not thinking it worth the trouble to carry him away. Now, that's the whole history. What the devil, captain, one cannot win all one's battles ! The great Pompey lost that of Pharsalia ; and Francis the First, who was, as I have heard say, as good as other folks, nevertheless lost the battle of Pavia."

"And I have the honour of assuring you, that I killed one of them with his own sword," safd Aramis, "for mine was broken at the first parry. Killed him, or poniarded him, sir, as is most agreeable to you."

"I did not know that," replied M. de Tréville, in a somewhat softened tone. "M. le Cardinal exaggerated, as I perceive."

"But pray, sir," continued Aramis, who, seeing his captain become appeased, ventured to risk a prayer—"pray, sir, do not say that Athos is wounded ; he would be in despair if that should come to the ears of the king ; and as the wound is very serious, seeing that after crossing the shoulder it penetrates into the chest, it is to be feared——"

At this instant the tapestry was raised, and a noble and handsome head, but frightfully pale, appeared under the fringe.

"Athos !" cried the two musketeers.

"Athos !" repeated M. de Tréville to himself.

"You have sent for me, sir," said Athos to M. de Tréville, in a feeble yet perfectly calm voice—"you have sent for me, as my comrades inform me, and I have hastened to receive your orders. I am here, monsieur ; what do you want with me ?"

And at these words the musketeer, in irreproachable costume, belted as usual, with a tolerably firm step, entered the cabinet. M. de Tréville, moved to the bottom of his heart by this proof of courage, sprang towards him.

"I was about to say to these gentlemen," added he, "that I forbid my musketeers to expose their lives needlessly; for brave men are very dear to the king, and the king knows that his musketeers are the bravest fellows on earth. Your hand, Athos!"

And without waiting for the answer of the newly-arrived to this proof of affection, M. de Tréville seized his right hand, and pressed it with all his might, without perceiving that Athos, whatever might be his self-command, allowed a slight murmur of pain to escape him, and, if possible, grew paler than he was before.

The door had remained open, so strong was the excitement produced by the arrival of Athos, whose wound, though kept as secret as possible, was known to all. A burst of satisfaction hailed the last words of the captain ; and two or three heads, carried away by the enthusiasm of the moment, appeared through the openings of the tapestry. M. de Tréville was about to reprehend this infraction of the rules of etiquette, when he felt the hand of Athos stiffen within his, and, upon turning his eyes towards him, perceived he was about to faint. At the same instant Athos, who had rallied all his energies to contend against pain, at length overcome by it, fell upon the floor as if he was dead.

"A surgeon!" cried M. de Tréville, "mine! the king's! the best that can be found!—a surgeon! or, *sang Dieu!* my brave Athos will die!"

At the cries of M. de Tréville, the whole assemblage rushed into the cabinet without his thinking of shutting the door against any one, and all crowded round the wounded man. But all this eager attention might have been useless if the doctor so loudly called for had not chanced to be in the hotel. He pushed through the crowd, approached Athos, still insensible, and, as all this noise and commotion inconvenienced him greatly, he required, as the first and most urgent thing, that the musketeer should be carried into another chamber. Immediately M. de Tréville opened the door, and pointed the way to Porthos and Aramis, who bore their comrade in their arms. Behind this group walked the surgeon, and as the surgeon passed through, the door closed.

The cabinet of M. de Tréville, generally held so sacred, became in an instant the recipient of the antechamber. Every one spoke, harangued, and vociferated, swearing, cursing, and consigning the cardinal and his guards to all the devils.

An instant after, Porthos and Aramis re-entered, the surgeon and M. de Tréville alone remaining with the wounded man.

At length M. de Tréville himself returned. Athos had recovered his senses ; the surgeon declared that the situation of the musketeer had nothing in it to render his friends uneasy, his weakness having been purely and simply aused by loss of blood.

Then M. de Tréville made a sign with his hand, and all retired except

D'Artagnan, who did not forget that he had an audience, and, with the tenacity of a Gascon, remained in his place.

When all had gone out, and the door was closed, M. de Tréville, on turning round, found himself alone with the young man. The stirring event which had just passed had in some degree broken the thread of his ideas. He inquired what was the will of his persevering visitor. D'Artagnan then repeated his name, and in an instant, recovering all his remembrances of the present and the past, M. de Tréville was in possession of the current circumstances.

"Pardon me," said he, smiling, "pardon me, my dear compatriot, but I had perfectly forgotten you. But what help is there for it! a captain is nothing but a father of a family, charged with even a greater responsibility than the father of an ordinary family. Soldiers are great children; but as I maintain that the orders of the king, and more particularly the orders of M. the Cardinal, should be executed——"

D'Artagnan could not restrain a smile. By this smile, M. de Tréville judged that he had not to deal with a fool, and changing the subject, came straight to the point.

"I respected your father very much," said he. "What can I do for the son? Tell me quickly, my time is not my own."

"Monsieur," said D'Artagnan, "on quitting Tarbes, and coming hither, it was my intention to request of you, in remembrance of the friendship which you have not forgotten, the uniform of a musketeer; but after all that I have seen, during the last two hours, I have become aware of the value of such a favour, and tremble lest I should not merit it."

"Well, young man," replied M. de Tréville, "it is, in fact, a favour, but it may not be so far beyond your hopes as you believe, or rather as you appear to believe; but his majesty's decision is always necessary: and I inform you with regret, that no one becomes a musketeer without the preliminary ordeal of several campaigns, certain brilliant actions, or a service of two years i some regiment of less reputation than ours."

D'Artagnan bowed without replying, feeling his desire to don the musketeer's uniform vastly increased by the difficulties which he learnt preceded the attainment of it.

"But," continued M. de Tréville, fixing upon his compatriot a look so piercing, that it might be said he wished to read the thoughts of his heart; "but, on·account of my old companion, your father, as I have said, I will do something for you, young man. Our cadets from Béarn are not generally very rich, and I have no reason to think matters have much changed in this respect since I left the province. I dare say you have not brought too large a stock of money with you?"

D'Artagnan drew himself up with an air that plainly said, "I ask charity of no man."

"Oh! that's all very well, young man," continued M. de Tréville, "that's all very well. I am well acquainted with all those lofty airs; I myself came to Paris with four crowns in my purse, and would have fought with any one who would have dared to tell me I was not in a condition to purchase the Louvre."

D'Artagnan's carriage became still more imposing ; thanks to the sale of his horse, he commenced his career with four crowns more than M. de Tréville had possessed at the commencement of his.

"You ought, I say, then, to husband the means you have, however large the sum may be ; but you ought also to endeavour to perfect yourself in the exercises becoming a gentleman. I will write a letter to-day to the director of the Royal Academy, and to-morrow he will admit you without any expense to yourself. Do not refuse this little service. Our best born and richest gentlemen sometimes solicit it, without being able to obtain it. You will be learning riding, swordsmanship in all its branches, and dancing ; you will make some desirable acquaintances, and from time to time you can call upon me, just to tell me how you are going on, and to say whether I can be of further service to you."

D'Artagnan, stranger as he was to all the manners of a court, could not but perceive a little coldness in this reception.

"Alas ! sir," said he, "I cannot but perceive how sadly I miss the letter of introduction which my father gave me to present to you."

"I certainly am surprised," replied M. de Tréville, "that you should undertake so long a journey without that necessary viaticum, the only resource of us poor Béarnese."

"I had one, sir, and, thank God, such as I could wish, but it was perfidiously stolen from me."

He then related the adventure of Meung, described the unknown gentleman with the greatest minuteness, and all with a warmth and truthfulness that delighted M. de Tréville.

"This is all very strange," said M. de Tréville, after meditating a minute ; "you mentioned my name, then, aloud ?"

"Yes, sir, I certainly committed that imprudence ; but why should I have done otherwise ? A name like yours must be as a buckler to me on my way. Why should I not avail myself of it ?"

Flattery was at that period very current, and M. de Tréville loved incense as well as a king, or even a cardinal. He could not refrain from a smile of visible satisfaction, but this smile soon disappeared ; and returning to the adventure of Meung——

"Tell me," continued he, "had not this gentleman a slight scar on his cheek ?"

"Yes, such a one as would be made by the grazing of a ball."

"Was he not a fine-looking man ?"

"Yes."

"Of lofty stature ?"

"Yes."

"Of pale complexion and brown hair ?"

"Yes, yes, that is he ; how is it, sir, that you are acquainted with this man ? If ever I should meet him again, and I will find him, I swear,— were it in hell."

"He was waiting for a woman," continued Tréville.

"He, at least, departed immediately after having conversed for a minute with the one for whom he appeared to have been waiting."

" You did not gather the subject of their discourse ?"

" He gave her a box ; told her that that box contained her instruc‹ tions, and desired her not to open it before she arrived in London."

" Was this woman English ?"

" He called her Milady."

" It is he ! it must be he !" murmured Tréville ; " I thought he was still at Brussels !"

" Oh ! sir ; if you know who and what this man is," cried D'Artagnan, " tell me who he is, and whence he is.   I will then release you from all your promises—even that of procuring my admission into the Musketeers ; for, before everything, I am desirous to avenge myself."

" Beware, young man !" cried De Tréville ; " if you see him coming on one side of the street, pass by on the other ! Do not cast yourself against such a rock ; he would break you like glass."

" That thought will not prevent me," replied D'Artagnan, " if ever I should happen to meet with him."

" In the meantime, if you will take my advice, you will not seek him," said Tréville.

All at once, the Captain stopped, as if struck by a sudden suspicion. This great hatred which the young traveller manifested so loudly for this man, who—a rather improbable thing—had stolen his father's letter from him !—Was there not some perfidy concealed under this hatred ? —might not this young man be sent by his Eminence ?—might he not have come for the purpose of laying a snare for him ?—this pretended D'Artagnan ! was he not an emissary of the cardinal's whom he sought to introduce into his house, to place near him, and win his confidence, and afterwards to bring about his ruin, as had been practised in a thousand other instances ?   He fixed his eyes upon D'Artagnan, even more earnestly than before.   He was moderately reassured, however, by the aspect of that countenance, full of shrewd intelligence and affected humility.

I know he is a Gascon, reflected he ; but he may be one for the cardinal as well as for me.   Let us try him.—" My friend," said he, slowly, " I wish, as the son of an ancient friend—for I consider this story of the lost letter perfectly true—I wish, I say, in order to repair the coldness you may have remarked in my reception of you, to make you acquainted with the secrets of our policy.—The king and the cardinal are the best of friends ; their apparent bickerings are only feints to deceive fools.   I am not willing that a compatriot, a handsome cavalier, a brave youth, quite fit to make his way, should become the dupe of all these artifices, and fall into the snare, after the example of so many others, who have been ruined by it.   Be assured that I am devoted to both these all-powerful masters, and that my earnest endeavours have no other aim than the service of the king, and that of the cardinal, one of the most illustrious geniuses that France has ever produced.

" Now, young man, regulate your conduct accordingly ; and if you entertain, whether from your family, your relations, or even from your instincts, any of these enmities which we see constantly breaking out against the cardinal, bid me adieu, and let us separate. I will aid you in many ways, but without attaching you to my person. I hope that my frankness, at least, will make you my friend ; for you are the only young man to whom I have hitherto spoken as I have done to you."

Tréville said to himself :

" If the cardinal has set this young fox upon me, he will certainly not have failed, he, who knows how bitterly I execrate him, to tell his spy that the best means of making his court to me is to rail at him ; therefore in spite of all my protestations, if it be as I suspect, my cunning gossip here will launch out in abuse of his Eminence."

It, however, proved otherwise. D'Artagnan answered, with the greatest simplicity :

" I am come to Paris with exactly such intentions, sir. My father advised me to stoop to nobody but the King, Monsieur the Cardinal, and you—whom he considered the three first personages in France."

D'Artagnan added M. de Tréville to the others, as may be perceived ; but he thought this adjunction would do no harm.

" I hold, therefore, M. the Cardinal in the greatest veneration," continued he ; " and have the greatest respect for his actions. So much the better for me, sir, if you speak to me, as you say, with frankness— for then you will do me the honour to esteem the resemblance of our opinions ; but if you have entertained any doubt, as naturally you may, I feel that I am ruining myself by speaking the truth. But I still trust you will not esteem me the less for it, and that is my object beyond all others."

M. de Tréville was surprised to the greatest degree. So much pene- tration—so much frankness—created admiration, but did not entirely remove his suspicions ; the more this young man was superior to others, the more he was to be dreaded, if he meant to deceive him. Never- theless, he pressed D'Artagnan's hand, and said to him :

" You are an honest youth ; but, at the present moment, I can only do for you that which I just now offered. My hotel will be always open to you. Hereafter, being able to ask for me at all hours, and, conse- quently to take advantage of all opportunities, you will probably obtain that which you desire."

" That is to say, sir," replied D'Artagnan, " that you will wait till I have proved myself worthy of it. Well ! be assured," added he, with the familiarity of a Gascon, " you shall not wait long." And he bowed on retiring, as if he considered the future was left in his own hands.

" But, wait a minute," said M. de Tréville, stopping him. " I pro- mised you a letter for the director of the Academy ; are you too proud to accept it, young gentleman ?"

" No, sir," said D'Artagnan ; " and I will answer for it that this one shall not fare like the other. I will guard it so carefully, that I will be sworn it shall arrive at its address, and woe be to him who shall attempt to take it from me !"

M. de Tréville smiled at this little flourish ; and, leaving his young companion in the embrasure of the window, where they had talked together, he seated himself at a table, in order to write the promised letter of recommendation. Whilst he was doing this, D'Artagnan, having no better employment, amused himself with beating a march upon the window, and with looking at the musketeers, who went away, one after another, following them with his eyes till they disappeared at the turning of the street.

M. de Tréville, after having written the letter, sealed it ; and, rising, approached the young man, in order to give it to him. But, at the very moment that D'Artagnan stretched out his hand to receive it, M. de Tréville was highly astonished to see his *protégé* make a sudden spring, become crimson with passion, and rush from the cabinet, crying—"Ah! *Sang Dieu !* he shall not escape me this time !"

"Who? who?" asked M. de Tréville.

"He, my thief !" replied D'Artagnan. "Ah ! the traitor !" and he disappeared.

"The devil take the madman !" murmured M. de Tréville, "unless," added he, "this is a cunning mode of escaping, seeing that he has failed in his purpose !"

CHAPTER IV.

THE SHOULDER OF ATHOS, THE BALDRICK OF PORTHOS, AND THE HANDKERCHIEF OF ARAMIS.

D'ARTAGNAN, in a state of fury, crossed the antechamber at three bounds, and was darting towards the stairs, which he reckoned upon descending four at a time, when, in his heedless course, he ran headforemost against a musketeer, who was coming out of one of M. de Tréville's back rooms, and striking his shoulder violently, made him utter a cry, or rather a howl.

"Excuse me," said D'Artagnan, endeavouring to resume his course, "excuse me, but I am in a hurry."

Scarcely had he descended the first stair, when a hand of iron seized him by the belt and stopped him.

"You are in a hurry," said the musketeer, as pale as a sheet ; "under that pretence, you run against me ; you say, 'Excuse me !' and you believe that that is sufficient? Not at all, my young man. Do you fancy that because you have heard M. de Tréville speak to us a little cavalierly to-day, that other people are to treat us as he speaks to us? Undeceive yourself, my merry companion, you are not M. de Tréville."

"Ma foi !" replied D'Artagnan, recognising Athos, who, after the dressing performed by the doctor, was going to his own apartment, "ma foi ! I did not do it intentionally, and, not doing it intentionally, I said, 'Excuse me !' It appears to me that that is quite enough. I repeat to you, however, and this time, *parole d'honneur,*—I think, perhaps, too often,—that I am in great haste—great haste. Leave your hold then, I beg of you, and let me go where my business calls me."

"Monsieur," said Athos, letting him go, "you are not polite ; it is easy to perceive that you come from a distance."

D'Artagnan had already strode down three or four stairs, when Athos' last remark stopped him short.

"Morbleu, monsieur !" said he, "however far I may come, it is not you who can give me a lesson in good manners, I warn you."

"Perhaps !" said Athos.

"Ah ! if I were not in such haste, and if I were not running after some one," said D'Artagnan.

"Mister gentleman in a hurry, you can find me without running after me ; me ! do you understand me ?"

"And where, I pray you ?"

"Near the Carmes Deschaux."

"At what hour ?"

"About noon."

"About noon ; that will do, I will be there."

"Endeavour not to make me wait, for at a quarter past twelve I will cut off your ears as you run."

"Good !" cried D'Artagnan, "I will be there ten minutes before twelve."

And he set off running as if the devil possessed him, hoping that he might yet find the unknown, whose slow pace could not have carried him far.

But, at the street-gate Porthos was talking with the soldier on guard. Between the two talkers there was just room for a man to pass. D'Artagnan thought it would suffice for him, and he sprang forward like a dart between them. But D'Artagnan had reckoned without the wind. As he was about to pass, the wind blew out Porthos' long cloak, and D'Artagnan rushed straight into the middle of it. Without doubt, Porthos had reasons for not abandoning this part of his vestments, for, instead of quitting his hold of the flap in his hand, he pulled it towards him, so that D'Artagnan rolled himself up in the velvet, by a movement of rotation explained by the persistency of Porthos.

D'Artagnan, hearing the musketeer swear, wished to escape from under the cloak which blinded him, and endeavoured to make his way up the folds of it. He was particularly anxious to avoid marring the freshness of the magnificent baldrick we are acquainted with ; but on timidly opening his eyes, he found himself with his nose fixed between the two shoulders of Porthos, that is to say, exactly upon the baldrick.

Alas ! how most of the things in this world have nothing in their favour but appearances !—the baldrick was glittering with gold in the front, but was nothing but simple buff behind. Vain-glorious as he was, Porthos could not afford to have an entirely gold-worked baldrick, but had, at least, half one ; the care on account of the cold, and the necessity for the cloak became intelligible.

"Vertubleu !" cried Porthos, making strong efforts to get rid of D'Artagnan, who was wriggling about his back, "the fellow must be mad to run against people in this manner !"

"Excuse me!" said D'Artagnan, reappearing under the shoulder of the giant, "but I am in such haste—I was running after some one, and——"

"And do you always forget your eyes when you happen to be in a hurry?" asked Porthos.

"No," replied D'Artagnan, piqued, "no, and thanks to my eyes, I can see what other people cannot see."

Whether Porthos understood him or did not understand him, giving way to his anger,—

"Monsieur," said he, "you stand a chance of getting chastised if you run against musketeers in this fashion."

"Chastised, monsieur!" said D'Artagnan, "the expression is strong."

"It is one that becomes a man accustomed to look his enemies in the face."

"Ah! pardieu! I know full well that you don't turn your back to yours!"

And the young man, delighted with his joke, went away laughing loudly.

Porthos foamed with rage, and made a movement to rush after D'Artagnan.

"Presently, presently," cried the latter, "when you haven't your cloak on."

"At one o'clock then, behind the Luxembourg."

"Very well, at one o'clock, then," replied D'Artagnan, turning the angle of the street.

But neither in the street he had passed through, nor in the one which his eager glance pervaded, could he see any one ; however slowly the unknown had walked, he was gone on his way, or perhaps had entered some house. D'Artagnan inquired of every one he met with, went down to the ferry, came up again by the Rue de Seine, and the Croix Rouge ; but nothing, absolutely nothing ! This chase was, however, advantageous to him in one sense, for in proportion as the perspiration broke from his forehead, his heart began to cool.

He began to reflect upon the events that had passed ; they were numerous and inauspicious ; it was scarcely eleven o'clock in the morning, and yet this morning had already brought him into disgrace with M. de Tréville, who could not fail to think the manner in which D'Artagnan had left him a little cavalier.

Besides this, he had drawn upon himself two good duels with two men, each capable of killing three D'Artagnans, with two musketeers, in short, with two of those beings whom he esteemed so greatly, that he placed them in his mind and heart above all other men.

Appearances were sad. Sure of being killed by Athos, it may easily be understood that the young man was not very uneasy about Porthos. As hope, however, is the last thing extinguished in the heart of man, he finished by hoping that he might survive, although terribly wounded in both these duels, and in case of surviving, he made the following reprehensions upon his own conduct.

What a hare-brained, stupid fellow I am! That brave and unfortunate Athos was wounded exactly on that shoulder against which I must run head-foremost, like a ram. The only thing that astonishes me is that he did not strike me dead at once : he had good cause to do so, the pain I gave him must have been atrocious. As to Porthos,—oh ! as to Porthos, ma foi ! that's a droll affair !

And, in spite of himself, the young man began to laugh aloud, looking round carefully, however, to see if his solitary laugh, without an apparent cause, in the eyes of passers-by, offended no one.

As to Porthos, that is certainly droll, but I am not the less a giddy fool. Are people to be run against without warning ? No ! and have I any right to go and peep under their cloaks to see what is not there ? He would have pardoned me, he would certainly have pardoned me, if I had not said anything to him about that cursed baldrick, in ambiguous words, it is true, but rather drolly ambiguous ! Ah ! cursed Gascon that I am, I get from one hobble into another. "Friend D'Artagnan," continued he, speaking to himself with all the amenity that he thought due to himself, "if you escape, of which there is not much chance, I would advise you to practise perfect politeness for the future. You must henceforth be admired and quoted as a model of it. To be obliging and polite does not necessarily make a man a coward. Look at Aramis now : Aramis is mildness and grace personified. Well ! did ever any body dream of saying that Aramis is a coward ? No, certainly not, and from this moment I will endeavour to model myself after him. Ah ! that's strange ! here he is !"

D'Artagnan, walking and soliloquising had arrived within a few steps of the Hotel d'Arguillon, and in front of that hotel perceived Aramis chatting gaily with three gentlemen of the king's guards. On his part Aramis perceived D'Artagnan ; but as he had not forgotten that it was before this young man that M. de Tréville had been so angry in the morning, and that a witness of the rebuke the musketeers had received was not likely to be at all agreeable, he pretended not to see him. D'Artagnan, on the contrary, quite full of his plans of conciliation and courtesy, approached the young men, with a profound bow, accompanied by a most gracious smile. Aramis bowed his head slightly, but did not smile. All four, besides, immediately broke off their conversation.

D'Artagnan was not so dull as not to perceive that he was not wanted ; but he was not sufficiently broken into the fashions of the world to know how to extricate himself gallantly from a false position, as that of a man generally is who comes up and mingles with people he is scarcely acquainted with, and in a conversation that does not concern him. He was seeking in his mind, then, for the least awkward means of retreat, when he remarked that Aramis had let his handkerchief fall, and, by mistake, no doubt, had placed his foot upon it, and it appeared a favourable opportunity to repair his intrusion : he stooped, and with the most gracious air he could assume, drew the handkerchief from under the foot of the musketeer, in spite of the efforts the latter made to detain it, and holding it out to him, said :

" I believe, monsieur, that this is a handkerchief you would be sorry to lose ?"

The handkerchief was, in fact, richly embroidered, and had a coronet and arms at one of its corners. Aramis blushed excessively, and snatched rather than took the handkerchief from D'Artagnan's hand.

" Ah ! ah !" cried one of the guards, " will you persist in saying, most discreet Aramis, that you are not on good terms with Madame de Bois-Tracy, when that gracious lady has the kindness to lend you her handkerchief ?"

Aramis darted at D'Artagnan one of those looks which inform a man that he has acquired a mortal enemy ; then, resuming his mild air,—

" You are deceived, gentlemen," said he, " this handkerchief is not mine, and I cannot fancy why monsieur has taken it into his head to offer it to me rather than to one of you, and as a proof of what I say, here is mine in my pocket."

So saying, he pulled out his own handkerchief, which was likewise a very elegant handkerchief, and of fine cambric, though cambric was then dear, but a handkerchief with embroidery and without arms, only ornamented with a single cipher, that of the musketeer.

This time D'Artagnan was not hasty, he perceived his mistake ; but the friends of Aramis were not at all convinced by his assertion, and one of them, addressing the young musketeer with affected seriousness,—

" If it were as you pretend it is," said he, " I should be forced, my dear Aramis, to reclaim it myself ; for, as you very well know, Bois-Tracy is an intimate friend of mine, and I cannot allow the property of his wife to be sported as a trophy."

" You make the demand badly," replied Aramis ; "and whilst acknowledging the justice of your reclamation, I refuse it on account of the form."

" The fact is," hazarded D'Artagnan timidly, " I did not see the handkerchief fall from the pocket of M. Aramis. He had his foot upon it, that is all, and I thought from his having his foot upon it, the handkerchief was his."

" And, you were deceived, my dear sir," replied Aramis, coldly, very little sensible to the reparation ; then turning towards that one of the guards who had declared himself the friend of Bois-Tracy ;—" Besides," continued he, " I have reflected, my dear intimate friend of Bois-Tracy, that I am not less tenderly his friend than you can possibly be, so that decidedly this handkerchief is as likely to have fallen from your pocket as mine ?"

" No, upon my honour !" cried his majesty's guard.

" You are about to swear upon your honour and I upon my word, and then it will be pretty evident that one of us will have lied. Now, here, Montaran, we will do better than that, let each take a half."

" Of the handkerchief ?"

" Yes."

" Perfectly just," cried the two other guards,—" the judgment of King Solomon ! Aramis, you certainly are cram-full of wisdom !"

The young men burst into a loud laugh, and, as may be supposed, the affair had no other consequence. In a moment or two the conversation ceased, and the three guards and the musketeer, after having cordially shaken hands, separated, the guards going one way, and Aramis another.

"Now is my time to make my peace with this gentleman," said D'Artagnan to himself, having stood on one side during the whole of the latter part of the conversation ; and with this good feeling drawing near to Aramis, who was going without paying any attention to him,—

"Monsieur," said he, "you will excuse me, I hope."

"Ah ! monsieur," interrupted Aramis, "permit me to observe to you, that you have not acted in this affair as a man of good breeding ought to have done."

"What, monsieur !" cried D'Artagnan, "you suppose——"

"I suppose, monsieur, that you are not a fool, and that you knew very well, although coming from Gascony, that people do not tread upon pocket-handkerchiefs without a reason. What the devil ! Paris is not paved with cambric !"

"Monsieur, you act wrongly in endeavouring to mortify me," said D'Artagnan, with whom the natural quarrelsome spirit began to speak more loudly than his pacific resolutions. "I am from Gascony, it is true ; and since you know it, there is no occasion to tell you that Gascons are not very enduring, so that when they have begged to be excused once, were it even for a folly, they are convinced that they have done already at least as much again as they ought to have done."

"Monsieur, what I say to you about the matter," said Aramis, " is not for the sake of seeking a quarrel. Thank God ! I am not a spadasin, and, being a musketeer but for a time, I only fight when I am forced to do so, and always with great repugnance ; but this time the affair is serious, for here is a lady compromised by you."

"By us, you mean," cried D'Artagnan.

"Why did you so injudiciously restore me the handkerchief ?"

"Why did you so awkwardly let it fall ?"

"I have said, monsieur, that the handkerchief did not fall from my pocket."

"Well, and by saying so, you have lied twice, monsieur, for I saw it fall."

"Oh, oh ! you take it up in that way, do you, Master Gascon ? Well, I will teach you how to behave yourself."

"And I will send you back to your mass-book, Master Abbé. Draw, if you please, and instantly——"

"Not so, if you please, my good friend, not here, at least. Do you not perceive that we are opposite the Hotel d'Arguillon, which is full of the cardinal's creatures ? How do I know that it is not his eminence who has honoured you with the commission to bring him in my head ? Now I entertain a ridiculous partiality for my head, it seems to suit my shoulders so admirably. I have no objection to killing you, depend upon that, but quietly, in a snug remote place, where you will not be able to boast of your death to anybody."

" I agree, monsieur, but do not be too confident. Take away your handkerchief ; whether it belongs to you or another, you may, perhaps, stand in need of it."

" Monsieur is a Gascon ?" asked Aramis.

" Yes. Monsieur does not postpone an interview through prudence ?"

" Prudence, monsieur, is a virtue sufficiently useless to musketeers, I know, but indispensable to churchmen ; and as I am only a musketeer provisionally, I hold it good to be prudent. At two o'clock, I shall have the honour of expecting you at the hotel of M. de Tréville. There I will point out to you the best place and time."

The two young men bowed and separated, Aramis ascending the street which led to the Luxembourg, whilst D'Artagnan, perceiving the appointed hour was approaching, took the road to the Carmes-Deschaux, saying to himself, " Decidedly I can't draw back ; but at least, if I am killed, I shall be killed by a musketeer !"

CHAPTER V.

THE KING'S MUSKETEERS AND THE CARDINAL'S GUARDS.

D'ARTAGNAN was acquainted with nobody in Paris. He went, therefore, to his appointment with Athos, without a second, determined to be satisfied with those his adversary should choose. Besides, his intention was formed to make the brave musketeer all suitable apologies, but without meanness or weakness, fearing that that might result from this duel which generally results from an affair of the kind, when a young and vigorous man fights with an adversary who is wounded and weakened : if conquered, he doubles the triumph of his antagonist ; if a conqueror, he is accused of foul play and want of courage.

Now, we must have badly painted the character of our adventurer, or our readers must have already perceived that D'Artagnan was not a common man ; therefore, whilst repeating to himself that his death was inevitable, he did not make up his mind to die so quietly as another, less courageous and less moderate than he, might have done in his place. He reflected upon the different characters of the men he had to fight with, and began to view his situation more clearly. He hoped, by means of loyal excuses, to make a friend of Athos, whose nobleman air and austere courage pleased him much. He flattered himself he should be able to frighten Porthos with the adventure of the baldrick, which he might, if not killed upon the spot, relate to everybody—a recital which, well managed, would cover Porthos with ridicule ; as to the astute Aramis, he did not entertain much dread of him, and if he should be able to get so far as him, he determined to despatch him in good style, or, at least, by hitting him in the face, as Cæsar recommended his soldiers to do to those of Pompey, damage the beauty of which he was so proud for ever.

In addition to this, D'Artagnan possessed that invincible stock of resolution which the counsels of his father had implanted in his heart—Endure nothing from any one but the king, the cardinal, and M. de Tréville. He flew, then, rather than walked, towards the convent of the Carmes Déchaussés, or rather Dechaux, as it was called at that period, a sort of building without a window, surrounded by barren fields, an accessory to the Pré-aux-Clercs, and which was generally employed as the place for the rencontres of men who had no time to lose.

When D'Artagnan arrived in sight of the bare spot of ground which extended along the foot of the monastery, Athos had been waiting about five minutes, and twelve o'clock was striking ; he was, then, as punctual as the Samaritan woman, and the most rigorous casuist with regard to duels could have nothing to say.

Athos, who still suffered grievously from his wound, though it had been dressed by M. de Tréville's surgeon at nine, was seated on a post and waiting for his adversary with that placid countenance and that noble air which never forsook him. At sight of D'Artagnan, he arose and came politely a few steps to meet him. The latter, on his side, saluted his adversary with hat in hand, and his feather even touching the ground.

"Monsieur," said Athos, "I have engaged two of my friends as seconds ; but these two friends are not yet come, at which I am astonished, as it is not at all their custom to be behindhand."

"I have no seconds on my part, monsieur," said D'Artagnan ; "for, having only arrived yesterday in Paris, I as yet know no one but M. de Tréville, to whom I was recommended by my father, who has the honour to be, in some degree, one of his friends."

Athos reflected for an instant.

"You know no one but M. de Tréville ?" he asked.

"No, monsieur ; I only know him."

"Well, but then," continued Athos, speaking partly to himself, " well, but then, if I kill you, I shall have the air of a boy-slayer."

"Not too much so," replied D'Artagnan, with a bow that was not deficient in dignity, " not too much so, since you do me the honour to draw a sword with me whilst suffering from a wound which is very painful."

"Very painful, upon my word, and you hurt me devilishly, I can tell you ; but I will take the left hand—I usually do so in such circumstances. Do not fancy that I favour you—I use both hands equally; and it will be even a disadvantage to you—a left-handed man is very troublesome to people who are not used to it. I regret I did not inform you sooner of this circumstance."

"You are truly, monsieur," said D'Artagnan, bowing again, "of a courtesy, for which, I assure you, I am very grateful."

"You confuse me," replied Athos, with his gentlemanly air ; "let us talk of something else, if you please. Ah, *sang Dieu !* how you have hurt me ! my shoulder quite burns."

"If you would permit me——," said D'Artagnan, with timidity.

"What, monsieur ?"

"I have a miraculous balsam for wounds—a balsam given to me by my mother, and of which I have made a trial upon myself."

"Well?"

"Well, I am sure that in less than three days this balsam would cure you ; and at the end of three days, when you would be cured—well, sir, it would still do me a great honour to be your man."

D'Artagnan spoke these words with a simplicity that did honour to his courtesy, without throwing the least doubt upon his courage.

"*Pardieu*, monsieur !" said Athos, " that's a proposition that pleases me ; not that I accept it, but it savours of the gentleman a league off. It was thus that spoke the gallant knights of the time of Charlemagne, in whom every knight ought to seek his model.   Unfortunately, we do not live in the time of the great emperor ; we live in the times of Monsieur the Cardinal, and three days hence, however well the secret might be guarded, it would be known, I say, that we were to fight, and our combat would be prevented.   I think these fellows will never come."

" If you are in haste, monsieur," said D'Artagnan, with the same simplicity with which a moment before he had proposed to him to put off the duel for three days, " if you are in haste, and if it be your will to despatch me at once, do not inconvenience yourself— I am ready."

"Well, that is again well said," cried Athos, with a gracious nod to D'Artagnan, that did not come from a man without brains. and certainly not from a man without a heart. "Monsieur, I love men of your kidney, and I foresee plainly that, if we don't kill each other, I shall hereafter have much pleasure in your conversation.   We will wait for these gentlemen, if you please ; I have plenty of time, and it will be more correct. Ah ! here is one of them, I think."

In fact, at the end of the Rue Vanguard, the gigantic form of Porthos began to appear.

"What !" cried D'Artagnan, " is your first second M. Porthos ?"

"Yes. Is that unpleasant to you ?"

" Oh, not at all."

" And here comes the other."

D'Artagnan turned in the direction pointed to by Athos, and perceived Aramis.

" What !" cried he, in an accent of greater astonishment than before, " is your second witness M. Aramis ?"

" Doubtless he is. Are you not aware that we are never seen one without the others, and that we are called in the musketeers and the guards, at court and in the city, Athos, Porthos, and Aramis, or the three inseparables ?   And yet, as you come from Dax or Pau——",

" From Tarbes," said D'Artagnan.

" It is probable you are ignorant of this circumstance," said Athos.

"*Ma foi !*" replied D'Artagnan, " you are well named, gentlemen, and my adventure, if it should make any noise, will prove at least that your union is not founded upon contrasts."

In the meantime Porthos had come up, waved his hand to Athos, and then turning towards D'Artagnan, stood quite astonished.

Permit us to say, in passing, that he had changed his baldrick, and was without his cloak.

" Ah, ah !" said he, " what does this mean ?"

" This is the gentleman I am going to fight with," said Athos, pointing to D'Artagnan with his hand, and saluting him with the same gesture.

" Why, it is with him I am also going to fight," said Porthos.

" But not before one o'clock," replied D'Artagnan.

"Well, and I also am going to fight with that gentleman," said Aramis, coming on to the ground as he spoke.

" But not till two o'clock," said D'Artagnan, with the same calmness.

" But what are you going to fight about, Athos ?" asked Aramis.

" *Ma foi !* I don't very well know ; he hurt my shoulder. And you, Porthos ?"

" *Ma foi !* I am going to fight, because I am going to fight," answered Porthos, colouring deeply.

Athos, whose keen eye lost nothing, perceived a faintly sly smile pass over the lips of the young Gascon, as he replied :

" We had a short discussion upon dress."

" And you, Aramis ?" asked Athos.

" Oh, ours is a theological quarrel," replied Aramis, making a sign to D'Artagnan to keep secret the cause of their dispute.

Athos saw a second smile on the lips of D'Artagnan.

" Indeed ?" said Athos.

" Yes ; a passage of St. Augustin, upon which we could not agree," said the Gascon.

" By Jove ! this is a clever fellow," murmured Athos.

"And now you are all assembled, gentlemen," said D'Artagnan, " permit me to offer you my excuses."

At this word *excuses*, a cloud passed over the brow of Athos, a haughty smile curled the lip of Porthos, and a negative sign was the reply of Aramis.

" You do not understand me, gentlemen," said D'Artagnan, throwing up his head, the sharp and bold lines of which were at the moment gilded by a bright sun ray. " I ask to be excused in case I should not be able to discharge my debt to all three ; for M. Athos has the right to kill me first, which must abate your valour in your own estimation, M. Porthos, and render yours almost null, M. Aramis. And now, gentlemen, I repeat, excuse me, but on that account only, and—guard !"

At these words, with the most gallant air possible, D'Artagnan drew his sword.

The blood had mounted to the head of D'Artagnan, and at that moment he would have drawn his sword against all the musketeers in the kingdom, as willingly as he now did against Athos, Porthos, and Aramis.

It was a quarter past mid-day. The sun was in its zenith, and the spot chosen for the theatre of the duel was exposed to its full power.

" It is very hot," said Athos, drawing his sword in his turn, "and yet I cannot take off my doublet ; for I just now felt my wound begin to bleed again, and I should not like to annoy monsieur with the sight of blood which he has not drawn from me himself."

"That is true, monsieur," replied D'Artagnan, "and, whether drawn by myself or another, I assure you I shall always view with regret the blood of so brave a gentleman ; I will therefore fight in my doublet, as you do."

"Come, come, enough of compliments," cried Porthos ; "please to remember we are waiting for our turns."

"Speak for yourself, when you are inclined to utter such incongruities," interrupted Aramis. "For my part, I think what they say is very well said, and quite worthy of two gentlemen."

"When you please, monsieur," said Athos, putting himself on guard. "I waited your orders," said D'Artagnan, crossing swords.

But scarcely had the two rapiers sounded on meeting, when a company of the guards of his Eminence, commanded by M. de Jussac, turned the angle of the convent.

"The cardinal's guards ! the cardinal's guards !" cried Aramis and Porthos at the same time. "Sheathe swords ! gentlemen ! sheathe swords !"

But it was too late. The two combatants had been seen in a position which left no doubt of their intentions.

"Hola !" cried Jussac, advancing towards them, and making a sign to his men to do so likewise, "hola ! musketeers, fighting here, then, are you ? And the edicts, what is become of them ?"

"You are very generous, gentlemen of the guards," said Athos, with acrimony, for Jussac was one of the aggressors of the preceding day. "If we were to see you fighting, I can assure you that we would make no effort to prevent you. Leave us alone then, and you will enjoy a little amusement without cost to yourselves."

"Gentlemen," said Jussac, "it is with great regret that I pronounce the thing impossible. Duty before everything. Sheathe, then, if you please, and follow us."

"Monsieur," said Aramis, parodying Jussac, "it would afford us great pleasure to obey your polite invitation, if it depended upon ourselves ; but, unfortunately, the thing is impossible : M. de Tréville has forbidden it. Pass on your way, then ; it is the best thing you can do."

This raillery exasperated Jussac.

"We will charge upon you, then," said he, "if you disobey."

"There are five of them," said Athos, half aloud, "and we are but three ; we shall be beaten again, and must die on the spot, for, on my part, I declare I will never appear before the captain again as a conquered man."

Athos, Porthos, and Aramis, instantly closed in, and Jussac drew up his soldiers.

This short interval was sufficient to determine D'Artagnan on the part he was to take ; it was one of those events which decide the life of a man ; it was a choice between the king and the cardinal ; the choice made, it must be persisted in. To fight was to disobey the law, to risk his head, to make at once an enemy of a minister more powerful than the king himself; all this the young man perceived, and yet, to his praise we speak it, he did not hesitate a second. Turning towards Athos and his friends,—

"Gentlemen," said he, "allow me to correct your words, if you please. You said you were but three, but it appears to me we are four."

"But you are not one of us," said Porthos.

"That's true," replied D'Artagnan ; "I do not wear the uniform, but I am in spirit. My heart is that of a musketeer ; I feel it, monsieur, and that impels me on."

"Withdraw, young man," cried Jussac, who, doubtless, by his gestures and the expression of his countenance, had guessed D'Artagnan's design. "You may retire, we allow you to do so. Save your skin ; begone quickly."

D'Artagnan did not move.

"Decidedly you are a pretty fellow," said Athos, pressing the young man's hand.

"Come, come, decide one way or the other," replied Jussac.

"Well," said Porthos to Aramis, "we must do something."

"Monsieur is very generous," said Athos.

But all three reflected upon the youth of D'Artagnan, and dreaded his inexperience.

"We should only be three, one of whom is wounded, with the addition of a boy," resumed Athos, "and yet it will be not the less said we were four men."

"Yes, but to yield !" said Porthos.

"That's rather difficult," replied Athos.

D'Artagnan comprehended whence a part of this irresolution arose.

"Try me, gentlemen," said he, "and I swear to you by my honour that I will not go hence if we are conquered."

"What is your name, my brave fellow ?" said Athos.

"D'Artagnan, monsieur."

"Well, then ! Athos, Porthos, Aramis, and D'Artagnan, forward !" cried Athos.

"Come, gentlemen, have you made your minds up ?" cried Jussac, for the third time.

"It is done, gentlemen," said Athos.

"And what do you mean to do ?" asked Jussac.

"We are about to have the honour of charging you," replied Aramis, lifting his hat with one hand, and drawing his sword with the other.

"Oh ! you resist, do you !" cried Jussac.

"*Sang Dieu !* does that astonish you ?"

And the nine combatants rushed upon each other with a fury which, however, did not exclude a certain degree of method.

Athos fixed upon a certain Cahusac, a favourite of the cardinal's ; Porthos had Bicarat, and Aramis found himself opposed to two adversaries. As to D'Artagnan, he sprang towards Jussac himself.

The heart of the young Gascon beat as if it would burst through his side, not from fear, God be thanked,—he had not the shade of it,—but with emulation ; he fought like a furious tiger, turning ten times round his adversary, and changing his ground and his guard twenty times. Jussac was, as was then said, a fine blade, and had had much practice ; nevertheless, it required all his skill to defend himself against an adversary, who, active and energetic, departed every instant from received rules, attacking him on all sides at once, and yet parrying like a man who had the greatest respect for his own epidermis.

This contest at length exhausted Jussac's patience. Furious at being held in check by him whom he had considered a boy, he became warm, and began to commit faults. D'Artagnan, who, though wanting in practice, had a profound theory, redoubled his agility. Jussac, anxious to put an end to this, springing forward, aimed a terrible thrust at his adversary, but the latter parried it ; and whilst Jussac was recovering himself, glided like a serpent beneath his blade, and passed his sword through his body. Jussac fell like a dead mass.

D'Artagnan then cast an anxious and rapid glance over the field of battle.

Aramis had killed one of his adversaries, but the other pressed him warmly. Nevertheless, Aramis was in a good situation, and able to defend himself.

Bicarat and Porthos had just made counter-hits ; Porthos had received a thrust through his arm, and Bicarat one through his thigh. But neither of the wounds was serious, and they only fought the more earnestly for them.

Athos, wounded again by Cahusac, became evidently paler, but did not give way a foot : he had only changed his sword-hand, and fought with his left hand.

According to the laws of duelling at that period, D'Artagnan was at liberty to assist the one he pleased. Whilst he was endeavouring to find out which of his companions stood in greatest need, he caught a glance from Athos. This glance was of sublime eloquence. Athos would have died rather than appeal for help ; but he could look, and with that look ask assistance. D'Artagnan interpreted it ; with a terrible bound, he sprang to the side of Cahusac, crying :

" To me, monsieur ! guard, or I will slay you !"

Cahusac turned ; it was time, for Athos, whose great courage alone supported him, sank upon his knee.

" *Sang Dieu !*" cried he to D'Artagnan," do not kill him, young man, I beg of you ; I have an old affair to settle with him, when I am cured and sound again. Disarm him only—make sure of his sword ; that's it, that's it ! well done ! very well done !"

This exclamation was drawn from Athos by seeing the sword of Cahusac fly twenty paces from him. D'Artagnan and Cahusac sprang forward at the same instant, the one to recover, the other to obtain the sword ; but D'Artagnan, being the more active, reached it first, and placed his foot upon it.

Cahusac immediately ran to that of one of the guards that Aramis had killed, and returned towards D'Artagnan ; but on his way he met Athos, who, during this relief which D'Artagnan had procured him, had recovered his breath, and who, for fear that D'Artagnan should kill his enemy, wished to resume the fight.

D'Artagnan perceived that it would be disobliging Athos not to leave him alone ; and in a few minutes Cahusac fell, with a sword-thrust through his throat.

At the same instant Aramis placed his sword-point on the breast of his fallen enemy, and compelled him to ask for mercy.

There only then remained Porthos and Bicarat. Porthos made a thousand fanfaronnades, asking Bicarat what o'clock it could be, and offering him his compliments upon his brother's having just obtained a company in the regiment of Navarre ; but, joke as he might, he gained no advantage—Bicarat was one of those iron men who never fall dead.

Nevertheless, it was necessary to put an end to the affair. The watch might come up, and take all the combatants, wounded or not, royalists or cardinalists. Athos, Aramis, and D'Artagnan surrounded Bicarat, and required him to surrender. Though alone against all, and with a wound in his thigh, Bicarat wished to hold out ; but Jussac, who had risen upon his elbow, cried out to him to yield. Bicarat was a Gascon, as D'Artagnan was ; he turned a deaf ear, and contented himself with laughing ; and, between two parries, finding time to point to a spot of earth with his sword, —

" Here," cried he, parodying a verse of the Bible, " here will Bicarat die, the only one of those who are with him !"

" But there are four against you ; leave off, I command you."

" Ah ! if you command me, that's another thing," said Bicarat ; " you being my brigadier, it is my duty to obey."

And, springing backward, he broke his sword across his knee, to avoid the necessity of surrendering it, threw the pieces over the convent wall, and crossed his arms, whistling a cardinalist air.

Bravery is always respected, even in an enemy. The musketeers saluted Bicarat with their swords, and returned them to their sheaths. D'Artagnan did the same ; then, assisted by Bicarat, the only one left standing, he bore Jussac, Cahusac, and that one of Aramis's adversaries who was only wounded, under the porch of the convent. The fourth, as we have said, was dead. They then rang the bell, and, carrying away four swords out of five, they took their road, intoxicated with joy, towards the hotel of M. de Tréville.

They walked arm in arm, occupying the whole width of the street, and accosting every musketeer they met, so that it in the end became a triumphal march. The heart of D'Artagnan swam in delight ; he marched between Athos and Porthos, pressing them tenderly.

" If I am not yet a musketeer," said he to his new friends, as he passed through the gateway of M. de Tréville's hotel, " at least I have entered upon my apprenticeship, haven't I ?"

CHAPTER VI.

HIS MAJESTY KING LOUIS XIII.

THIS affair made a great noise. M. de Tréville scolded his musketeers in public, and congratulated them in private; but as no time was to be lost in gaining the king, M. de Tréville made all haste to the Louvre. But he was too late: the king was closeted with the cardinal, and M. de Tréville was informed that the king was busy, and could not receive him. In the evening, M. de Tréville attended the king's play-table. The king was winning, and, as the king was very avaricious, he was in an excellent humour; thus, perceiving M. de Tréville at a distance—

"Come here, monsieur le capitaine," said he, "come here, that I may scold you. Do you know that his eminence has just been to make fresh complaints against your musketeers, and that with so much emotion, that his eminence is indisposed this evening? Why, these musketeers of yours are very devils!"

"No, sire," replied Tréville, who saw at the first glance which way things would take—"no, sire; on the contrary, they are good creatures, as meek as lambs, and have but one desire, I'll be their warranty; and that is, that their swords may never leave their scabbards but in your majesty's service. But what are they to do? the guards of monsieur the cardinal are for ever seeking quarrels with them, and for the honour of the corps even, the poor young men are obliged to defend themselves."

"Listen to M. de Tréville," said the king, "listen to him! would not one say he was speaking of a religious community! In truth, my dear captain, I have a great mind to take away your commission, and give it to Mademoiselle de Chemerault, to whom I promised an abbey. But don't fancy that I am going to take you on your bare word; I am called Louis the Just, Monsieur de Tréville, and by-and-by, by-and-by, we will see."

"Ah! it is because I have a perfect reliance upon that justice that I shall wait patiently and quietly the good pleasure of your majesty."

"Wait, then, monsieur, wait," said the king; "I will not detain you long."

In fact, fortune changed, and as the king began to lose what he had won, he was not sorry to find an excuse for leaving off. The king then arose a minute after, and putting the money which lay before him into his pocket, the major part of which arose from his winnings—

"La Vieuville," said he, "take my place; I must speak to M. de Tréville on an affair of importance. Ah, I had eighty louis before me; put down the same sum, so that they who have lost may have nothing to complain of—justice before everything." Then turning towards M. de Tréville, and walking with him towards the embrasure of a window—

"Well, monsieur," continued he, "you say it is his eminence's guards who have sought a quarrel with your musketeers?"

"Yes, sire, as they always do."

" And how did the thing happen ? let us see, for you know, my dear captain, a judge must hear both sides."

" Good lord ! in the most simple and natural manner possible. Three of my best soldiers, whom your majesty knows by name, and whose devotedness you have more than once appreciated, and who have, I dare affirm to the king, his service much at heart ; three of my best soldiers, I say—MM. Athos, Porthos, and Aramis—had made a party of pleasure with a young cadet from Gascony, whom I had introduced to them the same morning. The party was to take place at St. Germain, I believe, and they had appointed to meet at the Carmes-Deschaux, when they were disturbed by M. de Jussac, MM. Cahusac, Bicarat, and two other guards, who certainly did not go there in such a numerous company without some ill intention against the edicts."

" Ah, ah ! you incline me to think so," said the king : " there is no doubt they went thither to fight themselves."

" I do not accuse them, sire ; but I leave your majesty to judge what five armed men could possibly be going to do in such a retired spot as the environs of the Convent des Carmes."

" You are right, Tréville—you are right !"

" Then, upon seeing my musketeers, they changed their minds, and forgot their private hatred for the hatred *de corps ;* for your majesty cannot be ignorant that the musketeers, who belong to the king, and to nobody but the king, are the natural enemies of the guards, who belong to the cardinal."

" Yes, Tréville, yes !" said the king, in a melancholy tone ; " and it is very sad, believe me, to see thus two parties in France, two heads to royalty. But all this will come to an end, Tréville, will come to an end. You say, then, that the guards sought a quarrel with the musketeers ?"

" I say that it is probable that things have fallen out so, but I will not swear to it, sire. You know how difficult it is to discover the truth ; and unless a man be endowed with that admirable instinct which causes Louis XIII. to be termed the Just——"

" You are right, Tréville ; but they were not alone, your musketeers —they had a youth with them ?"

" Yes, sire, and one wounded man ; so that three of the king's musketeers—one of whom was wounded, and a youth—not only maintained their ground against five of the most terrible of his eminence's guards, but absolutely brought four of them to the earth."

" Why, this is a victory !" cried the king, glowing with delight, " a complete victory !"

" Yes, sire ; as complete as that of the bridge of Cè."

" Four men, one of them wounded, and a youth, say you ?"

" One scarcely attained the age of a young man ; but who, however, behaved himself so admirably on this occasion, that I will take the liberty of recommending him to your majesty."

" What is his name ?"

" D'Artagnan, sire ; he is the son of one of my oldest friends—the son of a man who served under your father of glorious memory, in the partisan war."

"And you say that this young man behaved himself well? Tell me how, De Tréville—you know how I delight in accounts of war and fights."

And Louis XIII. twisted his moustache proudly, placing his hand upon his hip.

"Sire," resumed Tréville, "as I told you, M. d'Artagnan is little more than a boy, and as he has not the honour of being a musketeer, he was dressed as a private citizen; the guards of M. the Cardinal, perceiving his youth, and still more that he did not belong to the corps, pressed him to retire before they attacked."

"So you may plainly see, Tréville," interrupted the king, "it was they who attacked?"

"That is true, sire; there can be no more doubt on that head. They called upon him then to retire, but he answered that he was a musketeer at heart, entirely devoted to your majesty, and that he would therefore remain with messieurs the musketeers."

"Brave young man!" murmured the king.

"Well, he did remain with them; and your majesty has in him so firm a champion, that it was he who gave Jussac the terrible sword-thrust which has made M. the Cardinal so angry."

"He who wounded Jussac!" cried the king—"he, a boy! Tréville, that's impossible!"

"It is as I have the honour to relate it to your majesty."

"Jussac, one of the first swordsmen in the kingdom?"

"Well, sire, for once he found his master."

"I should like to see this young man, Tréville—I should like to see him; and if anything can be done—well, we will make it our business."

"When will your majesty deign to receive him?"

"To-morrow, at mid-day, Tréville."

"Shall I bring him alone?"

"No; bring me all four together; I wish to thank them all at once. Devoted men are so rare, Tréville, we must recompense devotedness."

"At twelve o'clock, sire, we will be at the Louvre."

"Ah! by the back staircase, Tréville, by the back staircase; it is useless to let the cardinal know."

"Yes, sire."

"You understand Tréville; an edict is still an edict—it is forbidden to fight, after all."

"But this encounter, sire, is quite out of the ordinary conditions of a duel; it is a brawl, and the proof is that there were five of the cardinal's guards against my three musketeers and M. d'Artagnan."

"That is true," said the king; "but never mind, Tréville, come still by the back staircase."

Tréville smiled. But as it was already something to have prevailed upon this child to rebel against his master, he saluted the king respectfully, and, with this agreement, took leave of him.

That evening the three musketeers were informed of the honour which was granted them. As they had long been acquainted with the king, they were not much excited by the circumstance; but D'Artagnan, with his Gascon imagination, saw in it his future fortune, and passed the night in golden dreams. As early, then, as eight o'clock he was at the apartment of Athos.

D'Artagnan found the musketeer dressed and ready to go out. As the hour to wait upon the king was not till twelve, he had made a party with Porthos and Aramis to play a game at tennis, in a tennis-court situated near the stables of the Luxembourg. Athos invited D'Artagnan to follow them; and, although ignorant of the game, which he had never played, he accepted the invitation, not knowing what to do with his time from nine o'clock in the morning, as it then scarcely was, till twelve.

The two musketeers were already there, and were playing together. Athos, who was very expert in all bodily exercises, passed with D'Artagnan to the opposite side, and challenged them; but at the first effort he made, although he played with his left hand, he found that his wound was yet too recent to allow of such exertion. D'Artagnan remained, therefore, alone; and as he declared he was too ignorant of the game to play it regularly, they only continued giving balls to each other, without counting; but one of these balls, launched by Porthos' Herculean hand, passed so close to D'Artagnan's face, that he thought if, instead of passing near, it had hit him, his audience would have been probably lost, as it would have been impossible for him to have presented himself before the king. Now, as upon this audience, in his Gascon imagination, depended his future life, he saluted Aramis and Porthos politely, declaring that he would not resume the game until he should be prepared to play with them on more equal terms; and he went and took his place near the cord and in the gallery.

Unfortunately for D'Artagnan, among the spectators was one of his eminence's guards, who, still irritated by the defeat of his companions, which had happened only the day before, had promised himself to seize the first opportunity of avenging it. He believed this opportunity was now come, and addressing his neighbour,—

"It is not astonishing," said he, "that that young man should be afraid of a ball; he is doubtless a musketeer apprentice."

D'Artagnan turned round as if a serpent had stung him, and fixed his eyes intensely upon the guard who had just made this insolent speech.

"*Pardieu!*" resumed the latter, twisting his moustache, "look at me as long as you like, my little gentleman, I have said what I have said."

"And as since that which you have said is too clear to require any explanation," replied D'Artagnan, in a low voice, "I beg you will follow me."

"And when?" asked the guard, with the same jeering air.

"Immediately, if you please."

"And you know who I am, without doubt?"

" I ! no, I assure you I am completely ignorant ; nor does it much concern me."

" You're in the wrong there ; for if you knew my name, perhaps you would not be in such a hurry."

" What is your name, then ?"

" Bernajoux, at your service."

" Well, then, Monsieur Bernajoux," said D'Artagnan, quietly, " I will wait for you at the door."

" Go on, monsieur, I will follow you."

" Do not appear to be in a hurry, monsieur, so as to cause it to be observed that we go out together ; you must be aware that for that which we have in hand company would be inconvenient."

" That's true," said the guard, astonished that his name had not produced more effect upon the young man.

In fact, the name of Bernajoux was known to everybody, D'Artagnan alone excepted, perhaps ; for it was one of those which figured most frequently in the daily brawls, which all the edicts of the cardinal had not been able to repress.

Porthos and Aramis were so engaged with their game, and Athos was watching them with so much attention, that they did not even perceive their young companion go out, who, as he had told his eminence's guard he would, stopped outside the door ; an instant after, the guard descended. As D'Artagnan had no time to lose, on account of the audience of the king, which was fixed for mid-day, he cast his eyes around, and seeing that the street was empty,—

" *Ma foi !*" said he to his adversary, "it is fortunate for you, although your name is Bernajoux, to have only to deal with an apprentice musketeer ; never mind, be content, I will do my best.—Guard !"

" But," said he whom D'Artagnan thus provoked, " it appears to me that this place is very ill-chosen, and that we should be better behind the Abbey St. Germain or in the Pré-aux-Clercs."

" What you say is very sensible," replied D'Artagnan ; " but unfortunately, I have very little time to spare, having an appointment at twelve precisely. Guard ! then, monsieur, guard !"

Bernajoux was not a man to have such a compliment paid to him twice. In an instant his sword glittered in his hand, and he sprang upon his adversary, whom, from his youth, he hoped to intimidate.

But D'Artagnan had on the preceding day gone through his apprenticeship. Fresh sharpened by his victory, full of the hopes of future favour, he was resolved not to give back a step ; so the two swords were crossed close to the hilts, and as D'Artagnan stood firm, it was his adversary who made the retreating step ; but D'Artagnan seized the moment at which, in this movement, the sword of Bernajoux deviated from the line ; he freed his weapon, made a lunge, and touched his adversary on the shoulder. D'Artagnan immediately made a step backwards and raised his sword ; but Bernajoux cried out that it was nothing, and rushing blindly upon him, absolutely spitted himself upon D'Artagnan's sword. As, however, he did not fall, as he did not declare himself conquered, but only broke away towards the hotel of M. de Trémouille, in whose service he had a relation, D'Artagnan was ignorant of the seriousness of the last wound his adversary had received, pressed him warmly, and without doubt would soon have completed his work with a third blow, when the noise which arose from the street being heard in the tennis-court, two of the friends of the guard, who had seen him go out after exchanging some words with D'Artagnan, rushed, sword in hand, from the court, and fell upon the conqueror. But Athos, Porthos, and Aramis quickly appeared in their turn, and the moment the two guards attacked their young companion, drove them back. Bernajoux now fell, and as the guards were only two against four, they began to cry, " To the rescue ! the hotel de Trémouille !" At these cries, all who were in the hotel rushed out, falling upon the four companions, who, on their side, cried aloud, " To the rescue ! musketeers !"

This cry was generally attended to ; for the musketeers were known to be enemies to the Cardinal, and were beloved on account of the hatred they bore to his enemies. Thus the guards of other companies than those which belonged to the Red Duke, as Aramis had called him, in general, in these quarrels took part with the king's musketeers. Of three guards of the company of M. Dessessart, who were passing, two came to the assistance of the four companions, whilst the other ran towards the hotel of M. de Tréville, crying :—" To the rescue ! musketeers ! to the rescue !" As usual, this hotel was full of soldiers of this corps who hastened to the succour of their comrades ; the *mêlée* became, general, but strength was on the side of the musketeers ; the Cardinal's guards and M. de la Trémouille's people retreated into the hotel, the doors of which they closed just in time to prevent their enemies from entering with them. As to the wounded man, he had been taken in at once, and, as we have said, in a very bad state.

Excitement was at its height among the musketeers and their allies, and they even began to deliberate whether they should not set fire to the hotel to punish the insolence of M. de la Trémouille's domestics, in daring to make a *sortie* upon the king's musketeers. The proposition had been made, and received with enthusiasm, when fortunately eleven o'clock struck ; D'Artagnan and his companions remembered their audience, and as they would very much have regretted that such a feat should be performed without them, they succeeded in quieting their coadjutors. The latter contented themselves with hurling some paving stones against the gates, but the gates were too strong ; they then grew tired of the sport ; besides, those who must be considered as the leaders of the enterprise had quitted the group and were making their way towards the hotel of M. de Tréville, who was waiting for them, already informed of this fresh disturbance.

" Quick, to the Louvre," said he, " to the Louvre without losing an instant, and let us endeavour to see the king before he is prejudiced by the Cardinal : we will describe the thing to him as a consequence of the affair of yesterday, and the two will pass off together."

M. de Tréville, accompanied by his four young men, directed his course towards the Louvre ; but to the great astonishment of the captain of the musketeers, he was informed that the king was gone stag-hunting in the forest of St. Germain. M. de Tréville required this intelligence to be repeated to him twice, and each time his companions saw his brow become darker.

" Had his majesty," asked he, " any intention of holding this hunting party yesterday ?"

" No, your excellency," replied the valet de chambre, " the grand veneur came this morning to inform him that he had marked down a stag. He, at first, answered that he would not go, but could not resist his love of sport, and set out after dinner."

" Has the king seen the Cardinal ?" asked M. de Tréville.

" Most probably he has," replied the valet de chambre, " for I saw the horses harnessed to his eminence's carriage this morning, and when I asked where he was going, I was told to St. Germain."

" He is beforehand with us," said M. de Tréville. " Gentlemen, I will see the king this evening ; but as to you, I do not advise you to risk doing so."

This advice was too reasonable, and, moreover, came from a man who knew the king too well, to allow the four young men to dispute it. M. de Tréville recommended them each to retire to his apartment, and wait for news from him.

On entering his hotel, M. de Tréville thought it best to be first in making the complaint. He sent one of his servants to M. de la Trémouille with a letter, in which he begged of him to eject the Cardinal's guard from his house, and to reprimand his people for their audacity in making *sortie* against the king's musketeers. But M. de la Trémouille, already prejudiced by his esquire, whose relation, as we already know, Bernajoux was, replied that it was neither for M. de Tréville nor the musketeers to complain, but on the contrary, he, whose people the musketeers had assaulted and whose hotel they had endeavoured to burn. Now, as the debate between these two nobles might last a long time, each becoming, naturally, more firm in his own opinion, M. de Tréville thought of an expedient, which might terminate it quietly ; which was to go himself to M. de la Trémouille.

He repaired, then, immediately to his hotel, and caused himself to be announced.

The two nobles saluted each other politely, for if no friendship existed between them, there was at least esteem. Both were men of courage and honour ; and as M. de la Trémouille, a protestant, and seeing the king seldom, was of no party, he did not, in general, carry any bias into his social relations. This time, however, his address, although polite, was colder than usual.

" Monsieur !" said M. de Tréville, " we fancy that we have each cause to complain of the other, and I am come to endeavour to clear up this affair."

" I have no objection," replied M. de la Trémouille, " but I warn you that I have inquired well into it, and all the fault lies with your musketeers."

" You are too just and reasonable a man, monsieur!" said De Tréville, " not to accept the proposal I am about to make to you."

" Make it, monsieur.   I am attentive."

" How is M. Bernajoux, your esquire's relation ?"

" Why, monsieur, very ill, indeed !   In addition to the sword-thrust in his arm, which is not dangerous, he has received another right through his lungs, of which the doctor speaks very unfavourably."

" But is the wounded man sensible ?"

" Perfectly."

" Can he speak ?"

" With difficulty, but he can speak."

" Well, monsieur, let us go to him ; let us adjure him, in the name of the God before whom he is called upon, perhaps quickly, to appear, to speak the truth.   I will take him for judge in his own cause, monsieur, and will believe what he will say."

M. de la Trémouille reflected for an instant, then, as it was difficult to make a more reasonable proposal, agreed to it.

Both descended to the chamber in which the wounded man lay. The latter, on seeing these two noble lords who came to visit him, endeavoured to raise himself up in his bed, but he was too weak, and, exhausted by the effort, he fell back again almost insensible.

M. de la Trémouille approached him, and made him respire some salts, which recalled him to life.   Then M. de Tréville, unwilling that it should be thought that he had influenced the wounded man, requested M. de la Trémouille to interrogate him himself.

That which M. de Tréville had foreseen, happened.   Placed between life and death, as Bernajoux was, he had no idea for a moment of concealing the truth ; and he described to the two nobles the affair exactly as it had passed.

This was all that M. de Tréville wanted ; he wished Bernajoux a speedy recovery, took leave of M. de la Trémouille, returned to his hotel, and immediately sent word to the four friends that he awaited their company to dinner.

M. de Tréville received very good company, quite anti-cardinalist, though.   It may easily be understood, therefore, that the conversation, during the whole of dinner, turned upon the two checks that his eminence's guards had received.   Now, as D'Artagnan had been the hero of these two fights, it was upon him that all the felicitations fell, which Athos, Porthos, and Aramis abandoned to him ; not only as good comrades, but as men who had so often had their turn, that they could very well afford him his.

Towards six o'clock, M. de Tréville announced that it was time to go to the Louvre ; but as the hour of audience granted by his majesty was past, instead of claiming the *entrée* by the back-stairs, he placed himself with the four young men in the antechamber.   The king was not yet returned from hunting.   Our young men had been waiting about half an hour, mingled with the crowd of courtiers, when all the doors were thrown open, and his majesty was announced.

At this announcement, D'Artagnan felt himself tremble to the very marrow of his bones. The instant which was about to follow would, in all probability, decide his future life. His eyes, therefore, were fixed in a sort of agony upon the door through which the king would pass.

Louis XIII. appeared, walking fast; he was in hunting costume covered with dust, wearing large boots, and had a whip in his hand. At the first glance, D'Artagnan judged that the mind of the king was stormy.

This disposition, visible as it was in his majesty, did not prevent the courtiers from ranging themselves upon his passage. In royal ante-chambers, it is better to be looked upon with an angry eye, than not to be looked upon at all. The three musketeers, therefore, did not hesitate to make a step forward; D'Artagnan, on the contrary, remained concealed behind them ; but although the king knew Athos, Porthos, and Aramis personally, he passed before them without speaking or look-ing,—indeed, as if he had never seen them before. As for M. de Tréville, when the eyes of the king fell upon him, he sustained the look with so much firmness, that it was the king who turned aside ; after which his majesty, grumbling, entered his apartment.

"Matters go but badly," said Athos, smiling ; "and we shall not be made knights of the order this time."

"Wait here ten minutes," said M. de Tréville ; "and if, at the ex-piration of ten minutes, you do not see me come out, return to my hotel, for it will be useless for you to wait for me longer."

The four young men waited ten minutes, a quarter of an hour, twenty minutes ; and, seeing that M. de Tréville did not return, went away very uneasy as to what was going to happen.

M. de Tréville entered the king's closet boldly, and found his ma-jesty in a very ill humour, seated on a *fauteuil*, beating his boot with the handle of his whip ; which, however, did not prevent his asking, with the greatest coolness, after his majesty's health.

"Bad ! monsieur,—bad ! *je m'ennuie !*" (I grow weary.)

This was, in fact, the worst complaint of Louis XIII., who would sometimes take one of his courtiers to a window, and say, " Monsieur So-and-so, *ennuyons-nous ensemble.*" (Let us weary one another.)

"How ! your majesty is becoming dull ! Have you not enjoyed the pleasures of the chase to-day ?"

"A fine pleasure, indeed, monsieur ! Upon my soul, everything de-generates ; and I don't know whether it is the game leaves no scent, or the dogs that have no noses. We started a stag of ten-tine ; we chased him for six hours, and when he was near being taken—when St. Simon was already putting his horn to his mouth to sound the *halali*—crack, all the pack takes the wrong scent, and sets off after a two-tine. I shall be obliged to give up hunting, as I have given up hawking. Ah ! I am an unfortunate king, Monsieur de Tréville ! I had but one gerfalcon, and he died the day before yesterday."

" Indeed, sire, I enter into your annoyance perfectly ; the misfortune is great ; but I think you have still a good number of falcons, sparrow-hawks, and tiercets."

" And not a man to instruct them. Falconers are declining ; I know no one but myself who is acquainted with the noble art of venery. After me it will be all over, and people will hunt with gins, snares, and traps. If I had but the time to form pupils ! but there is M. le Cardinal always at hand, who does not leave me a moment's repose ; who talks to me perpetually about Spain, about Austria, about England ! Ah ! *à propos* of M. le Cardinal, Monsieur de Tréville, I am vexed with you."

This was the place at which M. de Tréville waited for the king. He knew the king of old, and he knew that all these complaints were but a preface—a sort of excitation to encourage himself—and that he had now come to his point at last.

"And in what have I been so unfortunate as to displease your majesty?" asked M. de Tréville, feigning the most profound astonishment.

" Is it thus you perform your charge, monsieur ?" continued the king, without directly replying to De Tréville's question ; " is it for this I name you captain of my musketeers, that they should assassinate a man, disturb a whole quarter, and endeavour to set fire to Paris, without your saying a word ? But yet," continued the king, " without doubt, my haste accuses you wrongfully ; without doubt the rioters are in prison, and you come to tell me justice is done."

" Sire," replied M. de Tréville, calmly, " I come to demand it of you."

" And against whom, pray ?" cried the king.

" Against calumniators," said M. de Tréville.

" Ah ! this is something new," replied the king. " Will you tell me that your three damned musketeers, Athos, Porthos, and Aramis, and your cadet from Béarn, have not fallen, like so many furies, upon poor Bernajoux, and have not maltreated him in such a fashion that probably by this time he is dead ? Will you tell me that they did not lay siege to the hotel of the Duc de la Trémouille, and that they did not endeavour to burn it ?—which would not, perhaps, have been a great misfortune in time of war, seeing that it is nothing but a nest of Huguenots ; but which is, in time of peace, a frightful example. Tell me, now—can you deny all this ?"

" And who has told you this fine story, sire?" asked De Tréville, quietly.

" Who has told me this fine story, monsieur ? Who should it be but him who watches whilst I sleep, who labours whilst I amuse myself, who conducts everything at home and abroad—in Europe as well as in France ?"

" Your majesty must speak of God, without doubt," said M. de Tréville ; " for I know no one but God that can be so far above your majesty."

" No, monsieur ; I speak of the prop of the state—of my only servant—of my only friend—of M. le Cardinal."

"His eminence is not his holiness, sire."

"What do you mean by that, monsieur?"

"That it is only the Pope that is infallible, and that this infallibility does not extend to the cardinals."

"You mean to say that he deceives me—you mean to say that he betrays me? You accuse him, then? Come, speak—confess freely that you accuse him!"

"No, sire; but I say that he deceives himself; I say that he is ill-informed; I say that he has hastily accused your majesty's musketeers, towards whom he is unjust, and that he has not obtained his information from good sources."

"The accusation comes from M. de la Trémouille,—from the duke himself. What do you answer to that?"

"I might answer, sire, that he is too deeply interested in the question to be a very impartial evidence; but so far from that, sire ' know the duke to be a loyal gentleman, and I refer the matter to him,—but upon one condition, sire."

"What is that?"

"It is, that your majesty will make him come here, will interrogate him yourself, *tête-à-tête*, without witnesses, and that I shall see your majesty as soon as you have seen the duke."

"What then! and you will be bound," cried the king, "by what M. de la Trémouille shall say?"

"Yes, sire."

"You will abide by his judgment?"

"Doubtless, I will."

"And you will submit to the reparation he may require?"

"Certainly."

"La Chesnaye!" cried the king; "La Chesnaye!"

Louis XIII.'s confidential valet de chambre, who never left the door, entered in reply to the call.

"La Chesnaye," said the king, "let some one go instantly and find M. de la Trémouille; I wish to speak with him this evening."

"Your majesty gives me your word that you will not see any one between M. de la Trémouille and me?"

"Nobody—by the word of a gentleman."

"To-morrow then, sire?"

"To-morrow, monsieur."

"At what o'clock, please your majesty?"

"At whatsoever time you like."

"But I should be afraid of awakening your majesty, if I came too early."

"Awaken me! Do you think I ever sleep, then? I sleep no longer, monsieur. I sometimes dream, that's all. Come, then, as early as you like—at seven o'clock: but beware, if you and your musketeers are guilty."

"If my musketeers are guilty, sire, the guilty shall be placed in your majesty's hands, who will dispose of them at your good pleasure.

Does your majesty require anything further? Speak, I am ready to obey."

"No, monsieur, no ; I am not called Louis the Just without reason. To-morrow, then, monsieur,—to-morrow."

"Till, then, God preserve your majesty."

However ill the king might sleep, M. de Tréville slept still worse ; he had ordered his three musketeers and their companion to be with him at half-past six in the morning. He took them with him, without encouraging them or promising them anything, and without concealing from them that their favour, and even his own, depended upon this cast of the dice.

When arrived at the bottom of the back-stairs, he desired them to wait. If the king was still irritated against them, they would depart without being seen ; if the king consented to see them, they would only have to be called.

On arriving at the king's private antechamber, M. de Tréville found La Chesnaye, who informed him that they had not been able to find M. de la Trémouille on the preceding evening at his hotel, that he came in too late to present himself at the Louvre, that he had only that moment arrived, and that he was then with the king.

This circumstance pleased M. de Tréville much, as he thus became certain that no foreign suggestion could insinuate itself between M. de la Trémouille's deposition and himself.

In fact, ten minutes had scarcely passed away, when the door of the king's closet opened, and M. de Tréville saw M. de la Trémouille come out ; the duke came straight up to him, and said :

" M. de Tréville, his majesty has just sent for me in order to inquire respecting the circumstances which took place yesterday at my hotel. I have told him the truth, that is to say, that the fault lay with my people, and that I was ready to offer you my excuses. Since I have the good fortune to meet you, I beg you to receive them, and to consider me always as one of your friends."

"Monsieur le Duc," said M. de Tréville, " I was confident of your loyalty, that I required no other defender before his majesty than yourself. I find that I have not been mistaken, and I am gratified to think that there is still one man in France of whom may be said, without disappointment, what I have said of you."

" That's well said," said the king, who had heard all these compliments through the open door ; " only tell him, Tréville, since he wishes to be considered as your friend, that I also wish to be one of his, but he neglects me ; that it is nearly three years since I have seen him, and that I never do see him unless I send for him. Tell him all this for me, for these are things which a king cannot say himself."

" Thanks, sire, thanks," said M. de la Trémouille ; " but your majesty may be assured that it is not those—I do not speak of M. de Tréville— that it is not those whom your majesty sees at all hours of the day that are the most devoted to you."

"Ah ! you heard what I said? so much the better, duke, so much the better," said the king, advancing towards the door. "Ah ! that's you, Tréville. Where are your musketeers ? I told you the day before yesterday to bring them with you, why have you not done so ?"

" They are below, sire, and with your permission La Chesnaye will tell them to come up."

" Yes, yes, let them come up immediately ; it is nearly eight o'clock, and at nine I expect a visit. Go, monsieur le duc, and return often. Come in, Tréville."

The duke bowed and retired. At the moment he opened the door, the three musketeers and D'Artagnan, conducted by La Chesnaye, appeared at the top of the staircase.

" Come in, my braves," said the king, " come in ; I am going to scold you."

The musketeers advanced, bowing, D'Artagnan following closely behind them.

" How the devil !" continued the king, " seven of his eminence's guards placed *hors de combat* by you four in two days ! That's too many, gentlemen, too many ! If you go on so, his eminence will be forced to renew his company in three weeks, and I to put the edicts in force in all their rigour. One, now and then, I don't say much about ; but seven in two days, I repeat, it is too many, it is far too many !"

" Therefore, sire, your majesty sees that they are come quite contrite and repentant to offer you their excuses."

" Quite contrite and repentant ! Hem !" said the king, " I place no confidence in their hypocritical faces ; in particular, there is one yonder of a Gascon look. Come hither, monsieur."

D'Artagnan, who understood that it was to him this compliment was addressed, approached, assuming a most deprecating air.

" Why, you told me he was a young man ? This is a boy, Tréville, a mere boy ! Do you mean to say that it was he who bestowed that severe thrust upon Jussac ? And those two equally fine thrusts upon Bernajoux ?"

" Truly !"

" Without reckoning," said Athos, " that if he had not rescued me from the hands of Cahusac, I should not now have the honour of making my very humble reverences to your majesty."

" Why this Béarnais is a very devil ! Ventre-saint-gris ! Monsieur de Tréville, as the king my father would have said. But at this sort of work, many doublets must be slashed and many swords broken. Now Gascons are always poor, are they not ?"

" Sire, I can assert that they have hitherto discovered no gold mines in their mountains ; though the Lord owes them this miracle in recompense of the manner in which they supported the pretensions of the king, your father."

" Which is to say, that the Gascons made a king of me, myself, seeing that I am my father's son, is it not, Tréville ? Well, in good faith, I don't say nay to it. La Chesnaye, go and see if, by rummaging all my pockets, you can find forty pistoles ; and if you can find them, bring them to me. And now, let us see, young man, with your hand upon your conscience, how did all this come to pass ?"

D'Artagnan related the adventure of the preceding day in all its details : how, not having been able to sleep for the joy he felt in the expectation of seeing his majesty, he had gone to his three friends three hours before the hour of audience ; how they had gone together to the fives-court, and how, upon the fear he had manifested of receiving a ball in the face, he had been jeered at by Bernajoux, who had nearly paid for his jeer with his life, and M. de la Trémouille, who had nothing to do with the matter, with the loss of his hotel.

"This is all very well," murmured the king ; "yes, this is just the account the duke gave me of the affair. Poor cardinal ! seven men in two days, and those of his very best ! but that's quite enough, gentlemen ; please to understand, that's enough : you have taken your revenge, for the Rue Ferou, and even exceeded it ; you ought to be satisfied."

"If your majesty is so," said Tréville, "we are."

"Oh, yes, I am," added the king, taking a handful of gold from La Chesnaye, and putting it into the hand of D'Artagnan. "Here," said he, "is a proof of my satisfaction."

At this period, the ideas of pride which are in fashion in our days, did not yet prevail. A gentleman received, from hand to hand, money from the king, and was not the least in the world humiliated. D'Artagnan put his forty pistoles into his pocket without any scruple ; on the contrary, thanking his majesty greatly.

"There," said the king, looking at a clock, "there, now, as it is half-past eight, you may retire ; for, as I told you, I expect some one at nine. Thanks for your devotedness, gentlemen. I may continue to rely upon it, may I not ?"

"Oh, sir !" cried the four companions, with one voice, "we would allow ourselves to be cut to pieces in your majesty's service !"

"Well, well, but keep whole : that will be better, and you will be more useful to me. Tréville," added the king, in a low voice, as the others were retiring, "as you have no room in the musketeers, and as we have besides decided that a noviciate is necessary before entering that corps, place this young man in the company of the guards of M. Dessessart, your brother-in-law. Ah! Pardieu ! I enjoy beforehand the face the cardinal will make ; he will be furious ! but I don't care ; I am doing what is right."

And the king waved his hand to Tréville, who left him and rejoined the musketeers, whom he found sharing the forty pistoles with D'Artagnan.

And the cardinal, as his majesty had said, was really furious, so furious that during eight days he absented himself from the king's play-table, which did not prevent the king from being as complacent to him as possible, or whenever he met him from asking in the kindest tone :

"Well, monsieur the cardinal, how fares it with that poor Jussac, and that poor Bernajoux of yours ?"

CHAPTER VII.

THE INTERIOR OF "THE MUSKETEERS."

WHEN D'Artagnan was out of the Louvre, and consulted his friends upon the use he had best make of his share of the forty pistoles, Athos advised him to order a good repast at the Pomme-de-Pin, Porthos to engage a lackey, and Aramis to provide himself with a suitable mistress.

The repast was carried into effect that very day, and the lackey waited at table. The repast had been ordered by Athos, and the lackey furnished by Porthos. He was a Picard, whom the glorious musketeer had picked up on the bridge De la Tournelle, making his rounds and spitting in the water.

Porthos pretended that this occupation was a proof of a reflective and contemplative organisation, and he had brought him away without any other recommendation. The noble carriage of this gentleman, on whose account he believed himself to be engaged, had seduced Planchet —that was the name of the Picard :—he felt a slight disappointment, however, when he saw that the place was already taken by a compeer named Mousqueton, and when Porthos signified to him that the state of his household, though great, would not support two servants, and that he must enter into the service of D'Artagnan. Nevertheless, when he waited at the dinner given by his master, and saw him take out a handful of gold to pay for it, he believed his fortune made, and returned thanks to Heaven for having thrown him into the service of such a Crœsus ; he preserved this opinion even after the feast, with the remnants of which he repaired his long abstinences. But when in the evening he made his master's bed, the chimæras of Planchet faded away. The bed was the only one in the apartments, which consisted of an antechamber and a bedroom. Planchet slept in the antechamber upon a coverlet taken from the bed of D'Artagnan, and which D'Artagnan from that time made shift without.

Athos, on his part, had a valet whom he had trained in his service in a perfectly peculiar fashion, and who was named Grimaud. He was very taciturn, this worthy signor. Be it understood we are speaking of Athos. During the five or six years that he had lived in the strictest intimacy with his companions, Porthos and Aramis, they could remember having often seen him smile, but had never heard him laugh. His words were brief and expressive—conveying all that was meant— and no more : no embellishments, no embroidery, no arabesques. His conversation was a fact without any episodes.

Although Althos was scarcely thirty years old, and was of great personal beauty, and intelligence of mind, no one knew that he had ever had a mistress. He never spoke of women. He certainly did not prevent others from speaking of them before him, although it was easy to perceive that this kind of conversation, in which he only mingled by bitter words and misanthropic remarks, was perfectly disagreeable to him. His reserve, his roughness, and his silence made almost an old man of him ; he had then, in order not to disturb his habits, accustomed

Grimaud to obey him upon a simple gesture, or upon the mere movement of his lips.   He never spoke to him but upon most extraordinary occasions.

Sometimes Grimaud, who feared his master as he did fire, whilst entertaining a strong attachment to his person, and a great veneration for his talents, believed he perfectly understood what he wanted, flew to execute the order received, and did precisely the contrary.   Athos then shrugged his shoulders, and without putting himself in a passion, gave Grimaud a good thrashing.   On these days he spoke a little.

Porthos, as we have seen, was of a character, exactly opposite to that of Athos : he not only talked much, but he talked loudly ; little caring, we must render him that justice, whether anybody listened to him or not ; he talked for the pleasure of talking, and for the pleasure of hearing himself talk ; he spoke upon all subjects except the sciences, alleging in this respect, the inveterate hatred he had borne to the learned from his childhood.   He had not so noble an air as Athos, and the consciousness of his inferiority in this respect had, at the commencement of their intimacy, often rendered him unjust towards that gentleman, whom he endeavoured to eclipse by his splendid dress.   But with his simple musketeer's uniform and nothing but the manner in which he threw back his head and advanced his foot, Athos instantly took the place which was his due, and consigned the ostentatious Porthos to the second rank.   Porthos consoled himself by filling the antechamber of M. de Tréville and the guard-room of the Louvre with the accounts of his *bonnes fortunes*, of which Athos never spoke, and at the present moment, after having passed from the noblesse of the robe to the noblesse of the sword, from the lawyer's dame to the baroness, there was question of nothing less with Porthos than a foreign princess, who was enormously fond of him.

An old proverb says, " Like master like man." Let us pass then from the valet of Athos to the valet of Porthos, from Grimaud to Mousqueton.

Mousqueton was a Norman, whose pacific name of Boniface his master had changed into the infinitely more sonorous one of Mousqueton. He had entered Porthos's service upon condition that he should only be clothed and lodged, but in a handsome manner ; he claimed but two hours a day to himself, to consecrate to an employment which would provide for his other wants.   Porthos agreed to the bargain ; the thing suited him wonderfully well.   He had doublets for Mousqueton cut out of his old clothes and cast-off cloaks, and thanks to a very intelligent tailor, who made his clothes look as good as new by turning them, and whose wife was suspected of wishing to make Porthos descend from his aristocratic habits, Mousqueton made a very good figure when attending on his master.

As for Aramis, of whom we believe we have sufficiently explained the character, a character besides which, like that of his companions, we shall be able to follow in its development, his lackey was called Bazin. Thanks to the hopes which his master entertained of some day entering into orders, he was always clothed in black, as became the servant of a churchman. This was a Berrichon of from thirty-five to forty years of age, mild, peaceable, sleek, employing the leisure his master left him in the perusal of pious works, providing rigorously for two, a dinner of few dishes, but excellent. For the rest, he was dumb, blind, and deaf, and of unimpeachable fidelity.

And now that we are acquainted, superficially at least, with the masters and the valets, let us pass on to the dwellings occupied by each of them.

Athos dwelt in the Rue Férou, within two steps of the Luxembourg : his apartments consisted of two small chambers, very nicely fitted up, in a furnished house, the hostess of which, still young, and still really handsome, cast tender glances uselessly at him. Some fragments of great past splendour appeared here and there upon the walls of this modest lodging ; a sword, for example, richly damascened, which belonged by its make to the times of Francis I., the hilt of which alone, incrusted with precious stones, might be worth two hundred pistoles, and which, nevertheless, in his moments of greatest distress, Athos had never pledged or offered for sale. This sword had long been an object of ambition for Porthos. Porthos would have given ten years of his life to possess this sword.

One day, when he had an appointment with a duchess, he endeavoured even to borrow it of Athos. Athos, without saying anything, emptied his pockets, got together all his jewels, purses, aiguillettes, and gold chains, and offered them all to Porthos ; but as to the sword, he said, it was sealed to its place, and should never quit it, until its master should himself quit his lodgings. In addition to the sword there was a portrait representing a nobleman of the time of Henry III., dressed with the greatest elegance, and who wore the order of the Holy Ghost ; and this portrait had with Athos certain resemblances of lines, certain family likenesses, which indicated that this great noble, a knight of the orders of the king, was his ancestor.

Besides these, a casket of magnificent goldsmith's work, with the same arms as the sword and the portrait, formed a middle ornament to the mantel-piece, which assorted badly with the rest of the furniture. Athos always carried the key of this coffer about him, but he one day opened it before Porthos, and Porthos was convinced that this coffer contained nothing but letters and papers,—love letters and family papers, no doubt.

Porthos lived in apartments, large in size, and of a very sumptuous appearance, in the Rue du Vieux-Colombier. Every time he passed with a friend before his windows, at one of which Mousqueton was sure to be placed in full livery, Porthos raised his head and his hand, and said, "*That is my abode !*" But he was never to be found at home, he never invited anybody to go up with him, and no one could form an idea of what these sumptuous apartments contained in the shape of real riches.

As to Aramis, he dwelt in a little lodging composed of a boudoir, an eating-room, and a bed-room, which room, situate, as the others were, on the ground-floor, looked out upon a little, fresh, green garden, shady and impenetrable to the eyes of his neighbours.

With regard to D'Artagnan, we know how he was lodged, and we have already made acquaintance with his lackey, Master Planchet.

D'Artagnan, who was by nature very curious, as people generally are who possess the genius of intrigue, did all he could to make out who Athos, Porthos, and Aramis really were ; for under these *noms de guerre*, each of these young men concealed his family name. Athos in particular, who savoured of the noble a league off. He addressed himself then to Porthos, to gain information respecting Athos and Aramis, and to Aramis, in order to learn something of Porthos.

Unfortunately Porthos knew nothing of the life of his silent companion but that which had transpired. It was said he had met with great crosses in an affair of the heart, and that a frightful treachery had for ever poisoned the life of this gallant young man. What could this treachery be ? All the world was ignorant of it.

As to Porthos, except his real name, which no one but M. de Tréville was acquainted with, as well as with those of his two comrades, his life was very easily known. Vain and indiscreet, it was as easy to see through him as through a crystal. The only thing to mislead the investigator would have been for him to believe all the good he said of himself.

With respect to Aramis, whilst having the air of having nothing secret about him, he was a young fellow made up of mysteries, answering little to questions put to him about others, and eluding those that concerned himself. One day, D'Artagnan, having for a long time interrogated him about Porthos, and having learned from him the report which prevailed concerning the *bonne fortune* of the musketeer with a princess, wished to gain a little insight into the amorous adventures of his interlocutor.

" And you, my dear companion," said he, " you who speak of the baronesses, countesses, and princesses of others ?"

" Pardieu ! I spoke of them because Porthos talked of them himself, because he has cried all these fine things before me. But, be assured, my dear Monsieur d'Artagnan, that if I had obtained them from any other source, or if they had been confided to me, there exists no confessor more discreet than I am."

" Oh ! I don't doubt that," replied D'Artagnan ; " but it seems to me that you are tolerably familiar with coats of arms, a certain embroidered handkerchief, for instance, to which I owe the honour of your acquaintance ?"

This time Aramis was not angry, but assumed the most modest air, and replied in a friendly tone :

" My dear friend, do not forget that I wish to belong to the church, and that I avoid all mundane opportunities. The handkerchief you saw had not been given to me, but it had been forgotten, and left at my house by one of my friends. I was obliged to pick it up, in order not to compromise him and the lady he loves. As for myself, I neither have nor desire to have a mistress, following, in that respect, the very judicious example of Athos, who has none, any more than I have."

" But, what the devil ! you are not an abbé, you are a musketeer !"

" A musketeer for a time, my friend, as the cardinal says, a musketeer against my will, but a Churchman at heart, believe me. Athos and Porthos dragged me into this to occupy me. I had, at the moment of being ordained, a little difficulty with——But that would not interest you, and I am taking up your valuable time."

" Oh ! not at all ; it interests me very much," cried D'Artagnan, " and at this moment, I have absolutely nothing to do."

" Yes, but I have my breviary to repeat," answered Aramis ; " then some verses to compose, which Madame d'Aiguillon begged of me. Then I must go to Rue St. Honoré, in order to purchase some rouge for Madame de Chevreuse : so you see, my dear friend, that if you are not in a hurry, I am."

And Aramis held out his hand in a cordial manner to his young companion, and took leave of him.

Notwithstanding all the pains he took, D'Artagnan was unable to learn any more concerning his young friends. He formed, therefore, the resolution of believing in the present all that was said of their past, hoping for more certain and extended revelations from the future. In the meanwhile, he looked upon Athos as an Achilles, Porthos as an Ajax, and Aramis as a Joseph.

As to the rest, the life of our four young friends was joyous enough. Athos played, and that generally unfortunately. Nevertheless, he never borrowed a sou of his companions, although his purse was ever at their service ; and when he had played upon honour, he always awakened his creditor by six o'clock the next morning, to pay the debt of the preceding evening.

Porthos played by fits : on the days he won he was insolent and ostentatious ; if he lost, he disappeared completely for several days, after which he reappeared with a pale face and thinner person, but with money in his purse.

As to Aramis, he never played. He was the worst musketeer and the most unconvivial companion imaginable. He had always something or other to do. Sometimes, in the midst of dinner, when every one, under the attraction of wine and in the warmth of conversation, believed they had two or three hours longer to enjoy themselves at table, Aramis looked at his watch, arose with a bland smile, and took leave of the company, to go, as he said, to consult a casuist with whom he had an appointment. At other times he would return home to write a treatise, and requested his friends not to disturb him.

At this Athos would smile, with his charming, melancholy smile, which so became his noble countenance, and Porthos would drink, swearing that Aramis would never be anything but a village *curé*.

Planchet, D'Artagnan's valet, supported his good fortune nobly ; he received thirty sous per day, and during a month he returned home gay as a chaffinch, and affable towards his master. When the wind of adversity began to blow upon the housekeeping of Rue des Fossoyeurs, that is to say, when the forty pistoles of King Louis XIII. were consumed, or nearly so, he commenced complaints which Athos thought nauseous, Porthos unseemly, and Aramis ridiculous. Athos advised D'Artagnan to dismiss the fellow, Porthos was of opinion that he should give him a good thrashing first, and Aramis contended that a master should never attend to anything but the civilities paid him.

" This is all very easy for you to say," replied D'Artagnan ; " for you Athos, who live like a dumb man with Grimaud, who forbid him to speak, and consequently never exchange ill words with him ; for you, Porthos, who carry matters in such magnificent style, and are a god for your valet Mousqueton ; and for you, Aramis, who, always abstracted by your theological studies, inspire your servant Bazin, a mild, religious man, with a profound respect ; but for me, who am without any settled means, and without resources,—for me, who am neither a musketeer, nor even a guard, what am I to do to inspire either affection, terror, or respect in Planchet ?"

" The thing is serious," answered the three friends ; " it is a family affair ; it is with valets as with wives, they must be placed at once upon the footing in which you wish them to remain. Reflect upon it."

D'Artagnan did reflect, and resolved to thrash Planchet in the interim, which was executed with the conscience that D'Artagnan placed in everything ; then, after having well beaten him, he forbade him to leave his service without his permission ; for, added he, "the future cannot fail to mend ; I inevitably look for better times. Your fortune is therefore made if you remain with me, and I am too good a master to allow you to miss such a chance by granting you the dismissal you require."

This manner of acting created much respect for D'Artagnan's policy among the musketeers. Planchet was equally seized with admiration, and said no more about going away.

The life of the four young men had become common ; D'Artagnan, who had no settled habits of his own, as he came from his province into the midst of a world quite new to him, fell easily into the habits of his friends.

They rose about eight o'clock in the winter, about six in summer, and went to take the orderly word and see how things went on at M. de Tréville's. D'Artagnan, although he was not a musketeer, performed the duty of one with remarkable punctuality : he went on guard, because he always kept company with that one of his friends who mounted his. He was well known at the hotel of the musketeers, where every one considered him a good comrade ; M. de Tréville, who had appreciated him at the first glance, and who bore him a real affection, never ceased recommending him to the king.

On their side, the three musketeers were much attached to their young comrade. The friendship which united these four men, and the want they felt of seeing each other three or four times a-day, whether for duel, business, or pleasure, caused them to be continually running after one another like shadows, and the inseparables were constantly to be met with seeking each other, from the Luxembourg to the Place Saint-Sulpice, or from the Rue du Vieux-Colombier to the Luxembourg.

In the meanwhile the promises of M. de Tréville went on prosperously. One fine morning the king commanded M. le Chevalier Desessarts to admit D'Artagnan as a cadet in his company of guards. D'Artagnan, with a sigh, donned this uniform, which he would have exchanged for that of a musketeer, at the expense of ten years of his existence. But M. de Tréville promised this favour after a novitiate of two years, a novitiate which might, besides, be abridged if an opportunity should present itself for D'Artagnan to render the king any signal service, or to distinguish himself by some brilliant action. Upon this promise D'Artagnan retired, and the next day entered upon his duties.

Then it became the turn of Athos, Porthos, and Aramis to mount guard with D'Artagnan, when he was on duty. By admitting D'Artagnan, the company of M. le Chevalier Desessarts thus received four instead of one.

CHAPTER VIII.

A COURT INTRIGUE.

IN the meantime, the forty pistoles of King Louis XIII., like all other things of this world, after having had a beginning had an end, and after this end our four companions began to be somewhat embarrassed. At first Athos supported the association for a time with his own means. Porthos succeeded him, and thanks to one of these disappearances to which he was accustomed, he was able to provide for the wants of all for a fortnight ; at last it became Aramis's turn, who performed it with a good grace, and who succeeded, as he said, by selling some theological books, in procuring a few pistoles.

They then, as they had been accustomed to do, had recourse to M. de Tréville, who made some advances on their pay ; but these advances could not go far with three musketeers who were already much in arrears, and a guard who as yet had no pay at all.

At length, when they found they were likely to be quite in want, they got together, as a last effort, eight or ten pistoles, with which Porthos went to the gaming-table. Unfortunately he was in a bad vein ; he lost all, together with twenty-five pistoles upon his parole.

Then the inconvenience became distress ; the hungry friends, followed by their lackeys, were seen haunting the quays and guard-rooms, picking up among their friends abroad all the dinners they could meet with ; for, according to the advice of Aramis, it was prudent to sow repasts right and left in prosperity in order to reap a few in time of need.

Athos was invited four times, and each time took his friends and their lackeys with him ; Porthos had six occasions, and contrived in the same manner that his friends should partake of them ; Aramis had eight of them. He was a man, as must have been already perceived, who made but little noise, and yet was much sought after.

As to D'Artagnan, who as yet knew nobody in the capital, he only found one breakfast of chocolate at the house of a priest who was his countryman, and one dinner at the house of a cornet of the guards. He took his army to the priest's, where they devoured as much provision as would have lasted him for two months ; and to the cornet's, who performed wonders ; but, as Planchet said, " People only eat once at a time, even although they eat much."

D'Artagnan then felt himself humiliated in having only procured one meal and a half for his companions, as the breakfast at the priest's could only be counted as half a repast, in return for the feasts which Athos, Porthos, and Aramis had procured him. He fancied himself a burden to the society, forgetting in his perfectly juvenile good faith, that he had fed this society for a month, and he set his mind actively to work. He reflected that this coalition of four young, brave, enterprising, and active men ought to have some other object than swaggering walks, fencing lessons, and practical jokes, more or less sensible.

In fact, four men, such as they were, four men devoted to each other, from their purses to their lives, four men always supporting each other, never yielding, executing singly or together the resolutions formed in common ; four arms threatening the four cardinal points, or turning towards a single point, must inevitably, either subterraneously, in open day, by mining, in the trench, by cunning, or by force, open themselves a way towards the object they wished to attain, however well it might be defended, or however distant it might seem. The only thing that astonished D'Artagnan was, that his friends had never yet thought of this.

He was thinking alone, and seriously racking his brain to find a direction for this single force four times multiplied, with which he did not doubt, as with the lever for which Archimedes sought, they should succeed in moving the world, when some one tapped gently at his door. D'Artagnan awakened Planchet and desired him to go and see who was there.

Let not the reader, from this phrase—"D'Artagnan awakened Planchet," suppose that it was night, or that the day was not yet come. No, it had just struck four. Planchet, two hours before, had asked his master for some dinner, and he had answered him with the proverb, " He who sleeps dines." And Planchet dined sleeping.

A man was introduced of a common mien, with the appearance of a bourgeois.

Planchet, by way of dessert, would have liked to hear the conversation, but the bourgeois declared to D'Artagnan that that which he had to say being important and confidential, he desired to be left alone with him.

D'Artagnan dismissed Planchet, and requested his visitor to be seated.

There was a moment of silence, during which the two men looked at each other, as if to make a preliminary acquaintance, after which D'Artagnan bowed as a sign that he was attentive.

"I have heard speak of M. d'Artagnan as of a very brave young man," said the bourgeois, "and this reputation, which he justly enjoys, has determined me to confide a secret to him."

"Speak, monsieur, speak," said D'Artagnan, who instinctively scented something advantageous.

The bourgeois made a fresh pause and continued :

"I have a wife who is seamstress to the queen, monsieur, and who is not deficient in either good conduct or beauty. I was induced to marry her, about three years ago, although she had but very little dowry, because M. Laporte, the queen's cloak-bearer, is her godfather, and patronises her."

"Well, monsieur ?" asked D'Artagnan.

"Well !" resumed the bourgeois, "well ! monsieur, my wife was carried off, yesterday morning, as she was coming out of her work-room."

"And by whom was your wife carried off ?"

"I know nothing certain about the matter, monsieur, but I suspect some one."

"And who is the person you suspect ?"

"A man who pursued her a long time ago."

"The devil !"

"But allow me to tell you, monsieur," continued the citizen, "that I am convinced that there is less love than policy in all this."

"Less love than policy," replied D'Artagnan, with a very serious air, "and what do you suspect ?"

"I do not know whether I ought to tell you what I suspect."

"Monsieur, I beg you to observe that I ask you absolutely nothing. It is you who have come to me. It is you who have told me that you had a secret to confide to me. Act then as you think proper ; there is still time to withhold it."

"No, monsieur, no ; you appear to be an honest young man, and I will place confidence in you. I believe, then, that love has nothing to do with the carrying off of my wife, as regards herself, but that it has been done on account of the amours of a much greater lady than she is."

"Ah ! ah ! can it be on account of the amours of Madame de Bois-Tracy ?" said D'Artagnan, wishing to have the air, in the eyes of the bourgeois, of being acquainted with the affairs of the court.

"Higher, monsieur, higher."

"Of Madame d'Aiguillon ?"

"Still higher."

"Of Madame de Chevreuse ?"

"Higher ; much higher !"

"Of the —— ?" D'Artagnan stopped.

"Yes, monsieur," replied the terrified bourgeois, in a tone so low that he was scarcely audible.

"And with whom?"

"With whom can it be, if not with the duke of —— ?"

"The duke of ——"

"Yes, monsieur," replied the bourgeois, giving a still lower intonation to his voice.

"But how do you know all this?"

"How do I know it?"

"Yes, how do you know it? No half-confidence, or ——, you understand!"

"I know it from my wife, monsieur,—from my wife herself."

"Who knows it—she herself,—from whom?"

"From M. Laporte. Did I not tell you that she was the goddaughter of M. Laporte, the confidential man of the queen? Well, M. Laporte placed her near her majesty, in order that our poor queen might at least have some one in whom she could place confidence, abandoned as she is by the king, watched as she is by the cardinal, betrayed as she is by everybody."

"Ah! ah! it begins to develop itself," said D'Artagnan.

"Now my wife came home four days ago, monsieur: one of her conditions was that she should come and see me twice a week; for, as I had the honour to tell you, my wife loves me dearly; my wife, then, came and confided to me that the queen, at this very moment, entertained great fears."

"Indeed!"

"Yes. M. le Cardinal, as it appears, pursues her and persecutes her more than ever. He cannot pardon her the history of the Saraband. You know the history of the Saraband?"

"Pardieu! know it!" replied D'Artagnan, who knew nothing about it, but who wished to appear to know everything that was going on.

"So that now it is no longer hatred, but vengeance."

"Indeed!"

"And the queen believes ——"

"Well, what does the queen believe?"

"She believes that some one has written to the Duke of Buckingham in her name."

"In the queen's name?"

"Yes, to make him come to Paris; and when once come to Paris, to draw him into some snare."

"The devil! But your wife, monsieur, what has she to do with all this?"

"Her devotion to the queen is known, and they wish either to remove her from her mistress, or to intimidate her, in order to obtain her majesty's secrets, or to seduce her and make use of her as a spy."

"That is all very probable," said D'Artagnan; "but the man who has carried her off,—do you know him?"

"I have told you that I believe I know him."

" His name ?"

" I do not know that ; what I do know is that he is a creature of the cardinal's, his *âme damnée.*"

" But you have seen him ?"

" Yes, my wife pointed him out to me one day."

" Has he anything remarkable about him, by which he may be recognised ?"

" Oh ! certainly ; he is a noble of very lofty carriage, black hair, swarthy complexion, piercing eye, white teeth, and a scar on his temple."

" A scar on his temple," cried D'Artagnan ; " and with that, white teeth, a piercing eye, dark complexion, black hair, and haughty carriage ; why, that's my man of Meung."

" He is your man, do you say ?"

" Yes, yes ; but that has nothing to do with it. No, I am mistaken ; that simplifies the matter greatly ; on the contrary, if your man is mine, with one blow I shall obtain two revenges, that's all ; but where is this man to be met with ?"

" I cannot inform you."

" Have you no information respecting his dwelling ?"

" None ; one day, as I was conveying my wife back to the Louvre, he was coming out as she was going in, and she showed him to me."

" The devil ! the devil !" murmured D'Artagnan ; " all this is vague enough ; from whom did you learn the abduction of your wife ?"

" From M. Laporte."

" Did he give you any of the particulars ?"

" He knew none himself."

" And you have learned none from any other quarter ?"

" Yes, I have received ——"

" What ?"

" I fear I am committing a great imprudence.

" You still keep harping upon that ; but I beg leave to observe to you this time that it is too late now to retreat."

" I do not retreat, mordieu !" cried the bourgeois, swearing to keep his courage up. " Besides, by the word of Bonacieux ——"

" Your name is Bonacieux ?" interrupted D'Artagnan.

" Yes, that is my name."

" You said then, by the word of Bonacieux ! Pardon me for interrupting you, but it appears to me that that name is familiar to me."

" Very possibly, monsieur. I am your *propriétaire.*"

" Ah ! ah !" said D'Artagnan, half rising and bowing ; " you are m, *propriétaire ?*"

" Yes, monsieur, yes. And as it is three months since you came, and engaged as you must be in your important occupations, you have forgotten to pay me my rent ; as, I say, I have not tormented you a single instant, I thought you would appreciate my delicacy."

" How can it be otherwise, my dear Bonacieux ?" replied D'Artagnan ;

"trust me, I am fully grateful for such conduct, and if, as I have told you, I can be of any service to you ——"

"I believe you, monsieur, I believe you ; and as I was about to say, by the word of Bonacieux ! I have confidence in you."

" Finish, then, that which you were about to say."

The bourgeois took a paper from his pocket, and presented it to D'Artagnan.

" A letter ?" said the young man.

" Which I received this morning."

D'Artagnan opened it, and as the day was beginning to decline, he drew near to the window to read it, and the bourgeois followed him.

"'Do not seek for your wife,' "read D'Artagnan ; "'she will be restored to you when there is no longer occasion for her. If you make a single step to find her you are lost.'"

" That's pretty positive," continued D'Artagnan ; " but, after all, it is but a threat."

" Yes ; but that threat terrifies me. I am not a man of the sword at all, monsieur ; and I am afraid of the Bastille."

" Hum!" said D'Artagnan. " I have no greater regard for the Bastille than you. If it were nothing but a sword-thrust ——"

" I have depended upon you on this occasion, monsieur."

" You have ?"

" Seeing you constantly surrounded by musketeers of a very superb appearance, and knowing that these musketeers belonged to M. de Tréville, and were consequently enemies of the cardinal, I thought that you and your friends, whilst rendering justice to our poor queen, would not be displeased at having an opportunity of giving his eminence an ill-turn."

" Without doubt."

" And then I thought that owing me three months' rent, which I have said nothing about ——"

" Yes, yes ; you have already given me that reason, and I find it excellent."

" Reckoning still further, that as long as you do me the honour to remain in my house, that I shall never name to you your future rent."

" Very kind !"

" And adding to this, if there be need of it, meaning to offer you fifty pistoles, if, against all probability, you should be short at the present moment."

" Admirable ! but you are rich then, my dear Monsieur Bonacieux?"

" I am comfortably off, monsieur, that's all : I have scraped together some such thing as an income of two or three thousand crowns in the mercery business, but more particularly in venturing some funds in the last voyage of the celebrated navigator, Jean Moquet : so that you understand, monsieur,——But !" cried the bourgeois.

" What !" demanded D'Artagnan.

" Whom do I see yonder ?"

" Where ?"

" In the street, fronting your window, in the embrasure of that door ! a man enveloped in a cloak."

" It is he !" cried D'Artagnan and the bourgeois at the same time, having each recognised his man.

" Ah ! this time," cried D'Artagnan, springing to his sword, '' this time he does not escape me !"

Drawing his sword from the sheath, he rushed out of the apartment.

On the staircase he met Athos and Porthos, who were coming to see him. They separated, and D'Artagnan rushed between them like lightning.

" Where the devil are you going?" cried the two musketeers in a breath ?

" The man of Meung !", replied D'Artagnan, and disappeared.

D'Artagnan had more than once related to his friends his adventure with the unknown, as well as the apparition of the beautiful foreigner to whom this man had confided some important missive.

The opinion of Athos was that D'Artagnan had lost his letter in the skirmish. A gentleman, in his opinion, and according to D'Artagnan's portrait of him the unknown must be a gentleman, a gentleman would be incapable of the baseness of stealing a letter.

Porthos saw nothing in all this but a love-meeting, given by a lady to a cavalier, or by a cavalier to a lady, which had been disturbed by the presence of D'Artagnan and his yellow horse.

Aramis said that as these sorts of affairs were mysterious, it was better not to attempt to unravel them.

They understood then, from the few words which escaped from D'Artagnan, what affair was in hand, and as they thought that after having overtaken his man or lost sight of him, D'Artagnan would return to his rooms again, they went in.

When they entered D'Artagnan's chamber, it was empty ; the *propriétaire* dreading the consequences of the rencontre which was, doubtless, about to take place between the young man and the unknown, had, consistently with the character he had given himself, judged it most prudent to decamp.

CHAPTER IX.

D'ARTAGNAN BEGINS TO DEVELOP HIMSELF.

As Athos and Porthos had foreseen, at the expiration of half-an-hour D'Artagnan returned. He had this time again missed his man, who had disappeared as if by enchantment. D'Artagnan had run, sword in hand, through all the neighbouring streets, but had found nobody resembling the man he sought for ; then he did that by which, perhaps, he ought to have begun, which was to knock at the door against which the unknown was leaning ; but it had proved useless to knock ten or twelve times running, for no one answered, and some of the neighbours, who put their noses out of their windows, or were brought to their doors by the noise, had assured him that that house, all the openings of which were tightly closed, had been for six months completely uninhabited.

Whilst D'Artagnan was running through the streets and knocking at doors, Aramis had joined his companions, so that on returning home D'Artagnan found the meeting complete.

" Well !" cried the three musketeers all together, on seeing D'Artagnan enter with his brow covered with perspiration, and his face clouded with anger.

" Well !" cried he, throwing his sword upon the bed ; " this man must be the devil in person ; he has disappeared like a phantom, like a shade, like a spectre."

" Do you believe in apparitions ?" asked Athos, of Porthos.

" I never believe in anything I have not seen, and as I never have seen an apparition, I don't believe in them."

" The Bible," said Aramis, " makes our belief in them a law ; the shade of Samuel appeared to Saul, and it is an article of faith that I should be very sorry to see any doubt thrown upon, Porthos."

"At all events, man or devil, body or shadow, illusion or reality, this man is born for my damnation, for his flight has caused us to miss a glorious affair, gentlemen, an affair by which there were a hundred pistoles, and perhaps more to be gained."

" How is that ?" cried Porthos and Aramis in a breath.

As to Athos, faithful to his system of mutism, he satisfied himself with interrogating D'Artagnan by a look.

"Planchet," said D'Artagnan, to his domestic, who just then insinuated his head through the half-open door, in order to catch some fragments of the conversation, "go down to my *propriétaire*, M. Bonacieux, and tell him to send me half-a-dozen bottles of Beaugency wine; I prefer that."

" Ah ! ah ! what, are you in credit with your *propriétaire*, then ?" asked Porthos.

" Yes," replied D'Artagnan, " from this very day, and mind ! if the wine be not good, we will send to him to find better."

" We must use, and not abuse," said Aramis sententiously.

" I always said that D'Artagnan had the longest head of the four," said Athos, who, after having uttered his opinion, to which D'Artagnan replied with a bow, immediately resumed his habitual silence.

" But, come, tell us, what is this about ?" asked Porthos.

" Yes," said Aramis, " impart it to us, my dear friend, unless the honour of any lady be hazarded by this confidence ; in that case you would do better to keep it to yourself."

" Be satisfied," replied D'Artagnan, " the honour of no one shall have to complain of that which I have to tell you."

He then related to his friends, word for word, all that had passed between him and his landlord, and how the man who had carried off the wife of his worthy *propriétaire* was the same with whom he had had a difference at the hostelry of the Franc-Meunier.

" Your affair is not a bad one," said Athos, after having tasted the wine like a connoisseur, and indicated by a nod of his head that he thought it good, " and fifty or sixty pistoles may be got out of this good man. Then, there only remains to ascertain whether these fifty or sixty pistoles are worth the risk of four heads."

" But please to observe," cried D'Artagnan, " that there is a woman in the affair, a woman carried off, a woman who is doubtless threatened, tortured perhaps, and all because she is faithful to her mistress."

" Beware, D'Artagnan, beware," said Aramis, " you grow a little too warm, in my opinion, about the fate of Madame Bonacieux. Woman was created for our destruction, and it is from her we inherit all our miseries."

At this speech of Aramis the brow of Athos became clouded, and he bit his lips.

" It is not Madame Bonacieux about whom I am anxious," cried D'Artagnan, " but the queen, whom the king abandons, whom the cardinal persecutes, and who sees the heads of all her friends fall one after the other."

" Why does she love what we hate most in the world, the Spaniards and the English ?"

" Spain is her country," replied D'Artagnan ; " and it is very natural that she should love the Spanish, who are the children of the same soil as herself. As to the second reproach, I have heard say that she does not love the English, but an Englishman."

" Well, and by my faith !" said Athos, " it must be confessed that this Englishman was worthy of being loved. I never saw a man with a nobler air than his."

" Without reckoning that he dresses as nobody else can," said Porthos. " I was at the Louvre on the day that he scattered his pearls ; and, pardieu ! I picked up two that I sold for ten pistoles each. Do you know him, Aramis ?"

" As well as you do, gentlemen ; for I was among those who seized him in the garden at Amiens, into which M. Putange, the queen's equerry, introduced me. I was at school at the time, and the adventure appeared to me to be cruel for the king."

" Which would not prevent me," said D'Artagnan, " if I knew where the duke of Buckingham was, to take him by the hand and conduct him to the queen, were it only to enrage the cardinal ; for our true, our only, our eternal enemy, gentlemen, is the cardinal, and if we could find means to play him a sharp turn, I confess that I would voluntarily risk my head in doing it."

" And did the mercer," rejoined Athos, " tell you, D'Artagnan, that the queen thought that Buckingham had been brought over by a forged letter ?"

" She is afraid so."

" Wait a minute, then," said Aramis.

" What for ?" demanded Porthos.

" Go on. I am endeavouring to remember some circumstances."

" And now I am convinced," said D'Artagnan, " that this abduction of the queen's woman is connected with the events of which we are speaking ; and perhaps with the presence of Monsieur de Buckingham at Paris."

" The Gascon is full of ideas," said Porthos, with admiration.

" I like to hear him talk," said Athos, " his *patois* amuses me."

" Gentlemen," cried Aramis, " listen to this."

" Listen to Aramis," said his three friends.

" Yesterday I was at the house of a doctor of theology whom I some- times consult about my studies."

Athos smiled.

" He resides in a quiet quarter," continued Aramis : " his tastes and his profession require it. Now, at the moment that I left his house—"

Here Aramis stopped.

" Well," cried his auditors ; " at the moment you left his house ?"

Aramis appeared to make a strong inward effort, like a man who, in the full relation of a falsehood, finds himself stopped by some unfore- seen obstacle ; but the eyes of his three companions were fixed upon him, their ears were wide open, and there were no means of retreating.

" This doctor has a niece," continued Aramis.

" A niece ! has he ?" said Porthos.

" A very respectable lady," said Aramis.

The three friends burst into a loud laugh.

" Ah ! if you laugh, or doubt what I say," replied Aramis, " you shall know nothing."

" We are as staunch believers as Mahometans, and as mute as cata- falques," said Athos.

" I will go on then," resumed Aramis. " This niece comes sometimes to see her uncle ; and, by chance, was there yesterday at the same time that I was, and I could do no less than offer to conduct her to her car- riage."

" Oh ! oh ! Then this niece of the doctor's keeps a carriage, does she ?" interrupted Porthos, one of whose faults was a great incontinence of tongue ; " a very nice acquaintance, my friend !"

" Porthos," replied Aramis, " I have had occasion to observe to you, more than once, that you are very indiscreet ; and that is injurious to you among the women."

" Gentlemen, gentlemen," cried D'Artagnan, who began to get a glimpse of the result of the adventure, " the thing is serious ; endeavour, then, not to joke, if possible. Go on, Aramis, go on."

" All at once, a tall, dark gentleman,—just like yours, D'Artagnan."

" The same, perhaps," said he.

" Possibly," continued Aramis,—" came towards me, accompanied by five or six men, who followed at about ten paces behind him ; and, in the politest tone, ' Monsieur the Duke,' said he to me, ' and you, ma- dame,' continued he, addressing the lady, who had hold of my arm,—"

" The doctor's niece ?"

" Hold your tongue, Porthos," said Athos ; " you are insupportable."

"' Be so kind as to get into this carriage ; and that without offering the slightest resistance, or making the least noise.' "

"He took you for Buckingham !" cried D'Artagnan.

"I believe so," replied Aramis.

"But the lady ?" asked Porthos.

"He took her for the queen !" said D'Artagnan.

"Just so," replied Aramis.

"The Gascon is the devil !" cried Athos ; "nothing escapes him."

"The fact is," said Porthos, "Aramis is of the same height, and something of the shape of the duke ; but it nevertheless appears to me that the uniform of a musketeer——"

"I wore a very large cloak," said Aramis.

"In the month of July ; the devil !" said Porthos. "Is the doctor afraid you should be recognised ?"

"I can comprehend that the spy may have been deceived by the person ; but the face——"

"I had a very large hat on," said Aramis.

"Oh ! good lord !" cried Porthos, "what precautions to study theology !"

"Gentlemen, gentlemen," said D'Artagnan, "do not let us lose our time in jesting ; let us separate, and let us seek the mercer's wife ; that is the key of the intrigue."

"A woman of such inferior condition ! can you believe so ?" said Porthos, protruding his lip with contempt.

"She is goddaughter to Laporte, the confidential valet of the queen. Have I not told you so, gentlemen ? Besides, it has perhaps been a scheme of her majesty's to have sought, on this occasion, for support so lowly. High heads expose themselves sometimes ; and the cardinal is far-sighted."

"Well," said Porthos, "in the first place make a bargain with the mercer ; and a good bargain, too."

"That's useless," said D'Artagnan ; "for I believe if he does not pay us, we shall be well enough paid by another party."

At this moment a sudden noise of footsteps was heard upon the stairs, the door was thrown violently open, and the unfortunate mercer rushed into the chamber in which the council was held.

"Save me ! gentlemen ! save me !" cried he. "There are four men come to arrest me ; save me ! for the love of heaven, save me !"

Porthos and Aramis arose.

"A moment," cried D'Artagnan, making them a sign to replace their half-drawn swords : "on this occasion we don't require courage ; we must exercise prudence."

"And yet," cried Porthos, "we will not leave——"

"You will leave D'Artagnan to act as he thinks proper ; he has, I repeat, the longest head of the four, and for my part, I declare I obey him. Do as you think best D'Artagnan."

At this moment the four guards appeared at the door of the antechamber, but seeing four musketeers standing, and their swords by their sides, they hesitated to advance further.

"Come in, gentlemen, come in ; you are here in my apartment, and we are all faithful servants of the king and Monsieur le Cardinal."

"Then, gentlemen, you will not oppose our executing the orders we have received ?" asked the one who appeared to be the leader of the party.

"On the contrary, gentlemen, we would assist you if it were necessary."

"*What* does he say ?" grumbled Porthos.

"That you are a simpleton," said Athos ; "hold your tongue."

"But you promised me,"—said the poor mercer, in a very low voice.

"We can only save you by being free ourselves," replied D'Artagnan, in a rapid, low tone, "and if we appear inclined to defend you, they will arrest us with you."

"It seems—nevertheless——"

"Come in, gentlemen ! come in !" said D'Artagnan ; "I have no motive for defending monsieur. I saw him to-day for the first time, and he can tell you on what occasion ; he came to demand the rent of my lodging. Is not that true, M. Bonacieux ? Answer ?"

"That's the very truth," cried the mercer ; "but monsieur does not tell you——"

"Silence, with respect to me ! silence, with respect to my friends !— silence about the queen above all, or you will ruin everybody without saving yourself. Now, gentlemen, you are at liberty to take away this man !"

And D'Artagnan pushed the half-stupefied mercer among the guards, saying to him—

"You are a shabby old fellow, my dear !—you come to demand money of me ! of a musketeer !—to prison with him !—gentlemen, once more, take him to prison, and keep him under key as long as possible— that will give me time to pay him."

The sbirri were full of thanks, and took away their prey.

At the moment they were going down, D'Artagnan laid his hand on the shoulder of their leader.

"Shall I not have the pleasure of drinking to your health, and you to mine ?" said D'Artagnan, filling two glasses with the Beaugency wine which he had obtained from the liberality of M. Bonacieux.

"That will do me great honour," said the leader of the sbirri, "and I consent thankfully."

"Then to yours, monsieur—what is your name ?"

"Boisrenard."

"Monsieur Boisrenard !"

"To yours, my good sir—in your turn, what is your name, if you please ?"

"D'Artagnan."

"To yours, Monsieur d'Artagnan."

" And above all others," cried D'Artagnan, as if carried away by his enthusiasm, " to that of the king and the cardinal."

The leader of the sbirri would perhaps have doubted the sincerity of D'Artagnan if the wine had been bad, but the wine was good, and he was convinced.

" Why, what a devil of a villany have you performed there," said Porthos, when the alguazil-in-chief had rejoined his companions, and the four friends were left alone.   " Shame ! shame ! for four musketeers to allow an unfortunate devil who cried out for help to be arrested from amongst them.   And a gentleman to hob-nob with a bailiff !"

" Porthos," said Aramis, " Athos has already told you, you are a simpleton, and I am quite of his opinion. D'Artagnan, you are a great man, and when you occupy M. de Tréville's place, I will come and ask your influence to secure me an abbey."

" Well ! I am quite lost !" said Porthos, " do *you* approve of what D'Artagnan has done ?"

" Parbleu ! indeed I do !" said Athos, " I not only approve of what he has done, but I congratulate him upon it."

" And now, gentlemen," said D'Artagnan, without stopping to explain his conduct to Porthos—" all for one, one for all, that is our device, is it not ?"

" And yet !" said Porthos.

" Hold out your hand and swear !"cried Athos and Aramis at once.

Overcome by example, grumbling to himself, nevertheless, Porthos stretched out his hand, and the four friends repeated with one voice the formula dictated by D'Artagnan.

" All for one, one for all."

" That's well !   Now let every one retire to his own home," said D'Artagnan, as if he had done nothing but command all his life—" and attention ! for from this moment we are at feud with the cardinal."

CHAPTER X.

A MOUSE-TRAP IN THE SEVENTEENTH CENTURY.

THE invention of the mouse-trap does not date from our days ; as soon as societies, in forming, had invented any kind of police, that police in its turn, invented mouse-traps.

As perhaps our readers are not familiar with the slang of the Rue de Jerusalem, and that it is fifteen years since we applied this word, for the first time, to this thing, allow us to explain to them what a mouse-trap is.

When in a house, of whatever kind it may be, an individual suspected of any crime be arrested, the arrest is held secret ; four or five men are placed in ambuscade in the first apartment, the door is opened to all that knock, it is closed after them, and they are arrested : so that at the end of two or three days they have in their power almost all the familiars of the establishment. And that is a mouse-trap.

The apartment of Master Bonacieux then became a mouse-trap, and whoever appeared there was taken and interrogated by the cardinal's people. It must be observed that as a private passage led to the first floor, in which D'Artagnan lodged, those who called to see him were exempted from this.

Besides, nobody came thither but the three musketeers; they had all been engaged in earnest search and inquiries, but had discovered nothing. Athos had even gone so far as to question M. de Tréville, a thing which, considering the habitual mutism of the worthy musketeer, had very much astonished his captain. But M. de Tréville knew nothing, except that the last time he had seen the cardinal, the king and the queen, the cardinal looked very thoughtful, the king uneasy, and the redness of the queen's eyes denoted that she had been deprived of sleep, or had been weeping. But this last circumstance was not at all striking, as the queen, since her marriage, had slept badly and wept much.

M. de Tréville requested Athos, whatever might happen, to be observant of his duty to the king, but more particularly to the queen, begging him to convey his desires to his comrades.

As to D'Artagnan, he did not stir from his apartment. He converted his chamber into an observatory. From his windows he saw all come who were caught; then, having removed some of the boarding of his floor, and nothing remaining but a simple ceiling between him and the room beneath, in which the interrogatories were made, he heard all that passed between the inquisitors and the accused.

The interrogatories, preceded by a minute search operated upon the persons arrested, were almost all thus conceived.

"Has Madame Bonacieux sent anything to you for her husband, or any other person?

"Has Monsieur Bonacieux sent anything to you for his wife, or for any other person?

"Has either the one or the other confided anything to you by word of mouth?"

"If they were acquainted with anything, they would not question people in this manner," said D'Artagnan to himself. "Now, what is it they want to know? Why, if the Duke of Buckingham is in Paris, and if he has not had, or is not to have, some interview with the queen."

D'Artagnan was satisfied with this idea, which, after all he had heard, was not wanting in probability.

In the meanwhile, the mouse-trap continued in operation, as likewise did D'Artagnan's vigilance.

On the evening of the day after the arrest of poor Bonacieux, as Athos had just left D'Artagnan, to go to M. de Tréville's, as nine o'clock had just struck, and as Planchet, who had not yet made the bed, was beginning his task, a knocking was heard at the street-door; the door was instantly opened and shut: some one was taken in the mouse-trap.

D'Artagnan flew to his hole, and laid himself down on the floor at full length to listen.

Cries were soon heard, and then moans, which someone appeared to be endeavouring to stifle. There were no interrogatories.

" The devil !" said D'Artagnan to himself, "it's a woman—they are searching her—she resists—they use force—the scoundrels !"

In spite of all his prudence, D'Artagnan restrained himself with great difficulty from taking a part in the scene that was going on below.

" But I tell you that I am the mistress of the house, gentlemen ! I tell you I am Madame Bonacieux—I tell you I belong to the queen !" said the unfortunate woman.

" Madame Bonacieux !" murmured D'Artagnan ; " can I have been so lucky as to have found what everybody is seeking for ?"

The voice became more and more indistinct ; a tumultuous movement shook the wainscoting. The victim resisted as much as a woman could resist four men.

" Pardon, gentlemen,—par——" murmured the voice, which could now be only heard in inarticulate sounds.

" They are binding her, they are going to drag her away," cried D'Artagnan to himself, springing up from the floor. " My sword ! good, it is by my side. Planchet !"

" Monsieur."

" Run and seek Athos, Porthos, and Aramis. One of the three will certainly be at home, perhaps all three are. Tell them to arm, to come here, and be quick ! Ah ! I remember, Athos is at M. De Tréville's.

" But where are you going, monsieur, where are you going ?"

" I am going down by the window, in order to be there the sooner," cried D'Artagnan : " on your part, put back the boards, sweep the floor, go out at the door, and run where I bid you."

" Oh ! monsieur ! monsieur ! you will kill yourself," cried Planchet.

" Hold your tongue, you stupid fellow," said D'Artagnan, and laying hold of the window-frame, he let himself gently down, and the height not being great, he did not sustain the least injury.

He then went straight to the door and knocked, murmuring :

" I will go myself and be caught in the mouse-trap, but woe be to the cats that shall pounce upon such a mouse !"

The knocker had scarcely sounded under the hand of the young man than the tumult ceased, steps approached, the door was opened, and D'Artagnan, sword in hand, rushed into the apartment of Master Bonacieux, the door of which, doubtless, acted upon by a spring, closed after him.

Then those who dwelt in Bonacieux's unfortunate house, together with the nearest neighbours, heard loud cries, stamping of feet, clashing of swords, and breaking of furniture. Then, a moment after, such as, surprised by this tumult, had gone to their windows to learn the cause of it, could see the door open, and four men, clothed in black, not come out of it, but fly, like so many frightened crows, leaving on the ground, and on the corners of the furniture, feathers from their wings; that is to say, portions of their clothes and fragments of their cloaks.

D'Artagnan was conqueror, without much trouble, it must be confessed, for only one of the alguazils was armed, and defended himself for form's sake. It is true that the three others had endeavoured to knock the young man down with chairs, stools, and crockery ware ; but two or three scratches made by the Gascon's blade terrified them. Ten minutes had sufficed for their defeat, and D'Artagnan remained master of the field of battle.

The neighbours who had opened their windows, with *sang froid* peculiar to the inhabitants of Paris in these times of perpetual riots and disturbances, closed them again as soon as they saw the four men in black fly away : their instinct telling them that, for the moment, all was over.

Besides, it began to grow late, and then, as at the present day, people went to bed early in the quarter of the Luxembourg.

On being left alone with Madame Bonacieux, D'Artagnan turned towards her ; the poor woman reclined, where she had been left, upon a *fauteuil*, in a half-fainting state. D'Artagnan examined her with a rapid but an earnest glance.

She was a charming woman, of about twenty-five years of age, dark hair, blue eyes, and a nose slightly turned up, admirable teeth, and a complexion marbled with rose and opal. There, however, stopped the signs which might have confounded her with a lady of rank. The hands were white, but without delicacy : the feet did not bespeak the woman of quality. Fortunately, D'Artagnan was, as yet, not acquainted with such niceties.

Whilst D'Artagnan was examining Madame Bonacieux, and was, as we have said, close to her, he saw on the ground a fine cambric handkerchief, which he mechanically picked up, and at the corner of which he recognised the same cipher that he had seen on the handkerchief which had nearly caused him and Aramis to cut each other's throats.

From that time D'Artagnan had been cautious with respect to handkerchiefs with arms on them, and he therefore placed the one he had just picked up in Madame Bonacieux's pocket.

At that moment Madame Bonacieux recovered her senses. She opened her eyes, looked around her with terror, saw that the apartment was empty, and that she was alone with her liberator. She immediately held out her hands to him with a smile—Madame Bonacieux had the sweetest smile in the world !

"Ah ! monsieur !" said she, "you have saved me : permit me to thank you."

"Madame," said D'Artagnan, "I have only done what every gentleman would have done in my place—you owe me no thanks."

"Oh ! yes, monsieur, oh ! yes ; and I hope to prove to you that you have not served an ingrate. But what could these men, whom I at first took for robbers, want with me, and why is M. Bonacieux not here ?"

" Madame, those men were much more dangerous than any robbers could have been, for they are the agents of M. the Cardinal : and as to your husband, M. Bonacieux, he is not here, because he was yesterday evening taken away to the Bastille."

" My husband in the Bastille !" cried Madame Bonacieux. "Oh ! good God ! what can he have done ? Poor dear man ! he is innocence itself !"

And something like a faint smile glided over the still terrified features of the young woman.

" What has he done, madame?" said D'Artagnan. " I believe that his only crime is to have at the same time the good fortune and the misfortune to be your husband."

" But, monsieur, you know then ——"

" I know that you have been carried off, madame."

" And by whom ? Do you know ? Oh ! if you know, tell me !"

" By a man of from forty to forty-five years of age, with black hair, a dark complexion, and a scar on his left temple."

" That is he, that is he ; but his name ?"

" Ah ! his name ? I do not know that."

" And did my husband know I had been carried off ?"

" He was informed of it by a letter written to him by the ravisher himself."

" And does he suspect," said Madame Bonacieux, with some embarrassment, " the cause of this event ?"

" He attributed it, I believe, to a political cause."

" I suspected so myself at first, and now I think entirely as he does. My dear M. Bonacieux has not then for an instant suspected me ?"

" So far from it, madame, he was too proud of your prudence, and particularly of your love."

A second smile stole almost imperceptibly over the rosy lips of the pretty young woman.

" But," continued D'Artagnan, " how did you escape ?"

" I took advantage of a moment at which they left me alone ; and as I knew from this morning what to think of my abduction, with the help of the sheets, I let myself down from the window ; then, as I concluded my husband would be at home, I hastened hither."

" To place yourself under his protection ?"

" Oh ! no, poor dear man ! I knew very well that he was incapable of defending me ; but, as he could be otherwise useful to us, I wished to inform him."

" Of what ?"

" Oh ! that is not my secret ; I must not, therefore, tell you."

" Besides," said D'Artagnan, " (pardon me madame, if, guard as I am, I remind you of prudence)—besides, I believe we are not here in a very proper place for imparting confidences. The men I have put to flight will return reinforced ; if they find us here, we are lost. I have sent for three of my friends, but who knows whether they may be at home ?"

" Yes ! yes ! you are right," cried the terrified Madame Bonacieux ; " let us fly ! let us save ourselves."

At these words she passed her arm under that of D'Artagnan, and pulled him forward, eagerly.

" But whither shall we fly ?—whither escape to ?"

" Let us in the first place get away from this house ; when clear of it we shall see."

And the young woman and the young man, without taking the trouble to shut the door after them, descended the Rue des Fossoyeurs rapidly, turned into the Rue des Fossés-Monsieur-le-Prince, and did not stop till they came to the Place-Saint-Sulpice.

" And now, what are we to do, and whither do you wish me to conduct you ?" asked D'Artagnan.

" I am quite at a loss how to answer you, I confess," said Madame Bonacieux ; " my intention was to inform M. Laporte, by means of my husband, in order that M. Laporte might tell us exactly what has taken place at the Louvre in the course of the last three days, and whether there were any danger in presenting myself there."

" But I," said D'Artagnan, " can go and inform M. Laporte."

" No doubt you could ; only there is one misfortune in it, and that is that M. Bonacieux is known at the Louvre, and would be allowed to pass ; whereas you are not known there, and the gate would be closed against you."

" Ah ! bah !" said D'Artagnan ; " there is no doubt you have at some wicket of the Louvre a concierge who is devoted to you, and who, thanks to a pass-word, would——"

Madame Bonacieux looked earnestly at the young man.

" And if I give you this pass-word," said she, " would you forget it as soon as you had made use of it ?"

" Parole d'honneur ! by the faith of a gentleman !" said D'Artagnan, with an accent so truthful, no one could mistake it.

" Then, I believe you ; you appear to be a brave young man ; besides, your fortune, perhaps, is at the end of your devotedness."

" I will do, without a promise, and voluntarily, all that I can do to serve the king and be agreeable to the queen : dispose of me, then, as a friend."

" But I ?—where shall I go in the meanwhile ?"

" Do you know no one from whose house M. Laporte can come and fetch you ?"

" No, I know no one to whom I dare trust."

" Stop," said D'Artagnan ; " we are near Athos's door. Yes, here it is."

" Who is this Athos ?"

" One of my friends."

" But, if he should be at home, and see me ?"

" He is not at home, and I will carry away the key, after having placed you in his apartment."

" But if he should return ?"

"Oh ! he won't return ; and if he should, he will be told that I have brought a lady with me, and that lady is in his apartment."

"But that will compromise me sadly, you know ?"

"Of what consequence can it be to you ?—nobody knows you ; besides, we are in a situation in which we must not be too particular."

"Come, then, let us go to your friend's house ; where does he live ?"

"Rue Ferou, within two steps."

"Come, then !"

And both resumed their way. As D'Artagnan had foreseen, Athos was not at home ; he took the key, which was customarily given him as one of the family, ascended the stairs, and introduced Madame Bonacieux into the little apartment of which we gave a description.

"Here, make yourself at home," said he ; "wait here, fasten the door within, and open it to nobody unless you hear three taps like these ;" and he tapped thrice ; "two taps close together and pretty hard, the other at a considerable distance and more light."

"That is all well," said Madame Bonacieux ; "now, in my turn, let me give you my orders."

"I am all attention."

"Present yourself at the wicket of the Louvre, on the side of the Rue de l'Echelle, and ask for Germain."

"Well ; and then ?"

"He will ask you what you want, and you will answer by these two words—Tours and Bruxelles. He will immediately be at your command."

"And what shall I order him to do ?"

"To go and fetch M. Laporte, the queen's *valet de chambre*."

"And when he shall have informed him, and M. Laporte is come ?"

"You will send him to me."

"That is all very well ; but where and how shall I see you again ?"

"Do you, then, wish much—to see me again ?"

"Certainly, I do."

"Well, let that care be mine, and be at ease."

"I depend upon your word."

"You may."

D'Artagnan bowed to Madame Bonacieux, darting at her the most loving glance that he could possibly concentrate upon her charming little person ; and whilst he descended the stairs, he heard the door closed and double-locked. In two bounds he was at the Louvre : as he entered the wicket of l'Echelle, ten o'clock struck. All the events we have described had taken place within half an hour.

Everything fell out as Madame Bonacieux said it would. On hearing the password, Germain bowed : in a few minutes Laporte was at the lodge ; in two words D'Artagnan informed him where Madame Bona-cieux was. Laporte assured himself, by having it twice repeated, of the exactitude of the address, and set off at a run. He had, however, scarcely got ten steps before he returned

" Young man," said he to D'Artagnan, " I have a piece of advice to give you."

" What is it ?"

" You may get into trouble by what has taken place."

" Do you think so ?"

" Yes. Have you any friend whose clock is too slow ?"

" What then ?"

" Go and call upon him, in order that he may give evidence of your having been with him at half-past nine. In a court of justice, that is called an *alibi*."

D'Artagnan found this advice prudent ; he took to his heels, and was soon at M. de Tréville's ; but instead of passing to the saloon with the rest of the world, he required to be introduced to M. de Tréville's closet. As D'Artagnan so constantly frequented the hotel, no difficulty was made in complying with his request, and a servant went to inform M. de Tréville that his young compatriot, having something important to communicate, solicited a private audience. Five minutes after, M. de Tréville was asking D'Artagnan what he could do to serve him, and what caused his visit at so late an hour.

" Pardon me, monsieur," said D'Artagnan, who had profited by the moment he had been left alone to put back M. de Tréville's clock three quarters of an hour, " but I thought, as it was yet only twenty minutes past nine, it was not too late to wait upon you."

" Twenty minutes past nine !" cried M. de Tréville, looking at the clock ; " why, that's impossible !"

" Look, rather, monsieur," said D'Artagnan, " the clock shows it."

" That's true," said M. de Tréville ; " I should have thought it had been later. But what can I do for you ?"

Then D'Artagnan told M. de Tréville a long history about the queen. He expressed to him the fears he entertained with respect to her majesty ; he related to him what he had heard of the projects of the cardinal with regard to Buckingham ; and all with a tranquillity and sereneness of which M. de Tréville was the more the dupe, from having himself, as we have said, observed something fresh between the cardinal, the king, and the queen.

As ten o'clock was striking, D'Artagnan left M. de Tréville, who thanked him for his information, recommended him to have the service of the king and queen always at heart, and returned to the saloon. But at the foot of the stairs, D'Artagnan remembered he had forgotten his cane : he consequently sprang up again, re-entered the closet, with a turn of his finger set the clock right again, that it might not be perceived the next day that it had been put wrong, and certain from that time that he had a witness to prove his *alibi*, he ran down stairs and soon gained the street.

CHAPTER XI.

THE PLOT THICKENS.

His visit to M. de Tréville being paid, D'Artagnan took his pensive but longest way homewards.

On what was D'Artagnan thinking, that he strayed thus from his path, gazing at the stars in the heavens, and sometimes sighing, sometimes smiling?

He was thinking of Madame Bonacieux. For an apprentice musketeer, the young woman was almost a loving ideality. Pretty, mysterious, initiated in almost all the secrets of the court, which spread such a charming gravity over her pleasing features, she was suspected of not being insensible, which is an irresistible charm for novices in love of the other sex; still further, D'Artagnan had delivered her from the hands of the demons who wished to search and ill-treat her; and this important service had established between them one of those sentiments of gratitude which so easily take another character.

D'Artagnan already fancied himself, so rapid is the progress of our dreams upon the wings of imagination, accosted by a messenger from the young woman, who brought him some billet appointing a meeting, a gold chain, or a diamond. We have observed that young cavaliers received presents from their king without shame; let us add that, in these times of lax morality, they had no more delicacy with respect to their mistresses, and that the latter almost always left them valuable and durable remembrances, as if they endeavoured to conquer the fragility of their sentiments by the solidity of their gifts.

Men then made their way in the world by the means of women without blushing. Such as were only beautiful gave their beauty; whence, without doubt, comes the proverb, "That the most beautiful girl in the world can give no more than she has." Such as were rich, gave in addition a part of their money; and a vast number of heroes of that gallant period may be cited who would neither have won their spurs in the first place, nor their battles afterwards, without the purse, more or less furnished, which their mistress fastened to the saddle-bow.

D'Artagnan possessed nothing; provincial diffidence, that slight varnish, that ephemeral flower, that down of the peach, had been borne to the winds by the but little orthodox counsels which the three musketeers gave their friend. D'Artagnan, following the strange custom of the times, considered himself at Paris as on a campaign, and that neither more nor less than if he had been in Flanders,—Spain yonder, woman here. In each there was an enemy to contend with, and contributions to be levied.

But, we must say, at the present moment D'Artagnan was governed by a much more noble and disinterested feeling. The mercer had told him he was rich; the young man might easily guess that, with so weak a man as M. Bonacieux, it was most likely the young wife kept the purse. But all this had no influence upon the feeling produced by the sight of Madame Bonacieux, and interest remained nearly foreign to this commencement of love, which had been the consequence of it. We say nearly, for the idea that a young, handsome, kind and witty woman is at the same time rich, takes nothing from the charm of this beginning of love, but, on the contrary, strengthens it.

There are in affluence a crowd of aristocratic cares and caprices which are highly becoming to beauty. A fine and white stocking, a silken robe, a lace kerchief, a pretty slipper on the foot, a tasty ribbon on the head, do not make an ugly woman pretty, but they make a pretty woman beautiful, without reckoning the hands which gain by all this ; the hands, among women particularly, to be beautiful must be idle.

Then D'Artagnan, as the reader, from whom we have not concealed the state of his fortune, very well knows,—D'Artagnan was not a millionnaire ; he hoped to become one some day, but the time which in his own mind he fixed upon for this happy change was still far distant. In the meanwhile, how disheartening to see the woman one loves long for those thousands of nothings which constitute a woman's happiness, and be unable to give her those thousands of nothings ! At least, when the woman is rich and the lover is not, that which he cannot offer she offers to herself ; and although it is generally with her husband's money that she procures herself this indulgence, the gratitude for it seldom reverts to him.

Then D'Artagnan, disposed to become the most tender of lovers, was at the same time a very devoted friend. In the midst of his amorous projects upon the mercer's wife, he did not forget his friends. The pretty Madame Bonacieux was just the woman to walk with in the Plaine St. Denis, or in the fair of Saint-Germain, in company with Athos, Porthos, and Aramis, to whom D'Artagnan would be so proud to display such a conquest. Then, when people walk for any length of time they become hungry, at least D'Artagnan had fancied so several times lately ; and they could enjoy some of those little charming dinners, in which we, on one side, touch the hand of a friend, and on the other, the foot of a mistress. Besides, on pressing occasions, in extreme difficulties, D'Artagnan would become the preserver of his friends.

And Monsieur Bonacieux, whom D'Artagnan had pushed into the hands of the sbirri, denying him aloud, although he had promised in a whisper to save him ! We are compelled to admit to our readers, that D'Artagnan thought nothing about him in any way ; or that, if he did think of him, it was only to say to himself that he was very well where he was, wherever it might be. Love is the most selfish of all the passions.

Let our readers, however, be satisfied ; if D'Artagnan forgets his host, or appears to forget him, under the pretence of not knowing where he has been taken to, we will not forget him, and we know where he is. But for the moment, let us do as the amorous Gascon did ; we will see after the worthy mercer presently.

D'Artagnan, reflecting on his future loves, addressing himself to the beautiful night, and smiling at the stars, reascended the Rue Cherche-Midi, or Chasse-Midi, as it was then called. As he found himself in the quarter in which Aramis lived, he took it into his head to pay his friend a visit, in order to explain to him why he had sent Planchet to him, with a request that he would come instantly to the Mouse-trap. Now, if Aramis was at home when Planchet came to his abode, he had doubtless hastened to the Rue des Fossoyeurs, and finding nobody there but his two other companions, perhaps they would not be able to conceive what all this meant. This mystery required an explanation ; at least, so D'Artagnan thought.

And he likewise whispered to himself that he thought this was an opportunity for talking about pretty little Madame Bonacieux, of whom his head, if not his heart, was already full. We must never look for discretion in first love. First love is accompanied by such excessive joy, that unless this joy be allowed to overflow, it will stifle you.

Paris for two hours past had been dark, and began to be deserted. Eleven o'clock struck by all the clocks of the Faubourg Saint-Germain ; it was delightful weather ; D'Artagnan was passing along a lane upon the spot where the Rue d'Assas is now situated, respiring the balmy emanations which were borne upon the wind from the Rue Vaugirard, and which arose from the gardens refreshed by the dews of evening and the breeze of night. From a distance sounded, deadened, however, by good shutters, the songs of the tipplers enjoying themselves in the cabarets in the plain. When arrived at the end of the lane, D'Artagnan turned to the left. The house in which Aramis dwelt was situated between the Rue Cassette and the Rue Servandoni.

D'Artagnan had just passed the Rue Cassette, and already perceived the door of his friend's house, shaded by a mass of sycamores and clematis, which formed a vast arch opposite the front of it, when he perceived something like a shadow issuing from the Rue Servandoni. This something was enveloped in a cloak, and D'Artagnan at first believed it was a man ; but by the smallness of the form, the hesitation of the progress, and the indecision of the step, he soon discovered that it was a woman. Further, this woman, as if not certain of the house she was seeking, lifted up her eyes to look around her, stopped, went a little back, and then returned again. D'Artagnan was perplexed.

" If I were to go and offer her my services !" thought he. " By her step she must be young, perhaps pretty. Oh ! yes. But a woman who wanders about the streets at this hour seldom does so but to meet her lover. Peste ! to go and disturb an assignation would not be the best means of commencing an acquaintance."

The young woman, however, continued advancing slowly, counting the houses and windows. This was neither a long nor a difficult affair ; there were but three hotels, in this part of the street, two windows looking out upon that street, and one of them was that of a pavilion parallel to that which Aramis occupied, the other was that of Aramis himself.

" Pardieu !" said D'Artagnan to himself, to whose mind the niece of the theologian reverted ; " Pardieu ! it would be droll if this late flying dove should be in search of our friend's house. But, by my soul, that seems more than probable. Ah ! my dear friend Aramis, this time, I will find you out."

And D'Artagnan, making himself as small as he could, concealed himself in the darkest side of the street, near a stone bench placed at the back of a niche.

The young woman continued to advance, for, in addition to the lightness of her step, which had betrayed her, she had just emitted a little cough which announced a clear sweet voice. D'Artagnan believed this cough to be a signal.

Nevertheless, whether this cough had been answered to by an equivalent signal, which had removed the resolution of the nocturnal seeker, or whether she had recognized that she had arrived at the end of her journey, she boldly drew near to Aramis's shutter, and tapped at three equal intervals with her bent finger.

" This is all very fine, friend Aramis," murmured D'Artagnan. " Ah ! master hypocrite ! this is the way you study theology, is it ?"

The three blows were scarcely struck, when the inward casement was opened, and a light appeared through the apertures of the shutter.

" Ah ! ah !" said the listener, " not through doors, but through windows ! Ah ! ah ! this was an expected visit. We shall see the windows open, and the lady enter by escalade ! Very pretty !"

But to the great astonishment of D'Artagnan, the shutter remained closed. Still more, the light which had shone out for an instant disappeared, and all was dark again.

D'Artagnan thought this could not last long, and continued to look with all his eyes, and listen with all his ears.

He was right : at the end of some seconds two sharp taps were heard in the interior ; the young woman of the street replied by a single tap, and the shutter was opened a little way.

It may be judged whether D'Artagnan looked or listened with avidity. Unfortunately the light had been removed into another chamber. But the eyes of the young man were accustomed to the night. Besides, the eyes of Gascons have, as it is asserted, like those of cats, the faculty of seeing in the dark.

D'Artagnan then saw that the young woman took from her pocket a white object, which she unfolded quickly, and which took the form of a handkerchief. She made her interlocutor observe the corner of this unfolded object.

This immediately recalled to D'Artagnan's mind the handkerchief which he had found at the feet of Madame Bonacieux, which had reminded him of that which he had dragged from under Aramis's foot.

" What the devil could that handkerchief mean ?"

Placed where he was, D'Artagnan could not perceive the face of Aramis ; we say Aramis, because the young man entertained no doubt that it was his friend who held this dialogue from the interior with the lady of the exterior ; curiosity prevailed over prudence, and taking advantage of the preoccupation in which the sight of the handkerchief appeared to have plunged the two personages now on the scene, he stole from his hiding place, and quick as lightning, but stepping with utmost caution, he went and placed himself close to the angle of the wall, from which his eye could plunge into the interior of the apartment.

Upon gaining this advantage, D'Artagnan was near uttering a cry of surprise ; it was not Aramis who was conversing with the nocturnal visitor, it was a woman ! D'Artagnan, however, could only see enough to recognise the form of her vestments, not enough to distinguish her features.

At the same instant the woman of the apartment drew a second handkerchief from her pocket, and exchanged it for that which had just been shown to her. Then some words were pronounced by the two wcmen. At length the shutter was closed : the woman who was outside the window turned round, and passed within four steps of D'Artagnan, pulling down the hood of her cloak ; but the precaution was too late, D'Artagnan had already recognised Madame Bonacieux.

Madame Bonacieux ! The suspicion that it was she had crossed the mind of D'Artagnan when she drew the handkerchief from her pocket ; but what probability was there that Madame Bonacieux, who had sent for M. Laporte, in order to be reconducted to the Louvre, should be running about the streets of Paris, at half-past eleven at night, at the risk of being carried off a second time ?

It must be, then, for some affair of importance : and what is the affair of the greatest importance to a pretty woman of twenty-five ? Love.

But was it on her own account or on account of another person that she exposed herself to such hazards ? This was a question the young man asked himself, whom the demon of jealousy already gnawed to the heart, neither more nor less than a settled lover.

There was, besides, a very simple means of satisfying himself whither Madame Bonacieux was going : that was to follow her. This means was so simple, that D'Artagnan employed it quite naturally and instinctively.

But at the sight of the young man, who detached himself from his wall like a statue walking from its niche, and at the noise of the steps which she heard resound behind her, Madame Bonacieux uttered a little cry and fled.

D'Artagnan ran after her. It was not a very difficult thing for him to overtake a woman embarrassed with her cloak. He came up to her before she had traversed a third of the street. The unfortunate woman was exhausted, not by fatigue, but by terror, and when D'Artagnan placed his hand upon her shoulder, she sank upon one knee, crying in a choking voice :

" Kill me, if you please, you shall know nothing !"

D'Artagnan raised her by passing his arm round her waist ; but as he felt by her weight she was on the point of fainting, he made haste to reassure her by protestations of devotedness. These protestations were nothing for Madame Bonacieux, for such protestations may be made with the worst intentions in the world ; but the voice was all. Madame Bonacieux thought she recognised the sound of that voice ; she opened her eyes, cast a quick glance upon the man who had terrified her so, and at once perceiving it was D'Artagnan, she uttered a cry of joy.

"Oh! it is you! it is you! thank God! thank God!"

"Yes, it is I!" said D'Artagnan, "it is I, whom God has sent to watch over you."

"Was it with that intention you followed me?" asked the young woman, with a coquettish smile, whose somewhat bantering character resumed its influence, and with whom all fear had disappeared from the moment in which she recognised a friend in one she had taken for an enemy.

"No," said D'Artagnan; "no, I confess it: it was chance that threw me in your way; I saw a female knocking at the window of one of my friends."

"Of one of your friends?" interrupted Madame Bonacieux.

"Without doubt; Aramis is one of my most intimate friends."

"Aramis! who is he?"

"Come, come, you won't tell me you don't know Aramis?"

"This is the first time I ever heard his name pronounced."

"It is the first time, then, that you ever went to that house?"

"Certainly it is."

"And you did not know that it was inhabited by a young man?"

"No."

"By a musketeer?"

"Not at all."

"It was not him, then, you came to seek?"

"Not the least in the world. Besides, you must have seen that the person I spoke to was a woman."

"That is true; but this woman may be one of the friends of Aramis."

"I know nothing of th t."

"Since she lodges with him."

"That does not concern me."

"But who is she?"

"Oh! that is not my secret."

"My dear Madame Bonacieux, you are charming; but at the same time you are one of the most mysterious women."

"Do I lose much by that?"

"No; you are, on the contrary, adorable!"

"Give me your arm, then."

"Most willingly. And now?"

"Now conduct me."

"Where?"

"Where I am going."

"But where are you going?"

"You will see, because you will leave me at the door."

"Shall I wait for you?"

"That will be useless."

"You will return alone, then?"

"Perhaps I may, perhaps I may not."

" But will the person who shall accompany you afterwards be a man or a woman ?"

" I don't know yet."

" But I will know it !"

" How ?"

" I will wait for your coming out."

" In that case, adieu !"

" Why so ?"

" I do not want you."

" But you have claimed——"

" The aid of a gentleman, not the watchfulness of a spy."

" The word is rather hard."

" How are they called who follow others in spite of them ?"

" They are indiscreet."

" The word is too mild."

" Well, madame, I perceive I must act as you please."

" Why did you deprive yourself of the merit of doing so at once ?"

" Is there no merit in repentance ?"

" And you do really repent ?"

" I know nothing about it myself. But what I know is, that I promise to do all you wish if you will allow me to accompany you where you are going."

" And you will leave me afterwards ?"

" Yes."

" Without waiting for my coming out again ?"

" No."

" Parole d'honneur ?"

" By the faith of a gentleman."

" Take my arm, then, and let us go on."

D'Artagnan offered his arm to Madame Bonacieux, who willingly took it, half laughing, half trembling, and both gained the top of Rue la Harpe. When arrived there the young woman seemed to hesitate, as she had before done in the Rue Vaugirard. She, however, appeared by certain signs, to recognize a door ; and approaching that door,—

" And now, monsieur," said she, " it is here I have business ; a thousand thanks for your honourable company, which has saved me from all the dangers to which, alone, I might have been exposed. But the moment is come to keep your word : I am arrived at the place of my destination."

" And you will have nothing to fear on your return ?"

" I shall have nothing to fear but robbers."

" And is that nothing ?"

" What could they take from me ?—I have not a denier about me."

" You forget that beautiful handkerchief, with the coat of arms."

" Which ?"

" That which I found at your feet, and replaced in your pocket !"

" Silence ! silence ! imprudent man ! Do you wish to destroy me ?"

"You see very plainly that there is still danger for you, since a single word makes you tremble ; and you confess that if that word were heard you would be ruined. Come, come, madame !" cried D'Artagnan, seizing her hands, and surveying her with an ardent glance ; "come ! be more generous—trust to me ; have you not read in my eyes, that there is nothing but devotion and sympathy in my heart ?"

"Yes," replied Madame Bonacieux ; "therefore, ask my own secrets, and I will tell them to you ; but those of others,—that is quite another thing."

"It is all very well," said D'Artagnan. " I shall discover them ; as these secrets may have an influence over your life, these secrets must become mine."

"Beware of what you do !" cried the young woman, in a manner so serious as made D'Artagnan start, in spite of himself. " Oh ! meddle in nothing which concerns me ; do not seek to assist me in that which I am accomplishing. And this I ask of you in the name of the interest with which I inspire you ; in the name of the service you have rendered me, and which I never shall forget while I have life. Rather place faith in what I tell you. Take no more concern about me ; I exist no longer for you, any more than if you had never seen me."

"Must Aramis do as much as I, madame ?" said D'Artagnan, deeply piqued.

"This is the second or third time, monsieur, that you have repeated that name, and yet I have told you that I do not know him."

"You do not know the man at whose shutter you went and knocked ? Indeed, madame, you think me too credulous !"

"Confess, now, that it is for the sake of making me talk that you invent this history, and create this personage."

"I invent nothing, madame : I create nothing : I only speak the exact truth."

"And you say that one of your friends lives in that house."

"I say so, and I repeat it for the third time ; that house is that in which one of my friends live ; and that friend is Aramis."

"All this will be cleared up at a later period," murmured the young woman ; "no, monsieur, be silent."

"If you could see my heart," said D'Artagnan, "you would there read so much curiosity that you would pity me ; and so much love, that you would instantly satisfy my curiosity. We have nothing to fear from those who love us."

"You speak very quickly of love, monsieur !" said the young woman, shaking her head.

"That is because love has come suddenly upon me, and for the first time ; and because I am only twenty years old."

The young woman looked at him furtively.

"Listen ; I am already upon the scent," resumed D'Artagnan. " About three months ago I was near having a duel with Aramis, concerning a handkerchief resembling that you showed to the female in the house ; for a handkerchief marked in the same manner, I am sure."

"Monsieur," said the young woman, "you fátigue me very much, I assure you, by your questions."

"But you, madame! prudent as you are, think, if you were to be arrested with that handkerchief, and that handkerchief were to be seized, would you not be compromised?"

"In what way : are not the initials mine—C. B.—Constance Bonacieux?"

"Or Camille de Bois-Tracy."

"Silence, monsieur! once again, silence! Ah! since the dangers I incur on my own account cannot stop you, think of those you may yourself run!"

"Danger for me?"

"Yes ; there is risk of imprisonment, risk of life, in knowing me."

"Then I will not leave you."

"Monsieur!" said the young woman, supplicating him, and clasping her hands together ; "monsieur, in the name of heaven, by the name of a soldier, by the courtesy of a gentleman, depart !—there !—there is midnight striking !—that is the hour at which I am expected."

"Madame," said the young man, bowing ; "I can refuse nothing asked of me thus ; be satisfied, I will depart."

"But, you will not follow me ; you will not watch me?"

"I will return home instantly."

"Ah! I was quite sure you were a good and brave young man," said Madame Bonacieux, holding out her hand to him, and placing the other upon the knocker of a little door almost hidden in the wall.

D'Artagnan seized the hand that was held out to him, and kissed it ardently.

"Ah! I wish I had never seen you!" cried D'Artagnan, with that ingenuous roughness which women often prefer to the affectations of politeness, because it betrays the depth of the thought, and proves that feeling prevails over reason.

"Well!" resumed Madame Bonacieux, in a voice that was almost caressing, and pressing the hand of D'Artagnan, who had not left hold of hers, "well! I will not say as much as you do : what is lost for to-day, may not be lost for ever. Who knows, when I shall be some day at liberty, that I may not satisfy your curiosity?"

"And, will you make the same promise to my love?" cried D'Artagnan, beside himself with joy.

"Oh! as to that, I do not engage myself ; that depends upon the sentiments you may inspire me with."

"Then, to-day, madame——"

"Oh! to-day, I have got no further than gratitude."

"Ah! you are too charming," said D'Artagnan, sorrowfully ; "and you abuse my love."

"No, I use your generosity ; that's all. But be of good cheer ; with certain people, everything comes round."

"Oh! you render me the happiest of men! Do not forget this evening—do not forget that promise."

" Be satisfied, in time and place I will remember everything. Well ! now then, go ; go, in the name of Heaven ! I was expected exactly at midnight, and I am late."

" By five minutes."

" Yes ; but in certain circumstances, five minutes are five ages."

" When one loves."

" Well ! and who told you I had not to do with some one in love !"

" It is a man, then, that expects you ?" cried D'Artagnan,—" a man !"

" Oh, Lord ! oh, Lord ! there is the discussion going to begin again !" said Madame Bonacieux, with a half-smile, which was not quite free from a tinge of impatience.

" No, no ; I am going, I am going ; I believe in you, and I would have all the merit of my devotedness, if that devotedness were even a stupidity. Adieu, madame, adieu !"

And as if he only felt the strength to detach himself from the hand he held by a violent effort, he sprang away, running, whilst Madame Bonacieux knocked, as she had done at the shutter, three light and regular taps ; then, when he had gained the angle of the street, he returned : the door had been opened, and shut again—the mercer's pretty wife had disappeared.

D'Artagnan pursued his way ; he had given his word not to watch Madame Bonacieux, and if his life had depended upon the spot to which she was going, or the person who should accompany her, D'Artagnan would have returned home, since he had promised that he would do so. In five minutes he was in the Rue des Fossoyeurs.

" Poor Athos !" said he ; " he will never guess what all this means. He will have fallen asleep waiting for me, or else he will have returned home, where he will have learned that a woman had been there. A woman at Athos's house ! After all," continued D'Artagnan, "there was certainly one in Aramis's house. All this is very strange ; I should like to know how it will all end."

" Badly ! monsieur—badly !" replied a voice, which the young man recognised as that of Planchet ; for, soliloquising aloud, as very pre-occupied people do, he had entered the alley, at the bottom of which were the stairs which led to his chamber.

" How, badly ? What do you mean by that, you stupid fellow ?" asked D'Artagnan ; " what has happened, then ?"

" All sorts of misfortunes."

" What ?"

" In the first place, M. Athos is arrested."

" Arrested ! Athos arrested ! What for ?"

" He was found in your lodging,—they took him for you."

" And by whom was he arrested ?"

" By the guards whom the black men you put to flight fetched."

" Why did he not tell them his name ? Why did he not tell them he knew nothing about this affair ?"

" He took care not to do so, monsieur ; on the contrary, he came up to me, and said, ' It is your master that wants his liberty at this moment, and not I, since he knows everything, and I know nothing. They will believe he is arrested, and that will give him time ; in three days I will tell them who I am, and they cannot fail to set me at liberty again."

" Bravo, Athos ! noble heart !" murmured D'Artagnan. " I know him well there ! And what did the *sbirri* do ?"

" Four conveyed him away, I don't know where—to the Bastille or For l'Evêque ; two remained with the black men, who rummaged every place out, and took all the papers ; the two last mounted guard at the door during this examination ; then, when all was over, they went away, leaving the house empty and the doors open."

" And Porthos and Aramis ?"

" I could not find them ; they did not come."

" But they may come from one moment to the other, for you left word that I wanted them ?"

" Yes, monsieur."

" Well, don't stir, then ; if they come, tell them what has happened. Let them wait for me at the Pomme de Pin ; here it would be dangerous —the house may be watched. I will run to M. de Tréville's to tell him all this, and will join them there."

" Very well, monsieur," said Planchet.

" But you will remain, will you not? You are not afraid ?" said D'Artagnan, coming back to recommend courage to his lackey.

" Be satisfied, monsieur," said Planchet ; " you do not know me yet. I am brave when I set about it—I have only to begin ; besides, I am a Picard."

" Then that's understood," said D'Artagnan ; " you would rather be killed than desert your post ?"

" Yes, monsieur ; and there is nothing I would not do to prove to monsieur that I am attached to him."

" Good !" said D'Artagnan to himself. " It appears that the method I have adopted with this boy is decidedly a good one ; I shall employ it upon occasion."

And with all the swiftness of his legs, already a little fatigued, how-ever, with the exercise of the day and night, D'Artagnan directed his course towards M. de Tréville's.

M. de Tréville was not at his hotel ; his company was on guard at the Louvre ; he was at the Louvre with his company.

He must get at M. de Tréville ; it was of importance that he should be informed of what was going on. D'Artagnan resolved to endeavour to get into the Louvre. His costume of a guard in the company of M. des Essarts would, he thought, be a passport for him.

He therefore went down the Rue des Petits Augustins, and came up to the quay, in order to take the Pont Neuf. He had an idea of passing over by the ferry-boat ; but, on gaining the river-side, he had mechani-cally put his hand into his pocket, and perceived that he had not where-withal to pay the ferryman.

As he gained the top of the Rue Guénegaud, he saw two persons coming out of the Rue Dauphine whose appearance very much struck him. One was a man, and the other a woman : the latter very much like Madame Bonacieux in size and step, the former could be nobody but Aramis.

Besides, the woman had on that black cloak whose outline D'Artagnan could still see reflected upon the shutter of the Rue de Vaugirard, and upon the door of the Rue de la Harpe.

And still further, the man wore the uniform of a musketeer.

The woman's hood was pulled down, and the man held a handkerchief to his face ; both, this double precaution indicated—both had an interest in not being known then.

They took the bridge ; that was D'Artagnan's road, as D'Artagnan was going to the Louvre ; D'Artagnan followed them.

He had not gone twenty steps before he became convinced that the woman was really Madame Bonacieux, and the man Aramis.

He felt himself doubly betrayed—by his friend, and by her whom he already loved as a mistress. Madame Bonacieux had declared to him, by all that was holy, that she did not know Aramis ; and, a quarter of an hour after having made this assertion, he found her hanging on the arm of Aramis.

D'Artagnan did not reflect that he had only known the mercer's pretty wife for three hours ; that she owed him nothing but a little gratitude for having delivered her from the black men who wished to carry her off, and that she had promised him nothing. He considered himself to be an outraged, betrayed, and ridiculed lover ; blood and anger mounted to his face—he was resolved to unravel the mystery.

The young man and woman perceived they were watched, and re-doubled their speed. D'Artagnan determined upon his course : he passed them, then returned, so as to meet them exactly before the *Samaritaine*, which was illuminated by a lamp, which threw its light over all that part of the bridge.

D'Artagnan stopped before them, and they stopped before him.

"What do you want, monsieur ?" demanded the musketeer, drawing back a step, and with a foreign accent, which proved to D'Artagnan that he was deceived in one part of his conjectures at least.

"It is not Aramis !" cried he.

"No, monsieur, it is not Aramis ; and by your exclamation I perceive you have mistaken me for another, and pardon you."

"You pardon me !" cried D'Artagnan.

"Yes," replied the unknown. "Allow me, then, to pass on, since it is not with me you have anything to do."

"You are right, monsieur, it is not with you I have anything to do ; it is with madame, here."

"With madame ! You do not know her !" replied the stranger.

"You are deceived, monsieur ; I know her very well."

"Ah," said Madame Bonacieux, in a tone of reproach, "ah, monsieur, I had the promise of a soldier and the word of a gentleman ; I thought I might have depended upon them !"

"And I, madame !" said D'Artagnan, embarrassed—"you promised me——"

"Take my arm, madame," said the stranger, "and let us proceed on our way."

D'Artagnan, however, stupefied, cast down, annihilated by all that happened so strangely to him, still stood, with his arms crossed, before the musketeer and Madame Bonacieux.

The musketeer advanced two steps, and pushed D'Artagnan aside with his hand.

D'Artagnan made a spring backwards, and drew his sword.

At the same time, and with the rapidity of lightning, the unknown drew his.

"In the name of heaven, milord !" cried Madame Bonacieux, throwing herself between the combatants, and seizing the swords with her hands.

"Milord !" cried D'Artagnan, enlightened by a sudden idea, "milord ! Pardon me, monsieur, but are you not——"

"Milord, the Duke of Buckingham !" said Madame Bonacieux, in an undertone ; "and now you may ruin us all."

"Milord—madame, I ask a hundred pardons ! but I love her, milord, and was jealous ; you know what it is to love, milord. Pardon me, and then tell me how I can risk my life to serve your grace ?"

"You are a brave young man !" said Buckingham, holding out his hand to D'Artagnan, who pressed it respectfully. "You offer me your services ; with the same frankness I accept them. Follow us at a distance of twenty paces, to the Louvre, and if any one watches us, slay him !"

D'Artagnan placed his naked sword under his arm, allowed the duke and Madame Bonacieux to proceed twenty steps, and then followed them, ready to execute the instructions of the noble and elegant minister of Charles I.

But fortunately he had no opportunity to give the duke this proof of his devotion, and the young woman and the handsome musketeer entered the Louvre by the wicket of the Echelle, without meeting with any interruption.

As for D'Artagnan, he immediately repaired to the cabaret of the Pomme-de-Pin, where he found Porthos and Aramis, who were waiting for him. But, without giving them any explanation of the alarm and inconvenience he had caused them, he told them that he had terminated the affair alone, in which he had, for a moment, thought he should stand in need of their assistance.

And now, carried away as we are by our history, we must leave our three friends to return each to his own home, and follow the Duke of Buckingham and his guide through the labyrinths of the Louvre.

CHAPTER XII.

GEORGE VILLIERS, DUKE OF BUCKINGHAM.

MADAME BONACIEUX and the duke entered the Louvre without difficulty : Madame Bonacieux was known to belong to the queen, the duke wore the uniform of the musketeers of M. de Tréville, who were, as we have said, that evening on guard. Besides, Germain was in the interests of the queen, and, if anything should happen, Madame Bonacieux would only be accused of having introduced her lover into the Louvre. She took the risk upon herself ; to be sure her reputation was jeopardised, but of what value in the world was the reputation of the little wife of a mercer ?

Once entered into the interior of the court, the duke and the young woman kept along the wall for about twenty-five steps ; this space passed, Madame Bonacieux pushed a little side-door, open by day, but generally closed at night. The door yielded : both entered, and found themselves in darkness ; but Madame Bonacieux was acquainted with all the turnings and windings of this part of the Louvre, destined for the people of the household. She closed the door after her, took the duke by the hand, advanced a little, feeling her way, came to a balustrade, put her foot upon the bottom step, and began to ascend a flight of stairs ; the duke counted two stories. She then turned to the right, followed the course of a long corridor, redescended a story, went a few steps further, introduced a key into a lock, opened a door, and pushed the duke into an apartment lighted only by a night-lamp, saying, "Remain here, milord-duke ; some one will come." She then went out by the same door, which she locked, so that the duke found himself literally a prisoner.

Nevertheless, isolated as he was, we must say that the Duke of Buckingham did not experience an instant of fear : one of the salient sides of his character was the seeking of adventures and a love of the romantic. Brave, even rash, and enterprising, this was not the first time he had risked his life in such attempts ; he had learnt that the pretended message from Anne of Austria, upon the faith of which he had come to Paris, was a snare, and instead of regaining England, he had, abusing the position in which he had been placed, declared to the queen that he would not go back again without having seen her. The queen had at first positively refused, but at length became afraid that the duke, if exasperated, would commit some rashness. She had already decided upon seeing him and urging his immediate departure, when, on the very evening of coming to this decision, Madame Bonacieux, who was charged with going to fetch the duke and conducting him to the Louvre, was carried off. During two days it was not known what had become of her, and everything remained in suspense. But when once free, and placed in communication with Laporte, matters resumed their course, and she accomplished the perilous enterprise which, but for her abduction, would have been executed three days earlier.

Buckingham, on being left alone, walked towards a mirror. His musketeer's uniform became him wonderfully well.

At thirty-five, which was then his age, he passed, with just title, for the handsomest gentleman and the most elegant cavalier of France or England.

The favourite of two kings, immensely rich, all powerful in a kingdom which he threw into disorder at his fancy, and calmed again at his caprice, George Villiers, Duke of Buckingham, passed through one of those fabulous existences which remain in the course of centuries as an astonishment for posterity.

Thus, sure of himself, convinced of his own power, certain that the laws which rule other men could not reach him, he went straight to the object he aimed at, even were this object so elevated and so dazzling that it would have been madness for any other even to have contemplated it. It was thus he had succeeded in gaining access several times to the beautiful and haughty Anne of Austria, and making himself loved by her, by astonishing her.

George Villiers then placed himself before the mirror, as we have said, restored the undulations to his beautiful hair, which the weight of his hat had disordered, turned his moustache, and, with a heart swelling with joy, happy and proud of being near the moment he had so long sighed for, he smiled upon himself with pride and hope.

At this moment a door concealed in the tapestry opened, and a woman appeared. Buckingham saw this apparition in the glass ; he uttered a cry—it was the queen !

Anne of Austria was then from twenty-six to twenty-seven years of age—that is to say, she was in the full splendour of her beauty.

Her carriage was that of a queen or a goddess ; her eyes, which cast the brilliancy of emeralds, were perfectly beautiful, and yet were, at the same time, full of sweetness and majesty.

Her mouth was small and rosy, and although her under-lip, like that of the princes of the house of Austria, protruded slightly beyond the other, it was eminently lovely in its smile, but as profoundly disdainful in the expression of contempt.

Her skin was admired for its velvety softness, her hands and arms were of surpassing beauty, all the poets of the time singing them as incomparable.

Lastly, her hair, which, from being light in her youth, had become chestnut, and which she wore curled very plain, and with much powder, admirably set off her face, in which the most rigid critic could only have descried a little less rouge, and the most fastidious statuary a little more fineness in the nose.

Buckingham remained for a moment dazzled ; never had Anne of Austria appeared to him so beautiful, amidst balls, fêtes, or carousals, as she appeared to him at this moment, dressed in a simple robe of white satin, and accompanied by Donna Estafania, the only one of her Spanish women that had not been driven from her by the jealousy of the king, or by the persecutions of the cardinal.

Anne of Austria made two steps forward ; Buckingham threw himself at her feet, and before the queen could prevent him, kissed the hem ot her robe.

" Duke, you already know that it is not I who have caused you to be written to."

"Yes, yes, madame ! yes, your majesty !" cried the duke ; " I know that I must have been mad, senseless, to believe that snow would become animated or marble warm ; but what then ! they who love easily believe in love ;—besides, this voyage is not a loss, since I see you."

" Yes," replied Anne, " but you know why and how I see you, milord ! I see you out of pity for yourself ; I see you because, insensible to all my sufferings, you persist in remaining in a city where, by remaining, you run the risk of your own life, and make me run the risk of my honour ; I see you to tell you that everything separates us. the depths of the sea, the enmity of kingdoms, the sanctity of vows. It is sacrilege to struggle against so many things, milord. In short, I see you to tell you that we must never see each other again."

" Speak on, madame, speak on, queen," said Buckingham ; "the sweetness of your voice covers the harshness of your words. You talk ot sacrilege ! why, the sacrilege is the separation of two hearts formed by God for each other."

" Milord," cried the queen, " you forget that I have never told you I loved you."

" But you have never told me that you did not love me, and truly, to speak such words to me would be, on the part of your majesty, too great an ingratitude. For tell me, where can you find a love like mine, a love which neither time, nor absence, nor despair can extinguish ; a love which contents itself with a lost ribbon, a stray look, or a chance word ? It is now three years, madame, since I saw you for the first time, and during those three years I have loved you thus.

" Shall I tell you how you were dressed the first time I saw you ? shall I describe to you every one of the ornaments you wore ? Mark ! I see you now ; you were seated upon cushions, in the Spanish fashion ; you wore a robe of green satin embroidered with gold and silver, hanging sleeves, fastened up upon your beautiful arms, upon those lovely arms, with large diamonds ; you wore a close ruff, a small cap upon your head of the same colour as your robe, and in that cap a heron's feather.

" Oh, madame ! madame ! I shut my eyes, and I can see you such as you then were ; I open them again, and I see you such as you are now —a hundred times still more beautiful !"

" What folly !" murmured Anne of Austria, who had not the courage to find fault with the duke for having so well preserved her portrait in his heart ; " what folly to feed a useless passion with such remembrances !"

"And upon what then must I live ? I have nothing but remembrances. They are my happiness, my treasures, my hopes. Every time that I see you is a fresh diamond which I enclose in the casket of my heart.

This is the fourth which you have let fall and I have picked up ; for, in three years, madame, I have only seen you four times ; the first which I have just described to you, the second at the mansion of Madame de Chevreuse, the third in the gardens of Amiens."

" Duke," said the queen, blushing, " never name that evening."

" Oh, yes ! let me speak of it, on the contrary, let me speak of it ; that is the most happy and brilliant evening of my life ! Do you not remember what a beautiful night it was ? How soft and perfumed the air was ? and how lovely the blue star-enamelled sky was ?

" Ah ! that time, madame, I was able for one instant to be alone with you ; that time you were about to tell me all, the isolation of your life, the griefs of your heart. You leant upon my arm ; upon this, madame ! I felt, as leaning my head towards you, your beautiful hair touched my cheek, and every time that it did touch me, I trembled from head to foot. Oh, queen, queen ! you do not know what felicity from heaven, what joys from Paradise, are comprised in a moment like that ! I would give all my wealth, all my fortunes, all my glory, all the days I have to live, for such an instant, for a night like that ! for that night, madame, that night you loved me, I will swear it."

" Milord, yes, it is possible that the influence of the place, the charm of the beautiful evening, the fascination of your look, the thousand circumstances, in short, which sometimes unite to destroy a woman, were grouped around me on that fatal evening ; but, milord, you saw the queen come to the aid of the woman who faltered : at the first word you dared to utter, at the first freedom to which I had to reply, I summoned my attendants."

" Yes, yes ! that is true, and any other love but mine would have sunk beneath this ordeal, but my love came out from it more ardent and more eternal. You believed you should fly from me by returning to Paris, you believed that I should not dare to quit the treasure over which my master had charged me to watch. What to me were all the treasures in the world, or all the kings of the earth ! Eight days after I was back again, madame. That time you had nothing to say to me ; I had risked my life and my favour to see you but for a second ; I did not even touch your hand, and you pardoned me on seeing me so submissive and so repentant."

" Yes, but calumny seized upon all those follies in which I took no part, as you well know, milord. The king, excited by M. the Cardinal, made a terrible clamour ; Madame de Vernet was driven from me, Putange was exiled, Madame de Chevreuse fell into disgrace, and when you wished to come back as ambassador to France, the king himself, remember, milord, the king himself opposed it."

" Yes, and France is about to pay for her king's refusal with a war. I am not allowed to see you, madame, but you shall every day hear speak of me ! What object, think you, have this expedition to Ré and this league with the Protestants of Rochelle which I am projecting ? The pleasure of seeing you.

" I have no hope of penetrating sword in hand to Paris, I know that well ; but this war may bring round a peace, this peace will require a negotiator, that negotiator will be me. They will not dare to refuse me then, and I will see you, and will be happy for an instant. Thousands of men, it is true, will have to pay for my happiness with their lives, but what will that signify to me, provided I see you again! All this is perhaps madness, folly, but tell me what woman has a lover more truly in love? what queen has a servant more faithful or more ardent?"

" Milord ! milord ! you invoke in your defence things which accuse you more strongly : milord, all these proofs of love that you boast are little better than crimes."

" Because you do not love me, madame : if you loved me, you would view all this much otherwise : if you loved me, oh ! if you loved me, that would be happiness too great, and I should run mad. Ah ! Madame de Chevreuse, of whom you spoke but now, Madame de Chevreuse was less cruel than you. Holland loved her, and she responded to his love."

" Madame de Chevreuse was not a queen," murmured Anne of Austria, overcome in spite of herself by the expression of so profound a passion.

" You would love me, then, if you were not one; you, madame, say that you would love me then ? I am then to believe that it is the dignity of your rank alone that makes you cruel to me : I may then believe that if you had been Madame de Chevreuse, the poor Buckingham might have hoped ? Thanks for those sweet words ! oh, my lovely queen ! a hundred times, thanks !"

" Oh ! milord ! you have ill understood, wrongly interpreted ; I did not mean to say——"

" Silence! silence!" cried the duke ; " if I am happy in an error do not have the cruelty to deprive me of it. You have told me yourself, madame, that I have been drawn into a snare, and I, perhaps, shall leave my life in it ; for, although it be strange, I have for some time had a presentiment that I shall shortly die." And the duke smiled, with a smile at once sad and charming.

" Oh ! my God !" cried Anne of Austria, with an accent of terror which proved how much greater an interest she took in the duke than she ventured to tell.

" I do not tell you this, madame, to terrify you ; no, it is even ridiculous for me to name it to you, and, believe me, I take no heed of such dreams. But the words you have just spoken, the hope you have almost given me, will have richly paid all—were it my life."

" Oh ! but I," said Anne, " I, duke, have had presentiments likewise, I have had dreams. I dreamt that I saw you lying bleeding, wounded."

" In the left side, was it not, and with a knife !" interrupted Buckingham.

" Yes, it was so, milord, it was so, in the left side, and with a knife.

Who can possibly have told you I had had that dream; I have imparted it to no one but my God, and that in my prayers."

"I ask for no more ; you love me, madame ? it is enough."

"I love you ! I !"

"Yes, yes. Would God send the same dreams to you as to me, if
you did not love me? Should we have the same presentiments if our
existences were not associated by our hearts? You love me, my beautiful queen, and you will weep for me?"

"Oh ! my God ! my God!" cried Anne of Austria, "this is more
than I can bear ! In the name of Heaven, duke, leave me, go ! I do
not know whether I love you or do not love you, but what I know is
that I will not be a perjured woman. Take pity on me, then, and go.
Oh ! if you are struck in France, if you die in France, if I could
imagine that your love for me was the cause of your death, nothing
could console me, I should run mad. Depart, go then, I implore you !"

"Oh ! how beautiful you are thus! Oh ! how I love you !" said
Buckingham.

"Oh ! but go ! go ! I implore you, and come back hereafter ; come
back as ambassador, come back as minister, come back surrounded with
guards who will defend you, with servants who will watch over you,
and then—then I shall be no longer in fear for your days, and I shall
be happy in seeing you."

"Oh ! is this true, is it true what you say?"

"Yes."

"Oh ! then, some pledge of your indulgence, some object which,
coming from you, may assure me that I have not dreamt ; something
you have worn, and that I may wear in my turn,—a ring, a necklace,
a chain."

"Will you go then, will you go, if I give you that you ask for ?"

"Yes."

"This very instant ?"

"Yes."

"You will leave France, you will return to England ?"

"I will, I swear to you I will."

"Wait, then, wait."

And Anne of Austria re-entered her apartment, and came out again
almost immediately, holding a casket in her hand made of rosewood,
with her cipher upon it in gold letters.

"Here, milord, here," said she, "keep this in memory of me."

Buckingham took the casket, and fell a second time on his knees.

"You promised me you would go," said the queen.

"And I keep my word. Your hand, madame, your hand, and I
depart."

Anne of Austria stretched forth her hand, closing her eyes, and
leaning with the other upon Estafania, for she felt her strength ready to
fail her.

Buckingham applied his lips passionately to that beautiful hand, and
then rising said :

"Within six months if I am not dead, I shall have seen you again, madame; even if I have confounded the whole world for that object, I shall have seen you again."

Faithful to the promise he had made, with a desperate effort, he rushed out of the apartment.

In the corridor he met Madame Bonacieux, who waited for him, and who, with the same precautions and the same good fortune, conducted him out of the Louvre.

CHAPTER XIII.

MONSIEUR BONACIEUX.

THERE was in all this, as may have been observed, one personage concerned, of whom, notwithstanding his precarious position, we have appeared to take but very little notice; this personage is M. Bonacieux, the respectable martyr of the political and amorous intrigues which entangled themselves so nicely together at this gallant and chivalric period.

Fortunately, the reader may remember, or may not remember, fortunately, that we promised not to lose sight of him.

The officers who had arrested him, conducted him straight to the Bastille, where he passed tremblingly before a party of soldiers who were loading their muskets.

Thence, introduced into a half-subterranean gallery, he became, on the part of those who had brought him, the object of the grossest insults and the harshest treatment. The *sbirri* perceived that they had not to deal with a gentleman, and they treated him like a very beggar.

At the end of half-an-hour, or thereabouts, an officer came to put an end to his tortures, but not to his inquietudes, by giving the order for M. Bonacieux's being led to the chamber of interrogatories.

Ordinarily, prisoners were interrogated in their own cells, but they did not pay so much respect to M. Bonacieux.

Two guards attended the mercer, who made him traverse a court, and enter a corridor in which were three sentinels, opened a door and pushed him unceremoniously into an apartment, the whole furniture of which consisted of one table, one chair, and a commissary. The commissary was seated in the chair, and was busily writing upon the table.

The two guards led the prisoner towards the table, and, upon a sign from the commissary, drew back so far as to be unable to hear the examination.

The commissary, who had till this time held his head down over his papers, looked up to see what sort of person he had to do with. This commissary was a man of very repulsive mien, with a pointed nose, yellow and salient cheek-bones, small, but keen penetrating eyes, and an expression of countenance partaking of the polecat and the fox. His head, supported by a long and flexible neck, issued from his large black robe, balancing itself with a motion very much like that of the tortoise when drawing his head out of his shell.

He began by asking M. Bonacieux his name, prenames, age, condition, and abode.

The accused replied that his name was Jacques Michel Bonacieux, that he was fifty-one years old, was a retired mercer, and lived Rue des Fossoyeurs, No. 14.

The commissary then, instead of continuing to interrogate him, made him a long speech upon the danger there is for an obscure bourgeois to meddle with public matters.

He complicated this exordium by an exposition in which he painted the power and the acts of M. the Cardinal, that incomparable minister, that conqueror of past ministers, that example for ministers to come, —acts and power which no one would thwart with impunity.

After this second part of his discourse, fixing his hawk's-eye upon poor Bonacieux, he bade him reflect upon the seriousness of his situation.

The reflections of the mercer were already made ; he had consigned to the devil the instant at which M. Laporte had formed the idea of marrying him to his goddaughter, but more particularly that instant in which that goddaughter had been received lady of the *lingerie* to her majesty.

The character of M. Bonacieux was one of profound selfishness, mixed with sordid avarice, the whole seasoned with extreme cowardice The love with which his young wife had inspired him was a secondary sentiment, and was not strong enough to contend with the primitive feelings we have just enumerated.

Bonacieux reflected, in fact, upon what had just been said to him.

" But, M. le Commissaire," said he, timidly, " I beg you to believe that I know and appreciate more than anybody the merit of the incomparable eminence by whom we have the honour to be governed."

" Indeed ?" asked the commissary, with an air of doubt, " indeed ? if that is really the case, how came you in the Bastille ?"

" How I came there or rather why I came there," replied Bonacieux, " is what it is impossible for me to tell you, because I don't know myself ; but to a certainty it is not for having, knowingly at least, disobliged M. the Cardinal."

" You must, nevertheless, have committed a crime, since you are here, and are accused of high treason."

" Of high treason !" cried the terrified Bonacieux, " of high treason ! How is it possible for a poor mercer, who detests all Huguenots, and who abhors all Spaniards, to be accused of high treason ? Consider, monsieur, the thing is materially impossible."

" Monsieur Bonacieux," said the commissary, looking at the accused, as if his little eyes had the faculty of reading to the very depths of hearts, " Monsieur Bonacieux, you have a wife ?"

" Yes, monsieur," replied the mercer, in a tremble, feeling that that was the point at which affairs were likely to become perplexing,—"that is to say, I had one."

" What ? you had one ! what have you done with her then, if you have her no longer ?"

" She has been carried off from me, monsieur."

" Been carried off from you ?" said the commissary. " Ah !"

Bonacieux felt, when he heard this " Ah," that matters were becoming more and more perplexing.

" She has been carried off ?" resumed the commissary, " and do you know who the man is that has committed this outrage ?"

' I think I know him."

" Who is he ?"

" Remember that I affirm nothing, Monsieur le Commissaire, and that I only suspect."

" Whom do you suspect ? Come, answer freely."

M. Bonacieux was in the greatest perplexity possible : had he better deny everything or tell everything ? By denying all, it might be suspected that he must know too much to be so ignorant ; by confessing all, he should prove his good will. He decided then upon telling all.

" I suspect," said he, " a tall, dark man, of lofty carriage, who has the air of a great lord ; he has followed us several times, as I think, when I have waited for my wife at the wicket of the Louvre to fetch her home."

The commissary appeared to experience a little uneasiness.

" And his name ?" said he.

" Oh ! as to his name, I know nothing about it, but, if I were ever to meet him, I should know him in an instant, I will answer for it, even if he were among a thousand persons."

The face of the commissary grew still darker.

" You should recognise him among a thousand, say you ?" continued he.

" That is to say " cried Bonacieux, who saw he had gone wrong, " that is to say,——"

" You have answered that you should recognise him," said the commissary, " that is all very well, and enough for to-day ; before we proceed further, some one must be informed that you know the ravisher of your wife."

" But I have not told you that I know him !" cried Bonacieux in despair, " I told you, on the contrary——"

" Take away the prisoner," said the commissary to the two guards.

" Where must we place him ?" demanded the officer.

" In a dungeon."

" Which ?"

" Good Lord ! in the first you come to, provided it be a safe one," said the commissary, with an indifference which penetrated poor Bonacieux with horror.

" Alas ! alas !" said he to himself, " misfortune hangs over me ; my wife must have committed some frightful crime ; they believe that I am her accomplice, and will punish me with her . one must have spoken, she must have confessed everything, a woman is so weak ! A dungeon, the first he comes to ! that's it ! one night is soon passed over ; and to-morrow to the wheel, to the gallows ! Oh ! my God ! my God ! have pity on me !"

Without listening the least in the world to the lamentations of Master Bonacieux, lamentations to which, besides, they must have been pretty well accustomed, the two guards took the prisoner each by an arm, and led him away, whilst the commissary wrote a letter in haste, and des-patched it by an officer in waiting.

Bonacieux could not close his eyes ; not because his dungeon was so very disagreeable, but because his uneasiness was too great to allow him to sleep. He sat up all night upon his stool, starting at the least noise ; and when the first rays of the sun penetrated into his chamber, the dawn itself appeared to him to have taken a funeral tint.

All at once he heard his bolts drawn, and sprang up with a terrified bound, believing that they were come to fetch him to the scaffold ; so that when he saw purely and simply that it was only his commissary of the preceding evening, attended by his officer, he was ready to embrace them both.

"Your affair has become more complicated since yesterday evening, my good man, and I advise you to tell the whole truth ; for your repent-ance alone can remove the anger of the cardinal."

"Why, I am ready to tell everything," cried Bonacieux, "at least, all that I know. Interrogate me, I entreat you !"

"Where is your wife, in the first place ?"

"Why, did not I tell you she had been stolen away from me ?"

"Yes, but yesterday, at five o'clock in the afternoon, thanks to you, she escaped."

"My wife escaped !" cried Bonacieux. "Oh ! unfortunate creature ! Monsieur, if she has escaped, it is no fault of mine, I will swear."

"What business had you then to go into the chamber of M. d'Artag-nan, your neighbour, with whom you had a long conference, in the course of the day ?"

"Ah ! yes, Monsieur le Commissaire ; yes, that is true, and I confess that I was in the wrong. I did go to M. d'Artagnan's apartment."

"What was the object of that visit ?"

"To beg him to assist me in finding my wife. I believed I had a right to endeavour to recover her ; I was deceived, as it appears, and I ask your pardon for so doing."

"And what did M. D'Artagnan reply ?"

"M. D'Artagnan promised me his assistance ; but I soon found out that he was betraying me."

"You are imposing upon justice ! M. d'Artagnan made an agreement with you, and in virtue of that agreement put to flight the men of the police who had arrested your wife, and has placed her out of reach of all inquiries."

"M. d'Artagnan has carried off my wife ! What can that mean ?"

" Fortunately M. d'Artagnan is in our hands, and you shall be confronted with him."

" Ah ! ma foi ! I ask no better," cried Bonacieux ; " I shall not be sorry to see the face of an acquaintance."

" Bring in M. d'Artagnan," said the commissary to the guards.

The two guards led in Athos.

"Monsieur d'Artagnan," said the commissary, addressing Athos, " declare all that passed yesterday between you and monsieur here."

" But !" cried Bonacieux, "this is not M. d'Artagnan that you have brought before me !"

" What ! not M. d'Artagnan !" exclaimed the commissary.

" Not the least in the world like him," replied Bonacieux.

" What is this gentleman's name ?" asked the commissary.

" I cannot tell you ; I don't know him."

" How ! you don't know him ?"

" No."

" Did you never see him ?"

" Yes, I have seen him, but I don't know what his name is."

" Your name ?" asked the commissary.

" Athos," replied the musketeer.

" But that is not a man's name, that is the name of a mountain," cried the poor commissary, who began to feel a little bewildered.

" That is my name," said Athos, quietly.

" But you said that your name was D'Artagnan."

" Who, I ?"

" Yes, you."

" My guards said to me : ' You are Monsieur d'Artagnan ?' I answered, ' You think so, do you ?' My guards again exclaimed that they were sure I was. I did not think it worth while to contradict them. Besides, I might myself be deceived."

" Monsieur, you insult the majesty of justice."

" Not at all," said Athos, calmly.

" You are Monsieur d'Artagnan."

" You see, monsieur, that you persist in saying that I am."

" But, I tell you, Monsieur le Commissaire," cried Bonacieux, in his turn, " there is not the least doubt about the matter. M. d'Artagnan is my tenant, although he does not pay me my rent, and even better on that account ought I to know him. M. d'Artagnan is a young man, scarcely nineteen, and this gentleman must be thirty at least. M. d'Artagnan is in M. des Essart's guards, and monsieur is in the company of M. de Tréville's musketeers ; look at his uniform, Monsieur le Commissaire, look at his uniform !"

" That's true," murmured the commissary ; "pardieu ! that's true."

At this moment the door was opened quickly, and a messenger, introduced by one of the gate-keepers of the Bastille, gave a letter to the commissary.

" Oh ! unhappy woman !" cried the commissary.

" How ! what do you say ? of whom do you speak ? It is not of my wife, I hope !"

"On the contrary, it is of her. Your affair is becoming a pretty one."

"But," said the agitated mercer, "do me the pleasure, monsieur, to tell me how my own proper affair can become the worse by anything my wife does whilst I am in prison?"

"Because that which she does is part of a plan concerted between you, of an infernal plan!"

"I swear to you, Monsieur le Commissaire, that you are in the profoundest error, that I know nothing in the world about what my wife had to do; that I am entirely a stranger to what she has done, and that if she has committed any follies, I renounce her, I abjure her, I curse her!"

"Bah!" said Athos to the commissary, "if you have no more need of me, send me somewhere; your Monsieur Bonacieux is very unpleasant."

"Reconduct the prisoners to their dungeons," said the commissary, designating, by the same gesture, Athos and Bonacieux, "and let them be guarded more closely than ever."

"And yet," said Athos, with his habitual calmness, "if it be M. d'Artagnan who is concerned in this matter, I do not perceive too clearly how I can take his place."

"Do as I bade you," cried the commissary, "and preserve the profoundest secrecy! You understand me!"

Athos shrugged his shoulders, and followed his guards silently, whilst Monsieur Bonacieux uttered lamentations enough to break the heart of a tiger.

They led back the mercer to the same dungeon in which he had passed the night, and left him to himself during the day. Bonacieux wept away the hours like a true mercer, not being at all a man of the sword, as he himself informed us. In the evening, at the moment he had made his mind up to lie down upon the bed, he heard steps in his corridor. These steps drew near to his dungeon, the door was thrown open, and the guards appeared.

"Follow me," said an exempt, who came behind the guards.

"Follow you!" cried Bonacieux, "follow you, at this hour! Where, in the name of God?"

"Where we have orders to lead you."

"But that is not an answer, that."

"It is, nevertheless, the only one we can give you."

"Ah! my God! my God!" murmured the poor mercer, "now, indeed, I am lost!" And he followed the guards who came for him mechanically and without resistance.

He passed along the same corridor as before, crossed a first court, then a second side of the building; at length at the gate of the entrance-court he found a carriage surrounded by four guards on horseback. They made him get into this carriage, the exempt placed himself by his side, the door was locked, and they were left in a rolling prison. The carriage was put in motion as slowly as a funeral car. Through the closely fastened windows the prisoner could perceive the houses and the pavement, that was all ; but, true Parisian as he was, Bonacieux could recognise every street by the rails, the signs, and the lamps. At the moment of arriving at Saint Paul, the spot where such as were condemned at the Bastille were executed, he was near fainting and crossed himself twice. He thought the carriage was about to stop there. The carriage, however, passed on.

Further on, a still greater terror seized him on passing by the cemetery of Saint Jean, where state criminals were buried. One thing, however, reassured him : he remembered that before they were buried their heads were generally cut off, and he felt that his head was still on his shoulders. But when he saw the carriage take the way to La Grêve, when he perceived the pointed roof of the Hôtel de Ville, and the carriage passed under the arcade, he then thought all was over with him, wished to confess to the exempt, and upon his refusal, uttered such pitiable cries, that the exempt told him that if he continued to deafen him in that manner, he should put a gag in his mouth.

This measure somewhat reassured Bonacieux ; if they meant to execute him at La Grêve, it could scarcely be worth while to gag him, as they had nearly reached the place of execution. In fact, the carriage crossed the fatal spot without stopping. There remained then no other place to fear but the Croix-du-Trahoir ; the carriage was taking exactly the road to it.

This time there was no longer any doubt : it was at the Croix-du-Trahoir that obscure criminals were executed. Bonacieux had flattered himself in believing himself worthy of Saint Paul or of the Place de Grêve : it was at the Croix-du-Trahoir that his journey and his destiny were about to be ended ! He could not yet see that dreadful cross, but he felt as if it were in some sort coming to meet him. When he was within twenty paces of it, he heard a noise of people, and the carriage stopped. This was more than poor Bonacieux could endure, depressed as he was by the successive emotions which he had experienced : he uttered a feeble groan, which might have been taken for the last sigh of a dying man, and fainted.

CHAPTER XIV.

THE MAN OF MEUNG.

THE crowd was not produced by the expectation of a man who was to be hung, but by the contemplation of a man who was hung.

The carriage, which had been stopped for a minute, resumed its way passed through the crowd, threaded the Rue Saint Honoré, turned the Rue des Bons Enfans, and stopped before a low door.

The door opened, two guards received Bonacieux in their arms from the exempt, who supported him ; they carried him along an alley, up a flight of stairs, and deposited him in an antechamber.

All these movements had been effected, as far as he was concerned in them, mechanically. He had moved along as if in a dream ; he had a glimpse of objects as if through a fog ; his ears had perceived sounds without comprehending them ; he might have been executed at that moment without his making a single gesture in his own defence, or his uttering a cry to implore mercy.

He remained upon the bench, with his back leaning against the wall and his hands hanging down, exactly in the spot where the guards had placed him.

On looking round him, however, as he could perceive no threatening object, as nothing indicated that he ran any real danger, as the bench was comfortably covered with a well-stuffed cushion, as the wall was ornamented with beautiful Cordova leather, and as large red damask curtains, fastened back by gold clasps, floated before the window, he perceived by degrees that his fear was exaggerated, and he began to turn his head to the right and the left, upwards and downwards.

At this movement, which nobody opposed, he resumed a little courage, and ventured to draw up one leg and then the other ; at length, with the help of his two hands, he raised himself up upon the bench, and found himself upon his feet.

At this moment an officer of a sufficiently good appearance opened a door, continued to exchange some words with a person in the next chamber, and then came up to the prisoner :

" Is your name Bonacieux !" said he.

" Yes, Monsieur l'Officier," stammered the mercer, more dead than alive, " at your service."

" Come in," said the officer.

And he moved out of the way to let the mercer pass. The latter obeyed without reply, and entered the chamber, where he appeared to be expected.

It was a large cabinet, with the walls furnished with arms offensive and defensive, close and stifling ; and in which there was already a fire, although it was scarcely the end of September. A square table, covered with books and papers, upon which was unrolled an immense plan of the city of La Rochelle, occupied the centre of the apartment.

Standing before the chimney, was a man of middle height, of a haughty, proud mien ; with piercing eyes, a large brow, and a thin face, which was made still longer by a royal (or imperial, as it is now called), surmounted by a pair of moustaches. Although this man was scarcely thirty-six or thirty-seven years of age, hair, moustaches, and royal, all began to be grey. This man, except a sword, had all the appearance of a soldier ; and his buff boots, still slightly covered with dust, indicated that he had been on horseback in the course of the day.

This man was Armand Jean Duplessis, Cardinal de Richelieu, not such as he is now represented—broken down like an old man, suffering like a martyr, his body bent, his voice extinct—buried in a large *fauteuil*, as in an anticipated tomb ; no longer living but by the strength of his genius, and no longer maintaining the struggle with Europe but by the eternal application of his thoughts—but such as he really was at this period ; that is to say, an active and gallant cavalier, already weak of body, but sustained by that moral power which made of him one of the most extraordinary men that ever existed ; preparing, after having supported the Duke de Nevers in his duchy of Mantua, after having taken Nîmes, Castres, and Uzes—to drive the English from the isle of Ré, and lay siege to La Rochelle.

At first sight, nothing denoted the cardinal ; and it was impossible for those who did not know his face to guess in whose presence they were.

The poor mercer remained standing at the door, whilst the eyes of the personage we have just described were fixed upon him, and appeared to wish to penetrate even into the depths of the past.

" Is this that Bonacieux ?" asked he, after a moment of silence.

" Yes, monseigneur," replied the officer.

" That's well.   Give me those papers, and leave us."

The officer took the papers pointed out from the table, gave them to him who asked for them, bowed to the ground, and retired.

Bonacieux recognised, in these papers, his interrogatories of the Bastille.   From time to time, the man of the chimney raised his eyes from the writings, and plunged them like poniards into the heart of the poor mercer.

At the end of ten minutes' reading, and ten seconds of examination, the cardinal was satisfied.

" That head has never conspired," murmured he ; " but it matters not ; we will see, nevertheless."

" You are accused of high treason," said the cardinal, slowly.

" So I have been told already, monseigneur," cried Bonacieux, giving his interrogator the title he had heard the officer give him, " but I swear to you that I know nothing about it."

The cardinal repressed a smile.

" You have conspired with your wife, with Madame de Chevreuse, and with milord duke of Buckingham."

" In fact, monseigneur, I have heard her pronounce all those names."

" And on what occasion ?"

" She said that the Cardinal de Richelieu had drawn the Duke of Buckingham to Paris to ruin him and to ruin the queen."

" She said that ?" cried the cardinal, with violence.

" Yes, monseigneur, but I told her she was wrong to talk about such things ; and that his eminence was incapable——"

" Hold your tongue ! you are stupid," replied the cardinal.

" That's exactly what my wife said, monseigneur."

" Do you know who carried off your wife ?"

" No, monseigneur."

" You have suspicions, nevertheless ?"

" Yes, monseigneur ; but these suspicions appeared to be disagreeable to monsieur the commissary, and I no longer have them."

" Your wife has escaped ! Did you know that ?"

" No, monseigneur ; I learnt it since I have been in prison, and that from the conversation of monsieur the commissary—a very good kind of man."

The cardinal repressed another smile.

"Then you are ignorant of what is become of your wife since her flight."

"Absolutely, monseigneur ; but she has most likely returned to the Louvre."

"At one o'clock this morning she had not returned."

"Good God ! what can have become of her then ?"

"We shall know, be assured ; nothing is concealed from the cardinal ; the cardinal knows everything."

"In that case, monseigneur, do you believe the cardinal will be so kind as to tell me what has become of my wife ?"

"Perhaps he may ; but you must, in the first place, reveal to the cardinal all you know of your wife's relations with Madame de Chevreuse."

"But, monseigneur, I know nothing about them ; I have never seen her !"

"When you went to fetch your wife from the Louvre, did you always return directly home ?"

"Scarcely ever ; she had business to transact with linendrapers, to whose houses I conducted her."

"And how many were there of these linendrapers ?"

"Two, monseigneur."

"And where did they live?"

"One Rue de Vaugirard, the other Rue de la Harpe."

"Do you go into these houses with her ?"

"Never, monseigneur ; I waited at the door."

"And what excuse did she make for going in in this manner alone?"

"She gave me none ; she told me to wait, and I waited."

"You are a very complacent husband, my dear Monsieur Bonacieux," said the cardinal.

"He calls me his dear monsieur," said the mercer to himself. " Peste ! matters are going all right !"

"Should you know those doors again ?"

"Yes."

"Do you know the numbers ?"

"Yes."

"What are they ?"

"No. 25 in the Rue Vaugirard ; 75 in the Rue de la Harpe."

"That's well," said the cardinal.

At these words, he took up a silver bell, and rang it : the officer entered.

"Go," said he, in a subdued voice, "and find Rochefort ; tell him to come to me immediately, if he is returned."

"The count is here," said the officer, "and requests to speak with your eminence instantly."

"Let him come in, then ; let him come in, then !" said the cardinal, eagerly.

The officer sprang out of the apartment with that alacrity which all the servants of the cardinal displayed in obeying him.

" To your eminence !" murmured Bonacieux, rolling his eyes round in astonishment.

Five seconds had scarcely elapsed after the disappearance of the officer, when the door opened, and a new personage entered.

" It is he !" cried Bonacieux.

" He ! what he ?" asked the cardinal.

" The man that took away my wife !"

The cardinal rang a second time. The officer reappeared.

" Place this man in the care of h.s guards again, and let him wait till I send for him."

" No, monseigneur ! no ! it is not ne !" cried Bonacieux ; " no, I was deceived : this is quite a different man, and does not resemble him at all. Monsieur is, I am sure, a very good sort of man !"

" Take away that fool !" said the cardinal.

The officer took Bonacieux by the arm, and led him into the ante-chamber, where he found his two guards.

The newly-introduced personage followed Bonacieux impatiently with his eyes till he was gone out, and the moment the door closed, he advanced eagerly towards the cardinal, and said :

" They have seen each other !"

" Who ?" asked his eminence.

" He and she !"

" The queen and the duke ?" cried Richelieu,

" Yes."

" Where ?"

" At the Louvre."

" Are you sure of it ?"

" Perfectly sure."

" Who told you of it ?"

" Madame Lannoy, who is devoted to your eminence, as you know."

" Why did she not let me know sooner ?"

" Whether by chance or from mistrust, I don't know ; but the queen made Madame de Surgis sleep in her chamber, and detained her all day."

" Well, we are beaten ! Now let us try to take our revenge."

" I will assist you with all my heart, monseigneur ; be assured of that."

" How did it take place ?"

" At half-past twelve, the queen was with her women——"

" Where ?"

" In her bedchamber——"

" Go on."

" When some one came and brought her a handkerchief from her *dame de lingerie.*"

" And then !"

" The queen immediately exhibited strong emotion ; and notwithstanding that her face was covered with rouge, evidently turned pale——"

"Well, go on !"

"She, however, rose, and with a trembling voice : ' Ladies,' said she, wait for me ten minutes, I shall soon return.' She then opened the door of her alcove, and went out."

"Why did not Madame Lannoy come and inform you instantly ?"

"Nothing was certain ; besides, her majesty had said : ' Ladies, wait for me ;' and she did not dare to disobey the queen."

"How long did the queen remain out of the chamber ?"

"Three-quarters of an hour."

"Did none of her women accompany her ?"

"Only Donna Estefana."

"Did she afterwards return ?"

"Yes ; but to take a little rosewood casket, with her cipher upon it ; and went out again immediately."

"And when she finally returned, did she bring that casket with her ?"

"No."

"Does Madame Lannoy know what was in that casket ?"

"Yes ; the diamond studs which his majesty gave the queen."

"And she came back without this casket ?"

"Yes."

"Madame Lannoy, then, is of opinion that she gave them to Buckingham ?"

"She is sure of it."

"How can she be so ?"

"In the course of the day, Madame de Lannoy, in her quality of tire-woman of the queen, looked for this casket, appeared uneasy at not finding it, and at length asked the queen if she knew anything about it."

"And the queen ?"

"The queen became exceedingly red, and replied, that having on the preceding evening broken one of those studs, she had sent it to her gold-smith to be repaired."

"He must be called upon, and so ascertain if the thing be true or not."

"I have just been with him."

"And the goldsmith says ?——"

"The goldsmith has heard of nothing of the kind."

"Right ! right !　Rochefort, all is not lost ; and perhaps—perhaps—everything is for the best !"

"The fact is, that I do not doubt your eminence's genius——"

"Will repair the blunders of his agent—is that it ?"

"That is exactly what I was going to say, if your eminence had permitted me to fisinh my sentence."

"Do you know where the duchesse de Chevreuse and the duke of Buckingham are now concealed ?"

"No, monseigneur ; my people could tell me nothing on that head."

"But I know."

"You, monseigneur ?"

" Yes ; or at least I guess. They were, one in the Rue Vaugirard, No. 25 ; the other in the Rue de la Harpe, No. 75."

" Does your eminence command that they should be both instantly arrested ?"

" It will be too late ; they will be gone."

" But still, we can make sure that they are so."

" Take ten men of my guards, and search the house thoroughly."

" Instantly, monseigneur."

And Rochefort went hastily out of the apartment.

The cardinal, upon being left alone, reflected for an instant, and then rang the bell a third time. The same officer appeared.

" Bring the prisoner in again," said the cardinal.

Master Bonacieux was introduced afresh, and upon a sign from the cardinal the officer retired.

" You have deceived me !" said the cardinal, sternly.

" I !" cried Bonacieux ; " I ! deceive your eminence !"

" Your wife, when going to Rue de Vaugirard and Rue de la Harpe, did not go to meet linendrapers."

" Then whom did she go to meet, in the name of God ?"

" She went to meet the Duchesse de Chevreuse and the Duke of Buckingham."

" Yes," cried Bonacieux, recalling all his remembrances of the circumstances, " yes, that's it. Your eminence is right. I told my wife, several times, that it was surprising that linendrapers should live in such houses as those—in houses that had no signs—but she only always laughed at me.

"Ah ! monseigneur !" continued Bonacieux, throwing himself at his eminence's feet, " ah ! how truly you are the cardinal, the great cardinal, the man of genius whom all the world reveres."

The cardinal, however contemptible might be the triumph gained over so vulgar a being as Bonacieux, did not the less enjoy it for an instant ; then, almost immediately, as if a fresh thought had occurred, to the mercer, ——

" Rise, my good friend," said he ; " you are a worthy man."

" The cardinal has touched me with his hand ! I have touched the hand of the great man !" cried Bonacieux : " the great man has called me his friend !"

" Yes, my friend ; yes !" said the cardinal, with that paternal tone which he sometimes knew how to assume, but which deceived none who knew him ; " and as you have been unjustly suspected, well ! you must be indemnified : here ! take this purse of a hundred pistoles, and pardon me."

" I pardon you, monseigneur !" said Bonacieux, hesitating to take the purse, fearing, doubtless, that this pretended gift was but a joke. " But you are free to have me arrested, you are free to have me tortured, you are free to have me hung : you are the master, and I could not have the least word to say against it. Pardon you, monseigneur ! you cannot mean that !"

"Ah! my dear Monsieur Bonacieux, you are generous in this matter, and I thank you for it. Thus, then, you will take this bag, and you will go away without being too much dissatisfied with your treatment."

"I shall go away enchanted."

"Farewell, then; that is to say, for the present, for I hope we shall meet again."

"Whenever monseigneur wishes: I am always at his eminence's orders."

"And that will be frequently, I assure you, for I have found something extremely agreeable in your conversation."

"Oh! monseigneur!"

"Au revoir, Monsieur Bonacieux, au revoir!"

And the cardinal made him a sign with his hand, to which Bonacieux replied by bowing to the ground; he then went out backwards, and when he was in the antechamber, the cardinal heard him, in his enthusiasm, crying aloud, "Vive monseigneur! Vive son eminence! Vive le grand cardinal!" The cardinal listened with a smile to this vociferous manifestation of the feelings of Bonacieux; and then, when Bonacieux's cries were no longer audible,—

"Good!" said he, "that man would, henceforward, lay down his life for me."

And the cardinal began to examine with the greatest attention the map of La Rochelle, which, as we have said, lay open upon the table, tracing with a pencil the line in which the famous dyke was to pass, which, eighteen months later, shut up the port of the besieged city. As he was in the deepest of his strategic meditations, the door opened, and Rochefort returned.

"Well!" said the cardinal eagerly, rising with a promptitude which proved the degree of importance he attached to the commission with which he had charged the count.

"Well!" said the latter, "a young woman of about twenty-six or twenty-eight years of age, and a man of from thirty-five to forty, have lodged at the two houses pointed out by your eminence, but the woman left last night, and the man this morning."

"They were the persons!" cried the cardinal, looking at the clock; "and now it is too late to have them pursued: the duchess is at Tours, and the duke at Boulogne. It is at London they must be met with."

"What are your eminence's orders?"

"Not a word of what has passed; let the queen remain in perfect security; let her be ignorant that we know her secret; let her believe that we are in search of some conspiracy or other. Send me the keeper of the seals, Monsieur Séguier."

"And that man, what has your eminence done with him?"

"What man?" asked the cardinal.

"That Bonacieux."

"I have done with him all that could be done: I have made him a spy upon his wife."

The count de Rochefort bowed like a man who acknowledges as great the superiority of the master, and retired.

" Tell Vitray to come to me," said he, " and tell him to get ready for a journey."

The instant after, the man he required was before him, booted and spurred.

" Vitray," said he, " you will go, with all speed, to London. You must not stop an instant on the way. You will deliver this letter to Milady. Here is an order for two hundred pistoles ; call upon my treasurer and get the money. You shall have as much again if you are back within six days, and have executed your commission well."

The messenger, without replying a single word, bowed, took the letter, with the order for the two hundred pistoles, and retired.

These were the contents of the letter :

" Milady,—

" Be at the first ball at which the duke of Buckingham shall be present. He will wear on his doublet twelve diamond studs ; get as near to him as you can, and cut off two of them.

" As soon as these studs shall be in your possession, inform me."

CHAPTER XV.

MEN OF THE ROBE AND MEN OF THE SWORD.

ON the day after these events had taken place, Athos not having re-appeared, M. de Tréville was informed by D'Artagnan and Porthos of the circumstance. As to Aramis, he had asked for leave of absence for five days, and was gone, it was said, to Rouen, on family business.

M. de Tréville was the father of his soldiers. The lowest or the most unknown of them, as soon as he assumed the uniform of the company, was as sure of his aid and support as his brother himself could have been.

He repaired, then, instantly to the residence of the *lieutenant-criminel.* The officer who commanded the post of the Croix-Rouge was sent for, and by successive inquiries they found that Athos was at the time lodged in the For l'Evêque.

Athos had passed through all the examinations we have seen Bonacieux undergo.

We were present at the scene in which the two captives were confronted with each other. Athos, who had till that time said nothing, for fear that D'Artagnan, interrupted in his turn, should not have the time necessary : but from this moment Athos declared that his name was Athos, and not D'Artagnan. He added that he did not know either Monsieur or Madame Bonacieux ; that he had never spoken to the one or the other ; that he had come, at about ten o'clock in the evening, to pay a visit to his friend, M. D'Artagnan, but that till that hour he had been at M. de Tréville's, where he had dined ; " twenty witnesses," added he, " could attest the fact," and he named several distinguished gentlemen, and among them was M. the duke de la Trémouille.

The second commissary was as much bewildered as the first had been at the simple but firm declaration of the musketeer, upon whom he was anxious to take the revenge which men of the robe like at all times to gain over men of the sword ; but the name of M. de Tréville, and that of M. de la Trémouille, commanded a little reflection.

Athos was then sent to the cardinal, but unfortunately the cardinal was at the Louvre with the king.

It was precisely at this moment, at which M. de Tréville, on leaving the residence of the *lieutenant-criminel*, and that of the governor of the For l'Evêque, without being able to find Athos, arrived at the palace.

As captain of the musketeers, M. de Tréville had the right of *entrée* at all times.

It is well known how violent the king's prejudices were against the queen, and how carefully these prejudices were kept up by the cardinal, who, in affairs of intrigue, mistrusted women much more than men. One of the principal causes of this prejudice was the friendship of Anne of Austria for Madame de Chevreuse. These two women gave him more uneasiness than the war with Spain, the quarrel with England, or the embarrassment of the finances. In his eyes, and to his perfect conviction, Madame de Chevreuse not only served the queen in her political intrigues, but, which troubled him still more, in her love affairs.

At the first word the cardinal spoke of Madame de Chevreuse, who, though exiled to Tours, and who was believed to be in that city, had been at Paris, remained there five days, and had outwitted the police, the king flew into a furious passion. Although capricious and unfaithful, the king wished to be called Louis the Just and Louis the Chaste. Posterity will find a difficulty in understanding this character, which history explains only by facts and never by reasonings.

But when the Cardinal added, that not only Madame de Chevreuse had been in Paris, but, still further, that the queen had renewed with her, by the means of one of those mysterious correspondences which at that time was named a cabal, when he affirmed that he, the cardinal, was about to unravel the most closely twisted thread of this intrigue, when at the moment of arresting in the fact, with all the proofs about her, the queen's emissary to the exiled duchess, a musketeer, had dared to interrupt the course of justice violently, by falling, sword in hand, upon the honest men of the law charged with investigating impartially the whole affair, in order to place it before the eyes of the king. Louis XIII. could not contain himself, and he made a step towards the queen's apartment, with that pale and mute indignation, which, when it broke out, led this prince to the commission of the coldest cruelty.

And yet, in all this, the cardinal had not yet said a word about the duke of Buckingham.

At this instant M. de Tréville entered, cold, polite, and in irreproachable costume.

Rendered aware of what had passed by the presence of the cardinal, and the alteration in the king's countenance, M. de Tréville felt himself something like Samson before the Philistines.

Louis XIII. had already placed his hand on the button of the door ; at the noise of M. de Tréville's entrance he turned round.

"You arrive in good time, monsieur," said the king, who, when his passions were raised to a certain point, could not dissemble ; "I have learned some pretty things concerning your musketeers !"

"And I," said M. de Tréville, coldly, "I have some pretty things to inform your majesty of, concerning these men of the robe."

"What do you say ?" said the king, with hauteur.

"I have the honour to inform your majesty," continued M. de Tréville, in the same tone, "that a party of procureurs, commissaries, and men of the police, very estimable people, but very inveterate, as it appears, against the uniform, have taken upon themselves to arrest in a house, to lead away through the open street, and throw into the Fort l'Evêque, all upon an order which they have refused to show me, one of my, or rather your musketeers, sire, of irreproachable conduct, of an almost illustrious reputation, and whom your majesty knows favourably, M. Athos."

"Athos !" said the king, mechanically ; "yes, indeed, I know that name."

"Let your majesty remember," said M. de Tréville, "that M. Athos is the musketeer who, in the annoying duel which you are acquainted with, had the misfortune to wound M. de Cahusac so seriously. Apropos, monseigneur," continued De Tréville, addressing the cardinal, "M. de Cahusac is quite recovered, is he not ?"

"Thank you !" said the cardinal, biting his lips with anger.

"M. Athos, then, went to pay a visit to one of his friends, at the time absent," continued M. de Tréville, "to a young Béarnais, a cadet in his majesty's guards, the company of M. des Essarts, but scarcely had he arrived at his friend's, and taken up a book, whilst waiting his return, when a crowd of bailiffs and soldiers mixed, came and laid siege to the house, broke open several doors——"

The cardinal made the king a sign, which signified, "That was on account of the affair about which I spoke to you."

"Oh ! we all know that," interrupted the king ; "for all that was done for our service."

"Then," said Tréville, "it was also for your majesty's service, that one of my musketeers, who was innocent, has been seized ; that he has been placed between two guards, like a malefactor ; and that this gallant man, who has ten times shed his blood in your majesty's service, and is ready to shed it again, has been paraded through the midst of an insolent populace !"

"Bah !" said the king, who began to be shaken, "was it managed so ?"

"M. de Tréville," said the cardinal, with the greatest phlegm, "does not tell your majesty that this innocent musketeer, this gallant man, had only an hour before attacked, sword in hand, four commissaries of inquiry, who were delegated by me to examine into an affair of the highest importance."

"I defy your eminence to prove it," cried M. de Tréville, with his Gascon freedom and military roughness; "for one hour before, M. Athos, who, I will confide it to your majesty, is really a man of the highest quality, did me the honour, after having dined with me, to be conversing in the salon of my hotel, with M. the duke de la Trémouille and M. le comte de Châlus, who happened to be there."

The king looked at the cardinal.

"A *procès-verbal* attests it," said the cardinal, replying aloud to the mute interrogation of his majesty; "and the ill-treated people have drawn up the following, which I have the honour to present to your majesty."

"And is the *procès-verbal* of men of the robe to be placed in comparison with the word of honour of a man of the sword?" replied Tréville, haughtily.

"Come, come, Tréville, hold your tongue," said the king.

"If his eminence entertains any suspicion against one of my musketeers," said Tréville, "the justice of M. the Cardinal is sufficiently well known to induce me, myself, to demand an inquiry."

"In the house in which this judicial inquiry was made," continued the impassable cardinal, "there lodges, I believe, a young Béarnais, a friend of the musketeer's."

"Your eminence means M. D'Artagnan."

"I mean a young man whom you patronize, Monsieur de Tréville."

"Yes, your eminence, it is the same."

"Do you not suspect this young man of having given bad advice—"

"To M. Athos! to a man double his age?" interrupted M. de Tréville. "No, Monseigneur. Besides, M. D'Artagnan passed the evening at my hotel."

"Well," said the cardinal, "everybody seems to have passed the evening at your hotel!"

"Does your eminence doubt my word?" said De Tréville, with a brow flushed with anger.

"No, God forbid!" said the cardinal; "but only let me inquire at what hour he was with you?"

"Oh, that I can speak to positively, your eminence; for as he came in I remarked that it was but half-past nine by the clock, although I had believed it to be later."

"And at what hour did he leave your hotel?"

"At half-past ten; an hour after the event."

"Well, but," replied the cardinal, who could not for an instant suspect the loyalty of De Tréville, and who felt that the victory was escaping from his hands,—"well, but Athos *was* taken in the house of the Rue des Fossoyeurs."

"Is one friend forbidden to visit another? or a musketeer of my company to fraternize with a guard of M. des Essart's company?"

"Yes, when the house in which he fraternizes is suspected."

"That house is suspected, Tréville," said the king; "perhaps you were not aware of that?"

"Indeed, sire, I knew nothing of the circumstance. The house may be suspected, but I deny that it is so in the part of it inhabited by M. D'Artagnan; for I can affirm, sire, if I can believe what he says, that there does not exist a more devoted servant of your majesty, or a more profound admirer of Monsieur the Cardinal."

"Was it not this D'Artagnan who wounded, one day, Jussac, in that unfortunate encounter which took place near the convent of the Carmes Déchaussés?" asked the king, looking at the cardinal, who coloured with vexation.

"And the next day Bernajoux. Yes, sire, yes, it is the same. Your majesty has an excellent memory."

"Come, how shall we determine?" said the king.

"That concerns your majesty more than me," said the cardinal. "I should affirm the culpability."

"And I deny it," said De Tréville. "But his majesty has judges, and these judges will decide."

"That is best," said the king. "Send the case before the judges; it is their business to judge, and they will judge."

"Only," replied Tréville, "it is a sad thing that, in the unfortunate times in which we live, the purest life, the most incontestable virtue, cannot exempt a man from infamy and persecution. The army, I will answer for it, will be but little pleased at being exposed to rigorous treatment on account of affairs of police."

The expression was imprudent; but M. de Tréville launched it with a full knowledge of his cause. He was desirous of an explosion, because in that case the mine throws forth fire, and fire enlightens.

"Affairs of police!" cried the king, taking up De Tréville's words; "affairs of police! And what do you know about them, monsieur? Meddle with your musketeers, and do not annoy me in this way. It appears, according to your account, that if, unfortunately, a musketeer is arrested, France is in danger! Here's a piece of work about a musketeer! Why, I would arrest ten of them, *ventrebleu!* a hundred, even —all the company! and I would not allow a murmur!"

"From the moment they are suspected by your majesty," said Tréville, "the musketeers are guilty; therefore, you see me prepared to surrender my sword; for, after having accused my soldiers, there can be no doubt that M. the Cardinal will end by accusing me. It is best to constitute myself at once a prisoner with M Athos, who is already arrested, and with M. D'Artagnan, who most probably will be arrested."

"Gascon-headed man! will you have done?" said the king.

"Sire," replied Tréville, without lowering his voice in the least, "either order my musketeer to be restored to me, or let him be tried."

"He shall be tried," said the cardinal.

"Well, so much the better; for in that case I shall demand of his majesty permission to plead for him."

The king became afraid of an outbreak.

"If his eminence," said he, "had not personal motives——"

The cardinal saw what the king was about to say, and interrupted him:

"Pardon me," said he ; "but the instant your majesty considers me a prejudiced judge, I withdraw."

"Come," said the king, "will you swear by my father that M. Athos was at your residence during the event, and that he took no part in it ?"

"By your glorious father, and by yourself,—who are that which I love and venerate the most in the world,—I swear it !"

"Be so kind as to reflect, sire," said the cardinal. "If we release the prisoner thus, we shall never be able to know the truth."

"M. Athos will always be to be found," replied Tréville,—"always ready to answer, when it shall please the men of the long robe to interrogate him. He will not desert, Monsieur le Cardinal, be assured of that : I will answer for him."

"No, he will not desert," said the king ; "he can always be found, as M. de Tréville says. Besides," added he, lowering his voice, and looking with a suppliant air at the cardinal, "let us give them apparent security : there is policy in that."

This policy of Louis XIII.'s made Richelieu smile.

"Order it as you please, sire ; you possess the right of pardoning."

"The right of pardoning only applies to the guilty," said Tréville, who was determined to have the last word, "and my musketeer is innocent. It is not mercy, then, that you are about to accord, sire ; it is justice."

"And he is in the For l'Evêque ?" said the king.

"Yes, sire, in solitary confinement, in a dungeon, like the lowest criminal."

"The devil ! the devil !" murmured the king ;—"what must be done ?"

"Sign the order for his release, and all will be said," replied the cardinal. "I believe, with your majesty, that M. de Tréville's guarantee is more than sufficient."

Tréville bowed very respectfully, with a joy that was not unmixed with fear ; he would have preferred an obstinate resistance on the part of the cardinal, to this sudden yielding.

The king signed the order for enlargement, and Tréville carried it away without delay.

At the moment he was about to leave the presence, the cardinal gave him a friendly smile, and said :

"A perfect harmony seems to prevail in your musketeers, sire, between the leader and the soldiers, which must be good for the service, and advantageous to all."

"Now he will play me some dog's trick or other, and that immediately," said Tréville ; "there is no possibility of getting the last word with such a man. But let us be quick,—the king may change his mind

presently ; and, at all events, it is more difficult to replace a man in the
For l'Evêque, or the Bastille, who has got out, than to keep a prisoner
there who is in."

M. de Tréville made his entrance triumphantly into the For l'Evêque,
whence he delivered the musketeer, whose peaceful indifference had
not for a moment abandoned him.

The first time he saw D'Artagnan, " You have come off well," said he
to him ; "there is your Jussac thrust paid for. There still remains
that of Bernajoux, but you must not be too confident."

As to the rest, M. de Tréville had good reason to mistrust the cardinal, and to think that all was not over, for scarcely had the captain
of the musketeers closed the door after him, than his eminence said to
the king :

" Now that we are at length by ourselves, we will, if your majesty
pleases, converse seriously. Sire, Monsieur de Buckingham has been
in Paris five days, and only left it this morning."

CHAPTER XVI.

IN WHICH MONSIEUR SEGUIER, THE KEEPER OF THE SEALS, LOOKS MORE THAN ONCE FOR THE BELL, IN ORDER TO RING IT, AS HE DID BEFORE.

IT is impossible to form an idea of the impression these few words made
upon Louis XIII. He grew pale and red alternately ; and the cardinal
saw at once that he had recovered, by a single blow, all the ground he
had lost.

" M. de Buckingham in Paris !" cried he, " and what does he come
to do there ?"

" To conspire, no doubt, with your enemies the Huguenots and the
Spaniards."

" No, pardieu ! no ! To conspire against my honour, with Madame
de Chevreuse, Madame de Longueville, and the Condés."

" Oh ! sire, what an idea ! The queen is too prudent, and, besides,
loves your majesty too well."

" Woman is weak, monsieur le cardinal," said the king ; " and as to
loving me much, I have my own opinion respecting that love."

" I not the less maintain," said the cardinal, " that the duke of Buckingham came to Paris for a project purely political."

"And I am sure that he came for quite another purpose, monsieur
le cardinal, but if the queen be guilty, let her tremble !"

" Indeed," said the cardinal, " whatever repugnance I may have to
directing my mind to such a treason, your majesty compels me to think
of it. Madame de Lanney, whom, according to your majesty's command, I have frequently interrogated, told me this morning, that the
night before last her majesty sat up very late, that this morning she
wept much, and that she was writing all day."

" That's it !" cried the king ; " to him, no doubt. Cardinal, I must
have the queen's papers,"

" But how to take them, sire? It seems to me that neither your majesty nor I can charge ourselves with such a mission."

" How did they act with regard to La Maréchale d'Ancre?" cried the king, in the highest state of irritation ; " her *armoires* were thoroughly searched, and then she herself was searched."

" The Maréchale d'Ancre was no more than the Maréchale d'Ancre, a Florentine adventurer, sire, and that was all ; whilst the august spouse of your majesty is Anne of Austria, queen of France, that is to say, one of the greatest princesses in the world."

" She is not the less guilty, monsieur le duc ! The more she has forgotten the high position in which she was placed, the more degrading is her fall. It is long since, besides, that I have determined to put an end to all these petty intrigues of policy and love. She has also about her a certain Laporte."

" Who, I believe, is the mainspring of all this, I confess," said the cardinal.

" You think then, as I do, that she deceives me?" said the king.

" I believe, and I repeat it to your majesty, that the queen conspires against the power of the king, but I have not said against his honour."

" And I,—I tell you against both ; I tell you the queen does not love me ; I tell you she loves another ; I tell you she loves that infamous Buckingham ! Why did you not cause him to be arrested whilst he was in Paris?"

" Arrest the duke! arrest the prime minister of King Charles I. ! Think of it, sire ! What a scandal! And if then the suspicions of your majesty, which I still continue to doubt, should prove to have any foundation, what a terrible disclosure ! what a fearful scandal !"

" But as he acted like a vagabond or a thief, he should have been——"

Louis XIII. stopped, terrified at what he was about to say, whilst Richelieu, stretching out his neck, waited uselessly for the word which had died on the lips of the king.

" He should have been ?"

" Nothing," said the king, " nothing. But all the time he was in Paris, you, of course, did not lose sight of him ?"

" No, sire."

" Where did he lodge ?"

" Rue de la Harpe, No. 75."

" Where is that ?"

" By the side of the Luxembourg."

" And you are certain that the queen and he did not see each other ?"

" I believe the queen to have too high a sense of her duties, sire."

" But they have corresponded ; it is to him that the queen has been writing all the day ; monsieur le duc, I must have those letters !"

" Sire, notwithstanding ——"

" Monsieur le duc, at whatever price it may be, I will have them."

" I would, however, beg your majesty to observe——"

" Do you then also join in betraying me, monsieur le cardinal, by thus always opposing my will? Are you also in concert with Spain and England, with Madame de Chevreuse and the queen?"

" Sire," replied the cardinal, sighing, " I thought I was secure from such a suspicion.'

" Monsieur le cardinal, you have heard me; I will have those letters."

" There is but one means."

" What is that?"

" That would be to charge M. de Séguier, the keeper of the seals, with this mission. The matter enters completely into the duties of his post."

" Let him be sent for instantly."

" He is most likely at my hotel; I requested him to call, and when I came to the Louvre, I left orders, if he came, to desire him to wait."

" Let him be sent for instantly."

" Your majesty's orders shall be executed; but——"

" But what?"

" But the queen will perhaps refuse to obey."

" What, my orders?"

" Yes, if she is ignorant that these orders come from the king."

" Well, that she may have no doubt on that head, I will go and inform her myself."

" Your majesty will not forget that I have done everything in my power to prevent a rupture."

" Yes, duke, yes, I know you are very indulgent towards the queen, too indulgent, perhaps; we shall have occasion, I warn you, at some future period to speak of that."

" Whenever it shall please your majesty; but I shall be always happy and proud, sire, to sacrifice myself to the good harmony which I desire to see reign between you and the queen of France."

" It is all very well, cardinal, all very well; but, in the meantime, send for monsieur the keeper of the seals. I will go to the queen."

And Louis XIII. opening the door of communication, passed into the corridor which led to the apartments of Anne of Austria.

The queen was in the midst of her women, Madame de Guitant, Madame de Sable, Madame de Montbazon, and Madame de Guéméné. In a corner was the Spanish camériste, Donna Estefana, who had followed her from Madrid. Madame Guéméné was reading aloud, and everybody was listening to her with attention, with the exception of the queen, who had, on the contrary, desired this reading in order that she might be able, whilst feigning to listen, to pursue the thread of her own thoughts.

These thoughts, gilded as they were by a last reflection of love, were not the less sad. Anne of Austria, deprived of the confidence of her husband, pursued by the hatred of the cardinal, who could not pardon her for having repulsed a more tender feeling, having before her eyes the example of the queen mother, whom that hatred had tormented all her life, though Mary de Medici, if the memoirs of the time are to be believed, had begun by according to the cardinal that sentiment which

Anne of Austria always refused him ; Anne of Austria had seen fall around her her most devoted servants, her most intimate confidants, her dearest favourites. Like those unfortunate persons endowed with a fatal gift, she brought misfortune upon everything she touched ; her friendship was a fatal sign which called down persecution. Madame Chevreuse and Madame Vernet were exiled, and Laporte did not conceal from his mistress that he expected to be arrested every instant.

It was at the moment she was plunged in the deepest and darkest of these reflections, that the door of the chamber opened, and the king entered.

The reader was instantly silent, all the ladies rose, and there was a profound silence. As to the king, he made no demonstration of polite-ness, only stopping before the queen.

" Madame," said he, " you are about to receive a visit from the chan-cellor, who will communicate certain matters to you, with which I have charged him."

The unfortunate queen, who was constantly threatened with divorce, exile, and trial even, turned pale under her rouge, and could not refrain from saying :

" But why this visit, sire ? What can monsieur the chancellor have to say to me that your majesty could not say yourself ?"

The king turned upon his heel without reply, and almost at the same instant the captain of the guards, M. de Guitant, announced the visit of Monsieur the Chancellor.

When the chancellor appeared, the king had already gone out by another door.

The chancellor entered, half smiling, half blushing. As we shall pro-bably meet with him again in the course of our history, it would be quite as well for our readers to be made at once acquainted with him.

This chancellor was a pleasant man. It was Des Roches le Masle, canon of Nôtre Dame, and who had formerly been valet de chambre to the cardinal, who introduced him to his eminence as a perfectly devout man. The cardinal trusted him, and found his advantage in it.

There were many stories related of him, and amongst them this :

After a wild youth, he had retired into a convent, there to expiate, at least for some time, the follies of adolescence.

But, on entering this holy place, the poor penitent was unable to shut the door so close as to prevent the passions he fled from, from entering with him. He was incessantly attacked by them, and the superior, to whom he had confided this misfortune, wishing, as much as in him lay, to free him from them, had advised him, in order to conjure away the tempting demon, to have recourse to the bell-rope, and to ring with all his might. At the denunciating sound, the monks would be rendered aware that temptation was besieging a brother, and all the community would go to prayers.

This advice appeared good to the future chancellor. He conjured the evil spirit with abundance of prayers offered up by the monks. But the devil does not suffer himself to be easily dispossessed from a place in which he has fixed his garrison : in proportion as they redoubled the exorcisms he redoubled the temptations, so that day and night the bell was ringing full swing, announcing the extreme desire for mortification which the penitent experienced.

The monks had no longer an instant of repose. By day they did nothing but ascend and descend the steps which led to the chapel ; at night, in addition to complins and matins, they were further obliged to leap twenty times out of their beds and prostrate themselves on the floor of their cells.

It is not known whether it was the devil who gave way, or the monks who grew tired ; but within three months the penitent reappeared in the world with the reputation of being the most terrible *possessed* that ever existed.

On leaving the convent, he entered into the magistracy, became pre-sident *à mortier* in the place of his uncle, embraced the cardinal's party, which did not prove want of sagacity ; became chancellor, served his eminence with zeal in his hatred against the queen-mother, and his vengeance against Anne of Austria ; stimulated the judges in the affair of Chalais ; encouraged the essays of M. de Laffemas, *grand gibecier* of France ; then, at length, invested with the entire confidence of the car-dinal, a confidence which he had so well earned, he received the singular commission for the execution of which he presented himself in the queen's apartments.

The queen was still standing when he entered, but scarcely had she perceived him than she reseated herself in her *fauteuil*, and made a sign to her women to resume their cushions and stools, and, with an air of supreme hauteur, said :

" What do you desire, monsieur, and with what object do you present yourself here ?"

" To make, madame, in the name of the king, and without prejudice to the respect which I have the honour to owe to your majesty, a close perquisition into all your papers."

" How, monsieur ! a perquisition into my papers !—mine ! Truly, this is an unworthy proceeding !"

" Be kind enough to pardon me, madame ; but in this circumstance I am but the instrument which the king employs. Has not his majesty just left you ? and has he not himself desired you to prepare for this visit ?"

" Examine, then, monsieur ; I am a criminal, as it appears. Estefana, give the keys of my tables and my secretaires."

For form's sake the chancellor paid a visit to the pieces of furniture named, but he well knew that it was not in a piece of furniture that the queen would place the important letter she had written in the course of the day.

When the chancellor had opened and shut twenty times the drawers of the secretaires, it became necessary, whatever hesitation he might experience, it became necessary, I say, to come to the conclusion of the affair—that is to say, to search the queen herself. The chancellor advanced, therefore, towards Anne of Austria, and, with a very perplexed and embarrassed air—

" And now," said he, " it remains for me to make the principal perquisition."

" What is that ?" asked the queen, who did not understand, or, rather, was not willing to understand.

" His majesty is certain that a letter has been written by you in the course of the day ; he knows that it has not yet been sent to its address. This letter is not in your table-drawers, nor in your secretary ; and yet this letter must be somewhere."

" Would you dare to lift your hand to your queen ?" said Anne of Austria, drawing herself up to her full height, and fixing her eyes upon the chancellor with an expression almost threatening.

" I am an humble subject of the king, madame, and all that his majesty commands, I shall do."

" Well, that's true !'" said Anne of Austria ; " and the spies of the cardinal have served him faithfully. I have written a letter to-day ; that letter is not yet gone. The letter is here."

And the queen laid her beautiful hand on her bosom.

" Then give me that letter, madame," said the chancellor.

" I will give it to none but the king, monsieur," said Anne.

" If the king had desired that the letter should be given to him, madame, he would have demanded it of you himself, and if you do not give it up——"

" Well ?"

" He has, then, charged me to take it from you."

" How ! what do you say ?"

" That my orders go far, madame ; and that I am authorised to seek for the suspected paper, even on the person of your majesty."

" What horror !" cried the queen.

" Be kind enough, then madame, to act more compliantly."

" This conduct is infamously violent ! Do you know that, monsieur ?"

" The king commands it, madame ; excuse me."

" I will not suffer it ! no, no, I would rather die !" cried the queen, with whom the imperious blood of Spain and Austria began to rise.

The chancellor made a profound reverence ; then, with the intention quite patent of not drawing back a foot from the accomplishment of the commission with which he was charged, and as the attendant of an executioner might have done in the chamber of torture, he approached Anne of Austria, from whose eyes at the same instant sprang tears of rage.

The queen was, as we have said, of great beauty. The commission might, then, pass for delicate ; and the king had arrived, in his jealousy for Buckingham, at the point of being no longer jealous of any one.

Without doubt the Chancellor Séguier looked about at that moment for the rope of the famous bell ; but, not finding it, he summoned his resolution, and stretched forth his hands towards the place where the queen had acknowledged the paper was to be found.

Anne of Austria made one step backward, became so pale that it might be said she was dying, and, leaning with her left hand, to keep herself from falling, upon a table behind her, she with her right hand drew the paper from her bosom, and held it out to the keeper of the seals.

"There, monsieur, there is that letter!" cried the queen, with a broken and trembling voice; "take it, and deliver me from your odious presence."

The chancellor, who, on his part, trembled with an emotion easily to be conceived, took the letter, bowed to the ground, and retired.

The door was scarcely closed upon him, when the queen sank, half-fainting, into the arms of her women.

The chancellor carried the letter to the king without having read a single word of it. The king took it with a trembling hand, looked for the address, which was wanting, became very pale, opened it slowly, then, seeing by the first words that it was addressed to the King of Spain, he read it rapidly.

It was nothing but a plan of an attack against the cardinal. The queen pressed her brother and the Emperor of Austria to appear to be wounded, as they really were, by the policy of Richelieu, the eternal object of which was the abasement of the house of Austria; to declare war against France, and, as a condition of peace, to insist upon the dismissal of the cardinal; but as to love, there was not a single word about it in all the letter.

The king, quite delighted, inquired if the cardinal was still at the Louvre: he was told that his eminence awaited the orders of his majesty in the business cabinet.

The king went straight to him.

"There, duke," said he, "you were right, and I was wrong: the whole intrigue is political, and there is not the least question of love in this said letter. But, on the other hand, there is abundant question of you."

The cardinal took the letter, and read it with the greatest attention; then, when he had arrived at the end of it, he read it a second time.

"Well, your majesty," said he, "you see how far my enemies go; they threaten you with two wars if you do not dismiss me. In your place, in truth, sire, I should yield to such powerful instances; and, on my part, it would be a real happiness to withdraw from public affairs."

"What's that you say, duke?"

"I say, sire, that my health is sinking under these annoying struggles, and these never-ending labours. I say that, according to all probability, I shall not be able to undergo the fatigues of the siege of La Rochelle, and that it would be far better that you should appoint there, either M. de Condé, M. de Bassompierre, or some valiant gentleman whose business is war, and not me, who am a churchman, and who am constantly turned aside from my real vocation to look after matters for which I have no aptitude. You would be the happier for it at home, sire, and I do not doubt you would be the greater for it abroad."

"Monsieur le duc," said the king, "I understand you. Be satisfied, all who are named in that letter shall be punished as they deserve; and the queen herself shall not be forgotten."

"What do you say, sire? God forbid that the queen should suffer the least inconvenience or uneasiness on my account! She has always believed me, sire, to be her enemy, although your majesty can bear witness that I have always taken her part warmly, even against you. Oh! if she betrayed your majesty on the side of your honour, it would be quite another thing, and I should be the first to say, ' No grace, sire—no grace for the guilty!' Fortunately, there is nothing of the kind, and your majesty has just acquired a fresh proof of it."

"That is true, monsieur le cardinal," said the king, "and you were right, as you always are; but the queen, not the less, deserves all my anger."

"It is you, sire, who have now incurred hers; and even if she were to be seriously offended, I could well understand it; your majesty has treated her with a severity——"

"It is thus I will always treat my enemies and yours, duke, however high they may be placed, and whatever peril I may incur in acting severely towards them."

"The queen is my enemy, but is not yours, sire; on the contrary, she is a devoted, submissive, and irreproachable wife; allow me, then, sire, to intercede for her with your majesty."

"Let her humble herself, then, and come to me first."

"On the contrary, sire, set the example; you have committed the first wrong, since it was you who suspected the queen."

"What! I make advances first!" said the king, "never!"

Sire, I entreat you to do so."

Besides, in what manner can I make advances first?"

"By doing a thing which you know will be agreeable to her."

"What is that?"

"Give a ball; you know how much the queen loves dancing. I will answer for it, her resentment will not hold out against such an attention."

"Monsieur le Cardinal, you know that I do not like mundane pleasures."

"The queen will only be the more grateful to you, as she knows your antipathy for that amusement; besides, it will be an opportunity for her to wear those beautiful diamonds which you gave her recently, on her birthday, and with which she has since had no occasion to adorn herself."

"We shall see, Monsieur le Cardinal, we shall see," said the king, who, in his joy at finding the queen guilty of a crime which he cared little about, and innocent of a fault of which he had great dread, was ready to make up all differences with her; "we shall see, but, upon my honour, you are too indulgent towards her."

"Sire," said the cardinal, "leave severity to your ministers; clemency is a royal virtue; employ it, and you will find you derive advantage from it."

Upon which the cardinal, hearing the clock strike eleven, bowed lowly, demanding permission of the king to retire, and supplicating him to come to a good understanding with the queen.

Anne of Austria, who, in consequence of the seizure of her letter, expected reproaches, was much astonished the next day to see the king make s e attempts at reconciliation with her. Her first movement was repulsive, her womanly pride and her queenly dignity had both been so cruelly outraged, that she could not come round at the first advance ; but, overpersuaded by the advice of her women, she at last had the appearance of beginning to forget. The king took advantage of this favourable moment to tell her that he had the intention of shortly giving a fête.

A fête was so rare a thing for poor Anne of Austria, that at this announcement, as the cardinal had predicted, the last trace of her resentment disappeared, if not from her heart, at least from her countenance She asked upon what day this fête would take place, but the king replied that he must consult the cardinal upon that head.

In fact, every day the king asked the cardinal when this fête should take place, and every day the cardinal, under some pretence or other, deferred fixing it. Ten days passed away thus.

On the eighth day after the scene we have described, the cardinal received a letter with the London stamp, which only contained these lines :

" I have them, but I am unable to leave London for want of money ; send me five hundred pistoles, and four or five days after I have received them I shall be in Paris."

On the same day that the cardinal received this letter, the king put his customary question to him.

Richelieu counted on his fingers, and said to himself :

" She will arrive, she says, four or five days after having received the money ; it will require four or five days for the transmission of the money, four or five days for her to return, that makes ten days ; now, allowing for contrary winds, accidents, and a woman's weakness, we cannot make it, altogether, less than twelve days."

" Well, monsieur le duc," said the king, " have you made your calculations ?"

" Yes, sire, to-day is the 20th of September ; the *échevins* of the city give a fête on the 3rd of October. That will fall in wonderfully well ; you will not appear to have gone out of your way to please the queen."

Then the cardinal added :

" A propos, sire, do not forget to tell her majesty, the evening before the fête, that you should like to see how her diamond studs become her."

CHAPTER XVII.

BONACIEUX AT HOME.

IT was the second time the cardinal had mentioned these diamond studs to the king. Louis XIII. was struck with these repetitions, and began to fancy that this recommendation concealed some mystery.

More than once the king had been humiliated by the cardinal, whose police, without having yet attained the perfection of the modern police, was excellent, being better informed than himself even upon what was going on in his own household. He hoped, then, in a conversation with Anne of Austria, to obtain some information from that conversation, and afterwards, to come upon his eminence with some secret, which the cardinal either knew or did not know, but which, in either case, would raise him infinitely in the eyes of his minister.

He went then to the queen, and, according to custom, accosted her with fresh menaces against those who surrounded her. Anne of Austria hung down her head, allowed the torrent to flow on without replying, and hoped that it would end by stopping of itself; but this was not what Louis XIII. meant; Louis XIII. wanted a discussion, from which some light or other might break, convinced as he was that the cardinal had some after-thought, and was preparing for him one of those terrible surprises which his eminence was so skilful in getting up. He arrived at this end by his persistence in accusing.

" But," cried Anne of Austria, tired of these vague attacks; "but, sire, you do not tell me all that you have in your heart. What have I done, then? Let me know what crime I have committed? It is impossible that your majesty can make all this to-do about a letter written to my brother !"

The king, attacked in a manner so direct, did not know what to answer ; and he thought that this was the moment for expressing the desire which he was not to have made until the evening before the fête.

" Madame," said he, with dignity, " there will shortly be a ball at the Hôtel de Ville ; I wish that, to do honour to our worthy *échevins*, you should appear at it in ceremonial costume, and particularly ornamented with the diamond studs which I gave you on your birthday. That is my answer."

The answer was terrible. Anne of Austria believed that Louis XIII. knew all, and that the cardinal had persuaded him to employ this long dissimulation of seven or eight days, which, likewise, was characteristic. She became excessively pale, leant her beautiful hand upon a console, which hand appeared then like one of wax, and looking at the king, with terror in her eyes, she was unable to reply by a single syllable.

" You hear, madame," said the king, who enjoyed this embarrassment to its full extent, but without guessing the cause,—" You hear, madame ?"

" Yes, sire, I hear," stammered the queen.

" You will appear at this ball ?"

" Yes."

" And with those studs ?"

" Yes."

The queen's paleness, if possible increased ; the king perceived it and enjoyed it with that cold cruelty which was one of the worst sides of his character.

" Then that is agreed," said the king, " and that is all I had to say to you."

" But on what day will this ball take place ?" asked Anne of Austria.

Louis XIII. felt instinctively that he ought not to reply to this question, the queen having put it in an almost inaudible voice.

" Oh ! very shortly, madame," said he, " but I do not precisely recollect the date of the day ; I will ask the cardinal."

" It was the cardinal, then, who informed you of this *fête ?*"

" Yes, madame," replied the astonished king ; " but why do you ask that ?"

' It was he who told you to desire me to appear there with these studs ?"

" That is to say, madame——"

" It was he, sire, it was he !"

" Well ; and what does it signify whether it was **he or I** ? Is there any crime in this request ?"

" No, sire."

" Then you will appear ?"

" Yes, sire."

" That's well," said the king, retiring, " that's well, I depend upon you."

The queen made a courtsey, less from etiquette than because her knees were sinking under her.

" I am lost," murmured the queen, " lost ! for the cardinal knows all, and it is he who urges on the king, who as yet knows nothing, but will soon know everything. I am lost ! my God ! my God ! my God !"

She knelt upon a cushion and prayed, with her head buried between her palpitating arms.

In fact, her position was terrible. Buckingham had returned to London, Madame de Chevreuse was at Tours. More closely watched than ever, the queen felt certain that one of her women betrayed her, without knowing how to tell which. Laporte could not leave the Louvre ; she had not a soul in the world in whom she could confide.

Thus, whilst contemplating the misfortune which threatened her, and the abandonment in which she was left, she broke out into sobs and tears.

" Can I be of no service to your majesty ?" said all at once a voice full of sweetness and pity.

The queen turned sharply round, for there could be no deception in the expression of that voice : it was a friend who spoke thus.

In fact, at one of the doors which opened into the queen's apartment, appeared the pretty Madame Bonacieux ; she had been engaged in arranging the dresses and linen in a closet, when the king entered ; she could not get out, and had heard all.

The queen uttered a piercing cry at finding herself surprised, for in her trouble she did not at first recognise the young woman who had been given to her by Laporte.

" Oh ! fear nothing, madame !" said the young woman, clasping her hands, and weeping herself at the queen's sorrows ; " I am your majesty's, body and soul, and however far I may be from you, however inferior may be my position, I believe I have discovered a means of extricating your majesty from your trouble."

" You ! oh heavens ! you !" cried the queen ; " but look me in the face ; I am betrayed on all sides ; can I trust in you ?"

" Oh ! madame !" cried the young woman, falling on her knees, "upon my soul, I am ready to die for your majesty !"

This expression sprang from the very bottom of the heart, and, like the first, there was no mistaking it.

" Yes," continued Madame Bonacieux, " yes, there are traitors here ; but by the holy name of the Virgin, I swear that none is more devoted to your majesty than I am. Those studs, which the king speaks of, you gave them to the Duke of Buckingham, did. you not ? Those studs were in a little rosewood box, which he held under his arm ? Am I deceived ? Is it not so, madame ?"

" Oh ! my God ! my God !" murmured the queen, whose teeth chattered with fright.

" Well, those studs," continued Madame Bonacieux, " we must have them back again."

" Yes, without doubt, it must be so," cried the queen, " but how am I to act ? How can it be effected ?"

" Some one must be sent to the duke."

" But who ? who ? in whom can I trust ?"

" Place confidence in me, madame ; do me that honour, my queen, and I will find a messenger."

" But I must write."

" Oh, yes ; that is indispensable. Two words from the hand of your majesty and your own private seal."

" But these two words would bring about my condemnation, divorce, exile !"

" Yes, if they fell into infamous hands. But I will answer for these two words being delivered to their address."

" Oh ! my God ! I must then place my life, my honour, my reputation, all in your hands ?"

" Yes, yes, madame, you must, and I will save them all."

" But how,—tell me at least, how ?"

" My husband has been set at liberty these two or three days ; I have not yet had time to see him again. He is a worthy, honest man, who entertains neither love nor hatred for anybody. He will do anything I wish ; he will set out upon receiving an order from me, without knowing what he carries, and he will remit your majesty's letter, without even knowing it is from your majesty, to the address which shall be upon it."

The queen took the two hands of the young woman with a burst of emotion, gazed at her as if to read her very heart, and seeing nothing but sincerity in her beautiful eyes, embraced her tenderly.

"Do that," cried she, "and you will have saved my life, you will have saved my honour !"

"Oh! do not exaggerate the service I have the happiness to render your majesty ; I have nothing of your majesty's to save, who are only the victim of perfidious plots."

"That is true, that is true, my child," said the queen, "you are right."

"Give me then that letter, madame ; time presses."

The queen ran to a little table, upon which were pens, ink, and paper ; she wrote two lines, sealed the letter with her private seal, and gave it to Madame Bonacieux.

"And now," said the queen, "we are forgetting one very necessary thing."

"What is that, madame ?"

"Money."

Madame Bonacieux blushed.

"Yes, that is true," said she, "and I will confess to your majesty that my husband——"

"Your husband has none ; is that what you would say ?"

"Oh ! yes, he has some, but he is very avaricious, that is his fault. Nevertheless, let not your majesty be uneasy, we will find means."

"And I have none, neither," said the queen. Such as have read the Memoirs of Madame de Motteville will not be astonished at this reply. "But wait a minute."

Anne of Austria ran to her jewel-case,——

"Here," said she, "here is a ring of great value, as I have been assured ; it came from my brother, the king of Spain ; it is mine, and I am at liberty to dispose of it. Take this ring, make money of it, and let your husband set out."

"In an hour, you shall be obeyed, madame."

"You see the address," said the queen, speaking so low that Madame Bonacieux could hardly hear what she said,—"To Milord Duke of Buckingham, London."

"The letter shall be given to him himself."

"Generous girl !" cried Anne of Austria.

Madame Bonacieux kissed the hands of the queen, concealed the paper in the bosom of her dress, and disappeared with the lightness of a bird.

Ten minutes afterwards, she was at home ; as she told the queen, she had not seen her husband since his liberation, she was ignorant of the change that had taken place in him with respect to the cardinal, a change which had since been strengthened by two or three visits from the Count de Rochefort, who had become the best friend of Bonacieux, and had persuaded him that nothing culpable had been intended by the carrying off of his wife, but that it was only a piece of political pre-caution.

She found Bonacieux alone : the poor man was restoring, with much trouble, order in his house, the furniture of which he had found mostly broken, and his chests and drawers mostly empty, justice not being one of the three things which King Solomon named as leaving no traces of their passage.   As to the servant, she had run away at the moment of her master's arrest.   Terror had had such an effect upon the poor girl, that she had never ceased walking from Paris till she got to Burgundy, her native place.

The worthy mercer had, immediately upon entering his house, communicated to his wife the news of his happy return, and his wife had replied by congratulating him, and telling him that the first moment she could steal from her duties should be devoted to paying him a visit.

This first moment had been delayed five days, which, under any other circumstances, might have appeared rather long to Master Bonacieux ; but he had, in the visit he had made to the cardinal, and in the visits Rochefort had made him, ample subjects for reflection, and, as everybody knows, nothing makes time pass more quickly than reflection.

This was all so much the more so from Bonacieux's reflections all being *couleur de rose*.   Rochefort called him his friend, his dear Bonacieux, and never ceased telling him that the cardinal had a great respect for him.   The mercer fancied himself already in the high road to honours and fortune.

On her side, Madame Bonacieux had also reflected, but it must be admitted, upon something widely different from ambition : in spite of herself, her thoughts constantly reverted to that handsome young man, who was so brave, and appeared to be so much in love.   Married at eighteen to Monsieur Bonacieux, having always lived amongst her husband's friends, people very little susceptible of inspiring any sentiment whatever in a young woman whose heart was above her position, Madame Bonacieux had remained insensible to vulgar seductions : but at this period the title of gentleman had a particularly great influence with the bourgeoisie, or citizen class, and D'Artagnan was a gentleman ; besides, he wore the uniform of the guards, which, next to that of the musketeers, was most admired by the ladies.   He was, we repeat, handsome, young, and bold ; he spoke of love like a man who did love, and was anxious to be loved in return : there was certainly enough in all this to turn a head only twenty-three years old, and Madame Bonacieux had just attained that happy period of life.

The married couple then, although they had not seen each other for eight days, and that during that time serious events had taken place in which both were concerned, accosted each other with a degree of preoccupation : nevertheless, M. Bonacieux manifested real joy, and advanced towards his wife with open arms.

Madame Bonacieux presented her cheek to him.

" Let us talk a little," said she.

" How !" said Bonacieux, astonished.

" Yes ; I have something of great importance to tell you."

" True," said he, " and I have some questions sufficiently serious to put to you.   Describe to me how you were carried off."

"Oh! that's of no consequence just now," said Madame Bonacieux.

"And what does it allude to then? To my captivity!"

"I heard of it the day it happened; but as you were not guilty of any crime, as you were not guilty of any intrigue, as you, in short, knew nothing that could compromise yourself or anybody else, I attached no more importance to that event than it merited."

"You speak pretty much at your ease, madame," said Bonacieux, hurt at the little interest his wife seemed to take in him : "do you know that I was plunged during a whole day and a whole night in a dungeon of the Bastille?"

"Oh! a day and night soon pass away; let us return to the object that brings me here."

"What! to that which brings you home to me! Is it not the desire of seeing a husband again from whom you have been separated for a week?" asked the mercer, piqued to the quick.

"Yes, that first, and other things afterwards."

"Speak then."

"It is a thing of the highest interest, and upon which our future fortune perhaps depends."

"The complexion of our fortune has changed very much since I saw you, Madame Bonacieux, and I should not be astonished if, in the course of a few months, it were to excite the envy of many folks."

"Particularly if you obey the instructions I am about to give you."

"To me?"

"Yes, to you. There is a good and holy action to be performed, monsieur, and much money to be gained at the same time."

Madame Bonacieux knew that when naming money to her husband, she attacked him on his weak side. But a man, were he even a mercer, when he has talked for ten minutes with the Cardinal de Richelieu, is no longer the same man.

"Much money to be gained?" said Bonacieux, protruding his lip.

"Yes, much."

"About how much, pray?"

"A thousand pistoles, perhaps."

"Humph! What you have to ask of me then is serious!"

"It is indeed."

"What is to be done?"

"You must set out immediately; I will give you a paper which you must not part with on any account, and which you will deliver into the proper hands."

"And where am I to go to?"

"London."

"I go to London! You are joking, I have nothing to do in London."

"But others require that you should go there."

"But who are those others? I warn you that I will never again work in the dark, and that I will know not only to what I expose myself, but for whom I expose myself."

"An illustrious person sends you, an illustrious person awaits you :

the recompense will exceed your expectations, that is all I promise you."

" More intrigues ! nothing but intrigues ! Thank you, madame, I am aware of them now ; Monsieur le Cardinal has enlightened me on that head."

" The cardinal ?" cried Madame Bonacieux ; " have you seen the cardinal ?"

" He sent for me," answered the mercer, proudly.

" And you went ! you imprudent man !"

" Well, I can't say I had much choice in going or not going, for I was taken to him between two guards. I must also confess that as I did not then know his eminence, if I had been able to have declined the visit, I should have been delighted to have done so."

" He ill-treated you, then ? he threatened you ?"

" He gave me his hand, and he called me his friend—his friend ! do you hear that, madame ? I am the friend of the great cardinal !"

" Of the great cardinal !"

" Perhaps you would dispute his right to that title, madame ?"

" Oh ! I would dispute his right to nothing ; but I tell you that the favour of a minister is ephemeral, and that a man must be mad to attach himself to a minister ; there are powers above his which do not depend upon a man or the issue of an event, it is around these powers we should endeavour to range ourselves."

" I am sorry for it, madame, but I acknowledge no other power but that of the great man whom I have the honour to serve."

" You serve the cardinal ?"

" Yes, madame, and as his servant, I will not allow you to be concerned in plots against the safety of the state, or to assist in the intrigues of a woman who is not a Frenchwoman, and who has a Spanish heart. Fortunately, we have the great cardinal, his vigilant eye watches over and penetrates to the bottom of hearts."

Bonacieux was repeating, word for word, a sentence which he had heard the Count de Rochefort make use of ; but the poor wife, who had reckoned on her husband, and who, in that hope, had answered for him to the queen, did not tremble the less, both at the danger into which she had nearly cast herself, and at the helpless state to which she was reduced. Nevertheless, knowing the weakness of her husband, and more particularly his cupidity, she did not despair of bringing him round to her purpose.

" Ah ! you are a Cardinalist ! then, monsieur, are you ?" cried she, " and you serve the party who ill-treat your wife and insult your queen?"

" Private interests are as nothing before the interests of all. I am for those who save the state," said Bonacieux, emphatically.

This was another of the Count de Rochefort's sentences which he had retained, and which he sought an occasion to make use of.

" And what do you know about the state you talk of ?" said Madame Bonacieux, shrugging her shoulders. " Be satisfied with being a plain, straightforward bourgeois, and turn your attention to that side which holds out the greatest advantages."

" Eh ! eh !" said Bonacieux, slapping a plump, round bag, which returned a sound of money ; " what do you think of this, madam preacher ?"

" Where does that money come from ?"

" Can't you guess ?"

" From the cardinal ?"

" From him, and from my friend the Count de Rochefort."

" The Count de Rochefort ! why, it was he who carried me off !"

" Perhaps it was, madame."

" And you receive money from that man !"

" Did you not yourself tell me that that carrying off was entirely political ?"

" Yes, but that event had for its object to make me betray my mistress, to draw from me by tortures confessions that might have compromised the honour, and perhaps the life of my august mistress."

" Madame," replied Bonacieux, " your august mistress is a perfidious Spaniard, and what the cardinal does is well done."

" Monsieur," said the young woman, " I know you to be cowardly, avaricious, and weak, but I never till now believed you to be infamous !"

" Madame !" said Bonacieux, who had never seen his wife in a passion, and who retreated before this conjugal anger ; " Madame, what is that you say ?"

" I say you are a miserable mean creature !" continued Madame Bonacieux, who saw she was regaining some little influence over her husband. " You meddle with politics, do you ! And still more, with cardinalist politics ! Why, you are selling yourself, body and soul, to the devil, for money !"

" No, but to the cardinal."

" It's the same thing !" cried the young woman. " Who says Richelieu says Satan !"

" Hold your tongue ! hold your tongue, madam ; we may be overheard."

" Yes, you are right, I should be ashamed for anyone to know your baseness."

" But what do you require of me, then ; come, let us see !"

" I have told you : you must set out instantly, monsieur ; you must accomplish loyally the commission with which I deign to charge you, and on that condition I pardon everything, I forget everything ; and still further,"—and she held out her hand to him—" I give you my love again."

Bonacieux was a coward, and he was avaricious, but he loved his wife—he was softened. A man of fifty cannot long bear malice with a pretty wife of twenty-three. Madame Bonacieux saw that he hesitated.

" Come ! have you made your mind up ?" said she.

" But, my dear love ! reflect a little upon what you require of me.

London is far from Paris, very far, and perhaps the commission with which you charge me is not without dangers ?"

" Of what consequence is that, if you avoid them ?"

" Well, then, Madame Bonacieux," said the mercer, " well, then, I positively refuse : intrigues terrify me. I have seen the Bastille ; I —whew !—that's a frightful place, that Bastille! only to think of it makes my flesh crawl. They threatened me with torture ! Do you know what the torture is ? Wooden points that they stick in between your legs till your bones burst out ! No, positively I will not go. And, morbleu ! why do you not go yourself ? for, in truth, I think I have hitherto been deceived in you ; I really believe you are a man, and a violent one too."

" And you, you are a woman, a miserable woman, stupid and bruti-fied. You are afraid, are you ? Well, if you do not go this very in-stant, I will have you arrested by the queen's orders, and I will have you placed in that Bastille which you dread so much."

Bonacieux fell into a profound reflection ; he turned the two angers in his brain, that of the cardinal and that of the queen ; that of the cardinal predominated enormously.

" Have me arrested on the part of the queen," said he, " and I, I will appeal to his eminence."

At once, Madame Bonacieux saw that she had gone too far, and she was terrified at having communicated so much. She for a moment contemplated, with terror, that stupid countenance, impressed with the invincible resolution of a fool that is overcome by fear.

" Well, be it so !" said she. " Perhaps, when all is considered, you are right : in the long run, a man knows more about politics than a woman does, particularly such as, like you, Monsieur Bonacieux, have con-versed with the cardinal. And yet it is very hard," added she, " that a man upon whose affection I thought I might depend, treats me thus unkindly, and will not comply with any of my fancies."

" That is because your fancies might lead you too far," replied the triumphant Bonacieux, " and I mistrust them."

" Well, I will give it up, then, " said the young woman, sighing ; " it is as well as it is, say no more about it."

" Yes, at least you should tell me what I should have to do in Lon-don," replied Bonacieux, who remembered a little too late, that Roche-fort had desired him to endeavour to obtain his wife's secrets.

" It is of no use for you to know anything about it," said the young woman, whom an instinctive mistrust now impelled to draw back : " it was about one of those purchases that interest women, a purchase by which much might have been gained."

But the more the young woman excused herself, the more important Bonacieux conceived the secret to be which she declined to communi-cate to him. He resolved, then, that instant to hasten to the residence of the Count de Rochefort, and tell him that the queen was seeking for a messenger to send to London.

" Pardon me for leaving you, my dear Madame Bonacieux," said he ;

"but not knowing you would come to see me, I had made an engagement with a friend ; I shall soon return, and if you will wait only a few minutes for me, as soon as I have concluded my business with that friend, as it is growing late, I will come and conduct you back to the Louvre."

"Thank you, monsieur, you are not obliging enough to be of any use to me whatever," replied Madame Bonacieux ; "I shall return very safely to the Louvre by myself."

"As you please, Madame Bonacieux," said the ex-mercer, "shall I have the pleasure of seeing you soon again ?"

"Yes, next week, I hope my duties will afford me a little liberty, and I will take advantage of it to come and put things in order here, as they must, necessarily, be much deranged."

"Very well ; I shall expect you. You are not angry with me ?"

"Who, I ?—Oh ! not the least in the world."

"Till then, then ?"

"Till then, adieu !"

Bonacieux kissed his wife's hand and set off at a quick pace.

"Well !" said Madame Bonacieux when her husband had shut the street door, and she found herself alone, " there wanted nothing to complete that poor creature but being a cardinalist ! And I, who have answered for him to the queen ! I, who have promised my poor mistress ! Ah ! my God ! my God ! she will take me for one of those wretches with whom the palace swarms, and which are placed about her as spies ! Ah ! Monsieur Bonacieux ! I never did love you much, but now, it is worse than ever : I hate you ! and by my word, you shall pay for this !"

At the moment she spoke these words a rap on the ceiling made her raise her head, and a voice which reached her through the plaster, cried :

"Dear Madame Bonacieux, open the little passage-door for me, and I will come down to you."

CHAPTER XVIII.

THE LOVER AND THE HUSBAND.

"AH ! madame," said D'Artagnan, as he entered by the door which the young woman had opened for him, " allow me to tell you, that you have a bad sort of a husband there !"

"You have then overheard our conversation ?" asked Madame Bonacieux, eagerly, and looking at D'Artagnan with much uneasiness.

"The whole of it."

"But how, my God ! could you do that ?"

"By a mode of proceeding known to myself, and by which I likewise overheard the more animated conversation which you had with the cardinal's *sbirri*."

"And what did you understand by what you heard us say ?"

" A thousand things ; in the first place that, fortunately, your husband is a simpleton and a fool ; in the next place you are in trouble, of which I am very glad, as it gives me an opportunity of placing myself at your service, and God knows I am ready to throw myself into the fire for you ; and that the queen wants a brave, intelligent, devoted man to make a journey to London for her. I have, at least, two of the qualities you stand in need of,—and here I am."

Madame Bonacieux made no reply, but her heart beat with joy, and secret hope shone in her eyes.

" And what pledge can you give me," asked she, " if I consent to confide this message to you ?"

" My love for you. Speak ! command ! What must I do ?"

" My God ! my God !" murmured the young woman, " ought I to confide such a secret to you, monsieur ? You are almost a boy !"

" I suppose, then, you require some one to answer for me ?"

" I admit that that would reassure me greatly."

" Do you know Athos ?"

" No."

" Porthos ?"

" No."

" Aramis ?"

" No ; who are these gentlemen ?"

" Three of the king's musketeers. Do you know M. de Tréville, their captain ?"

" Oh ! yes, him, I know him ; not personally, but from having heard the queen speak of him more than once as a brave and loyal gentleman."

" You are not afraid that he would betray you for the sake of the cardinal ?"

" Oh ! no, certainly."

" Well, reveal your secret to him, and ask him, whether, however important, however valuable, however terrible it may be, you may not safely confide it to me."

" But this secret is not mine, and I cannot reveal it in this manner."

" Why, you were going to confide it to M. Bonacieux," said D'Artagnan, with an offended tone.

" As we confide a letter to the hollow of a tree, to the wing of a pigeon, or the collar of a dog."

" And yet me ;—you see plainly that I love you."

" You say so."

" I am an honourable man."

" I believe so."

" I am brave."

" Oh ! I am sure of that."

" Then, put me to the proof."

Madame Bonacieux looked at the young man, restrained for a minute by a last hesitation ; but there was such an ardour in his eyes, such persuasion in his voice, that she felt herself drawn on to place confidence in him. Besides, she was in one of those circumstances in which everything must be risked for the sake of everything. The queen also might be as much injured by too much discretion as by too much confidence—and—let us admit it, the involuntary sentiment which she felt for her young protector, compelled her to speak.

"Listen," said she, "I yield to your protestations, I yield to your assurances. But I swear to you, before God who hears us, that if you betray me, and my enemies pardon me, I will kill myself, whilst accusing you of my death."

"And I, I swear to you before God, madame," said D'Artagnan, "that if I am taken whilst accomplishing the orders you give me, I will die sooner than do anything, or say anything, that may compromise any one."

Then the young woman confided to him the terrible secret of which chance had already communicated to him a part, in front of the *Samaritaine.*

This was their mutual declaration of love.

D'Artagnan was radiant with joy and pride. This secret which he possessed, this woman whom he loved ! Confidence and love made him a giant.

"I will go," said he, "I will go at once."

"How ! you will go !" said Madame Bonacieux; "and your regiment, your captain ?"

"By my soul, you have made me forget all that, dear Constance ! Yes, you are right, I must obtain leave of absence."

"There is still another obstacle," murmured Madame Bonacieux, sorrowfully.

"Whatever it may be," cried D'Artagnan, after a moment of reflection, "I shall surmount it, be assured."

"How ?"

"I will go this very evening to M. de Tréville, whom I will request to ask this favour for me of his brother-in-law, M. des Essarts."

"But still, there is another thing."

"What is that ?" asked D'Artagnan, seeing that Madame Bonacieux hesitated to continue.

"You have, perhaps, no money ?"

"Perhaps is too much," said D'Artagnan, smiling.

"Then," replied Madame Bonacieux, opening a cupboard and taking from it the very bag which half an hour before her husband had caressed so affectionately, "take this bag."

"The cardinal's !" cried D'Artagnan, breaking into a loud laugh, he having heard, as may be remembered, thanks to his broken floor, every syllable of the conversation between the mercer and his wife.

"The cardinal's," replied Madame Bonacieux ; "you see it makes a very respectable appearance."

"Pardieu !" cried D'Artagnan, "it will be a doubly amusing affair to save the queen with the cardinal's money !"

" You are an amiable and a charming young man !" said Madame Bonacieux. " Be assured you will not find her majesty ungrateful."

" Oh ! I am already more than recompensed !" cried D'Artagnan. " I love you ; you permit me to tell you that I do ; that is already more happiness than I dared to hope for."

" Silence !" said Madame Bonacieux, starting.

" What !"

" Some one is talking in the street."

" It is the voice of——"

" Of my husband !   Oh ! yes ; I recognised it !

D'Artagnan ran to the door and drew the bolt.

" He shall not come in before I am gone," said he ; " and when I am gone, you can open the door for him."

" But I ought to be gone, too. And the disappearance of this money, how am I to justify it, if I am here ?"

" You are right ; we must go out."

" Go out?   How?   He will see us if we go out."

" Then you must come up into my room."

" Ah !" said Madame Bonacieux, " you speak that in a tone that ter-rifies me !"

Madame Bonacieux pronounced these words with tears in her eyes. D'Artagnan saw those tears, and much disturbed, softened, he threw himself at her feet.

" In my apartment you will be as safe as in a temple ; I give you my word of a gentleman."

" Let us go, then, I place full confidence in you, my friend !"

D'Artagnan drew back the bolt with precaution, and both, light as shadows, glided through the interior door into the passage, ascended the stairs as quietly as possible, and entered D'Artagnan's apartment.

Once in his apartment, for greater security, the young man barri-caded the door. They both went up to the window, and, through a slit in the shutter, they saw M. Bonacieux talking with a man in a cloak.

At the sight of this man, D'Artagnan started, half drew his sword, and sprang towards the door.

It was the man of Meung.

" What are you going to do ?" cried Madame Bonacieux ; " you will ruin us all !"

" But I have sworn to kill that man !" said D'Artagnan.

" At this time your life is devoted, and does not belong to you ! In the name of the queen I forbid you to throw yourself into any danger which is foreign to that of your voyage !"

" And do you command nothing in your own name ?"

" In my name ?" said Madame Bonacieux, with great emotion ; " in my name I beg you ! But listen ; they appear to be speaking of me."

D'Artagnan drew near the window, and listened.

M. Bonacieux had opened his door, and seeing the apartment empty, had returned to the man in the cloak, whom he had left alone for an instant.

"She is gone," said he; "she must be gone back to the Louvre."

"You are sure," replied the stranger, "that she did not suspect the intention you went out with?"

"No," replied Bonacieux, with a self-sufficient air, "she is too superficial a woman."

"Is the young guardsman at home?"

"I do not think he is; as you see, his shutter is closed, and there is no light through the chinks of the shutters."

"That's true; but it's as well to be certain."

"How can we be so?"

"By knocking at his door."

"Go."

"I will ask his servant."

Bonacieux went into the house again, passed through the same door that had afforded a passage for the two fugitives, went up to D'Artagnan's door, and knocked.

No one answered. Porthos, to make a greater display, had that evening borrowed Planchet. As to D'Artagnan, he took care not to give the least sign of existence.

At the moment the finger of Bonacieux sounded on the door, the two young people felt their hearts bound within them.

"There is nobody within," said Bonacieux.

"Never mind; let us walk into your apartment; we shall be better there than in the doorway."

"Oh! Good God!" whispered Madame Bonacieux, "we shall hear no more."

"On the contrary," said D'Artagnan, "we shall hear the better."

D'Artagnan raised the three or four boards which made another Dionysius's ear of his chamber, spread a carpet, went down upon his knees, and made a sign to Madame Bonacieux to do as he did, stooping down towards the opening.

"You are sure there is nobody there?" said the unknown.

"I will answer for it," said Bonacieux.

"And you think that your wife——"

"Is returned to the Louvre."

"Without speaking to anyone but yourself?"

"I am sure of it."

"Please to understand, that is an important point."

"Then the news I brought you is valuable?"

"Very, my dear Bonacieux; I don't attempt to deny it."

"Then the cardinal will be pleased with me?"

"No doubt he will."

"The great cardinal!"

"Are you sure, that in her conversation with you, your wife mentioned no proper names?"

"I don't think she did."

"She did not name Madame de Chevreuse, the Duke of Buckingham, or Madame de Vernet?"

" No ; she only told me she wished to send me to London, to further the interests of an illustrious personage."

" Oh ! the traitor !" murmured Madame Bonacieux.

" Silence !" whispered D'Artagnan, taking a hand, which, without thinking of it, she suffered him to retain.

" Never mind," continued the man in the cloak ; " it was very silly of you not to have feigned to accept the mission ; you would now be in possession of the letter ; the state, which is now threatened, would be safe ; and you——"

" And I ?"

" Well, you ! The cardinal would have given you letters of nobility."

" Did he tell you so ?"

" Yes, I know that he meant to afford you that agreeable surprise."

" Be satisfied," replied Bonacieux ; " my wife adores me, and there is still plenty of time."

" The silly fool !" murmured Madame Bonacieux.

" Silence !" said D'Artagnan, pressing her hand more closely.

" What do you mean by its being still time ?" asked the man in the cloak.

" I will go to the Louvre, I will ask for Madame Bonacieux, I will tell her I have reflected upon the matter, I will renew the affair, I will obtain the letter, and I will run directly to the cardinal's."

" Well ! begone then ! make all possible haste : I will shortly come back to learn the result of your plan."

The unknown went out.

" Base old fool !" said Madame Bonacieux, addressing this affectionate epithet to her husband.

" Silence, once more !" said D'Artagnan, pressing her hand still more warmly.

A terrible howling interrupted these reflections of D'Artagnan and Madame Bonacieux. It was her husband, who had discovered the disappearance of his money bag, and was screaming out, " Thieves ! thieves !"

" Oh ! good God," cried Madame Bonacieux, " he will rouse the whole quarter."

Bonacieux cried for a long time ; but, as such cries, on account of their frequency, did not attract much notice in the Rue des Fossoyeurs, and as lately the mercer's house had not been in very good repute, finding that nobody came, he went out, crying aloud, his voice being heard fainter and fainter, in the direction of the Rue du Bac.

" Now he is gone, it is your turn to get out," said Madame Bonacieux : " courage, my friend, but, above all, prudence, and think what you owe to the queen !"

" To her and to you !" cried D'Artagnan. " Be satisfied, lovely Constance. I shall prove worthy of her gratitude ; but shall I likewise return worthy of your love ?"

The young woman only replied by the beautiful glow which mounted to her cheeks. A few seconds after, D'Artagnan went out in his turn, enveloped likewise in a large cloak, which ill-concealed the sheath of a long sword.

Madame Bonacieux followed him with her eyes, with that long, fond look with which a woman accompanies the man she loves ; but when he had turned the angle of the street, she fell on her knees, and clasping her hands,—

"Oh! my God !" cried she, "protect the queen, protect me !"

CHAPTER XIX.

PLAN OF THE CAMPAIGN.

D'ARTAGNAN went straight to the hotel of M. de Tréville. He had reflected that in a few minutes the cardinal would be warned by this cursed unknown, who appeared to be his agent, and he judged, with reason, he had not a moment to lose.

The heart of the young man overflowed with joy. An opportunity presented itself to him in which there would be both glory and money to be gained, and, as a far higher encouragement still, which had brought him into close intimacy with a woman he adored. This chance did then for him, at once, more than he would have dared to ask of Providence.

M. de Tréville was in his saloon with his habitual court of gentlemen. D'Artagnan, who was known as a familiar of the house, went straight to his cabinet, and sent word to him that he wished to see him upon an affair of importance.

D'Artagnan had been there scarcely five minutes when M. de Tréville entered. At the first glance, and by the joy which was painted on his countenance, the worthy captain plainly perceived that something fresh and extraordinary was on foot.

All the way he came, D'Artagnan was consulting with himself whether he should place confidence in M. de Tréville, or whether he should only ask him to give him *carte blanche* for a second affair. But M. de Tréville had always been so perfectly his friend, had always been so devoted to the king and queen, and hated the cardinal so cordially, that the young man resolved to tell him everything.

"Did you ask for me, my young friend ?" said M. de Tréville.

"Yes, monsieur," said D'Artagnan, "you will pardon me, I hope, for having disturbed you, when you know the importance of my business."

"Speak, then, I am attentive."

"It concerns nothing less," said D'Artagnan, lowering his voice, "than the honour, perhaps the life, of the queen."

"What do you say ?" asked M. de Tréville, glancing round to see if they were alone, and then fixing his interrogative look upon D'Artagnan.

"I say, monsieur, that chance has rendered me master of a secret—"

"Which you will keep, I hope, young man, sacred as your life."

" But which I must impart to you, monsieur, for you alone can assist me in the mission I have just received from her majesty."

" Is this secret your own ?"

" No, monsieur, it is her majesty's."

" Are you authorised by her majesty to communicate it to me ?"

" No, monsieur, for on the contrary, I am desired to preserve the profoundest mystery."

" Why, then, are you about to betray it with respect to me ?"

" Because, as I said, without you I can do nothing, and I was afraid that you would refuse me the favour I am come to ask, if you were not acquainted with the object for which I requested it of you."

" Keep your secret, young man, and tell me what you wish."

" I wish you to obtain for me, from M. des Essarts, leave of absence for a fortnight."

" When ?"

" This very night."

" You are leaving Paris ?"

" I am going on a mission."

" May you tell me whither ?"

" To London."

" Has any one an interest in preventing your arriving there ?"

" The cardinal, I believe, would give anything in the world to prevent my success."

" And you are going alone ?"

" I am going alone ?"

" In that case you will not get beyond Bondy ; I tell you so, by the word of De Tréville."

" How so, monsieur ?"

" You will be assassinated."

" And I shall die in the performance of my duty."

" Yes, but please to recollect your mission will not be accomplished."

" That is true !" replied D'Artagnan.

" You may take my word," continued Tréville, " in enterprises of this kind, in order that one may arrive, four must set out."

" Ah ! you are right, monsieur," said D'Artagnan ; " but you know Athos, Porthos, and Aramis, and you know if I can dispose of them."

" Without confiding to them the secret which I was not willing to know ?"

" We are sworn, once for ever, implicit confidence and devotedness against all proof ; besides, you can tell them that you have full confidence in me, and they will not be more incredulous than you."

" I can send to each of them leave of absence for a fortnight, that is all : Athos, whose wound still gives him inconvenience, to go to the waters of Forges ; to Porthos and Aramis to accompany their friend, whom they are not willing to abandon in such a painful position. The sending of their leave of absence will be proof enough that I authorise their voyage."

" Thanks, monsieur ! you are a hundred times kind !"

" Begone then, find them instantly, and let all be done to night. Ha !
but first write your request to M. des. Essarts. You, perhaps, had a
spy at your heels, and your visit, if it should ever be known to the cardinal, will be thus legitimated."

D'Artagnan drew up his request, and M. de Tréville, on receiving it,
assured him that by two o'clock in the morning, the four leaves of
absence should be at the respective domiciles of the travellers.

" Have the goodness to send mine to Athos's residence. I should
dread some disagreeable encounter if I were to go home."

" I will. Adieu ! and a prosperous voyage ! Apropos !" said M. de
Tréville, calling him back.

D'Artagnan returned.

" Have you any money ?"

D'Artagnan tapped the bag he had in his pocket.

" Enough ?" asked M. de Treville.

" Three hundred pistoles."

" Oh ! plenty ; that would carry you to the end of the world : begone
then."

D'Artagnan bowed to M. de Tréville, who held out his hand to him ;
D'Artagnan pressed it with a respect mixed with gratitude. Since his
first arrival at Paris, he had had constant occasion to honour this excellent man, whom he had always found worthy, loyal, and great.

His first visit was for Aramis, at whose residence he had not been
since the famous evening on which he had followed Madame Bonacieux.
Still further, he had seen the young musketeer but seldom, but every
time he had seen him, he had remarked a deep sadness imprinted on
his countenance.

He found Aramis this evening, sitting up, but melancholy and
thoughtful ; D'Artagnan risked a question or two about this prolonged
melancholy ; Aramis pleaded as his excuse a commentary upon the
eighteenth chapter of St. Augustin, that he was forced to write in Latin,
for the following week, and which preoccupied him a good deal.

After the two friends had been chatting a few instants, a servant
from M. de Tréville entered, bringing a sealed packet.

" What is that," asked Aramis.

" The leave of absence monsieur has asked for," replied the lackey.

" For me ! I have asked for no leave of absence !"

" Hold your tongue, and take it," said D'Artagnan. " And you, my
friend, there is a demi-pistole for your trouble ; you will tell M. de Tréville that M. Aramis is very much obliged to him. Go."

The lackey bowed to the ground and departed.

" What does all this mean ?" asked Aramis.

" Pack up all you want for a journey of a fortnight, and follow me."

" But I cannot leave Paris, just now, without knowing——"
Aramis stopped.

" What is become of her ? I suppose you mean——" continued
D'Artagnan.

" Become of whom ?" replied Aramis.

" The lady who was here, the lady of the embroidered handkerchief."

" Who told you there was a lady here?" replied Aramis, becoming as pale as death.

" I saw her."

" And you know who she is?"

" Well, I think I can give a pretty good guess, at least."

" Then," said Aramis, " since you appear to know so many things, can you tell me what is become of that lady?"

" I presume that she is gone back to Tours."

" To Tours? yes, that may be; you evidently know her. But why did she return to Tours without telling me anything about it?"

" Because she was in fear of being arrested."

" Why did she not write to me then?"

" Because she was afraid of compromising you."

" D'Artagnan, you restore me to life?" cried Aramis. " I fancied myself despised, betrayed. I was so delighted to see her again! I could not have believed she would risk her liberty for me, and yet for what other cause could she have returned to Paris?"

" For the cause which, to-day, carries us to England."

" And what is this cause?" demanded Aramis.

" Oh! you'll know it some day, Aramis; but, at present, I must beg leave to imitate the discretion of *the doctor's niece.*"

Aramis smiled, as he remembered the tale he had related to his friends on a certain evening.

" Well, then, since she has left Paris, and you are sure of it, D'Artagnan, nothing prevents me, and I am ready to follow you. You say we are going——"

" To Athos's residence, now, and if you will come thither, I beg you to make haste, for we have lost much time already. Apropos, inform Bazin."

" Will Bazin go with us?" asked Aramis.

" Perhaps so. At all events, it is best that he should follow us to Athos's."

Aramis called Bazin, and after having ordered him to join them at Athos's residence: " Let us go, then," said he, taking his cloak, sword, and three pistols, opening uselessly two or three drawers to see if he could not find some stray coin or other. When well assured this search was superfluous, he followed D'Artagnan, wondering to himself how this young guardsman should know so well who the lady was to whom he had given hospitality, and that he should know better than he did what was become of her.

Only, as they went out, Aramis placed his hand upon the arm of D'Artagnan, and looking at him earnestly,—

" You have not spoken of this lady?" said he.

" To nobody in the world."

" Not even to Athos or Porthos?"

" I have not breathed a syllable to them."

" That's well!"

And, at ease on this important point, Aramis continued his road with D'Artagnan, and both soon arrived at Athos's dwelling.

They found him holding his leave of absence in one hand, and M. de Tréville's note in the other.

" Can you explain to me what this leave of absence and this letter, which I have just received mean ?" said the astonished Athos :——" My dear Athos, I wish, as your health absolutely requires it, that you should rest for a fortnight. Go, then, and take the waters of Forges, or any that may be more agreeable to you, and re-establish yourself as quickly as possible.—Your affectionate De Tréville."

" Well ; this leave of absence and that letter mean that you must follow me, Athos."

" To the waters of the Forges ?"

" There or elsewhere."

" In the king's service ?"

" Either the king's or the queen's ; are we not their majesties' servants ?"

At that moment Porthos entered.

" *Pardieu !*" said he ; " here is a strange thing has happened ! Since when, I wonder, in the musketeers, did they grant men leave of absence without its being asked for ?"

" Since," said D'Artagnan, " they have friends who ask it for them."

" Ah, ah !" said Porthos, " it appears there's something fresh afoot ?"

" Yes, we are going——" said Aramis.

" Going ! to what country ?" demanded Porthos.

" *Ma foi !* I don't know much about it," said Athos ; " ask D'Artagnan here."

" To London, gentlemen," said D'Artagnan.

" To London !" cried Porthos ; " and what the devil are we going to do in London ?"

" That is what I am not at liberty to tell you, gentlemen ; you must trust to me."

" But, in order to go to London, a man should have some money ; and I have none."

" Nor I," said Aramis.

" Nor I," said Porthos.

" Well, I have," added D'Artagnan, pulling out his treasure from his pocket, and placing it on the table. There are in this bag three hundred pistoles. Let each take seventy-five, which will be quite enough to take us to London and back. Besides, we may be sure that all of us will not arrive at London."

" Why so ?"

" Because, according to all probability, some of us will be left on the road."

" What is this, then, a campaign upon which we are entering ?"

" And a most dangerous one. I give you fair notice."

" Ah ! ah ! but if we do risk being killed," said Porthos, " at least I should like to know what for."

" You would be all the wiser !" said Athos.

" And yet," said Aramis, " I am somewhat of Porthos's opinion."

" Is the king accustomed to give you such reasons ? No. He says to you, very simply : 'Gentlemen, there is fighting going on in Gascony or in Flanders ; go and fight ;' and you go there. Why ? You need give yourselves no uneasiness about that."

" D'Artagnan is right," said Athos ; "here are our three leaves of absence, which came from M. de Tréville ; and here are three hundred pistoles, which came from I don't know where. So let us go and get killed where we are told to go. Is life worth the trouble of so many questions ? D'Artagnan, I am ready to follow you."

" And I," said Porthos.

" And I, also," said Aramis. " And, indeed, I am not sorry to quit Paris ; I stood in need of a little distraction."

" Well, you will have distractions enough, gentlemen, be assured," said D'Artagnan.

" And, now, when are we to go ?" asked Athos.

" Immediately," replied D'Artagnan ; "we have not a minute to lose."

" Hola ! Grimaud, Planchet, Mousqueton, Bazin !" cried the four young men, calling their lackeys, " clean my boots, and fetch the horses from the hotel."

Each musketeer was accustomed to leave at the general hotel, as at a barrack, his own horse and that of his lackey.

Planchet, Grimaud, Mousqueton, and Bazin set off at full speed.

" Now let us lay down the plan of the campaign," said Porthos. " Where do we go first ?"

" To Calais," said D'Artagnan ; " that is the most direct line to London."

" Well," said Porthos, " this is my advice——"

" Speak,—what is it ?"

" Four men travelling together would be suspicious ; D'Artagnan will give each of us his instructions ; I will go by the way of Boulogne, to clear the way ; Athos will set out two hours after, by that of Amiens ; Aramis will follow us by that of Noyou ; as to D'Artagnan, he will go by what route he thinks best, in Planchet's clothes, whilst Planchet will follow us like D'Artagnan, in the uniform of the guards."

" Gentlemen," said Athos, " my opinion is that it is not proper to allow lackeys to have anything to do in such an affair : a secret may, by chance, be betrayed by gentlemen ; but it is almost always sold by lackeys."

" Porthos's plan appears to me to be impracticable," said D'Artagnan, " inasmuch as I am myself ignorant of what instructions I can give you. I am the bearer of a letter, that is all. I have not, and I cannot make three copies of that letter, because it is sealed : we must then, as it appears to me, travel in company. This letter is here, in this pocket ;" and he pointed to the pocket which contained the letter. " If I should be killed, one of you must take it, and pursue the route ; if he be killed, it will be another's turn, and so on ; provided a single one arrives, that is all that is required."

"Bravo, D'Artagnan ! your opinion is mine," cried Athos. "Besides, we must be consistent ; I am going to take the waters, you will accompany me ; instead of taking the waters of Forges, I go and take sea waters ; I am free to do so. If any one wishes to stop us, I will show M. de Tréville's letter, and you will show your leaves of absence ; if we are attacked, we will defend ourselves ; if we are tried, we will stoutly maintain that we were only anxious to dip ourselves a certain number of times in the sea. They would have an easy bargain of four isolated men ; whereas four men together make a troop. We will arm our four lackeys with pistols and musketoons ; if they send an army out against us, we will give battle, and the survivor, as D'Artagnan says, will carry the letter."

"Well said," cried Aramis ; "you don't often speak, Athos ; but when you do speak, it is like Saint John of the Golden Mouth. I agree to Athos's plan. And you, Porthos?"

"I agree to it, too," said Porthos, "if D'Artagnan approves of it. D'Artagnan being bearer of the letter, is naturally the head of the enterprise ; let him decide, and we will execute."

"Well !" said D'Artagnan ; "I decide that we should adopt Athos's plan, and that we set off in half an hour."

"Agreed !" shouted the three musketeers in chorus.

And every one, stretching out his hand to the bag, took his seventy-five pistoles, and made his preparations to set out at the time appointed.

CHAPTER XX.

THE JOURNEY.

AT two o'clock in the morning, our four adventurers left Paris by the barrier St. Denis ; as long as it was dark they remained silent ; in spite of themselves they felt the influence of the obscurity, and apprehended ambushes everywhere.

With the first rays of the sun their tongues became loosened ; with day their gaiety revived ; it was like the eve of a battle, the heart beat, the eyes laughed, and they felt that the life they were perhaps going to lose, was, after all, worth something.

Besides, the appearance of the caravan was formidable ; the black horses of the musketeers, their martial carriage, with the squadron-like step of these noble companions of the soldier, would have betrayed the most strict incognito. The lackeys followed, armed to the teeth.

All went well till they arrived at Chantilly, which place they reached about eight o'clock in the morning. They stood in need of breakfast ; and alighted at the door of an auberge, recommended by a sign representing St. Martin giving half his cloak to a poor man. They ordered the lackeys not to unsaddle the horses, and to hold themselves in readiness to set off again immediately.

They entered the common room and placed themselves at table. A gentleman, who had just arrived by the route of Dammartin, was seated at the same table, and was taking his breakfast. He opened the conversation by talking of rain and fine weather; the travellers replied, he drank to their good health, and the travellers returned his politeness.

But at the moment Mousqueton came to announce that the horses were ready, and they were rising from table, the stranger proposed to Porthos to drink the health of the cardinal. Porthos replied that he asked no better, if the stranger in his turn, would drink the health of the king. The stranger cried that he acknowledged no other king but his eminence. Porthos told him he was drunk, and the stranger drew his sword.

"You have committed a piece of folly," said Athos, "but it can't be helped; there is no drawing back; kill the fellow, and rejoin us as soon as you can."

And all three mounted their horses, and set out at a good pace, whilst Porthos was promising his adversary to perforate him with all the thrusts known in the fencing schools.

"There goes one!" cried Athos, at the end of five hundred paces.

"But why did that man attack Porthos, rather than any other of us?" asked Aramis.

"Because Porthos talking louder than the rest, he took him for the leader of the party." said D'Artagnan.

"I always said that this cadet from Gascony was a well of wisdom," murmured Athos.

And the travellers continued their route.

At Beauvais they stopped two hours, as well to breathe their horses a little, as to wait for Porthos. At the end of the two hours, as Porthos did not come, and as they heard no news of him, they resumed their journey.

At a league from Beauvais, where the road was confined between two high banks, they fell in with eight or ten men who, taking advantage of the road being unpaved in this spot, appeared to be employed in digging holes and filling up the ruts with mud.

Aramis, not liking to soil his boots with this artificial mortar, apostrophized them rather sharply. Athos wished to restrain him, but it was too late. The labourers began to jeer the travellers, and by their insolence disturbed the equanimity even of the cool Athos, who urged on his horse against one of them.

The men all immediately drew back to the ditch, from which each took a concealed musket; the result was that our seven travellers were outnumbered in weapons. Aramis received a ball, which passed through his shoulder, and Mousqueton another ball which lodged in the fleshy part which prolongs the lower portion of the loins. Mousqueton alone fell from his horse, not because he was severely wounded, but from not being able to see the wound, he judged it to be more serious than it really was.

"It is an ambuscade !" shouted D'Artagnan, "don't waste a charge ! forward !"

Aramis, wounded as he was, seized the mane of his horse, which carried him on with the others. Mousqueton's horse rejoined them, and galloped by the side of his companions.

"That will serve us for a relay," said Athos.

"I would rather have had a hat," said D'Artagnan, "mine was carried away by a ball. By my faith, it is very fortunate that the letter was not in it."

"Well, but they'll kill poor Porthos, when he comes up," said Aramis.

"If Porthos were on his legs, he would have rejoined us by this time," said Athos, "my opinion is that when they came to the point, the drunken man proved to be sober enough."

They continued at their best speed for two hours, although the horses were so fatigued, that it was to be feared they would soon decline the service.

The travellers had chosen cross-roads, in the hope that they might meet with less interruption ; but at Crèvecœur, Aramis declared he could proceed no farther. In fact, it required all the courage which he concealed beneath his elegant form and polished manners to bear him so far. He every minute grew more pale, and they were obliged to support him on his horse. They lifted him off, at the door of a cabaret, left Bazin with him, who besides, in a skirmish, was more embarrassing than useful, and set forward again in the hope of sleeping at Amiens.

"Morbleu !" said Athos, as soon as they were again in motion, "reduced to two masters and Grimaud and Planchet ! Morbleu ! I won't be their dupe, I will answer for it ; I will neither open my mouth nor draw my sword between this and Calais. I swear by——"

"Don't waste time in swearing," said D'Artagnan, "let us gallop, if our horses will consent to it."

And the travellers buried their rowels in their horses' flanks, who, thus vigorously stimulated, recovered their energies. They arrived at Amiens at midnight, and alighted at the auberge of the Lis d'Or.

The host had the appearance of as honest a man as any on earth ; he received the travellers with his candlestick in one hand and his cotton night-cap in the other ; he wished to lodge the two travellers each in a charming chamber, but, unfortunately, these charming chambers were at the opposite extremities of the hotel, and D'Artagnan and Athos declined them. The host replied that he had no other worthy of their excellencies ; but his guests declared they would sleep in the common chamber, each upon a mattress, which might be thrown upon the ground. The host insisted, but the travellers were firm, and he was obliged to comply with their wishes.

They had just prepared their beds and barricaded their door within, when some one knocked at the yard-shutter ; they demanded who was there, and, upon recognising the voices of their lackeys, opened the shutter.

In fact, it was Planchet and Grimaud.

"Grimaud can take care of the horses," said Planchet ; "if you are willing, gentlemen, I will sleep across your doorway, and you will then be certain that nobody can come to you."

"And what will you sleep upon ?" said D'Artagnan.

"Here is my bed," replied Planchet, producing a bundle of straw.

"Come, then," said D'Artagnan, "you are right, mine host's face does not please me at all, it is too civil by half."

"Nor me neither," said Athos.

Planchet got up through the window, and installed himself across the doorway, whilst Grimaud went and shut himself up in the stable, undertaking that, by five o'clock in the morning, he and the four horses should be ready.

The night passed off quietly enough, it is true ; till about two o'clock in the morning, when somebody endeavoured to open the door, but as Planchet awoke in an instant, and cried, "Who is there ?" this same somebody replied he was mistaken, and went away.

At four o'clock in the morning, there was a terrible riot in the stables. Grimaud had tried to waken the stable-boys, and the stable-boys had set upon him and beaten him. When they opened the window they saw the poor lad lying senseless, with his head split by a blow with a fork-handle.

Planchet went down into the yard, and proceeded to saddle the horses. But the horses were all knocked up. Mousqueton's horse, which had travelled for five or six hours without a rider the day before, alone might have been able to pursue the journey ; but, by an inconceivable error, a veterinary surgeon, who had been sent for, as it appeared, to bleed one of the host's horses, had bled Mousqueton's.

This began to be annoying. All these successive accidents were, perhaps, the result of chance ; but they might, quite as probably, be the fruits of a plot. Athos and D'Artagnan went out, whilst Planchet was sent to inquire if there were not three horses to be sold in the neighbourhood. At the door stood two horses, fresh, strong, and fully equipped. These would just have suited them. He asked where the masters of them were, and was informed that they had passed the night in the auberge, and were then settling with the master.

Athos went down to pay the reckoning, whilst D'Artagnan and Planchet stood at the street-door. The host was in a lower and back chamber, to which Athos was requested to go.

Athos entered without the least mistrust, and took out two pistoles to pay the bill. The host was alone, seated before his desk, one of the drawers of which was partly open. He took the money which Athos offered to him, and, after turning and turning it over and over in his hands, suddenly cried out that it was bad, and that he would have him and his companions arrested as coiners.

"You scoundrel!" cried Athos, stepping towards him, "I'll cut your ears off!"

But the host stooped, took two pistols from the half-open drawer, pointed them at Athos, and called out for help.

At the same instant, four men, armed to the teeth, entered by lateral doors, and rushed upon Athos.

"I am taken!" shouted Athos, with all the power of his lungs; "Go on, D'Artagnan! spur, spur!" and he fired two pistols.

D'Artagnan and Planchet did not require twice bidding : they unfastened the two horses that were waiting at the door, leaped upon them, buried their spurs in their sides, and set off at full gallop.

"Do you know what has become of Athos?" asked D'Artagnan of Planchet, as they galloped on.

"Ah, monsieur," said Planchet, "I saw one fall at each of his shots, and he appeared to me, through the glass door, to be fighting with his sword with the others."

"Brave Athos!" murmured D'Artagnan; "and to think that we are compelled to leave him, whilst the same fate awaits us, perhaps, two paces hence! Forward, Planchet, forward! you are a brave fellow!"

"Did not I tell you, monsieur," replied Planchet, "that we Picards are found out by being used? Besides, I am in my own country here, and that puts me on my mettle!"

And both, with free use of the spur, arrived at St. Omer without drawing bit. At St. Omer they breathed their horses with their bridles passed under their arms, for fear of accident, and ate a morsel in their hands, standing in the road, after which they departed again.

At a hundred paces from the gates of Calais, D'Artagnan's horse sank under him, and could not by any means be got up again, the blood flowing from both his eyes and his nose. There still remained Planchet's horse, but, after he stopped, he remained quite still, and could not be urged to move a step.

Fortunately, as we have said, they were within a hundred paces of the city; they left their two nags upon the high road, and ran towards the port. Planchet called his master's attention to a gentleman who had just arrived with his lackey, and preceded them by about fifty paces.

They made all speed to come up to this gentleman, who appeared to be in great haste. His boots were covered with dust, and he inquired if he could not instantly cross over to England.

"Nothing would be more easy," said the captain of a vessel ready to set sail; "but this morning an order arrived that no one should be allowed to cross without express permission from the cardinal."

"I have that permission," said the gentleman, drawing a paper from his pocket; "here it is."

"Have it examined by the governor of the port," said the captain, "and give me the preference."

"Where shall I find the governor?"

"At his country-house."

"Where is that situated?"

" At a quarter of a league from the city.   Look, you may see it from here—at the foot of that little hill, that slated roof."

" Very well," said the gentleman.

And, with his lackey, he took the road to the governor's country-house.

D'Artagnan and Planchet followed the gentleman at a distance, not to be noticed ; but when he was out of the city, D'Artagnan quickly came up with him, just as he was entering a little wood.

" Monsieur," said D'Artagnan, " you appear to be in great haste ?"

" No one can be more so, monsieur."

" I am sorry for that," said D'Artagnan ; " for, as I am in great haste likewise, I wished to beg you to render me a service."

" What service ?"

" To let me go first."

" That's impossible," said the gentleman ; " I have travelled sixty leagues in forty-four hours, and by to-morrow, at mid-day, I must be in London."

" I have performed the same distance in forty hours, and by to-morrow, at ten o'clock in the morning, I must be in London."

" Very sorry, monsieur ; but I was here first, and will not go second."

" I am sorry too, monsieur ; but I arrived second, and will go first."

" The king's service !" said the gentleman..

" My own service !" said D'Artagnan.

" But this is a needless quarrel you are fastening upon me, as I think."

" Parbleu ! what do you desire it to be ?"

" What do you want ?"

" Would you like to know ?"

" Certainly."

" Well, then, I want that order of which you are the bearer, seeing that I have not one of my own, and must have one."

" You are joking, I presume."

" I seldom joke."

" Let me pass !"

" You shall not pass."

" My brave young man, I will blow out your brains.   Hola, Lubin ! my pistols !"

" Planchet," called out D'Artagnan, " take care of the lackey ; I will manage the master."

Planchet, emboldened by the first exploit, sprang upon Lubin, and, being strong and vigorous, he soon got him on the broad of his back, and placed his knee upon his breast.

" Go on with your affair, monsieur," cried Planchet ; " I have finished mine."

Seeing this, the gentleman drew his sword, and sprang upon D'Artagnan ; but he had more than he expected to deal with.

In three seconds, D'Artagnan had wounded him three times, exclaiming at each thrust:

" One for Athos ! one for Porthos ! and one for Aramis !"

At the third hit the gentleman fell heavily to the ground.

D'Artagnan believed him to be dead, or at least insensible, and went towards him for the purpose of taking the order ; but at the moment he stretched out his hand to search for it, the wounded man, who had not dropped his sword, plunged the point into his breast, crying :

" And one for you !"

" And one for me ! the best for the last !" cried D'Artagnan, in a rage, nailing him to the earth with a fourth thrust through his body.

This time the gentleman closed his eyes and fainted. D'Artagnan searched his pockets, and took from one of them the order for the passage. It was in the name of the Count de Wardes.

Then, casting a glance on the handsome young man, who was scarcely twenty-five years of age, and whom he was leaving in his gore, deprived of sense, and perhaps dead, he gave a sigh to that unaccountable destiny which leads men to destroy each other for the interests of people who are strangers to them, and who often do not even know they exist.

But he was soon roused from these reflections by Lubin, who uttered loud cries, and screamed for help with all his might.

Planchet grasped him by the throat, and pressed as hard as he could.

" Monsieur," said he, " as long as I hold him in this manner, he can't cry, I'll be bound ; but as soon as I leave go, he will howl again as loud as ever. I have found out that he's a Norman, and Normans are all obstinate."

In fact, tightly held as he was, Lubin endeavoured still to get out a cry.

" Stay !" said D'Artagnan, and, taking out his handkerchief, he gagged him.

" Now," said Planchet, " let us bind him to a tree."

This being properly done, they drew the Count de Wardes close to his servant ; and as night was approaching, and as the wounded man and the bound man were at some little distance within the wood, it was evident they were likely to remain there till the next day.

" And now," said D'Artagnan, " to the governor's house."

" But you appear to me to be wounded," said Planchet.

"Oh, that's nothing ! Let us despatch that which is most pressing first, and we will attend to my wound afterwards ; besides, I don't think it seems a very dangerous one."

And they both set forward as fast as they could towards the country-house of the worthy functionary.

The Count de Wardes was announced, and D'Artagnan was introduced.

" You have an order, signed by the cardinal ?"

" Yes, monsieur," replied D'Artagnan ; " here it is."

" Ah, ah ! it is quite regular and explicit," said the governor.

" Most likely," said D'Artagnan ; " I am one of his most faithful servants."

"It appears that his eminence is anxious to prevent some one from crossing to England ?"

"Yes ; a certain D'Artagnan, a Béarnese gentleman, who left Paris in company of three of his friends, with the intention of going to London."

"Do you know him personally ?" asked the governor.

"Whom ?"

"This D'Artagnan."

"Oh, yes, perfectly well."

"Describe him to me, then."

"Nothing more easy."

And D'Artagnan gave, feature for feature, and in every way, the most minute description of the Count de Wardes.

"Is he accompanied by any one ?"

"Yes, by a lackey, named Lubin."

' We will keep a sharp look out for them ; and if we lay hands upon them, his eminence may be assured they shall be reconducted to Paris under a good escort."

"And by doing so, monsieur the governor," said D'Artagnan, "you will have merited well of the cardinal."

"Shall you see him on your return ?"

"Doubtless I shall."

"Tell him, I beg you, that I am his humble servant."

"I will not fail."

And, delighted with this assurance, the governor signed the passport, and delivered it to D'Artagnan, who lost no time in useless compliments, but thanked the governor, bowed, and departed.

When once out, he and Planchet set off as fast as they could, and, by making a detour, avoided the wood, and re-entered the city by another gate.

The vessel was quite ready to sail, and the captain waiting in the port.

"Well ?" said he, on perceiving D'Artagnan.

"Here is my pass, examined," said the latter.

"And that other gentleman ?"

"He will not go to-day," said D'Artagnan ; "but here, I'll pay you for us two."

"In that case we will be gone," said the captain.

"Yes, as soon as you please," replied D'Artagnan.

He leaped, with Planchet, into the boat, and five minutes after they were on board. And it was time ; for they had scarcely sailed half a league, when D'Artagnan saw a flash and heard a detonation—it was the cannon which announced the closing of the port.

He had now leisure to look to his wound. Fortunately, as D'Artagnan had thought, it was not dangerous : the point of the sword had met with a rib, and glanced along the bone ; still further, his shirt had stuck to the wound, and he had lost but very little blood.

D'Artagnan was worn out with fatigue. A mattress was laid upon the deck for him ; he threw himself upon it, and fell fast asleep.

At break of day they were still three or four leagues from the coast of England: the breeze had been so light during the night, they had made but little way.

At ten o'clock the vessel cast anchor in the port of Dover, and at half-past ten D'Artagnan placed his foot on English land, crying:
"Here I am at last!"

But that was not all, they had to get to London. In England the post was well served; D'Artagnan and Planchet took post-horses with a postilion, who rode before them; and in a few hours were in the capital.

D'Artagnan did not know London, he was not acquainted with one word of English: but he wrote the name of Buckingham on a piece of paper, and every one to whom he showed it pointed out to him the way to the duke's hotel.

The duke was at Windsor hunting with the king.

D'Artagnan inquired for the confidential valet of the duke, who having accompanied him in all his voyages, spoke French perfectly well; he told him that he came from Paris, on an affair of life and death, and that he must speak with his master instantly.

The confidence with which D'Artagnan spoke convinced Patrick, which was the name of this minister; he ordered two horses to be saddled, and himself went as guide to the young guardsman. As for Planchet, he had been lifted from his horse as stiff as a rush; the poor lad's strength was almost exhausted. D'Artagnan seemed to be made of iron.

On their arrival at the castle they inquired for the duke, and learned that he was hawking with the king in the marshes, at some distance.

They were quickly on the spot named, and Patrick almost at the moment caught the sound of his master's voice, recalling his falcon.

"Whom must I announce to my lord duke?" asked Patrick.

"The young man who one evening sought a quarrel with him on the Pont Neuf, opposite the *Samaritaine.*"

"Rather a singular introduction?"

"You will find that it is as good as another."

Patrick galloped off, reached the duke, and announced to him, in the terms directed, that a messenger awaited him.

Buckingham at once remembered the circumstance, and suspecting that something was going on in France, of which it was necessary he should be informed, he only took the time to inquire where the messenger was, and recognising the uniform of the guards, he put his horse into a gallop, and rode straight up to D'Artagnan; Patrick, discreetly, keeping in the back ground.

"No misfortune has happened to the queen?" cried Buckingham, the instant he came up, throwing all his fear and love into the question.

"I believe not; nevertheless, I believe she is in some great peril from which your grace alone can extricate her."

"I!" cried Buckingham. "What is it? I should be but too happy to render her any service! Speak! speak!"

"Take this letter," said D'Artagnan.

"This letter ! from whom does this letter come ?"

"From her majesty, as I think."

"From her majesty !" said Buckingham, becoming so pale that D'Artagnan feared he would faint,—and he broke the seal.

"What is this rent !" said he, showing D'Artagnan a place where it had been pierced through.

"Ah ! ah ?" said D'Artagnan, "I did not see that ; it was the sword of the Count de Wardes that made that hole when he ran it into my breast."

"Are you wounded ?" asked Buckingham, as he opened the letter.

"Oh ! nothing ! milord, only a scratch," said D'Artagnan.

"Just Heavens ! what have I read !" cried the duke. "Patrick, remain here, or rather join the king, wherever he may be, and tell his majesty that I hereby beg him to excuse me, but an affair of the greatest importance calls me to London. Come, monsieur, come !"—and both set off towards the capital at full gallop.

CHAPTER XXI.

THE COUNTESS DE WINTER.

As they rode along, the duke endeavoured to draw from D'Artagnan, not what had passed, but what D'Artagnan himself knew. By adding all that he heard from the mouth of the young man to his own remembrances, he was enabled to form a pretty exact idea of a position of the seriousness of which, in addition, the queen's letter, however short and explicit, rendered him quite aware. But that which astonished him most was, that the cardinal, so deeply interested in preventing this young man from setting his foot on the soil of England, had not succeeded in arresting him on the road. It was then, and upon the manifestation of this astonishment, that D'Artagnan related to him the precaution taken, and how, thanks to his three friends, whom he had left scattered on the road, he had succeeded in coming off with a single sword-thrust, which had pierced the queen's letter, and for which he had repaid M. de Wardes in such terrible coin. Whilst he was listening to this account, which was delivered with the greatest simplicity, the duke looked from time to time at the young man with astonishment, as if he could not comprehend how so much prudence, courage, and devotedness were allied with a countenance evidently not more than twenty years of age.

The horses went like the wind, and in an incredibly short time they were in London. D'Artagnan imagined that on arriving in the city the duke would slacken his pace, but it was not so : he kept on his way, heedless of whom he rode against. In fact, in crossing the city, two or three accidents of this kind happened ; but Buckingham did not even turn his head to see what became of those he had knocked down,

D'Artagnan followed him amidst cries which very much resembled curses.

On entering the court of his hotel, Buckingham sprang from his horse and, without taking heed of the noble animal, threw the bridle on his neck, and sprang towards the vestibule. D'Artagnan did the same, with a little more concern, however, for the fine creatures, whose merits he fully appreciated; but he had the satisfaction to see three or four grooms run from the stables, and take charge of them.

The duke walked so fast that D'Artagnan had some trouble in keeping up with him. He passed through several apartments of an elegance of which even the greatest nobles of France had not even an idea, and arrived at length in a bed-chamber which was at once a miracle of taste and of splendour. In the alcove of this chamber was a door practised in the tapestry, which the duke opened with a small gold key, which he wore suspended from his neck by a chain of the same metal. From discretion, D'Artagnan remained behind; but at the moment of Buckingham's passing through the door, he turned round, and seeing the hesitation of the young man,—

"Come in! come in!" cried he, "and if you have the good fortune to be admitted to her majesty's presence, tell her what you have seen."

Encouraged by this invitation, D'Artagnan followed the duke, who closed the door after them.

He found himself with the duke in a small chapel covered with a tapestry of Persian silk worked with gold, and brilliantly lit with a vast number of wax lights. Over a species of altar, and beneath a canopy of blue velvet, surmounted by white and red plumes, was a full-length portrait of Anne of Austria, so perfect in its resemblance, that D'Artagnan uttered a cry of surprise on beholding it: it might be believed that the queen was about to speak.

Upon the altar, and beneath the portrait, was the casket containing the diamond studs.

The duke approached the altar, fell on his knees as a priest might have done before a crucifix, and opened the casket.

"There," said he, drawing from the casket a large bow of blue ribbon all sparkling with diamonds; "here," said he, "are the precious studs which I have taken an oath should be buried with me. The queen gave them to me, the queen requires them back again; her will be done, like that of God, in all things."

Then he began to kiss, one after the other, those dear studs with which he was about to part.—All at once, he uttered a terrible cry.

"What is the matter?" exclaimed D'Artagnan, anxiously, "what has happened to you, milord?"

"All is lost! all is lost!" cried Buckingham, turning as pale as death; "two of the studs are wanting! there are but ten of them!"

"Can you have lost them, milord, or do you think they have been stolen?"

"They have been stolen !" replied the duke, "and it is the cardinal who has dealt me this blow. See, the ribbons which held them have been cut with scissors."

"If milord suspects they have been stolen—perhaps the person who stole them still has them."

"Let me reflect," said the duke—"The only time I wore these studs was at a ball given by the king a week ago at Windsor. The Countess de Winter, with whom I had had a quarrel, became reconciled to me at that ball. That reconciliation was nothing but the vengeance of a jealous woman. I have never seen her from that day. The woman is an agent of the cardinal's."

"Why then, he has agents throughout the whole world !" cried D'Artagnan.

"Yes, yes," said Buckingham, gnashing his teeth with rage, "he is a terrible antagonist !—But when is this ball to take place ?"

"On Monday next."

"On Monday next ! Still five days before us ; that's more time than we want. Patrick !" cried the duke, opening the door of the chapel, "Patrick !"

His confidential valet, who had that moment returned, appeared at his call.

"My jeweller and my secretary."

The valet de chambre went out with a mute promptitude that showed he was accustomed to obey implicitly and without reply.

But although the jeweller had been mentioned first, it was the secretary that first made his appearance, simply because he lived in the hotel. He found Buckingham seated at a table in his bed-chamber, writing orders with his own hand.

"Master Jackson," said he, "go instantly to the lord chancellor and tell him that I desire him to execute these orders. I wish them to be promulgated immediately."

"But, my lord, if the lord chancellor interrogates me upon the motives which may have led your grace to adopt such an extraordinary measure, what reply shall I make ?"

"That such is my pleasure, and that I answer for my will to no man."

"Will that be the answer," replied the secretary, smiling, "which he must transmit to his majesty, if, by chance, his majesty should have the curiosity to know why no vessel is to leave any of the ports of Great Britain ?"

"You are right, Master Jackson," replied Buckingham. "He will say, in that case, to the king, that I am determined on war, and that this measure is my first act of hostility against France."

The secretary bowed and retired.

"We are safe on that side," said Buckingham, turning towards D'Artagnan. "If the studs are not yet gone to Paris, they will not arrive till after you."

"How so, milord ?"

"I have just placed an embargo on all vessels at present in his majesty's ports, and, without particular permission, not one can lift an anchor."

D'Artagnan looked with stupefaction at a man who thus employed the unlimited power with which he was clothed by the confidence of a king, in the prosecution of his amours. Buckingham saw by the expression of the young man's face what was passing in his mind, and he smiled.

"Yes," said he, "yes, Anne of Austria is my true queen ; upon a word from her, I would betray my country, I would betray my king. I would betray my God. She asked me not to send the Protestants of La Rochelle the assistance I promised them : I have not done so. I broke my word, it is true ; but what signifies that ? I obeyed my love ; and have I not been richly paid for that obedience ? It was to that obedience I owe her portrait !"

D'Artagnan admired by what fragile and unknown threads the destinies of nations and the lives of men are sometimes suspended.

He was lost in these reflections when the goldsmith entered. He was an Irishman, one of the most skilful of his craft, and who himself confessed that he gained a hundred thousand livres a year by the Duke of Buckingham.

"Master O'Reilly," said the duke to him, leading him into the chapel, "look at these diamond studs, and tell me what they are worth a-piece."

The goldsmith cast a glance at the elegant manner in which they were set, calculated, one with another, what the diamonds were worth, and without hesitation :

"Fifteen hundred pistoles each, my lord," replied he.

"How many days would it require to make two studs exactly like them ? You see there are two wanting."

"A week, my lord."

"I will give you three thousand pistoles each for two, if I can have them by the day after to-morrow."

"My lord, you shall have them."

"You are a jewel of a man, Master O'Reilly ; but that is not all ; these studs cannot be trusted to anybody : it must be effected in the palace."

"Impossible, my lord ; there is no one but myself can execute them so that the new may not be distinguished from the old."

"Therefore, my dear master O'Reilly, you are my prisoner ; and if you wish ever so to leave my palace, you cannot ; so make the best of it. Name to me such of your workmen as you stand in need of, and point out the tools they must bring."

The goldsmith knew the duke ; he knew all observation would be useless, and instantly determined how to act.

"May I be permitted to inform my wife ?" said he.

"Oh ! you may even see her if you like, my dear master O'Reilly ; your captivity shall be mild, be assured ; and as every inconvenience deserves its indemnification, here is, in addition to the price of the studs, an order for a thousand pistoles, to make you forget the annoyance I cause you."

D'Artagnan could not get over the surprise created in him by this minister, who thus, open-handed, sported with men and millions.

As to the goldsmith, he wrote to his wife, sending her the order for the thousand pistoles, and charging her to send him, in exchange, his most skilful apprentice, an assortment of diamonds, of which he gave the names and the weight, and the necessary tools.

Buckingham led the goldsmith to the chamber destined for him, and which, at the end of half-an-hour, was transformed into a workshop. Then he placed a sentinel at each door, with an order to admit nobody, upon any pretence, but his valet-de-chambre, Patrick. We need not add that the goldsmith, O'Reilly, and his assistant, were prohibited from going out on any account.

All this being regulated, the duke turned to D'Artagnan.

"Now, my young friend," said he, "England is all our own. What do you wish for? What do you desire?"

"A bed, milord," replied D'Artagnan. "At present, I confess, that is the thing I stand most in need of."

Buckingham assigned D'Artagnan a chamber adjoining his own. He wished to have the young man at hand, not that he at all mistrusted him, but for the sake of having some one to whom he could constantly talk about the queen.

In one hour after, the ordinance was published in London that no vessel bound for France should leave the ports—not even the packet-boat with letters. In the eyes of everybody this was a declaration of war between the two kingdoms.

On the day after the morrow, by eleven o'clock, the two diamond studs were finished, and they were so completely imitated, so perfectly alike, that Buckingham could not tell the new ones from the old ones, and the most practised in such matters would have been deceived as he was.

He immediately called D'Artagnan.

"Here," said he to him, "are the diamond studs that you came to fetch, and be my witness that I have done all that human power could do."

"Be satisfied, milord; I will tell all that I have seen. But does your grace mean to give me the studs without the casket?"

"The casket would only encumber you. Besides, the casket is the more precious from being all that is left to me. You will say that I keep it."

"I will perform your commission, word for word, milord."

"And now," resumed Buckingham, looking earnestly at the young man, "how shall I ever acquit myself of the debt I owe you?"

D'Artagnan coloured up to the eyes. He saw that the duke was searching for a means of making him accept something, and the idea that the blood of himself and his friends was about to be paid for with English gold was strangely repugnant to him.

"Let us understand each other, milord," replied D'Artagnan, "and let us make things clear, in order that there may be no mistake. I am in the service of the King and Queen of France, and form part of the company of M. des Essarts, who, as well as his brother-in-law, M. de Tréville, is particularly attached to their majesties. What I have done, then, has been for the queen, and not at all for your grace. And, still further, it is very probable I should not have done anything of this, if it had not been to make myself agreeable to some one who is my lady, as the queen is yours."

"I understand," said the duke, smiling, "and I even believe that I know that other person ; it is——"

"Milord ! I have not named her !" interrupted the young man, warmly.

"That is true," said the duke, "and it is to this person I am bound to discharge my debt of gratitude."

"You have said, milord ; for truly, at this moment, when there is question of war, I confess to you that I see nothing in your grace but an Englishman, and, consequently, an enemy, whom I should have much greater pleasure in meeting on the field of battle than in the park at Windsor or the chambers of the Louvre ; all which, however, will not prevent me from executing, to the very point, my commission, or from laying down my life, if there be need of it, to accomplish it ; but I repeat it to your grace, without your having personally on that account more to thank me for in this second interview, than for that which I did for you in the first."

"We say, ' proud as a Scotchman,' " murmured the Duke of Buckingham.

"And we say, ' proud as a Gascon,' " replied D'Artagnan ; "the Gascons are the Scots of France."

D'Artagnan bowed to the duke, and was retiring.

"Well ! you are going away in that manner ? But where ? and how ?"

"That's true !"

"Fore Gad, these Frenchmen have no consideration !"

"I had forgotten that England was an island, and that you were the king of it."

"Go to the port, ask for the brig Sund, and give this letter to the captain ; he will convey you to a little port, where certainly you are not expected, and which is ordinarily only frequented by fishermen."

"What is the name of that port ?"

"Saint-Valery ; but listen. When you have arrived there, you will go to a mean auberge, without a name and without a sign, a mere fisherman's hut. You cannot be mistaken, there is but one."

"And then ?"

"You will ask for the host, and will repeat to him the word—*Forward !*"

"Which means ?"

"In French, *en avant ;* that is the password. He will give you a ready-saddled horse, and will point out to you the road you are to take.

You will find, in this manner, four relays on your route.   If you will
give, at each of these relays, your address in Paris, the four horses will
follow you thither.   You already know two of them, and you appeared
to appreciate them like a judge.   They were those we rode on, and you
may rely upon me for the others not being inferior to them.   These
horses are equipped for the field.   However proud you may be, you will
not refuse to accept one of them, and to request your three companions to accept the others : that is in order to make war against
us, besides.   The end excuses the means, as you Frenchmen say, does
it not ?"

"Yes, milord, I accept them," said D'Artagnan, "and, if it please God,
we will make a good use of your presents."

"Well, now, your hand, young man ; perhaps we shall soon meet on
the field of battle ; but, in the meantime, we shall part good friends,
I hope ?"

"Yes, milord ; but with the hope of soon becoming enemies ?"

"Be satisfied on that head ; I promise you."

"I depend upon your parole, milord."

D'Artagnan bowed to the duke, and made his way as quickly as
possible to the port.   Opposite the Tower he found the vessel that had
been named to him, delivered his letter to the captain, who, after
having it examined by the governor of the port, made immediate preparations to sail.

Fifty vessels were waiting to set out, in momentary expectation of
the removal of the prohibition.   When passing alongside of one of
them, D'Artagnan fancied he perceived on board of it the lady of Meung,
the same whom the unknown gentleman had styled milady, and whom
D'Artagnan had thought so handsome ; but thanks to the tide of the
river and a fair wind, his vessel passed so quickly that he had little
more than a glimpse of her.

The next day, about nine o'clock in the morning, he landed at St.
Valery.   D'Artagnan went instantly in search of the auberge, and easily
discovered it by the riotous noise which resounded from it : war between
England and France was then confidently talked of, and the sailors were
carousing in the hopes of it.

D'Artagnan made his way through the crowd, advanced towards the
host, and pronounced the word, "*Forward !*"   The host instantly made
him a sign to follow him, went out with him by a door which opened
into a yard, led him to the stable, where a ready-saddled horse awaited
him, and asked him if he stood in need of anything else.

"I want to know the route I am to follow," said D'Artagnan.

"Go from hence to Blangy, and from Blangy to Neufchâtel.   At
Neufchâtel, go to the auberge of the ' Herse d'Or,' give the password
to the host, and you will find, as you have done here, a horse ready-
saddled."

"Have I anything to pay ?" demanded D'Artagnan.

"Everything is paid," replied the host, "and liberally.   Begone then,
and may God conduct you safely."

"Amen !" cried the young man, and set off at full gallop.

In four hours from starting he was in Neufchâtel. He strictly followed the instructions he had received ; at Neufchâtel, as at St. Valery, he found a horse quite ready awaiting him ; he was about to remove the pistols from the saddle he had vacated to the one he was about to occupy, but he found the holsters furnished with similar pistols.

"Your address at Paris ?"

"Hotel of the Guards, company of Des Essarts."

"Enough," replied the interrogator.

"Which route must I take ?" demanded D'Artagnan, in his turn.

"That of Rouen ; but you will leave the city on your right. You must stop at the little village of Eccuis, in which there is but one auberge, 'l'Ecu de France.' Don't condemn it from appearances, you will find a horse in the stables quite as good as this."

"The same password ?"

"Exactly."

"Adieu, master !"

"A good journey, gentleman ! Do you want anything ?"

D'Artagnan shook his head in reply, and set off at full speed. At Eccuis, the same scene was repeated ; he found as provident a host and a fresh horse. He left his address as he had done before, and set off again, at the same pace, for Pontoise. At Pontoise he changed his horse for the last time, and at nine o'clock galloped into the yard of M. de Tréville's hotel. He had performed nearly sixty leagues in little more than twelve hours.

M. de Tréville received him as if he had seen him that same morning; only, when pressing his hand a little more warmly than usual, he informed him that the company of M. des Essarts was on duty at the Louvre, and that he might repair at once to his post.

CHAPTER XXII.

THE BALLET OF LA MERLAISON.

ON the morrow, nothing was talked of in Paris but the ball which Messieurs the Echevins of the city were to give to the king and queen, and in which the king and queen were to dance the famous La Merlaison, the king's favourite ballet.

The whole of the last week had been occupied in preparations at the Hôtel de Ville for this important evening. The city carpenters had erected scaffolds upon which the ladies invited were to be placed ; the city grocer had ornamented the chambers with two hundred flambeaux of white wax, which was a piece of luxury unheard of at that period ; and twenty violins were ordered, and the price paid for them fixed at double the usual rate, upon condition, said the report, that they should be played all night.

At ten o'clock in the morning, the Sieur de la Coste, ensign in the king's guards, followed by two exempts and several archers of that body, came to to the city greffier (registrar or secretary), named Clement, and demanded of him all the keys of the chambers and offices of the hotel. These keys were given up to him instantly ; and each of them had a ticket attached to it, by which it might be known, and from that moment the Sieur de la Coste was charged with the guarding of all the doors and all the avenues.

At eleven o'clock came in his turn Duhallier, captain of the guard, bringing with him fifty archers, who were distributed immediately, through the hotel, at the doors which had been assigned to them.

At three o'clock, arrived two companies of the guards, one French, the other Swiss. The company of French guards was composed half of M. Duhallier's men, and half of M. des Essart's men.

At nine o'clock, Madame la Première Presidente arrived. As, next to the queen, this was the most considerable personage of the fête, she was received by the city gentlemen, and placed in a box opposite to that which the queen was to occupy.

At ten o'clock, the king's collation, consisting of confitures and other delicacies, was prepared in the little chamber on the side of the church of St. Jean, in front of the silver buffet of the city, which was guarded by four archers.

At midnight, great cries and loud acclamations were heard ; it was the king, who was passing through the streets which led from the Louvre to the Hôtel de Ville, and which were all illuminated with coloured lamps.

Immediately Messieurs the Echevins, clothed in their cloth robes, and preceded by six sergeants, holding each a flambeau in his hand, went to attend upon the king, whom they met on the steps, where the provost of the merchants offered him the compliment of welcome ; a compliment to which his majesty replied by an apology for coming so late, but laying the blame upon M. the Cardinal, who had detained him till eleven o'clock, talking of affairs of state.

His majesty, in full dress, was accompanied by his royal highness Monsieur the count de Soissons, the Grand Prior, the Duke de Longueville, the Duke d'Elbœuf, the Count d'Harcourt, the Count de la Roche-Guyon, M. de Liancourt, M. de Baradas, the Count de Cramail, and the Chevalier de Souveray.

Everybody observed that the king looked dull and preoccupied.

A closet had been prepared for the king and another for monsieur. In each of these closets were placed masquerade habits. The same had been done with respect to the queen and Madame la Présidente. The nobles and ladies of their majesties' suites were to dress, two by two, in chambers prepared for the purpose.

Before entering his closet the king desired to be informed the moment the cardinal arrived.

Half an hour after the entrance of the king, fresh acclamations were heard : these announced the arrival of the queen. The *échevins* did as they had done before, and, preceded by their sergeants, went to receive their illustrious guest.

The queen entered the great hall ; and it was remarked, that, like the king, she looked dull, and moreover, fatigued.

At the moment she entered, the curtain of a small gallery which to that time had been closed, was drawn, and the pale face of the cardinal appeared, he being dressed as a Spanish cavalier. His eyes were fixed upon those of the queen, and a smile of terrible joy passed over his lips: —the queen did not wear her diamond studs.

The queen remained for a short time to receive the compliments of the city gentlemen and to reply to the salutations of the ladies.

All at once the king appeared at one of the doors of the hall. The cardinal was speaking to him in a low voice, and the king was very pale.

The king made his way through the crowd without a mask, and the ribbons of his doublet scarcely tied ; he went straight to the queen, and in an altered voice, said :

"Why, madame, have you not thought proper to wear your diamond studs, when you know it would have given me so much gratification ?"

The queen cast a glance around her, and saw the cardinal behind, with a diabolical smile on his countenance.

"Sire," replied the queen, with a faltering voice, "because, in the midst of such a crowd as this, I feared some accident might happen to them."

"And you were wrong, madame ! if I made you that present it was that you might adorn yourself with them. I tell you, again, you were wrong."

And the voice of the king was tremulous with anger : the company looked and listened with astonishment, comprehending nothing of what passed.

"Sire," said the queen, "I can send for them to the Louvre, where they are, and thus your majesty's wishes will be complied with."

"Do so, madame ! do so, and that at the quickest ; for within an hour the ballet will commence."

The queen bent in token of submission, and followed the ladies who were to conduct her to her closet. On his part. the king returned to his.

A moment of trouble and confusion ensued in the assembly. Everybody had remarked that something had passed between the king and queen, but both of them had spoken so low, that all out of respect had kept at a distance of several steps, so that nobody had heard anything. The violins began to sound with all their might, but nobody listened to them.

The king came out first from his closet; he was in a hunting costume of the most elegant description, and monsieur and the other nobles were dressed as he was. This was the costume that became the king the best, and when thus dressed, he really appeared the first gentleman of his kingdom.

The cardinal drew near to the king, and placed in his hand a small casket. The king opened it, and found in it two diamonds.

" What does this mean ?" demanded he of the cardinal.

" Nothing," replied the latter ; " only, if the queen has the studs, of which I very much doubt, count them, sire, and if you only find ten, ask her majesty who can have stolen from her the two studs that are here."

The king looked at the cardinal as if to interrogate him : but he had not time to address any question to him ; a cry of admiration burst from every mouth. If the king appeared to be the first gentleman of his kingdom, the queen was, without doubt, the most beautiful woman in France.

It is true that the habit of a huntress became her admirably ; she wore a beaver hat with blue feathers, a surtout of grey-pearl velvet, fastened with diamond clasps, and a petticoat of blue satin, embroidered with silver. On her left shoulder sparkled the diamond studs upon a bow of the same colour as the plumes and the petticoat.

The king trembled with joy and the cardinal with vexation ; nevertheless, distant as they were from the queen, they could not count the studs ; the queen had them ; the only question was, had she ten or twelve ?

At that moment the violins sounded the signal for the ballet. The king advanced towards Madame la Présidente, with whom he was to dance, and his highness monsieur with the queen. They took their places, and the ballet began.

The king figured opposite the queen, and every time that he passed by her, he devoured with his eyes those studs of which he could not ascertain the number. A cold sweat covered the brow of the cardinal.

The ballet lasted an hour, and had sixteen *entrées*.

The ballet ended amidst the applauses of the whole assemblage, and every one reconducted his lady to her place ; but the king took advantage of the privilege he had of leaving his lady, to advance eagerly towards the queen.

" I thank you, madame," said he, " for the deference you have shown to my wishes, but I think you want two of the studs, and I bring them back to you."

At these words he held out to the queen the two studs the cardinal had given him.

" How, sire !" cried the young queen, affecting surprise, " you are giving me then two more ; but then I shall have fourteen !"

In fact, the king counted them, and the twelve studs were all on her majesty's shoulder.

The king called the cardinal to him.

" What does this mean, Monsieur the Cardinal ?" asked the king in a severe tone.

" This means, sire," replied the cardinal, " that I was desirous of presenting her majesty with these two studs, and that not daring to offer them myself, I adopted these means of inducing her to accept them."

" And I am the more grateful to your eminence," replied Anne of Austria, with a smile that proved she was not the dupe of this in-

genious piece of gallantry, " from being certain these two studs have
cost you as dearly as all the others cost his majesty."

Then, after bowing to the king and the cardinal, the queen resumed
her way to the chamber in which she had dressed, and where she was to
take off her ball costume.

The attention which we have been obliged to give, during the commencement of the chapter, to the illustrious personages we have introduced in it, has diverted us for an instant from him to whom Anne of
Austria owed the extraordinary triumph she had obtained over the cardinal ; and who, confounded, unknown, lost in the crowd gathered at
one of the doors, looked on at this scene, comprehensible only to four
persons, the king, the queen, his eminence, and himself.

The queen had just regained her chamber, and D'Artagnan was about
to retire, when he felt his shoulder lightly touched ; he turned round,
and saw a young woman who made him a sign to follow her. The face
of this young woman was covered with a black velvet mask, but, notwithstanding this precaution, which was, in fact, taken rather against
others than against him, he at once recognised his usual guide, the
light and intelligent Madame Bonacieux.

On the evening before, they had scarcely seen each other for a moment at the apartment of the Swiss Germain, whither D'Artagnan had
sent for her. The haste which the young woman was in, to convey to
her mistress the excellent news of the happy return of her messenger,
prevented the two lovers from exchanging more than a few words.
D'Artagnan then followed Madame Bonacieux, moved by a double
sentiment, love and curiosity. During the whole of the way, and in proportion as the corridors became more deserted, D'Artagnan wished to
stop the young woman, seize her, and gaze upon her, were it only for a
minute ; but quick as a bird, she glided between his hands, and when
he wished to speak to her, her finger placed upon her mouth, with a
little imperative gesture full of grace, reminded him that he was under
the command of a power which he must blindly obey, and which forbade him even to make the slightest complaint ; at length, after winding about for a minute or two, Madame Bonacieux opened the door of
a closet, which was entirely dark, and led D'Artagnan into it. There
she made a fresh sign of silence, and opening a second door concealed
by a tapestry, and which opening spread at once a brilliant light, she
disappeared.

D'Artagnan remained for a moment motionless, asking himself where
he could be ; but soon a ray of light which penetrated through the
chamber, together with the warm and perfumed air which reached him
from the same aperture, the conversation of two or three ladies, in
a language at once respectful and elegant, and the word "majesty" two
or three times repeated, indicated clearly that he was in a closet
attached to the queen's chamber.

The young man waited the event quietly in comparative darkness.

The queen appeared to be cheerful and happy, which seemed to astonish the persons who surrounded her, and who were accustomed to see

her almost always sad and full of care. The queen attributed this joyous feeling to the beauty of the fête, to the pleasure she had experienced in the ballet, and as it is not permissible to contradict a queen, whether she smile or whether she weep, all rivalled each other in expatiating upon the gallantry of messieurs the *échevins* of the good city of Paris.

Although D'Artagnan did not at all know the queen, he soon distinguished her voice from the others, at first by a slightly foreign accent, and next by that tone of domination naturally impressed upon all sovereign expressions. He heard her approach, and withdraw from the partially open door, and twice or three times he even saw the shadow of a person intercept the light.

At length a hand and an arm, surpassingly beautiful in their form and whiteness, glided through the tapestry. D'Artagnan, at once, comprehended that this was his recompense : he cast himself on his knees, seized the hand, and touched it respectfully with his lips ; then the hand was withdrawn, leaving in his an object which he perceived to be a ring ; the door immediately closed, and D'Artagnan found himself again in complete darkness.

D'Artagnan placed the ring on his finger, and again waited : it was evident that all was not yet over. After the reward of his devotion that of his love was to come. Besides, although the ballet was danced, the evening's pleasures had scarcely begun : supper was to be served at three, and the clock of St. Jean had struck three-quarters past two.

The sound of voices diminished by degrees in the adjoining chamber ; the company was then heard departing ; then the door of the closet in which D'Artagnan was, was opened, and Madame Bonacieux entered quickly.

" You at last ?" cried D'Artagnan.

" Silence !" said the young woman, placing her hand upon his lips ; " Silence ! and begone the same way you came !"

" But where and when shall I see you again ?" cried D'Artagnan.

" A note which you will find at home will tell you. Begone ! begone !"

And at these words she opened the door of the corridor, and pushed D'Artagnan out of the closet. D'Artagnan obeyed like a child, without the least resistance or objection, which proved that he was downright really in love.

CHAPTER XXIII.

THE RENDEZVOUS.

D'ARTAGNAN ran home immediately, and although it was three o'clock in the morning, and he had some of the worst reputed quarters of Paris to pass through, he met with no misadventure. Every one knows that drunkards and lovers have a protecting deity.

He found the door of his passage open, sprang up the stairs, and knocked softly, in a manner agreed upon between him and his lackey.

Planchet,* whom he had sent home two hours before from the Hôtel de Ville, desiring him to be careful and sit up for him, opened the door to him.

"Has any one brought a letter for me ?" asked D'Artagnan eagerly.

"No one has *brought* a letter, monsieur," replied Planchet ; "but there is one come of itself."

"What do you mean by that, you stupid fellow ?"

"I mean to say that when I came in, although I had the key of your apartment in my pocket, and that key had never been out of my possession, I found a letter upon the green table-cover in your bed-chamber."

"And where is that letter ?"

"I left it where I found it, monsieur. It is not natural for letters to enter in this manner into people's houses. If the window had been open, even in the smallest way, I should think nothing of it ; but, no ; all was as close as possible. Beware, monsieur, there is certainly some magic in it."

Whilst Planchet was saying this, the young man had darted into his chamber, and seized and opened the letter ; it was from Madame Bonacieux, and was conceived in these terms :

"There are many thanks to be offered to you, and to be transmitted to you. Be this evening about ten o'clock, at St. Cloud, in front of the pavilion built at the corner of the hotel of M. d'Estrées.—C. B."

Whilst reading this letter, D'Artagnan felt his heart dilated and compressed by that delicious spasm which tortures and caresses the hearts of lovers.

It was the first billet he had received, it was the first rendezvous that had ever been granted him. His heart, swelled by the intoxication of joy, felt ready to dissolve away at the very gate of that terrestrial paradise called Love !

"Well, monsieur," said Planchet, who had observed his master grow red and pale successively ; "did I not guess truly ? is it not some bad business or other ?"

"You are mistaken, Planchet," replied D'Artagnan ; "and, as a proof, there is a crown to drink my health."

"I am much obliged to monsieur, for the crown he has given me, and I promise him I will obey his instructions exactly ; but it is not the less true that letters which come in this manner into shut-up houses—"

"Fall from heaven, my friend, fall from heaven."

"Then monsieur is satisfied ?" asked Planchet.

"My dear Planchet, I am the happiest of men !"

"And I may profit by monsieur's happiness, and may go to bed ?"

"Yes, go."

"May the blessings of heaven fall upon monsieur ; but it is not the less true that that letter——"

* There is no doubt the reader will ask, as the Translator does, "How came Planchet here?" We left him "stiff as a rush" from fatigue, being carried to bed in London. M. Dumas's errors from haste are very numerous ; I only say this, that they may not be laid at the door of the wrong party.—TRANS.

And Planchet retired, shaking his head with an air of doubt, which the liberality of D'Artagnan had not entirely removed.

Left alone, D'Artagnan read and re-read his billet, then he kissed and re-kissed twenty times the lines traced by the hand of his beautiful mistress. At length he went to bed, fell asleep, and had golden dreams.

At seven o'clock in the morning he arose and called Planchet, who, at the second summons, opened the door, his countenance not yet quite free from the anxiety of the preceding night.

"Planchet," said D'Artagnan, "I am going out for all day, perhaps; you are, therefore, your own master till seven o'clock in the evening; but at seven o'clock you must hold yourself in readiness with two horses."

"There!" said Planchet, "we are going again, it appears, to have our skins pierced through, and rubbed off in all directions!"

"You will take your musketoon and your pistols."

"There now! did I not say so?" cried Planchet. "I was sure of it; that cursed letter."

"Come, don't be afraid! you silly fellow; there is nothing in hand but a party of pleasure."

"Ah! like the charming journey the other day, when it rained billets, and produced a crop of steel-traps!"

"Well, if you are really afraid, Monsieur Planchet," resumed D'Artagnan, "I will go without you; I prefer travelling alone to having a companion who entertains the least fear."

"Monsieur does me wrong," said Planchet; "I thought he had seen me at work."

"Yes, but I did not know whether you had not worn out all your courage the first time."

"Monsieur shall see, upon occasion, that I have some left; only I beg monsieur not to be too prodigal of it, if he wishes it to last long."

"Do you believe you have still a certain amount of it to expend this evening?"

"I hope I have, monsieur."

"Well, then, I depend upon you."

"At the appointed hour I shall be ready; only I believed that monsieur had but one horse in the guard stables."

"Perhaps there is but one at this moment; but by this evening there will be four."

"It appears that our journey was a remounting journey then?"

"Exactly so," said D'Artagnan; and nodding to Planchet, he went out.

M. Bonacieux was standing at his door. D'Artagnan's intention was to go out without speaking to the worthy mercer; but the latter made so polite and friendly a salutation, that his tenant felt obliged, not only to stop, but to enter into conversation with him.

Besides, how is it possible to avoid a little condescension towards a husband, whose pretty wife has appointed a meeting with you that same evening at St. Cloud, opposite the pavilion of M. d'Estrées? D'Artagnan approached him with the most amiable air he could assume.

The conversation naturally fell upon the incarceration of the poor man. M. Bonacieux, who was ignorant that D'Artagnan had overheard his conversation with the unknown of Meung, related to his young tenant the persecutions of that monster, M. de Laffemas, whom he never ceased to qualify, during his account, with the title of the cardinal's executioner, and expatiated at great length upon the Bastille, the bolts, the wickets, the dungeons, the loop-holes, the gratings, and the instruments of torture.

D'Artagnan listened to him with exemplary complaisance, and when he had finished said :

" And Madame Bonacieux, do you know who carried her off? for I do not forget that I owe to that unpleasant circumstance the good fortune of having made your acquaintance."

" Ah !" said Bonacieux, " they took good care not to tell me that, and my wife, on her part, has sworn to me by all that's sacred, that she does not know. But you," continued M. Bonacieux, in a tone of perfect bonhomie, " what has become of you for several days past? I have not seen either you or any of your friends, and I don't think you could pick up all that dust on the pavement of Paris that I saw Planchet brush off your boots yesterday."

" You are right, my dear M. Bonacieux, my friends and I have been on a little journey."

" Far from Paris ?"

" Oh lord, no ! about forty leagues only. We went to take M. Athos to the waters of Forges, where my friends have remained."

" And you have returned, have you not ?" replied M. Bonacieux, giving to his countenance the most jocular air. " A handsome young fellow like you does not obtain long leaves of absence from his mistress ; and we were impatiently waited for at Paris, were we not ?"

" *Ma foi !*" said the young man, laughing, " I am fain to confess it, and so much the more readily, my dear Bonacieux, as I see there is no concealing anything from you. Yes, I was expected, and impatiently, I assure you."

A slight shade passed over the brow of Bonacieux, but so slight that D'Artagnan did not perceive it.

" And we are going to be recompensed for our diligence ?" said Bonacieux, with a trifling alteration in his voice—so trifling, indeed, that D'Artagnan did not perceive it any more than he had the shade which, an instant before, had darkened the countenance of the worthy man.

" Ah, I hope you are a true prophet !" said D'Artagnan, laughing.

" No ; that which I say is only that I may know whether you will be late."

" Why do you ask me that question, my dear host ? Do you intend to sit up for me ?"

" No ; only since my arrest and the robbery that was committed in my house, I am alarmed every time I hear a door opened, particularly in the night. What the deuce can you expect? I told you I was no man of the sword."

"Well, don't be alarmed if I come home at one, two, or three o'clock in the morning ; indeed, do not be alarmed if I do not come at all."

This time Bonacieux became so pale that D'Artagnan could not do otherwise than perceive it, and asked him what was the matter ?

"Nothing," replied Bonacieux, "nothing ; only since my misfortunes I have been subject to faintnesses, which seize me all at once, and I have just felt a cold shiver. Pay no attention to it ; you have nothing to occupy yourself with but being happy."

"Then I have full occupation, for I am so."

"Not yet—wait a little ; this evening, you said."

"Well, this evening will come, thank God ! And perhaps you look for it with as much impatience as I do ; perhaps this evening Madame Bonacieux will visit the conjugal domicile."

"Madame Bonacieux is not at liberty this evening," replied the husband seriously ; "she is detained at the Louvre this evening by her duties."

"So much the worse for you, my dear host, so much the worse for you ! When I am happy, I wish all the world to be so; but it appears that is not possible."

And the young man departed, laughing at the joke, which he thought he alone could comprehend.

"Ah, have your laugh out !" replied Bonacieux, in a sepulchral tone.

But D'Artagnan was too far off to hear him, and if he had heard him, in the disposition of mind he then enjoyed, he, certes, would not have remarked it.

He took his way towards the hotel of M. de Tréville : his visit of the day before had been very short and very little explicative.

He found M. de Tréville in the joy of his heart. He had thought the king and queen charming at the ball. It is true the cardinal had been particularly ill-tempered ; he had retired at one o'clock under the pretence of being indisposed. As to their majesties, they did not return to the Louvre till six o'clock.

"Now," said M. de Tréville, lowering his voice, and looking round to every corner of the apartment to see if they were alone, "now let us talk about you, my young friend ; for it is evident that your fortunate return has something to do with the joy of the king, the triumph of the queen, and the humiliation of the cardinal. You must take care of yourself."

"What have I to fear," replied D'Artagnan, "as long as I shall have the good fortune to enjoy the favour of their majesties ?"

"Everything, believe me. The cardinal is not the man to forget a mystification until he has settled his accounts with the mystifier; and the mystifier appears to me to have the air of being a certain young Gascon of my acquaintance."

"Do you believe that the cardinal knows as much as you do, and knows that I have been to London ?"

"The devil ! you said London ! Was it from London you brought that beautiful diamond that glitters on your finger? Beware, my dear

D'Artagnan ! a present from an enemy is not a good thing. Are there not some Latin verses upon that subject ? Stop !"

"Yes, doubtless," replied D'Artagnan, who had never been able to cram the first rudiments even of that language into his head, and who had by his ignorance driven his master to despair—"yes, doubtless there is one."

"There certainly is one," said M. de Tréville, who had a tincture of letters, "and M. Benserade was quoting it to me the other day. Stop a minute—ah, this is it : 'Timeo Danaos et dona ferentes,' which means, 'Beware of the enemy who makes you presents.'"

"This diamond does not come from an enemy, monsieur," replied D'Artagnan ; "it comes from the queen."

"From the queen ! oh, oh !" said M. de Tréville. "Why, it is, indeed, a true royal jewel, which is worth a thousand pistoles if it is worth a denier. By whom did the queen send you this jewel ?"

"She gave it to me herself."

"Where ?"

"In the closet adjoining the chamber in which she changed her toilet."

"How ?"

"Giving me her hand to kiss."

"What ! you have kissed the queen's hand ?" said M. de Tréville, looking earnestly at D'Artagnan.

"Her majesty did me the honour to grant me that favour."

"And that in the presence of witnesses ! Imprudent woman ! thrice imprudent !"

"No, monsieur ; be satisfied, nobody saw her," replied D'Artagnan, and he related to M. de Tréville how the affair had passed.

"Oh, the women, the women !" cried the old soldier. "I know them by their romantic imaginations ; everything that savours of mystery charms them. So you have seen the arm, that was all ; you would meet the queen and you would not know her ; she might meet you and she would not know who you were ?"

"No ; but thanks to this diamond," replied the young man.

"Listen to me," said M. de Tréville ; "shall I give you a good piece of advice—a piece of friendly advice ?"

"You will do me honour, monsieur," said D'Artagnan.

"Well, then, go to the nearest goldsmith's, and sell that diamond for the highest price you can get from him ; however much of a Jew he may be, he will give you at least eight hundred pistoles. Pistoles have no name, young man, and that ring has a terrible one, which may betray him who wears it."

"Sell this ring—a ring which comes from my sovereign ! never !" said D'Artagnan.

"Then at least turn the collet of it inside, you silly fellow ; for everybody must be aware that a cadet from Gascony does not find such gems in his mother's jewel-case."

"You think, then, I have something to dread ?" asked D'Artagnan.

" I mean to say, young man, that he who sleeps over a mine, the match of which is already lighted, may consider himself in safety in comparison with you."

"The devil!" said D'Artagnan, whom the positive tone of M. de Tréville began to make a little uneasy—" the devil! what must I do?"

" Be particularly, and at all times, on your guard. The cardinal has a tenacious memory and a long arm ; you may depend upon it, he will repay you by some ill turn."

" But what sort of one?"

" Eh! how can I tell? Has he not all the devil's tricks at command? The least that can be expected is that you will be arrested."

"What! will they dare to arrest a man in his majesty's service?"

"*Pardieu!* they did not scruple much in the case of Athos. At all events, young man, depend upon one who has been thirty years at court. Do not lull yourself in security, or you will be lost ; but, on the contrary—and it is I who tell you so—see enemies in all directions. If any one seeks a quarrel with you, shun it, were it with a child of ten years old ; if you are attacked by day or by night, fight, but retreat, without shame ; if you cross a bridge, feel every plank of it with your foot, lest one should give way beneath you ; if you pass before a house which is being built, look up, for fear a stone should fall upon your head ; if you stay out late, be always followed by your lackey, and let your lackey be armed, if, by-the-by, you can be sure of your lackey. Mistrust everybody, your friend, your brother, your mistress—your mistress in particular."

D'Artagnan blushed.

" Of my mistress," repeated he, mechanically ; " and why rather her than any other?"

" Because a mistress is one of the cardinal's favourite means—he has not one that is more expeditious ; a woman will sell you for ten pistoles, witness Dalila. You are acquainted with the Scriptures, eh?"

D'Artagnan thought of the appointment Madame Bonacieux had made with him for that very evening ; but we are bound to say, to the credit of our hero, that the bad opinion entertained by M. de Tréville of women in general, did not inspire him with the least suspicion of his pretty hostess.

" But, *àpropos*," resumed M. de Tréville, " what has become of your three companions?"

" I was about to ask you if you had heard no news of them."

" None whatever, monsieur."

" Well, I left them on my road : Porthos at Chantilly, with a duel on his hands ; Aramis at Crèvecœur, with a ball in his shoulder ; and Athos at Amiens, detained by an accusation of coining!"

" See there, now!" said M. de Tréville ; " and how the devil did you escape?"

" By a miracle, monsieur, I must acknowledge, with a sword-thrust in my breast, and by nailing M. le Comte de Wardes, on the bye-road to Calais, like a butterfly on a tapestry."

"There again! De Wardes, one of the cardinal's men, a cousin of Rochefort's. But stop, my friend, I have an idea."

"Speak, monsieur."

"In your place, I would do one thing."

"What, monsieur?"

"Whilst his eminence was seeking for me in Paris, I would take, without sound of drum or trumpet, the road to Picardy, and would go and make some inquiries concerning my three companions. What the devil! they merit richly that piece of attention on your part."

"The advice is good, monsieur, and to-morrow I will set out."

"To-morrow! and why not this evening?"

"This evening, monsieur, I am detained in Paris by an indispensable business."

"Ah, young man, young man! some love-passage or other! Take care, I repeat to you, take care! it is woman who was the ruin of us all, is the ruin of us all, and will be the ruin of us all, as long as the world stands. Take my advice, and set out this evening."

"It is impossible, monsieur."

"You have given your word, then?"

"Yes, monsieur."

"Ah, that's quite another thing; but promise me, if you should not happen to be killed to-night, that you will go to-morrow."

"I promise you, monsieur."

"Do you want money?"

"I have still fifty pistoles. That, I think, is as much as I shall want."

"But your companions?"

"I don't think they can be in need of any. We left Paris with each seventy-five pistoles in his pocket."

"Shall I see you again before your departure?"

"I think not, monsieur, unless anything fresh should happen."

"Well, a pleasant journey to you, then."

"Thank you, monsieur."

And D'Artagnan left M. de Tréville, penetrated more than ever by his paternal solicitude for his musketeers.

He called successively at the abodes of Athos, Porthos, and Aramis. Neither of them had returned. Their lackeys likewise were absent, and nothing had been heard of either masters or servants.

He would have inquired after them at their mistress's, but he was neither acquainted with Porthos's nor Aramis's, and as to Athos, he had not one.

As he passed the Hôtel des Gardes, he took a glance into the stables. Three out of the four horses were already arrived. Planchet, all astonishment, was busy grooming them, and had already finished two.

"Ah, monsieur," said Planchet, on perceiving D'Artagnan, "how glad I am to see you."

"Why so, Planchet?" asked the young man.

"Do you place confidence in our landlord, M. Bonacieux?"

" I ? Not the least in the world."

" Oh ! you do quite right, monsieur."

" But, why do you ask ?"

" Because, while you where talking with him, I watched you without listening to you ; and, monsieur, his countenance changed so, two or three times !"

" Bah !"

" Preoccupied as monsieur was with the letter he had received, he did not observe that ; but I, whom the strange fashion in which that letter came into the house had placed on my guard, I did not lose a movement of his features."

" And you found it ?"

" Traitorous, monsieur."

" Indeed !"

" Still more ; as soon as monsieur had left, and disappeared round the corner of the street, M. Bonacieux took his hat, shut his door, and set off at a quick pace in an opposite direction."

" It seems you are right, Planchet ; all this appears to be a little mysterious ; and be assured that we will not pay him our rent until the matter shall be categorically explained to us."

" Monsieur jokes, but monsieur will see."

" What would you have, Planchet?—It is written, that what must be must !"

" Monsieur has not then renounced his excursion for this evening ?"

" Quite the contrary, Planchet ; the more ill-will I have reason to entertain towards M. Bonacieux, the more punctual I shall be in keeping the appointment made with me in that letter which makes you so uneasy."

" Then that is monsieur's determination ?"

" Most decidedly, my friend ; at nine o'clock, then, be ready here, at the hotel, I will come and take you."

Planchet seeing there was no longer any hope of making his master renounce his project, heaved a profound sigh, and set to work to groom the third horse.

As to D'Artagnan, being at bottom a prudent youth, instead of returning home, he went and dined with the Gascon priest, who, at the time of the distress of the four friends, had given them a breakfast of choco

---

CHAPTER XXIV.

THE PAVILION.

At nine o'clock D'Artagnan was at the Hôtel des Gardes ; he found Planchet under arms.   The fourth horse had arrived.

Planchet was armed with his musketoon and a pistol.   D'Artagnan had his sword, and placed two pistols in his belt ; then both mounted, and departed quietly.   It was quite dark, and no one saw them go out.

Planchet took his place behind his master, and kept at a distance of about ten paces from him.

D'Artagnan crossed the quays, went out by the gate of La Conference, and proceeded along the road, much more beautiful then than it is now, which leads to St. Cloud.

As long as he was in the city, Planchet kept at the respectful distance he had imposed upon himself; but as soon as the road began to be more lonely and dark, he drew softly nearer; so that when they entered the Bois de Boulogne, he found himself riding quite naturally side by side with his master. In fact, we must not dissemble, that the oscillation of the tall trees, and the reflection of the moon in the dark underwood, gave him serious uneasiness. D'Artagnan could not help perceiving that something more than usual was passing in the mind of his lackey, and said :—

"Well, Master Planchet! what is the matter with us now?"

"Don't you think, monsieur, that woods are like churches?"

"How so, Planchet!"

"Because we dare not speak aloud in one or the other."

"But why do you not dare to speak aloud, Planchet?—because you are afraid?"

"Afraid of being heard?—yes, monsieur."

"Afraid of being heard! Why there is nothing improper in our conversation, my dear Planchet, and no one could find fault with it."

"Ah, monsieur!" replied Planchet, recurring to his besetting idea, "that M. Bonacieux has something vicious in his eyebrows, and something very unpleasant in the play of his lips."

"What the devil makes you think of Bonacieux now?"

"Monsieur, we think of what we can, and not of what we will."

"Because you are a coward, Planchet."

"Monsieur, we must not confound prudence with cowardice; prudence is a virtue."

"And you are very virtuous, are you not, Planchet?"

"Monsieur, is not that the barrel of a musket which glitters yonder? Had we not better lower our heads?"

"In truth," murmured D'Artagnan, to whom M. de Tréville's recommendation recurred, "in truth, this animal will end by making me afraid." And he put his horse into a trot.

Planchet followed the movements of his master, as if he had been his shadow, and was soon trotting by his side.

"Are we going to continue this pace all night?" asked Planchet.

"No, for you, on your part, are at your journey's end."

"I, monsieur, am arrived! and monsieur?"

"Why, I am going a few steps farther."

"And does monsieur intend to leave me here alone?"

"You certainly are afraid, Planchet?"

"No; but I only beg leave to observe to monsieur, that the night will be very cold, that chills bring on rheumatism, and that a lackey who has the rheumatism makes but a poor servant, particularly to a master as active as monsieur."

"Well, if you are cold, Planchet, you can go into one of those caba-rets that you see yonder, and be waiting for me at the door by six o'clock in the morning."

"Monsieur, I have eaten and drunk respectfully the crown you gave me this morning ; so that I have not a sou left, in case I should be cold."

"Here's half a pistole. To-morrow morning, then."

D'Artagnan sprang from his horse, threw the bridle to Planchet, and departed at a quick pace, folding his cloak round him.

"Good Lord, how cold I am !" cried Planchet, as soon as he had lost sight of his master ; and in such haste was he to warm himself, that he went straight to a house set out with all the attributes of a suburban auberge, and knocked at the door.

In the meantime D'Artagnan, who had plunged into a bye-path, con-tinued his route, and gained St. Cloud ; but instead of following the high street, he turned behind the château, reached a sort of retired lane, and found himself soon in front of the pavilion named. It was situated in a very private spot. A high wall, at the angle of which was the pavilion, ran along one side of this lane, and on the other was a little garden, connected with a poor cottage, which was protected from pas-sengers by a hedge.

He gained the place appointed, and as no signal had been given him by which to announce his presence, he waited.

Not the least noise was to be heard, it might be imagined that he was a hundred miles from the capital. D'Artagnan leant against the hedge, after having cast a glance behind him. Beyond that hedge, that garden, and that cottage, a dark mist enveloped with its folds that im-mensity in which sleeps Paris, a vast void from which glittered a few luminous points, the funeral stars of that hell !

But for D'Artagnan all aspects were clothed happily, all ideas wore a smile, all darknesses were diaphanous. The appointed hour was about to strike.

In fact, at the end of a few minutes, the belfry of St. Cloud let fall slowly ten strokes from its sonorous jaws.

There was something melancholy in this brazen voice pouring out its lamentations amidst the night.

But every one of those hours which composed the expected hour. vibrated harmoniously to the heart of the young man.

His eyes were fixed upon the little pavilion situated at the angle of the wall, of which all the windows were closed with shutters, except one on the first story. Through this window shone a mild light which silvered the foliage of two or three linden trees, which formed a group outside the park. There could be no doubt that behind this little window, which threw forth such friendly beams, the pretty Madame Bonacieux expected him.

Wrapt in this sweet idea, D'Artagnan waited half an hour without the least impatience, his eyes fixed upon that charming little abode of which he could perceive a part of the ceiling with its gilded mouldings, attesting the elegance of the rest of the apartment.

The belfry of St. Cloud struck half-past ten.

This time, without at all knowing why, D'Artagnan felt a cold shiver run through his veins. Perhaps the cold began to affect him, and he took a perfectly physical sensation for a moral impression.

Then the idea seized him that he had read incorrectly, and that the appointment was for eleven o'clock. He drew near to the window, and placing himself so that a ray of light should fall upon the letter as he held it, he drew it from his pocket, and read it again ; but he had not been mistaken, the appointment was for ten o'clock.

He went and resumed his post, beginning to be pretty uneasy at this silence and this solitude.

Eleven o'clock struck !

D'Artagnan began now really to fear that something had happened to Madame Bonacieux. He clapped his hands three times, the ordinary signal of lovers ; but nobody replied to him—not even an echo.

He then thought, with a touch of vexation, that perhaps the young woman had fallen asleep whilst waiting for him.

He approached the wall, and endeavoured to climb up it ; but the wall had been recently pointed, and he could obtain no hold.

At that moment he thought of the trees, upon whose leaves the light still shone, and as one of them drooped over the road, he thought that from its branches he might succeed in getting a glimpse of the interior of the room.

The tree was easy to climb. Besides, D'Artagnan was but twenty years old, and consequently had not yet forgotten his school-boy habits. In an instant he was among the branches, and his keen eyes plunged through the transparent window into the interior of the pavilion.

It was a strange thing, and one which made D'Artagnan tremble from the sole of his foot to the root of his hair, to find that this soft light, this calm lamp, enlightened a scene of fearful disorder : one of the windows was broken, the door of the chamber had been beaten in, and hung, split in two, on its hinges ; a table, which had been covered with an elegant supper, was overturned ; the decanters, broken in pieces, and the fruits crushed, strewed the floor ; everything in the apartment gave evidence of a violent and desperate struggle ; D'Artagnan even fancied he could recognize amidst this strange disorder, fragments of garments, and some bloody spots staining the cloth and the curtains.

He hastened down into the street, with a frightful beating at his heart ; he wished to see if he could find any other traces of violence.

The little soft light continued to shine in the calm of the night. D'Artagnan then perceived, a thing that he had not before remarked, for nothing had led him to the examination, that the ground, trampled here, and hoof-marked there, presented confused traces of men and horses. Besides, the wheels of a carriage, which appeared to have come from Paris, had made a deep impression in the soft earth, which did not extend beyond the pavilion, but turned again towards Paris.

At length D'Artagnan, in following up his researches, found near the wall a woman's torn glove ; which glove, wherever it had not touched the muddy ground, was of irreproachable freshness. It was one of those perfumed gloves that lovers like to snatch from a pretty hand.

As D'Artagnan pursued his investigations, at every fresh discovery a more abundant and more icy sweat broke in large drops from his forehead ; his heart was oppressed by a horrible anguish, his respiration was broken and short ; and yet he said, to reassure himself, that this pavilion, perhaps, had nothing in common with Madame Bonacieux ; that the young woman had made an appointment with him before the pavilion, and not in the pavilion ; that she might have been detained in Paris by her duties, or perhaps by the jealousy of her husband.

But all these reasons were combated, destroyed, overthrown, by that feeling of intimate pain which, on certain occasions, takes possession of our being, and cries to us, so as to be understood unmistakably, that some great misfortune is hanging over us.

Then D'Artagnan became almost wild ; he ran along the high road, took the path he had before taken, and, coming to the ferry, closely interrogated the boatman.

About seven o'clock in the evening, the boatman said he had taken over a young woman, enveloped in a black mantle, who appeared to be very anxious not to be seen ; but, entirely on account of her precautions, the boatman had paid more attention to her, and discovered that she was young and pretty.

There was then, as there is now, a crowd of young and pretty women who came to St. Cloud, and who had great reasons for not being seen, and yet D'Artagnan did not for an instant doubt that it was Madame Bonacieux whom the boatman had remarked.

D'Artagnan took advantage of the lamp which burned in the cabin of the boatman to read the billet of Madame Bonacieux once again, and satisfy himself that he had not been mistaken, that the appointment was at St. Cloud and not elsewhere, before the pavilion of M. d'Estrées and not in another street.

Everything conspired to prove to D'Artagnan that his presentiments had not deceived him, and that a great misfortune had happened.

He again ran back to the château ; it appeared to him that something might have happened at the pavilion in his absence, and that fresh information awaited him.

The lane was still empty, and the same calm soft light shone from the window.

D'Artagnan then thought of that silent, obscure cottage ; some one from it might have seen, no doubt, and might tell of something.

The gate of the enclosure was shut, but he leaped over the hedge, and in spite of the barking of a chained-up dog, went up to the cabin.

No one answered to his first knocking. A silence of death reigned in the cabin as in the pavilion ; the cabin, however, was his last resource ; he knocked again.

It soon appeared to him that he heard a slight noise within, a timid noise, which seemed itself to tremble lest it should be heard.

Then D'Artagnan ceased to knock, and prayed with an accent so full of anxiety and promises, terror and cajolery, that his voice was of a nature to reassure the most fearful. At length an old, worm-eaten shutter was opened, or rather pushed ajar, but closed again as soon as the light from a miserable lamp which burned in the corner had shone upon the baldrick, sword-belt, and pistol pummels of D'Artagnan. Nevertheless, rapid as the movement had been, D'Artagnan had had time to get a glimpse of the head of an old man.

"In the name of Heaven!" cried he, "listen to me : I have been waiting for some one who is not come ; I am dying with anxiety. Has anything particular happened in the neighbourhood ? Speak !"

The window was again opened slowly, and the same face appeared again : only it was still more pale than before.

D'Artagnan related his history simply, with the omission of names : he told how he had an appointment with a young woman before that pavilion, and how, not seeing her come, he had climbed the linden tree, and by the light of the lamp, had seen the disorder of the chamber.

The old man listened attentively, making a sign only that it all was so ; and then, when D'Artagnan had ended, he shook his head with an air that announced nothing good.

"What do you mean ?" cried D'Artagnan, "in the name of Heaven, tell me, explain yourself."

"Oh ! monsieur," said the old man, "ask me nothing ; for if I told you what I have seen, certainly no good would befall me."

"You have then seen something?" replied D'Artagnan. "In that case, in the name of Heaven," continued he, throwing him a pistole, "tell me what you have seen, and I will pledge you the word of a gentleman that not one of your words shall escape from my heart."

The old man read so much truth and so much grief in the face of the young man, that he made him a sign to listen, and repeated in a low voice :

" It was scarcely nine o'clock when I heard a noise in the street, and was wondering what it could be, when on coming to my door, I found that somebody was endeavouring to open it. As I am very poor, and am not afraid of being robbed, I went and opened the gate and saw three men at a few paces from it. In the shade was a carriage with two horses, and a man held three saddle horses. These horses evidently belonged to the three men, who were dressed as cavaliers.

" ' Ah ! my worthy gentlemen,' cried I, ' what do you want ?'

" ' Have you a ladder?' said the one who appeared to be the leader of the party.

" ' Yes, monsieur, the one with which I gather my fruit.'

" ' Lend it to us, and go into your house again ; there is a crown for the annoyance we have caused you. Only remember this, if you speak a word of what you may see or what you may hear (for you will look and you will listen, I am quite sure, however we may threaten you), you are lost.'

"At these words he threw me a crown, which I picked up, and he took the ladder.

"After shutting the gate behind them, I pretended to return to the house, but I immediately went out at a back door, and stealing along in the shade of the hedge, I gained yonder clump of elder, from which I could hear and see everything.

"The three men brought the carriage up quietly, and took out of it a little man, stout, short, elderly, and commonly dressed in clothes of a dark colour, who ascended the ladder very carefully, looked suspiciously in at the window of the pavilion, came down as quietly as he had gone up, and whispered :

"'It is she !'

"Immediately he who had spoken to me approached the door of the pavilion, opened it with a key he had in his hand, closed the door and disappeared, whilst at the same time the other two men ascended the ladder. The little old man remained at the coach door, the coachman took care of his horses, the lackey held the saddle horses.

"All at once great cries resounded in the pavilion, and a woman came to the window, and opened it, as if to throw herself out of it ; but as soon as she perceived the other two men, she fell back and they got into the chamber.

"Then I saw no more ; but I heard the noise of breaking furniture. The woman screamed and cried for help. But her cries were soon stifled ; two of the men appeared, bearing the woman in their arms, and carried her to the carriage, into which the little old man got after her. The leader closed the window, came out an instant after at the door, and satisfied himself that the woman was in the carriage : his two companions were already on horseback ; he sprang into his saddle, the lackey took his place by the coachman, the carriage went off at a quick pace, escorted by the three horsemen, and all was over :—from that moment I have neither seen nor heard anything."

D'Artagnan, entirely overcome by this terrible story, remained motionless and mute, whilst all the demons of anger and jealousy were howling in his heart.

"But, my good gentleman," resumed the old man, upon whom this mute despair certainly produced a greater effect than cries and tears would have done ; "do not take on so, they did not kill her from you, that's a comfort."

"Do you know anything," said D'Artagnan, "of the man who led this infernal expedition ?"

"I don't know him at all."

"But, as you spoke to him you must have seen him."

"Oh ! it's a description of him you want ?"

"Exactly so."

"A tall, dark man, with black moustaches, dark eyes, and looked like a gentleman."

"That's the man !" cried D'Artagnan, "again he, for ever he ! He is my demon, to all appearance. And the other ?"

"Which ?"

"The short one."

"Oh! he was not a gentleman, I'll answer for it; besides, he did not wear a sword, and the others treated him with no consideration."

"Some lackey," murmured D'Artagnan. "Poor girl! poor girl! what have they done with you?"

"You have promised to be secret, my good monsieur?" said the old man.

"And I repeat my promise; be satisfied, I am a gentleman. A gentleman has but his word, and I have given you mine."

With a heavy heart, D'Artagnan again bent his way towards the ferry. Sometimes he hoped it could not be Madame Bonacieux, and that he should find her next day at the Louvre; sometimes he feared she had had an intrigue with another, who, in a jealous fit, had surprised her and carried her off. His mind was torn by doubt, grief, and despair.

"Oh! if I had my three friends here!" cried he, "I should have, at least, some hopes of finding her; but who knows what is become of them themselves?"

It was past midnight; the next thing was to find Planchet. D'Artagnan went successively into all the cabarets in which there was a light, but could not meet with Planchet in any of them.

At the sixth he began to reflect that the search was rather hazardous. D'Artagnan had appointed six o'clock in the morning with his lackey, and wherever he might be, he was doing as he had bidden him.

Besides, it came into the young man's mind, that by remaining in the environs of the spot on which this sad event had passed, he should, perhaps, have some light thrown upon the mysterious affair. At the sixth cabaret, then, as we said, D'Artagnan stopped, asked for a bottle of wine of the best quality, and placing himself in the darkest corner of the room, determined thus to wait till daylight; but this time again his hopes were disappointed, and although he listened with all his ears, he heard nothing, amidst the oaths, coarse jokes, and abuse which passed between the labourers, servants, and carters, who comprised the honourable society of which he formed a part, which could put him at all upon the traces of her who had been stolen from him. He was compelled, then, after having swallowed the contents of his bottle, to pass the time as well as to avoid suspicion, to fall into the easiest position in his corner, and to sleep, whether well or ill. D'Artagnan, be it remembered, was only twenty years old, and at that age sleep has its imprescriptible rights, which it imperiously insists upon, even in the saddest hearts.

Towards six o'clock, D'Artagnan awoke with that uncomfortable feeling which generally follows a bad night. He was not long in making his toilette; he examined himself to see if advantage had not been taken of his sleep, and having found his diamond ring on his finger, his purse in his pocket, and his pistols in his belt, he got up, paid for his wine, and went out to try if he could have any better luck in his search after his lackey than he had had the night before. The first thing he perceived through the damp grey mist was honest Planchet, who, with the two horses in hand, awaited him at the door of a little blind cabaret, before which D'Artagnan had passed without even suspecting its existence.

CHAPTER XXV.
PORTHOS.

INSTEAD of returning directly home, D'Artagnan alighted at the door of M. de Tréville, and ran quickly up the stairs. This time he was determined to relate all that had passed. He would doubtless give him good advice in the whole affair; and besides, as M. de Tréville saw the queen almost every day, he might be able to get from her majesty some intelligence of the poor young woman, whom they were doubtless making pay very dearly for her devotedness to her mistress.

M. de Tréville listened to the young man's account with a seriousness which proved that he saw something else in this adventure besides a love affair; and when D'Artagnan had finished:

" Hum !" said he, " all this savours of his eminence, a league off."

" But, what is to be done ?" said D'Artagnan.

" Nothing, absolutely nothing, at present, but quitting Paris, as I told you, as soon as possible. I will see the queen; I will relate to her the details of the disappearance of this poor woman, of which she is, no doubt, ignorant. These details will guide her on her part, and, on your return, I shall perhaps have some good news to tell you."

D'Artagnan knew that, although a Gascon, M. de Tréville was not in the habit of making promises, and that when by chance he did promise, he generally more than kept his word. He bowed to him, then, full of gratitude for the past and for the future, and the worthy captain, who, on his side, felt a lively interest in this young man, so brave and so resolute, pressed his hand kindly, whilst wishing him a pleasant journey.

Determined to put the advice of M. de Tréville in practice instantly, D'Artagnan directed his course towards the Rue des Fossoyeurs, in order to superintend the packing of his valise. On approaching the house, he perceived M. Bonacieux, in morning costume, standing at his door. All that the prudent Planchet had said to him the preceding evening recurred to the mind of D'Artagnan, who looked at him with more attention than he had done before. In fact, in addition to that yellow, sickly paleness which indicates the insinuation of the bile in the blood, and which might, besides, be accidental, D'Artagnan remarked something perfidiously significant in the play of the wrinkled features of his countenance. A rogue does not laugh in the same way that an honest man does; a hypocrite does not shed the same sort of tears as fall from the eyes of a man of good faith. All falsehood is a mask, and however well made the mask may be, with a little attention we may always succeed in distinguishing it from the true face.

It appeared, then, to D'Artagnan, that M. Bonacieux wore a mask, and likewise that that mask was very disagreeable to look upon.

In consequence of this feeling of repugnance, he was about to pass without speaking to him, but, as he had done the day before, M. Bonacieux accosted him.

" Well, young man," said he, " we appear to pass rather gay nights ! Seven o'clock in the morning ! Peste ! you seem to reverse ordinary customs, and come home at the hour when other people are going out."

" No one can reproach you for anything of the kind, Master Bonacieux," said the young man ; " you are a model for regular people. It is true that when a man possesses a young and pretty wife, he has no need to seek happiness elsewhere ; happiness comes to meet him, does it not, Monsieur Bonacieux ?"

Bonacieux became as pale as death, and grinned a ghastly smile.

" Ah ! ah !" said Bonacieux, " you are a jocular companion ! But where the devil were you gadding last night, my young master ? It does not appear to be very clean in the cross-roads."

D'Artagnan glanced down at his boots, all covered with mud, but that same glance fell upon the shoes and stockings of the mercer, and it might have been said they had been dipped in the same mud-heap ; both were stained with splashes of mud of the same appearance.

Then a sudden idea crossed the mind of D'Artagnan. That little stout man, short and elderly, that sort of lackey, dressed in dark clothes, treated without consideration by the men wearing swords who composed the escort, was Bonacieux himself ! The husband had presided over the carrying off of his wife !

A terrible inclination immediately took possession of D'Artagnan to seize the mercer by the throat and strangle him ; but, as we have said, he was, occasionally, a very prudent youth, and he restrained himself. The revolution, however, which had appeared upon his countenance, was so visible, that Bonacieux was terrified at it, and he endeavoured to draw back a step or two, but being before the flap of the door, which was shut, the obstacle compelled him to keep his place.

" Ah ! ah ! but you are joking, my worthy man !" said D'Artagnan. " It appears to me that if my boots want a sponge, your stockings and shoes stand in equal need of a brush. May you not have been philandering a little also, Master Bonacieux ? Oh ! the devil ! that's unpardonable in a man of your age, and who, besides, has such a pretty young wife as yours is !"

" Oh lord ! no," said Bonacieux ; " but yesterday I went to Saint Mandé, to make some inquiries after a servant, as I cannot possibly do without one, and the roads were so bad that I brought back all this mud, which I have not yet had time to remove."

The place named by Bonacieux as that which had been the object of his journey was a fresh proof in support of the suspicions D'Artagnan had conceived. Bonacieux had named Mandé, because Mandé was in an exactly opposite direction to Saint Cloud. This probability afforded him his first consolation. If Bonacieux knew where his wife was, the mercer might, at any time, by employing extreme means, be forced to open his teeth, and allow his secret to escape. The question, then, only was to change this probability into a certainty.

"I beg your pardon, my dear Monsieur Bonacieux, if I don't stand upon ceremony," said D'Artagnan, "but nothing makes one so thirsty as want of sleep; I am parched with thirst; allow me to take a glass of water in your apartment; you know that is never refused among neighbours!"

And without waiting for the permission of his host, D'Artagnan went quickly into the house, and cast a rapid glance at the bed. The bed had not been slept in. Bonacieux had not been to bed. He had only been back an hour or two; he had accompanied his wife to the place of her confinement, or else, at least, to the first relay.

"Many thanks to you, Master Bonacieux," said D'Artagnan, emptying his glass: "that is all I wanted of you. I will now go up into my room, I will make Planchet brush my boots, and when he has done, I will, if you like, send him to you to brush your shoes."

And he left the mercer quite astonished at his singular farewell, and asking himself if he had not been a little inconsiderate.

At the top of the stairs he found Planchet in a great fright.

"Ah! monsieur!" cried Planchet, as soon as he perceived his master, "here is more trouble! I thought you would never come in!"

"What's the matter now, Planchet?"

"Oh! I give you a hundred, I give you a thousand times to guess, monsieur, the visit I have received in your absence."

"When?"

"About half an hour ago, whilst you were at M. de Tréville's."

"Who has been here? Come, speak."

"M. de Cavois."

"M. de Cavois?"

"In person."

"The captain of his eminence's guards?"

"Himself."

"Did he come to arrest me?"

"I have no doubt he did, monsieur, for all his carnying manner."

"Was he so polite, then?"

"All honey, monsieur."

"Indeed!"

"He came, he said, on the part of his eminence, who wished you well, and to beg you to follow him to the Palais-Cardinal."*

"What did you answer him?"

"That the thing was impossible, seeing that you were not at home, as he might perceive."

"Well, what did he say then?"

"That you must not fail to call upon him in the course of the day; and then he added, in a low voice, 'Tell your master that his eminence is very well disposed towards him, and that his fortune perhaps depends upon this interview.'"

* M. Dumas calls it the Palais-Royal, but it was called the Palais-Cardinal before Richelieu had given it to the king: indeed, I doubt whether it was built at all at the period of this story.—TRANS.

" The snare is not very skilfully set for the cardinal," replied the young man, smiling.

" Oh ! yes, I saw the snare, and I answered you would be quite in despair, on your return.

" ' Where is he gone to ?' asked M. de Cavois.

" ' To Troyes, in Champagne,' I answered.

" ' And when did he set out ?'

" ' Yesterday evening.' "

" Planchet, my friend," interrupted D'Artagnan, " you are really a jewel of a man."

" You will understand, monsieur, I thought there would be still time, if you wish, to see M. de Cavois, to contradict me by saying you were not yet gone ; the falsehood would then lie at my door, and as I am not a gentleman, I may be allowed to lie."

" Be of good heart, Planchet, you shall preserve your reputation as a man of truth ; in a quarter of an hour we will set off."

" That's just the advice I was going to give, monsieur : and where are we going, may I ask, without being too curious ?"

" Pardieu ! in the opposite direction to that which you said I was gone. Besides, are you not as anxious to learn news of Grimaud, Mousqueton, and Bazin, as I am to know what has become of Athos, Porthos, and Aramis ?"

" Oh ! yes, monsieur," said Planchet, " and I will go as soon as you please ; indeed, I think provincial air will suit us much better just now than the air of Paris. So then——"

" So then, pack up our necessaries, Planchet, and let us be off. On my part, I will go out with my hands in my pockets, that nothing may be suspected. You can join me at the Hôtel des Gardes. Apropos, Planchet, I think you are right with respect to our host, and that he is decidedly a frightfully low wretch."

" Ah ! monsieur ! you may take my word when I tell you anything. I am a physiognomist, I assure you !"

D'Artagnan went out first, as had been agreed upon ; then, in order that he might have nothing to reproach himself with, he directed his steps towards the residences of his three friends : no news had been received of them ; only a letter, all perfumed, and of an elegant writing in small characters, was come for Aramis. D'Artagnan took charge of it. Ten minutes afterwards, Planchet joined him at the stables of the Hôtel des Gardes. D'Artagnan, in order that there might be no time lost, had saddled his horse himself.

" That's well," said he to Planchet, when the latter added the portmanteau to the equipment ; " now saddle the other three horses."

" Do you think, then, monsieur, that we shall travel faster with two horses a-piece ?" said Planchet, with his cunning air.

" No master joker," replied D'Artagnan, " but with our four horses we may bring back our three friends, if we should have the good fortune to find them living."

" Which must be a great chance," replied Planchet, " but we must not despair of the mercy of God."

" Amen !" cried D'Artagnan, getting into his saddle.

As they went from the Hôtel des Gardes, they separated, leaving the street at opposite ends, one having to quit Paris by the barrier of La Villette, and the other by the barrier Mont-Martre, with an understanding to meet again beyond St. Denis, a strategetic manœuvre which, having been executed with equal punctuality, was crowned with the most fortunate results. D'Artagnan and Planchet entered Pierrefitte together.

Planchet was more courageous, it must be admitted, by day than by night. His natural prudence, however, never forsook him for a single instant ; he had forgotten not one of the incidents of the first journey, and he looked upon everybody he met on the road as an enemy. It followed that his hat was for ever in his hand, which procured him some severe reprimands from D'Artagnan, who feared that his excess of politeness would lead people to think he was the lackey of a man of no consequence.

Nevertheless, whether the passengers were really touched by the urbanity of Planchet, or whether this time nobody was posted on the young man's road, our two travellers arrived at Chantilly without any accident, and alighted at the hotel of the Grand Saint Martin, the same they had stopped at on their first journey.

The host, on seeing a young man followed by a lackey with two led horses, advanced respectfully to the door. Now, as they had already travelled eleven leagues, D'Artagnan thought it time to stop, whether Porthos were or were not in the hotel. And then perhaps it would not be prudent to ask at once what had become of the musketeers. It resulted from these reflections that D'Artagnan, without asking intelligence of any kind, alighted, recommended the horses to the care of his lackey, entered a small room destined to receive such as wished to be alone, and desired the host to bring him a bottle of his best wine, and as good a breakfast as possible, a desire which further corroborated the high opinion the aubergiste, had formed of the traveller at first sight.

D'Artagnan was therefore served with a miraculous celerity. The regiment of the guards was recruited among the first gentlemen of the kingdom, and D'Artagnan, followed by a lackey with four magnificent horses, could not fail to make a sensation. The host desired to wait upon him himself, which D'Artagnan perceiving, ordered two glasses to be brought, and commenced the following conversation :

" Ma foi ! my good host," said D'Artagnan, filling the two glasses, "I asked for a bottle of your best wine, and if you have deceived me, you will be punished by that you have sinned in, for, seeing that I hate drinking by myself, you shall drink with me. Take your glass then, and let us drink. But what shall we drink to, so as to avoid wounding any susceptibility ? Let us drink to the prosperity of your establishment."

" Your lordship does me much honour," said the host, " and I thank you sincerely for your kind wish,"

"But don't mistake," said D'Artagnan, "there is more selfishness in my toast than perhaps you may think; for it is only in prosperous establishments that one is well received; in hotels that do not flourish, everything is in confusion, and the traveller is a victim to the embarrassments of his host: now I travel a great deal, particularly on this road, and I wish to see all aubergistes making a fortune."

"I was thinking," said the host, "that it was not the first time I had had the honour of seeing monsieur."

"Bah! I have passed, perhaps, ten times through Chantilly, and out of the ten times, I have stopped three or four times at your house at least. Why I was here only ten or twelve days ago; I was conducting some friends, musketeers, one of whom, by-the-bye, had a dispute with a stranger, an unknown, a man who sought a quarrel with him for I don't know what."

"Ah! exactly so!" said the host; "I remember it perfectly. Is it not M. Porthos, that your lordship means?"

"Yes; that is my companion's name. Good heavens! my dear host; I hope nothing has happened to him?"

"Your honour must have observed that he could not continue his journey."

"Why, to be sure, he promised to rejoin us, and we have seen nothing of him."

"He has done us the honour to remain here."

"What! he has done you the honour to remain here?"

"Yes, monsieur, in this hotel; and we are even a little uneasy——"

"On what account?"

"Certain expenses he has been at."

"Well: but whatever expenses he may have incurred, I am sure he is in a condition to pay them."

"Ah! monsieur, you infuse balm into my mind! We have made considerable advances; and this morning only the surgeon declared that if M. Porthos did not pay him, he should look to me, as it was I who had sent for him."

"What, is Porthos wounded, then?"

"I cannot tell you, monsieur."

"What! you cannot tell me! surely you ought to be able to tell me better than any other person."

"Yes; but in our situation we must not say all we know; particularly when we have been warned that our ears should answer for our tongues."

"Well! can I see Porthos?"

"Certainly, monsieur. Take the stairs on your right; go up the first flight, and knock at No. 1. Only warn him that it is you."

"Warn him! why should I do that?"

"Because, monsieur, some mischief might happen to you."

"Of what kind, in the name of wonder?"

"M. Porthos may imagine you belong to the house, and in a fit of passion might run his sword through you, or blow out your brains."

" What have you done to him, then ?"

" We asked him for money."

" The devil !—ah ! I can understand that ; it is a demand that Porthos takes very ill when he is not in funds ; but I know he ought to be so at present."

" We thought so too, monsieur ; as our concern is carried on very regularly, and we make our bills every week, at the end of eight days we presented our account ; but it appeared we had chosen an unlucky moment, for at the first word on the subject, he sent us to all the devils ; it is true he had been playing the day before."

" Playing the day before !—and with whom ?"

" Lord ! who can say, monsieur ? With some gentleman who was travelling this way, to whom he proposed a game of lansquenet."

" That's it, then ! and the foolish fellow has lost all he had ?"

" Even to his horse, monsieur ; for when the gentleman was about to set out, we perceived that his lacquey was saddling M. Porthos's horse, as well as his master's. When we observed this to him, he told us to trouble ourselves with our own business, as this horse belonged to him. We also informed M. Porthos of what was going on ; but he told us we were scoundrels, to doubt a gentleman's word ; and that as he had said the horse was his, there could be no doubt that it was so."

" That's Porthos all over !" murmured D'Artagnan.

" Then," continued the host, " I replied that from the moment we seemed not destined to come to a good understanding with respect to payment, I hoped that he would have, at least, the kindness to grant the favour of his custom to my brother host of the Aigle d'Or ; but M. Porthos replied, that my hotel being the best, he should remain where he was.

" This reply was too flattering to allow me to insist on his departure. I confined myself then to begging him to give up his chamber, which is the handsomest in the hotel, and to be satisfied with a pretty little closet on the third floor. But to this M. Porthos replied, that as he every moment expected his mistress, who was one of the greatest ladies of the court, I might easily comprehend that the chamber he did me the honour to occupy in my house was itself very mean for the visit of such a personage.

" Nevertheless, whilst acknowledging the truth of what he said, I thought proper to insist ; but without even giving himself the trouble to enter into any discussion with me, he took one of his pistols, laid it on his table, day and night, and said that at the first word that should be spoken to him about removing, either within the house or out of it, he would blow out the brains of the person who should be so imprudent as to meddle with a matter which only concerned himself. So from that time, monsieur, nobody enters his chamber but his servant."

" What ! Mousqueton is here, then ?"

" Oh ! yes, monsieur ; five days after your departure, he came back, and in a very bad condition, too ; it appears that he had met with dis-agreeables, likewise, on his journey. Unfortunately he is more nimble than his master ; so that for the sake of his master, he sets us all at defiance ; and as he thinks we might refuse what he asked for, he takes all he wants without asking at all."

" Well, it's a fact," said D'Artagnan, " I always observed a great degree of intelligence and devotedness to his master in Mousqueton."

" Very possibly, monsieur : but suppose if I should happen to be brought in contact, only four times a year, with such intelligence and devotedness,—why, I should be a ruined man !"

" No ! for Porthos will pay you."

" Hum !" said the host, in a doubting tone.

" Why, it is not to be imagined that the favourite of a great lady will be allowed to be inconvenienced for such a paltry sum as he owes you."

" If I durst say what I believe on that head——"

" What you believe ?"

" I ought rather to say : what I know."

" What you know ?"

" Aye ; even what I am sure of."

" Well : tell me what this is you are so sure of ?"

" I would say, that I know this great lady."

" You ?"

" Yes ; I."

" And how did you become acquainted with her ?"

" Oh ! monsieur, if I could believe I might trust in your discretion."

" Speak : by the word of a gentleman, you shall have no cause to repent of your confidence."

" Well, monsieur, you may conceive that uneasiness makes us do many things."

" What have you done ?"

" Oh ! nothing that I had not a right to do in the character of a creditor."

" Go on !"

" Instead of putting the letter in the post, which is never safe, I took advantage of one of my lads being going to Paris, and I ordered him to convey the letter to this duchess himself. This was fulfilling the intentions of M. Porthos, who had desired us to be so careful of this letter, was it not ?"

" Nearly so."

" Well, monsieur, do you know who this great lady is ?"

" No ; I have heard Porthos speak of her, that's all."

" Do you know who this pretended duchess is ?"

" I repeat to you, I don't know her."

" Why, she is the wife of a procureur of the Châtelet, monsieur, named Madame Coquenard ; who, although she is at least fifty, still gives herself jealous airs. It struck me as very odd, that a princess should live in the Rue aux Ours."

" But how do you know all this ?"

" Because she flew into a great passion on receiving the letter, say-

ing that M. Porthos was a fickle, inconstant man, and that she was sure
it was on account of some woman he had received this wound."

" What, has he been wounded then ?"

" Oh ! good Lord ! what have I said ?"

" You said that Porthos was wounded."

" Yes, but he has forbidden me so strictly to say so !"

" And why so ?"

" Zounds ! monsieur, only because he had boasted that he would perforate the stranger with whom you left him in dispute where he pleased,
whereas the stranger, on the contrary, in spite of all his rhodomontades,
quickly brought him on his back. Now, as M. Porthos, is a very vain-
glorious man, he insists that nobody shall know he has received this
wound, except the duchess, whom he endeavoured to interest by an
account of his adventure."

" It is a wound, then, that confines him to his bed ?"

" Ah ! and something like a wound, too ! I assure you. Your friend's
soul must stick pretty tight to his body."

" Were you there, then ?"

" Monsieur, I followed them from curiosity, so that I saw the combat
without the combatants seeing me.'

" And what took place ?"

" Oh ! the affair was not long, I assure you. They placed themselves
in guard : the stranger made a feint and a lunge, and that so rapidly,
that when M. de Porthos came to the *parade*, he had already three
inches of steel in his breast. He immediately fell backwards. The
stranger placed the point of his sword at his throat ; and M. Porthos,
finding himself at the mercy of his adversary, allowed himself to be
conquered. Upon which the stranger asked his name, and learning
that it was Porthos, and not M. D'Artagnan, he assisted him to rise,
brought him back to the hotel, mounted his horse, and disappeared.

" So it was with M. D'Artagnan this stranger meant to quarrel ?"

" It appears so."

" And do you know what has become of him ?"

" No; I never saw him until that moment ; and have not seen him
since."

" Very well ! now I know all that I wish to know. Porthos's chamber
is, you say, on the first story, No. 1 ?"

" Yes, monsieur, the handsomest in the auberge ; a chamber that I
could have had occupied ten times over."

"Well, well, be satisfied," said D'Artagnan, laughing ; " Porthos will
pay you with the money of the Duchess Coquenard."

" Oh ! monsieur, procureuse or duchess, if she will but draw her purse-
strings, it will be all the same ; but she positively answered that she was
tired of the exigencies and infidelities of M. Porthos, and that she would
not send him a denier."

" And did you convey this answer to your guest ?"

" We took good care not to do that ; he would have found out how
we had delivered the letter."

" So that he is still in expectation of his money ?"

" Oh! mon Dieu! yes, monsieur! Yesterday he wrote again, but it was his servant who this time put his letter in the post."

" Do you say the procureuse is old and ugly ?"

" Fifty at least, monsieur, and not at all handsome, according to Pathaud's account."

" In that case, you may be quite at ease : she will soon be softened; besides, Porthos cannot owe you much."

" How, not much! Twenty good pistoles, already, without reckoning the doctor. Bless you, he denies himself nothing ; it may easily be seen he has been accustomed to live pretty well."

" Never mind! if his mistress abandons him, he will find friends, I will answer for it. So, my dear host, be not uneasy, and continue to take all the care of him that his situation requires."

" Monsieur has promised me not to open his mouth about the procureuse, and not to say a word of the wound ?"

" That's a thing agreed upon ; you have my word."

" Oh! he would kill me! I am sure he would!"

" Don't be afraid : he is not so much of a devil as he appears to be."

Saying these words, D'Artagnan went upstairs, leaving his host a little better satisfied with respect to two things in which he appeared to be very much interested—his debt and his life.

At the top of the stairs, upon the most conspicuous door of the corridor, was traced in black ink a gigantic "No. 1;" D'Artagnan knocked, and upon being desired to come in, entered the chamber.

Porthos was in bed, and was playing a game at lansquenet with Mousqueton, to keep his hand in, whilst a spit loaded with partridges was turning before the fire, and, at each side of a large chimney-piece, over two chafing-dishes, were boiling two stew-pans, from which exhaled a double odour of *gibelotte* and *matelotte*, very grateful to the olfactory nerves. In addition to this, he perceived that the top of a wardrobe and the marble of a commode were covered with empty bottles.

At the sight of his friend, Porthos uttered a loud cry of joy ; and Mousqueton, rising respectfully, yielded his place to him, and went to give an eye to the two stew-pans, of which he appeared to have the particular inspection.

"Ah! pardieu! is that you!" said Porthos to D'Artagnan. "You are right welcome, my dear fellow!—I hope you will excuse my not coming to meet you. But," added he, looking at D'Artagnan, with a certain degree of uneasiness, " you know what has happened to me ?"

" Not exactly."

" Has the host told you nothing, then?"

" I asked after you, and came up as soon as I could."

Porthos seemed to breathe more freely.

"And what has happened to you, my dear Porthos ?" continued D'Artagnan.

" Why, on making a thrust at my adversary, whom I had already hit three times, and with whom I meant to finish by a fourth, I put my foot on a stone, slipped, and strained my knee,"

" Indeed !"

" Honour ! Luckily for the rascal, for I should have left him dead on the spot, I assure you."

" And what became of him ?"

" Oh! I don't know ; he had enough, and set off without waiting for the rest.   But you, my dear D'Artagnan, what has happened to you?"

" So that this strain of the knee," continued D'Artagnan, " my dear Porthos, keeps you here in bed ?"

" Mon Dieu ! that's all ; I shall be about again in a few days."

" Why did you not have yourself conveyed to Paris?   Living here must be cruelly wearisome."

" That was my intention ; but, my dear friend, I have one thing to confess to you."

" What's that ?"

" It is, that, as I found it cruelly wearisome, as you say, and as I had the seventy-five pistoles in my pocket which you had distributed to me, in order to amuse myself, I invited a gentleman who was travelling this way to walk up, and proposed a cast of dice to him.   He accepted my challenge, and, *ma foi!* my seventy-five pistoles quickly passed from my pocket to his, without reckoning my horse, which he won into the bargain.   But you, I want to know about you, D'Artagnan ?"

" What can you expect, my dear Porthos ; a man is not privileged in all ways," said D'Artagnan ; " you know the proverb : 'Unlucky at play, lucky in love.'   You are too fortunate in your love, for play not to take its revenge ; what consequence can the reverses of fortune be to you?—have you not, happy rogue as you are, have you not your duchess, who cannot fail to come to your assistance ?"

" Well ! you see, my dear D'Artagnan, with what ill luck I play," replied Porthos ; "with the most careless air in the world I wrote to her to send me fifty louis, or so, of which I stood absolutely in need, on account of my accident."

" Well !"

" Well ! she must be at her country-seat, for she has not answered me."

" Indeed !"

" No ; so I yesterday addressed another letter to her, still more pressing than the first ; but you are come, my dear fellow, let us speak of you.   I confess I began to be very uneasy on your account."

" But your host behaves very well towards you, as it appears, friend Porthos," said D'Artagnan, directing the sick man's attention to the full stewpans and the empty bottles.

" So, so !" replied Porthos.   " It is not above four days ago since the impertinent jackanapes gave me his bill, and I was forced to turn both him and his bill out of the door ; so that I am here something in the fashion of a conqueror, holding my position, as it were, by conquest. So, you see, being in constant fear of being forced in that position, I am armed to the teeth."

" And yet," said D'Artagnan, laughing, " it appears to me that from time to time you must make sorties." And he again pointed to the bottles and the stewpans.

"No, not I, unfortunately!" said Porthos. "This miserable strain confines me to my bed, but Mousqueton forages, and brings in provisions. Friend Mousqueton, you see that we have a reinforcement arrived, and we must have an increase of provisions."

"Mousqueton," said D'Artagnan, "you must render me a service."

"Of what kind, monsieur?"

"You must give your receipt to Planchet; I may be besieged in my turn, and I shall not be sorry for him to be able to let me enjoy the same advantages with which you gratify your master."

"Lord, monsieur! there is nothing more easy," said Mousqueton, with a modest air. "It only requires to be sharp, that's all. I was brought up in the country, and my father, in his leisure time, was something of a poacher."

"And how did he occupy the rest of his time?"

"Monsieur, he carried on a trade, which I have always found pretty productive."

"What was that?"

"As it was a time of war between the Catholics and the Huguenots, and as he saw the Catholics exterminate the Huguenots and the Huguenots exterminate the Catholics, and all in the name of religion, he adopted a mixed belief, which permitted him to be sometimes a Catholic, sometimes a Huguenot. Now, he was accustomed to walk, with his fowling-piece on his shoulder, behind the hedges which border the roads, and when he saw a Catholic coming alone, the Protestant religion immediately prevailed in his mind. He lowered his gun in the direction of the traveller; then, when he was within ten paces of him, he commenced a conversation which almost always ended by the traveller's abandoning his purse to save his life. I must at the same time say that when he saw a Huguenot coming, he felt himself urged with such an ardent Catholic zeal that he could not understand how, a quarter of an hour before, he had been able to have any doubts upon the superiority of our holy religion. For my part, I am, monsieur, a Catholic; my father, faithful to his principles, having made my elder brother a Huguenot."

"And what was the end of this worthy man?" asked D'Artagnan.

"Oh! of the most unfortunate kind, monsieur. One day he was surprised in a hollow way between a Huguenot and a Catholic, with both of whom he had before had to do, and who both knew him again; so they united against him and hung him on a tree; then they came and boasted of their fine exploit in the cabaret of the next village, where my brother and I were drinking."

"And what did you do?" said D'Artagnan.

"We let them tell their story out," replied Mousqueton. Then, as in leaving the cabaret they took different directions, my brother went and hid himself on the road of the Catholic, and I on that of the Huguenot. Two hours after, all was over; we had done the business of both of them, admiring the foresight of our poor father, who had taken the pre-caution to bring each of us up in a different religion."

" Well, I must allow, as you say, your father must have been a very intelligent fellow. And you say in his leisure moments the worthy man was a poacher ?"

" Yes, monsieur, and it was he who taught me to lay a snare and ground a line. The consequence is that when I saw our shabby host wanted to feed us upon lumps of fat meat fit for labourers, which did not at all suit such delicate stomachs as ours, I had recourse to a little of my old trade. Whilst walking near the wood of Monsieur le Prince, I laid a few snares in the runs ; and whilst reclining on the banks of his highness's pieces of water, I slipped a few lines into his fish-ponds. So that now, thanks be to God ! we do not want, as monsieur can testify, for partridges, rabbits, carp, or eels—all light, wholesome food, suitable for sick persons."

" But the wine," said D'Artagnan, " who furnishes the wine ? That, at least, must be your host ?"

" That is to say yes and no."

" How yes and no ?"

" He furnishes it, it is true, but he does not know that he has that honour."

" Explain yourself, Mousqueton, your conversation is full of instruc-tive things."

" This is it, monsieur. It has so chanced that I met with a Spaniard in my peregrinations, who had seen many countries, and among them the New World."

" What the deuce connection can the New World have with the bottles which are on the commode and the press ?"

" Patience, monsieur, everything will come in its turn."

" You are right, Mousqueton, I leave it to you."

" This Spaniard had in his service a lackey who had accompanied him in his voyage to Mexico. This lackey was my compatriot, and we became the more intimate for there being many resemblances of cha-racter between us. We loved sporting of all kinds better than any-thing, so that he related to me how, in the plains of the Pampas, the natives hunt the tiger and the wild bull with simple running nooses, which they throw round the necks of those terrible animals. At first I would not believe that they could attain such a degree of skill as to throw to a distance of twenty or thirty paces the end of a cord with such nicety ; but in face of the proof I was obliged to acknowledge the truth of the recital. My friend placed a bottle at the distance of thirty paces, and at each cast he caught the neck of the bottle in his running-noose. I practised this exercise, and as nature has endowed me with some faculties, at this day I can throw the *lasso* with any man in the world. Well, do you understand, monsieur? Our host has a well-furnished cellar, the key of which never leaves him ; only this cellar has a loop-hole. Now, through this loop-hole I throw my *lasso*, and as I now know which part of the cellar the best wine is in, that's my point for sport. Thus you see, monsieur, what the New World has to do with the bottles which are on the commode and the clothes-press. Now, will you taste our wine, and, without prejudice, say what you think of it ?"

"Thank you, my friend, thank you ; unfortunately I have just breakfasted."

"Well," said Porthos, "arrange your table, Mousqueton, and whilst we breakfast, D'Artagnan will relate to us what has happened to him during the ten days since he left us."

"Willingly," said D'Artagnan.

Whilst Porthos and Mousqueton were breakfasting with the appetites of convalescents, and with that brotherly cordiality which unites men in misfortune, D'Artagnan related how Aramis, being wounded, was obliged to stop at Crèvecœur, how he had left Athos fighting at Amiens with four men who accused him of being a coiner, and how he, D'Artagnan, had been forced to run the Count de Wardes through the body in order to reach England.

But there the confidence of D'Artagnan stopped : he only added, that on his return from Great Britain, he had brought back four magnificent horses, one for himself, and one for each of his companions ; then he informed Porthos that the one which was intended for him was already installed in the stable of the hotel.

At this moment Planchet entered, to inform his master that the horses were sufficiently refreshed, and that it would be possible to sleep at Clermont.

As D'Artagnan was tolerably reassured with regard to Porthos, and as he was anxious to obtain news of his two other friends, he held out his hand to the wounded man, and told him he was about to resume his route in order to prosecute his researches. For the rest, as he reckoned upon returning through Chantilly, if, in seven or eight days, Porthos were still at the hotel of the Grand St. Martin, he would call for him on his way.

Porthos replied that, according to all probability, his sprain would not permit him to depart yet awhile. Besides, it was necessary he should stay at Chantilly, to wait for the answer from his duchess.

D'Artagnan wished that that answer might be prompt and favourable ; and after having again recommended Porthos to the care of Mousqueton, and paid his expenses at the hotel, he resumed his route with Planchet, who was already relieved of one of his led horses.

CHAPTER XXVI.

ARAMIS'S THESIS.

D'ARTAGNAN had said nothing to Porthos of his wound or of his procureuse. Our Béarnais was a prudent lad, however young he might be. Consequently he had appeared to believe all that the vain-glorious musketeer had told him ; convinced that no friendship will hold out against a surprised secret, particularly when pride is deeply interested in that secret ; besides, we feel always a sort of mental superiority over those with whose lives we are better acquainted than they are aware of. Now, in his projects of intrigue for the future, and determined as he was to make his three friends the instruments of his fortune, D'Artagnan was not sorry at getting in his grasp beforehand the invisible strings by which he reckoned upon moving them.

And yet, as he journeyed along, a profound sadness weighed upon his heart ; he thought of that young and pretty Madame Bonacieux, who was to have paid him so richly for all his devotedness ; but, let us hasten to say that this sadness possessed the young man less from the regret of the happiness he had missed, than from the fear he entertained that some serious misfortune had befallen the poor woman. For himself, he had no doubt she was a victim of the cardinal's vengeance, and, as was well known, the vengeance of his eminence was terrible. How he had found grace in the eyes of the minister, was what he himself was ignorant of, but, without doubt, what M. de Cavois would have revealed to him, if the captain of the guards had met with him at home.

Nothing makes time pass more quickly or more shortens a journey than a thought which absorbs in itself all the faculties of the organisation of him who thinks. The external existence then resembles a sleep of which this thought is the dream. By its influence, time has no longer measure, space has no longer distance. We depart from one place and arrive at another—that is all. Of the interval passed through, nothing remains in the memory but a vague mist in which a thousand confused images of trees, mountains, and landscapes are lost. It was as a prey to this hallucination that D'Artagnan travelled, at whatever pace his horse pleased, the six or eight leagues that separated Chantilly from Crèvecœur, without his being able to remember, on his arrival in the village, any of the things he had passed or met with on the road.

There only his memory returned to him, he shook his head, perceived the cabaret at which he had left Aramis, and putting his horse to the trot, he shortly pulled up at the door.

This time it was not a host, but a hostess who received him : D'Artagnan was a physiognomist, his eye took in at a glance the plump, cheerful countenance of the mistress of the place, and he at once perceived there was no occasion for dissembling with her, or of fearing anything on the part of one blessed with such a joyous physiognomy.

"My good dame," asked D'Artagnan, "can you tell me what is become of one of my friends, whom we were obliged to leave here about twelve days ago ?"

"A handsome young man, three or four and twenty years old, mild, amiable, and well made ?"

"Exactly the man : wounded, moreover, in the shoulder ?"

"Just so.—Well, monsieur, he is still here !"

"Ah ! Pardieu ! my dear dame," said D'Artagnan, springing from his horse, and throwing the bridle to Planchet, "you restore me to life; where is this dear Aramis? let me embrace him! I am quite anxious to see him again."

"I beg your pardon, monsieur, but I doubt whether he can see you at this moment."

"Why so? Has he got a lady with him?"

"Jesus! what do you mean by that? Poor lad! No, monsieur, he has not got a lady with him!"

"With whom is he, then?"

"With the curé of Montdidier and the superior of the Jesuits of Amiens."

"Good heavens!" cried D'Artagnan, "is the poor fellow worse, then?"

"Oh! no, monsieur, quite the contrary; but after his illness grace touched him, and he determined to enter into orders."

"Oh! that's it!" said D'Artagnan, "I had forgotten that he was only a musketeer for the time."

"Is monsieur still anxious to see him?"

"More so than ever."

"Well, monsieur has only to take the right-hand staircase in the yard and knock at No. 5, on the second floor."

D'Artagnan walked quickly in the direction pointed out, and found one of those exterior staircases that are still to be seen in the yards of our old-fashioned auberges. But there was no getting thus at the place of sojourn of the future abbé; the defiles of the chamber of Aramis were neither more nor less guarded than the gardens of Armida: Bazin was stationed in the corridor, and barred his passage with so much the more intrepidity, that, after many years of trial, Bazin found himself near arriving at a result of which he had ever been ambitious.

In fact, the dream of poor Bazin had always been to serve a churchman, and he awaited with impatience the moment, always contemplated in the future, when Aramis would throw aside the uniform and assume the cassock. The daily renewed purpose of the young man, that the moment would not long be delayed, had alone kept him in the service of a musketeer, a service in which, he said, his soul was in constant jeopardy.

Bazin was then at the height of joy. According to all probability, this time his master would not retract. The union of physical pain with moral uneasiness had produced the effect so long desired; Aramis, suffering at once in body and mind, had at length fixed his eyes and his thoughts upon religion, and he had considered as a warning from heaven the double accident which had happened to him, that is to say, the sudden disappearance of his mistress and the wound in his shoulder.

It may be easily understood, that in the present disposition of his master, nothing could be more disagreeable to Bazin than the arrival of D'Artagnan, which might cast his master back again into that vortex of mundane affairs that had so long carried him away. He resolved then to defend the door bravely; and as, betrayed by the mistress of the auberge, he could not say that Aramis was absent, he endeavoured to prove to the new comer that it would be the height of indiscretion to disturb his master in his pious conference, which had commenced with the morning, and would not be, as Bazin said, terminated before night.

But D'Artagnan took very little heed of the eloquent discourse of Master Bazin, and as he had no desire to support a polemic discussion with his friend's valet, he simply moved him out of the way with one hand, and with the other turned the handle of the door, No. 5.

The door opened, and D'Artagnan penetrated into the chamber.

Aramis, in a black gown, his head enveloped in a sort of round, flat cap, not much unlike a calotte, was seated before an oblong table, covered with rolls of paper and enormous volumes in folio ; at his right hand was placed the superior of the Jesuits, and on his left the curé of Montdidier. The curtains were half drawn, and only admitted the mysterious light calculated for beatific reveries. All the mundane objects that generally strike the eye on entering the room of a young man, particularly when that young man is a musketeer, had disappeared as if by enchantment, and, for fear, no doubt, that the sight of them might bring his master back to ideas of this world, Bazin had laid his hands upon sword, pistols, plumed hat, and embroideries and laces of all kinds and sorts.

But in their stead and place, D'Artagnan thought he perceived in an obscure corner a discipline cord suspended from a nail in the wall.

At the noise made by D'Artagnan in entering, Aramis lifted up his head and beheld his friend. But to the great astonishment of the young man, the sight of him did not produce much effect upon the musketeer, so completely was his mind detached from the things of this world.

" Good day to you, dear D'Artagnan ; believe me, I am very glad to see you."

" So am I delighted to see you," said D'Artagnan, " although I am not yet sure that it is Aramis I am speaking to."

" To himself, my friend, to himself ! but what makes you doubt ?"

" I was afraid I had made a mistake in the chamber, and that I had found my way into the apartment of some churchman ; then another error seized me on seeing you in company with these gentlemen—I was afraid you were dangerously ill."

The two men in black, who guessed D'Artagnan's meaning, darted at him a glance which might have been thought threatening ; but D'Artagnan took no heed of it.

" I disturb you, perhaps, my dear Aramis," continued D'Artagnan, " for by what I see, I am led to believe you are confessing to these gentlemen."

Aramis coloured imperceptibly.

" You disturb me ! oh ! quite the contrary, dear friend, I swear ; and as a proof of what I say, permit me to declare I am rejoiced to see you safe and sound."

" Ah ! he'll come round !" thought D'Artagnan, " that's not bad !"

" For this gentleman, who is my friend, has just escaped from a seri-

6us danger," continued Aramis with unction, pointing to D'Artagnan with his hand, and addressing the two ecclesiastics.

" Give God praise, monsieur," replied they, bowing.

" I have not failed to do so, your reverences," replied the young man, returning their salutation.

" You arrive very àpropos, D'Artagnan," said Aramis, "and by taking part in our discussion, may assist us with your intelligence. M. le Principal of Amiens, M. le Curé of Montdidier, and I, are arguing upon certain theological questions, with which we have been much interested ; I shall be delighted to have your opinion."

" The opinion of the man of the sword can have very little weight," replied D'Artagnan, who began to get uneasy at the turn things were taking, " and you had better be satisfied, believe me, with the knowledge of these gentlemen."

The two men in black bowed in their turn.

" On the contrary," replied Aramis, "your opinion will be very valuable ; the question is this : Monsieur le Principal thinks that my thesis ought to be dogmatic and didactic."

" Your thesis ! are you then making a thesis ?"

" Without doubt," replied the Jesuit : " in the examination which precedes ordination, a thesis is always requisite."

" Ordination !" cried D'Artagnan, who could not believe what the hostess and Bazin had successively told him ; and he gazed, half stupefied, upon the three persons before him.

" Now," continued Aramis, taking the same graceful position in his easy chair that he would have assumed in a *ruelle*, and complacently examining his hand, which was as white and plump as that of a woman, and which he held in the air to cause the blood to descend from it, " now, as you have heard, D'Artagnan, M. le Principal is desirous that my thesis should be dogmatic, whilst I, for my part, would rather it should be ideal.   This is the reason why M. le Principal has proposed to me the following subject, which has not yet been treated upon, and in which I perceive there is matter for magnificent developments :—
' *Utraque manus in benedicendo clericis inferioribus necessaria est.*' "

D'Artagnan, whose erudition we are well acquainted with, evinced no more interest on hearing this quotation, than he had of that of M. de Tréville, in allusion to the presents he fancied he had received from the Duke of Buckingham.

" Which means," resumed Aramis, that he might perfectly understand the matter ; " ' The two hands are indispensable for priests of the inferior orders, when they bestow the benediction.' "

" An admirable subject !" cried the Jesuit.

" Admirable and dogmatic !" repeated the curate, who, about as strong as D'Artagnan with respect to Latin, carefully watched the Jesuit, in order to keep step with him, and repeated his words like an echo.

As to D'Artagnan, he remained perfectly insensible to the enthusiasm of the two men in black.

"Yes, admirable! *prorsus admirabile!*" continued Aramis; "but which requires a profound study of both the Scriptures and the Fathers. Now, I have confessed to these learned ecclesiastics, and that in all humility, that the duties of mounting guard and the service of the king have caused me to neglect study a little. I should find myself therefore, more at my ease, *facilius natans,* in a subject of my own choice, which would be to these hard theological questions what morals are to metaphysics in philosophy."

D'Artagnan began to be tired, and so did the *curé.*

"See what an exordium!" cried the Jesuit.

"Exordium," repeated the *curé,* for the sake of saying something. "*Quemadmodum inter cælorum immensitatem.*"

Aramis cast a glance upon D'Artagnan, to see what effect all this produced; and found his friend gaping enough to split his jaws.

"Let us speak French, worthy father," said he to the Jesuit, "M. D'Artagnan will enjoy our conversation the more."

"Yes," replied D'Artagnan; "I am fatigued with riding, and all this Latin confuses me."

"Certainly," replied the Jesuit, a little thrown out, whilst the *curé* greatly delighted, turned upon D'Artagnan a look full of gratitude: "well, let us see what is to be derived from this gloss."

"Moses, the servant of God—he was but a servant, please to understand! Moses blessed with the hands; he held out both his arms, whilst the Hebrews beat their enemies, and then he blessed them with his two hands. Besides, what does the gospel say: '*Imponite manus,*' and not '*manum*.' place the hands and not the hand."

"Place the hands," repeated the *curé,* with the proper gesture.

"St. Peter, on the contrary, of whom the popes are the successors," continued the Jesuit: "'*Porrige digitos*.' present the fingers. Do you see that, now?"

"Certes," replied Aramis, in a pleased tone, "but the thing is subtle."

"The fingers!" resumed the Jesuit, "St. Peter blessed with the fingers. The pope, therefore, blesses with the fingers. And with how many fingers does he bless? With *three* fingers, to be sure, one for the Father, one for the Son, and one for the Holy Ghost."

All crossed themselves; D'Artagnan thought it was proper to follow this example.

"The pope is the successor of St. Peter, and represents the three divine powers; the rest, *ordines inferiores,* of the ecclesiastical hierarchy, bless in the name of the holy archangels and angels. The most humble clerks, such as our deacons and sacristans, bless with *goupillons* (brushes for sprinkling holy water), which resemble an infinite number of blessing fingers. There is the subject simplified. *Argumentum omni denudatum ornamento.* I could make of that subject two volumes of the size of this——" and, in his enthusiasm, he struck a St. Chrysostom in folio, which made the table bend beneath its weight.

D'Artagnan trembled.

" Certes," said Aramis, " I do justice to the beauties of this thesis ; but, at the same time, I perceive it would be overwhelming for me. I had chosen this text;—tell me, dear D'Artagnan, if it is not to your taste : ' *Non inutile est desiderium in oblatione :*' or, still better, ' A little regret is not unsuitable in an offering to the Lord.' "

" Stop there !" cried the Jesuit, " for that thesis touches closely upon heresy : there is a proposition almost like it in the *Augustinus* of the heresiarch Jansenius, whose book will, sooner or later, be burnt by the hands of the hangman. Take care, my young friend ; you are inclining towards false doctrines, my young friend, you will be lost !"

" You will be lost," said the *curé*, shaking his head sorrowfully.

" You approach that famous point of free-will, which is a mortal rock. You face the insinuations of the Pelagians and the demi-Pelagians."

" But, my reverend——" replied Aramis, a little amazed by the shower of arguments that poured upon his head.

" How will you prove," continued the Jesuit, without allowing him to speak, " that we ought to regret the world when we offer ourselves to God ? Listen to this dilemma : God is God, and the world is the devil. To regret the world is to regret the devil ; that is my conclusion."

" And, that is mine, also," said the *curé*.

" But for Heaven's sake——" resumed Aramis.

" *Desideras diabolum,* unhappy man," cried the Jesuit.

" He regrets the devil ! Ah ! my young friend," added the *curé*, groaning, " do not regret the devil, I implore you !"

D'Artagnan felt himself bewildered ; he appeared to be in a mad-house, and that he was becoming as mad as those he saw. He was, however, forced to hold his tongue, from not comprehending half the language they employed.

" But listen to me, then," resumed Aramis, with politeness mingled with a little impatience. " I do not say I regret ; no, I will never pronounce that sentence, which would not be orthodox."

The Jesuit raised his hands towards heaven, and the curate did the same.

" No, but pray grant me that it is acting with an ill grace to offer to the Lord only that with which we are perfectly disgusted ? Don't you think so, D'Artagnan ?"

" *Pardieu !* I think so, indeed," cried he.

The Jesuit and the *curé* quite started from their chairs.

" This is the point I start from, it is a syllogism ; the world is not wanting in attractions, I quit the world, then I make a sacrifice ; now, the Scripture says positively, 'Make a sacrifice unto the Lord.' "

" That is true," said his antagonists.

" And then," said Aramis, pinching his ear, to make it red, as he rubbed his hands to make them white, " and then I made a certain rondeau upon it last year, which I showed to M. de Voiture, and that great man paid me a thousand handsome compliments upon it."

" A rondeau !" said the Jesuit, disdainfully.

"A rondeau !" said the *curé*, mechanically.

"Repeat it ! repeat it !" cried D'Artagnan ; "it will make a little change."

"Not so, for it is religious," replied Aramis ; "it is theology in verse."

"The devil !" said D'Artagnan.

"Here it is," said Aramis, with a little look of diffidence, which, however, was not exempt from a shade of hypocrisy :

> "Vous qui pleurez un passé plein de charmes,
> Et qui trainez des jours infortunés,
> Tous vos malheurs se verront terminés,
> Quand à Dieu seul vous offrirez vos larmes,
> 　　　Vous qui pleurez !

> You who weep for pleasures fled,
> Whilst dragging on a life of care,
> All your woes will melt in air,
> If at God's feet your tears you shed,
> 　　　You who weep !"

D'Artagnan and the *curé* appeared pleased.　The Jesuit persisted in his opinion.

"Beware of a profane taste in your theological style.　What says Augustin on this subject : *Severus sit clericorum verbo.*"

"Yes, let the sermon be clear," said the *curé*.

"Now," hastily interrupted the Jesuit, on seeing that his acolyte was going astray, "now, your thesis would please the ladies ; it would have the success of one of M. Patru's pleadings."

"I hope to God it may !" cried Aramis, transported.

"There it is," cried the Jesuit ; "the world still speaks within you in a loud voice, *altissimâ voce.* You follow the world, my young friend, and I tremble lest grace prove not efficacious."

"Be satisfied, my reverend father, I can depend upon myself."

"Mundane presumption !"

"I know myself, father ; my resolution is irrevocable."

"Then you persist in continuing that thesis ?"

"I feel myself called upon to treat that, and no other ; I will see about the continuation of it, and to-morrow I hope you will be satisfied with the corrections I shall have made in consequence of your advice."

"Work slowly," said the *curé ;* "we leave you in an excellent tone of mind."

"Yes, the ground is all sown," said the Jesuit, "and we have not to fear that one portion of the seed may have fallen upon stone, another upon the highway, or that the birds of heaven have eaten the rest, *aves cœli comederunt illam.*"

"Plague stifle you and your Latin !" said D'Artagnan, who began to feel all his patience exhausted.

"Farewell, my son," said the *curé*, "till to-morrow."

"Till to-morrow, my rash young friend," said the Jesuit.　"You promise to become one of the lights of the Church ; Heaven grant that this light prove not a devouring fire !"

D'Artagnan, who, for an hour past, had been gnawing his nails with impatience, was beginning to attack the flesh.

The two men in black rose, bowed to Aramis and D'Artagnan, and advanced towards the door. Bazin, who had been standing listening to all this controversy with a pious jubilation, sprang towards them, took the breviary of the *curé* and the missal of the Jesuit, and walked respectfully before them, to clear their way.

Aramis conducted them to the foot of the stairs, and then immediately came up again to D'Artagnan, whose senses were still in a state of confusion.

When left alone, the two friends at first observed an embarrassed silence ; it, however, became necessary for one of them to break it the first, and as D'Artagnan appeared determined to leave that honour to his companion—

" You see," said Aramis, " that I am returned to my original ideas."

" Yes ; efficacious grace has touched you, as that gentleman said just now."

" Oh, these plans of retreat have been formed for a long time ; you have often heard me speak of them, have you not, my friend ?"

" Yes ; but I must confess that I always thought you were joking."

" With such sort of things ! Oh, D'Artagnan !"

" The devil ! Why, people joke with death."

" And people are wrong, D'Artagnan ; for death is the door which leads to perdition or to salvation."

" Granted ; but, if you please, let us not theologise, Aramis ; you must have had enough for to-day ; as for me, I have almost forgotten the little Latin I have ever known. Then I confess to you that I have eaten nothing since ten o'clock this morning, and I am devilish hungry."

" We will dine directly, my friend ; only you must please to remember that this is Friday : now, on such a day I cannot eat meat or see it eaten. If you can be satisfied with my dinner, it consists of cooked tetragones and fruits."

" What do you mean by tetragones ?" asked D'Artagnan, eagerly.

" I mean spinach," replied Aramis ; " but, on your account, I will add some eggs, and that is a serious infraction of the rule, for eggs are meat, since they engender chickens."

" This feast is not very succulent ; but never mind, I will put up with it for the sake of remaining with you."

" I am grateful to you for the sacrifice" said Aramis ; " but if your body be not greatly benefited by it, your soul will, be assured."

" And so, Aramis, you are decidedly going into the church ? What will our two friends say ? What will M. de Tréville say ? They will treat you as a deserter, I warn you."

" I do not enter the church—I re-enter it ; I deserted the church for the world, for you know that I committed violence upon myself when I became a musketeer."

" Who—I ? I know nothing about it."

"You don't know how I quitted the seminary?"

"Not at all."

"This is my history, then ; besides, the Scriptures say, ' Confess your-selves to one another,' and I confess to you, D'Artagnan."

"And I give you absolution beforehand ; you see, I am a good sort of a man."

"Do not jest with holy things, my friend."

"Go on, then ; I'll listen."

"I had been at the seminary from nine years old ; in three days I should have been twenty ; I was about to become an abbé, and all was told.

"One evening, I had gone, according to custom, to a house which I frequented with much pleasure ; when one is young, what can be ex-pected?—one is weak. An officer who saw me, with a jealous eye, reading the 'Lives of the Saints' to the mistress of the house, entered suddenly, and without being announced. That evening I had translated an episode of Judith, and had just communicated my verses to the lady, who made me all sorts of compliments, and, leaning on my shoulder, was reading them a second time. Her *pose*, which, I must admit, was rather free, wounded this gentleman's feelings. He said nothing, but when I went out he followed, and quickly came up with me.

"' Monsieur l'Abbé,' said he, ' do you like blows with a cane ?'

"' I cannot say, monsieur,' answered I ; ' no one has ever dared to give me any.'

"' Well, listen to me, then, Monsieur l'Abbé : if you venture again into the house in which I have met you this evening, I will dare, myself, Monsieur l'Abbé.'

"I really think I must have been frightened ; I became very pale, I felt my legs fail me, I sought for a reply, but could find none—I was silent.

"The officer waited for this reply, and, seeing it so long coming, he burst into a laugh, turned upon his heel, and re-entered the house.

"I returned to my seminary.

"I am a gentleman born—my blood is warm, as you may have re-marked, my dear D'Artagnan ; the insult was terrible, and, however unknown to the rest of the world, I felt it live and fester at the bottom of my heart. I informed my superiors that I did not feel myself suffi-ciently prepared for ordination, and, at my request, the ceremony was postponed for a year.

"I sought out the best fencing-master in Paris ; I made an agreement with him to take a.lesson every day, and every day during a year I took that lesson. Then, on the anniversary of the day on which I had been insulted, I hung my cassock on a peg, assumed the costume of a cavalier, and went to a ball given by a lady friend of mine, and to which I knew my man was invited. It was Rue des Francs-Bourgeois, close to La Force.

"As I expected, my officer was there. I went up to him, as he was singing a love ditty and looking tenderly at a lady, and interrupted him exactly in the middle of the second couplet,

"'Monsieur,' said I, 'is it still unpleasant to you that I should frequent a certain house of La Rue Payenne? And would you still bestow a caning upon me if I took it into my head to disobey you?'

"The officer looked at me with astonishment, and then said :

"'What is your business with me, monsieur? I do not know you.'

"'I am,' said I, 'the little abbé, who reads the "Lives of the Saints," and translates Judith into verse.'

"'Ah, ah! I recollect now,' said the officer, in a jeering tone ; 'well, what do you want with me?'

"'I want you to spare time to take a walk with me.'

"'To-morrow morning, if you like, and with the greatest pleasure.

"'No, not to-morrow morning, but immediately, if you please.'

"'If you absolutely insist upon it——'

"'I do—I insist upon it.'

"'Come, then. Ladies,' said the officer, 'do not disturb yourselves ; allow me time just to kill this gentleman, and I will return and finish the last couplet.

"We went out. I took him to the Rue Payenne, to exactly the same spot where, a year before, at the very same hour, he had paid me the compliment I have related to you. It was a superb moonlight night. We immediately drew, and at the first pass I laid him stark dead."

"The devil!" cried D'Artagnan.

"Now," continued Aramis, "as the ladies did not see the singer come back, and as he was found in the Rue Payenne, with a great sword-wound through his body, it was supposed that I had accommodated him thus, and the matter created some scandal, which obliged me to renounce the cassock for a time. Athos, whose acquaintance I made about that period, and Porthos, who had, in addition to my lessons, taught me some effective tricks of fence, prevailed upon me to solicit the uniform of a musketeer. The king entertained great regard for my father, who had fallen at the siege of Arras, and the uniform was granted. You may understand that the moment is arrived for me to re-enter into the bosom of the church."

"And why to-day, rather than yesterday, or to-morrow? What has happened to you to-day, to create all these melancholy ideas?"

"This wound, my dear D'Artagnan, has been a warning to me from Heaven."

"This wound? Bah! it is nearly healed, and I am sure that it is not that which at the present moment gives you the most pain."

"What do you think it is, then?" said Aramis, blushing.

"You have one in your heart, Aramis, one deeper and more painful, a wound made by a woman."

The eye of Aramis kindled, in spite of himself.

"Ah," said he, dissembling his emotion under a feigned carelessness, "do not talk of such things. What! I think of such things, and suffer love-pains? *Vanitas vanitatum!* According to your idea, then, my brain is turned! And for whom?—for some grisette, some fille-de-chambre, with whom I have trifled in some garrison! Fie!"

"I crave your pardon, my dear Aramis, but I thought you aimed higher."

"Higher? And who am I, to nourish such ambition?—a poor musketeer, a beggar and unknown, who hates slavery, and finds himself ill-placed in the world."

"Aramis, Aramis!" cried D'Artagnan, looking at his friend with an air of doubt.

"Dust I am, and to dust I return. Life is full of humiliations and sorrows," continued he, becoming still more melancholy; "all the ties which attach him to life break in the hand of man, particularly the golden ties. Oh, my dear D'Artagnan," resumed Aramis, giving to his voice a slight tone of bitterness, "trust me, conceal your wounds when you have any; silence is the last joy of the unhappy. Beware of giving any one the clue to your griefs; the curious suck our tears as flies suck the blood of a wounded hart."

"Alas! my dear Aramis," said D'Artagnan, in his turn heaving a profound sigh, "that is my history you are relating!"

"How?"

"Yes; a woman whom I love, whom I adore, has just been torn from me by force. I do not know where she is; I have no means of ascertaining where she has been taken to. She is perhaps a prisoner; she is perhaps dead!"

"Yes, but you have at least this consolation, that you can say to yourself she has not quitted you voluntarily; that if you learn no news of her, it is because all communication with you is interdicted: whilst I——"

"Whilst what?"

"Nothing," replied Aramis, "nothing."

"So you renounce the world, then, for ever; that is a settled thing; a resolution decreed?"

"For ever! You are my friend to-day, to-morrow you will be no more to me than a shadow; or rather, even, you will no longer exist for me. As for the world, it is a sepulchre, and nothing else."

"The devil! All this is very sad."

"What is to be said? My vocation commands me, it carries me away." D'Artagnan smiled, but made no answer. Aramis continued:

"And yet, whilst I do belong to the earth, I should wish to speak of you and of our friends."

"And on my part," said D'Artagnan, "I should have wished to speak of you, but I find you so completely detached from everything! Love you cry fie upon! friends are shadows! the world is a sepulchre!"

"Alas! you will find it so yourself," said Aramis, with a sigh.

"Well, then let us say no more about it," said D'Artagnan; "and let us burn this letter, which, no doubt, announces to you some fresh infidelity of your grisette or your fille-de-chambre."

"What letter?" cried Aramis, eagerly.

"A letter which was sent to your abode in your absence, and which was given to me for you."

" But from whom is that letter ?"

"Oh ! from some heart-broken waiting-woman, some desponding grisette ; from Madame de Chevreuse's fille-de-chambre, perhaps, who was obliged to return to Tours with her mistress, and who, in order to appear smart and attractive, stole some perfumed paper, and sealed her letter with a duchess's coronet."

" What do you say ?"

" Well ! I really think I must have lost it," said the young man, maliciously, whilst pretending to search for it. " But fortunately the world is a sepulchre ; the men, and consequently the women, are but shadows, and love is a sentiment upon which you cry fie ! fie !"

" D'Artagnan ! D'Artagnan !" cried Aramis, " you are killing me !"

"Well ! here it is at last !" said D'Artagnan, as he drew the letter from his pocket.

Aramis sprang towards him, seized the letter, read it, or rather devoured it, his countenance absolutely beaming with delight.

" This same waiting-maid seems to have an agreeable style," said the messenger, carelessly.

" Thanks, D'Artagnan, thanks !" cried Aramis, almost in a state of delirium. "She was forced to return to Tours ; she is not faithless ; she still loves me ! Dear friend, let me embrace you ; happiness almost stifles me !"

And the two friends began to dance round the venerable St. Chrysostom, kicking about famously the sheets of the thesis, which had fallen on the floor.

At that moment Bazin entered with the spinach and the omelette.

" Be off, you scoundrel !" cried Aramis, throwing his *calotte* in his face ; "return to whence you came ; take back those horrible vegetables, and that poor kickshaw ! Order a larded hare, a fat capon, a *gigot à l'ail* and four bottles of the best old Burgundy !"

Bazin, who looked at his master, without comprehending the cause of this change, in a melancholy manner, allowed the omelette to slip into the spinach, and the spinach on to the floor.

" Now is the moment to consecrate your existence to the King of Kings," said D'Artagnan, " if you persist in offering him a civility. *Non inutile desiderium oblatione.*"

" Get to the devil with your Latin. Let us drink, my dear D'Artagnan, *morbleu!* let us drink while the wine is fresh, let us drink heartily, and whilst we do so, tell me something about what is doing in the world yonder."

CHAPTER XXVII.

THE WIFE OF ATHOS.

" WELL, we have now to search for Athos," said D'Artagnan to the vivacious Aramis, when he had informed him of all that had passed since their departure from the capital, and that a good dinner had made one of them forget his thesis and the other his fatigue.

"Do you think, then, that any harm can have happened to him?" asked Aramis. "Athos is so cool, so brave, and handles his sword so skilfully."

"There is no doubt of all that ; nobody has a higher opinion of the courage and skill of Athos than I have ; but I like better to hear my sword clang against lances than against staves : I fear lest Athos should have been beaten down by a mob of serving-men : those fellows strike hard, and don't leave off in a hurry. This is my reason for wishing to set out again as soon as I possibly can."

"I will try to accompany you," said Aramis, "though I scarcely feel in a condition to mount on horseback. Yesterday I undertook to employ that cord which you see hanging against the wall, but pain prevented my continuing the pious exercise."

"That's the first time I ever heard of anybody trying to cure gun-shot wounds with a cat-o'-nine-tails ; but you were ill, and illness renders the head weak ; therefore you may be excused."

"When do you mean to set out?"

"To-morrow, at daybreak : sleep as soundly as you can to-night, and to-morrow, if you are strong enough, we will take our departure together."

"Till to-morrow, then," said Aramis ; "for, iron-nerved as you are, you must stand in need of repose."

The next morning, when D'Artagnan entered Aramis's chamber, he found him standing at the window.

"What are you looking at there?" asked D'Artagnan.

"Ma foi ! I am admiring three magnificent horses which the stable lads are leading about : it would be a pleasure worthy of a prince to travel upon such horses."

"Well, my dear Aramis, you may enjoy that pleasure, for one of those three horses is yours."

"Ah ! bah ! which of them ?"

"Which of the three you like, I have no preference."

"And the rich caparison, is that mine too?"

"Without doubt it is."

"You are laughing, D'Artagnan."

"No ; I have left off laughing now you speak French again."

"What, those rich holsters, that velvet housing, that saddle studded with silver, are they all mine?"

"Yours, and nobody else's, as the horse which is pawing the ground in eagerness is mine, and the other horse which is caracoling belongs to Athos."

"Peste ! they are three superb animals !"

"I am glad they please you."

"Why, it must have been the king who made you such a present?"

"To a certainty, it was not the cardinal ; but don't trouble yourself about where they come from, be satisfied that one of them is your property."

"I choose that which the red-headed boy is leading."

" Have it then."

" Vive Dieu ! That is enough to drive away all my pains ; I could ride upon him with thirty balls in my body. What handsome stirrups ! Hola ! Bazin, come here this minute."

Bazin made his appearance at the door, dull and spiritless.

" Furbish my sword, put my hat to rights, brush my cloak, and load my pistols !" said Aramis.

" That last order is useless," interrupted D'Artagnan : " there are loaded pistols in your holsters."

Bazin sighed.

" Come, master Bazin, make yourself easy ; people gain the kingdom of Heaven in all conditions of life."

" Monsieur was already such a good theologian," said Bazin, almost weeping ; " he might have become a bishop, perhaps a cardinal."

" Well ! but my poor Bazin, reflect a little ; of what use is it to be a churchman, pray ? You do not avoid going to war by that means ; you see the cardinal is about to make the next campaign, helm on head and partisan in hand ; and M. de Nogaret de la Valette, what do you say of him ? he is a cardinal likewise ; ask his lackey how often he has had to prepare lint for him."

" Alas !" signed Bazin, " I very well know, monsieur, that everything is turned topsy-turvy in the world now-a-days."

Whilst this dialogue was going on, the two young men and the poor lackey went down into the yard.

" Hold my stirrup, Bazin," cried Aramis.

And Aramis sprang into his saddle with his usual grace and light-ness ; but, after a few vaults and curvets of the noble animal, his rider felt his pains come on so insupportably, that he turned pale, and be-came unsteady in his seat. D'Artagnan, who, foreseeing such an event, had kept his eye on him, sprang towards him, caught him in his arms, and assisted him to his chamber.

" That's well, my dear Aramis, take care of yourself," said he, " I will go alone in search of Athos."

" You are a man of brass," replied Aramis.

" No : I have good luck, that is all ; but how do you mean to pass your time till I come back ? no more theses, no more glosses upon the fingers, or upon benedictions, hem !"

Aramis smiled : " I will make verses," said he.

" Yes, I dare say ; verses perfumed with the odour of the billet from the attendant of Madame de Chevreuse. Teach Bazin prosody, that will console him. As to the horse, ride him a little every day, till you become accustomed to him and recover your strength."

" Oh ! make yourself easy on that head," replied Aramis, " you will find me ready to follow you."

They took leave of each other, and in ten minutes, after commending his friend to the cares of the hostess and Bazin, D'Artagnan was trotting along in the direction of Amiens.

How was he going to find Athos, even should he find him at all ?

The position in which he had left him was critical ; he might, very probably, have succumbed. This idea, whilst darkening his brow, drew
several sighs from him, and caused him to formulate to himself a few
vows of vengeance. Of all his friends, Athos was the eldest, and the
least resembling him in appearance, in his tastes and sympathies.
And yet he entertained a marked preference for this gentleman. The
noble and distinguished air of Athos, those flashes of greatness, which
from time to time broke out from the shade in which he voluntarily
kept himself, that unalterable equality of temper which made him the
most pleasant companion in the world, that forced and malign gaiety,
that bravery which might have been termed blind if it had not been
the result of the rarest coolness,—such qualities attracted more than
the esteem, more than the friendship of D'Artagnan, they attracted his
admiration.

Indeed, when placed beside M. de Tréville, the elegant and noble
courtier, Athos, in his most cheerful days, might advantageously sustain a comparison : he was but of middle height ; but his person was
so admirably shaped, and so well proportioned, that more than once,
in his struggles with Porthos, he had overcome the giant whose physical
strength was proverbial amongst the musketeers : his head, with piercing
eyes, a straight nose, a chin cut like that of Brutus,—had altogether
an indefinable character of grandeur and grace ; his hands, of which he
took little care, were the envy of Aramis, who cultivated his with almond
paste and perfumed oil ; the sound of his voice was at once penetrating
and melodious, and then, that which was inconceivable in Athos, who
was always retiring, was that delicate knowledge of the world, and of
the usages of the most brilliant society, those manners of a high family
which appeared, as if unconsciously to himself, in his least actions.

If a repast were on foot, Athos presided over it better than any other,
placing every guest exactly in the rank which his ancestors had earned
for him, or that he had made for himself. If a question in heraldry
were started, Athos knew all the noble families of the kingdom, their
genealogy, their alliances, their arms, and the origin of their arms.
Etiquette had no minutiæ which were unknown to him ; he knew what
were the rights of the great landowners ; he was profoundly versed in
venery and falconry, and had, one day, when conversing on this great
art, astonished even Louis XIII. himself, who took a pride in being considered a past-master in it.

Like all the great nobles of that period, he rode and fenced to perfection. But still further, his education had been so little neglected, even
with respect to scholastic studies, so rare at this time among gentlemen,
that he smiled at the scraps of Latin which Aramis sported, and which
Porthos pretended to understand ; twice or thrice even, to the great
astonishment of his friends, he had, when Aramis allowed some rudi-
mental error to escape him, replaced a verb in its right tense and a
noun in its case ; besides all which, his probity was irreproachable, in
an age in which soldiers compounded so easily with their religion and
their consciences, lovers with the rigorous delicacy of our days, and the

poor with God's seventh commandment. This Athos, then, was a very extraordinary man.

And yet this nature so distinguished, this creature so beautiful, this essence so fine, was seen to turn insensibly towards material life, as old men turn towards physical and moral imbecility. Athos in his hours of privation—and these hours were frequent—was extinguished as to the whole of the luminous portion of him, and his brilliant side disappeared as if in profound darkness.

Then the demi-god having vanished, he remained scarcely a man. His head hanging down—his eye dull—his speech slow and painful, Athos would look for hours together at his bottle, his glass, or at Grimaud, who, accustomed to obey him by signs, read in the faint glance of his master his least desire, and satisfied it immediately. If the four friends were assembled at one of these moments, a word, thrown forth occasionally with a violent effort, was the share Athos furnished to the conversation. In exchange for his silence, Athos alone drank enough for four, and without appearing to be otherwise affected by wine, than by a more marked contraction of the brow, and by a deeper sadness.

D'Artagnan, whose inquiring disposition we are acquainted with, had not—whatever interest he had in satisfying his curiosity on this subject —been able to assign any cause for these fits, or for the periods of their recurrence. Athos never received any letters, Athos never had concerns with which all his friends were unacquainted.

It could not be said that it was wine which produced this sadness, for, in truth, he only drank to combat this sadness, which wine only, as we have said, rendered still darker. This excess of bilious humour could not be attributed to play, for, unlike Porthos, who accompanied the variations of chance with songs or oaths, Athos, when he had won, remained as impassible as when he had lost. He had been known, in the circle of the musketeers, to win in one night three thousand pistoles ; lose to the gold embroidered belt of gala days ; re-win all this, with the addition of a hundred louis, without his beautiful eyebrow being heightened or lowered half a line, without his hands losing their pearly hue, without his conversation, which was cheerful that evening, ceasing for a moment to be calm and agreeable.

Neither was it, as with our neighbours the English, an atmospheric influence which darkened his countenance, for the sadness generally became more intense towards the fine season of the year : June and July were the terrible months with Athos.

On account of the present he had no care, he shrugged his shoulders when people spoke of the future ; his secret then was with the past, as D'Artagnan had often vaguely said.

This mysterious shade spread over his whole person, rendered still more interesting the man whose eyes or mouth had never, even in the most complete intoxication, revealed anything, however skilfully questions had been put to him.

"Well," thought D'Artagnan, "poor Athos is perhaps at this moment dead, and dead by my fault, for it was I who dragged him into this affair, of which he did not know the origin, of which he will be ignorant of the result, and from which he can derive no advantage."

"Without reckoning, monsieur," added Planchet to his master's audibly expressed reflections, "that we perhaps owe our lives to him. Do you remember how he cried : 'On, D'Artagnan ! on ! I am taken ?' And when he had discharged his two pistols, what a terrible noise he made with his sword ! One might have said that twenty men, or rather twenty mad devils, were fighting."

And these words redoubled the eagerness of D'Artagnan, who excited his horse, which stood in need of no excitement, and they proceeded at a rapid pace. About eleven o'clock in the morning they perceived Amiens, and at half-past eleven they were at the door of the cursed auberge.

D'Artagnan had often meditated against the perfidious host one of those hearty vengeances which offer consolation whilst being hoped for. He entered the hostelry with his hat pulled over his eyes, his left hand on the pummel of the sword, and cracking his whip with his right hand.

"Do you remember me ?" said he to the host, who advanced, bowing, towards him.

"I have not that honour, monseigneur," replied the latter, his eyes being dazzled by the brilliant style in which D'Artagnan travelled.

"What ! do you mean to say you don't know me ?"

"No, monseigneur."

"Well ! two words will refresh your memory. What have you done with that gentleman against whom you had the audacity, about twelve days ago, to make an accusation of passing bad money ?"

The host became as pale as death ; D'Artagnan having assumed a threatening attitude, and Planchet having modelled himself upon his master.

"Ah ! monseigneur ! do not mention it," cried the host, in the most pitiable voice imaginable ; "ah ! seigneur, how dearly have I paid for that fault ! Unhappy wretch as I am !"

"That gentleman, I say, what is become of him ?"

"Deign to listen to me, monseigneur, and be merciful ! Sit down, I beg !"

D'Artagnan, mute with anger and uneasiness, took a seat in the threatening attitude of a judge ; Planchet looking fiercely over the back of his *fauteuil*.

"Here is the history, monseigneur," resumed the trembling host, "for I now recollect you : it was you who rode off at the moment I had that unfortunate difference with the gentleman you speak of."

"Yes, it was I ; so you may plainly perceive that you have no mercy to expect if you do not tell me the whole truth."

"Condescend to listen to me, and you shall know it all."

"I am listening to you."

"I had been warned by the authorities that a celebrated coiner of bad money would arrive at my auberge, with several of his companions, all disguised as guards or musketeers. I was furnished with a description of your horses, your lackeys, your countenances,—nothing was omitted."

"Go on! go on!" said D'Artagnan, who quickly conceived whence such an exact description had come.

"I took then, in conformity with the orders of the authorities, who sent me a reinforcement of six men, such measures as I thought necessary to get possession of the persons of the pretended coiners."

"Again!" said D'Artagnan, whose ears were terribly wounded by the repetition of this word *coiners*.

"Pardon me, monseigneur, for saying such things, but they form my excuse. The authorities had terrified me, and you know that an aubergiste must keep on good terms with the authorities."

"But, once again, that gentleman, where is he? What is become of him? is he dead? is he living?"

"Patience, monseigneur, we are coming to it. There happened then that which you know, and of which your precipitate departure," added the host, with a *finesse* that did not escape D'Artagnan, "appeared to authorise the issue. That gentleman, your friend, defended himself desperately. His lackey, who, by an unforeseen piece of ill-luck, had quarrelled with the people belonging to the authorities, disguised as stable-lads——"

"Miserable scoundrel!" cried D'Artagnan, "you were all in the plot then! and I really don't know what prevents me from exterminating you all!"

"Alas! monsieur, you will soon see we were not so. Monsieur, your friend (I ask pardon for not calling him by the honourable name which no doubt he bears, but we do not know that name), monsieur, your friend, having placed two men *hors de combat* with his pistols, retreated fighting with his sword, with which he disabled one of my men, and stunned me with a blow of the flat side of it."

"But, you infernal villain! when will you come to the end?" cried D'Artagnan; "Athos, what is become of Athos?"

"Whilst fighting and retreating, as I have told monseigneur, he found the door of the cellar stairs behind him, and as the door was open, he took out the key, and barricaded himself inside. As we were sure of finding him there, we left him alone."

"Yes," said D'Artagnan, "you did not particularly wish to kill him, and so were satisfied with detaining him a prisoner."

"Good God! a prisoner, monseigneur? Why, he imprisoned himself, and I will be upon my oath, he did. In the first place he had made rough work of it; one man was killed on the spot, and two others were severely wounded. The dead man, and the two that were wounded, were carried off by their companions, and I have heard nothing of either the one or the other since. As for myself, as soon as I recovered my senses, I went to M. the governor, to whom I related all that had passed, and whom I asked what I should do with my prisoner. But M. the governor was all astonishment; he told me he knew nothing about the matter, that the orders I had received did not come from him, and that if I had the audacity to mention his name as being concerned in this disturbance he would have me hanged. It appears that I made a mistake, monsieur, that I had arrested the wrong person, and that he whom I ought to have arrested had escaped."

"But Athos !" cried D'Artagnan, whose impatience was increased by the state of abandonment in which the authorities left the matter ; "Athos ! where is he ?"

"As I was anxious to repair the wrongs I had done the prisoner," resumed the aubergiste, "I took my way straight to the cellar, in order to set him at liberty. Ah ! monsieur, he was no longer a man, he was a devil ! To my offer of liberty, he replied that it was nothing but a snare, and that before he came out he intended to impose his own conditions. I told him, very humbly—for I could not conceal from myself the scrape I had got into by laying hands on one of his majesty's musketeers—I told him I was quite ready to submit to his conditions."

"'In the first place,' said he, 'I insist upon having my lackey placed with me, fully armed.' We hastened to obey this order ; for you will please to understand, monsieur, we were disposed to do everything your friend could desire. M. Grimaud (he told us his name, he did, although he does not talk much), M. Grimaud, then, went down to the cellar, wounded as he was ; then his master, having received him, barricaded the door afresh, and ordered us to remain quietly in our own bar."

"Well, but where is Athos now?" cried D'Artagnan.

"In the cellar, monsieur."

"What ! you good-for-nothing scoundrel ! What ! have you kept him in the cellar all this time?"

"Merciful heaven ! No, monsieur ! We keep him in the cellar ! You do not know what he is about in the cellar ! Ah ! if you could but persuade him to come out, monsieur, I should owe you the gratitude of my whole life ; I should adore you as my patron saint !"

"Then he is there ? I shall find him there ?"

"Without doubt you will, monsieur ; he persists in remaining there. We every day pass through the loop-hole some bread at the end of a fork, and some meat when he asks for it ; but alas ! it is not of bread and meat that he makes the greatest consumption. I once endeavoured to go down with two of my servants, but he flew into a terrible rage. I heard the noise he made in loading his pistols, and his servant in loading his musketoon. Then, when we asked them what were their intentions, the master replied that he had forty charges to fire, and that he and his lackey would fire to the last one, before he would allow a single soul of us to set foot in the cellar. Upon this I went and complained to the governor, who replied, that I only had what I deserved, and that it would teach me to insult honourable gentlemen who took up their abode in my house."

"So that from that time——" replied D'Artagnan, totally unable to refrain from laughing at the pitiable face of the host.

"So that from that time, monsieur," continued the latter, "we have led the most miserable life imaginable ; for you must know, monsieur, that all our provisions are in the cellar ; there is our wine in bottles, and our wine in the piece ; beer, oil, grocery, bacon, and large sausages ; and as we are prevented from going down, we are forced to refuse food and drink to the travellers who come to the house, so that our hostelry is daily going to ruin. If your friend remains another week in my cellar I shall be a ruined man."

"And not more than justice, neither, you stupid man ; could you not perceive by our appearance that we were people of quality, and not coiners,—say ?"

"Yes, monsieur, you are right," said the host. "But, hark ! hark ! there he is in a passion again !"

"Somebody has disturbed him, no doubt," said D'Artagnan.

"But he must be disturbed," cried the host ; "here are two English gentlemen just arrived."

"Well ?"

"Well ! the English like good wine, as you may know, monsieur ; these have asked for the best. My wife then requested permission of M. Athos to go into the cellar to satisfy these gentlemen ; and he, as usual, has refused. Ah ! good heaven ! there is the Sabbath louder than ever !"

D'Artagnan, in fact, heard a great noise on the side next the cellar. He rose, and, preceded by the host, wringing his hands, and followed by Planchet with his musketoon, ready for action, he approached the scene of action.

The two gentlemen were exasperated ; they had had a long ride, and were dying with hunger and thirst.

"But this is a tyranny !" cried one of them, in very good French, though with a foreign accent, "that this madman will not allow these good people access to their own wine ! Nonsense ! let us break open the door, and if he is too far gone in his madness, well ! we will kill him !"

"Softly, gentlemen !" said D'Artagnan, drawing his pistols from his belt, "there is nobody to be killed, if you please !"

"Good ! good !" cried Athos, from the other side of the door, "let them just come in, these devourers of little children, and we shall see !"

Brave as they appeared to be, the two English gentlemen looked at each other hesitatingly ; it might be said that there was in that cellar one of those hungry ogres, the gigantic heroes of popular legends, into whose cavern nobody could force their way with impunity.

There was a moment of silence ; but at length the two Englishmen felt ashamed to draw back, and the more angry one descended the five or six steps which led to the cellar, and gave a kick against the door enough to split a wall.

"Planchet," said D'Artagnan, cocking his pistols, "I will take charge of the one at the top, you look to the one below. Now, gentlemen, if it's battle you want, you shall have it."

" Good God !" cried the hollow voice of Athos, " I can hear D'Artagnan, I think."

" Yes !" cried D'Artagnan, exalting his voice, in his turn, " I am here, my friend !"

" Ah ! ah ! then," replied Athos, " we will give it to these breakers-in of doors !"

The gentlemen had drawn their swords, but they found themselves taken between two fires ; they still hesitated an instant ; but, as before, pride prevailed, and a second kick split the door from bottom to top.

" Stand on one side, D'Artagnan, stand on one side," cried Athos, " I am going to fire !"

" Gentlemen !" exclaimed D'Artagnan, whom reflection never abandoned, " gentlemen, think of what you are about ! Patience, Athos ! You are running your heads into a very silly affair ; you will be riddled. My lackey and I will have three shots at you, and you will get as many from the cellar ; you will then have our swords, with which, I can assure you, my friend and I can play tolerably well. Let me conduct your business and my own. You shall soon have something to drink ; I give you my word."

" If there is any left," grumbled the jeering voice of Athos.

The host felt a cold sweat creep down his back.

" What ! if there is any left !" murmured he.

" What, the devil ! there must be plenty left," replied D'Artagnan : " be satisfied of that ; these two can never have drunk all the cellar. Gentlemen, return your swords to their scabbards."

" We will, provided you replace your pistols in your belt."

" Willingly."

And D'Artagnan set the example. Then turning towards Planchet, he made him a sign to uncock his musketoon.

The Englishmen, overcome by these peaceful proceedings, sheathed their swords, grumblingly. The history of Athos's imprisonment was then related to them ; and as they were really gentlemen, they pronounced the host in the wrong.

" Now, gentlemen," said D'Artagnan, " go up to your room again ; and in ten minutes, I will answer for it, you shall have all you desire."

The Englishmen bowed, and went upstairs.

" Now I am alone, my dear Athos," said D'Artagnan, " open the door, I beg of you."

" Instantly," said Athos.

Then was heard a great noise of fagots being removed, and of the groaning of posts ; these were the counterscarps and bastions of Athos, which the besieged demolished himself.

An instant after, the broken door was removed, and the pale face of Athos appeared, who with a rapid glance took a survey of the environs.

D'Artagnan threw himself on his neck and embraced him tenderly ; he then endeavoured to draw him from his moist abode, but, to his surprise, perceived that Athos staggered.

"Why, you are wounded?" said he.

"I! not at all; I am dead drunk, that's all, and never did a man set about getting so better. Vive dieu! my good host! I must at least have drunk for my part a hundred and fifty bottles."

"Misericorde!" cried the host, "if the lackey has drunk only half as much as the master, I am a ruined man."

"Grimaud is a well-bred lackey; he would never think of faring in the same manner as his master; he only drank from the butt: hark! I don't think he put the fosset in again. Do you hear it? It is running now."

D'Artagnan burst into a loud laugh, which changed the trembling of the host into a burning fever.

In the meantime, Grimaud appeared in his turn behind his master, with his musketoon on his shoulder, and his head shaking like one of those drunken satyrs in the pictures of Rubens. He was moistened before and behind with a liquid which the host recognised as his best olive oil.

The *cortége* crossed the public room and proceeded to take possession of the best apartment in the house, which D'Artagnan occupied by authority.

In the meantime the host and his wife hurried down with lamps into the cellar, which had so long been interdicted to them, and where a frightful spectacle awaited them.

Beyond the fortifications through which Athos had made a breach in order to get out, and which were composed of fagots, planks, and empty casks, heaped up according to all the rules of the strategic art, they found, swimming in puddles of oil and wine, the bones and fragments of all the hams they had eaten; whilst a heap of broken bottles filled the whole left-hand corner of the cellar, and a tun, the cock of which was left running, was yielding, by this means, the last drop of its blood. "The image of devastation and death," as the ancient poet says, "reigned as over a field of battle."

Of sixty large sausages, that had been suspended from the joists, scarcely any remained.

Then the lamentations of the host and hostess pierced the vault of the cellar. D'Artagnan himself was moved by them; Athos did not even turn his head.

But to grief succeeded rage. The host armed himself with a spit, and rushed into the chamber occupied by the two friends.

"Some wine!" said Athos, on perceiving the host.

"Some wine!" cried the stupefied host, "some wine! why you have drunk more than a hundred pistoles' worth!—I am a ruined man, lost! destroyed!"

"Bah!" said Athos, "why we were always dry."

"If you had been contented with drinking, why, well and good; but you have broken all the bottles."

"You pushed me upon a heap which rolled down. That was your fault."

" All my oil is lost !"

" Oil is a sovereign balm for wounds, and my poor Grimaud here
was obliged to dress those you had inflicted on him."

" All my sausages gnawed !"

" There is an enormous number of rats in that cellar."

" You shall pay me for all this," cried the exasperated host.

" You triple ass !" said Athos, rising ; but he sank down again immediately ; he had tried his strength to the utmost. D'Artagnan came to
his relief, with his whip in his hand.

The host drew back and burst into tears.

" This will teach you," said D'Artagnan, " to treat the guests God
sends you in a more courteous fashion."

" God ! say the devil !"

" My dear friend," said D'Artagnan, " if you stun us in this manner,
we will all four go and shut ourselves up in your cellar, and see if the
mischief be as great as you say."

" Oh ! gentlemen ! gentlemen !" said the host, " I have been wrong.
I confess it, but, pardon to every sin ! you are a gentleman and I am a
poor aubergiste, you will have pity on me."

" Ah ! if you speak in that way," said Athos, " you will break my heart,
and the tears will flow from my eyes as the wine flowed from the cask.
We are not such devils as we appear to be. Come hither, and let us talk
the matter over."

The host approached with hesitation.

" Come hither, I say, and don't be afraid," continued Athos. " At the
moment I was about to pay you, I had placed my purse on the table."

" Yes, monsieur."

" That purse contained sixty pistoles, where is it ?"

" Deposited in the justice's office : they said it was bad money."

" Very well ; get me my purse back and keep the sixty pistoles."

" But monseigneur knows very well that justice never lets go that
which it once lays hold of. If it were bad money, there might be some
hopes ; but unfortunately they are all good pieces."

" Manage the matter as well as you can, my good man ; it does not
concern me, the more so as I have not a livre left."

" Come," said D'Artagnan, " let us try further ; Athos's horse, where
is that ?"

" In the stable."

" How much is it worth ?"

" Fifty pistoles at most."

" It's worth eighty, take it, and there ends the matter."

" What !" cried Athos, " are you selling my horse ? my Bajazet ? and
pray upon what shall I make my campaign ? upon Grimaud ?"

" I have brought you another," said D'Artagnan.

" Another."

" And a magnificent one, too !" cried the host.

" Well, since there is another finer and younger, why, you may take
the old one, and let us have some wine."

"Which ?" asked the host, quite cheerful again.

"Some of that at the bottom, near the laths ; there are twenty-five bottles of it left, all the rest were broken by my fall. Bring up six of them."

"Why, this man is a tun !" said the host aside ; "if he only remains here a fortnight, and pays for what he drinks, my affairs will soon be right again."

"And don't forget," said D'Artagnan, "to bring up four bottles of the same sort for the two English gentlemen."

"And now," said Athos, "whilst they are bringing up the wine, tell me, D'Artagnan, what has become of the others, come !"

D'Artagnan related how he had found Porthos in bed with a strained knee, and Aramis at a table between two theologians. As he finished, the host entered with the wine and a ham, which, fortunately for him, had been left out of the cellar.

"That's well !" said Athos, filling his glass and that of his friend ; "here's to Porthos and Aramis ! but you, D'Artagnan, what is the matter with you, and what has happened to you personally ? You don't look happy !"

"Alas !" said D'Artagnan, "it is because I am the most unfortunate of all !"

"You ! unfortunate !" said Athos ; "come ! how the devil can you be unfortunate ? let us see that."

"Presently !" said D'Artagnan.

"Presently ! and why presently ? Now, that's because you think I am drunk, D'Artagnan. But, take this with you, my ideas are never so clear as when I have had plenty of wine. Speak, then, I am all ears.

D'Artagnan related his adventure with Madame Bonacieux. Athos listened to him with perfect immobility of countenance ; and, when he had finished,—

"Trifles, all that ;" said Athos, "nothing but trifles !" That was Athos's expression.

"You always say trifles, my dear Athos !" said D'Artagnan, "and that comes very ill from you, who have never been in love."

The drink-deadened eye of Athos flashed, but it was only for a moment—it became dull and vacant as before.

"That's true," said he quietly, "for my part I have never loved."

"Acknowledge then, you stone-hearted man," said D'Artagnan, "that you have no right to be so hard upon us whose hearts are tender."

"Tender hearts ! wounded hearts !" said Athos.

"What do you say ?"

"I say that love is a lottery, in which he who wins, wins death ! You are very fortunate to have lost, believe me, my dear D'Artagnan. And if I may be allowed to advise you, it will be to lose always."

"Oh ! but she seemed to love me so !"

"She seemed, did she ?"

"Oh ! she did love me !"

"You boy ! why, there lives not a man who has not believed, as you do, that his mistress loved him, and there lives not a man who has not been deceived by his mistress."

"Except you, Athos, who never had one."

"That's true," said Athos, after a moment's silence, "that's true! I never had one! I!—I !—Drink !"

"But then, philosopher as you are," said D'Artagnan, "it is your duty to instruct me, to support me; I stand in need of being taught and consoled."

"Consoled! for what?"

"For my misfortune."

"Your misfortune is laughable," said Athos, shrugging his shoulders; "I should like to know what you would say if I were to relate to you a real tale of love !"

"Which concerns you?"

"Either me or one of my friends, what matters?"

"Tell it, Athos, tell it."

"Drink! I shall tell it better if I drink."

"Drink and relate, then."

"Not a bad idea!" said Athos, emptying and filling his glass, "the two things go marvellously well together."

"I am all attention," said D'Artagnan.

Athos collected himself, and in proportion as he did so, D'Artagnan saw that he became paler; he was at that period of intoxication in which vulgar drinkers fall and sleep. He kept himself upright and dreamed, without sleeping. This somnambulism of drunkenness had something frightful in it.

"You particularly wish it?" asked he.

"I beg you will," said D'Artagnan.

"Be it done then, as you desire. One of my friends, please to observe, not myself," said Athos, interrupting himself with a melancholy smile; "one of the counts of my province, that is to say, of Berry, noble as a Dandolo or a Montmorency, at twenty-five years of age, fell in love with a girl of sixteen, beautiful as fancy can paint. Through the ingenuousness of her age beamed an ardent mind, a mind not of the woman, but of the poet; she did not please, she intoxicated; she lived in a small town with her brother, who was a curé. Both had recently come into the country; they came nobody knew whence; but when seeing her so lovely and her brother so pious, nobody thought of asking whence they came. They were said, however, to be of good extraction. My friend, who was lord of the country, might have seduced her, or he might have seized her forcibly, at his will, for he was master; who would have come to the assistance of two strangers, two unknown persons? Unfortunately, he was an honourable man, he married her. The fool! the ass! the idiot !"

"How so, if he loved her?" asked D'Artagnan.

"Wait!" said Athos. "He took her to his château, and made her the first lady in the province; and, in justice, it must be allowed, she supported her rank becomingly."

"Well?" asked D'Artagnan, quite excited.

"Well, one day when she was hunting with her husband," continued Athos, in a low voice, and speaking very quickly, "she fell from her horse and fainted ; the count flew to her help, and as she appeared to be oppressed by her clothes, he ripped them open with his poniard, and in so doing laid bare her shoulder : and now, guess, D'Artagnan," said Athos, with a maniacal burst of laughter, "guess what she had upon her shoulder."

"How can I tell?" said D'Artagnan.

"A fleur-de-lis !" said Athos. "She was branded !"

And Athos emptied at a single draught the glass he held in his hand.

"Horror !" cried D'Artagnan. "What *do* you tell me ?"

"Truth ! my friend,—the angel was a demon : the poor young girl had been a thief !"

"And what did the count do ?"

"The count was of the highest noblesse ; he had, on his estates, the right of high and low justice ; he tore the dress of the countess to pieces, he tied her hands behind her, and hanged her on a tree !"

"Heavens ! Athos ! a murder !" cried D'Artagnan.

"Yes, a murder,—no more "—said Athos, as pale as death. "But, methinks, they let me want wine !" and he seized the last bottle that was left, by the neck, put it to his mouth, and emptied it at a single draught as he would have emptied an ordinary glass.

Then he let his head sink upon his two hands, whilst D'Artagnan stood up before him, terrified, stupefied.

"That has cured me of beautiful, poetical, and loving women," said Athos, after a considerable pause, raising his head, and forgetting to continue the apologue of the count,—"God grant you as much !—Drink !"

"Then she is dead ?" stammered D'Artagnan.

"Parbleu !" said Athos. "But hold out your glass. Some ham, my man !" cried Athos ; "we don't half drink !"

"And her brother ?" added D'Artagnan timidly.

"Her brother ?" replied Athos.

"Yes, the priest."

"Oh ! I inquired after him for the purpose of hanging him likewise, but he was beforehand with me, he had quitted the curacy instantly."

"Was it ever known who this miserable fellow was ?"

"He was doubtless the first lover, and the accomplice of the fair lady, a worthy man, who had pretended to be a curé, for the purpose of getting his mistress married, and securing her a position. He has been hanged and quartered before this time, I hope."

"Good God ! good God !" cried D'Artagnan, quite stunned by the relation of this horrible adventure.

"Taste some of this ham, D'Artagnan ; it is exquisite," said Athos, cutting a slice, which he placed on the young man's plate. "What a pity it is there were only four like this in the cellar, I should have drunk fifty bottles more."

D'Artagnan could no longer endure this conversation, which had terrified away his senses ; he felt quite bewildered, and allowing his head to sink upon his hand, he pretended to sleep.

" These young fellows can none of them drink," said Athos, looking at him with pity, " and yet this is one of the best of them, too !"

CHAPTER XXVIII.

THE RETURN.

D'ARTAGNAN was astounded by the terrible confidence of Athos ; and yet many things appeared very obscure to him in this partial revelation ; in the first place, it had been made by a man quite drunk, to one who was half-drunk, and yet, in spite of the uncertainty which the vapour of three or four bottles of Burgundy carries with it to the brain, D'Artagnan, when awaking on the following morning, had every word of Athos's as present to his memory as if they fell from his mouth ; they had been impressed upon his mind. All this doubt only gave rise to a more lively desire of arriving at a certainty, and he went into his friend's chamber with a fixed determination of renewing the conversation of the preceding evening ; but he found Athos quite himself again, that is to say, the most shrewd and impenetrable of men. Besides which, the musketeer, after having exchanged a hearty shake of the hand with him, broached the matter first.

" I was pretty drunk yesterday, D'Artagnan," said he, " I can tell that by my tongue, which was swollen and hot this morning, and by my pulse, which was very tremulous ; I would lay a wager I uttered a thousand absurdities."

And whilst saying this he looked at his friend with an earnestness that embarrassed him.

" No," replied D'Artagnan, " if I recollect well what you said, it was nothing out of the common way."

" Indeed ! you surprise me, I thought I had related a most lamentable history to you ?" And he looked at the young man as if he would read to the very depths of his heart.

" Ma foi !" said D'Artagnan, " it would appear that I was more drunk than you, since I remember nothing of the kind."

But this did not deceive Athos, and he resumed :

" You cannot have failed to remark, my dear friend, that every one has his particular kind of drunkenness, sad or gay ; my drunkenness is always sad, and when I am thoroughly intoxicated my mania is to relate all the dismal histories which my foolish nurse infused into my brain. That is my failing : a capital failing, I admit ; but, with that exception, I am a good drinker.'

Athos spoke this in so natural a manner, that D'Artagnan was shaken in his conviction.

" Oh ! it is that, then," replied the young man, anxious to find out the truth, " it is that, then, I remember, as we remember a dream,—we were speaking of hanging people."

"Ah ! you see how it is," said Athos, becoming still paler, but yet attempting to laugh, " I was sure it was so—the hanging of people is my night-mare."

"Yes, yes," replied D'Artagnan, " I remember now ; yes, it was about —stop a minute—yes, it was about a woman."

"That's it," replied Athos, becoming almost livid, " that is my grand history of the fair lady, and when I relate that, I must be drunk indeed."

"Yes, that was it," said D'Artagnan, " the history of a tall, fair lady, with blue eyes."

"Yes, who was hanged."

"By her husband, who was a nobleman of your acquaintance," continued D'Artagnan, looking intently at Athos.

"Well, you see how a man may compromise himself when he does not know what he says," replied Athos, shrugging his shoulders as if he thought himself an object of pity. " I certainly never will get drunk again, D'Artagnan,—it is too bad a habit."

D'Artagnan remained silent.

Then Athos, changing the conversation all at once,—

" By-the-bye, I thank you for the horse you have brought me," said he.

" Is it to your mind ?" asked D'Artagnan.

"Yes ; but it is not a horse for hard work."

" You are mistaken ; I have ridden him nearly ten leagues in less than an hour and a half, and he appeared no more distressed than if he had only made the tour of the Place Saint Sulpice."*

"Ah, ah ! you begin to awaken my regret."

"Regret ?"

" Yes ; I have parted with him."

" How ?"

" Why, here is the simple fact : this morning I awoke at six o'clock, you were still fast asleep, and I did not know what to do with myself ; I was still stupid from our yesterday's debauch. As I came into the public room, I saw one of our Englishmen bargaining with a dealer for a horse, his own having died yesterday from bleeding. I drew near, and found he was bidding a hundred pistoles for a fine chestnut nag. ' Pardieu !' said I ; ' my good gentleman, I have a horse to sell, too.'

" ' Aye, and a very fine one ! I saw him yesterday—your friend's lackey was leading him.'

" ' Do you think he is worth a hundred pistoles ?'

" ' Yes ; will you sell him to me for that sum ?'

" ' No ; but I will play with you for him.'

" ' You will play with me ?'

" ' Yes.

* I endeavour to translate as faithfully as is consistent with spirit, therefore beg the reader not to hold me responsible for such wonders as this ; as a pretty good English horseman, I must confess I never met with such a horse : all these circumstances are exaggerated.—TRANS.

" ' At what ? '

" ' At dice.'

" No sooner said than done, and I lost the horse.   Ah, ah ! but please to observe I won back the caparison," cried Athos.

D'Artagnan looked much disconcerted.

" This vexes you ?" said Athos.

" Well, I must confess it does," replied D'Artagnan.   " That horse was to have assisted in making us known in the day of battle.   It was a pledge—a remembrance.   Athos, you have done very wrong."

" But, my dear friend, put yourself in my place," replied the musketeer.   " I was hipped to death : and still further, upon my honour, I don't like English horses.   If all the consequence is to be recognised, why the saddle will suffice for that ; it is quite remarkable enough.   As to the horse, we can easily find some excuse for its disappearance. What the devil ! a horse is mortal ; suppose mine had had the glanders, or the farcy ?'

D'Artagnan could not smile.

" It vexes me greatly," continued Athos, " that you attach so much importance to these animals, for I am not yet at the end of my story."

" What else have you done ?"

" After having lost my own horse, nine against ten—see how near ! —I formed an idea of staking yours."

" Yes—but you stopped at the idea, I hope ?"

" No ; for I put it in execution that very minute."

" And the consequence ?" said D'Artagnan, in great anxiety.

" I threw, and I lost."

" What, my horse ?"

" Your horse ; seven against eight ; a point short—you know the proverb."

" Athos, you are not in your right senses,—I swear you are not."

" My dear lad, it was yesterday, when I was telling you silly stories, that you ought to have told me that, and not this morning.   I lost him, then, with all his appointments and furniture."

" Really, this is frightful !"

" Stop a minute ; you don't know all yet.   I should make an excellent gambler if I were not too hot-headed ; but I became so, just as if I were drinking ; well, I was hot-headed then——"

" Well, but what else could you play for,—you had nothing left ?"

" Oh ! yes, yes, my friend ; there was still that diamond left which sparkles on your finger, and which I had observed yesterday."

" This diamond !" said D'Artagnan, placing his hand eagerly on his ring

" And as I am a connoisseur in such things, having had a few of my own once, I estimated it at a thousand pistoles."

" I hope," said D'Artagnan, half dead with fright, " you made no mention of my diamond ?"

" On the contrary, my dear friend, this diamond became our only resource ; with it I might regain our horses and their furniture, and, still further, money to pay our expenses on the road."

"Athos, you make me tremble !" cried D'Artagnan.

" I mentioned your diamond then to my adversary, who had likewise remarked it. What the devil ! do you think you can wear a star from heaven on your finger and nobody observe it ? Impossible !"

"Oh ! go on, go on !" said D'Artagnan ; "for upon my honour, you will kill me with your careless coolness !"

" We divided, then, this diamond into ten parts, of a hundred pistoles each."

"You are laughing at me, and want to try me !" said D'Artagnan, whom anger began to take by the hair, as Minerva takes Achilles, in the *Iliad.*

" No, I am not joking, mordieu ! I should like to have seen you in my place ! I had been fifteen days without seeing a human face, and had been left to brutalise myself with the company of nothing but bottles."

" That was no reason for staking my diamond !" replied D'Artagnan, closing his hand with a nervous spasm.

" But hear the end. Ten throws of a hundred pistoles each—ten throws, without revenge ; in thirteen throws I lost all—in thirteen throws. The number thirteen was always fatal to me ; it was on the 13th of the month of July that——"

" Ventrebleu !" cried D'Artagnan, rising from the table, the history of the present day making him forget that of the preceding one.

" Patience, patience !" said Athos ; "I had a plan. The Englishman was an original ; I had seen him conversing that morning with Grimaud, and Grimaud had told me that he had made him proposals to enter into his service. I staked Grimaud—the silent Grimaud—divided into ten portions."

" Well, what next ?" said D'Artagnan, laughing in spite of himself.

" Grimaud himself, understand ! and with the ten parts of Grimaud, which are not worth a ducatoon, I won back the diamond. Tell me, now, whether you don't think persistence is a virtue ?"

" Ma foi ! but this is a droll story," cried D'Artagnan, a little consoled, and holding his sides with laughter.

" You may easily guess, that finding the luck turned, I again staked the diamond."

" The devil !" said D'Artagnan, becoming again angry.

" I won back your furniture, then your horse, then my furniture, then my horse, and then I lost again   To make short, I regained your furniture and then mine. That's where we left off. That was a superb throw, so I left off there."

D'Artagnan breathed as if the whole hostelry had been removed from off his chest.

" Then I understand," said he, timidly, "the diamond is safe ?"

" Intact, my dear friend ; *plus* the furniture of your Bucephalus and mine."

"But what is the use of horse-furniture without horses?"

"I have an idea concerning them."

"Athos, you keep me in a fever."

"Listen to me. You have not played for a long time, D'Artagnan."

"Neither have I any inclination to play."

"Swear to nothing. You have not played for a long time, I said; you ought, then, to have a good hand."

"Well, what then?"

"Well! the Englishman and his companion are still here. I remarked that he regretted the horse-furniture very much. You appear to think much of your horse. In your place, now, I would stake the furniture against the horse."

"But he will not be satisfied with one equipment."

"Stake both, pardieu! I am not selfish, if you are."

"You would do so?" said D'Artagnan, undecided, so strongly did the confidence of Athos begin to prevail, unknown to himself.

"Parole d'honneur, in one single throw."

"But having lost the horses, I am particularly anxious to preserve the furniture."

"Stake your diamond, then!"

"This! No, thank you! that's quite another thing. Never! never!"

"The devil!" said Athos. "I would propose to you to stake Planchet, but as that has already been done, the Englishman would not, perhaps, be willing."

"Decidedly, my dear Athos, I should like better not to risk anything."

"That's a pity," said Athos, coolly; "the Englishman is overflowing with pistoles. Good lord! try one throw; one throw is soon thrown!"

"And if I lose?"

"You will win, I tell you."

"But if I lose?"

"Well, you will surrender the furniture."

"I will try one throw," said D'Artagnan.

Athos went in search of the Englishman, whom he found in the stable, examining the furniture with a greedy eye. The opportunity was good. He proposed the conditions—the two furnitures against one horse, or a hundred pistoles, to choose. The Englishman calculated fast: the two furnitures were worth three hundred pistoles to them: he consented.

D'Artagnan threw the dice with a trembling hand, and turned up the number three; his paleness terrified Athos, who, however, contented himself with saying:

"That's a sad throw, comrade; you will have the horses fully equipped, monsieur."

The Englishman, quite triumphant, did not even give himself the trouble to shake the dice; he threw them on the table without looking at them, so sure was he of victory; D'Artagnan himself had turned on one side to conceal his ill-humour.

"There ! there ! there !" said Athos, with his quiet tone ; "that throw of the dice is extraordinary. I have only witnessed such a one four times in my life. Two aces, gentlemen !"

The Englishman looked, and was seized with astonishment ; D'Artagnan looked, and was seized with pleasure.

"Yes," continued Athos, "four times only : once at the house of M. Créquy ; another time at my own house in the country, in my château at——, when I had a château; a third time at M. de Tréville's, where it surprised us all ; and the fourth time at a cabaret, where it fell to my lot, and where I lost a hundred louis and a supper on it."

"Then monsieur takes his horse back again," said the Englishman.

"Certainly," said D'Artagnan.

"Then there is no revenge ?"

"Our conditions said no revenge, you will please to recollect."

"That is true ; the horse shall be restored to your lackey, monsieur."

"A moment !" said Athos ; "with your permission, monsieur, I wish to speak a word with my friend."

"If you please."

Athos drew D'Artagnan on one side.

"Well, tempter ! what more do you want with me ?" said D'Artagnan ; "you want me to throw again, do you not ?"

"No ; I would wish you to reflect a little before you decide."

"Upon what ?"

"You mean to take your horse, do you not ?"

"Without doubt, I do."

"You are wrong, then. I would take the hundred pistoles ; you know you have staked the furniture against the horse or a hundred pistoles, at your choice."

"Yes."

"Well, then, I would take the hundred pistoles."

"And I will take the horse."

"In which, I repeat, you are wrong. What is the use of one horse for us two ? I could not get up behind : we should look like the two sons of Amyon, who have lost their brother. You cannot think of humiliating me by riding by my side, prancing along upon that magnificent charger. For my part, I should not hesitate a moment, but take the hundred pistoles. We want money to carry us back to Paris."

"I am much attached to that horse, Athos."

"And there, again, you are wrong ; a horse slips and injures a joint, a horse stumbles and breaks his knees to the bone, a horse eats out of a manger in which a glandered horse has eaten ; there is a horse, or rather a hundred pistoles, lost : a master must feed his horse, whilst, on the contrary, the hundred pistoles feed their master."

"But how shall we get back to Paris ?"

"Upon our lackeys' horses, pardieu ! Never think of our steeds ; anybody may see by our carriage that we are people of condition."

"Very pretty figures we shall cut upon ponies, whilst Aramis and Porthos will be caracolling upon their war steeds !"

"Aramis and Porthos !" cried Athos, and laughed more loudly than was his custom.

"What are you laughing at ?" asked D'Artagnan, who did not at all comprehend the hilarity of his friend.

"Never mind !—do, one thing or the other," said Athos.

"Your advice then is——"

"To take the hundred pistoles, D'Artagnan ; with the hundred pistoles we can live well to the end of the month: we have undergone a great deal of fatigue, remember, and a little rest will do us no harm."

"I rest ! oh, no, Athos, the moment I am in Paris, I shall prosecute my researches after that unfortunate woman."

"Well, you may be assured that your horse will not be half so serviceable to you for that purpose as the good louis d'or ;—take the hundred pistoles, my friend, take the hundred pistoles !"

D'Artagnan only required one reason, to be satisfied. This last reason appeared convincing. Besides, he feared that by resisting longer he should appear selfish in the eyes of Athos: he acquiesced, then, and chose the hundred pistoles, which the Englishman paid down immediately.

They then determined to depart. Peace with the landlord, in addition to Athos's old horse, cost six pistoles ; D'Artagnan and Athos took the nags of Planchet and Grimaud, and the two lackeys started on foot, carrying the saddles on their heads.

However ill our two friends were mounted, they soon got far in advance of their servants, and arrived at Crèvecœur. From a distance they perceived Aramis, seated in a melancholy manner at his window, looking out, like *Sister Anne*, at the dust in the horizon.

"Holo ! ha ! Aramis ! what the devil are you doing there !" cried they.

"Ah ! is that you, D'Artagnan, and you, Athos ?" said the young man. "I was reflecting upon the rapidity with which the blessings of this world leave us, and my English horse, which has just disappeared amidst a cloud of dust, has furnished me with a living image of the fragility of the things of the earth. Life itself may be resolved into three words : *Erat, est, fuit.*"

"Which means——" said D'Artagnan, who began to suspect the truth.

"Which means, that I have just been duped ; sixty louis for a horse, which, by the manner in which he goes, can do at least five leagues an hour."

D'Artagnan and Athos burst into a loud laugh.

"My dear D'Artagnan," said Aramis, "don't be too angry with me, I beg of you, necessity has no law ; besides, I am the person punished, as that rascally horse-dealer has robbed me of fifty pistoles at least. Ah ! you fellows are good managers ! you ride on your lackey's horses, and have your own gallant steeds led along carefully by hand, at short stages."

At the same instant a market-cart, which had for some minutes appeared upon the Amiens road, pulled up at the auberge, and

Planchet and Grimaud got out of it with the saddles on their heads. The carter was going to Paris, and had agreed, on condition of being prevented from feeling thirst upon the road, to convey the lackeys and their burdens thither.

"How is all this?" said Aramis, on seeing them arrive—"nothing but saddles?"

"Now, do you understand?" said Athos.

"Oh, yes! all alike. I retained my furniture by instinct. Hola! Bazin! bring my new saddle, and carry it with those of these gentlemen."

"And what have you done with your curés?" asked D'Artagnan.

"Why, I invited them to a dinner the next day," replied Aramis; "they have some capital wine here; please to observe that in passing, I did my best to make them drunk;—then the curé forbade me to quit my uniform, and the Jesuit entreated me to get him made a musketeer."

"Without a thesis!" cried D'Artagnan, "without a thesis! for my part, I request the thesis may be suppressed!"

"From that time," continued Aramis, "I have lived very agreeably. I have begun a poem in verse of one syllable! that is rather difficult, but the merit in all things consists in the difficulty. The matter is tasty. I will read the first canto to you; it has four hundred verses, and lasts a minute."

"Ma foi! my dear Aramis!" said D'Artagnan, who detested verses almost as much as he did Latin; "add to the merit of the difficulty that of the brevity, and you are sure that your poem will at least have two merits."

"Ah; but you will see," continued Aramis, "that it breathes irreproachable passion.—And so, my friends, we are returning to Paris? Bravo! I am ready, we are going to rejoin that good fellow, Porthos! so much the better. You can't think how I have missed him, the great simpleton. He would not sell his horse; not for a kingdom! I think I can see him now, mounted upon his superb animal and seated in his handsome saddle, looking like the Great Mogul!"

They made a halt for an hour, to refresh their horses: Aramis discharged his bill, placed Bazin in the cart with his comrades, and they set forward to join Porthos.

They found him up, less pale than when D'Artagnan left him, and seated at a table, on which, though he was alone, was spread enough for four persons; this dinner consisted of viands nicely dressed, choice wines, and superb fruit.

"Ah! pardieu!" said he, rising, "you come in the nick of time; gentlemen, I was just beginning the potage, and you will dine with me."

"Oh, oh!" said D'Artagnan, "these bottles are not the fruits of Mousqueton's *lasso!* besides, here is a *fricandeau piqué*, and a *filet de bœuf!*"

"I am recruiting myself," said Porthos, "I am recruiting myself;—

nothing weakens a man more than these cursed strains. Did you ever suffer from a strain, Athos?"

"Never!—only I remember that when in our affair of the Rue Férou, I received a sword-wound, which at the end of fifteen or eighteen days produced exactly the same effect."

"But this dinner was not intended for you alone, Porthos?" said Aramis.

"No," said Porthos, "I expected some gentlemen of the neighbourhood, who have just sent me word they could not come; you will take their places, and I shall not lose by the exchange. Holo, Mousqueton! seats, and order the number of bottles to be doubled."

"Do you know what we are eating here?" said Athos, at the expiration of about ten minutes.

"Pardieu!" replied D'Artagnan, "for my part I am eating *veau piqué aux cardons* and *à-la moelle.*"

"And I some *filets d'agneau,*" said Porthos.

"And I a *blanc de volaille,*" said Aramis.

"You are all mistaken, gentlemen," answered Athos, with a serious countenance; "you are all eating horse-flesh."

"Eating what?" said D'Artagnan.

"Horse-flesh!" said Aramis, with a look of disgust.

Porthos alone made no reply.

"Yes, real horse; are we not, Porthos, eating a horse? and perhaps his saddle."

"No, no, gentlemen, I have kept the furniture," said Porthos.

"Ma foi!" said Aramis, "we are all bad alike; one would think we acted upon agreement."

"What could I do?" said Porthos; "this horse made my visitors ashamed of theirs, and I don't like to humble people!"

"Then your duchess is still taking the waters?" asked D'Artagnan.

"Yes, still," replied Porthos. "And the governor of the province, one of the gentlemen I expected to-day, seemed to have such a wish for him, that I gave him to him."

"Gave him?" cried D'Artagnan.

"Lord! yes, gave it to him, you can't call it anything but a gift," said Porthos, "for the animal was worth at least a hundred and fifty louis, and the stingy fellow would only give me eighty!"

"Without the saddle?" said Aramis.

"Yes, without the saddle."

"You will please to observe, gentlemen," said Athos, "that Porthos has made the best bargain of any of us."

And then commenced a roar of laughter in which they all joined, to the astonishment of poor Porthos: but when he was informed of the cause of their hilarity, his laughter, according to custom, was more vociferous than anybody's.

"So, then, there is one comfort, we are all in cash," said D'Artagnan.

"Well, for my part," said Athos, "I found Aramis' Spanish wine so good, that I sent on a hamper of sixty bottles of it with the lackeys; that has weakened my purse not a little."

"And I," said Aramis, "you can imagine that I had given almost my last sou to the church of Montdidier and the Jesuits of Amiens ; that I, moreover, had formed engagements which I ought to have kept. I have ordered masses for myself, and for you, gentlemen, which will be said, gentlemen, and for which I have not the least doubt you will be very much the better."

"And I," said Porthos, "do you think my strain cost me nothing ? without reckoning Mousqueton's wound, on account of which the surgeon was obliged to come twice a day, and who charged me double on account of Mousqueton's having allowed himself to be wounded in a part which people generally only show to an apothecary ; so I advised him to try never to get wounded there any more."

"Aye, aye !" said Athos, exchanging a smile with D'Artagnan and Aramis ; "it is very clear you acted nobly with regard to the poor lad ; that is like a good master."

"In short," said Porthos, "when all my expenses are paid, I shall have, at most, thirty crowns left."

"And I about ten pistoles," said Aramis.

"Well, then, it appears that we are the Crœsuses of the society. How much have you left of your hundred pistoles, D'Artagnan ?"

"Of my hundred pistoles ? Why, in the first place, I gave you fifty."

"You did ?"

"Pardieu ! yes."

"Ah ! yes, so you did ; I recollect now."

"Then I paid the host six."

"What an animal that host was ! Why did you give him six pistoles ?"

"Why, you told me to give them to him yourself !"

"Ah ! so I did ; but I am too good-natured. In brief, how much have you left ?"

"Twenty-five pistoles," said D'Artagnan.

"And I," said Athos, taking some small change from his pocket, "I——"

"You ? why, nothing !"

"Ma foi ! so little that it is not worth reckoning with the general stock."

"Now, then, let us calculate how much we possess in all."

"Porthos ?"

"Thirty crowns."

"Aramis ?"

"Ten pistoles."

"And you, D'Artagnan ?"

"Twenty-five."

"That makes in all ?" said Athos.

"Four hundred and seventy-five livres !" said D'Artagnan, who reckoned like an Archimedes.

"Then on our arrival in Paris, we shall still have four hundred, besides the furniture," said Porthos.

"But our troop horses?" said Aramis.

"Well! of the four lackeys' horses we will make two for the masters, for which we will draw lots; with the four hundred livres, we will make the half of one for one of the unmounted, and then we will give the turnings out of our pockets to D'Artagnan, who has a steady hand, and will go and play in the first *tripet* we come to. There, that's arranged."

"Let us finish the dinner, then," said Porthos; "it is getting cold."

The friends, having set their minds at ease with regard to the future, did honour to the repast, the remains of which were abandoned to MM. Mousqueton, Bazin, Planchet, and Grimaud.

On arriving in Paris, D'Artagnan found a letter from M. de Tréville, which informed him that, at his request, the king had promised that he should be admitted to the company of the musketeers.

As this was the height of D'Artagnan's worldly ambition, apart, be it well understood, from his desire of finding Madame Bonacieux, he ran, full of joy, to seek his comrades, whom he had left only half an hour before, but whom he found very sad and deeply preoccupied. They were assembled in council at the residence of Athos, which always indicated an event of some seriousness. M. de Tréville had intimated to them that, it being his majesty's fixed intention to open the campaign on the 1st of May, they must immediately get ready all their appointments.

The four philosophers looked at each other in a state of bewilderment. M. de Tréville never joked in matters relating to discipline.

"And what do you reckon your appointments will cost?" said D'Artagnan.

"Oh, we can scarcely venture to say. We have made our calculations with Spartan economy, and we each require fifteen hundred livres."

"Four times fifteen make sixty—ah! six thousand livres," said Athos.

"For my part, I think," said D'Artagnan, "with a thousand livres each—I do not speak as a Spartan, but as a procureur——"

This word procureur roused Porthos.

"Stop!" said he, "I have an idea."

"Well, that's something; for my part, I have not the shadow of one," said Athos, coolly; "but as to D'Artagnan, the idea of belonging to *ours*, gentlemen, has driven him out of his senses. A thousand livres! for my part, I declare I want two thousand."

"Four times two make eight, then," said Aramis; "it is eight thousand that we want to complete our appointments, of which appointments, it is true, we have already handsome saddles."

"Besides," said Athos, waiting till D'Artagnan, who went to thank M. de Tréville, had shut the door, "besides, there is that beautiful ring which beams from the finger of our friend. What the devil! D'Artagnan is too good a comrade to leave his brothers in embarrassment whilst he wears the ransom of a king on his finger."

CHAPTER XXIX.

HUNTING FOR THE EQUIPMENTS.

THE most preoccupied of the four friends was certainly D'Artagnan, although D'Artagnan, in his quality of guard, would be much more easily equipped than messieurs the musketeers, who were all very high ; but our Gascon cadet was, as may have been observed, of a provident and almost avaricious character, and with that (explain the contradiction if you can) so vainglorious as almost to rival Porthos. To this preoccupation of his vanity, D'Artagnan, at this moment, joined an uneasiness much less selfish. Notwithstanding all his inquiries respecting Madame Bonacieux, he could obtain no intelligence of her. M. de Tréville had spoken of her to the queen ; the queen was ignorant where the mercer's young wife was, but had promised to have her sought for. But this promise was very vague, and did not at all reassure D'Artagnan.

Athos did not laeve his chamber ; he made up his mind not to take a single step to provide for his equipment.

" We have still a fortnight before us," said he to his friends ; " well, if, at the end of a fortnight, I have found nothing, or, rather, if nothing has come to find me, as I am too good a Catholic to kill myself with a pistol-bullet, I will seek a good cause of quarrel with four of his eminence's guards or with eight Englishmen ; I will fight until one of them has killed me, which, considering the number, cannot fail to happen. It will then be said of me that I died for the king, so that I shall have performed my duty without the expense of equipment."

Porthos continued to walk about, with his hands behind him, tossing his head, and repeating :

" I shall follow up my idea."

Aramis, anxious, and negligently dressed, said nothing.

It may be seen by these disastrous details that desolation reigned in the community.

The lackeys, on their part, like the coursers of Hippolytus, shared the sadness of their masters. Mousqueton collected a store of crusts ; Bazin, who had always been inclined to devotion, never quitted the churches ; Planchet watched the flight of flies ; and Grimaud, whom the general distress could not induce to break the silence imposed by his master, heaved sighs enough to soften stones.

The three friends—for, as we have said, Athos had sworn not to stir a foot to equip himself—the three friends went out early in the morning, and returned late at night. They wandered about the streets, looking at the pavement as if to see whether the passengers had not left a purse behind them. They might have been supposed to be following tracks, so attentive were they wherever they went. When they met they looked desolately at each other, as much as to say, " Have you found anything ?"

However, as Porthos had first found an idea, and had thought of it earnestly afterwards, he was the first to act. He was a man of execution, this worthy Porthos. D'Artagnan perceived him one day walking towards the church of St. Leu, and followed him instinctively ; he entered, after having twisted his moustache and elongated his royal, which always announced, on his part, the most conquering resolutions. As D'Artagnan took some precautions to conceal himself, Porthos believed he had not been seen. D'Artagnan entered behind him, Porthos went and leaned against the side of a pillar ; D'Artagnan, still unperceived, supported himself against the other side of it.

There happened to be a sermon, which made the church very full. Porthos took advantage of this circumstance to ogle the women : thanks to the cares of Mousqueton, the exterior was far from announcing the distress of the interior : his hat was a little napless, his feather was a little faded, his gold lace was a little tarnished, his laces were a trifle frayed ; but in the obscurity of the church these things were not seen, and Porthos was still the handsome Porthos.

D'Artagnan observed, on the bench nearest to the pillar against which Porthos leaned, a sort of ripe beauty, rather yellow and rather dry, but erect and haughty, under her black hood. The eyes of Porthos were furtively cast upon this lady, and then roved about at large over the nave.

On her side, the lady, who from time to time blushed, darted with the rapidity of lightning a glance towards the inconstant Porthos, and then immediately the eyes of Porthos were sent wandering over the church anxiously. It was plain that this was a mode of proceeding that piqued the lady in the black hood to the quick, for she bit her lips till they bled, scratched the top of her nose, and could not sit still in her seat.

Porthos, seeing this, retwisted his moustache, elongated his royal a second time, and began to make signals to a beautiful lady who was near the choir, and who not only was a beautiful lady, but, still further, no doubt, a great lady, for she had behind her a negro boy, who had brought the cushion on which she knelt, and a female servant who held the coat-of-arms-marked bag, in which was placed the book from which she read the mass.

The lady with the black hood followed through all their wanderings the looks of Porthos, and perceived that they stopped upon the lady with the velvet cushion, the little negro, and the maid-servant.

During all this time Porthos played close ; it was almost imperceptible motions of his eyes, fingers placed upon the lips, little assassinating smiles, which really did assassinate the disdained beauty.

Then she uttered, in form of *mea culpa*, and striking her breast, a *hum !* so vigorous that everybody, even the lady with the red cushion, turned round towards her. Porthos paid no attention ; nevertheless, he understood it all, but was as deaf as the pillar he leaned against.

The lady with the red cushion produced a great effect—for she was very handsome—upon the lady with the black hood, who saw in her a rival really to be dreaded ; a great effect upon Porthos, who thought her much more pretty than the lady with the black hood ; a great effect upon D'Artagnan, who recognised in her the lady of Meung, of Calais, and Dover, whom his persecutor, the man with the scar, had saluted by the name of milady.

D'Artagnan, without losing sight of the lady of the red cushion, continued to watch the proceedings of Porthos, which amused him greatly; he directly guessed that the lady of the black hood was the procureur's wife of the Rue aux Ours, which was the more probable from the church of St. Leu being contiguous to that locality.

He guessed, likewise, that Porthos was taking his revenge for the defeat of Chantilly, when the procureuse had proved so refractory with respect to her purse.

But, amidst all this, D'Artagnan remarked also that not one countenance responded to the gallantries of Porthos. There was nothing but chimeras and illusions; but for real love, for true jealousy, is there any reality but illusions and chimeras?

The sermon over, the procureuse advanced towards the *bénitier;* Porthos went before her, and, instead of a finger, dipped his whole hand in. The procureuse smiled, thinking that it was for her that Porthos put himself to this expense; but she was cruelly and promptly undeceived: when she was only about three steps from him, he turned his head round, fixing his eyes invariably upon the lady of the red cushion, who had risen and was approaching, followed by her black boy and her fille-de-chambre.

When the lady of the red cushion came close to Porthos, Porthos drew his dripping hand from the *bénitier.* The fair *dévote* touched the great hand of Porthos with her delicate fingers, smiled, made the sign of the cross, and left the church.

This was too much for the procureuse; she entertained no doubt that there was an affair of gallantry between this lady and Porthos. If she had been a great lady she would have fainted; but as she was only a procureuse, she contented herself with saying to the musketeer, with concentrated fury:

"Eh, Monsieur Porthos, you don't offer *me* any holy water?"

Porthos, at the sound of that voice, started like a man awakened from a sleep of a hundred years.

"Ma—madame!" cried he; "is that you? How is your husband, our dear Monsieur Coquenard? Is he still as stingy as ever? Where can my eyes have been not to have even perceived you during the two hours the sermon has lasted?"

"I was within two paces of you, monsieur," replied the procureuse; "but you did not perceive me, because you had no eyes but for the pretty lady to whom you just now gave the holy water."

Porthos pretended to be confused.

"Ah," said he, "you have remarked."

"I must have been blind if I had not."

"Yes," said Porthos, "that is a duchess of my acquaintance, with whom I have great trouble to meet, on account of the jealousy of her husband, and who sent me word that she should come to-day, solely for the purpose of seeing me in this poor church, buried in this vile quarter."

"Monsieur Porthos," said the procureuse, "will you have the kindness to offer me your arm for five minutes ? I have something to say to you."

"Certainly, madame," said Porthos, winking to himself, as a gambler does who laughs at the dupe he is about to pluck.

At that moment D'Artagnan passed in pursuit of milady ; he cast a passing glance at Porthos, and beheld this triumphant look.

"Eh, eh !" said he, reasoning to himself according to the strangely easy morality of that gallant period, "there is one, at least, in the road to be equipped in time."

Porthos, yielding to the pressure of the arm of the procureuse, as a barque yields to the rudder, arrived at the Cloisters Saint Magloire, a very unfrequented passage, enclosed with a turnstile at each end. In the daytime nobody was seen there but mendicants devouring their crusts, and children playing.

"Ah, Monsieur Porthos," cried the procureuse, when she was assured that no one a stranger to the population of the locality could either see or hear her, "ah, Monsieur Porthos, you are a great conqueror, it appears !"

"Who—I, madame?" said Porthos, drawing himself up proudly ; "how so ?"

"Look at the proofs of it, just now, and the holy water ! But that must be a princess, at least, that lady with her negro boy and her maid !"

"Pardieu ! madame, you are deceived ; she is simply a duchess."

"And that running footman who waited at the door, and that carriage with a coachman in grand livery, who sat waiting on his seat ?"

Porthos had seen neither the footman nor the carriage, but, with the eye of a jealous woman, Madame Coquenard had seen everything.

Porthos regretted that he had not at once made the lady of the red cushion a princess.

"Ah, you are quite the pet of the ladies, Monsieur Porthos !" resumed the procureuse, with a sigh.

"Why, you may well imagine that, with the person with which nature has endowed me, I am not in want of ladies' favours."

"Good Lord ! how quickly men forget !" cried the procureuse, raising her eyes towards heaven.

"Still less quickly than the women, in my opinion," replied Porthos ; "as a proof, I, madame, I may say I was your victim ; when wounded, dying, I was abandoned by the surgeons ; I, the offspring of a noble family, who placed reliance upon your friendship, I was near dying of my wounds at first, and of hunger afterwards, in a beggarly auberge at Chantilly, without your ever deigning once to reply to the burning letters I addressed to you."

"But, Monsieur Porthos," murmured the procureuse, who began to feel that, to judge by the conduct of the great ladies of the time, she was wrong.

"I ! who had sacrificed the Countess de Penaflor on your account !"

" Well, I know you did."

" The Baronne de——"

" Monsieur Porthos, do not overwhelm me quite !"

" The Countess de——"

" Monsieur Porthos, be generous !"

" You are right, madame, and I will not finish."

" But it was my husband who would not hear of lending."

" Madame Coquenard," said Porthos, " remember the first letter you wrote me, and which I preserve engraven in my memory."

The procureuse uttered a groan.

" Besides," said she, " the sum you required me to borrow was rather large ; you said you wanted a thousand livres !"

" Madame Coquenard, I gave you the preference.   I had but to write to the Duchess de—— ; but I won't repeat her name, for I am incapable of compromising a woman ; but this I know, that I had but to write to her, and she would have sent me fifteen hundred."

The procureuse let fall a tear.

" Monsieur Porthos," said she, " I can assure you you have severely punished me; and if in the time to come you should find yourself in a similar situation, you have but to apply to me."

" Fie, madame, fie !" said Porthos, as if disgusted ; " let us not talk about money, if you please ; it is humiliating."

" Then you no longer love me ?" said the procureuse, slowly and sadly.

Porthos maintained a majestic silence.

" And that is the only reply you make me ?   Alas ! I but too well understand."

" Think of the offence you have committed towards me, madame ! it remains *here !*" said Porthos, placing his hand on his heart, and pressing it strongly.

" I will repair it ; indeed I will, my dear Porthos."

" Besides, what did I ask of you ?" resumed Porthos, with a movement of the shoulders full of *bonhommie*.   " A loan, nothing more !   After all, I am not an unreasonable man.   I know you are not rich, Madame Coquenard, and that your husband is obliged to bleed his poor clients to squeeze a few paltry crowns from them.   Oh ! if you were a duchess, a marquise, or a countess, it would be quite a different thing ; it would be unpardonable."

The procureuse was piqued.

" Please to know, Monsieur Porthos," said she, " that my strong box, strong box of a procureuse as it may be, is better filled than those of your ruined minxes."

" That, then, doubles the offence," said Porthos, disengaging his arm from that of the procureuse ; " for, if you are rich, Madame Coquenard, then there is no excuse for your refusal."

" When I said rich," replied the procureuse, who saw that she had gone too far, " you must not take the word for the letter. I am not precisely rich, I am only pretty well off."

"Hold, madame," said Porthos, "let us say no more upon the subject, I beg of you. You don't know me,—all sympathy is extinct between us."

"Ungrateful man as you are !"

"Ah ! I advise you to complain !" said Porthos.

"Begone, then, to your beautiful duchess, I will detain you no longer."

"And she is not to be despised, in my opinion."

"Now, Monsieur Porthos, once more, and this is the last ! do you love me still ?"

"Alas ! madame," said Porthos, in the most melancholy tone he could assume, "when we are about to enter upon a campaign, a campaign in which my presentiments tell me I shall be killed——"

"Oh ! don't talk of such things !" cried the procureuse, bursting into tears.

"Something whispers me so," continued Porthos, becoming still more and more melancholy.

"Rather say that you have a new love affair."

"No, not so : I speak frankly to you. No new object affects me ; and I even feel here, at the bottom of my heart, something which speaks for you. But in a fortnight's time, as you know, or as you do not know, this fatal campaign is to open ; I shall be fearfully engaged in providing for my equipment. Then I am obliged to make a journey to my family, in the lower part of Brittany, to obtain the sum necessary for my departure."

Porthos observed a last struggle between love and avarice.

"And as," continued he, "the duchess you saw at the church has estates near to those of my family, we mean to make the journey together. Journeys, you know, appear much shorter when we travel two in company."

"Have you no friends in Paris, then, Monsieur Porthos ?" said the procureuse.

"I thought I had," said Porthos, resuming his melancholy air ; "but I have been bitterly taught that I was mistaken."

"You have some, Monsieur Porthos, you have some !" cried the procureuse, in a transport that surprised even herself ; "come to our house to-morrow. You are the son of my aunt, consequently my cousin ; you come from Noyon, in Picardy ; you have several law-suits and no procureur. Can you recollect all that ?"

"Perfectly, madame."

"Come at dinner-time."

"Very well."

"And be upon your guard before my husband, who is rather shrewd, notwithstanding his seventy-six years."

"Seventy-six years ! Peste ! that's a fine age !" replied Porthos.

"A great age, you mean, Monsieur Porthos. Yes, the poor man may be expected to leave me a widow, every hour," continued she, throwing a significant glance at Porthos. "Fortunately, by our marriage-contract, the survivor takes everything."

" Everything ?"

" Yes, all."

" You are a woman of precaution, I see, my dear Madame Coque-nard," said Porthos, squeezing the hand of the procureuse tenderly.

" We are, then, reconciled, dear Monsieur Porthos ?" said she, sim-pering.

" For life," said Porthos, in the same manner.

" Till we meet again, then, dear traitor !"

" Till we meet again, my forgetful charmer !"

" To-morrow, my angel !"

" To-morrow, flame of my life !"

CHAPTER XXX.

D'ARTAGNAN AND THE ENGLISHMAN.

D'ARTAGNAN followed milady, without being perceived by her ; he saw her get into her carriage, and heard her order the coachman to drive to St. Germain.

It was useless to endeavour to keep pace on foot with a carriage drawn by two powerful horses : D'Artagnan returned then to the Rue Férou.

In the Rue de Seine he met with Planchet, who had stopped before the house of a pastrycook, and was contemplating with ecstasy, a cake of the most appetising appearance.

He ordered him to go and saddle two horses in M. de Tréville's stables, one for himself, D'Artagnan, and one for Planchet. M. de Tréville, on all common occasions, had allowed him the liberty to do so.

Planchet proceeded towards the Rue du Colombier, and D'Artagnan towards the Rue Férou. Athos was at home, emptying in solitary sad-ness one of his bottles of the famous Spanish wine he had brought back with him from his journey into Picardy. He made a sign for Grimaud to bring a glass for D'Artagnan, and Grimaud obeyed, still as silently as usual.

D'Artagnan related to Athos all that had passed at the church be-tween Porthos and the procureuse, and how their comrade was probably by that time in a fair way to be equipped.

" As for me," replied Athos, to this recital, " I am quite at my ease ; it will not be women that will defray the expense of my equip-ment."

" The more to blame you ; handsome, well-bred, noble as you are, my dear Athos, neither princesses nor queens would be secure !"

" How young this D'Artagnan is !" said Athos, shrugging his shoulders, and making a sign to Grimaud to bring another bottle.

At that moment Planchet put his head modestly in at the half-open door, and told his master that the horses were ready.

" What horses ?" asked Athos.

"Two horses that M. de Tréville lends me when I please, and with which I am now going to take a ride to St. Germain."

"Well, and what are you going to do at St. Germain?"

Then D'Artagnan described the meeting which, on his side, he had had at the church, and how he had found that lady who, with the seigneur in the black cloak, and with the scar near his temple, filled his mind constantly.

"That is to say, you are in love with this lady as you were with Madame Bonacieux," said Athos, shrugging his shoulders contemptuously, as if he pitied human weakness.

"I? not at all!" said D'Artagnan, "I am only curious to unravel the mystery to which she is attached. I do not know why, but I have a strong feeling that this woman, perfectly unknown to me as she is, and unknown to her as I am, has an influence over my life."

"Well, perhaps you are right," said Athos; "I do not know a woman that is worth the trouble of being sought for when she is once lost. Madame Bonacieux is lost, so much the worse for her."

"No, Athos, no, you are mistaken," said D'Artagnan; "I love my poor Constance more than ever, and if I knew the place in which she is, were it at the end of the world, I would go and free her from the hands of her enemies; but I cannot find out where she is, all my researches have proved in vain. What is to be said? I must divert my attention by something!"

"Amuse yourself, then, with milady, my dear D'Artagnan; I wish you may with all my heart, if that will amuse you."

"Hear me, Athos," said D'Artagnan, "instead of shutting yourself up here as if you were under arrest, get on horseback, and come and take a ride with me to St. Germain."

"My dear fellow," said Athos, "I ride horses when I have any; when I have none, I walk on foot."

"Well, on my part," said D'Artagnan, smiling at the misanthropy of Athos, which from any other person would certainly have offended him, "for my part, I ride what I can get; I am not so proud as you, Athos. So, *au revoir*, my proud, melancholy friend."

"*Au revoir*," said the musketeer, making a sign to Grimaud to uncork the bottle he had just brought.

D'Artagnan and Planchet got into the saddle, and took the road to St. Germain.

As he rode along, that which Athos had said respecting Madame Bonacieux, recurred to the mind of the young man. Although D'Artagnan was not of a very sentimental character, the mercer's pretty wife had made a real impression upon his heart. As he said, he was ready to go to the end of the world to seek her: but the world being round, it has many ends, so that he did not know which way to turn; in the meantime, he was going to try to find out who milady was. Milady had spoken to the man in the black cloak, therefore she knew him. Now, in the opinion of D'Artagnan, it was certainly the man in the black cloak who had carried off Madame Bonacieux the second time, as he had carried her off the first.   D'Artagnan then only half lied, which is lying but little, when he said that by going in search of milady, he at the same time went in search of Constance.

Thinking of all this, and from time to time giving a touch of the spur to his horse, D'Artagnan completed his short journey, and arrived at St. Germain.   He had just passed by the pavilion in which ten years later Louis XIV. was to be born.   He rode up a very quiet street, looking to the right and the left to see if he could catch any vestige of his beautiful Englishwoman, when from the terrace in front of a pretty house, which, according to the fashion of the time, had no window towards the street, he saw a face peep out with which he thought he was acquainted.   This person walked along the terrace, which was ornamented with flowers.   Planchet made out who it was first.

"Eh ! monsieur !" said he, addressing D'Artagnan, " don't you remember that face which is gaping about yonder ?"

" No," said D'Artagnan, " and yet I am certain it is not the first time I have seen it."

" Parbleu ! I believe it is not," said Planchet ; "why, it is poor Lubin, the lackey of the Count de Wardes—he whom you so well accommodated a month ago, at Calais, on the road to the governor's country-house !"

"So it is !" said D'Artagnan ; " I know him now.   Do you think he would recollect you ?"

" Ma foi ! monsieur, he was in such trouble, that I don't think he can have retained a very clear recollection of me."

" Well, go and get into conversation with him, and make out, if you can, whether his master is dead or not."

Planchet dismounted, and went straight up to Lubin, who did not at all remember him, and the two lackeys began to chat with the best understanding possible ; whilst D'Artagnan turned the two horses into a lane, and went round the house, coming back to watch the conference from behind a hedge of nut-trees.

At the end of an instant's observation he heard the noise of a carriage, and speedily saw that of milady stop opposite to him.   He could not be mistaken—milady was in it.   D'Artagnan stooped down upon the neck of his horse, in order that he might see without being seen.

Milady put her charming fair head out at the window, and gave her orders to her female attendant.

The latter, a pretty girl of about twenty years of age, active and lively, the true soubrette of a great lady, jumped from the step—upon which, according to the custom of the time, she was seated,—and took her way towards the terrace upon which D'Artagnan had perceived Lubin.

D'Artagnan followed the soubrette with his eyes, and saw her go towards the terrace.   But it happened that some one in the house called Lubin, so that Planchet remained alone, looking in all directions for his master.

The femme de chambre approached Planchet, whom she took for Lubin, and holding out a little billet to him.

" For your master," said she.

" For my master ?" replied Planchet, in astonishment.

" Yes—and of consequence,—take it quickly."

Thereupon she ran towards the carriage, which had turned round towards the way it came, jumped upon the step, and the carriage drove off.

Planchet turned the billet on all sides ; then, accustomed to passive obedience, he jumped down from the terrace, ran towards the lane, and at the end of twenty paces met D'Artagnan, who, having seen all, was coming to him.

" For you, monsieur," said Planchet, presenting the billet to the young man.

" For me !" said D'Artagnan,—" are you sure of that ?"

" Pardieu ! monsieur, I can't be more sure. The soubrette said ' *For your master.*' I have no other master but you ; so—a pretty little lass, ma foi ! is that soubrette !"

D'Artagnan opened the letter, and read these words :

"A person who takes more interest in you than she is willing to confess, wishes to know on what day it will suit you to walk in the forest ? To-morrow, at the Hôtel du Champ du Drap d'Or, a lackey in black and red will wait for your reply."

" Oh ! oh !" said D'Artagnan, "this is rather warm ; it appears that milady and I are anxious about the health of the same person. Well, Planchet, how is the good M. de Wardes ! he is not dead, then ?"

" Oh, no, monsieur, he is as well as a man can be with four sword-wounds in his body ; for you, without question, inflicted four upon the dear gentleman, and he is still very weak, having lost almost all his blood. As I said, monsieur, Lubin did not know me, and told me our adventure from one end to the other."

" Well done, Planchet ! you are the king of lackeys. Now jump up on your horse, and let us overtake the carriage."

They soon effected this. At the end of five minutes they perceived the carriage drawn up by the road-side : a cavalier, richly dressed, was close to the coach-door.

The conversation between milady and the cavalier was so animated, that D'Artagnan stopped on the other side of the carriage without any one but the pretty soubrette being aware of his presence.

The conversation took place in English,—a language which D'Artagnan could not understand ; but, by the accent, the young man plainly saw that the beautiful Englishwoman was in a great rage : she terminated it by an action which left no doubt as to the nature of this conversation—this was a blow with her fan, applied with such force that the little feminine weapon flew into a thousand pieces.

The cavalier broke into a loud laugh, which appeared to exasperate milady still more.

D'Artagnan thought this was the moment to interfere ; he approached the other door, and taking off his hat respectfully,—

" Madame," said he, " will you permit me to offer you my services ?

It appears to me that this cavalier has made you very angry. Speak one word, madame, and I take upon myself to punish him for his want of courtesy."

At the first word, milady turned round, looking at the young man with astonishment ; and when he had finished,—

"Monsieur," said she, in very good French, "I should with great confidence place myself under your protection, if the person with whom I quarrel were not my brother."

"Ah ! excuse me, then," said D'Artagnan, "you must be aware that I was ignorant of that, madame !"

"What is that stupid fellow troubling himself about?" cried the cavalier, whom milady had designated as her brother, stooping down to the height of the coach window,—"why does not he go about his own business?"

"Stupid fellow yourself !" said D'Artagnan, stooping in his turn on the neck of his horse, and answering on his side through the carriage-window. "I do not go on, because it pleases me to stop here."

The cavalier addressed some words in English to his sister.

"I speak to you in French," said D'Artagnan ; "be kind enough, then, to reply to me in the same language. You are madame's brother, I learn,—be it so ; but, fortunately, you are not mine."

It might be thought that milady, timid as women are in general, would have interposed in this commencement of mutual provocations, in order to prevent the quarrel from going too far ; but, on the contrary, she threw herself back in her carriage, and called out coolly to the coachman, "Go on—home !"

The pretty soubrette cast an anxious glance at D'Artagnan, whose good looks seemed to have made an impression upon her.

The carriage went on, and left the two men in face of each other ; no material obstacle separated them.

The cavalier made a movement, as if to follow the carriage; but D'Artagnan, whose anger, already excited, was much increased by recognising in him the Englishman of Amiens, who had won his horse and was very near winning his diamond of Athos, caught at his bridle and stopped him.

"Well, monsieur !" said he ; "you appear to be more stupid than I am, for you forget there is a little quarrel to arrange between us two."

"Ah ! ah !" said the Englishman ; "is it you, my master ? It seems you must always be playing some game or other."

"Yes ; and that reminds me that I have a revenge to take. We will see, my dear monsieur, if you can handle a sword as skilfully as you can a dice-box."

"You see plainly that I have no sword," said the Englishman. "Do you wish to play the braggart with an unarmed man?"

"I hope you have a sword at home ; but, at all events, I have two, and, if you like, I will throw with you for one of them."

"Quite unnecessary," said the Englishman ; "I am well furnished with such sorts of playthings."

" Very well ! my worthy gentleman," replied D'Artagnan ; " pick out the longest, and come and show it to me this evening."

" Where ?"

" Behind the Luxembourg ; that's a charming spot for such amusements as the one I propose to you."

" That will do ; I will be there."

" Your hour ?"

" Six o'clock."

" Apropos, you have probably one or two friends ?"

" Humph ! I have three who would be honoured by joining in the sport with me."

" Three ! that's fortunate ! That falls out oddly ! Three is just my number !"

" Now then, who are you ?" asked the Englishman.

" I am M. d'Artagnan, a Gascon gentleman, serving in the guards, in the company of M. des Essarts. And you ?"

" I am the Lord de Winter, Baron of Scheffield."

" Well, then, I am your servant, monsieur le baron," said D'Artagnan, " though you have names rather difficult to recollect."

And touching his horse with the spur, he cantered back to Paris.

As he was accustomed to do in all cases of any consequence, D'Artagnan went straight to the residence of Athos.

He found Athos reclining upon a large sofa, where he was waiting, as he said, for his equipment to come and find him.

He related to Athos all that had passed, except the letter to M. de Wardes.

Athos was delighted to find he was going to fight an Englishman. We are aware that that was his dream.

They immediately sent their lackeys for Porthos and Aramis, and, on their arrival, made them acquainted with the affair in hand.

Porthos drew his sword from the scabbard, and made passes at the wall, springing back from time to time, and making contortions like a dancer.

Aramis, who was constantly at work at his poem, shut himself up in Athos's closet, and begged not to be disturbed before the moment of drawing swords.

Athos, by signs, desired Grimaud to bring another bottle of wine.

And D'Artagnan employed himself in arranging a little plan, of which we shall hereafter see the execution, and which promised him some agreeable adventure, as might be seen by the smiles which from time to time passed over his countenance, the thoughtfulness of which they enlivened.

CHAPTER XXXI.

ENGLISH AND FRENCH.

THE hour being come, they, with their four lackeys, repaired to a spot behind the Luxembourg given up to the feeding of goats. Athos threw a piece of money to the goat-keeper to remove his flock to a distance. The lackeys were charged to act as sentinels.

A silent party soon drew near to the same enclosure, penetrated into it, and joined the musketeers : then, according to the English custom, the presentations took place.

The Englishmen were all men of rank ; consequently, the extraordinary names of their adversaries were, for them, not only a matter of surprise, but of uneasiness.

" But, after all this," said Lord de Winter, when the three friends had been named, " we do not know who you are ; as gentlemen, we cannot fight with such ; why, they are nothing but shepherds' names."

" Therefore your lordship may suppose they are only assumed names," said Athos.

" Which only gives us a greater desire to know the real ones," replied milord.

" You gambled very willingly with us without knowing our names," said Athos, " as is plain by your having won our horses."

" That is true, but we then only risked our pistoles ; this time we risk our blood : we play with anybody, but we only fight with our equals."

" And that is but just," said Athos, and he took aside that one of the four Englishmen with whom he was to fight, and communicated his name in a low voice.

Porthos and Aramis did the same.

" Does that satisfy you ?" said Athos to his adversary ; " do you think me sufficiently noble to do me the honour of crossing swords with me ?"

" Yes, monsieur," said the Englishman, bowing.

" Well ! now shall I tell you another thing ?" said Athos, coolly.

" What is that ?" replied the Englishman.

" Why, that is, that you would have acted much more wisely if you had not required me to make myself known."

" Why so ?"

" Because I am believed to be dead, and have reasons for wishing nobody should know I am living, so that I shall be obliged to kill you to prevent my secret getting wind."

The Englishman looked at Athos, believing that he was joking, but Athos was not joking the least in the world.

" Gentlemen," said Athos, addressing at the same time his companions and their adversaries, " are we ready ?"

" Yes !" answered the Englishmen and the Frenchmen, as with one voice.

" Guard, then !" cried Athos.

And immediately eight swords glittered in the rays of the setting sun, and the combat began with an animosity very natural to men who had been twice enemies.

Athos fenced with as much calmness and method as if he had been practising in a school.

Porthos, corrected, no doubt, of his too great confidence by his adventure of Chantilly, played with *finesse* and prudence.

Aramis, who had the third canto of his poem to finish, made all the despatch of a man very much pressed for time.

Athos, the first, killed his adversary : he hit him but once, but, as he had foretold, that hit was a mortal one—the sword passed through his heart.

Porthos, the second, stretched his upon the grass, with a wound through his thigh ; and as the Englishman, without making any further resistance, then surrendered his sword, Porthos took him up in his arms and carried him to his carriage.

Aramis pushed his so vigorously, that after going back fifty paces, he finished by fairly taking to his heels, and disappeared amid the hooting of the lackeys.

As to D'Artagnan, he fought purely and simply on the defensive ; and when he saw his adversary pretty well fatigued with a vigorous sidethrust he twisted the sword from his grasp, and sent it glittering into the air. The baron finding himself disarmed, gave two or three paces back, but in this movement, his foot slipped and he fell.

D'Artagnan was over him at a bound, and pointing his sword to his throat,—

"I could kill you, milord," said he to the Englishman ; "you are completely at my mercy, but I spare your life for the sake of your sister."

D'Artagnan was at the height of joy ; he had realised the plan which he had fancied, the development of which had produced the smiles upon his face we mentioned.

The Englishman, delighted at having to do with a gentleman of such a kind disposition, pressed D'Artagnan in his arms and paid a thousand compliments to the three musketeers, and, as Porthos's adversary was already installed in the carriage, and as Aramis's had run away, they had nothing to think about but the defunct.

As Porthos and Aramis were undressing him in the hope of finding his wound not mortal, a large purse dropped from his clothes. D'Artagnan picked it up and held it out to Lord de Winter.

"What the devil would you have me to do with that ?" said the Englishman.

"You can restore it to his family," said D'Artagnan.

"His family will care vastly about such a trifle as that ! his family will inherit fifteen thousand louis a year from him : keep the purse for your lackeys."

D'Artagnan put the purse into his pocket.

"And now, my young friend, if you will permit me, I hope to give you that name," said Lord de Winter, "on this very evening, if agreeable to you, I will present you to my sister, Lady Clarik ; for I am desirous that she should take you into her good graces ; and as she is not in bad odour at court, she may perhaps, on some future day, speak a word that will not prove useless to you."

D'Artagnan blushed with pleasure, and bowed a sign of assent.

At this time Athos came up to D'Artagnan :

" What do you mean to do with that purse ?" whispered he.

" Why, I meant to pass it over to you, my dear Athos."

" Me ! why to me ?"

" The devil ! why you killed him, didn't you ?   They are the *spolia opima.*"

" I, the heir of an enemy !" said Athos, " for whom then do you take me ?"

" It is the custom in war," said D'Artagnan, " why should it not be the custom in a duel ?"

" Even on the field of battle, I have never done that."

Porthos shrugged his shoulders ; Aramis by a movement of his lips applauded the opinion of Athos.

" Then," said D'Artagnan, " let us give the money to the lackeys, as Lord de Winter desired us to do."

" Yes," said Athos, " let us give the money to the lackeys, but not to our lackeys, to the lackeys of the Englishmen."

Athos took the purse, and threw it into the hand of the coach·man.

" For you and your comrades," said he.

This greatness of spirit in a man who was quite destitute, struck even Porthos, and this trait of French generosity, repeated by Lord de Winter and his friend, was highly applauded by every one, except MM. Grimaud, Bazin, Mousqueton, and Planchet.

Lord de Winter, on quitting D'Artagnan, gave him his sister's address ; she lived, No. 6, Place Royale, then the fashionable quarter, and undertook to call and take him with him in order to introduce him. D'Artagnan appointed eight o'clock at Athos's residence.

This introduction to Lady Clarik occupied the head of our Gascon greatly.   He remembered in what a strange manner this woman had hitherto been mixed up in his destiny.   According to his conviction, she was some creature of the cardinal's, and yet he felt himself invincibly drawn towards her by one of those sentiments for which we cannot account.   His only fear was that milady would recognise in him the man of Meung and of Dover.   Then she knew that he was one of the friends of M. de Tréville, and, consequently, that he belonged body and soul to the king, which would make him lose a part of his advantage, since when known to milady as he knew her, he played only an equal game with her.   As to the commencement of an intrigue between her and M. de Wardes, our presumptuous hero gave but little heed to that, although the marquis was young, handsome, rich, and high in the cardinal's favour.   It is not for nothing we are but twenty years old, particularly if we were born at Tarbes.

D'Artagnan began by making his most splendid toilette ; then returned to Athos's, and, according to custom, related everything to him.

Athos listened attentively to his projects ; then, shook his head, and recommended prudence to him with a shade of bitterness.

"What !" said he, "you have just lost one woman, who, you say, was good, charming, perfect, and here you are, running headlong after another !"

D'Artagnan felt the truth of this reproach.

"I loved Madame Bonacieux with my heart, whilst I only love milady with my head," said he ; "by getting introduced to her, my principal object is to ascertain what part she plays at court."

"The part she plays at court, pardieu ! it is not difficult to divine that, after all you have told me. She is some emissary of the cardinal's ; a woman who will draw you into a snare, in which you will leave your head."

"The devil ! my dear Athos, you view things on the dark side, methinks."

"D'Artagnan, I mistrust women : can it be otherwise ! I bought my experience dearly—particularly fair women. Milady is fair, you say ?"

"She has the most beautiful light hair imaginable !"

"Ah ! my poor D'Artagnan !" said Athos.

"Well, but listen to me : I want to be enlightened on a subject : then, when I shall have learned what I desire to know, I will withdraw."

"Be enlightened !" said Athos, phlegmatically.

Lord de Winter arrived at the appointed time, but Athos, being warned of his coming, went into the other chamber. He found D'Artagnan alone then, and as it was nearly eight o'clock, he took the young man with him.

An elegant carriage waited below, and as it was drawn by two excellent horses, they were soon at the Place Royale.

Milady Clarik received D'Artagnan ceremoniously. Her hotel was remarkably sumptuous ; and, whilst the most part of the English had quitted, or were about to quit France, on account of the war, milady had just been laying out much money upon her residence ; which proved that the general measure which drove the English from France, did not affect her.

"You see," said Lord de Winter, presenting D'Artagnan to his sister, "a young gentleman who has held my life in his hands, and who has not abused his advantage, although we had been twice enemies, although it was I who insulted him, and although I am an Englishman. Thank him then, madame, if you have any affection for me."

Milady frowned slightly, a scarcely visible cloud passed over her brow, and so peculiar a smile appeared upon her lips, that the young man who saw and observed this triple shade, almost shuddered at it.

The brother did not perceive this ; he had turned round to play with milady's favourite monkey, which had pulled him by the doublet.

"You are welcome, monsieur," said milady, in a voice whose singular sweetness contrasted with the symptoms of ill-humour which D'Artagnan had just remarked,—"you have to-day acquired eternal rights to my gratitude."

The Englishman then turned round, and described the combat without omitting a single detail. Milady listened with the greatest attention, and yet it was easily to be perceived, whatever effort she made to conceal her impressions, that this recital was not agreeable to her. The blood rose to her head, and her little foot worked with impatience beneath her robe.

Lord de Winter perceived nothing of this. When he had finished, he went to a table upon which was a salver with Spanish wine and glasses. He filled two, and by a sign, invited D'Artagnan to drink.

D'Artagnan knew it was considered disobliging by an Englishman to refuse to pledge him ; therefore, drew near to the table, and took the second glass. He did not, however, lose sight of milady, and in a mirror perceived the change that took place in her face. Now that she believed herself to be no longer observed, a sentiment which resembled ferocity animated her countenance. She bit her handkerchief with all her might.

That pretty little soubrette that D'Artagnan had already observed, then came in ; she spoke some words to Lord de Winter in English ; and he immediately requested D'Artagnan's permission to retire, excusing himself on account of the urgency of the business that called him away, and charging his sister to obtain his pardon.

D'Artagnan exchanged a shake of the hand with Lord de Winter, and then returned to milady. Her countenance, with surprising mobility, had recovered its gracious expression, but some little red spots upon her handkerchief indicated that she had bitten her lips till the blood came. Those lips were magnificent ! they might be said to be of coral.

The conversation took a cheerful turn. Milady appeared to be entirely recovered. She told D'Artagnan that Lord de Winter was her brother-in-law, and not her brother ; she had married a younger brother of the family, who had left her a widow with one child. This child was the only heir to Lord de Winter, if Lord de Winter did not marry. All this showed D'Artagnan that there was a veil which enveloped something, but he could not yet see under this veil.

In addition to this, after half an hour's conversation, D'Artagnan was convinced that milady was his compatriot ; she spoke French with an elegance and a purity that left no doubt on that head.

D'Artagnan was profuse in gallant speeches and protestations of devotedness. To all the simple things which escaped our Gascon, milady replied with a smile of kindness. The hour for retiring arrived. D'Artagnan took leave of milady, and left the salon the happiest of men.

Upon the stairs he met the pretty soubrette, who brushed gently against him as she passed, and then, blushing to the eyes, asked his pardon for having touched him, in a voice so sweet, that the pardon was granted instantly.

D'Artagnan came again on the morrow, and was still better received than on the day before. Lord de Winter was not at home, and it was milady who this time did all the honours of the evening. She appeared to take a great interest in him, asked him whence he came, who were his friends, and whether he had not at some times thought of attaching himself to M. le Cardinal.

D'Artagnan who, as we have said, was exceedingly prudent for a young man of twenty, then remembered his suspicions regarding milady ; he launched into an eulogy of his eminence, and said that he should not have failed to enter into the guards of the cardinal instead of the king's guards, if he had happened to know M. de Cavois instead of M. de Tréville.

Milady changed the conversation without any appearance of affectation, and asked D'Artagnan in the most careless manner possible, if he had never been in England.

D'Artagnan replied that he had been sent thither by M. de Tréville, to treat for a number of horses, and that he had brought back four as specimens.

Milady, in the course of her conversation, twice or thrice bit her lips ; she had to deal with a Gascon who played close.

At the same hour as the preceding evening D'Artagnan retired. In the corridor he again met the pretty Kitty ; that was the name of the soubrette. She looked at him with an expression of kindness which it was impossible to mistake. But D'Artagnan was so preoccupied by the mistress, that he remarked nothing but her.

D'Artagnan came again on the morrow and the day after that, and each day milady gave him a more gracious welcome.

Every evening, either in the antechamber, the corridor, or on the stairs, he met the pretty soubrette. But, as we have said, D'Artagnan paid no attention to this.

CHAPTER XXXII.

A PROCUREUR'S DINNER.

HOWEVER brilliant had been the part played by Porthos in the duel, it had not made him forget the dinner of his procureuse.

On the morrow he received the last polishing brush from the hand of Mousqueton, and took his way towards the Rue aux Ours, with the step of a man who was doubly in favour with fortune.

His heart beat, but not like D'Artagnan's, with a young and impatient love. No, a more material interest stirred his blood : he was about at last to pass that mysterious threshold, to climb those unknown stairs by which, one by one, the old crowns of Master Coquenard had ascended. He was about to see, in reality, a certain coffer, of which he had twenty times beheld the image in his dreams ; a coffer, long and deep, locked, bolted, fixed in the wall ; a coffer of which he had so often heard speak, and which the hands, a little wrinkled, it is true, but still not without elegance, of the procureuse were about to open to his admiring looks.

And then he, a wanderer on the earth, a man without fortune, a man without family, a soldier accustomed to auberges, cabarets, taverns, and parades, a lover of wine forced to depend upon chance treats,—he was about to partake of family meals, to enjoy the pleasures of a comfortable establishment, and to give himself up to those little attentions, which the harder one is the more they please, as the old soldiers say.

To come in quality of a cousin, and seat himself every day at a good table, to smooth the yellow, wrinkled brow of the old procureur, to pluck the clerks a little by teaching them *bassette, passe-dix,* and *lansquenet,* in their utmost *finesse,* and by winning of them, by way of fee for the lesson he would give them in an hour, their savings of a month—all this was enormously delightful in prospect to Porthos.

The musketeer could not forget the evil reports which then prevailed, and which indeed have survived them, of the procureurs of the period : meanness, stinginess, fasts ; but as, after all, excepting some few acts of economy, which Porthos had always found very unseasonable, the procureuse had been tolerably liberal—that is, be it understood, for a procureuse—he hoped to see a household of a highly comfortable kind.

And yet, at the very door, the musketeer began to entertain some doubts ; the approach was not such as to prepossess people ; an ill-smelling, dark passage, a staircase half lighted by bars through which stole a glimmer from a neighbouring yard ; on the first floor a low door studded with enormous nails, like the principal gate of the Grand Châtelet.

Porthos knocked with his finger ; a tall, pale clerk, with a face shaded by a forest of unclipped hair, opened the door, and bowed with the air of a man forced to respect in another lofty stature, which indicated strength, the military dress, which indicated rank, and a ruddy countenance, which indicated being accustomed to good living.

Another shorter clerk behind the first, another taller clerk behind the second, another stripling of twelve years old behind the third—in all, three clerks and a half, which, for the time, argued a very extensive cliency.

Although the musketeer was not expected before one o'clock, the procureuse had been upon the watch ever since twelve, reckoning that the heart, or perhaps the stomach of her lover, would bring him before his time.

Madame Coquenard therefore entered the office from the house at the same moment that her guest entered from the stairs, and the appearance of the worthy lady relieved him from an awkward embarrassment. The clerks surveyed him with great curiosity, and he, not knowing well what to say to this ascending and descending scale, remained mute.

" It is my cousin !" cried the procureuse ; "come in ! come in ! my dear Monsieur Porthos !"

The name of Porthos produced its effect upon the clerks, who began to laugh ; but Porthos turned sharply round, and every countenance quickly recovered its gravity.

They arrived in the closet of the procureur, after having passed through the antechamber in which the clerks were, and the office in which they ought to have been ; this last apartment was a sort of dark room, covered with waste paper. On leaving the office, the kitchen was on the right, and they entered the principal room, or, as we should now say, drawing-room.

All these chambers, which communicated with each other, did not inspire Porthos with the most favourable ideas. Words might be heard at a distance through all these open doors ; and then, whilst passing, he had cast a rapid, investigating glance into the kitchen, and he was obliged to confess to himself, to the shame of the procureuse, and his own regret, that he did not see that fire, that bustle, which, while a good repast is about to be produced, prevails generally in that sanctuary of good living.

The procureur had without doubt been warned of his visit, as he expressed no surprise at the sight of Porthos, who advanced towards him with a sufficiently familiar air, and saluted him courteously.

"We are cousins, it appears, Monsieur Porthos ?" said the procureur, rising, by supporting his weight upon the arms of his cane-chair.

The old man, enveloped in a large black doublet, in which the whole of his slender body was concealed, was brisk and dry ; his little grey eyes shone like carbuncles, and appeared, with his grinning mouth, to be the only part of his face in which life survived. Unfortunately, the legs began to refuse their service to this bony machine ; during the last five or six months that this weakness had been felt, the worthy procureur had nearly become the slave of his wife.

The cousin was received with resignation, that was all. Master Coquenard firm upon his legs, would have declined all relationship with M. Porthos.

"Yes, monsieur, we are cousins," said Porthos, without being disconcerted, as he had never reckoned upon being received enthusiastically by the husband.

"By the female side, I believe ?" said the procureur, maliciously.

Porthos did not feel the ridicule of this, and took it for a piece of simplicity at which he laughed in his large moustache. Madame Coquenard, who knew that a simple procureur was a very rare variety in the species, smiled a little, and coloured a great deal.

Master Coquenard had, from the arrival of Porthos, frequently cast his eyes with great uneasiness upon a large chest placed in front of his oak desk. Porthos comprehended that this chest, although it did not correspond in shape with that which he had seen in his dreams, must be the blessed coffer, and he congratulated himself that the reality was several feet higher than the dream.

Monsieur Coquenard did not carry his genealogical investigations any further ; but, withdrawing his anxious look from the chest, and fixing it upon Porthos, he contented himself with saying : "Monsieur, our cousin, will do us the favour of dining with us once before his departure for the campaign, will he not, Madame Coquenard ?"

This time, Porthos received the blow right in his stomach, and felt it. It appeared, likewise, that Madame Coquenard was not less affected by it on her part, for she added :

"My cousin will not return if he finds that we do not treat him kindly ; but, otherwise, he has so little time to pass in Paris, and consequently to spare to us, that we must entreat him to give us every instant he can call his own previously to his departure."

"Oh my legs ! my poor legs ! where are you ?" murmured Coquenard, and he endeavoured to smile.

This succour, which Porthos received at the moment in which he was attacked in his gastronomic hopes, inspired much gratitude in the musketeer for the procureuse.

The hour of dinner soon arrived. They passed into the eating-room, a large dark apartment situated opposite to the kitchen.

The clerks who, as it appeared, had smelt unusual perfumes in the house, were of military punctuality, and stood with their stools in their hands, quite ready to sit down. Their jaws moved preliminarily with fearful threatenings.

"Indeed !" thought Porthos, casting a glance at the three hungry clerks, for the lad was not, as might be expected, admitted to the honours of the master's table ; "indeed ! in my cousin's place, I would not keep such gluttonous-looking fellows as these ! Why, they have the appearance of shipwrecked sailors who have had nothing to eat for six weeks."

Monsieur Coquenard entered, pushed along upon his chair with castors by Madame Coquenard, whom Porthos assisted in rolling her husband up to the table.

He had scarcely entered when he began to agitate his nose and his jaws after the example of his clerks.

"Oh, oh !" said he ; "here is a potage which is rather inviting !"

"What the devil can they smell so extraordinary in this potage ?" said Porthos, at the sight of a pale *bouillon*, abundant, but perfectly free from meat, and upon the surface of which a few crusts swam about, as wide apart as the islands of an archipelago.

Madame Coquenard smiled, and upon a sign from her every one eagerly took his seat.

Master Coquenard was served first, then Porthos ; afterwards Madame Coquenard filled her own plate, and distributed the crusts without *bouillon* to the impatient clerks. At this moment the door of the dining-room opened of itself with a creak, and Porthos perceived the little clerk, who, not being allowed to take part in the feast, ate his dry bread in the passage, by which he gave it the double relish of the odour which came from the dining-room and the kitchen.

After the potage the maid brought in a boiled fowl, a piece of magnificence which caused the eyes of the usual guests to dilate in a manner that threatened injury to them.

"One may see that you love your family, Madame Coquenard," said the procureur, with a smile that was almost tragic : "you are certainly treating your cousin very handsomely !"

The poor fowl was thin, and covered with one of those thick bristly skins through which the teeth cannot penetrate with all their efforts. The fowl must have been sought for a long time on the perch, to which it had retired to die of old age.

"The devil!" thought Porthos, "this is poor work! I respect old age; but I don't think much of it boiled or roasted."

And he looked round to see if anybody partook of his opinion; but, on the contrary, he saw nothing but eager eyes which were devouring, in anticipation, that sublime fowl which was the object of his contempt.

Madame Coquenard drew the dish towards her, skilfully detached the two great black feet, which she placed upon her husband's plate; cut off the neck, which, with the head, she put on one side for herself; raised the wing for Porthos, and then returned to the servant who had brought it in, the animal, otherwise intact, and which had disappeared before the musketeer had had time to examine the variations which disappointment produces upon faces, according to the characters and temperaments of those who experience it.

In the place of the fowl, a dish of haricot beans made its appearance; an enormous dish, in which some bones of mutton, which, at first sight, might have been supposed to have some meat on them, pretended to show themselves.

But the clerks were not the dupes of this deceit, and their lugubrious looks settled down into resigned countenances.

Madame Coquenard distributed this dish to the young men with the moderation of a good housewife.

The time for taking wine was come. Master Coquenard poured, from a very small stone bottle, the third of a glass to each of the young men, served himself in about the same proportion, and passed the bottle to Porthos and Madame Coquenard.

The young men filled up their third of a glass with water; then, when they had drunk half the glass, they filled it up again, and continued to do so; which brought them, by the end of the repast, to the swallowing of a drink which, from the colour of the ruby, had passed to that of a pale topaz.

Porthos ate his wing of the fowl very timidly, and shuddered when he felt the knee of the procureuse under the table, as it came in search of his. He also drank half a glass of this sparingly served wine, and found it to be nothing but that horrible Montreuil, the terror of all practised palates.

Master Coquenard saw him swallowing this wine undiluted, and sighed deeply.

"Will you eat any of these beans, cousin Porthos?" said Madame Coquenard, in that tone which says, "Take my advice, don't touch them."

"Devil take me if I taste one of them!" murmured Porthos; and then aloud:

"Thank you, my dear cousin, I have no more appetite."

A general silence prevailed. Porthos was quite at a loss. The procureur repeated several times :

"Ah ! Madame Coquenard ! accept my compliments ; your dinner has been a real feast. Lord ! how I have eaten !"

Master Coquenard had eaten his potage, the black feet of the fowl, and the only mutton bone on which there was the least appearance of meat.

Porthos fancied they were mystifying him, and began to curl his moustache and knit his eyebrow ; but the knee of Madame Coquenard came, and gently advised him to be patient.

This silence and this interruption in serving, which were unintelligible to Porthos, had, on the contrary, a terrible meaning for the clerks ; upon a look from the procureur, accompanied by a smile from Madame Coquenard, they arose slowly from table, folded their napkins more slowly still, bowed, and retired.

"Go, young men ; go and promote digestion by working," said the procureur gravely.

The clerks being gone, Madame Coquenard rose and took from a buffet a piece of cheese, some preserved quinces, and a cake which she had herself made of almonds and honey.

Master Coquenard knitted his eyebrows because there were too many good things ; Porthos bit his lips because there was not enough for a man's dinner. He looked to see if the dish of beans were gone ; the dish of beans had disappeared.

"A positive feast !" cried Master Coquenard, turning about in his chair ; "a real feast, *epulæ epulorum;* Lucullus dines with Lucullus."

Porthos looked at the bottle, which was near him, and hoped that with wine, bread and cheese, he might make a dinner, but wine was wanting, the bottle was empty ; Monsieur and Madame Coquenard did not seem to observe it.

"This is very fine !" thought Porthos to himself, "I am prettily caught !"

He passed his tongue over a spoonful of preserves, and stuck his teeth into the sticky pastry of Madame Coquenard.

"Now," said he, "the sacrifice is consummated ! Ah ! if I had not the hopes of having a peep with Madame Coquenard into her husband's chest !"

Master Coquenard, after the luxuries of such a repast, which he called an excess, felt the want of a siesta. Porthos began to hope that the thing would take place at the present sitting, and in that same locality ; but the procureur would listen to nothing ; he would be taken to his chamber, and was not satisfied till he was close to his chest, upon the edge of which, for still greater precaution, he placed his feet.

The procureuse took Porthos into an adjoining chamber, and they began to lay the basis of reconciliation.

"You can come and dine three times a week," said Madame Coquenard.

"Thanks, madame !" said Porthos, "but I don't like to abuse your kindness ; besides, I must think of this equipment."

"That's true," said the procureuse, groaning—"that unfortunate equipment!"

"Alas! yes," said Porthos, "it is so."

"But of what, then, does the equipment of your corps consist, Monsieur Porthos?"

"Oh! of many things," said Porthos, "the musketeers are, as you know, picked soldiers, and they require many things that are useless to the guards or the Swiss."

"But yet, detail them to me."

"Why, they may amount to ——" said Porthos, who preferred discussing the total to taking them one by one.

The procureuse waited tremblingly.

"To how much?" said she, "I hope it does not exceed——" She stopped, speech failed her.

"Oh! no," said Porthos, "it does not exceed two thousand five hundred livres; I even think that, with economy, I could manage it with two thousand livres."

"Good God!" cried she, "two thousand livres! why that is a fortune!"

Porthos made a most significant grimace; Madame Coquenard understood it.

"I only wished to know the detail," said she, "because having many relations in business, I was almost sure of obtaining things at a hundred per cent. less than you could get them yourself."

"Ah! ah!" said Porthos, "if that is what you meant to say?"

"Yes, my dear Monsieur Porthos; thus, for instance, don't you, in the first place want a horse!"

"Yes, a horse."

"Well, then! I can just suit you."

"Ah!" said Porthos, brightening, "that's well as regards my horse, then; but I must have the horse appointments complete, which are composed of objects that a musketeer alone can purchase, and which will not amount, besides, to more than three hundred livres."

"Three hundred livres; then put down three hundred livres," said the procureuse, with a sigh.

Porthos smiled; it may be remembered that he had the saddle which came from Buckingham; these three hundred livres then he reckoned upon putting snugly into his pocket.

"Then," continued he, "there is a horse for my lackey and my valise; as to my arms it is useless to trouble you about them, I have them."

"A horse for your lackey?" resumed the procureuse, hesitatingly; "but that is doing things in a very noble style, my friend."

"Well, madame!" said Porthos, haughtily; "do you take me for a beggar?"

"No, no; I only thought that a pretty mule made sometimes as good an appearance as a horse, and it seemed to me that by getting a pretty mule for Mousqueton——"

"Well, agreed for a pretty mule," said Porthos; "you are right, I have seen very great Spanish nobles, whose whole suite were mounted on mules. But then you understand, Madame Coquenard, a mule with feathers and bells."

" Be satisfied," said the procureuse.

" Then there remains the valise."

" Oh ! don't let that disturb you," cried Madame Coquenard, " my husband has five or six valises, you shall choose the best ; there is one in particular, which he prefers himself whenever he travels, large enough to hold all the world."

" Your valise is then empty ?" asked Porthos, with simplicity

" Certainly it is empty," replied the procureuse, really simply, on her part.

" Ah ! but the valise I want," cried Porthos, " is a well-filled one, my dear."

Madame uttered fresh sighs. Molière had not written his scene in L'Avare then. Madame Coquenard has then the *pas* of Harpagan.

In short, the rest of the equipment was successively debated in the same manner ; and the result of the sitting was, that Madame Coquenard should give eight hundred livres in money, and should furnish the horse and the mule, which should have the honour to carry Porthos and Mousqueton to glory.

These conditions being agreed to, Porthos took leave of Madame Coquenard. The latter wished to detain him by darting certain tender glances ; but Porthos urged the commands of duty, and the procureuse was obliged to give place to the king.

The musketeer returned home as hungry as a hunter.

CHAPTER XXXIII.

SOUBRETTE AND MISTRESS.

IN the meantime, in spite of the cries of his conscience and the wise counsels of Athos, D'Artagnan became hourly more in love with milady ; thus he never failed to pay his diurnal court to her, and the self-satisfied Gascon was convinced that, sooner or later, she could not fail to respond to him.

One day when he arrived, with his head in the air, and as light at heart as a man who is in expectation of a shower of gold, he found the soubrette under the gateway of the hotel ; but this time the pretty Kitty was not contented with touching him as he passed ; she took him gently by the hand.

" Good !" thought D'Artagnan, "she is charged with some message for me from her mistress ; she is about to appoint some meeting which she had not courage to speak of." And he looked down at the pretty girl with the most triumphant air imaginable.

" I wish to say three words to you, Monsieur le Chevalier," stammered the soubrette.

"Speak, my dear, speak," said D'Artagnan; "I am all attention."

"Here? That's impossible; that which I have to say is too long, and, still more, too secret."

"Well, what is to be done?"

"If Monsieur le Chevalier would follow me?" said Kitty, timidly.

"Where you please, my pretty little dear."

"Come, then."

And Kitty, who had not let go the hand of D'Artagnan, led him up a little dark, winding staircase, and, after ascending about fifteen steps, opened a door.

"Come in here, Monsieur le Chevalier," said she; "here we shall be alone, and can talk safely."

"And whose chamber is this, my pretty-faced friend?"

"It is mine, Monsieur le Chevalier; it communicates with my mistress's by that door. But you need not fear; she will not hear what we say; she never goes to bed before midnight."

D'Artagnan cast a glance around him. The little apartment was charming for its taste and neatness; but, in spite of himself, his eyes were directed to that door which Kitty said led to milady's chamber.

Kitty guessed what was passing in the mind of the young man, and heaved a deep sigh.

"You love my mistress, then, very dearly, Monsieur le Chevalier?" said she.

"Oh, more than I can say, Kitty! I am mad for her!"

Kitty breathed a second sigh.

"Alas! monsieur," said she, "that is a great pity!"

"What the devil do you see so pitiable in it?" said D'Artagnan.

"Because, monsieur," replied Kitty, "my mistress does not love you at all."

"Hein!" said D'Artagnan, "can she have charged her to tell me so?"

"Oh, no, monsieur; out of the regard I have for you, I have taken upon myself to tell you so."

"I am much obliged, my dear Kitty, but for the intention only; for the information, you must agree, is not likely to be very pleasant."

"That is to say, you don't believe what I have told you, is it not?"

"We have always some difficulty in believing such things, my pretty dear, were it only from self-love."

"Then you don't believe me?"

"Why, I confess that, unless you give me some proof of what you advance——

"What do you think of this?"

And Kitty drew a little note from her bosom.

"For me?" said D'Artagnan, seizing the letter.

"No; for another."

"For another?"

"Yes."

"His name! his name!" cried D'Artagnan.

"Read the address."

" Monsieur le Comte de Wardes."

The remembrance of the scene at St. Germain presented itself to the mind of the presumptuous Gascon ; as quick as thought he tore open the letter, in spite of the cry which Kitty uttered on seeing what he was going to do, or, rather, what he was doing.

" Oh, good Lord ! Monsieur le Chevalier," said she, " what are you doing ?"

" Who—I ?" said D'Artagnan ; "nothing ;" and he read :

" You have not answered my first note ; are you indisposed, or have you forgot the glances you favoured me with at the ball of Madame de Guise ? You have an opportunity now, count ; do not allow it to escape."

D'Artagnan became very pale : he was wounded in his self-love ; he thought that it was in his love.

" Poor, dear Monsieur D'Artagnan !" said Kitty, in a voice full of compassion, and pressing the young man's hand again.

" You pity me, my kind little creature ?" said D'Artagnan.

" That I do, and with all my heart ; for I know what it is to be in love."

" You know what it is to be in love ?" said D'Artagnan, looking at her for the first time with much attention.

" Alas ! yes."

" Well, then, instead of pitying me, you would do much better to assist me in revenging myself of your mistress."

" And what sort of revenge would you take ?"

" I would triumph over her, and supplant my rival."

" I will never help you in that, Monsieur le Chevalier," said Kitty, warmly.

" Why not ?"

" For two reasons."

" What are they ?"

" The first is, that my mistress will never love you."

" How do you know that ?"

" You have offended her to the very heart.

" I ?—in what can I have offended her ? I, who, ever since I have known her, have lived at her feet like a slave ! Speak, I beg of you !"

" I will never confess that but to the man————who should read to the bottom of my soul !"

D'Artagnan looked at Kitty for the second time. The young girl was of a freshness and beauty which many duchesses would have purchased with their coronets.

" Kitty," said he, " I will read to the bottom of your soul whenever you like ; don't let that disturb you ;" and he gave her a kiss, at which the poor girl became as red as a cherry.

" Oh, no," said Kitty, " it is not me you love—it is my mistress you love ; you told me so only just now."

" And does that hinder you from telling me the second reason ?"

" The second reason, Monsieur le Chevalier," replied Kitty, emboldened by the kiss in the first place, and still further by the expression of the eyes of the young man, " is—that in love, every one for herself !"

Then only D'Artagnan remembered the languishing glances of Kitty, her constantly meeting him in the antechamber, the corridor, or on the stairs, those touches of the hand every time she did meet him, and her deep sighs ; but, absorbed by his desire to please the great lady, he had disdained the soubrette : he whose game is the eagle, takes no heed of the sparrow.

But this time our Gascon saw at a glance all the advantage that might be derived from the love which Kitty had just confessed so innocently—or so boldly : the interception of letters addressed to the Count de Wardes, intelligences on the spot, entrance at all hours into Kitty's chamber, which was contiguous to her mistress's. The perfidious deceiver was, as may plainly be perceived, already sacrificing in idea the poor girl to obtain milady, whether she would or not.

" Well," said he to the young girl, " are you willing, my dear Kitty, that I should give you a proof of that love of which you doubt ?"

" What love ?" asked the girl.

" Of that which I am ready to feel for you."

" And what is that proof ?"

" Are you willing that I should this evening pass with you the time I generally spend with your mistress ?"

" Oh, yes !" said Kitty, clapping her hands, " very willing."

" Well, then, come here, my dear," said D'Artagnan, establishing himself in a *fauteuil*, " come, and let me tell you that you are the prettiest soubrette I ever saw !"

And he did tell her so much, and so well, that the poor girl, who asked nothing better than to believe him, did believe him. Nevertheless, to D'Artagnan's great astonishment, the pretty Kitty defended herself with resolution.

In such conversations time passes very rapidly. Twelve o'clock struck, and almost at the same time the bell was rung in milady's chamber.

" Good God !" cried Kitty, " there is my mistress calling me ! Go, go directly !"

D'Artagnan rose, took his hat as if it had been his intention to obey ; then, opening quickly the door of a large closet, instead of that of the staircase, he plunged into the midst of robes and lady's dressing-gowns.

" What are you doing ?" cried Kitty.

D'Artagnan, who had secured the key, shut himself up in the closet without any reply.

" Well," cried milady, in a sharp voice, " are you asleep, that you don't answer when I ring ?"

And D'Artagnan heard the door of communication opened violently.

" Here am I, milady ! here am I !" cried Kitty, springing forward to meet her mistress.

Both went into the bedroom, and, as the door of communication remained open, D'Artagnan could hear milady for some time scolding her maid. She was at length, however, appeased, and the conversation turned upon him whilst Kitty was assisting her mistress to undress.

"Well," said milady, "I have not seen our Gascon this evening."

"What, milady! has he not been?" said Kitty. "Can he be inconstant before being happy?"

"Oh, no; he must have been prevented by M. de Tréville or M. des Essarts. I understand my game, Kitty; I have him safe!"

"What will you do with him, madame?"

"What will I do with him? Oh, Kitty, there is something between that man and me that he is quite ignorant of: he was very near making me lose my credit with his eminence. Oh, I will be revenged for that!"

"I thought madame loved him?"

"I love him? I detest him! A simple fool, who held the life of Lord de Winter in his hands and did not kill him, by which I missed three hundred thousand livres a year!"

"That's true," said Kitty; "your son was the only heir of his uncle, and until his coming of age you would have had the enjoyment of his fortune."

D'Artagnan shuddered to his very marrow at hearing this apparently sweet creature reproach him with that sharp voice, which she took such pains to conceal in conversation, for not having killed a man whom he had seen load her with kindnesses.

"For all this," continued milady, "I should long ago have revenged myself on him, if, and I don't know why, the cardinal had not requested me to conciliate him."

"Oh, yes; but madame has not favoured the little woman he was so fond of?"

"What! the mercer's wife of the Rue des Fossoyeurs? Has he not already forgotten she ever existed? Fine vengeance that, *ma foi!*"

A cold sweat broke from D'Artagnan's brow. Why, this woman was a monster! He resumed his listening, but unfortunately the toilet was ended.

"That will do," said milady; "go into your own room, and to-morrow endeavour again to obtain me an answer to the letter I gave you."

"For M. de Wardes?" said Kitty.

"To be sure; for M. de Wardes."

"Now, there is one," said Kitty, "who appears to me to be quite a different sort of man to that poor M. d'Artagnan."

"Go to bed, mademoiselle," said milady; "I don't like comments."

D'Artagnan heard the door close, then the noise of two bolts by which milady fastened herself in; on her side, but as softly as possible, Kitty turned the key of the lock, and then D'Artagnan opened the closet-door.

"Oh good Lord!" said Kitty, in a low voice, "what is the matter with you? How pale you are!"

"The abominable creature!" murmured D'Artagnan.

"Silence, silence! begone!" said Kitty; "there is nothing but a wainscot between my chamber and milady's ; every word that is uttered in one can be heard in the other."

" That's exactly the reason I won't go," said D'Artagnan.

" What !" said Kitty, blushing.

" Or, at least, I will go—later ;" and he put his arm round her waist.

D'Artagnan's love for Kitty was little more than an idea of vengeance upon milady. With a little more heart, he might have been contented with this new conquest ; but the principal features of his character were ambition and pride. It must, however, be confessed, in his justi-fication, that the first use he made of the influence he had obtained over Kitty was, to endeavour to find out what had become of Madame Bonacieux ; but the poor girl swore upon the crucifix to D'Artagnan, that she was entirely ignorant on that head, her mistress never admit-ting her into half her secrets, only she believed she was able to say she was not dead.

As to the cause which was near making milady lose the confidence of the cardinal, Kitty knew nothing about it ; but this time D'Artagnan was better informed than she was : as he had seen milady on board a vessel at the moment he was leaving England, he suspected that it was, almost without a doubt, on account of the diamond studs.

But what was clearest in all this was, that the true hatred, the pro-found hatred, the inveterate hatred of milady, was increased by his not having killed her brother-in-law.

D'Artagnan came the next day to milady's, and finding her in a very ill-humour, had no doubt that it was having no answer from M. de Wardes that provoked her thus. Kitty came in, but milady was very cross with her. The poor girl ventured a glance at D'Artagnan, which said—See how I suffer on your account !

Towards the end of the evening, however, the beautiful lioness be-came milder, she smilingly listened to the soft speeches of D'Artagnan, and even gave him her hand to kiss.

D'Artagnan, at parting, scarcely knew what to think ; but as he was a youth not easily imposed upon, whilst continuing to pay his court to milady, he determined to carry out the little plan he had framed in his mind.

He found Kitty at the gate, and, as on the preceding evening, went up to her chamber. Kitty had been accused of negligence, and con-sequently severely scolded. Milady could not at all comprehend the silence of the Count de Wardes, and she ordered Kitty to come at nine o'clock in the morning to take a third letter.

D'Artagnan made Kitty promise to bring him that letter on the fol-lowing morning ; the poor girl promised all her lover desired : she was mad.

Things passed as they had done the night before : D'Artagnan con-cealed himself in his closet, milady called, undressed, sent away Kitty, and shut the door. As before, likewise, D'Artagnan returned home at five o'clock in the morning.

At eleven o'clock Kitty came to him : she held in her hand a fresh billet from milady. This time the poor girl did not even hesitate at giving up the note to D'Artagnan ; she belonged, body and soul, to her handsome soldier.

D'Artagnan opened the letter, and read as follows :

"This is the third time I have written to you, to tell you that I love you. Beware that I do not write to you a fourth time, to tell you that I detest you.

"If you repent of the manner in which you have acted towards me, the young girl who brings you this will tell you how a man of spirit may obtain his pardon."

D'Artagnan coloured and grew pale several times whilst reading this billet.

"Oh! you love her still," said Kitty, who had not taken her eyes off the young man's countenance for an instant.

"No, Kitty, you are mistaken : I do not love her ; but I will revenge myself for her contempt of me."

"Oh! yes, I know what sort of vengeance! you told me that !"

"Of what consequence can it be to you, Kitty ; you know it is you alone I love."

"How can I be sure of that ?"

"By the scorn I will throw upon her."

D'Artagnan took a pen and wrote :

"Madame—Until the present moment, I could not believe that it was to me your two first letters were addressed, so unworthy did I feel myself of such an honour ; besides, I was so seriously indisposed, that I could not, in any case, have replied to them.

"But now I am forced to believe in the excess of your kindness, since not only your letter, but your servant, assures me that I have the good fortune to be beloved by you.

"She has no occasion to teach me the way in which a man of spirit may obtain his pardon ; I will come and ask mine at eleven o'clock this evening.

"To delay it a single day would be, in my eyes, now, to commit a fresh offence——He whom you have rendered the happiest of men,

"COMTE DE WARDES."

This note was in the first place a forgery ; it was likewise an indelicacy ; it was even, according to our present manners, something like an infamous action ; but at that period, people were not so scrupulous. Besides, D'Artagnan from her own admission, knew milady to be treacherous in matters of more importance, and could entertain no respect for her. And yet, notwithstanding this want of respect, he felt an uncontrollable passion for this woman boiling in his veins. Passion drunk with contempt ; but passion or thirst, as the reader pleases.

D'Artagnan's plan was very simple ; by Kitty's chamber he gained that of his mistress; he would take advantage of the first moment of surprise, shame and terror; he might fail, but something must be left to chance. In eight days the campaign was to open, and he would be compelled to leave Paris : D'Artagnan had no time for a prolonged love siege.

"There," said the young man, handing Kitty the letter, sealed and addressed, "give that to milady ; it is the Count de Wardes' reply."

Poor Kitty became as pale as death ; she suspected what the letter contained.

"Listen my dear girl," said D'Artagnan, "you cannot but perceive that all this must end, some way or other ; milady may discover that you gave the first billet to my lackey instead of to De Wardes'; that it is I who have opened the others which ought to have been opened by him ; milady will then turn you out of doors, and you know she is not the woman to let her vengeance stop there."

" Alas !" said Kitty, "for whom have I exposed myself to all that ?"

" For me, I well know, my sweet girl," said D'Artagnan. " But I am grateful."

" But what does this note contain ?"

" Milady will tell you."

"Ah ! you do not love me," cried Kitty, " and I am very wretched !"

In spite of the caresses with which D'Artagnan endeavoured to console her, Kitty wept for some time before she could be persuaded to give her mistress the note ; but she yielded at last.

CHAPTER XXXIV.

IN WHICH THE EQUIPMENT OF ARAMIS AND PORTHOS IS TREATED OF.

SINCE the four friends had been in search of their equipments, there had been no fixed meeting. They dined without each other, wherever they might happen to be, or rather, where they could find a dinner. Duty, likewise, on its part, took up a considerable portion of that precious time which was gliding away so rapidly. Only they had agreed to meet once a week, about one o'clock, at the residence of Athos, seeing that he, in agreement with the vow he had formed, did not pass over the threshold of his door.

This was the same day as that on which Kitty went to D'Artagnan.

Soon as Kitty left him, D'Artagnan directed his steps towards the Rue Férou.

He found Athos and Aramis philosophising. Aramis had some slight inclination to resume the cassock. Athos, according to his system, neither encouraged nor dissuaded him. Athos was an advocate that every one should be left to his own free will. He never gave advice but when it was asked ; and even then he required to be asked twice.

" People in general," he said, " only asked advice not to follow it ; or if they did follow it, it was for the sake of having some one to blame for having given it."

Porthos arrived a minute after D'Artagnan, and the four friends were all assembled.

The four countenances expressed four different feelings : that of Porthos, tranquillity ; that of D'Artagnan, hope ; that of Aramis, uneasiness ; that of Athos, carelessness.

At the end of a moment's conversation, in which Porthos hinted that a lady of elevated rank had condescended to relieve him from his embarrassment, Mousqueton entered.—He came to request his master to come home instantly ; his presence was very urgent.

"Is it my equipment ?"

"Yes, and no," replied Mousqueton.

"Well, but can't you speak ?"

"Come home, monsieur !"

Porthos rose, saluted his friends, and followed Mousqueton.

An instant after, Bazin made his appearance at the door.

"What do you want with me, my friend ?" said Aramis, with that mildness of language which was observable in him every time that his ideas were directed towards the church.

"A man wishes to see monsieur at home," replied Bazin.

"A man ! what man ?"

"A mendicant."

"Give him alms, Bazin, and bid him pray for a poor sinner."

"But this mendicant insists upon speaking to you, and pretends that you will be very glad to see him."

"Has he sent no particular message for me?"

"Yes, if M. Aramis hesitates to come," he said, "tell him I am from Tours."

"From Tours !" cried Aramis, "a thousand pardons, gentlemen, but no doubt this man brings me the news I expected.'

And rising, he went off at a quick pace.

There then only remained Athos and D'Artagnan.

"I believe these fellows have managed their business. What do you think, D'Artagnan ?" said Athos.

"I know that Porthos was in a fair way," replied D'Artagnan ; "and as to Aramis, to tell you the truth, I have never been uneasy on his account ; but you, my dear Athos, you, who so generously distributed the Englishman's pistoles, which were your legitimate property, what do you mean to do ?"

"I am satisfied with having killed that man, my good lad, seeing that it is blessed bread to kill an Englishman ; but if I had pocketed his pistoles, they would have weighed me down like a remorse."

"Athos ! Athos ! you have truly inconceivable ideas !"

"Well, leave that !—What do you think of M. de Tréville's telling me, when he did me the honour to call upon me yesterday, that you associated with the suspected English, whom the cardinal protects ?"

"That is to say, I visit an Englishwoman ; the one I named to you."

"Oh ! aye ! the fair woman, on whose account I gave you advice, which, naturally, you took care not to adopt."

" I gave you my reasons."

" Yes ; you look to the connection for your equipment, I think you said."

" Not at all ! I have acquired a certain knowledge that that woman was concerned in the carrying off of Madame Bonacieux."

" Yes, I understand now ; to find one woman you make love to another : it is the longest road, but certainly the most amusing."

D'Artagnan was on the point of telling Athos all ; but one consideration restrained him. Athos was a gentleman, and was punctilious in all that concerned honour, and there were in all the plans which our lover had devised with regard to milady, he was sure, certain things that would not obtain his approbation : he was therefore silent, and as Athos was the least curious of any man on earth, D'Artagnan's confidence stopped there.

We will therefore leave the two friends, who had nothing important to communicate to each other, to follow Aramis.

Upon being informed that the person who wanted to speak to him came from Tours, we have seen with what rapidity the young man followed, or rather went before Bazin ; he ran without stopping from the Rue Férou to Rue de Vaugirard.

On entering, he found a man of short stature and intelligent eyes, but covered with rags.

" Did you ask for me ?" said the musketeer.

" I wish to speak with Monsieur Aramis : is that your name, monsieur ?"

" Yes : you have brought me something ?"

" Yes, if you can show me a certain embroidered handkerchief ?"

" Here it is," said Aramis, taking a small key from his breast, and opening a little ebony box inlaid with mother-of-pearl ; " here it is, look !"

" That is right," replied the mendicant ; " dismiss your lackey."

In fact, Bazin, curious to know what the mendicant could want with his master, kept pace with him as well as he could, and arrived almost at the same time he did ; but this quickness was not of much use to him ; at the hint from the mendicant, his master made him a sign to retire, and he was obliged to obey.

Bazin being gone, the mendicant cast a rapid glance around him, in order to be sure that nobody could either see or hear him, and opening his ragged vest, badly held together by a leather strap, he began to unsew the upper part of his doublet, from which he drew a letter.

Aramis uttered a cry of joy at the sight of the seal, kissed the superscription with an almost religious respect, and opened the epistle, which contained what follows :

" MY FRIEND,—It is the will of fate that we should be still for some time separated ; but the delightful days of youth are not lost beyond return. Perform your duty in camp ; I will do mine elsewhere. Accept that which the bearer brings you : make the campaign like a handsome true gentleman, and think of me, who tenderly kiss your dear black eyes !

"Adieu ! or rather, *au revoir !*"

The mendicant continued to unsew his garments ; and drew from amidst his rags a hundred and fifty Spanish double pistoles, which he laid down on the table ; then he opened the door, bowed, and went out before the young man, stupefied by his letter, had ventured to address a word to him.

Aramis then re-perused the letter, and perceived there was a post-script.

"P.S. You may behave politely to the bearer, who is a count and a grandee of Spain."

"Golden dreams !" cried Aramis.   "Oh, beautiful life ! yes, we are young, yes, we shall yet have happy days !   Oh ! my love, my blood, my life ! all, all, all, all are thine, my adored mistress !"

And he kissed the letter with passion, without even vouchsafing a look at the gold which sparkled on the table.

Bazin scratched at the door, and as Aramis had no longer any reason to exclude him, he bade him come in.

Bazin was stupefied at the sight of the gold, and forgot that he came to announce D'Artagnan, who, curious to know who the mendicant could be, came to Aramis's residence on leaving that of Athos.

Now, as D'Artagnan used no ceremony with Aramis, seeing that Bazin forgot to announce him, he announced himself.

"The devil ! my dear Aramis," said D'Artagnan, "if these are the prunes that are sent to you from Tours, I beg you will make my compliments to the gardener who gathers them."

"You are mistaken, friend D'Artagnan," said Aramis, always on his guard, "this is from my bookseller, who has just sent me the price of that poem in one-syllable verse which I began yonder."

"Ah ! indeed," said D'Artagnan, "well, your bookseller is very generous, that's all I can say."

"How, monsieur ?" cried Bazin, "a poem sell so dear as that ! it is incredible !   You can write as much as you like, you may become equal to M. Voiture and M. Benserade.   I like that.   A poet is as good as an abbé.   Ah, Monsieur Aramis ! become a poet, I beg of you."

"Bazin, my friend," said Aramis, "I believe you are interfering with my conversation."

Bazin perceived he was wrong ; he bowed and went out.

"Ah !" said D'Artagnan with a smile, "you sell your productions at their weight in gold ; you are very fortunate, my friend, but take care, or else you will lose that letter which is peeping out from your doublet, and which comes, no doubt, from your bookseller likewise."

Aramis blushed to the eyes, crammed in the letter, and rebuttoned his doublet,

"My dear D'Artagnan," said he, "if you please, we will join our friends; as I am rich, we will to-day begin to dine together again, expecting that you will be rich in your turn."

"Ma foi !" said D'Artagnan, with great pleasure. " It is long since we have had a good dinner together ; and I, for my part, have a some-what hazardous expedition for this evening, and shall not be sorry, I confess, to fortify myself with a few glasses of good old Burgundy."

" Agreed, as to the old Burgundy ; I have no objection to that," said Aramis, from whom the letter and the gold had removed, as by magic, his ideas of retreat.

And having put two or three double pistoles into his pocket to answer the calls of the moment, he placed the others in the ebony box, inlaid with mother-of-pearl, in which was the famous handkerchief, which served him as a talisman.

The two friends repaired to Athos's dwelling ; and he, faithful to his vow of not going out, took upon him to order dinner to be brought to them ; as he was perfectly acquainted with the details of gastronomy, D'Artagnan and Aramis made no difficulty in abandoning this impor-tant care to him.

They went to find Porthos, and at the corner of the Rue Bac met Mousqueton, who, with a most pitiable air, was driving before him a mule and a horse.

D'Artagnan uttered a cry of surprise, which was not quite free from joy.

" There's my yellow horse, Aramis," cried he ; " look at that horse !"

" Oh, the frightful brute !" said Aramis.

"Well," replied D'Artagnan, " upon that very horse I came to Paris."

"What, does monsieur know this horse ?" said Mousqueton.

" It is of a singular colour," said Aramis ; " I never saw one with such a hide in my life."

" I can well believe you did not," replied D'Artagnan, " and that was how I got three crowns for him ; it must have been for his hide, for, certes, the carcase is not worth eighteen livres. But how did this horse come into your hands, Mousqueton ?"

" Pray," said the lackey, " say nothing about it, monsieur ; it is a frightful trick played us by the husband of our duchess !"

" How has it come about, Mousqueton ?"

" Why, we are looked upon with a rather favourable eye, by a lady of quality, the Duchess of————— ; but, your pardon ; my master has commanded me to be discreet ; she had forced us to accept, as a little keepsake, a magnificent Spanish genet and an Andalusian mule, which were beautiful to look upon ; the husband heard of the affair ; on their way he seized the two magnificent beasts which were being sent to us, and substituted these horrible animals in their places."

" Which you are taking back to him, I suppose ?" said D'Artagnan.

" Exactly so, monsieur !" replied Mousqueton ; " you may well believe that we will not accept such steeds as these in exchange for those which had been promised to us."

" No, pardieu ! though I should like to have seen Porthos upon my yellow horse ; that would give me an idea of how I looked on my arrival in Paris. But don't let us hinder you, Mousqueton ; go, and perform your master's orders. Is he at home ?"

"Yes, monsieur," said Mousqueton, "but in a very ill humour. Go on !" and he continued his way towards the Quai des Grands Augustins, whilst the two friends went to ring at the bell of the unfortunate Porthos. He, having seen them crossing the yard, took care not to answer ; and they rang in vain.

In the meanwhile Mousqueton continued on his way, and crossing the Pont Neuf, still driving the two sorry animals before him, he reached the Rue aux Ours. When arrived there, he fastened, according to the orders of his master, both the horse and mule to the knocker of the procureur's door ; then, without taking any heed of their future fate, he returned to Porthos, and told him that his commission was completed.

In a short time the two unfortunate beasts, who had not eaten anything since the morning, made such a noise with the knocker, that the procureur ordered his boy-clerk to go and inquire in the neighbourhood to whom this horse and mule belonged.

Madame Coquenard recognised her present, and could not at first comprehend this restitution ; but the visit of Porthos soon enlightened her. The anger which fired the eyes of the musketeer, in spite of his efforts to suppress it, terrified his sensitive lover. In fact, Mousqueton had not concealed from his master that he had met D'Artagnan and Aramis, and that D'Artagnan, in the yellow horse, had recognised the Béarnais pony upon which he had come to Paris, and which he had sold for three crowns.

Porthos went away after having appointed a meeting with the procureuse in the cloisters of St. Magloire. The procureur, seeing he was going, invited him to dinner ; an invitation which the musketeer refused with an air of majesty.

Madame Coquenard repaired trembling to the cloisters of St. Magloire, for she guessed the reproaches that awaited her there ; but she was fascinated by the lofty airs of Porthos.

All that which a man, wounded in his self love, could let fall in the shape of imprecations and reproaches upon the head of a woman, Porthos let fall upon the bowed head of his procureuse.

"Alas !" said she, " I did all for the best. One of our clients is a horsedealer ; he owes money to the office, and was backward in his pay. I took the mule and the horse for what he owed us ; he assured me that they were two noble steeds."

" Well, madame," said Porthos, "if he owed you more than five crowns, your horsedealer is a thief."

" There is no harm in endeavouring to buy things cheap, Monsieur Porthos," said the procureuse, seeking to excuse herself.

"No, madame, but they who so earnestly try to buy things cheap, ought to permit others to seek more generous friends."

And Porthos, turning on his heel, made a step to retire.

" Monsieur Porthos ! Monsieur Porthos !" cried the procureuse, " I have been wrong, I confess it, I ought not to have driven a bargain when the matter was to equip a cavalier like you."

Porthos, without reply, retreated a second step.

The procureuse fancied she saw him in a brilliant cloud, all surrounded by duchesses and marquises, who cast bags of money at his feet.

" Stop ! in the name of heaven ! Monsieur Porthos," cried she ; " stop, and let us talk."

" Talking with you brings me misfortune," said Porthos.

" But, tell me, what do you ask ?"

" Nothing, for that amounts to the same thing as if I asked you for something."

The procureuse hung herself upon the arm of Porthos, and, in the violence of her grief, she cried out :

" Monsieur Porthos, I am ignorant of all such matters. How should I know what a horse is ? How should I know what horse-furniture is ?"

" You should have left it to me, then, madame, who do know what they are : but you would be parsimonious, and, consequently, lend at usury."

" I have done wrong, Monsieur Porthos, but I will repair that wrong, upon my word of honour I will."

" And how will you do that ?" asked the musketeer.

" Listen to me. This evening M. Coquenard is going to the house of M. Le Duc de Chaulnes, who has sent for him. It is upon a consultation, which will last three hours at least ; come, we shall be alone, and can make up our accounts."

" Ah ! now that is speaking to the purpose, my dear !"

" You pardon me, then ?"

" We shall see," said Porthos, majestically.

And they separated, both saying : " Till this evening."

" The devil !" thought Porthos, as he walked away, " it appears I am getting nearer to Monsieur Coquenard's strong box at last."

CHAPTER XXXV.

A GASCON A MATCH FOR CUPID.

ON the morning following the evening so fondly anticipated by both Porthos and D'Artagnan, Athos sat chewing the cud of recollections, in which the bitter somewhat predominated over the sweet, when his meditations were pleasingly interrupted by the appearance of D'Artagnan. We say pleasingly, for two reasons : first, that Athos took particular pleasure in the society of the frank, shrewd Gascon ; and, secondly, that though the circumstances of his early life had cast a tinge of melancholy over his tone of mind, and altered his habits of existence, there was still a spirit of comparative youth and natural buoyancy of temperament, which made him hail, as a relief, the society of a man he esteemed so greatly as he did D'Artagnan.

As to the Gascon, he was in exuberant spirits, but spirits which, to the cool, observant eye of Athos, seemed rather feverish than natural ; his eye sparkled, his tongue was voluble, his laugh was loud, but there was occasionally a nervous twitching of the muscles of the mouth, and, altogether, an uneasiness which denoted that his spirits resembled rather the excitement produced by opium or wine, than the overflowing cheerfulness of youth and peace of mind.

" This seems to have been an auspicious night with you, D'Artagnan," said Athos. " Did you visit your fascinating Englishwoman ?"

" Oh, yes," replied D'Artagnan, rubbing his hands ; " and my revenge is complete."

" Ah ?" said Athos, gravely. " Beware ! revenge is an awkward passion to indulge in ; they who employ it find it a double-edged weapon, which, in the recoil, frequently wounds the hand that wields it."

" Mordioux ! I must confess that I am not quite at ease. Milady has a deal more of a Circe than a Venus in her, however beautiful I think her. Her very love and its expression have something mysterious in them."

" Well, we know she was a spy of the Cardinal's," said Athos. " The Cardinal does not usually employ lovable people ; few of us would like to take either Le Père Joseph or his *âme damnée*, Rochefort, to our bosoms as confidential friends ; and a woman must be still more to be dreaded. With men, we can be on our guard ; against women, never."

" Peste !" said D'Artagnan ; " that is it. I almost trembled while I loved. She has the strangest expression in her eyes I ever met with. Though merely grey eyes, their brilliancy is astonishing ; but that brilliancy is more of the nature of the flash of a meteor, than of the moonlike lustre we love in women's eyes. But I will tell you all, and then you may judge for yourself." And with his usual readiness and fluency, the Gascon related to his attentive friend the adventures of the evening.

In the first place he recapitulated all that our readers know concerning the lady's warm letters to De Wardes, and D'Artagnan's forged reply.

At this period Athos's brow became clouded. In general, the eye of Athos seemed to turn towards D'Artagnan as the weary look of the town drudge seeks a break between the line of houses where he can catch a glimpse of green fields and golden sunshine ; but now, it was serious to sternness.

"My dear friend, this is not like you. You are, naturally, no assassin ; though anxious to win the fight, you would never forget that honour should be dearer to a combatant than victory. But look at the consequence of this victory ; for the sake of a momentary gratification, you secure yourself an enemy, and no mean one, depend upon it."

" Oh," said D'Artagnan, " I have felt all that—but—but, Athos, you know what it is to be under the influence of a beautiful, artful woman."

The brow of Athos again darkened.

" But proceed," added he, gravely.

" Well, at my usual time, about nine o'clock, I presented myself, and was almost flattered into hope by my reception. I had never seen her look handsomer ; her spirits were good, her laugh was cheerful, and there was none of that constrained, affected air of politeness of which I had before seen so much. But then the devil of jealousy did not fail to whisper to me that all this arose from the anticipation of gratified love, and was not in any way due to me or my presence. But passion is a bad reasoner ; and I said to myself, ' Well, she may love De Wardes, but if she will take all this pains to make herself agreeable to me, I must go for something, and she may not take the deception very ill.' Besides, he was hard to be courted ; I was a willing slave."

" There, your usually acute philosophy was at fault, D'Artagnan. As a soldier, you ought to know there is more honour from a contested victory, than from a too easy surrender. But go on."

" Well, I perceived my billet had done its work. Kitty was ordered to bring in sherbet. Her mistress's good-humour extended even to her ; she spoke more kindly to her than usual, but I could see poor Kitty was insensible to it all—her heart seemed full of the idea of my purposed revenge. As I witnessed the play of natural feeling in the countenance of one of these women, and beheld the artful blandishments of that of the other, I was not only tempted to think that fortune had made a mistake in their relative positions, but even felt my heart waver, and turn, instinctively, from art to nature. But I was committed, and had no means of honourable retreat before victory.

" At ten o'clock milady began to be uneasy. I could plainly see what was the matter. She arose, walked about, sat down again, her eyes seeming constantly to reproach the sluggish progress of the pendulum. At length, as the time drew near, there was no mistaking her ; her looks said, distinctly as words, You have been very agreeable, but it is quite time you were gone. I arose, took my hat, bowed upon her hand, even ventured to kiss it, all which she not only allowed, but I was astonished to find her beautiful fingers return the respectful pressure of mine. And yet, though the fascination still continued, I was not for a moment deceived ; there was no partiality for me, not even coquetry in it.

" ' She must love him devilishly,' thought I, as I descended the stairs.

" But my poor little Kitty could not find it in her heart to come down to meet me ; I was obliged to grope my way up the back staircase alone.

" On reaching the soubrette's little apartment, I found her seated with her head leaning on her hands, weeping bitterly. She did not notice my entrance, but when I went, in a kindly manner, to take her hand, she broke into an agony of sobbing. I soon found, from her reproaches, that milady, in the delirium of her joy, had revealed to her the contents of the supposed De Wardes's billet, and, as a reward for the manner in which she had performed her commission, had given her a purse of money.

" Kitty, on regaining her chamber, had thrown this purse contemptuously into a corner, where it lay, disgorging three or four pieces of gold upon the carpet.

"My heart smote me more than I like to own, but my plan lay too much at my heart ; the only honest thing I could do towards Kitty was to give her clearly to understand that I could not draw back, that I must go on ; only adding, as a sedative, that I was now actuated solely by revenge.

"From some little remains of modesty, milady had ordered all the lights to be extinguished, even in her own chamber, and M. de Wardes was to depart before day, in darkness.

"I had not been many minutes with Kitty before we heard milady enter her chamber, and I quickly ensconced myself in my closet ; indeed, Kitty had scarcely pushed me in, when her mistress's little bell rang. Kitty replied to the summons, taking care to shut the door after her ; but the wainscot was so thin I could hear almost all both the women said.

"Milady appeared intoxicated with joy. She made Kitty repeat the minutest details of her pretended interview with De Wardes ; to which poor Kitty returned but broken answers, and I really expected, from her tone, she would begin to cry. And yet, so selfish is happiness, milady was too much engrossed by her own joy, to mark the distress of her poor attendant.

"A few minutes before the appointed hour, milady had all the lights put out in her chamber, and dismissed Kitty to hers, with an injunction to introduce the count the moment he arrived.

"You may suppose I did not keep Kitty waiting long.

"Seeing through a chink of my hiding place that all was darkness, I was at the door of milady's chamber before Kitty had closed it.

"'What is that noise?' said milady.

"'It is I, De Wardes,' replied I, in a suppressed voice.

"'Well, why does he not come in?' said milady.

"Shaking off poor Kitty, with as much kindness as I could, I made my way into milady's chamber. And here, dear Athos, I must confess that I scarcely knew which predominated, love or jealousy. I had no idea what a man's feelings would be when he has passionate protestations of love poured into his ears, and knows that they are addressed to a rival. Oh, what a keen, remorseless tooth has jealousy ! Her love for De Wardes seems boundless."

"Call it not love, D'Artagnan," said Athos, "it is a desecration of the word ; such natures as hers may be susceptible of coarse passion, but know nothing of love."

"Well, call it what you will, she is intensely in earnest, as you may judge. At parting, she forced this ring upon my finger, with a request that I would return her a token of responding affection to-day ; and people don't give such jewels as this away lightly. My heart smote me, and I wished to refuse it. She, however, would not hear of that, but replied, 'No, no ; keep that ring for my sake ; you will render me likewise a greater service than you are aware of by doing so,'—and her voice was agitated as she spoke. What the latter part of her speech meant, I don't know ; but she is full of mysteries. I remembered the ring ; it is, as you see, a magnificent sapphire, surrounded by brilliants. At that moment I felt ready to reveal everything, but, very strangely, she added :

" ' Poor dear angel ! whom the monster of a Gascon was so near killing.'

" Comfortable, this ! to know I was the monster.

" ' Do you suffer much from your wounds ?' continued she.

" ' Yes, a great deal,' said I, scarcely knowing what to answer.

" ' Be satisfied,' murmured she ; ' I will avenge you, and cruelly.'

" ' Peste !' thought I to myself ; ' the time for confidence has not yet come.' At our parting, which was a passionate one, another interview was agreed upon for next week."

" Your milady is doubtless an infamous creature. But since you mentioned it, my attention has been engrossed by your ring," said Athos.

" I saw you were looking at it ; it is handsome, is it not ?" said D'Artagnan.

" Yes," said Athos, "magnificent. It reminds me of a family jewel ; I did not think two sapphires of such a fine water existed. And she gave you that ring, do you say."

" Yes, my beautiful Englishwoman, or rather Frenchwoman, for I am sure she was born in France, took it from her own finger and forced it on to mine."

" Let me look at it," said Athos ; and, as he took it and examined it, he became very pale. He tried it on his little finger, which it fitted as if made for it.

A shade of anger and vengeance passed across his usually calm brow.

" It is impossible it can be she," said he. " How could this ring come into the possession of Lady Clarik ? And yet it is difficult suppose such a resemblance should exist between two jewels."

" Do you know this ring ?" said D'Artagnan.

" I thought I did," replied Athos ; "but, no doubt, was mistaken."

And he returned D'Artagnan the ring, without, however, ceasing to look at it.

" Pray," said Athos, after a minute, " either take off that ring, or turn the collet inside ; it recalls such recollections that I cannot keep my head cool enough to converse with you. But stop, let me look at that ring again ; the one I mentioned to you had one of its faces scratched."

D'Artagnan took off the ring, giving it again to Athos.

Athos started. " Look ?" said he, " is it not strange ?" and he pointed out to D'Artagnan the scratch he had remembered.

" But from whom did this ring come to you, Athos ?"

" From my mother, who inherited it from her mother."

" And you—sold it ?" asked D'Artagnan, hesitatingly.

" No," replied Athos, with a singular smile ; " I gave it away in a love affair, as it has been given to you."

D'Artagnan became pensive in his turn ; it appeared as if there were abysses in milady's soul whose depths were dark and unknown. He took back the ring, but put it into his pocket, and not on to his finger.

"D'Artagnan," said Athos, taking his hand, "you know I love you; if I had a son, I could not love him better. Take my advice, renounce this woman."

"You are right," said D'Artagnan. "I have done with her; she terrifies me."

"Shall you have the courage?" said Athos.

"I shall," replied D'Artagnan; "and instantly."

"In truth, my young friend, you will act rightly, and God grant that this woman, who has scarcely entered into your life, may not leave a terrible trace in it!"

And Athos bowed to D'Artagnan, like a man who wishes to be left alone with his thoughts.

On reaching home, D'Artagnan found Kitty waiting for him.

She was sent by her mistress to the false De Wardes. Her mistress was mad with love; she wished to know when her lover would meet her again. And poor Kitty, pale and trembling, awaited D'Artagnan's reply. The counsels of his friend, joined to the cries of his own heart, made him determine, now his pride was saved and his vengeance satisfied, not to see milady again. As a reply, he wrote the following letter:

"Do not depend upon me, madame, for the next meeting; since my convalescence I have so many affairs of this kind on my hands, that I am forced to regulate them a little. When your turn comes, I shall have the honour to inform you of it. I kiss your hands.

"DE WARDES."

Not a word about the ring. Was the Gascon determined to keep it as a weapon against milady; or else, let us be frank, did he not reserve the jewel as a last resource for the equipment? We should be wrong to judge of the actions of one period from the point of view of another. That which would now be considered as disgraceful to a gentleman, was at that time quite a simple and natural affair, and the cadets of the best families were frequently kept by their mistresses. D'Artagnan gave the open letter to Kitty, who at first was unable to comprehend it, but who became almost wild with joy on reading it a second time. She could scarcely believe in her happiness: and whatever might be, considering the violent character of milady, the danger which the poor girl incurred in giving this billet to her mistress, she ran back to the Place Royale as fast as her legs could carry her.

Milady opened the letter with eagerness: but at the first words she read she became livid; she crushed the paper in her hand, and turning with flashing eyes upon Kitty,—

"What is this letter?" cried she.

"The answer to madame's," replied Kitty, all in a tremble.

"Impossible!" cried milady; "it is impossible a gentleman could have written such a letter to a woman." Then all at once, starting,—

"My God!" cried she, "can he have——" and she stopped. She ground her teeth ; she was of the colour of ashes. She endeavoured to go towards the window for air, but she could only stretch forth her arms, her legs failed her, and she sank into a *fauteuil*. Kitty, fearing she was going to faint, hastened towards her, and was beginning to open her dress ; but milady started up, pushing her away.

"What do you want with me ?" said she ; "and why do you place your hand on me ?"

"I thought you were going to faint, milady," answered the terrified girl.

"I faint ! I ! I ! do you take me for a weak, silly woman, then ? When I am insulted I do not faint, I avenge myself !"

And she made a sign for Kitty to leave the room.

CHAPTER XXXVI.

DREAM OF VENGEANCE.

THAT evening milady gave orders that when M. D'Artagnan came as usual, he should be immediately admitted. But he did not come.

The next day Kitty went to see the young man again, and related to him all that had passed on the preceding evening : D'Artagnan smiled; this jealous anger of milady was his revenge.

That evening milady was still more impatient than on the preceding one ; she renewed the order relative to the Gascon ; but, as before, she expected him in vain.

The next morning, when Kitty presented herself at D'Artagnan's residence, she was no longer joyous and alert, as she had been on the two preceding days, but on the contrary, as sad as possible.

D'Artagnan asked the poor girl what was the matter with her, but she, as her only reply, drew a letter from her pocket and gave it to him.

This letter was in milady's handwriting, only this time it was addressed to M. D'Artagnan, and not to M. de Wardes.

He opened it, and read as follows :

"DEAR MONSIEUR D'ARTAGNAN—It is wrong thus to neglect your friends, particularly at the moment you are about to leave them for so a long time. My brother-in-law and myself expected you yesterday and the day before, but in vain. Will it be the same this evening ?

"Your very grateful ,
"LADY CLARIK."

"That's all very simple," said D'Artagnan ; "I expected this letter. My credit rises by the fall of that of the Count de Wardes."

"And will you go ?" asked Kitty.

"Listen to me, my dear girl," said the Gascon, who sought for an excuse in his own eyes for breaking the promise he had made Athos; "you must understand it would be impolitic not to accept such a positive invitation. Milady, at not seeing me come again, would not be able to understand what could cause the interruption of my visits, and might suspect something : who could say how far the vengeance of such a woman would go ?"

" Oh dear ! oh dear !" said Kitty, "you know how to represent things in such a way that you are always in the right. You are going now to pay your court to her again, and if, this time, you succeed in pleasing her in your own name and with your own face, it will be much worse than before."

Instinct caused poor Kitty to guess a part of what was going to happen.

D'Artagnan reassured her as well as he could, and promised to remain insensible to the seductions of milady.

He desired Kitty to tell her mistress that he could not be more grateful for her kindnesses than he was, and that he would be obedient to her orders : but he did not dare to write, for fear of not being able, to such experienced eyes as those of milady, to disguise his writing sufficiently.

As nine o'clock struck, D'Artagnan was at the Place Royale. It was evident that the servants who waited in the antechamber were warned, for as soon as D'Artagnan appeared, before even he had asked if milady were visible, one of them ran to announce him.

" Show him in," said milady, in a quick tone, but so piercing that D'Artagnan heard her in the antechamber.

He was introduced.

" I am at home to nobody," said milady ; "observe, to nobody."

The servant went out.

D'Artagnan cast an inquiring glance at milady. She was pale, and her eyes looked red, either from tears or want of sleep. The number of lights had been intentionally diminished, but the young woman could not conceal the traces of the fever which had devoured her during the last two days.

D'Artagnan approached her with his usual gallantry. She then made an extraordinary effort to receive him, but never did a more distressed countenance give the lie to a more amiable smile.

To the questions which D'Artagnan put concerning her health,—

" Ill !" replied she, " very ill !"

" Then," replied he, " my visit is ill-timed ; you, no doubt, stand in need of repose, and I will not intrude longer."

" No, no," said milady : "on the contrary. Stay, Monsieur D'Artagnan, your agreeable company will divert me."

"Oh! oh!" thought D'Artagnan. "She has never been so kind before. I must be on my guard."

Milady assumed the most agreeable air possible, and conversed with more than her usual brilliancy. At the same time the fever, which for an instant abandoned her, returned to give lustre to her eyes, colour to her cheeks, and vermilion to her lips. D'Artagnan was again in the presence of the Circe who had before surrounded him with her enchantments. His love, which he believed to be extinct, but which was only asleep, awoke again in his heart. Milady smiled, and D'Artagnan felt that he could damn himself for that smile. There was a moment at which he felt something like remorse.

By degrees, milady became more communicative. She asked D'Artagnan if he had a mistress.

"Alas!" said D'Artagnan, with the most sentimental air he could assume, "can you be cruel enough to put such a question to me; to me, who, from the moment I saw you, have only breathed and sighed by you and for you!"

Milady smiled with a strange smile.

"Then you do love me?" said she.

"Have I any need to tell you so? can you have failed to perceive it?"

"Perhaps I have; but you know, the more hearts are worth the capture, the more difficult they are to be won."

"Oh! difficulties do not affright me," said D'Artagnan. "I shrink before nothing but impossibilities."

"Nothing is impossible," replied milady, "to true love."

"Nothing, madame?"

"Nothing," replied milady.

"The devil!" thought D'Artagnan. "The note is changed. Can she be going to fall in love with me, by chance, this fair inconstant, and be disposed to give me myself another sapphire like that which she gave me for De Wardes."

D'Artagnan drew his seat nearer to milady's.

"Well, now, let us see what you would do to prove this love of which you speak."

"All that could be required of me. Order—I am ready."

"For everything?"

"For everything," cried D'Artagnan, who knew beforehand that he had not much to risk in engaging himself thus.

"Well, now let us talk a little seriously," said milady, in her turn drawing her *fauteuil* nearer to D'Artagnan's chair.

"I am all attention, madame," said he.

Milady remained thoughtful and undecided for a moment; then, as if appearing to have formed a resolution,—

"I have an enemy," said she.

"You, madame!" said D'Artagnan, affecting surprise; "is that possible? My God! good and beautiful as you are!"

"A mortal enemy."

"Indeed!"

"An enemy, who has insulted me so cruelly, that between him and me it is war to the death. May I reckon on you as an auxiliary?"

D'Artagnan at once perceived what the vindictive creature was coming to.

"You may, madame," said he, with emphasis. "My arm and my life are yours, as my love is."

" Then," said milady, " since you are as generous as you are loving—"
She stopped.

'Well ?" demanded D'Artagnan.

" Well," replied milady, after a moment of silence, " from the present time cease to talk of impossibilities."

" Do not overwhelm me with happiness !" cried D'Artagnan, throwing himself on his knees, and covering with kisses the hands she did not attempt to withdraw.

"Avenge me of that infamous De Wardes," said milady to herself, "and I shall soon know how to get rid of you, double fool, living sword-blade !"

" Fall voluntarily into my arms," said D'Artagnan, likewise to himself, "after having abused me with such effrontery, hypocritical, dangerous woman, and afterwards I will laugh at you with him whom you wish me to kill."

D'Artagnan lifted up his head.

" I am ready," said he.

"You have understood me, then, dear Monsieur D'Artagnan," said milady.

" I could understand one of your looks."

"Then you would employ on my account your arm, which has already acquired so much renown ?"

" Instantly !"

" But on my part," said milady, " how should I repay such a service ? I know what lovers are ; they are men who do nothing for nothing."

" You know the only reply that I desire," said D'Artagnan, " the only one worthy of you and of me !"

And he drew nearer to her.

She did not retreat.

" Interested man !" cried she, smiling.

" Ah !" cried D'Artagnan, really carried away by the passion this woman had the power to kindle in him, " Ah ! that is because my happiness appears so impossible to me : and I have such fear that it should fly away from me like a dream, that I pant to make a reality of it."

" Well ! merit this pretended happiness, then !"

" I am at your orders," said D'Artagnan.

" Quite certain ?" said milady, with a last doubt.

" Only name to me the base man that has brought tears into your beautiful eyes !"

" Who told you that I had been weeping ?" said she.

" It appeared to me——"

" Such women as I am don't weep," said milady.

" So much the better ! Come, tell me what his name is ?"

" Remember that his name is all my secret."

" Yet I must know his name."

" Yes, you must ; see what confidence I have in you !"

"You overwhelm me with joy.   What is his name?"

"You know him."

"Indeed."

"Yes."

"It is surely not one of my friends?" replied D'Artagnan, affecting hesitation, in order to make her believe him ignorant.

"If it were one of your friends, you would hesitate then?" cried milady ; and a threatening glance darted from her eyes.

"Not if it were my own brother!" cried D'Artagnan, as if carried away by his enthusiasm.

Our Gascon advanced this without risk, for he knew all that was meant.

"I love your devotedness," said milady.

"Alas ! do you love nothing else in me?" asked D'Artagnan.

"I love you also, you !" said she, taking his hand.

And the warm pressure made D'Artagnan tremble, as if by the touch, that fever which consumed milady was communicated to him.

"You love me ! you!" cried he.   "Oh! if that were so, I should lose my reason !"

And he folded her in his arms.   She made no effort to remove her lips from his kisses, only she did not respond to them.

Her lips were cold ; it appeared to D'Artagnan that he had embraced a statue.

He was not the less intoxicated with joy, electrified by love ; he almost believed in the tenderness of milady ; he almost believed in the crime of De Wardes.   If De Wardes had at that moment been under his hand, he would have killed him.

Milady seized the desired moment.

"His name is——" said she, in her turn.

"De Wardes ; I know it," cried D'Artagnan.

"And how do you know it?" asked milady, seizing both his hands, and endeavouring to read with her eyes to the bottom of his heart.

D'Artagnan felt he had allowed himself to be carried away, and that he had committed an error.

"Tell me ! tell me ! tell me, I say," repeated milady, "how do you know it ?"

"How do I know it?" said D'Artagnan.

"Yes."

"I know it, because, yesterday, M. de Wardes, in a salon where I was, showed a ring which he said he had of you."

"Miserable scoundrel !" cried milady.

The epithet, as may be easily understood, resounded to the very bottom of the heart of D'Artagnan.

"Well ?" continued she.

"Well, I will avenge you of this 'miserable scoundrel,'" replied D'Artagnan, giving himself the airs of Don Japhet of Armenia.

"Thanks ! my brave friend !" cried milady ; "and when shall I be avenged ?"

"To-morrow—immediately—when you please !"

Milady was about to cry out, "immediately;" but she reflected that such precipitation would not be very gracious towards D'Artagnan.

Besides, she had a thousand precautions to take, a thousand counsels to give to her defender, in order that he might avoid explanations with the count before witnesses. All this was answered by an expression of D'Artagnan's.

"To-morrow," said he, "you will be avenged, or I shall be dead !"

"No!" said she, "you will avenge me; but you will not be dead. He is a contemptible fellow."

"Towards women he may be, but not towards men. I know something of him."

"But it seems you had not much to complain of your fortune in your contest with him ?"

"Fortune is a courtesan ; though favourable yesterday, she may turn her back to-morrow."

"Which means that you now hesitate ?"

"No, I do not hesitate ; God forbid ! But would it be just to allow me to go to a possible death, without having given me at least something more than hope ?"

Milady answered by a glance which, said, "Is that all, speak then ?" And then accompanying the glance with explanatory words,—

"That is but too just," said she, tenderly.

"Oh ! you are an angel !" exclaimed the young man.

"Then all is agreed ?" said she.

"Except that which I ask of you, dear love !"

"But when I tell you that you may rely on my tenderness ?"

"I cannot wait till to-morrow."

"Silence ! I hear my brother : it will be useless for him to find you here."

She rang the bell, and Kitty appeared.

"Go out this way," said she, opening a small private door, "and come back at eleven o'clock ; we will then terminate this conversation ; Kitty will conduct you to my chamber."

The poor girl was near fainting at hearing these words.

"Well ! mademoiselle ! what are you thinking about, standing there like a statue ? Do as I bid you ; show the chevalier the way ; and this evening, at eleven o'clock,—you have heard what I said."

"It appears that these appointments are all made for eleven o'clock," thought D'Artagnan : "that's a settled custom."

Milady held out her hand to him, which he kissed tenderly.

"But," said he, as he retired as quickly as possible from the reproaches of Kitty, "but I must not play the fool :—this is certainly a very bad woman, I must be upon my guard."

CHAPTER XXXVII.

MILADY'S SECRET.

D'ARTAGNAN left the hotel instead of going up at once to Kitty's chamber, as she endeavoured to persuade him to do, and that for two reasons : the first, because by this means he should escape reproaches, recriminations, and prayers ; the second, because he was not sorry to have an opportunity of examining his own thoughts, and endeavouring, if possible, to fathom those of this woman.

What was most clear in the matter was that D'Artagnan loved milady like a madman, and that she did not love him at all.   In an instant D'Artagnan perceived that the best way in which he could act would be to go home and write milady a long letter, in which he would confess to her that he and De Wardes were, up to the present moment, the same, and that consequently he could not undertake, without committing suicide, to kill the Count de Wardes.   But he also was spurred on by a ferocious desire of vengeance ; he wished to subdue this woman in his own name ; and as this vengeance appeared to him to have a certain sweetness in it, he could not make up his mind to renounce it.

He walked six or seven times round the Place Royale, turning, at every ten steps to look at the light in milady's apartment, which was to be seen through the blinds ; it was evident that this time the young woman was not in such haste to retire to her apartment as she had been the first.

At length the light disappeared.

With this light was extinguished the last irresolution in the heart of D'Artagnan: he recalled to his mind the details of the first night, and, with a beating heart and a brain on fire, he re-entered the hotel and flew towards Kitty's chamber.

The poor girl pale as death, and trembling in all her limbs, wished to delay her lover ; but milady, with her ear on the watch, had heard the noise D'Artagnan had made, and, opening the door,—

" Come in," said she.

All this was of such incredible immodesty, of such monstrous effrontery, that D'Artagnan could scarcely believe what he saw or what he heard.   He imagined himself to be drawn into one of those fantastic intrigues which we meet with in our dreams.

He, however, darted not the less quickly towards milady, yielding to that magnetic attraction which the loadstone exercises over iron.

As the door closed after them, Kitty rushed towards it.   Jealousy, fury, offended pride, all the passions, in short, that dispute the heart of an outraged woman in love, urged her to make a revelation ; but she reflected that she would be totally lost if she confessed having assisted in such a machination. and, above all, that D'Artagnan would also be lost to her for ever.   This last thought of love counselled her to make this last sacrifice.

D'Artagnan, on his part, had gained the summit of all his wishes : it was no longer a rival that was beloved, it was he himself that was apparently beloved. A secret voice whispered to him, at the bottom of his heart, that he was but an instrument of vengeance, that he was only caressed till he had given death ; but pride, but self-love, but madness silenced this voice, and stifled its murmurs. And then our Gascon, with that large quantity of conceit which we know he possessed, compared himself with De Wardes, and asked himself why, after all, he should not be beloved for himself?

He was absorbed entirely by the sensations of the moment. Milady was no longer, for him, that woman of fatal intentions who had for a moment terrified him ; she was an ardent, passionate mistress, returning his love in full measure.

But milady, who had not the same motives for forgetfulness that D'Artagnan had, was the first to return to reality, and asked the young man if the means which were on the morrow to bring on the rencontre between him and De Wardes were already arranged in his mind.

But D'Artagnan, whose ideas had taken quite another course, forgot himself like a fool, and answered gallantly, that that was not the time to think about duels and sword-thrusts.

This coldness for the only interests that occupied her mind terrified milady, whose questions became more pressing.

Then D'Artagnan, who had never seriously thought of this impossible duel, endeavoured to turn the conversation, but he could not succeed. Milady kept him within the limits she had traced beforehand with her irresistible spirit and her iron will.

D'Artagnan fancied himself very cunning when advising milady to renounce, by pardoning De Wardes, the furious projects she had formed.

But at the first word she started, and exclaimed, in a sharp, bantering tone, which sounded strangely :

"Are you afraid, dear D'Artagnan ?"

"You cannot think me so, dear love !" replied D'Artagnan, "but now, suppose this poor Count de Wardes should be less guilty than you imagine him to be ?"

"At all events," said milady, seriously, "he has deceived me, and, from the moment he deceived me, he merited death."

"He shall die, then, since you condemn him !" said D'Artagnan, in so firm a tone that it appeared to milady the expression of a devotedness superior to every trial.

This reassured her.

When the faint light of dawn peeped through the blinds, milady warned D'Artagnan that it was time to depart, not forgetting to remind him of his promise to avenge her on the Count de Wardes.

"I am quite ready," said D'Artagnan ; "but, in the first place, I should like to be certain of one thing."

"And what is that ?" asked milady.

"That is, whether you really love me ?"

"You have little reason to ask such a question, I think."

"Well, perhaps you do, and I am yours, body and soul !"

" Thanks, my brave lover ; but as you are satisfied of my love, you must, in your turn, satisfy me of yours. Is not that just ?"

" Certainly ; but if you love me as much as you say," replied D'Artagnan, " do you not entertain a little fear on my account ?"

" What have I to fear ?"

" Why, that I may be dangerously wounded—killed even."

" Impossible !" cried milady ; " you are such a valiant man, and such an expert swordsman."

" You would not, then, prefer a means," resumed D'Artagnan, " which would equally avenge you, whilst rendering the combat useless ?"

Milady looked at her lover in silence ; the pale light of the first rays of day gave to her clear eyes a strangely frightful expression.

" Really," said she, " I believe you now begin to hesitate."

" No, I do not hesitate ; but I really pity this poor Count de Wardes, since you have ceased to love him. I think that a man must be so severely punished by the loss of your love, that he stands in need of no other chastisement."

" Who told you that I have loved him ?" asked milady, sharply.

" At least, I am now at liberty to believe, without too much fatuity, that you love another," said the young man, in a caressing tone, " and I repeat that I am really interested for the count."

" You are ?" asked milady.

" Yes, I."

" And on what account ?"

" Because I alone know——"

" What ?"

" That he is far from being, or rather having been, so guilty towards you as he appears to be."

" Indeed !" said milady, in an anxious tone ; " explain yourself, for I really cannot tell what you mean."

And she looked at D'Artagnan.

" Yes ; I am a man of honour," said D'Artagnan, determined to come to an end, " and since your love is mine, and I am satisfied I possess it —for I do possess it, do I not ?"

" Entirely ; go on."

" Well, I feel as if transformed—a confession weighs on my mind."

" A confession !"

" If I had the least doubt of your love I would not make it ; but you love me, do you not ?"

" Without doubt I do."

" Then if, through excess of love, I have rendered myself culpable towards you, you will pardon me ?"

" Perhaps."

D'Artagnan assumed his most winning smile, but it had no effect ; he had alarmed milady, and she involuntarily turned from him.

" This confession," said she, growing paler and paler, " what is this confession !"

" You gave De Wardes a meeting on Thursday last, in this very room, did you not ?"

" Who—I ? No, certainly not !" said milady, in a tone of voice so firm, and with a countenance so unchanged, that if D'Artagnan had not been in such perfect possession of the fact, he would have doubted.

" Do not say that which is not true, my angel," said D'Artagnan, smiling ; " that would be useless."

" What do you mean ? Speak ! you terrify me to death."

" Be satisfied ; you are not guilty towards me—I have already pardoned you."

" What next ? what next ?"

" De Wardes cannot boast of anything."

" How is that ? You told me yourself that that ring——"

" That ring I have ! The Count de Wardes of last Thursday and the D'Artagnan of to-day are the same person !"

The imprudent young man expected a surprise, mixed with shame— a slight storm, which would resolve itself into tears ; but he was strangely deceived, and his error was not of long duration.

Pale and trembling, milady repulsed D'Artagnan's attempted embrace by a violent blow on the chest, as she sprang from him.

It was then broad daylight.

In his eagerness to detain her, D'Artagnan had grasped her dress ; but the frail cambric could not stand against two such strong wills—it was torn from her fair round shoulders, and, to his horror and astonishment, D'Artagnan recognised upon one of them, indelibly branded, the mark which is impressed by the ignominious hand of the executioner.

" Great God !" cried D'Artagnan, loosing his hold, and remaining mute, motionless, and frozen.

But milady felt herself denounced by his terror even. He had doubtless seen all. The young man now knew her secret, her terrible secret —the secret she concealed even from her maid with such care, the secret of which all the world, excepting he, was ignorant.

She turned upon him, no longer like a furious woman, but like a wounded panther.

" Ah, wretch !" cried she, " thou hast basely betrayed me ! and still more, thou hast my secret ! Thou shalt die !"

And she flew to a little inlaid casket which stood upon the toilet, opened it with a feverish and trembling hand, drew from it a small poniard with a golden haft and a sharp thin blade, and then threw herself with a bound upon D'Artagnan.

Although the young man was, as we know, brave, he was terrified at that wild countenance, those terribly dilated pupils, those pale cheeks, and those bleeding lips. He drew back to the other side of the room as he would have done from a serpent which was crawling towards him, and his sword coming in contact with his nervous hand, he drew it, almost unconsciously, from the scabbard.

But, without taking any heed of the sword, milady endeavoured to get near enough to him to stab him, and did not stop till she felt the sharp point at her throat.

She then endeavoured to seize the sword with her hands ; but D'Artagnan kept it free from her grasp, and continued to present the point, sometimes at her eyes, sometimes at her breast, whilst he aimed at making his retreat by the door which led to Kitty's apartment.

Milady during this time continued to strike at him with her dagger with horrible fury, screaming in a superhuman manner.

As all this, however, bore some resemblance to a duel, D'Artagnan soon began to recover himself.

"Very well, pretty lady, very well," said he ; "but, pardieu ! if you don't calm yourself, I will mark you with a second fleur-de-lis upon one of those pretty cheeks !"

"Scoundrel ! infamous scoundrel !" howled milady.

But D'Artagnan, still keeping on the defensive, drew near to Kitty's door. At the noise they made, she in overturning the furniture in her efforts to get at him, he in screening himself behind the furniture to keep out of her reach, Kitty, in great alarm, opened the door. D'Artagnan, who had constantly manœuvred to gain this point, was not at more than three paces from it. With one spring he flew from the chamber of milady into that of the maid, and, quick as lightning, he slammed-to the door, and placed all his weight against it, whilst Kitty bolted it.

Then milady attempted to tear down the door-case, with a strength apparently above that of a woman ; but finding she could not accomplish this, she, in her fury, stabbed at the door with her poniard, the point of which repeatedly glittered through the wood. Every blow was accompanied with terrible imprecations.

"Quick, Kitty, quick !" said D'Artagnan, in a low voice, as soon as the bolts were fast, "let me get out of the hotel ; for if we leave her time to turn round, she will have me killed by the servants !"

"But you can't go out so," said Kitty ; "you have hardly any clothes on."

"That's true," said D'Artagnan, then first thinking of the costume he appeared in—"that's true ; but dress me as well as you are able, only make haste ; think, my dear girl, it's life and death !"

Kitty was but too well aware of that. In a moment she muffled him up in a large flowered robe, a capacious hood, and a cloak ; she gave him some slippers, in which he placed his naked feet, and then conducted him down the stairs. It was time : milady had already rung her bell, and roused the whole hotel ; the porter was drawing the cord at the moment milady cried from her window :

"Don't open the gate ! don't open the gate !"

The young man sprang out whilst she was still threatening him with an impotent gesture. At the moment she lost sight of him, milady sank back fainting into her chamber.

CHAPTER XXXVIII.

HOW, WITHOUT INCOMMODING HIMSELF, ATHOS FOUND HIS EQUIPMENT.

D'ARTAGNAN was so completely bewildered that, without taking any heed of what would become of Kitty, he ran at full speed across half Paris, and did not stop till he came to Athos' door. The confusion of his mind, the terror which spurred him on, the cries of some of the patrol who started in pursuit of him, and the shouting of the people, who, notwithstanding the early hour, were going to their work, only made him precipitate his course.

He crossed the court, ran up the two flights to Athos' apartments, and knocked at the door enough to break it down.

Grimaud came, rubbing his half-open eyes, to answer this noisy summons, and D'Artagnan sprang with such violence into the room as nearly to overturn the astonished lackey.

In spite of his habitual mutism, the poor lad this time found his speech.

"Holloa, there !" cried he ; "what do you want, you strumpet ? What's your business here, you hussey ?"

D'Artagnan threw off his hood, and disengaged his hands from the folds of the cloak ; and, at sight of the moustaches and the naked sword, the poor devil perceived he had to deal with a man. He then concluded it must be an assassin.

"Help ! murder ! help !" cried he.

"Hold your tongue, you stupid fellow !" said the young man ; "I am D'Artagnan—don't you know me ? Where is your master ?"

"You, Monsieur D'Artagnan !" cried Grimaud, "impossible !"

"Grimaud," said Athos, coming out of his apartment in a *robe de chambre*, "Grimaud, I thought I heard you permitting yourself to speak ?"

"Ah, monsieur, but——"

"Silence !"

Grimaud contented himself with pointing D'Artagnan out to his master with his finger.

Athos recognised his comrade, and, phlegmatic as he was, he burst into a laugh that was quite excused by the masquerade before his eyes : petticoats falling over his shoes, sleeves tucked up, and moustaches stiff with agitation.

"Don't laugh, my friend !" cried D'Artagnan ; "for Heaven's sake, don't laugh, for, upon my soul, it's no laughing matter !"

And he pronounced these words with such a solemn air and with such a real appearance of terror, that Athos eagerly seized his hand, crying :

"Are you wounded, my friend ? How pale you are !"

"No, but I have just met with a terrible adventure ! Are you alone, Athos ?"

"Parbleu ! who do you expect to find with me at this hour ?"

"Well, well !" and D'Artagnan rushed into Athos' chamber,

" Come, speak !" said the latter, closing the door and bolting it, that they might not be disturbed. " Is the king dead ? Have you killed the cardinal ? Why, you are quite beside yourself ! Come, come, tell me ; I am dying with curiosity and uneasiness !"

" Athos," said D'Artagnan, getting rid of his female garments, and appearing in his shirt, " prepare yourself to hear an incredible, an un-heard-of history."

" Well, but put on that *robe de chambre* first," said the musketeer to his friend.

D'Artagnan got into the robe as quickly as he could, taking one sleeve for the other, so greatly was he still agitated.

" Well ?" said Athos.

" Well," replied D'Artagnan, inclining his mouth to Athos' ear, and lowering his voice, " milady is marked with a fleur-de-lis upon her shoulder !"

" Ah !" cried the musketeer, as if he had received a ball in his heart.

" Are you sure," said D'Artagnan, " are you *sure* that the *other* is dead ?"

" *The other ?*" said Athos, in so inward a voice that D'Artagnan scarcely heard him.

" Yes ; she of whom you told me one day at Amiens."

Athos uttered a groan, and let his head sink into his hands.

" This one is a woman of from twenty-six to twenty-eight years of age."

" Fair," said Athos, " is she not ?"

" Very."

" Blue and clear eyes, of a strange brilliancy, with black eyelids and eyebrows ?"

" Yes."

" Tall, well-made ? She has lost a tooth, next to the eye-tooth on the left ?"

" Yes."

" The fleur-de-lis is small, red in colour, and looks as if endeavours had been made to efface it with paste of some kind ?"

" Yes."

" But you say she is an Englishwoman ?"

" She is called Milady, but, notwithstanding that, she may be a Frenchwoman. Lord de Winter is only her brother-in-law."

" I will see her, D'Artagnan !"

" Beware, Athos, beware ; you endeavoured to kill her ; she is a woman to return you the like, and not to fail, I promise you."

" She will not dare to say anything ; that would be to denounce her-self."

" She is capable of anything or everything. Did you ever see her furious ?"

" No," said Athos.

" A tigress ! a panther ! Ah ! my dear Athos, I am greatly afraid I have drawn a terrible vengeance on both of us !"

D'Artagnan then related all : the mad passion of milady and her menaces of death to him.

"You are right, and upon my soul, I would give my life for a hair," said Athos. "Fortunately, the day after to-morrow we leave Paris. We are going, according to all probability, to La Rochelle, and once gone——"

"She will follow you to the end of the world, Athos, if she recognises you ; let her then exhaust her vengeance on me alone !"

"My dear friend ! of what consequence is it if she kills me ?" said Athos, "do you, perchance, think I set any great store by life ?"

"There is something horribly mysterious under all this, Athos ; this woman is one of the cardinal's spies, I am sure of that."

"In that case take care of yourself. If the cardinal does not hold you in high admiration for the affair of London, he entertains a great hatred for you ; but as, considering everything, he cannot accuse you openly, and as hatred must be satisfied, particularly when it's a cardinal's hatred, take care of yourself ! If you go out, do not go out alone ; when you eat, use every precaution ; mistrust, in short, everything, even your own shadow."

"Fortunately," said D'Artagnan, "all this will be only necessary till after to-morrow evening, for when once with the army, we shall have, I hope, only men to dread."

"In the meantime," said Athos, "I renounce my plan of seclusion, and wherever you go, I will go with you : you must return to the Rue des Fossoyeurs ; I will accompany you."

"Yes, but however near it may be, I cannot go thither in this guise."

"That's true," said Athos, and he rang the bell.

Grimaud entered.

Athos made him a sign to go to D'Artagnan's residence, and bring back some clothes. Grimaud replied, by another sign, that he understood perfectly, and set off.

"All this will not advance your equipment," said Athos, "for, if I am not mistaken, you have left the best of your apparel at milady's, and she will certainly not have the politeness to return it to you. Fortunately, you have the sapphire."

"The sapphire is yours, my dear Athos ! Did you not tell me it was a family jewel ?"

"Yes, my father gave two thousand crowns for it, as he once told me ; it formed part of the nuptial present he made my mother ; and it is magnificent. My mother gave it to me, and I, fool as I was, instead of keeping the ring as a holy relic, gave it to this wretched woman."

"Then, my friend, take back this ring, to which, it is plain, you attach much value."

"I take back the ring, after it has passed through the hands of that infamous creature ! never ! that ring is defiled, D'Artagnan."

"Sell it, then."

" Sell a diamond which was the gift of my mother. I must confess I should consider that as a profanation."

" Pledge it, then ; you can borrow at least a thousand crowns on it. With that sum you can extricate yourself from your present difficulties ; and when you are full of money again, you can redeem it, and take it back cleansed from its ancient stains, as it will have passed through the hands of usurers."

Athos smiled.

" You are a capital companion, D'Artagnan," said he ; " your never-failing cheerfulness raises poor souls in affliction. Agreed, let us pledge the ring, but upon one condition."

" What is that ?"

" That there shall be five hundred crowns for you, and five hundred crowns for me."

" Don't think of such a thing, Athos ; I don't want the half of such a sum. I who am still only in the guards, and by selling my saddles, I shall get it. What do I want ? A horse for Planchet, that's all. Besides, you forget that I have a ring likewise."

" To which you attach more value than I do to mine ; at least, I have thought it seemed so."

" Yes, for in any extreme circumstance it might not only extricate us from some great embarrassment, or even a great danger ; it is not only a valuable diamond, it is an enchanted talisman."

" I don't at all understand you, but I believe all you say to be true. Let us return to my ring, or rather to yours ; you shall take half the sum that will be advanced upon it, or I will throw it into the Seine ; and I doubt, as was the case with Polycrates, whether any fish will be sufficiently complaisant to bring it back to us."

" Well, I will take it, then," said D'Artagnan.

At this moment Grimaud returned, accompanied by Planchet ; the latter, anxious about his master, and curious to know what had happened to him, took advantage of the opportunity, and brought his clothes himself.

D'Artagnan dressed himself, and Athos did the same. When about to go out, the latter made Grimaud the sign of a person taking an aim, and the lackey immediately took down his musketoon, and got ready to follow his master.

They arrived without accident at the Rue des Fossoyeurs. Bonacieux was standing at the door ; he cast one of his ill-meaning, bantering looks at D'Artagnan as he passed him,—

" Make haste, my dear lodger," said he ; " there is a very pretty girl waiting for you upstairs ; and, you know, women don't like to be made to wait."

" That's Kitty !" said D'Artagnan to himself, and darted into the passage.

In fact, upon the landing leading to the chamber, and crouching against the door, he found the poor girl, all in a tremble. As soon as she perceived him.—

"You promised to protect me ; you promised to save me from her anger," said she ; "remember, it was you who ruined me !"

"Yes, yes, to be sure, Kitty," said D'Artagnan ; "be at ease, my girl. But what happened after my departure ?"

"How can I tell !" said Kitty. "The lackeys were brought by the cries she made,—she was mad with passion ; there exist no imprecations she did not utter against you. Then I thought she would remember it was through my chamber you had gone into hers, and that then she would suppose I was your accomplice ; so I took what little money I had and the best of my things, and I got away as fast as I could."

"Poor dear girl ! But what can I do with you ? I am going away the day after to-morrow."

"Do what you please, monsieur le chevalier ; help me out of Paris ; help me out of France !"

"I cannot take you, however, to the siege of La Rochelle," said D'Artagnan.

"No ; but you can place me in one of the provinces, with some lady of your acquaintance ; in your own country, for instance."

"My dear little love ! in my country the ladies do without chambermaids. But, stop ; I can manage your business for you. Planchet, go and find M. Aramis ; request him to come here directly. We have something very important to say to him."

"I understand," said Athos ; "but why not Porthos ? I should have thought that his duchess——"

"Oh ! Porthos' duchess is dressed by her husband's clerks," said D'Artagnan, laughing. "Besides, Kitty would not like to live in the Rue aux Ours."

"I do not care where I live," said Kitty, "provided I am well concealed, and she does not know where I am."

"And now, Kitty, when we are about to separate, and you are no longer jealous of me——"

"Monsieur le chevalier, far off or near, be where I may, I shall always love you."

"Where the devil will constancy take up its abode next ?" said Athos to himself.

"And I also," said D'Artagnan ; "I also shall always love you ; be sure of that. But now, answer me ; I attach great importance to the question I am about to put to you. Did you never hear talk of a young woman who was carried off one night ?"

"There now !—Oh ! monsieur le chevalier, do you love that woman still ?"

"No, no ; it is one of my friends who loves her—M. Athos ; this gentleman here."

"I ?" cried Athos, with an accent like that of a man who perceives he was about to tread upon an adder.

"You, to be sure !" said D'Artagnan, pressing Athos' hand. "You know the interest we both take in this poor little Madame Bonacieux. Besides, Kitty will tell nothing ; will you, Kitty ? You understand, my dear girl," continued D'Artagnan, "she is the wife of that frightful baboon you saw at the door as you came in."

" Oh ! mon Dieu ! you remind me of my fright ! if he should have known me again !"

" What ! know you again ! Did you ever see that man before ?"

" He came twice to milady's."

" That's it. About what time ?"

" Why, about fifteen or eighteen days ago."

" Exactly so."

" And yesterday evening he came again."

" Yesterday evening ?"

" Yes, just before you came."

" My dear Athos, we are enveloped in a network of spies ! And do you believe he knew you again, Kitty ?"

" I pulled down my hood as soon as I saw him, but perhaps it was too late."

" Go down, Athos, he mistrusts you less than me, and see if he be still at his door."

Athos went down and returned immediately.

" He is gone," said he, " and the house door is shut."

" He is gone to make his report, and to say that the pigeons are at this moment all in the dovecote."

" Well, then, let us all fly away," said Athos, " and leave nobody here but Planchet, to bring us news."

" A minute. But Aramis, whom we have sent for !"

" That's true," said Athos, " we must wait for Aramis."

At that moment Aramis arrived.

The matter was all explained to him, and the friends gave him to understand that among all his high connections he must find a place for Kitty.

Aramis reflected for a minute, and then said, colouring :—" Will it be really rendering you a service, D'Artagnan ?"

" I shall be grateful to you all my life."

" Very well ; Madame de Bois-Tracy asked me, for one of her friends who resides in the provinces, I believe, for a trustworthy femme de chambre ; and if you can, my dear D'Artagnan, answer for mademoiselle——"

" Oh! monsieur, be assured that I shall be entirely devoted to the person who will give me the means of quitting Paris."

" Then," said Aramis, " this falls out very well."

He placed himself at the table, and wrote a little note which he sealed with a ring, and gave the billet to Kitty.

" And now, my dear girl," said D'Artagnan, " you know that it is not good for any of us to be here. Therefore let us separate. We shall meet again in better days, depend upon it."

" Dicers' oaths !" said Athos, whilst D'Artagnan went to conduct Kitty downstairs.

An instant afterwards the three young men separated, agreeing to meet again at four o'clock at Athos' residence, and leaving Planchet to guard the house.

Aramis returned home, and Athos and D'Artagnan went about pledging the sapphire.

As the Gascon had foreseen, they found no difficulty in obtaining three hundred pistoles upon the ring. Still further, the Jew told them that if they would sell it to him, as it would make a magnificent pendant for ear-rings, he would give five hundred pistoles for it.

Athos and D'Artagnan, with the activity of two soldiers, and the knowledge of two connoisseurs, hardly required three hours to purchase the entire equipment of the musketeer. Besides, Athos was very easy, and a noble to his fingers' ends. Whenever a thing suited him, he directly paid the price asked for it, without thinking to ask for any abatement. D'Artagnan would have remonstrated at this, but Athos put his hand upon his shoulder, with a smile, and D'Artagnan understood that it was all very well for such a little Gascon gentleman as himself to drive a bargain, but not for a man who had the bearing of a prince. The musketeer met with a superb Andalusian horse, black as jet, nostrils of fire, legs clean and elegant, rising six. He examined him, and found him sound and without blemish ; he was asked a thousand livres for him.

He might, perhaps, have been bought for less ; but whilst D'Artagnan was discussing the price with the dealer, Athos was counting the money down on the table.

Grimaud had a stout, short Picard cob, which cost three hundred livres.

But when the saddle and arms for Grimaud were purchased, Athos had not a sou left of his hundred and fifty pistoles. D'Artagnan offered his friend a part of his share, which he should return when convenient.

But Athos only replied to this proposal by shrugging his shoulders.

"How much did the Jew say he would give for the sapphire, if he purchased it ?" said Athos.

"Five hundred pistoles."

"That is to say, two hundred more ! a hundred pistoles for you, and a hundred pistoles for me. Well, now, that would be a real fortune to us, my friend ; let us go back to the Jew's again."

"What ! will you—— ?"

"This ring would certainly only recall very bitter remembrances ; then we shall never be masters of three hundred pistoles to redeem it ; so that we really should lose two hundred pistoles by the bargain. Go and tell him the ring is his, D'Artagnan, and bring back the two hundred pistoles with you."

"Reflect, Athos !"

"Ready money is dear for the time that passes, and we must learn how to make sacrifices. Go, D'Artagnan, go ; Grimaud will accompany you with his musquetoon."

Half an hour afterwards, D'Artagnan returned with the two thousand livres, and without having met with any accident.

It was thus Athos found at home resources which he did not expect.

CHAPTER XXXIX.

A VISION.

At four o'clock the four friends were all assembled at Athos' apartments. Their anxiety about their equipments had all disappeared, and each countenance only preserved the expression of its own secret inquietudes; for behind all present happiness is concealed a fear for the future.

Suddenly Planchet entered, bringing two letters for D'Artagnan.

The one was a little billet, genteelly folded, with a pretty seal in green wax, on which was impressed a dove bearing a green branch.

The other was a large square epistle, resplendent with the terrible arms of his eminence the cardinal duke.

At the sight of the little letter the heart of D'Artagnan bounded, for he believed he had seen that writing before : and although he had seen that writing but once, the memory of it remained at the bottom of his heart.

He therefore seized the little letter, and opened it eagerly.

" Be," said the letter, " on Thursday next, at seven o'clock in the evening, on the road to Chaillot, and look carefully into the carriages that pass ; but if you have any consideration for your own life or that of those who love you, do not speak a single word, do not make a movement which may lead any one to believe you have recognised her, who exposes herself to everything for the sake of seeing you but for an instant."

No signature.

" That's a snare," said Athos ; " don't go, D'Artagnan."

" And yet," replied D'Artagnan, " I think I recognise the writing."

" That may be forged," said Athos ; " between six and seven o'clock, the road of Chaillot is quite deserted ; you might as well go and ride in the forest of Bondy."

" But suppose we all go," said D'Artagnan ; " what the devil ! they won't devour us all four ; four lackeys, horses, arms, and all !"

" And, besides, it will be a good opportunity for displaying our new equipments," said Porthos.

" But, if it is a woman that writes," said Aramis, " and that woman desires not to be seen, remember, you compromise her, D'Artagnan ; which is not behaving like a gentleman."

" We will remain in the background ; and he will advance alone."

" Yes, but a pistol-shot is easily fired from a carriage, however fast it may be going."

" Bah !" said D'Artagnan, " they will miss me ; if they fire, we will ride after the carriage, and exterminate those who may be in it. They must be enemies."

" He is right," said Porthos ; " battle . besides, it will be a good opportunity to try our new arms."

" Let us enjoy that pleasure," said Aramis, in his mild and careless manner.

" As you please," said Athos.

" Gentlemen," said D'Artagnan, " it is half-past four, and we have scarcely time to be on the road of Chaillot by six."

" Besides, if we go out late, nobody will see us," said Porthos, "and that will be a pity. Let us get ready, gentlemen."

" But this second letter," said Athos, " you forget that ; it appears to me, however, that the seal denotes that it deserves to be opened ; for my part, I declare, D'Artagnan, I think it of much more consequence than the little piece of waste paper you have so cunningly slipped into your bosom."

D'Artagnan blushed.

" Well," said he, " let us see, gentlemen, what are his eminence's commands," and D'Artagnan unsealed the letter, and read :

" M. D'Artagnan, of the King's Guards, company Des Essarts, is expected at the Palais-Cardinal, this evening at eight o'clock.
      " LA HOUDENIERE, Captain of the Guards."

" 'The devil !" said Athos ; " here's a rendezvous much more serious than the other."

" I will go to the second, after attending the first," said D'Artagnan, " one is for seven o'clock, and the other for eight : there will be time for both."

" Hum ! Now, I would not go at all," said Aramis ; " a gallant knight cannot decline an appointment made by a lady ; but a prudent gentleman may excuse himself from not waiting on his eminence, particularly when he has reason to believe he is not invited for courteous purposes."

" I am of Aramis' opinion," said Porthos.

" Gentlemen," replied D'Artagnan, " I have already received by M. de Cavois a similar invitation from his eminence ; I neglected it, and on the morrow a serious misfortune happened to me !—Constance disappeared. Whatever may ensue, I will go."

" If you are determined," said Athos, " do so."

" Yes, but the Bastille ?" said Aramis.

" Bah ! you will get me out. if they put me there," said D'Artagnan.

" To be sure we will," replied Aramis and Porthos, with admirable promptness and decision, as if that were the simplest thing in the world, —" to be sure we will get you out, if there ; but in the mean time, as we are to set off the day after to-morrow, you would do much better not to risk this Bastille."

" Let us do better than that," said Athos, " do not let us leave him during the whole evening ; let each of us wait at a gate of the palace with a musketeer behind him ; if we see any carriage with closed windows, and of at all suspicious appearance, come out, let us fall upon it : it is a long time since we have had a skirmish with the guards of Monsieur le Cardinal ; M. de Tréville must think us dead."

" To a certainty, Athos," said Aramis, " you were meant to be a general ; what do you think of the plan, gentlemen ?"

" Admirable !" replied the young men in chorus.

" Well !" said Porthos, " I will run to the hotel, and engage our com-rades to hold themselves in readiness by eight o'clock, the rendezvous, the Place du Palais-Cardinal ; in the mean time, you see that the lackeys saddle the horses."

" I have no horse," said D'Artagnan, " but that is of no consequence, I can take one of M. de Tréville's."

" That is not worth while," said Aramis, " you can have one of mine."

" One of yours ! how many have you, then ?" asked D'Artagnan.

" Three," replied Aramis smiling.

" Certes," cried Athos, " you are the best mounted poet of France or Navarre."

" Well, but Aramis, you don't want three horses ? I cannot compre-hend what induced you to buy three !"

" Therefore I only purchased two," said Aramis.

" The third then fell from the clouds, I suppose ?"

" No, the third was brought to me this very morning by a groom out of livery, who would not tell me in whose service he was, and who said he had received orders from his master."

" Or his mistress," interrupted D'Artagnan.

" That makes no difference," said Aramis, colouring ; " and who affirmed, as I said, that he had received orders from his mistress to place the horse in my stable, without informing me whence it came."

" It is only to poets that such things happen," said Athos gravely.

" Well, in that case, we can manage famously," said D'Artagnan ; " which of the two horses will you ride ; that which you bought, or the one that was given to you ?"

" That which was given to me, without doubt,—you cannot for a moment imagine, D'Artagnan, that I should commit such an offence towards——"

" The unknown giver," interrupted D'Artagnan.

" Or the mysterious benefactress," said Athos.

" The one you bought will then become useless to you ?"

" Nearly so."

" And you selected it yourself ?"

" With the greatest care : the safety of the horseman, you know, depends almost always upon the goodness of his horse."

" Well, let me have it at the price it cost you ?"

" I was going to make you the offer, my dear D'Artagnan, giving you all the time necessary for repaying me such a trifle."

" How much did it cost you ?"

" Eight hundred livres."

" Here are forty double pistoles, my dear friend," said D'Artagnan, taking the sum from his pocket ; " I know that is the coin in which you were paid for your poems."

" You are full of money, then ?" said Aramis.

" Money !—rolling in it, my dear fellow !"

And D'Artagnan chinked the remainder of his pistoles in his pocket.

"Send your saddle, then, to the hotel of the musketeers, and your horse can be brought back with ours."

"Very well ; but it is already five o'clock, so make haste."

A quarter of an hour afterwards, Porthos appeared at the end of the Rue Férou, mounted upon a very handsome genet; Mousqueton followed him upon an Auvergne horse, small, but very good-looking : Porthos was resplendent with joy and pride.

At the same time, Aramis made his appearance at the other end of the street, upon a superb English charger ; Bazin followed him upon a roan, leading a splendid, vigorous Mecklenburg horse ; this last was D'Artagnan's.

The two musketeers met at the gate ; Athos and D'Artagnan watched their approach from the window.

"The devil," cried Aramis, "you have a magnificent horse there, Porthos."

"Yes," replied Porthos, "it is the one that ought to have been sent to me at first ; a bad joke of the husband's substituted the other ; but the good man has been punished since, and I have obtained full satisfaction."

Grimaud then led up his master's horse ; D'Artagnan and Athos came down, got into their saddles, and all four set forward : Athos upon a horse he owed to a woman, Aramis on a horse he owed to his mistress, Porthos on a horse he owed to the procureuse, and D'Artagnan on a horse he owed to his good fortune, the best mistress possible.

The lackeys followed.

As Porthos had foreseen, the cavalcade produced a good effect ; and if Madame Coquenard had met Porthos, and seen what a superb appearance he made upon his handsome Spanish genet, she would not have regretted the bleeding she had inflicted upon the strong box of her husband.

Near the Louvre the four friends met with M. de Tréville, who was returning from St. Germain ; he stopped them to offer his compliments upon their appointments, which in an instant drew round them a hundred gapers.

D'Artagnan took advantage of the circumstance to speak to M. de Tréville of the letter with the great red seal, and the cardinal's arms ; we beg it to be understood that he did not breathe a word concerning the other.

M. de Tréville approved of the resolution he had adopted, and assured him, that if on the morrow he did not appear, he himself would undertake to find him, let him be where he might.

At this moment the clock of La Samaritaine struck six : the four friends pleaded an engagement, and took leave of M. de Tréville.

A short gallop brought them to the road of Chaillot ; the day began to decline, carriages were passing and repassing ; D'Artagnan, keeping at some distance from his friends, darted a scrutinizing glance into every carriage that appeared, but saw no face with which he was acquainted.

At length, after waiting a quarter of an hour, and just as twilight was beginning to thicken, a carriage appeared, coming at a quick pace on the road of Sèvres ; a presentiment instantly told D'Artagnan that this carriage contained the person who had appointed the rendezvous ; the young man was himself astonished to find his heart beat so violently. Almost instantly a female head was put out at the window, with two fingers placed upon her mouth, either to enjoin silence or to send him a kiss ; D'Artagnan uttered a slight cry of joy : this woman, or rather this apparition, for the carriage passed with the rapidity of a vision, was Madame Bonacieux.

By an involuntary movement, and in spite of the injunction given, D'Artagnan put his horse into a gallop, and in a few strides overtook the carriage ; but the window was close shut, the vision had disappeared.

D'Artagnan then remembered the injunction : " If you value your own life, or that of those who love you, remain motionless, and as if you had seen nothing."

He stopped, therefore, trembling, not for himself, but for the poor woman who had evidently exposed herself to great danger by appointing this rendezvous.

The carriage pursued its way, still going at a great pace, till it dashed into Paris, and disappeared.

D'Artagnan remained fixed to the spot, astounded, and not knowing what to think. If it was Madame Bonacieux, and if she was returning to Paris, why this fugitive interview, why this simple exchange of a glance, why this last kiss ? If, on the other side, it was not she, which was still quite possible, for the little light that rendered a mistake easy ; if it was not she, might it not be the commencement of some machination against him with the bait of this woman, for whom his love was known ?

His three companions joined him. All had plainly seen a woman's head appear out at the window, but none of them, except Athos, knew Madame Bonacieux. The opinion of Athos was that it was Madame Bonacieux ; but less preoccupied by that pretty face than D'Artagnan, he had fancied he saw a second head, a man's head, in the carriage.

" If that be the case," said D'Artagnan, "they are doubtless transporting her from one prison to another. But what can they intend to do with the poor creature, and how shall I ever meet her again ?"

" My friend," said Athos, gravely, "remember that it is the dead alone with whom we are not likely to meet again on this earth. You know something of that, as well as I do, I think. Now, if your mistress is not dead, if it is her we have just seen, you will meet with her again some day or other. And perhaps, my God !" added he, with that misanthropic tone which was peculiar to him, " perhaps sooner than you wish."

Half-past seven had struck, the carriage was twenty minutes behind the time appointed. D'Artagnan's friends reminded him that he had a visit to pay, but at the same time calling it to his observation that there was still time to retract.

But D'Artagnan was at the same time impetuous and curious. He had made up his mind that he would go to the Palais-Cardinal, and that he would learn what his eminence had :o say to him : nothing could turn him from his purpose.

They reached the Rue St. Honoré, and in the Place du Palais-Cardinal they found the twelve convoked musketeers, walking about in expectation of their comrades. There only they made :hem acquainted with the matter in question.

D'Artagnan was well known in the honourable corps of the king's musketeers, in which it had been stated that he was, one day, to take his place : he was considered, beforehand, as their comrade. It resulted from these antecedents that every one entered heartily into the purpose for which they met ; besides, it would not be unlikely that they should have an opportunity of playing either the cardinal or his people an ill turn, and for such expeditions these worthy gentlemen were always ready.

Athos divided them into three groups, assumed the command of one, gave the second to Aramis, and the third to Porthos, and then each group went and took a position for watching, near an entrance.

D'Artagnan, on his part, entered boldly at the front gate.

Although he felt himself ably supported, the young man was not without a little uneasiness as he ascended the great staircase, step by step. His conduct towards milady bore a strong resemblance to treachery, and he was very suspicious of the political relations which existed between that woman and the cardinal; still further, De Wardes, whom he had treated so ill, was one of the creatures of his eminence, and D'Artagnan knew, that whilst his eminence was terrible to his enemies, he was strongly attached to his friends.

"If De Wardes has related all our affair to the cardinal, which is not to be doubted, and if he has recognised me, which is probable, I may consider myself almost as a condemned man," said D'Artagnan, shaking his head. "But why has he waited till now? Humph ! that's all plain enough : milady has laid her complaint against me with that hypocritical grief which renders her so interesting, and this last offence has made the cup overflow."

"Fortunately," added he, "my good friends are down yonder, and they will not allow me to be carried away easily. Nevertheless, M. de Tréville's company of musketeers alone cannot maintain a war against the cardinal, who disposes of the forces of all France, and before whom the queen is without power and the king without will. D'Artagnan, my friend, you are brave, you are prudent, you have excellent qualities, but the women will ruin you !"

He came to this melancholy conclusion as he entered the antechamber. He placed his letter in the hands of the usher on duty, who led him into the waiting-room, and passed on into the interior of the palace.

In this waiting-room were five or six of the cardinal's guards, who recognised D'Artagnan, and knowing that it was he who had wounded Jussac, they looked upon him with a smile of singular meaning.

This smile appeared to D'Artagnan to be of bad augury : only, as our Gascon was not easily intimidated, or rather, thanks to a great pride natural to the men of his country, he did not allow himself easily to see that which was passing in his mind, when that which was passing at all resembled fear, he placed himself haughtily in front of messieurs the guards, and waited with his hand on his hip, in an attitude by no means deficient in majesty.

The usher returned and made a sign to D'Artagnan to follow him It appeared to the young man that the guards, on seeing him depart, whispered among themselves.

He followed a corridor, crossed a grand saloon, entered a library, and found himself in the presence of a man seated at a desk and writing.

The usher introduced him and retired without speaking a word. D'Artagnan remained standing and examined this man.

D'Artagnan at first believed that he had to do with some judge examining his papers, but he perceived that the man of the desk wrote or rather corrected lines of unequal length, scanning the words on his fingers ; he saw then that he was in face of a poet. At the end of an instant the poet closed his manuscript, upon the cover of which was written, *Mirame, a tragedy in five acts*, and raised his head.

D'Artagnan recognised the cardinal.

CHAPTER XL.

A TERRIBLE VISION.

THE cardinal leant his elbow on his manuscript, his cheek upon his hand, and looked intently at the young man for a moment. No one had a more searching eye than the Cardinal de Richelieu, and D'Artagnan felt this glance penetrate his veins like a fever.

He, however, kept a good countenance, holding his hat in his hand, and awaiting the good pleasure of his eminence, without too much assurance, but without too much humility.

" Monsieur," said the cardinal, " are you a D'Artagnan from Béarn !"

" Yes, monseigneur," replied the young man.

" There are several branches of the D'Artagnans at Tarbes, and in its environs," said the cardinal ; " to which do you belong ?"

" I am the son of him who served in the religious wars under the great King Henry, the father of his gracious majesty."

" That is well. It is you who set out, seven or eight months ago, from your country to try your fortune in the capital ?"

" Yes, monseigneur."

" You came through Meung, where something befell you, I don't very well know what, but still something."

" Monseigneur," said D'Artagnan, " this was what happened to me——"

" Of no consequence, of no consequence !" resumed the cardinal with a smile, which indicated that he knew the story as well as he who wished to relate it ; "you were recommended to M. de Tréville, were you not?"

" Yes, monseigneur, but in that unfortunate affair at Meung——"

" The letter was lost," replied his eminence ; " yes, I know that ; but M. de Tréville is a skilful physiognomist, who knows men at first sight ; and he placed you in the company of his brother-in-law, M. des Essarts, leaving you to hope, that one day or other you should enter the musketeers."

" Monseigneur is quite correctly informed," said D'Artagnan.

" Since that time many things have happened to you : you were walking one day behind the Chartreux, when it would have been better for you if you had been elsewhere ; then you took with your friends a journey to the waters of Forges ; they stopped on the road, but you continued yours. That is all very simple, you had business in England."

" Monseigneur," said D'Artagnan, quite confused, " I went——"

" Hunting at Windsor, or elsewhere : that concerns nobody. I am acquainted with the circumstances, because it is my position to know everything. On your return, you were received by an august personage, and I perceive with pleasure that you preserve the souvenir she gave you."

D'Artagnan placed his hand upon the queen's diamond, which he wore, and quickly turned the collet inwards ; but it was too late.

" The day after that, you received a visit from Cavois," resumed the cardinal : " he went to desire you to come to the palace ; you did not return that visit, and you were wrong."

" Monseigneur, I feared I had incurred the anger of your eminence."

" How could that be, monsieur ? Could you incur my anger by having followed the orders of your superiors with more intelligence and courage than another would have done ? It is the people who do not obey that I punish, and not those who, like you, obey but too well.—As a proof, remember the date of the day on which I caused you to be informed that I desired you to come to me, and seek in your memory for what happened to you that very night."

That was the very evening on which the carrying off of Madame Bonacieux took place ; D'Artagnan trembled ; and he likewise recollected that half an hour before the poor woman had passed close to him, without doubt, carried away by the same power that had caused her disappearance.

" In short," continued the cardinal, " as I have heard nothing of you for some time past, I wished to know what you were doing ; besides, you owe me some thanks ; you must yourself have remarked how much you have been considered in all the circumstances."

D'Artagnan bowed with respect.

" That," continued the cardinal, " arose not only from a feeling of natural equity, but likewise from a plan I have marked out with respect to you."

D'Artagnan became more and more astonished.

" I wished to explain this plan to you on the day you received my first invitation ; but you did not come. Fortunately nothing is lost by this delay, and you are now about to hear it. Sit down, there, before me, M. D'Artagnan ; you are quite gentleman enouh not to listen standing."

And the cardinal pointed with his finger to a chair for the young man, who was so astonished at what was passing, that he awaited a second sign from his interlocutor before he obeyed.

" You are brave, Monsieur D'Artagnan," continued his eminence ; " you are prudent, which is still better. I like men of head and heart. Don't be afraid," said he, smiling, " by men of heart, I mean men of courage ; but young as you are, and scarcely entering into the world, you have powerful enemies ; if you do not take great heed, they will destroy you !"

"Alas ! monseigneur !" replied the young man, "very easily, no doubt; for they are strong and well supported : whilst I am alone !"

" Yes, that's very true ; but alone as you are, you have already done much, and will still do more, I don't doubt. And yet you have need, I believe, to be guarded in the adventurous career you have undertaken ; for, if I mistake not, you came to Paris with the ambitious idea of making your fortune."

" I am at the age of extravagant hopes, monseigneur," said D'Artagnan.

" There are no extravagant hopes but for fools, monsieur, and you are a man of understanding. Now, what would you say to an ensigncy in my guards, and a company after the campaign ?"

" Ah ! monseigneur !"

" You accept it, do you not ?"

" Monseigneur," replied D'Artagnan, with an embarrassed air.

" What ! do you decline it ?" cried the cardinal, with astonishment.

" I am in his majesty's guards, monseigneur, and I have no reason to be dissatisfied."

" But it appears to me that my guards are also his majesty's guards, and whoever serves in a French corps serves the king."

" Monseigneur, your eminence has ill understood my words."

" You want a pretext, do you not ? I comprehend. Well, you have this excuse. Advancement, the opening campaign, the opportunity which I offer you, so much for the world ; as regards yourself, safe protection : for it is fit you should know, Monsieur D'Artagnan, that I have received heavy and serious complaints against you ; you do not consecrate your days and nights to the king's service alone."

D'Artagnan coloured.

" In fact," said the cardinal, placing his hand upon a bundle of papers, " I have here a whole pile which concerns you. I know you to be a man of resolution, and your services, well directed, instead of leading you to ill, might be very advantageous to you. Come, reflect, and decide."

" Your goodness confounds me, monseigneur," replied D'Artagnan, " and I am conscious of a greatness of soul in your eminence that makes me mean as an earth-worm ; but since monseigneur permits me to speak freely——"

D'Artagnan paused.

" Yes—speak."

" Then, I will presume to say, that all my friends are in the king's musketeers and guards, and, by an inconceivable fatality, all my enemies are in the service of your eminence ; I should, therefore, be ill received here and ill regarded there, if I accepted that which monseigneur offers me."

" Do you happen to entertain the proud idea that I have not yet made you an offer equal to your merit ?" asked the cardinal, with a smile of disdain.

" Monseigneur, your eminence is a hundred times too kind on my account, and, on the contrary, I think I have not proved myself worthy of your goodness. The siege of La Rochelle is about to be resumed, monseigneur ; I shall serve under the eye of your eminence, and if I have the good fortune to conduct myself at that siege in such a manner as to attract your attention—then I shall at least leave behind me some brilliant action to justify the protection with which you honour me. Everything is best in its time, monseigneur ; hereafter, perhaps, I shall have the right of giving myself : at present, I shall appear to sell myself."

" That is to say, you refuse to serve me, monsieur," said the cardinal, with a tone of vexation, through which, however, might be seen a sort of esteem ; " remain free, then, and preserve your hatreds and your sympathies."

" Monseigneur——"

" Well ! well !" said the cardinal, " I don't wish you any ill ; but you must be aware that it is quite trouble enough to defend and reward our friends ; we owe nothing to our enemies ; and let me give you a piece of advice : take good care of yourself, Monsieur D'Artagnan, for, from the moment I withdraw my hand from you, I would not give an obole for your life."

" I will try to do so, monseigneur," replied the Gascon, with a noble confidence.

" Remember at a later period, and at a certain moment, if any mischance should happen to you," said Richelieu, with earnestness, " that it was I who came to seek you, and that I did all in my power to prevent this misfortune befalling you."

" I shall entertain, whatever may happen," said D'Artagnan, placing his hand upon his breast and bowing, " an eternal gratitude towards your eminence for that which you now do for me."

" Well, let it be then, as you have said, Monsieur D'Artagnan ; we shall see each other again after the campaign : I will have my eye upon you, for I shall be there," replied the cardinal, pointing with his finger to a magnificent suit of armour he was to wear, " and on our return, well —we will settle our account !"

" Ah ! monseigneur !" cried D'Artagnan, " spare me the weight of your anger ; remain neuter, monseigneur, if you find that I act as a gentleman ought to act."

" Young man," said Richelieu, " if I am able to say to you again once more what I have said to you to-day, I promise you to do so."

This last expression of Richelieu's conveyed a terrible doubt ; it alarmed D'Artagnan more than a menace would have done, for it was a warning. The cardinal, then, was seeking to preserve him from some misfortune which threatened him. He opened his mouth to reply, but, with a haughty gesture, the cardinal dismissed him.

D'Artagnan went out, but at the door his heart almost failed him, and he felt inclined to return. But the noble and severe countenance of Athos crossed his mind : if he made the compact with the cardinal which he required, Athos would no more give him his hand, Athos would renounce him.

It was this fear that restrained him, so powerful is the influence of a truly great character on all that surrounds it.

D'Artagnan descended by the staircase at which he had entered, and found Athos and the four musketeers waiting his appearance, and beginning to grow uneasy. With a word D'Artagnan reassured them, and Planchet ran to inform the other post that it was useless to keep guard longer, as his master had come out safe from the Palais-Cardinal.

When they reached Athos' residence, Aramis and Porthos inquired eagerly the cause of this strange interview ; but D'Artagnan confined himself to telling them that M. de Richelieu had sent for him to propose to him to enter into his guards with the rank of ensign, and that he had refused.

" And you were quite right," cried Aramis and Porthos, with one voice.

Athos fell into a profound reverie and answered nothing. But when they were alone,—

" You have done that which you ought to have done, D'Artagnan," said Athos,—" but yet, perhaps, you have done wrong."

D'Artagnan sighed deeply, for this voice responded to a secret voice of his soul, which told him that great misfortunes awaited him.

The whole of the next day was spent in preparations for departure ; D'Artagnan went to take leave of M. de Tréville. At that time it was believed that the separation of the musketeers and the guards would be but momentary, the king holding his parliament that very day, and proposing to set out the day after. M. de Tréville contented himself with asking D'Artagnan if he could do anything for him, but D'Artagnan answered that he was supplied with all he wanted.

That night assembled all the comrades of the guards of M. des Essarts and the company of the musketeers of M. de Tréville, who had been accustomed to associate together. They were parting to meet again when it should please God, and if it should please God. The night, then, was a somewhat riotous one, as may he imagined ; in such cases extreme preoccupation being only to be combated by extreme carelessness.

At the first sound of the morning trumpet the friends separated, the musketeers hastening to the hotel of M. de Tréville, the guards to that of M. des Essarts. Each of the captains then led his company to the Louvre, where the king passed them in review.

The king was dull, and appeared ill, which took off a little from his usual lofty carriage. In fact, the evening before, a fever had seized him in the midst of the parliament, whilst he was holding his bed of justice. He had, not the less, decided upon setting out that same evening, and, in spite of the remonstrances that had been offered to him, he persisted in having the review, hoping, by setting it at defiance, to conquer the disease which began to lay hold of him.

The review over, the guards set forward alone on their march, the musketeers waiting for the king, which allowed Porthos time to go and take a turn, in his superb equipment, in the Rue aux Ours.

The procureuse saw him pass in his new uniform and upon his fine horse. She loved Porthos too dearly to allow him to part thus : she made him a sign to dismount and come to her. Porthos was magnificent, his spurs jingled, his cuirass glittered, his sword knocked proudly against his ample limbs. This time the clerks evinced no inclination to laugh, such a real ear-clipper did Porthos appear.

The musketeer was introduced to M. Coquenard, whose little grey eye sparkled with anger at seeing his cousin all blazing new. Nevertheless, one thing afforded him inward consolation ; it was expected by everybody that the campaign would be a severe one : he whispered a hope to himself that this beloved relation might be killed in the course of it.

Porthos paid his compliments to M. Coquenard, and bade him farewell ; Monsieur Coquenard wished him all sorts of prosperities. As to Madame Coquenard, she could not restrain her tears, but no evil impressions were taken from her grief, as she was known to be very much attached to her relations, about whom she was constantly having serious disputes with her husband.

But the real adieux were made in Madame Coquenard's chamber ; they were heartrending!

As long as the procureuse could follow him with her eyes, she waved her handkerchief to him, leaning so far out of the window as to lead people to believe she was about to precipitate herself after her musketeer. Porthos received all these attentions like a man accustomed to such demonstrations : only, on turning the corner of the street, he lifted his hat gracefully, and waved it to her as a sign of adieu.

On his part, Aramis wrote a long letter. To whom? Nobody knew. Kitty, who was to set out that evening for Tours, was waiting in the next chamber.

Athos sipped the last bottle of his Spanish wine.

In the meantime, D'Artagnan was defiling with his company. On arriving at the Faubourg St. Antoine, he turned round to look gaily at the Bastille ; but as it was the Bastille alone he looked at, he did not observe milady, who, mounted upon a light chestnut horse, pointed him out with her finger to two ill-looking men who came close up to the ranks to take notice of him. To a look of interrogation which they made, milady replied by a sign that that was the person. Then, certain that there could be no mistake in the execution of her orders, she turned her horse and disappeared.

The two men followed the company, and at leaving the Faubourg St. Antoine, mounted two horses properly equipped, which a servant out of livery was holding in expectation of their coming.

CHAPTER XLI.

THE SIEGE OF LA ROCHELLE.

THE siege of La Rochelle was one of the great political events of the reign of Louis XIII., and one of the great military enterprises of the cardinal. It is then interesting, and even necessary, that we should say a few words about it, particularly as many details of this siege are connected in too important a manner with the history we have undertaken to relate, to allow us to pass it over in silence.

The political views of the cardinal, when he undertook this siege, were considerable. Let us expose them first, and then pass on to the private ones, which, perhaps, had not less influence upon his eminence than the former.

Of the important cities given up by Henry IV. to the Huguenots as places of safety, there only remained La Rochelle. It became necessary, therefore, to destroy this last bulwark of Calvinism, a dangerous leaven, with which the ferments of civil revolt and foreign war were constantly mingling.

Spaniards, English and Italian malcontents, adventurers of all nations, and soldiers of fortune of every or of no sect, flocked at the first summons to the standards of the Protestants, and organised themselves like a vast association, whose branches diverged at leisure over all parts of Europe.

La Rochelle, which had derived a new importance from the ruin of the other Calvinist cities, was then the focus of dissentious and ambitious views. Moreover, its port was the last port in the kingdom of France open to the English, and by closing it against England, our eternal enemy, the cardinal completed the work of Joan of Arc and the Duke de Guise.

Thus Bassompierre, who was at once a Protestant and a Catholic—a Protestant by conviction and a Catholic as commander of the order of the Holy Ghost; Bassompierre, who was a German by birth, and a Frenchman at heart ; in short, Bassompierre, who had a distinguished command at the siege of La Rochelle, said, on charging at the head of several other Protestant nobles like himself :

" You will see, gentlemen, that we shall be fools enough to take La Rochelle."

And Bassompierre was right : the cannonade of the Isle of Ré presaged to him the dragonnades of the Cévennes ; the taking of La Rochelle was the preface to the revocation of the Edict of Nantes.

But, we have hinted, that by the side of these views of the levelling and simplifying minister, and which belong to history, the chronicler is forced to recognise the little aims of the lover and the jealous rival.

Richelieu, as every one knows, had been in love with the queen : was this love a simple political affair, or was it naturally one of those profound passions which Anne of Austria inspired in those who approached her ? That we are not able to say ; but, at all events, we have seen, by the anterior developments of this history, that Buckingham had had the advantage over him, and in two or three circumstances, particularly that of the diamond studs, had, thanks to the devotedness of the three musketeers, and the courage and conduct of D'Artagnan, cruelly mystified him.

It was, then, Richelieu's object, not only to get rid of an enemy of France, but to avenge himself of a rival ; but this vengeance ought to be great and striking, and worthy in every way of a man who held in his hand, as his weapon for combat, the forces of a whole kingdom.

Richelieu knew that whilst combating England he was combating Buckingham—that when triumphing over England, he triumphed over Buckingham ; in short, that in humiliating England in the eyes of Europe, he humiliated Buckingham in the eyes of the queen.

On his side, Buckingham, whilst pretending to maintain the honour of England, was moved by interests exactly similar to those of the cardinal. Buckingham, also, was pursuing a private vengeance. Buckingham could not, under any pretence, be admitted into France as an ambassador : he wished to enter it as a conqueror.

It resulted from this, that the veritable stake of this game, which two of the most powerful kingdoms played for the good pleasure of two men in love, was simply—a kind look from Anne of Austria.

The first advantage had been gained by Buckingham. Arriving unexpectedly in sight of the Isle of Ré, with ninety vessels, and nearly twenty thousand men, he had surprised the Count de Toirac, who commanded for the king in the isle ; he had, after a sanguinary conflict, effected his landing.

Allow us to observe, in passing, that in this fight perished the Baron de Chantal ; that the Baron de Chantal left a little orphan girl of eighteen months old, and that this little girl was afterwards Madame de Sévigné.

The Count de Toirac entered into the citadel St. Martin with his garrison, and threw a hundred men into a little fort, called the fort of La Prée.

This event had hastened the resolutions of the cardinal ; and till the king and he could take the command of the siege of La Rochelle, which was determined on, he had sent Monsieur to direct the first operations, and had ordered all the troops he could dispose of to march towards the theatre of war. It was of this detachment, sent as a vanguard, that our friend D'Arragnan formed a part.

The king, as we have said, was to follow as soon as his bed of justice had been held ; but on rising from his bed of justice on the 28th of June, he felt himself attacked by fever.   He was, notwithstanding, anxious to set out; but his illness becoming more serious, he was forced to stop at Villeroi.

Now, whenever the king stopped, the musketeers stopped.   It resulted that D'Artagnan, who was as yet purely and simply in the guards, found himself, for the time at least, separated from his good friends, Athos, Aramis, and Porthos.   This separation, which was no more than an unpleasant circumstance, would have certainly become a cause of serious uneasiness, if he had been able to guess by what unknown dangers he was surrounded.

He, however, arrived without accident in the camp established before La Rochelle, on the 10th of the month of September of the year 1627.

Everything was in the same state ; the Duke of Buckingham and his English, masters of the Isle of Ré, continued to besiege, but without success, the citadel of St. Martin and the fort of La Prée ; and hostilities with La Rochelle had commenced, two or three days before, about a fort which the Duke d'Angoulême had caused to be constructed near the city.

The guards, under the command of M. des Essarts, took up their quarters at the Minimes ; but, as we know, D'Artagnan, preoccupied by the ambition of passing into the musketeers, had formed but few friendships among his comrades, and he felt himself isolated, and given up to his own reflections.

His reflections were not very cheerful.   From the time of his arrival in Paris, he had been mixed up with public affairs ; but his own private affairs had not made any great progress, as regarded either love or fortune.   As to love, the only woman he could have loved was Madame Bonacieux ; and Madame Bonacieux had disappeared, without his being able to discover what had become of her.   With respect to fortune, he had made himself—he, humble as he was—an enemy of the cardinal, that is to say, of a man before whom trembled the greatest men of the kingdom, beginning with the king.

That man had the power to crush him, and yet he had not done it.   For a mind so perspicuous as that of D'Artagnan, this indulgence was a light by which he caught a glimpse of a better future.

And then he had made himself another enemy ; not so much to be feared, he thought, but, nevertheless, he instinctively felt not to be despised : the enemy was milady.

In exchange for all this, he had acquired the protection and goodwill of the queen ; but the favour of the queen was, at the present time, an additional cause of persecution ; and her protection, it was pretty well known, protected the objects of it very badly,—as instanced in Chalais and Madame Bonacieux.

What he had clearly gained in all this was the diamond, worth five or six thousand livres, which he wore on his finger ; and even this diamond, supposing that D'Artagnan, in his projects of ambition, wished to keep it, to make it some day a pledge for the gratitude of the queen, had not, in the meanwhile, since he could not part with it, more value than the stones he trod under his feet.

We say than the stones he trod under his feet, for D'Artagnan made these reflections whilst walking solitarily along a pretty little road which led from the camp to the village of Angoutin. Now, these reflections had led him further than he intended, and the day was beginning to decline, when, by the last ray of the setting sun, he thought he saw the barrel of a musket glitter from behind a hedge.

D'Artagnan had a quick eye, and a prompt understanding. He naturally supposed that that musket had not come there of itself, and that he who bore it had not concealed himself behind a hedge with any friendly intentions. He determined, therefore, to direct his course as clear from it as he could, when, on the opposite side of the road, from behind a rock, he perceived the extremity of another musket-barrel.

This was evidently an ambuscade.

The young man cast a glance at the first musket, and saw, with a certain degree of inquietude, that it was levelled in his direction ; but as soon as he perceived that the orifice of the barrel was motionless, he threw himself upon the ground : at the same instant the gun was fired, and he heard the whistling of a ball pass over his head.

No time was to be lost. D'Artagnan sprang up with a bound, and at the same instant the ball from the other musket tore up the stones on the very place on the road where he had thrown himself with his face to the ground.

D'Artagnan was not one of those uselessly brave men who seek a ridiculous death, in order that it may be said of them that they did not give way a single step ; besides, courage was out of the question here, —D'Artagnan had fallen into a premeditated ambuscade.

" If there should be a third shot," said he, " I am a lost man."

He immediately, therefore, took to his heels, and ran towards the camp, with the swiftness of the young men of his country, so renowned for their agility ; but whatever might be his speed, the first that fired, having had time to reload, fired a second shot, and this time so well aimed, that it struck his hat, and carried it ten paces from him.

As he, however, had no other hat, he picked up this as he ran, and arrived at his quarters, very pale and quite out of breath. He sat down without saying a word to anybody, and began to reflect.

This event might have three causes :

The first and the most natural was, that it might be an ambuscade of the Rochellais, who might not have been sorry to kill one of his majesty's guards ; in the first place, because it would be an enemy the less, and that this enemy might have a well-furnished purse in his pocket.

D'Artagnan took his hat, examined the hole made by the ball, and shook his head. The ball was not a musket-ball—it was an arquebuss-ball. The justness of the aim had first given him the idea that a particular kind of weapon had been employed. This could not, then, be a military ambuscade, as the ball was not of the regular calibre.

This might be a kind remembrance of Monsieur le Cardinal. It may be observed that at the very moment when, thanks to the ray of the sun, he perceived the gun-barrel, he was thinking with astonishment on the forbearance of his eminence with respect to him.

But D'Artagnan again shook his head. For people towards whom he had but to put forth his hand, his eminence had rarely recourse to such means.

It might be a vengeance of milady's—that was the most probable !

He endeavoured in vain to remember the faces or dress of the assassins ; he had escaped so rapidly, that he had not had leisure to remark anything.

"Ah ! my poor friends !" murmured D'Artagnan ; "where are you ? How sadly I want you !"

D'Artagnan passed a very restless night. Three or four times he started up, imagining that a man was approaching his bed for the purpose of poniarding him. Nevertheless, day dawned without darkness having brought any accident.

But D'Artagnan justly suspected that that which was deferred was not lost.

D'Artagnan remained all day in his quarters, assigning as a reason to himself that the weather was bad.

At nine o'clock next morning, the drums beat to arms. The Duke of Orleans visited the posts. The guards were under arms, and D'Artagnan took his place in the midst of his comrades.

Monsieur passed along the front of the line ; then all the superior officers approached him to pay their compliments, M. des Essarts, captain of the guards, as well as the others.

At the expiration of a minute or two, it appeared to D'Artagnan that M. des Essarts made him a sign to come to him ; he waited for a fresh gesture on the part of his superior, for fear he might be mistaken ; but this gesture being repeated, he left the ranks, and advanced to receive his orders.

"Monsieur is about to ask for some men of good courage for a dangerous mission, but which will do honour to those who shall accomplish it, and I made you a sign in order that you might hold yourself in readiness."

"Thanks ! captain !" replied D'Artagnan, who wished for nothing better than an opportunity for distinguishing himself under the eye of the lieutenant-general.

In fact, the Rochellais had made a sortie during the night, and had retaken a bastion of which the royal army had gained possession two days before ; the matter was to ascertain, by reconnoitring, how the enemy guarded this bastion.

At the end of a few minutes, Monsieur raised his voice, and said :

"I want, for this mission, three or four volunteers, led by a man who can be depended upon."

"As to the man to be depended upon, I have him under my hand, monseigneur," said M. des Essarts, pointing to D'Artagnan ; "and as to the four or five volunteers, monseigneur has but to make his intentions known, and the men will not be wanting."

"Four men of good will who will risk being killed with me !" said D'Artagnan, raising his sword.

Two of his comrades of the guards immediately sprang forward, and two other soldiers having joined them, the number was deemed sufficient ; D'Artagnan declined all others, being unwilling to injure the chance of honour of those who came forward first.

It was not known whether, after the taking of the bastion, the Rochellais had evacuated it or left a garrison in it ; the object then was to examine the place near enough to ascertain the thing.

D'Artagnan set out with his four companions, and followed the trench : the two guards marched abreast with him, and the two soldiers followed behind.

They arrived thus, screened by the lining of the trench, till they came within a hundred paces of the bastion ! There, on turning round, D'Artagnan perceived that the two soldiers had disappeared.

He thought that, beginning to be afraid, they had stayed behind.

At the turning of the counterscarp they found themselves within about sixty paces of the bastion. They saw no one, and the bastion seemed abandoned.

The three composing our forlorn hope were deliberating whether they should proceed any further, when all at once a circle of smoke enveloped the giant of stone, and a dozen balls came whistling round D'Artagnan and his companions.

They knew all they wished to know ; the bastion was guarded. A longer stay in this dangerous spot would have been useless imprudence : D'Artagnan and his two companions turned their backs, and commenced a retreat which looked very much like a flight.

On arriving at the angle of the trench which was to serve them as a rampart, one of the guards fell ; a ball passed through his breast. The other, who was safe and sound, continued his way towards the camp.

D'Artagnan was not willing to abandon his companion thus, and stooped down to raise him and assist him in regaining the lines ; but at this moment two shots were fired ; one ball hit the head of the already wounded guard, and the other was flattened against a rock, after having passed within two inches of D'Artagnan.

The young man turned quickly round, for this attack could not come from the bastion, which was masked by the angle of the trench ; the idea of the two soldiers who had abandoned him occurred to his mind, and with them that of the assassins of two evenings before ; he resolved then, this time, to know what he had to trust to, and fell upon the body of his comrade as if he had been dead.

He quickly saw two heads appear above an abandoned work, within thirty paces of him ; they were the heads of the two soldiers. D'Artagnan had not been deceived, these two men had only followed him for the purpose of assassinating him, hoping that the young man's death would be placed to the account of the enemy.

Only, as he might be wounded and might denounce their crime, **they** came up to him with the purpose of making sure of him ; fortunately, deceived by D'Artagnan's trick, they neglected to reload their guns.

When they were within ten paces of him, D'Artagnan, who, in falling had taken care not to leave hold of his sword, sprang up close to them.

The assassins comprehended that if they fled towards the camp without having killed their man, they should be accused by him ; therefore, their first idea was to pass over to the enemy. One of them took his gun by the barrel, and used it as he would a club ; he aimed a terrible blow at D'Artagnan, who avoided it by springing on one side ; but by this movement he left a passage free to the bandit, who darted off towards the bastion. As the Rochellais who guarded the bastion were ignorant of the intentions of the man they saw coming towards them, they fired upon him, and he fell, struck by a ball, which broke his shoulder.

In the mean time, D'Artagnan had thrown himself upon the other soldier, attacking him with his sword ; the conflict was not long ; the wretch had nothing to defend himself with but his discharged arquebuss; the sword of the guard slipped down the barrel of the now useless weapon, and passed through the thigh of the assassin, who fell.

D'Artagnan immediately placed the point of his sword at his throat.

" Oh, do not kill me !" cried the bandit. " Pardon, pardon ! my officer ! and I will tell you all."

" Is your secret of enough importance for me to spare your life for it ?" asked the young man, withholding his arm.

" Yes ! if you think existence worth anything to a man of twenty as you are, and who may hope for everything, being handsome and brave, as you are."

" Wretch !" cried D'Artagnan, " speak, and speak quickly ! who employed you to assassinate me ?"

" A woman whom I don't know ; but who is called milady."

" But if you don't know this woman, how do you know her name ?"

" My comrade knows her, and called her so ; it was with him she agreed, and not with me ; he even has in his pocket a letter from that person, who attaches great importance to you, as I have heard him say."

" But how did you become concerned in this villanous affair ?"

" He proposed to me to undertake it with him, and I agreed."

" And how much did she give you for this fine enterprise ?"

" A hundred louis."

" Well, come !" said the young man, laughing, " she thinks I am worth something ! A hundred louis ! Well, that was a temptation for two miserable creatures like you ; so I understand you accepted it, and I grant you my pardon ; but upon one condition !"

" What is that ?" said the soldier, uneasy at perceiving that all was not over.

" That you will go and fetch me the letter your comrade has in his pocket."

"Why," cried the bandit, "that is only another way of killing me, how can I go and fetch that letter under the fire of the bastion?"

"You must, however, make up your mind to go and fetch it, or you shall die by my hand."

"Pardon! Monsieur, have pity on me! In the name of that young lady you love, and whom you perhaps think is dead, but is not!" cried the bandit, throwing himself upon his knees, and leaning upon his hand, for he began to lose his strength with his blood.

"And how do you know there is a young woman that I love, or that I thought that woman dead?" asked D'Artagnan.

"By that letter which my comrade had in his pocket."

"You see, then," said D'Artagnan, "that I must have that letter; so no more delay, no more hesitation; or else, whatever may be my repugnance to soiling my sword a second time with the blood of a wretch like you, I swear by the word of a gentleman——"

And at these words D'Artagnan made so menacing a gesture that the wounded man sprang up.

"Stop, stop!" cried he, regaining strength from terror, "I will go—I will go!"

D'Artagnan took the soldier's arquebuss, made him go on before him, and urged him towards his companion by pricking him behind with his sword.

It was a frightful thing to see this unfortunate being, leaving a long track of blood upon the ground he passed over, pale with approaching death, endeavouring to drag himself along without being seen, to the body of his accomplice, which lay at twenty paces from him.

Terror was so strongly painted on his face, covered with a cold sweat, that D'Artagnan took pity on him, and casting upon him a look of contempt,—

"Stop!" said he, "I will show you the difference between a man of true courage and such a base creature as you; stay where you are, I will go myself."

And, with a light step, an eye on the watch, observing the movements of the enemy, and taking advantage of the accidents of the ground, D'Artagnan succeeded in reaching the second soldier.

There were two means of gaining his object; to search him on the spot, or to carry him away, making a buckler of his body, and searching him in the trench.

D'Artagnan preferred the second means, and lifted the assassin on to his shoulders at the moment the enemy fired.

A slight shock, the dull noise of three balls which penetrated the flesh, a last cry, a convulsion of agony, proved to D'Artagnan that he who had endeavoured to assassinate him had saved his life.

D'Artagnan regained the trench, and threw the body down by the wounded man, who was as pale as death.

The search was instantly commenced; a leather pocket-book, a purse, in which was evidently a part of the sum which the bandit had received, with a dice-box and dice, formed the heritage of the dead man.

He left the box and dice where he found them, threw the purse to the wounded man, and eagerly opened the pocket-book.

Amongst some unimportant papers he found the following letter ; that which he had sought at the risk of his life :

" Since you have lost sight of that woman, and she is now in safety in the convent, at which you should never have allowed her to arrive, try, at least, not to miss the man ; if you do, you know that my hand reaches far, and that you shall repay me very dearly the hundred louis you have had of me."

No signature. Nevertheless it was plain the letter came from milady. He consequently kept it as a piece of evidence, and, being in safety behind the angle of the trench, he began to interrogate the wounded man. He confessed that he had undertaken, with his comrade, the same that was killed, to carry off a young woman, who was to leave Paris by the barrier of La Vilette ; but having stopped to drink at a cabaret, they had missed the carriage by ten minutes.

" But what were you to have done with that woman ?" asked D'Artagnan, with great agitation.

" We were to have conveyed her to an hotel in the Place Royale," said the wounded man.

" Yes ! yes !" murmured D'Artagnan ; " that's the place ; milady's own residence !"

The young man tremblingly felt what a terrible thirst of vengeance urged this woman on to destroy him, as well as all who loved him, and how well she must be acquainted with the affairs of the court, since she had discovered everything. There could be no doubt she owed this information to the cardinal.

But amidst all this he perceived, with a feeling of real joy, that the queen must have discovered the prison in which poor Madame Bonacieux expiated her devotedness, and that she had freed her from that prison. And the letter he had received from the young woman, with her passing along the road of Chaillot like an apparition, were now explained.

From that time, also, as Athos had predicted, it became possible to find Madame Bonacieux, and a convent was not impregnable.

This idea completely restored clemency to his heart. He turned towards the wounded man, who had watched with intense anxiety all the various expressions of his countenance, and holding out his arm to him,—

" Come," said he, " I will not abandon you thus. Lean upon me, and let us return to the camp."

" Yes," said the man, who could scarcely believe in such magnanimity, " but is not that to have me hanged ?"

" You have my word," said he ; " for the second time I give you your life."

The wounded man sank upon his knees, to again kiss the feet of his preserver; but D'Artagnan, who had no longer a motive for staying so near the enemy, cut short the evidences of his gratitude.

The guard who had returned at the first discharge had announced the death of his four companions. They were therefore much astonished and delighted, in the regiment, when they saw the young man come back safe and sound.

D'Artagnan explained the sword-wound of his companion by a sortie which he improvised. He described the death of the other soldier, and the perils they had encountered. This recital was for him the occasion of a veritable triumph. The whole army talked of this expedition for a day, and Monsieur paid him his compliments upon it. Besides this, as every great action bears its own recompense with it, the great action of D'Artagnan had for result the restoration of the tranquillity he had lost. In fact, D'Artagnan believed that he might indulge in a little tranquillity, as of his two enemies, one was killed, and the other devoted to his interests.

This tranquillity proved one thing, which was, that D'Artagnan was not yet perfectly acquainted with milady.

CHAPTER XLII.

THE ANJOU WINE.

AFTER the most disheartening news of the king's health, a report of his convalescence began to prevail in the army; and as he was very anxious to be in person at the siege, it was said that as soon as he could mount on horseback he would set forward.

In the meantime, Monsieur, who knew that, from one day to the other, he might expect to be removed from his command by the Duke d'Angoulême, Bassompierre, or Schomberg, who were all eager for his post, did but little, lost his days in wavering, and did not dare to attempt any great enterprise to drive the English from the Isle of Ré, where they still besieged the citadel St. Martin and the fort of La Prée, whilst, on their side, the French were besieging La Rochelle.

D'Artagnan, as we have said, had become more tranquil, as always happens after a past danger, particularly when that danger seems to have vanished; he only felt one uneasiness, and that was at not hearing from his three friends.

But one morning at the commencement of the month of November, everything was explained to him by this letter, dated from Villeroi:—

"Monsieur D'Artagnan,

"MM. Athos, Porthos, and Aramis, after having had an entertainment at my house, and enjoyed themselves very much, created such a disturbance, that the provost of the castle, a very rigid man, has ordered them to be confined for some days; but I accomplish the order they have given me, by forwarding to you a dozen bottles of my Anjou wine, with which they are much pleased: they are desirous that you should drink to their health in their favourite wine. I have done accordingly, and am, monsieur, with great respect,

" Your very humble and obedient servant,

" GODEAU,

" Messman of the Musketeers."

" That's all well !" cried D'Artagnan, "they think of me in their pleasures, as I thought of them in my troubles. Well, I will certainly drink to their health with all my heart, but I will not drink alone."

And D'Artagnan went among the guards, with whom he had formed greater intimacy than with the others, to invite them to enjoy with him this present of delicious Anjou wine which had been sent him from Villeroi.

One of the two guards was engaged that evening, and another the next : so that the meeting was fixed for the day after that.

D'Artagnan, on his return, sent the twelve bottles of wine to the *buvette* of the guards, with strict orders that great care should be taken of it ; and then, on the day appointed, as the dinner was fixed for twelve o'clock, D'Artagnan sent Planchet, at nine in the morning, to assist in preparing everything for the entertainment.

Planchet, very proud of being raised to the dignity of *maître d'hôtel*, thought he would get all ready like an intelligent man, and with this view called in the assistance of the lackey of one of his master's guests, named Fourreau, and the false soldier who had endeavoured to kill D'Artagnan, and who, belonging to no corps, had entered into the service of D'Artagnan, or rather of Planchet, since D'Artagnan had saved his life.

The hour of the banquet being come, the two guests arrived, took their places, and the dishes were arranged upon the table. Planchet waited, towel on arm ; Fourreau uncorked the bottles, and Brisemont, which was the name of the convalescent, poured the wine, which was a little shaken by its journey, carefully into glass decanters. Of this wine, the first bottle being a little thick at the bottom, Brisemont poured the lees into a glass, and D'Artagnan desired him to drink it, for the poor devil had not half recovered his strength.

The guests, after having eaten the soup, were about to lift the first glass of wine to their lips, when all at once the cannon sounded from Fort Louis and Fort Neuf ; the guards, imagining this to be caused by some unexpected attack, either of the besieged or the English, sprang to their swords ; D'Artagnan, not less forward than they, did so likewise, and all ran out, in order to repair to their posts.

But scarcely were they out of the *buvette*, than they were made aware of the cause of this noise : cries of " Vive le Roi ! Vive Monsieur le Cardinal !" resounded on every side, and the drums were beaten in all directions.

In short, the king, impatient as we have said he was, had come by forced marches, and had arrived at that moment with all his household and a reinforcement of ten thousand troops : his musketeers preceded, and followed him. D'Artagnan, placed in line with his company, saluted with an expressive gesture his three friends, whose eyes soon discovered him, and M. de Tréville, who recognised him at once.

The ceremony of the arrival over, the four friends were soon together.

" Pardieu !" cried D'Artagnan, " you could not have arrived in better time ; the dinner cannot have had time to get cold ! can it, gentlemen?" added the young man, turning to the two guards, whom he introduced to his friends.

" Ah ! ah !" said Porthos, " it appears we are feasting, then !"

" I hope," said Aramis, " there are no women of your party."

" Is there any drinkable wine in your tavern ?" asked Athos.

" Well, pardieu ! there is your own, my dear friend," replied D'Artagnan.

" Our wine !" said Athos, astonished.

" Yes, that you sent me."

" We send you wine ?"

" Yes ; nonsense, you know what I mean ; the wine from the hills of Anjou."

" Yes, I know what wine you mean."

" The wine you prefer."

" Doubtless, when I can get neither champagne nor chambertin."

" Well ! in the absence of champagne and chambertin, you must content yourselves with that."

" And so, connoisseurs in wine as we are, we have sent you some Anjou wine, eh ! have we ?" said Porthos.

" Not exactly, it is the wine that was sent me on your account."

" On our account ?" said the three musketeers.

" Did you send this wine, Aramis ?" said Athos.

" No ; and you, Porthos ?"

" No ; and you, Athos ?"

" Well, but if it was not you, it was your messman," said D'Artagnan.

" Our messman !"

" Yes, your messman, Godeau, the messman of the musketeers."

" Ma foi ! never mind where it comes from," said Porthos, " let us taste it, and if it is good, let us drink it."

" No," said Athos, " don't let us drink wine which comes from an unknown source."

" You are right, Athos," said D'Artagnan. " Did none of you order Godeau to send me some wine ?"

" No ! and yet you say he has sent you some as from us ?"

" Here is his letter," said D'Artagnan, and he presented the note to his comrades.

" That is not his writing !" said Athos, " I know it ; before we left Villeroi, I settled the accounts of the regiment."

" It is a false letter altogether," said Porthos, " we have not been confined."

" D'Artagnan," said Aramis, in a reproachful tone, " how could you believe that we had made a disturbance ?"

D'Artagnan grew pale, and a convulsive trembling shook all his limbs.

"Thou alarmest me!" said Athos, who never used *thee* and *thou* but upon very particular occasions, "what has happened?"

"Hasten! hasten! my friend!" cried D'Artagnan, "a horrible suspicion crosses my mind! can this be another vengeance on the part of that woman?"

It was now Athos' turn to become pale.

D'Artagnan rushed towards the *buvette*, the three musketeers and the two guards following him.

The first object that met the eyes of D'Artagnan, on entering the *buvette*, was Brisemont, stretched upon the ground and rolling in horrible convulsions.

Planchet and Fourreau, as pale as death, were endeavouring to render him assistance; but it was plain that all assistance was useless: all the features of the dying man were distorted with agony.

"Ah!" cried he, on perceiving D'Artagnan, "ah! this is frightful! you pretend to pardon me, and you poison me!"

"I!" cried D'Artagnan, "I, wretched man! what can you mean by that?"

"I say that it was you who gave me the wine, I say that it was you who desired me to drink it, I say you wished to avenge yourself on me, and I say that it is horrible!"

"Do not think so, Brisemont," said D'Artagnan; "do not think so; I swear to you, I protest——"

"Oh! but God is above! God will punish you! My God! grant that he may one day suffer what I suffer!"

"Upon the Gospel," said D'Artagnan, throwing himself down by the dying man, "I swear to you that the wine was poisoned and that I was going to drink of it as you did."

"I do not believe you," cried the soldier, and he expired amidst horrible tortures.

"Frightful! frightful!" murmured Athos, whilst Porthos broke the bottles and Aramis gave orders, a little too late, that a confessor should be sent for.

"Oh! my friends," said D'Artagnan, "you come once more to save my life, not only mine, but that of these gentlemen. Gentlemen," continued he, addressing the guards, "I request you will be silent with regard to this adventure; great personages may have had a hand in what you have seen, and, if talked about, the evil would only recoil upon us."

"Ah! monsieur!" stammered Planchet, more dead than alive, "ah! monsieur! what an escape I have had!"

"How, sirrah! you were going to drink my wine, were you!"

"To the health of the king, monsieur; I was going to drink a small glass of it, if Fourreau had not told me I was called."

"Alas!" said Fourreau, whose teeth chattered with terror, "I wanted to get him out of the way that I might drink by myself!"

"Gentlemen," said D'Artagnan, addressing the guards, "you may easily comprehend that such a feast can but be very dull, after what has taken place; so accept my excuses, and put off the party till another day, I beg of you."

The two guards courteously accepted D'Artagnan's excuses, and perceiving that the four friends desired to be alone, retired.

When the young guardsman and the three musketeers were without witnesses, they looked at each other with an air which plainly expressed that every one of them perceived the seriousness of their situation.

" In the first place," said Athos, " let us leave this chamber; the dead are not agreeable company, particularly when they have died a violent death."

" Planchet," said D'Artagnan, " I commit the body of this poor devil to your care. Let him be interred in holy ground. He committed a crime, it is true; but he repented of it."

And the four friends quitted the room, leaving Planchet and Fourreau the charge of paying the mortuary honours to Brisemont.

The host gave them another chamber, and served them with fresh eggs and some water, which Athos went himself to draw at the fountain. In a few words, Porthos and Aramis were informed of past events.

" Well !" said D'Artagnan to Athos, " you see, my dear friend, that this is war to the death !"

Athos shook his head.

" Yes, yes," replied he, " I perceive that plainly; but do you really believe it is she ?"

" I am sure of it."

" Nevertheless, I confess I still doubt."

" But the fleur-de-lis on her shoulder ?"

" She is some Englishwoman who has committed a crime in France, and has been branded in consequence."

" Athos, she is your wife, I tell you," repeated D'Artagnan; " only reflect how much your description agrees with mine."

" Yes, but I should think the other must be dead, I hanged her so effectually."

It was D'Artagnan who now shook his head in his turn.

" But, in either case, what is to be done ?" said the young man.

" It is impossible to remain thus, with a sword hanging eternally over one's head," said Athos; " we must emancipate ourselves from this position."

" Well, but how ?"

" Listen; you must try to have an interview with her, and enter into an explanation with her; say to her :—' Peace or war, my word of honour of a gentleman never to say anything of you, never to do anything against you :—on your side, a solemn oath to remain neuter with respect to me; if not, I will apply to the chancellor, I will apply to the king, I will apply to the hangman, I will move the courts against you, I will denounce you as branded, I will bring you to trial, and if you are acquitted—well !—by the honour of a gentleman I will kill you, at the corner of some wall, as I would a mad dog.'"

" I like the means well enough," said D'Artagnan, " but where and how to meet with her ?"

" Time, dear friend, time brings round opportunity, opportunity is the martingal of man : the more we have ventured, the more we gain when we know how to wait."

" Yes, but to wait surrounded by assassins and poisoners."

" Bah !" said Athos, " God has preserved us hitherto, God will preserve us still."

" Yes, we ; we, besides, are men ; and everything considered, it is our lot to risk our lives ; but she," added he in an undertone.

" What she ?" asked Athos.

" Constance ?"

" Madame Bonacieux ! ah ! that's true," said Athos, " my poor friend, I had forgotten you were in love."

" Well, but," said Aramis, " have you not learned by the letter you found on the assassin, that she is in a convent ? She may be very comfortable in a convent ; and as soon as the siege of Rochelle is terminated, I promise you, on my part——"

" Good !" cried Athos, " good ! yes, Aramis, we all know that your views have a religious tendency."

" I am only a musketeer for the time," said Aramis, humbly.

" Aye, it is some time since he heard from his mistress," said Athos, in a low voice ; " but take no notice, we know all about that."

" Well !" said Porthos, " it appears to me that the means are very simple."

" What are they ?" said D'Artagnan.

" Don't you say she is in a convent ?" replied Porthos.

" Yes."

" Well, as soon as the siege is over, we'll carry her off from that convent."

" But we must first learn what convent she is in."

" That's true," said Porthos.

" But, I think I have it," said Athos.   " Don't you say, D'Artagnan, that it is the queen who has made choice of the convent for her ?"

" I believe so, at least."

" In that case, Porthos will assist us."

" How, I pray you ?"

" Why, by your marquise, your duchess, your princess ; she must have a long arm."

" Hush !" said Porthos, placing a finger on his lips, " I believe her to be a cardinalist ; she must know nothing of the matter."

" Then," said Aramis, " I take upon myself to obtain intelligence of her."

" You, Aramis !" cried the three friends, " how ?"

" By the queen's almoner, with whom I am very intimately acquainted," said Aramis, colouring.

And upon this assurance, the four friends, who had finished their modest repast, separated, with the promise of meeting again that evening ; D'Artagnan returned to the Minimes, and the three musketeers repaired to the king's quarters, where they had to prepare their lodging.

CHAPTER XLIII.

THE AUBERGE OF THE COLOMBIER ROGUE.

In the meanwhile, the king, although scarcely arrived, who was in such haste to face the enemy, and who, with more reason than the cardinal, showed his hatred for Buckingham, commanded every disposition to be made to drive the English from the Isle of Ré, and afterwards to press the siege of La Rochelle ; but, notwithstanding his earnest wish, he was delayed by the dissensions which broke out between MM. Bassompierre and Schomberg, against the Duke d'Angoulême.

MM. Bassompierre and Schomberg were marshals of France, and claimed their right of commanding the army under the orders of the king ; but the cardinal, who feared that Bassompierre, a Huguenot at heart, might press the English and Rochellais, his brothers in religion, but feebly, supported the Duke d'Angoulême, whom the king, at his instigation, had named lieutenant-general. The result was, that, to avoid seeing MM. Bassompierre and Schomberg desert the army, a separate command was forced to be given to each ; Bassompierre took up his quarters to the north of the city, between La Leu and Dompierre : the Duke d'Angoulême to the east, from Dompierre to Perigny ; and M. de Schomberg to the south, from Perigny to Angoutin.

The quarters of monsieur were at Dompierre. The quarters of the king were sometimes at Etre, sometimes at La Jairie. The cardinal's quarters were upon the downs, at the bridge of La Pierre, in a simple house without any entrenchment.

So that monsieur watched Bassompierre ; the king, the Duke d'Angoulême ; and the cardinal, M. de Schomberg.

As soon as this organization was established, they set about driving the English from the isle.

The conjuncture was favourable : the English, who require, above everything, good living, in order to be good soldiers, only eating salt meat and bad biscuit, had many sick in their camp ; still further, the sea, very bad at this period of the year on all the coasts of the ocean, destroyed every day some little vessel or other, and the shore, from the point of L'Arguillon to the trenches, was, at every tide, literally covered with the wrecks of pinnaces, roberges, and feluccas ; it resulted, that even if the king's troops remained quietly in their camp, it was evident that some day or other, Buckingham, who only continued in the isle from obstinacy, would be obliged to raise the siege.

But as M. de Toirac gave information that everything was preparing in the enemy's camp for a fresh assault, the king judged that it would be best to put an end to the affair, and gave the necessary orders for a decisive action.

It not being our intention to make a journal of the siege, but, on the contrary only to describe such of the events of it as are connected with the history we are relating, we will content ourselves with saying in two words that the expedition succeeded, to the great astonishment of the king, and the great glory of Monsieur le Cardinal. The English, repulsed foot by foot, beaten in all the rencounters, and defeated in the passage of L'Ile de Loix, were obliged to re-embark, leaving on the field of battle two thousand men, among whom were five colonels, three lieutenant-colonels, two hundred and fifty captains, and twenty gentlemen of rank, four pieces of cannon, and sixty colours, which were taken to Paris by Claude de St. Simon, and suspended with great pomp in the vaults of Nôtre Dame.

Te Deums were sung in the camp, and afterwards throughout France.

The cardinal was left master of carrying on the siege without having, at least at the present, anything to fear on the part of the English.

But, as we have just said, this repose was but for the moment.

An envoy of the Duke of Buckingham, named Montague, was taken, and proof was obtained of a league between the empire, Spain, England, and Lorraine.

This league was directed against France.

Still further, in Buckingham's quarters, which he had been forced to abandon more precipitately than he expected, papers were found which confirmed this league, and which, as the cardinal asserts in his memoirs, strongly compromised Madame de Chevreuse, and consequently the queen.

It was upon the cardinal that all the responsibility fell, for there is no being a despotic minister without responsibility ; all, therefore, of the vast resources of his genius were at work night and day, and engaged in listening to the least report that was to be heard in any of the great kingdoms of Europe.

The cardinal was acquainted with the activity, and, more particularly, with the hatred, of Buckingham ; if the league which threatened France triumphed, all his influence would be lost ; Spanish policy and Austrian policy would have their representatives in the cabinet of the Louvre, where they had as yet but partisans ; and he, Richelieu, the French minister, the national minister, would be ruined. The king, who, whilst obeying him like a child, hated him as a child hates his master, would abandon him to the personal vengeance of monsieur and the queen ; he would then be lost, and France, perhaps, with him. All this must be guarded against.

Thus, couriers, becoming every instant more numerous, succeeded each other, day and night, in the little house of the bridge of La Pierre, in which the cardinal had established his residence.

These were monks who wore the frock with such an ill grace, that it was easy to perceive they belonged to the church militant ; women, a little inconvenienced by their costume of pages, and whose large trousers could not entirely conceal their rounded forms : and peasants with blackened hands and fine limbs, savouring of the man of quality a league off.

In addition to these there were less agreeable visits, for two or three times reports were spread that the cardinal had nearly been assassinated.

It is true that the enemies of the cardinal said that it was he himself who set these bungling assassins to work, in order to have, if wanted, the right of using reprisals :—but we must not believe everything ministers say, nor everything their enemies say.

But these attempts did not prevent the cardinal, to whom his most inveterate detractors have never denied personal bravery, from making nocturnal excursions, sometimes to communicate to the Duke d'Angoulême some important orders ; sometimes to go and confer with the king ; and sometimes to have an interview with a messenger whom he did not wish to see at home.

On their part, the musketeers, who had not much to do with the siege, were not under very strict orders, and led a joyous life. This was the more easy for our three companions in particular, as being friends of M. de Tréville's, they obtained from him permission to be absent after the closing of the camp.

Now, one evening, when D'Artagnan, who was in the trenches, was not able to accompany them, Athos, Porthos, and Aramis, mounted upon their battle-steeds, enveloped in their war-cloaks, with their hands upon their pistol-butts, were returning from a *buvette* which Athos had discovered two days before upon the route to La Jairie, called the Colombier Rouge, following the road which led to the camp, and quite upon their guard, as we have stated, for fear of an ambuscade, when at about a quarter of a league from the village of Boinar, they fancied they heard the sound of horses approaching them. They immediately all three halted, closed in, and waited, occupying the middle of the road. At the end of an instant, and as the moon broke from behind a cloud, they saw, at a turning of the road, two horsemen who, on perceiving them, stopped in their turn, appearing to deliberate whether they should continue their route or go back. The hesitation created some suspicion in the three friends, and Athos, advancing a few paces in front of the others, cried in a firm voice :

" Who goes there ?"

" Who goes there, yourselves ?" replied one of the horsemen.

" That is not an answer," replied Athos. " Who goes there ? Answer, or else we charge."

" Beware of what you are about, gentlemen !" said a clear voice, which appeared accustomed to command.

" It is some superior officer, making his night-rounds," said Athos, " What do you mean to do, gentlemen ?"

" Who are you ?" said the same voice in the same commanding tone ; " answer in your turn, or you may repent of your disobedience."

" King's musketeers," said Athos, still more convinced that he who interrogated them had the right to do so.

" Of what company ?"

" Company of Tréville."

" Advance, and render me an account of what you are doing here at this time of night."

The three companions advanced rather humbly, for all were now convinced that they had to do with some one more powerful than themselves, leaving Athos the post of speaker.

" Your pardon, mon officier !" said Athos ; " but we were ignorant of whom we were speaking to, and you may see that we were keeping good guard."

" Your name ?" said the officer, a part of whose face was covered by his cloak.

" But yourself, monsieur," said Athos, who began to be annoyed by this inquisition, " give me, I beg you, the proof that you have the right to question me."

" Your name ?" repeated the cavalier a second time, letting his cloak fall, and leaving his face uncovered.

" Monsieur le Cardinal !" cried the stupefied musketeer.

" Your name ?" cried the cardinal for the third time.

" Athos !" said the musketeer.

The cardinal made a sign to his attendant, who drew near to him,—

" These three musketeers shall follow us," said he in an under voice, " I am not willing it should be known I have left the camp ; and by following us we shall be certain they will tell nobody."

" We are gentlemen, monseigneur," said Athos, " require our parole, and give yourself no uneasiness. Thank God ! we can keep a secret."

" You have a quick ear, Monsieur Athos," said the cardinal ; " but now listen to this ; it is not from mistrust that I request you to follow me, but for my security ; your companions are, no doubt, MM. Porthos and Aramis."

" Yes, your eminence," said Athos, whilst the two musketeers who had remained behind, advanced, hat in hand.

" I know you, gentlemen," said the cardinal, " I know you ; I know you are not quite my friends, and I am sorry you are not so ; but I know you are brave and loyal gentlemen, and that confidence may be placed in you. Monsieur Athos, do me, then, the honour to accompany me, you and your two friends, and then I shall have an escort to excite envy in his majesty, if we should meet him."

The three musketeers bowed to the necks of their horses.

" Well, upon my honour," said Athos, " your eminence is right in taking us with you ; we have seen several ill-looking faces on the road, and we have even had a quarrel at the Colombier Rouge with four of those faces."

" A quarrel, and what for, gentlemen ?" said the cardinal ; "you know I don't like quarrelers."

" And that is the reason why I have the honour to inform your eminence of what has happened ; for you might learn it from others, and upon a false account, believe us to be in fault."

"What have been the results of your quarrel?" said the cardinal, knitting his brow.

"My friend Aramis, here, has received a slight sword-wound in the arm, but not enough to prevent him, as your eminence may see, from mounting to the assault to-morrow, if your eminence orders an escalade."

"But you are not the men to allow sword-wounds to be inflicted upon you thus," said the cardinal; "come, be frank, gentlemen, you have given a good account of some persons; confess, you know I have the right of giving absolution."

"Who? I! monseigneur?" said Athos. "I did not even draw my sword, but I took him who offended me round the body, and threw him out of the window; it appears that in falling," continued Athos, with some hesitation, "he broke his thigh."

"Ah! Ah!" said the cardinal; "and you, Monsieur Porthos?"

"I, monseigneur, knowing that duelling is prohibited, I seized a bench, and gave one of these brigands such a blow, that I believe his shoulder is broken."

"Very well!" said the cardinal; "and you, Monsieur Aramis?"

"For my part, monseigneur, being of a very mild disposition, and being likewise, of which monseigneur, perhaps, is not aware, about to enter into orders, I endeavoured to appease my comrades, when one of these wretches gave me a wound with a sword, treacherously, across my left arm; then I admit my patience failed me; I drew my sword in my turn, and as he came back to the charge, I fancied I felt that in throwing himself upon me, he let it pass through his body: I only know, for a certainty, that he fell, and that he appeared to be borne away with his two companions."

"The devil, gentlemen!" said the cardinal, "three men placed *hors de combat* in a cabaret squabble! you don't do your work by halves; and pray what was this quarrel about?"

"These fellows were drunk," said Athos, "and knowing there was a lady who had arrived at the cabaret this evening, they wanted to force her door."

"Force her door!" said the cardinal, "and for what purpose?"

"To do her violence, without doubt," said Athos; "I have had the honour of informing your eminence that these men were drunk."

"And was this lady young and handsome?" asked the cardinal, with a certain degree of anxiety.

"We did not see her, monseigneur," said Athos.

"You did not see her! ah! very well," replied the cardinal, quickly: "you acted quite rightly in defending the honour of a woman; and as I am going to the Colombier Rouge myself, I shall know whether you nave told me truth or not."

"Monseigneur," said Athos, haughtily, "we are gentlemen, and to save our heads we would not be guilty of a falsehood."

"Therefore, I do not doubt what you say, Monsieur Athos, I do not

doubt it for a single instant ; but," added he, to change the conversation, " was this lady alone ?"

" The lady had a cavalier shut up with her," said Athos, " but as
notwithstanding the noise, this cavalier did not show himself, it is to
be presumed that he is a coward."

" Judge not rashly, says the Gospel," replied the cardinal.

Athos bowed.

" And now, gentlemen, that's all very well," continued the cardinal.
" I know what I wish to know ; follow me."

The three musketeers passed behind his eminence, who again enveloped his face in his cloak, and put his horse in motion ; keeping
at from eight to ten paces in advance of his companions.

They soon arrived at the silent, solitary auberge ; no doubt the host
knew what illustrious visitor he expected, and had consequently sent
intruders out of the way.

At ten paces from the door the cardinal made a sign to his attendant
and the three musketeers to halt ; a saddled horse was fastened to the
window-shutter, the cardinal knocked three times, and in a peculiar
manner.

A man, enveloped in a cloak, came out immediately, and exchanged
some rapid words with the cardinal ; after which he mounted his horse,
and set off in the direction of Surgères, which was likewise that of
Paris.

" Advance, gentlemen," said the cardinal.

" You have told me the truth, gentlemen," said he, addressing the
musketeers, " and it will not be my fault if our rencontre of this evening be not advantageous to you : in the meantime, follow me."

The cardinal alighted, the three musketeers did so likewise ; the cardinal threw the bridle of his horse to his attendant, the three musketeers fastened their horses to the shutter.

The host stood at the door ; for him, the cardinal was only an officer
coming to visit a lady.

" Have you any chamber on the ground floor where these gentlemen can wait, near a good fire?" said the cardinal.

The host opened the door of a large room, in which an old bad stove
had just been replaced by a large and excellent chimney.

" I have this, monsieur," said he.

" That will do," replied the cardinal ; " come in, gentlemen, and
be kind enough to wait for me ; I shall not be more than half an
hour."

And whilst the three musketeers entered the ground-floor room, the
cardinal, without asking further information, ascended the staircase like
a man who has no need of having his road pointed out to him.

CHAPTER XLIV.

THE UTILITY OF STOVE-PIPES.

IT was evident that without suspecting it, and actuated solely by their chivalric and adventurous character, our three friends had just rendered a service to some one the cardinal honoured with his particular protection.

Now, who could that some one be? That was the question the three musketeers put to each other ; then, seeing that none of the replies could throw any light on the subject, Porthos called the host, and asked for dice.

Porthos and Aramis placed themselves at the table and began to play. Athos walked about, in a contemplative mood.

Whilst thinking and walking, Athos passed and repassed before the pipe of the stove, broken in half, the other extremity of which passed into the upper chamber ; and every time he passed, he heard a murmur of words, which at length fixed his attention. Athos went close to it, and distinguished some words that appeared to merit so great an interest that he made a sign to his friends to be silent, remaining himself bent with his ear directed to the opening of the lower orifice.

" Listen, milady," said the cardinal, " the affair is important ; sit down, and let us talk it over."

" Milady !" murmured Athos.

" I am listening to your eminence with the greatest attention," replied a female voice that made the musketeer start.

" A small vessel, with an English crew, whose captain is mine, awaits you at the mouth of the Charente, at Fort de la Pointe ; he will set sail to-morrow morning."

" I must go thither to-night, then ?"

" Instantly ! that is to say, when you have received my instructions. Two men, whom you will find at the door, on going out, will serve you as escort ; you will allow me to leave first, and, half an hour after, you can go away in your turn."

" Yes, monseigneur. Now let us return to the mission with which you wish to charge me, and as I desire to continue to merit the confidence of your eminence, deign to expose it to me in clear and precise terms, so that I may not commit any error."

There was an instant of profound silence between the two interlocutors ; it was evident the cardinal was weighing beforehand the terms in which he was about to speak, and that milady was collecting all her faculties to comprehend the things he was about to say, and to engrave them in her memory when they should be spoken.

Athos took advantage of this moment to tell his two companions to fasten the door on the inside, and to make them a sign to come and listen with him.

The two musketeers, who loved their ease, brought a chair for each of themselves and one for Athos. All three then sat down with their heads together, and their ears on the watch.

" You will go to London," continued the cardinal ; "when arrived in London you will seek Buckingham."

" I must beg your eminence to observe," said milady, " that since the affair of the diamond studs, about which the duke always suspected me, his grace has been very mistrustful of me."

" Well, this time," said the cardinal, " it is not the question to steal his confidence, but to present yourself frankly and loyally as a negotiator."

" Frankly and loyally," repeated milady, with an unspeakable expression of duplicity.

" Yes, frankly and loyally," replied the cardinal, in the same tone ; " all this negotiation must be carried on openly."

" I will follow your eminence's instructions to the letter ; I only wait your giving them."

" You will go to Buckingham on my part, and you will tell him I am acquainted with all the preparations he has made, but that they give me no uneasiness, since, at the first step he takes, I will ruin the queen."

" Will he believe that your eminence is in a position to accomplish the threat you make him ?"

" Yes, for I have the proofs."

" I must be able to present these proofs to his appreciation."

" Without doubt ; and you will tell him I will publish the account of Bois-Robert and of the Marquis de Beautru, upon the interview which the duke had at the residence of Madame la Connétable with the queen, on the evening Madame la Connétable gave a masked *fête* ; you will tell him, in order that he may not doubt of anything, that he came there in the costume of the Great Mogul, which the Chevalier de Guise was to have worn, and that he purchased this exchange for the sum of three thousand pistoles."

" Very well, monseigneur."

" All the details of his coming into and going out of the palace, on the night when he introduced himself in the character of an Italian fortune-teller, you will tell him, in order that he may not doubt the correctness of my information : that he had under his cloak a large white robe, sown over with black tears, death's heads, and cross-bones ; for, in case of a surprise, he was to pass for the Phantom of the White Lady, who, as all the world knows, appears at the Louvre every time any great event is about to be accomplished."

" Is that all, monseigneur ?"

" Tell him also that I am acquainted with all the details of the adventure at Amiens, that I will have a little romance made of it, wittily turned, with a plan of the garden, and portraits of the principal actors in that nocturnal romance."

" I will tell him that."

" Tell him, further, Montague is in my power, that Montague is in the Bastille ; no letters were found upon him, it is true, but that nature may make him say much of what he knows, and even—what he does not know."

" Exactly."

" Then add, that his grace has, in his precipitation to quit the Isle of
Ré, forgotten and left behind him in his lodging a certain letter from
Madame de Chevreuse, which singularly compromises the queen, inas-
much as it proves not only that her majesty can love the enemies of
France, but that she can conspire with the enemies of France. You
recollect perfectly all I have told you, do you not ?"

" Your eminence will judge : the ball of Madame la Connétable ; the
night at the Louvre ; the evening at Amiens ; the arrest of Montague ;
the letter of Madame de Chevreuse."

" That's it," said the cardinal—" that's it ; you have an excellent
memory, milady."

" But," resumed the lady to whom the cardinal had addressed this
flattering compliment, " if, in spite of all these reasons, the duke does
not give way, and continues to menace France ?"

" The duke is in love to madness, or rather to folly," replied Richelieu,
with great bitterness ; " like the ancient paladins, he has only undertaken this war to obtain a look from his lady-love. If he becomes
certain that this war will cost the honour, and perhaps the liberty of
the lady of his thoughts, as he says, I will answer for it he will look at
it twice."

" And yet," said milady, with a persistence that proved she wished to
see clearly to the end of the mission with which she was about to be
charged, " and yet, if he persists ?"

" If he persists ?" said the cardinal ; " that is not probable."

" It is possible," said milady.

" If he persists——." His eminence made a pause, and resumed :
" If he persists--well, then I shall hope for one of those events which
change the destinies of states."

" If your eminence would quote to me some one of these events in
history," said milady, " perhaps I should partake of your confidence in
the future."

" Well, here, then, for example," said Richelieu. " When in 1610,
for a cause almost similar to that which moves the duke, the King
Henry IV., of glorious memory, was about, at the same time, to invade
Flanders and Italy to attack Austria on both sides—well, did there not
happen an event which saved Austria ? Why should not the King of
France have the same chance as the emperor ?"

" Your eminence means, I presume, the knife-stab of the Rue de la
Féronnerie ?"

" Exactly so," said the cardinal.

" Does not your eminence fear that the punishment inflicted upon
Ravaillac may deter any one who might entertain the idea of imitating
him ?"

" There will be, in all times and in all countries, particularly if religious divisions exist in those countries, fanatics who ask nothing better
than to become martyrs. Aye, and observe, it just recurs to me that
the Puritans are furious against Buckingham, and their preachers
designate him as the Anti-Christ."

" Well ?" said milady.

" Well," continued the cardinal, in an indifferent tone, " the only thing to be sought for, at this moment, is some woman, handsome, young and clever, who has cause of quarrel with the duke. The duke has had many affairs of gallantry, and if he has succeeded in many amours by his promises of eternal constancy, he must likewise have sown the seeds of many hatreds by his eternal infidelities."

" No doubt," said milady, coolly, " such a woman may be found."

" Well, such a woman, who would place the knife of Jacques Clement, or of Ravaillac, in the hands of a fanatic, would save France."

" Yes, but she would be the accomplice of an assassination."

" Were the accomplices of Ravaillac, or of Jacques Clement, ever known ?"

" No, for perhaps they were too high for any one to dare to look for them where they were ; the Palais de Justice would not be burnt down for everybody, monseigneur."

" You think, then, that the fire at the Palais de Justice was not caused by chance ?" asked Richelieu, in the tone with which he would have put a question of no importance.

" I, monseigneur ?" replied milady ; " I think nothing—I quote a fact, that is all; only I say that if I were named Mademoiselle de Montpensier, or the Queen Mary de Medici, I should take less precautions than I take, being simply called Lady Clarik."

" That is but just," said Richelieu ; " what do you require, then ?"

" I require an order which would ratify beforehand all that I should think proper to do for the greatest good of France."

" But, in the first place, this woman I have described must be found, who is desirous of avenging herself upon the duke."

" She is found," said milady.

" Then the miserable fanatic must be found, who will serve as an instrument of God's justice."

" He will be found."

" Well," said the cardinal, " then it will be time to claim the order which you just now required."

" Your eminence is right," replied milady ; " and I have been wrong in seeing in the mission with which you honour me, anything but that which it really is—that is to say, to announce to his grace, on the part of your eminence, that you are acquainted with the different disguises by the means of which he succeeded in approaching the queen during the *fête* given by Madame la Connétable ; that you have proofs of the interview granted at the Louvre by the queen to a certain Italian astrologer, who was no other than the Duke of Buckingham ; that you have ordered a little romance of a satirical nature to be written upon the adventures of Amiens, with a plan of the gardens in which those adventures took place, and portraits of the actors who figured in them ; that Montague is in the Bastille, and that the torture may make him say things he remembers, and even things he has forgotten ; that you possess a certain letter from Madame de Chevreuse, found in his grace's lodging, which singularly compromises not only her who wrote it, but her in whose name it was written. Then, if he persists, notwithstanding all this, as that is, as I have said, the limit of my mission, I shall have nothing to do but to pray God to work a miracle for the salvation of France. That is it, is it not, monseigneur, and I shall have nothing else to do?"

" That is it," replied the cardinal, drily.

" And now," said milady, without appearing to remark the change of the duke's tone towards her, " now that I have received the instructions of your eminence as concerns your enemies, monseigneur will permit me to say a few words to him of mine?"

" Have you enemies, then?" asked Richelieu.

" Yes, monseigneur, enemies against whom you owe me all your support, for I made them by serving your eminence."

" Who are they?" replied the duke.

" In the first place, there is a little intriguing woman, named Bonacieux."

" She is in the prison of Nantes."

" That is to say, she was there," replied milady; " but the queen has obtained an order from the king, by means of which she has been conveyed to a convent."

" To a convent?" said the duke.

" Yes, to a convent."

" And what convent?"

" I don't know : the secret has been well kept."

" But I will know !"

" And your eminence will tell me in what convent that woman is?"

" I see nothing inconvenient in that," said the cardinal.

" Well, now I have an enemy much more to be dreaded by me than this little Madame Bonacieux."

" Who is that?"

" Her lover."

" What is his name?"

" Oh, your eminence knows him well," cried milady, carried away by her anger. " He is the evil genius of both of us : it is he who, in a rencounter with your eminence's guards, decided the victory in favour of the king's musketeers ; it is he who gave three desperate wounds to De Wardes, your emissary, and who caused the affair of the diamond studs to fail ; it is he who, knowing it was I who had Madame Bonacieux carried off, has sworn my death."

" Ah, ah !" said the cardinal, " I know whom you mean."

" I mean that wretch D'Artagnan."

" He is a bold fellow," said the cardinal.

" And it is because he is a bold fellow that he is the more to be feared."

" I must have," said the duke, " a proof of his connection with Buckingham."

" A proof !" cried milady ; " I will find you ten."

" Well, then, it becomes the simplest thing in the world ; get me that proof, and I will send him to the Bastille."

" So far good, monseigneur ; but afterwards ?"

" When once in the Bastille, there is no afterwards !" said the cardinal, in a low voice. " Ah, pardieu !" continued he, " if it were as easy for me to get rid of my enemy as it is easy to get rid of yours, and if it were against such people you required impunity !"

" Monseigneur," replied milady, "a fair exchange—existence for existence, man for man ; give me one, I will give you the other."

" I don't know what you mean, nor do I even desire to know what you mean," replied the cardinal ; " but I wish to please you, and see nothing inconvenient in giving you what you ask for with respect to so mean a creature ; the more so as you tell me this paltry D'Artagnan is a libertine, a duellist, and a traitor."

" An infamous scoundrel, monseigneur, an infamous scoundrel !"

" Give me paper, a pen, and some ink, then," said the cardinal.

" Here they are, monseigneur."

There was a moment of silence, which proved that the cardinal was employed in seeking the terms in which he should write the note, or else in writing it. Athos, who had not lost a word of the conversation, took his two companions by the hand, and led them to the other end of the room.

" Well," said Porthos, " what do you want, and why do you not let us listen to the end of the conversation ?"

" Hush !" said Athos, speaking in a low voice ; " we have heard all it was necessary we should hear ; besides, I don't prevent you from listening, but I must be gone."

" You must be gone !" said Porthos ; "and if the cardinal asks for you, what answer can we make ?"

" You will not wait till he asks ; you will speak first, and tell him that I am gone on the look out, because certain expressions of our host's have given me reason to think the road is not safe ; I will say two words about it to the cardinal's attendant likewise ; the rest concerns myself, don't be uneasy about that."

" Be prudent, Athos," said Aramis.

" Be easy on that head," replied Athos, " you know I am cool enough."

Porthos and Aramis resumed their places by the stove pipe.

As to Athos, he went out without any mystery, took his horse which was tied with those of his friends to the fastenings of the shutters, in four words convinced the attendant of the necessity of a van-guard for their return, carefully examined the priming of his pistols, drew his sword, and took, like a forlorn hope, the road to the camp.

CHAPTER XLV.

A CONJUGAL SCENE.

As Athos had foreseen. it was not long before the cardinal came down; he opened the door of the room in which the musketeers were, and found Porthos playing an earnest game at dice with Aramis. He cast a rapid glance round the room, and perceived that one of his men was missing.

"What is become of M. Athos?" asked he.

"Monseigneur," replied Porthos, "he is gone as a scout, upon some words of our host, which made him believe the road was not safe."

"And how have you amused yourself, M. Porthos?"

"I have won five pistoles of Aramis, monseigneur."

"Well, now will you return with me?"

"We are at your eminence's orders."

"To horse, then, gentlemen; for it is getting late."

The attendant was at the door, holding the cardinal's horse by the bridle. At a short distance, a group of two men and three horses appeared in the shade; these were the two men who were to conduct milady to the fort of La Pointe, and superintend her embarkation.

The attendant confirmed to the cardinal what the two musketeers had already said with respect to Athos. The cardinal made an approving gesture, and retook his route with the same precautions he had used in coming.

Let us leave him to follow the road to the camp protected by his attendant and the two musketeers, and return to Athos.

For some distance he maintained the pace at which he started, but when out of sight, he turned his horse to the right, made a circuit, and came back within twenty paces of a high hedge, to watch the passage of the little troop; having recognised the laced hats of his companions and the golden fringe of the cardinal's cloak, he waited till the horsemen had turned the angle of the road, and having lost sight of them, he returned at a gallop to the auberge, which was opened to him without hesitation.

The host recognised him.

"My officer," said Athos, "has forgotten to give a piece of very important information to the lady, and has sent me back to repair his forgetfulness."

"Go up," said the host, "she is still in her chamber."

Athos availed himself of the permission, ascended the stairs with his lightest step, gained the landing, and through the open door perceived milady putting on her hat.

He went straight into the chamber and closed the door after him.

At the noise he made in bolting it, milady turned round.

Athos was standing before the door, enveloped in his cloak, with his hat pulled down over his eyes.

"Who are you? and what do you want?" cried she.

" Humph !" murmured Athos, " it is certainly she !"

And letting fall his cloak, and raising his hat, he advanced towards milady.

" Do you know me, madame ?" said he.

Milady made one step forward, and then drew back, as if she had seen a serpent.

" So far well," said Athos, " I perceive you know me."

" The Count de la Fère !" murmured milady, becoming exceedingly pale, and drawing back till the wall prevented her going any further.

" Yes, milady," replied Athos, " the Count de la Fère in person, who comes expressly from the other world to have the pleasure of paying you a visit. Sit down, madame, and let us talk, as the cardinal said."

Milady, under the influence of inexpressible terror, sat down without uttering a word.

" You certainly are a demon sent upon the earth !" said Athos. " Your power is great, I know ; but you also know that with the help of God men have often conquered the most terrible demons. You have once before thrown yourself in my path ! I thought I had crushed you, madame ; but either I was deceived, or hell has resuscitated you !"

Milady, at these words, which recalled frightful remembrances, hung down her head, with a suppressed groan.

" Yes, hell has resuscitated you," continued Athos, " hell has made you rich, hell has given you another name, hell has almost made you another countenance ; but it has neither effaced the stains from your soul nor the brand mark from your body !"

Milady arose as if moved by a powerful spring, and her eyes flashed lightning. Athos remained sitting.

" You believed me to be dead, did you not, as I believed you to be ? and the name of Athos as well concealed the Count de la Fère, as the name of milady Clarik concealed Anne de Beuil ! Was it not so you were called when your honoured brother married us ? Our position is truly a strange one," continued Athos, laughing, " we have only lived up to the present time because we believed each other to be dead, and because a remembrance is less oppressive than a living creature, though a remembrance is sometimes a devouring thing !"

" But," said Milady, in a hollow, faint voice, " what brings you back to me ? and what do you want with me ?"

" I wish to tell you, that whilst remaining invisible to your eyes, I have not lost sight of you."

" You know what I have done and been ?"

" I can relate to you, day by day, your actions, from your entrance into the service of the cardinal to this evening."

A smile of incredulity passed over the pale lips of milady.

" Listen ! It was you who cut off the two diamond studs from the shoulder of the Duke of Buckingham ; it was you who had Madame Bonacieux carried off ; it was you who, in love with De Wardes, and thinking to pass the night with him, opened the door to M. D'Artagnan ;

it was you who, believing that De Wardes had deceived you, wished to have him killed by his rival ; it was you who, when this rival had discovered your infamous secret, wished to have him killed in his turn by two assassins, whom you sent in pursuit of him ; it was you who, finding the balls had missed their mark, sent poisoned wine with a forged letter, to make your victim believe that that wine came from his friends ; in short, it was you who have but now, in this chamber, seated in this chair I now fill, made an engagement with the Cardinal de Richelieu to cause the Duke of Buckingham to be assassinated, in exchange for the promise he has made you to allow you to assassinate D'Artagnan !"

Milady was livid.

" You must be Satan !" cried she.

" Perhaps," said Athos ; " but, at all events, listen well to this. Assassinate the Duke of Buckingham, or cause him to be assassinated, I care very little about that ! I don't know him : besides, he is an Englishman ; but do not touch with the tip of your finger a single hair of D'Artagnan, who is a faithful friend, whom I love and defend, or, I swear to you by the head of my father, the crime which you shall have endeavoured to commit, or shall have committed, shall be the last."

" M. d'Artagnan has cruelly insulted me," said milady, in a hollow tone ; " M. d'Artagnan shall die !"

" Indeed ! is it possible to insult you, madame ?" said Athos, laughing ; " he has insulted you, and he shall die !"

" He shall die !" replied milady ; " she first, he afterwards."

Athos was seized with a kind of vertigo ; the sight of this creature, who had nothing of the woman about her, recalled devouring remembrances ; he thought that one day, in a less dangerous situation than the one in which he was now placed, he had already endeavoured to sacrifice her to his honour; his desire for blood returned, burning his brain, and pervading his frame like a raging fever ; he arose in his turn, reached his hand to his belt, drew forth a pistol, and cocked it.

Milady, pale as a corpse, endeavoured to cry out ; but her swollen tongue could utter no more than a hoarse sound, which had nothing human in it, and seemed the rattle of a wild beast : fixed against the dark tapestry, she appeared with her hair in disorder, like a horrid image of terror.

Athos slowly raised his pistol, stretched out his arm, so that the weapon almost touched milady's forehead, and then, in a voice the more terrible from having the supreme calmness of a fixed resolution :

" Madame," said he, " you will this instant deliver to me the paper the cardinal signed ; or, upon my soul, I will blow your brains out."

With another man, milady might have preserved some doubt ; but she knew Athos : nevertheless, she remained motionless.

" You have one second to decide," said he.

Milady saw by the contraction of his countenance that the trigger was about to be pulled ; she reached her hand quickly to her bosom, drew out a paper, and held it towards Athos.

" Take it," said she, " and be accursed !"

Athos took the paper, returned the pistol to his belt, approached the lamp, to be assured that it was the paper, unfolded it, and read :

" It is by my order, and for the good of the state, that the bearer of this has done what he has done.

" December 3rd, 1627. " RICHELIEU."

" And now," said Athos, resuming his cloak, and putting on his hat, " now that I have drawn your teeth, viper, bite if you can."

And he left the chamber without once looking behind him.

At the door he found the two men, and the spare horse which they held.

" Gentlemen," said he, " monseigneur's order is, you know, to conduct that woman, without losing time, to the fort of La Pointe, and never to leave her till she is on board."

As these orders agreed effectively with the order they had received, they bowed their heads in sign of assent.

With regard to Athos, he leaped lightly into the saddle, and set out at full gallop ; only, instead of following the road, he took across the fields, urging his horse to the utmost, and stopping occasionally to listen.

In one of those halts, he heard the steps of several horses on the road. He had no doubt it was the cardinal and his escort. He immediately made a new point in advance, rubbed his horse down with some heath and leaves of trees, and came and placed himself across the road, at about two hundred paces from the camp.

" Who goes there ?" cried he, as soon as he perceived the horsemen.

" That is our brave musketeer, I think," said the cardinal.

" Yes, monseigneur," said Porthos, " it is he."

" Monsieur Athos," said Richelieu, " receive my thanks for the good guard you have kept. Gentlemen, we are arrived ; take the gate on the left ; the watchword is, ' Roi et Ré.' "

On saying these words, the cardinal saluted the three friends with an inclination of his head, and took the right hand, followed by his attendant ; for, that night, he himself slept in the camp.

" Well !" said Porthos and Aramis, together, as soon as the cardinal was out of hearing ; " well ! he signed the paper she required !"

" I know he did," said Athos, " since here it is."

And the three friends did not exchange a single word till they got to their quarters, except to give the watchword to the sentinels.

They sent Mousqueton to tell Planchet that his master was requested, the instant he left the trenches, to come to the quarters of the musketeers.

Milady, as Athos had foreseen, on finding the two men that awaited her, made no difficulty in following them ; she had had for an instant an inclination to be reconducted to the cardinal, and relate everything to him ; but a revelation, on her part, would bring about a revelation on the part of Athos ; she might say that Athos had hung her ; but then Athos would tell that she was branded : she thought it was best to preserve silence, to set off discreetly, to accomplish her difficult mission with her usual skill ; and then, all things being performed to the satisfaction of the cardinal, to come back and claim her vengeance.

In consequence, after having travelled all night, at seven o'clock she was at fort La Pointe ; at eight o'clock she had embarked ; and at nine the vessel, which, with letters of marque from the cardinal, was supposed to be sailing for Bayonne, raised anchor, and steered its course towards England.

CHAPTER XLVI.

THE BASTION SAINT-GERVAIS.

ON arriving at the lodging of his three friends, D'Artagnan found them assembled in the same chamber : Athos was meditating, Porthos was twisting his moustaches, Aramis was reading prayers in a charming little *livre d'heures*, bound in blue velvet.

"Pardieu !" said he, "gentlemen ! I hope what you have to tell me is worth the trouble ; or else, I warn you, I will not pardon you for making me come here instead of getting a little rest, after a night spent in taking and dismantling a bastion. Ah ! why were you not there, gentlemen ; it was warm work !"

"We were in a place where it was not very cold !" replied Porthos, giving his moustache a twist which was peculiar to him.

"Hush !" said Athos.

"Oh ! oh !" said D'Artagnan, comprehending the slight frown of the musketeer ; "it appears there is something fresh abroad."

"Aramis," said Athos, "you went to breakfast the day before yesterday, at the auberge of the Parpaillot, I believe ?"

"Yes."

"How did you fare ?"

"For my part, I ate but little ; the day before yesterday was a fish day, and they had nothing but meat."

"What !" said Athos, "no fish at a sea-port ?"

"They say," said Aramis, resuming his pious studies, "that the dyke which the cardinal is making, drives them all out into the open sea."

"But that is not quite what I mean to ask you," replied Athos : "I want to know if you were left alone, and nobody interrupted you."

"Why, I think there were not many intruders ; yes, Athos, I know what you mean, we shall do very comfortably at the Parpaillot."

"Let us go to the Parpaillot, then ; for here the walls are like sheets of paper."

D'Artagnan, who was accustomed to his friend's manner of acting, and who perceived immediately by a word, a gesture, or a sign from him, that the circumstances were serious, took Athos' arm, and went out without saying anything ; Porthos followed, chatting with Aramis.

On their way they met with Grimaud : Athos made him a sign to come with them : Grimaud, according to custom, obeyed in silence ; the poor lad had nearly come to the pass of forgetting how to speak.

They arrived at the *buvette* of the Parpaillot : it was seven o'clock in the morning, and daylight began to appear : the three friends ordered breakfast, and went into a room in which, the host said, they would not be disturbed.

Unfortunately, the hour was badly chosen for a private conference ; the morning drum had just been beaten ; every one shook off the drowsiness of night, and, to dispel the humid morning air, came to take a drop at the *buvette :* dragoons, Swiss, guards, musketeers, light-horsemen, succeeded each other with a rapidity which might answer the purpose of the host very well, but agreed badly with the views of the four friends. Thus they replied very curtly to the salutations, healths, and jokes of their companions.

" I see how it will be," said Athos ; " we shall get into some prettv quarrel or other, and we don't stand in need of one just now. D'Artagnan, tell us what sort of a night you have had, and we will describe ours afterwards."

" Ah ! yes," said a light-horseman, with a glass of *eau-de-vie* in his hand, which he degustated slowly ; " ah ! yes ! I hear you gentlemen of the guards have been in the trenches to-night, and that you did not get much the best of the Rochellais."

D'Artagnan looked at Athos to know if he ought to reply to this intruder, who mixed unasked in their conversation.

" Well !" said Athos, " don't you hear M. de Busigny, who does you the honour to ask you a question ? Relate what has passed during the night, since these gentlemen desire it.'

" Have you not taken a bastion ?" said a Swiss, who was drinking rum out of a beer glass.

" Yes, monsieur," said D'Artagnan, bowing, " we have had that honour : we even have, as you may have heard, introduced a barrel of powder under one of the angles, which, in blowing up, made a very pretty breach ; without reckoning that, as the bastion was not of yesterday, all the rest of the building was much shaken."

" And what bastion is it ?" asked a dragoon, with his sabre run through a goose, which he was taking to be cooked.

" The bastion Saint-Gervais," replied D'Artagnan, " from behind which the Rochellais annoyed our workmen."

" Was the affair hot ?"

" Yes, moderately so ; we lost five men, and the Rochellais eight or ten."

" Balzempleu !" said the Swiss, who, notwithstanding the admirable collection of oaths possessed by the German language, had acquired a habit of swearing in French.

" But it is probable," said the light-horseman, " that they will send pioneers this morning to reinstate the bastion."

" Yes, that's probable," said D'Artagnan.

"Gentlemen," said Athos, " I have a wager to propose."

"Ah! ah! a wager!" cried the Swiss.

"What is it?" said the light-horseman.

"Stop a bit," said the dragoon, placing his sabre like a spit upon the two large iron dogs which held the fire in the chimney—"Stop a bit, I am in it. You master host! a dripping pan immediately, that I may not lose a drop of the fat of this estimable bird."

"You are quite right," said the Swiss; "Goose-grease is good with pastry."

"There!" said the dragoon. "Now, for the wager. We are all attention, M. Athos."

"Ah! now for the wager!" said the light-horseman.

"Well, Monsieur de Busigny, I will bet you," said Athos, "that my three companions, MM. Porthos, Aramis, and D'Artagnan, and myself, will go and breakfast in the bastion St. Gervais, and we will remain there an hour, by the watch, whatever the enemy may do to dislodge us."

Porthos and Aramis looked at each other; they began to comprehend.

"Well, but," said D'Artagnan, in Athos' ear, " you are going to get us all killed without mercy."

"We are much more likely to be killed," said Athos, "if we do not go."

"Ma foi! gentlemen," said Porthos, turning round upon his chair, and twisting his moustache, "that's a fair bet, I hope."

"I take it," said M. de Busigny; "now let us fix the stake."

"Why, you are four, gentlemen," said Athos, "and we are four; a dinner for eight,—will that do?"

"Capitally," replied M. de Busigny.

"Perfectly well," said the dragoon.

"That's just the thing," said the Swiss. The fourth auditor, who, during all this conversation had played a mute part, made a sign of the head to show that he acquiesced in the proposition.

"The breakfast for these gentlemen is ready," said the host.

"Well, bring it in," said Athos.

The host obeyed. Athos called Grimaud, pointed to a large basket which lay in a corner, and made a sign to him to wrap the viands up in the napkins.

Grimaud perceived that it was to be a breakfast on the grass, took the basket, packed up the viands, added the bottles, and then took the basket on his arm.

"But where are you going to eat my breakfast?" said the host.

"Of what consequence is that to you, if you are paid for it?" said Athos, and he threw two pistoles majestically on to the table.

"Shall I give you the change, mon officier?" said the host.

"No, only add two bottles of champagne, and the difference will be for the napkins."

The host had not quite so good a bargain as he at first hoped for, but he made amends by slipping in two bottles of Anjou wine instead of two bottles of champagne.

"Monsieur de Busigny," said Athos, "will you be so kind as to set your watch with mine, or permit me to regulate mine by yours?"

"Which you please, monsieur!" said the light-horseman, drawing from his fob a very handsome watch, surrounded with diamonds; "half-past seven," said he.

"Thirty-five minutes after seven," said Athos, "by which you perceive I am five minutes faster than you."

And bowing to all the astonished persons present, the young men took the road to the bastion St. Gervais, followed by Grimaud, who carried the basket, ignorant of where he was going, but, in the passive obedience which Athos had taught him, not even thinking of asking.

As long as they were within the camp, the four friends did not exchange one word; besides, they were followed by the curious, who hearing of the wager, were anxious to know how they would come out of it. But when once they had passed the line of circumvallation, and found themselves in the open plain, D'Artagnan, who was completely ignorant of what was going forward, thought it was time to demand an explanation.

"And now, my dear Athos," said he, "do me the kindness to tell me where we are going?"

"Why, you see, plainly enough, we are going to the bastion."

"But what are we going to do there?"

"Why, you know, equally well, we are going to breakfast there."

"But why did we not breakfast at the Parpaillot?"

"Because we have some very important matters to communicate to each other, and it was impossible to talk five minutes in that auberge without being annoyed by all those importunate fellows, who keep coming in, saluting you, and addressing you; yonder," said Athos, pointing to the bastion, "they will, at least, not come and disturb us."

"It appears to me," said D'Artagnan, with that prudence which allied itself in him so naturally with excessive bravery, "it appears that we could have found some retired place on the downs or the sea shore."

"Where we should have been seen all four conferring together, so that at the end of a quarter of an hour the cardinal would have been informed by his spies that we were holding a council."

"Yes," said Aramis, "Athos is right : *Animadvertuntur in desertis.*"

"A desert would not have been amiss," said Porthos, "but the matter was where to find it."

"There is no desert where a bird cannot pass over one's head, where a fish cannot leap out of the water, where a rabbit cannot come out of its burrow, and I believe that bird, fish, and rabbit would be all spies of the cardinal. Better, then, follow up our enterprise, from which, besides, we cannot retreat without shame ; we have made a wager, which could not be foreseen, and of which I defy any one to guess the true cause ; we are going, in order to win it, to remain an hour in the bastion. We either shall be or shall not be attacked. If we are not, we shall have all the time to talk, and nobody will hear us, for, I will answer for it the walls of the bastion have no ears ; if we are attacked, we will talk of our affairs just the same, and whilst defending ourselves, we shall cover ourselves with glory. You see that everything is to our advantage."

"Yes," said D'Artagnan, "but I think there is very little doubt that one of us will catch a ball."

"Well !" replied Athos, " I am sure you ought to know that the balls most to be dreaded are not from open enemies."

" But, for such an expedition, we surely ought to have brought our muskets."

" You are stupid, friend Porthos, why should we load ourselves with a useless burden ?"

" For my part, I don't think a good musket, twelve cartridges, and a powder flask very useless things, in face of an enemy."

" Well," replied Athos, "have you not heard what D'Artagnan said ?"

" What did he say to the purpose ?"

" D'Artagnan said that in the attack of last night, eight or ten Frenchmen were killed, and as many Rochellais."

" What then ?"

" The bodies were not plundered, were they ?—it appears the conquerors had something else to do."

" Well ?"

" Well ! we shall find their muskets, their cartridges, and their flasks, and instead of four musketoons and twelve balls, we shall have fifteen guns and a hundred charges to fire."

" Oh ! Athos !" said Aramis, " truly, thou art a great man."

Porthos bowed, in sign of agreement. D'Artagnan alone did not appear to be quite satisfied.

Grimaud, no doubt, shared the misgivings of the young man, for, seeing that they continued to advance towards the bastion, a circumstance which he had not at first suspected, he pulled his master by the skirt of his coat.

" Where are we going ?" asked he by a gesture.

Athos pointed to the bastion.

" But," said the still silent Grimaud, in the usual dialect current between him and his master, " we shall leave our skins behind us."

Athos raised his eyes, and pointed with his finger towards heaven.

Grimaud put his basket on the ground, and sat down with a shake of the head.

Athos took a pistol from his belt, looked to see if it was properly primed, cocked it, and placed the muzzle close to Grimaud's ear.

Grimaud was on his legs again, as if by magic. Athos then made him a sign to take up his basket, and to walk on first. Grimaud obeyed. All that Grimaud gained by this pantomime of a minute, was to pass from the rear-guard to the van-guard.

When arrived at the bastion, the four friends turned round.

More than three hundred soldiers of all kinds were assembled at the gate of the camp ; and in a separate group might be distinguished M. de Busigny, the dragoon, the Swiss, and the fourth wagerer.

Athos took off his hat, placed it on the end of his sword, and waved it in the air.

All the spectators returned him his salute, accompanying this politeness with a loud hurrah ! which was audible at the bastion.

After which, they all four disappeared in the bastion, Grimaud having preceded them.

CHAPTER XLVII.

THE COUNCIL OF THE MUSKETEERS.

As Athos had foreseen, the bastion was only occupied by a dozen of dead bodies, French and Rochellais.

"Gentlemen," said Athos, who had assumed the command of the expedition, "whilst Grimaud is laying out the breakfast, let us begin by collecting the guns and cartridges together ; we can talk whilst performing that necessary task.   These gentlemen," added he, pointing to the bodies, "cannot hear us."

"But we could throw them into the ditch," said Porthos, "after having assured ourselves they have nothing in their pockets."

"Yes," said Athos, "that's Grimaud's business."

"Well, then," cried D'Artagnan, "pray, let Grimaud search them, and throw them over the walls at once."

"I desire he will do no such thing," said Athos, "they may be useful to us."

"These bodies useful to us ? Why, Athos, you are mad !" said Porthos.

"Judge not rashly, say the Gospel and the cardinal," replied Athos ; "how many guns, gentlemen ?"

"Twelve," replied Aramis.

"How many cartridges ?"

"A hundred."

"That's quite as many as we shall want : let us load the guns."

The four musketeers went to work, and as they were loading the last musket, Grimaud announced that the breakfast was ready.

Athos replied, still by gestures, that that was well, and indicated to Grimaud, by pointing to a kind of pepper-castor, that he was to stand as sentinel.   Only, to alleviate the tediousness of the duty, Athos allowed him to take a loaf, two cutlets, and a bottle of wine.

"And now, to table," said Athos.

The four friends sat down upon the ground, with their legs crossed, like Turks or tailors.

"And now," said D'Artagnan, "as there is no longer a fear of being overheard, I hope you are going to let me into this momentous secret."

"I hope, at the same time, to procure you amusement and glory, gentlemen," said Athos.   "I have induced you to take a very pleasant walk ; here is a delicious breakfast, and five hundred persons yonder, as you may see through the loop holes, taking us for heroes or madmen, two classes of imbeciles sufficiently resembling each other."

"But the secret! the secret!" said D'Artagnan.

"The secret is," said Athos, "that I saw milady last night."

D'Artagnan was lifting a glass to his lips, but at the name of milady, his hand shook so, that he was obliged to put the glass on the ground again, for fear of spilling the contents.

"You saw your wi——"

"Hush!" interrupted Athos, "you forget, D'Artagnan, you forget that these gentlemen are not so initiated as you are in my family affairs. I have seen milady."

"Where?" demanded D'Artagnan.

"Within two leagues of this place, at the auberge of the Colombier Rouge."

"In that case, I am a lost man," said D'Artagnan.

"Not quite so yet," replied Athos; "for by this time she must have left the shores of France."

D'Artagnan breathed again.

"But, after all," asked Porthos, "who is milady?"

"A very charming woman!" said Athos, sipping a glass of sparkling wine. "A scoundrel of a host!" cried he, "he has given us Anjou wine instead of Champagne, and fancies we know no better! Yes," continued he, "a very charming woman, who entertained kind views towards our friend D'Artagnan, who, on his part, has given her some offence for which she endeavoured to revenge herself, a month ago, by having him killed by two musket shots; a week ago by trying to poison him; and yesterday, by demanding his head of the cardinal."

"What! by demanding my head of the cardinal?" cried D'Artagnan, pale with terror.

"Yes, that is as true as the Gospel," said Porthos; "I heard her with my own ears."

"So did I," said Aramis.

"Then," said D'Artagnan, letting his arm fall, as if overcome by discouragement, "it is useless to struggle any longer; I may as well blow my brains out, and put an end to the matter at once."

"That's the last folly to be committed," said Athos, "seeing that that is the only one for which there is no remedy."

"But I can never escape," said D'Artagnan, "with such enemies. First, there is my unknown man of Meung; then De Wardes, to whom I have given three wounds; next milady, whose secret I have discovered; and, last and worst, the cardinal, whose vengeance I have balked."

"Well," said Athos, "that only makes four; and we are four—one for one."

"Pardieu! if we may believe the signs Grimaud is making, we are about to have to do with a very different number of folks."

"What's the matter, Grimaud?" said Athos. "Considering the seriousness of the circumstance, I permit you to speak, my friend; but be laconic, I beg. What do you see?"

" A 'troop."

" Of how many persons ?"

" Twenty men."

" What sort of men ?"

" Sixteen pioneers, four soldiers."

" How far distant ?"

" Five hundred paces."

" Good ! We have just time to finish this fowl, and to drink one glass of wine to your health, D'Artagnan !"

" To your health," repeated Porthos and Aramis.

" Well, then, to my health ! although I am very much afraid that your good wishes will not be of great service to me."

" Bah !" said Athos, "God is great, as the followers of Mahomet say ; and the future is in His hands."

Then, swallowing the contents of his glass, which he put down close to him, Athos arose carelessly, took the musket next to him, and drew near to one of the loop-holes.

Porthos, Aramis, and D'Artagnan followed his example. As to Grimaud, he received orders to place himself behind the four friends, in order to reload their weapons.

At the expiration of a minute the troop appeared ; they advanced along a sort of narrow channel of the trench, which kept up a means of communication between the bastion and the city.

" Pardieu !" said Athos, " it was hardly worth while to disturb ourselves for twenty fellows, armed with pickaxes, mattocks, and shovels ! Grimaud had only need have made them a sign to go away, and I am convinced they would have left us alone."

" I doubt that," replied D'Artagnan ; " for they are advancing very resolutely. Besides, in addition to the pioneers, there are four soldiers and a brigadier armed with muskets."

" That's because they don't see us," said Athos.

" Ma foi !" said Aramis, " I must confess I feel a great repugnance to fire on these poor devils of bourgeois."

" He is a bad priest," said Porthos, " who feels pity for heretics !"

" In truth," said Athos, " Aramis is right,—I will warn them."

" What the devil are you going about ?" cried D'Artagnan, " you will be shot !"

But Athos took no heed of his advice ; and, mounting on the breach, with his musket in one hand, and his hat in the other :

" Gentlemen," said he, addressing the soldiers and the pioneers, who, astonished at his appearance, stopped at fifty paces from the bastion, and bowing courteously to them ; " gentlemen, a few friends and myself are about to breakfast in this bastion. Now, you know nothing is more disagreeable than being disturbed when one is at breakfast. We request you, then, if you really have business here, to wait till we have finished our repast, or to come again a short time hence ; unless, which would be far better, you form the salutary resolution to quit the side of the rebels, and come and drink with us to the health of the king of France.'

"Take care, Athos !" cried D'Artagnan ; "don't you see they are preparing to fire ?"

"Yes, yes," said Athos ; "but they are only bourgeois,—very bad marksmen, and who will be sure not to hit me."

In fact, at the same instant, four shots were fired, and the balls were flattened against the wall round Athos, but not one hit him.

Four shots replied to them, almost instantaneously, but much better aimed than those of the aggressors ; three soldiers fell dead, and one of the pioneers was wounded.

"Grimaud," said Athos, still on the breach, "another musket !"

Grimaud immediately obeyed. On their part, the three friends had reloaded their arms ; another discharge followed the second ; the brigadier and two pioneers fell dead ; the rest of the troop took to flight.

"Now, gentlemen, a sortie !" cried Athos.

And the four friends rushed out of the fort, gained the field of battle, picked up the four soldiers' muskets and the half-pike of the brigadier ; and, convinced that the fugitives would not stop till they got to the city, turned again towards the bastion, bearing with them the trophies of their victory.

"Reload the muskets, Grimaud," said Athos, "and we, gentlemen, will go on with our breakfast, and resume our conversation. Where were we ?"

"You were saying," said D'Artagnan, "that after having demanded my head of the cardinal, milady had left the shores of France. Where is she going to ?" added he, considerably interested in the itinerary milady followed.

"She is going into England," said Athos.

"With what view ?"

"With the view of assassinating, or causing to be assassinated, the Duke of Buckingham."

D'Artagnan uttered an exclamation of surprise and astonishment.

"But this is infamous !" cried he.

"As to that," said Athos, "I beg you to believe that I care very little about it. Now you have done, Grimaud, take our brigadier's half-pike, tie a napkin to it, and plant it at the top of our bastion, that these rebels of Rochellais may see that they have to deal with brave and loyal soldiers of the king."

Grimaud obeyed without replying. An instant afterwards, the white flag was floating over the heads of the four friends : a thunder of applause saluted its appearance : half the camp was at the barrier.

"But why do you care so little whether Buckingham be killed or not? The duke is our friend."

"The duke is an Englishman, the duke is fighting against us ; let her do what she likes with the duke ; I care no more about him than an empty bottle."

And Athos threw fifteen paces from him an empty bottle, from which he had poured the last drop into his glass.

"Aye, but stop a minute, I will not give up Buckingham thus," said D'Artagnan, "he gave us some very fine horses."

"And, moreover, very handsome saddles," said Porthos, who at the moment wore the lace of his on his cloak.

"Besides," said Aramis. "God desires the conversion, and not the death of a sinner."

"*Amen!*" said Athos, "and we will return to that subject presently, if such be your pleasure : but that which, for the moment, engaged my attention most earnestly, and I am sure you will understand me, D'Artagnan, was the getting from this woman a kind of signed carte-blanche, which she had extorted from the cardinal, and by means of which she could with impunity get rid of you and perhaps of us."

"But this creature must be a demon !" said Porthos, holding out his plate to Aramis, who was cutting up a fowl.

"And this carte-blanche," said D'Artagnan, "this carte-blanche, does it remain in her hands ?"

"No, it passed into mine ; I will not say without trouble, for if I did I should tell a lie."

"My dear Athos, I shall give over counting the number of times I am indebted to you for my life."

"Then it was to go to her you left us ?" said Aramis.

"Exactly so."

"And you have that letter of the cardinal's ?"

"Here it is," said Athos.

And he took the invaluable paper from the pocket of his uniform. D'Artagnan unfolded it with a hand, the trembling of which he did not even attempt to conceal, and read :

"It is by my order and for the good of the state, that the bearer of the present has done what he has done.

"5 December, 1627.   "RICHELIEU."

"In fact," said Aramis, "it is an absolution in all its forms."

"That paper must be torn to pieces," said D'Artagnan, who fancied he read in it his sentence of death.

"On the contrary," said Athos, "it must be preserved carefully ; I would not give this paper for as many gold pieces as would cover it."

"And what is she going to do now ?" asked the young man.

"Why," replied Athos, carelessly, "she is probably going to write to the cardinal that a damned musketeer, named Athos, has taken her *protection* from her by force ; she will advise him, in the same letter, to get rid of his two friends, Aramis and Porthos, at the time he disposes of him. The cardinal will remember that these are the same men that have so often crossed his path ; and then, some fine morning, he will arrest D'Artagnan, and for fear he should feel lonely, he will send us to keep him company in the Bastille."

"It appears to me you are making but very dull jokes, friend Athos," said Porthos.

" I am not joking."

" Do you know," said Porthos, " that to twist that damned milady's neck would be a less sin than to twist those of these poor devils of Huguenots, who have committed no other crimes than singing the Psalms in French that we sing in Latin ?"

" What says the abbé ?" asked Athos, quietly.

" I say I am entirely of Porthos's opinion," replied Aramis.

" And I am sure I am so too," said D'Artagnan.

" Fortunately, she is a good way off," said Porthos, " for I confess she would make me very uncomfortable if she were here."

" She makes me uncomfortable in England as well as in France," said Athos.

" She makes me uncomfortable wherever she is," said D'Artagnan.

" But, when you had her in your power, why did you not drown her, or strangle her, or hang her?" said Porthos, " it is only the dead that don't come back again."

" You think so, do you, Porthos ?" replied the musketeer, with a sad smile, which D'Artagnan alone understood.

" I have an idea," said D'Artagnan.

" What is it ?" said the musketeers.

" To arms !" cried Grimaud.

The young men sprang up, and seized their muskets.

This time, a small troop advanced, consisting of from twenty to five and twenty men ; but they were no longer pioneers, they were soldiers of the garrison.

" Shall we return to the camp?" said Porthos, " I don't think the sides are equal."

" Impossible, for three reasons," replied Athos, " the first is, that we have not finished breakfast ; the second is, that we have still some very important things to talk about ; and the third is, that it yet wants ten minutes before the hour will be elapsed."

" Well, then," said Aramis, " we must form a plan of battle."

" That's very simple," replied Athos, " as soon as the enemy are within musket-shot we must fire upon them ; if they continue to advance, we must fire again, we fire as long as we have loaded guns : if such as then remain of the troop persist in coming to the assault, we will allow the besiegers to go into the ditch, and then we will push down upon their heads that strip of wall which seems only to keep its perpendicular by a miracle."

" Bravo !" cried Porthos ; " decidedly, Athos, you were born to be a general, and the cardinal, who fancies himself a great captain, is nothing to you."

" Gentlemen," said Athos, " no divided attention, I beg ; let each one pick out his man."

" I cover mine," said D'Artagnan.

" And I mine," said Porthos.

" And I *idem*," said Aramis.

" Fire ! then," said Athos.

The four muskets made but one report, but four men fell.

The drum immediately beat, and the little troop advanced in charging step.

Then the shots were repeated, without regularity, but always aimed with the same correctness. Nevertheless, as if they had been aware of the numerical weakness of the friends, the Rochellais continued to advance in quick time.

Upon every three shots at least two men fell ; but the march of those left untouched was not slackened.

When arrived at the foot of the bastion, there was still more than a dozen of the enemy ; a last discharge welcomed them, but did not stop them ; they jumped into the ditch, and prepared to scale the breach.

" Now, my friends," said Athos, " finish them at a blow : to the wall ! to the wall !"

And the four friends, seconded by Grimaud, pushed with the barrels of their muskets an enormous sheet of the wall, which bent over as if acted upon by the wind, and, becoming detached from its base, fell with a horrible crash into the ditch. Then a fearful cry was heard, a cloud of dust mounted towards heaven,—and all was over !

" Can we have destroyed them all, from the first to the last ?" said Athos.

" Ma foi ! it appears so," said D'Artagnan.

" No," cried Porthos ; " there go three or four, limping away."

In fact, three or four of these unfortunate men, covered with dirt and blood, were flying along the hollow way, and at length regained the city : these were all that were left of the little troop.

Athos looked at his watch.

" Gentlemen," said he, " we have been here an hour, and our wager is won ; but we will be fair players : besides, D'Artagnan has not told us his idea yet."

And the musketeer, with his usual coolness, went and reseated himself before the remains of the breakfast.

" My idea ?" said D'Artagnan.

" Yes ; you said you had an idea," said Athos.

" Oh ! I remember now," said D'Artagnan. " Well, I will go into England a second time ; I will go and find M. Buckingham.'

" You shall not do that, D'Artagnan," said Athos, coolly.

" And why not ? Have I not been there once ?"

" Yes ; but at that period we were not at war : at that period M. de Buckingham was an ally, and not an enemy. What you now contemplate doing would amount to treason."

D'Artagnan perceived the force of this reasoning, and was silent.

" But," said Porthos, " I think I have an idea, in my turn."

" Silence for M. Porthos's idea !" said Aramis.

" I will ask leave of absence of M. de Tréville, on some pretext or other, which you must find out, as I am not very clever at pretexts. Milady does not know me ; I will get access to her without her suspecting me, and when I catch my beauty alone, I will strangle her."

"Well," replied Athos, "I am not far from approving the idea of M. Porthos."

"For shame ! for shame !" said Aramis—"kill a woman ? No, listen to me ; I have the best idea."

"Let us see your idea, Aramis," said Athos, who entertained much deference for the young musketeer.

"We must acquaint the queen."

"Ah, ma foi ! yes," said Porthos and D'Artagnan at the same time ; "we are coming nearer to it now."

"Acquaint the queen !" said Athos ; "and how will you do that ? Have we any relations with the court ? Could we send any one to Paris without its being known in the camp ? From hence to Paris it is a hundred and forty leagues ; before our letter was at Angers we should be in a dungeon."

"As to remitting a letter with safety to her majesty," said Aramis, colouring, "I will take that upon myself. I know a clever person at Tours——"

Aramis stopped on seeing Athos smile.

"Well, do you not adopt this means, Athos ?" said D'Artagnan.

"I do not reject it altogether," said Athos ; "but I wish to remind Aramis that he cannot quit the camp, and that nobody but one of our-selves is safe ; that two hours after the messenger has set out, all the capuchins, all the alguazils, all the black caps of the cardinal, will know your letter by heart, and you and your clever person will be arrested."

"Without reckoning that the queen would save M. de Buckingham, but would take no heed of us."

"Gentlemen," said D'Artagnan, "what Porthos says is full of sense."

"Ah, ah ! but what's going on in the city yonder ?" said Athos.

"They are beating the *générale.*"

The four friends listened, and all plainly heard the sound of the drum.

"You will see, they are going to send a whole regiment against us," said Athos.

"You don't think of holding out against a whole regiment, do you ?" said Porthos.

"Why not ?" said the musketeer. "I feel myself quite in a humour for it ; and I would hold out before a whole army if we had had the precaution to bring a dozen more bottles of wine."

"Upon my word, the drum draws near," said D'Artagnan.

"Let it come," said Athos. "It is a quarter of an hour's journey from hence to the city, consequently a quarter of an hour's journey from the city hither ; that is more than time enough for us to devise a plan. If we go from this place, we shall never find another so suitable. Ah ! stop ! I have it, gentlemen—the right idea has just occurred to me."

"Tell us what it is, then."

"Allow me to give Grimaud some indispensable orders."

Athos made a sign for his lackey to draw near.

"Grimaud," said Athos, pointing to the bodies which lay under the wall of the bastion, "take those gentlemen, set them up against the wall, put their hats upon their heads, and their guns in their hands."

"Oh, the great man !" cried D'Artagnan ; "I comprehend now."

"You comprehend ?" said Porthos.

"And do you comprehend, Grimaud ?" said Aramis.

Grimaud made a sign in the affirmative.

"That's all that's necessary," said Athos ; "now for my idea."

"I should like, however, to comprehend," said Porthos.

"Not at all necessary."

"Athos' idea ! Athos' idea !" cried Aramis and D'Artagnan at the same time.

"This milady—this woman—this creature—this demon, has a brother-in-law, as I think you have told me, D'Artagnan ?"

"Yes, I know him very well ; and I also believe that he has not a very warm affection for his sister-in-law."

"There is no harm in that ; if he detested her, it would be all the better," replied Athos.

"In that case, we are as well off as we wish."

"And yet," said Porthos, "I should like to comprehend what Grimaud is about."

"Silence, Porthos !" said Aramis.

"What is her brother's name ?"

"Lord de Winter."

"Where is he now ?"

"He returned to London at the first rumour of the war."

"Well, that's just the man we want," said Athos ; "it is him we must warn. We will have him informed that his sister-in-law is on the point of having some one assassinated, and we beg of him not to lose sight of her. There is in London, I hope, some establishment like that of the Madelonnettes, or of the Filles Repenties. He must place his sister in one of these, and we shall be in peace."

"Yes," said D'Artagnan, "until she gets out again."

"Ah, ma foi !" said Athos, "you require too much, D'Artagnan ; I have given you all I had, and I beg leave to tell you that that is the bottom of my sack."

"But I think it would be still better," said Aramis, "to inform the queen and M. de Winter at the same time."

"Yes ; but who is to carry the letter to Tours, and who to London ?"

"I answer for Bazin," said Aramis.

"And I for Planchet," said D'Artagnan.

"Aye," said Porthos, "if we cannot leave the camp, our lackeys may."

"To be sure they may, and this very day we will write the letters," said Aramis ; "give them money, and set them forward."

"We will give them money ?" replied Athos. "Have you any money, then ?"

The four friends looked at each other, and a cloud came over the brows which but lately had been so cheerful.

" Quick ! quick !" cried D'Artagnan, " I see black points and red points moving yonder. What ! did you talk of a regiment, Athos ? It is an army !"

" Ma foi ! yes," said Athos, " there they are. Think of the sneaks coming without beat of drum or sound of trumpet. Ah, ah ! have you finished, Grimaud ?"

Grimaud made a sign in the affirmative, and pointed to a dozen bodies which he had set up in the most picturesque attitudes : some ported arms, others seemed to be taking aim, and the remainder appeared merely to be sword in hand.

" Bravo !" said Athos ; " that does honour to your imagination."

" Aye, I dare say it's all very well," said Porthos, " but I should like to comprehend."

" Let us decamp first, and you can comprehend afterwards."

"Stop one minute, gentlemen ; give Grimaud time to collect the breakfast things."

"Ah, ah !" said Aramis, " the black points and the red points are visibly enlarging ; I am of D'Artagnan's opinion—we have no time to lose to regain our camp."

" Ma foi !" said Athos, " I have nothing more to say against a retreat ; we betted upon one hour, and we have stayed an hour and a half. Nothing can be said ; let us be off, gentlemen, let us be off ?"

Grimaud went on before with the basket ; the four friends followed, at about ten paces behind him.

" What the devil shall we do now, gentlemen ?" cried Athos.

" Have you forgotten anything ?" said Aramis.

" The white flag, morbleu ! we must not leave a flag in the hands of the enemy, even if that flag be but a napkin."

And Athos ran back to the bastion, mounted the platform, and bore off the flag ; but as the Rochellais were arrived within musket range, they opened a terrible fire upon this man, who appeared to expose himself for pleasure's sake.

But Athos might be said to bear a charmed life : the balls passed and whistled all round him ; not one hit him.

Athos waved his flag, turning his back to the city guards, and saluting those of the camp. On both sides loud cries arose—on the one side cries of anger, on the other cries of enthusiasm.

A second discharge followed the first, and three balls, by passing through it, made the napkin really a flag. Cries were heard from the camp, " Come down ! come down !"

Athos came down ; his friends, who anxiously awaited him, saw him return with joy.

" Come along, Athos, come along !" cried D'Artagnan ; " now we have found everything except money, it would be stupid to be killed."

But Athos continued to march majestically, whatever observations his companions made ; and they, finding their observations useless, regulated their pace by his.

Grimaud and his basket were far in advance, out of the reach of the balls.

At the end of an instant, a furious firing was heard.

"What's that?" asked Porthos, "what are they firing at now? I hear no balls, and I see nobody!"

"They are firing upon Grimaud's dead company," replied Athos.

"But the dead cannot return their fire."

"Certainly not; they will then fancy it is an ambuscade, they will deliberate, and by the time they have found out the joke we shall be out of the reach of their balls. That renders it useless to get a pleurisy by too much haste."

"Oh, I comprehend now," said the astonished Porthos.

"That's lucky," said Athos, shrugging his shoulders.

On their part, the French, on seeing the four friends return in common marching step, uttered cries of enthusiasm.

At length a fresh discharge was heard, and this time the balls came rattling among the stones around the friends, and whistling sharply in their ears. The Rochellais had at last taken possession of the bastion.

"These Rochellais are bungling fellows," said Athos; "how many have we killed of them—a dozen?"

"Or fifteen."

"How many did we crush under the wall?"

"Eight or ten."

"And in exchange for all that not even a scratch! Ah! but what is the matter with your hand, D'Artagnan? It bleeds, seemingly."

"Oh, it's nothing," said D'Artagnan.

"A spent ball?"

"Not even that."

"What is it, then?"

We have said that Athos loved D'Artagnan like a child, and this sombre and inflexible character felt the anxiety of a parent for the young man.

"Only grazed a little," replied D'Artagnan; "my fingers were caught between two stones, that of the wall and that of my ring, and the skin was broken."

"That comes of wearing diamonds, my master," said Athos, disdainfully.

"Ah, to be sure," cried Porthos, "there is a diamond; why the devil, then, do we plague ourselves about money, when there is a diamond?"

"Stop a bit!" said Aramis.

"Well thought of, Porthos; this time you have an idea."

"Certainly I have," said Porthos, drawing himself up at Athos' compliment; "as there is a diamond, let us sell it."

"But," said D'Artagnan, "it is the queen's diamond."

"The stronger reason why it should be sold," replied Athos: "the queen saving M. de Buckingham, her lover, nothing more just; the queen saving us, her friends, nothing more moral; let us sell the diamond. What says Monsieur l'Abbé. I don't ask Porthos; his opinion has been given."

"Why, I think," said Aramis, colouring as usual, "that his ring not coming from a mistress, and, consequently, not being a love-token, D'Artagnan may sell it."

"My dear Aramis, you speak like theology personified. Your opinion, then, is——"

"That the diamond may be sold."

"Well, then," said D'Artagnan, gaily, "let us sell the diamond, and say no more about it."

The fusilade continued ; but the friends were out of reach, and the Rochellais only fired for the discharge of their consciences.

"Ma foi ! it was time that idea came into Porthos' head—here we are at the camp ; therefore, gentlemen, not a word more of this affair. We are observed—they are coming to meet us ; we shall be borne in in triumph."

In fact, as we have said, the whole camp was in motion. More than two thousand persons had assisted, as at a spectacle, at this fortunate but wild undertaking of the four friends, an undertaking of which they were far from suspecting the real motive. Nothing was heard but cries of "Vivent les mousquetaires ! vivent les gardes !" M. de Busigny was the first to come and shake Athos by the hand, and acknowledge that the wager was lost. The dragoon and the Swiss followed him, and all their comrades followed the dragoon and the Swiss. There was nothing but felicitations, pressures of the hand, and embraces ; there was no end to the inextinguishable laughter at the Rochellais. The tumult at length became so great that the cardinal fancied there must be some riot, and sent La Houdinière, his captain of the guards, to inquire what was going on.

The affair was described to the messenger with all the effervescence of enthusiasm.

"Well ?" asked the cardinal, on seeing La Houdinière return.

"Well, monseigneur," replied the latter, "three musketeers and a guard laid a wager with M. de Busigny, that they would go and breakfast in the Bastion St. Gervais, and whilst breakfasting, they held it for two hours against the enemy, and have killed I don't know how many Rochellais."

"Did you inquire the names of those three musketeers ?"

"Yes, monseigneur."

"What are their names ?"

"MM. Athos, Porthos, and Aramis "

"Still my three brave fellows !" murmured the cardinal. "And the guard ?"

"M. D'Artagnan."

"Still my young scapegrace. Positively, these four men must be mine."

That same evening, the cardinal spoke to M. de Tréville of the exploit of the morning, which was the talk of the whole camp. M. de Tréville, who had received the account of the adventure from the mouths of the heroes of it, related it in all its details to his eminence, not forgetting the episode of the napkin.

"That's well! Monsieur de Tréville," said the cardinal; "pray let that napkin be sent to me. I will have three fleur-de-lis embroidered on it in gold, and will give it to your company as a standard."

"Monseigneur," said M. de Treville, "that will hardly be doing justice to the guards; M. D'Artagnan is not mine; he serves under M. des Essarts."

"Well, then, take him," said the cardinal; "when four men are so much attached to each other, it is only fair that they should serve in the same company."

That same evening, M. de Tréville announced this good news to the three musketeers and D'Artagnan, inviting all four to breakfast with him next morning.

D'Artagnan was beside himself with joy. We know that the dream of his life had been to become a musketeer. The three friends were likewise greatly delighted.

"Ma foi!" said D'Artagnan to Athos, "that was a triumphant idea of yours! As you said, we have acquired glory, and were enabled to carry on a conversation of the greatest importance."

"Which we can resume now without anybody suspecting us, for, with the help of God, we shall henceforth pass for cardinalists."

That evening D'Artagnan went to present his compliments to M. des Essarts, and inform him of his promotion.

M. des Essarts, who esteemed D'Artagnan, made him offers of service, as this change would bring on expenses for equipment.

D'Artagnan respectfully declined, but thinking the opportunity a good one, he begged him to have the diamond he put into his hand valued, as he wished to turn it into money.

The next day, by two o'clock, M. des Essarts' valet came to D'Artagnan's lodging, and gave him a bag containing seven thousand livres.

This was the price of the queen's diamond.

CHAPTER XLVIII.

A FAMILY AFFAIR.

ATHOS had discovered the word: *family affair.* A family affair was not subject to the investigation of the cardinal; a family affair concerned nobody; people might employ themselves in a family affair before all the world.

Thus Athos had discovered the word: family affair.

Aramis had discovered the idea: the lackeys.

Porthos had discovered the means: the diamond.

D'Artagnan alone had discovered nothing; he, ordinarily the most inventive of the four: but it must be also said that the name alone of milady paralysed him.

Ah! yes, but we were mistaken; he had discovered a purchaser for his diamond.

The breakfast at M. de Tréville's was as gay and cheerful as possible. D'Artagnan already wore his uniform ; for being nearly of the same size as Aramis, and Aramis being so liberally paid by the bookseller who purchased his poem, as to allow him to have bought double of everything, he yielded his friend a complete equipment.

D'Artagnan would have been at the height of his wishes, if he had not constantly seen milady, like a dark cloud, hovering in the horizon.

After breakfast, it was agreed that they should meet again in the evening at Athos' lodgings, and would there terminate the affair.

D'Artagnan passed the day in exhibiting his musketeer's uniform in every street of the camp.

In the evening, at the appointed hour, the four friends met ; there only remained three things to be decided upon :—

What they should write to milady's brother ;

What they should write to the clever person at Tours ;

And which should be the lackeys to carry the letters.

Every one offered his own : Athos talked of the discretion of Grimaud, who never spoke a word but when his master unlocked his mouth. Porthos boasted of the strength of Mousqueton, who was big enough to thrash four men of ordinary size. Aramis, confiding in the address of Bazin, made a pompous eulogium upon his candidate ; and D'Artagnan had entire faith in the bravery of Planchet, and reminded them of the manner in which he had conducted himself in the ticklish affair of Boulogne.

These four virtues disputed the prize for a length of time, and gave birth to magnificent speeches, which we do not repeat here, for fear they should be deemed too long.

"Unfortunately," said Athos, "he whom we send must possess in himself alone the four qualities united."

"But where is such a lackey to be found ?"

"Not to be found !" cried Athos ; "I know that ; take Grimaud then."

"Take Mousqueton !"

"Take Bazin !"

"Take Planchet ; Planchet is brave and shrewd ; they are two qualities out of the four."

"Gentlemen," said Aramis, "the principal question is not to know which of our four lackeys is the most discreet, the strongest, the cleverest, or the most brave ; the matter is to know which loves money the best."

"What Aramis says is very sensible," replied Athos ; "we must speculate upon the faults of people, and not upon their virtues. Monsieur l'Abbé, you are a great moralist !"

"Doubtless," said Aramis ; "for we not only require to be well served, in order to succeed, but, moreover, not to fail ; for, in case of failure, heads are in question, not for our lackeys——"

"Speak lower, Aramis," said Athos.

"That's correct ; not for the lackeys," resumed Aramis, "but for the masters ! Are our lackeys sufficiently devoted to us to risk their lives for us ? No."

" Ma foi !" said D'Artagnan, " I would almost answer for Planchet."

" Well, my dear friend, add to his natural devotedness a good sum of money, and then, instead of answering for him once, answer for him twice."

" Why, good God ! you will be deceived just the same," said Athos, who was an optimist when things were concerned, and a pessimist when men were in question. " They will promise everything for the sake of the money, and on the road fear will prevent them from acting. Once taken, they will be pressed ; when pressed, they will confess everything. What the devil, we are not children ! To go to England " (Athos lowered his voice), " all France (covered with the spies and creatures of the cardinal) must be crossed ; a pass for embarkation must be obtained ; and the party must be acquainted with English, to inquire the way to London. Really, I think the thing is very difficult !"

" Not at all," cried D'Artagnan, who was anxious the matter should be accomplished ; " on the contrary, I think it is very easy. It would be, no doubt. Parbleu ! if we write to Lord de Winter about affairs of vast importance, of the horrors of the cardinal——".

" Speak lower !" said Athos.

" Of the intrigues and secrets of state," continued D'Artagnan, complying with the recommendation ; " there can be no doubt we shall be all broken on the wheel ; but, for God's sake, do not forget, as you yourself said, Athos, that we only write to him concerning a family affair ; that we only write to him to entreat that as soon as milady arrives in London, he will put it out of her power to injure us. I will write to him then nearly in these terms."

" Let us see," said Athos, assuming a critical look.

" Monsieur, and dear friend——"

" Ah ! yes ! ' dear friend ' to an Englishman," interrupted Athos ; " capitally commenced ! Bravo, D'Artagnan ! Only with that word you would be quartered, instead of being broken on the wheel."

" Well ! perhaps. I will say, then, monsieur, quite short."

" You may even say, milord," replied Athos, who stickled for propriety.

" Milord, do you remember the little goat pasture of the Luxembourg ?"

" Good, the Luxembourg ! It might be believed to be an allusion to the queen-mother ! That's ingenious," said Athos.

" Well, then ! we will put simply, ' Milord, do you remember a certain little inclosure where your life was spared ?' "

" My dear D'Artagnan, you will never make anything but a very bad secretary. ' Where your life was spared !' For shame ! that's unworthy. A man of spirit is not to be reminded of such services. A benefit reproached is an offence committed."

" The devil," said D'Artagnan, " you are insupportable ! If the letter must be written under your censure, I renounce the task."

"And you will do right. Handle the musket and the sword, my dear fellow ; you will come off splendidly at those two exercises ; but pass the pen over to M. l'Abbé, that's his province."

"Aye, aye," said Porthos, "pass the pen over to Aramis, who writes theses in Latin."

"Well, so be it," said D'Artagnan, "draw up this note for us, Aramis ; but, by our holy father the pope ! be concise, for I shall prune you in my turn, I warn you."

"I ask no better," said Aramis, with that ingenuous air of confidence which every poet has in himself ; "but let me be properly acquainted with the subject ; I have heard, by this means and that, that this sister-in-law was a vile woman ; I have obtained a proof of it by listening to her conversation with the cardinal."

"Lower ! sacre bleu !" said Athos.

"But," continued Aramis, "the details escape me."

"And me also," said Porthos.

D'Artagnan and Athos looked at each other for some time in silence. At length, Athos, after apparently serious reflection, and becoming more pale than usual, made a sign of assent to D'Artagnan, who by it understood he was at liberty to speak.

"Well, this is what you have to say," said D'Artagnan : "'Milord, your sister-in-law is an infamous woman, who has wished to have you killed, that she might inherit your wealth. But she could not marry your brother, being already married in France, and having been——' " D'Artagnan stopped, as if seeking for the word, and looking at Athos.

"Repudiated by her husband."

"Because she had been branded," continued D'Artagnan.

"Bah !" cried Porthos, "impossible ! What do you say, she wanted to have her brother-in-law killed ?"

"Yes."

"And she was previously married ?" asked Aramis.

"Yes."

"And her husband found out that she had a fleur-de-lis on her shoulder ?" cried Porthos.

"Yes."

These three yeses had been pronounced by Athos, each with a deeper intonation.

"And who has seen this fleur-de-lis ?" said Aramis.

"D'Artagnan and I, or rather, to observe the chronological order, I and D'Artagnan," replied Athos.

"And does the husband of this frightful creature still live ?" said Aramis.

"He still lives."

"Are you quite sure of it ?"

"I am he."

There was a moment of cold silence, during which every one was affected, according to his nature.

"This time," said Athos, first breaking the silence, " D'Artagnan has given us an excellent programme, and the letter must be written at once."

"The devil ! you are right, Athos," said Aramis, "and it is rather a difficult matter.   M. the Chancellor himself would be puzzled how to write such a letter, and yet M. the Chancellor draws up a *procès-verbal* very agreeably.   Never mind ! be silent, I will try."

Aramis accordingly took the pen, reflected for a few moments, wrote eight or ten lines, in a charming, little, female hand, and then, with a voice soft and slow, as if each word had been scrupulously weighed, he read the following :

"MILORD

"The person who writes these few lines had the honour of crossing swords with you in the little enclosure of the Rue d'Enfer.   As you have several times since declared yourself the friend of that person, he thinks it his duty to respond to that friendship by sending you important advice.   Twice you have nearly been the victim of a near relation whom you believe to be your heir, because you are ignorant that before she contracted a marriage in England, she was already married in France.   But the third time, which is this, you may succumb.   Your relation left La Rochelle for England during the night.   Watch her arrival, for she has great and terrible projects.   If you require to know positively what she is capable of, read her past history upon her left shoulder."

"Well, now that will do wonderfully well," said Athos ; "really, my dear Aramis, you have the pen of a secretary of state.   Lord de Winter will now be upon his guard, if the letter should reach him ; and even if it should fall into the hands of the cardinal, we shall not be compromised.   But as the lackey who goes may make us believe he has been to London and may stop at Châtelherault, let us give him only half the sum promised him with the letter, with an agreement that he shall have the other half in exchange for the reply.   Have you the diamond?" continued Athos.

"I have what is still better : I have the value of it," said D'Artagnan, throwing the bag upon the table.   At the sound of the gold, Aramis raised his eyes, and Porthos started : as to Athos, he remained impassible.

"How much is there in that little bag ?"

"Seven thousand livres, in louis of twelve francs."

"Seven thousand livres !" cried Porthos; "that poor little diamond was worth seven thousand livres ?"

"It appears so," said Athos, "since here they are ; I don't suppose that our friend D'Artagnan has added any of his own to the amount."

"But gentlemen, in all this," said D'Artagnan, "we do not think of the queen.   Let us take some heed of the welfare of her dear Buckingham.   That is the least we owe her."

"That's true," said Athos, "but that falls to Aramis."

"Well," replied the latter, blushing, "what must I say ?"

"Oh ! that's simple enough," replied Athos ; " write a second letter for that clever personage that lives at Tours."

Aramis resumed his pen, reflected a little, and wrote the following lines, which he immediately submitted to the approbation of his friends :

" My dear cousin."

"Ah ! ah !" said Athos, " this clever person is your relation then ?"

" Cousin-german."

" Go on, to your cousin, then !"

Aramis continued :

" MY DEAR COUSIN,—His eminence the cardinal, whom God pre-serve for the happiness of France and the confusion of the enemies of the kingdom, is on the point of putting an end to the heretic rebellion of La Rochelle ; it is probable that the succour of the English fleet will never even arrive in sight of the place ; I will even venture to say that I am certain M. de Buckingham will be prevented from setting out by some great event. His eminence is the most illustrious politician of times past, of times present, and probably of times to come. He would extinguish the sun, if the sun incommoded him. Give these happy tidings to your sister, my dear cousin. I have dreamed that that cursed Englishman was dead. I cannot recollect whether it was by steel or by poison ; only of this I am sure, I have dreamed he was dead, and you know my dreams never deceive me. Be assured, then, of seeing me soon return."

." Capital," cried Athos : " you are the king of poets, my dear Aramis; you speak like the Apocalypse, and you are as true as the Gospel. There is nothing now to do but to put the address to this letter."

" That's soon done," said Aramis.

He folded the letter fancifully, and took up his pen and wrote :

" To Mademoiselle Michon, seamstress, Tours."

The three friends looked at each other and laughed : they were caught.

"Now," said Aramis, "you will please to understand, gentlemen, that Bazin alone can carry this letter to Tours ; my cousin knows nobody but Bazin, and places confidence in nobody but him : any other person would fail. Besides, Bazin is ambitious and learned ; Bazin has read history, gentlemen, he knows that Sixtus Quintus became pope after having kept pigs ; well ! as he means to enter the church at the same time as myself, he does not despair of becoming pope in his turn, or at least a cardinal ; you can understand that a man who has such views, will never allow himself to be taken, or if taken, will undergo martyrdom rather than speak."

" Very well," said D'Artagnan, " I consent to Bazin, with all my heart, but grant me Planchet ; milady had him one day turned out of doors, with sundry blows of a good stick, to accelerate his motions ; now Planchet has an excellent memory, and I will be bound that sooner than relinquish any possible means of vengeance, he will allow himself to be beaten to death. If your affairs of Tours are your affairs, Aramis those of London are mine. I request, then, that Planchet may be chosen, more particularly as he has already been to London with me, and knows how to speak very correctly : *London, sir, if you please, and my master, Lord D'Artagnan ;* with that, you may be satisfied, he can make his way, both going and returning."

" In that case," said Athos, " Planchet must receive seven hundred livres for going, and seven hundred livres for coming back ; and Bazin, three hundred livres for going, and three hundred livres for returning ; that will reduce the sum to five thousand livres ; we will each take a thousand livres to be employed as seems good to each, and we will leave a fund of a thousand livres, under the guardianship of Monsieur l'Abbé here, for extraordinary occasions or common wants. Will that do?"

" My dear Athos," said Aramis, " you speak like Nestor, who was, as every one knows, the wisest among the Greeks."

" Well, then," said Athos, " it is agreed ; Planchet and Bazin shall go : everything considered, I am not sorry to retain Grimaud ; he is accustomed to my ways, and I am particular ; yesterday's affair must have shaken him a little, his voyage would overset him quite."

Planchet was sent for, and instructions were given him ; the matter had been named to him by D'Artagnan, who had, in the first place, pointed out the money to him, then the glory, and then the danger.

" I will carry the letter in the lining of my coat," said Planchet ; "and if I am taken I will swallow it."

" Well, but then you will not be able to fulfil your commission," said D'Artagnan.

" You will give me a copy of it this evening, which I shall know by heart before the morning."

D'Artagnan looked at his friends, as if to say, "Well, what did I promise you ?"

" Now," continued he, addressing Planchet, " you have eight days to get an interview with Lord de Winter, you have eight days to return in, in all sixteen days ; if, on the sixteenth day after your departure, at eight o'clock in the evening, you are not here, no money, even if it be but five minutes past eight——"

" Then, monsieur," said Planchet, " you must buy me a watch."

" Take this," said Athos, with his usual careless generosity, giving him his own, " and be a good lad. Remember, if you talk, if you babble, if you get drunk, you risk your master's head, who has so much confidence in your fidelity, and who answers for you. But remember, also, that if, by your fault, any evil happens to M. D'Artagnan, I will find you, wherever you may be, and that for the purpose of ripping up your belly."

" Oh, monsieur !" said Planchet, humiliated by the suspicion, and, moreover, terrified at the calm air of the musketeer.

" And I," said Porthos, rolling his large eyes, "remember, I will skin you alive."

" Ah ! monsieur !"

"And I," said Aramis, with his soft melodious voice, "remember that I will roast you at a slow fire like a savage."

"Ah ! monsieur !"

And Planchet began to weep : we will not venture to say whether it was from terror, created by the threats, or from tenderness, at seeing four friends so closely united.

D'Artagnan took his hand.

"See, Planchet," said he, "these gentlemen only say this out of affection for me; at bottom, they all respect you."

"Ah, monsieur," said Planchet ; "I will succeed, or I will consent to be cut in quarters ; and if they do cut me in quarters, be assured that not a morsel of me will speak."

It was determined that Planchet should set out the next day, at eight o'clock in the morning, in order, as he had said, that he might, during the night, learn the letter by heart. He gained just twelve hours by this engagement ; he was to be back on the sixteenth day, by eight o'clock in the evening.

In the morning, as he was mounting on horseback, D'Artagnan, who felt at the bottom of his heart a partiality for the duke, took Planchet aside.

"Listen," said he to him ; "when you have given the letter to Lord de Winter, and he has read it, you will further say to him, 'Watch over his grace Lord Buckingham, for they wish to assassinate him.' But this, Planchet, is so serious and important, that I have not informed my friends that I would intrust this secret to you ; and, for a captain's commission I would not write it."

"Be satisfied, monsieur," said Planchet, "you shall see whether confidence can be placed in me or not."

And, mounted on an excellent horse, which he was to leave at the end of twenty leagues, to take the post, Planchet set off at a gallop, his spirits a little depressed by the triple promise made him by the musketeers ; but otherwise as light-hearted as possible.

Bazin set out the next day for Tours, and was allowed eight days to perform his commission in.

The four friends, during the period of these two absences, had, as may well be supposed, the eye on the watch, the nose to the wind, and the ear on the listen. Their days were passed in endeavouring to catch all that was said, in observing the proceedings of the cardinal, and in looking out for all the couriers that arrived. More than once an involuntary trembling seized them when called upon for any unexpected service. They had, besides, to look constantly to their own proper safety ; milady was a phantom which, when it had once appeared to people, did not allow them to sleep very quietly.

On the morning of the eighth day, Bazin, fresh as ever, and smiling according to custom, entered the cabaret of Parpaillot as the four friends were sitting down to breakfast, saying, as had been agreed upon :

"Monsieur Aramis, here is the answer from your cousin."

The four friends exchanged a joyful glance. half of the work was done ; it is true, however, that it was the shortest and the most easy part.

Aramis, blushing in spite of himself, took the letter, which was in a large, coarse hand, and not particular for its orthography.

"Good God !" cried he, laughing, "I quite despair of my poor Michon; she will never write like M. de Voiture."

"What do you mean by poor Michon ?" said the Swiss, who was chatting with the four friends when the letter arrived.

"Oh, pardieu ! less than nothing,' said Aramis ; "a little charming seamstress, whom I love dearly, and from whose hand I requested a few lines as a sort of keepsake."

"The devil !" said the Swiss, "if the lady is as great as her writing is large, you are a lucky fellow, comrade !"

Aramis read the letter, and passed it to Athos.

"See what she writes to me, Athos," said he.

Athos cast a glance over the epistle, and to disperse all the suspicions that might have been created, read aloud :

"My cousin,—My sister and I are skilful in interpreting dreams, and even entertain great fear of them; but of yours it may be said, I hope, every dream is an illusion. Adieu ! Take care of yourself ; and act so that we may, from time to time, hear you spoken of.

"Aglae Michon."

"And what dream does she mean ?" asked the dragoon, who had approached during the reading.

"Yes ; what's the dream ?" said the Swiss.

"Well, pardieu !" said Aramis, "it was only this,—I had a dream, and I related it to her."

"Yes, yes," said the Swiss ; "it's simple enough to relate a dream when you have one ; but I never dream."

"You are very fortunate," said Athos, rising ; "I wish I could say as much !"

"Never !" replied the Swiss, enchanted that a man like Athos could envy him anything. "Never ! never !"

D'Artagnan, seeing Athos rise, did so likewise, took his arm, and went out.

Porthos and Aramis remained behind to encounter the quolibets of the dragoon and the Swiss.

As to Bazin, he went and laid down on a truss of straw ; and as he had more imagination than the Swiss, he dreamed that Aramis, having become pope, adorned his head with a cardinal's hat.

But, as we have said, Bazin had not, by his fortunate return, removed more than a part of the uneasiness which weighed upon the four friends. The days of expectation are long, and D'Artagnan, in particular, would have wagered that the days were forty-four hours long. He forgot the necessary slowness of the navigation, he exaggerated to himself the power of milady. He gave to this woman, who appeared to him equal to a demon, auxiliaries as supernatural as herself; at the least noise, he imagined that he was about to be arrested, and that Planchet was being brought back to be confronted with himself and his friends. Still further : his confidence in the worthy Picard, at one time so great, diminished day by day. This anxiety became so great, that it even extended to Aramis and Porthos. Athos alone remained impassible, as if no danger hovered over him, and as if he respired his usual atmosphere.

On the sixteenth day, in particular, these signs were so visible in D'Artagnan and his two friends, that they could not remain quiet in one place, and they wandered about, like ghosts, on the road by which Planchet was expected.

"Really," said Athos, "you are not men, but children, to let a woman terrify you so ! And what does it amount to, after all ? To be imprisoned. Well, but we should be taken out of prison ; Madame Bonacieux got out. To be decapitated? Why, every day in the trenches, we go cheerfully to expose ourselves to worse than that, for a bullet may break a leg, and I am convinced a surgeon would give us more pain in cutting off a thigh, than an executioner would in cutting off a head. Wait quietly, then ; in two hours, in four, in six hours at latest, Planchet will be here : he promised to be here, and I have very great faith in Planchet's promises, I think him a very good lad."

"But if he does not come ?" said D'Artagnan.

"Well, if he does not come, it will be because he has been delayed, that's all. He may have fallen from his horse, he may have slipped down on the deck, he may have travelled so fast against the wind as to have produced a violent cold. Eh! gentlemen, let us reckon upon accidents ! Life is a chaplet of little miseries, which the philosopher unstrings with a smile. Be philosophers, as I am, gentlemen ; sit down to the table and let us drink ; nothing makes the future look so bright as surveying it through a glass of chambertin."

"That's all very well," replied D'Artagnan, "but I am tired of fearing, when I open a fresh bottle, that the wine may come from her ladyship's cellar."

"You are very diffident," said Athos ; "such a beautiful woman !"

"A woman of mark !" said Porthos, with his loud laugh.

Athos started, passed his hand over his brow to remove the drops of perspiration that burst forth, and rose in his turn with a nervous movement he could not repress.

The day, however, passed away, and the evening came on slowly, but it did come ; the buvettes were filled with drinkers. Athos, who had pocketed his share of the diamond, seldom quitted the Parpaillot. He had found in M. de Busigny, who, by-the-by, had given them a magnificent dinner, a partner worthy of his company. They were playing together, as usual, when seven o'clock struck ; the patrols were heard passing to double the posts : at half-past seven the retreat was sounded.

"We are lost," said D'Artagnan in Athos' ear.

"You mean to say we have lost," said Athos, quietly, drawing four pistoles from his pocket, and throwing them on the table. "Come, gentlemen," said he, "they are beating the tattoo—to bed, to bed!"

And Athos went out of the Parpaillot, followed by D'Artagnan. Aramis came behind, giving his arm to Porthos. Aramis mumbled verses to himself, and Porthos, from time to time, pulled a hair or two from his moustache, in sign of despair.

But, all at once, a shadow appeared in the darkness, the outline of which was familiar to D'Artagnan, and a well-known voice said:

"Monsieur, I have brought your cloak; it is chilly this evening."

"Planchet!" cried D'Artagnan, beside himself with joy.

"Planchet!" repeated Aramis and Porthos.

"Well, yes, Planchet, to be sure," said Athos, "what is there so astonishing in that? He promised to be back by eight o'clock, and eight is just now striking. Bravo! Planchet, you are a lad of your word, and if ever you leave your master, I will promise you a place in my service."

"Oh! no, never," said Planchet, "I will never leave M. D'Artagnan."

At the same time D'Artagnan felt that Planchet slipped a note into his hand.

D'Artagnan felt a strong inclination to embrace Planchet as he had embraced him on his departure; but he feared lest this mark of affection bestowed upon his lackey in the open street might appear extraordinary to passengers, and he restrained himself.

"I have a note," said he to Athos and his friends.

"That's well," said Athos, "let us go home and read it."

The note burned in the hand of D'Artagnan; he wished to increase their speed; but Athos took his arm and passed it under his own, and the young man was forced to regulate his pace by that of his friend.

At length they reached the tent, lit a lamp, and whilst Planchet stood at the entrance, that the four friends might not be surprised, D'Artagnan, with a trembling hand, broke the seal and opened the so anxiously expected letter.

It contained half a line in a hand perfectly British, and of a conciseness as perfectly Spartan.

> "*Thank you, be easy.*"

"Which means what?"

"Thank you, be easy," said D'Artagnan.

Athos took the letter from the hands of D'Artagnan, drew near to the lamp, set fire to it, and did not leave hold of it till it was reduced to ashes.

Then, calling Planchet,—

"Now, my lad," said he, "you may claim your seven hundred livres, but you did not run much risk with such a note as that."

"I am not to blame for having tried every means to compress it," said Planchet.

"Well!" cried D'Artagnan, "tell us all about it."

"Lord, monsieur, that's a long job !"

"You are right, Planchet," said Athos ; " besides, the tattoo has been sounded, and we should be observed if we kept a light burning longer than the others."

"So be it," said D'Artagnan. "Go to bed, Planchet, and sleep soundly."

" Ma foi, monsieur ! that will be the first time I have done so these sixteen days !"

" Or I either !" said D'Artagnan.

" Or I either !" said Porthos.

" Or I either !" said Aramis.

"Well ! if I must tell you the truth !—or I either !" said Athos.

CHAPTER XLIX.

FATALITY.

IN the meantime, milady, drunk with passion, roaring on the deck like a lioness that has been embarked, had been tempted to throw herself into the sea that she might regain the coast, for she could not get rid of the idea that she had been insulted by D'Artagnan, and threatened by Athos, and had left France without being revenged of both. This idea soon became so insupportable to her, that at the risk of whatever terrible consequences might result to herself from it, she implored the captain to put her on shore ; but the captain, eager to escape from his false position, placed between French and English cruisers, like the bat between the mice and the birds, was in great haste to gain the coast of England, and positively refused to obey what he took for a woman's caprice, promising his passenger, who had been particularly recommended to him by the cardinal, to land her, if the sea and the French permitted him, at one of the ports of Brittany, either at Lorient or Brest ; but the wind was contrary, the sea bad, they laveered, and kept off shore. Nine days after leaving the Charente, pale with fatigue and vexation, milady saw only the blue coasts of Finisterre appear.

She calculated that to cross this corner of France and return to the cardinal, it would take her at least three days ; and another day for landing, and it would make four; add these to the nine others, that would be thirteen days lost—thirteen days—during which so many important events might pass in London. She reflected, likewise, that the cardinal would be furious at her return, and, consequently, would be more disposed to listen to the complaints made against her than to the accusations she brought against others.

She allowed the vessel to pass Lorient and Brest without repeating her request to the captain, who, on his part, took care not to remind her of it. Milady, therefore, continued her voyage, and on the very day that Planchet embarked at Portsmouth for France, the messenger of his eminence entered the port in triumph.

All the city was agitated by an extraordinary movement—four large vessels, recently built, had just been launched.   Standing on the jetty, his clothes richly laced with gold, glittering, as was customary with him, with diamonds and precious stones, his hat ornamented with a white feather which drooped upon his shoulder, Buckingham was seen surrounded by a staff almost as brilliant as himself.

It was one of those rare and beautiful days in which England remembers that there is a sun.   The star of day, pale, but nevertheless still splendid, was declining towards the horizon, empurpling at once the heavens and the sea with bands of fire, and casting upon the towers and the old houses of the city a last ray of gold, which made the windows sparkle like the reflection of a conflagration.   Milady, on respiring that sea-breeze, so much more lovely and balsamic as the land is approached, whilst contemplating all the power of those preparations she was commissioned to destroy, all the power of that army which she was to combat alone—she, a woman—with a few bags of gold, compared herself mentally to Judith, the terrible Jewess, when she penetrated into the camp of the Assyrians, and beheld the enormous mass of chariots, horses, men, and arms, which a gesture of her hand was to dissipate like a cloud of smoke.

They entered the road, but as they drew near, in order to cast anchor, a little cutter, formidably armed, approached the merchant vessel, in appearance a guard-coast, and dropping its boat into the sea, the latter directed its course to the ladder.   This boat contained an officer, a mate, and eight rowers—the officer alone got on board, where he was received with all the deference inspired by the uniform.

The officer conversed a few instants with the captain, gave him several papers, of which he was the bearer, to read, and, upon the order of the merchant-captain, the whole crew of the vessel, both passengers and sailors, were called upon deck.

When this species of summons was made, the officer inquired aloud the point of the brig's departure, of its route, of its landings, and to all these questions the captain replied without difficulty and without hesitation.   Then the officer began to pass in review all the persons, one after the other, and stopping when he came to milady, surveyed her very closely, but without addressing a single word to her.

He then went up to the captain, again said a few words to him ; and, as if from that moment the vessel was under his command, he ordered a manœuvre which the crew executed immediately.   Then the vessel resumed its course, still escorted by the little cutter, which sailed side by side with it, menacing it with the mouths of its six cannon ; the boat followed in the wake of the ship, a speck near the enormous mass.

During the examination of my lady by the officer, as may well be imagined, milady, on her part, was not less scrutinising in her glances. But, however great was the power of this woman, with eyes of flame, in reading the hearts of those whose secrets she wished to divine, she met this time with a countenance of such impassibility, that no discovery followed her investigation.   The officer who had stopped before her, and studied her with so much care, might have been about twenty-five or twenty-six years of age ; he was of pale complexion, with clear blue eyes, rather deeply set ; his mouth, fine and well cut, remained motionless in its correct lines ; his chin, strongly marked, denoted that strength of will which, in the ordinary Britannic type, denotes mostly nothing but obstinacy ; a brow a little receding, as is proper for poets, enthusiasts, and soldiers, was scarcely shaded by short thin hair, which, like the beard which covered the lower part of his face, was of a beautiful, deep chestnut colour.

When they entered the port, it was already night. The fog increased the darkness, and formed round the stern-lights and the lanterns of the jetty a circle like that which surrounds the moon when the weather threatens to become rainy. The air they breathed was heavy, humid, and cold.

Milady, that woman so courageous and firm, shivered in spite of herself.

The officer desired to have milady's packages pointed out to him, and ordered them to be placed in the boat : when this operation was completed, he invited her to descend by offering her his hand.

Milady looked at this man, and hesitated.

"Who are you, sir," asked she, "who have the kindness to occupy yourself so particularly on my account?"

"You may perceive, madame, by my uniform, that I am an officer in the English navy," replied the young man.

"But is it the custom for the officers in the English navy to place themselves at the service of their female compatriots, when they land in a port of Great Britain, and carry their gallantry so far as to conduct them ashore?"

"Yes, milady, it is the custom, not from gallantry but prudence, that in time of war, foreigners are conducted to particular hotels, in order that they may remain under the *surveillance* of the government, until perfect information be obtained relative to them."

These words were pronounced with the most exact politeness, and the most perfect calmness. Nevertheless, they had not the power of convincing milady.

"But I am not a foreigner, sir," said she, with an accent as pure as ever was heard between Portsmouth and Manchester ; "my name is Lady Clarik, and this measure——"

"This measure is general, madam ; and you will endeavour in vain to evade it."

"I will follow you, then, sir."

And accepting the hand of the officer, she commenced the descent of the ladder, at the foot of which the boat waited. The officer followed her. A large cloak was spread at the stern ; the officer requested her to sit down upon this cloak, and placed himself beside her.

"Row on !" said he, to the sailors.

The eight oars fell at once into the sea, making but one single sound, giving one single stroke, and the boat seemed to fly over the surface of the waters.

At the expiration of five minutes they gained the land.

The officer sprang out of the boat, and offered his hand to milady A carriage was in waiting.

" Is this carriage for us ?" asked milady.

" Yes, madame," replied the officer.

" The hotel, then, is at some distance ?"

" At the other end of the town."

" Very well," said milady ; and she got resolutely into the carriage.

The officer saw that the baggage was fastened carefully behind the carriage ; and this operation being performed, he took his place beside milady, and shut the door.

Immediately, without any order being given, or his place of destina-tion indicated, the coachman set off at a rapid pace, and plunged intc the streets of the town.

So strange a reception naturally gave milady ample matter for re-flection ; so, seeing that the young officer did not seem at all disposed for conversation, she reclined in her corner of the carriage ; and, one after the other, passed in review all the suppositions which presented themselves to her mind.

At the end of a quarter of an hour, however, surprised at the length of the journey, she leant forward towards the window to see whither she was being conducted. Houses were no longer to be seen ; trees appeared in the darkness like great black phantoms running after one another.

Milady shuddered with apprehension.

" But we are no longer in the town, sir," said she.

The young officer preserved profound silence.

" I beg you to understand, sir, I will go no further, unless you tell me whither you are taking me."

This threat obtained no reply.

" Oh ! but this is outrageous !" cried milady. " Help ! help ! help !"

No voice replied to hers ; the carriage continued to roll on with rapidity ; the officer appeared a statue.

Milady looked at the officer with one of those terrible expressions peculiar to her countenance, and which so rarely failed of their effect ; anger made her eyes flash in the darkness.

The young man remained impassible.

Milady endeavoured to open the door, in order to throw herself out.

" Take care, madam," said the young man, coldly, " you will kill your-self if you attempt to jump out."

Milady reseated herself, foaming with rage ; the officer leant forward, looked at her in his turn, and appeared surprised to see that face, but just before so beautiful, distorted with passion and become almost hideous. The artful creature at once comprehended that she was injuring her-self by allowing him thus to read her soul ; she collected her features, and in a complaining voice said :

" In the name of heaven, sir ! tell me if it is to you, if it is to your government, if it is to an enemy I am to attribute the violence that is done me ?"

"No violence will be offered to you, madame, and what happens to you is the result of a very simple measure which we are obliged to adopt with all who land in England."

"Then you don't know me, sir ?"

"It is the first time I have had the honour of seeing you."

"And, upon your honour, you have no cause of hatred against me ?"

"None, I swear to you."

There was so much serenity, coolness, mildness even, in the voice of the young man, that milady felt reassured.

At length, after a journey of near an hour, the carriage stopped before an iron gate, which enclosed an avenue leading to a château severe in form, massive and isolated. Then, as the wheels rolled over a fine gravel, milady could hear a vast roaring ; which she at once recognised as the noise of the sea, dashing against some steep coast.

The carriage passed under two arched gateways, and at length stopped in a large, dark, square court ; almost immediately, the door of the carriage was opened, the young man sprang lightly out and presented his hand to milady, who leant upon it, and in her turn alighted with tolerable calmness.

"Still, then, I am a prisoner," said milady, looking around her, and bringing back her eyes with a most gracious smile to the young officer ; "but I feel assured it will not be for long," added she ; "my own conscience and your politeness, sir, are the guarantees of that."

However flattering this compliment was, the officer made no reply ; but drawing from his belt a little silver whistle, such as boatswains use in ships of war, he whistled three times, with three different modulations :—immediately several men appeared, who unharnessed the smoking horses, and put the carriage into a coach-house.

The officer then, with the same calm politeness, invited the lady to enter the house. She, with a still smiling countenance, took his arm, and passed with him under a low arched door, which, by a vaulted passage, lighted only at the farther end, led to a stone staircase, turning round an angle of stone : they then came to a massive door, which, after the introduction of a key into the lock, by the young officer, turned heavily upon its hinges, and disclosed the chamber destined for milady.

With a single glance the prisoner took in the apartment in its minutest details. It was a chamber whose furniture was at once proper for a prisoner or a free man ; and yet, bars at the windows and outside bolts at the door decided the question in favour of the prison.

In an instant all the strength of mind of this creature, though drawn from the most vigorous sources, abandoned her ; she sank into a large chair, with her arms crossed, her head hanging down, and expecting every instant to see a judge enter to interrogate her.

But no one entered except two marines, who brought in her trunks and packages, deposited them in a corner of the room, and retired without speaking.

The officer presided over all these details with the same calmness milady had observed in him, never pronouncing a word, and making himself obeyed by a gesture of his hand or a sound of his whistle.

It might have been said that between this man and his inferiors spoken language did not exist, or had become useless.

At length milady could hold out no longer ; she broke the silence :

"In the name of Heaven, sir !" cried she, " what does all this that is passing mean ? Put an end to my doubts ; I have courage enough for any danger I can foresee, for every misfortune which I can comprehend Where am I, and why am I here ? if I am free, why these bars and these doors ? If I am a prisoner, what crime have I committed ?"

"You are here in the apartment destined for you, madam. I received orders to go and take charge of you at sea, and to conduct you to this château ; this order I believe, I have accomplished, with all the exactness of a soldier, but also with the courtesy of a gentleman. There terminates, at least to the present moment, the duty I had to fulfil towards you, the rest concerns another person."

"And who is that other person ?" asked milady, warmly ; " can you not tell me his name ?"

At the moment a great jingling of spurs was heard upon the stairs ; some voices passed, and faded away, and the sound of one footstep approached the door.

"That person is here, madam," said the officer, leaving the entrance open, and drawing himself up in an attitude of respect.

At the same time the door opened ; a man appeared in the opening. He was without a hat, wore a sword, and carried a handkerchief in his hand.

Milady thought she recognised this shadow in the shade ; she supported herself with one hand upon the arm of the chair, and advanced her head as if to meet a certainty.

The stranger advanced slowly, and as he advanced, after entering into the circle of light projected by the lamp, milady involuntarily drew back.

Then, when she had no longer any doubt :

"What ! my brother," cried she, in a state of stupor, " is it you ?"

"Yes, fair lady !" replied Lord de Winter, making a bow, half courteous, half ironical—" it is I, myself."

"But this château, then ?"

"Is mine."

"This chamber ?"

"Is yours."

"I am your prisoner, then ?"

"Nearly so."

"But this is a frightful abuse of power !"

"No high-sounding words ! let us sit down and chat quietly, as brother and sister ought to do."

Then, turning towards the door, and seeing that the young officer was waiting for his last orders :

"That is all quite well," said he, " I thank you ; now leave us alone, Master Felton."

CHAPTER L.

CHAT BETWEEN A BROTHER AND SISTER.

DURING the time that Lord de Winter took to shut the door, close a shutter, and draw a chair near to his sister-in-law's *fauteuil*, milady, anxiously thoughtful, plunged her glance into the depths of possibility, and discovered all the plan, of which she could not even get a glance as long as she was ignorant into whose hands she had fallen. She knew her brother to be a worthy gentleman, a bold hunter, an intrepid player, enterprising with women, but by no means remarkable for his skill in the business of intrigues. How had he discovered her arrival? caused her to be seized? Why did he detain her?

Athos had dropped some words which proved that the conversation she had had with the cardinal had fallen into strange ears; but she could not suppose that he had dug a counter mine so promptly and so boldly. She rather feared that her preceding operations in England might have been discovered. Buckingham might have guessed that it was she who had cut off the two studs, and avenged himself for that little treachery; but Buckingham was incapable of going to any excess against a woman, particularly if that woman was supposed to have acted from a feeling of jealousy.

This supposition appeared to her the most reasonable; it seemed that they wanted to revenge the past, and not to go to meet the future. At all events, she congratulated herself upon having fallen into the hands of her brother-in-law, with whom she reckoned she could deal very easily, rather than into the hands of a direct and intelligent enemy.

"Yes, let us chat, brother," said she, with a kind of cheerfulness, decided as she was to draw from the conversation, in spite of all the dissimulation Lord de Winter could bring to it, the information of which she stood in need to regulate her future conduct.

"You were, then, determined to come to England again," said Lord de Winter, "in spite of the resolutions you so often manifested in Paris never to set your foot more on British ground?"

Milady replied to this question by another question.

"Before everything," said she, "how happen you to have watched me so closely, as to be beforehand aware, not only of my arrival, but still more, of the day, the hour, and the port, at which I should arrive?"

Lord de Winter adopted the same tactics as milady, thinking that as his sister-in-law employed them they must be the best.

"But tell me, my dear sister," replied he, "what are you come to do in England?"

"Come for! why to see you," replied milady, without knowing how much she aggravated, by this reply, the suspicions which D'Artagnan's letter had given birth to in the mind of her brother-in-law, and only desiring to gain the good will of her auditor by a falsehood.

"Humph! to see me?" said De Winter, as if doubtingly.

"To be sure, to see you. What is there astonishing in that?"

"And you had no other object in coming to England but to see me,"

" No."

" So it was for my sake alone you have taken the trouble to cross the channel ?"

" For your sake only."

" The deuce ! what tenderness, my sister !"

" Why, am I not your nearest relation ?" demanded milady, with a tone of the most touching ingenuousness.

" And my only heir, are you not ?" said Lord de Winter in his turn, fixing his eyes on those of milady.

Whatever command she had over herself, milady could not help starting, and as, in pronouncing the last words, Lord de Winter placed his hand upon the arm of his sister, this start did not escape him.

In fact, the blow was direct and severe. The first idea that occurred to milady's mind was that she had been betrayed by Kitty, and that she had described to the baron the interested aversion of which she had imprudently allowed some marks to escape her before her servant ; she also recollected the furious and imprudent attack she had made upon D'Artagnan when he spared the life of her brother.

" I do not comprehend, my lord," said she, to gain time and make her adversary speak out. " What do you mean to say ? Is there any secret meaning concealed beneath your words ?"

" Oh ! good lord ! no," said Lord de Winter, with an apparent *bonhomie*, " you wish to see me, and you come to England. I learn this desire, or rather I suspect that you feel it, and, in order to spare you all the annoyances of a nocturnal arrival in a port, and all the fatigues of landing, I send one of my officers to meet you, I place a carriage at his orders, and he brings you hither to this castle, of which I am governor, whither I come every day, and where, in order to satisfy our mutual desire of seeing each other, I have prepared you a chamber. What is there more astonishing in all that I have said to you, than in that which you have told me ?"

" No, all that I think astonishing is that you should be aware of my coming."

" And yet that is the most simple thing in the world, my dear sister : have you not observed that the captain of your little vessel, on entering the road, sent forward, to obtain permission to enter the port, a little boat bearing his log-book and the register of his crew ? I am commandant of the port, they brought me that book. I recognised your name in it. My heart told me what your mouth has just confirmed, that is to say, with what view you have exposed yourself to the dangers of so perilous a sea, or at least so troublesome at this moment, and I sent my cutter to meet you. You know the rest."

Milady comprehended that Lord de Winter lied, and was only the more alarmed.

" Brother," continued she, " was not that Milord Buckingham whom I saw on the jetty, this evening, as we entered the port ?"

" Himself. Ah ! I can understand how the sight of him struck you," replied Lord de Winter : " you came from a country where he must be very much talked of, and I know that his armaments against France greatly engage the attention of your friend the cardinal."

"My friend the cardinal!" cried milady, seeing that, upon this point as upon the other, Lord de Winter seemed perfectly well informed.

"Is he not your friend?" replied the baron, negligently; "ah! I crave your pardon, I thought he was; but we will return to my lord duke presently, let us not depart from the sentimental turn our conversation had taken: you came, you say, to see me?"

"Yes."

"Well! I reply to you that you shall be attended to to the height of your wishes, and that we shall see each other every day."

"Am I then to remain here eternally?" demanded milady with terror.

"Do you find yourself ill-lodged, sister? Ask for anything you want, and I will hasten to have you furnished with it."

"But I have neither my women, nor my servants."

"You shall have all that, madame. Tell me on what footing your household was established by your first husband, and, although I am only your brother-in-law, I will arrange it upon a similar one."

"My first husband!" cried milady, looking at Lord de Winter, with eyes almost starting from their sockets.

"Yes, your French husband; I don't speak of my brother. If you have forgotten, as he is still living, I can write to him, and he will send me information on the subject."

A cold sweat burst from the brow of milady.

"You are joking!" said she in a hollow, broken voice.

"Do I look as if I were?" asked the baron, rising and going a step backward.

"Or rather you insult me," continued she, pressing with her stiffened hands the two arms of her chair, and raising herself up upon her wrists.

"I insult you!" said Lord de Winter with contempt; "in truth, madame, do you think that can be possible?"

"In truth, sir," said milady, "you must be either drunk or mad: leave the room, sir, and send me a woman."

"Women are very indiscreet, sister! cannot I serve you as a waiting maid? by that means, all our secrets would be kept in the family."

"Insolent wretch!" cried milady, and, as if acted upon by a spring, she rushed towards the baron, who awaited her attack with his arms crossed, but one hand upon the hilt of his sword.

"Come! come!" said he, "I know you are accustomed to assassinate people, but I shall defend myself, I give you notice, even against you."

"No doubt you would!" said she; "you have all the appearance of being coward enough to lift your hand against a woman."

"Perhaps I have, and I have an excuse, for mine would not be the first man's hand that has been placed upon you, I imagine."

And the baron pointed with a slow and accusing gesture to the left shoulder of milady, which he almost touched with his finger.

Milady uttered a deep inward shriek, and retreated to a corner of the room, like a panther which draws back to take its spring.

"Oh! groan and shriek as much as you please," cried Lord de Winter, "but don't try to bite, for I warn you the thing would be to your prejudice ; there are here no procureurs who regulate successions beforehand ; there is no knight-errant to come and seek a quarrel with me, on account of the fair lady I detain a prisoner ; but I have judges quite ready, who will quickly dispose of a woman so shameless, as, although already married, to come and steal, a bigamist, into the bed of my brother, and these judges, I warn you, will soon pass you over to a hangman that will make both your shoulders alike."

The eyes of milady darted such flashes, that although he was a man, and armed, before an unarmed woman, he felt the chill of fear glide through his whole frame ; he, however, not the less continued, but with increasing warmth :

"Yes, I can very well understand that after having inherited the fortune of my brother, it would be very agreeable to you to be my heir likewise ; but know, beforehand, if you kill me, or cause me to be killed, my precautions are taken : not a penny of what I possess will pass into your hands. Were you not already rich enough, you who possess nearly a million ? and could you not stop your fatal career, if you did not do evil for the supreme delight of doing it ? Oh ! be assured, if the memory of my brother were not sacred to me, you should rot in a state dungeon, or satisfy the curiosity of sailors at Tyburn : I will be silent, but you must endure your captivity quietly : in fifteen or twenty days I shall set out for La Rochelle, with the army ; but before my departure, a vessel which I will see sail, will take you hence and convey you to our colonies of the south ; and be assured that you shall be accompanied by one who will blow your brains out at the first attempt you may make to return to England or to the Continent."

Milady listened with an attention that dilated her inflamed eyes.

"Yes, at present," continued Lord de Winter, "you will remain in this castle : the walls of it are thick, the doors strong, and the bars solid ; besides which your window opens immediately over the sea : the men of my crew, who are devoted to me for life and death, mount guard around this apartment, and watch all the passages that lead to the castle-yard ; and even if you gained the yard, there would still be three iron gates for you to pass through. The word given is positive ; a step, a gesture, a word, on your part, denoting an effort to escape, and you are to be fired upon ; if they kill you, English justice will be under an obligation to me for having saved it trouble. Ah ! I see your features are resuming their calmness, your countenance is recovering its assurance : fifteen days, twenty days, say you, bah ! I have an inventive mind, before that is expired some idea will occur to me ; I have an infernal spirit, I shall meet with a victim. Before fifteen days are gone by, you say to yourself, I shall be away from here ! Well, try !"

Milady, finding her thoughts betrayed, dug her nails into her flesh, to subdue every emotion that might give to her physiognomy any expression beyond that of pain.

Lord de Winter continued :

"The officer who commands here in my absence you have already seen, and therefore know him ; he knows how, as you must have observed, to obey an order, for you did not, I am sure, come from Portsmouth hither without endeavouring to make him speak. What did you say to him ? Could a statue of marble have been more impassible and more mute ? You have already tried the power of your seductions upon many men, and, unfortunately, you have always succeeded ; but I give you leave to try them upon this one : pardieu ! if you succeed with him, I pronounce you the demon himself."

He went towards the door and opened it hastily.

"Call Master Felton," said he. "Wait a minute longer, and I will introduce him to you."

There followed between these two personages a strange silence, during which the sound of a slow and regular step was heard approaching ; shortly a human form appeared in the shade of the corridor, and the young lieutenant, with whom we are already acquainted, stopped at the door, to receive the orders of the baron.

"Come in, my dear John," said Lord de Winter, "come in, and shut the door."

The young officer entered.

"Now," said the baron, "look at this woman : she is young, she is beautiful, she possesses all earthly seductions. Well, she is a monster, who, at twenty-five years of age, has been guilty of as many crimes as you could read of in a year in the archives of our tribunals : her voice prejudices her hearers in her favour, her beauty serves as a bait to her victims, her body even pays what she promises—I must do her that justice : she will endeavour to seduce you, perhaps she will endeavour to kill you. I have extricated you from misery, Felton, I have caused you to be named lieutenant, I once saved your life, you know on what occasion ; I am for you not only a protector, but a friend ; not only a benefactor, but a father : this woman is come back again into England for the purpose of conspiring against my life ; I hold this serpent in my power ; well ! I call upon you, and say to you : Friend Felton, John, my child, guard me, and more particularly guard yourself against this woman : swear by your hopes of salvation to keep her safely for the chastisement she has merited. John Felton, I trust in thy word ! John Felton, I put faith in thy loyalty !"

"My lord," said the young officer, summoning to his mild countenance all the hatred he could find in his heart ; "my lord, I swear all shall be done as you desire."

Milady received this look like a resigned victim : it was impossible to imagine a more submissive or a more mild expression than that which prevailed on her beautiful countenance. Lord de Winter himself could scarcely recognise the tigress who, a minute before, appeared preparing for fight.

"She is not to leave this chamber, understand, John ; she is not to correspond with any one, she is to speak to no one but you—if you will do her the honour to address a word to her."

" That is quite sufficient, my lord !   I have sworn."

" And now, madam, try to make your peace with God, for you are adjudged by men !"

Milady let her head sink, as if crushed by this sentence. Lord de Winter went out, making a sign to Felton, who followed him, shutting the door after him.

One instant after, the heavy step of a marine was heard in the corridor ; his axe in his girdle and his musket on his shoulder, he commenced his watch.

Milady remained for some minutes in the same position, for she thought they might perhaps be examining her through the keyhole ; she then slowly raised her head, which had resumed its formidable expression of menace and defiance, ran to the door to listen, looked out of her window, and, returning to bury herself again in her large *fauteuil*,—

She reflected.

CHAPTER LI.

OFFICER.

In the meanwhile, the cardinal looked anxiously for news from England ; but no news arrived but such as were annoying and threatening.

Although La Rochelle was invested, however certain success might appear, thanks to the precautions taken, and above all to the dyke, which prevented the entrance of any vessel into the besieged city, the blockade might last for a long time yet ; which was a great affront to the king's arms, and a great inconvenience to the cardinal, who had no longer, it is true, to embroil Louis XIII. with Anne of Austria, for that affair was done, but he had to accommodate matters between M. de Bassompierre and the Duke d'Angoulême.

As to Monsieur, who had begun the siege, he left to the cardinal the task of finishing it.

The city, notwithstanding the incredible perseverance of its mayor, had attempted a sort of mutiny to surrender ; the mayor had hung the mutineers. This execution quieted the ill-disposed, who resolved to allow themselves to die of hunger, this death always appearing to them more slow and less sure than strangulation.

On their side, from time to time, the besiegers took the messengers which the Rochellais sent to Buckingham, or the spies which Buckingham sent to the Rochellais. In one case or the other, the trial was soon over. M. le Cardinal pronounced the single word—Hanged ! The king was invited to come and see the hanging. The king came languidly, placing himself in a good situation to see all the details : this amused him sometimes a little, and made him endure the siege with patience ; but it did not prevent his getting very tired, or from talking at every moment of returning to Paris ; so that if the messengers and the spies had failed, his eminence, notwithstanding all his imagination, would have found himself very much embarrassed.

Nevertheless, time passed on, and the Rochellais did not surrender; the last spy that was taken was the bearer of a letter. This letter told Buckingham that the city was at an extremity; but instead of adding, "If your succour does not arrive within fifteen days, we will surrender," it added, quite simply, "If your succour does not arrive within fifteen days, we shall be all dead with hunger when it does arrive."

The Rochellais, then, had no hope but in Buckingham—Buckingham was their Messiah. It was evident that if they one day learnt in a certain manner that they must not reckon upon Buckingham, their courage would fail with their hope.

He looked, then, with great impatience for the news from England which would announce to him that Buckingham would not come.

The question of carrying the city by assault, though often debated in the council of the king, had been always rejected. In the first place, La Rochelle appeared impregnable; then the cardinal, whatever he might have said, very well knew that the horror of the blood shed in this rencounter, in which Frenchmen would combat against Frenchmen, was a retrograde movement of sixty years impressed upon his policy, and the cardinal was at that period what we now call a man of progress. In fact, the sacking of La Rochelle, and the assassination of three or four thousand insurgents who would allow themselves to be killed, would resemble too closely, in 1628, the Massacre of St. Bartholomew in 1572; and then, above all this, this extreme measure, to which the king, good Catholic as he was, was not at all repugnant, always fell before this argument of the besieging generals,—La Rochelle is impregnable except by famine.

The cardinal could not drive from his mind the fear he entertained of his terrible emissary, for he comprehended the strange qualities of this woman, sometimes a serpent, sometimes a lion. Had she betrayed him? Was she dead? He knew her well enough in all cases to know that, whilst acting for him or against him, as a friend or an enemy, she would not remain motionless without great impediments; but whence did these impediments arise? That was what he could not know.

And yet he reckoned, and with reason, on milady. He had divined in the past of this woman the terrible things which his red mantle alone could cover; and he felt that, from one cause or another, this woman was his own, as she could look to no other but himself for a support superior to the danger which threatened her.

He resolved, then, to carry on the war alone, and to look for no success foreign to himself, but as we look for a fortunate chance. He continued to press the raising of the famous dyke, which was to starve La Rochelle; in the meanwhile, he cast his eyes over that unfortunate city, which contained so much deep misery and so many heroic virtues, and recalling the saying of Louis XI., his political predecessor, as he himself was the predecessor of Robespierre, he repeated this maxim of Tristan's gossip: "Divide to reign."

Henry IV., when besieging Paris, had loaves and provisions thrown over the walls; the cardinal had little notes thrown over, in which he represented to the Rochellais how unjust, selfish, and barbarous was the conduct of their leaders ; these leaders had corn in abundance, and would not let them partake of it ; they adopted as a maxim,—for they, too, had maxims,—that it was of very little consequence that women, children, and old men should die, so long as the men who were to defend the walls remained strong and healthy.　Up to that time, whether from devotedness, or from want of power to react against it, this maxim, without being generally adopted, was, nevertheless, passed from theory to practice ; but the notes did it injury.　The notes reminded the men that the children, women, and old men whom they allowed to die, were their sons, their wives, and their fathers ; and that it would be more just for every one to be reduced to the common misery, in order that one same position should give birth to unanimous resolutions.

These notes had all the effect that he who wrote them could expect, in that they induced a great number of the inhabitants to open private negotiations with the royal army.

But at the moment when the cardinal saw his means already fructify, and applauded himself for having put it in action, an inhabitant of Rochelle, who had contrived to pass the Royal lines, God knows how, such was the watchfulness of Bassompierre, Schomberg, and the Duke d'Angoulême, themselves watched over by the cardinal—an inhabitant of Rochelle, we say, entered the city, coming from Portsmouth, and saying, that he had seen a magnificent fleet ready to sail within a week. Still further, Buckingham announced to the mayor, that at length the great league was about to declare itself against France, and that the kingdom would be at once invaded by the English, Imperial and Spanish armies.　This letter was read publicly in all the places of the city, copies were put up at the corners of the streets, and they even who had begun to open negotiations interrupted them, being resolved to await the succour so pompously announced.

This unexpected circumstance brought back Richelieu's former inquietudes, and forced him, in spite of himself, once more to turn his eyes to the other side of the sea.

During this time, exempt from these inquietudes of its only and true leader, the royal army led a joyous life, neither provisions nor money being wanting in the camp ; all the corps rivalled each other in audacity and gaiety.　To take spies and hang them, to make hazardous expeditions upon the dyke or the sea, to imagine wild plans, and to execute them coolly, such was the pastime which made the army find these days short, which were not only so long for the Rochellais, a prey to famine and anxiety, as even for the cardinal, who blockaded them so closely.

Sometimes when the cardinal, always on horseback, like the lowest gendarme of the army, cast a pensive glance over those works, so slowly keeping pace with his wishes, which the engineers, brought from all the corners of France, were executing under his orders, if he met a musketeer of the company of Tréville, he drew near and looked at him in a peculiar manner, and not recognising in him one of our four companions, he turned his penetrating look and profound thoughts in another direction.

One day, on which, oppressed with a mortal weariness of mind, without hope in the negotiations with the city, without news from England, the cardinal went out, without any other aim but to go out, accompanied only by Cahusac and La Houdinière, strolling along the beach. Mingling the immensity of his dreams with the immensity of the ocean, he arrived, his horse going at a foot's pace, on a hill, from the top of which he perceived, behind a hedge, reclining on the sand, and catching in its passage one of those rays of the sun so rare at this period of the year, seven men surrounded by empty bottles. Four of these men were our musketeers, preparing to listen to a letter one of them had just received. This letter was so important, that it made them abandon their cards and their dice on the drum-head.

The other three were occupied in opening an enormous flagon of Collicure wine ; these were the lackeys of these gentlemen.

The cardinal was, as we have said, in very low spirits, and nothing, when he was in that state of mind, increased his depression so much as gaiety in others. Besides, he had another strange fancy, which was always to believe that the causes of his sadness created the gaiety of others. Making a sign to La Houdinière and Cahusac to stop, he alighted from his horse, and went towards these suspected merry companions, hoping, by means of the sand which deadened the sound of his steps, and of the hedge which concealed his approach, to catch some words of this conversation which appeared so interesting ; at ten paces from the hedge he recognised the talkative Gascon, and as he had already perceived that these men were musketeers, he did not doubt that the three others were those called the inseparables, that is to say, Athos, Porthos, and Aramis.

It may be supposed that his desire to hear the conversation was augmented by this discovery ; his eyes took a strange expression, and with the step of a tiger-cat, he advanced towards the hedge ; but he had not been able to catch more than a few vague syllables without any positive sense, when a sonorous and short cry made him start, and attracted the attention of the musketeers.

" Officer !" cried Grimaud.

"You are speaking, you scoundrel !" said Athos, rising upon his elbow, and fascinating Grimaud with his angry look.

Grimaud therefore added nothing to his speech, but contented himself with pointing his index finger in the direction of the hedge, denouncing by this gesture the cardinal and his escort.

With a single bound the musketeers were on their feet, and saluted with respect.

The cardinal seemed furious.

" It appears that messieurs the musketeers keep guard," said he. " Are the English expected by land, or do the musketeers consider themselves superior officers ?"

" Monseigneur," replied Athos, for, amidst the general fright he alone

had preserved the noble calmness and coolness that never forsook him,
—"monseigneur, the musketeers, when they are not on duty, or when
their duty is over, drink and play at dice, and they are certainly superior
officers for their lackeys."

"Lackeys!" grumbled the cardinal; "lackeys, who have the word given
to warn their masters when any one passes, are not lackeys, they are
sentinels."

"Your Eminence may perceive that, if we had not taken this precaution, we should have been exposed to allowing you to pass without presenting you our respects, or offering you our thanks for the favour you
have done us in uniting us. D'Artagnan," continued Athos, "you, who
but lately were so anxious for such an opportunity for expressing your
thanks to monseigneur, here it is, avail yourself of it."

These words were pronounced with that imperturbable phlegm which
distinguished Athos in the hour of danger, and with that excessive
politeness which made of him, at certain moments, a king more majestic
than kings by birth.

D'Artagnan came forward and stammered out a few words of gratitude, which soon expired under the gloomy looks of the cardinal.

"It does not signify, gentlemen," continued the cardinal, without
appearing to be in the least diverted from his first intention by the incident which Athos had started—"it does not signify, gentlemen; I do
not like simple soldiers, because they have the advantage of serving in
a privileged corps, thus to play the great lords; discipline is the same
for them as for everybody else."

Athos allowed the cardinal to finish his sentence completely, and,
bowing in sign of assent, he resumed in his turn:

"Discipline, monseigneur, has, I hope, in no way been forgotten by
us. We are not on duty, and we believe that not being on duty we were
at liberty to dispose of our time as we pleased. If we are so fortunate
as to have some particular duty to perform for your Eminence, we are
ready to obey you. Your Eminence may perceive," continued Athos,
knitting his brow, for this sort of investigation began to annoy him,
"that we have not come out without our arms."

And he showed the cardinal, with his finger, the four muskets, piled
near the drum upon which were the cards and dice.

"Your Eminence may believe," added D'Artagnan, "that we would
have come to meet you, if we could have supposed it was monseigneur
coming towards us with so few attendants."

The cardinal bit his moustache, and even his lips a little.

"Do you know what you look like, all together, as you are, armed, and
guarded by your lackeys?" said the cardinal: "you look like four con-
spirators."

"Oh! so far, monseigneur, that's true," said Athos; "we do conspire,
as your Eminence might have seen the other day, only we conspire
against the Rochellais."

"Aye! aye! *messieurs les politiques!*" replied the cardinal, knitting
his brow in his turn, "the secret of many unknown things might per-

haps be found in your brains, if we could read in them, as you were reading that letter which you concealed as soon as you saw me coming."

The colour mounted to the face of Athos, and he made a step towards his Eminence.

"We might be led to think that you really suspected us, monseigneur, and that we were undergoing a real interrogatory; if it be so, we trust your Eminence will deign to explain yourself, and we should then at least be acquainted with our real position."

"And if it were an interrogatory," replied the cardinal, "others besides you have undergone such, Monsieur Athos, and have replied to them."

"Thus, I have told your Eminence that you had but to question us, and we are ready to reply."

"What was that letter you were about to read, Monsieur Aramis, and which you so promptly concealed?"

"A woman's letter, monseigneur."

"Ah! yes, I understand, we must be discreet with this sort of letters; but nevertheless, we may show them to a confessor, and, you know, I have taken orders."

"Monseigneur," said Athos, with a calmness the more terrible, from his risking his head when he made this reply, "the letter is a woman's letter, but it is neither signed Marion de Lorme, nor Madame d'Arguillon."

The cardinal became as pale as death; a fiery gleam darted from his eyes; he turned round as if to give an order to Cahusac and Houdinière. Athos saw the movement; he made a step towards the muskets, upon which the other three friends had fixed their eyes as men ill-disposed to allow themselves to be taken. The cardinal's party consisted of only three; the musketeers, lackeys included, numbered seven; he judged that the match would be so much the less equal, if Athos and his companions were really plotting; and by one of those rapid turns which he always had at command, all his anger faded away into a smile.

"Well! well!" said he, "you are brave young men, proud in daylight, faithful in darkness; we can find no fault with you for watching over yourselves, when you watch so carefully over others. Gentlemen, I have not forgotten the night in which you served me as an escort to the Colombier Rouge : if there were any danger to be apprehended on the road I am going, I would request you to accompany me ; but as there is none, remain where you are, finish your bottles, your game, and your letter. Adieu, gentlemen!"

And remounting his horse, which Cahusac led to him, he saluted them with his hand, and rode away.

The four young men, standing and motionless, followed him with their eyes, without speaking a single word, until he had disappeared.

Then they looked at each other.

The countenances of all gave evidence of terror; for, notwithstanding the friendly adieu of his Eminence, they plainly perceived that the cardinal went away with rage in his heart.

Athos alone smiled with a self-possessed, disdainful smile.

When the cardinal was out of hearing and sight,—

"That Grimaud kept bad watch!" cried Porthos, who had a great inclination to vent his ill-humour on somebody.

Grimaud was about to reply to excuse himself. Athos lifted his finger, and Grimaud was silent.

"Would you have given up the letter, Aramis?" said D'Artagnan.

"I!" said Aramis, in his most flute-like tone; "I had made up my mind; if he had insisted upon the letter being given up to him, I would have presented the letter to him with one hand, and with the other I would have run my sword through his body."

"I expected as much," said Athos; "and that was why I threw myself between you and him. In good truth, this man is very much to blame to talk in this manner to other men; one would say he had never had to do with any but women and children."

"My dear Athos, I admire your behaviour very much, but nevertheless, we were in the wrong, after all."

"How, in the wrong!" said Athos. "Whose, then, is the air we breathe? Whose is the ocean upon which we look? Whose is the sand upon which we were reclining? Whose is that letter of your mistress's? Do these belong to the cardinal? Upon my honour, this man fancies the world belongs to him; there you stood, stammering, stupefied, annihilated! one might have supposed that the Bastille appeared before you, and that the gigantic Medusa had converted you into stone. Is being in love conspiring? You are in love with a woman whom the cardinal has caused to be shut up, and you wish to get her out of the hands of his Eminence; that's a match you are playing with the cardinal: this letter is your game, why should you expose your game to your adversary? That is never done. Let him find it out if he can! We can find out his!"

"Well, that's all very sensible, Athos," said D'Artagnan.

"In that case, let there be no more question of what's past, and let Aramis resume the letter from his cousin, where the cardinal interrupted him."

Aramis drew the letter from his pocket, the three friends surrounded him, and the three lackeys grouped themselves again near the wine-jar.

"You had only read a line or two," said D'Artagnan; "begin the letter again, then."

"Willingly," said Aramis.

"MY DEAR COUSIN,—I think I shall make up my mind to set out for Stenay, where my sister has placed our little servant in the convent of the Carmelites; this poor child is quite resigned, as she knows she cannot live elsewhere without the salvation of her soul being in danger. Nevertheless, if the affairs of your family are arranged, as we hope they will be, I believe she will run the risk of being damned, and will return to those she regrets, particularly as she knows they are always thinking of her. In the meanwhile, she is not very wretched ; what she most desires is a letter from her intended. I know that such sort of provisions pass with difficulty through convent gratings ; but after all, as I have given you proofs, my dear cousin, I am not unskilled in such affairs, and I will take charge of the commission. My sister thanks you for your good and eternal remembrance. She has experienced much inquietude ; but she is now at length a little re-assured, having sent her secretary yonder, in order that nothing may happen unexpectedly.

"Adieu, my dear cousin ; let us hear from you as often as you can, that is to say, as often as you can with safety. I embrace you.

" MARY MICHON."

"Oh ! what do I not owe you, Aramis ?" said D'Artagnan. " Dear Constance ! I have at length, then, intelligence of you ; she lives, she is in safety in a convent, she is at Stenay ! Where is Stenay, Athos ?"

" Why, a few leagues from the frontiers of Alsace, in Lorraine ; the siege once over, we shall be able to make a tour in that direction."

"And that will not be long, it is to be hoped," said Porthos ; "for they have this morning hung a spy who confessed that the Rochellais had come to the leather of their shoes. Supposing, that after having eaten the leather they eat the soles, I cannot see anything else they have left, unless they eat one another."

" Poor fools !" said Athos, emptying a glass of excellent Bordeaux wine, which, without having, at that period, the reputation it now enjoys, merited it no less : " poor fools ! as if the Catholic religion was not the most advantageous and the most agreeable of all religions ! It's all one," resumed he, after having smacked his tongue against his palate, " they are brave fellows ! But what the devil are you about, Aramis ?" continued Athos ; " why, you are squeezing that letter into your pocket !"

" Yes," said D'Artagnan, " Athos is right, it must be burnt ; and yet if we burn it, who knows whether Monsieur le Cardinal has not a secret to interrogate ashes ?"

" He must have one," said Athos.

" What will you do with the letter, then ?" asked Porthos.

" Come here, Grimaud," said Athos. " As a punishment for having spoken without permission, my friend, you will please to eat this piece of paper ; then to recompense you for the service you will have rendered us, you shall afterwards drink this glass of wine ; here is the letter, first, eat heartily."

Grimaud smiled ; and with his eyes fixed upon the glass which Athos held in his hand, he ground the paper well between his teeth, and then swallowed it.

" Bravo ! Master Grimaud !" said Athos, " and now take this; that's well ! we dispense with your saying thank you."

Grimaud silently swallowed the glass of Bordeaux wine : but his eyes raised towards heaven spoke, during the whole time this delicious occupation lasted, a language which, for being mute, was not the less expressive.

" And now," said Athos, " unless Monsieur le Cardinal should form the ingenious idea of ripping up Grimaud, I think we may be pretty much at our ease respecting the letter."

In the meantime his Eminence continued his melancholy ride, murmuring between his moustaches :

" These four men must positively be mine."

CHAPTER LII.

THE FIRST DAY OF CAPTIVITY.

LET us return to milady, whom a glance thrown upon the coast of France has made us lose sight of for an instant.

We shall find her still in the despairing attitude in which we left her, plunged in an abyss of dismal reflections, a dark hell, at the gate of which she has almost left hope behind ; for, for the first time she doubts, for the first time she fears.

On two occasions her fortune has failed her, on two occasions she has found herself discovered and betrayed ; and on these two occasions, it was before the fatal genius, sent doubtlessly by Heaven to combat her, that she has succumbed : D'Artagnan has conquered her ; her, that invincible power of evil.

He has deceived her in her love, humbled her in her pride, thwarted her in her ambition, and now he ruins her fortune, deprives her of liberty, and even threatens her life. Still more, he has lifted the corner of her mask, that ægis with which she covered herself, and which rendered her so strong.

D'Artagnan has turned aside from Buckingham, whom she hates as she hates all she has loved, the tempest with which Richelieu threatened him in the person of the queen. D'Artagnan had passed himself upon her as De Wardes, for whom she had conceived one of those tigress-like fancies common to women of her character. D'Artagnan knows that terrible secret which she has sworn no one shall know without dying. In short, at the moment in which she has just obtained from Richelieu a *carte blanche* by the means of which she is about to take vengeance on her enemy, this precious paper is torn from her hands, and it is D'Artagnan who holds her prisoner, and is about to send her to some filthy Botany Bay, some infamous Tyburn of the Indian Ocean.

All this she owes to D'Artagnan, without doubt ; from whom can come so many disgraces heaped upon her head, if not from him ? He alone could have transmitted to Lord de Winter all these frightful secrets, which he has discovered, one after another, by a train of fatalities. He knows her brother-in-law, he must have written to him.

What hatred she distils ! There, motionless, with her burning, fixed glances in her desert apartment, how well the outbursts of passion, which at times escape from the depths of her chest with her respiration, accompany the sound of the surge which rises, growls, roars, and breaks itself, like an eternal and powerless despair, against the rocks upon which is built this dark and lofty castle ! How many magnificent projects of vengeance she conceives by the light of the flashes which her tempestuous passion casts over her mind, against Madame Bonacieux, against Buckingham, but, above all, against D'Artagnan—projects lost in the distance of the future !

Yes, but in order to avenge herself she must be free ; and to be free, a prisoner has to pierce a wall, detach bars, cut through a floor—all undertakings which a patient and strong man may accomplish, but before which the feverish irritations of a woman must give way. Besides, to do all this, time is necessary,—months, years—and she has ten or twelve days, as Lord de Winter, her fraternal and terrible gaoler, told her.

And yet, if she were a man, she would attempt all this, and, perhaps, might succeed ; why, then, did heaven make the mistake of placing that manlike soul in that frail and delicate body ?

The first moments of her captivity were terrible ; a few convulsions of rage which she could not suppress paid her debt of feminine weakness to nature. But by degrees she overcame the outbursts of her mad passion ; the nervous tremblings which agitated her frame disappeared, and she remained folded within herself, like a fatigued serpent reposing.

"Why, I must have been mad to allow myself to be carried away so," says she, plunging into the glass, which reflects back to her eyes the burning glance by which she appears to interrogate herself. "No violence ; violence is the proof of weakness. In the first place, I have never succeeded by that means ; perhaps if I employed my strength against women, I should have a chance to find them weaker than myself, and consequently to conquer them. But it is with men that my struggle is, and I am but a woman for them. Let us struggle like a woman, then ; my strength is in my weakness."

Then, as if to render an account to herself of the changes she could impose upon her countenance, so mobile and so expressive, she made it take all expressions, from that of passionate anger, which convulsed her features, to that of the most sweet, most affectionate, and most seducing smile. Then her hair assumed successively, under her skilful hands, all the undulations she thought might assist the charms of her face. At length she murmured, satisfied with herself :

"Come, nothing is lost. I am still beautiful."

It was then nearly eight o'clock in the evening. Milady perceived a bed ; she calculated that the repose of a few hours would not only refresh her head and her ideas, but still further, her complexion. A better idea, however, came into her mind, before going to bed. She had heard something said about supper. She had already been an hour in this apartment ; they could not be long before they brought her her repast. The prisoner was determined not to lose any time ; she resolved to make that very evening some attempts to ascertain the nature of the ground she had to work upon, by studying the characters of the people to whose guardianship she was committed.

A light appeared under the door ; this light announced the reappearance of her gaolers. Milady, who had arisen, threw herself quickly into the *fauteuil*, her head thrown back, her beautiful hair unbound and dishevelled, her bosom half bare beneath her crumpled laces, one hand on her heart and the other hanging down.

The bolts were drawn, the door groaned upon its hinges, steps sounded in the chamber and drew near.

" Place that table there," said a voice, which the prisoner recognised as the voice of Felton.

The order was obeyed.

" You will bring lights, and relieve the sentinel," continued Felton.

And this double order which the young man gave to the same individuals, proved to milady that her servants were the same men as her guards—that is to say, soldiers.

Felton's orders were, for the rest, executed with a silent rapidity that gave a good idea of the state in which he kept up discipline.

At length Felton, who had not looked at milady, turned towards her.

" Ah ! ah !" said he, " she is asleep, that's well ; when she wakes she can sup."   And he made some steps towards the door.

" But, my lieutenant !" said a soldier, a little less stoical than his officer, and who had approached milady, " this woman is not asleep."

" What ! not asleep !" said Felton, " what is she doing then ?"

" She has fainted away ; her face is very pale, and I have listened in vain ; I can't hear her breathe."

" You are right," said Felton, after having looked at milady from the spot on which he stood, without moving a step towards her : " Go and tell Lord de Winter that his prisoner has fainted.   The case not having been foreseen, I don't know what to do."

The soldier went out to obey the orders of his officer ; Felton sat down upon the *fauteuil* which was by chance near the door, and waited without speaking a word, without making a gesture.   Milady possessed that great art, so much studied by women, of looking through her long eye-lashes without appearing to open the lids ; she perceived Felton, who sat with his back towards her.   She continued to look at him during nearly ten minutes, and in these ten minutes the impassible guardian never turned round once.

She then thought that Lord de Winter would come, and by his presence give fresh strength to her gaoler : her first trial was lost ; she acted like a woman who reckons upon her resources ; she consequently raised her head, opened her eyes, and sighed deeply.

At this sigh Felton turned round.

" Ah ! you have awakened again, madame," he said ; " then I have nothing more to do here.   If you want anything, you can ring."

" Oh ! my God ! my God ! how I have suffered," said milady, in that harmonious voice, which, like that of the ancient enchantresses, charmed all those they wished to destroy.

And she assumed, upon sitting up in the *fauteuil*, a still more grace-ful and voluptuous position than that she had exhibited when reclining.

Felton rose.

" You will be served thus, madame, three times a day," said he ; "in the morning at nine o'clock, in the day at one o'clock, and in the evening at eight. If that does not suit you, you can point out what other hours you prefer, and in this respect your wishes will be complied with."

" But am I to remain always alone in this vast and dismal chamber ?" asked milady.

" A woman of the neighbourhood has been sent for, who will be to-morrow at the castle, and will return as often as you desire her presence."

" I thank you, sir," replied the prisoner, humbly.

Felton made a slight bow, and directed his steps towards the door. At the moment he was about to go out, Lord de Winter appeared in the corridor, followed by the soldier who had been sent to inform him of the fainting of milady. He held a phial of salts in his hand.

" Well, what's going on here ?" said he, in a jeering voice, on seeing the prisoner sitting up, and Felton about to go out. " Is this dead woman come to life again already ? Pardieu, Felton, my lad, did you not perceive that you were taken for a novice, and that the first act was being performed of a comedy of which we shall doubtless have the pleasure of following out all the developments ?"

" I imagined that might be the case, my lord," said Felton ; "but as the prisoner is a woman, after all, I wished to pay her the attention that every man of gentle birth owes to a woman, if not on her account, at least on my own."

Milady shuddered through her whole system. These words of Felton's passed like ice through her veins.

" So," replied De Winter, laughing, "that beautiful hair so skilfully dishevelled, that white skin and that languishing look, have not yet seduced you, you heart of stone ?"

" No, my lord," replied the impassible young man ; "your lordship may be assured that it requires more than the tricks and coquetry of a woman to corrupt me."

" In that case, my brave lieutenant, let us leave milady to find out something else, and go to supper ; but remember she has a fruitful imagination, and the second act of the comedy will not be long after the first."

And at these words Lord de Winter passed his arm through that of Felton, and led him out, laughing.

" Oh ! I will be a match for you !" murmured milady between her teeth : " be assured of that, you poor should-be monk, you poor con-verted soldier, who have cut your uniform out of a monk's frock !"

" Apropos," resumed De Winter, stopping at the door, " you must not, milady, let this check take away your appetite. Taste that fowl and those fish ; 'pon honour, they are not poisoned. I agree very well with my cook, and he is not to be my heir, I have full and perfect confidence in him. Do as I do. Adieu! dear sister! till your next fainting fit!"

This was all that milady could endure : her hands became clenched, she ground her teeth inwardly, her eyes followed the motion of the door as it closed behind Lord de Winter and Felton, and the moment she was alone a fresh fit of despair seized her ; she cast her eyes upon the table, saw the glittering of a knife, rushed towards it and clutched it ; but her disappointment was cruel : the blade was blunt, and of flexible silver.

A burst of laughter resounded from the other side of the ill-closed door, and the door was reopened.

"Ha ! ha ! ha !" cried Lord de Winter ; "Ha ! ha ! ha ! don't you see, my brave Felton ! don't you see what I told you? That knife was for you, my lad ; she would have killed you. Observe, this is one of her peculiarities, to get rid thus, after one fashion or another, of all the people who inconvenience her. If I had listened to you, the knife would have been pointed and of steel. Then it would have been all over with Felton ; she would have cut your throat, and, after that, the throat of everybody else. Look at her, John, see how well she knows how to handle a knife."

In fact, milady still held the harmless weapon in her clenched hand, but these last words, this supreme insult, relaxed her hands, her strength, and even her will. The knife fell to the ground.

"You were right, my lord," said Felton, with a tone of profound disgust, which sounded to the very bottom of the heart of milady ; " you were right, my lord ; I was in the wrong."

And both left the room afresh.

But this time milady lent a more attentive ear than the first, and she heard their steps die away in the distance of the corridor.

"I am lost," murmured she ; "I am lost ! I am in the power of men upon whom I can have no more influence than upon statues of bronze or granite ; they know me by heart, and are cuirassed against all my weapons. It is, however, impossible that this should end as they have decreed !"

In fact, as this last reflection, this instinctive return to hope indicated, sentiments of weakness or fear did not dwell long in her ardent spirit. Milady sat down to table, ate of several dishes, drank a little Spanish wine, and felt all her resolution return.

Before she went to bed, she had commented upon, analyzed, turned on all sides, examined on all points, the words, the gestures, the signs, and even the silence of her interlocutors, and from this profound, skilful, and anxious study, it resulted that Felton was, everything considered, the more vulnerable of her two persecutors.

One expression above all recurred to the mind of the prisoner :

" If I had listened to you," Lord de Winter had said to Felton.

Felton then had spoken in her favour, since Lord de Winter had not been willing to listen to Felton.

" Weak or strong," repeated milady, " that man has a spark of pity in his soul ; of that spark I will make a flame that shall devour him.

" As to the other, he knows me, he fears me, and knows what he has to expect of me, if ever I escape from his hands, it is useless then to attempt anything with him.

" But, Felton, that's another thing ; he is a young, ingenuous, pure man, who seems virtuous ; him there are means of destroying."

And milady went to bed and fell asleep, with a smile upon her lips. Any one who had seen her sleeping, might have said she was a young girl dreaming of the crown of flowers she was to wear on her brow at the next fête.

CHAPTER LIII.

THE SECOND DAY OF CAPTIVITY.

MILADY dreamed that she at length had D'Artagnan in her power, that she was present at his execution, and it was the sight of his odious blood, flowing beneath the axe of the executioner, which spread that charming smile upon her lips.

She slept as a prisoner sleeps who is rocked by his first hope.

In the morning, when they entered her chamber, she was still in bed. Felton remained in the corridor ; he brought with him the woman of whom he had spoken the evening before, and who had just arrived ; this woman entered, and approaching milady's bed, offered her services.

Milady was habitually pale ; her complexion might therefore deceive a person who saw her for the first time.

" I am in a fever," said she ; " I have not slept a single instant during all this long night—I am in frightful pain : are you likely to be more humane to me than others were to me yesterday ? All I ask is, permission to remain in bed."

" Would you like to have a physician sent for ?" said the woman.

Felton listened to this dialogue without speaking a word.

Milady reflected, that the more people she had around her, the more she should have to work upon, and the more strict would be the watch Lord de Winter kept over her ; besides, the physician might declare the malady was feigned, and milady, after having lost the first trick of the game, was not willing to lose the second.

" Go and fetch a physician !" said she ; " what could be the good of that ? These gentlemen declared yesterday that my illness was a comedy ; it would be just the same to-day, no doubt ; for, since yesterday evening they have had plenty of time to send for a doctor."

" Then," said Felton, who became impatient, " say yourself, madame, what treatment you wish to be pursued."

" Eh ! how can I tell? My God ! I know that I am in pain, that's all : give me anything you like, it is of very little consequence to me."

" Go and fetch Lord de Winter," said Felton, tired of these eternal complaints.

" Oh ! no, no !" cried milady ; " no, sir, do not call him, I conjure you.   I am well, I want nothing ; do not call him."

She gave so much vehemence, such prevailing eloquence to this ex-clamation, that Felton, in spite of himself, advanced some steps into the room.

" He is come !" thought milady.

" If you *really* are in pain," said Felton, "a physician shall be sent for ; and if you deceive us, well ! why it will be the worse for you, but at least we shall not have to reproach ourselves with anything."

Milady made no reply, but turning her beautiful head round upon her pillow, she burst into tears, and uttered heart-breaking sobs.

Felton surveyed her for an instant with his usual impassibility ; then, seeing that the crisis threatened to be prolonged, he went out ; the woman followed him, and Lord de Winter did not appear.

" I fancy I begin to see my way," murmured milady, with a savage joy, burying herself under the clothes to conceal from anybody who might be watching her, this burst of inward satisfaction.

Two hours passed away.

" Now it is time that the malady should be over," said she ; " let me rise, and obtain some success this very day ; I have but ten days, and this evening two of them will be gone."

In the morning, when the woman and Felton came, they had brought her breakfast ; now she thought they could not be long before they came to clear the table, and that Felton would then come back.

Milady was not deceived: Felton reappeared, and without observing whether she had or had not touched her repast, he made a sign that the table should be carried out of the room, it being brought in ready covered.

Felton remained behind : he held a book in his hand.

Milady, reclining in a *fauteuil*, near the chimney, beautiful, pale, and resigned, looked like a holy virgin awaiting martyrdom.

Felton approached her, and said :

" Lord de Winter, who is a Catholic, as well as yourself, madame, thinking that the privation of the rites and ceremonies of your church might be painful to you, has consented that you should read every day the ordinary of *your mass*, and here is a book which contains the ritual of it."

At the manner in which Felton laid the book upon the little table near which milady was sitting, at the tone in which he pronounced the two words *your mass*, at the disdainful smile with which he accom-panied them, milady raised her head, and looked more attentively at the officer.

Then, by that plain arrangement of the hair, by that costume of extreme simplicity, by the brow polished like marble, but as hard and impenetrable as it, she recognised one of those dark Puritans she had so often met with, as well at the court of King James as that of the king of France, where, in spite of the remembrance of the Saint Bartholo-mew, they sometimes came to seek refuge,

She then had one of those sudden inspirations which people of genius alone have in great crises, in supreme moments which are to decide their fortunes or their lives.

Those two words, *your mass*, and a simple glance cast upon Felton, revealed to her all the importance of the reply she was about to make.

But, with that rapidity of intelligence which was peculiar to her, this reply, ready arranged, presented itself to her lips :

" I !" said she, with an accent of disdain in unison with that which she had remarked in the voice of the young officer, " I, sir ; *my mass!* Lord de Winter, the corrupted Catholic, knows very well that I am not of his religion, and this is a snare he wishes to lay for me !"

" And of what religion are you, then, madame ?" asked Felton, with an astonishment which, in spite of the empire he held over himself, he could not entirely conceal.

" I will tell it," cried milady, with a feigned exultation, " on the day when I shall have suffered sufficiently for my faith."

The look of Felton revealed to milady the full extent of the space she had opened for herself by this single word.

The young officer, however, remained mute and motionless ; his look alone had spoken.

" I am in the hands of mine enemies," continued she, with that tone of enthusiasm which she knew was familiar to the Puritans : " well, let my God save me, or let me perish for my God! That is the reply I beg you to make to Lord de Winter. And as to this book," added she, pointing to the ritual with her finger, but without touching it, as if she must be contaminated by the touch, " you may carry it back and make use of it yourself ; for, doubtless, you are doubly the accomplice of Lord de Winter ; the accomplice in his persecutions, the accomplice in his heresies."

Felton made no reply, took the book with the same appearance of repugnance which he had before manifested, and retired pensively.

Lord de Winter came towards five o'clock in the evening ; milady had had time, during the whole day, to trace her plan of conduct. She received him like a woman who had already recovered all her advantages.

" It appears," said the baron, seating himself in the *fauteuil* opposite to that occupied by milady, and stretching out his legs carelessly upon the hearth, " it appears we have made a little apostasy !"

" What do you mean, sir ?"

" I mean to say that, since we last met, you have changed your religion ; you have not, by chance, married a Protestant for a third husband, have you ?"

" Explain yourself, my lord," replied the prisoner, with majesty ; " for, though I hear your words, I declare I do not understand them."

" Then it is, that you have no religion at all ; I like that best," replied Lord de Winter, laughing.

" It is certain that that is most accordant with your own principles," replied milady, coldly.

" Well, I confess it is all perfectly the same to me."

" Oh ! you need not avow this religious indifference, my lord, your debaucheries and crimes would gain credit for it."

" What ! you talk of debaucheries, Madame Messalina ! Lady Macbeth ! Either I misunderstand you, or, pardieu ! you are pretty impudent !"

" You only speak thus because you know you are listened to, sir," coldly replied milady ; " and you wish to interest your gaolers and your hangmen against me."

" My gaolers ! and my hangmen ! Heyday, madame ! you are getting quite into a poetical tone, and the comedy of yesterday is turning this evening to a tragedy. As to the rest, in eight days you will be where you ought to be, and my task will be completed."

" Infamous task ! impious task !" cried milady, with the exultation of a victim provoking the judge.

" Parole d'honneur !" said De Winter, rising, " I think the hussey is going mad ! Come, come, calm yourself, Madame Puritan, or I'll remove you to a dungeon. Pardieu ! it's my Spanish wine that has got into your head, is it not ? But, never mind, that sort of intoxication is not dangerous, and will have no consequences."

And Lord de Winter retired swearing, which at that period was a very cavalierlike habit.

Felton was, in fact, behind the door, and had not lost one word of this scene.

Milady had guessed as much.

" Yes, go ! go !" said she to her brother ; " the consequences are drawing near, on the contrary ; but you, weak fool ! will not see them until it will be too late to shun them."

Silence was re-established—two hours passed away ; milady's supper was brought in, and she was found deeply engaged in saying her prayers aloud ; prayers which she had learnt of an old servant of her second husband's, a most austere Puritan. She appeared to be in ecstasy, and did not pay the least attention to what was going on around her. Felton made a sign that she should not be disturbed ; and when all was arranged, he went out quietly with the soldiers.

Milady knew she might be watched, so she continued her prayers to the end ; and it appeared to her that the soldier who was on duty at her door did not march with the same step, and seemed to listen.

For the moment she required no more ; she arose, placed herself at table, ate but little, and drank only water.

An hour after, her table was cleared ; but milady remarked that this time Felton did not accompany the soldiers.

He feared, then, to see her too often.

She turned towards the wall to smile ; for there was in this smile such an expression of triumph, that this single smile would have betrayed her.

She allowed, therefore, half an hour to pass away ; and as at that moment all was silence in the old castle, as nothing was heard but the éternal murmur of the waves—that immense respiration of the ocean—with her pure, harmonious, and powerful voice, she began the first couplet of the psalm then in greatest favour with the Puritans :

> "Thou leavest thy servants, Lord !
> To see if they be strong,
> But soon thou dost afford
> Thy hand to conduct them along."

These verses were not excellent—very far from it, even ; but, as it is well known, the Puritans did not pique themselves upon their poetry.

Whilst singing, milady listened. The soldier on guard at her door stopped, as if he had been changed into stone. Milady was then able to judge of the effect she had produced.

Then she continued her singing with inexpressible fervour and feeling ; it appeared to her that the sounds spread to a distance beneath the vaulted roofs, and carried with them a magic charm to soften the hearts of her gaolers. It, however, likewise appeared that the soldier on duty—a zealous Catholic, no doubt, shook off the charm, for through the door,—

" Hold your tongue, madam !" said he ; " your song is as dismal as a *De profundis ;* and if, besides the pleasure of being in garrison here, we must hear such things as these, no mortal can hold out."

"Silence !" then said another stern voice, which milady recognised as that of Felton ; " what business is it of yours, you stupid fellow ! Did anybody order you to prevent that woman from singing ? No ; you were told to guard her—to fire at her if she attempted to fly. Keep her there ; if she flies, kill her ; but don't exceed your orders."

An expression of unspeakable joy lightened the countenance of milady ; but this expression was fleeting as the reflection of lightning, and, without appearing to have heard the dialogue, of which she had not lost a word, she began again, giving to her voice all the charm, all the power, all the seduction, the demon had bestowed upon it :

> " For all my tears and all my cares,
> My exile and my chains,
> I have my youth, I have my prayers,
> And God who counts my pains."

Her voice, of immense power and of sublime expression, gave to the rude, unpolished poetry of these psalms a magic and an effect which the most exalted Puritans rarely found in the songs of their brethren, and which they were forced to ornament with all the resources of their imagination. Felton believed he heard the singing of the angel who consoled the three Hebrews in the furnace.

Milady continued :

> " But the day of our liberation
> Will come, just and powerful Sire !
> And if it cheat our expectation,
> To death and martyrdom we can still aspire."

This verse, into which the terrible enchantress threw her whole soul, completed the trouble which had seized the heart of the young officer ;

he opened the door quickly, and milady saw him appear, pale as usual, but with his eyes inflamed and almost wild.

"Why do you sing thus, and with such a voice?" said he.

"I crave your pardon, sir," said milady, with mildness; "I forgot that my songs are out of place in this mansion. I have, perhaps, offended you in your religious opinions; but it was without wishing to do so, I assure you. Pardon me, then, a fault which is perhaps great, but which certainly was involuntary."

Milady was so beautiful at this moment—the religious ecstasy in which she appeared to be plunged gave such an expression to her countenance, that Felton was so dazzled that he fancied he beheld the angel whom he had just before only heard.

"Yes, yes," said he, "you disturb—you agitate the people who inhabit the castle."

And the poor, senseless young man was not aware of the incoherence of his words, whilst milady was reading, with her lynx's eyes, the very depths of his heart.

"I will be silent, then," said milady, casting down her eyes, with all the sweetness she could give to her voice, with all the resignation she could impress upon her manner.

"No, no, madame," said Felton; "only do not sing so loud, particularly at night."

And at these words Felton, feeling that he could not long maintain his severity towards his prisoner, rushed out of the room.

"You have done right, lieutenant," said the soldier; "such songs disturb the mind; and yet we become accustomed to them—her voice is so beautiful!"

CHAPTER LIV.

THE THIRD DAY OF CAPTIVITY.

FELTON had fallen, but there was still another step to be taken—he must be retained, or, rather, he must be left quite alone; and milady but obscurely perceived the means which could lead to this result.

Still more must be done: he must be made to speak, in order that he might be spoken to; for milady very well knew that her greatest seduction was in her voice, which so skilfully ran over the whole gamut of tones, from human speech to celestial language.

And yet, in spite of all this seduction, milady might fail; for Felton was forewarned, and that against the least chance. From that moment she watched all his actions, all his words, to the simplest glance of his eyes, to his gestures, even to a respiration that could be interpreted as a sigh; in short, she studied everything, as a skilful comedian does, to whom a new part has been assigned in a line he has not been accustomed to.

With Lord de Winter her plan of conduct was more easy; she had laid that down the preceding evening. To remain silent and dignified in his presence ; from time to time to irritate him by an affected disdain, by a contemptuous word ; to provoke him to threats and violence, which would produce a contrast with her own resignation—such was her plan. Felton would see all ; perhaps he would say nothing, but he would see.

In the morning, Felton came as usual ; but milady allowed him to preside over all the preparations for the breakfast without addressing a word to him. At the moment he was about to retire, she was cheered with a ray of hope, for she thought he was about to speak ; but his lips moved without any sound passing from his mouth, and, making a powerful effort over himself, he sent back to his heart the words that were about to escape from his lips, and went out.

Towards mid-day, Lord de Winter came to her apartment.

It was a tolerably fine winter's day, and a ray of that pale English sun, which lightens but does not warm, passed through the bars of her prison.

Milady was looking out at the window, and pretended not to hear the door as it opened.

"Ah, ah !" said Lord de Winter, "after having played comedy, after having played tragedy, we are now playing melancholy, eh ?"

The prisoner made no reply.

"Yes, yes," continued Lord de Winter, "I understand—you would like very well to be at liberty on that beach ! you would like very well to be in a good ship, dancing upon the waves of that emerald-green sea ; you would like very well, either on land or on the ocean, to lay for me one of those nice little ambuscades you are so skilful in planning. Patience, patience ! in four days' time the shore will be beneath your foot, the sea will be open to you—more open than will, perhaps, be agreeable to you ; for in four days England will be relieved of your presence."

Milady joined her hands, and raising her fine eyes towards heaven—

"Lord, Lord !" said she, with an angelic meekness of gesture and tone, "pardon this man, as I myself pardon him !"

"Yes, pray, accursed woman !" cried the baron ; "your prayer is so much the more generous from your being, I swear to you, in the power of a man who will never pardon you !" And he left the room.

At the moment he went out, a piercing glance darted through the opening of the nearly-closed door, and she perceived Felton, who drew quickly on one side to prevent being seen by her.

Then she threw herself upon her knees, and began to pray.

"My God, my God !" said she, "you know in what holy cause I suffer ; give me, then, the strength to support my sufferings."

The door opened gently ; the beautiful supplicant pretended not to hear the noise, and, in a voice broken by tears, she continued :

"God of vengeance ! God of goodness ! will you allow the frightful projects of this man to be accomplished ?"

Then only she feigned to hear the sound of Felton's steps and, rising quick as thought, she blushed, as if ashamed of being surprised on her knees.

"I do not like to disturb those who pray, madame," said Felton, seriously ; "do not disturb yourself on my account, I beseech you."

"How do you know I was praying, sir ?" said milady, in a voice interrupted by sobs. "You were deceived, sir ; I was not praying."

"Do you think, then, madame," replied Felton, in the same serious voice, but with a more mild tone, "do you think I assume the right of preventing a creature from prostrating herself before her Creator? God forbid ! God forbid ! Besides, repentance becomes the guilty ; whatever crimes they may have committed, for me the guilty are sacred at the feet of God !"

"Guilty !—I ?" said milady, with a smile which might have disarmed the angel of the last judgment. "Guilty ! oh, my God, thou knowest whether I am guilty ! Say I am condemned, sir, if you please ; but you know that God, who loves martyrs, sometimes permits the innocent to be condemned."

"Were you condemned, were you innocent, were you a martyr," replied Felton, "the greater would be the necessity for prayer ; and I myself will aid you with my prayers."

"Oh, you are a just man !" cried milady, throwing herself on her knees at his feet ; "I can hold out no longer, for I fear I shall be wanting in strength in the moment at which I shall be forced to undergo the struggle, and confess my faith. Listen, then, to the supplication of a despairing woman. You are abused, sir, but that is not the question ; I only ask you one favour, and if you grant it me, I will bless you in this world and in the next."

"Speak to the master, madame," said Felton ; "happily, I am neither charged with the power of pardoning nor punishing ; it is upon one higher placed than I am that God has laid this responsibility."

"To you—no, to you alone ! Listen to me, rather than contribute to my destruction, rather than contribute to my ignominy."

"If you have merited this shame, madame, if you have incurred this ignominy, you must submit to it as an offering to God."

"What do you say ? Oh, you do not understand me ! When I speak of ignominy, you think I speak of some punishment or other, of imprisonment or death ! Would to heaven it were no more ! Of what consequence to me is imprisonment or death ?"

"It is I who no longer understand you, madame," said Felton.

"Or, rather, who pretend not to understand me, sir !" replied the prisoner, with a smile of doubt.

"No, madame, upon the honour of a soldier, upon the faith of a Christian."

"What ! you are ignorant of Lord de Winter's designs upon me ?"

"I am unacquainted with them."

"Impossible ; you are his confidant !"

"I never lie, madame."

"Oh, he conceals them too little for you not to divine them."

"I seek to divine nothing, madame ; I wait till I am confided in, and, apart from that which Lord de Winter has said to me before you, he has confided nothing to me."

"Why, then," cried milady, with an incredible tone of truthfulness, "why, then, you are not his accomplice—you do not know that he destines me to a disgrace which all the punishments of the world cannot equal in horror?"

"You are deceived, madame," said Felton, blushing; "Lord de Winter is not capable of such a crime."

"Good !" said milady to herself; "without knowing what it is, he calls it a crime !"

Then aloud :

"The friend of the infamous is capable of everything."

"Whom do you call the infamous?" asked Felton.

"Are there, then, in England two men to whom such an epithet can be applied?"

"You mean George Villiers?" said Felton, whose looks became agitated.

"Whom Pagans and infidel Gentiles call Duke of Buckingham," replied milady ; "I could not have thought that there was an Englishman in all England, who would have required so long an explanation to make him understand of whom I was speaking."

"The hand of the Lord is stretched over him," said Felton, "he will not escape the chastisement he deserves."

Felton did but express, with regard to the duke, the feeling of execration which all the English had vowed to him whom the Catholics themselves called the extortioner, the pillager, the *débauché;* and whom the Puritans styled simply Satan.

"Oh ! my God ! my God !" cried milady ; "when I supplicate you to pour upon this man the chastisement which is his due, you know that it is not my own vengeance I pursue, but the deliverance of a whole nation that I implore !"

"Do you know him, then?" asked Felton.

"At length he interrogates me !" said milady to herself, at the height of joy at having obtained so quickly such a result.—"Oh ! know him ! yes ! to my misfortune, to my eternal misfortune !" and milady wrung her hands, as if arrived at the very paroxysm of grief.

Felton no doubt felt within himself that his strength was abandoning him, and he made several steps towards the door ; but the prisoner, whose eye was never off him, sprang in pursuit of him, and stopped him.

"Sir," cried she, "be kind, be clement, listen to my prayer ; that knife, which the fatal prudence of the baron deprived me of, because he knows the use I would make of it ; oh ! hear me to the end ! that knife, give it to me for a minute only, for mercy's, for pity's sake ! I will embrace your knees ! you shall shut the door that you may be certain I contemplate no injury to you ! my God ! to you ! the only just, good, and compassionate being I have met with !—to you ! my saviour, perhaps ! one minute, that knife, one minute, a single minute, and I will restore it to you through the grating of the door ; only one minute, Master Felton, and you will have saved my honour !"

" To kill yourself !" cried Felton, with terror, forgetting to withdraw his hands from the hands of the prisoner ; "to kill yourself ?"

" I have told, sir," murmured milady, lowering her voice, and allowing herself to sink overpowered to the ground, " I have told my secret ! He knows all ! My God, I am lost !"

Felton remained standing, motionless and undecided.

" He still doubts," thought milady, "I have not been earnest enough."

Some one was heard in the corridor, milady recognised the step of Lord de Winter.

Felton recognised it also, and made a step towards the door.

Milady sprang towards him.

" Oh ! not a word," said she in a concentrated voice, "not a word of all that I have said to you to this man, or I am lost, and it would be you—you——"

Then as the steps drew near she became silent, for fear of being heard, applying, with a gesture of infinite terror, her beautiful hand to Felton's mouth.

Felton gently pushed milady from him, and she sank into a chair.

Lord de Winter passed before the door without stopping, and the sound of his footsteps soon died away in the distance.

Felton, as pale as death, remained some instants with his ear turned and listening ; then, when the sound was quite extinct, he breathed like a man awaking from a dream, and rushed out of the apartment.

" Ah !" said milady, listening in her turn to the noise of Felton's steps, which faded away in a direction opposite to those of Lord de Winter ; "ah ! at length thou art mine !"

Then her brow darkened.

" If he tells the baron," said she, " I am lost, for the baron, who knows very well that I shall not kill myself, will place me before him, with a knife in my hand, and he will discover that all this despair is but played."

She went, and placed herself before the glass, and looked at herself attentively ; never had she appeared more beautiful.

" Yes ! yes !" said she, smiling, "but he won't tell him !"

In the evening Lord de Winter accompanied the supper.

" Sir," said milady, "is your presence an indispensable accessory of my captivity ! could you not spare me the increase of tortures which your visits inflict upon me ?"

" How ! my dear sister !" said Lord de Winter, "did not you sentimentally inform me, with that pretty mouth of yours, so cruel to me to-day, that you came to England solely for the pleasure of seeing me at your ease, an enjoyment of which you told me you so sensibly felt the privation, that you had risked everything for it,—bad seas, tempests, and captivity ? Well ! here I am, be satisfied : besides, this time, my visit has a motive."

Milady trembled—she thought Felton had told all ; perhaps, never in her life had this woman, who had experienced so many opposite and powerful emotions, felt her heart beat so violently.

She was seated ; Lord de Winter took a chair, drew it towards her, and sat down close beside her ; then taking a paper out of his pocket, he unfolded it slowly.

"Here," said he, "I want to show you the kind of passport which I have drawn up, and which will serve you henceforward as a numero of order in the life I consent to leave you."

Then, turning his eyes from milady to the paper, he read

"'Order to conduct to —— ;' the name is blank," interrupted Lord de Winter ; "if you have any preference you can point it out to me ; and if it be not within a thousand leagues of London, attention will be paid to your wishes. I will begin again, then : 'Order to conduct to ——, the person named Charlotte Backson, branded by the justice of the kingdom of France, but liberated after chastisement ; she is to dwell in this place, without ever going more than three leagues from it. In case of any attempt to escape, the penalty of death is to be applied. She will receive five shillings per day, for lodging and food.'"

"That order does not concern me," replied milady, coldly, "since it bears another name than mine."

"A name !—have you a name, then ?"

"I bear that of your brother."

"Aye, but you are mistaken ; my brother is only your second husband, and your first is still living. Tell me his name, and I will put it in the place of the name of Charlotte Backson. No ?—you will not ?— you are silent ? Well ! then you must be registered as Charlotte Backson."

Milady remained silent ; only this time it was no longer from affectation, but from terror : she believed the order to be about to be executed ; she thought that Lord de Winter had hastened her departure ; she thought she was condemned to set off that very evening. Everything, in her mind, was lost for an instant, when all at once, she perceived that no signature was attached to the order. The joy she felt at this discovery was so great she could not conceal it.

"Yes, yes," said Lord de Winter, who perceived what was passing in her mind ; "yes, you look for the signature, and you say to yourself, 'All is not lost, for that order is not signed ; it is only shown to me to terrify me ; that's all.' You are mistaken ; to-morrow this order will be sent to the Duke of Buckingham ; after to-morrow, it will return signed by his hand and marked with his seal ; and four-and-twenty hours afterwards, I will answer for its being carried into execution. Adieu, madame ; that is all I had to say to you."

"And I reply to you, sir, that this abuse of power, this exile under a false name, are infamous !"

"Would you like better to be hung in your true name, milady? You know that the English laws are inexorable on the abuse of marriage ! speak freely : although my name, or rather that of my brother, would be mixed up with the affair, I will risk the scandal of a public trial, to make myself certain of getting rid of you."

Milady made no reply, but became as pale as a corpse.

"Oh! I see you prefer peregrination. That's well, milady; and there is an old proverb that says 'Travelling forms youth.' Ma foi! you are not wrong, after all; and life is sweet. That's the reason why I take such care you shall not deprive me of mine. There only remains, then, the question of the five shillings to be settled; you think me rather parsimonious—don't you? That's because I don't care to leave you the means of corrupting your gaolers. Besides, you will always have your charms left to seduce them with. Employ them, if your check with regard to Felton has not disgusted you with attempts of that kind."

"Felton has not told him," said milady to herself; "nothing is lost, then."

"And now, madame, till I see you again. To-morrow I will come and announce to you the departure of my messenger."

Lord de Winter rose, saluted her ironically, and left the room.

Milady breathed again; she had still four days before her; four days would quite suffice to complete the seduction of Felton.

A terrible idea, however, rushed into her mind; she thought that Lord de Winter would, perhaps, send Felton himself to get the order signed by the Duke of Buckingham; in that case, Felton would escape her; for, in order to secure success, the magic of a continuous seduction was necessary. Nevertheless, as we have said, one circumstance re-assured her—Felton had not spoken.

As she would not appear to be agitated by the threats of Lord de Winter, she placed herself at table and ate.

There, as she had done the evening before, she fell on her knees and repeated her prayers aloud. As on the evening before, the soldier stopped his march to listen to her.

Soon after, she heard lighter steps than those of the sentinel, which came from the bottom of the corridor, and stopped before her door.

"That is he," said she.

And she began the same religious chant which had so strongly excited Felton the evening before.

But, although her voice, sweet, full, and sonorous, vibrated as harmo-niously and as affectingly as ever, the door remained shut. It appeared, however, to milady, that in one of the furtive glances she darted, from time to time, at the grating of the door, she thought she saw the ardent eyes of the young man through the narrow opening. But whether this was a reality or not, he had, this time, sufficient self-com-mand not to enter.

Only, a few instants after she had finished her religious song, milady thought she heard a profound sigh;—then the same steps she had heard approach, departed slowly, and as if with regret.

CHAPTER LV.

THE FOURTH DAY OF CAPTIVITY.

THE next day, when Felton entered milady's apartments, he found her standing, mounted upon a chair, holding in her hands a cord made by means of torn cambric handkerchiefs, twisted into a kind of rope one with another, and tied at the ends ; at the noise Felton made in entering, milady leaped lightly to the ground, and endeavoured to conceal behind her the improvised cord she held in her hand.

The young man was still more pale than usual, and his eyes, reddened by want of sleep, denoted that he had passed a feverish night.

Nevertheless, his brow was armed with a sternness more severe than ever.

He advanced slowly towards milady, who had sat down, and taking an end of the murderous rope, which by mistake or else by design, she allowed to appear,—

"What is this, madame ?" he asked, coldly.

"That ? Nothing," said milady, smiling with that painful expression which she knew so well how to give to her smile ; "*ennui* is the mortal enemy of prisoners ; I was *ennuyée*, and I amused myself with twisting that rope."

Felton turned his eyes towards the part of the wall of the apartment before which he had found milady standing in the chair in which she was now seated, and over her head he perceived a gilt-headed screw, fixed in the wall, for the purpose of hanging up clothes or arms.

He started, and the prisoner saw that start ; for, though her eyes were cast down, nothing escaped her.

"What were you doing, standing in that chair ?" asked he.

"Of what consequence can that be to you ?" replied milady.

"But," replied Felton, "I wish to know."

"Do not question me," said the prisoner, "you know that we true Christians are forbidden to speak falsely."

"Well, then," said Felton, "I will tell you what you were doing, or rather what you were going to do ; you were going to complete the fatal work you cherish in your mind : remember, madame, if our God forbids us to speak falsely, he much more severely forbids us to commit suicide."

"When God sees one of his creatures persecuted unjustly, placed between suicide and dishonour, believe me, sir," replied milady in a tone of deep conviction, "God pardons suicide : for, then, suicide becomes martyrdom."

"You say either too much or too little ; speak, madame, in the name of Heaven, explain yourself."

"That I may relate my misfortunes to you, for you to treat them as fables ; that I may tell you my projects, for you to go and denounce them to my persecutor : no, sir ; besides, of what importance is the life or death of a condemned wretch to you ? You are only responsible for my body, are you ? and provided you produce a carcase that may be recognised as mine, they will require no more of you ; nay, perhaps even, you will have a double reward."

"I, madame ! I !" cried Felton ; "to suppose that I should ever accept the price of your life !—Oh ! you cannot think what you say !"

"Let me act as I please, Felton, let me act as I please," said milady, becoming excited ; "every soldier must be ambitious, must he not ? You are now a lieutenant—you will follow me to the grave with the rank of captain.'

"What have I then done to you," said Felton, much agitated, "that you should load me with such a responsibility before God and before men ? In a few days you will be away from this place ; your life, madame, will then no longer be under my care, and," added he with a sigh, "then you can do what you will with it.'

"So," cried milady, as if she could not resist giving utterance to a holy indignation, "you, a pious man, you, who are called a just man, you ask but one thing—and that is that you may not be inculpated, annoyed, by my death !"

"It is my duty to watch over your life, madame, and I will watch over it."

"But do you understand the mission you are fulfilling ? A sufficiently cruel one if I am guilty, but what name can you give it, what name will the Lord give it, if I am innocent ?"

"I am a soldier, madame, and perform the orders I have received."

"Do you believe, then, that at the last day of judgment God will separate blind executioners from iniquitous judges ? You are not willing that I should kill my body, and you make yourself the agent of him who would kill my soul !"

"But I repeat it again to you," replied Felton, in great emotion, "no danger threatens you ; I will answer for Lord de Winter as for myself.'

"Senseless man !" cried milady, "poor senseless man ! who dares to answer for another man, when the wisest, when those most after God's own heart, hesitate to answer for themselves ; and who ranges himself on the side of the strongest and the most fortunate, to crush the weakest and the most unfortunate."

"Impossible, madame, impossible," murmured Felton, who felt to the bottom of his heart the justness of this argument : "a prisoner, you shall not recover your liberty by my means ; living, you shall not lose your life by my means !"

"Yes," cried milady, "but I shall lose that which is much dearer to me than life, I shall lose my honour, Felton ; and it is you, you whom I make responsible, before God and before men, for my shame and my infamy."

This time Felton, impassible as he was, or appeared to be, could not resist the secret influence which had already taken possession of him ; to see this woman, so beautiful, fair as the brightest vision, to see her by turns overcome with grief and threatening, to resist at once the ascendancy of grief and beauty, it was too much for a visionary, it was too much for a brain weakened by the ardent dreams of an ecstatic faith, it was too much for a heart corroded by the love of heaven that burns, by the hatred of men that devours.

Milady saw the trouble, she felt by intuition the flame of the opposing passions which burned with the blood in the veins of the young fanatic ; and, like a skilful general, who, seeing the enemy ready to surrender, marches towards him with a cry of victory, she rose, beautiful as an antique priestess, inspired like a Christian virgin, her arms extended, her throat uncovered, her hair dishevelled, holding with one hand her robe modestly drawn over her breast, her look illumined by that fire which had already created such disorder in the veins of the young Puritan, she stepped towards him, crying out with a vehement air, and in her melodious voice, to which, on this occasion, she communicated a terrible energy :

> " Let his victim to Baal be sent,
> To the lions the martyr be thrown.
> Thy God shall teach thee to repent !
> From th' abyss he'll give ear to my moan."

Felton stood before this strange apparition, like one petrified.

" Who art thou ? who art thou ?" cried he, clasping his hands : "art thou a messenger from God, art thou a minister from hell, art thou an angel or a demon, callest thou thyself Eloa or Astarte ?"

" Do you not know me, Felton ? I am neither an angel nor a demon, I am a daughter of earth, I am a sister of thy faith, that is all."

" Yes ! yes !" said Felton, " I doubted, but now I believe !"

" You believe, and still you are an accomplice of that child of Belial, who is called Lord de Winter ! You believe, and yet you leave me in the hands of my enemies, of the enemy of England, of the enemy of God ! You believe, and yet you deliver me up to him who fills and defiles the world with his heresies and debaucheries, to that infamous Sardanapalus ; whom the blind call the Duke of Buckingham, and whom true believers name Antichrist ! '

" I deliver you up to Buckingham ! I ! what mean you by that ?"

" They have eyes," cried milady, " and they will not see ; they have ears, and they will not hear."

" Yes ! yes !" said Felton, passing his hands over his brow, covered with sweat, as if to remove his last doubt ; " yes, I recognise the voice which speaks to me in my dreams ; yes, I recognise the features of the angel that appears to me every night, crying to my soul, which cannot sleep : 'Strike, save England, save thyself, for thou wilt die without having disarmed God !'—Speak ! speak !" cried Felton, " I can understand you now."

A flash of terrible joy, but rapid as thought, gleamed from the eyes of milady

However fugitive this homicide flash, Felton saw it, and started as if its light had revealed the abysses of this woman's heart. He recalled, all at once, the warnings of Lord de Winter, the seductions of milady, her first attempts after her arrival ; he drew back a step, and hung down his head, without, however, ceasing to look at her : as if, fascinated by this strange creature, he could not remove his eyes from her eyes.

Milady was not a woman to misunderstand the meaning of this hesitation. Under her apparent emotions, her icy coolness never abandoned her. Before Felton replied, and before she should be forced to resume this conversation, so difficult to be sustained in the same exalted tone, she let her hands fall, and as if the weakness of the woman overpowered the enthusiasm of the inspired fanatic,—

"But no," said she, "it is not for me to be the Judith to deliver Bethulia from this Holofernes. The sword of the eternal is too heavy for my arm. Allow me then to avoid dishonour by death, let me take refuge in martyrdom. I do not ask you for liberty, as a guilty one would, nor for vengeance, as a pagan would. Let me die, that is all I supplicate you, I implore you on my knees : let me die, and my last sigh shall be a blessing for my saviour."

At hearing that voice, so sweet and suppliant, at viewing that look, so timid and downcast, Felton reproached himself. By degrees the enchantress had clothed herself with that magic adornment which she assumed and threw aside at will, that is to say, beauty, meekness, and tears, and above all, the irresistible attraction of mystical voluptuousness, the most devouring of all voluptuousness.

"Alas !" said Felton, "I can do but one thing, which is, to pity you, if you prove to me you are a victim ! Lord de Winter alleges cruel accusations against you. You are a Christian, you are my sister in religion ; I feel myself drawn towards you, I, who have never loved any one but my benefactor, I, who have met with nothing but traitors and impious men. But you, madame, so beautiful in reality, you, so pure in appearance, must have committed great iniquities for Lord de Winter to pursue you thus."

"They have eyes," repeated milady, with an accent of indescribable grief, "and they will not see ; they have ears, and they will not hear."

"But," cried the young officer, "speak ! speak, then !"

"Confide my shame to you," cried milady, with the blush of modesty upon her countenance,—"for often the crime of one becomes the shame of another ; confide my shame to you, a man, and I a woman ! Oh !" continued she, placing her hand modestly over her beautiful eyes, "never ! never !—I could not !"

"But to me, to a brother ?" said Felton.

Milady looked at him for some time with an expression which the young man took for doubt, but which, however, was nothing but observation, or rather the will to fascinate.

Felton, in his turn a suppliant, clasped his hands.

"Well, then," said milady, " I confide in my brother, I will dare to——"

At this moment the steps of Lord de Winter were heard ; but this time the terrible brother-in-law of milady did not content himself, as on the preceding day, with passing before the door and going away again ; he stopped, exchanged two words with the sentinel, then the door opened, and he appeared.

During these two words, Felton drew back suddenly, and when Lord de Winter entered, he was at several paces from the prisoner.

The baron entered slowly, carrying a scrutinising glance from milady to the young officer.

"You have been a long time here, John," said he, "has this woman been relating her crimes to you? In that case I can comprehend the length of the conversation."

Felton started, and milady felt she was lost if she did not come to the assistance of the disconcerted Puritan.

"Ah! you fear your prisoner should escape," said she ; "well! ask your worthy gaoler what favour I was but this instant soliciting of him."

"You were soliciting a favour?" said the baron suspiciously

"Yes, my lord," replied the young man, in some confusion.

"And what favour, pray?" asked Lord de Winter.

"A knife, which she would return to me through the grating of the door, a minute after she had received it," replied Felton.

"There is some one then concealed here, whose throat this amiable lady is desirous of cutting," said De Winter, in an ironical, contemptuous tone.

"There is myself," replied milady.

"I have given you the choice between America and Tyburn," replied Lord de Winter, "choose Tyburn, milady ; believe me, the cord is more certain than the knife."

Felton grew pale, and made a step forward, remembering that at the moment he entered, milady had a rope in her hand.

"You are right," said she, "I have often thought of it ;" then she added, in a low voice, "and I will think of it again."

Felton felt a shudder run to the marrow of his bones ; probably Lord de Winter perceived this emotion.

"Mistrust yourself, John," said he ; "I have placed reliance upon you, my friend, beware ; I have warned you ! But be of good courage, my lad, in three days we shall be delivered from this creature, and where I shall send her to, she can hurt nobody."

"You hear him !" cried milady with vehemence, so that the baron might believe she was addressing heaven, and that Felton might understand she was addressing him.

Felton hung down his head and appeared buried in thought.

The baron took the young officer by the arm, turning his head over his shoulder, so as not to lose sight of milady till he was gone out.

"Alas !" said the prisoner, when the door was shut, "I am not so far advanced as I expected, I fear. De Winter has changed his usual stupidity into a prudence hitherto foreign to him :—it is the desire of vengeance, and new desires form a man ! As to Felton, he hesitates. Ah ! he is not a man like that cursed D'Artagnan. A Puritan only adores virgins, and he adores them by clasping his hands. A musketeer loves women, and he loves them by clasping his arms round them."

Milady waited then with much impatience, for she feared the day would pass away without her seeing Felton again. But, in an hour after the scene we have just related, she heard some one speaking in a low voice at the door; soon after the door opened, and she perceived Felton.

The young man advanced into the room with a quick step, leaving the door open behind him, and making a sign to milady to be silent; his face was much agitated.

"What do you want with me?" said she.

"Listen," replied Felton in a low voice; "I have just sent away the sentinel, that I might remain here, without its being known I was come here, that I might speak to you without having that I say to you overheard by others. The baron has just related a frightful history to me."

Milady assumed her smile of a resigned victim, and shook her head.

"Either you are a demon," continued Felton, "or the baron, my benefactor, my father, is a monster. I have known you four days, I have loved him four years; I therefore may hesitate between you; but be not alarmed at what I say, I want to be convinced. To-night, after twelve, I will come and see and listen to you, and you will convince me."

"No, Felton, no, my brother, the sacrifice is too great, and I feel what it must cost you. No, I am lost, do not be lost with me. My death will be much more eloquent than my life, and the silence of the corpse will convince you much better than the words of the prisoner."

"Be silent, madame," cried Felton, "and do not speak to me thus: I came to entreat you to promise me upon your honour, to swear to me by what you hold most sacred, that you will make no attempt upon your life.'

"I will not promise," said milady, "for no one has more respect for a promise or an oath than I have, and if I make a promise I must keep it."

"Well," said Felton, "only promise till after you have seen me again. If, when you have seen me again, you still persist——, well! then you shall be free, and I myself will give you the weapon you desire."

"Well!" said milady, "for your sake I will wait."

"Swear it."

"I swear I will, by our God. Are you satisfied?"

"I am," said Felton, "till night, then."

And he darted out of the room, shut the door, and waited in the corridor, the soldier's half-pike in his hand, and as if he had mounted guard in his place.

When the soldier returned, Felton gave him back his weapon.

Then, through the grating to which she had drawn near, milady saw the young man cross himself with a delirious fervour, and depart in an apparent transport of joy.

As for her, she returned to her place with a smile of savage contempt upon her lips, and repeated, blaspheming, that terrible name of God, by which she had just sworn without ever having learnt to know Him.

" My God !" said she, "what a senseless fanatic ! my God, it is I, I
and he, who will help me to avenge myself."

CHAPTER LVI.

THE FIFTH DAY OF CAPTIVITY.

MILADY had however achieved a half-triumph, and the success obtained
doubled her strength.

It was not a difficult thing to conquer, as she had hitherto done, men
prompt to allow themselves to be seduced, and whom the gallant education of a court led quickly into her snares ; milady was handsome
enough not to find much resistance on the part of the flesh, and she was
sufficiently skilful to prevail over all the obstacles of the mind.

But this time she had to contend with a wild nature, concentrated
and insensible by the power of austerity ; religion and its observances
had made Felton a man inaccessible to ordinary seductions. There
fermented in that heated brain plans so vast, projects so tumultuous,
that there remained no room for any capricious or material love, that
sentiment which is fed by leisure and grows with corruption. Milady
had then made a breach, with her false virtue, in the opinion of a man
horribly prejudiced against her, and by her beauty in the heart of a
man hitherto chaste and pure. In short, she had acquired a knowledge
of her means, till this instance unknown to herself, by this experiment,
made upon the most rebellious subject that nature and religion could
submit to her study.

Many a time, nevertheless, during the evening, she despaired of fate
and of herself : she did not invoke God, we very well know, but she had
faith in the genius of evil, that immense sovereignty which reigns in all
the details of human life, and by which, as in the Arabian fable, a single
pomegranate seed is sufficient to reconstruct a ruined world.

Milady, being well prepared for the reception of Felton, was able to
erect her batteries for the next day. She knew she had only two days
left ; that when once the order was signed by Buckingham—and Buckingham would sign it the more readily from its bearing a false name,
and that he could not, therefore, recognise the woman in question—
once this order signed, we say, the baron would make her embark immediately, and she knew very well that women condemned to transportation employ arms much less powerful in their seductions than the
pretendedly virtuous woman whose beauty is enlightened by the sun of
the world, which style of beauty the voice of fashion lauds, and whom a
halo of aristocracy gilds with its enchanting splendours. To be a woman
condemned to a painful and disgraceful punishment is no impediment
to beauty, but it is an obstacle to the regaining of power. Like all
persons of real genius, milady was acquainted with what suited her
nature and her means. Poverty was destruction to her—degradation
took away two-thirds of her greatness. Milady was only a queen among
queens. The pleasure of satisfied pride was necessary for her domina-

tion. To command inferior beings was rather a humiliation than a pleasure for her.

She should certainly return from her exile—she did not doubt that a single instant ; but how long might this exile last ? For an active, ambitious nature, like that of milady, days not spent in mounting are inauspicious days ! what word, then, can be found to describe those in which they descend ? To lose a year, two years, three years, is to talk of an eternity ; to return after the death or disgrace of the cardinal, perhaps ; to return when D'Artagnan and his friends, happy and trium-phant, should have received from the queen the reward they had well acquired by the services they had rendered her—these were devouring ideas that a woman like milady could not endure. For the rest, the storm which raged within her doubled her strength, and she would have burst the walls of her prison if her body had been able to take for a single instant the proportions of her mind.

Then that which spurred her on additionally in the midst of all this was the remembrance of the cardinal. What must the mistrustful, rest-less, suspicious cardinal think of her silence ; the cardinal, not merely her only support, her only prop, her only protector in the present, but still further, the principal instrument of her future fortune and ven-geance? She knew him—she knew that at her return it would be in vain to tell him of her imprisonment, in vain to enlarge upon the suffer-ings she had undergone—the cardinal would reply, with the sarcastic calmness of the sceptic, strong at once by power and genius, " You should not have allowed yourself to be taken."

Then milady collected all her energies, murmuring in the depths of her soul the name of Felton, the only beam of light that penetrated to her in the hell into which she was fallen ; and, like a serpent which folds and unfolds its rings to ascertain its strength, she enveloped Felton beforehand in the thousand meshes of her inventive imagination.

Time, however, passed away ; the hours, one after another, seemed to awaken the clock as they passed, and every blow of the brass hammer resounded upon the heart of the prisoner. At nine o'clock, Lord de Winter made his customary visit, examined the window and the bars, sounded the floor and the walls, looked to the chimney and the doors, without, during this long and minute examination, he or milady pro-nouncing a single word.

Doubtless both of them understood that the situation had become too serious to lose time in useless words and aimless passion.

" Well," said the baron, on leaving her, "you will not escape this night !"

At ten o'clock, Felton came and placed the sentinel ; milady recog-nised his step. She was as well acquainted with it now as a mistress is with that of the lover of her heart, and yet milady at the same time de-tested and despised this weak fanatic.

That was not the appointed hour—Felton would not come in.

Two hours after, as the clock struck twelve, the sentinel was relieved.

This time it was the hour, and from this moment milady waited with impatience.

The new sentinel commenced his walk in the corridor.

At the expiration of ten minutes Felton came.

Milady was all attention.

" Listen," said the young man to the sentinel ; " on no pretence leave the door, for you know that last night my lord punished a soldier for having quitted his post for an instant, although I, during his absence, watched in his place."

" Yes, I know he did," said the soldier.

" I recommend you, therefore, to keep the strictest watch. For my part, I am going to pay a second visit to this woman, who, I fear, entertains sinister intentions upon her own life, and I have received orders to watch her."

" Good !" murmured milady ; " the austere Puritan has learnt to lie !"

As to the soldier, he only smiled.

" Zounds ! lieutenant," said he, " you are not very unlucky in being charged with such commissions, particularly if my lord has authorised you to look in her bed !"

Felton blushed ; under any other circumstances he would have reprimanded the soldier for indulging in such a joke, but his conscience murmured too highly to allow his mouth to dare to speak.

" If I call, come in," said he ; " if any one comes, call me."

" I will, lieutenant," said the soldier.

Felton entered milady's apartment. Milady arose.

" You are come, then !" said she.

" I promised you I would come," said Felton, " and I am come."

" You promised me other things besides."

" What ? my God !" said the young man, who, in spite of his self-command, felt his knees tremble, and the sweat start from his brow.

" You promised to bring a knife, and to leave it with me after our conversation."

" Say no more of that, madame," said Felton ; " there is no situation, however terrible it may be, which can authorise one of God's creatures to inflict death upon itself. I have reflected, and I cannot, must not be capable of such a sin."

" Ah ! you have reflected !" said the prisoner, sitting down in her fauteuil, with a smile of disdain ; " and I also have reflected !"

" Upon what ? To what purpose ?"

" That I can have nothing to say to a man who does not keep his word."

" Oh ! my God !" murmured Felton.

" You may retire," said milady ; " I shall not speak."

" Here is the knife !" said Felton, drawing from his pocket the weapon which, according to his promise, he had brought, but which he hesitated to give to the prisoner.

" Let me see it," said milady.

" For what purpose ?"

" Upon my honour I will instantly return it to you ; you shall place it on that table, and you may remain between it and me."

Felton held the weapon to milady, who examined the temper of it attentively, and who tried the point on the tip of her finger

"Well," said she, returning the knife to the young officer, "this is fine and good steel ; you are a faithful friend, Felton."

Felton took back the weapon, and laid it upon the table, as had been agreed.

Milady followed him with her eyes, unable to refrain from a gesture of satisfaction.

"Now," said she, "listen to me."

The recommendation was useless : the young officer stood upright before her, awaiting her words, as if to devour them.

"Felton," said milady, with a solemnity full of melancholy, " if your sister, the daughter of your father, said to you :

"Still young, unfortunately handsome, I was dragged into a snare, I resisted ; ambushes and violences were multiplied around me, I resisted ; the religion I serve, the God I adore, were blasphemed because I called upon that religion and that God ; I resisted ; then outrages were heaped upon me, and as my soul was not subdued, it was determined to defile my body for ever. In short——"

Milady stopped, and a bitter smile passed over her lips.

"In short," said Felton, "in short, what did they do ?"

"At length, one evening, my enemy resolved to paralyse the resistance he could not conquer ; one evening he mixed a powerful narcotic with my water. Scarcely had I finished my repast, when I felt myself sink by degrees into a strange torpor. Although I was without suspicion, a vague fear seized me, and I endeavoured to struggle against sleep : I arose ; I endeavoured to run to the window, and call for help, but my limbs refused their office. It appeared as if the ceiling sank upon my head, and crushed me with its weight ; I stretched out my arms, I endeavoured to speak ; I could only utter inarticulate sounds, and irresistible faintness came over me ; I supported myself by a fauteuil, feeling that I was about to fall, but this support was soon useless, for my weak arms. I fell upon one knee, then upon both. I tried to pray, but my tongue was frozen ; God, doubtless, neither heard nor saw me, and I sank down upon the floor, a prey to a sleep which resembled death.

"Of all that passed in that sleep, or the time which glided away whilst it lasted, I have no remembrance ; the only thing I recollect is, that I awoke in bed, in a round chamber, the furniture of which was sumptuous, and into which light only penetrated by an opening in the ceiling. No door gave entrance to the room : it might be called a magnificent prison.

"It was a long time before I was able to make out what place I was in, or to take account of the details I describe : my mind appeared to strive in vain to shake off the heavy darkness of the sleep from which I could not rouse myself. I had vague perceptions of a space travelled over, of the rolling of a carriage, of a horrible dream, in which my strength had become exhausted ; but all this was so dark and so indistinct in my mind, that these events seemed to belong to another life than mine, and yet mixed with mine by a fantastic duality.

"At times, the state into which I was fallen appeared so strange, that I thought I was dreaming. I arose tremblingly, my clothes were near me on a chair ; I neither remembered having undressed myself, nor going to bed. Then by degrees the reality broke upon me, full of modest terrors : I was no longer in the house I had dwelt in. As well as I could judge by the light of the sun, the day was already two-thirds gone. It was the evening before that I had fallen asleep ; my sleep then must have lasted twenty-four hours ! What had taken place during this long sleep ?

" I dressed myself as quickly as possible ; my slow and stiff motions all attested that the effects of the narcotic were not all yet dissipated. The chamber was evidently furnished for the reception of a woman ; and the most finished coquette could not have formed a wish which, on casting her eyes round the apartment, she would not have found accomplished.

" Certainly, I was not the first captive that had been shut up in this splendid prison ; but you may easily comprehend, Felton, that the more superb the prison the greater was my terror.

" Yes, it was a prison, for I endeavoured in vain to get out of it. I sounded all the walls in the hopes of discovering a door, but every-where the walls returned a full and flat sound.

" I made the tour of the room at least twenty times, in search of an outlet of some kind ; there was none—I sank exhausted with fatigue and terror into a fauteuil.

" In the meantime, night came on rapidly, and with night my terrors increased : I did not know whether I had better remain where I was seated ; it appeared that I was surrounded with unknown dangers, into which I was about to fall at every instant. Although I had eaten no-thing since the evening before, my fears prevented my feeling hunger.

" No noise from without, by which I could measure the time, reached me ; I only supposed it must be seven or eight o'clock in the evening, for we were in the month of October, and it was quite dark.

" All at once, the noise of a door turning on its hinges made me start ; a globe of fire appeared above the glazed opening of the ceiling, casting a strong light into my chamber, and I perceived with terror that a man was standing within a few paces of me.

" A table, with two covers, bearing a supper ready prepared, stood, as if by magic, in the middle of the apartment.

" That man was he who had pursued me during a whole year, who had vowed my dishonour, and who, by the first words that issued from his mouth, gave me to understand he had accomplished it the preced-ing night."

" Infamous villain !" murmured Felton.

" Oh, yes, infamous villain !" cried milady, seeing the interest which the young officer, whose soul seemed to hang on her lips, took in this strange recital.

" Oh, yes, the infamous villain ! he believed that, by having triumphed over me in my sleep, all was completed ; he came, hoping that I should . accept my shame, as my shame was consummated ; he came to offer his fortune in exchange for my love.

" All that the heart of a woman could contain of haughty contempt and disdainful words I poured out upon this man.   Doubtless he was accustomed to such reproaches, for he listened to me calm and smiling, with his arms crossed over his breast ; then, when he thought I had said all, he advanced towards me ; I sprang towards the table, I seized a knife, I placed it to my breast.

" ' Make one step more,' said I, ' and, in addition to my dishonour, you shall have my death to reproach yourself with !'

" There was no doubt, in my look, my voice, my whole person, that truth of gesture, of *pose*, and action which carries conviction to the most perverse minds, for he stopped.

" ' Your death !' said he ; ' oh, no, you are too charming a mistress to allow me to consent to lose you thus, after what has happened.   Adieu, my charmer ; I will wait to pay you my next visit till you are in a better humour.'

" At these words, he blew a whistle : the globe of fire which lighted the room reascended and disappeared ; I found myself again in complete darkness.   The same noise of the door opening and shutting was repeated the instant afterwards, the flaming globe descended afresh, and I was completely alone.

" This moment was frightful ; if I had had any doubts of my misfortune, these doubts had vanished in an overwhelming reality : I was in the power of a man whom I not only detested, but despised ; of a man capable of anything, and who had already given me a fatal proof of what he was able to do."

" But who, then, was this man ?" asked Felton.

" I passed the night in a chair, starting at the least noise ; for towards midnight the lamp went out, and I again was in darkness.   But the night passed away without any fresh attempt on the part of my persecutor ; day came—the table had disappeared, only I had still the knife in my hand.

" This knife was my only hope.

" I was worn out with fatigue ; want of sleep inflamed my eyes ; I had not ventured to sleep a single instant.   The light of day reassured me ; I went and threw myself on the bed, without parting with the liberator knife, which I concealed under my pillow.

" When I awoke, a fresh table was served.

" This time, in spite of my terrors, in spite of my agony, I began to feel a devouring hunger—it was forty-eight hours since I had taken any nourishment ; I ate some bread and some fruit ; then, remembering the narcotic mixed with the water I had drunk, I would not touch that which was placed on the table, but filled my glass at a marble fountain fixed in the wall, over my toilet.

" And yet, notwithstanding these precautions, I remained for some time in a terrible agitation of mind. But my fears were ill-founded ; I passed the day without experiencing anything of the kind I dreaded.

" I took the precaution to half empty the carafe, in order that my suspicions might not be noticed.

" The evening came on, and with it darkness ; but, however profound was this darkness, my eyes began to be accustomed to it : I saw the table sink through the floor ; a quarter of an hour after, it reappeared, bearing my supper ; and in an instant, thanks to the lamp, my chamber was once more lighted.

" I was determined to eat only such objects as could not possibly have anything soporific introduced into them : two eggs and some fruit composed my repast, then I drew another glass of water from my protecting fountain, and drank it.

" After swallowing a mouthful or two, it appeared to me not to have the same taste that it had in the morning ; a suspicion instantly seized me—I stopped, but I had already drunk half a glassful of it.

" I threw the rest away with horror, and waited, with the dew of fear upon my brow.

" There was no doubt that some invisible witness had seen me draw the water from that fountain, and had taken advantage of my confidence in it, the better to assure my ruin, so coolly resolved upon, so cruelly pursued.

" Half an hour had not passed when the same symptoms began to appear ; only, as I had only drunk half a glass of the water, I contended longer, and, instead of falling entirely asleep, I sank into a state of drowsiness, which left me a perception of what was passing around me, whilst depriving me of the strength either to defend myself or to fly.

" I dragged myself towards the bed, to seek the only defence I had left—my preserver knife—but I could not reach the bolster ; I sank on my knees, my hands clasped round one of the bed-posts ; then I felt that I was lost."

Felton became frightfully pale, and a convulsive tremor crept through his whole body.

" And what was most terrible," continued milady, her voice altered, as if she still experienced the same agony as at that awful minute, " was that at this time I retained a consciousness of the danger that threatened me ; was that my soul, if I may say so, waked in my sleeping body ; was that I saw, was that I heard. It is true that all was like a dream, but it was not the less frightful.

" I saw the lamp ascend, and leave me in darkness ; then I heard the so well-known creaking of the door, although I had heard that door open but twice.

" I felt instinctively that some one approached me : it is said that the doomed wretch in the deserts of America thus feels the approach of the serpent.

" I endeavoured to make an effort, I attempted to cry out ; by an incredible effort of will I even raised myself up, but only to sink down again immediately, and to fall into the arms of my persecutor."

"Tell me who this man was !" cried the young officer.

Milady saw at a single glance all the painful feelings she inspired in Felton, by dwelling on every detail of her recital ; but she would not spare him a single pang. The more profoundly she wounded his heart, the more certainly he would avenge her. She continued, then, as if she had not heard his exclamation, or as if she thought the moment was not yet come to reply to it.

" Only this time it was no longer an inert body, without feeling, that the villain had to deal with ; I have told you that, without being able to regain the complete exercise of my faculties, I retained the sense of my danger. I struggled, then, with all my strength, and doubtless opposed, weak as I was, a long resistance, for I heard him cry out :

" ' These miserable Puritans ! I knew very well that they tired out their executioners, but I did not think they had been so strong against their lovers !'

"Alas ! this desperate resistance could not last long ; I felt my strength fail, and this time it was not my sleep that enabled the villain to prevail, but my swooning."

Felton listened without uttering any word or sound but a kind of inward expression of agony ; the sweat streamed down his marble brow, and his hand, under his coat, tore his breast in nervous excitement.

" My first impulse, on coming to myself, was to feel under my pillow for the knife I had not been able to reach ; if it had not been useful for defence, it might at least serve in expiation.

" But on taking this knife, Felton, a terrible idea occurred to me. I have sworn to tell you all, and I will tell you all ; I have promised you the truth—I will tell it, were it to destroy me."

" The idea came into your mind to avenge yourself on this man, did it not ?" cried Felton.

" Yes," said milady. " The idea was not that of a Christian, I knew ; but, without doubt, that eternal enemy of our souls, that lion roaring constantly around us, breathed it into my mind. In short, what shall I say to you, Felton ?" continued milady, in the tone of a woman accusing herself of a crime. " This idea occurred to me, and did not leave me ; it is of this homicidal thought that I now bear the punishment."

" Continue ! continue !" said Felton ; " I am eager to see you attain your vengeance !"

" Oh, I resolved that it should take place as soon as possible ; I had no doubt he would return the following night. During the day I had nothing to fear.

" When the hour of breakfast came, therefore, I did not hesitate to eat and drink. I determined to make believe to sup, but to take nothing ; I was forced, then, by the nourishment of the morning, to combat the fast of the evening.

" Only I concealed a glass of water, which formed part of my breakfast, thirst having been the chief of my sufferings when I had remained forty-eight hours without eating or drinking.

"The day passed away, without having any other influence on me than to strengthen the resolution I had formed ; only I took care that my face should not betray the thoughts of my heart, for I had no doubt I was watched ; several times, even, I felt a smile upon my lips. Felton, I dare not tell you at what idea I smiled ; you would hold me in horror——"

"Go on ! go on !" said Felton ; "you see plainly that I listen, and that I am anxious to know the end."

"Evening came, the ordinary events were accomplished : during the darkness, as before, my table was covered, then the lamp was lighted, and I sat down to table ; I only ate some fruit ; I pretended to pour out water from the carafe, but I only drank that which I had saved in my glass ; the substitution was made so carefully that my spies, if I had any, could have no suspicion of it.

"After supper, I exhibited the same marks of languor as on the preceding evening ; but this time, as if I yielded to fatigue, or as if I had become familiarised with danger, I dragged myself towards my bed, let my robe fall, and got in.

"I found my knife where I had placed it, under my pillow, and, whilst feigning to sleep, my hand grasped the handle of it convulsively.

"Two hours passed away without anything fresh occurring this time. Oh, my God ! who could have said so the evening before ! I began to fear that he would not come !

"At length I saw the lamp rise softly, and disappear in the depths of the ceiling ; my chamber was filled with darkness and obscurity, but I made a strong effort to penetrate this darkness and obscurity.

"Nearly ten minutes passed ; I heard no other noise but the beating of my own heart.

"I implored heaven that he might come.

"At length I heard the well-known noise of the door which opened and shut ; I heard, notwithstanding the thickness of the carpet, a step which made the floor creak ; I saw, notwithstanding the darkness, a shadow which approached my bed."

"Make haste ! make haste !" said Felton ; "do you not see that every one of your words burns me like molten lead !"

"Then," continued milady, "then I collected all my strength, I recalled to my mind that the moment of vengeance, or, rather, of justice, had struck. I looked upon myself as another Judith : I gathered myself up, my knife in my hand, and when I saw him near me, stretching out his arms to find his victim, then, with the last cry of agony and despair, I struck him in the middle of his breast.

"The miserable villain ! he had foreseen all ! his breast was covered with a coat of mail : the knife was bent against it !

"'Ah ! ah !' cried he, seizing my arm, and wresting from me the weapon that had so ill seconded my design, 'you want to take my life, do you, my pretty Puritan ! but that's more than dislike, that's ingratitude ! Come, come, calm yourself, my sweet girl ! I thought you were become kinder. I am not one of those tyrants who detain women by force. You don't love me ; with my usual fatuity, I doubted of it ; now I am convinced. To-morrow you shall be free.

"I had but one wish, and that was that he should kill me.

"'Beware !' said I, 'for my liberty is your dishonour.'

"'Explain yourself, my pretty Sibyl.'

"'Yes ; for no sooner shall I have left this place, than I will tell everything ; I will proclaim the violence you have used towards me ; I will describe my captivity. I will denounce this palace of infamy. You are placed on high, my lord, but tremble ! Above you there is the king ; above the king there is God !'

"However perfect master he was over himself, my persecutor allowed a movement of anger to escape him. I could not see the expression of his countenance, but I felt the arm upon which my hand was placed, tremble.

"'Then you shall not leave this place,' said he.

"'So be it,' cried I, 'then the place of my punishment will be that of my tomb. So be it, I will die here, and you will see if a phantom that accuses is not more terrible than a living being that threatens !'

"'You shall have no weapon left in your power.'

"'There is a weapon which despair has placed within the reach of every creature that has the courage to make use of it. I will allow myself to die with hunger.'

"'Come, come,' said the wretch, 'is not peace much better than such a war as that ? I will restore you to liberty this moment ; I will proclaim you a piece of immaculate virtue ; I will name you the Lucretia of England.'

"'And I will say that you are the Sextus ; I will denounce you before men as I have denounced you before God ; and if it be necessary that, like Lucretia, I should sign my accusation with my blood, I will sign it.'

"'Ah !' said my enemy, in a jeering tone, 'that's quite another thing. Ma foi ! everything considered, you are very well off here, you shall want for nothing, and if you choose to die of hunger—why, that will be your own fault.'

"At these words he retired ; I heard the door open and shut, and I remained overwhelmed, still less, I confess it, by my grief than by the shame of not having avenged myself.

"He kept his word. All the day, all the next night passed away, without my seeing him again. But I also kept my word with him, and I neither ate nor drank ; I was, as I had told him, resolved to die of hunger.

"I passed the day and the night in prayer, for I hoped that God would pardon me my suicide.

"The second night the door opened ; I was lying on the floor, for my strength began to abandon me.

"At the noise I raised myself up on one hand.

"'Well !' said a voice which vibrated in too terrible a manner in my ear not to be recognised ; 'well ! are we softened a little, will we not pay for our liberty with a single promise of silence? Come, I am a good sort of a prince,' added he, 'and although I am not very partial to Puritans, I do them justice, as well as to female Puritans, when they are pretty. Come, take a little oath for me on the cross, I won't ask anything more of you.'

"'Upon the cross,' cried I, rising up, for at that abhorred voice I had recovered all my strength; 'upon the cross! I swear that no promise, no menace, no force, no torture shall close my mouth; upon the cross! I swear to denounce you everywhere as a murderer, as a despoiler of honour, as a base coward; upon the cross! I swear, if I ever leave this place, to call down vengeance upon you from the whole human race.'

"'Beware!' said the voice, in a threatening accent that I had never yet heard, 'I have an extraordinary means, which I will not employ but in the last extremity, to close your mouth, or at least to prevent any one from believing a word you may utter.'

"I mustered all my strength to reply to him with a burst of laughter.

"He saw that, from that time, it was an exterminal war, a war to the death between us.

"'Listen,' said he, 'I give you the rest of the night and the day of tomorrow; reflect, promise to be silent, and riches, consideration, even honour shall surround you; threaten to speak, and I will condemn you to infamy.'

"'You,' cried I, 'you!'

"'To interminable, ineffaceable infamy!'

"'You,' repeated I. Oh! I declare to you, Felton, ı thought him mad!

"'Yes, I!' replied he.

"'Oh! leave me,' said I, 'begone, if you do not desire to see me dash my head against that wall, before your eyes!'

"'Very well! it is your own doing; till to-morrow evening, then!'

"'Till to-morrow evening, then,' replied I, allowing myself to fall, and biting the carpet with rage.

Felton leant for support upon a piece of furniture, and milady saw, with the joy of a demon, that his strength would fail him, perhaps before the end of her recital.

CHAPTER LVII.

MEANS FOR CLASSICAL TRAGEDY.

AFTER a moment of silence employed by milady in observing the young man who listened to her, milady continued her recital.

"It was nearly three days since I had eaten or drunk anything, I suffered frightful torments; at times there passed before me clouds which pressed my brow, which veiled my eyes; this was delirium.

"When the evening came, I was so weak that at every time that I fainted I thanked God, for I thought I was about to die.

" In the midst of one of these faintings, I heard the door open ; terror recalled me to myself.

" He entered the apartment, followed by a man in a mask ; he was masked likewise ; but I knew his step, I knew his voice, I knew him by that imposing carriage that hell has bestowed upon his person for the curse of humanity.

" ' Well !' said he to me, ' have you made your mind up to take the oath I have requested of you ?'

" ' You have said it, Puritans have but one word ; mine you have heard, and that is to pursue you on earth to the tribunal of men, in heaven to the tribunal of God.'

" ' You persist, then ?'

" ' I swear it before the God who hears me ; I will take the whole world as a witness of your crime, and that until I have found an avenger.'

" ' You are a prostitute,' said he, in a voice of thunder, ' and you shall undergo the punishment of prostitutes ! Disgraced in the eyes of the world you shall invoke, try to prove to that world that you are neither guilty nor mad !'

" Then, addressing the man who accompanied him :

" ' Executioner,' said he, ' do your duty.'

" Oh ! his name, his name !" cried Felton, "tell it me !"

" Then, in spite of my cries, in spite of my resistance, for I began to comprehend that there was a question of something worse than death, the executioner seized me, threw me on the floor, fastened me with his bonds, and suffocated by sobs, almost without sense, invoking God, who did not listen to me, I uttered all at once a frightful cry of pain and shame ; a burning fire, a red hot iron, the iron of the executioner, was imprinted on my shoulder."

Felton uttered a groan.

" Here," said milady, rising with the majesty of a queen—" here, Felton, behold the new martyrdom invented for a pure young girl, the victim of the brutality of a villain. Learn to know the heart of men, and henceforth make yourself less easily the instrument of their unjust vengeances."

Milady, with a rapid gesture, opened her robe, tore the cambric that covered her bosom, and red with feigned anger and simulated shame, showed the young man the ineffaceable impression which dishonoured that beautiful shoulder.

" But," cried Felton, "that is a fleur-de-lis which I see there."

" And therein consisted the infamy," replied milady. "The brand of England !—it would be necessary to prove what tribunal had imposed it on me, and I could have made a public appeal to all the tribunals of the kingdom ; but the brand of France !——oh ! by it, by it I was really branded indeed !"

This was too much for Felton.

Pale, motionless, overwhelmed by this frightful revelation, dazzled by the superhuman beauty of this woman, who unveiled herself before him with an immodesty which appeared to him sublime, he ended by falling on his knees before her, as the early Christians did before those pure and holy martyrs whom the persecution of the emperors gave up in the circus to the sanguinary lubricity of the populace. The brand disappeared, the beauty alone remained.

"Pardon! pardon!" cried Felton, "oh! pardon!"

Milady read in his eyes, love! love!

"Pardon for what?" asked she.

"Pardon me for having joined with your persecutors."

Milady held out her hand to him.

"So beautiful! so young!" cried Felton, covering that hand with his kisses.

Milady let one of those looks fall upon him which make a slave of a king.

Felton was a Puritan; he abandoned the hand of this woman to kiss her feet.

He no longer loved her, he adored her.

When this crisis was past, when milady appeared to have resumed her self-possession, which she had never lost; when Felton had seen her cover again with the veil of chastity those treasures of love which were only concealed from him to make him desire them the more ardently,—

"Ah! now," said he, "I have only one thing to ask of you, that is, the name of your true executioner, for, for me there is but one; the other was an instrument, that was all."

"What, brother!" cried milady, "must I name him again, have you not yet divined who he is?"

"What!" cried Felton, "he!—again he!—always he! What!—the truly guilty?"

"The truly guilty," said milady, "is the ravager of England, the persecutor of true believers, the base ravisher of the honour of so many women, he who, to satisfy a caprice of his corrupt heart, is about to make England shed so much blood, who protects the Protestants to-day and will betray them to-morrow——"

"Buckingham! it is, then, Buckingham!" cried Felton, in a high state of exasperation.

Milady concealed her face in her hands, as if she could not endure the shame which this name recalled to her.

"Buckingham, the executioner of this angelic creature!" cried Felton. "And thou hast not hurled thy thunder at him, my God! and thou hast left him noble, honoured, powerful, for the ruin of us all!"

"God abandons him who abandons himself," said milady.

"But he will draw down upon his head the punishment reserved for the damned!" said Felton, with increasing warmth; "he wills that human vengeance should precede heavenly justice."

"Men fear him and spare him."

"I!" said Felton, "I do not fear him, nor will I spare him!"

The soul of milady was as if bathed in an infernal joy.

"But how can Lord de Winter, my protector, my father," asked Felton, "possibly be mixed up with all this ?"

" Listen, Felton," resumed milady, " for by the side of base and contemptible men, there are often found great and generous natures. I had an affianced husband, a man whom I loved, and who loved me ; a heart like yours, Felton, a man like you. I went to him and told him all ; he knew me, that man did, and did not doubt an instant. He was a nobleman, a man equal to Buckingham, in every respect. He said nothing, he only girded on his sword, enveloped himself in his cloak, and went straight to Buckingham Palace."

" Yes, yes," said Felton ; " I understand how he would act ; but with such men it is not the sword, it is the poniard that should be employed."

" Buckingham had left England the day before, sent ambassador to Spain, to demand the hand of the Infanta for king Charles I., who was then only Prince of Wales. My affianced husband returned.

" ' Hear me,' said he ; ' this man is gone, and for the moment has, consequently, escaped my vengeance ; but let us be united, as we were to have been, and then leave it to Lord de Winter to maintain his own honour and that of his wife.' "

" Lord de Winter !" cried Felton.

" Yes," said milady, " Lord de Winter ; and now you can understand it all, can you not ? Buckingham remained nearly a year absent. A week before his return Lord de Winter died, leaving me his sole heir. Whence came the blow ? God who knows all, knows without doubt ; but as for me, I accuse nobody."

" Oh ! what an abyss ! what an abyss !" cried Felton.

" Lord de Winter died without revealing anything to his brother. The terrible secret was to be concealed till it burst, like a clap of thunder, over the head of the guilty. Your protector had seen with pain this marriage of his elder brother with a portionless girl. I was sensible that I could look for no support from a man disappointed in his hopes of an inheritance. I went to France, with a determination to remain there for the rest of my life. But all my fortune is in England. Communication being closed by the war, I was in want of everything. I was then obliged to come back again. Six days ago I landed at Portsmouth."

" Well ?" said Felton.

" Well. Buckingham heard by some means, no doubt, of my return. He spoke of me to Lord de Winter, already prejudiced against me ; and told him that his sister-in-law was a prostitute, a branded woman. The noble and pure voice of my husband was no longer there to defend me. Lord de Winter believed all that was told him, with so much the more facility from its being his interest to believe it. He caused me to be arrested, had me conducted hither, and placed me under your guard. You know the rest. The day after to-morrow he banishes me, he transports me ; the day after to-morrow he exiles me among the infamous. Oh ! the scheme is well laid ! the plot is clever ! my honour will not survive it ! You see, then, Felton, I can do nothing but die ! Felton, give me that knife !"

And, at these words, as if all her strength was exhausted, milady sank weak and languishing into the arms of the young officer, who, intoxicated with love, anger, and hitherto unknown sensations of delight, received her with transport, pressed her against his heart, all trembling at the breath from that charming mouth, bewildered by the contact with that beautiful bosom.

"No, no," said he, "no, you shall live honoured and pure, you shall live to triumph over your enemies."

Milady put him from her slowly with her hand, whilst drawing him nearer with her look ; but Felton, in his turn, embraced her more closely, imploring her like a divinity.

"Oh, death ! death !" said she, lowering her voice and her eyelids ; "oh, death rather than shame ! Felton, my brother, my friend, I conjure you !"

"No," cried Felton, "no ; you shall live, and you shall be avenged."

"Felton, I bring misfortune to all who surround me ! Felton, abandon me ! Felton, let me die !"

"Well, then, we will live and die together !" cried he, gluing his lips to those of the prisoner.

Several strokes resounded on the door ; this time milady really pushed him away from her.

"Hark !" said she ; "we have been overheard ; some one is coming ! all is over ! we are lost !"

"No," said Felton ; "it is only the sentinel warning me that they are about to change guard."

"Then run to the door and open it yourself."

Felton obeyed, this woman was now his whole thought, his whole soul.

He found a sergeant commanding a watch patrol.

"Well ! what is the matter ?" asked the young lieutenant.

"You told me to open the door if I heard any one cry out," said the soldier ; "but you forgot to leave me the key. I heard you cry out, without understanding what you said. I tried to open the door, but it was locked inside ; then I called the sergeant."

"And here I am," said the sergeant.

Felton, quite bewildered, almost mad, stood speechless.

Milady plainly perceived that it was now her turn to come forward : she ran to the table, and seizing the knife which Felton had laid down,—

"And by what right will you prevent me from dying ?" said she.

"Great God !" exclaimed Felton, on seeing the knife glitter in her hand.

At that moment a burst of ironical laughter resounded through the corridor. The baron, attracted by the noise, in his robe-de-chambre, his sword under his arm, stood in the doorway.

"Ah ! ah !" said he ; "here we are, arrived at the last act of the tragedy. You see, Felton, the drama has gone through all the phases I named ; but be at ease, no blood will flow."

Milady perceived that all was lost unless she gave Felton an immediate and terrible proof of her courage.

" You are mistaken, my lord, blood will flow ; and may that blood fall back on those who cause it to flow !"

Felton uttered a cry, and rushed towards her ; he was too late ; milady had stabbed herself.

But the knife had fortunately, we ought to say skilfully, come in contact with the steel busk, which at that period, like a cuirass, defended the chests of the women ; it had glided down it, tearing the robe, and had penetrated slantingly between the flesh and the ribs.

Milady's robe was not the less stained with blood in a second.

Felton snatched away the knife.

" See, my lord," said he, in a deep, gloomy tone, " here is a woman who was under my guard, and who has killed herself !"

" Be at ease, Felton," said Lord de Winter, " she is not dead ; demons do not die so easily. Be at ease, and go and wait for me in my chamber."

" But, my lord !——"

" Go, sir, I command you."

At this injunction from his superior, Felton obeyed ; but, in going out, he put the knife into his bosom.

As to Lord de Winter, he contented himself with calling the woman who waited on milady, and when she was come, he recommended the prisoner, who was still fainting, to her care, and left her alone with her.

But as, all things considered, notwithstanding his suspicions, the wound might be serious, he immediately sent off a man and horse to fetch a doctor.

CHAPTER LVIII.

ESCAPE.

As Lord de Winter had thought, milady's wound was not dangerous. So soon as she was left alone with the woman whom the baron had summoned to her assistance, she opened her eyes.

It was, however, necessary to affect weakness and pain ; not a very difficult task for so finished an actress as milady. Thus the poor woman was completely the dupe of the prisoner, whom, notwithstanding her entreaties to the contrary, she persisted in watching during the remainder of the night.

But the presence of this woman did not prevent milady from thinking.

There was no longer a doubt that Felton was convinced : Felton was hers. If an angel appeared to that young man as an accuser of milady, he would take him, in the disposition of mind he was then in, for a messenger from the demon.

Milady smiled at this thought, for Felton was from that time her only hope—her only means of safety.

But Lord de Winter might have suspected him—Felton himself might now be watched !

Towards four o'clock in the morning, the doctor arrived ; but since the time milady had stabbed herself, however short, the wound had closed. The doctor could, therefore, measure neither the direction nor the depth of it ; he only satisfied himself that, by milady's pulse, the case was not serious.

In the morning, milady, under the pretence of not having slept well in the night, and wanting rest, sent away the woman who attended her.

She had one hope ; which was, that Felton would appear at the breakfast hour ; but Felton did not come.

Were her fears realised ? Was Felton, suspected by the baron, about to fail her at the decisive moment ? She had only one day left. Lord de Winter had announced her embarkation for the 23rd, and it was now the morning of the 22nd.

Nevertheless, she still waited patiently till the hour for dinner.

Although she had eaten nothing in the morning, the dinner was brought in at its usual time ; milady then perceived with terror that the uniform of the soldiers that guarded her was changed.

Then she ventured to ask what had become of Felton.

She was told that he had left the castle an hour before, on horseback. She inquired if the baron was still at the castle. The soldier replied that he was, and that he had given orders to be informed if the prisoner wished to speak to him.

Milady replied that she was too weak at present, and that her only desire was to be left alone.

The soldier went out, leaving the dinner-table covered.

Felton was sent away ; the marines were removed ; Felton was then mistrusted !

This was the last blow to the prisoner.

Left alone, she got up. The bed in which she had remained from prudence, and that she might be believed to be seriously wounded, burnt her like a bed of fire. She cast a glance at the door : the baron had had a plank nailed over the grating ; he no doubt feared that, by this opening, she might still, by some diabolical means, succeed in corrupting her guards.

Milady smiled with joy. She was free now to give way to her transports without being observed. She traversed her chamber with the fury of a mad woman, or of a tigress shut up in an iron cage. Certes, if the knife had been left in her power, she would now have thought, not of killing herself, but of killing the baron.

At six o'clock, Lord de Winter came in : he was armed at all points. This man, in whom milady, till that time, had only seen a sufficiently simple gentleman, had become an admirable gaoler : he appeared to foresee everything, to divine everything, to prevent everything.

A single look at milady informed him of all that was passing in her mind.

"Aye !" said he, " I see ; but you shall not kill me to-day ; you have no longer a weapon ; and besides, I am on my guard. You began to pervert my poor Felton ; he was yielding to your infernal influence ; but I will save him,—he will never see you again,—all is over. Get your clothes together, to-morrow you shall go. I had fixed the embarkation for the 24th ; but I have reflected that the more promptly the affair takes place, the more certain it will be. To-morrow, by twelve o'clock, I shall have the order for your exile, signed—' Buckingham.' If you speak a single word to any one before being on ship-board, my sergeant will blow your brains out ; he has orders to do so ; if, when on board, you speak a single word to any one before the captain permits you, the captain will have you thrown into the sea,—that is agreed upon.

"*Au revoir*, then,—that is all I have to say to-day. To-morrow I will see you again, to take my leave of you." And at these words the baron went out. Milady had listened to all this menacing tirade with a smile of disdain on her lips, but rage in her heart.

The supper was served ; milady felt that she stood in need of all her strength ; she did not know what might take place during this night, which approached so menacingly ; for large masses of cloud rolled over the face of the heavens, and distant lightning announced a storm.

The storm came on about ten o'clock : milady felt a consolation in seeing nature partake of the disorder of her heart ; the thunder growled in the air like the passion and anger in her thoughts : it appeared to her that the blast as it swept along dishevelled her brow, as it bowed the branches of the trees and bore away their leaves ; she howled as the hurricane howled, and her voice was lost in the great voice of nature, who also seemed to groan with despair.

All at once she heard a tap at her window, and by the help of a flash of lightning she saw the face of a man appear behind the bars.

She ran to the window and opened it.

"Felton !" cried she,—" I am saved !"

"Yes !" said Felton ; " but be silent ! be silent ! I must have time to file through these bars. Only take care that I am not seen through the grating of the door."

"Oh ! it is a proof that the Lord is on our side, Felton," replied milady ; " they have closed up the grating with a board."

"That is well, God has made them senseless !" said Felton.

"But what must I do ?" asked milady.

"Nothing ! nothing ! only shut the window. Go to bed, or at least lie down in your clothes ; as soon as I have done I will knock on one of the panes of glass. But are you strong enough to follow me ?"

"Oh ! yes !"

"Your wound ?"

"Gives me pain, but will not prevent my walking."

"Be ready, then, at the first signal."

Milady shut the window, extinguished the lamp, and went, as Felton had desired her, to lie down on the bed. Amidst the moaning of the storm she heard the grinding of the file upon the bars, and by the light of every flash she perceived the shadow of Felton through the window.

She passed an hour apparently, unable to breathe, panting, with a cold sweat upon her brow, and her heart oppressed by frightful agony at every movement she heard in the corridor.

There are hours which last a year.

At the expiration of an hour, Felton tapped again.

Milady sprang out of bed and opened the window. Two bars removed formed an opening large enough for a man to pass through.

" Are you ready ?" asked Felton.

" Yes. Must I take anything with me ?"

" Money, if you have any."

" Yes, fortunately, they have left me all I had."

" So much the better, for I have expended all mine in hiring a vessel."

" Here !" said milady, placing a bag full of louis in Felton's hands.

Felton took the bag and threw it to the foot of the wall.

" Now," said he, " will you come ?"

" I am ready."

Milady mounted upon a chair, and passed the upper part of her person through the window ; she saw the young officer suspended over the abyss by a ladder of ropes. For the first time, an emotion of terror reminded her that she was a woman. The dark space frightened her.

" I expected this," said Felton.

" Oh ! it's nothing ! it's nothing !" said milady ; " I will descend with my eyes shut."

" Have you confidence in me ?" said Felton.

" How can you ask me such a question ?"

" Put your two hands together. Cross them—that's right !"

Felton tied her two wrists together with an handkerchief, and then over the handkerchief with a cord.

" What are you doing ?" asked milady with surprise.

" Pass your arms around my neck, and fear nothing."

" But I shall make you lose your balance, and we shall both be dashed to pieces."

" Don't be afraid ; I am a sailor."

Not a second was to be lost; milady passed her arms round Felton's neck, and let herself slip out of the window. Felton began to descend the ladder slowly, step by step ; notwithstanding the weight of their bodies, the blast of the hurricane made them wave in the air.

All at once Felton stopped.

" What is the matter ?" asked milady.

" Silence," said Felton, " I hear footsteps."

" We are discovered !"

There was a silence of several seconds.

" No," said Felton, " it is nothing."

" But what noise was that then ?"

" That of the patrol going their round."

" Where is their round ?"

" Just under us."

" They will discover us !"

" No ; if it does not lighten, they will not."

" But they will run against the ladder."

" Fortunately it is too short by six feet."

" Here they are ! my God !"

" Silence !"

Both remained suspended, motionless and breathless, within twenty paces of the ground, whilst the patrol passed beneath them, laughing and talking.

This was a terrible moment for the fugitives.

The patrol passed : the noise of their retreating footsteps and the murmur of their voices soon died away.

" Now," said Felton, " we are safe !"

Milady breathed a deep sigh and fainted.

Felton continued to descend. When arrived at the bottom of the ladder, and he found no more support for his feet, he clung with his hands ; at length, arrived at the last step, he hung by his hands and touched the ground. He stooped down, picked up the bag of money, and carried it in his teeth. Then he took milady in his arms and set off briskly in the direction opposite to that which the patrol had taken. He soon left the path of the rounds, descended across the rocks, and when arrived on the edge of the sea, whistled.

A similar signal replied to him, and five minutes after, a boat appeared, rowed by four men.

The boat approached as near as it could to the shore, but there was not depth of water enough for it to touch ; and Felton walked into the sea up to his middle, being unwilling to trust his precious burden to anybody.

Fortunately the storm began to die away, but still the sea was disturbed ; the little boat bounded over the waves like a nutshell.

" To the sloop," said Felton, " and row quickly."

The four men bent to their oars, but the sea was too rough to let them take much hold of it.

They, however, left the castle behind : that was the principal thing. The night was extremely dark, it was almost impossible to distinguish the shore from the boat, it was therefore less likely to distinguish the boat from the shore.

A black point floated on the sea—that was the sloop.

Whilst the boat was advancing with all the speed its four rowers could give it, Felton untied the cord, and then the handkerchief which bound milady's hands together. When her hands were loosed, he took some sea-water and sprinkled it over her face.

Milady breathed a sigh and opened her eyes.

"Where am I ?" said she.

" Saved," replied the young officer.

"Oh ! saved ! saved !" cried she. " Yes, there are the heavens, here is the sea ! the air I breathe is the air of liberty ! Ah ! thanks, Felton, thanks !"

The young man pressed her to his heart.

" But what is the matter with my hands ?" asked milady : " it seems as if my wrists had been crushed in a vice ?"

Milady held out her arms, and her wrists appeared bruised.

" Alas !" said Felton, looking at those beautiful hands and shaking his head sorrowfully.

" Oh ! it's of no consequence ! it's nothing !" cried milady ; " I remember now."

Milady looked around her, as if in search of something.

" It is there," said Felton, touching the bag of money with his foot.

They drew near to the sloop. A sailor on watch hailed the boat, the boat replied.

" What vessel is that ?" asked milady.

" The one I have hired for you."

" Where is it to take me to ?"

" Where you please, after you have put me on shore at Portsmouth."

" What are you going to do at Portsmouth ?" asked milady.

" To accomplish the orders of Lord de Winter," said Felton, with a gloomy smile.

" What orders ?" said milady.

" Do you not understand ?" asked Felton.

" No ; explain yourself, I beg."

" As he mistrusted me, he determined to guard you himself, and sent me in his place to get Buckingham to sign the order for your transportation."

" But if he mistrusted you, how could he confide such an order to you ?"

" How could I be supposed to know what I was the bearer of ?"

" That's true ! And you are going to Portsmouth !"

" I have no time to lose : to-morrow is the 23rd, and Buckingham sets sail to-morrow with his fleet."

" He sets sail to-morrow ! Where for ?"

" For La Rochelle."

" He must not sail !" cried milady, forgetting her usual presence of mind.

" Be satisfied," replied Felton ; " he will not sail."

Milady started with joy ; she could read to the depths of the heart of this young man ; the death of Buckingham was there written at full length.

" Felton——" cried she, " you are as great as Judas Maccabeus ! If you die, I will die with you ; that is all I am able to say to you."

" Silence !" cried Felton ; " we are arrived."

They were, in fact, close to the sloop.

Felton ascended first, and gave his hand to milady, whilst the sailors supported her, for the sea was still much agitated.

An instant after they were on the deck.

"Captain," said Felton, "this is the person of whom I spoke to you, and whom you must convey safe and sound to France."

"For a thousand pistoles," said the captain.

"I have paid you five hundred of them."

"That's correct," said the captain.

"And here are the other five hundred," replied milady, placing her hand upon the bag of gold.

"No," said the captain, "I make but one bargain; and I have agreed with this young man that the other five hundred shall not be due to me till we arrive at Boulogne."

"And shall we arrive there?"

"Safe and sound," said the captain; "as true as my name's Jack Butler."

"Well!" said milady, "if you keep your word, instead of five hundred, I will give you a thousand pistoles"

"Hurrah! for you, then, my pretty lady," cried the captain; "and may God often send me such passengers as your ladyship."

"In the meanwhile," said Felton, "convey me to the little bay of—— you know it was agreed you should put in there."

The captain replied by ordering the necessary manœuvres, and towards seven o'clock in the morning the little vessel cast anchor in the bay that had been named.

During this passage, Felton related everything to milady; how, instead of going to London, he had hired the little vessel; how he had returned; how he had scaled the wall by fastening cramps in the interstices of the stones as he ascended, to give him foothold: and how, when he had reached the bars, he fastened his ladder; milady knew the rest.

On her side, milady was going to endeavour to encourage Felton in his project; but at the first words that issued from her mouth, she plainly saw that the young fanatic stood more in need of being moderated than urged on.

It was agreed that milady should wait for Felton till ten o'clock; if he did not return by ten o'clock, she was to sail without him.

In that case, and supposing he was at liberty, he was to rejoin her in France, at the convent of the Carmelites, at Bethune.

CHAPTER LIX.

WHAT TOOK PLACE AT PORTSMOUTH ON THE 23RD AUGUST, 1628.

FELTON took leave of milady as a brother about to go for a mere walk takes leave of his sister, kissing her hand.

His whole person appeared in its ordinary state of calmness; only an unusual fire beamed from his eyes, like the effects of a fever; his brow was more pale than it generally was; his teeth were clenched, and his speech had a short dry accent, which indicated that something dark was at work within him.

As long as he remained in the boat which conveyed him to land, he kept his face towards milady, who, standing on the deck, followed him with her eyes. Both felt relieved from the fear of pursuit ; nobody ever came into milady's apartment before nine o'clock ; and it would require three hours to go from the castle to London.

Felton jumped on shore, climbed the little ascent which led to the top of the beach, saluted milady a last time, and took his course towards the city.

At the end of a hundred paces, the ground began to decline again, and he could, on turning round, only see the mast of the sloop.

He immediately ran in the direction of Portsmouth, which he saw at nearly half a league before him, standing out in the haze of the morning, with its houses and towers.

Beyond Portsmouth, the sea was covered with vessels, whose masts, like a forest of poplars, bent with each breath of the wind.

Felton, in his rapid walk, repassed in his mind all which two years of meditations and a long residence among partisans furnished of accusations, true or false, against the favourite of James I. and Charles I.

When he compared the public crimes of this minister, startling crimes, European crimes, if so we may say, with the private and unknown crimes with which milady had charged him, Felton found that the more culpable of the two men which formed the character of Buckingham was the one of whom the public knew not the life. This was because his love, so strange, so new, and so ardent, made him view the infamous and imaginary accusations of Lady de Winter as we view, through a magnifying glass, as frightful monsters, atoms in reality imperceptible by the side of an ant.

The rapidity of his walk heated his blood still more; the idea that he left behind him, exposed to a frightful vengeance, the woman he loved, or rather that he adored as a saint, the emotion he had experienced, present fatigue, all together exalted his mind above human feeling.

He entered Portsmouth about eight o'clock in the morning ; the whole population was on foot ; drums were beating in the streets and in the port ; the troops about to be embarked were marching towards the sea.

Felton arrived at the palace of the Admiralty, covered with dust, and streaming with perspiration. His countenance, usually so pale, was purple with heat and passion. The sentinel wanted to repulse him, but Felton called to the officer of the post, and drawing from his pocket the letter of which he was the bearer,—

"A pressing message from the Lord de Winter," said he.

At the name of Lord de Winter, who was known to be one of his grace's most intimate friends, the officer of the post gave orders for Felton to be allowed to pass, who, besides, wore the uniform of a naval officer.

Felton darted into the palace.

At the moment he entered the vestibule, another man was entering likewise, covered with dust, and out of breath, leaving at the gate a post-horse, which, as soon as he had alighted from it, sank down exhausted.

Felton and he addressed Patrick, the duke's confidential valet-dechambre, at the same moment. Felton named Lord de Winter, the unknown would not name anybody, and asserted that it was to the duke alone he should make himself known. Each was anxious to gain admission before the other.

Patrick, who knew Lord de Winter was in affairs of duty and in relations of friendship with the duke, gave the preference to him who came in his name. The other was forced to wait, and it was easily to be seen how he cursed the delay.

The valet-de-chambre led Felton through a large hall, in which waited the deputies from La Rochelle, headed by the Prince de Soubise, and introduced him into a closet, where Buckingham, just out of the bath, was finishing his toilet, on which, as at all times, he bestowed extraordinary attention.

"Lieutenant Felton, on the part of the Lord de Winter,' said Patrick.

"From Lord de Winter !" repeated Buckingham ; "let him come in."

Felton entered. At that moment Buckingham was throwing upon a couch a rich robe-de-chambre worked with gold, to put on a blue velvet doublet embroidered with pearls.

"Why did not the baron come himself?" demanded Buckingham ; "I expected him this morning."

"He desired me to tell your grace," replied Felton, "that he very much regretted not having that honour, but that he was prevented by the guard he is obliged to keep at the castle."

"Yes, I know," said Buckingham ; "he has a prisoner."

"It is of that prisoner I wish to speak to your grace," replied Felton.

"Well, then, speak !"

"That which I have to say of her can only be heard by yourself, my lord !"

"Leave us, Patrick," said Buckingham, "but remain within sound of the bell. I will call you presently."

Patrick went out.

"We are alone, sir," said Buckingham ; "speak !"

"My lord," said Felton, "the Baron de Winter wrote to you the other day to request you to sign an order of embarkation relative to a young woman named Charlotte Backson."

"Yes, sir, and I answered him, that if he would bring or send me that order, I would sign it."

"Here it is, my lord."

"Give it to me," said the duke.

And, taking it from Felton, he cast a rapid glance over the paper, and perceiving that it was the one that had been mentioned to him, he placed it on the table, took a pen, and prepared to sign it.

"I ask your pardon, my lord," said Felton, stopping the duke ; "but does your grace know that the name of Charlotte Backson is not the true name of this young woman ?"

" Yes, sir, I do know it," replied the duke, dipping the pen in the ink.

" Then your grace knows her real name?" asked Felton, in a sharp tone.

" Yes, I know that too;" and the duke put the pen to the paper. Felton grew pale.

" And, knowing that real name, my lord," replied Felton, " will you sign it all the same?"

" Doubtless, I will," said Buckingham, " and rather twice than once."

" I cannot believe," continued Felton, in a voice that became more sharp and rough, " that your grace knows that it is to Lady de Winter this relates."

" I do know it, perfectly well, although I must confess I am astonished that you know it."

" And will your grace sign that order without remorse?"

Buckingham looked at the young man with much *hauteur*.

" Do you know, sir, that you are asking me very strange questions, and that it is very silly, on my part, to answer them?"

" Reply to them, my lord," said Felton; " the circumstances are more serious than perhaps you imagine."

Buckingham reflected that the young man, coming from Lord de Winter, perhaps spoke in his name, and softened his manner a little.

" Doubtless, without any remorse," said he, " the baron knows, as well as myself, that Lady de Winter is a very guilty woman, and it is treating her very favourably to remit her punishment to transportation."

The duke put his pen to the paper again.

" You will not sign that order, my lord!" said Felton, making a step towards the duke.

" I will not sign this order!" said Buckingham, " and why not?"

" Because you will consult your own conscience, and you will do justice to my lady."

" I should do justice to my lady by sending her to Tyburn," said the duke; " my lady is an infamous woman."

" My lord, Lady de Winter is an angel; you know that she is, and I demand her liberty of you."

" Why, the man must be mad to talk to me in this manner!" said Buckingham.

" My lord, excuse me! I speak as I am able; I restrain myself all I can. But, my lord, think of what you are about to do, and beware of going too far!"

" What do you say? God pardon me!" cried Buckingham, " I really think the man threatens me!"

" No, my lord, I still pray, and I say to you: one drop of water suffices to make the full vase overflow, one slight fault may draw down punishment upon the head spared amidst many crimes."

" Master Felton," said Buckingham, " you will please to withdraw, and place yourself under arrest immediately."

" You shall hear me to the end, my lord. You have seduced this young girl, you have outraged, defiled her; repair your crimes towards her, let her go free, and I will require nothing else of you."

" You will require !" said Buckingham, looking at Felton with astonishment, and dwelling upon each syllable of the words as he pronounced them.

" My lord," continued Felton, becoming more excited as he spoke—"my lord, beware ! all England is tired of your iniquities ; my lord, you have abused the royal power, which you have almost usurped ; my lord, you are held in horror by God and men ; God will punish you hereafter, but I will punish you here !"

" Well ! this is too much !" cried Buckingham, making a step towards the door.

Felton barred his passage.

" I ask it humbly of you, my lord," said he ; "sign the order for the liberation of Lady de Winter ; reflect, she is a woman you have dishonoured.'

" Withdraw, sir," said Buckingham, " or I will call my attendant, and have you placed in irons."

" You shall not call," said Felton, throwing himself between the duke and the bell placed upon a *gueridon* incrusted with silver : " beware, my lord, you are in the hands of God !"

" In the hands of the devil, you mean !" cried Buckingham, raising his voice so as to attract the notice of his people, without absolutely calling.

" Sign, my lord, sign the liberation of Lady de Winter," said Felton, holding a paper to the duke.

" What, by force ! you are joking ! hilloa ! Patrick !"

" Sign, my lord !"

" Never."

" Never ?"

" Who waits there ?" cried the duke aloud, and at the same time sprang towards his sword.

But Felton did not give him time to draw it ; he held the knife with which milady had stabbed herself, open in his bosom ; at one bound he was upon the duke.

At that moment Patrick entered the room, crying :

" A letter from France, my lord."

" From France !" cried Buckingham, forgetting everything on thinking from whom that letter came.

Felton took advantage of this moment, and plunged the knife into his side up to the handle.

" Ah ! traitor !" cried Buckingham, " thou hast killed me !"

" Murder !" screamed Patrick.

Felton cast his eyes round for means of escape, and seeing the door free, he rushed into the next chamber, in which, as we said, the deputies from La Rochelle were waiting, crossed it as quickly as possible, and precipitated himself towards the staircase ; but upon the first step he met Lord de Winter, who, seeing him pale, confused, livid, and stained with blood both on his hands and face, seized him, crying :

" I knew it ! I guessed it ! but too late by a minute, unfortunate, unfortunate that I am !"

Felton made no resistance ; Lord de Winter placed him in the hands of the guards, who led him, whilst awaiting fresh orders, to a little terrace looking out upon the sea : and then the baron hastened to the duke.

At the cry uttered by the duke and the scream of Patrick, the man whom Felton had met in the antechamber, rushed into the closet.

He found the duke reclining upon a sofa, with his hand pressed upon the wound.

"Laporte," said the duke in a faint voice, "Laporte, do you come from her ?"

"Yes, monseigneur," replied the faithful cloak-bearer of Anne of Austria, "but too late perhaps."

"Silence ! Laporte, you may be overheard : Patrick, let no one enter : oh ! I cannot tell what she says to me ! my God ! I am dying !"

And the duke fainted.

In the meanwhile, Lord de Winter, the deputies, the leaders of the expedition, the officers of Buckingham's household, had all made their way into the chamber : cries of despair resounded on all sides. The news which filled the palace with tears and groans soon became known, and was spread throughout the city.

The report of a cannon announced that something new and unexpected had taken place.

Lord de Winter tore his hair in agony.

"Too late by a minute !" cried he, "too late by a minute ! oh ! my God ! my God ! what a misfortune !"

He had been informed at seven o'clock in the morning that a ladder of ropes was floating from one of the windows of the castle ; he had hastened to milady's chamber, found it empty, the window open, and the bars filed, had remembered the verbal caution D'Artagnan had transmitted to him by his messenger, had trembled for the duke, and running to the stable, without taking time to have a horse saddled, had jumped upon the first he came to, had galloped off at full speed, had alighted in the courtyard, had ascended the stairs precipitately, and on the top step, as we have said, had met Felton.

The duke, however, was not dead ; he recovered a little, opened his eyes, and hope revived in all hearts.

"Gentlemen," said he, "leave me alone with Patrick and Laporte,— Ah ! is that you, De Winter ! you sent me a strange madman, this morning ; see what a state he has placed me in !"

"Oh, my lord !" cried the baron, "I shall never console myself for it."

"And you would be quite wrong, my dear De Winter," said Buckingham, holding out his hand to him, "I do not know the man who deserves being regretted during the whole life of another man—but leave us, I pray you."

The baron went out sobbing with grief.

There only remained in the closet of the wounded duke, Laporte and Patrick. A doctor was being sought for, but none was yet found.

"You will live, milord, you will live!" repeated the faithful servant of Anne of Austria, on his knees before the duke's sofa.

"What has she written to me?" said Buckingham, feebly, streaming with blood, and suppressing his agony to speak of her he loved; "what has she written to me? read me her letter."

"Oh! milord!" said Laporte.

"Obey, Laporte; do you not see I have no time to lose?"

Laporte broke the seal, and placed the paper before the eyes of the duke; but Buckingham in vain endeavoured to make out the writing.

"Read!" said he, "read! I cannot see, read then! for soon, perhaps, I shall not hear, and I shall die without knowing what she has written to me."

Laporte made no more difficulty, and read:

"MILORD,—By that which, since I have known you, I have suffered by you and for you, I conjure you, if you have any care for my repose, to interrupt those great armaments which you are preparing against France, to put an end to a war, of which it is publicly said religion is the ostensible cause, and of which, it is generally whispered, your love for me is the concealed and real cause. This war may not only bring great catastrophes upon England and France, but misfortunes upon you, milord, for which I should never console myself.

"Be careful of your life, which is menaced, and which will be dear to me from the moment I am not obliged to see an enemy in you.

"Your affectionate
"ANNE."

Buckingham collected all his remaining strength to listen to the reading of the letter; then, when it was ended, as if he had met with a bitter disappointment,—

"Have you nothing else to say to me, yourself, Laporte?" asked he.

"Yes, milord! the queen charged me to tell you to be very careful, for she has been informed that your assassination would be attempted."

"And is that all? is that all?" replied Buckingham, impatiently.

"She likewise charged me to tell you that she still loved you."

"Ah!" said Buckingham, "God be praised! my death, then, will not be to her as the death of a stranger!"

Laporte burst into tears.

"Patrick," said the duke, "bring me the casket in which the diamond studs were kept."

Patrick brought the object desired, which Laporte recognised as having belonged to the queen.

"Now the *sachet* of white satin, upon which her cipher is embroidered in pearls."

Patrick again obeyed.

"Here, Laporte," said Buckingham, "these are the only remembrances I ever received from her, this silver casket and these letters. You will restore them to her majesty: and as a last memorial"—(he looked round for some valuable object)—" you will add——"

He still sought ; but his eyes, darkened by death, met with nothing but the knife which had fallen from the hand of Felton, still smoking with the blood spread over its blade.

"And you will add to them this knife," said the duke, pressing the hand of Laporte. He had just strength enough to place the *sachet* at the bottom of the silver casket, and to let the knife fall into it, making a sign to Laporte that he was no longer able to speak ;—and then, in a last convulsion, with which he had not the power to contend, he slipped off the sofa on the floor.

Patrick uttered a loud cry.

Buckingham endeavoured to smile a last time ; but death arrested his wish, which remained engraven on his brow like a last kiss of love.

At this moment the duke's surgeon arrived, quite terrified ; he was already on board the admiral's ship, from which he had been obliged to be fetched.

He approached the duke, took his hand, held it for an instant in his own, and letting it fall,—

"All is useless," said he, "he is dead."

"Dead ! dead !" screamed Patrick.

At this cry all the crowd came again into the apartment, and throughout the palace and town there was nothing but consternation and tumult.

As soon as Lord de Winter saw Buckingham was dead, he ran to Felton, whom the soldiers still guarded on the terrace of the palace.

"Miserable wretch !" said he, to the young man, who since the death of Buckingham had regained that coolness and self-possession which never after abandoned him ; "miserable wretch ! what hast thou done?"

"I have avenged myself!" said he.

"Avenged yourself!" said the baron ; "rather say that you have served as an instrument to that accursed woman ; but I swear to you, that this crime shall be her last crime."

"I don't know what you mean," replied Felton, quietly ; "and I am ignorant of whom you are speaking, my lord : I killed the Duke of Buckingham because he twice refused you yourself to appoint me captain ; I have punished him for his injustice, that is all."

De Winter, quite stupefied, looked on while the soldiers bound Felton, and could not tell what to think of such insensibility.

One thing alone, however, threw a shade over the pallid brow of Felton. At every noise he heard, the simple Puritan fancied he recognised the step and voice of milady coming to throw herself into his arms, to accuse herself, and meet death with him.

All at once he started—his eyes became fixed upon a point of the sea, which the terrace upon which he was overlooked ; with the eagle glance of a sailor, he had recognised there, where another would have only seen a gull hovering over the waves, the sail of the sloop, which was directed towards the coast of France.

He grew deadly pale, placed his hand upon his heart, which was breaking, and at once perceived all the treachery.

" One last favour, my lord !" said he, to the baron.

" What is that ?" replied his lordship.

" What o'clock is it ?"

The baron drew out his watch.

" It wants ten minutes to nine."

Milady had advanced her departure by an hour and a half ; as soon as she heard the cannon which announced the fatal event, she had ordered the anchor to be weighed.

The vessel was making way under a blue sky at a great distance from the coast.

" God has so willed it !" said he, with the resignation of a fanatic ; but without, however, being able to take his eyes from that ship, on board of which he doubtless fancied he could distinguish the white phantom of her to whom he had sacrificed his life.

De Winter followed his look, observed his feelings, and guessed all.

" Be punished *alone*, in the first place, miserable man !" said Lord de Winter to Felton, who was being dragged away with his eyes turned towards the sea, " but I swear to you, by the memory of my brother whom I loved so much, that your accomplice is not saved."

Felton hung down his head without pronouncing a syllable.

As to Lord de Winter he descended the stairs rapidly, and went straight to the port.

CHAPTER LX.

IN FRANCE.

THE first fear of the King of England, Charles I., on learning the death of the duke, was that such terrible news might discourage the Rochellais ; he endeavoured, says Richelieu in his memoirs, to conceal it from them as long as possible, closing all the ports of his kingdom, and carefully keeping watch that no vessel should go out until the army which Buckingham was getting together had set sail, taking upon himself, in default of Buckingham, to superintend its departure.

He carried the strictness of this order so far as to detain in England the ambassadors of Denmark, who had taken leave, and the ordinary ambassador of Holland, who was to take back to the port of Flushing the Indian merchantmen of which Charles I. had made restitution to the United Provinces.

But as he did not think of giving this order till five hours after the event, that is to say, till two o'clock in the afternoon, two vessels had already left the port : the one bearing, as we know, milady, who already anticipating the event, was further confirmed in that belief by seeing the black flag flying at the mast-head of the admiral's ship.

As to the second vessel, we will tell hereafter whom it carried, and how it set sail.

During all this time, nothing fresh occurred in the camp at La Rochelle ; only the king, who grew weary everywhere, but perhaps a little more so in the camp than in any other place, resolved to go incognito and spcnd the festival of St. Louis at St. Germain's, and asked the cardinal to order him an escort of twenty musketeers only. The cardinal, who sometimes became weary of the king, granted this leave of absence with great pleasure to his royal lieutenant, who promised to return about the 15th of September.

M. de Tréville, upon being informed by his eminence, maue up his portmanteau, and as, without knowing the cause, he knew the great desire and even imperative want that his friends had to return to Paris, he fixed upon them, of course, to form part of the escort.

The four young men heard the news a quarter of an hour after M. de Tréville, for they were the first to whom he communicated it. It was then that D'Artagnan appreciated the favour the cardinal had conferred upon him by making him at last pass into the musketeers, for without that circumstance he would have been forced to remain in the camp, whilst his companions left it.

It must be admitted that this impatience to return towards Paris had for cause the danger which Madame Bonacieux would run of meeting at the Convent of Bethune with milady, her mortal enemy. Aramis, therefore, had written immediately to Marie Michon, the seamstress at Tours, who had such fine acquaintances, to obtain from the queen authority for Madame Bonacieux to leave the convent, and to retire either into Lorraine or Belgium. They had not long to wait for an answer ; a week after, Aramis received the following letter :

" MY DEAR COUSIN,—With this you will receive the order from my sister to withdraw our little servant from the convent of Bethume, the air of which you think does not agree with her. My sister sends you this order with great pleasure, for she is very partial to the little girl, and to whom she intends to be more serviceable hereafter.

" I salute you,
" MARIE MICHON."

In this letter was enclosed an order conceived in these terms :

" The superior of the Convent of Bethune will place in the hands of the person who shall present this note to her, the novice who entered the convent upon my recommendation, and under my patronage.

" At the Louvre, August 10th, 1628. " ANNE."

It may be easily imagined how the relationship between Aramis and a seamstress who called the queen her sister amused the young men ; but Aramis, after having blushed up to the eyes at the gross jokes of Porthos, begged his friends not to revert to the subject again, declaring that if another single word were said to him about it, he would never again implore his cousin to interfere in such affairs.

There was no further question, therefore, of Marie Michon among the four musketeers, who, besides, had what they wanted : that was, the order to withdraw Madame Bonacieux from the convent of the Carmelites of Bethune. It was true that this order would not be of great use to them whilst they were in camp at La Rochelle, that is to say, at the other end of France ; therefore, D'Artagnan was going to ask leave of absence of M. de Tréville, confiding to him candidly the importance of his departure, when the news was transmitted to him, as well as to his three friends, that the king was about to set out for Paris with an escort of twenty musketeers, and that they formed part of the escort.

Their joy was great. The lackeys were sent on before with the baggage, and they set out on the morning of the 16th.

The cardinal accompanied his majesty from Surgères to Mauzé, and there the king and his minister took leave of each other with great demonstrations of friendship.

The king, however, who sought amusement, whilst travelling as fast as possible, for he was anxious to be in Paris by the 23rd, stopped from time to time to fly the pie, a pastime for which the taste had been formerly communicated to him by De Luynes, and for which he had always preserved a great predilection. Out of the twenty musketeers, sixteen, when the thing happened, rejoiced greatly at this relaxation, but the other four cursed it heartily. D'Artagnan, in particular, had a perpetual buzzing in his ears, which Porthos explained thus :

"A very great lady told me that that means somebody is talking of you somewhere."

At length the escort passed through Paris on the 23rd, in the night; the king thanked M. de Tréville, and permitted him to distribute leaves of absence for four days, upon condition that the favoured parties should not appear in any public place, under penalty of the Bastille.

The four first leaves granted, as may be imagined, were to our four friends. Still further, Athos obtained of M. de Tréville six days instead of four, and introduced into these six days two more nights, for they set out on the 24th, at five o'clock in the evening, and, as a further kindness, M. de Tréville post-dated the leave to the 25th in the morning.

"Good Lord !" said D'Artagnan, who, as we have often said, never doubted of anything—"it appears to me that we are making a great trouble of a very simple thing : in two days, and by knocking up two or three horses (which I care little about, as I have plenty of money) I am at Bethune, I present my letter from the queen to the superior, and I bring back the dear treasure I go to seek, not into Lorraine, not into Belgium, but to Paris ; where she will be much better concealed, particularly whilst the cardinal is at La Rochelle. Well, once returned from the campaign, half by the protection of her cousin, half in favour of what we have personally done for her, we shall obtain from the queen what we desire. Remain, then, where you are, and do not exhaust yourselves with useless fatigue : myself and Planchet. that is all that such a simple expedition as this requires."

To this Athos replied quietly :

"We, also, have money left ; for I have not yet drunk all my share of the diamond, and Porthos and Aramis have not eaten all theirs. We are, therefore, in a condition to knock up four horses as well as one. But consider, D'Artagnan," added he, in a tone so solemn that it made the young man shudder, "consider that Bethune is a city at which the cardinal has appointed to meet a woman, who, wherever she goes, brings misery with her. If you had only to deal with four men, D'Artagnan, I would allow you to go alone ; you have to do with that woman—we will go, and I hope to God that, with our four lackeys, we may be in sufficient number."

"You terrify me, Athos !" cried D'Artagnan ; "my God ! what do you fear ?"

"Everything !" replied Athos.

D'Artagnan examined the countenances of his companions, which, like that of Athos, wore an impression of deep anxiety, and they continued their route as fast as their horses could carry them, but without adding another word.

On the evening of the 25th, as they were entering Arras, and as D'Artagnan was dismounting at the auberge of the Herse d'Or to drink a glass of wine, a horseman came out of the posting-yard, where he had just had a relay, starting off at a gallop, and with a fresh horse, and taking the road to Paris. At the moment he was passing through the gateway into the street, the wind blew open the cloak in which he was enveloped, although it was in the month of August, and lifted his hat, which the traveller seized with his hand at the moment it had left his head, and pulled it down eagerly over his eyes.

D'Artagnan, who had his eyes fixed upon this man, became very pale, and let his glass fall.

"What is the matter, monsieur ?" said Planchet. "Oh, come, gentlemen, gentlemen ! my master is ill !"

The three friends hastened towards D'Artagnan, but, instead of finding him ill, met him running towards his horse. They stopped him at the door.

"Where the devil are you going to now, in this fashion ?" cried Athos.

"It is he !" cried D'Artagnan, pale with passion, and with the sweat on his brow, "it is he ! let me overtake him !"

"He ! but what he ?" asked Athos.

"He—that man !"

"What man ?"

"That cursed man, my evil genius, whom I have always met with when threatened by some misfortune—he who accompanied the horrible woman when I met her for the first time—he whom I was seeking when I offended our Athos—he whom I saw on the very morning Madame Bonacieux was carried off ! I have seen him ! that is he ! I recognised him when his cloak blew open !"

"The devil !" said Athos, musingly.

"To horse, gentlemen ! to horse ! let us pursue him ; we shall overtake him !"

"My dear friend," said Aramis, "remember that it is in an opposite direction to that in which we are going, that he has a fresh horse, and ours are fatigued, so that we shall disable our own horses without a chance of overtaking him. Let the man go, D'Artagnan ; let us save the woman."

"Monsieur, monsieur !" cried a stableman, running out and looking after the unknown—"monsieur, here is a paper which dropped out of your hat ! monsieur !"

"Friend," said D'Artagnan, " a half-pistole for that paper !"

"Ma foi ! monsieur, with great pleasure ! here it is !"

The stableman, delighted with the good day's work he had done, went into the yard again ; D'Artagnan unfolded the paper.

"Well ?" eagerly demanded all his three friends.

"Nothing but one word !" said D'Artagnan.

"Yes," said Aramis, "but that one word is the name of some town or village."

"*Armentières !*" read Porthos ; "Armentières—I don't know such a place."

"And that name of a town or village is written in her hand !" cried Athos.

"Come on, then ! come on, then !" said D'Artagnan ; "let us keep that paper carefully—perhaps I have not thrown away my half-pistole. To horse, my friends, to horse !"

And the four friends galloped off on the road to Bethune.

CHAPTER LXI.

THE CONVENT OF THE CARMELITES AT BETHUNE.

GREAT criminals bear about them a kind of predestination which makes them surmount all obstacles, which makes them escape all dangers, till the moment which a wearied Providence has marked as the rock of their impious fortunes.

It was thus with milady. She passed through the cruisers of both nations, and arrived at Boulogne without accident.

When landing at Portsmouth, milady was an Englishwoman, whom the persecutions of the French drove from La Rochelle ; when landing at Boulogne, after a two days' passage, she passed for a Frenchwoman, whom the English persecuted at Portsmouth, out of their hatred for France.

Milady had, likewise, the best of passports—her beauty, her noble appearance, and the liberality with which she distributed her pistoles. Freed from the usual formalities by the affable smile and gallant manners of an old governor of the port, who kissed her hand, she only remained long enough at Boulogne to put into the post a letter, conceived in the following terms :

"To his Eminence Monseigneur the Cardinal de Richelieu, in his camp before Rochelle.

"Monseigneur, let your eminence be reassured : his grace the Duke of Buckingham *will not set out* for France.

"Boulogne, evening of the 25th.

                                           "MILADY DE . . . ."

"P.S.—According to the desire of your eminence, I am going to the Convent of the Carmelites of Bethune, where I will await your orders."

Accordingly, that same evening, milady commenced her journey; night overtook her; she stopped, and slept at an auberge; at five o'clock the next morning she again proceeded, and in three hours after entered Bethune.

She inquired for the Convent of the Carmelites, and went to it immediately.

The superior came out to her; milady showed her the cardinal's order; the abbess assigned her a chamber, and had breakfast served.

All the past was effaced from the eyes of this woman, and her looks, fixed on the future, beheld nothing but the high fortunes reserved for her by the cardinal, whom she had so successfully served, without his name being in any way mixed up with the sanguinary affair. The ever-new passions which consumed her gave to her life the appearance of those clouds which float in the heavens, reflecting sometimes azure, sometimes fire, sometimes the opaque blackness of the tempest, and which leave no traces upon the earth behind them but devastation and death.

After breakfast, the abbess came to pay her a visit. There is very little amusement in the cloister, and the good superior was eager to make acquaintance with her new pensioner.

Milady wished to please the abbess. Now this was a very easy matter for a woman so really superior as she was: she endeavoured to be agreeable, and she was charming, winning the good superior by her varied conversation and by the graces spread over her whole person.

The abbess, who was the daughter of a noble house, took particular delight in histories of the court, which so seldom travel to the extremities of the kingdom, and which, above all, have so much difficulty in penetrating the walls of convents, at whose gates the noise of the world appears to die away.

Milady, on the contrary, was quite conversant in all aristocratic intrigues, amidst which she had constantly lived for five or six years; she made it her business, then, to amuse the good abbess with the mundane practices of the court of France, mixed with the extravagant devotions of the king; she made for her the scandalous chronicle of the lords and ladies of the court, whom the abbess knew perfectly by name; touched lightly on the amours of the queen and the Duke of Buckingham, talking a great deal to induce her auditor to talk a little.

But the abbess contented herself with listening and smiling, without replying a word. Milady, however, saw that this style of conversation amused her very much, and continued; only she now turned her chat in the direction of the cardinal.

But she was greatly embarrassed—she did not know whether the abbess was a royalist or a cardinalist; she therefore confined herself to a prudent middle course. But the abbess, on her part, maintained a reserve still more prudent, contenting herself with making a profound inclination of the head every time that the fair traveller pronounced the name of his eminence.

Milady began to conceive she should soon grow weary of a convent life ; she resolved then, to risk something, in order that she might know how to act afterwards. Desirous of seeing how far the discretion of the good abbess would go, she began to tell a story, obscure at first, but very circumstantial afterwards, of the cardinal, relating the amours of the minister with Madame d'Aiguillon, Marion de Lorme, and several other women of gallantry.

The abbess listened more attentively, grew animated by degrees, and smiled.

" Good !" thought milady ; " she takes a pleasure in my conversation. If she is a cardinalist, she has no fanaticism in her partiality."

She then went on to describe the persecutions exercised by the cardinal upon his enemies. The abbess only crossed herself, without approving or disapproving.

This confirmed milady in her opinion that the abbess was rather a royalist than a cardinalist ; milady, therefore, continued, heightening her narrations more and more.

" I am very little acquainted with all these matters," said the abbess at length ; " but however distant from the court we may be, however remote from the interests of the world we may be placed, we have very sad examples of what you have related ; and one of our pensioners has suffered much from the vengeance and persecution of Monsieur le Cardinal."

" One of your pensioners !" said milady ; " oh, my God ! poor woman, I pity her, then !"

" And you have reason to do so, for she is much to be pitied : imprisonment, menaces, ill-treatment, she has suffered everything. But after all," resumed the abbess, " Monsieur le Cardinal has, perhaps, plausible motives for acting thus ; and though she has the look of an angel, we must not always judge people by appearances."

" Good !" said milady to herself ; " who knows ! I am about, perhaps, to discover something here ; I am in the vein."

And she tried to give her countenance an appearance of perfect candour.

" Alas !" said milady, " I know it is so. It is said that we must not trust to the physiognomy ; but in what, then, shall we place confidence, if not in the most beautiful work of the Lord ? As for me, I shall be deceived all my life, perhaps, but I shall always have faith in a person whose countenance inspires me with sympathy."

" You would, then, be tempted to believe," said the abbess, " that this young person was innocent ?"

" M. le Cardinal does not always pursue crimes," said she ; " there are certain virtues that he pursues more severely than certain offences."

" Permit me, madame, to express my surprise," said the abbess.

"Upon what occasion?" said milady, with the utmost ingenuousness.

"Upon the language you hold."

"What do you find so astonishing in that language ?" said milady, smiling.

"You are the friend of the cardinal, for he sends you hither, and yet——"

"And yet I speak ill of him," replied milady, finishing the thought of the superior.

"At least, you don't speak well of him."

"That is because I am not his friend," said she, sighing, "but his victim !"

"Well, but this letter by which he recommends you to me ?"

"Is an order for me to confine myself to a sort of prison, from which he will release me by one of his satellites."

"But why have you not fled ?"

"Whither should I go ? Do you believe there is a spot on the earth which the cardinal cannot reach, if he takes the trouble to stretch forth his hand ? If I were a man, certainly that would be possible, but what can a woman do ? This young pensioner of yours, has she endeavoured to fly ?"

"No, that is true ; but she—that is another thing, for I believe she is detained in France by some love affair."

"Ah," said milady, with a sigh, "if she is in love, she is not altogether wretched."

"Then," said the abbess, looking at her with increasing interest, "I behold another poor persecuted woman ?"

"Alas ! yes," said milady.

The abbess looked at her for an instant with uneasiness, as if a fresh thought had arisen in her mind.

"You are not an enemy of our holy faith ?" said she, hesitatingly.

"Who—I ?" cried milady—"I a Protestant ! Oh no ! I attest the God who hears us, that, on the contrary, I am a fervent Catholic !"

"Then, madame," said the abbess, smiling, "be reassured ; the house in which you are shall not be a very hard prison, and we will do all in our power to make you in love with your captivity. You will find here, moreover, the young woman of whom I spoke, who is persecuted, no doubt, in consequence of some court intrigue. She is amiable and well-behaved.'

"What is her name ?"

"She was sent to me by some one of high rank, under the name of Kitty. I have not endeavoured to discover her other name."

"Kitty !" cried milady ; "what ! are you sure ?"

"That she is called so ? Yes, madame. Do you know her ?"

Milady smiled to herself at the idea which had occurred to her, that this might be her old waiting-maid. There was connected with the remembrance of this girl a remembrance of anger ; and a desire of vengeance disordered the features of milady, but which, however, immediately recovered the calm and benevolent expression which this woman of a hundred faces had for a moment allowed them to lose.

"And when can I see this young lady, for whom I already feel so great a sympathy ?" asked milady.

"Why, this evening," said the abbess : "to-day even. But you have been travelling these four days, as you told me : this morning you rose at five o'clock ; you must stand in need of repose. Go to bed and sleep, at dinner time we will call you."

Although milady would very willingly have gone without sleep, sustained as she was by all the excitements that a fresh adventure awakened in her heart, ever thirsting for intrigues, she nevertheless accepted the offer of the superior : during the last fifteen days she had experienced so many and such various emotions, that if her frame of iron was still capable of supporting fatigue, her mind required repose.

She therefore took leave of the abbess, and went to bed, softly rocked by the ideas of vengeance which the name of Kitty had naturally brought back to her thoughts. She remembered that almost unlimited promise which the cardinal had given her if she succeeded in her enterprise. She had succeeded, D'Artagnan was then in her power !

One thing alone frightened her ; that was, the remembrance of her husband, the Count de la Fère, whom she had thought dead, or at least expatriated, and whom she found again in Athos, the best friend of D'Artagnan.

But also, if he was the friend of D'Artagnan, he must have lent him his assistance in all the proceedings by the means of which the queen had defeated the projects of his eminence ; if he was the friend of D'Artagnan, he was the enemy of the cardinal ; and she, doubtless, should succeed in enveloping him in the folds of the vengeance by which she hoped to destroy the young musketeer.

All these hopes were so many sweet thoughts for milady ; so, rocked by them, she soon fell asleep.

She was awakened by a soft voice, which sounded at the foot of her bed. She opened her eyes, and saw the abbess, accompanied by a young woman, with light hair and a delicate complexion, who fixed upon her a look full of benevolent curiosity.

The face of the young woman was entirely unknown to her ; each examined the other with great attention, whilst exchanging the customary compliments ; both were very handsome, but of quite different styles of beauty. Milady, however, smiled on observing that she excelled the young woman by far in her high air and aristocratic bearing. It is true that the habit of a novice, which the young woman wore, was not very advantageous in a contest of this kind.

The abbess introduced them to each other ; then, when this formality was gone through, as her duties called her to the church, she left the two young women alone.

The novice, seeing milady remained in bed, was about to follow the example of the superior ; but milady stopped her.

"How, madame," said she, "I have scarcely seen you, and you already wish to deprive me of your company, upon which I had reckoned a little, I must confess, during the time I have to pass here?"

"No, madame," replied the novice, "only I thought I had chosen my time ill: you were asleep—you are fatigued."

"Well," said milady, "what can people who are asleep wish for? a happy awakening. This awakening you have given me; allow me then to enjoy it at my ease;" and taking her hand, she drew her towards the chair by the bedside.

The novice sat down.

"How unfortunate I am!" said she; "I have been here six months, without the shadow of an amusement; you arrive, and your presence was likely to afford me delightful company, and I expect, according to all probability, from one moment to another, to leave the convent?"

"Are you then going soon?" asked milady.

"At least I hope so," said the novice, with an expression of joy which she made no effort to disguise.

"I think I learned you had suffered persecutions from the cardinal," continued milady; "that would have been another motive for sympathy between us."

"What I have heard then from our good mother is true; you have likewise been a victim of that wicked priest?"

"Hush!" said milady; "let us not, even here, speak thus of him: almost all my misfortunes arise from my having said nearly what you have said, before a woman whom I thought my friend, and who betrayed me. Are you also the victim of a treachery?"

"No," said the novice, "but of my devotedness; of a devotedness to a woman I loved, for whom I would have laid down my life, for whom I would still do so."

"And who has abandoned you, is that it?"

"I have been sufficiently unjust to believe so; but during the last two or three days I have obtained proof to the contrary, for which I thank God! for it would have cost me very dear to think she had forgotten me. But you, madame, you appear to be free; and if you were inclined to fly, it only rests with yourself to do so."

"Whither would you have me go, without friends, without money, in a part of France with which I am unacquainted, and where I have never been before."

"Oh!" cried the novice, "as to friends, you would have them wherever you went, you appear so good and are so beautiful!"

"That does not prevent," replied milady, softening her smile so as to give it an angelic expression, "my being alone or being persecuted."

"Hear me," said the novice; "we must trust in heaven; there always comes a moment when the good you have done pleads your cause before God; and, see, perhaps it is a happiness for you, humble and powerless as I am, that you have met with me: for, if I leave this place; well! I have powerful friends, who, after having exerted themselves on my account, may also exert themselves for you."

"Oh! when I said I was alone," said milady, hoping to make the novice speak by speaking of herself, "it is not for want of some highly-placed friends; but these friends themselves tremble before the cardinal: the queen herself does not dare to oppose the terrible minister: I have proof that her majesty, notwithstanding her excellent heart, has more than once been obliged to abandon persons who had served her, to the anger of his eminence."

"Trust me, madame, the queen may appear to have abandoned those persons; but we must not put faith in appearances: the more they are persecuted, the more she thinks of them; and often, when they the least expect it, they receive proofs of a kind remembrance."

"Alas!" said milady, "I believe so: the queen is so good!"

"Oh! you know her, then! that lovely and noble queen, by your speaking of her thus!" cried the novice warmly.

"That is to say," replied milady, driven into her intrenchments, "that I have not the honour of knowing her personally; but I know a great number of her most intimate friends; I am acquainted with M. de Putange; I met M. Dujart in England; I know M. de Tréville."

"M. de Tréville!" exclaimed the novice, "do you know M. de Tréville?"

"Yes, perfectly well, intimately even."

"What, the captain of the king's musketeers?"

"Yes, the captain of the king's musketeers."

"Oh! why then, only see!" cried the novice, "we shall soon be well acquainted, almost friends; "if you know M. de Tréville, you must have visited him?"

"Often!" said milady, who having entered this track, and perceiving that falsehood succeeded, was determined to carry it on.

"If you have visited him, you must have met some of his musketeers?"

"All such as he is in the habit of receiving!" replied milady, for whom this conversation began to have a real interest.

"Name a few of those you know, and you will find they are my friends."

"Well!" said milady, a little embarrassed, "I know M. de Sauvigny, M. de Courtviron, M. de Ferrusac."

The novice let her speak, but observing she stopped,—

"Don't you know," said she, "a gentleman of the name of Athos?"

Milady became as pale as the sheets in which she was reclining, and mistress as she was of herself, could not help uttering a cry, seizing the hand of the novice, and devouring her with her looks.

"What is the matter? Good God!" asked the poor woman; "have I said anything that has hurt your feelings?"

"No, no; but the name struck me; because I also have known that gentleman, and it appeared strange to me to meet with a person who appears to know him well."

"Oh, yes, well! very well! not only him, but some of his friends: MM. Porthos and Aramis!"

"Indeed! you know them, likewise! I know them," cried milady, who began to feel a chill penetrate to her heart.

"Well! if you know them, you know that they are good and worthy gentlemen ; why do you not apply to them, if you stand in need of support ?"

" That is to say," stammered milady, "I am not really very intimate with any of them ; I know them from having heard one of their friends, a Monsieur D'Artagnan, say a great deal about them."

" You know M. d'Artagnan !" cried the novice, in her turn seizing the hands of milady, and fixing her eyes upon her.

Then, remarking the strange expression of milady's countenance—

" Pardon me, madame," said she, " you know him, by what title ?"

"Why," replied milady, considerably embarrassed, " why, by the title of friend."

" You are deceiving me, madame," said the novice ; " you have been his mistress !"

" It is you who have been his mistress, madame," cried milady, in her turn.

" I !" said the novice.

"Yes, you ; I know you now : you are Madame Bonacieux."

The young woman drew back in surprise and terror.

" Oh, do not deny it ! answer !" continued milady.

" Well! yes, madame !" said the novice ; " are we rivals ?"

The countenance of milady was illumined by so savage a joy, that under any other circumstances, Madame Bonacieux would have fled away in terror ; but she was absorbed by her jealousy.

" Speak, madame !" resumed Madame Bonacieux, with an energy of which she might not have been thought to be capable, " have you been, or are you, his mistress ?"

"Oh, no !" cried milady, with a tone that admitted no doubt of her truth ; "never ! never !"

" I believe you," said Madame Bonacieux ; " but why, then, did you cry out so ?"

" Do you not understand ?" said milady, who had already overcome her agitation, and recovered all her presence of mind.

"How can I understand ? I know nothing."

"Can you not understand that M. d'Artagnan, being my friend, might take me into his confidence ?"

" Indeed !"

" Do you not perceive that I know all ? Your being carried off from the little house at St. Germain, his despair, that of his friends, and their useless inquiries up to this moment ! How could I help being astonished, when, without having the least expectation of such a thing, I meet you face to face ; you, of whom we have so often spoken together, you, whom he loves with all his soul ; you, whom he had taught me to love before I had seen you ! Ah ! dear Constance, I have found you then, I see you at last !"

And milady stretched out her arms to Madame Bonacieux, who, convinced by what she had just said, saw nothing in this woman, whom an instant before she had believed to be her rival, but a sincere and devoted friend,

" Oh ! pardon me ! pardon me !" cried she, sinking upon the shoulders of milady ; " pardon me ! I love him so dearly !"

These two women held each other for an instant in a close embrace. Certes, if milady's strength had been equal to her hatred, Madame Bonacieux would have never escaped alive from that embrace.

But not being able to stifle her, she smiled upon her.

" Oh ! dear, pretty, good little creature !" said milady, " how delighted I am to have found you ! Let me look at you !" And, whilst saying these words, she absolutely devoured her with her eyes. " Oh ! yes, it is you indeed ! From what he has told me, I know you now ; I recognise you perfectly."

The poor young woman could not possibly suspect what was passing of frightful cruelty behind the rampart of that pure brow, behind those brilliant eyes, in which she read nothing but interest and compassion.

" Then you know what I have suffered," said Madame Bonacieux, " since he has told you what he has suffered : but to suffer for him is happiness."

Milady replied mechanically, " Yes, that is happiness."

She was thinking of something else.

" And then," continued Madame Bonacieux, " my punishment is drawing to a close : to-morrow, this evening perhaps, I shall see him again ; and then the past will no longer exist."

" This evening ?" asked milady, roused from her reverie by these words ; " what do you mean ? Do you expect any news from him ?"

" I expect him himself."———" Him himself ! D'Artagnan here !"

" Yes, him himself !'

" But that's impossible ! He is at the siege of La Rochelle, with the cardinal ; he will not return before the taking of the city."

" Ah ! you fancy so ; but is there anything impossible for my D'Artagnan, the noble and loyal gentleman ?"

" Oh, I cannot believe you !"

" Well, read, then !" said the unhappy young woman, in the excess of her pride and joy, presenting a letter to milady.

" Humph ! the writing of Madame de Chevreuse !" said milady to herself. " Ah ! I always thought there was some intelligence carried on on that side !" And she greedily read the following few lines :

" MY DEAR CHILD.—Hold yourself in readiness. *Our friend* will see you soon, and he will only see you to release you from that imprisonment in which your safety required you should be concealed. Prepare, then, for your departure, and never despair of us.

" Our charming Gascon has just proved himself as brave and faithful as ever. Tell him that certain parties are grateful to him for the warning he has given."

" Yes, yes, " said milady, " the letter is precise. Do you know what that warning was ?"

" No ; I only suspect he has warned the queen against some fresh machinations of the cardinal."

"Yes, that's it, no doubt !" said milady, returning the letter to Madame Bonacieux, and allowing her head to sink in a pensive manner upon her bosom.

At that moment the galloping of a horse was heard.

"Oh !" cried Madame Bonacieux, darting to the window : "can it be he !"

Milady remained still in bed, petrified by surprise ; so many unexpected things happened to her all at once, that for the first time she was at a loss.

"Ho ! ho !" murmured she ; "can it be he ?" And she remained in bed with her eyes fixed.

"Alas ! no," said Madame Bonacieux : "it is a man I don't know ; and yet he seems to be coming here. Yes, he has checked his horse—he stops at the gate—he rings."

Milady sprang out of bed.

"Are you sure it is not he ?" said she.

"Oh ! yes—very sure !"

"Perhaps you did not see him plainly."

"Oh ! if I were to see the plume of his hat, the end of his cloak, I should know him !"

Milady continued to dress herself.

"Never mind ! The man is coming here, do you say ?"

"Yes, he is come in."

"He must come either to you or to me."

"Good God ! how agitated you seem !"

"Yes, I admit I am so. I have not your confidence ; I am in dread of the cardinal."

"Hush !" said Madame Bonacieux ; "somebody is coming."

In fact, the door opened, and the superior entered.

"Do you come from Boulogne ?" demanded she of milady.

"Yes, I do," replied she, endeavouring to recover her self-possession; "Who wants me ?"

"A man who will not tell his name, but who comes from the cardinal."

"And who wishes to speak with me ?" asked milady.

"Who wishes to speak to a lady recently come from Boulogne."

"Then let him come in, if you please."

"Good God ! good God !" cried Madame Bonacieux ; "can it be any bad news ?"

"I am afraid so."

"I will leave you with this stranger · but as soon as he is gone, if you will permit me, I will return."

"Certainly ! I beg you will."

The superior and Madame Bonacieux retired.

Milady was left alone, with her eyes fixed upon the door. An instant after, the jingling of spurs was heard upon the stairs, steps drew near, the door opened, and a man appeared.

Milady uttered a cry of joy : this man was the Count de Rochefort, the *âme damnée* of the cardinal.

CHAPTER LXII.

TWO VARIETIES OF DEMONS.

"Ah!" cried milady and Rochefort together, "is that you?"

"Yes it is."

"And you come?"—asked milady.

"From La Rochelle—and you?"

"From England."

"Buckingham?"

"Dead or desperately wounded, as I left without being able to obtain anything of him. A fanatic has just assassinated him."

"Ah!" said Rochefort, with a smile; "this is a fortunate chance —one that will delight his eminence! Have you informed him of it?"

"I wrote to him from Boulogne. But what brings you here?"

"His eminence was uneasy, and sent me to inquire after you."

"I only arrived yesterday."

"And what have you been doing since yesterday?"

"I have not lost my time."

"Oh! I have no fear of that."

"Do you know whom I have found here?"

"No."

"Guess."

"How can I?"

"That young woman whom the queen took out of prison."

"The mistress of that fellow D'Artagnan?"

"Yes, Madame Bonacieux, with whose retreat the Cardinal was unacquainted."

"Upon my word!" said De Rochefort, "here is a chance that may be paired with the other! Truly, Monsieur le Cardinal is a privileged man!"

"Imagine my astonishment," continued milady, "when I found myself face to face with this woman?"

"Does she know you?"

"No."

"Then she looks upon you as a stranger?"

Milady smiled.

"I am her best friend."

"Upon my honour, it is only you, my fair countess, that can perform such miracles!"

"And it is well I can, chevalier," said milady; "for do you know what is going on here?"

"No."

"She is about to be taken away to-morrow, or the day after, with an order from the queen."

"Indeed! And who is going to do that?"

"D'Artagnan and his friends."

"They certainly will go so far, we shall be obliged to put them into the Bastille at last."

"Why is it not done already?"

"Why, because M. le Cardinal has a weakness with respect to these men which I cannot at all account for."

"Indeed!"

"Yes."

"Well then! tell him this, Rochefort: tell him that our conversation at the auberge of the Colombier Rouge was overheard by these four men; tell him that, after his departure, one of them came up to me, and took from me, by violence, the safe-conduct which he had given me tell him they warned Lord de Winter of my passage to England; that this time they had nearly made me fail in my mission, as they did in the affair of the studs; tell him that, among these four men, two only are to be feared,—D'Artagnan and Athos; tell him that the third, Aramis, is the lover of Madame de Chevreuse; he may be left alone, we know his secret, and it may be useful; as to the fourth, Porthos, he is a fool, a simpleton, a blustering booby, not worth troubling himself about."

"But these four men must be now at the siege of La Rochelle?"

"I thought so too, but a letter which Madame Bonacieux has received from Madame la Connétable, and which she has had the imprudence to show me, leads me to believe that these four men, on the contrary, are on the road hither to take her away."

"The devil! what's to be done?"

"What did the cardinal say with respect to me?"

"I was to take your despatches, written or verbal, to return post; and when he shall know what you have done, he will think of what you have to do."

"I must then remain here?"

"Here, or in the environs."

"You cannot take me with you?"

"No; the order is imperative: near the camp, you might be recognised; and your presence, you must be aware, would compromise the cardinal."

"Then I must wait here or in this neighbourhood?"

"Only tell me, beforehand, where you will wait for commands from the cardinal: let me know always where to find you."

"But, observe, it is probable I may not be able to remain here."

"Why not?"

"You forget that my enemies may arrive at any minute."

"That's true; but then, is this little woman to escape his eminence?"

"Bah!" said milady, with a smile that only belonged to herself, "did not I tell you I was her best friend?"

"Ah! that's true, likewise; I may then tell the cardinal, with respect to this little woman——"

"That he may be at ease."

"Is that all?"

" He will know what that means."

" He will guess, at least.　Now, then, what had I better do?"

" Set off back again directly; it appears to me that the news you bear is worth the trouble of a little diligence."

" My chaise broke down coming into Lilliers."

" I am glad of that."

" Why, glad of of that?"

" Yes, I am; I want your chaise."

" And how shall I travel, then?——"

" On horseback."

" You talk very much at your ease; a hundred and eighty leagues?"

" What's that?"

" Well, that may be done; and then?"

" Then? why, in passing through Lilliers you will send me your chaise, with an order to your servant to place himself at my disposal."

" Well."

" You have, no doubt, about you some order from the cardinal?"

" I have my *full power.*"

" Show it to the abbess, and tell her that some one will come and fetch me, either to-day or to-morrow, and that I am to follow the person who presents himself in your name."

" Very well."

" Don't forget to treat me harshly, in speaking of me to the abbess."

" To what purpose?"

" I am a victim of the cardinal.　I must inspire confidence in that poor little Madame Bonacieux."

" That's true.　Now, will you make me a report of all that has happened?"

" Why, I have related the events to you, you have a good memory, repeat what I have told you;—a paper may be lost."

" You are right; only let me know where to find you, that I may not lose my time in hunting for you about the neighbourhood."

"That's correct; wait a minute."

" Do you want a map?"

" Oh! I know this country well?"

" You? when were you here before?"

" I was brought up here."

" Indeed!"

" It is worth something, you see, to have been brought up somewhere."

"You will wait for me, then?"

" Let me reflect a little: aye, that will do, at Armentières."

" Where is that Armentières?"

" A little town upon the Lys; I shall only have to cross the river, and I shall be in a foreign country."

" Just so! but it is understood you will only cross the river in case of danger."

" Certainly not."

"And in that case, how shall I know where you are?"

"You do not want your lackey."

"No."

"Is he to be depended on?"

"Perfectly."

"Give him to me, then; nobody knows him; I will leave him at the place I may quit, and he will conduct you to me."

"And you say you will wait for me at Armentières?"

"At Armentières."

"Write that name on a piece of paper, lest I should forget it; there is no fear of compromising yourself in that; a name of a town, is it not?"

"Eh! who knows? never mind," said milady, writing the name upon half a sheet of paper; "I will commit myself."

"That will do," said Rochefort, taking the paper from milady, folding it, and placing it in the lining of his hat; "besides, to make sure, I will do as children do, for fear of losing the paper, repeat the name as I go along. Now, is that all?"

"I believe so."

"Let us see; Buckingham dead, or grievously wounded; your conversation with the cardinal overheard by the four musketeers; De Winter warned of your arrival at Portsmouth; D'Artagnan and Athos to the Bastille; Aramis the lover of Madame de Chevreuse; Porthos a fool; Madame Bonacieux found again; to send you the chaise as soon as possible; to place my lackey at your disposal; to make you out to be a victim of the cardinal, in order that the abbess may entertain no suspicion; Armentières, on the banks of the Lys. Is that all correct?"

"In good truth, my dear chevalier, you are a miracle of memory. Apropos, add one thing——"

"What is that?"

"I saw some very pretty woods which come close to the convent garden; say that I may be permitted to walk in those woods; who knows? perhaps I shall stand in need of a back door to go out at."

"You think of everything."

"And you forget one thing."

"What's that?"

"To ask me if I want any money."

"That's true, how much do you want?"

"All you have in gold."

"I have five hundred pistoles, or thereabouts."

"I have as much; with a thousand pistoles we may face everything. Empty your pockets."

"There it is, then."

"That's well! when do you start?"

"In an hour—time to eat a morsel, during which I shall send some one to look for a post-horse."

"All well! Adieu, chevalier!"

"Adieu, countess!"

" Commend me to the cardinal !"

" Commend me to Satan !"

Milady and Rochefort exchanged a smile and separated.

An hour afterwards, Rochefort set out at his horse's best speed ; five hours after that he passed through Arras.

Our readers already know that he was recognised by D'Artagnan, and how that recognition, by inspiring fear in the four musketeers, had given fresh activity to their journey.

CHAPTER LXIII.

THE DROP OF WATER.

ROCHEFORT had scarcely departed, when Madame Bonacieux re-entered. She found milady with a smiling countenance.

" Well," said the young woman, " what you dreaded has happened ; this evening, or to-morrow, the cardinal will send some one to take you away !"

" Who told you that, my dear ?" asked milady.

" I heard it from the mouth of the messenger himself."

" Come and sit down close to me," said milady ; "and let me be assured no one can hear us."

" Why do you take all these precautions ?"

" You shall know."

Milady arose, went to the door, opened it, looked in the corridor, and then returned and seated herself close to Madame Bonacieux.

" Then," said she, " he has well played his part."

" Who has ?"

" He who just now presented himself to the abbess as a messenger from the cardinal."

" It was, then, a part he was playing ?"

" Yes, my dear."

" That man, then, was not——"

" That man," said milady, lowering her voice, " is my brother !"

" Your brother !" said Madame Bonacieux.

" Mind, no one must know this secret, my dear, but yourself. If you reveal it to any one, whatever, I shall be lost, and perhaps you likewise !"

" Oh ! good God !"

" Listen to me ; this is what has happened. My brother, who was coming to my assistance, to take me away, by force, if it were necessary, met with the emissary of the cardinal, who was coming in search of me. He followed him. When arrived at a solitary and retired part of the road, he drew his sword and required the messenger to deliver up to him the papers of which he was the bearer ; the messenger resisted ; my brother killed him."

" Oh !" said Madame Bonacieux, with a shudder.

" Remember, that was the only means. Then my brother determined to substitute cunning for force. He took the papers, and presented himself here as the emissary of the cardinal, and in an hour or two a carriage will come to take me away by the orders of his eminence."

"I understand : your brother sends this carriage."

"Exactly so ; but that is not all. That letter you have received, and which you believe to be from Madame de Chevreuse——"

"Well ?"

"It is a forgery."

"How can that be ?"

"Yes, a forgery ; it is a snare to prevent your making any resistance when the persons come to fetch you."

"But it is D'Artagnan that will come !"

"Do not deceive yourself. D'Artagnan and his friends are detained at the siege of La Rochelle."

"How do you know that ?"

"My brother met some emissaries of the cardinal in the uniform of musketeers. You would have been summoned to the gate, you would have thought you went to meet friends, you would have been carried off, and conducted back again to Paris."

"Oh ! good God ! My senses fail me amidst such a chaos of iniquities. I feel, if this continues," said Madame Bonacieux, raising her hands to her forehead, "I shall go mad !"

"Stop——"

"What ?"

"I hear a horse's steps , it is my brother setting off again. I should like to offer him a last salute. Come ?"

Milady opened the window, and made a sign to Madame Bonacieux to join her. The young woman complied.

Rochefort passed at a gallop.

"Adieu, brother !" cried milady.

The chevalier raised his head, saw the two young women, and without stopping, waved his hand in a friendly way to milady.

"Dear, good George !" said she, closing the window with an expression of countenance full of affection and melancholy.

And she resumed her seat, as if plunged in reflections entirely personal.

"Dear lady," said Madame Bonacieux, "pardon me for interrupting you : but what do you advise me to do? Good Heaven ! You have more experience than I have. Speak ; I will listen to your advice with the greatest gratitude."

"In the first place," said milady, "it is possible that I may be deceived, and D'Artagnan and his friends may really come to your assistance."

"Oh ! that would be too much !" cried Madame Bonacieux ; "so much happiness is not destined for me !"

"Then, you perceive it would be only a question of time, a sort of race, which should arrive first. If your friends are the more speedy, you will be saved ; if the satellites of the cardinal are so, you will be lost !"

"Oh! yes, yes! lost beyond redemption! What am I to do? what am I to do?"

"There would be a very simple means, very natural——"

"What? Speak!"

"To wait, concealed in the neighbourhood, until you have satisfied yourself who the men were who came to ask for you."

"But where can I wait?"

"Oh! there is no difficulty in that; I shall stop and conceal myself at a few leagues from hence, until my brother can rejoin me. Well! I can take you with me; we can conceal ourselves, and wait together."

"But I shall not be allowed to go; I am almost a prisoner here."

"As I am supposed to go in consequence of an order from the cardinal, no one will believe you are anxious to follow me."

"Well?"

"Well! the carriage is at the door, you bid me adieu, you get upon the step to embrace me a last time; my brother's servant, who comes to fetch me, is told how to proceed; he makes a sign to the postilion, and we set off at a gallop."

"But D'Artagnan! D'Artagnan! if he should come!"

"Well! shall we not know it?"

"How?"

"Nothing more easy. We will send my brother's servant back to Bethune, and, as I told you we can trust in him, he shall assume a disguise, and place himself in front of the convent. If the emissaries of the cardinal arrive, he will take no notice; if they are M. D'Artagnan and his friends, he will bring them to us."

"He knows them, then?"

"Doubtless he does. Has he not seen M. D'Artagnan at my house?"

"Oh! yes, yes, you are right; in this way all may go well—all may be for the best; but do not go far from this place."

"Seven or eight leagues at most; we will keep on the frontiers, for instance; and at the first alarm, we can leave France."

"And what can we do there?"

"Wait."

"But if they come?"

"My brother's carriage will be here first."

"If I should happen to be at any distance from you when the carriage comes for you; at dinner or supper, for instance?"

"Do one thing."

"What is that?"

"Tell your good superior, that in order that we may be as much together as possible, you beg her to allow you to take your meals with me."

"Will she permit it?"

"What inconvenience can it be to her?"

"Oh, delightful! in this way we shall not be separated for an instant."

"Well! go down to her then, to make your request. I feel my head a little confused; I will take a turn in the garden."

" Do ; and where shall I find you ?"

" Here, within an hour."

" Here, in an hour ; oh ! you are so kind ! and I am so grateful !"

" How can I avoid interesting myself for one who is so beautiful, and so amiable ? Besides, are you not the beloved of one of my best friends ?"

" Dear D'Artagnan, oh ! how he will thank you !"

" I hope so. Now then, all is agreed ; let us go down."

" You are going into the garden ?"

" Yes."

" Go along this corridor, down a little staircase, and you are in it."

" That will do—thank you !"

And the two women parted, exchanging affectionate smiles.

Milady had told the truth—her head was confused ; for her ill-arranged plans clashed against each other like a chaos. She required to be alone in order to bring her thoughts a little in order. She saw vaguely into futurity : but she stood in need of a little silence and quiet to give all her ideas, at present in confusion, a distinct form and a regular plan.

What was most pressing was, to get Madame Bonacieux away, and convey her to a place of safety, and there, matters so falling out, make her a hostage. Milady began to have doubts of the issue of this terrible duel, in which her enemies showed as much perseverance as she did inveterate animosity.

Besides, she felt as we feel when a storm is coming on—that this issue was near, and could not fail to be terrible.

The principal thing for her then was, as we have said, to keep Madame Bonacieux in her power. Madame Bonacieux was the very life of D'Artagnan ; more than his life, was the life of the woman he loved ; this was, in case of ill fortune, a means of treating and obtaining good conditions.

Now, this point was settled : Madame Bonacieux, without any suspicion, accompanied her ; and, once concealed with her at Armentières, it would be easy to make her believe that D'Artagnan was not come to Bethune. In a fortnight, at most, Rochefort would be back again ; during that fortnight, besides, she should have time to think how she could best be revenged upon the four friends. She entertained no fear of being dull, thank God ! for she should enjoy the sweetest pastime events could offer to a woman of her character—the perfecting of a cruel vengeance.

Whilst revolving all this in her mind, she cast her eyes around her, and arranged the topography of the garden in her head. Milady was like a good general, who contemplates at the same time victory and defeat, and who is quite prepared, according to the chances of the battle, to march forward, or to beat a retreat.

At the end of an hour, she heard a soft voice calling her ; it was Madame de Bonacieux's. The good abbess had naturally consented to her request ; and as a commencement, they were to sup together.

On reaching the courtyard, they heard the noise of a carriage, which stopped at the gate.

Milady listened.

"Do you hear anything?" said she.

"Yes, the rolling of a carriage."

"It is the one my brother sends for us."

"Oh! my God!"

"Come; come! courage!"

The bell of the convent gate was rung—milady was not mistaken.

"Go up to your chamber," said she to Madame Bonacieux; "you have perhaps some jewels you would like to take with you."

"I have his letters," said she.

"Well! go and fetch them, and come to my apartment; we will snatch some supper; we shall perhaps travel part of the night, and must keep our strength up."

"Great God!" said Madame Bonacieux, placing her hand upon her bosom: "my heart beats so I cannot walk."

"Courage, my dear, courage! remember that in a quarter of an hour you will be safe; and think that what you are about to do is for his sake."

"Yes, yes, everything for his sake. You have restored my courage by a single word; go up, I will be with you directly."

Milady ran up to her apartment quickly; she there found Rochefort's lackey, and gave him his instructions.

He was to wait at the gate; if, by chance, the musketeers should appear, the carriage was to set off as fast as possible, pass round the convent, and go and wait for milady at a little village which was situated at the other side of the wood. In this case milady was to cross the garden and gain the village on foot. We have already said milady was perfectly acquainted with this part of France.

If the musketeers did not appear, things were to go on as had been agreed; Madame Bonacieux was to get into the carriage as if to bid her adieu, and she was to take away Madame Bonacieux.

Madame Bonacieux came in; and, to remove all suspicion, if she had any, milady repeated to the lackey, before her, the latter part of her instructions.

Milady made some questions about the carriage; it was a chaise with three horses, driven by a postilion; Rochefort's lackey preceded it, as a courier.

Milady was wrong in fearing that Madame Bonacieux would have any suspicions; the poor young woman was too pure to suppose that any female could be guilty of such perfidy; besides, the name of the Countess de Winter, which she had heard the abbess pronounce, was perfectly unknown to her, and she was even ignorant that a woman had had so great and so fatal a share in the misfortune of her life.

"You see," said she, when the lackey was gone out, "everything is ready. The abbess suspects nothing, and believes that I am fetched by the orders of the cardinal. The man is gone to give his last orders; take a mouthful to eat, drink half a glass of wine, and let us be gone."

"Yes," said Madame Bonacieux, mechanically; "let us be gone."

Milady made her a sign to sit down before her, poured out a small glass of Spanish wine for her, and helped her to the wing of a chicken.

"See!" said she, "if everything is not propitious; here is night coming on; by daybreak we shall have gained our retreat, and nobody can have any suspicion where we are. Come, courage!—take something."

Madame Bonacieux ate a few mouthfuls mechanically, and just touched the glass with her lips.

"Come! come!" said milady, lifting hers to her mouth, "do as I do."

But, at the moment the glass touched her lips, her hand remained suspended; she heard something on the road which sounded like the rattling of a distant gallop, and which drew nearer; and, almost at the same time, she heard the neighing of horses.

This noise acted upon her joy like the storm which awakens the sleeper in the midst of a happy dream; she grew pale, and ran to the window, whilst Madame Bonacieux, rising all in a tremble, supported herself upon her chair to avoid falling.

Nothing was yet to be seen, only they heard the galloping draw nearer.

"Oh! my God!" said Madame Bonacieux, "what is that noise?"

"That of either our friends or our enemies," said milady, with her terrible coolness; "stay where you are, I will tell you."

Madame Bonacieux remained standing, mute, motionless, and pale as a statue.

The noise became stronger, the horses could not be more than a hundred paces distant; if they were not yet to be seen, it was because the road made an elbow. The noise became so distinct that the horses might be counted by the sound of their hoofs.

Milady looked as if her eyes would start; it was just light enough to allow her to see those who were coming.

All at once, at the turning of the road, she saw the glitter of laced hats and the waving of feathers; she counted two, then five, then eight horsemen; one of them preceded the rest by double the length of his horse.

Milady uttered a stifled groan. In the first horseman she recognised D'Artagnan.

"Oh! heavens! oh! heavens!" cried Madame Bonacieux, "what is it? what is it?"

"It is the uniform of the cardinal's guards, not an instant to be lost! Let us fly! let us fly!"

"Oh! yes! let us fly!" repeated Madame Bonacieux, but without being able to make a step, fixed to the spot she stood on by terror.

They heard the horsemen pass under the windows.

"Come, then! why, come then!" cried milady, endeavouring to drag her along by the arm. "Thanks to the garden, we yet can fly; I have the key; but, make haste! in five minutes it will be too late!"

Madame Bonacieux endeavoured to walk, made two steps, and sank upon her knees.

Milady endeavoured to raise and carry her, but could not succeed.

At this moment they heard the rolling of the carriage, which at the approach of the musketeers, set off at a gallop. Then three or four shots were fired.

"For the last time, will you come?" cried milady.

"Oh! heaven! oh! heaven! you see my strength fails me, you see plainly I cannot walk: fly alone!"

"Fly alone! and leave you here! no, no, never!" cried milady.

All at once she remained still, a livid flash darted from her eyes; she ran to the table, poured into Madame Bonacieux' glass the contents of a ring, which she opened with singular quickness.

It was a grain of a reddish colour, which melted immediately.

Then, taking the glass with a firm hand,—

"Drink," said she, "this wine will give you strength, drink!"

And she put the glass to the lips of the young woman, who drank mechanically.

"This is not the way that I wished to avenge myself," said milady, replacing the glass upon the table with an infernal smile, "but, *ma foi!* we do what we can!"

And she rushed out of the room.

Madame Bonacieux saw her go without being able to follow her; she was like those people who dream they are pursued, and who in vain endeavour to walk.

A few moments passed, a great noise was heard at the gate; every instant Madame Bonacieux expected to see milady; but she did not return.

Several times, with terror, no doubt, the cold sweat burst from her burning brow.

At length she heard the grating of the hinges of the opening gates, the noise of boots and spurs resounded on the stairs; there was a great murmur of voices, which continued to draw near, and amongst which it appeared to her she heard her own name pronounced.

All at once she uttered a loud cry of joy, and darted towards the door, she had recognised the voice of D'Artagnan.

"D'Artagnan! D'Artagnan!" cried she, "is it you? This way! this way!"

"Constance! Constance?" replied the young man, "where are you? where are you?"

At the same moment, the door of the cell yielded to a shock, rather than was opened; several men rushed into the chamber; Madame Bonacieux had sunk into a *fauteuil*, without the power of moving.

D'Artagnan threw a yet smoking pistol from his hand, and fell on his knees before his mistress; Athos replaced his in his belt; Porthos and Aramis, who held their drawn swords in their hands, returned them to their scabbards.

" Oh ! D'Artagnan ! my beloved D'Artagnan ! thou art come, then, at last, thou hast not deceived me ! it is indeed thee !"

"Yes, yes, dear Constance ! united at last !"

"Oh ! it was in vain *she* told me you would not come. I hoped silently ; I was not willing to fly ; oh ! how rightly I have done ! how happy I am !"

At this word *she*, Athos, who had seated himself quietly, started up.

"*She !* what she ?" asked D'Artagnan.

" Why, my companion ; she who, from friendship for me, wished to take me from my persecutors, she who, mistaking you for the cardinal's guards, has just fled away."

"Your companion !" cried D'Artagnan, becoming more pale than the white veil of his mistress, "of what companion are you speaking, dear Constance ?"

" Of her whose carriage was at the gate, of a woman who calls herself your friend, of a woman to whom you have told everything."

" But her name, her name !" cried D'Artagnan ; "my God ! can you not remember her name ?"

" Yes, it was pronounced before me once ; stop——but—it is very strange——oh ! my God ! my head swims—I cannot see !"

" Help ! help ! my friends ! her hands are icy cold," cried D'Artagnan, " she will faint ! great God, she is losing her senses !"

Whilst Porthos was calling for help with all the power of his strong voice, Aramis ran to the table to get a glass of water ; but he stopped at seeing the horrible alteration that had taken place in the countenance of Athos, who, standing before the table, his hair rising from his head, his eyes fixed in stupor, was looking at one of the glasses and appeared a prey to the most horrible doubt.

" Oh !" said Athos, "oh ! no, it is impossible ! God would not permit such a crime !"

" Water ! water !" cried D'Artagnan, "water !"

" Oh ! poor woman ! poor woman !" murmured Athos, in a broken voice.

Madame Bonacieux opened her eyes under the kisses of D'Artagnan.

" She revives !" cried the young man. "Oh ! my God ! my God ! I thank thee !"

" Madame !" said Athos, " madame, in the name of heaven, whose empty glass is this ?"

" Mine, monsieur," said the young woman in a dying voice.

" But who poured out the wine for you that was in this glass ?"

" *She.*"

" But who was that *she ?*"

" Oh ! I remember," said Madame Bonacieux, " *the Countess de Winter.*"

The four friends uttered one and the same cry, but that of Athos dominated over all the rest.

At that moment the countenance of Madame Bonacieux became

livid, a fearful agony pervaded her frame, and she sank panting into the arms of Porthos and Aramis.

D'Artagnan seized the hands of Athos with an anguish difficult to be described.

" What ! what ! do you believe ?"   His voice was stifled by sobs.

" I believe everything," said Athos, biting his lips till the blood sprang, to avoid sighing.

" D'Artagnan ! D'Artagnan ! where art thou ? Do not quit me, thou seest that I am dying !" cried Madame Bonacieux.

D'Artagnan let fall the hands of Athos which he still held clasped in both his own, and hastened to her.

Her beautiful face was distorted with agony, her glassy eyes were fixed, a convulsive shuddering shook her whole body, the sweat flowed from her brow.

" In the name of heaven, run, call ; Aramis ! Porthos ! call for help !"

" Useless !" said Athos, " useless ! for the poison which *she* pours out there is no counter-poison !"

" Yes ! yes ! help ! help !" murmured Madame Bonacieux, "help !"

Then, collecting all her strength, she took the head of the young man between her hands, looked at him for an instant as if her whole soul passed in that look, and, with a sobbing cry, pressed her lips to his.

" Constance ! Constance !" cried D'Artagnan wildly.

A sigh escaped from the mouth of Madame Bonacieux, and dwelt for an instant on the lips of D'Artagnan—that sigh was the soul so chaste and so loving reascending to heaven.

D'Artagnan held nothing but a corpse pressed in his arms.

The young man uttered a cry and fell by the side of his mistress as pale and as senseless as she was.

Porthos wept, Aramis pointed towards heaven, Athos made the sign of the cross.

At that moment a man appeared in the doorway almost as pale as those in the chamber, looked round him and saw Madame Bonacieux dead, and D'Artagnan fainting.

He appeared just at that moment of stupor which follows great catastrophes.

" I was not deceived," said he ; "here is M. d'Artagnan, and you are his friends, Messieurs Athos, Porthos, and Aramis."

The persons whose names were thus pronounced looked at the stranger with astonishment, all three thought they knew him.

" Gentlemen," resumed the new comer, " you are, as I am, in search of a woman, who," added he, with a terrible smile, " must have passed this way, for I see a corpse !"

The three friends remained mute, for although the voice as well as the countenance reminded them of some one they had seen, they could not remember under what circumstances.

" Gentlemen," continued the stranger, "since you do not recognise a man who probably owes his life to you twice, I must name myself : I am the Lord de Winter, brother-in-law of that woman."

The three friends uttered a cry of surprise.

Athos rose, and offering him his hand,—

"You are welcome, milord," said he, "you are one of us."

" I set out five hours after her from Portsmouth," said Lord de Winter. " I arrived three hours after her at Boulogne, I missed her by twenty minutes at St. Omer ; at last at Lilliers I lost all trace of her. I was going about at hazard, inquiring of everybody, when I saw you gallop past ; I recognised M. d'Artagnan. I called to you, but you did not answer me ; I wished to follow you, but my horse was too much fatigued to permit me to overtake you. And yet, it appears that in spite of all your diligence you have arrived too late."

"You see !" said Athos, pointing to Madame Bonacieux dead, and to D'Artagnan, whom Porthos and Aramis were endeavouring to recal to life.

"Are they then both dead ?" asked Lord de Winter, sternly.

" No," replied Athos, "fortunately M. d'Artagnan has only fainted."

" Ah ! I am glad to hear that !" said Lord de Winter.

At that moment D'Artagnan opened his eyes.

He tore himself from the arms of Porthos and Aramis, and threw himself like a madman on the corpse of his mistress.

Athos rose, walked towards his friend with a slow and solemn step, embraced him tenderly, and as he burst into violent sobs, he said to him, with his noble and persuasive voice :

"Friend, be a man !—women weep for the dead, men avenge them !"

"Oh, yes !" cried D'Artagnan, "yes ! if it be to avenge her, I am ready to follow you."

Athos took advantage of this moment of strength which the hope of vengeance restored to his unfortunate friend, to make a sign to Porthos and Aramis to go and fetch the superior.

They met her in the corridor, in great trouble and agitation at such strange events ; she called for some of the nuns, who against all rules, found themselves in the presence of five men.

" Madame," said Athos, passing his arm under that of D'Artagnan, " we abandon to your pious care the body of that unfortunate woman. She was an angel on earth before being an angel in heaven. Treat her as one of your sisters. We will return some day to pray over her grave !"

D'Artagnan concealed his face in the bosom of Athos, and sobbed aloud.

"Weep !" said Athos, "weep ! thou poor heart, full of love, youth, and life ! Alas ! would that I were able to weep as thou dost !"

And he drew away his friend, affectionate as a father, consoling as a priest, great as a man who has suffered much.

All five, followed by their lackeys, leading their horses, took their way to the town of Bethune, whose faubourg they perceived, and stopped before the first auberge they came to.

"But," said D'Artagnan, "shall we not pursue that woman ?"

"Presently," said Athos ; "I have measures to take."

"She will escape us," replied the young man ; "she will escape us ; and it will be your fault, Athos."

"I will be accountable for her," said Athos.

D'Artagnan had so much confidence in the word of his friend, that he hung down his head, and entered the auberge, without making a reply.

Porthos and Aramis looked at each other without comprehending whence Athos derived this assurance.

Lord de Winter believed he spoke in this manner to soothe the grief of D'Artagnan.

"Now, gentlemen," said Athos, when he had ascertained there were five chambers disengaged in the hotel, "let every one retire to his own apartment ; D'Artagnan requires to be alone, to weep and to sleep. I take charge of everything, be all of you at ease."

"It appears, however," said Lord de Winter, "that if there be any measures to be taken against the countess, it particularly concerns me : she is my sister-in-law."

"And I," said Athos—"*she is my wife !*"

D'Artagnan smiled, for he was satisfied Athos was sure of his vengeance, when he revealed such a secret as that ; Porthos and Aramis looked at each other, and changed colour. Lord de Winter thought Athos was mad.

"Now, all retire to your chambers," said Athos, "and leave me to act. You must perceive that in my quality of a husband this concerns me in particular. Only, D'Artagnan, if you have not lost it, give me the piece of paper which fell from that man's hat, upon which is written the name of the village of——"

"Ah !" said D'Artagnan, "I comprehend now ; that name written in her hand."

"You see, then," said Athos, "there is a God in heaven, still !"

CHAPTER LXIV.

THE MAN WITH THE RED CLOAK.

THE despair of Athos had given place to a concentrated grief, which only rendered more lucid the brilliant mental faculties of that extraordinary man.

Possessed by one single thought, that of the promise he had made, and of the responsibility he had taken upon himself, he retired the last to his chamber, begged the host to procure him a map of the province, bent over it, examined every line traced upon it, perceived that there were four different roads from Bethune to Armentières, and called all the four valets.

Planchet, Grimaud, Bazin, and Mousqueton presented themselves, and received clear, positive, and serious orders from Athos.

They were to set out for Armentières the next morning at daybreak, and to go to Armentières—each by a different route. Planchet, the most intelligent of the four, was to follow that by which the carriage had gone, upon which the four friends had fired, and which was accompanied, as may be remembered, by Rochefort's servant.

Athos set the lackeys to work first, because, since these men had been in the service of himself and his friends, he had discovered in each of them different and essential qualities.

Then, lackeys who ask questions inspire less mistrust than masters ; and meet with more sympathies among those they address.

Besides, milady knew the masters, and did not know the lackeys ; whilst, on the contrary, the lackeys knew milady perfectly well.

All four were to meet the next day, at eleven o'clock ; if they had discovered milady's retreat, three were to remain on guard, the fourth was to return to Bethune, to inform Athos, and serve as a guide to the four friends.

These dispositions arranged, the lackeys retired.

Athos then arose from his chair, girded on his sword, enveloped himself in his cloak, and left the hotel : it was nearly ten o'clock. At ten o'clock in the evening, it is well known, the streets in provincial towns are very little frequented ; Athos, nevertheless, was visibly anxious to find some one of whom he could ask a question. At length he met a belated passenger, went up to him, and spoke a few words to him ; the man he addressed drew back with terror, and only answered the musketeer by an indication. Athos offered the man half a pistole to accompany him, but the man refused.

Athos then plunged into the street the man had pointed to with his finger ; but arriving at four cross roads, he stopped again, visibly embarrassed. Nevertheless, as the cross roads offered him a better chance than any other place of meeting somebody, he stood still. In a few minutes a night-watch passed. Athos repeated to him the same question he had asked the first person he had met ; the night-watch evinced the same terror, refused, in his turn, to accompany Athos, and only pointed with his hand to the road he was to take.

Athos walked in the direction indicated, and reached the faubourg, situated at the extremity of the city, opposite to that by which he and his friends had entered it. There he again appeared uneasy and embarrassed, and stopped for the third time.

Fortunately a mendicant passed, who coming up to Athos to ask charity, Athos offered him half-a-crown to accompany him where he was going. The mendicant hesitated at first, but at the sight of the piece of silver which shone in the darkness, he consented, and walked on before Athos.

When arrived at the angle of a street, he pointed to a small house, isolated, solitary, and dismal. Athos went towards the house, whilst the mendicant, who had received his reward, hobbled off as fast as his legs could carry him.

Athos went round the house before he could distinguish the door, amidst the red colour in which it was painted ; no light appeared through the chinks of the shutters, no noise gave reason to believe that it was inhabited—it was dark and silent as the tomb.

Three times Athos knocked without receiving any answer, At the third knock, however, steps were heard inside ; the door at length was opened, and a man of high stature, pale complexion, and black hair and beard, appeared.

Athos and he exchanged some words in a low voice, then the tall man made a sign to the musketeer that he might come in. Athos imme· diately took advantage of the permission, and the door was closed after them.

The man whom Athos had come so far to seek, and whom he had found with so much trouble, introduced him into his laboratory, where he was engaged in fastening together with iron wire the dry bones of a skeleton. All the frame was adjusted, except the head, which lay upon the table.

All the rest of the furniture indicated that the inhabitant of this house was engaged in the study of the natural sciences ; there were large bottles filled with serpents, ticketed according to their species ; dried lizards shone like emeralds set in great squares of black wood ; and bunches of wild, odoriferous herbs, doubtless possessed of virtues unknown to common men, were fastened to the ceiling and hung down in the corners of the apartment.

But there was no family, no servant ; the tall man inhabited this house alone.

Athos cast a cold and indifferent glance upon the objects we have described, and, at the invitation of him he came to seek, he sat down near him.

Then he explained to him the cause of his visit, and the service he required of him ; but scarcely had he expressed his request, than the unknown, who remained standing before the musketeer, drew back with signs of terror, and refused. Then Athos took from his pocket a small paper, upon which were written two lines, accom· panied by a signature and a seal, and presented them to him who had given too prematurely these signs of repugnance. The tall man had scarcely read these lines, seen the signature, and recognised the seal, when he bowed to denote that he had no longer any objection to make, and that he was ready to obey.

Athos required no more ; he arose, bowed, went out, returned by the same way he came, re-entered the hotel, and went to his apart- ment.

At daybreak D'Artagnan came to him, and asked him " What was to be done ?"

"Wait !" replied Athos.

Some minutes after, the superior of the convent sent to inform the musketeers that the burial would take place at mid-day. As to the poisoner, they had heard no tidings of her whatever ; only she must have made her escape through the garden, upon the sand of which her footsteps could be traced, and the door of which had been found shut : the key had disappeared.

At the hour appointed, Lord de Winter and the four friends repaired to the convent : the bells tolled, the chapel was open, but the grating of the choir was closed. In the middle of the choir the body of the victim, clothed in her novitiate dress, was exposed. On each side of the choir, and behind the gratings opening upon the convent, was assembled the whole community of the Carmelites, who listened to the divine service, and mingled their chants with the chants of the priests, without seeing the profane, or being seen by them.

At the door of the chapel D'Artagnan felt his courage fail again, and returned to look for Athos, but Athos had disappeared.

Faithful to his mission of vengeance, Athos had requested to be conducted to the garden; and there upon the sand, following the light steps of this woman, who had left a bloody track wherever she had gone, he advanced towards the gate which led into the wood, and, causing it to be opened, he went out into the forest.

Then all his suspicions were confirmed—the road by which the carriage had disappeared went round the forest. Athos followed the road for some time with his eyes fixed upon the ground ; slight stains of blood, which came from the wound inflicted upon the man who accompanied the carriage as a courier, or from one of the horses, were to be seen on the road. At the end of about three-quarters of a league, within fifty paces of Festubert, a larger bloodstain appeared ; the ground was trampled by horses. Between the forest and this accursed spot, a little behind the trampled ground, was the same track of small feet as in the garden ; the carriage, then, had stopped here. At this spot milady had come out of the wood, and got into the carriage.

Satisfied with this discovery, which confirmed all his suspicions, Athos returned to the hotel, and found Planchet impatiently waiting for him.

Everything was as Athos had foreseen.

Planchet had followed the road ; like Athos, he had discovered the stains of blood ; like Athos, he had remarked the spot where the horses had stopped ; but he had gone further than Athos, so that at the village of Festubert, whilst drinking at an auberge, he had learned, without asking a question, that the evening before, at about half-past eight, a wounded man, who accompanied a lady travelling in a post-chaise, had been obliged to stop, being unable to go any further. The wound was attributed to thieves who had stopped the chaise in the wood. The man remained in the village ; the lady had had a relay of horses, and continued her journey.

Planchet went in search of the postilion who had driven her, and found him. He had taken the lady as far as Fromelles, and from Fromelles she had set out for Armentières. Planchet took the cross-road, and by seven o'clock in the morning he was at Armentières.

There was but one hotel, that of the post. Planchet went and presented himself as a lackey out of place, who was in search of a situation.

He had not chatted ten minutes with the people of the auberge before he learned that a lady had come there about eleven o'clock the night before, alone ; had engaged a chamber, had sent for the master of the hotel, and told him that she was desirous to remain for some time in that neighbourhood.

Planchet did not want to know any more. He hastened to the rendezvous, found the lackeys at their posts, placed them as sentinels at all the issues of the hotel, and came to find Athos, who had just received his information when his friends returned.

All their countenances were melancholy and anxious, even the mild countenance of Aramis.

"What is to be done ?" said D'Artagnan.

"Wait," replied Athos.

Every one went to his own apartment.

At eight o'clock in the evening Athos ordered the horses to be saddled, and had Lord de Winter and his friends informed that they must prepare for the expedition.

In an instant all five were ready. Every one examined his arms, and put them in order. Athos came down the last, and found D'Artagnan already mounted, and growing impatient.

"Patience !" cried Athos ; " one of our party is still wanting."

The four horsemen looked round them with astonishment, for they sought uselessly in their minds who this other person they wanted could be.

At this moment Planchet brought out Athos' horse ; the musketeer leaped lightly into the saddle.

"Wait for me," cried he; "I will soon be back ;" and set off at a gallop.

In a quarter of an hour he returned, accompanied by a tall man, masked, and enveloped in a large red cloak.

Lord de Winter and the three musketeers looked at each other inquiringly. None of them could give the others any information, for all were ignorant who this man could be ; nevertheless, they felt convinced that this ought to be so, as it was done by Athos.

At nine o'clock, guided by Planchet, the little cavalcade set out, taking the route the carriage had taken.

It was a melancholy sight, that of these six men, travelling in silence, each plunged in his own thoughts, sad as despair, dark as punishment.

CHAPTER LXV.

TRIAL.

IT was a stormy and dark night ; vast clouds covered the heavens, concealing the stars ; the moon would not rise much before midnight.

Occasionally, by the light of a flash of lightning, which gleamed along the horizon, the road appeared before them, white and solitary ; the flash extinct, all remained in darkness.

At every instant Athos was forced to restrain D'Artagnan, constantly in advance of the little troop, and to beg him to keep his rank, which, at the end of a minute, he again departed from. He had but one thought, which was to go forward, and he went.

They passed in silence through the little village of Festubert, where the wounded servant was, and then skirted the wood of Richebourg; when arrived at Herlier, Planchet, who led the column, turned to the left.

Several times Lord de Winter, Porthos, or Aramis, endeavoured to enter into conversation with the man in the red cloak; but to every interrogation put to him he bowed, without making any reply. The travellers then comprehended that there must be some reason why the unknown preserved such a silence, and said no more to him.

The storm came on, the flashes succeeded each other more rapidly, the thunder began to growl, and the wind, the precursor of a hurricane, whistled in the plumes and the hair of the horsemen.

The cavalcade trotted on more sharply.

A little before they came to Fromilles the storm burst in all its fury upon them; they unfolded their cloaks. They had still three leagues to travel, and they performed it amidst torrents of rain.

D'Artagnan took off his hat, and could not be persuaded to make use of his cloak: he found ease in feeling the water trickle over his burning brow, and down his feverish body.

At the moment the little troop had passed Goskal, and were approaching the port, a man, sheltered beneath a tree, left the trunk of it, with which he had been confounded in the darkness, and advanced into the middle of the road, with his finger on his lips.

Athos recognised Grimaud.

"What's the matter?" cried Athos; "has she left Armentières?"

Grimaud made a sign in the affirmative. D'Artagnan ground his teeth.

"Silence, D'Artagnan!" said Athos. "I have charged myself with this affair; it is for me, then, to interrogate Grimaud."

"Where is she?" asked Athos.

Grimaud stretched out his hands in the direction of the Lys.

"Far from here?" asked Athos.

Grimaud showed his master his forefinger bent.

"Alone?" asked Athos.

Grimaud made a sign that she was.

"Gentlemen," said Athos, "she is alone, within half a league of us, in the direction of the river."

"That's well," said D'Artagnan; "lead us on, Grimaud."

Grimaud took his course across the country, and acted as a guide to the cavalcade.

At the end of about five hundred paces they came to a rivulet, which they forded.

By the aid of the lightning they could perceive the village of Enguinghem.

" Is she there ?" asked D'Artagnan of Athos.

Grimaud shook his head negatively.

" Silence, then !" cried Athos.

And the troop continued their route.

Another flash enlightened all around them ; Grimaud extended his arm, and by the blue splendour of the serpent of fire they distinguished a little isolated house, on the banks of the river, within a hundred paces of a ferry.

A light was seen at one window.

" This is the place," said Athos.

At this moment a man, who had been crouching in a ditch, jumped up and came towards them. It was Mousqueton ; he pointed with his finger to the window with the light in it.

" She is there," said he.

" And Bazin ?" asked Athos.

" Whilst I kept my eye on the window, he guarded the door."

" All is well !" said Athos ; " you are good and faithful servants."

Athos sprang from his horse, gave the bridle to Grimaud, and advanced towards the window, after having made a sign to the rest of the troop to go towards the door.

The little house was surrounded by a low quickset hedge of two or three feet high ; Athos sprang over the hedge, and went up to the window, which was without shutters, but had the half-curtain drawn closely.

He got upon the skirting-stone to enable him to look over the curtain.

By the light of a lamp he saw a woman enveloped in a mantle of a dark colour, seated upon a joint-stool near the dying embers of a fire ; her elbows were placed upon a mean table, and she leant her head upon her two hands, which were white as ivory.

He could not distinguish her countenance, but a sinister smile passed over the lips of Athos ; he could not be deceived—it was the woman he sought.

At this moment one of the horses neighed ; milady raised her head, saw the pale face of Athos close to the window, and screamed with terror.

Athos, perceiving that she knew him, pushed the window with his knee and hand ; it yielded—the frame and glass were broken to shivers.

And Athos, like the spectre of vengeance, sprang into the room.

Milady rushed to the door and opened it ; but, still more pale and menacing than Athos, D'Artagnan stood on the sill of it.

Milady drew back, uttering a cry ; D'Artagnan, believing she might have means of flight, and fearing she should escape, drew a pistol from his belt ; but Athos raised his hand.

"Put back that weapon, D'Artagnan," said he ; "this woman must be judged, not assassinated. Wait but a little, my friend, and you shall be satisfied. Come in, gentlemen."

D'Artagnan obeyed, for Athos had the solemn voice and the powerful gesture of a judge sent by the Lord himself. Behind D'Artagnan, entered Porthos, Aramis, Lord de Winter, and the man in the red cloak.

The four lackeys guarded the door and the window.

Milady had sunk into a chair, with her hands extended, as if to conjure away this terrible apparition. On perceiving her brother-in-law, an agonised cry of surprise and fright burst from her lips.

" What do you want ?" screamed milady.

"We want," said Athos, " Charlotte Backson, who first was called Countess de la Fère, and afterwards Lady de Winter, Baroness de Scheffield."

" That is I ! that is I !" murmured milady, in extreme terror ; " what do you want with me ?"

" We want to judge you according to your crime," said Athos ; " you shall be free to defend yourself ; justify yourself if you can. Monsieur D'Artagnan, it is for you to accuse her first."

D'Artagnan advanced.

" Before God and before men," said he, " I accuse this woman of having poisoned Constance Bonacieux, who died yesterday evening."

He turned towards Porthos and Aramis.

" We bear witness to this," said the two musketeers, with one voice.

D'Artagnan continued :

" Before God and before men, I accuse this woman of having attempted to poison me, in wine which she sent me from Villeroi, with a forged letter, as if that wine came from my friends. God preserved me, but a man named Brisemont died in my place."

" We bear witness to this," said Porthos and Aramis, in the same manner as before.

" Before God and before men, I accuse this woman of having urged me to murder the Baron de Wardes ; and of having employed assassins to shoot me ; from whom I was again preserved by God's providence : but, as none can bear witness to these facts, I attest them myself.—I have done," and M. d'Artagnan passed to the other side of the room, to Porthos and Aramis.

" It is your turn, milord," said Athos.

The baron came forward.

" Before God and before men," said he, " I accuse this woman of having been the means of the assassination of the Duke of Buckingham."

" The Duke of Buckingham assassinated !" cried all present, with one voice.

" Yes," said the baron,—" assassinated. Upon receiving the warning letter you wrote to me, I caused this woman to be arrested, and gave her in charge to a loyal servant ; she corrupted this man, she placed the poniard in his hand, she made him kill the duke ; and at this moment, perhaps, the assassin is paying with his head for the crime of this fury !"

A shudder crept through the frames of the judges at the revelation of such unheard-of crimes.

"That is not all," resumed Lord de Winter ; "my brother, who made you his heir, died in three hours, of a strange disorder, which left livid traces behind it all over the body. Sister, how did your husband die ?"

"Horror ! horror !" cried Porthos and Aramis.

"Assassin of Buckingham, assassin of Felton, assassin of my brother, I demand justice upon you, and I swear that if it be not granted to me, I will execute it myself."

And Lord de Winter ranged himself by the side of D'Artagnan, leaving the place free for another accuser.

Milady let her head sink between her two hands, and endeavoured to recall her ideas, which whirled about in a mortal vertigo.

"It is my turn," said Athos, himself trembling as the lion trembles at the sight of the serpent ; "it is my turn. I married that woman when she was a young girl ; I married her in opposition to the wishes of all my family ; I gave her my wealth, I gave her my name ; and one day I discovered that this woman was branded ; this woman was marked with a fleur-de-lis on her left shoulder."

"Oh !" said milady, "I defy you to find any tribunal which pronounced such an infamous sentence against me. I defy you to find him who executed it."

"Silence !" cried a hollow voice. "It is for me to reply to that !" And the man in the red cloak came forward in his turn.

"What man is that ? what man is that ?" cried milady, suffocated by terror, her hair unknotting, and rising over her livid countenance as if alive.

All eyes were turned towards this man ; for to all except Athos he was unknown.

And even Athos looked at him with as much stupefaction as the rest, for he could not conceive how he could in any way be mixed up with the horrible drama which was then being unfolded.

After having approached milady with a slow and solemn step, so that the table alone separated them, the unknown took off his mask.

Milady for some time examined with increasing terror that pale face, enframed in its black hair, beard and whiskers, the only expression of which was icy impassibility—all at once,—

"Oh ! no, no !" cried she, rising and retreating to the very wall ;— "no, no ! it is an infernal apparition ! It cannot be he ! Help, help !" screamed she, turning towards the wall, as if she would tear an opening with her hands.

"Who are you, then ?" cried all the witnesses of this scene.

"Ask that woman," said the man in the red cloak ; "for you may plainly see she knows me !"

"The executioner of Lille ! the executioner of Lille !" cried milady, a prey to wild terror, and clinging with her hands to the wall to avoid falling.

Every one drew back, and the man in the red cloak remained standing alone in the middle of the room.

"Oh ! pardon ! pardon !" cried the miserable woman, falling on her knees.

The unknown waited for silence, and then,—

"I told you so ; I was sure she would know me," resumed he. "Yes, I am the executioner of Lille, and this is my history : "

All eyes were fixed upon this man, whose words were listened to with anxious attention.

"That woman was formerly a young maiden as beautiful as she is now. She was a nun in the convent of the Benedictines of Templemar. A young priest, of a simple and trustful heart, performed the duties of the church of that convent. She undertook his seduction, and succeeded : she would have seduced a saint.

"Their vows were sacred and irrevocable. Their connection could not last long without ruining both. She prevailed upon him to leave the country ; but to leave the country, to fly together, to reach another part of France, where they might live at ease, because unknown, money was necessary ; neither of them had any The priest stole the sacred vases, and sold them ; but as they were preparing to escape together, they were both arrested.

"Within a week she seduced the son of the gaoler, and got away. The young priest was condemned to ten years of imprisonment, and to be branded. I was executioner of the city of Lille, as this woman has said, and the guilty man, gentlemen, was my brother !

"I then swore that this woman who had ruined him, who was more than his accomplice, since she had induced him to commit the crime, should at least share his punishment. I suspected where she was concealed. I followed her, I caught her, I bound her, and I impressed the same disgraceful mark upon her that I had branded upon my poor brother.

"The day after my return to Lille, my brother, in his turn, succeeded in making his escape ; I was accused of complicity, and was condemned to remain in his place till he should be again a prisoner. My poor brother was ignorant of this sentence ; he rejoined this woman ; they fled together into Berry, and there he obtained a little curacy. This woman passed for his sister.

"The lord of the estate upon which the church of the curacy was situated, saw this pretended sister, and became enamoured of her ; so much so, that he offered to marry her. Then she left him she had ruined, for him she was destined to ruin, and became the Countess de la Fère——"

All eyes were turned towards Athos, whose real name that was, and who made a sign with his head that all was true that the executioner had said.

"Then," resumed he, "mad, desperate, determined to get rid of an existence from which she had taken away everything, both honour and happiness, my poor brother returned to Lille, and learning the sentence which had condemned me in his place, surrendered himself, and hung himself that same night, from the iron bar of the loophole of his prison.

" To render justice to them who had condemned me, they kept their word.   As soon as the identity of my brother was proved, I was set at liberty.

" That is the crime of which I accuse her ; that is the cause of her being branded."

" Monsieur d'Artagnan," said Athos, " what is the penalty you demand against this woman ?"

" The punishment of death," replied D'Artagnan.

" Milord de Winter," continued Athos, " what is the penalty you demand against this woman ?"

" The punishment of death," replied Lord de Winter.

" Messieurs Porthos and Aramis," again said Athos, " you who are her judges, what is the sentence you pronounce upon this woman ?"

" The punishment of death," replied the musketeers, in a stern, hollow voice.

Milady uttered a frightful shriek, and dragged herself along several paces towards her judges upon her knees.

Athos stretched out his hand towards her.

" Charlotte Backson, Countess de la Fère, Milady de Winter," said he, " your crimes have wearied men on earth and God in heaven. If you know any prayer, say it ; for you are condemned, and you shall die."

At these words, which left no hope, milady raised herself up to her full height, and endeavoured to speak, but her strength failed her ; she felt that a powerful and implacable hand seized her by the hair, and dragged her away as irrevocably as fatality drags man : she did not, therefore, even attempt to make the least resistance, and went out of the cottage.

Lord de Winter, D'Artagnan, Athos, Porthos, and Aramis, went out close behind her and the executioner. The lackeys followed their masters, and the chamber was left solitary, with its broken window, its open door, and its smoky lamp burning dimly on the table.

CHAPTER LXVI.

EXECUTION.

IT was near midnight ; the moon, lessened by its decline and reddened by the last traces of the storm, arose behind the little town of Armentières, which showed against its pale light the dark outline of its houses, and the outline of its high belfry.   In front of them the Lys rolled its waters like a river of melted lead ; whilst on the other side was a black mass of trees, cutting a stormy sky, invaded by large coppery clouds, which created a sort of twilight amidst the night.   On the left was an old abandoned mill, with its motionless wings, from the ruins of which an owl threw out its shrill, periodical, and monotonous cry.   On the right and on the left of the road, which the dismal *cortège* pursued, appeared a few low, stunted trees, which looked like deformed dwarfs crouching down to watch men travelling at this sinister hour.

From time to time a broad sheet of lightning opened the horizon in its whole width, darted like a serpent over the black mass of trees, and, like a terrible scimitar, divided the heavens and the waters into two parts. Not a breath of wind now disturbed the heavy atmosphere. A death-like silence oppressed all nature, the soil was humid and glittering with the rain which had recently fallen, and the refreshed herbs threw forth their perfume with additional energy.

Two of the lackeys now led, or rather dragged, along milady by her arms ; the executioner walked behind them, and Lord de Winter, D'Artagnan, Porthos, and Aramis walked behind the executioner. Planchet and Bazin came last.

The two lackeys led milady to the banks of the river. Her mouth was mute ; but her eyes spoke with their inexpressible eloquence, supplicating by turns each of those she looked at.

Being a few paces in advance, she whispered to the lackeys :

"A thousand pistoles to each of you, if you will assist my escape ; but if you deliver me up to your masters, I have, near at hand, avengers who will make you pay for my death very dearly."

Grimaud hesitated ; Mousqueton trembled in all his members.

Athos, who heard milady's voice, came sharply up ; Lord de Winter did the same.

"Change these lackeys," said he, "she has spoken to them, they are no longer safe."

Planchet and Bazin were called forward, and took the places of Grimaud and Mousqueton.

When they arrived on the banks of the river, the executioner approached milady, and bound her hands and feet.

Then she broke silence to cry out :

"You are base cowards, miserable assassins, ten men combined to murder one woman ; beware ! if I am not saved I shall be avenged."

"You are not a woman," said Athos, coldly and sternly, "you do not belong to the human species : you are a demon escaped from hell, to which place we are going to send you back again."

"Ah ! you virtuous men !" said milady, "but please to remember that he who shall touch a hair of my head is himself an assassin."

"The executioner can kill, madame, without being on that account an assassin," said the man in the red cloak, striking upon his immense sword ; "this is the last judge ; that is all : *Nachrichter*, as our neighbours, the Germans, say."

And as he bound her whilst saying these words, milady uttered two or three wild cries, which produced a strange and melancholy effect in flying away into the night, and losing themselves in the depths of the woods.

"If I am guilty, if I have committed the crimes you accuse me of," shrieked milady, "take me before a tribunal ; you are not judges ; you cannot condemn me !"

21

"Why, I did offer you Tyburn," said Lord de Winter; "why did you not accept it?'

"Because I am not willing to die!" cried milady, struggling, "because I am too young to die!"

"The woman you poisoned at Bethune was still younger than you, madame, and yet she is dead," said D'Artagnan.

"I will enter a cloister, I will become a nun," said milady.

"You were in a cloister," said the executioner, "and you left it to destroy my brother."

Milady uttered a cry of terror, and sank upon her knees.

The executioner took her up in his arms, and was carrying her towards the boat.

"Oh! my God!" cried she, "my God! are you going to drown me?"

These cries had something so heartrending in them, that M. d'Artagnan, who had been at first the most eager in pursuit of milady, sank down on the stump of a tree, and leant down his head, covering his ears with the palms of his hands; and yet, notwithstanding, he could not help hearing her cry and threaten.

D'Artagnan was the youngest of all these men; his heart failed him.

"Oh! I cannot behold this frightful spectacle!" said he; "I cannot consent that this woman should die thus!"

Milady heard these few words, and caught at a shadow of hope.

"D'Artagnan! D'Artagnan!" cried she, "remember that I loved you!'

The young man rose, and made a step towards her.

But Athos arose, likewise, drew his sword, and placed himself between them.

"One step further, M. d'Artagnan," said he, "and, dearly as I love you, we cross swords."

M. d'Artagnan sank on his knees and prayed.

"Come!" continued Athos, "executioner, do your duty."

"Willingly, monseigneur," said the executioner; "for, as I am a good Catholic, I firmly believe I am acting justly in performing my functions on this woman."

"That's well."

Athos made a step towards milady.

"I pardon you," said he, "the ill you have done me; I pardon you for my blasted future, my lost honour, my defiled love, and my salvation for ever compromised by the despair into which you have cast me. Die in peace!"

Lord de Winter advanced in his turn.

"I pardon you," said he, "the poisoning of my brother, the assassination of his grace the Duke of Buckingham; I pardon you the death of poor Felton, I pardon you the attempts upon my own person. Die in peace."

"And I," said M. d'Artagnan. "Pardon me, madame, for having by a trick, unworthy of a gentleman, provoked your anger; and I, in exchange, pardon you the murder of my poor love, and your cruel vengeance against me. I pardon you, and I weep for you. Die in peace."

"I am lost !" murmured milady, in English ; "I must die !"

Then she rose up herself, and cast around her one of those piercing looks which seemed to dart from an eye of flame.

She saw nothing.

She listened, and she heard nothing.

"Where am I to die?" said she.

"On the other bank," replied the executioner.

Then he placed her in the boat, and as he was going to set foot in it himself, Athos handed him a purse of gold.

"Here," said he, "is the pay for the execution, that it may be plain we act as judges."

"That is correct," said the executioner ; "and now in her turn, let this woman see that I am not fulfilling my trade, but my duty."

And he threw the money into the river.

The boat moved off towards the left-hand shore of the Lys, bearing the guilty woman and the executioner ; all the others remained on the right-hand bank, where they fell on their knees.

The boat glided along the ferry-rope under the shadow of a pale cloud which hung over the water at the moment.

The troop of friends saw it gain the opposite bank ; the persons cut the red-tinted horizon with a black shade.

Milady, during the passage, had contrived to untie the cord which fastened her feet ; on coming near to the bank, she jumped lightly on shore and took to flight.

But the soil was moist : on gaining the top of the bank, she slipped and fell upon her knees.

She was struck, no doubt, with a superstitious idea : she conceived that heaven denied its succour, and she remained in the attitude she had fallen in, with her head drooping and her hands clasped.

Then they saw from the other bank the executioner raise both his arms slowly, a moonbeam fell upon the blade of the large sword, the two arms fell with a sudden force ; they heard the hissing of the scimitar and the cry of the victim, then a truncated mass sank beneath the blow.

The executioner then took off his red cloak, spread it upon the ground, laid the body in it, threw in the head, tied all up with the four corners, lifted it on to his back, and got into the boat again.

When arrived in the middle of the stream, he stopped the boat, and suspending his burden over the water,—

"Let the justice of God be done !" cried he with a loud voice.

And he let the body drop into the depths of the waters, which closed over it.

Within three days the four musketeers were in Paris ; they had not exceeded their leave of absence, and that same evening went to pay their customary visit to M. de Tréville.

"Well, gentlemen," said the brave captain, "I hope you have enjoyed your excursion."

"Prodigiously!" replied Athos, for himself and his companions.

CHAPTER LXVII.

CONCLUSION.

ON the sixth of the following month, the king, in compliance with the promise he had made the cardinal to return to La Rochelle, left his capital still in amazement at the news which began to spread of Buckingham's assassination.

Although warned that the man she had loved so much was in great danger, the queen, when his death was announced to her, would not believe the fact, and even imprudently exclaimed:

"It is false: he has just written to me!"

But the next day she was obliged to receive this fatal intelligence as truth; Laporte, detained in England, as every one else had been, by the orders of Charles I., arrived, and was the bearer of the duke's last dying present to the queen.

The joy of the king was great, he did not even give himself the trouble to dissemble it, and displayed it with affectation before the queen. Louis XIII., like all weak minds, was miserably wanting in generosity.

But the king soon again became dull and indisposed; his brow was not one of those that are clear for long together: he felt that by returning to his camp, he was about to resume his state of slavery; nevertheless, he did return.

The cardinal was for him the fascinating serpent, and he was the bird which flies from branch to branch, without being able to escape.

The return to La Rochelle, therefore, was profoundly dull. Our four friends, in particular, astonished their comrades; they travelled together, side by side, with spiritless eyes and heads depressed. Athos alone, from time to time, raised his expansive brow; a flash kindled in his eyes, and a bitter smile passed over his lips; then, like his comrades, he sank again into his reveries.

As soon as the escort arrived in any city, when they had conducted the king to his quarters, the four friends either retired to their own, or to some secluded cabaret, where they neither drank nor played; they only conversed in a low voice, looking around attentively that no one overheard them.

One day, when the king had halted to fly the pie, and the four friends, according to their custom, instead of following the sport, had stopped at a cabaret on the high road, a man, coming from La Rochelle on horseback, pulled up at the door to drink a glass of wine, and darted a searching glance into the chamber in which the four musketeers were sitting.

'Hilloa! Monsieur d'Artagnan!' said he, "is not that you I see yonder?"

D'Artagnan raised his head and uttered a cry of joy. It was the man he called his phantom, it was his unknown of Meung, of the Rue des Fossoyeurs and of Arras.

D'Artagnan drew his sword, and sprang towards the door.

But this time, instead of avoiding him, the unknown jumped from his horse, and advanced to meet D'Artagnan.

"Ah ! monsieur !" said the young man, "I have met with you, then, at last ! this time, I will answer for it, you shall not escape me !"

"Neither is it my intention, monsieur, for this time I was seeking you ; in the name of the king, I arrest you."

"How ! what do you say ?" cried D'Artagnan.

"I say that you must surrender your sword to me, monsieur, and that without resistance ; the safety of your head depends upon your compliance."

"Who are you, then ?" demanded D'Artagnan, lowering the point of his sword, but without yet surrendering it.

"I am the Chevalier de Rochefort," answered the other, "the equerry of monsieur the Cardinal de Richelieu, and I have orders to conduct you to his eminence."

"We are returning to his eminence, Monsieur le Chevalier," said Athos, advancing ; "and you will please to accept the word of M. d'Artagnan, that he will go straight to La Rochelle."

"I must place him in the hands of guards who will take him to the camp."

"We will be his guards, monsieur, upon our words, as gentlemen ; but, upon our words as gentlemen, likewise," added Athos, knitting his brow, "M. d'Artagnan shall not leave us."

The Chevalier de Rochefort cast a glance backward, and saw that Porthos and Aramis had placed themselves between him and the gate ; he therefore was convinced that he was completely at the mercy of these four men.

"Gentlemen," said he, "if M. d'Artagnan will surrender his sword to me, and join his word to yours, I will be satisfied with your promise to convey M. d'Artagnan to the quarters of monseigneur the cardinal."

"You have my word, monsieur, and here is my sword."

"This suits me the better," said Rochefort, "as I wish to continue my journey."

"If it is for the purpose of rejoining milady," said Athos, coolly, "it is useless, you will not find her."

"What is become of her then ?" asked Rochefort, eagerly.

"Come back with us to the camp and you shall know."

Rochefort remained for a moment undecided, then, as they were only a day's journey from Surgères, to which place the cardinal was to come to meet the king, he resolved to follow Athos's advice and go with them. Besides, this return presented him the advantage of watching over his prisoner.

They resumed their route.

On the morrow, at three o'clock in the afternoon, they arrived at

Surgères. The cardinal there awaited Louis XIII. The minister and the king exchanged numerous caresses, felicitating each other upon the fortunate chance which had freed France from the inveterate enemy who set on all Europe against her. After which, the cardinal, who had been informed that D'Artagnan was arrested, and who was anxious to see him, took leave of the king, inviting him to come the next day to view the labours of the dyke, which were completed.

On returning in the evening to his quarters at the bridge of La Pierre, the cardinal found D'Artagnan, without his sword, and the three mus-keteers armed, standing before the door of the house.

This time, as he was well attended, he looked at them sternly, and made a sign with his eye and hand for D'Artagnan to follow him.

D'Artagnan obeyed.

"We shall wait for you, D'Artagnan," said Athos, loud enough for the cardinal to hear him.

His eminence bent his brow, stopped for an instant, and then kept on his way, without uttering a single word.

D'Artagnan entered after the cardinal, and behind D'Artagnan the door was guarded.

His eminence went to the chamber which served him as a closet, and made a sign to Rochefort to bring in the young musketeer.

Rochefort obeyed and retired.

D'Artagnan remained alone in front of the cardinal ; this was his second interview with Richelieu, and he afterwards confessed that he felt well assured it would be his last.

Richelieu remained standing, leaning against the mantelpiece ; a table was between him and D'Artagnan.

"Monsieur," said the cardinal, "you have been arrested by my orders."

"So I have been informed, monseigneur."

"Do you know why ?"

"No, monseigneur, for the only thing for which I could be arrested is still unknown to your eminence."

Richelieu looked steadfastly at the young man.

"Indeed !" said he, "what does that mean ?"

"If monseigneur will have the goodness to tell me, in the first place, what crimes are imputed to me, I will then tell your eminence what I have really done."

"Crimes are imputed to you that have brought down much more lofty heads than yours, monsieur," said the cardinal.

"What are they, monseigneur ?" said D'Artagnan, with a calmness that astonished the cardinal himself.

"You are charged with having corresponded with the enemies of the kingdom ; you are charged with having surprised state secrets ; you are charged with having endeavoured to thwart the plans of your general."

"And who charges me with this, monseigneur ?" said D'Artagnan, who had no doubt the accusation came from milady—"a woman branded by the justice of the country—a woman who has espoused one man in

France and another in England—a woman who poiscned her second husband, and who attempted both to poison and assassinate me !"

" What is all this, monsieur ?" cried the cardinal, astonished ; " and what woman are you speaking of thus ?"

" Of Milady de Winter," replied D'Artagnan—" yes, of Milady de Winter, of whose crimes your eminence is doubtless ignorant, because you have honoured her with your confidence."

" Monsieur," said the cardinal, " if Milady de Winter has committed the crimes you lay to her charge, she shall be punished."

" She is punished, monseigneur.'

" And who has punished her ?"

" We have.'

" Is she in prison ?"

" She is dead."

" Dead !" repeated the cardinal, who could not believe what he heard -" dead ! Did you say she was dead ?"

" Three times she attempted to kill me, and I pardoned her ; but she murdered the woman I loved. Then my friends and I took her, tried her, and condemned her."

D Artagnan then related the poisoning of Madame Bonacieux in the convent of the Carmelites of Bethune, the trial in the solitary house, and the execution on the banks of the Lys.

A shudder crept through the body of the cardinal, who, it may be observed, was not easily made to shudder.

But all at once, as if undergoing the influence of a secret thought, the countenance of the cardinal, till that moment gloomy, cleared up by degrees, and recovered perfect serenity.

" So,' said the cardinal, in a tone that contrasted strongly with the severity of his words, " you have constituted yourselves judges, without remembering that they who punish without license to punish, are assassins ?"

" Monseigneur, I swear to you that I never for an instant had the intention of defending my head against you ; I willingly will submit to any punishment your eminence may please to inflict upon me ; I do not hold life dear enough to be afraid of death."

" Yes, I know you are a man of a stout heart, monsieur," said the cardinal, in an almost kind tone ; " I can therefore tell you beforehand you shall be tried, and even condemned."

" Another might reply that he had his pardon in his pocket. I will content myself with saying, Issue your orders, monseigneur ; I am ready."

" Your pardon ?" said Richelieu, surprised.

" Yes, monseigneur," said D'Artagnan.

" And signed by whom—by the king ?"

And the cardinal pronounced these words with a singular expression of contempt.

" No ; by your eminence."

" By me ? You must be mad, monsieur !"

" Monseigneur will doubtless recognise his own writing."

And D'Artagnan presented to the cardinal the precious piece of paper which Athos had forced from milady, and which he had given to D'Artagnan, to serve him as a safeguard.

His eminence took the paper, and read in a slow voice, dwelling upon every syllable :

" It is by my orders that the bearer of this paper has done what he has just done.

"At the camp of Rochelle, this fifth of August, 1628.

" RICHELIEU."

The cardinal, after having read these two lines, sank into a profound reverie ; but he did not return the paper to D'Artagnan.

" He is meditating what sort of punishment he shall put me to death by," said D'Artagnan to himself. " Let him ; *ma foi !* he shall see how a gentleman can die !"

The young musketeer was then in an excellent disposition to suffer heroically.

Richelieu still continued thinking, twisting and untwisting the paper in his hands.

At length he raised his head, fixed his eagle look upon that loyal, open, and intelligent countenance, read upon that face, furrowed with tears, all the sufferings he had endured in the course of the last month, and reflected for the third or fourth time how much that youth of twenty-one years of age had before him, and what resources his activity, his courage, and his shrewd understanding might offer to a good master.

In another respect the crimes, the strength of mind, and the infernal genius of milady had more than once terrified him ; he felt something like a secret joy at having got rid of this dangerous accomplice.

He slowly tore the paper which D'Artagnan had generously placed in his hand.

" I am lost !" said D'Artagnan to himself.

And he bowed profoundly before the cardinal, like a man who says, " Lord, thy will be done !"

The cardinal went up to the table, and, without sitting down, wrote a few lines upon a parchment of which two-thirds were already filled up, and affixed his seal to it.

" That is my condemnation," thought D'Artagnan ; " he will spare me the *ennui* of the Bastille, or the tediousness of a trial. That's very kind of him."

" Here, monsieur," said the cardinal to the young man, " I have aken from you one signed blank to give you another. The name is wanting in this commission ; you can write it yourself."

D'Artagnan took the paper hesitatingly, and cast his eyes over it ; it was a lieutenant's commission in the musketeers.

D'Artagnan fell at the feet of the cardinal.

" Monseigneur," said he, " my life is yours—henceforward dispose of it. But this favour which you bestow upon me I do not merit ; I have three friends who are more meritorious and more worthy——"

"You are a brave youth, D'Artagnan," interrupted the cardinal, tapping him familiarly on the shoulder, charmed at having subdued this rebellious nature. "Do with this commission what you will ; only remember that, though the name be a blank, it was to you that I gave it."

"I shall never forget it," replied D'Artagnan ; "your eminence may be certain of that."

The cardinal turned round, and said in a loud voice :

"Rochefort !"

The chevalier, who no doubt was near the door, entered immediately.

"Rochefort," said the cardinal, "you see M. d'Artagnan—I receive him among the number of my friends ; embrace, then, and be prudent, if you have any wish to preserve your heads."

Rochefort and D'Artagnan saluted coolly ; but the cardinal was there observing them with his vigilant eye.

They left the chamber at the same time.

"We shall meet again, shall we not, monsieur?"

"When you please,' said D'Artagnan.

"An opportunity will offer itself," replied Rochefort.

"What's that ?" said the cardinal, opening the door.

The two men smiled at each other, shook hands, and bowed to his eminence.

"We were beginning to grow impatient," said Athos.

"Well, here I am, my friends," replied D'Artagnan, "not only free, but in favour."

"Tell us all about it."

"This evening."

Accordingly, that same evening D'Artagnan repaired to the quarters of Athos, whom he found in a fair way of emptying a bottle of Spanish wine, an occupation which he religiously went through every night.

He related all that had taken place between the cardinal and himself, and, drawing the commission from his pocket,—

"Here, my dear Athos," said he, "this belongs to you naturally."

Athos smiled with one of his sweet and expressive smiles.

"My friend," said he, "for Athos this is too much, for the Count de la Fère it is too little ; keep the commission—it is yours ; alas ! you have purchased it dearly enough."

D'Artagnan left Athos' chamber, and went to that of Porthos.

He found him clothed in a magnificent dress covered with splendid embroidery, admiring himself before a glass.

"Ah, ah ! is that you, friend D'Artagnan ?" exclaimed he ; "how do you think these garments fit me, eh ?"

"Wonderfully well," said D'Artagnan ; "but I am come to offer you a dress which will become you still better."

"What's that ?" asked Porthos.

"That of a lieutenant of musketeers."

D'Artagnan related to Porthos the substance of his interview with the cardinal, and, taking the commission from his pocket,

"Here, my friend," said he, "write your name upon it, and become my officer."

Porthos cast his eyes over the commission, and returned it to D'Artagnan, to the great astonishment of the young man.

"Yes," said he, "yes, that would flatter me very much, but I should not have time enough to enjoy the distinction. During our expedition to Bethune the husband of my duchess died, so that, my dear friend, the coffer of the defunct holding out its arms to me, I shall marry the widow; look here, I at this moment was trying on my wedding suit. No, keep the lieutenancy, my dear fellow, keep it."

And he returned the commission to D'Artagnan.

The young man then entered the apartment of Aramis.

He found him kneeling before a *prie-Dieu*, with his head leaning upon an open book of prayer.

He described to him his interview with the cardinal, and, for the third time drawing his commission from his pocket,

"You, our friend, our intelligence, our invisible protector," said he, "accept this commission ; you have merited it more than any of us by your wisdom and your counsels, always followed by such happy results."

"Alas ! my dear friend," said Aramis, "our late adventures have disgusted me with life and with the sword; this time my determination is irrevocably taken : after the siege I shall enter the house of the Lazarists. Keep the commission, D'Artagnan—the profession of arms suits you ; you will be a brave and adventurous captain."

D'Artagnan, his eye moist with gratitude, though beaming with joy, went back to Athos, whom he found still at table, contemplating the charms of his last glass of Malaga by the light of his lamp.

"Well," said he, "and they likewise have refused me !"

"That, my dear friend, is because nobody is more worthy than yourself."

And he took a pen, wrote the name of D'Artagnan on the commission, and returned it to him.

"I shall then no longer have friends," said the young man; "alas ! nothing but bitter recollections."

And he let his head sink upon his hands, whilst two large tears rolled down his cheeks.

"You are young," replied Athos, "and your bitter recollections have time to be changed into sweet remembrances."

EPILOGUE.

LA ROCHELLE, deprived of the assistance of the English fleet, and of the reinforcements promised by Buckingham, surrendered after a siege of a year On the 28th of October, 1628, the capitulation was signed.

The king made his entrance into Paris on the 23rd of December of the same year He was received in triumph, as if he came from conquering an enemy, and not Frenchmen. He entered by the Faubourg St Jacques under verdant triumphal arches.

D'Artagnan took possession of his rank. Porthos left the service, and in the course of the following year married Madame Coquenard; the so much coveted coffer contained 800,000 livres.

Mousqueton had a magnificent livery, and enjoyed the satisfaction he had been ambitious of all his life—that of standing behind a gilded carriage.

Aramis, after a journey into Lorraine, disappeared all at once, and ceased to write to his friends; they learned, at a later period, by Madame de Chevreuse, who told it to two or three of her intimates, that he had taken the habit in a convent of Nancy.

Bazin became a lay brother.

Athos remained a musketeer under the command of D'Artagnan till the year 1631, at which period, after a journey which he made to Couraine, he also quitted the service, under the pretext of having inherited a small property in Roussillon.

Grimaud followed Athos.

D'Artagnan fought three times with Rochefort, and wounded him at each encounter

"I shall most likely kill you at the fourth," said he to him, holding out his hand to assist him to rise.

"We had much better leave off as we are, both for you and for me," answered the wounded man. "Corbleu! I am much more your friend than you think; for, from our very first encounter, I could, by saying a word to the cardinal, have had your throat cut!"

They this time embraced heartily, and without retaining any malice.

Planchet obtained from Rochefort the rank of sergeant in the guards.

M. Bonacieux lived on very quietly, perfectly ignorant what had become of his wife, and caring very little about the matter. One day he had the imprudence to intrude himself upon the memory of the cardinal; the cardinal had him informed that he would provide for him, so that he should never want for anything in future.   In fact, M. Bonacieux having left his house at seven o'clock in the evening to go to the Louvre, never appeared again in the Rue des Fossoyeurs ; the opinion of those who seemed to be the best informed was, that he was fed and lodged in some royal castle, at the expense of his generous eminence.

THE END.

Twenty Years After

CONTENTS.

TWENTY YEARS AFTER.

CHAPTER I.

THE SHADE OF CARDINAL RICHELIEU,

IN one of the rooms of the Palais Royal, in old times styled the
Palais Cardinal, there sat a man in deep reverie, his head supported on his hands, leaning over a table, the corners of which
were of silver-gilt, and which was covered with letters and papers.
Behind this figure was a vast fireplace glowing with heat; large
masses of wood blazed and crackled on the gilded andirons, and
the flames shone upon the superb habiliments of the solitary inhabitant of the chamber, illumined in the foreground by a candelabra
filled with wax-lights.

Any one who had happened at that moment to contemplate that
red simar—the gorgeous robe of office—and the rich lace—or who
gazed upon that pale brow, bent in anxious meditation, might, in
the solitude of that apartment, combined with the silence of the
ante-chambers, and the measured paces of the guards upon the
landing-place, have fancied that the shade of Cardinal Richelieu
still lingered in his accustomed haunt.

But it was, alas! only the ghost of former greatness. France
enfeebled, the authority of her sovereign rejected, her nobles returning to their former turbulence and insolence, her enemies
within her frontiers—all proved that Richelieu was no longer in
existence.

In truth, that the red simar which occupied his wonted place
was his no longer, was still more strikingly obvious from the isolation which seemed, as we have observed, more appropriate to a
phantom than to a living creature—from the corridors, deserted

by courtiers, and courts crowded with guards—from that spirit of bitter ridicule, which, arising from the streets below, penetrated through the very windows of that room, which resounded with the murmurs of a whole city leagued against the minister, as well as from the distant and incessant sounds of guns firing—let off, happily, without other end or aim, except to show to the guards, the Swiss troops, and the military who surrounded the Palais Royal,* that the people were possessed of arms.

The shade of Richelieu was Mazarin. Now Mazarin was alone and defenceless—as he well knew.

"Foreigner!" he ejaculated, "Italian! that is their mean word of reproach—the watchword with which they assassinated, hanged, and made away with Concini, and—if I gave them their way—they would assassinate, hang, and make away with me in the same manner, although they have nothing to complain of, except a tax or two now and then. Idiots! ignorant of their real enemies, they do not perceive that it is not the Italian who speaks French badly, but those who can say fine things to them in the purest Parisian accent, who are their real foes.

"Yes, yes," Mazarin continued, whilst his wonted smile, full of subtlety, gave a strange expression to his pale lips; "yes, these noises prove to me, indeed, that the destiny of favourites is precarious; but ye should know that I am no ordinary favourite. No! the Earl of Essex, 'tis true, wore a splendid ring, set with diamonds, given him by his royal mistress; whilst I—I have nothing but a simple circlet of gold, with a cypher on it and a date; but that ring has been blessed in the chapel of the Palais Royal,† so they will never ruin me, as they would do; and whilst they shout 'Down with Mazarin!' I, unknown and unperceived by them, incite them to cry out, 'Long live the Duke de Beaufort' one day; another, 'Long live the Prince de Condé;' and again, 'Long live the Parliament!'" And, at this word, the smile on the Cardinal's lips assumed an expression of hatred, of which his mild countenance seemed incapable. "The parliament! We shall soon see how to dispose," he continued, "of the parliament! Both Orleans and Montargis are ours. It will be a work of time! but those who have begun by crying out, 'Down with Mazarin!' will finish by shouting out, Down with all the people I have mentioned, each in his turn.

* The Palais Royal ceased to be called the Palais Cardinal before this epoch.
† It is said that Mazarin, who, though a cardinal, had not taken such vows as to prevent it, was secretly married to Anne of Austria.—*La Porte's Memoirs.*

"Richelieu, whom they hated during his lifetime, and whom they now praise after his death, was even less popular than I am. Often was he driven away—oftener still had he a dread of being sent away. The queen will never banish me; and even were I obliged to yield to the populace, she would yield with me; if I fly, she will fly; and then we shall see how the rebels will get on without either king or queen.

"Oh, were I not a foreigner! were I but a Frenchman! would I were even merely a gentleman!"

The position of the Cardinal was, indeed, critical, and several recent events added to his difficulties. Discontent had long pervaded the lower ranks of society in France. Crushed and impoverished by taxation—imposed by Mazarin, whose avarice impelled him to grind them down to the very dust—the people, as the Advocate-General Talon described it, had nothing left to them except their souls; and as those could not be sold by auction, they began to murmur. Patience had in vain been recommended to them, by reports of brilliant victories gained by France; laurels, however, were not meat and drink; and the people had for some time been in a state of discontent.

Had this been all, it might not, perhaps, have greatly signified; for, when the lower classes alone complained, the court of France, separated as it was from the poor by the intervening classes of the gentry and the *bourgeoisie*, seldom listened to their voice; but, unluckily, Mazarin had had the imprudence to attack the magistrates, and had sold no less than ten appointments in the Court of Requests, at a high price; and, as the officers of that court paid very dear for their places, and as the addition of twelve new colleagues would necessarily lower the value of each place, the old functionaries formed an union amongst themselves, and, enraged, swore on the Bible not to allow of this addition to their number, but to resist all the persecutions which might ensue; and should any one of them chance to forfeit his post by this resistance, to combine to indemnify him for his loss.

Now the following occurrences had taken place between the two contending parties.

On the seventh of January between seven and eight hundred tradesmen had assembled in Paris to discuss a new tax which was to be levied on house property. They deputed ten of their number to wait upon the Duke of Orleans, who, according to custom, affected popularity. The duke received them, and they informed him that they were resolved not to pay this tax, even if they were obliged to defend themselves against the collectors of it by force of arms.   They were listened to with great politeness by the duke, who held out hopes of more moderate measures; promised them to speak in their behalf to the queen; and dismissed them with the ordinary expression of royalty—" We shall see what we can do."

Two days afterwards these same magistrates appeared before the Cardinal, and the spokesman among them addressed Mazarin with so much fearlessness and determination, that the minister was astounded, and sent the deputation away with the same answer as it had received from the Duke of Orleans—that he would see what could be done : and, in accordance with that intention, a council of state was assembled, and the superintendent of finance was summoned.

This man, named Emery, was the object of popular detestation —in the first place, because he *was* superintendent of finance, and every superintendent of finance deserved to be hated ; in the second place, because he rather deserved the odium which he had incurred.

He was the son of a banker at Lyons, named Particelli, who, after becoming a bankrupt, chose to change his name to Emery; and Cardinal Richelieu, having discovered in young Emery great financial aptitude, had introduced him with a strong recommendation to Louis XIII. under his assumed name, in order that he might be appointed to the post which he subsequently held.

" You surprise me !" exclaimed the monarch.   " I am rejoiced to hear you speak of Monsieur d'Emery as calculated for a post which requires a man of probity.   I was really afraid that you were going to force that villain Particelli upon me."

" Sire," replied Richelieu, " rest assured that Particelli—the man to whom your majesty refers—has been hanged."

" Ah, so much the better !" exclaimed the king.   " It is not for nothing that I am styled Louis the Just"—and he signed Emery's appointment

This was the same Emery who had become eventually superintendent of finance.

He was sent for by the ministers, and he came before them pale and trembling, declaring that his son had very nearly been assassinated the day before near the palace.   The mob had insulted him on account of the ostentatious luxury of his wife, whose house was hung with red velvet, edged with gold fringe.   This lady was the daughter of Nicholas de Camus, who had arrived in Paris with twenty francs in his pocket—had become secretary of state—and had accumulated wealth enough to divide nine millions of francs among his children, and to keep forty thousand for himself.

The fact was, that Emery's son had run a great chance of being suffocated; one of the rioters having proposed to squeeze him until he gave up all the gold he had swallowed. Nothing therefore was settled that day, as Emery's head was not steady enough for business after such an occurrence.

Other disturbances had followed this outrage.

Matthew Mole, chief president of the parliament, and esteemed equal in courage to Condé and De Beaufort, had been insulted and threatened. The queen, in going to mass at Notre Dame, as she always did on Saturdays, was followed by more than two hundred women, demanding justice. These poor creatures had no bad intentions. They wished only to be allowed to fall on their knees before their sovereign, and that they might move her to compassion; but they were prevented by the royal guard, and the queen proceeded on her way, haughtily disdainful of their entreaties.

At length parliament was convoked—the authority of the king was to be maintained.

One day—it was the morning of that when my story begins—the king, Louis XIV., then ten years of age, went in state, under pretext of returning thanks for his recovery from the small-pox, to Notre Dame. He took the opportunity of calling out his guard, the Swiss troops, and the Musketeers, and he had planted them round the Palais Royal, on the quays, and on the Pont Neuf. After mass, the young monarch drove to the parliament house, where, upon the throne, he hastily confirmed not only the edicts which he had already passed, but issued new ones; each one, according to Cardinal de Retz, more ruinous than the others—a proceeding which drew forth a strong remonstrance from the chief president Mole—whilst President Blancmesnil and Councillor Broussel raised their voices in indignation against fresh taxes.

The king returned amidst the silence of a vast multitude to the Palais Royal. All minds were uneasy—most were foreboding—many of the people using threatening language.

At first, indeed, they were doubtful whether the king's visit to the parliament had been in order to lighten or to increase their burdens; but scarcely was it known that the taxes were even to be increased, than cries of "Down with Mazarin!" "Long live Broussel!" "Long live Blancmesnil!" resounded through the city. All attempts to disperse the groups now collected in the streets, or to silence their exclamations, were vain. Orders had just been given to the royal guard, and to the Swiss Guards, not only to stand firm, but to send out patrols to the streets of Saint

Denis and Saint Martin, where the people thronged, and where they were the most vociferous, when the Mayor of Paris was announced at the Palais Royal.

He was shown in directly : he came to say that if these offensive precautions were not discontinued, in two hours Paris would be under arms.

Deliberations were being held, when a lieutenant in the Guards, named Comminges, made his appearance, with his clothes all torn, his face streaming with blood. The queen, on seeing him, uttered a cry of surpise, and asked him what was going on.

As the mayor had foreseen, the sight of the Guards had exas-perated the mob. The tocsin was sounded. Comminges had arrested one of the ringleaders, and had ordered him to be hanged near the cross of Du Trahoir; but, in attempting to execute this command, the soldiery were attacked in the market-place with stones and halberds : the delinquents all escaped to the Rue des Lombards, and rushed into a house. They broke open the doors, and searched the dwelling, but in vain. Comminges, wounded by a stone which had struck him on the forehead, had left a picquet in the street, and returned to the Palais Royal, followed by a menacing crowd, to tell his story.

This account confirmed that of the mayor. The authorities were not in a condition to contend with a serious revolt. Mazarin endeavoured to circulate among the people a report that troops had only been stationed on the quays, and on the Pont Neuf, on account of the ceremonial of the day, and that they would soon withdraw. In fact, about four o'clock they were all concentrated about the Palais Royal, the courts and ground floors of which were filled with Musketeers and Swiss Guards, and there awaited the event of all this disturbance.

Such was the state of affairs at the very moment when we introduced our readers into the study of Cardinal Mazarin—once that of Cardinal Richelieu. We have seen in what state of mind he listened to the murmurs from below, which even reached him in his seclusion, and to the guns, the firing of which resounded in that room. All at once he raised his head : his brow slightly con-tracted, like that of a man who has formed a resolution ; he fixed his eyes upon an enormous clock which was about to strike ten, and taking up a whistle, of silver gilt, which was placed on the table near him, he whistled twice.

A door hidden in the tapestry opened noiselessly, and a man in black stood behind the chair on which Mazarin sat.

"Bernouin," said the Cardinal, not turning round, for, having whistled, he knew that it was his valet-de-chambre who was behind him, "what Musketeers are there in the palace?"

"The Black Musketeers, my lord."

"What company?"

"Treville's company."

"Is there any officer belonging to this company in the ante chamber?"

"Lieutenant d'Artagnan."

"A man on whom we can depend, I hope."

"Yes, my lord."

"Give me a uniform of one of these Musketeers, and help me to dress."

The valet went out as silently as he came in, and appeared in a few minutes, bringing the dress which was asked for.

The Cardinal, in deep thought, and in silence, began to take off the robes of state which he had assumed in order to be present at the sitting of parliament, and to attire himself in the military coat, which he wore with a certain degree of easy grace, owing to his former campaigns in Italy. When he was completely dressed, he said:

"Bring Monsieur d'Artagnan hither."

The valet went out of the room, this time by the centre door, but still as silently as before: one might have fancied him an apparition.

When he was left alone, the Cardinal looked at himself in the glass with a feeling of self-satisfaction. Still young—for he was scarcely forty-six years of age—he possessed great elegance of form, and was above the middle height; his complexion was brilliant and beautiful; his glance full of expression; his nose, though large, was well proportioned; his forehead broad and majestic; his hair, of a chestnut colour, was rather frizzed; his beard, which was darker than his hair, was turned carefully with a curling-iron, a practice which greatly improved it. After a short time the Cardinal arranged his shoulder-belt, then looked with great complacency at his hands, which were very beautiful, and of which he took the greatest care; and throwing on one side the large kid gloves which he tried on at first, as belonging to the uniform, he put on others of silk only. At this instant the door opened.

"Monsieur d'Artagnan," said the valet-de-chambre.

An officer, as he spoke, entered the apartment. He was a man between thirty-nine and forty years of age, of a small but well-proportioned figure; thin, with an intellectual and animated physiognomy; his beard black, and his hair turning grey, as often

happens when people have found this life either too gay or too
sad, more especially when they happen to be of a dark complexion.

D'Artagnan advanced a few steps into the apartment. How
perfectly he remembered his former entrance into that very room.
Seeing, however, no one there except a Musketeer of his own
troop, he fixed his eyes upon the supposed soldier, in whose dress,
nevertheless, he recognised, at the first glance, the Cardinal.

The lieutenant remained standing in a dignified but respectful
posture ; such as became a man of good birth, who had in the
course of his life been frequently in the society of the highest
nobles.

The Cardinal looked at him with a glance, cunning rather than
serious ; yet he examined his countenance with attention, and after
a momentary silence, said :

" You are Monsieur d'Artagnan ?"

" I am that individual," replied the officer.

Mazarin gazed once more at a countenance full of intelligence,
the play of which had been nevertheless subdued by age and experience ; and D'Artagnan received the penetrating glance like
one who had formerly sustained many a searching look, very different, indeed, from those which were inquiringly directed towards
him at that instant.

" Sir," resumed the Cardinal, " you are to come with me, or
rather I am to go with you."

" I am at your commands, my lord," returned D'Artagnan.

" I wish to visit in person the outposts which surround the
Palais Royal ; do you suppose that there is any danger in so
doing ?"

" Danger, my lord !" exclaimed D'Artagnan, with a look of astonishment ; " what danger ?"

" I am told that there is a general insurrection."

" The uniform of the King's Musketeers carries a certain respect
with it ; and even if that were not the case, I would engage, with
four of my men, to put to flight an hundred of these clowns."

" Did you witness the injuries sustained by Comminges ?"

" Monsieur de Comminges is in the Guards, and not in the
Musketeers——"

" Which means, I suppose, that the Musketeers are better soldiers than the Guards." The Cardinal smiled as he spoke.

" Every one likes his own uniform best, my lord."

" Myself excepted ;" and again Mazarin smiled ; " for you perceive that I have left off mine, and put on yours."

"Lord bless us! this is modesty, indeed," cried D'Artagnan. "Had I such a uniform as your Eminence possesses, I protest I should be mighty content; and I would take an oath never to wear any other costume——"

"Yes, but for to-night's adventure, I don't suppose my dress would have been a very safe one. Give me my felt hat, Bernouin."

The valet instantly brought to his master a regimental hat with a wide brim. The Cardinal put it on in a military style.

"Your horses are already saddled in their stables, are they not?" he said, turning to D'Artagnan.

"Yes, my lord."

"Well, let us set out."

"How many men does your Eminence wish to escort you?"

"You say that with four men you will undertake to disperse a hundred low fellows; as it may happen that we shall have to encounter two hundred, take eight——"

"As many as my lord wishes."

"I shall follow you. This way—light us down stairs, Bernouin."

The valet held a wax-light; the Cardinal took a key from his bureau, and, opening the door of a secret stair, descended into the court of the Palais Royal.

CHAPTER II.

A NIGHTLY PATROL.

In ten minutes Mazarin and his party were traversing the street "Les Bons Enfans," behind the theatre built by Richelieu expressly for the play of *Mirame*, and in which Mazarin, who was an amateur of music, but not of literature, had introduced into France the first opera that was ever acted in that country.

The appearance of the town denoted the greatest agitation. Numberless groups paraded the streets; and, whatever D'Artagnan might think of it, it was obvious that the citizens had, for the night, laid aside their usual forbearance, in order to assume a warlike aspect. From time to time noises came in the direction of the public markets. The report of fire-arms was heard near the Rue St. Denis, and occasionally church bells began to ring indiscriminately, and at the caprice of the populace. D'Artagnan, meantime, pursued his way with the indifference of a man upon whom such acts of folly made no impression. The Cardinal envied his composure, which he ascribed to the habit of encountering danger.　On approaching an outpost near the Barrière des Sergens, the sentinel cried out, "Who's there?" and D'Artagnan answered —having first asked the word of the Cardinal—"Louis and Rocroy."　After which he inquired if Lieut. Comminges were not the commanding officer at the outpost.　The soldier replied by pointing out to him an officer who was conversing, on foot, with his hand upon the neck of a horse on which the individual to whom he was talking sat.　Here was the officer whom D'Artagnan was seeking.

"Here is Monsieur Comminges," said D'Artagnan, returning to the Cardinal.　He instantly retired, from a respectful delicacy; it was, however, evident that the Cardinal was recognised by both Comminges and the other officer on horseback.

"Well done, Guitant," cried the Cardinal to the equestrian; "I see plainly, that notwithstanding the sixty-four years which have passed over your head, you are still the same man, active and zealous.　What were you saying to this youngster?"

"My lord," replied Guitant, "I was observing that we live in strange times, and that to-day's events are very like those in the days of the Ligue, of which I heard so much in my youth.　Are you aware that the mob have even suggested throwing up barricades in the Rue Saint Denis and the Rue Saint Antoine?"

"And what was Comminges saying to you in reply, dear Guitant?"

"My lord," said Comminges, "I answered that to compose a Ligue, only one ingredient was wanting—in my opinion an essential one—a Duc de Guise—moreover, no one ever does the same thing twice over."

"No, but they mean to make a Fronde, as they call it," said Guitant.

"And what is a Fronde?" inquired Mazarin.

"My lord, a Fronde is the name that the discontented give to their party."

"And what is the origin of this name?"

"It seems that some days since, Counsellor Backaumont remarked at the palace that rebels and agitators reminded him of schoolboys slinging stones from the moats round Paris—young urchins who run off the moment the constable appears, only to return to their diversion the instant that his back is turned.　So they have picked up the word, and the insurrectionists are called 'Frondeurs;' and yesterday every article sold was 'à la Fronde;' bread 'à la Fronde,' hats 'à la Fronde,' to say nothing of gloves, pocket-handkerchiefs, and fans—but listen——"

At that moment a window opened, a man began to sing—

> "A breeze from the Fronde
> Blew to-day :
> I think that it blows
> Against Mazarin."

"Insolent wretch !" cried Guitant.

"My lord," said Comminges, who, irritated by his wounds, wished for revenge, and longed to give back blow for blow, "shall I fire off a ball to punish that jester, and to warn him not to sing so much out of tune in future ?"

And, as he spoke, he put his hand on the holster of his uncle's saddle-bow.

"Certainly not—certainly not !" exclaimed Mazarin. "Diavolo ! my dear friend, you are going to spoil everything—everything is going on famously. I know the French as well as if I had made them myself from first to last. They sing—let them pay the piper. During the Ligue, about which Guitant was speaking just now, the people chaunted nothing except the Mass, so everything went to destruction. Come, Guitant, come along, and let's see if they keep watch at the Quinze-Vingts as at the Barrière des Sergens."

And, waving his hand to Comminges, he rejoined D'Artagnan, who instantly put himself at the head of his troop, followed by the Cardinal, Guitant, and the rest of the escort.

"Just so," muttered Comminges, looking after Mazarin. "True, I forgot—provided he can get money out of the people, that is all he wants."

The street of Saint Honoré, when the Cardinal and his party passed through it, was crowded by an assemblage, who, standing in groups, discussed the edicts of that memorable day—they pitied the young king, who was unconsciously ruining his country, and threw all the odium of his proceedings on Mazarin. Addresses to the Duke of Orleans and to Condé were suggested. Blancmesnil and Broussel seemed in high favour.

D'Artagnan passed through the very midst of this discontented multitude, just as if his horse and he had been made of iron. Mazarin and Guitant conversed together in whispers. The musketeers, who had already discovered who Mazarin was, followed in profound silence. In the street of Saint Thomas-du-Louvre, they stopped at that barrier which was distinguished by the name of Quinze-Vingts. Here Guitant spoke to one of the subalterns, and asked him how matters went on.

"Ah, captain !" said the officer, "everything is quiet hereabouts —if I did not know that something is going on in yonder house !"

And he pointed to a magnificent hotel, situated on the very spot whereon the Vaudeville now stands.

"In that hotel?—it is the Hotel Rambouillet," cried Guitant.

"I really don't know what hotel it is—all I do know is that I observed some suspicious-looking people go in there——"

"Nonsense!" exclaimed Guitant, with a burst of laughter, "those men must be poets."

"Come, Guitant, speak, if you please, respectfully of these gentlemen," said Mazarin; "don't you know that I was in my youth a poet? I wrote verses in the style of Beuserade——"

"You, my lord?"

"Yes, I—shall I repeat to you some of my verses?"

"Just as you please, my lord. I do not understand Italian."

"Yes, but you understand French;" and Mazarin laid his hand upon Guitant's shoulder. "My good, my brave Guitant, whatsoever command I may give you in that language—in French—whatever I may order you to do, will you not do it?"

"Certainly. I have already answered that question in the affirmative; but that command must come from the queen herself."

"Yes! ah, yes!" (Mazarin bit his lips as he spoke.) "I know your devotion to her majesty."

"I have been a captain in the Queen's Guards for twenty years," was the reply.

D'Artagnan, in the meantime, had taken the head of his detachment without a word, and with that ready and profound obedience which marks the character of an old soldier.

He led the way towards the hut of Saint Roche. The Rue Richelieu and the Rue Villedot were then, owing to their vicinity to the ramparts, less frequented than any others in that direction, for the town was thinly inhabited thereabouts. He therefore chose these streets to pass through in preference to those more crowded.

"Who is in command here?" asked the Cardinal.

"Villequier," said Guitant.

"Diavolo! Speak to him yourself, for ever since you were deputed by me to arrest the Duc de Beaufort, this officer and I have been on bad terms. He laid claim to that honour as captain of the Royal Guards."

Guitant accordingly rode forward, and desired the sentinel to call Monsieur de Villequier.

"Ah! so you are here!" cried the officer, in a tone of ill-humour habitual to him; "what the devil are you doing here?"

"I wish to know—can you tell me, pray—is there anything fresh happening in this part of the town?"

"What do you mean? People cry out, 'Long live the king! down with Mazarin'—that's nothing new—no, we've been used to those acclamations for some time."

"And you sing chorus," replied Guitant, laughing.

"Faith, I've half a mind to do it. In my opinion the people are right: and cheerfully would I give up five years of my pay—which I am never paid, by the way—to make the king five years older."

"Really! And pray what is to come to pass supposing the king were five years older than he is?"

"As soon as ever the king comes of age, he will issue his commands himself, and 'tis far pleasanter to obey the grandson of Henry IV. than the grandson of Peter Mazarin. S'death! I would die willingly for the king; but supposing I happened to be killed on account of Mazarin, as your nephew was near being to-day, there could be nothing in Paradise—so well off as I have been in this world—that could console me for being a martyr."

"Well, well, Monsieur de Villequier," here Mazarin interposed, "I shall take care that the king hears of your loyalty. Come, gentlemen," he addressed the troop, "let us return."

"Stop," exclaimed Villequier; "so, Mazarin is here! so much the better. I have been wanting for a long time to tell him what I think of him. I'm obliged to you, Guitant, for this opportunity."

He turned away, and went off to his post, whistling a tune, then popular among the party called the 'Fronde,' whilst Mazarin returned, in a pensive mood, towards the Palais Royal. All that he had heard from these three different men, Comminges, Guitant, and Villequier, confirmed him in his conviction that in case of serious tumults there would be no one on his side except the queen: and then, Anne of Austria had so often deserted her friends, that her support seemed very precarious. During the whole of this nocturnal ride, during the whole time that he was endeavouring to understand the various characters of Comminges, Guitant, and Villequier, Mazarin was, in truth, studying more especially one man. This man — who had remained immovable when menaced by the mob—not a muscle of whose face was altered either by Mazarin's witticisms, or by the jests of the multitude—seemed to the Cardinal a peculiar being, who, having participated in past events similar to those which were now occurring, was calculated to cope with those which were on the eve of taking place.

The name of D'Artagnan was not altogether new to Mazarin, who, although he had not arrived in France before the year 1634,

or 1635, that is to say, about eight or nine years after the events
which we have related in a preceding narrative,* fancied that he
had heard it pronounced, in reference to one who was said to be a
model of courage, address, and loyalty.

Possessed by this idea, the Cardinal resolved to know all about
D'Artagnan immediately; of course he could not inquire from
D'Artagnan himself who he was, and what had been his career;
he remarked, however, in the course of conversation, that the
Lieutenant of Musketeers spoke with a Gascon accent. Now the
Italians and the Gascons are too much alike, and know each other
too well, ever to trust to what any one of them may say of himself;
so, on reaching the walls which surrounded the Palais Royal, the
Cardinal knocked at a little door, and after thanking D'Artagnan,
and requesting him to wait in the court of the Palais Royal, he
made a sign to Guitant to follow him in.

"My dear friend," said the Cardinal, leaning, as they walked
through the gardens, on his friend's arm, "you told me just now
that you had been twenty years in the queen's service."

"Yes, 'tis true; I have," returned Guitant.

"Now, my dear Guitant, I have often remarked that in addition
to your courage—which is indisputable, and to your fidelity—
which is invincible, you possess an admirable memory."

"You have found that out, have you, my lord? Deuce take it—
all the worse for me!"

"How?"

"There's no doubt but that one of the chief qualities in a courtier
is to know when to forget."

"But you, Guitant, are not a courtier. You are a brave soldier,
one of the few remaining veterans of the days of Henry IV.—alas!
how few exist still!——"

"Plague on't, my lord—have you brought me here to get my
horoscope out of me?"

"No—I only brought you here to ask you," returned Mazarin,
smiling, "if you have taken any particular notice of our Lieutenant
of Musketeers?"

Monsieur D'Artagnan? I do not care to notice him particularly; he's an old acquaintance. He's a Gascon. De Treville
knows him, and esteems him greatly, and De Treville, as you
know, is one of the queen's greatest friends. As a soldier the man
ranks well: he did his duty, and even more than his duty, at the
siege of Rochelle—as well as at Suze and Perpignan."

---

* In the "Three Musketeers."

"But you know, Guitant; we poor ministers often want men with other qualities besides courage ; we want men of talent.   Pray was not Monsieur d'Artagnan, in the time of the Cardinal, mixed up in some intrigue from which he came out, according to report, rather cleverly ?"

"My lord, as to the report you allude to"—Guitant perceived that the Cardinal wished to make him speak out—" I know nothing but what the public knows.   I never meddle in intrigues ; and if I occasionally become a confidant in the intrigues of others, I am sure your Eminence will approve of my keeping them secret."

Mazarin shook his head.

"Ah !" he said ; "some ministers are very fortunate, and find out all that they wish to know."

"My lord," replied Guitant, "such ministers do not weigh men in the same balance ; they get their information on war from the warriors ; on intrigues, from the politician.   Consult some politician of the period of which you speak, and if you pay well for it, you will certainly get to know all you want."

Mazarin, with a grimace which he always made when spoken to about money—" People must be paid—one can't do otherwise," he said.

"Does my lord seriously wish me to name any one who has been mixed up in the cabals of that day ?"

"By Bacchus !" rejoined Mazarin, impatiently, "it's about an hour ago since I asked you a question about D'Artagnan, wooden-headed as you are."

"There is one man for whom I can answer, if he will speak out."

"That's my concern ; I must make him speak."

"Ah ! my lord, 'tis not easy to make people say what they don't wish to let out."

"Pooh ! patience (we're coming to it at last).   Well, this man. Who is he ?"

"The Comte de Rochefort."

"The Comte de Rochefort !"

"Unfortunately he has disappeared these four or five years, and I don't know where he is."

"*I* know, Guitant," said Mazarin.

"Well, then, how is it that your Eminence complained just now of want of information on some points ?"

"You think," resumed Mazarin, "that Rochefort——"

"He was Cardinal Richelieu's creature, my lord.   I warn you, however, his services will be expensive.   The Cardinal was lavish to his underlings."

"Yes, yes, Guitant," said Mazarin; Richelieu was a great man, a very great man, but he had that defect. Thanks, Guitant; I shall benefit by your advice this very evening."

Here they separated, and bidding adieu to Guitant in the court of the Palais Royal, Mazarin approached an officer who was walking up and down within that enclosure.

It was D'Artagnan, who was waiting for him.

"Come hither," said Mazarin, in his softest voice, "I have an order to give you."

D'Artagnan bent low, and following the Cardinal up the secret staircase, soon found himself in the study whence he had first set out.

The Cardinal seated himself before his bureau, and taking a sheet of paper, wrote some lines upon it, whilst D'Artagnan remained standing, imperturbable, and without showing either impatience or curiosity. He was like a military automaton acting (or, rather, obeying the will of others) upon springs.

The Cardinal folded and sealed his letter.

"Monsieur d'Artagnan," he said, "you are to take this despatch to the Bastille, and to bring back here the person whom it concerns. You must take a carriage and an escort, and guard the prisoner carefully."

D'Artagnan took the letter, touched his hat with his hand, turned round upon his heel, like a drill-serjeant, and, a moment afterwards, was heard in his dry and monotonous tone, commanding, "Four men and an escort, a carriage and a horse." Five minutes afterwards the wheels of the carriage and the horses' shoes were heard resounding on the pavement of the court-yard.

CHAPTER III.

OLD ANIMOSITIES.

D'ARTAGNAN arrived at the Bastille just as it was striking half-past eight. His visit was announced to the governor, who, on hearing that he came from the Cardinal, went to meet him, and received him at the top of the great flight of steps outside the door. The governor of the Bastille was Monsieur du Tremblay, the brother of the famous Capuchin, Joseph, that fearful favourite of Richelieu's, who went by the name of the Gray Cardinal.

During the period that the Duc de Bassompierre passed in the

Bastille—where he remained for twelve whole years—when his companions, in their dreams of liberty, said to each other, "As for me, I shall go out of prison at such a time," and another, at such and such a time, the duke used to answer, "As for me, gentlemen, I shall leave only when Monsieur du Tremblay leaves;" meaning that at the death of the Cardinal, Du Tremblay would certainly lose his place at the Bastille, and then De Bassompierre would regain his at court.

His prediction was nearly being fulfilled, but in a very different way to that which De Bassompierre supposed; for, after the death of Richelieu, everything went on, contrary to expectation, in the same way as before; and Bassompierre had little chance of leaving his prison.

Monsieur du Tremblay received D'Artagnan with extreme politeness, and invited him to sit down with him to supper, of which he was himself about to partake.

"I should be delighted to do so," was the reply; "but if I am not much mistaken, the words, 'In haste,' are written on the envelope of the letter which I brought."

"You are right," said Du Tremblay. "Holloa, major, tell them to order number 256 to come down stairs."

The unhappy wretch who entered into the Bastille ceased, as he crossed the threshold, to be a man, and became a number.

D'Artagnan shuddered at the noise of the keys; he therefore remained on horseback, having no inclination to dismount, and sat looking at the bars, at the thick strong windows, and the immense walls which he had hitherto only seen from the other side of the moat, and by which he had, for twenty years, been awe-struck.

A bell sounded.

"I must leave you," said Du Tremblay; "I am sent for to sign the release of the prisoner. I shall be happy to meet you again, sir."

"May the devil annihilate me if I return thy wish!" murmured D'Artagnan, smiling as he pronounced the imprecation; "I declare I feel quite ill, after only being five minutes in the court-yard. Go to—go to! I should rather die upon straw, than hoard up five hundred a-year by being governor of the Bastille."

He had scarcely finished this soliloquy before the prisoner arrived. On seeing him D'Artagnan could hardly suppress an exclamation of surprise. The prisoner did not seem, however, to recognise the Musketeer.

"Gentlemen," thus D'Artagnan addressed the four Musketeers,

"I am ordered to exercise the greatest possible care in guarding the prisoner; and, since there are no locks to the carriage, I shall sit beside him. Monsieur de Lillebonne, lead my horse by the bridle, if you please." As he spoke, he dismounted, gave the bridle of his horse to the Musketeer, and placing himself by the side of the prisoner, said, in a voice perfectly composed, 'To the Palais Royal, at a full trot.'"

The carriage drove on, and D'Artagnan, availing himself of the darkness in the archway under which they were passing, threw himself into the arms of the prisoner.

"Rochefort!" he exclaimed; "you—is it you; you, indeed? I am not mistaken?"

"D'Artagnan!" cried Rochefort.

"Ah! my poor friend!" resumed D'Artagnan, "not having seen you for four or five years, I concluded that you were dead."

"I'faith," said Rochefort, "there's no great difference, I think, between a dead man and one who has been buried alive; now I have been buried alive, or very nearly so."

"And for what crime are you imprisoned in the Bastille?"

"Do you wish me to speak the truth to you?"

"Yes."

"Well, then, I don't know."

"Have you any suspicion of me, Rochefort?"

"No! on the honour of a gentleman; but I cannot be imprisoned for the reason alleged—it is impossible."

"What reason?" asked D'Artagnan.

"For stealing."

"For stealing! you—Rochefort—you are laughing at me. It is impossible that it could have been that, my dear Rochefort, which was alleged against you; it is a mere pretext; but you will, perhaps, soon know on what account you have been in prison."

"Ah, indeed! I forgot to ask you—where are you taking me?"

"To the Cardinal."

"What does he want with me?"

"I do not know. I did not even know that you were the person whom I was sent to fetch."

"Impossible! You—a favourite of the minister!"

"A favourite! no, indeed!" cried D'Artagnan. "Ah, my poor friend! I am just as poor a Gascon as when I saw you at Meung, twenty-two years ago, you know; alas!" and he concluded his speech with a deep sigh.

"Nevertheless, you come as one in authority."

"Because I happened to be in the antechamber when the Cardinal called me, just by chance. I am still a lieutenant in the Musketeers, and have been so these twenty years."

"Then no misfortune has happened to you?"

"And what misfortune could happen to me? To quote some Latin verses which I have forgotten, or rather, never known well, 'the thunderbolt never falls on the valleys;' and I am a valley, dear Rochefort, and one of the lowest that can be."

"Then Mazarin is still Mazarin?"

"The same as ever, my friend; it is said that he is married to the queen."

"Married?"

"If not her husband, he is unquestionably her lover."

"You surprise me; to resist Buckingham, and yield to Mazarin."

"Just like the women," replied D'Artagnan, coolly.

"Like women—but not like queens."

"Egad! queens are the weakest of their sex, when we come to such matters as these."

The count then made several minute inquiries after his friends. The Duc de Beaufort, was he still in prison? To this D'Artagnan answered in the affirmative.

"And," said the prisoner, "what talk is there of war with Spain?"

"With Spain—no," answered D'Artagnan; "but with Paris."

"What do you mean?" cried Rochefort.

"Do you hear the guns, pray? The citizens are amusing themselves in the meantime."

"And you—do you really think that anything could be done with these *bourgeois?*"

"Yes, they might do well, if they had any leader to unite them in one body."

"How miserable not to be free!"

"Don't be downcast. Since Mazarin has sent for you, it is because he wants you. I congratulate you! Many a long year has passed since any one has wanted to employ me; so you see in what a situation I am."

"Make your complaints known; that's my advice."

"Listen, Rochefort; let's make a compact. We are friends, are we not?"

"Egad! I bear the traces of our friendship—three cuts from your sword."

"Well, if you should be restored to favour, don't forget me."

"On the honour of a Rochefort; but you must do the like for me."

" There's my hand—I promise."

" Therefore, whenever you find any opportunity of saying something in my behalf——"

" I shall say it ; and you ?"

" I shall do the same."

" Apropos, are we to speak about your friends as well—Athos,
Porthos, and Aramis ? or have you forgotten them ?"

" Almost !"

" What's become of them ?"

" I don't know; we separated, as you know.   They are alive,
and that's all I can say about them.   From time to time I hear of
them indirectly, but in what part of the world they are, devil take
me if I know.   No, on my honour, I have not a friend in the
world but you. Rochefort."

" And the illustrious—what's the name of the lad whom I made
a sergeant in Piedmont's regiment ?"

" Planchet ?"

" The illustrious Planchet.   What's become of him ?"

" I shouldn't wonder if he is not at the head of the mob at this
very moment.   He married a woman who keeps a confectioner's
shop in the Rue des Lombards ; for he's a lad that was always
fond of sweetmeats ; he's now a citizen of Paris.   You'll see that
that queer fellow will be a sheriff before I shall be a captain."

" Come, dear D'Artagnan, look up a little—courage.   It is when
one is lowest on the wheel of fortune, that the wheel turns round
and raises us.   This evening your destiny begins to change."

" Amen !" exclaimed D'Artagnan, stopping the carriage.

He got out, and remounted his steed, not wishing to arrive at
the gate of the Palais Royal in the same carriage with the
prisoner.

In a few minutes the party entered the court-yard, and D'Artagnan led the prisoner up the great staircase, and across the
corridor and ante-chamber.

As they stopped at the door of the Cardinal's study, D'Artagnan
was about to be announced, when Rochefort slapped him on his
shoulder.

" D'Artagnan, let me confess to you what I've been thinking
about during the whole of my drive, as I looked out upon the
parties of citizens who perpetually crossed our path, and looked at
you and your four men, with their flambeaux."

" Speak out," answered D'Artagnan.

" I had only to cry out ' Help !' for you and your companions
to be cut to pieces, and then I should have been free."

"Why didn't you do it?" asked the lieutenant.

"Come, then!" cried Rochefort. "We swore friendship! Ah! Had any one but you been there—I don't say——"

D'Artagnan bowed.

But the impatient voice of Mazarin summoned Rochefort to the room where the minister awaited him. "Tell Monsieur D'Artagnan to wait outside—I don't require him yet," said the Cardinal.

Rochefort, rendered suspicious and cautious by these words, entered the apartment, where he found Mazarin sitting at the table, dressed in his ordinary garb, and as one of the prelates of the Church, his costume being similar to that of the abbés in that day, excepting that his scarf and stockings were violet.

As the door was closed, Rochefort cast a glance towards Mazarin, which was answered by one, equally furtive, from the minister.

There was little change in the Cardinal; still dressed with sedulous care, his hair well arranged and well curled, his person perfumed—he looked, owing to his extreme taste in dress, only half his age. But Rochefort, who had passed five years in prison, had become old in the lapse of years; the dark locks of this estimable friend of the defunct Cardinal de Richelieu were now white; the deep bronze of his complexion had been succeeded by a mortal paleness, which betokened debility. As he gazed at him, Mazarin shook his head slightly, as much as to say, "This is a man who does not appear to me fit for much."

After a pause, which appeared an age to Rochefort, Mazarin, however, took from a bundle of papers a letter, and showing it to the count, he said:

"I find here a letter in which you sue for liberty, Monsieur de Rochefort. You are in prison, then?"

Rochefort trembled in every limb at this question. "But I thought," he said, "that your Eminence knew that circumstance better than any one——"

"I? Oh no! There's a mass of prisoners in the Bastille who were sent there in the time of Monsieur de Richelieu—I don't even know their names."

"Yes, but in regard to myself, my lord, it cannot be so, for I was removed from the Chatelet to the Bastille owing to an order from your Eminence."

"You think you were."

"I am certain of it."

"Ah, yes! I think I remember it. Did you not once refuse to undertake a journey to Brussels for the queen?"

"Ah! ah!" exclaimed Rochefort. "There is the true reason! Idiot as I am, though I have been trying to find it out for five years, I never found it out."

"But I do not say that it was the cause of your imprisonment. I merely ask you, did you not refuse to go to Brussels for the queen, whilst you had consented to go there to do some service for the late Cardinal?"

"That is the very reason that I refused to go back again to Brussels. I was there at a fearful moment. I was sent there to intercept a correspondence between Chalais and the archduke, and even then, when I was discovered, I was nearly torn to pieces. How could I then return to Brussels?"

"Well, then, since the best motives are liable to misconstruction, the queen saw in your refusal nothing but a refusal—a distinct refusal; she had also much to complain of you during the lifetime of the Cardinal—yes,—her majesty the queen——"

Rochefort smiled contemptuously.

"Since I was a faithful servant, my lord, to Cardinal Richelieu during his life, it stands to reason that now, after his death, I should serve you well, in defiance of the whole world."

"With regard to myself, Monsieur de Rochefort," replied Mazarin, "I am not like Monsieur de Richelieu, all-powerful. I am but a minister, who wants no servants, being myself nothing but a servant of the queen's. Now, the queen is of a sensitive nature; hearing of your refusal to obey her, she looked upon it as a declaration of war; and as she considers you as a man of superior talent, and therefore dangerous, she desired me to make sure of you—that is the reason of your being shut up in the Bastille—but your release can be managed. You are one of those men who can comprehend certain matters : and have understood them, and can act with energy——"

"Such was Cardinal Richelieu's opinion, my lord."

"The Cardinal," interrupted Mazarin, "was a great politician, and there was his vast superiority over me. I am a straightforward, simple man; that's my great disadvantage. I am of a frankness of character quite French."

Rochefort bit his lips in order not to smile.

"Now to the point. I want friends. I want faithful servants. When I say I want, I mean the queen wants them. I do nothing without her commands; pray, understand that—not like Monsieur de Richelieu, who went on just as he pleased—so I shall never be a great man, as he was; but, to compensate for that, I shall be a good man, Monsieur de Rochefort, and I hope to prove it to you."

Rochefort knew well the tones of that soft voice, in which there was sometimes a sort of gentle lisp, like the hissing of a viper.

"I am disposed to believe your Eminence," he replied; "but have the kindness not to forget that I have been five years in the Bastille, and that no way of viewing things is so false as through the grating of a prison."

"Ah, Monsieur de Rochefort! have I not told you already that I had nothing to do with that. The queen—cannot you make allowances for the pettishness of a queen and a princess? But that has passed away as suddenly as it came, and is forgotten."

"I can easily suppose, sir, that her majesty has forgotten it amid the fêtes and the courtiers of the Palais Royal, but I, who have passed those years in the Bastille——"

"Ah! *mon Dieu!* my dear Monsieur de Rochefort! do you absolutely think that the Palais Royal is the abode of gaiety? No. We have had great annoyances there. As for me, I play my game fair and above board, as I always do. Let us come to some conclusion. Are you one of us, Monsieur de Rochefort?"

"I am very desirous of being so, my lord; but I am totally in the dark about everything. In the Bastille one talks politics only with soldiers and gaolers, and you have not an idea, my lord, how little those sort of people really know of the state of affairs; I am of Monsieur de Bassompierre's party. Is he still one of the seventeen peers of France?"

"He is dead, sir;—'tis a great loss. His devotion to the queen was great; and men of loyalty are scarce."

"I think so, forsooth," said Rochefort; "and when you find any of them you send them off to the Bastille. However, there are plenty of them in the world, but you don t look in the right direction for them, my lord."

"Indeed! explain to me. Ah! my dear Monsieur de Rochefort, how much you must have learned during your intimacy with the late Cardinal! Ah! he was a great man!"

"Will your Eminence be angry if I read you a lesson?"

"I! never! you know you may say anything to me. I try to be beloved, and not to be feared."

"Well, I myself, on the wall of my cell, scratched with a nail, a proverb, which says, 'Like master, like servant.'"

"Pray, what does that mean?"

"It means that Monsieur de Richelieu was able to find trusty servants—dozens and dozens of them."

"He! the point aimed at by every poignard! Richelieu, who passed his life in warding off blows which were for ever aimed at him!"

"But he *did* ward them off," said De Rochefort, "and the reason was, that though he had bitter enemies he possessed also true friends.   I have known persons," he continued,—for he thought he might avail himself of the opportunity of speaking of D'Artagnan—"who, by their sagacity and address, have deceived the penetration of Cardinal Richelieu ; who, by their valour, have got the better of his guards and his spies ; persons without money, without support, without credit, yet who have preserved to the crowned head its crown, and made the Cardinal ask for pardon."

"Ah," cried Mazarin, with his wonted grace, "could I but find such men !"

"My lord, there has stood for six years at your very door a man such as I describe, and during those six years he has been unappreciated and unemployed by you."

"Who is it ?"

"It is Monsieur d'Artagnan, a Gascon, who has done all this, saved his queen, and made Monsieur de Richelieu confess, that in point of talent, address, and political skill, he was to him only a tyro."

"Tell me how it all happened."

"No, my lord, the secret is not mine ; it is a secret which concerns the queen.   In what he did, this man had three colleagues, three brave men, such men as you were wishing for just now."

"And were these four men attached to each other, true in heart, really united ?"

"As if they had been one man, as if their four hearts had pulsated in one breast."

"You pique my curiosity, dear Rochefort ; pray tell me the whole story."

"That is impossible ; but I will tell you a true story, my lord."

"Pray do so—I delight in stories," cried the Cardinal.

"Listen then," returned Rochefort, as he spoke endeavouring to read, in that subtle countenance, the Cardinal's motive.   "Once upon a time there lived a queen—a powerful monarch—who reigned over one of the greatest kingdoms of the universe ; and a minister ; and this minister wished much to injure the queen, whom once he had loved too well.   (Do not try, my lord, you cannot guess who it is ; all this happened long before you came into the country where this queen reigned.)   There came to the court an ambassador so brave, so magnificent, so elegant, that every woman lost her heart to him ; and the queen had even the indiscretion to give him certain ornaments so rare, that they could never be replaced by any like them.

"As these ornaments belonged to the king, the minister persuaded his majesty to insist upon the queen's appearing in them as part of her jewels, at a ball which was soon to take place. There is no occasion to tell you, my lord, that the minister knew for a fact that these ornaments had been sent after the ambassador, who was far away, beyond seas. This illustrious queen had fallen low as the least of her subjects—fallen from her high estate."

"Indeed !"

"Well, my lord, four men resolved to save her. These four men were not princes, neither were they dukes, neither were they men in power, they were not even rich men. They were four honest soldiers, each with a good heart, a good arm, and a sword at the service of those who wanted it. They set out. The minister knew of their departure, and had planted people on the road to prevent them ever reaching their destination. Three of them were overwhelmed and disabled by numerous assailants, one of them alone arrived at the port, having either killed or wounded those who wished to stop him. He crossed the sea, and brought back the set of ornaments to the great queen, who was able to wear them on her shoulder on the appointed day, and this very nearly ruined the minister. What think you of that trait, my lord ?"

"It is splendid," said Mazarin.

"Well, I know ten such men."

"And was Monsieur d'Artagnan one of these four men ?" inquired the Cardinal.

"It was he who conducted the enterprise."

"And who were the others ?"

"I leave it to Monsieur d'Artagnan to name them, my lord."

"You suspect me, Monsieur de Rochefort; I want him, and you, and all to aid me."

"Begin by telling me why, my lord; for after five or six years of imprisonment, it is natural to feel some curiosity as to one's destination."

"You, my dear Monsieur de Rochefort, shall have the post of confidence; you shall go to Vincennes, where Monsieur de Beaufort is confined; you will guard him well for me."

"My lord," replied Rochefort, "to go out of the Bastille in order to go into Vincennes is only to change one's prison."

"Say at once that you are on the side of Monsieur de Beaufort —that will be the most sincere line of conduct," said Mazarin.

"My lord, I have been so long shut up, that I am only of one party—I am for fresh air. Employ me in any other way; employ me even actively—but let it be on the high roads."

"My dear Monsieur de Rochefort," Mazarin replied in a tone of raillery, "you think yourself still a young man—your spirit is still juvenile, but your strength fails you. Believe me, you ought now to take rest. Here!"

"You decide, then, nothing about me, my lord?"

"On the contrary, I have come to a decision about you."

Bernouin came into the room.

"Call an officer of justice," he said; "and stay close to me," he added in a low tone.

The officer entered—Mazarin wrote a few words, which he gave to this man—then he bowed.

"Adieu, Monsieur de Rochefort," he said.

Rochefort bent low.

"I see, my lord, that I am to be taken back to the Bastille."

"You are sagacious."

"I shall return thither, my lord, but you are wrong not to employ me."

"You? the friend of my greatest foes? don't suppose that you are the only person who can serve me, Monsieur de Rochefort. I shall find many as able men as you are."

"I wish you may, my lord," replied De Rochefort.

He was then reconducted by the little staircase, instead of passing through the antechamber where D'Artagnan was waiting. In the court-yard the carriage and the four Musketeers were ready, but he looked around in vain for his friend.

"Ah!" he muttered to himself, "things are changed indeed;" yet he jumped into the carriage with the alacrity of a man of five-and-twenty.

CHAPTER IV.

ANNE OF AUSTRIA AT THE AGE OF FORTY-SIX.

WHEN left alone with Bernouin, Mazarin was, for some minutes, lost in thought. He had gained much information, but not enough.

"My lord, have you any commands?" asked Bernouin.

"Yes, yes," replied Mazarin. "Light me; I am going to the queen."

Bernouin took up a candlestick, and led the way.

There was a secret communication between the Cardinal's apartments and those of the queen; and through this corridor* Mazarin passed whenever he wished to visit Anne of Austria.

* This secret passage is still to be seen in the Palais Royal.

In the bedroom in which this passage ended Bernouin encountered Madame de Beauvais, like himself entrusted with the secret of these subterranean love affairs; and Madame de Beauvais undertook to prepare Anne of Austria, who was in her oratory with the young king, Louis XIV., to receive the Cardinal.

Anne, reclining in a large easy chair, her head supported by her hand, her elbow resting on a table near her, was looking at her son, who was turning over the leaves of a book filled with pictures of battles. This celebrated woman fully understood the art of being dull with dignity. It was her practice to pass hours either in her oratory, or in her room, without either reading or praying.

When Madame de Beauvais appeared at the door, and announced the Cardinal, the child, who had been engrossed in the pages of Quintus Curtius, enlivened as they were by engravings of Alexander's feats of arms, frowned, and looked at his mother,—

"Why," he said, "does he enter without asking first for an audience?"

Anne coloured slightly.

"The prime minister," she said, "is obliged, in these unsettled times, to inform the queen of all that is happening from time to time, without exciting the curiosity or remarks of the court."

"But Richelieu never came in, in this manner," said the pertinacious boy.

"How can you remember what Monsieur de Richelieu did? You were too young to know that."

"I do not remember what he did; but I have inquired, and I have been told all about it."

At this very moment Mazarin entered. The king rose immediately, took his book, closed it, and went to lay it down on the table, near which he continued standing, in order that Mazarin might be obliged to stand also.

Mazarin contemplated these proceedings with a thoughtful glance. They explained what had occurred that evening.

He bowed respectfully to the king, who gave him a somewhat cavalier reception, but a look from his mother reproved him for the hatred which, from his infancy, Louis XIV. had entertained towards Mazarin, and he endeavoured to receive with a smile the minister's homage.

"It is time that the king should retire to rest," said the queen, speaking to Madame de Beauvais—for Anne was surprised at this early visit from Mazarin, who scarcely ever came into her apartments until every one had withdrawn for the night.

The queen had several times already told her son that he ought to go to bed; and, several times, Louis had coaxingly insisted on staying where he was; but now he made no reply, but turned pale, and bit his lips with anger.

In a few minutes Laporte came into the room. The child went directly to him without kissing his mother.

"Well, Louis," said Anne, "why do you not kiss me?"

"I thought you were angry with me, madam; you sent me away."

"I do not send you away; but you have had the small-pox, and I am afraid that sitting up late may tire you."

"You had no fears of my being tired when you ordered me to go to the palace to-day to pass the odious decrees, which have raised up murmurs among the people."

"Sire!" interposed Laporte, in order to turn the subject—"to whom does your majesty wish me to give the candle?"

"To any one, Laporte," the child said; and then added, in a loud voice, "to any one but Mancini."

Now Mancini was a nephew of Mazarin's, and was as much hated by Louis as the Cardinal himself, although placed near his person by the minister.

And the king went out of the room, without either embracing his mother, or even bowing to the Cardinal.

"Good," said Mazarin. "I am glad to see that his majesty is brought up with a hatred of dissimulation."

The queen, however, asked, with some impatience, what important business had brought the Cardinal there that evening.

Mazarin sank into a chair, with the deepest melancholy painted on his countenance.

"It is likely," he replied, "that we shall soon be obliged to separate, unless you love me well enough to follow me into Italy."

"Why," cried the queen; "how is that?"

"Because, as they say in the opera of Thisbe—'The whole world conspires to break our bonds.'"

"You jest, sir!" answered the queen, endeavouring to assume something of her former dignity.

"Alas! I do not, madam," rejoined Mazarin. "Mark well what I say. The whole world conspires to break our bonds. Now as you are one of the whole world, I mean to say that you also desert me."

"Cardinal!"

"Heavens! did I not see you the other day smile on the Duke of Orleans? or rather at what he said?"

"And what was he saying?"

"He said this, madam. 'Mazarin is a stumbling-block. Send him away, and all will be well.'"

"What do you wish me to do?"

"Oh, madam—you are the queen!"

"Queen, forsooth! when I am at the mercy of every scribbler in the Palais Royal, who covers waste paper with nonsense, or of every country squire in the kingdom."

"Nevertheless, you have still the power of banishing from your presence those whom you do not like!"

"That is to say, whom *you* do not like," returned the queen.

"I!—persons whom *I* do not like!"

"Yes, indeed. Who sent away Madame de Chevreuse?"

"A woman of intrigue; who wanted to keep up against me the spirit of cabal which she had raised against M. de Richelieu."

"Then who dismissed Madame de Hautefort?"

"A prude, who told you every night as she undressed you, that it was a sin to love a priest; just as if one were a priest, because one happens to be a cardinal."

"Who ordered Monsieur de Beaufort to be arrested?"

"An incendiary; the burden of whose song was his intention to assassinate me. My enemies, madam, ought to be yours, and your friends my friends."

"My friends, sir!" The queen shook her head. "Alas! I have none. In vain do I look about me for friends. I have no influence over any one. Monsieur* is led by his favourite to-day, Choisy; to-morrow it will be La Rivière, or some one else. The prince is led by Madame de Longueville, who is, in her turn, led by the Prince de Marsillac, her lover. Monsieur de Conti is under the influence of the deputy, who is the slave of Madame de Guemenée."

"Do you know Monsieur de Rochefort?" said Mazarin.

"One of my bitterest enemies—the faithful friend of Cardinal Richelieu."

"I know that, and we sent him to the Bastille," said Mazarin.

"Is he at liberty?" asked the queen.

"No; still there—but I only speak of him in order that I may introduce the name of another man. Do you know Monsieur d'Artagnan?" he added, looking steadfastly at the queen.

Anne of Austria received the blow with a beating heart.

"Has the Gascon been indiscreet?" she murmured; then said aloud:

* The Duke of Orleans.

"D'Artagnan! stop an instant; that name is certainly familiar to me. D'Artagnan! there was a Musketeer who was in love with one of my women, poor young creature! she was poisoned on my account."

"That's all you know of him?" asked Mazarin.

The queen looked at him, surprised.

"You seem, sir," she remarked, "to be making me undergo a course of interrogations."

"Which you answer according to your own fancy," replied Mazarin.

"Tell me your wishes, and I will comply with them."

The queen spoke with some impatience.

"Well then, madam, not a day passes in which I do not suffer affronts from your princes and your lordly servants; every one of them automata who do not perceive that I hold the spring which makes them move, nor do they see that beneath my quiet demeanour there is the scoff of an injured and irritated man, who has sworn to himself to master them one of these days. We have arrested Monsieur de Beaufort, but he is the least dangerous among them. There is the Prince de Condé——"

"The hero of Rocroy! do you think of *him*?"

"Yes, madam, often and often; but *pazienza*, as we say in Italy. Next, after Monsieur de Condé, comes the Duke of Orleans."

"What are you saying? The first prince of the blood—the king's uncle!"

"No! not the first prince of the blood, not the king's uncle, but the base conspirator, the soul of every cabal, who pretends to lead the brave people who are weak enough to believe in the honour of a prince of the blood—not the prince nearest to the throne, not the king's uncle, I repeat, but the murderer of Chalais, of Montmorency, and of Cinq-Mars, who is playing now the same game that he played long ago, and who fancies he shall gain an advantage, instead of having an opponent who frowns, he has one before him, face to face, who smiles. But he is mistaken. I shall not leave so near the queen that source of discord with which the deceased cardinal so often caused the anger of the king to boil over."

Anne blushed, and buried her head in her hands.

"What am I to do?" she said, bowed down beneath the voice of her tyrant.

"Endeavour to remember the names of those faithful servants who crossed the Channel, in spite of Monsieur de Richelieu— tracking the roads along which they passed by their blood—to bring back to your majesty certain jewels given by her to Bucking-ham."

Anne arose, full of majesty, and, as if touched by a spring, started up, and looking at the Cardinal with the haughty dignity which, in the days of her youth, had made her so powerful, "You insult me, sir," she said.

"I wish" continued Mazarin, finishing, as it were, the speech which this sudden movement of the queen had cut short; "I wish, in fact, that you should now do for your husband what you for-merly did for your lover."

"Again, that accusation?" cried the queen; "I thought that calumny was stifled or extinct. You have spared me till now; but since you speak of it, once for all I tell you——"

"Madam, what I wish is, to know all," said Mazarin, astounded by this returning courage.

"I will tell you all," replied Anne. "Listen: there were, in truth, at that epoch, four devoted hearts, four loyal spirits, four faithful swords who saved more than my life—my honour——"

"Ah! you confess it," exclaimed Mazarin.

"Is it only the guilty whose honour is at the sport of others, sir; and cannot women be dishonoured by appearances? However, I swear I was not guilty; I swear it by——"

The queen looked around her for some sacred object by which she could swear; and taking out of a cupboard, hidden in the tapestry, a small coffer of rosewood, set in silver, and laying it on the altar—

"I swear," she said, "by these sacred relics that Buckingham was not my lover."

"What relics are those by which you swear?" asked Mazarin, smiling. "I am incredulous."

The queen untied from around her throat a small golden key which hung there, and presented it to the Cardinal.

"Open," she said, "sir, and look for yourself."

Mazarin opened the coffer; a knife, covered with rust, and two letters, one of which was stained with blood, alone met his gaze.

"What are these things?" he asked.

"What are these things?" replied Anne, with queen-like dignity, and extending towards the open coffer an arm, despite the lapse of years, still beautiful. "These two letters are the only letters that I ever wrote to him. That knife is the knife with which Felton stabbed him. Read the letters, and see if I have lied, or spoken the truth."

But Mazarin, notwithstanding this permission, instead of reading the letters, took the knife which the dying Buckingham had snatched out of the wound, and sent by Laporte to the queen. The blade was red, for the blood had become rust; after a momentary examination, during which the queen became as white as the cloth which covered the altar on which she was leaning, he put it back into the coffer with an involuntary shudder.

"It is well, madam; I believe your oath."

"No, no, read," exclaimed the queen indignantly; "read, I command you, for I am resolved that everything shall be finished to-night, and never will I recur to this subject again. Do you think," she said, with a ghastly smile, "that I shall be inclined to re-open this coffer to answer any future accusations?"

Mazarin, overcome by this determination, read the two letters. In one the queen asked for the ornaments back again. This letter had been conveyed by D'Artagnan, and had arrived in time. The other was that which Laporte had placed in the hands of the Duke of Buckingham, warning him that he was about to be assassinated; this had arrived too late.

"It is well, madam," said Mazarin; "nothing can be said to this testimony."

"Sir," replied the queen, closing the coffer, and leaning her hand upon it, "if there is anything to be said, it is that I have always been ungrateful to the brave men who saved me—that I have given nothing to that gallant officer, D'Artagnan, you were speaking of just now, but my hand to kiss, and this diamond."

As she spoke she extended her beautiful hand to the Cardinal, and showed him a superb diamond which sparkled on her finger.

"It appears," she resumed, "that he sold it—he sold it in order to save me another time—to be able to send a messenger to the duke to warn him of his danger—— He sold it to Monsieur des Essarts, on whose finger I remarked it. I bought it from him, but it belongs to D'Artagnan. Give it back to him, sir; and since you have such a man in your service, make him useful.

"And now," added the queen, her voice broken by her emotion, "have you any other question to ask me?"

"Nothing"—the Cardinal spoke in the most conciliatory manner —"except to beg of you to forgive my unworthy suspicions. I love you so tenderly that I cannot help being jealous—even of the past."

A smile, which was indefinable, passed over the lips of the queen.

"Since you have no further interrogations to make, leave me, I beseech you," she said. "I wish, after such a scene, to be alone."

Mazarin bent low before her.

"I shall retire, madam; do you permit me to return?"

"Yes, to-morrow."

The Cardinal took the queen's hand, and pressed it, with an air of gallantry, to his lips.

Scarcely had he left her than the queen went into her son's room, and inquired from Laporte if the king was in bed. Laporte pointed to the child, who was asleep.

Anne ascended the steps aside of the bed, and kissed softly the placid forehead of her son; then she retired as silently as she came, merely saying to Laporte:

"Try, my dear Laporte, to make the king more courteous to Monsieur le Cardinal, to whom both he and I are under such great obligations."

CHAPTER V.

THE GASCON AND THE ITALIAN.

MEANWHILE the Cardinal returned to his own room; and after asking Bernouin, who stood at the door, whether anything had occurred during his absence, and being answered in the negative, he desired that he might be left alone.

When he was alone, he opened the door of the corridor, and then that of the ante-chamber. There D'Artagnan was asleep upon a bench.

The Cardinal went up to him, and touched his shoulder. D'Artagnan started, awakened himself, and, as he awoke, stood up exactly like a soldier under arms.

"Monsieur D'Artagnan," said the Cardinal, sitting down on a *fauteuil*, "you have always seemed to me to be a brave and an honourable man."

"Possibly," thought D'Artagnan; "but he has taken a long time to let me know his thoughts;" nevertheless he bent down to the very ground in gratitude for Mazarin's compliment.

"Monsieur d'Artagnan," continued Mazarin, "you have performed sundry exploits in the last reign."

"Your Eminence is too good to remember that. It is true I fought with tolerable success."

"I don't speak of your warlike exploits, Monsieur," said Mazarin; "although they gained you much reputation, they were surpassed by others."

D'Artagnan pretended astonishment.

"Well, you do not reply?" resumed Mazarin.

"I am waiting, my lord, till you tell me of what exploits you speak."

"I speak of certain adventures. I speak of the adventure referring to the queen—of the ornaments, of the journey you made with three of your friends."

"Ha, ho-o!" thought the Gascon; "is this a snare, or not? Let me be on my guard."

And he assumed a look of stupidity which Mendori or Bellerose, two of the first actors of the day, might have envied him.

"Bravo," cried Mazarin; "they told me that you were the man I wanted. Come, let us see what you will do for me!"

"Everything that your Eminence may please to command me," was the reply.

"You will do for me what you have done for the queen?"

"Certainly," D'Artagnan said to himself, "he wishes to make me speak out. He's not more cunning than De Richelieu was! Devil take him!" Then he said aloud:

"The queen, my lord! I don't comprehend."

"You don't comprehend that I want you and your three friends to be of use to me?"

"What friends, my lord?"

"Your three friends—the friends of former days."

"Of former days, my lord! In former days I had not only three friends, I had fifty—at twenty, one calls every one one's friend."

"Well, sir," returned Mazarin; "prudence is a fine thing, but to-day you might regret having been too prudent."

"My lord, Pythagoras made his disciples keep silence for five years, that they might learn to hold their tongues."

"But you have been silent for twenty years, sir. Speak, now, for the queen herself releases you from your promise."

"The queen!"

"Yes, the queen! And as a proof of what I say she commanded me to show you this diamond, which she thinks you know."

And so saying, Mazarin extended his hand to the officer, who sighed as he recognised the ring which had been given to him by the queen on the night of the ball at the Hôtel de Ville.

"'Tis true. I remember well that diamond."

"You see, then, that I speak to you in the queen's name. Answer me without acting as if you were on the stage—your interests are concerned in your doing so. Where are your friends?"

"I do not know, my lord. We have parted company this long time; all three have left the service."

"Where can you find them, then?"

"Wherever they are, that's my business."

"Well, now what are your conditions if I employ you?"

"Money, my lord; as much money as what you wish me to undertake will require."

"The devil he does! Money! and a large sum!" said Mazarin. "Pray are you aware that the king has no money now in his treasury?"

"Do then as I did, my lord. Sell the crown diamonds. Trust me, don't let us try to do things cheaply. Great undertakings are badly done with small means."

"Well," returned Mazarin, "we will satisfy you."

"Richelieu," thought D'Artagnan, would have given me five hundred pistoles in advance."

"You will then be at my service?" asked Mazarin.

"And what are we to do?"

"Make your mind easy; when the time for action comes, you shall be in full possession of what I require from you; wait till that time arrives, and find out your friends."

"My lord, possibly they are not in Paris. I must, perhaps, make a long journey to find them out. Travelling is dear, and I am only a poor lieutenant in the Musketeers; besides, I have been in the service for twenty-two years, and have accumulated nothing but debts."

Mazarin remained some moments in deep thought, as if he combated with himself; then, going to a large cupboard closed with a triple lock, he took from it a bag of silver, and weighing it twice in his hands before he gave it to D'Artagnan—

"Take this," he said, with a sigh, "'tis for your journey."

D'Artagnan bowed, and plunged the bag into the depth of an immense pocket.

"Well, then, all is settled; you are to set off," said the Cardinal.

"Yes, my lord."

"Apropos, what are the names of your friends?"

"The Count de la Fère, formerly styled Athos; Monsieur du Valon, whom we used to call Porthos; the Chevalier d'Herblay— now the Abbe d'Herblay—whom we used to call Aramis——"

The Cardinal smiled.

"Younger sons," he said, "who enlisted in the Musketeers under feigned names in order not to lower their family names. Long rapiers, but light purses, you know."

"If, God willing, these rapiers should be devoted to the service of your Eminence," said D'Artagnan, "I shall venture to express a wish—which is, that, in its turn, the purse of your Eminence may become light, and theirs heavy—for with these three men, your Eminence may rouse all Europe, if you like."

"These Gascons," said the Cardinal, laughing, "almost beat the Italians in effrontery."

"— At all events," answered D'Artagnan, with a smile similar to the Cardinal's, "they beat them when they draw their swords."

He then withdrew, and as he passed into the court-yard he stopped near a lamp, and dived eagerly into the bag of money.

"Crown pieces only, silver pieces! I suspected it. Ah, Mazarin! Mazarin! thou hast no confidence in me! so much the worse for thee—harm may come of it!"

Meanwhile the Cardinal was rubbing his hands in great satisfaction.

"A hundred pistoles! a hundred pistoles! for a hundred pistoles I have discovered a secret for which Richelieu would have paid a thousand crowns: without reckoning the value of that diamond"—he cast a complacent look at the ring, which he had kept, instead of restoring it to D'Artagnan—"which is worth, at least, ten thousand francs."

He returned to his room, and, after depositing the ring in a casket filled with brilliants of every sort—for the Cardinal was a connoisseur in precious stones—he called to Bernouin to undress him, regardless of the noises, or of the firing of guns which continued to resound through Paris, although it was now nearly midnight.

CHAPTER VI.

D'ARTAGNAN IN HIS FORTIETH YEAR.

YEARS have elapsed, many events have happened, alas! since, in our romance of "The Three Musketeers," we took leave of D'Artagnan, at No. 12 Rue des Fossoyeurs. D'Artagnan had not failed in his career, but circumstances had been adverse to him. So long as he was surrounded by his friends, he retained his youth and the poetry of his character. His was one of those fine, ingenuous natures which assimilate themselves easily to the dispositions of others. Athos imparted to him his greatness of soul; Porthos, his enthusiasm; Aramis, his elegance. Had D'Artagnan continued his intimacy with these three men, he would have become a superior character. Athos was the first to leave him, in order that he might retire to a small property which he had inherited near Blois. Porthos, the second, to marry an attorney's wife; and lastly, Aramis, the third, to take orders, and become an abbé. From that day D'Artagnan felt lonely and powerless, without courage to pursue a career in which he could only distinguish himself on condition that each of his three companions should endow him with one of the gifts which each had received from heaven.

Notwithstanding his commission in the Musketeers, D'Artagnan felt completely solitary. For a time the delightful remembrance of Madame Bonacieux left on his character a certain poetic tinge, perishable, and, like all other recollections in this world, these impressions were, by degrees, effaced. A garrison life is fatal even to the most aristocratic organisations; and, imperceptibly, D'Artagnan, always in the camp, always on horseback, always in garrison, became (I know not how in the present age one would express it) a complete trooper. His early refinement of character was not only not lost, but was even greater than ever; but it was now applied to the little, instead of to the great things of life—to the material condition of the soldier—comprised under the heads of a good lodging, a good table, a good hostess. These important advantages D'Artagnan found to his own taste in the Rue Tiquetonne, at the sign of the Roe, where a pretty Flemish woman, named Madeleine, presided.

In the evening, after his conversation with Mazarin, he returned to his lodgings, absorbed in reflection. His mind was full of the fine diamond which he had once called his own, and which he had seen on the minister's finger that night.

"Should that diamond ever fall into my hands again," such was his reflection, "I should turn it at once into money; I should buy, with the proceeds, certain lands around my father's chateau, which is a pretty place—well enough—but with no land to it at all, except a garden about the size of the Cemetery des Innocents; and I should wait, in all my glory, till some rich heiress, attracted by my good looks, chose to marry me. Then I should like to have three sons; I should make the first a nobleman, like Athos; the second a good soldier, like Porthos; the third an excellent abbé, like Aramis. Faith! that would be a far better life than I lead now; but Monsieur Mazarin is a mean wretch, who won't dispossess himself of his diamond in my favour."

On entering the Rue Tiquetonne he heard a tremendous noise, and found a dense crowd near the house.

"Oh! oh!" said he, "is the hotel on fire?" On approaching the hotel of the Roe, he found, however, that it was in front of the next house that the mob was collected. The people were shouting, and running about with torches. By the light of one of these torches, D'Artagnan perceived men in uniform.

He asked what was going on.

He was told that twenty citizens, headed by one man, had attacked a carriage, which was escorted by a troop of the Cardinal's bodyguard; but, a reinforcement having come up, the assailants had been put to flight, and the leader had taken refuge in the hotel, next to his lodgings; the house was now being searched.

In his youth, D'Artagnan had often headed the *bourgeoisie* against the military, but he was cured of all those hot-headed propensities; besides, he had the Cardinal's hundred pistoles in his pocket: so he went into the hotel without saying a word; he found Madeleine alarmed for his safety, and anxious to tell him all the events of the evening, but he cut her short by ordering her to put his supper in his room, and to give him with it a bottle of good Burgundy.

He took his key and his candle, and went upstairs to his bedroom. He had been contented, for the convenience of the house, to lodge on the fourth story; and truth obliges us even to confess that his chamber was just above the gutter and below the roof. His first care on entering it was to lock up in an old bureau with a new lock, his bag of money, and then as soon as supper was ready, he sent away the waiter who brought it up, and sat down to table.

Not to reflect on what had passed, as one might fancy. No—D'Artagnan considered that things are never well done when they are not reserved to their proper time. He was hungry; he supped, he went to bed. Neither was he one of those who think that the silence of the night brings good counsel with it. In the night he slept, but in the morning, refreshed and calm, he was inspired with the clearest views of everything. It was long since he had had any reason for his morning's inspiration, but he had always slept all night long. At daybreak he awoke, and made a turn round his room.

"In '43," he said, "just before the death of the late Cardinal, I received a letter from Athos. Where was I then? Let me see. Oh! at the siege of Besançon! I was in the trenches. He told me—let me think—what was it? That he was living on a small estate—but where? I was just reading the name of the place when the wind blew my letter away—I suppose to the Spaniards;

there's no use in thinking any more about Athos. Let me see,—
with regard to Porthos, I received a letter from him, too. He
invited me to a hunting party on his property in the month of
September, 1646. Unluckily, as I was then in Bearn, on account
of my father's death, the letter followed me there. I had left
Bearn when it arrived, and I never received it until the month of
April, 1647; and as the invitation was for September, 1646, I
couldn't accept it. Let me look for this letter; it must be with
my title-deeds."

D'Artagnan opened an old casket, which stood in a corner of
the room, and which was full of parchments, referring to an estate,
during a period of two hundred years lost to his family. He
uttered an exclamation of delight, for the large handwriting of
Porthos was discernible, and beneath it some lines traced by his
worthy spouse.

D'Artagnan eagerly searched for the date of this letter; it was
dated from the Chateau du Vallon.

Porthos had forgotten that any other address was necessary; in
his pride he fancied that every one must know the Chateau du
Vallon.

"Devil take the vain fellow," said D'Artagnan. "However, I
had better find him out first, since he can't want money. Athos
must have become an idiot by this time from drinking. Aramis
must be absorbed in his devotional exercises."

He cast his eyes again on the letter. There was a postscript.

"I write by the same courier to our worthy friend Aramis in his
convent."

"In his convent! what convent? There are about two hundred
in Paris, and three thousand in France; and then, perhaps, on
entering the convent he has changed his name. Ah! if I were
but learned in theology, I should recollect what it was he used to
dispute about with the Curate of Montdidier and the Superior of
the Jesuits, when we were at Crevecour; I should know what
doctrine he leans to, and I should glean from that what saint he
has adopted as his patron.

"Well, suppose I go back to the Cardinal and ask him for a
passport into all the convents one can find; even into the nun-
neries? It would be a curious idea, and maybe I should find my
friend under the name of Achilles. But, no! I should lose myself
in the Cardinal's opinion. Great people only thank you for doing
for them what's impossible; what's possible, they say, they can do
themselves, and they are right."

So he was perfectly ignorant either where to find Aramis any

more than Porthos, and the affair was becoming a matter of great
perplexity, when he fancied he heard a pane of glass break in his
room window.   He thought directly of his bag, and rushed from
the inner room where he was sleeping.   He was not mistaken; as
he entered his bedroom, a man was getting in by the window.

"Ah! you scoundrel!" cried D'Artagnan, taking the man for a
thief, and seizing his sword.

"Sir," cried the man.   "In the name of heaven put your sword
back into the sheath, and don't kill me unheard.   I'm no thief,
but an honest citizen, well off in the world, with a house of my
own.   My name is—ah! but surely you are Monsieur D'Artagnan?"

"And thou—Planchet!" cried the lieutenant.

"At your service, sir," said Planchet, overwhelmed with joy;
"and I'm still capable of serving you."

"Perhaps so," replied D'Artagnan.   "But why the devil dost
thou run about the tops of houses at seven o'clock of the morning
in the month of January?"

"Sir," said Planchet, "you must know; but, perhaps, you ought
not to know——"

"Tell us what," returned D'Artagnan, "but first put a napkin
against the window, and draw the curtains."

"Sir," said the prudent Planchet, "in particular, are you on
good terms with Monsieur de Rochefort?"

"Perfectly; one of my dearest friends."

"Ah! so much the better!"

"But what has De Rochefort to do with this manner you have
of invading my room?"

"Ah, sir! I must tell you that Monsieur de Rochefort is——"
Planchet hesitated.

"Egad, I know where he is," said D'Artagnan.   "He's in the
Bastille!"

"That is to say, he was there," replied Planchet.   "But in returning thither last night, when fortunately you did not accompany
him, as his carriage was crossing the Rue de la Ferronnerie, his
guards insulted the people, who began to abuse them.   The prisoner thought this a good opportunity for escape; he called out
his name, and cried for help.   I was there.   I heard the name of
Rochefort.   I remembered him well.   I said in a loud voice that
he was a prisoner, a friend of the Duc de Beaufort, who called
for help.   The people were infuriated; they stopped the horses,
and cut the escort to pieces, whilst I opened the doors of the
carriage, and Monsieur de Rochefort jumped out and was lost
amongst the crowd.   At this moment a patrol passed by.   I was

obliged to sound a retreat towards the Rue Tiquetonne; I was pursued, and took refuge in a house next to this, where I have been concealed till this morning on the top of the house, between two mattresses. I ventured to run along the gutters, and——"

"Well," interrupted D'Artagnan, "I am delighted that De Rochefort is free; but as for thee, if thou shouldst fall into the hands of the king's servants, they will hang thee without mercy. Nevertheless, I promise thee thou shalt he hidden here, though I risk by concealing thee neither more nor less than my lieutenancy, if it was found out that I gave a rebel an asylum."

"Ah! sir, you know well I would risk my life for you."

"Thou mayst add that thou hast risked it, Planchet. I have not forgotten all I owe thee. Sit down there, and eat in security. I see thee cast expressive glances at the remains of my supper."

"Yes, sir; for all I've had since yesterday was a slice of bread and butter with preserve on it. Although I don't despise sweet things in proper time and place, yet I found that supper rather light."

"Poor fellow!" said D'Artagnan. "Well, come; set to."

"Ah, sir! you are going to save my life a second time," cried Planchet.

And he seated himself at the table, and ate as he did in the merry days of the Rue des Fossoyeurs, whilst D'Artagnan walked to and fro, and thought how he could make use of Planchet under present circumstances. While he turned this over in his mind, Planchet did his best to make up for lost time at table.

At last he uttered a sigh of satisfaction, and paused, as if he had partially appeased his hunger.

"Come," said D'Artagnan, who thought that it was now a convenient time to begin his interrogations, "dost thou know where Athos is?"

"No, sir," replied Planchet.

"The devil thou dost not! Dost know where Porthos is?"

"No—not at all."

"And Aramis?"

"Not in the least."

"The devil! the devil! the devil!"

"But, sir," said Planchet, with a look of surprise, "I know where Bazin is."

"Where is he?"

"At Nôtre Dame."

"What has he to do at Nôtre Dame?"

"He is bedell."

"Bazin bedell at Nôtre Dame! He must know where his master is!"

"Without doubt he must."

D'Artagnan thought for a moment, then took his sword, and put on his cloak ready to go out.

"Sir," said Planchet, in a mournful tone, "do you abandon me thus to my fate! Think, if I am found out here, the people of the house, who have not seen me enter it, must take me for a thief."

"True," said D'Artagnan. "Let's see. Canst thou speak any patois?"

"I can do something better than that, sir; I can speak Flemish."

"Where the devil didst thou learn it?"

"In Artois, where I fought for two years. Listen, sir. Gooden morgen, mynheer, ith ben begeeray le weeten the ge sond heets omstand."

"Which means?

"Good day, sir! I am anxious to know the state of your health."

"He calls that knowing a language! but, never mind, that will do capitally."

D'Artagnan opened the door, and called out to a waiter to desire Madeleine to come upstairs.

When the landlady made her appearance, she expressed much astonishment at seeing Planchet.

"My dear landlady," said D'Artagnan, "I beg to introduce to you your brother, who is arrived from Flanders, and whom I am going to take into my service."

"My brother?"

"Wish your sister good morning, Master Peter."

"Wilkom, suster," said Planchet.

"Goeden day, broder," replied the astonished landlady.

"This is the case," said D'Artagnan: "this is your brother, Madeleine; you don't know him, perhaps, but I know him; he has arrived from Amsterdam. You must dress him up during my absence. When I return, which will be in about an hour, you must offer him to me as a servant, and, upon your recommendation, though he doesn't speak a word of French, I take him into my service. You understand?"

"That is to say, I guess your wishes; and that is all that's necessary," said Madeleine.

"You are a precious creature, my pretty hostess, and I'm obliged to you."

The next moment D'Artagnan was on his way to Nôtre Dame.

CHAPTER VII.

TOUCHES UPON THE DIFFERENT EFFECTS WHICH HALF A PISTOLE
MAY PRODUCE UPON A BEDELL AND A CHORISTER.

D'ARTAGNAN, as he passed the Pont Neuf, congratulated himself
upon having found Planchet again; for at that time an intelligent
servant was essential to him; nor was he sorry that through Planchet, and the situation which he held in the Rue des Lombards, a
connection with the *bourgeoisie* might be commenced, at that critical period when that class were preparing to make war with the
court party. It was like having a spy in the enemy's camp. In
this frame of mind, grateful for the accidental meeting with Planchet, pleased with himself, D'Artagnan reached Nôtre Dame. He
ran up the steps, entered the church, and addressing a verger who
was sweeping the chapel, asked him if he knew Monsieur Bazin.

"Monsieur Bazin, the bedell," said the verger. "Yes; there he
is, attending mass, in the chapel of the Virgin."

D'Artagnan nearly jumped for joy—he had despaired of finding
Bazin; but now, he thought, since he held one of the threads, he
should be pretty sure to reach the other end of the clue.

He knelt down just opposite to the chapel, in order not to lose
sight of his man; and as he had almost forgotten his prayers, and
had omitted to take a book with him, he made use of his time in
gazing at Bazin.

Bazin wore his dress, it may be observed, with equal dignity and
saintly propriety. It was not difficult to understand that he had
gained the summit of his ambition, and that the silver-mounted
wand which he brandished was, in his eyes, as honourable a distinction as the marshal's baton, which Condé threw, or did not
throw, into the enemy's line of battle at Fribourg. His person
had undergone a change, analogous to the change in his dress;
his figure was rounded, and, as it were, canonized. The striking
points of his face were effaced; he had still a nose; but his cheeks,
fattened out, each took off a portion of it into themselves; his
chin was joined to his throat; his eyes were swelled up with the
puffiness of his cheeks; his hair, cut straight in holy guise, covered
his forehead as far as his eyebrows.

The officiating priest was just finishing the mass, whilst D'Artagnan was looking at Bazin; he pronounced the words of the holy
sacrament, and retired, giving the benediction, which was received
by the kneeling communicants, to the astonishment of D'Artagnan,

who recognised in the priest the Coadjutor* himself, the famous
Jean François Goneli, who at that time, having a presentiment of
the part he was to play, was beginning to court popularity by alms-
giving. It was to this end that he performed from time to time
some of those early masses which the common people generally
alone attended.

D'Artagnan knelt as well as the rest, received his share of the
benediction, and made the sign of the cross; but when Bazin
passed in his turn, with his eyes raised to heaven, and walking, in
all humility, the very last, D'Artagnan pulled him by the hem of
his robe.

Bazin looked down and started as if he had seen a serpent.

"Monsieur d'Artagnan!" he cried; "Vade retra, Satanas!"

"So, my dear Bazin," said the officer, laughing, "this is the way
you receive an old friend."

"Sir," replied Bazin, "the true friends of a Christian are those
who aid him in working out his salvation; not those who hinder
him in so doing."

"I don't understand you, Bazin; nor can I see how I can be a
stumbling-block in the way of your salvation," said D'Artagnan.

"You forget, sir, that you very nearly ruined for ever that of my
master; and that it was owing to you that he was very nearly being
damned eternally for remaining a Musketeer, whilst his true vocation was for the church."

"My dear Bazin, you ought to perceive," said D'Artagnan,
"from the place in which you find me, that I am much changed
in everything. Age produces good sense, and, as I doubt not but
that your master is on the road to salvation, I want you to tell me
where he is, that he may help me to mine."

"Rather say—to take him back with you into the world. Fortunately, I don't know where he is."

"How!" cried D'Artagnan; "you don't know where Aramis is?"

"Formerly," replied Bazin, "Aramis was his name of perdition.
By Aramis is meant Simara, which is the name of a demon.
Happily for him, he has ceased to bear that name."

D'Artagnan saw clearly that he should get nothing out of this
man, who was evidently telling a falsehood in his pretended ignorance of the abode of Aramis, but whose falsehoods were bold and
decided.

"Well, Bazin," said D'Artagnan, "since you do not know where
your master lives, let us speak of it no more; let us part good
friends. Accept this half-pistole to drink to my health."

* A sacerdotal office.

"I do not drink"—Bazin pushed away with dignity the officer's hand—"'tis good only for the laity."

"Incorruptible!" murmured D'Artagnan; "I am unlucky;" and whilst he was lost in thought, Bazin retreated towards the sacristy, where he was only, as he thought, secure by shutting the door and closing himself in.

D'Artagnan was still in deep thought, when some one touched him on the shoulder. He turned, and uttered an exclamation of surprise.

"You here, Rochefort?" he said in a low voice.

"Hush!" returned Rochefort. "Do you know that I am at liberty?"

"I knew it from the fountain-head—from Planchet. And what brought you here?"

"I came to thank God for my happy deliverance," said Rochefort.

"And nothing more? I suppose that is not all."

"To take my orders from the Coadjutor, and to see if we cannot plague Mazarin a little."

"A bad plan; you'll be shut up again in the Bastille."

"Oh, as to that, I shall take care, I assure you. The air, the fresh free air, is so good; besides"—and Rochefort drew a deep breath as he spoke—"I am going into the country to make a tour."

"Stop," cried D'Artagnan; "I, too, am going."

"And if I may, without impertinence, ask—where are you going?"

"To seek my friends. To find out Athos, Porthos, and Aramis."

"And when do you set out?"

"I am now on my road."

"Good luck to you."

"And to you—a good journey."

"Perhaps we shall meet on our road. Adieu! till we meet again! Apropos, should Mazarin speak to you about me, tell him that I have requested you to acquaint him that in a short time he will see whether I am, as he says, too old for action."

And Rochefort went away with one of those diabolical smiles which used formerly to make D'Artagnan shudder, but D'Artagnan could now see it without anguish, and, smiling in his turn, with an expression of melancholy, which the recollections called up by that smile, could, perhaps, alone give to his countenance, he said:

"Go, demon, do what thou wilt! it matters little to me. There is not a second Constance in the world."

On his return into the cathedral, D'Artagnan saw Bazin, who was conversing with the sacristan. Bazin was making with his spare, little, short arms, ridiculous gestures. D'Artagnan perceived that he was enforcing prudence with respect to himself.

D'Artagnan slipped out of the cathedral, and placed himself in ambuscade at the corner of the Rue des Canettes; it was impossible that Bazin could go out of the cathedral without his seeing him.

In five minutes Bazin made his appearance, looking in every direction to see if he were observed, but he saw no one. Tranquilised by appearances, he ventured to walk on through the Rue Nôtre Dame. Then D'Artagnan rushed out of his hiding-place, and arrived in time to see Bazin turn down the Rue de la Juiverie, and enter, in the Rue de la Calandre, a respectable-looking house; and this D'Artagnan felt no doubt was the habitation of the worthy bedell. Afraid of making any inquiries at this house, D'Artagnan entered a small tavern at the corner of the street, and asked for a cup of hypocras. This beverage required a good half-hour to prepare it, and D'Artagnan had time, therefore, to watch Bazin unsuspected.

He perceived in the tavern a pert boy between twelve and fifteen years of age, whom he fancied he had seen not twenty minutes before, under the guise of a chorister. He questioned him; and as the boy had no interest in deceiving, D'Artagnan learned that he exercised from six o'clock in the morning until nine, the office of chorister; and from nine o'clock till midnight that of a waiter in the tavern.

Whilst he was talking to this lad, a horse was brought to the door of Bazin's house. It was saddled and bridled. Almost immediately Bazin came downstairs.

"Look!" said the boy, "there's our bedell, who is going a journey."

"And where is he going?" asked D'Artagnan.

"Forsooth, I don't know."

"Half a pistole if you can find out," said D'Artagnan.

"For me?" cried the child, his eyes sparkling with joy, "if I can find out where Bazin is going? 'Tis not difficult. You are not joking—are you?"

"No, on the honour of an officer; there is the half pistole;" and he showed him the seductive coin, but did not give it him.

"I shall ask him."

"Just the very way not to know. Wait till he is set out, and then, marry, come up—ask, and find out. The half-pistole is ready;" and he put it back again into his pocket.

"I understand," said the child, with that jeering smile which marks especially the "gamin de Paris." "Well, we must wait."

They had not long to wait. Five minutes afterwards Bazin set off on a full trot, urging on his horse by the blows of a paraphine, which he was in the habit of using instead of a riding-whip.

Scarcely had he turned the corner of the Rue de la Juiverie, then the boy rushed after him like a blood-hound on full scent.

Before five minutes had elapsed the child returned.

"Well!" said D'Artagnan.

"Well!" answered the boy; "the thing is done."

"Where is he gone?"

"The half-pistole is for me?"

"Doubtless; answer me."

"I want to see it. Give it me, that I may see that it is not false."

"There it is."

The child put the piece of money into his pocket.

"And now, where is he gone?" inquired D'Artagnan.

"He is gone to Noisy."

"How dost thou know?"

"Ah, faith! there was no great cunning necessary. I knew the horse which he rode; it belonged to the butcher who lets it out now and then to M. Bazin. Now, I thought as much that the butcher would not let his horse out like that without knowing where it went to. And he answered, 'that Monsieur Bazin went to Noisy. 'Tis his custom. He goes two or three times a-week.'"

"Dost thou know Noisy well?"

"I think so, truly; my nurse lives there."

"Is there a convent at Noisy?"

"Isn't there a grand one—a convent of Jesuits."

"What's thy name?"

"Friquet."

D'Artagnan wrote down the child's name in his tablets.

"Please, sir," said the boy, "do you think I can get any more half-pistoles any way?"

"Perhaps," replied D'Artagnan.

And, having got out all he wanted, he paid for the hypocras, which he did not drink, and went quickly back to the Rue Tiquetonne.

CHAPTER VIII.

HOW D'ARTAGNAN, ON GOING TO A DISTANCE TO FIND OUT ARAMIS,
DISCOVERS THAT HIS FRIEND WAS RIDING BEHIND PLANCHET.

THE plan adopted by D'Artagnan was soon perfected. He resolved not to reach Noisy in the day, for fear of being recognised :
he had therefore plenty of time before him, for Noisy is only three
or four leagues from Paris, on the road to Meaux.

He began his day by breakfasting very substantially—a bad beginning when one wants to employ the head, but an excellent precaution when one wants to work the body ; and about two o'clock
he had his two horses saddled, and followed by Planchet, he
quitted Paris by the Barrière de la Villette.

At about a league and a half from the city, D'Artagnan, finding
that in his impatience he had set out too soon, stopped to give the
horses breathing time. The inn was full of disreputable-looking
people, who seemed as if they were on the point of commencing
some nightly expedition. A man, wrapped in a cloak, appeared
at the door; but seeing a stranger, he beckoned to his companions,
and two men who were drinking in the inn went out to speak to
him.

D'Artagnan, on his side, went up to the landlady—praised her
wine—which was a horrible production from the country of Montreuil—and heard from her that there were only two houses of importance in the village ; one of these belonged to the Archbishop
of Paris, and was at that time the abode of his niece, the Duchess
of Longueville; the other was a convent of Jesuits, and was the
property—a by no means unusual circumstance—of these worthy
fathers.

At four o'clock D'Artagnan recommenced his journey. He
proceeded slowly, and in a deep reverie. Planchet was also lost
in thought, but the subject of their reflections was not the same.

One word which their landlady had pronounced had given a
particular turn to D'Artagnan's deliberations—this was the name
of Madame de Longueville.

That name was, indeed, one to inspire imagination, and to produce thought. Madame de Longueville was one of the highest
ladies in the realm ; she was also one of the greatest beauties at
the court. She had formerly been suspected of an intimacy of too
tender a nature with Coligny—who, for her sake, had been killed
in a duel, in the Place Royale, by the Duc de Guise. She was

now connected by a bond of a political nature with the Prince de Marsillac, the eldest son of the old Duc de Rochefoucauld, whom she was trying to inspire with an enmity towards the Duc de Condé, her brother-in-law, whom she now hated mortally.

D'Artagnan thought of all these matters. He remembered how, at the Louvre, he had often seen, as she passed by him in the full radiance of her dazzling charms, the beautiful Madame de Longueville. He thought of Aramis, who, without possessing any greater advantages than he had, had formerly been the lover of Madame de Chevreux, who had been in another court what Madame de Longueville was in that day; and he wondered how it was that there should be in the world people who succeed in every wish—some in ambition, others in love—whilst others, either from chance or from ill-luck, or from some natural defect or impediment, remain only halfway on the road towards the goal of their hopes and expectations.

He was confessing to himself that he belonged to the latter class of persons, when Planchet approached, and said :

" I will lay a wager, your honour, that you and I are thinking of the same thing."

" I doubt it, Planchet," replied D'Artagnan—" but what are you thinking of?"

" I am thinking, sir, of those desperate-looking men who were drinking in the inn where we rested."

" Always cautious, Planchet."

" 'Tis instinct, your honour."

" Well, what does your instinct tell you now?"

" Sir, my instinct told me that those people were assembled there for some bad purpose; and I was reflecting on what my instinct had told me, in the darkest corner of the stable, when a man, wrapped in a cloak, and followed by two other men, came in."

" Ah !"

" One of these two men said, ' He must certainly be at Noisy, or be coming there this evening, for I've seen his servant.'

" ' Art thou sure?' said the man in the cloak.

" ' Yes, my prince.'"

" My prince !" interrupted D'Artagnan.

" Yes, ' my prince'—but listen. ' If he is here'—this is what the other man said—' let's see decidedly what to do with him.'

" ' What to do with him ?' answered the prince.

" ' Yes, he's not a man to allow himself to be taken anyhow—he'll defend himself.'

" ' Well—we must try to take him alive. Have you cords to
bind him with, and a gag to stop his mouth?'

" ' We have.'

" ' Remember that he will most likely be disguised as a horseman.'

" ' Yes, yes, my lord—don't be uneasy.'

" ' Besides, I shall be there.'

" ' You will assure us that justice——'

" ' Yes, yes—I answer for all that,' the prince said.

" ' Well, then, we'll do our best.' Having said that, they went
out of the stable."

"Well—what matters all that to us?" said D'Artagnan ; "this is
one of those attempts that happen every day."

"Are you sure that we are not its objects?"

"We—why?"

"Just remember what they said ;" and Planchet recapitulated
what he had just stated.

"Alas ! my dear Planchet," said D'Artagnan, sighing, "we are
unfortunately no longer in those times in which princes would
care to assassinate me. Those were good old days : never fear—
these people owe us no grudge."

"Is your honour sure?"

"I can answer for it they do not."

"Well—we won't speak of it any more, then ;" and Planchet
took his place in D'Artagnan's suite with that sublime confidence
which he had always had in his master, and which fifteen years of
separation had not destroyed.

They had travelled onwards about half a mile, when Planchet
came close up to D'Artagnan.

"Stop, sir ; look yonder," he whispered ; "don't you see, in the
darkness, something pass by, like shadows? I fancy I hear
horses' feet."

"Impossible !" returned D'Artagnan. "The ground is soaked
in rain ; yet I fancy, as thou sayest, that I see something."

At this moment the neighing of a horse struck upon his ear—
coming through darkness and space.

"There are men somewhere about ; but that's of no consequence
to us," said D'Artagnan ; "let us ride onwards."

At about half-past eight o'clock they reached the first houses in
Noisy ; every one was in bed, and not a light was to be seen in
the village. The obscurity was broken only now and then by the
dark lines of the roofs of houses. Here and there a dog barked
behind a door, or an affrighted cat fled precipitately from the

midst of the pavement, to take refuge behind a heap of faggots, from which retreat her eyes shone like carbuncles. These were the only living creatures that seemed to inhabit the village.

Towards the middle of the town, commanding the principal open space, rose a dark mass, separated from the rest of the world by two lanes, and overshadowed in the front by enormous lime-trees. D'Artagnan looked attentively at the building.

"This," he said to Planchet, "must be the archbishop's château, the abode of the fair Madame de Longueville; but the convent, where is that?"

"The convent, your honour, is at the end of the village; I know it well."

"Well, then, Planchet, gallop up to it, whilst I tighten my horse's girth, and come back and tell me if there is a light in any of the Jesuits' windows."

In about five minutes Planchet returned.

"Sir," he said, "there is one window of the convent lighted up."

"Hem! If I were a 'Frondeur,'" said D'Artagnan, "I should knock here, and should be sure of a good supper. If I were a monk, I should knock yonder, and should have a good supper there, too; whereas, 'tis very possible that, between the castle and the convent, we shall sleep on hard beds, dying with hunger and thirst."

"Yes," added Planchet, "like the famous ass of Buridan. Shall I knock?"

"Hush!" replied D'Artagnan; "the light in the window is extinguished."

"Do you hear nothing?" whispered Planchet.

"What is that noise?"

There came a sound like a whirlwind, and at the same time two troops of horsemen, each composed of ten men, sallied forth from each of the lanes which encompassed the house, and surrounded D'Artagnan and Planchet.

"Heyday!" cried D'Artagnan, drawing his sword, and taking refuge behind his horse; "are you not mistaken? is it us you wish to attack—us?"

"Here he is! we have him now," said the horsemen, rushing on D'Artagnan with naked swords.

"Don't let him escape," said a loud voice.

"No, my lord; be assured, we shall not."

D'Artagnan thought it was now time for him to join in the conversation.

"Hallo, gentlemen!" he called out in his Gascon accent, "what do you want—what do you demand?"

"Thou wilt soon know," shouted a chorus of horsemen.

"Stop, stop !" cried he whom they had addressed as "my lord ;" "'tis not his voice."

"Ah ! just so, gentlemen ! pray do people get into passions at random at Noisy ?　Take care, for I warn you that the first man that comes within the length of my sword—and my sword is long —I rip him up."

The chieftain of the party drew near.

"What are you doing here ?" he asked, in a lofty tone, and like one accustomed to command.

"And you—what are *you* doing here ?" replied D'Artagnan.

"Be civil, or I shall beat you ; for, although one may not choose to proclaim one's self, one insists on respect suitable to one's rank."

"You don't choose to discover yourself, because you are the leader of an ambuscade," returned D'Artagnan ; "but with regard to myself, who am travelling quietly with my own servant, I have not the same reasons as you have to conceal my name !"

"Enough ! enough ! what is your name ?"

"I shall tell you my name in order that you may know where to find me, my lord, or my prince, as it may suit you best to be called," said our Gascon, who did not choose to seem to yield to a threat.　"Do you know Monsieur D'Artagnan ?"

"Lieutenant in the king's regiment of Musketeers ?" said the voice ; "you are Monsieur D'Artagnan ?"

"I am."

"Then you are come here to defend him ?"

"Him ? whom ?　Him ?"

"Him whom we are seeking."

"It seems," said D'Artagnan, "that whilst I thought I was coming to Noisy, I have entered, without suspecting it, into the kingdom of mysteries."

"Come," replied the same lofty tone, "answer ! Are you waiting for him underneath these windows ? Did you come to Noisy to defend him ?"

"I am waiting for no one," replied D'Artagnan, who was beginning to be angry.

"Well, well," rejoined the leader, "there's no doubt 'tis a Gascon who is speaking, and therefore not the man we are looking for.　We shall meet again, Master D'Artagnan ; let us go onwards, gentlemen."

And the troop, angry and complaining, disappeared in the darkness, and took the road to Paris.　D'Artagnan and Planchet remained for some moments still on the defensive ; then, as the noise of the horsemen became more and more distant, they sheathed their swords.

"Thou seest, simpleton," said D'Artagnan to his servant, "that they wished no harm to us."

"But to whom, then ?"

"I'faith ! I don't know, nor care. What I care for now, is to make my way into the Jesuits' convent; so, to horse, and let us knock at their door. Happen what will—devil take them—they won't eat us."

And he mounted his horse. Planchet had just done the same, when an unexpected weight fell upon the back of his horse, which sank down.

"Hey ! your honour !" cried Planchet, "I've a man behind me."

D'Artagnan turned round, and saw, plainly, two human forms upon Planchet's horse.

"'Tis then the devil that pursues us !" he cried, drawing his sword, and preparing to attack the new foe.

"No, no, dear D'Artagnan," said the figure, "'tis not the devil, 'tis Aramis ; gallop fast, Planchet, and when you come to the end of the village, go to the left."

And Planchet, with Aramis behind him, set off full gallop, followed by D'Artagnan, who began to think he was dreaming some incoherent and fantastic dream.

CHAPTER IX.

THE ABBÉ D'HERBLAY

At the extremity of the village Planchet turned to the left, in obedience to the orders of Aramis, and stopped underneath the window which had a light in it. Aramis alighted, and knocked three times with his hands. Immediately the window was opened, and a ladder of rope was let down from it.

"My friend," said Aramis, "if you like to ascend, I shall be delighted to receive you."

"Pass on before me, I beg of you."

"As the late Cardinal used to say to the late king—only to show you the way, sire." And Aramis ascended the ladder quickly, and reached the window in an instant.

D'Artagnan followed, but less nimbly, showing plainly that this mode of ascent was not one to which he was accustomed.

"Sir," said Planchet, when he saw D'Artagnan on the summit of the ladder, "this way is easy for Monsieur Aramis, and even for you; in case of necessity I might also climb up, but my two horses cannot mount the ladder."

"Take them to yonder shed, my friend," said Aramis, pointing to a building in the plain, "there you will find hay and straw for them; then come back here, and knock thrice, and we will give you out some provisions. Marry, forsooth, people don't die of hunger here."

And Aramis, drawing in the ladder, closed the window. D'Artagnan then looked around him attentively.

Never was there an apartment at the same time more warlike and more elegant. At each corner there were trophies, presenting to the view swords of all sorts, and four great pictures representing in their ordinary military costume the Cardinal de Lorraine, the Cardinal de Richelieu, the Cardinal de la Valette, and the Archbishop of Bordeaux. Exteriorly nothing in the room showed that it was the habitation of an abbé. The hangings were of damask, the carpets came from Alençon, and the bed, more especially, had more the look of a fine lady's couch, with its trimmings of fine lace, and its embroidered counterpane, than of a man who had made a vow that he would endeavour to gain heaven by fasting and mortification.

Whilst D'Artagnan was engaged in contemplation the door opened, and Bazin entered; on perceiving the Musketeer he uttered an exclamation which was almost a cry of despair.

"My dear Bazin," said D'Artagnan, "I am delighted to see with what wonderful composure you tell a lie even in a church!"

"Sir," replied Bazin, "I have been taught by the good Jesuit fathers, that it is permitted to tell a falsehood when it is told in a good cause."

"So far well," said Aramis; "we are dying of hunger. Serve us up the best supper you can, and especially give us some good wine."

Bazin bowed low, and left the room.

"Now we are alone, dear Aramis," said D'Artagnan, "tell me how the devil did you manage to light upon the back of Planchet's horse?"

"Eh! faith!" answered Aramis, "as you see, from heaven."

"From heaven!" replied D'Artagnan, shaking his head; "you have no more the appearance of coming from thence than you have of going there."

"My friend," said Aramis, with a look of imbecility on his face which D'Artagnan had never observed whilst he was in the Musketeers, "if I did not come from heaven, at least I was leaving paradise, which is almost the same."

"Here, then, is a puzzle for the learned," observed D'Artagnan; "until now they have never been able to agree as to the situation of paradise: some place it on Mount Ararat, others between the Tigris and the Euphrates; it seems that they have been looking very far off for it, while it was actually very near. Paradise is at Noisy le See, upon the site of the archbishop's château. People do not go out from it by the door, but by the window; one doesn't descend here by the marble steps of a peristyle, but by the branches of a lime tree; and the angel with a flaming sword who guards this elysium, seems to have changed his celestial name of Gabriel into that of the more terrestrial one of the Prince de Marsillac."

Aramis burst out into a fit of laughter.

"You were always a merry companion, my dear D'Artagnan," he said, "and your witty Gascon fancy has not deserted you. Yes, there is something in what you say; nevertheless, do not believe that it is Madame de Longueville with whom I am in love."

"A plague on't! I shall not do so. After having been so long in love with Madame de Chevreuse, you would not lay your heart at the feet of her mortal enemy!"

"Yes," replied Aramis, with an absent air, "yes, that poor duchess! I once loved her much, and, to do her justice, she was very useful to us. Eventually she was obliged to leave France. He was a relentless enemy, that damned Cardinal," continued Aramis, glancing at the portrait of the old minister. "He had even given orders to arrest her, and would have cut off her head, had she not escaped with her waiting-maid—poor Kitty! The duchess escaped in man's clothes, and a couplet was made upon her"—and Aramis hummed a few lines of a well-known song of the day.

"Bravo!" cried D'Artagnan, "you sing charmingly, dear Aramis. I do not perceive that singing masses has altered your voice."

"My dear D'Artagnan," replied Aramis, "you understand, when I was a Musketeer I mounted guard as seldom as I could; now, when I am an abbé, I say as few masses as I can. But to return to our duchess."

"Which? the Duchesse de Chevreuse or the Duchesse de Longueville?"

"Have I not already told you that there is nothing between me and the Duchesse de Longueville? little flirtations, perhaps, and that's all. No, I spoke of the Duchesse de Chevreuse; did you see her after her return from Brussels, after the king's death?"

"Yes, she is still beautiful."

"Yes," said Aramis, "I saw her also at that time. I gave her good advice, by which she did not profit. I ventured to tell her that Mazarin was the lover of Anne of Austria. She wouldn't believe me, saying, that she knew Anne of Austria, who was too proud to love such a worthless coxcomb. She since plunged into the cabal headed by the Duke of Beaufort; and the 'coxcomb' arrested De Beaufort, and banished Madame de Chevreuse."

"You know," resumed D'Artagnan, "that she has had leave to return to France?"

"Yes, she is come back, and is going to commit some fresh folly or another; she is much changed."

"In that respect unlike you, my dear Aramis, for you are still the same; you have still your beautiful dark hair, still your elegant figure, still your feminine hands, which are admirably suited to a prelate."

"Yes," replied Aramis, "I am extremely careful of my appearance. Do you know that I am growing old; I am nearly thirty-seven."

"Mind, Aramis"—D'Artagnan smiled as he spoke—"since we are together again, let us agree on one point, what age shall we be in future?"

"How?"

"Formerly, I was your junior by two or three years, and, if I am not mistaken, I am turned forty years old."

"Indeed! Then 'tis I who am mistaken, for you have always been a good chronologist. By your reckoning I must be forty-three at least. The devil I am! Don't let it out at the Hotel Rambouillet, it would ruin me," replied the abbé.

"Don't be afraid, I shall not," said D'Artagnan.

"And now let us go to supper," said Aramis, seeing that Bazin had returned and prepared the table.

The two friends sat down, and Aramis began to cut up fowls, partridges, and hams with admirable skill.

"The deuce!" cried D'Artagnan; "do you live in this way always?"

"Yes, pretty well. The Coadjutor has given me dispensations from fasting on the *jours maigres*, on account of my health; then I have engaged as my cook, the cook who lived with Lafollome— you know whom I mean?—the friend of the Cardinal, and the famous epicure whose grace after dinner used to be—'Good Lord, do me the favour to make me digest what I have eaten.'"

"Nevertheless, he died of indigestion, in spite of his grace," said D'Artagnan.

"What can you expect?" replied Aramis, in a tone of resignation; "a man must fulfil his destiny."

"If it be not an indelicate question," resumed D'Artagnan, "are you grown rich?"

"Oh, heaven! no. I make about twelve thousand francs a year, without counting a little benefice which the prince gave me."

"And how do you make your twelve thousand francs?—by your poems?"

"No, I've given up poetry, except now and then to write a drinking song, some gay sonnet, or some innocent epigram; I make sermons, my friend."

"How! sermons? Do you preach them?"

"No; I sell them to those of my cloth who wish to become great orators."

"Ah, indeed! and you have not been tempted by the hopes of reputation yourself?"

"I should, my dear D'Artagnan, have been so, but nature said 'No.' When I am in the pulpit, if by chance, a pretty woman looks at me, I look at her again; if she smiles, I smile also. Then I speak at random; instead of preaching about the torments of hell, I talk of the joys of paradise. An event took place in the Church of St. Louis au Marais. A gentleman laughed in my face. I stopped short to tell him that he was a fool; the congregation went out to get stones to stone me with; but whilst they were away, I found means to conciliate the priests who were present, so that my foe was pelted instead of me. 'Tis true that he came the next morning to my house, thinking that he had to do with an abbé—like all other abbés."

"And what was the end of the affair?"

"We met in the Place Royale—Egad, you know about it."

"Was I not your second?" cried D'Artagnan.

"You were—you know how I settled the matter!"

"Did he die?"

"I don't know. But, at all events, I gave him absolution 'in articulo mortis.' 'Tis enough to kill the body, without killing the soul."

A long silence ensued after this disclosure. Aramis was the first to break it.

"What are you thinking of, D'Artagnan?" he began.

"I was thinking, my good friend, that when you were a Musketeer you turned your thoughts incessantly to the Church, and now that you are an Abbé you are perpetually longing to be a Musketeer."

"'Tis true—man, as you know," said Aramis, "is a strange animal, made up of contradictions. Since I became an abbé I dream of nothing but battles. I practise shooting all day long, with an excellent master whom we have here."

"How! here?"

"Yes, in this convent—we have always a 'maître d'armes' in a convent of Jesuits."

"Then you would have killed the Prince de Marsillac if he had attacked you singly?"

"Certainly," replied Aramis, "with the greatest ease."

"Well, dear Aramis, you ask me why I have been searching for you. I sought you, in order to offer you a way of killing Monsieur de Marsillac whenever you please—prince though he may be. Are you ambitious?"

"As ambitious as Alexander."

"Well, my friend, I bring you the means of being rich, powerful, and free, if you wish. Have you, my dear Aramis, thought sometimes of those happy days of our youth that we passed laughing, and drinking, and fighting each other for play?"

"Certainly—and more than once regretted them—'twas a happy time."

"Well, these happy days may return; I am commissioned to find out my companions, and I began by you—who were the very soul of our society."

Aramis bowed rather with respect than pleasure at the compliment.

"To meddle in politics," he exclaimed, in a languid voice, leaning back in his easy chair. "Ah! dear D'Artagnan! see how regularly I live—and how easy I am here. We have experienced the ingratitude of 'the great,' as you know."

"'Tis true," replied D'Artagnan. "Yet the great sometimes repent of their ingratitude."

"In that case, it would be quite another thing. Come! let's be merciful to every sinner; besides, you are right in another respect, which is, in thinking that if we were to meddle in politics, there could not be a better time than this."

"How can you know that? You would never interest yourself in politics?"

"Ah? without caring about them myself, I live among those who are much occupied in them. Poet as I am, I am intimate with Sarazin—who is devoted to the Prince de Conti, and with Monsieur de Bois-Robert, who, since the death of Cardinal Richelieu, is of all or any party, so that political discussions have not altogether been uninteresting to me."

"I have no doubt of it," said D'Artagnan.

"Now, my dear friend, don't look upon all I tell you as merely the statement of a monk—but of a man who resembles an echo —repeating simply what he hears. I understand that Mazarin is, at this very moment, extremely uneasy as to the state of affairs; that his orders are not respected like those of our former bugbear, the deceased Cardinal, whose portrait you see here;—for whatever may be thought of him, it must be allowed that Richelieu was a great man."

"I shall not contradict you there," said D'Artagnan.

"My first impressions were favourable to the minister; but, as I am very ignorant of those sort of things, and as the humility which I profess obliges me not to rest on my own judgment, but to ask the opinion of others, I have inquired—Eh?—my friend——"

Aramis paused.

"Well?—what?" asked his friend.

"Well—I must mortify myself. I must confess that I was mistaken; Monsieur de Mazarin is not a man of genius, as I thought: he is a man of no origin—once a servant of Cardinal Bentivoglio, and he got on by intrigue. He is an upstart, a man of no name, who will only be the tool of a party in France. He will amass wealth, he will injure the king's revenue, and pay to himself the pensions which Richelieu paid to others. He is neither a gentleman in manner nor in feeling, but a sort of buffoon, a punchinello, a pantaloon. Do you know him?—I do not?"

"Hem!" said D'Artagnan, "there is some truth in what you say, —but you speak of him, not of his party, nor of his resources."

"It is true—the queen is for him."

—"Something in his favour."

"But he will never have the king."

—"A mere child."

"A child who will be of age in four years. Then he has neither the parliament nor the people with him—they represent the wealth of the country; nor the nobles, nor the princes—who are the military power of France; but perhaps I am wrong in speaking thus to you, who have evidently a leaning to Mazarin."

"I!" cried D'Artagnan, "not in the least."

"You spoke of a mission."

"Did I?—I was wrong then—no, I said what you say—there is a crisis at hand. Well! let's fly the feather before the wind, let us join with that side to which the wind will carry it, and resume our adventurous life. We were once four valiant knights—four hearts fondly united; let us unite again, not our hearts, which have never been severed, but our courage and our fortunes. Here's a good opportunity for getting something better than a diamond."

" You are right, D'Artagnan ; I held a similar project, but, as I have not your fruitful and vigorous imagination, the idea was suggested to me. Every one nowadays wants auxiliaries ; propositions have been made to me, and I confess to you frankly, that the Coadjutor has made me speak out."

" The Prince de Conti ! the Cardinal's enemy ?"

" No !—the king's friend."

" But the king is with Mazarin."

" He is, but not willingly—in appearance, not heart ; and that is exactly the snare that the king's enemies prepare for a poor child."

" Ah ! but this is, indeed, civil war which you propose to me, dear Aramis."

" War for the king."

" Yet the king will be at the head of the army on Mazarin's side."

" But his heart will be in the army commanded by the Duc de Beaufort."

" Monsieur de Beaufort ? He is at Vincennes."

" Did I name Monsieur de Beaufort ?" said Aramis.

" Monsieur de Beaufort or some one else. The prince, perhaps. But Monsieur de Conti is going to be made a Cardinal."

" Are there not warlike Cardinals ?" said Aramis.

" Do you see any great advantage in adhering to this party ?" asked D'Artagan.

" I foresee in it the aid of powerful princes."

—" With the enmity of the government."

" Counteracted by parliament and insurrections."

" That may be done, if they can separate the king from his mother."

" That may be done," said Aramis.

" Never !" cried D'Artagnan. " You, Aramis, know Anne of Austria better than I do. Do you think she will ever forget that her son is her safeguard, her shield, the pledge for her dignity, for her fortune, for her life ? Should she forsake Mazarin she must join her son, and go over to the prince's side ; but you know better than I do that there are certain reasons why she can never abandon Mazarin."

" Perhaps you are right," said Aramis thoughtfully ; " therefore I shall not pledge myself."

" To them, or to us, do you mean, Aramis ?"

" To no one."

" I am a priest," resumed Aramis. " What have I to do with politics ? I am not obliged to read any breviary. I have a little circle of holy abbés and pretty women; everything goes on smoothly; so certainly, dear friend, I shall not meddle in politics."

" Well, listen, my dear Aramis," said D'Artagnan; "your philosophy convinces me, on my honour. I don't know what devil of an insect stung me, and made me ambitious. I have a post by which I live; at the death of Monsieur de Treville, who is old, I may be a captain, which is a very pretty position for a poor Gascon. Instead of running after adventures, I shall accept an invitation from Porthos; I shall go and shoot on his estate. You know he has estates,—Porthos ?"

" I should think so, indeed. Ten leagues of wood, of marsh land and valleys; he is lord of the hill and the plain, and is now carrying on a suit for his feudal rights against the bishop of Noyon !"

" Good," said D'Artagnan to himself. " That's what I wanted to know. Porthos is in Picardy !"

Then aloud,—

" And he has taken his ancient name of Valon ?"

—" To which he adds that of Bracieux—an estate which has been a barony, by my troth."

" So that Porthos will be a baron."

" I don't doubt it. The 'Baroness Porthos' will be particularly charming."

And the two friends began to laugh.

" So," D'Artagnan resumed, "you will not become a partisan of Mazarin's."

—" Nor you of the Prince de Condé ?"

" No, lovers belong to no party, but remain friends; let us be neither Cardinalists nor Frondists."

" Adieu, then." And D'Artagnan poured out a glass of wine.

" To old times," he said.

" Yes," returned Aramis. " Unhappily those times are passed."

" Nonsense ! They will return," said D'Artagnan. " At all events, if you want me, remember the Rue Ticquetonne, hotel de la Chevrette."

—" And I shall be at the convent of Jesuits, from six in the morning to eight at night come by the door. From eight in the evening until six in the morning come in by the window. Go then, my friend," he added, " follow your career; Fortune smiles on you; do not let her flee from you. As for me, I remain in my humility and my indolence. Adieu!"

"Thus, 'tis quite decided," said D'Artagnan, "that what I have to offer you does not suit you?"

"On the contrary, it would suit me were I like any other man," rejoined Aramis, "but, I repeat, I am made up of contradictions. What I hate to-day, I adore to-morrow, and vice versâ. You see, that I cannot, like you for instance, settle on any fixed plan."

"Thou liest, subtle one," said D'Artagnan to himself. "Thou alone, on the contrary, knowest how to choose thy object, and to gain it stealthily."

The friends embraced. They descended into the plain by the ladder. Planchet met them close by the shed. D'Artagnan jumped on his saddle, then the old companions in arms again shook hands. D'Artagnan and Planchet spurred on their horses and took the road to Paris.

But after he had gone about two hundred steps, D'Artagnan stopped short, alighted, threw the bridle of his horse over the arm of Planchet, and took the pistols from his saddle-bow to fasten them to his girdle.

"What's the matter?" asked Planchet.

"This is the matter; be he ever so cunning, he shall never say that I was his dupe. Stand here, don't stir, turn your back to the road, and wait for me."

Having thus spoken, D'Artagnan cleared the ditch by the road side, and crossed the plain so as to wind round the village. He had observed between the house that Madame de Longueville inhabited and the convent of Jesuits, an open space surrounded by a hedge.

The moon had now risen, and he could see well enough to re-trace his road.

He reached the hedge, and hid himself behind it; in passing by the house where the scene which we have related took place, he remarked that the window was again lighted up, and he was convinced that Aramis had not yet returned to his own apartment, and that when he did return there, it would not be alone.

In truth, in a few minutes he heard steps approaching, and low whispers.

—Close to the hedge the steps stopped.

D'Artagnan knelt down near the thickest part of the hedge.

Two men—to the astonishment of D'Artagnan—appeared shortly: soon, however, his surprise vanished, for he heard the murmurs of a soft, harmonious voice; one of these two men was a woman disguised as a cavalier.

"Calm yourself, dear Réné," said the soft voice, "the same thing will never happen again. I have discovered a sort of subterranean passage which runs under the street, and we shall only have to raise one of the marble slabs before the door to open you an entrance and an outlet."

"Oh!" answered another voice, which D'Artagnan soon recognised as that of Aramis. "I swear to you, princess, that your reputation does not depend on precautions, and that I would risk my life rather than——"

"Yes, yes! I know you are brave and venturesome as any man in the world, but you do not belong to me alone; you belong to all our party. Be prudent! be sensible!"

"I always obey, madam, when I am commanded by so gentle a voice."

He kissed her hand tenderly.

"Ah!" exclaimed the cavalier with the soft voice.

"What's the matter?" asked Aramis.

"Do you not see that the wind has blown off my hat?"

Aramis rushed after the fugitive hat. D'Artagnan took advantage of the circumstance to find a place in the hedge not so thick, where his glance could penetrate to the supposed cavalier. At that instant, the moon, inquisitive, perhaps, like D'Artagnan, came from behind a cloud, and by her light D'Artagnan recognised the large blue eyes, the golden hair, and the classic head of the Duchesse de Longueville.

Aramis returned, laughing; one hat on his head, and the other in his hand; and he and his companion resumed their walk towards the convent.

"Good!" said D'Artagnan, rising and brushing his knees; "now I have thee—thou art a Frondeur, and the lover of Madame de Longueville."

CHAPTER X.

MONSIEUR PORTHOS DE VALON DE BRACIEUX DE PIERREFONDS.

THANKS to what Aramis had told him, D'Artagnan, who knew already that Porthos called himself de Valon, was now aware that he styled himself, from his estate, De Bracieux; and that he was, on account of this estate, engaged in a lawsuit with the bishop of Noyon.

At eight o'clock in the evening, he and Planchet again left the hotel of the Chevrette, quitting Paris by the Porte Saint Denis.

Their route lay through Daumartin—and then, taking one of two roads that branched off—to Compiègne, when it was necessary to inquire the situation of the estate of Bracieux.

They travelled always at night; and having learned at Villars-Cotterets that Porthos was at the property which he had lately bought, called Pierrefonds, they set out, taking the road which leads from Villars-Cotterets to Compiègne.

The morning was beautiful; and in this early spring-time the birds sang on the trees, and the sunbeams shone through the misty glades, like curtains of golden gauze.

In other parts of the forest the light could scarcely penetrate through the foliage; and the stems of two old oak-trees—the refuge of the squirrel, startled by the travellers—were in deep shadow.

There came up from all nature in the dawn of day a perfume of herbs, flowers, and leaves, which delighted the heart. D'Artagnan, sick of the closeness of Paris, thought that when a man had three names of his different estates joined one to another, he ought to be very happy in such a paradise; then he shook his head, saying, "If I were Porthos, and D'Artagnan came to make to me such a proposition as I am going to make to him, I know what I should say to it."

As to Planchet, he thought of nothing.

At the extremity of the wood D'Artagnan perceived the road which had been described to him; and at the end of the road he saw the towers of an immense feudal castle.

"Oh! oh!" he said, "I fancied this castle belonged to the ancient branch of Orleans. Can Porthos have negotiated for it with the Duc de Longueville?"

—"Faith!" exclaimed Planchet, "here's land in good condition; if it belongs to Monsieur Porthos, I shall wish him joy."

"Zounds!" cried D'Artagnan, "don't call him Porthos, nor even Valon: call him De Bracieux or De Pierrefonds; thou wilt ruin my mission otherwise."

As he approached the castle, which had first attracted his eye, D'Artagnan was convinced that it could not be there that his friend dwelt: the towers, though solid, and as if built yesterday, were open and broken. One might have fancied that some giant had cloven them with blows from a hatchet.

On arriving at the extremity of the castle, D'Artagnan found himself overlooking a beautiful valley, in which, at the foot of a charming little lake, stood several scattered houses, which, humble in their aspect, and covered, some with tiles and others with thatch, seemed to acknowledge as their sovereign lord a pretty château, built about the beginning of the reign of Henry IV., and surmounted by some stately weathercocks. D'Artagnan felt now no doubt of this being the dwelling of Porthos.

The road led straight up to this château, which, compared to its ancestor on the hill, was exactly what a fop of the coterie of the Duc d'Enghien would have been beside a knight in steel armour in the time of Charles VI. D'Artagnan spurred his horse on and pursued his road, followed by Planchet at the same pace.

In ten minutes D'Artagnan reached the end of an alley regularly planted with fine poplars, and terminating in an iron gate, the points and crossed bars of which were gilt. In the midst of this avenue was a nobleman dressed in green, and with as much gilding about him as the iron gate, riding on a tall horse. On his right hand and his left were two footmen, with the seams of their dresses laced. A considerable number of clowns were assembled, and rendered homage to their lord.

"Ah!" said D'Artagnan to himself, "can this be the Seigneur du Valon de Bracieux de Pierrefonds? Well-a-day! how he is wrinkled since he has given up the name of Porthos!"

"This cannot be Monsieur Porthos," observed Planchet, replying, as it were, to his master's thoughts. "Monsieur Porthos was six feet high; this man is scarcely five."

"Nevertheless," said D'Artagnan, "the people are bowing very low to this person."

As he spoke he rode towards the tall horse—to the man of importance and his valets. As he approached he seemed to recognise the features of this individual.

"Jesu!" cried Planchet, "can it be he?"

At this exclamation the man on horseback turned slowly, and with a lofty air; and the two travellers could see, displayed in all their brilliancy, the large eyes, the vermilion visage, and the eloquent smile of Mousqueton.

It was, indeed, Mousqueton—Mousqueton, as fat as a pig, rolling about with rude health, puffed out with good living, who, recognising D'Artagnan, and acting very differently from the hypocrite Bazin, slipped off his horse and approached the officer with his hat off; so that the homage of the assembled crowd was turned towards this new sun, which eclipsed the former luminary.

"Monsieur d'Artagnan! Monsieur d'Artagnan!" cried Mousqueton, his fat cheeks swelling out, and his whole frame perspiring with joy. "Monsieur d'Artagnan! oh! what joy for my lord and master De Valon de Bracieux de Pierrefonds!"

"Thou good Mousqueton! where is thy master?"

"You are on his property."

"But how handsome thou art—how fat! how thou'st prospered and grown stout!" and D'Artagnan could not restrain his astonishment at the change which good fortune had produced upon the once famished one.

"Hey? yes, thank God, I am pretty well," said Mousqueton.

"But dost thou say nothing to thy friend Planchet?"

"How? my friend Planchet? Planchet, art thou there?" cried Mousqueton, with open arms and eyes full of tears.

"My very self," replied Planchet; "but I wanted first to see if thou wert grown proud."

"Proud towards an old friend? never, Planchet! thou would'st not have thought so hadst thou known Mousqueton well."

"So far so well," answered Planchet, alighting, and extending his arms to Mousqueton, and the two servants embraced with an emotion which touched those who were present, and made them suppose that Planchet was a great lord in disguise, so greatly did they estimate the position of Mousqueton.

"And now, sir," resumed Mousqueton, when he had rid himself of Planchet, who had in vain tried to clasp his hands round his friend's back, "now, sir, allow me to leave you, for I could not permit my master to hear of your arrival from any one but myself; he would never forgive me for not having preceded you."

"This dear friend," said D'Artagnan, carefully avoiding to utter either the former name borne by Porthos, or his new one; "then he has not forgotten me?"

"Forgotten! he!" cried Mousqueton; "there's not a day, sir, that we don't expect to hear that you were made marshal, either instead of Monsieur de Gassion or of Monsieur de Bassompierre."

On D'Artagnan's lips there played one of those rare and melancholy smiles which seemed to come from the depth of his heart; the last trace of youth and happiness which had survived disappointment.

"And you—fellows," resumed Mousqueton, "stay near Monsieur le Comte d'Artagnan, and pay him every attention in your power, whilst I go to prepare my lord for his visit."

And mounting his horse, Mousqueton rode off down the avenue, on the grass, in an easy gallop.

"Ah! there!—there's something promising," said D'Artagnan. "No mysteries, no cloak to hide one's self in—no cunning policy here; people laugh outright, they weep for joy here. I see nothing but faces a yard broad; in short, it seems to me that Nature herself wears a holiday suit, and that the trees, instead of leaves and flowers, are covered with red and green ribbons, as on gala days."

"As for me," said Planchet, "I seem to smell from this place even a most delectable smell of roast meat, and to see the scullions in a row by the hedge, hailing our approach. Ah! sir, what a cook must Monsieur Pierrefonds have, when he was so fond of eating and drinking, even whilst he was only called Monsieur Porthos!"

"Say no more!" cried D'Artagnan. "If the reality corresponds with appearances, I'm lost; for a man so well off will never change his happy condition;—and I shall fail with him, as I have already done with Aramis."

CHAPTER XI.

HOW D'ARTAGNAN, IN DISCOVERING THE RETREAT OF PORTHOS, PERCEIVES THAT WEALTH DOES NOT PRODUCE HAPPINESS.

D'ARTAGNAN passed through the iron gate, and arrived in front of the château. He alighted,—as he saw a species of giant on the steps. Let us do justice to D'Artagnan; that, independent of every selfish wish, his heart palpitated with joy when he saw that tall form and martial demeanour, which recalled to him a good and brave man.

He ran to Porthos and threw himself into his arms; the whole body of servants, arranged in a circle at a respectful distance, looked on with humble curiosity. Mousqueton, at the head of them, wiped his eyes. Porthos put his arm in that of his friend.

"Ah! how delightful to see you again, dear friend," he cried, in a voice which was now changed from a baritone into a bass; "you've not then forgotten me?"

"Forgot you! oh! dear De Valon, does one forget the happiest days of one's youth—one's dearest friends—the dangers we have dared together? on the contrary, there is not an hour that we have passed together that is not present to my memory."

"Yes, yes," said Porthos, trying to give to his moustache a curl which it had lost whilst he had been alone. "Yes, we did some fine things in our time, and we gave that poor Cardinal some thread to unravel."

And he heaved a sigh.

"Under any circumstances," he resumed, "you are welcome, my dear friend; you will help me to recover my spirits; to-morrow we will hunt the hare on my plain, which is a superb tract of land, or we'll pursue the deer in my woods, which are magnificent. I have four harriers, which are considered the swiftest in our county, and a pack of hounds which are unequalled for twenty leagues round."

And Porthos heaved another sigh.

"But first," interposed D'Artagnan, "you must present me to Madame de Valon."

A third sigh from Porthos.

"I lost Madame de Valon two years ago," he said, "and you find me still in affliction on that account. That was the reason why I left my Château de Valon, near Corbeil, and came to my estate, Bracieux. Poor Madame de Valon!• her temper was uncertain, but she came at last to accustom herself to my ways and to understand my little wishes."

"So, you are free now—and rich?"

"Alas!" replied Porthos, "I am a widower, and have forty thousand francs a-year. Let us go to breakfast."

"I shall be happy to do so; the morning air has made me hungry."

"Yes," said Porthos, "my air is excellent."

They went into the château; there was nothing but gilding, high and low; the cornices were gilt, the mouldings were gilt, the legs and arms of the chairs were gilt. A table, ready set out, awaited them.

"You see," said Porthos, "this is my usual style."

"Devil take me!" answered D'Artagnan, "I wish you joy of it. The king has nothing like this."

"No," answered Porthos; "I hear it said that he is very badly fed by the Cardinal, Monsieur de Mazarin. Taste this cutlet, my dear D'Artagnan; 'tis off one of my sheep."

"You have very tender mutton, and I wish you joy of it," said D'Artagnan.

"Yes, the sheep are fed in my meadows, which are excellent pasture."

"Give me another cutlet."

"No, try this hare, which I had killed yesterday in one of my warrens."

"Zounds! what a flavour!" cried D'Artagnan; "ah! they are fed on thyme only, your hares."

"And how do you like my wine?" asked Porthos; "it is pleasant, isn't it?"

"Capital."

"It's nothing, however, but a wine of the country."

"Really."

"Yes, a small declivity to the south, yonder, on my hill, gives me twenty hogsheads."

"Quite a vineyard, hey?"

Porthos sighed for the fifth time—D'Artagnan had counted his sighs. He became curious to solve the problem.

"Well, now," he said, "it seems, my dear friend, that something vexes you; you are ill, perhaps? That health, which——"

"Excellent, my dear friend; better than ever. I could kill an ox with a blow of my fist."

"Well, then, family affairs, perhaps?"

"Family! I have, happily, only myself in the world to care for."

"But what makes you sigh?"

"My dear fellow," replied Porthos; "to be candid with you, I am not happy."

"You not happy, Porthos? You, who have a château, meadows, hills, woods—you who have forty thousand francs a-year—you not happy?"

"My dear friend all those things I have, but I am alone in the midst of them."

"Surrounded, I suppose, only by clod-hoppers, with whom you could not associate."

Porthos turned rather pale, and drank off a large glass of wine.

"No; but just think, there are paltry country squires who have all some title or another, and pretend to go back as far as Charlemagne, or at least to Hugh Capet. When I first came here, being the last comer, it was to me to make the first advances. I made them, but, you know, my dear friend, Madame de Valon——"

Porthos, in pronouncing these words, seemed to gulp down something.

"Madame de Valon was of doubtful gentility. She had in her first marriage (I don't think, D'Artagnan, I am telling you anything new) married a lawyer; they thought that 'nauseous;' you can understand that's a word bad enough to make one kill thirty thousand men. I have killed two, which has made people hold their tongues, but has not made me their friend. So that I have no society—I live alone: I am sick of it—my mind preys on itself."

D'Artagnan smiled. He now saw where the breastplate was weak, and prepared the blow.

"But now," he said, "that you are a widower, your wife's connections cannot injure you."

"Yes, but understand me; not being of a race of historic fame, like the De Coucys, who were content to be plain sirs, or the Rohans, who didn't wish to be dukes, all these people, who are all either vicomtes or comtes, go before me at church, in all the ceremonies, and I can say nothing to them. Ah! if I were merely a —"

"A baron, don't you mean?" cried D'Artagnan, finishing his friend's sentence.

"Ah!" cried Porthos; "would I were but a baron!"

"Well, my friend, I am come to give you this very title, which you wish for so much."

Porthos gave a jump which shook all the room; two or three bottles fell and were broken. Mousqueton ran thither, hearing the noise.

Porthos waved his hand to Mousqueton to pick up the bottles.

"I am glad to see," said D'Artagnan, "that you have still that honest lad with you."

"He's my steward," replied Porthos; "he will never leave me. Go away now, Mouston."

"So he's called Mouston," thought D'Artagnan; "'tis too long a word to pronounce, Mousqueton."

"Well," he said aloud, "let us resume our conversation later— your people may suspect something—there may be spies about. You can suppose, Porthos, what I have to say relates to important matters."

"Devil take them, let us walk in the park," answered Porthos, "for the sake of digestion."

"Egad," said D'Artagnan, "the park is like everything else, and there are as many fish in your pond as rabbits in your warren; you're a happy man, my friend, since you have retained your love of the chase, and acquired that of fishing."

"My friend," replied Porthos, "I leave fishing to Mousqueton —it is a vulgar pleasure; but I shoot sometimes, that is to say, when I am dull, and I sit on one of those marble seats, have my gun brought to me, my favourite dog, and I shoot rabbits."

"Really, how very amusing!"

"Yes," replied Porthos, with a sigh; "it *is* very amusing!"

D'Artagnan now no longer counted the sighs.

"However, what had you to say to me?" he resumed, "let us return to that subject."

"With pleasure," replied D'Artagnan; "I must, however, first frankly tell you that you must change your mode of life."

"How?"

"Go into harness again, gird on your sword, run after adventures, and leave, as in old times, a little of your fat on the roadside."

" Ah ! hang it !" said Porthos.

" I see you are spoiled, dear friend, you are corpulent, your arm has no longer that movement of which the late Cardinal's Guards had so many proofs."

" Ah ! my fist is strong enough, I swear," cried Porthos, extending a hand like a shoulder of mutton.

" So much the better."

" Are we then to go to war ?"

" By my troth, yes."

" Against whom ?"

" Are you a politician, my friend ?"

" Not in the least."

" Are you for Mazarin, or for the princes ?"

" I am for no one."

" That is to say you are for us. Well, I tell you that I come to you from the Cardinal."

This speech was heard by Porthos in the same sense as if it had still been in the year 1640, and related to the true Cardinal.

" Ho ! ho ! what are the wishes of his Eminence ?"

" He wishes to have you in his service. Rochefort has spoken of you—and since, the queen—and, to inspire us with confidence, she has even placed in Mazarin's hands that famous diamond— you know about it—that I had sold to Monsieur des Essarts, and of which I don't know how she regained possession."

" But it seems to me," said Porthos, " that she would have done much better to give it back to you."

" So I think," replied D'Artagnan ; " but kings and queens are strange beings, and have odd fancies ; nevertheless, since it is they who have riches and honours, one is devoted to them."

" Yes, one is devoted to them," repeated Porthos ; " and you, to whom are you devoted, now ?"

" To the king, the queen, and to the Cardinal ; moreover, I have answered for your devotion also ; for, notwithstanding your forty thousand francs a-year, and, perhaps, even for the very reason that you have forty thousand francs a-year, it seems to me that a little coronet would do well on your carriage, hey ?"

" Yes, indeed," said Porthos.

" Well, my dear friend, win it—it is at the point of our swords. We shall not interfere with each other—your object is a title ; mine, money. If I can get enough to rebuild Artagnan, which my ancestors impoverished by the Crusades, allowed to fall into ruins, and to buy thirty acres of land about it, it is all I wish. I shall retire, and die tranquilly there."

" For my part," said Porthos, " I wish to be made a baron."

"You shall be one."

"And have you not seen any of our other friends?"

"Yes; I have seen Aramis."

"And what does he wish? To be a bishop?"

"Aramis," answered D'Artagnan, who did not wish to undeceive Porthos. "Aramis, fancy! has become a monk and a Jesuit, and lives like a bear. My offers could not rouse him."

"So much the worse! He was a clever man—and Athos?"

"I have not yet seen him. Do you know where I shall find him?"

"Near Blois. He is called Bragelonne. Only imagine, my dear friend. Athos, who was of as high birth as the Emperor, and who inherits one estate which gives him the title of Comte, what is he to do with all those dignities—Comte de la Fère, Comte de Bragelonne?"

"And he has no children with all these titles?"

"Ah!" said Porthos, "I have heard that he had adopted a young man who resembles him greatly."

"What, Athos? Our Athos, who was as virtuous as Scipio? Have you seen him?"

"No."

"Well, I shall see him to-morrow, and tell him about you; but I am afraid, 'entre nous,' that his liking for wine has aged and degraded him."

"Yes, he used to drink a great deal," replied Porthos.

"And then he was older than any of us," added D'Artagnan.

"Some years only. His gravity made him look older."

"Well, then, if we can get Athos, all will be well. If we cannot, we will do without him. We two are worth a dozen."

"Yes," said Porthos, smiling at the remembrance of his former exploits; "but we four, altogether, would be equal to thirty-six; more especially as you say the work will not be easy. Will it last long?"

"By'r lady—two or three years, perhaps."

"So much the better," cried Porthos. "You have no idea, my friend, how my bones ache since I came here. Sometimes, on a Sunday, I take a ride in the fields, and on the property of my neighbours, in order to pick up some nice little quarrel, which I am really in want of, but nothing happens. Either they respect or they fear me, which is more likely; but they let me trample down the clover with my dogs, insult and obstruct every one, and I come back still more weary and low-spirited—that's all. At any rate, tell me—there's more chance of fighting at Paris, is there not?"

"In that respect, my dear friend, it's delightful. No more

edicts, no more of the Cardinal's Guards, no more De Jussacs, nor other bloodhounds. I'Gad! underneath a lamp, in an inn, any-where, they ask, ' Are you one of the Fronde ?' They unsheathe, and that's all that is said. The Duke de Guise killed Monsieur de Coligny in the Place Royale, and nothing was said of it."

" Ah, things go on well, then," said Porthos.

" Besides which, in a short time," resumed D'Artagnan, " we shall have set battles, cannonades, conflagrations, and there will be great variety."

" Well, then, I decide."

" I have your word, then ?"

" Yes, 'tis given. I shall fight heart and soul for Mazarin; but——"

" But !"

" But he must make me a baron."

" Zounds !" said D'Artagnan, " that's settled already. I answer for your barony."

On this promise being given, Porthos, who had never doubted his friend's assurance, turned back with him towards the castle.

CHAPTER XII.

IN WHICH IT IS SHOWN THAT IF PORTHOS WERE DISCONTENTED WITH HIS CONDITION, MOUSQUETON WAS COMPLETELY SATIS-FIED WITH HIS.

As they returned towards the castle, D'Artagnan thought of the miseries of poor human nature, always dissatisfied with what it has, always desirous of what it has not.

In the position of Porthos, D'Artagnan would have been per-fectly happy; and, to make Porthos contented, there was wanting —what ?—five letters to put before his three names, and a little coronet to paint upon the panels of his carriage !

" I shall pass all my life," thought D'Artagnan, " in seeking for a man who is really contented with his lot."

Whilst making this reflection, chance seemed, as it were, to give him the lie direct. When Porthos had left him to give some orders, he saw Mousqueton approaching. The face of the steward, despite one slight shade of care, light as a summer cloud, seemed one of perfect felicity.

" Here is what I am looking for," thought D'Artagnan ; " but alas! the poor fellow does not know the purpose for which I am here."

He then made a sign for Mousqueton to come to him.

"Sir," said the servant, "I have a favour to ask you."

"Speak out, my friend."

"I am afraid to do so. Perhaps you will think, sir, that prosperity has spoiled me?"

"Art thou happy, friend?" asked D'Artagnan.

"As happy as possible; and yet, sir, you may make me even happier than I am."

"Well, speak, if it depends on me."

"Oh, sir! it depends on you only."

"I listen—I am waiting to hear."

"Sir, the favour I have to ask of you is, not to call me 'Mousqueton,' but 'Mouston.' Since I have had the honour of being my lord's steward, I have taken the last name as more dignified, and calculated to make my inferiors respect me. You, sir, know how necessary subordination is in an establishment of servants."

D'Artagnan smiled. Porthos lengthened out his names—Mousqueton cut his short.

"Well, my dear Mouston," he said, "rest satisfied. I will call thee Mouston; and, if it will make thee happy, I would not 'tutoyer' you any longer."

"Oh!" cried Mousqueton, reddening with joy; "if you do me, sir, such an honour, I shall be grateful all my life—'tis too much to ask."

D'Artagnan was secretly touched with remorse—not at inducing Porthos to enter into schemes in which his life and fortune would be in jeopardy—for Porthos, in the title of baron had his object and reward; but poor Mousqueton, whose only wish was to be called Mouston—was it not cruel to snatch him from the delightful state of peace and plenty in which he was?

He was thinking on these matters when Porthos summoned him to dinner.

Whilst dessert was on the table the steward came in to consult his master upon the proceedings of the next day, and also with regard to the shooting party which had been proposed.

"Tell me, Mouston," said Porthos—"are my arms in good condition?"

"Your arms, my lord—what arms?"

"Zounds!—my weapons."

"What weapons?"

"My military weapons."

" Yes, my lord—I think so, at any rate."

" Make sure of it; and if they want it, have them rubbed up. Which is my best cavalry horse?"

" Vulcan."

" And the best hack?"

" Bayard."

" What horse dost thou choose for thyself?"

" I like Rustand, my lord; a good animal, whose paces suit me."

" Strong, think'st thou?"

" Half Norman, half Mecklenburger—will go night and day."

" That will do for us. See to these horses. Clean up, or make some one else clean, my arms. Then take pistols with thee, and a hunting-knife."

" Are we then going to travel, my lord?" asked Mousqueton, rather uneasy.

" Something better still, Mouston."

" An expedition, sir?" asked the steward, whose roses began to change into lilies.

" We are going to return to the service, Mouston," replied Porthos, still trying to restore his moustache to the military curl that it had lost.

" Into the service—the king's service?" Mousqueton trembled; even his fat smooth cheeks shook as he spoke, and he looked at D'Artagnan with an air of reproach; he staggered, and his voice was almost choked.

" Yes and no. We shall serve in a campaign, seek out all sorts of adventures; return, in short, to our former life."

These last words fell on Mousqueton like a thunderbolt. It was these terrible former days which made the present so delightful; and the blow was so great that he rushed out, overcome, and forgot to shut the door.

The two friends remained alone to speak of the future, and to build castles in the air. The good wine which Mousqueton had placed before them gave to D'Artagnan a perspective shining with quadruples and pistoles, and showed to Porthos a blue ribbon and a ducal mantle; they were, in fact, asleep on the table when the servants came to beg them to go to bed.

Mousqueton was, however, a little consoled by D'Artagnan, who the next day told him that in all probability war would always be carried on in the heart of Paris, and within reach of the Château de Valon, which was near Corbeil; of Bracieux, which was near Melun; and of Pierrefonds, which was between Compiègne and Villars-Cotterets.

"But—formerly—it appears," began Mousqueton, timidly.

"Oh," said D'Artagnan, "we don't now make war as we did formerly. To-day it's a sort of diplomatic arrangement; ask Planchet."

Mousqueton inquired, therefore, the state of the case of his old friend, who confirmed the statement of D'Artagnan. "But," he added, "in this war prisoners stand a chance of being hung."

"The deuce they do!" said Mousqueton; "I think I should like the siege of Rochelle better than this war then!"

Porthos, meantime, asked D'Artagnan to give him his instructions how to proceed on his journey.

"Four days," replied his friend, "are necessary to reach Blois; one day to rest there; three or four days to return to Paris. Set out, therefore, in a week, with your suite, and go to the Hotel de la Chevrette, Rue Tiquetonne, and wait for me there."

"That's agreed," said Porthos.

"As to myself, I shall go round to see Athos; for though I don't think his aid worth much, one must, with one's friends, observe all due politeness," said D'Artagnan.

The friends then took leave of each other on the very border of the estate of Pierrefonds, to which Porthos escorted his friend.

"At least," D'Artagnan said to himself, as he took the road to Villars-Cotterets, "At least I shall not be alone in my undertaking. That devil, Porthos, is a man of immense strength; still, if Athos joins us, well—we shall be three of us to laugh at Aramis—that little coxcomb with his good luck."

At Villars-Cotterets he wrote to the Cardinal :—

"My Lord,

I have already one man to offer to your eminence, and he is well worth twenty men. I am just setting out for Blois. The Comte de la Fère inhabits the castle of Bragelonne, in the environs of that city."

CHAPTER XIII.

TWO ANGELIC FACES.

The road was long, but the horses upon which D'Artagnan and Planchet rode had been refreshed in the well-supplied stables of the Lord of Bracieux; the master and servant rode side by side, conversing as they went, for D'Artagnan had, by degrees, thrown off the master, and Planchet had entirely ceased to assume the manners of a servant. He had been raised by circumstances to the rank of a confidant to his master. It was many years since D'Artagnan had opened his heart to any one; it happened, however, that these two men, on meeting again, assimilated perfectly. Planchet was, in truth, no vulgar companion in these new adventures; he was a man of good sense. Without seeking danger, he never shrank from an attack; in short, he had been a soldier, and arms ennoble a man; it was, therefore, on the footing of friends, that D'Artagnan and Planchet arrived in the neighbourhood of Blois.

Going along, D'Artagnan, shaking his head, said:

"I know that my going to Athos is useless and absurd; but I owe this step to my old friend, a man who had·in him materials for the most noble and generous of characters."

"Oh, Monsieur Athos was a noble gentleman," said Planchet, "was he not? Scattering money about him as Heaven scatters hail. Do you remember, sir, that duel with the Englishman in the inclosure Des Carmes? Ah! how lofty, how magnificent Monsieur Athos was that day, when he said to his adversary, 'You have insisted on knowing my name, sir; so much the worse for you, since I shall be obliged to kill you.' I was near him, those were his exact words; when he stabbed his foe as he said he would, and his adversary fell without saying, Oh! 'Tis a noble gentleman —Monsieur Athos."

"Yes, true as Gospel," said D'Artagnan, "but one single fault has swallowed up all these fine qualities."

"I remember well," said Planchet—"he was fond of drinking— in truth he drank, but not as other men did. One seemed, as he raised the wine to his lips, to hear him say, 'Come, juice of the grape, and chase away my sorrows.' And how he used to break the stem of a glass, or the neck of a bottle! There was no one like him for that."

"And now," replied D'Artagnan, "behold the sad spectacle that awaits us. This noble gentleman, with his lofty glance, this handsome cavalier, so brilliant in feats of arms, that every one was surprised that he held in his hand a sword only instead of a baton of command! Alas! we shall find him changed into a bent-down old man, with red nose, and eyes that water; we shall find him extended on some lawn, whence he will look at us with a languid eye, and, perhaps, not recognise us. God knows, Planchet, that I should fly from a sight so sad, if I did not wish to show my respect for the illustrious shadow of what was once the Comte de la Fère, whom we loved so much."

Planchet shook his head and said nothing.

" And then," resumed D'Artagnan, " to this decrepitude is probably added poverty—for he must have neglected the little that he had, and the dirty scoundrel, Grimaud, more taciturn than ever, and still more drunken than his master—stay, Planchet, all this breaks my heart to think of."

" I fancy myself there, and that I see him staggering and hear him stammering," said Planchet, in a piteous tone, " but at all events, we shall soon know the real state of things, for I think those lofty walls, reddened by the setting sun, are the walls of Blois."

" Probably ; and yon steeples, pointed and sculptured, that we catch a glimpse of yonder, are like what I have heard described of Chambord."

At this moment one of those heavy waggons, drawn by bullocks, which carry the wood cut in the fine forests of the country to the ports of the Loire, came out of a bye-road full of ruts, and turned on that which the two horsemen were following. A man carrying a long switch with a nail at the end of it, with which he urged on his slow team, was walking with the cart.

" Ho ! friend," cried Planchet.

" What's your pleasure, gentlemen ?" replied the peasant, with a purity of accent peculiar to the people of that district, and which might have put to shame the polished dwellers near the Sorbonne and the Rue de l'Université.

" We are looking for the house of Monsieur de la Fère," said D'Artagnan.

The peasant took off his hat on hearing this revered name.

" Gentlemen," he said, " the wood that I am carting is his—I cut it in his copse, and am taking it to the château."

D'Artagnan determined not to question this man ; he did not wish to hear from another what he had himself said to Planchet.

" The château," he said to himself ; " what château ? Ah, I understand : Athos is not a man to be thwarted ; he has obliged his peasantry, as Porthos has done his, to call him ' my lord,' and to call his paltry place a château. He had a heavy hand—that dear Athos—after drinking."

D'Artagnan, after asking the man the right way, continued his route, agitated, in spite of himself, at the idea of seeing once more that singular man whom he had so truly loved, and who had contributed so much by his advice and example to his education as a gentleman. He slackened the pace of his horse, and went on, his head drooping as if in deep thought.

Soon as the road turned, the Château de la Vallière appeared in view, then, a quarter of a mile further, a white house, encircled in sycamores, was visible at the further end of a group of trees, which spring had powdered with a snow of flowers.

On beholding this house, D'Artagnan, calm as he was in general, felt an unusual disturbance within his heart—so powerful during the whole course of his life were the recollections of his youth. He proceeded, nevertheless, and came opposite to an iron gate, ornamented in the taste which marked the works of that period.

Through the gate were seen kitchen-gardens, carefully attended to, a spacious court-yard, in which neighed several horses held by valets in various liveries, and a carriage drawn by two horses of the country.

"We are mistaken," said D'Artagnan; "this cannot be the house of Athos. Good heavens! suppose he is dead, and that this property now belongs to some one who bears his name. Alight, Planchet, and inquire, for I confess I have not courage to do so."

Planchet alighted.

"Thou must add," said D'Artagnan, "that a gentleman who is passing by wishes to have the honour of paying his respects to the Comte de la Fère, and if thou art satisfied with what thou hearest, then mention my name!"

Planchet obeyed these instructions. An old servant opened the door and took in the message which D'Artagnan had ordered Planchet to deliver, in case that his servant was satisfied that this was the Comte de la Fère whom they sought. Whilst Planchet was standing on the steps before the house he heard a voice say:

"Well, where is this gentleman, and why do they not bring him here?"

This voice—the sound of which reached D'Artagnan—re-awakened in his heart a thousand sentiments, a thousand remembrances that he had forgotten. He sprang hastily from his horse, while Planchet, with a smile on his lips, was advancing towards the master of the house.

"But I know him—I know the lad yonder," said Athos, appearing on the threshold.

"Oh, yes—Monsieur le Comte, you know me, and I know you. I am Planchet—Planchet, whom you know well." But the honest servant could say no more, so much was he overcome by this unexpected interview.

"What, Planchet, is Monsieur D'Artagnan here?"

"Here I am, my friend, dear Athos?" cried D'Artagnan in a faltering voice, and almost staggering from agitation.

At these words a visible emotion was expressed on the beautiful countenance and calm features of Athos. He rushed towards D'Artagnan, with his eyes fixed upon him, and clasped him in his arms. D'Artagnan, equally moved, pressed him also closely to him, while tears stood in his eyes. Athos then took him by the hand and led him into the drawing-room, where there were several people. Every one rose.

"I present to you," he said, "Monsieur le Chevalier D'Artagnan, lieutenant of His Majesty's Musketeers, a devoted friend, and one of the most excellent and brave gentlemen that I have ever known."

D'Artagnan received the compliments of those who were present in his own way ; and whilst the conversation became general, he looked earnestly at Athos.

Strange ! Athos was scarcely aged at all ! His fine eyes, no longer surrounded by that dark line which nights of dissipation draw round them, seemed larger and more liquid than ever. His face, a little elongated, had gained in calm dignity what it had lost in feverish excitement. His hand, always wonderfully beautiful and strong, was set off by a ruffle of lace, like certain hands by Titian and Vandyck. He was less stiff than formerly. His long dark hair, scattered here and there with gray locks, fell elegantly over his shoulders with a wavy curl ; his voice was still youthful, as if at only twenty-five years old ; and his magnificent teeth, which he had preserved white and sound, gave an indescribable charm to his smile.

Meanwhile, the guests, seeing that the two friends were longing to be alone, prepared to depart, when a noise of dogs barking resounded through the court-yard, and many persons said, at the same moment :

"Ah ! 'tis Raoul who is come home."

Athos, as the name of Raoul was pronounced, looked inquisitively at D'Artagnan, in order to see if any curiosity was painted on his face. But D'Artagnan was still in confusion, and turned round almost mechanically, when a fine young man of fifteen years of age, dressed simply, but in perfect taste, entered the room, raising, as he came, his hat, adorned with a long plume of red feathers.

Nevertheless, D'Artagnan was struck by the appearance of this new personage. It seemed to explain to him the change in Athos ; a resemblance between the boy and the man explained the mystery of this regenerated existence. He remained listening and gazing.

"Here you are, home again, Raoul," said the Comte.

"Yes, sir," replied the youth, with deep respect, "and I have performed the commission that you gave me."

"But what's the matter, Raoul?" said Athos, very anxiously. "You are pale and agitated."

"Sir," replied the young man; "it is on account of an accident which has happened to our little neighbour."

"To Mademoiselle de la Vallière?" asked Athos, quickly.

"What is it?" asked many persons present.

"She was walking with her nurse Marceline, in the place where the woodmen cut the wood, when, passing on horseback, I stopped. She saw me also, and in trying to jump from the end of a pile of wood on which she had mounted, the poor child fell, and was not able to rise again. She has, I fear, sprained her ankle."

"Oh, Heavens!" cried Athos. "And her mother, Madame de Saint-Remy, have they told her of it?"

"No, sir; Madame de Saint-Remy is at Blois, with the Duchess of Orleans. I am afraid that what was first done was unskilful and useless. I am come, sir, to ask your advice."

"Send directly to Blois, Raoul; or rather take your horse, and ride there yourself."

Raoul bowed.

"But where is Louisa?" asked the Comte.

"I have brought her here, sir, and I have deposited her in the charge of Charlotte, who, till better advice comes, has put the foot into iced water."

The guests now all took leave of Athos, excepting the old Duke de Barbé, who, as an old friend of the family of La Vallière, went to see little Louisa, and offered to take her to Blois in his carriage.

"You are right, sir," said Athos. "She will be better with her mother. As for you, Raoul, I am sure it is your fault; some giddiness or folly."

"No, sir, I assure you," muttered Raoul, "it is not."

"Oh, no, no, I declare it is not!" cried the young girl, while Raoul turned pale at the idea of his being, perhaps, the cause of her disaster.

"Nevertheless, Raoul, you must go to Blois, and you must make your excuses and mine to Madame de Saint-Remy."

The youth looked pleased. He again took in his strong arms the little girl, whose pretty golden head and smiling face rested on his shoulder, and placed her gently in the carriage; then, jumping on his horse with the elegance and agility of a first-rate esquire, after bowing to Athos and D'Artagnan, he went off close by the door of the carriage, in the inside of which his eyes were incessantly riveted.

CHAPTER XIV.

THE CASTLE OF BRAGELONNE.

WHILE this scene was going on, D'Artagnan remained with open mouth and a confused gaze. Everything had turned out so differently to what he expected, that he was stupefied with wonder.

Athos, who had been observing him and guessing his thoughts, took his arm, and led him into the garden.

"Whilst supper is being prepared," he said, smiling, "you will not, my friend, be sorry to have the mystery which so puzzles you cleared up."

"True, Monsieur le Comte," replied D'Artagnan, who felt that by degrees Athos was resuming that great influence which aristocracy had over him.

Athos smiled.

"First and foremost, dear D'Artagnan, we have no title such as Count here. When I call you 'chevalier,' it is in presenting you to my guests, that they may know who you are. But to you, D'Artagnan, I am, I hope, still dear Athos, your comrade, your friend. Do you intend to be ceremonious because you are less attached to me than you were?"

"Oh! God forbid!"

"Then let us be as we used to be; let us be open to each other. You are surprised at what you see here?"

"Extremely."

"But above all things, *I* am a marvel to you?"

"I confess it."

"I am still young, am I not? Should you not have known me again, in spite of my eight-and-forty years of age?"

"On the contrary, I do not find you the same person at all."

"Ah, I understand," cried Athos, with a slight blush. "Everything, D'Artagnan, even folly, has its limit."

"Then your means, it appears, are improved; you have a capital house, your own, I presume? You have a park, horses, servants."

Athos smiled.

"Yes; I inherited this little property when I quitted the army, as I told you. The park is twenty acres—twenty, comprising kitchen gardens and a common. I have two horses—I don't count my servant's short-tailed nag. My sporting dogs consist of two pointers, two harriers, and two setters. And then all this extravagance is not for myself," added Athos, laughing.

"Yes, I see, for the young man Raoul," said D'Artagnan. .

"You guess right, my friend; this youth is an orphan, deserted by his mother, who left him in the house of a poor country priest. I have brought him up. It is he who has worked in me the change you see : I was dried up like a miserable tree, isolated, attached to nothing on earth; it was only a deep affection which could make me take root again, and bind me to life. This child has caused me to recover what I had lost. I had no longer any wish to live for myself. I have lived for him. I have corrected the vices that I had. I have assumed the virtues that I had not. Precept is much, example is more. I may be mistaken, but I believe that Raoul will be as accomplished a gentleman as our degenerate age could display."

The remembrance of *my lady* recurred to D'Artagnan.

"And you are happy?" he said to his friend.

"As happy as it is allowed to one of God's creatures to be on this earth; but say out all you think, D'Artagnan, for you have not done so."

".You are too bad, Athos; one can hide nothing from you," answered D'Artagnan. "I wished to ask you if you ever feel any emotions of terror resembling——"

"Remorse ! I finish your phrase—yes and no. I do not feel remorse, because that woman, I believe, deserved her punishment. I do not feel remorse, because, had we allowed her to live, she would have persisted in her work of destruction. But I do not mean, my friend, that we were right in what we did. Perhaps all blood that is shed demands an expiation. Hers has been accomplished; it remains, possibly, for us to accomplish ours."

"I have sometimes thought as you do, Athos."

"She had a son, that unhappy woman ?"

"Yes."

"Have you ever heard of him ?"

"Never."

"He must be about twenty-three years of age," said Athos, in a low tone. "I often think of that young man, D'Artagnan."

"Strange ! for I had forgotten him," said the lieutenant.

Athos smiled—the smile was melancholy.

"And Lord de Winter—do you know anything about him ?"

"I know that he is in high favour with Charles I."

"The fortunes of that monarch are now at a low ebb. He shed the blood of Strafford : that confirms what I said just now—blood will have blood : and the queen ?"

"Henrietta of England is at the Louvre ?"

"Yes, and I hear in the greatest poverty. Her daughter, during the bitterest cold, was obliged, for want of fire, to remain in bed. Why did she not ask from any one of us a home instead of from Mazarin? She should have wanted for nothing."

"Have you ever seen the Queen of England?" inquired D'Artagnan.

"No, but my mother, as a child, saw her. My mother was maid of honour to Marie de Medici."

At this instant they heard the sound of horses' feet.

"'Tis Raoul, who is come back," said Athos; "and we can now hear how the poor child is. Well," he added, "I hope the accident has been of no consequence?"

"They don't yet know, sir, on account of the swelling; but the doctor is afraid some muscle may be injured."

At this moment a little boy, half-peasant, half-footboy, came to announce supper.

Athos led his guest into a dining-room of moderate size, the windows of which opened on one side on a garden—on the other on a hothouse, full of magnificent flowers.

D'Artagnan glanced at the dinner-service. The plate was magnificent, old, and belonging to the family. D'Artagnan stopped to look at a sideboard, on which was a superb ewer of silver.

"That workmanship is divine!" he exclaimed.

"Yes, a chef-d'œuvre of the great Florentine sculptor, Benvenuto Cellini," replied Athos.

"What battle does it represent?"

"That of Marignan, just at the point where one of my forefathers is offering his sword to Francis I., who had broken his. It was on that occasion that my ancestor, Emguerrand de la Fère was made a Knight of the Order of St. Michael; besides which the king, fifteen years afterwards, gave him also this ewer, and a sword which you may have seen formerly in my house, also a beautiful specimen of workmanship. Men were giants in those times," said Athos; "now we are pigmies in comparison. Let us sit down to supper. Call Charles," he added, addressing the boy who waited.

"My good Charles, I particularly recommend to your care Planchet, the 'laquais' of Monsieur D'Artagnan. He likes good wine; now you have the key of the cellar—he has slept a long time on a hard bed, so he won't object to a soft one—take care of him, I beg of you." Charles bowed and retired.

"You think of everything," said D'Artagnan; "and I thank you for Planchet, my dear Athos."

Raoul stared on hearing this name, and looked at the count to be quite sure that it was he whom the lieutenant thus addressed.

"That name sounds strange to you," said Athos, smiling; "it was my 'nom de guerre,' when Monsieur D'Artagnan, two other gallant friends, and myself performed some feats of arms at the siege of La Rochelle, under the deceased Cardinal and Monsieur de Bassompierre. My friend is still so kind as to address me by that old and dear appellation, which makes my heart glad when I hear it."

"'Tis an illustrious name," said the lieutenant, "and had one day triumphal honours paid to it."

"What do you mean, sir?" inquired Raoul.

"You have not forgotten Saint Gervais, Athos, and the napkin which was converted into a banner;" and he then related to Raoul the story of the bastion, and Raoul fancied he was listening to one of those deeds of arms belonging to days of chivalry, and recounted by Tasso and Ariosto.

"D'Artagnan does not tell you, Raoul," said Athos, in his turn, "that he was reckoned one of the best swordsmen of his time—a knuckle of iron, a wrist of steel, a sure eye, and a glance of fire— that's what his adversary met with from him. He was eighteen, only three years older than you are, Raoul, when I saw him at this work—pitted against tried men."

"And was Monsieur D'Artagnan the conqueror?" said the young man, with glistening eyes.

"I killed one man, I believe," replied D'Artagnan, with a look of inquiry directed to Athos; "another I disarmed, or wounded. I don't remember which——"

"Wounded," said Athos; "oh! you were a strong one."

The young man would willingly have prolonged this conversation all night, but Athos pointed out to him that his guest must need repose. D'Artagnan would fain have declared that he was not fatigued; but Athos insisted on his retiring to his chamber, conducted thither by Raoul.

CHAPTER XV.

ATHOS AS A DIPLOMATIST.

D'ARTAGNAN retired to bed—not to sleep, but to think over all that he had heard that evening. As he was good-hearted, and had once had for Athos a liking, which had grown into a sincere friendship,

he was delighted at thus meeting a man full of intelligence and
of moral strength, instead of a wretched drunkard.   He admitted,
without annoyance, the continued superiority of Athos over himself, devoid as he was of that jealousy which might have saddened
a less generous disposition : he was delighted also that the high
qualities of Athos appeared to promise favourably for his mission.
Nevertheless, it seemed to him that Athos was not, in all respects,
sincere and frank.   Who was the youth whom he had adopted,
and who bore so great a resemblance to him?   What could
explain Athos' having re-entered the world, and the extreme sobriety
which he had observed at table?   The absence of Guimaud, whose
name had never once been uttered by Athos, gave D'Artagnan uneasiness.   It was evident either that he no longer possessed the
confidence of his friend, or that Athos was bound by some invisible
chain, or that he had been forewarned of the lieutenant's visit.

He could not help thinking of M. Rochefort, whom he had
seen in Nôtre Dame ;—could De Rochefort have preceded him
with Athos?   Again, the moderate fortune which Athos possessed,
concealed, as it was, so skilfully, seemed to show a regard for appearances, and to betray a latent ambition, which might be easily
aroused.   The clear and vigorous intellect of Athos would render
him more open to conviction than a less able man would be.   He
would enter into the minister's schemes with the more ardour,
because his natural activity would be doubled by a dose of
necessity.

Resolved to seek an explanation on all these points on the following day, D'Artagnan, in spite of his fatigue, prepared for an
attack, and determined that it should take place after breakfast.
He determined to cultivate the good will of the youth Raoul, and,
either whilst fencing with him, or in shooting, to extract from his
simplicity some information which would connect the Athos of old
times with the Athos of the present.   But D'Artagnan, at the same
time, being a man of extreme caution, was quite aware what injury
he should do himself, if, by any indiscretion or awkwardness,
he should betray his manœuvring to the experienced eye of Athos.
Besides, to say the truth, whilst D'Artagnan was quite disposed to
adopt a subtle course against the cunning of Aramis, or the vanity
of Porthos, he was ashamed to equivocate with Athos, the true-
hearted, open Athos.   It seemed to him that if Porthos and
Aramis deemed him superior to them in the arts of diplomacy,
they would like him all the better for it, but that Athos, on the
contrary, would despise him.

" Ah ! why is not Guimaud, the taciturn Guimaud, here?" thought

D'Artagnan; "there are things which his silence would have shown me—his silence was eloquence!"

There was now a perfect stillness in the house. D'Artagnan had heard the doors shut, and the shutters barred; then the dogs became, in their turn, silent. At last, a nightingale, lost in a thicket of shrubs, had dropped off in the midst of its most melodious cadences, and fallen asleep. Not a single sound was heard in the castle, except that of a footstep, up and down in the chamber above,—as he supposed, the bed-room of Athos.

"He is walking about, and thinking," thought D'Artagnan, "but of what? It is impossible to know; everything else might be guessed, but not that."

At length Athos went to bed, apparently, for the noise ceased.

Silence, and fatigue together, overcame D'Artagnan, and sleep overtook him also. He was not, however, a good sleeper. Scarcely had dawn gilded his window-curtains, than he sprang out of bed, and opened the windows. Somebody, he perceived, was in the court-yard, but moving stealthily. True to his custom of never passing anything over that it was within his power to know, D'Artagnan looked out of window, and perceived the close red coat and brown hair of Raoul.

The young man was opening the door of the stable. He then, with noiseless haste, took out the horse that he had ridden on the previous evening, saddled and bridled it himself, and led the animal into the alley to the right of the kitchen-garden, opened a side-door which conducted him to a bridle-road, shut it after him, and D'Artagnan saw him pass by like a dart, bending, as he went, beneath pendant flowery branches of the maple-trees and acacias. The road, as D'Artagnan had observed, was the way to Blois.

"So!" thought the Gascon, "here's a young blade who has already his love affair, who doesn't at all agree with Athos in his hatred to the fair sex. He's not going to hunt, for he has neither dogs nor arms; he's not going on a message, for he goes secretly. Why does he go in secret? Is he afraid of me, or of his father? for I am sure the count is his father. By Jove! I shall know about that soon, for I shall speak out to Athos."

Day was now advanced: all the noises that had ceased the night before were re-awakened, one after the other. The bird in the branches, the dog in his kennel, the sheep in the field, the boats which were moored in the Loire, even, seemed to be animated, and, leaving the shore, to abandon themselves to the current of the stream. The Gascon gave a last twist to his moustache, a last turn to his hair, brushed, from habit, the brim of his hat with the sleeve of his doublet, and went downstairs. Scarcely had he descended the last step of the threshold than he saw Athos, bent down towards the ground, as if he were looking for a crown-piece in the dust.

"Good morning, my dear host," cried D'Artagnan.

"Good day to you; have you slept well?"

"Excellently well, Athos; but what are you looking for? you are, perhaps, a tulip fancier?"

"My dear friend, if I were, you should not laugh at me for being so. In the country, people alter; one gets to like, without knowing it, all those beautiful objects that God causes to spring from the bottom of the earth, and which are despised in cities. I was looking anxiously for some iris roots which I planted here, close to this reservoir, and which some one has trampled upon this morning. These gardeners are the most careless people in the world: in bringing the horse out of the water, they've allowed him to walk over the border."

D'Artagnan began to smile.

"Ah! you think so, do you?"

And he took his friend along the alley, where a number of tracks, like those which had trampled down the flower-beds, were visible.

"Here are the horse's hoofs again, it seems, Athos," he said carelessly.

"Yes, indeed; the marks are recent."

"Quite so," replied the lieutenant.

"Who went out this morning?" Athos asked uneasily. "Has any horse got loose from the stable!"

"Not likely," answered the Gascon; "these marks are regular."

"Where is Raoul?" asked Athos; "how is it that I have not seen him?"

"Hush?" exclaimed D'Artagnan, putting his finger on his lips; and he related what he had seen, watching Athos all the while.

"Ah! he's gone to Blois; the poor boy——"

"To do what?"

"Ah! to inquire after little La Vallière; she has sprained her foot, you know."

"You think he is?"

"I am sure of it," said Athos; "don't you see that Raoul is in love?"

"Indeed! with whom? with a child of seven years old?"

"Dear friend, at Raoul's age the heart is so ardent that it must expand towards some object or another, fancied or real; well, his love is half one—half the other. She is the prettiest little creature in the world, with flaxen hair, blue eyes—at once saucy and languishing."

"But what say you to Raoul's fancy?"

"Nothing; I laugh at Raoul; but this first desire of the heart is imperious. I remember, just at his age, how in love I was with a Grecian statue, which our good king, then Henry IV., gave my father, insomuch that I was mad with grief when they told me that the story of Pygmalion was nothing but a fable."

"'Tis want of occupation; you do not make Raoul work, so he takes his own way of employing himself."

"Exactly so; therefore I think of sending him away from this place."

"You will be wise to do so."

"No doubt of it; but it will break his heart. So long as three or four years ago, he used to adorn and adore his little idol, whom he will some day fall in love with in good earnest, if he remains here. The parents of little La Vallière have for a long time perceived, and been amused at it; but now they begin to look grave about it."

"Nonsense! however, Raoul must be diverted from this fancy; send him away, or you will never make a man of him."

"I think I shall send him to Paris."

"So!" thought D'Artagnan; and it seemed to him that the moment for attack had arrived.

"Suppose," he said, "we chalk out a career for this young man. I want to consult you about something."

"Do so."

"Do you think it is time to enter into the service?"

"But are you not still in the service? you—D'Artagnan?"

"I mean into active service. Our former life—has it still no attractions for you? should you not be happy to begin anew in my society, and in that of Porthos, the exploits of our youth?"

"Do you propose to me to do so, D'Artagnan?"

"Decidedly and honestly."

"On whose side?" asked Athos, fixing his clear benevolent glance on the countenance of the Gascon.

"Ah! devil take it, you speak in earnest——"

"And must have a definite answer. Listen, D'Artagnan. There is but one person—or rather, one cause—to whom a man like me can be useful—that of the king."

"Exactly," answered the Musketeer.

"Yes, but let us understand each other," returned Athos, seri-

ously. " If by the cause of the king you mean that of Monsieur
de Mazarin, we do *not* understand each other."

" I don't say, exactly," answered the Gascon, confused.

" Come, D'Artagnan, don't let us play a cunning game; your
hesitation, your evasion, tell me at once on whose side you are;
for that party no one dares openly to recruit, and when people
recruit for it, it is with a downcast head and low voice."

" Ah ! my dear Athos !"

" You know that I am not alluding to you ; you are the pearl of
brave and bold men. I speak of that spiteful and intriguing
Italian—of the pedant who has tried to put on his own head a
crown which he stole from under a pillow—of the scoundrel who
calls his party the party of the king—who wants to send the princes
of the blood to prison, not daring to kill them, as our great Cardinal—our Cardinal did—of the miser who weighs his gold pieces,
and keeps the clipped ones for fear, though he is rich, of losing
them at play next morning—of the impudent fellow who insults
the queen, as they say—so much the worse for her—and who is
going, in three months, to make war upon us, in order that he may
retain his pensions—is that the master whom you propose to me ?
Thanks, D'Artagnan."

" You are more impetuous than you were," returned D'Artagnan.
" Age has warmed, not chilled, your blood. Who told you that
that was the master I proposed to you ? Devil take it," he muttered to himself, " don't let me betray my secrets to a man not
inclined to receive them well."

" Well, then," said Athos, " what are your schemes ? what do
you propose ?"

" Zounds ! nothing can be more natural; you live on your
estate, happy in your golden mediocrity. Porthos has, perhaps,
sixty thousand francs income. Aramis has always fifty duchesses
who are quarrelling for the priest, as they quarrelled formerly for
the musketeer; but I—what have I in the world ? I have worn
my cuirass for these twenty years, kept down in this inferior rank,
without going forwarder or backwarder, without living. In fact, I
am dead. Well ! when there is some idea of being resuscitated—
you say he's a scoundrel—an impudent fellow—a miser—a bad
master ! By Jove ! I'm of your opinion; but find me a better
one, or give me the means of living."

Athos was, for a few moments, thoughtful.

" Good ! D'Artagnan is for Mazarin," he said to himself.

From that moment he became very guarded.

On his side D'Artagnan was more cautious also.

"You spoke to me," Athos resumed, "of Porthos; have you persuaded him to seek his fortune? but he has wealth, I believe, already?"

"Doubtless he has; but such is man, that he always wants something."

"What does Porthos wish for?"

"To be a baron."

"Ah! true! I forgot," said Athos, laughing.

"'Tis true!" thought the Gascon, "where has he heard it? Does he correspond with Aramis? Ah! if I knew that he did, I should know all."

The conversation was interrupted by the entrance of Raoul.

"Is our little neighbour worse?" asked Athos, seeing a look of vexation on the face of the youth.

"Ah, sir!" replied Raoul, "her fall is a very serious one; and without any apparent injury, the physician fears that she will be lame for life."

"That is terrible," said Athos.

"And what makes me wretched, sir, is that I am the cause of this misfortune."

"There's only one remedy, dear Raoul—that is, to marry her as a compensation," remarked D'Artagnan.

"Ah, sir!" answered Raoul, "you joke about a real misfortune; that is cruel, indeed."

The good understanding between the two friends was not in the least altered by the morning's skirmish. They breakfasted with a good appetite, looking now and then at poor Raoul, who, with moist eyes and a full heart, scarcely ate at all.

After breakfast two letters arrived for Athos, who read them with deep attention; whilst D'Artagnan could not restrain himself from jumping up several times, on seeing him read these epistles, in one of which, having a very strong light, he perceived the fine writing of Aramis. The other was in a feminine hand, long and crossed.

"Come," said D'Artagnan to Raoul—seeing that Athos wished to be alone—"come, let us take a turn in the fencing-gallery, that will amuse you."

And they both went into a low room, where there were foils, gloves, masques, breast-plates, and all the accessories for a fencing match.

In a quarter of an hour Athos joined them; and, at the same moment, Charles brought in a letter for D'Artagnan, which a messenger had just desired might be instantly delivered.

It was now the turn of Athos to take a sly look.

D'Artagnan read the letter with apparent calmness, and said, shaking his head,—

"See, dear friend, what the army is; my faith, you are, indeed, right not to return to it. Monsieur de Tréville is ill—so my company can't do without me; there! my leave is at an end!"

"Do you go back to Paris?" asked Athos, quickly.

"Egad! yes; but why don't you come there also?"

Athos coloured a little, and answered,—

"Should I go, I shall be delighted to see you there."

"Hallo, Planchet!" cried the Gascon from the door, "we must set out in ten minutes; give the horses some hay."

Then turning to Athos, he added—

"I seem to miss something here. I am really sorry to go away without having seen Grimaud."

"Grimaud!" replied Athos. "I'm surprised you have never asked after him. I have lent him to a friend——"

"Who will understand the signs he makes," returned D'Artagnan.

"I hope so."

The friends embraced cordially; D'Artagnan pressed Raoul's hand.

"Will you not come with me?" he said; "I shall pass by Blois."

Raoul turned towards Athos, who showed him by a secret sign that he did not wish him to go.

"Adieu, then, to both, my good friends," said D'Artagnan; "may God preserve you! as we used to say when we said good-bye to each other in the late Cardinal's time."

Athos waved his hand, Raoul bowed, and D'Artagnan and Planchet set out.

The count followed them with his eyes—his hands resting on the shoulders of the youth, whose height was almost equal to his own; but, as soon as they were out of sight, he said,—

"Raoul—we set out to-night for Paris."

"How!" cried the young man, turning pale.

"You may go and offer your adieux and mine to Madame de Saint-Remy. I shall wait for you here till seven."

The young man bent low, with an expression of sorrow and gratitude mingled, and retired, in order to saddle his horse.

As to D'Artagnan, scarcely, on his side, was he out of sight, than he drew from his pocket a letter, which he read over again.

"Return immediately to Paris.—T. M."

"The epistle is laconic," said D'Artagnan; "and if there had not been a postscript, probably I should not have understood it; but, happily, there is a postscript."

And he read that famous postscript, which made him forget the abruptness of the letter.

" P.S.   Go to the king's treasurer at Blois ; tell him your name, and show him this letter, you will receive two hundred pistoles."

" Assuredly," said D'Artagnan ; " I like this piece of prose, and the Cardinal writes better than I thought.   Come, Planchet, let us pay a visit to the king's treasurer, and then set off."

" Towards Paris, sir ?"

" Towards Paris."

And both set out on as hard a trot as their horses could go.

CHAPTER XVI.

THE DUC DE BEAUFORT.

THE circumstances which had hastened the return of D'Artagnan to Paris were the following :—

One evening, when Mazarin, according to custom, went to visit the queen, in passing the guard-chamber he heard loud voices there ; wishing to know on what the soldiers were conversing, he approached, with his wonted stealthy and wolf-like step—pushed open the door, and put his head close to the chink.

There was a dispute among the guards.

" I tell you," one of them was saying, " that if Coysel predicted that, 'tis as good as true ; I know nothing about it, but I've heard say that he's not only an astrologer, but a magician."

" Deuce take it, friend—if he's one of thy friends, thou wilt ruin him in saying so."

" Why ?"

" Because he may be tried for it."

" Ah ! absurd ! they don't burn sorcerers nowadays."

" No ?   'Tis not a long time since the late Cardinal burnt Urban Grandier though."

" My friend Urban Grandier wasn't a sorcerer ; he was a learned man.   He didn't predict the future ; he knew the past—often a much worse thing."

Mazarin nodded an assent ; but wishing to know what the prediction was about which they disputed, he remained in the same place.

" I don't say," resumed the guard, " that Coysel is not a sorcerer —but I say that if his prophecy gets wind, it's a sure way to prevent its coming true."

"How so?"

"Why, in this way—if Coysel says, loud enough for the Cardinal to hear him, on such or such a day such a prisoner will escape, 'tis plain that the Cardinal will take measures of precaution, and that the prisoner will not escape."

"Good Lord!" said another guard, who appeared asleep on a bench, but who had not lost a syllable of the conversation, "do you suppose that men can escape their destiny? If it is written yonder, in heaven, that the Duc de Beaufort is to escape, he will escape; and all the precautions of the Cardinal will not hinder it."

Mazarin started. He was an Italian, and therefore superstitious. He walked straight into the midst of the guards, who, on seeing him, were silent.

"What were you saying?" he asked, with his flattering manner, "that Monsieur de Beaufort had escaped—did you not?"

"Oh, no, my lord!" said the incredulous soldier. "He's well guarded now; we said, only, that he would escape."

"Who said so?"

"Repeat your story, Saint Laurent," replied the man, turning to the originator of the tale.

"My lord," said the guard, "I have simply mentioned the pro-phecy that I heard from a man named Coysel, who believes that be he ever so closely guarded, the Duke of Beaufort will escape before Whitsuntide."

"Coysel is a madman!" returned the Cardinal.

"No," replied the soldier, tenacious in his credulity; "he has foretold many things which have come to pass—for instance, that the queen would have a son; that Monsieur de Coligny would be killed in a duel with the Duc de Guise; and finally, that the Coad-jutor would be made Cardinal. Well! the queen has not only one son, but two; then, Monsieur de Coligny was killed, and——"

"Yes," said Mazarin; "but the Coadjutor is not yet made a Cardinal!"

"No, my lord—but he will be," answered the guard.

Mazarin made a grimace, as if he meant to say—"But he does not yet wear the Cardinal's cap;" then he added:

"So, my friend, it's your opinion that Monsieur de Beaufort will escape?"

"That's my idea, my lord; and if your Eminence were to offer to make me at this moment governor of the castle of Vincennes, I should refuse it. After Whitsuntide it would be another thing."

There is nothing so convincing as a firm conviction. It has an effect upon the most incredulous; and, far from being incredulous,

Mazarin was superstitious. He went away thoughtful and anxious, and returned to his own room, where he summoned Bernouin, and desired him to fetch there the next morning the special guard whom he had placed near Monsieur de Beaufort, and to awaken him whenever he should arrive on the following morning.

The guard had, in fact, touched the Cardinal in the tenderest point. During the whole five years in which the Duc de Beaufort had been in prison, not a day had passed in which the Cardinal had not felt a secret dread of his escape. It was not possible, as he knew well, to confine for the whole of his life the grandson of Henry IV., especially when this young prince was scarcely thirty years of age. But, however and whensoever he did escape, what hatred he must have cherished against him to whom he owed his long imprisonment; who had taken him rich, brave, glorious, beloved by women, feared by men, to cast off from his life its happiest years; for it is not existence, it is merely life, in prison. Meantime, Mazarin redoubled the surveillance over the duke. But, like the miser in the fable, he could not sleep near his treasure. Often he awoke in the night, suddenly, dreaming that he had been robbed of Monsieur de Beaufort. Then he inquired about him, and had the vexation of hearing that the prisoner played, drank, sang—but that whilst playing, drinking, singing, he often stopped short, to vow that Mazarin should pay dear for all the amusements which he had forced him to enter into at Vincennes.

So much did this one idea haunt the Cardinal, even in his sleep, that when, at seven in the morning, Bernouin came to arouse him, his first words were :—"Well—what's the matter? Has Monsieur de Beaufort escaped from Vincennes?"

"I do not think so, my lord," said Bernouin ; "but you will hear about him, for La Ramée is here, and awaits the commands of your Eminence."

"Tell him to come in," said Mazarin, arranging his pillows, so that he might receive him sitting, in bed.

The officer entered—a large fat man, with a good physiognomy. His air of perfect serenity made Mazarin uneasy.

"Approach, sir," said the Cardinal.

The officer obeyed.

"Do you know what they are saying here?"

"No, your Eminence."

"Well, they say that Monsieur de Beaufort is going to escape from Vincennes, if he has not done so already."

The officer's face expressed complete stupefaction. He opened, at once his great eyes and his little mouth, to inhale better the joke that his Eminence deigned to address to him, and ended by a burst of laughter, so violent, that his great limbs shook in his hilarity as they would have done in a fever.

"Escape! my lord—escape! Your Eminence does not then know where Monsieur de Beaufort is?"

"Yes, I do, sir; in the donjon of Vincennes."

"Yes, sir; in a room, the walls of which are seven feet thick, with grated windows, each bar being as thick as my arm."

"Sir," replied Mazarin, "with perseverance one may penetrate through a wall—with a watch-spring one may saw through an iron bar."

"Then my lord does not know that there are eight guards about him—four in his chamber, four in the ante-chamber—and they never leave him."

"But he leaves the room, he plays at tennis at the Mall?"

"Sir, those amusements are allowed; but if your Eminence wishes it, we will discontinue the permission."

"No, no," cried Mazarin, fearing that should his prisoner ever leave his prison he would be the more exasperated against him, if he thus retrenched his amusements,—he then asked with whom he played.

"My lord—either with the officers of the guard, with the other prisoners, or with me."

"Hum;" said the Cardinal, beginning to feel more comfortable. "You mean to say, then, my dear Monsieur la Ramée——"

"That unless Monsieur de Beaufort can contrive to metamorphose himself into a little bird, I answer for him."

"Take care—you assert a great deal," said Mazarin. "M. de Beaufort told the guards who took him to Vincennes, that he had often thought what he should do in case he were put into prison, and that he had found out forty ways of escaping."

"My lord—if among these forty there had been one good way, he would have been out long ago."

"Come, come; not such a fool as I fancied!" thought Mazarin. "But when you leave him, for instance?"

"Oh! when I leave him! I have, in my stead, a bold fellow who aspires to be His Majesty's special guard. I promise you, he keeps a good watch over the prisoner. During the three weeks that he has been with me, I have only had to reproach him with one thing—being too severe with the prisoners."

"And who is this Cerberus?"

"A certain Monsieur Grimaud, my lord."

"And what was he before he went to Vincennes?"

"He was in the country, as I was told by the person who recommended him to me."

"And who recommended this man to you?"

"The steward of the Duc de Grammont."

"He is not a gossip, I hope?"

"Lord a-mercy, my lord! I thought for a long time that he was dumb; he answers only by signs. It seems his former master accustomed him to that. The fact is, I fancy he got into some trouble in the country from his stupidity, and that he wouldn't be sorry in the royal livery to find impunity."

"Well, dear Monsieur la Ramée," replied the Cardinal, "let him prove a firm and faithful keeper, and we will shut our eyes upon his rural misdeeds, and put on his back a uniform to make him respectable, and in the pockets of that uniform some pistoles to drink to the king's health."

Mazarin was large in his promises—quite different to the virtuous Monsieur Grimaud, so be-praised by La Ramée; for he said nothing, and did much.

It was now nine o'clock. The Cardinal, therefore, got up, perfumed himself, dressed, and went to the queen to tell her what had detained him. The queen, who was scarcely more afraid of Monsieur de Beaufort than she was of the Cardinal himself, and who was almost as superstitious as he was, made him repeat word for word all La Ramée's praises of his deputy. Then, when the Cardinal had ended,—

"Alas! sir! why have we not a Grimaud near every prince?"

"Patience!" replied Mazarin, with his Italian smile; "that may happen one day; but in the meantime——"

"Well! in the meantime?"

"I shall take precautions."

And he wrote to D'Artagnan to hasten his return.

CHAPTER XVII.

DESCRIBES HOW THE DUC DE BEAUFORT AMUSED HIS LEISURE HOURS IN THE DONJON OF VINCENNES.

THE captive, who was the source of so much alarm to the Cardinal, and whose means of escape disturbed the repose of the whole court, was wholly unconscious of the terrors which he caused in the Palais Royal.

He had found himself so strictly guarded, that he soon perceived the fruitlessness of any attempt at escape. His vengeance, therefore, consisted in uttering curses on the head of Mazarin ; he even tried to make some verses on him, but soon gave up the attempt. For Monsieur de Beaufort had not only not received from Heaven the gift of versifying, but he had even the greatest possible difficulty in expressing himself in prose.

The duke was the grandson of Henry IV. and of Gabrielle d'Estrees—as good-natured, as brave, as proud, and, above all, as Gascon as his ancestor, but less educated. After having been for some time, after the death of Louis XIII., the favourite, the confidant, the first man in short, at the court, he had been obliged to yield his place to Mazarin, and he became the second in influence and favour ; and, eventually, as he was stupid enough to be vexed at this change of position, the queen had had him arrested, and sent to Vincennes, in charge of Guitant, who made his appearance in these pages in the beginning of this history, and whom we shall see again. By the queen, means by Mazarin.

During the five years of his seclusion, which would have improved and matured the intellect of any other man, M. de Beaufort, had he not affected to brave the Cardinal, to despise princes, and to walk alone, without adherents or disciples, would either have regained his liberty, or made partisans. But these considerations never occurred to the duke, and every day the Cardinal received fresh accounts of him, which were as unpleasant as possible to the minister.

After having failed in poetry, Monsieur de Beaufort tried drawing. He drew portraits with a piece of coal, of the Cardinal ; and as his talents did not enable him to produce a very good likeness, he wrote under the picture, that there might be no doubt of the original—" Portrait of the Illustrious Coxcomb Mazarin." Monsieur de Chavigny, the governor of Vincennes, waited upon the duke, to request that he would amuse himself in some other way, or, that, at all events, if he drew likenesses, he would not put mottoes to them. The next day the prisoner's room was full of pictures and of mottoes. Monsieur de Beaufort, in common with many other prisoners, was bent upon doing things which were prohibited ; and the only resource which the governor had was, one day when the duke was playing at tennis, to efface all these drawings, consisting chiefly of profiles. M. de Beaufort did not venture to draw the Cardinal's fat face.

The duke thanked Monsieur de Chavigny for having, as he said, cleaned his drawing-paper for him ; he then divided the walls of his room into compartments, and dedicated each of these compartments to some incident in Mazarin's life. In one was depicted the "Illustrious Coxcomb" receiving a shower of blows from Cardinal Bentivoglio, whose servant he had been; another the "Illustrious Mazarin," acting the part of Ignatius Loyola in a tragedy of that name; a third, the "Illustrious Mazarin" stealing the portfolio of prime minister from Monsieur de Chavigny, who had expected to have it; a fourth, the "Illustrious Coxcomb Mazarin" refusing to give Laporte, the young king's valet, clean sheets; and saying that it was quite enough for the king of France to have sheets every three months.

The governor, of course, thought proper to threaten his prisoner that if he did not give up drawing such pictures, he should be obliged to deprive him of all means of amusing himself in that manner. To this Monsieur de Beaufort replied, that since every opportunity of distinguishing himself in arms was taken from him, he wished to make himself celebrated in the fine arts; since he could not be a Bayard, he would become a Raphael, or a Michael Angelo. Nevertheless, one day when Monsieur de Beaufort was walking in the meadow, his fire was put out; his coal taken away, and all means of drawing completely destroyed.

The poor duke swore, fell into a rage, yelled, and declared that they wished to starve him to death, as they had starved the Maréchal Ornano, and the Grand Prior of Vendôme; but he refused to promise that he would not make any more drawings, and remained without any fire in the room all the winter.

His next act was to purchase a dog from one of his keepers. With this animal, which he called Pistache, he was often shut up for hours alone, superintending, as every one supposed, its education. At last, when Pistache was sufficiently well trained, Monsieur de Beaufort invited the governors and officers of Vincennes to attend a representation which he was going to have in his apartment.

The party assembled; the room was lighted with wax-lights, and the prisoner, with a bit of plaster he had taken out of the wall of his room, had traced a long white line, representing a cord, on the floor. Pistache, on a signal from his master, placed himself on this line, raised himself on his hind paws, and holding in his front paws a wand with which clothes used to be beaten, he began to dance upon the line with as many contortions as a rope-dancer. Having been several times up and down it, he gave the wand back to his master, and began, without hesitation, to perform the same revolutions over again.

The intelligent creature was received with loud applause.

The first part of the entertainment being concluded, Pistache was desired to say what o'clock it was ; he was shown Monsieur de Chavigny's watch ; it was then half-past six. The dog raised and dropped his paw six times ; the seventh he let it remain up-raised. Nothing could be better done ; a sun-dial could not have shown the hour with greater precision.

Then the question was put to him who was the best gaoler in all the prisons of France ?

The dog performed three evolutions round the circle, and laid himself, with the deepest respect, at the feet of Monsieur de Chavigny, who at first seemed inclined to like the joke, and laughed loud ; but a frown soon succeeded, and he bit his lips with vexation.

Then the duke put to Pistache this difficult question : who was the greatest thief in the world ?

Pistache went again the round of the circle, but stopped at no one ; and, at last, went to the door, and began to scratch and bark.

"See, gentlemen," said M. de Beaufort, "this wonderful animal, not finding here what I asked for, seeks it out of doors ; you shall, however, have his answer. Pistache, my friend, come here. Is not the greatest thief in the world, Monsieur (the king's secretary) La Camus, who came to Paris with twenty francs in his pocket, and who now possesses six millions ?"

The dog shook his head.

"Then is it not," resumed the duke, "the Superintendent Emery, who gave his son, when he was married, three hundred thousand francs and a house, compared to which the Tuileries are a heap of ruins and the Louvre a paltry building ?"

The dog again shook his head, as if to say "no."

"Then," said the prisoner, "let's think who it can be. Can it be, can it possibly be, the illustrious coxcomb, Mazarin de Piscina, hey ?"

Pistache made violent signs that it was, by raising and lowering his head eight or ten times successively.

"Gentlemen, you see," said the duke to those present, who dared not even smile, "that it is the 'illustrious coxcomb' who is the greatest thief in the world ; at least, according to Pistache."

"Let us go on to another of his exercises.

"Gentlemen !"—there was a profound silence in the room when the duke again addressed them—"do you not remember that the Duc de Guise taught all the dogs in Paris to jump for Mademoi-

selle de Pons, whom he styled 'the fairest of the fair?' Pistache
is going to show you how superior he is to all other dogs. Monsieur de Chavigny, be so good as to lend me your cane. Now
Pistache, my dear, jump the height of this cane for Madame
Montbazon."

The dog found no difficulty in it, and jumped joyfully for
Madame de Montbazon.

"But," interposed M. de Chavigny, "it seems to me that Pistache is only doing what other dogs have done when they jumped
for Mademoiselle de Pons.

"Stop," said the duke; "Pistache, jump for the queen." And
he raised his cane six inches higher.

The dog sprang, and in spite of the height, jumped lightly
over it.

"And now," said the duke, raising it still six inches higher,
"jump for the king."

The dog obeyed, and jumped quickly over the cane.

"Now, then," said the duke, and as he spoke, lowered the cane
almost level with the ground; "Pistache, my friend, jump for the
illustrious coxcomb, Mazarin de Piscina."

The dog turned his back to the cane.

"What," asked the duke, "what do you mean?" and he gave
him the cane again, first making a semicircle from the head to the
tail of Pistache. "Jump, then, Monsieur Pistache."

But Pistache, as at first, turned round on his legs, and stood with
his back to the cane.

Monsieur de Beaufort made the experiment a third time : but
this time Pistache rushed furiously on the cane and broke it with
his teeth.

Monsieur de Beaufort took the pieces out of his mouth, and
presented them with great formality to Monsieur de Chavigny,
saying that for that evening the entertainment was ended, but in
three months it should be repeated, when Pistache would have
learned some new tricks.

Three days afterwards Pistache was poisoned.

Then the duke said openly that his dog had been killed by a drug
with which they meant to poison him; and one day after dinner,
he went to bed, calling out that he had pains in the stomach, and
that Mazarin had poisoned him.

This fresh impertinence reached the ears of the Cardinal, and
alarmed him much. The donjon of Vincennes was considered very
unhealthy, and Madame de Rambouillet had said that the room in
which the Maréchal Ornano and the Grand Prior de Vendôme had

died was worth its weight in arsenic—a bon-mot which had great success. So the prisoner was henceforth to eat nothing that was not previously tasted, and La Ramée was, in consequence, placed near him as taster.

Every kind of revenge was practised upon the duke by the governor, in return for the insults of the innocent Pistache. De Chavigny, who, according to report, was a son of Richelieu's, and had been a creature of the late Cardinal's, understood tyranny. He took from the duke all the steel knives and silver forks, and replaced them with silver knives and wooden forks, pretending that, as he had been informed that the duke was to pass all his life at Vincennes, he was afraid of his prisoner's attempting suicide. A fortnight afterwards the duke, going to the tennis court, found two rows of trees about the size of his little finger planted by the roadside; he asked what they were for, and was told that they were to shade him from the sun on some future day. One morning the gardener went to him and told him, as if to please him, that he was going to plant a bed of asparagus for his use. Now, as every one knows, asparagus takes four years in coming to perfection, this civility infuriated Monsieur de Beaufort.

At last his patience was exhausted. He assembled his keepers, and, notwithstanding his well-known difficulty of utterance, addressed them as follows:

"Gentlemen! will you permit a grandson of Henry IV. to be overwhelmed with insults and ignominy? Odds fish! as my grandfather used to say—I once reigned in Paris; do you know that? I had the king and monsieur the whole of one day in my care. The queen at that time liked me, and called me the most honest man in the kingdom. Gentlemen and citizens, set me free; I shall go to the Louvre, and strangle Mazarin. You shall be my bodyguard. I will make you all captains, with good pensions! Odds fish!—on—march forward!"

But, eloquent as he might be, the eloquence of the grandson of Henry IV. did not touch those hearts of stone; not one man stirred, so Monsieur de Beaufort was obliged to be satisfied with calling them rascals, and cruel foes.

Sometimes, when Monsieur de Chavigny paid him a visit, the duke used to ask him what he should think if he saw an army of Parisians, all fully armed, appear at Vincennes to deliver him from prison.

"My lord," answered De Chavigny, with a low bow, "I have on the ramparts twenty pieces of artillery, and in my casemates thirty thousand guns. I should cannonade the troops as well as I could."

"Yes—but after you had fired off your thirty thousand guns, they would take the donjon; the donjon being taken, I should be obliged to let them hang you—for which I should be very unhappy, certainly."

And, in his turn, the duke bowed low to Monsieur de Chavigny.

" For myself, on the other hand, my lord," returned the governor, " the first rebel that should pass the threshold of my postern doors, I should be obliged to kill you with my own hand, since you were confided peculiarly to my care, and as I am obliged to give you up —dead or alive."

And he bowed low again to his highness.

These bitter and sweet pleasantries lasted ten minutes, or some-times longer; but always finished thus :

Monsieur de Chavigny, turning towards the door, used to call out :

" Hallo ! La Ramée !"

La Ramée came into the room.

"La Ramée, I recommend Monsieur le Duc to you, particu-larly; treat him as a man of his rank and family ought to be treated; therefore never leave him alone an instant."

La Ramée became therefore the duke's dinner guest, by com-pulsion—his eternal keeper—the shadow of his person; but La Ramée—gay, frank, convivial, fond of play, a great hand at tennis —had one defect in the duke's eyes—he was incorruptible.

One may be a jailer or a keeper, and at the same time a good father and husband. La Ramée adored his wife and children, whom now he could only catch a glimpse of from the top of the wall, when, in order to please him, they used to walk on the opposite side of the moat. 'Twas too brief an enjoyment, and La Ramée felt that the gaiety of heart which he had regarded as the cause of that health (of which it was, perhaps, rather the result) would not long survive such a mode of life.

He accepted, therefore, with delight, an offer made to him by his friend the steward of the Duc de Grammont, to give him a substitute; he also spoke of it to Monsieur de Chavigny, who promised that he would not oppose it in any way—that is, if he approved of the person proposed.

We consider it as useless to draw a physical or moral portrait of Grimaud : if—as we hope—our readers have not wholly forgotten the first part of this work, they must have preserved a clear idea of that estimable individual—who is wholly unchanged—except that he is twenty years older, an advance in life that has made him only more silent; although, since the alteration that had been working in himself, Athos had given Grimaud permission to speak.

But Grimaud had for twelve or fifteen years preserved an habitual silence, and a habit of fifteen or twenty years' duration becomes a second nature.

CHAPTER XVIII.

GRIMAUD BEGINS HIS FUNCTIONS.

GRIMAUD thereupon presented himself with his smooth exterior at the donjon of Vincennes. Now Monsieur de Chavigny piqued himself on his infallible penetration ; for that which almost proved that he was the son of Richelieu was his everlasting pretension ; he examined attentively the countenance of the applicant for place, and fancied that the contracted eyebrows, thin lips, hooked nose, and prominent cheek-bones of Grimaud, were favourable signs. He addressed about twelve words to him ; Grimaud answered in four.

"There's a promising fellow, and I have found out his merits," said Monsieur de Chavigny. "Go," he added, "and make yourself agreeable to Monsieur la Ramée, and tell him that you suit me in all respects."

Grimaud had every quality which could attract a man on duty who wishes to have a deputy. So, after a thousand questions which met with only a word in reply, La Ramée, fascinated by this sobriety in speech, rubbed his hands, and engaged Grimaud.

"My orders ?" asked Grimaud.

"They are these : never to leave the prisoner alone ; to keep away from him every sharp or piercing instrument—and to prevent his conversing any length of time with the keepers."

"Those are all ?" asked Grimaud.

"All, now," replied La Ramée.

"Good," answered Grimaud ; and he went right to the prisoner.

The duke was in the act of combing his beard, which he had allowed to grow as well as his hair, in order to reproach Mazarin with his wretched appearance and condition. But having, some days previously, seen from the top of the donjon, Madame de Montbazon pass in her carriage, and still cherishing an affection for that beautiful woman, he did not wish to be to her what he wished to be to Mazarin ; and, in the hope of seeing her again, had asked for a leaden comb, which was allowed him. The comb was to be a leaden one, because his beard, like that of most fair people, was rather red; he therefore dyed it when he combed it out.

As Grimaud entered he saw this comb on the tea-table; he took it up, and, as he took it, he made a low bow.

The duke looked at this strange figure with surprise. The figure put the comb in its pocket.

"Ho!—hey! what's that?" cried the duke, "and who is this creature?"

Grimaud did not answer, but bowed a second time.

"Art thou dumb?" cried the duke.

Grimaud made a sign that he was not.

"What art thou, then? Answer! I command thee!" said the duke.

"A keeper," replied Grimaud.

"A keeper!" reiterated the duke; "there was nothing wanting in my collection except this gallows-bird. Hallo! La Ramée! —some one!"

La Ramée ran in haste to obey the call.

"Who is this wretch who takes my comb and puts it in his pocket?" asked the duke.

"One of your guards, my prince—a man full of talent and merit—whom you will like, as I and Monsieur de Chavigny do, I am sure."

"Why does he take my comb?"

"Why do you take my lord's comb?" asked La Ramée.

Grimaud drew the comb from his pocket, and passing his fingers over the largest teeth, pronounced this one word—"Piercing."

"True," said La Ramée.

"What does the animal say?" asked the duke.

"That the king has forbidden your lordship to have any piercing instrument."

"Are you mad, La Ramée?—you yourself gave me this comb."

"I was very wrong, my lord; for in giving it to you I acted in opposition to my orders." The duke looked furiously at Grimaud.

"I perceive that that creature will become odious to me," he muttered.

Grimaud, nevertheless, was resolved, for certain reasons, not at once to come to a full rupture with the prisoner; he wanted to inspire, not a sudden repugnance, but a good, and sound, and steady hatred; he retired, therefore, and gave place to four guards who, having breakfasted, could attend on the prisoner.

A fresh practical joke had now occurred to the duke. He had asked for craw-fish for his breakfast on the following morning: he intended to pass the day in making a small gallows, and hang one of the finest of these fish in the middle of his room—the red colours evidently conveying an allusion to the Cardinal—so that he might have the pleasure of hanging Mazarin in effigy, without being accused of having hung anything except a craw-fish.

The day was employed in preparations for the execution. Everyone grows childish in prison; but the character of Monsieur de Beaufort was particularly disposed to become so. In the course of his morning's walk he collected two or three small branches from a tree, and found a small piece of broken glass, a discovery which delighted him. When he came home he formed his handkerchief into a loop.

Nothing of all this escaped Grimaud, but La Ramée looked on with the curiosity of a father who thinks that he may perhaps get an idea of a new toy for his children; the guards regarded it all with indifference. When everything was ready—the gallows hung in the middle of the room—the loop made—and when the duke had cast a glance upon the plate of craw-fish, in order to select the finest specimen among them, he looked round for his piece of glass —it had disappeared.

"Who has taken my piece of glass?" asked the duke, frowning.

Grimaud made a sign to denote that he had done so.

"How! thou, again! Why didst thou take it?"

"Yes—why?" asked La Ramée.

Grimaud, who held the piece of glass in his hand, said:
"Sharp."

"True, my lord!" exclaimed La Ramée. "Ah! deuce take it! we have got a precious lad."

"Monsieur Grimaud!" said the duke, "for your sake, I beg of you, never come within the reach of my fist!"

"Hush! hush!" cried La Ramée, "give me your gibbet, my lord, I will shape it out for you with my knife."

And he took the gibbet and shaped it out as neatly as possible.

"That's it," said the duke; "now make me a little hole in the floor whilst I go and fetch the culprit."

La Ramée knelt down and made a hole in the floor; meanwhile the duke hung the craw-fish up by a thread. Then he placed the gibbet in the middle of the room, bursting with laughter.

La Ramée laughed also, and the guards laughed in chorus; Grimaud, however, did not even smile. He approached La Ramée, and showing him the craw-fish, hung up by the thread,—

"Cardinal!"—he said.

"Hung by his Highness the Duc de Beaufort!" cried the prisoner, laughing violently, " and by Master Jacques Chrysostom La Ramée, the king's commissioner."

La Ramée uttered a cry of horror, and rushed towards the gibbet, which he broke at once, and threw the pieces out of the window. He was going to throw the craw-fish out also, when Grimaud snatched it from his hands.

"Good to eat !" he said ; and he put it into his pocket.

This scene so enchanted the duke that, at the moment, he forgave Grimaud for his part in it ; but on reflection, he hated him more and more, being convinced that he had some bad motive for his conduct.

The prisoner happened to remark among the guards one man, with a very good countenance ; and he favoured this man the more as Grimaud became the more and more odious to him. One morning he took this man on one side and had succeeded in speaking to him, when Grimaud entered, saw what was going on, approached the duke respectfully, but took the guard by the arm.

" Go away," he said.

The guard obeyed.

" You are insupportable," cried the duke : " I shall beat you." Grimaud bowed.

" I shall break every bone in your body," cried the duke. Grimaud bowed, and stepped back.

" Mr. Spy," cried the duke, more and more enraged, " I shall strangle you with my own hands."

And he extended his hands towards Grimaud, who merely thrust the guard out, and shut the door behind him. At the same time he felt the duke's arms on his shoulders, like two iron claws ; but instead either of calling out or defending himself, he placed his forefinger on his lips, and said in a low tone :

" Hush !"—smiling as he uttered the word.

A gesture, a smile, and a word from Grimaud, all at once, were so unusual, that his highness stopped short, astounded.

Grimaud took advantage of that instant to draw from his vest a charming little note, with an aristocratic seal, and presented it to the duke without a word.

The duke, more and more bewildered, let Grimaud loose, and took the note.

—" From Madame de Montbazon !" he cried.

Grimaud nodded assent.

The duke tore open the note, passed his hands over his eyes, for he was dazzled and confused, and read :

" My dear Duke,

" You may entirely confide on the brave lad who will give you this note; he has consented to enter into the service of your keeper, and to shut himself up at Vincennes with you, in order to prepare and assist your escape, which we are contriving. The moment of your deliverance is at hand; have patience and courage, and remember that, in spite of time and absence, all your friends continue to cherish for you the sentiments that they have professed.

" Yours wholly, and most affectionately,
" Marie de Montbazon."

" P.S. I sign my full name, for I should be vain if I could suppose that after five years of absence you would remember my initials."

The poor duke became perfectly giddy. What for five years he had been wanting,—a faithful servant—a friend—a helping hand—seemed to have fallen from heaven just when he expected it the least.

" Oh, dearest Marie! she thinks of me, then, after five years of separation! Heavens! there is constancy!" Then turning to Grimaud, he said:

" And thou, my brave fellow, thou consentest then to aid me?"

Grimaud signified his assent.

" What then shall we do? how proceed?"

" It is now eleven," answered Grimaud. " Let my lord at two o'clock ask leave to make up a game at tennis, with La Ramée, and let him send two or three balls over the ramparts."

" And then?"

" Your highness will approach the walls and call out to a man who works in the moat to send them back again."

" I understand," said the duke.

Grimaud made a sign that he was going away.

" Ah!" cried the duke, "will you not accept any money from me?"

" I wish my lord would make me one promise."

" What? speak!"

" 'Tis this—when we escape together, that I shall go everywhere, and be always first; for if my lord should be overtaken and caught, there's every chance of his being brought back to prison, whereas, if I'm caught, the least that can befall me—is to be hung."

" True; on my honour as a gentleman, it shall be as thou dost suggest."

" Now," resumed Grimaud, "I've only one thing more to ask, that your highness will continue to detest me."

"I shall try," said the duke.

At this moment La Ramée, after the interview which we have described with the Cardinal, entered the room. The duke had thrown himself—as he was wont to do in moments of dulness and vexation—on his bed. La Ramée cast an inquiring look around him.

"Well, my lord," said La Ramée, with his rude laugh; "you still set yourself against this poor fellow?"

"So 'tis you, La Ramée; in faith 'tis time you came back again. I threw myself on the bed, and turned my nose to the wall that I mightn't break my promise and strangle Grimaud. I feel stupid beyond everything to-day."

"Then let us have a match in the tennis court," exclaimed La Ramée.

"If you wish it."

"I am at your service, my lord."

"I protest, my dear La Ramée," said the duke, "that you are a charming person, and that I would stay for ever at Vincennes, to have the pleasure of your society."

"My lord," replied La Ramée, "I think if it depended on the Cardinal, your wishes would be fulfilled."

"How?"

"He sent for me to-day; in short, my lord, you are his nightmare."

The duke smiled with bitterness.

"Ah, La Ramée! if you would but accept my offers! I would make your fortune."

"How? you would no sooner have left prison than your goods would be confiscated."

"I shall no sooner be out of prison than I shall be master of Paris."

"Pshaw! pshaw! I cannot hear such things said as that; I see, my lord, I shall be obliged to fetch Grimaud."

"Well, then, let us go and have a game at tennis, La Ramée."

"My lord—I beg your highness's pardon—but I must beg for half an hour's leave of absence."

"Why?"

"Because Monseigneur Mazarin is a prouder man than your highness, though not of such high birth: he forgot to ask me to breakfast."

"Well, shall I send for some breakfast here?"

"No, my lord; I must tell you that the confectioner who lived opposite the Castle—Father Marteau, as they called him——"

" Well ?"

" Well, he sold his business a week ago to a confectioner from Paris—an invalid, ordered country air for his health."

" Well, what have I to do with that ?"

" Why, good lord ! this man, your highness, when he saw me stop before his shop, where he has a display of things which would make your mouth water, my lord, asked me to get him the custom of the prisoners in the donjon. ' I bought,' says he, 'the business of my predecessor, on the strength of his assurance that he supplied the Castle ; whereas, on my honour, Monsieur de Chavigny, though I've been here a week, has not ordered so much as a tartlet.' So, my lord, I am going to try his patés ; and, as I am fasting, you understand, I would, with your highness's leave——" And La Ramée bent low.

" Go, then, animal," said the duke ; " but remember, I only allow you half an hour."

" May I promise your custom to the successor of Father Marteau, my lord ?"

" Yes—if he does not put mushrooms in his pies—thou knowest that mushrooms from the wood of Vincennes are fatal to my family."

La Ramée went out, but in five minutes one of the officers of the guard entered, in compliance with the strict orders of the Cardinal, that the prisoner should never be left one moment.

But, during these five minutes, the duke had had time to read over again the note from Madame de Montbazon, which proved to the prisoner that his friends were concerting plans for his deliverance ; but in what way he knew not.

But his confidence in Grimaud, whose petty persecutions he now perceived were only a blind, increased, and he conceived the highest opinion of his intellect, and resolved to trust entirely to his guidance.

CHAPTER XIX.

IN WHICH THE CONTENTS OF THE PATÉS MADE BY THE SUCCESSOR OF FATHER MARTEAU ARE DESCRIBED.

IN half an hour La Ramée returned full of glee, like most men who have eaten, and more especially drunk, to their heart's content. The patés were excellent, and the wine delicious.

The weather was fine, and the game at tennis took place in the open air.

At two o'clock the tennis balls began, according to Grimaud's directions, to take the direction of the moat, much to the joy of La Ramée, who marked fifteen whenever the duke sent a ball into the moat; and very soon balls were wanting, so many had gone over. La Ramée then proposed to send some one to pick them up. But the duke remarked that it would be losing time; and going near the rampart himself, and looking over, he saw a man working in one of the numerous little gardens cleared out by the peasants on the opposite side of the moat.

"Hey, friend !" cried the duke.

The man raised his head, and the duke was about to utter a cry of surprise. The peasant, the gardener, was Rochefort, whom he believed to be in the Bastille.

"Well ! who's up there ?" said the man.

"Be so good as to send us back our balls," said the duke.

The gardener nodded, and began to throw up the balls, which were picked up by La Ramée and the guard. One, however, fell at the duke's feet; and seeing that it was intended for him, he put it into his pocket.

La Ramée was in ecstasies at having beaten a prince of the blood.

The duke went indoors, and retired to bed, where he spent, indeed, the greater part of every day, as they had taken his books away. La Ramée carried off all his clothes, in order to be certain that the duke would not stir. However, the duke contrived to hide the ball under his bolster, and as soon as the door was closed, he tore off the cover of the ball with his teeth, and found underneath it the following letter :

"MY LORD,

"Your friends watch over you, and the hour of your deliverance draws near. Ask to-morrow to have a pie made by the new confectioner opposite the castle, and who is no other than Noirmont, your former 'maître d'hotel.' Do not open the pie till you are alone. I hope you will be satisfied with its contents.

"Your highness's most devoted servant,

"In the Bastille, as elsewhere,

"COMTE DE ROCHEFORT."

The duke, who had latterly been allowed a fire, burned the letter, but kept the ball, and went to bed, hiding the ball under his bolster. La Ramée entered : he smiled kindly on the prisoner, for he was an excellent man who had taken a great liking for the captive prince. He endeavoured to cheer him up in his solitude.

"Ah, my friend !" cried the duke, "you are so good ; if I could but go, as you do, and eat patés and drink Burgundy at the house of Father Marteau's successor !"

"'Tis true, my lord," answered La Ramée, "that his patés are famous, and his wine magnificent."

"Good," said the duke to himself ; "it seems that one of master La Ramée's seven deadly sins is gluttony."

Then aloud :

"Well, my dear La Ramée ! the day after to-morrow is a holiday."

"Yes, my lord, Pentecost."

"Will you give me a lesson the day after to-morrow ?"

"In what ?"

"In gastronomy."

"Willingly, my lord."

"But tête-à-tête. The guards shall go to sup in the canteen of Monsieur de Chavigny—we'll have a supper here, under your direction."

"Hum !" said La Ramée.

The duke watched the countenance of La Ramée with an anxious glance.

"Well," he asked, "that will do ? Will it not ?"

"Yes, my lord, on one condition."

"What ?"

"That Grimaud should wait on us at table."

Nothing could be more agreeable to the duke ; however, he had presence of mind enough to exclaim :

"Send your Grimaud to the devil ! he'll spoil my feast. I see you distrust me."

"My lord, the day after to-morrow is Pentecost."

"Well ! what of that ?"

"I have already told you what that magician had predicted."

"And what was it ?"

"That the day of Pentecost would not pass without your highness being out of Vincennes."

"You believe in sorcerers, then, you fool !"

"I—I care for them, that—" and he snapped his fingers ; "but it is my Lord Giulio who cares for them—as an Italian, he is superstitious."

The duke shrugged his shoulders.

"Well, then," with a well-acted good humour, "I allow of Grimaud, but no one else—you must manage it all. Order whatever you like for supper—the only thing I specify is one of those pies ; and tell the confectioner that I will promise him my custom if he excels this time in his pies—not only now, but when I leave my prison."

"Then you think you shall leave it ?" said La Ramée.

"The devil !" replied the prince ; "surely at the death of Mazarin. I am fifteen years younger than he is. At Vincennes; 'tis true, one lives faster——''

"My lord," replied La Ramée, "my lord——''

"Or one dies sooner, so it comes to the same thing."

La Ramée was going out. He stopped, however, at the door for an instant.

"Whom does your highness wish me to send to you ?"

"Any one, except Grimaud."

"The officer of the guard, then ? with his chess-board ?"

"Yes."

Five minutes afterwards the officer entered, and the duke seemed to be immersed in the sublime combinations of chess.

It was midnight before he went to sleep that evening, and he awoke at daybreak. Wild dreams had disturbed his repose. He dreamed that he had been gifted with wings—he wished to fly away. For a time these wings had supported him ; but, when he had reached a certain height, this new aid had failed him. His wings were broken, and he seemed to sink into a bottomless abyss, whence he awoke, bathed in perspiration, and as much overcome as if he had really fallen. He fell asleep again, and another vision appeared. He was in a subterranean passage, by which he was to leave Vincennes. Grimaud was walking before him with a lantern. By degrees the passage narrowed, yet the duke continued his course. At last it became so narrow that the fugitive tried in vain to proceed. The sides of the walls seemed to close in, and to press against him. He made fruitless efforts to go on ; it was impossible. Nevertheless, he still saw Grimaud, with his lantern in front, advancing. He wished to call out to him, but could not utter a word. Then, at the other extremity, he heard the footsteps of those who were pursuing him. These steps came on— they came fast. He was discovered—all hopes of flight were gone. Still the walls seemed to be closing on him ; they appeared to be in concert with his enemies. At last he heard the voice of La Ramée. La Ramée took his hand, and laughed loud. He was captured again, and conducted to the low and vaulted chamber, in which Ornano, Puylaurens, and his uncle had died. Their three graves were there, rising above the ground, and a third was also there—yawning to receive a corpse.

The duke was obliged to make as many efforts to awaken as he had done to go to sleep; and La Ramée found him so pale and fatigued, that he inquired whether he was ill.

"What is the matter with your highness?" he asked.

"'Tis thy fault, thou simpleton," answered the duke. "With your idle nonsense yesterday, about escaping, you worried me so, that I dreamed that I was trying to escape, and broke my neck in doing so."

La Ramée laughed.

"Come," he said, "'tis a warning from heaven. Never commit such an imprudence as to try to escape, except in your dreams. Listen! your supper is ordered."

"Ah! and what is it to be? Monsieur, my major-domo, will there be a pie?"

"I think so indeed; as high as a tower."

"You told him it was for me?"

"Yes; and he said he would do his best to please your highness."

"Good!" exclaimed the duke, rubbing his hands.

"Devil take it, my lord! what a gourmand you are becoming. I haven't seen you with so cheerful a face these five years."

At this moment Grimaud entered, and signified to La Ramée that he had something to say to him.

The duke instantly recovered his composure.

"I forbade that man to come here," he said.

"'Tis my fault," replied La Ramée; "but he must stay here whilst I go to see Monsieur de Chavigny, who has some orders to give me."

And La Ramée went out. Grimaud looked after him; and when the door was closed, he drew out of his pocket a pencil and a sheet of paper.

"Write, my lord," he said.

"And what?"

Grimaud dictated.

"All is ready for to-morrow evening. Keep watch from seven till nine o'clock. Have two riding-horses quite ready. We shall descend by the first window in the gallery."

"What next?"

"Sign your name, my lord."

The duke signed.

"Now, my lord, give me, if you have not lost it, the ball—that which contained the letter."

The duke took it from under his pillow, and gave it to Grimaud. Grimaud gave a grim smile.

"Now," said the duke, "tell me what this famous raised pie is to contain."

"Two poignards, a knotted rope, and a poire d'angoisse."*

"Yes, I understand;—we shall take to ourselves the poignards and the rope," replied the duke.

"And make La Ramée eat the pear," answered Grimaud.

"My dear Grimaud, thou speakest seldom, but when thou dost speak, one must do thee justice—thy words are of gold."

CHAPTER XX.

ONE OF MARIE MICHON'S ADVENTURES.

WHILST these projects where being formed by the Duc de Beaufort and Grimaud, the Comte de la Fère and the Vicomte de Bragelonne were entering Paris by the Rue du Faubourg Saint Marcel.

They stopped at the sign of the Fox, in the Rue du Vieux Colombier, a tavern known for many years by Athos, and asked for two bed-rooms.

"You must dress yourself, Raoul," said Athos. "I am going to present you to some one. I wish you to look well, so arrange your dress with care."

"I hope, sir," replied the youth, smiling, "that there's no idea of a marriage for me ; you know my engagement to Louise ?"

Athos, in his turn, smiled also.

"No, don't be alarmed—although it is to a lady that I am going to present you--and I am anxious that you should love her——"

"What age is she ?" inquired the Vicomte de Bragelonne.

"My dear Raoul, learn once for all, that that is a question which is never asked. When you can find out a woman's age by her face it is useless to ask it; when you cannot do so it is indiscreet."

"Is she beautiful ?"

"During sixteen years she was deemed not only the prettiest but the most graceful woman in France."

This reply reassured the vicomte. A woman who had been a reigning beauty for sixteen years could not be the subject of any scheme for him. He retired to his toilet. When he reappeared, Athos received him with the same paternal smile as that which he

---

* This poire d'angoisse was a famous gag, in the form of a pear, which, being thrust into the mouth, by the aid of a spring, dilated so as to distend the jaws to their greatest width.

had often bestowed on D'Artagnan—but a more profound tenderness for Raoul was now visibly impressed upon his face.

Athos cast a glance at his feet, hands, and hair—those three
marks of race. The youth's dark hair was neatly parted, and hung
in curls, forming a sort of dark frame round his face—such was
the fashion of the day. Gloves of grey kid, matching the hat,
displayed the form of a slender and elegant hand; whilst his
boots, similar in colour to the hat and gloves, confined the feet,
small as those of a child of ten years old.

"Come," murmured Athos, "if she is not proud of him, she
will be hard to please."

It was three o'clock in the afternoon. The two travellers proceeded to the Rue St. Dominique, and stopped at the door of a
magnificent hotel, surmounted with the arms of De Luynes.

"'Tis here," said Athos.

He entered the hotel, and ascended the front steps, and address-
ing a footman who waited there in a grand livery, asked if the
Duchesse de Chevreuse was visible, and if she could receive the
Comte de la Fère?

The servant returned with a message to say that though the
duchess had not the honour of knowing Monsieur de la Fère, she
would receive him. He was accordingly announced.

Madame de Chevreuse, whose name appears so often in our
story—"The Three Musketeers"—without her actually having
appeared in any scene, was still a most beautiful woman. Although
about forty-four or forty-five years old, she scarcely seemed thirty-
eight. She still had her rich fair hair; her large, animated, intelligent eyes, so often opened by intrigue, so often closed by the
blindness of love. She had still her nymph-like form, so that
when her back was turned, she seemed to be still the girl who
had jumped with Anne of Austria over the moat of the Tuileries
in 1563. In all other respects she was the same mad creature
who threw over her amours such an air of originality as to make
them almost a proverb in her family.

She was in a little boudoir looking upon a garden, and hung
with blue damask, adorned by red flowers, with a foliage of gold;
and reclined upon a sofa, her head supported on the rich tapestry
which covered it. She held a book in her hand. and her arm was
supported by a cushion.

As the footman announced two strangers, she raised herself a
little and peeped out, with some curiosity.

Athos appeared.

He was dressed in violet-coloured velvet, trimmed with the

same colour. His shoulder-knots were of burnished silver; his mantle had no gold nor embroidery on it, and a simple plume of violet feathers adorned his hat; his boots were of black leather; and at his girdle hung that sword with a magnificent hilt that Porthos had so often admired in the Rue Feronnière. Splendid lace formed the falling collar of his shirt, and lace fell also over the tops of his boots.

In his whole person he bore such an impress of high condition, that Madame de Chevreuse half rose from her seat when she saw him, and made him a sign to sit down near her. He obeyed, the servant disappeared, and the door was closed.

There was a momentary silence, during which these two persons looked at each other attentively.

The duchess was the first to speak.

"Well, sir! I am waiting to hear what you wish to say to me—with impatience."

"And I, madame," replied Athos, "am looking with admiration."

"Sir," said Madame de Chevreuse, "you must excuse me, but I long to know to whom I am talking. You belong to the court, doubtless, yet I have never seen you at court. Have you been in the Bastille by any mischance?"

"No, madame, I have not; but perhaps I am on the road to it."

"Ah! then tell me who you are, and get along with you," replied the duchess, with the gaiety which made her so charming, "for I am sufficiently in bad odour there already, without compromising myself still more."

"Who I am, madame? My name has been mentioned to you —the Comte de la Fère—you do not know that name. I once bore another, which you knew; but you have certainly forgotten it."

"Tell it me, sir."

"Formerly," said the count, "I was Athos."

Madame de Chevreuse looked astonished. The name was not wholly forgotten, but mixed up and confused with some old recollections.

"Stop," she said.

And she placed her hands on her brow, as if to force the fugitive ideas it contained to be concentrated for a moment.

"Shall I help you, madame?" asked Athos.

"Yes, do," said the duchess.

"This Athos was connected with three young Musketeers, named Porthos, D'Artagnan, and——"

He stopped short.

"And Aramis," said the duchess, quickly.

"And Aramis; you have not forgotten that name."

"No," she said : poor Aramis ; a charming man, elegant, discreet, and a writer of poetry verses.   I am afraid he has turned out ill," she added.

"He has; he is an abbé."

"Ah, what a misfortune !" exclaimed the duchess, playing carelessly with her fan.   "Indeed, sir, I thank you; you have recalled one of the most agreeable recollections of my youth."

"Will you permit me, then, to recall another to you?"

"Anything relating to him?"

"Yes and no.   Aramis was intimate with a young needlewoman from Tours, a cousin of his, named Marie Michon."

"Ah, I knew her !" cried the duchess.   "It was to her he wrote from the siege of Rochelle, to warn her of a plot against the Duke of Buckingham."

"Exactly so; will you allow me to speak to you of her?"

"If," replied the duchess, with a meaning look, "you do not say too much against her."

"You encourage me, madame.   I shall continue," said Athos; and he began his narrative.

He alluded to events long gone by; to the journey in disguise of Marie Michon, the supposed needlewoman of Tours, but, in fact, the beautiful, intriguing, and at one time, all powerful Duchesse de Chevreuse, into Spain : he spoke of her rencontres and adventures; and he told her anecdotes of her life which seemed to her mind to be the revelations of a sorcerer rather than the disclosures of a mere man . . . .   These disclosures remain in mystery; they were succeeded by an exclamation of joy from Madame de Chevreuse.

"He is there ! my son ! the son of Marie Michon !   But I must see him instantly."

"Take care, madame," said Athos, "for he knows neither his father nor his mother."

"You have kept the secret ! you have brought him to see me, thinking to make me happy.   Oh, thanks ! thanks ! sir," cried Madame de Chevreuse, seizing his hand, and trying to put it to her lips; "you have a noble heart."

"I bring him to you, madame," said Athos, withdrawing his hand, "hoping that, in your turn, you will do something for him; till now I have watched over his education, and I have made him, I hope, an accomplished gentleman; but I am now obliged to return to the dangerous and wandering life of party faction.   To-morrow I plunge into an adventurous affair in which I may be killed.   Then it will devolve on you to push him on in that world where he is called on to occupy a place."

"Be assured," cried the duchess, "I shall do what I can. I have but little influence now, but all that I have shall be his. As to his title and fortune——"

"As to that, madame, I have made over to him the estate of Bragelonne, my inheritance, which will give him ten thousand francs a-year, and the title of vicomte ;—and now I will call him."

Athos moved towards the door ; the duchess held him back.

"Is he handsome ?" she asked.

Athos smiled.

"He resembles his mother."

And he opened the door, and desired the young man to come in.

The duchess could not forbear uttering a cry of joy on seeing so handsome a young cavalier, who surpassed all that her pride had been able to conceive.

"Vicomte, come here," said Athos ; "the duchess permits you to kiss her hand."

The youth approached with his charming smile, and his head bare, and, kneeling down, kissed the hand of the Duchesse de Chevreuse.

"Sir," he said, turning to Athos, "was it not in compassion to my timidity that you told me that this lady was the Duchesse de Chevreuse, and is she not the queen ?"

"No," said the duchess, extending her hand to him ; "no ; unhappily I am not the queen, for, if I were, I should do for you at once all that you deserve : but let us see ; whatever I may be," she added, her eyes glistening with delight, "let us see what profession you wish to follow ?"

Athos, standing, looked at them both with indescribable pleasure.

"Madame," answered the youth in his sweet voice, "it seems to me that there is only one career for a gentleman—that of the army. I have been brought up by Monsieur le Comte with the intention, I believe, of making me a soldier ; and he gave me reason to hope that, at Paris, he would present me to some one who would recommend me to the favour of the prince."

"Yes, I understand it well. Personally I am on bad terms with him, on account of the quarrels between Madame de Montbazon, my mother-in-law, and Madame de Longueville. But the Prince de Marsillac ! yes, indeed, that's the right thing. The Prince de Marsillac, my old friend—he will recommend our young friend to Madame de Longueville, who will give him a letter to her brother, the prince, who loves her too tenderly not to do what she wishes immediately."

"Well, that will do charmingly," said the count ; "but may I beg that the greatest haste may be made, for I have reasons for wishing the vicomte not to sleep longer than to-morrow night in Paris ?"

"Do you wish it known that you are interested about him, Monsieur le Comte ?"

"Better for him, in future, that he should be supposed never to have seen me."

"Oh, sir !" cried Raoul.

"You know, Bragelonne, " said Athos, "I never act without reflection.

"Well, comte, I am going instantly," interrupted the duchess, "to send for the Prince de Marsillac, who is, happily, in Paris just now. What are you going to do this evening ?"

"We intend to visit the Abbé Scarron, for whom I have a letter of introduction, and at whose house I expect to meet some of my friends."

"'Tis well ; I shall go there also, for a few minutes," said the duchess ; do not quit his *salon* until you have seen me."

Athos bowed, and took his departure.

CHAPTER XXI.

THE ABBÉ SCARRON.

THERE was once, in the Rue des Tournelles, a house known by all the sedan chairmen and footmen of Paris, and yet, nevertheless, this house was neither that of a great lord, nor of a rich man. There was neither dining, nor playing at cards, nor dancing in that house. Nevertheless, it was the rendezvous of all the great world, and all Paris went there. It was the abode of little Scarron.

There, in the home of that witty abbé, there was incessant laughter ; there all the news of the day had their source, and were so quickly transformed, misrepresented, and converted, some into epigrams, some into falsehoods, that every one was anxious to pass an hour with little Scarron, listening to what he said, and reporting it to others.

The diminutive Abbé Scarron, who, however, was only an abbé because he owned an abbey, and not because he was in orders, had formerly been one of the gayest prebendaries of the town of Maur, which he inhabited. But he had become lame ; every means had been in vain employed to restore the use of his limbs. He had been subjected to a severe discipline : at length he sent away all his doctors, declaring that he preferred the disease to the treatment, and came to Paris, where the fame of his wit had preceded him. There he had a chair made on his own plan ; and one day, visiting Anne of Austria in this chair, she asked him, charmed as she was with his wit, if he did not wish for a title.

" Yes, your majesty, there is a title which I covet much," replied Scarron.

" And what is that ?"

" That of being *your* invalid," answered Scarron.

So he was called the queen's invalid, with a pension of fifteen hundred francs.

From that lucky moment Scarron led a happy life, spending both income and principal. One day, however, an emissary of the Cardinal's gave him to understand that he was wrong in receiving the Coadjutor so often.

" And why ?" asked Scarron ; " is he not a man of good birth ?"

" Certainly."

" Agreeable ?"

" Undeniably."

" Witty ?"

" He has, unluckily, too much wit."

" Well, then, why do you wish me to give up seeing such a man ?"

" Because he is an enemy."

" Of whom ?"

" Of the Cardinal."

" How ?" answered Scarron ; " I continue to receive Monsieur Gilles Despreaux, who thinks ill of me, and you wish me to give up seeing the Coadjutor, because he thinks ill of another man."

Now, the very morning of which we speak, was that of his quarter-day's payment, and Scarron, as usual, had sent his servant to fetch his money at the pension-office, but he had returned, and said that the Government had no more money to give Monsieur Scarron.

It was a Thursday, the abbé's day of reception ; people went there in crowds. The Cardinal's refusal to pay the pension was known about the town in half an hour, and he was abused with vehemence.

—Athos made two visits in Paris ; at seven o'clock he and Raoul directed their steps to the Rue des Tournelles ; it was stopped up by porters, horses, and footmen. Athos forced his way through and entered, followed by the young man. The first person that struck him on his entrance was Aramis, planted near a great chair on castors, very large, covered with a canopy of tapestry, under which there moved, enveloped in a quilt of brocade, a little face, rather young, rather merry, but somewhat pallid,— whilst its eyes never ceased to express a sentiment at once lively, intellectual, and amiable.   This was the Abbé Scarron, always laughing, joking, complimenting,—yet suffering—and scratching himself with a little switch.

Around this kind of rolling tent pressed a crowd of gentlemen and ladies.   The room was neat and comfortably furnished. Large vallances of silk, embroidered with flowers of gay colours, which were rather faded, fell from the wide windows; the fitting-up of the room was simple, but in good taste.   Two men servants, well trained, attended on the company.   On perceiving Athos, Aramis advanced towards him, took him by the hand, and presented him to Scarron.   Raoul remained silent, for he was not prepared for the dignity of the "bel esprit."

After some minutes the door opened, and a footman announced Mademoiselle Paulet.

Athos touched the shoulder of the vicomte.

" Look at this lady, Raoul, she is an historic personage; it was to visit her that King Henry IV. was going, when he was assassinated."

Everyone thronged round Mademoiselle Paulet, for she was always much in fashion.   She was a tall woman, with a wavy and slender figure, and a forest of golden curls, such as Raphael was fond of, and as Titian has painted all his Magdalens with.   This fawn-coloured hair—or, perhaps, the sort of ascendancy which she had over other women—gave her the name of "La Lionne."

Mademoiselle Paulet took her accustomed seat; but before sitting down, she cast, in all her queen-like grandeur, a look round the room—and her eyes rested on Raoul.

Athos smiled.

" Mademoiselle Paulet has observed you, vicomte; go and bow to her; don't try to appear anything but what you are—a true country youth—on no account speak to her of Henry IV."

"When shall we two talk together ?" Athos then said to Aramis.

" Presently—there are not a sufficient number of people here yet—we shall be remarked."

At this moment the door opened, and in walked the Coadjutor.

At this name everyone looked round, for it was already a name very celebrated.   Athos did the same.   He knew the Abbé de Gondy only by report.

He saw a little dark man, ill-made and awkward with his hands in everything—except when drawing a sword and firing a pistol, and with something haughty and contemptuous in his face.

Scarron turned round towards him, and came to meet him in his chair.

"Well," said the Coadjutor on seeing him, "you are in disgrace, then, Abbé?"

This was the orthodox phrase. It had been said that evening a hundred times—and Scarron was at his hundredth "bon-mot" on the subject—he was very near stopping short, but one despairing effort saved him.

"Monsieur, the Cardinal Mazarin has been so kind as to think of me," he said.

"But how can you continue to receive us?" asked the Coadjutor; "if your income is lessened, I shall be obliged to make you a canon of Nôtre Dame."

"Oh, no," cried Scarron, "I should compromise you too much."

"Perhaps you have resources of which we are ignorant?"

"I shall borrow from the queen."

"But her Majesty has no property," interposed Aramis.

At this moment the door opened, and Madame de Chevreuse was announced. Everyone rose. Scarron turned his chair towards the door; Raoul blushed; Athos made a sign to Aramis, who went to hide himself in the inclosure of a window.

In the midst of all the compliments that awaited her on her entrance, the duchess seemed to be looking for some one: at last she found out Raoul, and her eyes sparkled; she perceived Athos, and became thoughtful; she saw Aramis in the seclusion of the window, and gave a start of surprise behind her fan.

"Apropos," she said, as if to drive away thoughts that pursued her in spite of herself, "how is poor Voiture; do you know, Scarron?"

"What! is Monsieur Voiture ill?" inquired a gentleman who had spoken to Athos in the Rue St. Honoré; "what is the matter with him?"

"He was acting—but forgot to take the precaution to have clean linen brought to change," said the Coadjutor, "so he took cold, and is going to die."

"Is he then so ill, dear Voiture?" asked Aramis, half hidden by the window curtain.

"He die!" cried Mademoiselle Paulet bitterly: "he! why he is surrounded by sultanas, like a Turk. Madame de Saintot has hastened to him with broth; La Renaudet warms his sheets; the Marquise de Rambouillet sends him his 'tisanes.'"

"You don't like him, my dear Parthenie," said Scarron.

"What an injustice, my dear invalid! I hate him so little, that I should be delighted to order masses for the repose of his soul."

"You are not called 'Lionne' for nothing," observed Madame de Chevreuse, "you bite most cruelly."

"You are unjust to a great poet, so it seems to me," Raoul ventured to say.

"A great poet! he! come, one may easily see, vicomte, that you are lately from the provinces, and have never seen him. A great poet! he is scarcely five feet high."

"Bravo! bravo!" cried a tall man with an enormous moustache and a long rapier, "bravo, fair Paulet, it is high time to put little Voiture is his right place. For my part I always thought his poetry detestable, and I think I know something about poetry."

"Who is this officer," inquired Raoul, of Athos, "who is speaking?"

"Monsieur de Scudery, the author of 'Delia,' and of 'Le Grand Cyrus,' which were composed partly by him, and partly by his sister, who is now talking to that pretty person yonder, near Monsieur Scarron."

Raoul turned, and saw two new faces just arrived. One was perfectly charming, delicate, pensive, shaded by beautiful dark hair, with eyes soft as velvet, like those lovely flowers—the heartsease, under which shine the golden petals. The other, of mature age, seemed to have the former one under her charge—and was cold, dry, and yellow—the true type of a duenna or a devotee.

Raoul resolved not to quit the room without having spoken to the beautiful girl with the soft eyes, who by a strange fancy—although she bore no resemblance—reminded him of his poor little Louise, whom he had left in the Château de la Vallière, and whom, in the midst of all the party, he had never one moment forgotten. Meantime Aramis had drawn near to the Coadjutor, who, smiling all the while, had contrived to drop some words into his ear. Raoul, following the advice of Athos, went towards them. Athos had now joined the other two, and they were in deep consultation as the youth approached them.

"'Tis a rouleau by Monsieur Voiture that Monsieur l'Abbé is repeating to me," said Athos in a loud voice, "and I confess I think it incomparable."

Raoul stayed only a few minutes near them, and then mingled in the group around Madame de Chevreuse.

"Well, then," asked Athos, in a low tone, as soon as the three friends were unobserved, "to-morrow?"

"Yes, to-morrow," said Aramis quickly, "at six o'clock."

"Where?"

"At St. Maude."

"Who told you?"

"The Count de Rochefort."

Some one drew near.

"And then philosophic ideas are wholly wanting in Voiture's works—but I am of the same opinion as the Coadjutor—he is a poet, a true poet." Aramis spoke so as to be heard by everybody.

"And I too," murmured the young lady with the velvet eyes; "I have the misfortune also to admire his poetry extremely."

"Monsieur Scarron, do me the honour," said Raoul, blushing, "to tell me the name of that young lady whose opinion seems so different to that of the others of the company generally."

"Ah! my young vicomte," replied Scarron, "I suppose you wish to propose to her an alliance, offensive and defensive."

Raoul blushed again.

"You asked the name of that young lady. She is called the fair Indian."

"Excuse me, sir," returned Raoul, blushing still more deeply, "I know no more than I did before. Alas! I am from the country."

"Which means that you know very little about the nonsense which flows here, down our streets. So much the better, young man! so much the better! Don't try to understand it—you will only lose your time."

"You forgive me then, sir," said Raoul; "and you will deign to tell me who is the person that you call the young Indian?"

"Certainly; one of the most charming persons that lives—Mademoiselle Frances d'Aubigné."

"Does she belong to the family of the celebrated Agrippus, the friend of Henry IV.?"

"His grand-daughter. She comes from Martinique, so I call her the beautiful Indian."

Raoul looked surprised, and his eyes met those of the young lady, who smiled.

The company went on speaking of the poet Voiture.

"Monsieur," said Mademoiselle d'Aubigné to Scarron, as if she wished to join in the conversation he was engaged in with Raoul, "do you not admire Monsieur Voiture's friends? Listen how they pull him to pieces, even whilst they praise him; one takes away from him all claim to good sense, another runs off with his poetry, another with his originality, another with his humour, another with his independence of character, another— but, good heavens! what will they leave him? as Mademoiselle de Scudery remarks."

Scarron and Raoul laughed. The fair Indian, astonished at the sensation her observations produced, looked down and resumed her air of ' naïveté.'

Athos—still within the enclosure of the window—watched this scene with a smile of disdain on his lips.

"Tell the Count de la Fère to come to me," said Madame de Chevreuse, "I want to speak to him."

"And I," said the Coadjutor, "want it to be thought that I do *not* speak to him. I admire, I love him—for I know his former adventures—but I shall not speak to him until the day after to-morrow."

"And what then?" asked Madame de Chevreuse.

"You shall know to-morrow evening," replied the Coadjutor, laughing.

Athos then drew near her.

"Monsieur le Comte," said the duchess, giving him a letter, "here is what I promised you; our young friend will be extremely well received."

"Madame, he is very happy in owing any obligation to you."

Madame de Chevreuse rose to depart.

"Vicomte," said Athos to Raoul, "follow the duchess; beg her to do you the favour to take your arm in going downstairs, and thank her as you descend."

The fair Indian approached Scarron.

"You are going already?" he said.

"One of the last, as you see; if you hear anything of Monsieur Voiture, be so kind as to send me word to-morrow."

"Oh!" said Scarron, "he may die now."

"Why?" asked the young girl with the velvet eyes.

"Certainly—his panegyric has been uttered."

They parted, laughing; she turning back to gaze at the poor paralytic man with interest, he looking after her with eyes of love.

So the invalid disappeared soon afterwards, and went into his sleeping-room; and one by one the lights in the salon of La Rue des Tournelles were extinguished.

CHAPTER XXII.

SAINT DENIS.

THE day had begun to break when Athos rose and dressed himself; it was plain, by the paleness still greater than usual, and by those traces which loss of sleep leaves on the face, that he must have passed almost the whole of the night without sleeping. Contrary to the custom of a man so firm and decided, there was this morning in his personal appearance something slow and irresolute. He was evidently occupying himself in preparations for the departure of Raoul; after employing nearly an hour in these cares, he opened the door of the room in which the Vicomte slept, and entered.

The sun, already high, penetrated into the room through the window, the curtains of which Raoul had neglected to close on the previous evening. He was still sleeping, his head gracefully reposing on his arm.

Athos approached and hung over the youth in an attitude full of tender melancholy; he looked long on this young man, whose smiling mouth, and half-closed eyes, bespoke soft dreams and light slumbers, as if his guardian angel watched over him with solicitude and affection. By degrees Athos gave himself up to the charms of his reverie in the proximity of youth, so pure, so fresh. His own youth seemed to re-appear, bringing with it all those soft remembrances, which are like perfumes more than thoughts. Between the past and the present there was an abyss. But imagination has the flight of an angel of light, and travels over the seas where we have been almost shipwrecked,—the darkness in which our associations are lost—the precipice, whence our happiness has been hurled and swallowed up. He remembered that all the first part of his life had been embittered by a woman, and he thought with alarm of the influence which love might possess over so fine, and, at the same time, so vigorous an organisation as that of Raoul.

In recalling all that he had suffered, he foresaw all that Raoul would suffer; and the expression of the deep and tender compassion which throbbed in his heart was pictured in the moist eye with which he gazed on the young man.

At this moment Raoul awoke, without a cloud on his face—without weariness or lassitude; his eyes were fixed on those of Athos, and he, perhaps, comprehended all that passed in the heart of the man who was awaiting his awakening as a lover awaits the awakening of his mistress, for his glance, in return, had all the tenderness of infinite love.

"You are there, sir," he said respectfully.

"Yes, Raoul," replied the count.

"And you did not awaken me?"

"I wished to leave you still to enjoy some moments of sleep, my child; you must be fatigued from yesterday."

"Oh, sir! how good you are!"

Athos smiled.

"How are you ?" he said.

"Perfectly well; quite rested, sir."

"You are still growing," Athos continued, with that charming and paternal interest felt by a grown man for a youth.

"Oh, sir! I beg your pardon," exclaimed Raoul, ashamed of so much attention; "in an instant, I shall be dressed."

Athos then called Olivain.

"Everything," said Olivain to Athos, "has been done according to your directions; the horses are waiting."

"And I was asleep !" cried Raoul; "whilst you, sir, you had the kindness to attend to all these details. Truly, sir, you overwhelm me with benefits !"

"Therefore you love me, a little, I hope," replied Athos, in a tone of emotion.

"Oh, sir! God knows that I love, I revere you."

"See that you forget nothing !" said Athos, appearing to look about him that he might hide his emotion.

"No, indeed, sir," answered Raoul.

The servant then approached Athos, and said, hesitatingly:

"Monsieur le Vicomte has no sword."

"'Tis well," said Athos. "I will take care of that."

They went downstairs; Raoul looking every now and then at the count to see if the moment of farewell was at hand, but Athos was silent. When they reached the steps, Raoul saw three horses.

"Oh, sir! then you are going with me ?"

"I shall conduct you part of the way," said Athos.

They set out, passing over the Pont Neuf; they pursued their way along the quay then called L'Abreuvoir Pepin, and went along by the walls of the Grand Châtelet. They proceeded to the Rue St. Denis.

After passing through the Porte Saint Denis, Athos looked at Raoul's horse, and said:

"Take care, Raoul! I have already often told you of this; you must not forget it, for it is a great defect in a rider. See! your horse is tired already, he froths at the mouth, whilst mine looks as if he had only just left the stable. You hold the bit too tight, and so make his mouth hard; so that you will not be able to make him manœuvre quickly. The safety of a cavalier often depends on the prompt obedience of his horse. In a week, remember, you will no longer be performing your manœuvres, as a practice, but on a field of battle."

Then, suddenly, in order not to give too sad an importance to this observation:

"See, Raoul!" he resumed; "what a fine plain for partridge shooting! I have remarked also another thing," said Athos, "which is, that in firing off your pistol, you hold your arm too much stretched out. This tension lessens the accuracy of the aim. So, in twelve times you thrice missed the mark."

"Which you, sir, struck twelve times," answered Raoul, smiling.

"Because I bent my arm, and rested my hand on my elbow—so—do you understand what I mean?"

"Yes, sir. I fired since in that manner, and was completely successful."

"What a cold wind!" resumed Athos. "A wintry blast. Apropos, if you fire—and you will do so, for you are recommended to a young General who is very fond of powder—remember in single combat (which often takes place in the cavalry) never to fire the first shot. He who fires the first shot rarely hits his man, for he fires with the apprehension of being disarmed before an armed foe; then, whilst he fires, make your horse rear; that manœuvre has saved my life several times."

"I shall do so, if only in gratitude for——"

"Eh!" cried Athos, "are not those poachers whom they have arrested yonder? They are. Then another important thing, Raoul; should you be wounded in a battle, and fall from your horse—if you have any strength left, disentangle yourself from the line that your regiment has formed; otherwise, it may be driven back, and you will be trampled to death by the horses. At all events, if you should be wounded, write to me the very instant, or make some one write to me. We are judges of wounds, we old soldiers," Athos added, smiling.

"Thank you, sir," answered the young man, much moved.

They arrived that very moment at the gate of the town, guarded by two sentinels.

"Here comes a young gentleman," said one of them, "who seems as if he were going to join the army."

"How do you find that out?" inquired Athos.

"By his manner, sir, and his age; he's the second to-day."

"Has a young man, such as I am, gone through this morning, then?" asked Raoul.

"Faith, yes, with a haughty presence and fine equipage; such as the son of a noble house would have."

"He was to be my companion on the journey, sir," cried Raoul. "Alas! he cannot make me forget what I shall have lost!"

Thus talking, they traversed the streets, full of people on account of the fête, and arrived opposite the old cathedral where the first mass was going on.

"Let us alight, Raoul," said Athos. "Olivain, take care of our horses, and give me my sword."

The two gentlemen then went into the church. Athos gave Raoul some of the holy water. A love as tender as that of a lover for his mistress dwells, undoubtedly, in some paternal hearts for a son.

"Come, Raoul," he said, "let us follow this man."

The verger opened the iron grating which guarded the royal tombs, and stood on the topmost step, whilst Athos and Raoul descended. The depths of the sepulchral descent were dimly lighted by a silver lamp, on the lowest step; and just below this lamp there was laid, wrapt in a large mantle of violet velvet, worked with fleurs-de-lis of gold, a catafalque resting upon trestles of oak.

The young man, prepared for this scene by the state of his own feelings, which were mournful, and by the majesty of the cathedral, which he had passed through, had descended in a slow and solemn manner, and stood with his head uncovered before these mortal spoils of the last king, who was not to be placed by the side of his forefathers until his successor should take his place there; and who appeared to abide on that spot, that he might thus address human pride, so sure to be exalted by the glories of a throne: "Dust of the earth! I await thee!"

There was a profound silence.

Then Athos raised his hand, and pointing to the coffin,—

"This temporary sepulchre is," he said, "that of a man of feeble mind; yet whose reign was full of great events; because, over this king watched the spirit of another man, even as this lamp keeps vigil over this coffin, and illumines it. He whose intellect was thus supreme, was, Raoul, the actual sovereign; the other, nothing but a phantom to whom he gave a soul; and yet, so powerful is majesty amongst us, this man has not even the honour of a tomb even at the feet of him in whose service his life was worn away. Remember, Raoul, this! If Richelieu made the king, by comparison, small, he made royalty great. The palace of the Louvre contains two things—the king, who must die—and royalty, which dieth not. The minister, so feared, so hated by his master, has descended into the tomb, drawing after him the king —whom he would not leave alone on earth, lest he should destroy what he had done. So blind were his contemporaries that they regarded the Cardinal's death as a deliverance; and I, even I, opposed the designs of the great man who held the destinies of France in his hands. Raoul, learn how to distinguish the king from royalty; the king is but a man; royalty is the gift of God. Whenever you hesitate as to whom you ought to serve, abandon the exterior, the material appearance, for the invisible principle : for the invisible principle is everything. Raoul, I seem to read your future destiny as through a cloud. It will be happier, I think, than ours has been. Different in your fate to us—you will have a king without a minister, whom you may serve, love, respect. Should the king prove a tyrant, for power begets tyranny, serve, love, respect royalty, that Divine right, that celestial spark which makes this dust still powerful and holy, so that we—gentlemen, nevertheless, of rank and condition—are as nothing in comparison with that cold corpse extended here."

"I shall adore God, sir," said Raoul. "I shall respect royalty, I shall serve the king, and I shall, if death be my lot, hope to die for the king, for royalty, and for God. Have I, sir, comprehended your instructions?"

Athos smiled.

"Yours is a noble nature," he said; "here is your sword."

Raoul bent his knee to the ground.

"It was worn by my father, a loyal gentleman. I have worn it in my turn, and it has sometimes not been disgraced when the hilt was in my hand, and the sheath at my side. Should your hand still be too weak to use this sword, Raoul, so much the better. You will have more time to learn to draw it only when it ought to be used."

"Sir," replied Raoul, putting the sword to his lips as he received it from the count, "I owe everything to you, and yet this sword is the most precious gift you have made me. I shall wear it, I swear to you, as a grateful man should do."

"'Tis well—arise, vicomte, embrace me."

Raoul rose, and threw himself with emotion into the count's arms.

"Adieu," faltered the count, who felt his heart die away within him; "adieu, and think of me."

"Oh! for ever and ever!" cried the youth; "oh! I swear to you, sir, should any harm happen to me, your name shall be the last that I shall utter — the remembrance of you, my last thought."

Athos hastened up-stairs to conceal his emotion, and regained, with hurried steps, the porch where Olivain was waiting with the horses.

"Olivain," said Athos, showing the servant Raoul's shoulder-belt; "tighten the buckle of this sword, which falls a little too low. You will accompany Monsieur le Vicomte till Grimaud has rejoined you. You know, Raoul, Grimaud is an old and zealous servant, he will follow you."

"Yes, sir," answered Raoul.

"Now to horse, that I may see you depart."

Raoul obeyed.

"Adieu, Raoul," said the count; "adieu, my dear boy!"

"Adieu, sir—adieu—my beloved protector!"

Athos waved his hand; he dared not trust himself to speak, and Raoul went away, his head uncovered. Athos remained motionless, looking after him until he turned the corner of the street.

Then the count threw the bridle of his horse into the hands of a peasant, mounted again the steps, went into the cathedral, there to kneel down in the darkest corner, and to pray.

CHAPTER XXIII.

ONE OF THE FORTY METHODS OF ESCAPE OF THE DUC DE BEAUFORT.

THE game at tennis, which, upon a sign from Grimaud, Monsieur de Beaufort had consented to play, began in the afternoon. The duke was in full force, and beat La Ramée completely.

Four of the guards, who were constantly near the prisoner, assisted in picking up the tennis balls. When the game was over, the duke, laughing at La Ramée for his bad play, offered these men two louis-d'or to go and drink his health, with their four other comrades.

The guards asked permission of La Ramée, who gave it to them, but not till the evening, however—until then he had business, and the prisoner was not to be left alone.

Six o'clock came, and, although they were not to sit down to table until seven o'clock, dinner was ready, and served up. Upon a side-board appeared the colossal pie with the duke's arms on it, and, seemingly, cooked to a turn, as far as one could judge by the golden colour which illumined the crust.

The rest of the dinner was to come.

Every one was impatient; La Ramée to sit down to table—the guards to go and drink—the duke to escape.

Grimaud alone was calm as ever. One might have fancied that Athos had educated him with a forethought of this great event.

There were moments when, looking at Grimaud, the duke asked himself if he was not dreaming, and if that marble figure was really at his service, and would become animate when the moment arrived for action.

La Ramée sent away the guards, desiring them to drink to the duke's health, and, as soon as they were gone, he shut all the doors, put the keys in his pocket, and showed the table to the prince with an air which meant——

"Whenever my lord pleases."

The prince looked at Grimaud—Grimaud looked at the clock —it was hardly a quarter past six. The escape was fixed to take place at seven o'clock. There were, therefore, three quarters of an hour to wait.

The duke, in order to delay a quarter of an hour, pretended to be reading something that interested him, and said he wished they would allow him to finish his chapter. La Ramée went up to him and looked over his shoulder to see what book it was that had so singular an influence over the prisoner as to make him put off taking his dinner.

It was "Cæsar's Commentaries," which La Ramée had lent him, contrary to the orders of the governor; and La Ramée resolved never again to disobey those injunctions.

Meantime he uncorked the bottles, and went to smell if the pie was good.

At half-past six the duke arose, and said very gravely :

"Certainly, Cæsar was the greatest man of ancient times."

"You think so, my lord?" answered La Ramée.

"Yes."

"Well, as for me, I prefer Hannibal."

"And why, pray, Master La Ramée?" asked the duke.

"Because he left no Commentaries," replied La Ramée, with his coarse laugh.

The duke offered no reply, but sitting down at the table, made a sign that La Ramée should also seat himself opposite to him. There is nothing so expressive as the face of an epicure who finds himself before a well-spread table : so La Ramée, when receiving his plate of soup from Grimaud, presented a type of perfect bliss.

The duke smiled.

"Zounds !" he said; "I don't suppose there is a happier man at this moment in the kingdom than you are !"

"You are right, my lord duke," answered the officer; "I don't know a pleasanter sight than a well-covered table; and when, added to that, he who does the honours is the grandson of Henry IV., you will, my lord duke, easily comprehend that the honour one receives doubles the pleasure one enjoys."

The duke bowed in his turn, and an imperceptible smile appeared on the face of Grimaud, who kept behind La Ramée.

"My dear La Ramée," said the duke, "you're the only man who can turn a compliment as you do."

"No, my lord duke," replied La Ramée, in the fulness of his heart; "I say what I think—there is no compliment in what I say to you——"

"Then you are attached to me?" asked the duke.

"To own the truth, I should be inconsolable if you were to leave Vincennes."

"A droll way of showing your affliction." The duke meant to say "affection."

"But, my lord," returned La Ramée; "what would you do if you got out? Every folly you committed would embroil you with the court, and they would put you into the Bastille, instead of Vincennes. Now, Monsieur de Chavigny is not amiable, I allow; but Monsieur du Tremblay is much worse."

"Indeed!" exclaimed the duke, who from time to time looked at the clock, the fingers of which seemed to move with a sickening slowness; "but what could you expect from the brother of a Capuchin monk, brought up in the school of Cardinal Richelieu?"

"Ah, my lord, it is a great happiness that the queen, who always wished you well, had a fancy to send you here, where there's a promenade and a tennis court, good air, and a good table."

"In short," answered the duke, "if I comprehend you, La Ramée, I am ungrateful for having ever thought of leaving this place?"

"Oh! my lord duke, 'tis the height of ingratitude; but your highness has never seriously thought of it?"

"Yes," returned the duke; "I must confess I do sometimes think of it."

"Still by one of your forty methods, your highness?"

"Yes—yes, indeed."

"My lord," said La Ramée, "now we are quite at our ease, and enjoying ourselves, pray tell me one of those forty ways invented by your highness."

"Willingly," answered the duke; "give me the pie!"

"I am listening," said La Ramée, leaning back in his arm-chair, and raising his glass of Madeira to his lips, and winking his eye that he might see the sun through the rich liquid that he was about to taste.

The duke glanced at the clock. In ten minutes it would strike seven.

Grimaud placed the pie before the duke, who took a knife with a silver blade to raise the upper crust; but La Ramée, who was afraid of any harm happening to this fine work of art, passed his knife, which had an iron blade, to the duke.

"Thank you, La Ramée," said the prisoner.

"Well, my lord! this famous invention of yours?"

"Must I tell you," replied the duke, "on what I most reckon, and what I determine to try first?"

"Yes, that one! my lord."

"Well—I should hope, in the first instance, to have as a keeper an honest fellow, like you."

"And you have one, my lord—well?"

"Having then a keeper like La Ramée, I should try also to have introduced to me by some friend a man who would be devoted to me, and who would assist me in my flight."

"Come, come," said La Ramée, "not a bad idea."

"Isn't it? For instance, the former serving man of some brave gentleman, an enemy himself to Mazarin, as every gentleman ought to be."

"Hush—don't let us talk politics, my lord!"

"Then my keeper will begin to trust this man, and to depend upon him; and then I shall have news from those without the prison walls."

"Ah, yes! but how can the news be brought to you?"

"Nothing easier—in a game of tennis. I send a ball into the moat; a man is there who picks it up; the ball contains a letter."

"The devil it does! The devil it does!" said La Ramée, scratching his head; "you are wrong to tell me that, my lord. I shall watch the men who pick up balls."

The duke smiled.

"But," resumed La Ramée, "that is only one way of corresponding."

"'Tis a good one, it seems to me."

"But not a sure one."

"Pardon me. For instance, I say to my friends, Be on a certain day, on a certain hour, at the other side of the moat, with two horses."

"Well, what then?"—La Ramée began to be uneasy—"unless the horses have wings to mount up to the ramparts and to come and fetch you."

"That's not needed. I have," replied the duke, "a way of descending from the ramparts."

" What ?"

" A ladder of ropes."

" Yes—but," answered La Ramée, trying to laugh, " a ladder or ropes can't be sent round a ball, like a letter."

" No; but it can come in another way—in a pie, for instance," replied the duke. " The guards are away. Grimaud is here alone ; and Grimaud is the man whom a friend has sent to second me in everything. The moment for my escape is fixed—seven o'clock. Well—at a few minutes to seven——"

" At a few minutes to seven ?" cried La Ramée, the cold sweat on his brow.

" At a few minutes to seven," returned the duke (suiting the action to the words), " I raise the crust of the pie. I find in it two poignards, a ladder of ropes, and a gag. I point one of the poignards at La Ramée's breast, and I say to him, ' My friend, I am sorry for it; but if thou stirrest, if thou utterest a cry, thou art a dead man !' "

The duke, in pronouncing these words, suited, as we have before said, the action to the words. He was standing near the officer, and he directed the point of the poignard in such a manner, close to La Ramée's heart, that there could be no doubt in the mind of that individual as to his determination. Meanwhile, Grimaud, still mute as ever, drew from the pie the other sword, the rope-ladder, and the gag.

La Ramée followed all these objects with his eyes ; his alarm every moment increasing.

" Oh, my lord !" he cried, with an expression of stupefaction in his face ; " you haven't the heart to kill me !"

" No ; not if thou dost not oppose my flight."

" But, my lord, if I let you escape, I am a ruined man."

" I shall compensate thee for the loss of thy place."

" You are determined to leave the château ?"

" By heaven and earth ! This evening I shall be free."

" And if I defend myself, or call, or cry out ?"

" I shall kill thee ; on the honour of a gentleman, I shall."

At this moment the clock struck.

" Seven o'clock !" said Grimaud, who had not spoken a word.

La Ramée made one movement, in order to satisfy his conscience. The duke frowned ; the officer felt the point of the poignard, which, having penetrated through his clothes, was close to his heart.

" Let us despatch," said the duke.

" My lord—one last favour."

" What ? speak—make haste."

" Bind my arms, my lord, fast."

" Why bind thee ?"

" That I may not be considered as your accomplice."

" Your hands ?" asked Grimaud.

" Not before me, behind me."

" But with what ? " asked the duke.

" With your belt, my lord," replied La Ramée.

The duke undid his belt and gave it to Grimaud, who tied La Ramée in such a way as to satisfy him.

" Your feet also," said Grimaud.

La Ramée stretched out his legs, Grimaud took a napkin, tore it into strips, and tied La Ramée's feet together.

" Now, my lord," said the poor man, " let me have the *poire d'angoisse.* I ask for it; without it I should be tried in a court of justice because I did not cry out. Thrust it into my mouth, my lord, thrust it in."

Grimaud prepared to comply with this request, when the officer made a sign as if he had something to say.

"Speak," said the duke.

" Now, my lord, do not forget, if any harm happens to me, on your account, that I have a wife and four children."

" Rest assured—put the gag in, Grimaud."

In a second La Ramée was gagged, and laid prostrate. Two or three chairs were thrown down, as if there had been a struggle. Grimaud then took from the pocket of the officer all the keys it contained, and first opened the door of the room in which they were, then shut it, and double-locked it, and both he and the duke proceeded rapidly down the gallery, which led to the little inclosure. At last they reached the tennis-court. It was completely deserted. No sentinels—no one at the windows.

The duke ran on to the rampart, and perceived, on the other side of the ditch, three cavaliers with two riding horses. The duke exchanged a signal with them. It was well for him that they were there.

Grimaud, meantime, undid the means of escape.

This was not, however, a rope-ladder, but a ball of silk cord, with a narrow board, which was to pass between the legs and to unwind itself by the weight of the person who sat astride upon the board.

" Go !" said the duke.

" The first, my lord ?" inquired Grimaud.

"Certainly. If I am caught, I risk nothing but being taken back again to prison. If they catch thee, thou wilt be hung."

" True," replied Grimaud.

And, instantly, Grimaud, sitting upon the board, as if on horseback, commenced his perilous descent.

The duke followed him with his eyes with involuntary terror. He had gone down about three-quarters of the length of the wall, when the cord broke. Grimaud fell—precipitated into the moat.

The duke uttered a cry, but Grimaud did not give a single moan. He must have been dreadfully hurt, for he did not stir from the place where he fell.

Immediately, one of the men who were waiting, slipped down into the moat, tied under Grimaud's shoulders the end of a cord, and the other two, who held the other end, drew Grimaud to them.

" Descend, my lord," said the man in the moat. " There are only fifteen feet more from the top down here, and the grass is soft."

The duke had already begun to descend. His task was the more difficult, as there was no board to support him. He was obliged to let himself down by his hands, and from a height of fifty feet. But, as we have said, he was active, strong, and full of presence of mind. In less than five minutes he arrived at the end of the cord. He was then only fifteen feet from the ground, as the gentleman below had told him. He let go the rope, and fell upon his feet, without receiving any injury.

He instantly began to climb up the slope of the moat, on the top of which he met De Rochefort. The other two gentlemen were unknown to him. Grimaud, in a swoon, was tied on to a horse.

" Gentlemen," said the duke, " I shall thank you later : now we have not a moment to lose. On, then ! on ! those who love me, follow me !"

And he jumped on his horse, and set off on full gallop, drawing in the fresh air, and crying out, with an expression of face which it would be impossible to describe :

" Free ! free ! free !"

CHAPTER XXIV.

THE TIMELY ARRIVAL OF D'ARTAGNAN IN PARIS.

At Blois D'Artagnan received the money paid to him by Mazarin for any future services he might render the Cardinal.

From Blois to Paris was a journey of four days for ordinary travellers, but D'Artagnan arrived on the third day at the Barrière

Saint Denis. In turning the corner of the Rue Montmartre, in order to reach the Rue Tiquetonne and the Hôtel de la Chevrette, where he had appointed Porthos to meet him, he saw, at one of the windows of the hotel, his friend Porthos, dressed in a sky-blue waistcoat, embroidered with silver, and gaping, till he showed all down his throat; whilst the people passing by admiringly gazed at this gentleman, so handsome and so rich, who seemed so weary of his riches and his greatness.

Porthos, seeing D'Artagnan, hastened to receive him on the threshold of the hotel.

" Ah ! my dear friend !" he cried, " what bad stabling for my horses here !"

" Indeed !" said D'Artagnan ; " I am most unhappy to hear it, on account of those fine animals."

" And I also—I was also wretchedly off," he answered, moving backwards and forwards as he spoke—" and had it not been for the hostess," he added, with his air of vulgar self-complacency, " who is very agreeable, and understands a joke, I should have got a lodging elsewhere."

" Yes, I understand," said D'Artagnan, " the air of La Rue Tiquetonne is not like that of Pierrefonds ; but console yourself, I shall soon conduct you to one much better."

Then, taking Porthos aside :

" My dear De Valon," he said, " here you are in full dress most fortunately, for I shall take you directly to the Cardinal's."

" Gracious me !—really !" cried Porthos, opening his great, wondering eyes.

" Yes, my friend."

" A presentation ?—indeed !"

" Does that alarm you ?"

" No ; but it agitates me."

" Oh ! don't be distressed ; you have not to deal with the other Cardinal ; and this one will not oppress you by his dignity."

" 'Tis the same thing—you understand me, D'Artagnan—a court."

" There's no court now. Alas !"

" The queen !"

" I was going to say, there's no longer a queen. The queen ! Be assured we shall not see her."

" But you, my friend ; are you not going to change your dress?"

" No, I shall go as I am. This travelling dress will show the Cardinal my haste to obey his commands."

They set out on Vulcan and Bayard, followed by Mousqueton on Phœbus, and arrived at the Palais Royal at about a quarter to seven. The streets were crowded, for it was the day of Pentecost —and the crowd looked in wonder at these two cavaliers; one as fresh as if he had come out of a bandbox, the other so covered with dust, that he looked as if he had come from a field of battle.

Mousqueton also attracted attention; and as the romance of Don Quixote was then the fashion, they said that he was Sancho, who, after having lost one master, had found two.

On reaching the palace, D'Artagnan sent in to his Eminence the letter in which he had been ordered to return without delay. He was soon ordered to enter into the presence of the Cardinal.

"Courage!" he whispered to Porthos, as they proceeded. "Do not be intimidated. Believe me, the eye of the eagle is closed for ever. We have only the vulture to deal with. Hold yourself up as stiff as on the day of the bastion of Saint Gervais; and do not bend too low to this Italian: that might give him a poor idea of us."

"Good!" answered Porthos. "Good!"

Mazarin was in his study, working at a list of pensions and benefices, of which he was trying to reduce the number. He saw D'Artagnan and Porthos enter with pleasure, yet showed no joy in his countenance.

"Ah! you, is it? Monsieur le Lieutenant, you have been very prompt. 'Tis well. Welcome to ye."

"Thanks, my lord. Here I am at your Eminence's service, as well as Monsieur de Valon, one of my old friends, who used to conceal his nobility under the name of Porthos."

Porthos bowed to the Cardinal.

"A magnificent cavalier," remarked Mazarin.

Porthos turned his head to the right and to the left, and drew himself up with a movement full of dignity.

"The best swordsman in the kingdom, my lord," said D'Artagnan.

Porthos bowed to his friend.

Mazarin was as fond of fine soldiers as, in later times, Frederick of Prussia used to be. He admired the strong hands, the broad shoulders, and steady eye of Porthos. He seemed to see before him the salvation of his administration, and of the kingdom, sculptured in flesh and bone. He remembered that the old association of Musketeers was composed of four persons.

"And your two other friends?" he asked.

Porthos opened his mouth, thinking it a good opportunity to put in a word in his turn; D'Artagnan checked him by a glance from the corner of his eye.

"They are prevented at this moment, but will join us later."

Mazarin coughed a little.

" And this gentleman, being disengaged, takes to the service willingly ?" he asked.

" Yes, my lord, and from complete devotion to the cause, for Monsieur de Bracieux is rich."

" Fifty thousand francs a-year," said Porthos.

These were the first words he had spoken.

" From pure zeal ?" resumed Mazarin, with his artful smile ; " from pure zeal and devotion, then ?"

" My lord has, perhaps, no faith in that word," said D'Artagnan.

" Have you, Monsieur le Gascon ?" asked Mazarin, supporting his elbows on his desk, and his chin on his hands.

" I," replied the Gascon, " I believe in devotion as a word at one's baptism, for instance, which naturally comes before one's proper name ; every one is naturally more or less devout, certainly ; but there should be, at the end of one's devotion, something to gain."

" Your friend, therefore, what does he wish for as the reward of his devotion ?"

D'Artagnan was about to explain that the aim and end of the zeal of Porthos, was, that one of his estates should be erected into a barony, when a great noise was heard in the antechamber ; at the same time the door of the study was burst open, and a man, covered with dust, rushed into it, exclaiming :

" My lord the Cardinal ! my lord the Cardinal !"

Mazarin thought that some one was going to assassinate him, and he drew back, pushing his chair on the castors. D'Artagnan and Porthos moved so as to plant themselves between the person entering and the Cardinal.

" Well, sir," exclaimed Mazarin, " what's the matter ? and why do you rush in here as if you were just going into a market-place ?"

" My lord," replied the messenger, " I wish to speak to your Eminence in secret. I am Monsieur du Poins, an officer in the guards, on duty at the donjon of Vincennes."

Mazarin, perceiving by the paleness and agitation of the messenger that he had something of importance to say, made a sign that D'Artagnan and Porthos should retire.

When they were alone :

" What I have to say is, my lord, that the Duc de Beaufort has contrived to escape from the Château of Vincennes."

Mazarin uttered a cry, and became paler than he who brought this news. He fell, almost fainting, back in his chair.

" Escaped ? Monsieur de Beaufort escaped ?"

" My lord, I saw him run off from the top of the terrace."

" And you did not fire on him ?"

" He was beyond reach of a shot."

" Monsieur de Chavigny—where was he ?"

" Absent."

" And La Ramée ?"

" He was found locked up in the prisoner's room, a gag in his mouth, and a poignard near him."

" But the man who was under him ?"

" Was an accomplice of the duke's, and escaped with him."

Mazarin groaned.

" My lord," said D'Artagnan, advancing towards the Cardinal, " it seems to me that your Eminence is losing precious time. It may still be possible to trace the prisoner. France is large; the nearest frontier is sixty leagues distant."

" And who is to pursue him ?" cried Mazarin.

" I ! Egad ! if my lord orders me to pursue the devil, I would do so, and seize him by the horns and bring him back again."

" And I, too," said Porthos.

" Go, then ; take what guards you find here, and pursue him."

" You command us, my lord, to do so ?"

" And I sign my orders," said Mazarin, taking a piece of paper, and writing some lines; " Monsieur de Valon, your barony is on the back of the Duc de Beaufort's horse ; you have nothing to do but to overtake it. As for you, my dear lieutenant, I promise you nothing; but if you bring him back to me, dead or alive, you shall ask all you wish."

" To horse, Porthos !" said D'Artagnan, taking his friend by the hand.

" Here I am," replied Porthos, with his sublime composure.

They descended the great staircase, taking with them all the guards that they found on their road, and crying out, " To horse ! To horse !" and they spurred on their horses, which set off along the Rue St. Honoré with the speed of a whirlwind.

" Well, baron ! I promised you some good exercise !" said the Gascon.

" Yes, my captain."

As they went, the citizens, awakened, left their doors, and the fierce dogs followed the cavaliers, barking. At the corner of the Cimetière Saint Jean, D'Artagnan upset a man : it was too slight an occurrence to delay people so eager to get on. The troop continued its course as if their steeds were winged.

Alas ! there are no unimportant events in this world ! and, we shall see, that this apparently slight one was near endangering the monarchy.

CHAPTER XXV.

AN ADVENTURE ON THE HIGH ROAD.

THE Musketeers rode the whole length of the Faubourg St. Antoine, and of the road to Vincennes, and soon found themselves out of the town, then in a forest, and then in sight of a village.

From the top of an eminence D'Artagnan perceived a group of people collected on the other side of the moat, in front of that part of the donjon which looks towards Saint Maur. He rode on, convinced that he should in that direction gain intelligence of the fugitive; and he learned from the people that composed that group, that the duke had been pursued without success; that his party consisted of four able men, and one wounded, and that they were two hours and a quarter in advance of their pursuers.

"Only four !" cried D'Artagnan, looking at Porthos; "baron, only four of them !"

Porthos smiled.

"And only two hours and a quarter before us, and we so well mounted, Porthos !"

Porthos sighed, and thought of all that was awaiting his poor horses.

The troop then pursued their course with their wonted ardour; but some of them could no longer sustain this rapidity; three of them stopped after an hour's march, and one fell down.

D'Artagnan, who never turned his head, did not perceive it. Porthos told him of it in his calm manner.

"If we can only keep two," said D'Artagnan, "it will be enough, since the duke's troop are only four in number."

And he spurred his horse on.

At the end of another two hours the horses had gone twelve leagues without stopping; their legs began to tremble; and the foam that they shed whitened the doublets of their masters.

"Let us rest here an instant to give these miserable creatures breathing time," said Porthos

"Let us rather kill them ! yes, kill them !" cried D'Artagnan; "I see fresh tracks; 'tis not a quarter of an hour since they passed this place."

In fact, the road was trodden by horses' feet, visible even in the approaching gloom of evening.

They set out; after a run of two leagues, Mousqueton's horse sank.

"Gracious me!" said Porthos, "there's Phœbus ruined."

"The Cardinal will pay you a hundred pistoles."

"I'm above that.

"Let us set out then again, on a full gallop."

"Yes, if we can."

But, at last, the lieutenant's horse refused to go on; he could not breathe; one last spur, instead of making him advance, made him fall.

"The devil!" exclaimed Porthos, "there's Vulcan foundered."

"Zounds!" cried D'Artagnan, "we must then stop! Give me your horse, Porthos! What the devil are you doing?"

"By Jove, I am falling, or rather Bayard is falling," answered Porthos.

All three then called out, "All's over."

"Hush!" said D'Artagnan.

"What is it?"

"I hear a horse, 'tis on before; it is at a hundred steps from hence, and in advance of us."

There was, in truth, the neighing of a horse heard.

"Sir," said Mousqueton, "at a hundred steps from us there's a little hunting seat."

"Mousqueton, my pistols."

"They are in my hand, sir."

"Porthos, keep yours in your saddle bags."

"I have them."

"Now, we require horses for the king's service."

"For the king's service," repeated Porthos.

"Then not a word, and to work!"

They went on, through the night, silent as phantoms; they saw a light shine in the midst of some trees.

"There is the house, Porthos," said the Gascon; "let me do what I please, and do you do what I do."

They glided from tree to tree, till they arrived at twenty steps from the house unperceived, and saw, by means of a lanthorn suspended under a hut, four fine horses. A groom was rubbing them down; near them were saddles and bridles.

"I want to buy thy horses," said D'Artagnan, approaching the groom.

"These horses are not to be sold," was the reply.

"I take them, then," said the lieutenant.

And he took hold of one within his reach; his two companions did the same thing.

"Sir," cried the groom, "they have just been six leagues, and have only been unharnessed about half an hour."

"Half an hour's rest is enough," replied the Gascon.

The groom called aloud for help. A kind of steward appeared, just as D'Artagnan and his companions were prepared to mount. The steward wished to expostulate.

"My dear friend," cried the lieutenant, "if you say a word I will blow out your brains."

"But sir," answered the steward, "do you know that these horses belong to Monsieur de Montbazon?"

"So much the better; they must be good animals, then."

"Sir, I shall call my people."

"And I mine; I've ten guards behind me; don't you hear them gallop; and I'm one of the king's Musketeers; come Porthos, come Mouston."

They all mounted the horses as quickly as possible.

"Here! here!" cried the steward; "the house servants with the carabines."

"On! on!" cried D'Artagnan; "there'll be firing! on!"

They all set off, swift as the winds.

"Here!" cried the steward, "here!" whilst the groom ran to a neighbouring building.

"Take care of your horses," said D'Artagnan to him.

"Fire!" replied the steward.

A gleam, like a flash of lightning, illumined the road, and, with the flash, was heard the whistling of balls, which were fired in the air.

"They fire like grooms," said Porthos; "in the time of the Cardinal, people fired better than that; do you remember the road to Crevecœur, Mousqueton?"

"Ah, sir! my left side still pains me."

"Are you sure we are on the right track, lieutenant?"

"Egad, didn't you hear—these horses belong to Monsieur de Montbazon: well, Monsieur de Montbazon is the husband of Madame de Montbazon——"

"And——"

"And Madame de Montbazon is the mistress of the Duc de Beaufort."

"Ah! I understand," replied Porthos; "she has ordered relays of horses."

"Exactly so."

"And we are pursuing the duke with the very horses he has just left?"

"My dear Porthos, you are really a man of superior understanding," said D'Artagnan, with a look as if he spoke against his conviction.

"Pooh!" said Porthos, "I am what I am."

They rode on for an hour, till the horses were covered with foam and dust.

"Zounds! what is yonder?" cried D'Artagnan.

"You are very lucky, if you see anything in such a night as this," said Porthos.

"Something bright."

"I, too," cried Mousqueton, "saw them also."

"Yes, a dead horse," said D'Artagnan, pulling up his horse, which shied: "it seems that they also are broken-winded as well as ourselves."

"I seem to hear the noise of a troop of horsemen," exclaimed Porthos, leaning over his horse's mane.

"Impossible!"

"They appear to be numerous."

"Then, 'tis something else."

"Another horse!" said Porthos.

"Dead?"

"No; dying."

"Saddled?"

"Yes, saddled and bridled."

"Then 'tis the fugitives."

"Courage, we have them!"

"But, if they are numerous," observed Mousqueton, "'tis not we who have them, but they who have us."

"Nonsense!" cried D'Artagnan, "they'll suppose us to be stronger than themselves, as we're in pursuit, they'll be afraid, and disperse."

"Certainly," remarked Porthos.

"Ah! do you see?" cried the lieutenant.

"The lights again! this time I too saw them," said Porthos.

"On! on! forward! forward!" cried D'Artagnan, in his stentorian voice, "we shall laugh over all this in five minutes."

And they darted on anew. The horses, excited by pain and emulation, raced over the dark road, in the midst of which was now seen a moving mass, more dense and obscure than the rest of the horizon.

CHAPTER XXVI.

THE RENCONTRE.

They rode on in this way for ten minutes. Suddenly, two dark forms seemed to separate from the mass, advanced, grew in size, and, as they grew larger and larger, assumed the appearance of two horsemen.

"Oh, oh !" cried D'Artagnan, "they're coming towards us."

"So much the worse for them," said Porthos.

"Who goes there ?" cried a hoarse voice.

The three horsemen made no reply, stopped not, and all that was heard was the noise of swords, drawn from the scabbards, and of the cocking of the pistols, with which the two phantoms were armed.

"Arm to the teeth," said D'Artagnan.

Porthos understood him, and he and the lieutenant each one took from his left hand a pistol, and armed himself each in his turn.

"Who goes there ?" was asked a second time. "Not a step forwarder, or you're dead men ?"

"Stuff !" cried Porthos, almost choked with dust. "Stuff and nonsense ! we have seen plenty of dead men in our time."

Hearing these words, the two shadows blockaded the road, and by the light of the stars might be seen the shining of their arms.

"Back !" cried D'Artagnan ; "or you are dead !"

Two shots were the reply to this threat ; but the assailants attacked their foes with such velocity that in a moment they were upon them ; a third pistol-shot was heard, aimed by D'Artagnan ; and one of his adversaries fell. As to Porthos he assaulted his with such violence, that although his sword was thrust aside, the enemy was thrown off his horse, and fell about ten steps from it.

"Finish ! Mouston—finish the work !" cried Porthos. And he darted on, beside his friend, who had already begun a fresh pursuit.

"Well ?" said Porthos.

"I've broken his skull," cried D'Artagnan. "And you——"

"I've only thrown him down ; but hark !"

Another shot of a carabine was heard. It was Mousqueton, who was obeying his master's command.

"On ! on !" cried D'Artagnan ; "all goes well ! we have the first throw."

"Ha ! ha !" answered Porthos ; "behold, other players appear."

And, in fact, two other cavaliers made their appearance detached, as it seemed, from the principal group ; they again disputed the road.

This time the lieutenant did not wait for the opposite party to speak.

"Stand aside," he cried ; "stand off the road."

"What do you want?" asked a voice.

"The duke!" Porthos and D'Artagnan roared out both at once.

A burst of laughter was the answer, but finished with a groan. D'Artagnan had, with his sword, cut the poor wretch in two who had laughed.

At the same time Porthos and his adversary fired on each other, and D'Artagnan turned to him:

"Bravo!—you've killed him, I think."

"No, wounded his horse only."

"But what ails my horse?"

"What ails your horse is, that he's falling down," replied Porthos.

In truth, the lieutenant's horse stumbled, and fell on his knees; then a rattling in his throat was heard, and he lay down to die. D'Artagnan swore loud enough to be heard in the skies above.

"Does your honour want a horse?" asked Mousqueton.

"Zounds! want one?" cried the Gascon.

"Here's one, your honour——"

"How the devil hast thou two horses?" asked D'Artagnan, jumping on one of them.

"Their masters are dead! I thought they might be useful, so I took them."

Meantime Porthos had reloaded his pistols.

"Be on the alert!" cried D'Artagnan. "Here are two other cavaliers."

As he spoke two horsemen advanced at full speed.

"Ho! your honour," cried Mosqueton, "the man you upset is getting up."

"Why didn't thou do as thou didst to the first man?" said Porthos

"I held the horses, my hands were full, your honour."

A shot was fired that moment—Mousqueton shrieked with pain.

"Ah, sir! I'm hit in the other side! exactly in the other! This hurt is just the fellow of that I had on the road to Amiens."

Porthos turned round like a lion—plunged on the dismounted cavalier, who tried to draw his sword; but, before it was out of the scabbard, Porthos, with the hilt of his, had hit him such a terrible blow on the head, that he fell like an ox beneath the butcher's knife.

Mousqueton, groaning, slipped down from his horse—his wound not allowing him to sit in his saddle.

On perceiving the cavaliers, D'Artagnan had stopped and charged his pistol afresh; besides. his horse, he found, had a carbine on the bow of the saddle.

" Here I am !" exclaimed Porthos. "Shall we wait, or shall we charge ?"

" Let us charge them," answered the Gascon.

"Charge !" said Porthos.

They spurred on their horses ; the other cavaliers were only twenty steps from them.

" For the king !" cried D'Artagnan.

"The king has no authority here !" answered a deep voice, which seemed to proceed from a cloud—so enveloped was the cavalier in a whirlwind of dust.

" 'Tis well; we will see if the king's name is not a passport everywhere," replied the Gascon.

"See !" answered the voice.

Two shots were fired at once ; one by D'Artagnan, the other by the adversary of Porthos. D'Artagnan's ball took off his enemy's hat. The ball fired by Porthos's foe went through the throat of his horse, which fell, groaning.

" Ah ! this," cried the voice, the tone of which was at once piercing and jeering—" this ! 'tis nothing but a butchery of horses, and not a combat between men. To the sword, sir !—the sword !"

And he jumped off his horse.

" To our swords !—be it so !" replied D'Artagnan—" that's just what I want."

D'Artagnan, in two steps, was engaged with the foe, whom, according to his custom, he attacked impetuously ; but he met this time with a skill and a strength of arm which made him pause. Twice he was obliged to step back ; his opponent stirred not one inch. D'Artagnan returned, and again attacked him.

Twice or thrice blows were struck on both sides without effect ; sparks were emitted from the swords, like water spouting out.

At last D'Artagnan thought it was time to try one of his favourite feints in fencing. He brought it to bear ; skilfully executed it with the rapidity of lightning; and struck the blow with a force which he fancied would prove irresistible.

The blow was parried.

" Sdeath !" he cried, with his Gascon accent.

At this exclamation his adversary bounded back, and, bending his bare head, tried to distinguish in the gloom, the features of the lieutenant.

As to D'Artagnan, afraid of some feint, he still stood on the defensive.

" Have a care," cried Porthos to his opponent ; " I've still two pistols charged."

"The more reason you should fire the first," cried his foe.

Porthos fired; a flash threw a gleam of light over the field of battle.

As the light shone on them, a cry was heard from the other two combatants.

" Athos !" exclaimed D'Artagnan.

" D'Artagnan !" ejaculated Athos.

Athos raised his sword—D'Artagnan lowered his.

" Aramis !" cried Athos—" don't fire !"

" Ha ! ha ! is it you, Aramis ?" said Porthos.

And he threw away his pistol.

Aramis pushed his back into his saddle bags, and sheathed his sword.

" My son !" exclaimed Athos, extending his hand to D'Artagnan. This was the name which he gave him in former days—in their moments of tender intimacy.

" Athos !" cried D'Artagnan, wringing his hands. " So you defend him ! And I, who have sworn to take him dead or alive, I am dishonoured—Ah !"

" Kill me !" replied Athos, uncovering his breast, " if your honour requires my death."

" Oh ! woe's me ! woe's me !" cried the lieutenant; " there's only one man in the world who could stay my hand; by a fatality that very man comes across my way. What shall I say to the Cardinal ?"

" You can tell him, sir," answered a voice, which was a voice of high command in that battle-field, " that he sent against me the only two men capable of getting the better of four men;—of fighting man to man, without discomfiture against the Count de la Fère and the Chevalier D'Herblay, and of surrendering only to fifty men !"

" The prince !" exclaimed at the same moment Athos and Aramis, unmasking as they spoke; " the Duc de Beaufort !" whilst D'Artagnan and Porthos stepped backwards.

" Fifty cavaliers !" cried the Gascon and Porthos.

" Look round you, gentlemen, if you doubt the facts," said the duke.

The two friends looked to the right—to the left; they were encompassed by a troop of horsemen.

" Hearing the noise of the fight," resumed the duke, " I fancied you had about twenty men with you, so I came back with those around me, tired of always running away, and wishing to draw my sword for my own cause; but you are only two."

"Yes, my lord; but, as you have said, two equal to twenty," said Athos.

"Come, gentlemen, your swords," said the duke.

"Our swords!" cried D'Artagnan, raising his head and regaining his self-possession—"Never!"

"Never," added Porthos.

Some of the men moved towards them.

"One moment, my lord," whispered Athos; and he said something in a low voice.

"As you will," replied the duke. "I am too much indebted to you to refuse your first request. Gentlemen," he said to his escort, "withdraw. Monsieur d'Artagnan, Monsieur de Valon, you are free."

The order was obeyed; D'Artagnan and Porthos then found themselves in the centre of a large circle.

"Now, D'Herblay," said Athos, "dismount, and come here."

Aramis dismounted, and went to Porthos; while Athos approached D'Artagnan. All the four were together.

"Friends!" said Athos; "do you regret that you have not shed our blood?"

"No," replied D'Artagnan; "I regret to see that we, hitherto united, are opposed to each other. Ah! nothing will ever go well with us now!"

"Oh! heaven! No, all is over!" said Porthos.

"Well—be on our side now," resumed Aramis.

"Silence, D'Herblay!" cried Athos; "such proposals are not to be made to gentlemen such as these. 'Tis a matter of conscience with them, as with us."

"Meantime, here we are, enemies!" said Porthos. "Grammercy! who would ever have thought it?"

D'Artagnan only sighed.

Athos looked at them both, and took their hands in his.

"Gentlemen!" he said, "this is a serious business, and my heart bleeds as if you had pierced it through and through. Yes, we are severed; there is the great—the sad truth! but we have not as yet declared war; perhaps we shall have to make certain conditions, therefore a solemn conference is indispensable."

"For my own part, I demand it," said Aramis.

"I accept it," interposed D'Artagnan, proudly.

Porthos bowed, as if in assent.

"Let us choose a place of rendezvous," continued Athos; "and, in a last interview, arrange our mutual position, and the conduct we are to maintain towards each other."

"Good !" the other three exclaimed.

"Well, then, the place ?"

"Will the Place Royale suit you ?" asked D'Artagnan.

"In Paris ?"

"Yes."

Athos and Aramis looked at each other.

"The Place Royale—be it so !" replied Athos.

"When ?"

"To-morrow evening, if you please."

"At what hour ?"

"At ten in the evening if that suits you—we shall be returned."

"Good."

"There," continued Athos, "either peace or war will be decided—our honour, at all events, will be secured."

"Alas !" murmured D'Artagnan, "our honour as soldiers is lost to us for ever ! Now, Porthos ; now we must hence, to bear back our shame on our heads to the Cardinal."

"And tell him," cried a voice, "that I am not too old to be still a man of action."

D'Artagnan recognised the voice of De Rochefort.

"Can I do anything for you, gentlemen," asked the duke.

"Be a witness that we have done what we have done."

"That shall be done, be assured. Adieu ! we shall meet soon, I trust, in Paris, where you shall have your revenge."

The duke, as he spoke, kissed his hand, spurred his horse into a gallop, and disappeared, followed by his troop, who were soon lost in distance and darkness.

D'Artagnan and Porthos were now alone with a man who held their two horses ; they thought it was Mousqueton, and went up to him.

"What do I see ?" cried the lieutenant. "Grimaud, is it thou?"

Grimaud signified that he was not mistaken.

"And whose horses are these ?" cried D'Artagnan.

"Who has given them to us ?" said Porthos.

"The Count de la Fère."

"Athos ! Athos !" muttered D'Artagnan, "you think of everyone ; you are indeed a gentleman ! Where art thou bound to Grimaud ?"

"To join the Vicomte de Bragelonne in Flanders, your honour."

They were taking the road towards Paris, when groans, which seemed to proceed from a ditch, attracted their attention.

"What is that ?" asked D'Artagnan.

"It is I, Mousqueton," said a mournful voice, while a sort of shadow arose out of the side of the road.

Porthos ran to him. "Art thou dangerously wounded, my dear Mouston?" he said.

"No, sir, but I am severely wounded."

"What can we do?" said D'Artagnan; "we must return to Paris."

"I will take care of Mousqueton," said Grimaud; and he gave his arm to his old comrade, whose eyes were full of tears, and Grimaud could not tell whether the tears were caused by his wounds, or by the pleasure of seeing him again.

D'Artagnan and Porthos went on, meantime, to Paris. They were passed by a sort of courier, covered with dust, the bearer of a letter from the duke to the Cardinal, giving testimony to the valour of D'Artagnan and Porthos.

Mazarin had passed a very bad night, when this letter was brought to him, announcing that the duke was free, and that he should henceforth raise up a mortal strife against him.

"What consoles me," said the Cardinal, after reading the letter, "is, that at least, in this chase, D'Artagnan has done me one good turn—he has destroyed Broussel. This Gascon is a precious fellow —even his mishaps are useful."

The Cardinal referred to that man whom D'Artagnan upset at the corner of the Cimetière Saint Jean, in Paris, and who was no other than the Councillor Broussel.

CHAPTER XXVII.

THE FOUR OLD FRIENDS PREPARE TO MEET AGAIN.

"WELL," said Porthos, seated in the court-yard of the Hôtel de la Chevrette, to D'Artagnan, who with a long and melancholy face had returned from the Palais Royal, "did he receive you ungraciously, my dear friend?"

"'Ifaith, yes! a hideous brute that Cardinal—what are you eating there, Porthos?"

"I am dipping a biscuit into a glass of Spanish wine—do the same."

"You are right. Gimblon, a glass of wine!"

"Well! how has all gone off?"

"Zounds! you know there's only one way of saying things; so I went in and I said: 'My lord, we were not the strongest party.'

"'Yes, I know that,' he said, 'but tell me the particulars.'

"You know, Porthos, I could not give him the particulars without naming our friends—to name them would be to commit them to ruin, so I merely said they were fifty and we were two."

"'There was firing, nevertheless, I heard,' he said; 'and your swords, they saw the light of day, I presume?'

"'That is, the night, my lord,' I answered.

"'Ah!' cried the Cardinal; 'I thought you were a Gascon, my friend.'

"'I am only a Gascon,' said I, 'when I succeed.' So the answer pleased, and he laughed."

"Well, not so bad a reception as I thought," remarked Porthos.

"No, no, but 'tis the manner in which he spoke. Gimblon, another bottle of wine—'tis almost incredible what a quantity of wine these biscuits will hold."

"Hem—didn't he mention me?" inquired Porthos.

"Ah! yes, indeed!" cried D'Artagnan, who was afraid of disheartening his friend by telling him that the Cardinal had not breathed a word about him; "yes, surely! he said——"

"He said?" resumed Porthos.

"Stop, I want to remember his exact words. He said, as to your friend, tell him that he may sleep in peace."

"Good, very good," said Porthos; "that means as clear as daylight that he intends still to make me a baron."

At this moment nine o'clock struck. D'Artagnan started.

"Ah, yes," said Porthos; "there is nine o'clock. We have a rendezvous, you remember, at the Place Royale."

"Ah! stop! hold your peace, Porthos—don't remind me of it, 'tis that which has made me so cross since yesterday. I shall not go."

"Why," asked Porthos.

"Why, suppose this appointment is only a blind? That there's something hidden beneath it?"

D'Artagnan did not believe Athos to be capable of a deception, but he sought an excuse for not going to the rendezvous.

"We must go," said the superb lord of Bracieux, "lest they should say we were afraid. We, who have faced fifty foes on the high road, can well meet two in the Place Royale."

"Yes, yes, but they took part with the princes without apprising us of it—perhaps the duke may try to catch us in his turn."

"Nonsense! He had us in his power, and let us go. Besides, we can be on our guard—let us take arms, and let Planchet go with us with his carbine."

"Planchet is a Frondeur," answered D'Artagnan.

"Devil take these civil wars! one can no more reckon on one's friends than on one's footmen," said Porthos ; " ah, if Mousqueton were here ! there's one who will never desert me !"

" So long as you are rich ! ah ! my friend ! 'tis not civil war that disunites us ! It is that we are, each of us, twenty years older ; it is that the honest emotions of youth have given place to the suggestions of interest—to the whispers of ambition—to the counsels of selfishness. Yes, you are right—let us go, Porthos ! but let us go well armed—were we not to go they would say we were afraid. Hollo ! Planchet, here ! saddle our horses—take your carbine."

" Whom are we going to attack, sir ?"

" No one—a mere matter of precaution," answered the Gascon.

" You know, sir, that they wished to murder that good Councillor Broussel, the father of the people ?"

" Really, did they ?" said D'Artagnan.

" Yes, but he has been avenged. He was carried home in the arms of the people. His house has been full ever since. He has received visits from the Coadjutor, from Madame de Longueville, and the Prince de Conti—Madame de Chevreuse and Madame de Vendome have left their names at his door."

" How did you hear this ?" inquired D'Artagnan.

" From a good source, sir—I heard it from Friquet."

" From Friquet ? I know that name——"

" A son of Monsieur de Broussel's servant, and a lad that I promise you, in a revolt, will not cast away his share to the dogs."

" Is he not a singing boy at Nôtre Dame ?" asked D'Artagnan.

" Yes, that's he, patronised by Bazin."

" Ah, yes, I know."

" What importance is this reptile of to you ?" asked Porthos.

" Gad !" replied D'Artagnan ; " he has already given me good information, and he may do the same again."

Whilst all this was going on, Athos and Aramis were entering Paris by the Faubourg St. Antoine. They had taken some refreshment on the road, and hastened on that they might not fail at the rendezvous. Bazin was their only attendant, for Grimaud had stayed behind to take care of Mousqueton. As they were passing onwards, Athos proposed that they should lay aside their arms and military costume, and assume a dress suited to the city.

" Oh, no, dear count !" cried Aramis, " is it not a warlike encounter that we are going to ?"

" What do you mean, Aramis ?"

" That the Place Royale is the termination to the main road to Vendomois, and nothing else."

" How, our friends ?"

"Are become our most dangerous enemies, Athos; let us be on our guard."

"Oh! my dear d'Herblay!"

"Who can say whether D'Artagnan has not betrayed us to the Cardinal? who can tell whether Mazarin may not take advantage of this rendezvous and seize us?"

Athos folded his arms, and his noble head fell drooping on his chest.

"What do you expect, Athos?" pursued Aramis; "such are men, and, remember, they are not always twenty years of age; let us take precautions, Athos!"

"But suppose they come unarmed? what a disgrace to us."

"Oh, never fear! besides, if they do, we can make an excuse; we come straight from a journey, and are insurgents, also."

"An excuse for us! to meet D'Artagnan with a false excuse! to have to make a false excuse to Porthos! Oh, Aramis!" continued Athos, shaking his head mournfully, "upon my soul, you make me the most miserable of men; you disenchant a heart not wholly dead to friendship. Go in whatsoever guise you will, for my part I shall go disarmed."

"No, for I will not allow you to do so. 'Tis not one man, 'tis not Athos only, 'tis not the Count de la Fère, whom you will ruin by this weakness, but a whole party to whom you belong, and who depend upon you."

"Be it then so," replied Athos, sorrowfully.

And they pursued their road in mournful silence.

Scarcely had they reached by the Rue de la Mule—the iron gate of the Place Royale—than they perceived three cavaliers, D'Artagnan, Porthos, and Planchet, the two former wrapped up in their military cloaks, under which their swords were hidden, and Planchet, his musket by his side. They were waiting at the entrance of the Rue St. Catherine, and their horses were fastened to the rings of the arcade. Athos, therefore, commanded Bazin to fasten up his horse and that of Aramis in the same manner.

They then advanced, two and two, and saluted each other politely.

"Now, where will it be agreeable to you that we hold our conference?" inquired Aramis, perceiving that people were stopping to look at them, supposing that they were going to engage in one of those far-famed duels still extant in the memory of the Parisians —and especially the inhabitants of the Place Royale.

"The gate is shut," said Aramis, "but if these gentlemen like a cool retreat, under the trees, and a perfect seclusion, I will get the key from the Hôtel de Rohan, and we shall be well situated."

D'Artagnan darted a look into the obscurity of the place. Porthos ventured to put his head between the railings, to try if his glance could penetrate the gloom.

"If you prefer any other place," said Athos, in his persuasive voice, "choose for yourselves."

"This place, if Monsieur d'Herblay can procure the key, is the best that we can have," was the answer.

Aramis went off at once, begging Athos not to remain alone within reach of D'Artagnan and Porthos; a piece of advice which was received with a contemptuous smile.

Aramis returned soon with a man from the Hôtel de Rohan, who was saying to him :

"You swear, sir, that it is not so ?"

"Stop," and Aramis gave him a louis d'or.

"Ah! you will not swear, my master," said the concierge, shaking his head.

"Well, one can never say what may happen ; at present these gentlemen are our friends."

"Yes, certainly," added Athos, "and the other two——"

"You hear that ?" said D'Artagnan to Porthos ; "he won't swear."

"No ?"

"No ; caution, therefore."

Athos did not lose sight of these two speakers. Aramis opened the gate, and faced round in order that D'Artagnan and Porthos might enter. In passing through the gate, the hilt of the lieutenant's sword was caught in the grating, and he was obliged to pull off his cloak ; in doing so he showed the butt-end of his pistols, and a ray of the moon was reflected on the shining metal.

"Do you see ?" whispered Aramis to Athos, touching his shoulder with one hand, and pointing with the other to the arms which the Gascon wore under his belt.

"Alas, I do !" replied Athos, with a deep sigh.

He entered third, and Aramis, who shut the gate after him, last. The two serving-men waited without, but, as if they likewise mistrusted each other, kept their respective distances.

CHAPTER XXVIII.

THE PLACE ROYALE.

They proceeded silently to the centre of the Place ; but as at this very moment the moon had just emerged from behind a cloud, it was considered that they might be observed if they remained on that spot, and they regained the shade of the lime-trees.

There were benches here and there—the four gentlemen stopped near them; at a sign from Athos, Porthos and D'Artagnan sat down, the two others stood in front of them.

After a few minutes of silent embarrassment, Athos spoke.

"Gentlemen," he said, "our presence here is a proof of our former friendship; not one of us has failed at this rendezvous; not one has, therefore, to reproach himself."

"Hear me, count," replied D'Artagnan; "instead of making compliments to each other, let us explain our conduct to each other, like men of right and honest hearts."

"I wish for nothing more; have you any cause of anger against me or Monsieur D'Herblay? If so, speak out," answered Athos.

"I have," replied D'Artagnan. "When I saw you at your château at Bragelonne, I made certain proposals to you, which you perfectly understood; instead of answering me as a friend, you played with me as a child: the friendship, therefore, that you boast of was not broken yesterday by the shock of our swords, but by your dissimulation at your castle."

"D'Artagnan!" said Athos, reproachfully.

"You asked for candour—there it is. You ask what I have against you—I say it. And I have the same sincerity to show you, if you wish, Monsieur D'Herblay; I acted in a similar way to you, and you also deceived me; I reproach you with nothing, however; 'tis only because Monsieur de la Fère has spoken of friendship that I question your conduct."

"And what do you find in it to blame?" asked Aramis, haughtily.

The blood mounted instantly to the temples of D'Artagnan, who rose, and replied:

"I consider it the conduct of a pupil of Jesuits."

On seeing D'Artagnan rise, Porthos rose also; these four men were, therefore, all standing at the same time, with a menacing aspect, opposite to each other.

Upon hearing D'Artagnan's reply, Aramis seemed about to draw his sword, when Athos prevented him.

"D'Artagnan," he said, "you come here to-night, still infuriated by our yesterday's adventure. I believed that your heart was sufficiently noble to enable a friendship of twenty years to be stronger than an affront of a quarter of an hour. Come, do you really think you have anything to say against me? say it then; if I am in fault, I will avow my fault."

The grave and harmonious tones of that beloved voice had still over D'Artagnan its ancient influence, whilst that of Aramis, which had become sharp and screaming in his moments of ill-humour, irritated him. He answered therefore :

"I think, Monsieur le Comte, that you had something to communicate to me at your château of Bragelonne, and that gentleman"—he pointed to Aramis—"had also something to tell me, when I was in his convent. At that time I was not concerned in the adventure during which you barricaded the road that I was going ; however, because I was prudent, you must not take me for a fool. If I had wished to widen the breach between those whom Monsieur D'Herblay chooses to receive with a rope-ladder, and those whom he receives with a wooden ladder, I could have spoken out."

"What are you meddling with?" cried Aramis, pale with anger, suspecting that D'Artagnan had acted as a spy on him, and had seen him with Madame de Longueville.

"I never meddle but with what concerns me, and I know how to make belief that I haven't seen what does not concern me ; but I hate hypocrites, and, among that number, I place musketeers who are abbés, and abbés who are musketeers ; and," he added, turning to Porthos, "here's a gentleman who is of the same opinion as myself."

Porthos, who had not spoken one word, answered merely by a word and a gesture.

He said "yes," and he put his hand on his sword. Aramis started back, and drew his. D'Artagnan bent forward, ready either to attack, or to stand on his defence.

Athos, at that moment, extended his hand with the air of supreme command which characterised him alone, drew out his sword and the scabbard at the same time, broke the blade in the sheath on his knee, and threw the pieces to his right. Then turning to Aramis :

"Aramis," he said, "break your sword in two."

Aramis hesitated.

"It must be done," said Athos ; then in a lower and more gentle voice, he added, "I wish it."

Then Aramis, paler than before, but subdued by these words, broke the flexible blade with his hands, and then, folding his arms, stood trembling with rage.

These proceedings made D'Artagnan and Porthos draw back. D'Artagnan did not draw his sword ; Porthos put his back into the sheath.

" Never !" exclaimed Athos, raising his right hand to heaven, " Never ! I swear before God, who seeth us, and who in the dark- ness of this night heareth us, never shall my sword cross yours, never my eye cast a glance of anger, nor my heart a throb of hatred, to you. We lived together, we loved, we hated together ; we shed, we mingled our blood together, and, too probably, I may still add, that there may be yet a bond between us closer even than that of friendship—perhaps there may be the bond of crime ; for we four, we once did condemn, judge, and slay a human being whom we had not any right to cut off from this world, although ap- parently fitter for hell than for this life. D'Artagnan, I have always loved you as my son ; Porthos, we slept six years side by side ; Aramis is your brother as well as mine, and Aramis has once loved you, as I love you now, and as I have ever loved you. What can Cardinal Mazarin be to us, who compelled such a man as Richelieu to act as we pleased ? What is such or such a prince to us, who have fixed on the queen's head the crown ? D'Artagnan, I ask your pardon for having yesterday crossed swords with you ; Aramis does the same to Porthos : now, hate me if you can ; but, for my own part, I shall ever, even if you do hate me, retain esteem and friendship for you ; repeat my words, Aramis, and then, if you desire it, and if they desire it, let us separate for ever from our old friends."

There was a solemn, though momentary, silence, which was broken by Aramis.

"I swear," he said, with a calm brow, and kindly glance, but in a voice still trembling with recent emotion, "I swear that I no longer bear animosity to those who were once my friends. I regret that I ever crossed swords with you, Porthos : I swear not only that it shall never again be pointed at your breast, but that in the bottom of my heart there will never in future be the slightest hostile sentiment ; now, Athos, come."

Athos was about to retire.

"Oh ! no ! no ! do not go away !" cried D'Artagnan, impelled by one of those irresistible impulses which showed the ardour of his nature, and the native uprightness of his character : "I swear that I would shed the last drop of my blood, and the last frag- ment of my limbs, to preserve the friendship of such a man as you, Athos—of such a man as you, Aramis." And he threw him- self into the arms of Athos.

"My son !" exclaimed Athos, pressing him in his arms.

"And as for me !" said Porthos, "I swear nothing, but I'm choked—forsooth ! If I were obliged to fight against you, I think

I should allow myself to be pierced through and through—for I never loved any one but you in the world;" and honest Porthos burst into tears, as he embraced Athos.

"My friends," said Athos, "this is what I expected from such hearts as yours—yes—I have said it, and I now repeat it! our destinies are irrevocably united, although we pursue different roads. I respect your convictions; and while we fight for opposite sides, let us remain friends. Ministers, princes, kings will pass away like a torrent; civil war, like a flame; but we—we shall remain; I have a presentiment that we shall."

"Yes," replied D'Artagnan, "let us still be Musketeers, and let us retain as our colours that famous napkin of the bastion Saint Gervais—on which the great Cardinal had three fleurs-de-lis embroidered."

"Be it so," cried Aramis. "Cardinalists, or Frondeurs, what matters it—let us meet again our capital seconds at a duel—our devoted friends in business—our merry companions in pleasure."

"And whenever," added Athos, "we meet in battle, at this word—'Place Royale!'—let us put our swords into our left hands, and shake hands with the right—even in the very thick of the carnage."

"You speak charmingly," said Porthos.

"And are the first of men!" added D'Artagnan. "You excel us all!"

Athos smiled with ineffable pleasure.

"'Tis then all settled—gentlemen, your hands—are you not pretty good Christians?"

"Egad!" said D'Artagnan, "by Heaven—yes."

"We should be so on this occasion, if only to be faithful to our oath," said Aramis.

"Ah, I'm ready to do what you will," cried Porthos—"to swear by Mahomet;—devil take me if I've ever been so happy as at this moment!"

And he wiped his eyes, still moist.

"Has not one of you a cross?" asked Athos.

Aramis smiled, and drew from his vest a cross of diamonds, which was hung round his neck by a cross of pearls. "Here is one," he said.

"Well," resumed Athos, "swear on this cross, which, in spite of its material, is still a cross; swear to be united in spite of everything, and for ever, and may this oath bind us to each other—and even, also, our descendants! Does this oath satisfy you?"

"Yes!" said they all with one accord.

"Ah ! traitor !" muttered D'Artagnan to himself, leaning towards Aramis, and whispering in his ear, "you have made us swear on the crucifix of a Frondeuse."

CHAPTER XXIX.

THE FERRY OVER THE OISE.

WE hope that the reader has not quite forgotten the young traveller whom we left on the road to Flanders.

In losing sight of his guardian, whom he had quitted, gazing after him in front of the royal Basilica, Raoul spurred on his horse, in order not only to escape from his own melancholy reflections, but also to hide from Olivain the emotion which his face might betray.

One hour's rapid progress, however, sufficed to disperse the gloomy fancies which had clouded the young man's bright anticipations ; and the hitherto unknown pleasure of freedom—a pleasure which has its sweetness even for those who have never suffered from dependence—seemed to gild for Raoul, not only both heaven and earth, but especially that blue, distant horizon of life which we call the future.

Nevertheless, after several attempts at conversation with Olivain, he foresaw that many long days passed thus would be very dull ; and the count's agreeable voice, his gentle and persuasive eloquence, recurred to his mind, at the various towns through which they journeyed, and about which he had no longer any one to give him those interesting details which he would have drawn from Athos, the most amusing and the best-informed of guides. Another recollection contributed also to sadden Raoul : on their arrival at Sonores, he had perceived, hidden between a screen of poplars, a little château, which so vividly recalled that of La Vallière to his mind, that he had halted for nearly ten minutes to gaze at it, and had resumed his journey with a sigh, too abstracted even to reply to Olivain's respectful inquiry about the cause of this fixed attention. The aspect of external objects is often a mysterious guide communicating with the fibres of memory, which, in spite of us, will arouse them at times ; this thread, like that of Ariadne, when once unravelled, will conduct one through a labyrinth of thought, in which one loses one's self in endeavouring to follow that phantom of the past which is called recollection.

Now the sight of this château had taken Raoul back fifty leagues westward, and had caused him to review his life from the moment when he had taken leave of little Louise to that in which he had seen her for the first time ; and every branch of oak, every weathercock seen on a roof of slates, reminded him, that instead of returning to the friends of his childhood, every instant removed him further from them, and that perhaps he had even left them for ever.

With a full heart and burning head, he desired Olivain to lead on the horses to a little inn, which he observed by the wayside within gun-shot range, a little in advance of the place they had reached.

As for himself, he dismounted, and remained under a beautiful group of chestnuts in flower, among which were murmuring multitudes of bees, and bade Olivain send the host to him with writing-paper and ink, to be placed on a table which he found there, conveniently ready for writing. Olivain obeyed and continued his road, while Raoul remained sitting with his elbow leaning on the table, from time to time gently shaking the flowers from his head, which fell upon him like snow, and gazing vaguely on the pretty landscape before him, dotted over with green fields and groups of trees.

Raoul had been there about ten minutes, during five out of which he was lost in reverie, when there appeared within the circle comprised in his wandering gaze a rubicund figure, who, with a napkin round his body, another under his arm, and a white cap upon his head, approached him, holding paper, pen, and ink in his hand.

"Ah! ah!" said the apparition, "every gentleman seems to have the same fancy, for, not a quarter of an hour ago, a young lad, well-mounted like you, as tall as you, and about your age, halted before this clump of trees, and had this table and this chair brought here, and dined here—with an old gentleman who seemed to be his tutor—upon a pie, of which they haven't left a mouthful, and a bottle of Mâcon wine, of which they haven't left a drop ; but fortunately we have still got some of the same wine, and some of the same pies left, and if your worship will only give your orders——"

"No friend," replied Raoul, smiling, "I am obliged to you, but at this moment I want nothing but the things for which I have asked ;—only I shall be very glad if the ink prove black, and the pen good ; upon these conditions, I will pay for the pen the price of the bottle, and for the ink the price of the pie."

"Very well, sir," said the host, "I'll give the pie and the bottle of wine to your servant, and in this way you will have the pen and ink into the bargain."

"Do as you like," said Raoul, who was beginning his apprenticeship with that particular class of society, who, when there were robbers on the high roads, were connected with them, and who, since highwaymen no longer exist, have advantageously supplied their place.

The host, his mind quite at ease about the bill, placed pen, ink, and paper upon the table. By a lucky chance the pen was tolerably good, and Raoul began to write. The host remained standing in front of him, looking with a kind of involuntary admiration at his handsome face, combining both gravity and sweetness of expression. Beauty has always been, and always will be, all-powerful.

"He's not a guest like the other one here just now," observed mine host to Olivain, who had rejoined his master to see if he wanted anything, "and your young master has no appetite."

"My master had appetite enough three days ago ; but what can one do ? he lost it the day before yesterday."

And Olivain and the host took their way together towards the inn. Olivain, according to the custom of grooms contented with their places, relating to the tavern-keeper all that he thought he could say about the young gentleman ; and Raoul wrote on thus :

"Sir,—After a four hours' march I stop to write to you, for I miss you every moment, and I am always on the point of turning my head as if to reply when you speak to me. I was so bewildered by your departure, and so overcome with grief at our separation, that I but very feebly expressed all the affection and the gratitude that I feel towards you. You will forgive me, sir, for your heart is of such a generous nature, that you can well understand all that passed in mine. I entreat you to write to me, for you form a part of my existence, and if I may venture to tell you so, I also feel anxious. It seemed to me as if you were yourself preparing for some dangerous undertaking, about which I did not dare to question you, since you had told me nothing. I have, therefore, as you see, great need to hear from you. Now that you are no longer beside me, I am afraid every moment of erring. You sustained me powerfully, sir, and I protest to you that to-day I feel very lonely. Will you have the goodness, sir, should you receive news from Blois, to send me a few lines about my little friend, Mademoiselle de la Vallière, about whose health, when we left, some anxiety was felt ? You can understand, honoured and dear guardian, how precious and indispensable to me is the remembrance of the time that I have passed with you. I hope that you will sometimes, too, think of me, and if at certain hours you should miss me, if you should feel any slight regret at my absence, I shall be overwhelmed with joy at the thought that you have appreciated my affection and my devotion for yourself, and that I have been able to prove them to you whilst I had the happiness of living with you."

After finishing this letter, Raoul felt more composed ; he looked well around him to see if Olivain and the host were not watching him, whilst he impressed a kiss upon the paper, a mute and touching caress, which the heart of Athos might well divine on opening the letter.

During this time Olivain had finished his bottle and eaten his pie ; the horses also were refreshed. Raoul motioned the host to approach, threw a crown down on the table, mounted his horse, and posted his letter at Senlis. The rest that had been thus afforded to men and horses enabled them to continue their journey without stopping. At Verbérie, Raoul desired Olivain to make some inquiry about the young man who was preceding them ; he had been observed to pass only three-quarters of an hour previously, but he was well-mounted, as the tavern-keeper had already said, and rode at a rapid pace.

"Let us try to overtake this gentleman," said Raoul to Olivain ; "like ourselves, he is on his way to join the army, and may prove agreeable company."

It was about four o'clock in the afternoon when Raoul arrived at Compiègne ; there he dined heartily, and again inquired about the young gentleman who was in advance of them. He had stopped, like Raoul, at the hotel of the Bell and Bottle, the best at Compiègne, and had started again on his journey, saying that he should sleep at Noyon.

"Well, let us sleep at Noyon," said Raoul.

"Sir," replied Olivain, respectfully, "allow me to remark, that we have already much fatigued the horses this morning. I think it would be well to sleep here, and to start again very early to-morrow. Eighteen leagues is enough for the first stage."

"The Count de la Fère wished me to hasten on," replied Raoul, "that I might rejoin the prince on the morning of the fourth day ; let us push on, then, to Noyon, it will be a stage similar to those that we travelled from Blois to Paris. We shall arrive at eight o'clock. The horses will have a long night's rest, and at five o'clock to-morrow morning we can be again on the road."

Olivain dared offer no opposition to this determination; but he followed his master grumbling.

"Go on, go on," said he, between his teeth, "expend your ardour the first day; to-morrow, instead of journeying twenty miles, you will do ten; the day after to-morrow, five, and in three days you will be in bed. There you must rest; all these young people are such braggarts."

It is easy to see that Olivain had not been taught in the school of the Planchets and the Grimauds. Raoul really felt tired; but he was desirous of testing his strength, and, brought up in the principles of Athos, and certain of having heard him speak a thousand times of stages of twenty-five leagues, he did not wish to fall short of his model. D'Artagnan, that man of iron, who seemed to be made of nerve and muscle only, had struck him with admiration. Therefore, in spite of all Olivain's remarks, he continued to urge on his steed more and more, and following a pleasant little path, leading to a ferry, and which he had been assured shortened the journey by the distance of one league, he arrived at the summit of a hill, and perceived the river flowing before him. A little troop of men on horseback were waiting on the edge of the stream, ready to embark. Raoul did not doubt that this was the gentleman and his escort: he called out to him, but he was too distant to be heard; then, in spite of the weariness of his beast, he made it gallop; but the rising ground soon deprived him of the sight of the travellers, and when he had again attained a new height, the ferry-boat had left the shore, and was making for the opposite bank. Raoul, seeing that he could not arrive in time to cross the ferry with the travellers, halted to wait for Olivain. At this moment a shriek was heard which seemed to come from the river. Raoul turned towards the side whence the cry had sounded, and shaded his eyes from the glare of the setting sun with his hand.

"Olivain!" he exclaimed, "what do I see below there?"

A second scream, more piercing than the first, now sounded.

"Oh, sir!" cried Olivain, "the rope which holds the ferry-boat has broken, and the boat is drifting away. But what do I see in the water? something struggling."

"Oh! yes," exclaimed Raoul, fixing his glance on one point in the stream, splendidly illumined by the setting sun, "a horse, a rider!"

"They are sinking!" cried Olivain in his turn.

It was true, and Raoul was convinced that some accident had happened, and that a man was drowning; he gave his horse its head, struck his spurs into its sides, and the animal, urged on by pain, and feeling that he had space open before him, bounded over a kind of paling which enclosed the landing-place, and fell into the river, scattering to a distance waves of white froth.

"Ah, sir!" cried Olivain, "what are you doing? Good God!"

Raoul was directing his horse towards the unhappy man in danger. This was, in fact, a custom familiar to him. Having been brought up on the banks of the Loire, he might have been said to have been cradled on its waves; a hundred times he had crossed it on horseback, a thousand times he had swum across. Athos, foreseeing the period when he should make a soldier of the viscount, had inured him to all these kinds of undertakings.

"Oh, heavens!" continued Olivain, in despair, "what would the count say if he only saw you?"

"The count would do as I do," replied Raoul, urging his horse vigorously forward.

"But I—but I," cried Olivain, pale and disconsolate, rushing about on the shore, "how shall I cross?"

"Leap, coward," cried Raoul, swimming on; then addressing the traveller, who was struggling twenty yards in advance of him, "Courage, sir," said he, "courage, we are coming to your aid."

Olivain advanced, retired, then made his horse rear—turned it, and then, struck to the core by shame, leapt, as Raoul had done, only repeating:

"I am a dead man; we are lost!"

In the meantime the ferry-boat floated away, carried down by the stream; and the shrieks of those whom it contained resounded more and more. A man with grey hair had thrown himself from the boat into the river, and was swimming vigorously towards the person who was drowning; but being obliged to go against the current, he advanced but slowly. Raoul continued his way, and was visibly gaining the shore; but the horse and its rider, of whom he did not lose sight, were evidently sinking. The nostrils of the horse were no longer above water, and the rider, who had lost the reins in struggling, fell with his head back and his arms extended. One moment longer, and all had disappeared.

"Courage," cried Raoul, "courage."

"Too late!" murmured the young man, "too late!"

The water passed over his head, and stifled his voice in his mouth.

Raoul sprang from his horse, to which he left the charge of its own preservation, and in three or four strokes was at the gentleman's side; he seized the horse at once by the curb, and raised its head above water. The animal then breathed more freely, and as if he comprehended that they had come to his aid, redoubled, his efforts. Raoul at the same time seized one of the young man's hands, and placed it on the mane, at which it grasped with the tenacity of a drowning man. Thus, sure that the rider would not release his hold, Raoul now only directed his attention to the horse, which he guided to the opposite bank, helping it to cut through the water, and encouraging it with words.

All at once the horse stumbled against a ridge, and then placed its foot on the sand.

"Saved!" exclaimed the man with grey hair, who sprang on land in his turn.

"Saved," mechanically repeated the young gentleman, releasing the mane, and gliding from the saddle into Raoul's arms; Raoul was but ten yards from the shore : he bore the fainting man there, and laying him down on the grass, unfastened the buttons of his collar, and unhooked his doublet. A moment later the grey-headed man was beside him. Olivain managed in his turn to land, after crossing himself repeatedly, and the people in the ferry-boat guided themselves as well as they were able towards the bank, with the aid of a hook which chanced to be in the boat.

Thanks to the attention of Raoul, and the man who accompanied the young gentleman, the colour gradually returned to the pale cheeks of the dying man, who opened two eyes at first bewildered, but who soon fixed his glance upon the person who had saved him.

"Ah, sir," he exclaimed, "it was you I wanted; without you I was a dead man—thrice dead."

"But one recovers, sir, as you see," replied Raoul, "and we shall but have had a bath."

"Oh! sir, what gratitude I feel," exclaimed the man with grey hair.

"Ah, there you are, my good D'Arminges, I have given you a great fright, have I not? but it is your own fault; you were my tutor, why did you not teach me to swim better?"

"Oh, sir!" replied the old man, "had any misfortune happened to you, I should never have dared to have shown myself to the marshal again."

"But how did the accident happen?" asked Raoul.

"Oh, sir, in the most natural manner possible," replied he to whom they had given the title of count. "We were about a third of the way across the river when the cord of the ferry-boat broke. Alarmed by the cries and the gestures of the boatmen, my horse sprang into the water. I swim badly, and dared not throw myself into the river. Instead of aiding the movements of my horse, I paralysed them; and I was just going to drown myself, with the best grace in the world, when you arrived just in time to pull me out of the water; therefore, sir, if you will agree, henceforth we are friends in life until death."

"Sir," replied Raoul, bowing, "I am entirely at your service, I assure you."

"I am called the Count de Guiche," continued the young man; "my father is the Maréchal de Grammont; and now that you know who I am, do me the honour to inform me who you are."

"I am the Viscount de Bragelonne," answered Raoul, blushing at being unable to name his father, as the Count de Guiche had done.

"Viscount, your countenance, your goodness, and your courage incline me towards you; my gratitude is already due to you—shake hands;—I ask your friendship."

"Sir," said Raoul, returning the count's pressure of the hand, "I like you already from my heart; pray regard me as a devoted friend, I beseech you."

"And now, where are you going, viscount?" inquired De Guiche.

"To the army, under the prince, count."

"And I too," exclaimed the young man, in a transport of joy.— "Oh, so much the better; we shall fire off the first pistol shot together."

"It is well—be friends," said the tutor; "young as you both are, you were perhaps born under the same star, and were destined to meet. And now," continued he, "you must change your clothes; your servants, to whom I gave directions the moment they had left the ferry-boat, ought to be already at the inn. Linen and wine are both being warmed—come."

The young men had no objection to make to this proposition; on the contrary, they thought it an excellent one. They mounted again at once, whilst looks of admiration passed between them. They were indeed two elegant horsemen, with figures slight and upright—two noble faces, with open foreheads—bright and proud looks—loyal and intelligent smiles.

De Guiche might have been about eighteen years of age; but he was scarcely taller than Raoul, who was only fifteen.

CHAPTER XXX.

SKIRMISHING.

The halt at Noyon was short, every one there being wrapt in profound sleep. Raoul had desired to be awakened should Grimaud have arrived—but Grimaud did not arrive. Doubtless, too, the horses, on their parts, appreciated the eight hours of repose, and the abundant stabling which was granted to them. The Count de Guiche was awakened at five o'clock in the morning by Raoul, who came to wish him good day. They had breakfast in haste, and at six o'clock had already gone ten miles.

The young count's conversation was most interesting to Raoul; therefore he listened much, whilst the count talked much. Brought up in Paris, where Raoul had been but once; at the court, which Raoul had never seen—his follies as page—two duels, which he had already found the means of fighting, in spite of the edicts against them, and more especially in spite of his tutor's vigilance —these things excited the greatest curiosity in Raoul. Raoul had only been at M. Scarron's house; he named to De Guiche the people whom he had seen there. De Guiche knew everybody:— Madame de Muillan, Mademoiselle D'Aubigné, Mademoiselle de Scudery, Mademoiselle Paulet, Madame de Chevreuse.—He criticised everybody humorously. Raoul trembled lest he should laugh among the rest at Madame de Chevreuse, for whom he entertained deep and genuine sympathy, bnt either instinctively, or from affection for the Duchesse de Chevreuse, he said everything possible in her favour. His praises increased Raoul's friendship for him twofold. Then came the question of gallantry and love affairs. Under this head also, Bragelonne had much more to hear than to tell. He listened attentively, and fancied that he discovered through three or four rather frivolous adventures, that the count, like himself, had a secret to hide in the depths of his heart.

De Guiche, as we have said before, had been educated at the court, and the intrigues of this court were known to him. It was the same court of which Raoul had so often heard the Count de la Fère speak, except that its aspect had much changed since the period when Athos had himself witnessed it; therefore everything which the Count de Guiche related was new to his travelling companion. The young count, witty and caustic, passed all the world in review; the queen herself was not spared, and Cardinal Mazarin came in for his share of ridicule.

The day passed away as rapidly as one hour. The count's tutor, a man of the world, and a 'bon vivant,' up to his eyes in learning, as his pupil described him, often recalled the profound erudition, the witty and caustic satire, of Athos to Raoul; but as regarded grace, delicacy, and nobility of external appearance, no one in these points was to be compared to the Count de la Fère.

The horses, which were better cared for than on the previous day, stopped at Arras at four o'clock in the evening. They were approaching the scene of war; and as bands of Spaniards sometimes took advantage of the night to make expeditions even as far as the neighbourhood of Arras, they determine to remain in this town until the morrow. The French army held all between Pont-à-Mare as far as Valenciennes, falling back upon Douai. The prince was said to be in person at Béthune.

The enemy's army extended from Cassel to Courtray; and as there was no species of violence or pillage which it did not commit, the poor people on the frontier quitted their isolated dwellings, and fled for refuge into the strong cities which held out a shelter to them. Arras was encumbered with fugitives. An approaching battle was much spoken of, the prince having manœuvred until that moment, only in order to await a reinforcement, which had just reached him.

The young men congratulated themselves on having arrived so opportunely. The evening was employed in discussing the war; the grooms polished the arms; the young men loaded the pistols in case of a skirmish, and they awoke in despair, having both dreamt that they had arrived too late to participate in the battle. In the morning it was rumoured that Prince Condé had evacuated Béthune, and fallen back upon Carvin, leaving, however, a strong garrison in the former city.

But as there was nothing positively certain in this report, the young men decided to continue their way towards Béthune, free, on the road, to diverge to the right, and to march to Carvin if necessary.

The count's tutor was well acquainted with the country; he consequently proposed to take a cross road, which lay between that of Lens and that of Béthune. They obtained information at Ablain, and a statement of their route was left for Grimaud. About seven o'clock in the morning they set out. De Guiche, who was young and impulsive, said to Raoul, "Here we are, three masters and three servants. Our valets are well armed, and yours seems to be tough enough."

"I have never seen him put to the test," replied Raoul, "but he is a Breton, which promises something."

" Yes, yes," resumed De Guiche; " I am sure he can fire a musket when required. On my side, I have two very sure men, who have been in action with my father. We, therefore, represent six fighting men : if we should meet a little troop of enemies, equal or even superior in number to our own, shall we charge them, Raoul ?"

" Certainly, sir," replied the viscount.

" Holloa ! young people—stop there !" said the tutor, joining in the conversation. "Zounds ! how do you arrange my instructions, pray, count ? You seem to forget the orders I received to conduct you safe and sound to his highness the prince ! Once with the army, you may be killed at your good pleasure; but, until that time, I warn you, that in my capacity of general of the army, I shall order a retreat, and turn my back on the first red coat I see."

De Guiche and Raoul glanced at each other, smiling.

They arrived at Ablain without accident. There they inquired, and learned that the prince had in reality quitted Béthune, and placed himself between Cambria and La Venthie. Therefore, leaving directions at every place for Grimaud, they took a cross road, which conducted the little troop upon the bank of a small stream flowing into the Lys. The country was beautiful, intersected by valleys as green as the emerald. Every here and there they passed little copses crossing the path which they were following. In anticipation of some ambuscade in each of these little woods, the tutor placed his two servants at the head of the band, thus forming the advance guard. Himself and the two young men represented the body of the army, whilst Olivain, with his rifle on his knee, and his eye on the watch, protected the rear.

They had observed for some time before them on the horizon a rather thick wood ; and when they had arrived at a distance of a hundred steps from it, Monsieur D'Arminges took his usual precautions, and sent on in advance the count's two grooms. The servants had just disappeared under the trees, followed by the tutor, and the young men were laughing and talking about a hundred yards off. Olivain was at the same distance in the rear, when suddenly there resounded five or six musket-shots. The tutor cried halt ; the young men obeyed, pulling up their steeds, and at the same moment the two valets were seen returning at a gallop.

The young men, impatient to learn the cause of the firing, spurred on towards the servants. The tutor followed them behind.

" Were you stopped ?" eagerly inquired the two youths.

" No," replied the servants, " it is even probable that we have not been seen ; the shots were fired about a hundred steps in advance of us, almost in the thickest part of the wood, and we returned to ask your advice."

"My advice," said Monsieur D'Arminges, "and, if needs be, my will is, that we beat a retreat. There may be an ambuscade concealed in this wood."

"Did you see nothing there ?" asked the count.

"I thought I saw," said one of the servants, "horsemen dressed in yellow, creeping along the bed of the stream."

"That's it," said the tutor. "We have fallen in with a party of Spaniards. Come back, sirs—back."

The two youths looked at each other, and at this moment a pistol-shot and several cries for help were heard. Another glance between the young men convinced them both that neither had any wish to go back, and as the tutor had already turned his horse's head, they both spurred on forward, Raoul crying, "Follow me, Olivain;" and Count de Guiche, "Follow, Urban and Blanchet." And before the tutor could recover his surprise, they had both disappeared into the forest. When they spurred their steeds, they held their pistols ready also. Five minutes after they arrived at the spot whence the noise had proceeded ; therefore, restraining their horses, they advanced cautiously.

"Hush," whispered De Guiche ; "these are cavaliers."

"Yes, three on horseback, and three who have dismounted."

"Can you see what they are doing ?"

"Yes, they appear to be searching a wounded or dead man."

"It is some cowardly assassination," said De Guiche.

"They are soldiers, though," resumed De Bragelonne.

"Yes, skirmishers ; that is to say, highway robbers."

"At them !" cried Raoul. "At them !" echoed De Guiche.

"Oh ! sirs, sirs ; in the name of Heaven !" cried the poor tutor.

But he was not listened to, and his cries only served to arouse the attention of the Spaniards.

The men on horseback at once rushed at the two youths, leaving the three others to complete the plunder of the two travellers ; for, on approaching nearer, instead of one extended figure, the young men discovered two. De Guiche fired the first shot at ten paces, and missed his man ; and the Spaniard, who had advanced to meet Raoul, aimed in his turn, and Raoul felt a pain in his left arm, similar to that of a blow from a whip. He let off his fire at but four paces. Struck in the breast, and extending his arms, the Spaniard fell back on the croup of his horse, which, turning round, carried him off.

Raoul, at this moment, perceived the muzzle of a gun pointed at him, and remembering the recommendation of Athos, he, with the rapidity of lightning, made his horse rear as the shot was fired. His horse bounded to one side, losing its footing, and fell, entangling Raoul's leg under its body. The Spaniard sprang forward, and seized the gun by its muzzle, in order to strike Raoul on the head by the butt-end. In the position in which Raoul lay, unfortunately, he could neither draw his sword from the scabbard, nor his pistols from their holsters. The butt-end of the musket hovered over his head, and he could scarcely restrain himself from closing his eyes, when, with one bound, De Guiche reached the Spaniard, and placed a pistol at his throat. " Yield !" he cried, " or you are a dead man." The musket fell from the soldier's hands, who yielded at the instant.

De Guiche summoned one of his grooms, and delivering the prisoner into his charge, with orders to shoot him through the head if he attempted to escape, he leaped from his horse and approached Raoul.

" Faith, sir," said Raoul, smiling, although his pallor somewhat betrayed the excitement consequent on a first affair—" you are in a great hurry to pay your debts, and have not been long under any obligation to me. Without your aid," continued he, repeating the count's words, " I should have been a dead man—thrice dead."

" My antagonist took flight," replied De Guiche, " and left me at liberty to come to your aid. But you are seriously wounded ? I see you are covered with blood !"

" I believe," said Raoul, " that I have got something like a scratch on the arm. If you will help me to drag myself from under my horse, I hope nothing need prevent us continuing our journey."

Monsieur D'Arminges and Olivain had already dismounted, and were attempting to raise the horse, which struggled in terror. At last Raoul succeeded in drawing his foot from the stirrup, and his leg from under the animal, and in a second he was on his feet again.

" Nothing broken ?" asked De Guiche.

" Faith, no, thank Heaven !" replied Raoul; " but what has become of the poor wretches whom these scoundrels were murdering ?"

" I fear we arrived too late. They had killed them and taken flight, carrying off their booty. My two servants are examining the bodies."

" Let us go and see whether they are quite dead, or if they can be recovered," suggested Raoul. "Olivain, we have come into possession of two horses, but I have lost my own; take the best of the two for yourself, and give me yours."

Saying this, they approached the spot where the victims lay.

CHAPTER XXXI.

THE MONK.

Two men lay extended on the ground; one bathed in his blood, and motionless, with his face towards the earth; he was dead. The other leant against the tree, supported there by the two valets, and was praying fervently, with clasped hands, and eyes raised to heaven. He had received a ball in his thigh, which had broken the upper part of it. The young men first approached the dead man.

"He is a priest," said Bragelonne, "he has worn the tonsure. Oh the scoundrels! to lift their hands against the minister of God."

"Come here, sir," said Urban, an old soldier who had served under the cardinal-duke in all his campaigns. "Come here, there is nothing to be done with him; whilst we may perhaps be able to save this one."

The wounded man smiled sadly. "Save me! oh no," said he; "but help me to die, you can."

"Are you a priest?" asked Raoul.

"No, sir."

"I ask, as your unfortunate companion appeared to me to belong to the church."

"He is the curate of Béthune, sir, and was carrying the holy vessels belonging to his church, and the treasure of the chapter, to a safe place, the prince having abandoned our town yesterday; and as it was known that bands of the enemy were prowling about the country, no one dared to accompany the good man, so I offered to do so."

"And, sir," continued the wounded man, "I suffer much, and would like, if possible, to be carried to some house."

"Where you can be relieved?" asked De Guiche.

"No, where I can confess myself."

"But perhaps you are not so dangerously wounded as you think," said Raoul.

"Sir," replied the wounded man, "believe me there is no time to lose; the ball has broken the thigh-bone, and entered the intestines."

"Are you a surgeon?" asked De Guiche.

"No, but I know a little about wounds, and mine is mortal. Try, therefore, either to carry me to some place where I may see a priest, or take the trouble to send one to me here. It is my soul that must be saved; as for my body, that is lost.

"Good God! good God!" added the wounded man, in an accent of terror which made the young man shudder; "you will not allow me to die without receiving absolution? that would be too terrible!"

"Calm yourself, sir," replied De Guiche. "I swear to you that you shall receive the consolation that you ask. Only tell us where we shall find a house at which we can demand aid, and a village from which we can fetch a priest."

"Thank you, and God will reward you! About half a mile from this, on the same road, there is an inn; and about a mile further on, after leaving the inn, you will reach the village of Greney. There you must find the curate; or if he is not at home, go to the convent of the Augustins, which is the last house on the right in the village, and bring me one of the brothers. Monk or priest, it matters not, provided he have received from our holy church the power of absolving 'in articulo mortis!'"

"Monsieur D'Arminges," said De Guiche, "remain beside this unfortunate man, and see that he is removed as gently as possible. The vicomte and myself will go and find a priest."

"Go, sir," replied the tutor; "but, in heaven's name, do not expose yourself to danger!"

"Do not fear. Besides, we are safe to-day; you know the axiom —*Non bis in idem.*"

"Courage, sir," said Raoul to the wounded man. "We are going to execute your wishes."

"May heaven prosper you!" replied the dying man, with an accent of gratitude impossible to describe.

The two young men galloped off in the direction mentioned to them, and ten minutes after reached the inn. Raoul, without dismounting, called to the host, and announced that a wounded man was about to be brought to his house, and begged him in the meantime to prepare everything necessary for dressing his wounds. He desired him also, should he know in the neighbourhood any doctor, surgeon, or operator, to fetch him, taking on himself the payment of the messenger. Raoul had already proceeded for more than a

mile, and had begun to descry the first houses of the village, the
red tiled roofs of which stood out strongly from the green trees
which surrounded them, when, coming towards them, mounted on
a mule, they perceived a poor monk, whose large hat and grey
worsted dress made them mistake him for an Augustine brother.
Chance for once had seemed to favour them in sending what they
were seeking for. He was a man about twenty-two or twenty-
three years old, but who appeared to be aged by his ascetic exercises. His complexion was pale, not of that deadly pallor which
is a beauty, but of a bilious, yellow hue ; his light colourless hair
was short, and scarcely extended beyond the circle formed by the
hat round his head, and his light blue eyes seemed entirely destitute
of any expression.

" Sir," began Raoul, with his usual politeness. " are you an ecclesiastic ?"

" Why do you ask me that ?" replied the stranger, with a coolness which was barely civil.

" Because we want to know," said De Guiche, haughtily.

The stranger touched his mule with his heel, and continued his
way.

In a second De Guiche had sprung before him and barred his
passage. " Answer, sir," exclaimed he ; " you have been asked
politely, and every question is worth an answer."

" I suppose I am free to say who I am, or not, to any kind of
people who choose to take a fancy to ask me ?"

It was with difficulty that De Guiche restrained the intense
desire he had of breaking the monk's bones.

" In the first place," he said, making an effort to control himself,
" we are not people who may be treated any how ; my friend there
is the Viscount of Bragelonne, and I am the Count de Guiche. Nor
is it from a matter of caprice that we asked you the question ; for
there is a wounded and dying man who demands the succour of
the Church. If you be a priest, I conjure you in the name of
humanity to follow me to aid this man ; if you be not, it is a different matter, and I warn you, in the name of courtesy, of which
you appear so utterly ignorant, that I shall chastise you for your
insolence."

The pale face of the monk became so livid, and his smile was
so strange, that Raoul, whose eyes were still fixed upon him, felt
as if this smile had struck to his heart like some insult.

" He is some Spanish or Flemish spy," said he, putting his
hand to his pistols. A glance, threatening and as transient as
lightning, replied to Raoul.

"Well, sir," said De Guiche, "are you going to reply?"

"I am a priest," said the young man.

"Then, father," said Raoul, forcing himself to give a respect to his speech which did not come from his heart, "if you are a priest, then you have an opportunity, as my friend has told you, of exercising your vocation. At the next inn you will find a wounded man, who has asked the assistance of a minister of God, attended on by our servants."

"I will go," said the monk.

And he touched his mule.

"If you do not go, sir," said De Guiche, "remember that we have two steeds quite able to catch your mule, and the power of having you seized wherever you may be; and then I swear your trial will be short; one can always find a tree and a cord."

The monk's eye again flashed, but that was all; he merely repeated his phrase, "I will go,"—and he went.

"Let us follow him," said De Guiche; "it will be the more sure plan."

"I was about to propose doing so," answered De Bragelonne.

In the space of five minutes the monk turned round to ascertain whether he was followed or not.

"You see," said Raoul, "we have done wisely."

"What a horrible face that monk has," said De Guiche.

"Horrible!" replied Raoul, "especially in expression."

"Yes, yes," said De Guiche, "a strange face; but these monks are subject to such degrading practices; the fasts make them pale; the blows of the discipline make them hypocrites; and their eyes become inflamed in weeping for the good things of this life which we enjoy, and which they have lost."

"Well," said Raoul, "the poor man will get his priest; but by heaven, the penitent appears to have a better conscience than the confessor. I confess I am accustomed to see priests of a very different appearance."

"Ah!" exclaimed De Guiche, "you must understand that this is one of those wandering brothers, who go begging on the high road, until some day a benefice falls down from heaven for them; they are mostly foreigners—Scotch, Irish, or Danish."

"What a misfortune for that poor wounded fellow to die under the hands of such a friar!"

"Pshaw!" said De Guiche. "Absolution comes not from him who administers it, but from God. However, let me tell you that I would rather die unshriven than have anything to say to such a confessor. You are of my opinion, are you not, viscount? and I see you playing with the pommel of your pistol, as if you had a great inclination to break his head."

"Yes, count, it is a strange thing, and one which might astonish you ; but I feel an indescribable horror at the sight of that man. Have you ever seen a snake rise up in your path ?"

"Never," answered De Guiche.

"Well, it has happened to me to do so in our Blaisois forests, and I remember that the first time I encountered one with its eyes fixed upon me, curled up, swinging its head, and pointing its tongue, that I remained fixed, pale, and as if fascinated, until the moment when the Count de la Fère——"

"Your father ?" asked De Guiche.

"No, my guardian," replied Raoul, blushing.

"Very well——"

"Until the moment when the Count de la Fère," resumed Raoul, "said, 'Come, Bragelonne, draw your sword ;' then only I rushed upon the reptile, and cut it in two ; just at the moment when it was rising on its tail and hissing ere it sprang upon me. Well, I vow I felt exactly the same sensation at the sight of that man when he said, 'Why do you ask me that ?' and looked at me."

"Then you regret that you did not cut your serpent in two morsels ?"

"Faith, yes, almost," said Raoul.

They had now arrived in sight of the little inn, and could see on the opposite side the procession bearing the wounded man, and guided by Monsieur d'Arminges. The youths spurred on.

"There is the wounded man," said De Guiche, passing close to the Augustine brother. "Be good enough to hurry yourself a little, sir monk."

As for Raoul, he avoided the monk the whole width of the road, and passed him, turning his head away in disgust.

The young men rode up to the wounded man to announce that they were followed by the priest. He raised himself to glance in the direction which they pointed out, saw the monk, and fell back upon the litter, his face being lightened up by joy.

"And now," said the youths, "we have done all we can for you ; and as we are in haste to join the prince's army we must continue our journey. You will excuse us, sir, but we are told that a battle is expected, and we do not wish to arrive the day after it."

"Go, my young sirs," said the sick man ; "and may you both be blessed for your piety. God protect you and all dear to you !"

"Sir," said De Guiche to his tutor, "we will precede you, and you can rejoin us on the road to Cambrin."

The host was at his door, and everything was prepared—bed, bandages, and lint.

"Everything," said he to Raoul, "shall be done as you desire; but will you not stop to have your wound dressed?"

"Oh, my wound—mine—it is nothing," replied the viscount; "it will be time to think about it when we next halt; only have the goodness, should you see a cavalier pass who should make inquiries from you about a young man mounted on a chestnut horse, and followed by a servant, to tell him, in fact, that you have seen me, but that I have continued my journey, and intend to dine at Mazingarbe, and to stop at Cambrin. This cavalier is my attendant."

"Would it not be safer and more sure that I should ask him his name, and tell him yours?" demanded the host.

"There is no harm in over-precaution. I am the Viscount de Bragelonne, and he is called Grimaud."

At this moment the wounded man passed on one side, and the monk on the other, the latter dismounting from his mule and desiring that it should be taken to the stables without being unharnessed.

"Come, count," said Raoul, who seemed instinctively to dislike the vicinity of the Augustine; "come, I feel ill here," and the two young men spurred on.

The litter, borne by the two servants, now entered the house. The host and his wife were standing on the steps of the staircase, whilst the unhappy man seemed to suffer dreadful pain, and yet only to be anxious to know if he was followed by the monk. At the sight of this pale, bleeding man, the wife grasped her husband's arm.

"Well, what's the matter?" asked the latter; "are you going to be ill just now?"

"No, but look," replied the hostess, pointing to the wounded man; "I ask you if you recognise him?"

"That man—wait a bit."

"Ah! I see that you know him," exclaimed the wife; "for you have become pale in your turn."

"In truth," cried the host, "misfortune has come upon our house; it is the executioner of Béthune!"

"The former executioner of Béthune!" murmured the young monk, shrinking back, and showing on his countenance the feeling of repugnance which his penitent inspired.

Monsieur D'Arminges, who was at the door, perceived his hesitation.

"Sir monk," said he, "whether he is now or has been an executioner, this unfortunate being is no less a man. Render to him, then, the last service he will ask from you, and your work will be all the more meritorious."

The monk made no reply, but silently wended his way to the room where the two valets had deposited the dying man on a bed. D'Arminges and Olivain, and the two grooms, then mounted their horses, and all four started off at a quick trot to rejoin Raoul and his companion. Just as the tutor and his escort disappeared in their turn, a new traveller stopped on the threshold of the inn.

"What does your worship want?" demanded the host, pale and trembling from the discovery he had just made.

The traveller made a sign as if he wished to drink, pointed to his horse, and gesticulated like a man who is rubbing something.

"Ah! diable," said the host to himself, "this man seems dumb. And where will your worship drink?"

"There," answered the traveller, pointing to a table.

"I was mistaken," said the host; "he's not quite dumb. And what else does your worship wish for?"

"To know if you have seen a young man pass, fifteen years of age, mounted on a chestnut horse, and followed by a groom."

"The Viscount de Bragelonne?"

"Just so."

"Then you are called Monsieur Grimaud?"

The traveller made a sign of assent.

"Well, then," said the host, "your young master has been here a quarter of an hour ago; he will dine at Mazingarbe, and sleep at Cambrin."

"How far from Mazingarbe?"

"Two miles and a half."

"Thank you."

Grimaud was drinking his wine silently, and had just placed his glass on the table to be filled a second time, when a fearful scream resounded from the room occupied by the monk and the dying man. Grimaud sprang up,—

"What is that?" said he; "whence that cry?"

"From the wounded man's room," replied the host.

"What wounded man?"

"The former executioner of Béthune, who has just been brought in here assassinated by the Spaniards, and who is now being confessed by an Augustine friar."

" The old executioner of Béthune ?" muttered Grimaud ; " a man between fifty-five and sixty, tall, strong, swarthy, black hair and beard."

" That is he—do you know him ?" asked the host.

" I have seen him once," replied Grimaud, a cloud darkening his countenance at the picture called up by his recollections.

At this instant a second cry, less piercing than the first, but followed by prolonged groaning, was heard.

" We must see what it is," said Grimaud.

If Grimaud was slow in speaking, we know that he was quick in action ; he sprang to the door and shook it violently, but it was bolted on the other side.

" Open the door," cried the host, " open it instantly, sir monk !" No reply.

" Unfasten it, or I will break in the panel," said Grimaud.

The same silence, and then, ere the host could oppose his design, Grimaud seized on some pincers which he perceived lying in a corner, and had forced the bolt. The room was inundated with blood, streaming through the mattresses upon which lay the wounded man speechless—the monk had disappeared.

" The monk !" cried the host ; " where is the monk ?"

Grimaud sprang towards an open window which looked into the court-yard.

" He has escaped by this means," exclaimed he.

" Do you think so ?" said the host, bewildered ; " boy, see if the mule belonging to the monk is still in the stable."

" There's no mule," replied the person to whom this question was addressed.

The host held up his hand, and looked around him suspiciously, whilst Grimaud knit his brows and approached the wounded man, whose worn, hard features awoke in his mind such awful recollections of the past.

" There can be no longer any doubt but that it is himself," said he.

" Does he still live ?" inquired the innkeeper.

Making no reply, Grimaud opened the poor man's jacket to feel if the heart beat, whilst the host approached in his turn ; but in a moment they both fell back, the host uttering a cry of horror, and Grimaud becoming pallid. The blade of a dagger was buried up to the hilt in the left side of the executioner.

" Run—run for help !" cried Grimaud, " and I will remain beside him here."

The host quitted the room in agitation ; and as for his wife, she had fled at the sound of her husband's cries.

CHAPTER XXXII.

GRIMAUD SPEAKS.

GRIMAUD was left alone with the executioner, who in a few moments opened his eyes.

" Help, help," he murmured ; " oh, God ! have I not a single friend in the world who will aid me either to live or to die ?"

" Take courage," said Grimaud ; " they are gone to find help."

" Who are you ?" asked the wounded man, fixing his half-opened eyes on Grimaud.

" An old acquaintance," replied Grimaud.

" You ?" and the wounded man sought to recall the features of the person who was before him to his mind.

" Under what circumstances did we meet ?" he asked again.

" One night, twenty years ago, my master fetched you from Béthune, and conducted you to Armentières."

" I know you well, now," said the executioner ; " you are one of the four grooms."

" Just so."

" Where do you come from now ?"

" I was passing by on the road, and drew up at this inn to rest my horse. They were relating to me how the executioner of Béthune was here, and wounded, when you uttered two piercing cries. At the first we ran to the door, and at the second forced it open."

" And the monk ?" exclaimed the executioner ; " did you see the monk ?"

" What monk ?"

" The monk that was shut in with me."

" No, he was no longer here ; he appears to have fled by that window. Was it he who struck you ?"

" Yes," said the executioner.

Grimaud moved, as if to leave the room.

" What are you going to do ?" asked the wounded man.

" He must be apprehended."

" Do not attempt it ; he has revenged himself, and has done well. Now I may hope that God will forgive me, since my crime has been expiated."

" Explain yourself," said Grimaud.

"—The woman, whom you and your masters made me kill——"

" Milady ?"

"Yes, milady; it is true you called her thus."

"Well, what has the monk to do with milady?"

"She was his mother."

Grimaud trembled, and stared at the dying man in a dull and stupid manner.

"His mother!" repeated he.

"Yes, his mother."

"But does he know this secret, then?"

"I mistook him for a monk, and revealed it to him in confession."

"Unhappy man," cried Grimaud, whose face was covered with sweat, at the bare idea of the evil results which such a revelation might cause—"unhappy man, you named no one, I hope?"

"I pronounced no name, for I knew none, except his mother's, as a young girl, and it was by this name that he recognised her; but he knows that his uncle was among her judges."

Thus speaking, he fell back exhausted. Grimaud, wishing to relieve him, advanced his hand towards the hilt of the dagger.

"Touch me not!" said the executioner; "if this dagger is withdrawn, I shall die."

Grimaud remained with his hand extended; then, striking his forehead, he exclaimed: "Oh! if this man should ever discover the names of the others, my master is lost."

"Haste! haste to him, and warn him," cried the wounded man, "if he still lives; warn his friends too. My death, believe me, will not be the end of this terrible adventure."

"Where was the monk going?" asked Grimaud.

"Towards Paris."

"Who stopped him?"

"Two young gentlemen, who were on their way to join the army, and the name of one of whom I heard his companion mention, the Viscount de Bragelonne."

"And it was this young man who brought the monk to you. Then it was the will of God that it should be so, and this it is which is so awful," continued Grimaud; "and yet that woman deserved her fate: do you not think so?"

"On one's death-bed the crimes of others appear very small in comparison with one's own," said the executioner; and he fell back exhausted, and closed his eyes.

At this moment the host re-entered the room, followed not only by a surgeon, but by many other persons, whom curiosity had attracted to the spot. The surgeon approached the dying man who seemed to have fainted.

"We must first extract the steel from the side," said he, shaking his head in a significant manner.

The prophecy which the wounded man had just uttered recurred to Grimaud, who turned away his head. The weapon, as we have already stated, was plunged into the body up to the hilt, and as the surgeon, taking it by the end, drew it from the wound, the wounded man opened his eyes, and fixed them in a manner truly frightful. When, at last, the blade had been entirely withdrawn, a red froth issued from the mouth of the wounded man, and a stream of blood sprang from the wound, when he at length drew breath; then, fixing his eyes on Grimaud, with singular expression, the dying man uttered the last death rattle, and expired.

Then Grimaud, raising the dagger from the pool of blood which was gliding along the room—to the horror of all present—made a sign to the host to follow him, paid him with a generosity worthy of his master, and again mounted his horse. Grimaud's first intentions had been to return to Paris, but he remembered the anxiety which his prolonged absence might occasion to Raoul, and, reflecting that there were now only two miles between Raoul and himself, that a quarter of an hour's riding would unite them, and that the going, returning, and explanation would not occupy an hour, he put spurs to his horse, and, ten minutes after, had reached the only inn of Mazingarbe.

Raoul was seated at table with the Count de Guiche and his tutor, when all at once the door opened, and Grimaud presented himself, travel-stained and dirty, still covered with the blood of the unfortunate executioner.

"Grimaud, my good Grimaud!" exclaimed Raoul, "here you are at last! Excuse me, sirs, this is not a servant, but a friend. How did you leave the count?" continued he; "does he regret me a little? Have you seen him since I left him? Answer, for I have many things to tell you, too; indeed, the last three days some odd adventures have happened,—but, what is the matter?—how pale you are!—and blood, too! what is this?"

"It is the blood of the unfortunate man whom you left at the inn, and who died in my arms."

"In your arms?—that man! But know you who he was?"

"I know that he was the old headsman of Béthune."

"You knew him? and he is dead?"

"Yes."

"Well, sir," said D'Arminges, "it is the common lot, and even an executioner is not exempted from it. I had a bad opinion of him the moment I saw his wound, and, since he asked for a monk, you know it was his own opinion too that death must ensue."

At the mention of the monk Grimaud turned pale.

"Come, come," continued D'Arminges, "to dinner;" for, like most men of his age and of his generation, he did not allow any sensibility to interfere with a repast.

"You are right, sir," said Raoul. "Come, Grimaud, order some dinner for yourself, and when you have rested a little, we can talk."

"No, sir, no," said Grimaud; "I cannot stop a moment; I must start for Paris again immediately."

"How now? you start for Paris? Explain yourself! do you intend to disobey me for a change?"

"I cannot explain myself, and must disobey, unless you wish me to leave his honour, the count, to be killed!"

"Grimaud, my friend," said the viscount, "will you leave me thus, in such anxiety? Speak, speak in Heaven's name!"

"I can tell you but one thing, sir, for the secret you wish to know is not my own. You met this monk, did you not?"

"Yes."

"You conducted him to the wounded man, and you had time to observe him, and perhaps you would know him again were you to meet him?"

"Yes! yes!" exclaimed both the young men.

"Very well! if ever you meet him again, wherever it may be, whether on the high road or in the street, or in a church, anywhere that he or you may be, put your foot on his neck and crush him without pity, without mercy, as you would crush a viper, a snake, an asp; destroy him, and leave him not till he is dead; the lives of five men are not safe, in my opinion, as long as he lives!"

And without adding another word, Grimaud, profiting by the astonishment and terror into which he had thrown his auditors, rushed from the room. Ten minutes later the gallop of a horse was heard on the road—it was Grimaud on his way to Paris. When once in the saddle, Grimaud reflected upon two things; the first that, at the pace he was going, his horse would not carry him ten miles; and secondly, that he had no money. But Grimaud's imagination was more prolific than his speech; and. therefore, at the first halt he sold his steed, and with the money obtained from the purchaser he took post-horses.

CHAPTER XXXIII.

A DINNER IN THE OLD STYLE.

THE second interview between the former Musketeers had not been so pompous and stiff as the first. Athos, with his superior understanding, wisely deemed that the table would be the most speedy and complete point of re-union, and at the moment when his friends, doubtful of his deportment and his sobriety, dared scarcely speak of some of their former good dinners, he was the first to propose that they should all assemble round some well-spread table, and abandon themselves unreservedly to their own natural character and manners, a freedom which had formerly contributed so much to the good understanding between them as to give them the name of the inseparables. For different reasons this was an agreeable proposition to them all, and it was therefore agreed that each should leave a very exact address, and that upon the request of any of the associates, a meeting should be convoked at a famous eating-house in the Rue de la Monnaie, of the sign of the Hermitage; the first rendezvous was fixed for the following Wednesday, at eight o'clock in the evening precisely.

On that day, in fact, the four friends arrived punctually at the said hour, each from his own abode. Porthos had been trying a new horse; D'Artagnan came from being on guard at the Louvre; Aramis had been to visit one of his penitents in the neighbourhood; and Athos, whose domicile was established in the Rue Guéne-gaud, found himself close at hand. They were therefore somewhat surprised to meet altogether at the door of the Hermitage; Athos starting out from the Pont Neuf, Porthos by the Rue du Roule, D'Artagnan by the Rue des Fossées St. Germain l'Auxerrois, and Aramis by the Rue de Bethisy.

The first words exchanged between the four friends, on account of the ceremony which each of them mingled with their demon-stration, were somewhat forced, and even the repast began with a kind of stiffness. Athos perceived this embarrassment, and by way of supplying a prompt remedy, called for four bottles of champagne.

At this order, given in Athos's habitually calm manner, the face of the Gascon relaxed, and Porthos' brow was smooth. Aramis was astonished. He knew that Athos not only never drank, but that more, he had a kind of repugnance to wine. This astonish-ment was doubled when Aramis saw Athos fill a bumper, and drink with his former enthusiasm. His companions following his example, in an instant the four bottles were empty, and this excellent specific succeeded in dissipating even the slightest cloud which might have rested on their spirits. Now the four friends began to speak loud, scarcely waiting till one had finished for another to begin, and to assume each his favourite attitude on or at the table. Soon—strange fact—Aramis unfastened two buttons of his doublet, seeing which, Porthos unhooked his entirely.

Battles, long journeys, blows given and received, sufficed for the first subject of conversation; which then turned upon the silent struggles sustained against him who was now called the great Cardinal.

"Faith," said Aramis, laughing, "we have praised the dead enough, let us revile the living a little. I should like to say something evil of Mazarin; is it allowed?"

"Go on—go on," replied D'Artagnan, laughing heartily, "relate your story, and I will applaud if it is a good one."

"A great prince," said Aramis, "with whom Mazarin sought an alliance, was invited by him to send him a list of the conditions on which he would do him the honour to negotiate with him. The prince, who had a great repugnance to treat with such an illbred fellow, made his list against the grain, and sent it. In this list there were three conditions which displeased Mazarin, and he offered the prince ten thousand crowns to renounce them."

"Ah, ah, ah!" exclaimed the three friends, "not a bad bargain; and there was no fear of being taken at his word; what did the prince then?"

"The prince immediately sent fifty thousand francs to Mazarin begging him never to write to him again, and offered twenty thousand francs more, on condition that he would never speak to him."

"What did Mazarin do?"

"He stormed?" suggested Athos.

"He beat the messenger?" cried Porthos.

"He accepted the money?" said D'Artagnan.

"You have guessed it," answered Aramis; and they all laughed so heartily, that the host appeared in order to inquire whether these gentlemen wanted anything; he thought they were fighting.

At last their hilarity was calmed, and—

"Faith!" exclaimed D'Artagnan to his two friends, "you may well wish ill to Mazarin; for I assure you, on his side, he wishes you no good."

"Pooh! really?" asked Athos. "If I thought that the fellow knew me by my name, I would be re-baptised, for fear I should be thought to know him."

"He knows you better by your actions than by your name; he is quite aware that there are two gentlemen who have greatly aided the escape of Monsieur de Beaufort, and he has instigated an active search for them, I can answer for it."

"By whom?"

"By me; and this morning he sent for me to ask me if I had obtained any information."

"And what did you reply?"

"That I had none yet; but that I was to dine to-day with two gentlemen, who would be able to give me some."

"You told him that?" said Porthos, his broad smile spreading over his honest face, "bravo! and you are not afraid of that, Athos?"

"No," replied Athos; "it is not the search of Mazarin that I fear."

"Now," said Aramis, "tell me a little what you do fear."

"Nothing for the present, at least, in good earnest."

"And with regard to the past?" asked Porthos.

"Oh! the past is another thing," said Athos, sighing; "the past and the future."

"Are you afraid for your young Raoul?" asked Aramis.

"Well," said D'Artagnan, "one is never killed in a first engagement."

"Nor in the second," said Aramis.

"Nor in the third," returned Porthos; "and even when one is killed, one rises again, the proof of which is, that here we are!"

"No," said Athos, "it is not Raoul about whom I am anxious, for I trust he will conduct himself like a gentleman; and if he is killed—well—he will die bravely; but hold—should such a misfortune happen—well——" Athos passed his hand across his pale brow.

"Well?" asked Aramis.

"Well, I shall look upon it as an expiation."

"Oh! ah!" said D'Artagnan; "I know what you mean."

"And I, too," added Aramis; "but you must not think of that, Athos; what is past is past."

"I don't understand," said Porthos.

"The affair at Armentières," whispered D'Artagnan.

"The affair at Armentières?" asked he again.

"Milady."

" Oh, yes !" said Porthos ; " true, I had forgotten it."

Athos looked at him intently.

" You have forgotten it, Porthos ?" said he.

" Faith ! yes, it is so long ago," answered Porthos.

" This thing does not, then, weigh on your conscience ?"

" Faith, no."

" And you, D'Artagnan ?"

" I—I own that when my mind returns to that terrible period, I have no recollection of anything but the stiffened corpse of that poor Madame Bonacieux.   Yes, yes," murmured he, " I have often felt regret for the victim, but never any remorse for the assassin."

Athos shook his head doubtfully.

" Consider," said Aramis, " if you admit divine Justice and its participation in the things of this world, that woman was punished by the will of heaven.   We were but the instruments—that is all."

" But as to free will, Aramis ?"

" How acts the judge ?   He has a free will, and he condemns fearlessly.   What does the executioner ?   he is master of his arm, and yet he strikes without remorse."

" The executioner !" muttered Athos, as if arrested by some recollection.

" I know that it is terrible," said D'Artagnan ; " but when I reflect that we have killed English, Rochellais, Spaniards, nay, even French, who never did us any other harm but to aim at and to miss us, whose only fault was to cross swords with us, and not to be able to ward us off quick enough—I can, on my honour, find an excuse for my share of the murder of that woman."

" As for me," said Porthos, " now that you have reminded me of it, Athos, I have the scene again before me, as if I was there ! Milady was there, as it were in your place." (Athos changed colour.)   " I—I was where D'Artagnan stands.   I wore a short sword which cut like a Damascus—you remember it, Aramis, for you——"

" And you, Aramis ?"

" Well, I think of it sometimes," said Aramis.   " And I swear to you all three, that had the executioner of Béthune—was he not of Béthune ?—yes, egad ! of Béthune !—not been there, I would have cut off the head of that infamous being without remembering who I am, and even remembering it.   She was a bad woman."

" And then," resumed Aramis, with the tone of philosophical indifference which he had assumed since he had belonged to the Church, and in which there was more atheism than confidence in God, " what is the use of thinking of all that ?   At the last hour we must confess this action, and God knows better than we can whether it is a crime, a fault, or a meritorious action. *I* repent of it? Egad! no. By honour, and by the holy cross, I only regret it because she was a woman."

"The most satisfactory part of the matter," said D'Artagnan, "is that there remains no trace of it."

"She had a son," observed Athos.

"Oh! yes; I know that," said D'Artagnan, "and you mentioned it to me; but who knows what has become of him? If the serpent be dead, why not its brood? Do you think that his uncle De Winter would have brought up that young viper? De Winter probably condemned the son as he had done the mother."

"Then," said Athos, "woe to De Winter, for the child had done no harm."

"May the devil take me if the child be not dead," said Porthos. "There is so much fog in that detestable country, at least so D'Artagnan declares."

Just as this conclusion arrived at by Porthos was about probably to bring back hilarity to the faces now more or less clouded, footsteps were heard on the stair, and some one knocked at the door.

"Come in," cried Athos.

"Please your honours," said the host, "a person, in a great hurry, wishes to speak to one of you."

"To which of us?" asked all the four friends.

"To him who is called the Count de la Fère."

"It is I," said Athos; "and what is the name of the person?"

"Grimaud."

"Ah!" exclaimed Athos, turning pale. "Returned already. What has happened, then, to Bragelonne?"

"Let him enter," cried D'Artagnan, "let him come up,"

But Grimaud had already mounted the staircase, and was waiting on the last step; so springing into the room, he motioned the host to leave it. The door being closed, the four friends waited in expectation. Grimaud's agitation, his pallor, the sweat which covered his face, the dust which soiled his clothes, all indicated that he was the messenger of some important and terrible news.

"Your honours," said he, "that woman had a child; that child has become a man; the tigress had a little one, the tiger has roused himself; he is ready to spring upon you—beware!"

Athos glanced around at his friends with a melancholy smile. Porthos turned to look at his sword which was hung up against the wall; Aramis seized his knife; D'Artagnan rose.

"What do you mean, Grimaud?" he exclaimed.

"That milady's son has left England; that he is in France on his road to Paris, if he be not here already."

"The devil he is!" said Porthos. "Are you sure of it?"

"Certain!" replied Grimaud.

This announcement was received in silence. Grimaud was so breathless, so exhausted, that he had fallen back upon a chair. Athos filled a glass with champagne, and gave it to him.

"Well, and after all," said D'Artagnan, "supposing that he lives, that he comes to Paris, we have seen many other such. Let him come."

"Yes," echoed Porthos, stroking his sword, suspended to the wall, "we can wait for him, let him come."

"Moreover, he is but a child," said Aramis.

Grimaud rose.

"A child!" he exclaimed. "Do you know what he has done —this child? Disguised as a monk, he discovered the whole history in confession from the executioner of Béthune, and having confessed him, after having learnt everything from him, he gave him absolution by planting this dagger into his heart. See, it is still red and wet, for it is not thirty hours ago since it was drawn from the wound."

And Grimaud threw the dagger on the table.

D'Artagnan, Porthos, and Aramis rose, and in one spontaneous motion rushed to their swords. Athos alone remained seated, calm and thoughtful.

"And you say he is dressed as a monk, Grimaud?"

"Yes, as an Augustine monk.'

"What sized man is he?"

"About my height, the host said; thin, pale, with light-blue eyes, and light hair."

"And he did not see Raoul?" asked Athos.

"Yes, on the contrary, they met, and it was the viscount himself who conducted him to the bed of the dying man."

Athos rose, in his turn, without speaking—went, and unhooked his sword.

"Heigh, sir," said D'Artagnan, trying to laugh; "do you know we look very much like silly women! How is it that we, four men, who have faced armies without blinking, begin to tremble at the sight of a child!"

"Yes," said Athos, "but this child comes in the name of Heaven."

And they hastily quitted the inn.

CHAPTER XXXIV.

A LETTER FROM CHARLES THE FIRST.

THE reader must now cross the Seine with us, and follow us to the door of the Carmelite Convent in the Rue St. Jacques. It is eleven o'clock in the morning, and the pious sisters have just finished saying a mass for the success of the armies of King Charles I. Leaving the church, a woman and a young girl dressed in black, the one as a widow and the other as an orphan, have re-entered their cell.

The woman kneels on a prie-Dieu of painted wood, and at a short distance from her stands the young girl, leaning against a chair, weeping.

The woman must have been handsome, but the traces of sorrow have aged her. The young girl is lovely, and her tears only embellish her; the lady appears to be about forty years of age, the girl about fourteen.

"Oh, God!" prayed the kneeling suppliant, "protect my husband, guard my son, and take my wretched life instead!"

"Oh, God!" murmured the girl, "leave me my mother!"

"Your mother can be of no use to you in this world, Henrietta," said the lady, turning round. "Your mother has no longer either throne or husband, nor son, nor money, nor friends—the whole world, my poor child, has abandoned your mother!" And she fell back, weeping, into her daughter's arms.

"Courage, take courage, my dear mother!" said the girl.

"Ah! 'tis an unfortunate year for kings," said the mother. "And no one thinks of us in this country, for each must think of his own affairs. As long as your brother was with me he kept me up; but he is gone, and can no longer send us news of himself, either to me or to your father. I have pawned my last jewels, sold all your clothes and my own to pay his servants, who refused to accompany him unless I made this sacrifice. We are now reduced to live at the expense of these daughters of Heaven; we are the poor succoured by God."

"But why not address yourself to your sister the queen?" asked the girl.

"Alas! the queen, my sister, is no longer queen, my child. Another reigns in her name. One day you will be able to understand how this is."

"Well, then, to the king, your nephew; shall I speak to him? You know how much he loves me, my mother."

"Alas! my nephew is not yet king, and you know Laporte has told us twenty times that he himself is in need of almost everything."

"Then let us pray to Heaven," said the girl.

The two women who thus knelt together in prayer were the daughter and granddaughter of Henry IV., the wife and daughter of Charles I.

They had just finished their double prayer, when a nun softly tapped at the door of the cell.

"Enter, my sister," said the queen.

"I trust your majesty will pardon this intrusion on her meditations, but a foreign lord has arrived from England, and waits in the parlour, demanding the honour of presenting a letter to your majesty."

"Oh! a letter! a letter from the king, perhaps. News from your father, do you hear, Henrietta—And the name of this lord?"

"Lord de Winter."

"Lord de Winter!" exclaimed the queen, "the friend of my husband. Oh, let him come in!"

And the queen advanced to meet the messenger, whose hand she seized affectionately, whilst he knelt down, and presented a letter to her contained in a gold case.

"Ah! my lord," said the queen, "you bring us three things which we have not seen for a long time. Gold, a devoted friend, and a letter from the king, our husband and master."

De Winter bowed again, unable to reply from excess of emotion.

On their side the mother and daughter retired into the embrasure of a window to read eagerly the following letter :

"DEAR WIFE,—We have now reached the moment of decision. I have concentrated here at Naseby camp all the resources which Heaven has left me ; and I write to you in haste from thence. Here I await the army of my rebellious subjects, and I am about to fight for the last time against them. If victorious, I shall continue the struggle ; if beaten, I am completely lost. I shall try, in the latter case (alas! in our position, one must provide for everything), I shall try to gain the coast of France. But can they, will they receive an unhappy king, who will bring such a sad story into a country already agitated by civil discord? Your wisdom and your affection must serve me as guides. The bearer of this letter will tell you, madam, what I dare not trust to the risk of miscarrying. He will explain to you the steps which I expect you to pursue. I charge him also with my blessing for my children, and with the sentiments of my heart for yourself, dear wife."

The letter bore the signature, not of "Charles, King," but of "Charles—still king."

"And let him be no longer king," cried the queen. "Let him be conquered, exiled, proscribed, provided he still lives. Alas! in these days the throne is too dangerous a place for me to wish him to keep it! But, my lord, tell me," she continued, "hide nothing from me—what is, in truth, the king's position? Is it as hopeless as he thinks?"

"Alas! madame—more hopeless than he thinks. His majesty has so good a heart, that he cannot understand hatred;—is so loyal, that he does not suspect treason! England is disturbed by a spirit of excitement, which, I greatly fear, blood alone can extinguish."

"But, Lord Montrose," replied the queen, "I have heard of his great and rapid successes, of battles gained. I heard it said that he was marching to the frontier to join the king."

"Yes, madame; but on the frontier he was met by Lesly, he had tired victory by means of superhuman undertakings. Now victory has abandoned him. Montrose, beaten at Philiphaugh, was obliged to disperse the remains of his army, and to fly disguised as a servant. He is at Bergen, in Norway."

"Heaven preserve him!" said the queen. "It is at least a consolation to know that some who have so often risked their lives for us are in safety. And now, my lord, that I see how hopeless the position of the king is, tell me with what you are charged on the part of my royal husband."

"Well, then, madame," said De Winter, "the king wishes you to try and discover the dispositions of the king and queen towards him."

"Alas! you know, the king is but still a child, and the queen is a woman weak enough too. Monsieur Mazarin is everything here."

"Does he desire to play the part in France that Cromwell plays in England?"

"Oh, no! He is a subtle and cunning Italian, who, though he may dream of crime, dares never commit it; and unlike Cromwell, who disposes of both Houses, Mazarin has had the queen to support him in his struggle with the parliament."

"—More reason, then, that he should protect a king pursued by his parliament."

The queen shook her head despairingly.

"If I judge for myself, my lord," she said, "the Cardinal will do nothing, and will even, perhaps, act against us. The presence of my daughter and myself in France is already irksome to him; much more so would be that of the king. My lord," added Henrietta, with a melancholy smile, "it is sad, and almost shameful, to be obliged to say that we have passed the winter in the Louvre without money, without linen—almost without bread, and often not rising from bed because we wanted fire."

"Horrible!" cried De Winter; "the daughter of Henry IV., and the wife of King Charles! Wherefore did you not apply then, madame, to the first person you saw from us?"

"Such is the hospitality shown to a queen by the minister, from whom a king would demand it."

"But I heard that a marriage between the Prince of Wales and Mademoiselle d'Orléans was spoken of," said De Winter.

"Yes, for an instant I hoped it was so. The young people felt a mutual esteem; but the queen, who at first sanctioned their affection, changed her mind, and Monsieur the Duc d'Orléans, who had encouraged the familiarity between them, has forbidden his daughter to think any longer about the union. Oh, my lord!" continued the queen, without restraining her tears, "it is better to fight as the king has done, and to die, as perhaps he will, than to live begging as I have."

"Courage, madame! courage! Do not despair! The interests of the French crown—endangered this moment—are to discourage civil rebellion in a nation so near to it. Mazarin, as a statesman, will understand the necessity of doing so."

"But are you sure," said the queen doubtfully, "that you have not been forestalled?"

"By whom?"

"By the Joyces, the Prinns, the Cromwells."

"By a tailor, by a coachmaker, by a brewer! Ah! I hope, madame, that the Cardinal will not enter into negotiations with such men!"

"Ah! what wishes he himself?" asked Madame Henrietta.

"Solely the honour of the king—of the queen."

"Well, let us hope that he will do something for the sake of their honour," said the queen. "A true friend's eloquence is so powerful, my lord, that you have reassured me. Give me your hand, and let us go to the minister; and yet," she added, "suppose he refuse, and that the king loses the battle!"

"His majesty will then take refuge in Holland, where I hear that his highness the Prince of Wales is."

"And can his majesty count upon many such subjects as yourself for his fight?"

"Alas! no, madame," answered De Winter; "but the case is provided for, and I am come to France to seek allies."

"Allies!" said the queen, shaking her head.

"Madame!" replied De Winter, "provided I can find some old friends of former times, I will answer for anything."

"Come, then, my lord," said the queen, with the painful doubt that is felt by those who have suffered much; "come, and may Heaven hear you."

CHAPTER XXXV.

CROMWELL'S LETTER.

AT the very moment when the queen quitted the convent to go to the Palais Royale, a young man dismounted at the gate of this royal abode, and announced to the guards that he had something of consequence to communicate to Cardinal Mazarin. Although the Cardinal was often tormented by fear, he was more often in need of counsel and information, and he was therefore sufficiently accessible. The true difficulty of being admitted was not to be found at the first door, and even the second was passed easily enough; but at the third watched, besides the guard and the doorkeepers, the faithful Bernouin, a Cerberus whom no speech could soften; no wand, even of gold, could charm.

It was, therefore, at the third door, that those who solicited or were bid to an audience, underwent a formal interrogatory.

The young man, having left his horse tied to the gate in the court, mounted the great staircase, and addressed the guard in the first chamber.

"Cardinal Mazarin?" said he.

"Pass on," replied the guard.

The cavalier entered the second hall, which was guarded by the Musketeers and doorkeepers.

"Have you a letter of audience?" asked a porter, advancing to the new arrival.

"I have one, but not from Cardinal Mazarin."

"Enter, and ask for Monsieur Bernouin," said the porter, opening the door of the third room. Whether he but held his usual post, or whether it might be by accident, but Monsieur Bernouin was found standing behind the door, and must have heard all that had passed.

" You seek me, sir?" said he.　" From whom may the letter be that you bear to his Eminence ?"

" From the General Oliver Cromwell," said the new comer. " Be so good as to mention this name to his Eminence, and to bring me word whether he will receive me—yes or no."

Saying which, he resumed the dark and proud bearing peculiar at that time to the Puritans.　Bernouin cast an inquisitorial glance at the person of the young man, and entered the cabinet of the Cardinal, to whom he transmitted the messenger's words.

" A man bringing a letter from Oliver Cromwell ?" said Mazarin. " And what kind of a man ?"

" A true Englishman, your Eminence.　Hair sandy-red—more red than sandy ; grey blue eyes—more gray than blue ; and for the rest, stiff and proud."

" Let him give in his letter."

" His Eminence asks for the letter," said Bernouin, passing back into the antechamber.

" His Eminence cannot see the letter without the bearer of it," replied the young man ; " but to convince you that I am really the bearer of a letter, see, here it is ; and add," continued he, " that I am not a simple messenger, but an envoy extraordinary."

Bernouin re-entered the cabinet, and returning in a few seconds, —" Enter, sir," said he.

The young man appeared on the threshold of the minister's closet ; in one hand holding his hat, in the other the letter.　Mazarin rose.　" Have you, sir," asked he, " a letter accrediting you to me ?"

" There it is my lord," said the young man.

Mazarin took the letter, and read it thus :

" Mr. Mordaunt, one of my secretaries, will remit this letter of introduction to his Eminence, the Cardinal Mazarin, in Paris. He is also the bearer of a second confidential epistle for his Eminence.

" OLIVER CROMWELL."

" Very well, Monsieur Mordaunt," said Mazarin, " give me the second letter, and sit down."

The young man drew from his pocket the second letter, presented it to the Cardinal, and sat down.　The Cardinal, however, did not unseal the letter at once, but continued to turn it again and again in his hand ; then, in accordance with his usual custom, and judging from experience that few people could hide anything from him, when he began to question them, fixing his eyes upon them at the same time, he thus addressed the messenger :

"You are very young, Monsieur Mordaunt, for this difficult task of ambassador, in which the oldest diplomatists sometimes fail."

"My lord, I am twenty-three years of age ; but your Eminence is mistaken in saying that I am young. I am older than your Eminence, although I possess not your wisdom. Years of suffering, in my opinion, count double, and I have suffered for twenty years."

"Ah, yes, I understand," said Mazarin ; "want of fortune, perhaps. You are poor—are you not?" Then he added to himself —"These English revolutionists are all beggars and ill-bred."

"My lord, I ought to have a fortune of three hundred a-year, but it has been taken from me."

"You are not then a man of the people?" said Mazarin, astonished.

"If I bore my title I should be a lord. If I bore my name, you would have heard one of the most illustrious names of England."

"What is your name, then?" asked Mazarin.

"My name is Mordaunt," replied the young man, bowing.

Mazarin now understood that Cromwell's envoy desired to retain his incognito. He was silent for an instant, and during that time he scanned the young man even more attentively than he had done at first. The messenger was unmoved.

"Devil take these Puritans," said Mazarin aside ; "they are cut out of marble." Then he added aloud, "But you have relations left to you?"

"I have one remaining, and three times I have presented myself to him to ask his support, and three times he has desired his servants to turn me away."

"Oh, mon Dieu! my dear Mr. Mordaunt," said Mazarin, hoping, by a display of affected pity, to catch the young man in a snare, "how extremely your history interests me ! You know not, then, anything of your birth, you have never seen your mother?"

"Yes, my lord; she came three times, while I was a child, to my nurse's house ; I remember the last time she came as well as if it were to-day."

"You have a good memory," said Mazarin.

"Oh! yes, my lord !" said the young man, with such peculiar emphasis that the Cardinal felt a shudder run through all his veins.

"And who brought you up?" he asked again.

"A French nurse, who sent me away when I was five years old, because no one paid her for me, telling me the name of a relation, of whom she had heard my mother often speak."

" What became of you ?"

" As I was weeping and begging on the high road, a minister from Kingston took me in, instructed me in the Calvinistic faith, taught me all he knew himself, and aided me in my researches after my family."

" And these researches ?"

" Were fruitless ; chance did everything."

" You discovered what had become of your mother ?"

" I learnt that she had been assassinated by my relation, aided by four friends, but I was already aware that I had been robbed of all my wealth, and degraded from my nobility, by King Charles I."

" Oh ! I now understand why you are in the service of Cromwell ; you hate the king. '

" Yes, my lord, I hate him !" said the young man.

Mazarin marked, with surprise, the diabolical expression with which the young man uttered these words ; as, in general, ordinary countenances are coloured by the blood—his face seemed dyed by hatred, and became livid.

" Your history is a terrible one, Mr. Mordaunt, and touches me keenly ; but, happily for you, you serve an all-powerful master, he ought to aid you in your search ; we have so many means of gaining information."

" My lord, to a dog of good breed it is only necessary to show but one end of a track, that he may be certain to reach the other end."

" But this relation whom you mentioned, do you wish me to speak to him ?" said Mazarin, who was anxious to make a friend about Cromwell's person.

" Thanks, my lord, I will speak to him myself ; he will treat me better the next time I see him."

" You have the means, then, of touching him ?"

" I have the means of making myself feared."

Mazarin looked at the young man, but, at the fire which shot from his glance, he bent down his head ; then, embarrassed how to continue such a conversation, he opened Cromwell's letter. It was lengthy, and began by alluding to the situation of England, and announcing that he was on the eve of a decisive engagement with King Charles, and certain of success. He then adverted to the hospitality and protection afforded by France to Henrietta Maria, and continued :

" As regards King Charles, the question must be viewed differently; in receiving and aiding him France will censure the acts of the English nation, and thus so essentially do harm to England, and especially to the progress of the Government which she reckons upon forming, so that such a proceeding will be equal to flagrant hostilities."

At this moment Mazarin became very uneasy at the turn which the letter was taking, and paused to glance under his eyes at the young man. The latter continued lost in thought. Mazarin resumed his reading of the General's worthy epistle, which ended by demanding perfect neutrality from France:

"A neutrality," it said, "which was solely to consist in excluding King Charles from the French territories, nor to aid a king so entirely a stranger, either by arms, money, or troops. Farewell, sir; should we not receive a reply in the space of fifteen days, I shall presume my letter will have miscarried.

"OLIVER CROMWELL."

"Mr. Mordaunt," said the Cardinal, raising his voice, as if to arouse the thinker, "my reply to this letter will be more satisfactory to General Cromwell if I am convinced that all are ignorant of my having given one; go, therefore, and await it at Boulogne-sur-Mer, and promise me to set out to-morrow morning."

"I promise, my lord," replied Mordaunt; "but how many days will your Eminence oblige me to await your reply?"

"If you do not receive it in ten days, you can leave."

Mordaunt bowed.

"It is not all, sir," continued Mazarin; "your private adventures have touched me to the quick; besides, the letter from Mr. Cromwell makes you an important person in my eyes as ambassador; come, tell me what can I do for you?"

Mordaunt reflected a moment, and, after some hesitation, was about to speak, when Bernouin entered hastily, and, bending down to the ear of the Cardinal, whispered to him:

"My lord, the Queen Henrietta Maria, accompanied by an English noble, is just entering the Palais Royale at this moment."

Mazarin made a bound from his chair, which did not escape the attention of the young man, and repressed the confidence he was about to make.

"Sir," said the Cardinal, "you have heard me? I fix on Boulogne because I presume that every town in France is indifferent to you; if you prefer another, name it; but you can easily conceive that, surrounded as I am by influences from which I can escape alone by means of discretion, I desire your presence in Paris to be ignored."

"I shall go, sir," said Mordaunt, advancing a few steps to the door by which he had entered.

"No, not that way I beg, sir," quickly exclaimed the Cardinal; "be so good as to pass by that gallery, by which you can gain the hall; I do not wish you to be seen leaving—our interview must be kept secret.

Mordaunt followed Bernouin, who conducted him through a neighbouring chamber, and left him with a doorkeeper showing him the way out.

CHAPTER XXXVI.

HENRIETTA MARIA AND MAZARIN.

THE Cardinal rose, and advanced in haste to receive the Queen of England. He showed the more respect to this queen, deprived of all pomp, and without followers, as he felt some self-reproach for his own want of heart and his avarice. But suppliants for favour know how to vary the expression of their features, and the daughter of Henry IV. smiled as she advanced to meet one whom she hated and despised.

"Ah!" said Mazarin to himself, "what a sweet face! does she come to borrow money of me?"

And he threw an uneasy glance at his strong box; he even turned inside the bevel of the magnificent diamond ring, the brilliancy of which drew every eye upon his hand, which indeed was handsome and white.

"Your Eminence," said the august visitor, "it was my first intention to speak of the affairs which have brought me here, to the queen, my sister, but I have reflected that political matters are more especially the concerns of men."

"Madame," said Mazarin, "be assured that your majesty overwhelms me with this flattering distinction."

"He is very gracious," thought the queen; "has he guessed my errand, then?"

"Give," continued the Cardinal, "your commands to the most respectful of your servants.'

"Alas, sir," replied the queen, "I have lost the habit of giving commands, and have adopted instead that of making petitions; I am come to petition you, too happy should my prayer be heard favourably."

"I listen, madame, with interest," said Mazarin.

, "Your Eminence, it concerns the war which the king, my husband, now sustains against his rebellious subjects. You are, perhaps, ignorant that they are fighting in England," added she, with a melancholy smile, "and that, in a short time, they will fight in a much more decided fashion than they have done hitherto."

"I am completely ignorant of it, madame," said the Cardinal, accompanying his words with a slight shrug of the shoulders; "alas, our own wars have quite absorbed the time and the mind of a poor, incapable, and infirm minister like myself."

"Well, then, your Eminence," said the queen, "I must inform you that Charles I., my husband, is on the eve of a decisive engagement. In case of a check——" (Mazarin made a slight movement) "one must foresee everything; in case of a check, he desires to retire into France, and to live here as a private individual. What do you say to this project?"

The Cardinal had listened without permitting a single fibre of his face to betray what he felt, and his smile remained as it ever was—false and flattering, and, when the queen finished speaking, he said:

"Do you think, madame, that France, agitated and disturbed as it is, would be a safe refuge for a dethroned king? How will the crown, which is so scarce firmly set on the head of Louis IV., support a double weight?"

"This weight was not so heavy when I was in peril," interrupted the queen, with a sad smile, "and I ask no more for my husband than has been done for me; you see that we are very humble monarchs, sir."

"Oh, you, madame, you," the Cardinal hastened to say, in order to cut short the explanations which he foresaw were coming, "with regard to you, that is another thing; a daughter of Henry IV., of that great, that sublime sovereign——"

"All which does not prevent you refusing hospitality to his son-in-law, sir! Nevertheless, you ought to remember that that great, that sublime monarch, when proscribed at one time, as my husband may be, demanded aid from England, and that England accorded it to him; and it is but just to say that Queen Elizabeth was not his niece."

"Peccato!" said Mazarin, writhing beneath this simple eloquence, "your majesty does not understand me; you judge my intentions wrongly, and that is because doubtless I explain myself ill in French."

"Speak Italian, sir: ere the Cardinal, your predecessor, sent our mother, Marie de Medicis, to die in exile, she taught us that language. If anything yet remains of that great, that sublime king, Henry, of whom you have just spoken, he would be much surprised at so little pity for his family being united to such a profound admiration of himself."

The perspiration hung in large drops upon Mazarin's brow.

"That admiration is, on the contrary, so great, so real, madame," returned Mazarin, without noticing the change of language offered to him by the queen, "that if the king, Charles I., whom Heaven protect from evil! came into France, I would offer him my house —my own house—but, alas! it would be but an unsafe retreat. Some day the people will burn that house, as they burnt that of the Maréchal d'Ancre. Poor Concino Concini! and yet he but desired the good of the people.'

"Yes, my lord, like yourself!" said the queen ironically.

Mazarin pretended not to understand the double meaning of his own sentence, but continued to compassionate the fate of Concino Concini.

"Well, then, your Eminence," said the queen, becoming impatient, "what is your answer?"

"Madame," cried Mazarin, more and more moved, "will your majesty permit me to give you counsel?"

"Speak, sir," replied the queen; "the counsels of so prudent a man as yourself ought certainly to be good."

"Madame, believe me, the king ought to defend himself to the last."

"He has done so, sir, and this last battle, which he encounters with resources much inferior to those of the enemy, proves that he will not yield without a struggle; but, in case he is beaten?"

"Well, madame, in that case my advice—I know that I am very bold to offer advice to your majesty—my advice is that the king should not leave his kingdom. Absent kings are very soon forgotten; if he passes over to France his cause is lost."

"But then," persisted the queen, "if such be your advice, and you have his interest at heart, send him some help of men and money, for I can do nothing for him: I have sold even to my last diamond to aid him. If I had had a single ornament left, I should have bought wood this winter to make a fire for my daughter and myself."

"Oh, madame," said Mazarin, "your Majesty knows not what you ask. On the day when foreign succour follows in the train of a king to replace him on his throne, it is an avowal that he no longer possesses the help and the love of his subjects."

"To the point, sir," said the queen, "to the point, and answer me, yes or no; if the king persists in remaining in England, will you send him succour? If he comes to France, will you accord him hospitality? What do you intend to do?—speak."

"I will go this instant and consult the queen, and we will refer the affair at once to the parliament."

"With which you are at war, is it not so? You will charge Broussel to report it. Enough, sir, enough. I understand you, or rather, I am wrong. Go to the parliament; for it was from this parliament, the enemy of monarchs, that the daughter of the great, the sublime Henry IV., whom you so much admire, received the only relief this winter, which prevented her from dying of hunger and cold!"

And with these words Henrietta rose in majestic indignation, whilst the Cardinal, raising his hands clasped towards her, exclaimed, "Ah, madame, madame, how little you know me, mon Dieu!"

"It signifies little," said Mazarin, when he was alone; "it gave me pain, and it is an ungracious part to play. But I have said nothing either to the one or to the other. Bernouin!"

Bernouin entered.

"See if the young man with the black doublet and the short hair, who was with me just now, is still in the palace."

Bernouin went out, and soon returned with Comminges, who was on guard.

"Your Eminence," said Comminges, "as I was re-conducting the young man for whom you have asked, he approached the glass door of the gallery, and gazed intently upon some object, doubtless the picture by Raphael, which is opposite the door. He reflected for a second, and then descended the stairs. I believe I saw him mount on a grey horse and leave the palace court. But is not your Eminence going to the queen?"

"For what purpose?"

"Monsieur de Guitant, my uncle, has just told me that her majesty has received news of the army."

"It is well—I will go."

Comminges had seen rightly, and Mordaunt had really acted as he had related. In crossing the gallery parallel to the large glass gallery, he perceived De Winter, who was waiting until the queen had finished her negotiation.

At this sight the young man stopped short, not in admiration of Raphael's picture, but as if fascinated at the sight of some terrible object. His eyes dilated, and a shudder ran through his body. One would have said that he longed to break through the wall of glass which separated him from his enemy; for if Comminges had seen with what an expression of hatred the eyes of this young man were fixed upon De Winter, he would not have doubted for an instant but that the English lord was his mortal foe.

But he stopped—doubtless to reflect; for, instead of allowing his first impulse, which had been to go straight to Lord De Winter, to carry him away, he leisurely descended the staircase, left the palace with his head down, mounted his horse, which he reined in at the corner of the Rue Richelieu, and with his eyes fixed on the gate, he waited until the queen's carriage had left the court.

He did not wait long, for the queen scarcely remained a quarter of an hour with Mazarin; but this quarter of an hour of expectation, appeared a century to him. At last the heavy machine, which was called a chariot in those days, came out, rumbling against the gates, and De Winter, still on horseback, bent again to the door to converse with her majesty.

The horses started into a trot, and took the road to the Louvre, which they entered. Before leaving the convent of the Carmelites, Henrietta had desired her daughter to attend her at the palace, which she had inhabited for a long time, and which she had only left because their poverty seemed to them more difficult to bear in gilded chambers.

Mordaunt followed the carriage, and when he had watched it drive under the sombre arches, he went and stationed himself under a wall over which the shadow was extended, and remained motionless, amidst the mouldings of Jean Goujon, like a bas-relievo representing an equestrian statue.

CHAPTER XXXVII.

HOW, SOMETIMES, THE UNHAPPY MISTAKE CHANCE FOR PROVIDENCE.

"WELL, madame," said De Winter, when the queen had dismissed her attendants.

"Well, my lord, what I had foreseen has come to pass."

"What? does the Cardinal refuse to receive the king? France refuse hospitality to an unfortunate prince? But it is for the first time, madame!"

" I did not say France, my lord, I said the Cardinal, and the Cardinal is not even a Frenchman."

" But did you see the queen?"

" It is useless," replied Henrietta; " the queen will not say yes when the Cardinal has said no. Are you not aware that this Italian directs everything, both in doors and out? And, moreover, I should not be surprised had we been forestalled by Cromwell; he was embarrassed whilst speaking to me, and yet quite firm in his determination to refuse. Then, did you not observe the agitation in the Palais Royale, the passing to and fro of busy people? Can they have received any news, my lord?"

" Not from England, madame. I made such haste that I am certain of not having been forestalled. I set out three days ago, passing miraculously through the Puritan army, and I took post-horses with my servant Tony: the horses upon which we were mounted were bought in Paris. Besides, the king, I am certain, awaits your majesty's reply before risking anything."

" You will tell him, my lord," resumed the queen, despairingly, " that I can do nothing: that I have suffered as much as himself —more than he has—obliged as I am to eat the bread of exile, and to ask hospitality from false friends who smile at my tears; and as regards his royal person, he must sacrifice it generously, and die like a king. I shall go and die by his side."

" Madame, madame!" exclaimed De Winter, " your majesty abandons yourself to despair; and yet, perhaps, there still remains some hope."

" No friends left, my lord; no other friends left in the whole world but yourself! Oh God!" exclaimed the poor queen, raising her eyes to heaven, " have you indeed taken back all the generous hearts which existed in the world?"

" I hope not, madame," replied De Winter, thoughtfully; " I once spoke to you of four men."

" What can be done with four men?"

" Four devoted, resolute men can do much, be assured, madame; and those of whom I speak have done much at one time."

" And these men were your friends?"

" One of them held my life in his hands, and gave it to me. I know not whether he is still my friend; but since that time I have remained his."

" And these men are in France, my lord?"

" I believe so."

" Tell me their names; perhaps I have heard them mentioned, and might be able to aid you in finding them."

" One of them was called the Chevalier d'Artagnan."

" Oh ! my lord, if I do not mistake, the Chevalier d'Artagnan is a lieutenant of the guards ; but take care, for I fear that this man is devoted entirely to the Cardinal."

" That would be a misfortune," said De Winter, " and I shall begin to think that we are really doomed."

" But the others," said the queen, who clung to this last hope as a shipwrecked man clings to the remains of his vessel : " the others, my lord !"

" The second—I heard his name by chance ; for before fighting us, these four gentlemen told us their names ; the second was called the Count de la Fère. As for the two others, I had so much the habit of calling them by nicknames, that I have forgotten their real ones."

" Oh, mon Dieu, it is a matter of great urgency to find them out," said the queen, " since you think these worthy gentlemen might be so useful to the king."

" Oh, yes," said De Winter, " for they are the same men."

" Well then, my lord, they must be found; but what can four men, or rather three men, do ?—for I tell you, you must not count on Monsieur d'Artagnan."

" It will be one valiant sword the less, but there will remain still three, without reckoning my own ; now four devoted men round the king to protect him from his enemies,—to be at his side in battle, to aid him in counsel, to escort him in flight, are sufficient— not to make the king a conqueror, but to save him if conquered ; and whatever Mazarin may say—once on the shores of France, your royal husband may find as many retreats and asylums as the sea-bird finds in storms."

" Seek them, my lord—seek these gentlemen ; and if they will consent to go with you to England, I will give to each a duchy the day that we re-ascend the throne, besides as much gold as would pave Whitehall. Seek them, my lord. Seek them, I conjure you."

" I will search for them well, madame," said De Winter, " and doubtless I shall find them—but time fails me. Has your majesty forgotten that the king expects your reply, and awaits it in agony ?"

" Then, indeed, we are lost," cried the queen, in the fulness of a broken heart.

At this moment the door opened, and the young Henrietta appeared ; then the queen, with that wonderful strength which is he theroism of a mother, repressed her tears, and motioned to De Winter to change the subject of conversation.

"What do you want, Henrietta?" she demanded.

"My mother," replied the young princess, "a cavalier has just entered the Louvre, and wishes to present his respects to your majesty; he arrives from the army, and has, he says, a letter to remit to you on the part of the Maréchal de Grammont, I think."

"Ah!" said the queen to De Winter, "he is one of my faithful adherents; but do you not observe, my dear lord, that we are so poorly served that it is my daughter who fills the office of introducer?"

"Madame, have pity on me," exclaimed De Winter; "you break my heart!"

"And who is this cavalier, Henrietta?" asked the queen.

"I saw him from the window, madame; he is a young man who appears scarcely sixteen years of age, and who is called the Viscount de Bragelonne."

The queen, smiling, made a sign with her head; the young princess opened the door, and Raoul appeared on the threshold.

Advancing a few steps towards the queen, he knelt down.

"Madame," said he, "I bear to your Majesty a letter from my friend the Count de Guiche, who told me he had the honour of being your servant; this letter contains important news, and the expression of his respect."

At the name of the Count de Guiche, a blush spread over the cheeks of the young princess, and the queen glanced at her with some degree of severity.

"You told me that the letter was from the Maréchal de Grammont, Henrietta!" said the queen.

"I thought so, madame," stammered the young girl.

"It is my fault, madame," said Raoul. "I did announce myself, in truth, as coming on the part of the Maréchal de Grammont; but being wounded in the right arm, he was unable to write, and therefore the Count de Guiche served as his secretary."

"There has been fighting, then?" asked the queen, motioning to Raoul to rise.

"Yes, madame," said the young man.

At this announcement of a battle having taken place, the young princess opened her lips as if to ask a question of interest; but her lips closed again without articulating a word, while the colour gradually faded from her cheeks.

The queen saw this, and doubtless her maternal heart translated this emotion, for addressing Raoul again,—

"And no evil has happened to the young Count de Guiche?" she asked; for not only is he our servant, as you say, sir, but more; he is one of our friends."

"No, madame," replied Raoul; "on the contrary, he gained great glory on that day, and had the honour of being embraced by his highness the prince on the field of battle."

The young princess clasped her hands; and then, ashamed of having been betrayed into such a demonstration of joy, she half turned away, and bent over a vase of roses, as if to inhale their odour.

"Let us see," said the queen, "what the count says." And she opened the letter and read:

"MADAME,—Being unable to have the honour of writing to you myself, by reason of a wound which I have received in the right hand, I have commanded my son, the Count de Guiche, who with his father, is equally your humble servant, to write to tell you that we have just gained the battle of Lens, and that this victory cannot fail to give great power to the Cardinal Mazarin and to the queen over the affairs of Europe. If her majesty will have faith in my counsels, she ought to profit by this event to address at this moment, in favour of her august husband, the court of France. The Viscount de Bragelonne, who will have the honour of remitting this letter to your majesty, is the friend of my son, to whom he owes his life; he is a gentleman in whom your Majesty can confide entirely, in the case when your majesty may have some verbal or written order to forward to me.

"I have the honour to be, with respect, &c.,

"MARÉCHAL DE GRAMMONT."

At the moment, when mention occurred of his having rendered a service to the count, Raoul· could not help turning his eyes towards the young princess, and then he saw in her eyes an expression of infinite gratitude to the young man; he no longer doubted that the daughter of King Charles the First loved his friend.

"The battle of Lens gained!" said the queen; "they are lucky indeed for me—they can gain battles! Yes, the Maréchal de Grammont is right; this will change the aspect of affairs; but I much fear it will do nothing for ours, even if it does not harm them. This is recent news, sir," continued she, "and I thank you for having made such haste to bring it to me; without this letter, I should not have heard it till to-morrow—perhaps after to-morrow—the last of all Paris."

"Madame," said Raoul, "the Louvre is but the second palace which this news has reached: it is as yet unknown to all, and I had sworn to the Count de Guiche to remit this letter to your Majesty ere even I should embrace my guardian."

"Your guardian! is he too a Bragelonne?" asked Lord de Winter. "I knew formerly a Bragelonne—is he still alive?"

"No, sir, he is dead; and I believe it is from him that my guardian, whose near relation be was, inherited the estate from which I take my name."

"And your guardian, sir," asked the queen, who could not help feeling some interest in the handsome young man before her, "what is his name?"

"The Count de la Fère, madame," replied the young man, bowing.

De Winter made a gesture of surprise, and the queen turned to him with a start of joy.

"The Count de la Fère!" cried De Winter in his turn. "Oh, sir, reply, I entreat you—is not the Count de la Fère a noble, whom I remember handsome and brave, a Musketeer under Louis XIII., and who must be now about forty-seven or forty-eight years of age?"

"Yes, sir, you are right in every respect."

"And who served under a borrowed name?"

"—Under the name of Athos. Latterly I heard his friend Monsieur d'Artagnan give him that name."

"That is it, madame, that is the same. God be praised! And he is in Paris?" continued he, addressing Raoul; then, turning to the queen—"We may still hope. Providence has declared for us, since I have found this brave man again in so miraculous a manner. And, sir, where does he reside, pray?"

"The Count de la Fère lodges in the Rue Guénegand, Hôtel du Grand Roi Charlemagne."

"Thanks, sir. Inform this dear friend that he may remain within. I shall go and see him immediately."

"Sir, I obey with pleasure, if her Majesty will permit me to depart."

"Go, Monsieur de Bragelonne," said the queen, "and be assured of our affection."

Raoul bent respectfully before the two princesses, and, bowing to De Winter, departed.

The queen and De Winter continued to converse for some time in low voices, in order that the young princess should not overhear them; but the precaution was needless; she was in deep converse with her own thoughts.

Then, when De Winter rose to take leave—

"Listen, my lord," said the queen; "I have preserved this diamond cross which came from my mother, and this order of

St. Michael, which came from my husband. They are worth about fifty thousand pounds. I had sworn to die of hunger rather than to part with these precious pledges ; but now that this ornament may be useful to him or to his defenders, everything must be sacrificed to the hope of it. Take them, and if you need money for your expedition, sell them fearlessly, my lord. But should you find the means of retaining them, remember, my lord, that I shall esteem you as having rendered the greatest service which a gentleman can render to a queen ; and in the day of my prosperity, he who brings me this order and this cross will be blessed by me and my children."

"Madame," replied De Winter, "your majesty will be served by a man devoted to you. I hasten to deposit these two objects in a safe place, nor should I accept them if the resources of our ancient fortune were left to us ; but our estates are confiscated, our ready money is exhausted, and we are reduced to turn into resources everything we possess. In an hour hence I shall be with the Count de la Fère, and to-morrow your majesty shall have a definitive answer."

The queen tendered her hand to Lord de Winter, who, kissing it respectfully, went out, traversing alone, unconducted, those large dark and deserted apartments, and brushing away tears which, blasé as he was by fifty years spent as a courtier, he could not help shedding at the spectacle of this royal distress, so dignified and yet so intense.

CHAPTER XXXVIII.

THE UNCLE AND THE NEPHEW.

THE horse and servant belonging to De Winter were waiting for him at the door ; he sauntered towards his abode very thoughtfully, looking behind him from time to time to contemplate the dark and silent façade of the Louvre. It was then that he saw a horseman, as it were, detach himself from the wall and follow him at a little distance. In leaving the Palais Royale he remembered to have observed a similar shadow.

"Tony," he said, motioning to his groom to approach.

"Here I am, my lord."

"Did you remark that man who is following us ?"

"Yes, my lord."

"Who is he ?"

"I do not know, only he has followed your grace from the Palais Royale, stopped at the Louvre to wait for you, and now leaves the Louvre with you."

"Some spy of the Cardinal," said De Winter to him aside. "Let us pretend not to notice that he is watching us."

And spurring on, he pursued the labyrinth of streets which led to his hotel, situated near the Marais, for having for so long a time lived near the Place Royale, Lord de Winter naturally returned to lodge near his ancient dwelling.

The unknown put his horse into a gallop.

De Winter dismounted at his hotel, went up into his apartment, intending to watch the spy; but as he was about to place his gloves and hat on a table, he saw reflected in a glass opposite to him a figure which stood on the threshold of the room. He turned round, and Mordaunt was before him.

There was a moment of frozen silence between these two men.

"Sir," said De Winter, "I thought I had already made you aware that I am weary of this persecution; withdraw, then, or I shall call, and have you turned out, as you were in London. I am not your uncle; I know you not."

"My uncle," replied Mordaunt, with his harsh and bantering tone, "you are mistaken; you will not have me turned out this time, as you did in London; you dare not. As for denying that I am your nephew, you will think twice about it, now that I have learnt some things of which I was ignorant a few days ago."

"And how doth it concern me what you have learnt?" said De Winter.

"Oh, it concerneth you much, my uncle, I am sure; and you will soon be of my opinion," added he, with a smile which sent a shudder through the veins of him whom he addressed. "When I presented myself before you for the first time in London, it was to ask you what had become of my wealth; the second time it was to demand who had sullied my name; and this time I come before you to ask a question far more terrible than any other: to ask you, my lord, what have you done with your sister—your sister, who was my mother?"

De Winter shrank back from the fire of those scorching eyes.

"Your mother?" he said.

"Yes, my lord, my mother," replied the young man, advancing into the room until he was face to face with Lord de Winter, and crossing his arms. "I have asked the headsman of Béthune," he said, his voice hoarse and his face livid with passion and grief; "and the headsman of Béthune gave me a reply."

De Winter fell back into a chair as if struck by a thunderbolt, and in vain attempted to answer.

"Yes," continued the young man, "all is now explained; with this key the abyss is opened. My mother had inherited an estate from her husband, and you have assassinated my mother; my name would have secured to me the paternal estate, and you have despoiled me of my name, you have deprived me of my fortune. I am no longer astonished that you knew me not. I am not surprised that you refused to recognise me. When a man is a robber, it is unbecoming to call him a nephew whom one has impoverished; when one is a murderer, to term that man whom one has made an orphan a relative."

These words produced a contrary effect to what Mordaunt had anticipated. De Winter remembered the monster that milady had been; he rose, dignified and calm, restraining by the severity of his look the wild glances of the young man.

"You desire to fathom this horrible secret?" said De Winter; "well, then, so be it. Know, then, what that woman was for whom to-day you come to call me to account. That woman had, in all probability, poisoned my brother, and in order to inherit from me she was about to assassinate me in my turn. I have proof of it. What say you to that?"

"I say that she was my mother."

"She caused the unfortunate Duke of Buckingham to be stabbed by a man who was, ere that, honest, good, and pure. What say you to that crime, of which I have the proof?"

"She was my mother!"

"On our return to France she had a young woman who was attached to one of her foes poisoned in the convent of the Augustines at Béthune. Will this crime persuade you of the justice of her punishment? of this I have the proofs."

"Silence, sir—she was my mother," exclaimed the young man, his face running with sweat, his hair, like Hamlet's, standing upon his forehead, and raging with fury; "she was my mother! her crimes, I know them not—her disorders, I know them not—her vices, I know them not. But this I know, that I had a mother, that five men leagued against one woman, murdered her clandestinely by night—silently—like cowards. I know that you were one of them, my uncle, and that you cried louder than the others —'she must die.' Therefore I warn you—and listen well to my words, that they may be engraved on your memory, never to be forgotten—this murder, which has robbed me of everything—this murder, which has deprived me of my name—this murder, which has impoverished me—this murder, which has made me corrupt, wicked, implacable—I shall summon you to account for it first, and then those who were your accomplices—when I discover them !"

With hatred in his eyes, foaming at his mouth, and his fist extended, Mordaunt had advanced one more step—a threatening, terrible step—towards De Winter. The latter put his hand to his sword, and said, with the smile of a man who for thirty years has jested with death :

"Would you assassinate me, sir ? Then I shall recognise you as my nephew, for you are a worthy son of such a mother."

"No," replied Mordaunt, forcing all the veins in his face, and the muscles of his body, to resume their usual places and to be calm; "no, I shall not kill you—at least, not at this moment, for without you I could not discover the others. But when I have found them, then tremble, sir. I have stabbed the headsman of Béthune—stabbed him without mercy or pity, and he was the least guilty of you all."

With these words the young man went out, and descended the stair sufficiently calm to pass unobserved; then, upon the lowest landing-place, he passed Tony leaning over the balustrade, waiting only for a call from his master to mount to his room.

But De Winter did not call; crushed, enfeebled, he remained standing, and with listening ear; then only, when he had heard the step of the horse going away, he fell back on a chair saying :

"My God, I thank Thee that he knows me alone."

CHAPTER XXXIX.

PATERNAL AFFECTION.

WHILE this terrible scene was passing at Lord de Winter's, Athos, seated near his window, his elbow on the table, and his head supported on his hand, was listening intently to Raoul's account of the adventures he met with on his journey, and the details of the battle

Listening to the relation of those first emotions so fresh and pure, the fine, noble face of Athos betrayed indescribable pleasure; he inhaled the tones of that young voice as harmonious music. He forgot all that was dark in the past, and that was cloudy in the future. It almost seemed as if the return of this much-loved boy had changed his fears into hopes. Athos was happy—happy as he had never been before.

"And you assisted and took part in this great battle, Bragelonne?" said the ancient Musketeer.

"Yes, sir."

"And it was a hard one?"

"His highness the prince charged eleven times in person."

"He is a great commander, Bragelonne."

"He is a hero, sir; I did not lose sight of him for an instant.
Oh! how fine it is to be called Condé, and to be so worthy of such
a name!"

"He is calm and radiant, is he not?"

"As calm as at parade; as radiant as at a fête. When we went
up to the enemy, it was slowly; we were forbidden to draw first,
and we were marching towards the Spaniards, who were on a
height with lowered muskets. When we arrived about thirty paces
from them, the prince turned round to the soldiers, 'Comrades,'
he said, 'you are about to suffer a furious discharge; but——.'
There was such dead silence that friends and enemies could have
heard these words; then raising his sword, 'Sound trumpets!' he
cried."

"Well, very good; you will do as much when the opportunity
occurs—will you, Raoul?"

"I know not, sir, but I thought it was very fine and grand!"

"Were you afraid, Raoul?" asked the count.

"Yes, sir," replied the young man naïvely; "I felt a great chill
at my heart, and at the word 'fire,' which resounded in Spanish
from the enemy's ranks, I closed my eyes and thought of you."

"In honest truth, Raoul?" said Athos, pressing his hand.

"Yes, sir; at that instant there was such a firing that one might
have supposed that the infernal regions were opened, and those
who were not killed felt the heat of the flames. I opened my
eyes, astonished at my being alive, or at least unhurt; a third of
the squadron were lying on the ground, mutilated and bloody.
At this moment I encountered the eye of the prince, and I had
but one thought, and that was that he was observing me. I
spurred on, and found myself in the enemy's ranks."

"And the prince was pleased with you?"

"He told me so, at least, sir, when he desired me to return to
Paris with Monsieur de Châtillon, who was charged to carry the
news to the queen, and to bring the colours we had taken. 'Go,'
said he, 'the enemy will not rally for fifteen days, and until that
time I have no need of your service. Go and see those whom
you love, and who love you, and tell my sister De Longueville that
I thank her for the present she made me of you.' And I came,

sir," added Raoul, gazing at the count with a smile of real affection, " for I thought you would be glad to see me again."

Athos drew the young man towards him, and pressed his lips to his brow, as he would have done to a young daughter.

" And now, Raoul," said he, " you are launched ; you have dukes for friends, a marshal of France for a godfather, a prince of the blood as commander, and on the day of your return you have been received by two queens ; it is rather well for a novice."

" Oh, sir !" said Raoul, suddenly, " you recall something to me, which, in my haste to relate my exploits, I had forgotten ; it is that there was with her Majesty the queen of England, a gentleman who, when I pronounced your name, uttered a cry of surprise and joy ; he said he was a friend of yours—asked your address, and is coming to see you."

" What is his name ?".

" I did not dare ask, sir ; he spoke elegantly, although I thought from his accent he was an Englishman."

" Ah !" said Athos, leaning down his head as if to remember who it could be. Then, when he raised it again, he was struck by the presence of a man who was standing at the open door, and was gazing at him with a compassionate air.

" Lord de Winter !" exclaimed the count.

" Athos, my friend !"

And the two gentlemen were for an instant locked in each other's arms ; then Athos, looking into his friend's face, and taking him by both hands, said:

" What ails you, my lord ? you appear as unhappy as I am happy."

" Yes, truly, dear friend ; and I may even say that the sight of you increases my dismay."

And De Winter glancing round him, Raoul quickly understood that the two friends wished to be alone, and he therefore left the room unaffectedly.

" Come, now that we are alone," said Athos, " let us talk of yourself."

" Whilst we are alone let us speak of ourselves," replied De Winter. " He is here."

" Who ?"

" Milady's son."

Athos, who was again struck by this name, which seemed to pursue him like an echo, hesitated for a moment, then slightly knitting his brows, he calmly said:

" I know it ; Grimaud met him between Béthune and Arras, and then came here to warn me of his presence."

" Does Grimaud know him, then ?"

" No ; but he was present at the deathbed of a man who knew him."

" The headsman of Béthune ?" exclaimed De Winter.

" You know about that ?" cried Athos, astonished.

" He has just left me," replied De Winter, " after telling me all. Ah ! my friend ! what a horrible scene ! Why did we not destroy the child with the mother ?"

" What need you fear ?" said Athos, recovering from the instinctive fear he had at first experienced, by the aid of reason ; " are we not here to defend ourselves ? Is this young man an assassin by profession—a murderer in cold blood ? He has killed the executioner of Béthune in an impulse of passion, but now his fury is assuaged."

De Winter smiled sorrowfully, and shook his head.

" Do you not then know the race ?" said he.

" Pooh !" said Athos, trying to smile in his turn. " It must have lost its ferocity in the second generation. Besides, my friend, Providence has warned us that we may be on our guard. All we can do is to wait. Let us wait ; and, as I said before, let us speak of yourself. What brings you to Paris ?"

" Affairs of importance which you shall know later. But what is this that I hear from Her Majesty the Queen of England ? Monsieur d'Artagnan is with Mazarin ! Pardon my frankness, dear friend. I neither hate nor blame the Cardinal, and your opinions will be held ever sacred by me ; do you happen to belong 'o this man ?"

" Monsieur D'Artagnan," replied Athos, " is in the service ; he is a soldier, and obeys the constituted authority. Monsieur D'Artagnan is not rich, and has need of his position as lieutenant to enable him to live. Millionaires like yourself, my lord, are rare in France."

" Alas !" said De Winter, " I am at this moment as poor as he is, if not poorer ; but to return to our subject."

" Well, then, you wish to know if I am of Mazarin's party. No. Pardon my frankness, also, my lord."

" I am obliged to you, count, for this pleasing intelligence ! You make me young and happy again by it. Ah ! so you are not a Mazarinist ? Delightful ! Indeed, you could not belong to him. But pardon me, are you free ?"

" What mean you by free ?"

" I mean to ask if you be not married ?"

" Ah ! as to that, no," replied Athos, laughing.

" Because that young man—so handsome, so elegant, so polished——"

" He is a child that I have adopted, and who does not even know who was his father."

" Very well—you are always the same, Athos, great and generous. Are you still friends with Monsieur Porthos and Monsieur Aramis ?"

" And add Monsieur D'Artagnan, too, my lord. We still remain four friends devoted to each other ; but when it becomes a question of serving the Cardinal, or of fighting, of being Mazarinists or Frondists, then we are only two. "

" Is Monsieur Aramis with D'Artagnan ?" asked Lord de Winter.

" No," said Athos : " Monsieur Aramis does me the honour to share my opinions."

" Could you put me in communication with your witty and agreeable friend ? Is he changed?"

" He has become an abbé, that is all."

" You alarm me ; his profession must have made him renounce any great undertakings."

" On the contrary," said Athos, smiling, " he has never been so much a musketeer as since he became an abbé, and you will find him a veritable soldier."

" Could you engage to bring him to me to-morrow morning at ten o'clock, on the Pont du Louvre ?"

" Oh, oh !" exclaimed Athos, smiling, " you have a duel in prospect."

" Yes, count, and a splendid duel, too ; a duel in which I hope you will take your part."

" Where are we to go to, my lord ?"

" To Her Majesty the Queen of England, who has desired me to present you to her."

" This is an enigma," said Athos ; " but it matters not ; from the moment that you have guessed the word, I ask no further. Will your lordship do me the honour to sup with me ?"

" Thanks, count, no," replied De Winter. " I own to you that that young man's visit has taken away my appetite, and will probably deprive me of sleep. What undertaking can have brought him to Paris ? It was not to meet me that he came, for he was ignorant of my journey. This young man terrifies me, my lord ; for there lies in him a sanguinary predisposition."

" What occupies him in England ?"

" He is one of Cromwell's most enthusiastic disciples."

"But what has attached him to this cause? His father and mother were Catholics, I believe?"

"His hatred of the king, who deprived him of his estates, and forbad him to bear the name of De Winter."

"And how is he now called?"

"Mordaunt."

"A puritan, yet, disguised as a monk, he travels alone in France."

"Do you say as a monk?"

"It was thus, and by mere accident—may God pardon me if I blaspheme!—that he heard the confession of the executioner of Béthune."

"Then I understand it all; he has been sent by Cromwell to Mazarin, and the queen guessed rightly; we have been forestalled. Everything is clear to me now. Adieu, count, till to-morrow."

"But the night is dark," said Athos, perceiving that Lord de Winter seemed more uneasy than he wished to show; "and you have no servant."

"I have Tony, a good but simple youth."

"Holloa there, Grimaud, Olivain, and Blaisois, call the viscount here, and take the musket with you."

Blaisois was the tall youth, half groom, half peasant, whom we saw at the Château de Bragelonne, whom Athos had christened by the name of his province.

"Viscount," said Athos to Raoul as he entered, "you will conduct my lord as far as his hotel, and permit no one to approach him."

"Oh! count," said De Winter, "for whom do you take me?"

"For a stranger who does not know Paris," said Athos, "and to whom the viscount will show the way."

De Winter shook him by the hand.

"Grimaud," said Athos, "put yourself at the head of the troop, and beware of the monk."

Grimaud shuddered, and nodding, awaited the departure, regarding the butt of his musket with silent eloquence. Then, obeying the orders given him by Athos, he headed the little procession, bearing the torch in one hand and the musket in the other, until it reached the door of De Winter's inn, when, striking on the door with his fist, he bowed to my lord without saying a word.

The same order was pursued in returning; nor did Grimaud's searching glance discover anything of a suspicious appearance, save a dark shadow in ambuscade at the corner of the Rue

Guénégaud of the Quai. He fancied also that in going he had already observed the street watcher who had attracted his attention. He pushed on towards him, but before he could reach it the shadow had disappeared into an alley, in which Grimaud deemed it scarcely prudent to pursue it.

The next day, on awaking, the count perceived Raoul by his bedside. The young man was already dressed, and was reading a new book by M. Chapelain.

"Already up, Raoul?" exclaimed the count.

"Yes, sir," replied Raoul, with a slight hesitation. "I did not sleep well."

"You, Raoul, not sleep well! then you must have something on your mind!" said Athos.

"Sir, you will, perhaps, think that I am in a great hurry to leave you, when I have only just arrived, but——"

"Have you only two days of leave, Raoul?"

"On the contrary, sir, I have ten; nor is it to the camp that I wish to go."

"Where then?" said Athos, smiling, "if it be not a secret. You are now almost a man, since you have made your first passage of arms, and have acquired the right to go where you will without telling me."

"Never, sir," said Raoul, "as long as I possess the happiness of having you for a protector, shall I deem I have the right of freeing myself from a guardianship which is so valuable to me. I have, therefore, the wish to go and pass a day only at Blois. You look at me, and are going to laugh at me."

"No; on the contrary, I am not inclined to laugh," said Athos, suppressing a sigh. "You wish to see Blois again; it is but very natural."

"Then you permit me to go, and you are not angry in your heart!" exclaimed Raoul joyously.

"Certainly; and why should I regret what will give you pleasure?"

"Oh! how kind you are," exclaimed the young man, pressing his guardian's hand; "and I can set out immediately?"

"When you like, Raoul."

"Sir," said Raoul, as he turned to leave the room, "I have thought of one thing, and that is about the Duchess of Chevreuse, so kind to me, and to whom I owe my introduction to the prince."

"And you ought to thank her, Raoul. Well, try the Hôtel de Luynes, Raoul, and ask if the duchess can receive you. I am glad to see that you pay attention to the usages of the world. You must take Grimaud and Olivain."

"Both, sir?" asked Raoul, astonished.

"Both."

Raoul went out, and when Athos heard his young, joyous voice calling to Grimaud and Olivain, he sighed.

"It is very soon to leave me," he thought, "but he follows the common lot. Nature has made us thus: she looks on before her. He certainly likes that child, but will he love me less because he loves others?"

And Athos confessed to himself that he was unprepared for so prompt a departure; but Raoul was so happy that this consideration effaced everything else from the mind of his guardian.

Everything was ready at ten o'clock for their journey, and as Athos was seeing Raoul mount, a groom rode up from the Duchess de Chevreuse. He was charged to tell the Count de la Fère that she had learnt the return of her youthful protégé, and also the manner he had conducted himself on the field, and she added that she should be very glad to offer him her congratulations.

"Tell her grace," replied Athos, "that the viscount has just mounted his horse to proceed to the Hôtel de Luynes."

Then, with renewed instructions to Grimaud, Athos signified to Raoul that he could set out, and ended by reflecting that it was, perhaps, better that Raoul should be away from Paris at that moment.

CHAPTER XL.

AGAIN A QUEEN DEMANDING HELP.

ATHOS had not failed to send early to Aramis, and had given his letter to Blaisois, the only serving-man whom he had left. Blaisois found Bazin donning his bedell's gown, his services being required that day at Nôtre Dame.

Athos had desired Blaisois to try to speak to Aramis himself. Blaisois, a tall, simple youth, who understood nothing but what he was desired, asked, therefore, for the Abbé d'Herblay, and in spite of Bazin's assurances that his master was not at home, he persisted in such a manner as to put Bazin into a passion. Blaisois seeing Bazin in clerical guise, was little discomposed at his denials, and wanted to pass at all risks, believing, too, that he with whom he had to do was endowed with the virtues of his cloth—namely, patience and Christian charity.

But Bazin, still the servant of a Musketeer, when once the blood mounted to his fat cheeks, seized a broomstick and began thumping Blaisois, saying:

"You insulted the Church; my friend, you have insulted the Church!"

At this moment Aramis, aroused by this unusual disturbance, cautiously opened the door of his room; and Blaisois, looking reproachfully at the Cerberus, drew the letter from his pocket, and presented it to Aramis.

"From the Count de la Fère," said Aramis. "All right." And he retired into his room without even asking the cause of so much noise.

Blaisois returned disconsolate to the hotel of the Grand Roi Charlemagne, and when Athos inquired if his commission was executed, he related his adventure.

"You foolish fellow!" said Athos, laughing. "And you did not tell him that you came from me?"

"No, sir."

At ten o'clock, Athos, with his habitual exactitude, was waiting on the Pont du Louvre, and was almost immediately joined by Lord de Winter.

They waited ten minutes, and then his lordship began to fear that Aramis was not coming to join them.

"Patience," said Athos, whose eyes were fixed in the direction of the Rue du Bac, "patience; I see an abbé giving a cuff to a man, and a bow to a woman—that must be Aramis."

It was he, in truth; having run against a young shopkeeper who was gaping at the crows, and who had splashed him, Aramis with one blow of his fist had distanced him ten paces.

At this moment one of his penitents passed, and as she was young and pretty, Aramis took off his cap to her, with his most gracious smile.

A most affectionate greeting, as one can well believe, took place between him and Lord de Winter.

"Where are we going?" inquired Aramis; "are we going to fight there, 'faith? I carry no sword this morning, and cannot return home to procure one."

"No," said Lord de Winter, "we are going to pay a visit to Her Majesty the Queen of England."

"Oh, very well," replied Aramis; then, bending his face down to Athos' ear, "what is the object of this visit?" continued he.

"I'faith, I know not; some evidence required from us, perhaps."

"May it not be about that cursed affair?" asked Aramis, "in

which case ⊥ do not greatly care to go, for it will be to pocket some reproofs; and since I am used to give it to so many, I do not like to receive it myself."

"If it were so," answered Athos, "we should not be taken there by Lord de Winter, for he would come in for his share; he was one of us."

"Truly—yes, let us go."

On arriving at the Louvre, Lord de Winter entered first; indeed, there was but one porter to receive them at the gate.

It was impossible, in daylight, for the impoverished state of the habitation, which avaricious charity had conceded to an unfortunate queen, to pass unnoticed by Athos, Aramis, and even the Englishman. Large rooms, completely denuded of furniture, bare walls, upon which, here and there, shone the old gold mouldings which had resisted time and neglect, windows with broken panes (which it was impossible to close fast), no carpets, nor guards, nor servants; this is what at first met the eyes of Athos, to which he, touching his companion's elbow, directed his attention by his glances.

"Mazarin is better lodged," said Aramis.

"Mazarin is almost king," answered Athos; "and Madame Henrietta is almost no longer queen."

"If you would condescend to be clever, Athos," observed Aramis, "I really do think you would be more so than poor Monsieur de Voiture."

Athos smiled.

The queen appeared to be impatiently expecting them, for at the first slight noise which she heard in the hall leading to her room, she came herself to the door to receive the courtiers of the days of misfortune.

"Enter and be welcome, gentlemen," she said.

The gentlemen entered and remained standing, but at a motion from the queen they seated themselves. Athos was calm and grave, but Aramis was furious; the sight of such royal misery exasperated him, and his eyes examined every new trace of poverty which presented itself.

"You are examining the luxury I enjoy?" said the queen, glancing sadly around her.

"Madame," replied Aramis, "I must ask your pardon, but I know not how to hide my indignation at seeing how a daughter of Henry IV. is treated at the court of France."

"Monsieur Aramis is not an officer?" asked the queen of Lord de Winter.

"That gentleman is the Abbé D'Herblay," replied he.

Aramis blushed. "Madame," he said, "I am an abbé, it is true, but I am so against my will; I never had a vocation for the bands; my cassock is fastened by one button only, and I am always ready to become a Musketeer again. This morning, being ignorant that I should have the honour of seeing your Majesty, I encumbered myself with this dress, but you will find me no less a man devoted to your Majesty's service, in whatever you see fit to command me."

"The Abbé D'Herblay," resumed De Winter, "is one of those gallant Musketeers belonging to his Majesty King Louis XIII., of whom I have spoken to you, madame." Then, turning towards Athos, he continued: "And this gentleman is that noble Count de la Fère, whose high reputation is so well known to your Majesty."

"Gentlemen," said the queen, "a few years ago I had around me gentlemen, treasures, and armies; and by the lifting of a finger all these were occupied in my service. To-day, look around you, and it may astonish you, that in order to accomplish a plan which is dearer to me than life, I have only Lord de Winter, the friend of twenty years, and you, gentlemen, whom I see for the first time, and whom I know but as my countrymen."

"It is enough," said Athos, bowing low, "if the life of three men can purchase yours, madame."

"I thank you, gentlemen. But hear me," continued she. "I am not only the most miserable of queens, but the most unhappy of mothers, the most despairing of wives. My children—two of them at least—the Duke of York and the Princess Elizabeth, are far away from me, exposed to the blows of the ambitious and our foes; my husband, the king, is leading in England so wretched an existence, that it is no exaggeration to say that he seeks death, as a thing to be desired. Hold! gentlemen, there is the letter conveyed to me by Lord de Winter. Read it."

Obeying the queen, Athos read aloud the letter, which we have already seen, in which King Charles demanded whether the hospitality of France would be accorded to him.

"Well?" asked Athos, when he had closed the letter.

"Well," said the queen, "it has been refused."

The two friends exchanged a smile of contempt.

"And now," said Athos, "what is to be done? I have the honour to inquire from your Majesty, what you desire Monsieur D'Herblay and myself to do in your service. We are ready."

"Ah! sir, you have a noble heart," exclaimed the queen, with a burst of gratitude ; whilst Lord de Winter turned to her with a. glance which said, " Did I not answer for them to you ?"

" But you, sir ?" said the queen to Aramis.

" I, madame," replied he, "follow Monsieur de la Fère where-ever he leads, even were it to death, without demanding where-fore ; but when it concerns your Majesty's service, then," added he, looking at the queen with all the grace of his former days, " I precede the count."

" Well, then, gentlemen," said the queen, "since it is thus,. and since you are willing to devote yourselves to the service of a. poor princess whom the whole world has abandoned, this is what is required to be done for me. The king is alone with a few gentlemen, whom he fears to lose every day ; surrounded by the Scotch, whom he distrusts, although he be himself a Scotchman. Since Lord de Winter left him I am distracted, sirs. I ask much,. too much perhaps, for I have no title to ask it. Go to England, join the king, be his friends, his protectors, march to battle at his side, and be near him in the interior of his house, where con-spiracies, more dangerous than the perils of war, increase every day. And in exchange of the sacrifice that you make, gentlemen,. I promise—not to reward you, I believe that word would offend you—but to love you as a sister, to prefer you next to my husband and my children, to every one. I swear it before Heaven."

And the queen raised her eyes solemnly upwards.

" Madame," said Athos, " when must we set out ?"

" You consent, then ?" exclaimed the queen, joyfully.

" Yes, madame ; only it seems to me that your Majesty goes. too far in engaging to load us with a friendship so far above our merit. We do service to God, madame, in serving a prince so unfortunate, and a queen so virtuous. Madame, we are yours, body and soul."

" Oh, sirs," said the queen, moved to tears, "this is the first time for five years that I have felt anything like joy and hope. God—who can read my heart, all the gratitude I feel—will reward you ! Save my husband ! Save the king, and although you care not for the price which is placed upon a good action in this world, leave me the hope that we shall meet again, when I may be able to thank you myself. In the meantime I remain here. Have you any counsel to give me ? From this moment I become your friend, and since you are engaged in my affairs, I ought to occupy myself in yours."

" Madame," replied Athos, " I have only to ask your majesty's. prayers."

" And I," said Aramis, " I am alone in the world, and have only your majesty to serve."

The queen held out her hand, which they kissed, and having two letters prepared for the king—one from herself, and one written by the Princess Henrietta—she gave one to Athos and the other to Aramis, lest, should they be separated by chance, they might make themselves known to the king; after which they withdrew.

At the foot of the staircase De Winter stopped.

" Not to arouse suspicions, gentlemen," said he, " go your way, and I will go mine, and this evening at nine o'clock we will assemble again at the gate St. Denis. We will travel on horseback as far as our horses can go, and afterwards we can take the post. Once more, let me thank you, my good friends, thank you in my own name, and in the queen's."

The three gentlemen then shook hands, Lord de Winter taking the Rue St. Honore, and Athos and Aramis remaining together.

" Well," said Aramis, when they were alone, " what do you think of this business, my dear count ?"

" Bad," replied Athos, " very bad."

" But you received it with enthusiasm."

" As I shall ever receive the defence of a great principle, my dear D'Herblay. Monarchs are only strong by the aid of the aristocracy, but aristocracy cannot exist without monarchs. Let us, then, support monarchy in order to support ourselves."

" We shall be murdered there," said Aramis. " I hate the English—they are coarse, like all people who drink beer."

" Would it be better to remain here ?" said Athos, " and take a turn in the Bastille, or in the dungeon of Vincennes, for having favoured the escape of Monsieur de Beaufort ? Oh ! i'faith, Aramis, believe me there is little left to regret. We avoid imprisonment, and we take the part of heroes—the choice is easy."

" It is true ; but in everything, friend, one must always return to the same question—a stupid one I admit—but very necessary ; have you any money ?"

" Something like a hundred pistoles, that my farmer sent to me the day before I left Bragelonne ; but out of that sum, I ought to leave fifty for Raoul—a young man must live respectably. I have then about fifty pistoles. And you ?"

" As for me, I am quite sure that after turning out all my pockets and emptying my drawers, I shall not find ten louis at home. Fortunately, Lord de Winter is rich."

" Lord de Winter is ruined for the moment, for Cromwell claims all his resources."

" Now is the time when Baron Porthos would be useful !"

" Now it is that I regret D'Artagnan."

" Let us entice them away."

" This secret, Aramis, does not belong to us; take my advice, then, and put no one into our confidence. And, moreover, in taking such a step, we should appear to be doubtful of ourselves. Let us regret to ourselves for our own sakes, but not speak of it."

" You are right; but what are you going to do till this evening; I have two things to postpone."

" And what are they ?"

" First, a thrust with the Coadjutor, whom I met last night at Madame de Rambouillet's, and whom I found particular in his remarks respecting me."

" Oh, fye—a quarrel between priests, a duel between allies !"

" What can I do, friend; he is a bully, and so am I; his cassock is a burden to him, and I think I have had enough of mine; in fact, there is so much resemblance between us, that I sometimes believe he is Aramis, and I am the Coadjutor. This kind of life fatigues and oppresses me; besides, he is a turbulent fellow who will ruin our party. I am convinced that if I gave him a box on the ear, such as I gave this morning to the little citizen who splashed me, it would change the appearance of things."

" And I, my dear Aramis," quietly replied Athos, " I think it would only change Monsieur de Retz's appearance. Take my advice, leave things as they are; besides, you are neither of you now your own masters; he belongs to the Fronde, and you to the Queen of England. But now we must part. I have one or two visits to make, and a letter to write. Call for me at eight o'clock, or shall I wait supper for you at seven ?"

" That will do very well," said Aramis. " I have twenty visits to make, and as many letters to write."

They then separated. Athos went to pay a visit to Madame de Vendôme, left his name at Madame de Chevreuse's, and wrote the following letter to D'Artagnan :

" DEAR FRIEND,—I am about to set off with Aramis on important business. I wished to make my adieux to you, but time did not allow me. Remember that I write to you now to repeat how much affection I have for you.

"Raoul is gone to Blois, and is ignorant of my departure; watch over him in my absence as much as you possibly can, and if by chance you receive no news of me three months hence, tell him to open a packet which he will find addressed to him in my bronze casket at Blois, and of which I send you the key.

"Embrace Porthos from Aramis and myself. Adieu, perhaps farewell."

At the hour agreed upon Aramis arrived; he was dressed as an officer, and had the old sword at his side which he had drawn so often, and which he was more than ever ready to draw.

"By-the-bye," he said, "I think that we are decidedly wrong to depart thus, without leaving a line for Porthos and D'Artagnan."

"The thing is done, dear friend," said Athos; "I foresaw that, and have embraced them both from you and myself."

"You are a wonderful man, my dear count," said Aramis; "you think of everything."

"Well, have you made up your mind to this journey?"

"Quite; and now that I reflect about it, I am glad to leave Paris at this moment."

"And so am I," replied Athos; "my only regret is not having seen D'Artagnan; but that rascal is so cunning, he might have guessed our project."

When supper was over Blaisois entered. "Sir," said he, "here is Monsieur d'Artagnan's answer."

"But I did not tell you there was an answer, stupid!" said Athos.

"And I set off without waiting for one, but he called me back and gave me this;" and he presented a little bag made of leather, round and ringing.

Athos opened it, and began by drawing from it a little note, written in these terms:

"My dear Count,—When one travels—and especially for three months—one has never enough money. Now, recalling our former time of distress, I send you the half of my purse; it is money to obtain which I made Mazarin sweat. Don't make a bad use of it I entreat you.

"As to what you say about not seeing you again, I believe not a word of it; with your heart and your sword one might pass through everything. Au revoir, then, and not farewell.

"It is unnecessary to say that from the day I saw Raoul I loved him; nevertheless, believe that I heartily pray to God that

I may not become his father, however much I might be proud of such a son.

" Jonis d'Artagnan.

" P.S.—Be it well understood that the fifty louis which I send are equally for Aramis as for you, and for you as for Aramis."

Athos smiled, and his fine eye was dimmed by a tear. D'Artagnan, who had loved him so tenderly, loved him still, Mazarinist though he was.

"There are the fifty louis, i'faith," said Aramis, emptying the purse on the table, " all bearing the effigy of Louis XIII. Well, what shall you do with this money, count; shall you keep it, or send it back ?"

" I shall keep it, Aramis; and even had I no need of it, I should still keep it. What is offered from a generous heart should be accepted generously. Take twenty-five of them, Aramis, and give me the remaining twenty-five."

"All right; I am glad to see that you are of my opinion. Then now shall we start ?"

"When you like ; but have you no groom ?"

"No! that idiot Bazin had the folly to make himself verger, as you know, and therefore cannot leave Nôtre Dame."

"Very well, take Blaisois, with whom I know not what to do since I have had Grimaud."

"Willingly," said Aramis.

At this moment Grimaud appeared at the door. "Ready," said he, with his usual curtness.

" Let us go then," said Athos.

The two friends mounted, as did their servants. At the corner of the Quai they encountered Bazin, who was running breathlessly.

"Oh, sir !" exclaimed he, "thank heaven I have arrived in time. Monsieur Porthos has just been to your house, and has left this for you, saying that the thing was important, and ought to be given to you before you left."

" Good," said Aramis, taking a purse which Bazin presented to him. "What is this ?"

"Wait, your reverence, there is a letter."

" You know that I have already told you that if you ever call me anything but chevalier I will break your bones. Give me the letter."

"How can you read ?" asked Athos; "it is as dark as in an oven."

"Wait," said Bazin, striking a light, and lighting a twisted wax-light, with which he lighted the church candles. By this light Aramis read the following epistle:

"My dear D'Herblay,—I learn from D'Artagnan, who has embraced me on the part of the Count de la Fère and yourself, that you are setting out on a journey which may perhaps last two or three months. As I know that you do not like to ask money of your friend, I offer to you. Here are two hundred pistoles, of which you can dispose, and return to me when an opportunity occurs. Do not fear that you put me to inconvenience; if I want money, I can send for some from one of my châteaux; at Bracieux alone I have twenty thousand francs in gold. So, if I do not send you more, it is because I fear you would not accept a large sum.

"I address you, because you know, that although I esteem him from my heart, I am a little awed by Count de la Fère; but it is understood, that what I offer to you I offer to him at the same time.

"I am, as I trust you do not doubt, your devoted
"De Valon de Bracieux de Pierrefonds."

"Well," said Aramis, "what do you say to that?"

"I say, my dear D'Herblay, that it is almost sacrilege to distrust Providence when one has such friends, and therefore we will divide the pistoles from Porthos, as we divided the louis sent by D'Artagnan."

The division being made by the light of Bazin's taper, the two friends continued their road, and a quarter of an hour later they had joined De Winter at the Porte St. Denis.

CHAPTER XLI.

IN WHICH IT IS PROVED THAT FIRST IMPULSES ARE ALWAYS BEST.

The three gentlemen took the road to Picardy—a road so well known to them, and which recalled to Athos and Aramis some of the most picturesque adventures of their youth.

"If Mousqueton were with us," observed Athos, on reaching the spot where they had had a dispute with the paviers, "how he would tremble at passing this! Do you remember, Aramis, that it was here he received that famous ball?"

" By my faith, I would allow him to tremble," replied Aramis ; " for even I feel a shudder at the recollection ; hold, just above that tree is the little spot where I thought I was killed."

It was soon time for Grimaud to recall the past.   Arriving before the inn at which his master and himself had made such an enormous repast, he approached Athos, and said, showing him the air-hole of the cellar :

" Sausages !"

Athos began to laugh, and this youthful folly of his appeared to be as amusing as if some one had related it of another person.

At last, after travelling two days and one night, they arrived at Boulogne towards the evening, favoured by magnificent weather. Boulogne was a strong position, and then almost a deserted town, built entirely on the heights, and what is now called the lower town did not then exist.

" Gentlemen," said De Winter, on reaching the gate of the town, " let us do here as at Paris—let us separate to avoid suspicion.   I know an inn, little frequented, but of which the host is entirely devoted to me.   I will go there, where I expect to find letters, and you go to the first tavern in the town, to L'Epée du Grand Henri for instance, refresh yourselves, and in two hours be upon the jetty—our boat is waiting there for us."

The matter being thus decided, the two friends found, about two hundred paces further, the tavern indicated to them.   The horses were fed, but not unsaddled ; the grooms up—for it was already late—and their two masters, impatient to return, appointed a place of meeting with them on the jetty, and desired them on no account to exchange a word with any one.   It is needless to say that this caution concerned Blaisois alone—it was long since it had become a useless one to Grimaud.

Athos and Aramis walked down towards the port.   From their dress, covered with dust, and from a certain easy manner by which a man accustomed to travel is always recognised, the two friends excited the attention of a few walkers.   There was more especially one upon whom their arrival had produced a decided impression. This man, who they had observed from the first for the same reason as they had themselves been remarked by others, walked in a melancholy way up and down the jetty.   From the moment he perceived them he did not cease to look at them, and seemed to burn with the wish to speak to them.

On reaching the jetty, Athos and Aramis stopped to look at a little boat fastened to a stake, and ready rigged as if waiting to start.

"That is, doubtless, our boat," said Athos.

"Yes," replied Aramis, "and the sloop sailing about there must be that which is to take us to our destination; now," continued he, "if only De Winter does not keep us waiting. It is not at all amusing here—there is not a single woman passing."

"Hush!" said Athos, "we are overheard."

In truth, the walker who, during the observations of the two friends, had passed and repassed behind them several times, stopped at the name of De Winter; but as his face betrayed no emotion at the mention of this name, it might have been by chance that he had stopped.

"Gentlemen," said the man, who was young and pale, bowing with much ease and politeness, "pardon my curiosity, but I see you come from Paris, or at least that you are strangers at Boulogne."

"We come from Paris, yes," replied Athos, with the same courtesy; "what is there at your service?"

"Sir," said the young man, "will you be so good as to tell me if it be true that Cardinal Mazarin is no longer minister?"

"That is a strange question," said Aramis.

"He is and he is not," replied Athos; "that is to say, he is dismissed by one-half of France; and that, by means of intrigues and promises, he makes the other half retain him; you will perceive that this may last a long time."

"However, sir," said the stranger, "he has neither fled, nor is in prison?"

"No, sir, not at this moment at least."

"Sirs, accept my thanks for your politeness," said the young man, retreating.

"What do you think of that interrogator?" asked Aramis.

"I think he is either a provincial person who is dull, or a spy wishing for information."

"And you replied to him with that notion?"

"Nothing warranted me to answer him otherwise: he was polite to me, and I was so to him."

"But if he be a spy——"

"What do you think a spy would be about here? We are not living in the time of Cardinal Richelieu, who would have closed the ports on a bare suspicion."

"It matters not; you were wrong to reply to him as you did," continued Aramis, following with his eyes the young man disappearing behind the cliffs.

"And you," said Athos, "you forget that you committed a very different kind of imprudence in pronouncing Lord de Winter's name.   Did you not see that at that name the young man stopped ?"

" More reason, then, when he spoke to you for sending him about his business."

" A quarrel ?" asked Athos.

" And since when have you become afraid of a quarrel ?"

" I am always afraid of a quarrel when I am expected at any place, and that such a quarrel might possibly prevent my reaching it.   Besides, let me own something to you.   I am anxious to see that young man nearer."

" And wherefore ?"

" Aramis, you will certainly laugh at me—you will say that I am always repeating the same thing—you will call me the most timorous of visionaries ; but to whom do you see a resemblance in that young man ?"

" In beauty, or on the contrary ?" asked Aramis, laughing.

" In ugliness, and as far as a man can resemble a woman ?"

" Ah, egad !" cried Aramis, " you have made me think.   No, in truth, you are no visionary, my dear friend, and now that I think of it—you—yes, i'faith, quite right—that delicate and compressed mouth, those eyes which seem always at the command of the intellect, and never of the heart !   Yes, it is one of Milady's bastards !"

" You laugh, Aramis."

" From habit, that is all ; for I swear to you, I should like no better than yourself to meet that viper in my path."

" Ah ! here is De Winter coming," said Athos.

" Good, one thing now is only wanting, and that is that our grooms should keep us waiting."

" No," said Athos, " I see them about twenty paces behind my lord.   I recognise Grimaud by his long legs and stiff gait.   Tony carries our muskets."

" Then we shall embark to-night?" asked Aramis, glancing towards the west, where the sun had left but one golden cloud, which, dipping into the ocean, appeared by degrees to be extinguished.

" Probably so," said Athos.

" Diable !" resumed Aramis ; " I have little fancy for the sea by day, but still less at night ; the sounds of the winds and waves, the frightful motion of the vessel—I confess that I prefer to be in the convent of Noisy."

Athos smiled sadly, for it was evident that he was thinking of other things as he listened to his friend, and he moved towards De Winter.

"What ails our friend?" said Aramis; "he resembles one of Dante's damned people, whose neck Satan has dislocated, and who always look at their heels. What the devil makes him look thus behind him?"

When De Winter perceived them, in his turn he advanced towards them with surprising rapidity.

"What is the matter, my lord?" said Athos; "and what puts you out of breath thus?"

"Nothing," replied De Winter, "nothing; and yet in passing the heights it seemed to me——" and he again turned round.

Athos glanced at Aramis.

"But let us go," continued De Winter; "let us be off; the boat must be waiting for us, and there is our sloop at anchor—do you see it there? I wish I were on board already,"—and he looked back again.

"He has seen him," said Athos, in a low tone to Aramis.

They had now reached the ladder which led to the boat. De Winter made the grooms who carried the arms, and the porters with the luggage, descend the first, and was about to follow them.

At this moment, Athos perceived a man walking on the sea shore parallel to the jetty, and hastening his steps as if to reach the other side of the port, scarcely twenty steps from the place of embarking. He fancied in the darkness that he recognised the young man who had questioned him. Athos now descended the ladder in his turn, without losing sight of the young man. The latter, to make a short cut, had appeared on a sluice.

"He certainly bodes us no good," said Athos; "but let us embark—once out at sea, let him come."

And Athos sprang into the boat, which was immediately pushed off, and which soon distanced the shore under the efforts of four strong rowers.

But the young man had begun to follow or rather to advance before the boat. She was obliged to advance between the point of the jetty, surmounted by a beacon, just lighted, and a rock which jutted out. They saw him in the distance climbing the rock, in order to look down upon the boat as she passed.

"Ay, but," said Aramis, "that young man is decidedly a spy."

"Which is the young man?" asked De Winter, turning round.

"He who followed us, and spoke to us, and awaits us there—see!"

De Winter turned, and followed the direction of Aramis's finger. The beacon bathed its light upon the little strait through which they were about to pass, and the rock where the young man stood with bare head and crossed arms.

" It is he !" exclaimed De Winter, seizing the arm of Athos ; " it is he ! I thought I recognised him, and I was not mistaken."

" Who—him ?" asked Aramis.

" Milady's son," replied Athos.

" The monk !" exclaimed Grimaud.

The young man heard the words, and bent so forward over the rock that one might have supposed he was about to precipitate himself from it.

" Yes, it is I, my uncle. I, the son of Milady—I, the monk—I, the secretary and friend of Cromwell—and I know you, both you and your companions."

There were in that boat three men, unquestionably brave, and whose courage no man would have dared to dispute; nevertheless, at that voice, that accent, and those gestures, they felt a shudder of terror run through their veins. As for Grimaud, his hair stood on end, and drops of sweat ran from his brow.

" Ah !" exclaimed Aramis, "that is the nephew, the monk, and the son of Milady, as he says himself."

" Alas ! yes," murmured De Winter.

" Then, wait," said Aramis ; and with the terrible coolness which on important occasions he showed, he took one of the muskets from Tony, shouldered and aimed it at the young man, who stood, like the accusing angel, upon the rock.

" Fire !" cried Grimaud, unconsciously.

Athos threw himself on the mouth of the gun, and arrested the shot which was about to he fired.

" The devil take you," said Aramis, "I had him so well at the point of my gun, I should have sent a ball into his breast."

" It is enough to have killed the mother," said Athos, hoarsely.

" The mother was a wretch, who struck at us all, and at those dear to us."

" Yes, but the son has done us no harm."

Grimaud, who had risen to watch the effect of the shot, fell back hopeless, wringing his hands.

The young man burst into a laugh.

" Ah, it is certainly you," he cried, "and I know you now."

His mocking laugh and threatening words passed over their heads, carried on by the breeze, until lost in the depths of the horizon. Aramis shuddered.

" Be calm !" exclaimed Athos, "for Heaven's sake ;—have we ceased to be men ?"

"No," said Aramis "but that being is a fiend ; and ask the uncle whether I was wrong to rid him of his nephew."

De Winter only replied by a groan.

"It was all up with him," continued Aramis; "ah, I much fear that, with your wisdom, you have made me commit a great folly."

Athos took Lord de Winter's hand, and tried to turn the conversation.

"When shall we land in England ?" he asked ; but De Winter seemed not to hear his words, and made no reply.

"Hold, Athos," said Aramis, "perhaps there is still time. See if he is still in the same place."

Athos turned round with an effort ; the sight of the young man was evidently painful to him, and there he still was, in fact, on the rock, the beacon shedding round him, as it were, a glory of light.

"Decidedly, Aramis," said Athos; "I think I was wrong not to let you fire."

"Hold your tongue," replied Aramis; "you will make me weep if it were possible."

At this moment they were hailed by a voice from the sloop, and a few seconds later, men, servants, and baggage were on deck. The captain had been only waiting his passengers, and hardly had they put foot on board ere her head was turned towards Hastings, where they were to disembark. At this instant the three friends turned, in spite of themselves, a last look on the rock, upon the menacing figure which pursued them and stood out boldly. Then a voice reached them once more, sending out this threat: "To our next meeting, sirs, in England."

CHAPTER XLII.

THE TE DEUM FOR THE VICTORY OF LENS.

THE bustle which had been observed by Henrietta Maria, and for which she had vainly sought to discover a reason, was occasioned by the battle of Lens, announced by the prince's messenger, the Duc de Châtillon, who had taken such a noble part in the engagement ; he was, besides, charged to hang twenty-five flags taken from the Lorraine party, as well as from the Spaniards, upon the arches of Nôtre Dame.

This news was decisive; it destroyed, in favour of the court, the struggle commenced with the parliament. The motive given for all the taxes summarily imposed, and to which the parliament had made opposition, was the necessity of sustaining the honour of France, and upon the uncertain hope of beating the enemy. Now, since the affair of Nordlingen, they had but experienced reverses; the parliament had a plea for calling Mazarin to account for all the victories—always promised and always deferred; but this time there had really been fighting, there had been a triumph and a complete one. And this all knew so well, that it was a double victory for the court—a victory interior and exterior, so that even when the young king learned the news, he exclaimed, "Ah, gentlemen of the parliament, we shall see what you will say now." Upon which the queen had pressed to her heart the royal child, whose haughty and unruly sentiments were in such harmony with her own. A council was called the same evening, but nothing transpired of what was decided. It was only known that on the following Sunday a "Te Deum" would be sung at Nôtre Dame in honour of the victory of Lens.

The following Sunday, then, the Parisians arose with joy; at that period a "Te Deum" was a grand affair; this kind of ceremony had not then been made an abuse of, and it produced a great effect. The shops were deserted, the houses closed; everyone wished to see the young king with his mother, and the famous Cardinal Mazarin, whom they hated so much, that no one wished to be deprived of his presence. Moreover, great liberty prevailed among this immense crowd; every opinion was openly expressed, and rung out, so to speak, insurrection, as the thousand bells of all the Paris churches rang out the "Te Deum." The police belonging to the city being formed by the city itself, nothing threatening presented itself to disturb the concert of universal hatred, or to freeze words between slandering lips.

Nevertheless, at eight o'clock in the morning, the regiment of the queen's guards, commanded by Guitant, under whom was his nephew Comminges, marched, preceded by drums and trumpets, to file off from the Palais Royale as far Nôtre Dame, a manœuvre which the Parisians witnessed tranquilly, delighted as they were with military music and brilliant uniforms.

Friquet had put on his Sunday clothes, under the pretext of having a cold, which he had managed to procure momentarily, by introducing an infinite number of cherry nuts into one side of his mouth, and had procured a whole holiday from Bazin. On leaving Bazin, Friquet started off to the Palais Royal, where. he

arrived at the moment of the turning out of the regiment of
guards, and as he had only gone there for the enjoyment of seeing
it and hearing the music, he took his place at their head, beating
the drum on two pieces of slate, and passing from that exercise
to that of the trumpet, which he counterfeited naturally with his
mouth in a manner which had more than once called forth the
praises of amateurs of imitative harmony.

This amusement lasted from the Barrière des Sergens to the
place of Nôtre Dame; and Friquet found in it true enjoyment;
but when at last the regiment separated, penetrated to the heart
of the city, and placed itself at the extremity of the Rue St.
Christophe, near the Rue Cocatrix, in which Broussel lived, then
Friquet remembered that he had not had breakfast; and after
thinking to which side he had best turn his steps in order to accomplish this important act of the day, he reflected deeply, and
decided that it should be Counsellor Broussel who should bear the
cost of his repast.

In consequence he took a start, arrived breathlessly at the
counsellor's door, and knocked violently.

His mother, the counsellor's old servant, opened it.

"What dost thou here, good-for-nothing?" she said, "and why
art thou not at Nôtre Dame?"

"I have been there, mother," said Friquet, "but I saw things
happen of which Master Broussel ought to be warned, and so
with Monsieur Bazin's permission—you know, mother, Monsieur
Bazin, the verger?—I came to speak to Monsieur Broussel."

"And what hast thou to say, boy, to Monsieur Broussel."

"I wish to tell him," replied Friquet, screaming with all his
might, "that there is a whole regiment of guards coming this way.
And, as I hear everywhere that at the court they are ill-disposed to
him, I wish to warn him, that he may be on his guard."

Broussel heard the scream of the young oddity; and, enchanted
with this excess of zeal, came down to the first floor, for he was,
in truth, working in his room on the second.

"Well!" said he, "friend—what matters the regiment of guards
to us, and art thou not mad to make such a disturbance?
Knowest thou not that it is the custom of these soldiers to act
thus, and that it is usual for the regiment to form themselves
into a hedge where the king passes?"

Friquet counterfeited surprise—and turning his new cap round
his fingers, said:

"It is not astonishing for you to know it, Monsieur Broussel,
who know everything;—but me, by the holy truth, I do not know

it, and I thought I would give you good advice :—you must not be angry with me for that, Monsieur Broussel."

"On the contrary, my boy; on the contrary, I am pleased with your zeal. Dame Nanette, see for those apricots which Madame de Longueville sent to us yesterday from Noisy, and give half-a-dozen of them to your son, with a crust of new bread."

"Oh, thank you, sir, thank you, Monsieur Broussel," said Friquet; "I am so fond of apricots!"

Broussel then proceeded to his wife's room, and asked for breakfast; it was nine o'clock. The counsellor placed himself at the window; the street was completely deserted; but in the distance was heard, like the noise of the tide rushing in, the deep hum of the populous waves which increased around Nôtre Dame.

This noise redoubled, when D'Artagnan, with a company of Musketeers, placed himself at the gates of Nôtre Dame to secure the service of the church. He had told Porthos to profit by this opportunity to see the ceremony; and Porthos, in full dress, mounted his finest horse, doing the part of an honorary Musketeer, as D'Artagnan had so often done formerly. The sergeant of this company, an old veteran of the Spanish wars, had recognised Porthos, his old companion, and very soon all those who served under him had been placed in possession of startling facts concerning the honour of the ancient Musketeers of Treville. Porthos had not only been well received by the company, but he was, moreover, looked upon with great admiration.

At ten o'clock the guns of the Louvre announced the departure of the king, and then a movement, similar to that of trees in a stormy wind bending and agitating their tops, ran through the multitude, which was compressed behind the immovable muskets of the guards. At last the king appeared with the queen in a gilded chariot. Ten other carriages followed, containing the ladies of honour, the officers of the royal household, and all the court.

"God save the king!" was the cry in every direction; the young monarch gravely put his head out of the window, looked sufficiently grateful, and even bowed slightly : at which the cries of the multitude were renewed.

Just as the court was being placed in the cathedral, a carriage, bearing the arms of Comminges, quitted the line of court carriages, and proceeded slowly to the end of the Rue St. Christophe, now entirely deserted. When it arrived there, four guards and a police officer, who accompanied it, mounted into the heavy machine, and closed the shutters; then, with a judicious admittance of the light, the policeman began to watch the length of the Rue Cocatrix, as if he was waiting for some one.

All the world was occupied with the ceremony, so that neither the chariot, nor the precautions taken by those who were within it, had been observed. Friquet, whose eye, always on the alert, could alone have discovered them, had gone to devour his apricots upon the entablature of a house in the square of Nôtre Dame. Thence, he saw the king, the queen, and Monsieur Mazarin, and heard the mass, as well as if he had been on service.

Towards the end of the service, the queen, seeing Comminges standing near her, waiting for a confirmation of the order she had given him before quitting the Louvre, said, in a whisper:

" Go, Comminges, and may God aid you !"

Comminges immediately left the church, and entered the Rue St. Christophe. Friquet, seeing this fine officer thus walk away, followed by two guards, amused himself by pursuing them, and did thus so much the more gladly, since the ceremony ended at that instant, and the king remounted his carriage.

Hardly had the police-officer observed Comminges at the end of the Rue Cocatrix, then he said one word to the coachman, who at once put his vehicle into motion, and drove up before Broussel's door. Comminges knocked at the door at the same moment, and Friquet was waiting behind Comminges until the door should be opened.

" What dost thou there, rascal ?" asked Comminges.

" I want to go into Master Broussel's house, captain," replied Friquet, in that coaxing tone which the " gamins" of Paris know so well how to assume when necessary.

" And on what floor does he live ?" asked Comminges.

" In the whole house," said Friquet; " the house belongs to him ; he occupies the second floor when he works, and descends to the first to take his meals; he must be at dinner now—it is noon."

" Good," said Comminges.

At this moment the door was opened, and having questioned the servant, the officer learnt that Master Broussel was at home, and at dinner.

Broussel was seated at the table with his family, having his wife opposite to him, his two daughters by his side, and his son, Louvières, whom we have already seen when the accident happened to the counsellor—an accident from which he had quite recovered—at the bottom of the table. The worthy man, restored to perfect health, was tasting the fine fruit which Madame de Longueville had sent to him.

At the sight of the officer, Broussel was somewhat moved; but seeing him bow politely, he rose and bowed also. Still, in spite of this reciprocal politeness, the countenances of the women betrayed some uneasiness; Louvières became very pale, and waited impatiently for the officer to explain himself.

"Sir," said Comminges, "I am the bearer of an order from the king."

"Very well, sir," replied Broussel; "what is this order?" And he held out his hand.

"I am commissioned to seize your person, sir," said Comminges, in the same tone, and with the same politeness; "and if you will believe me, you had better spare yourself the trouble of reading that long letter, and follow me."

A thunderbolt falling in the midst of these good people, so peacefully assembled there, would not have produced a more appalling effect. It was a terrible thing at that period to be imprisoned by the enmity of the king. Louvières sprang forward to take his sword, which was on a chair in a corner of the room; but a glance from the worthy Broussel, who in the midst of it all did not lose his presence of mind, checked this action of despair. Madame Broussel, separated by the width of the table from her husband, burst into tears, and the young girls clung to their father's arms.

"Come, sir," said Comminges, "make haste, you must obey the king."

"Sir," said Broussel, "I am in bad health, and cannot give myself up a prisoner in this state; I ask time."

"It is impossible," said Comminges; "the order is strict, and must be put into execution this instant."

"Impossible!" said Louvières; "sir, beware of driving us to despair."

"Impossible!" cried a shrill voice from the bottom of the room.

Comminges turned and saw Dame Nanette, her eyes flashing with anger, and a broom in her hand.

"My good Nanette, be quiet, I beseech you," said Broussel.

"Me! keep quiet while my master is arrested; he, the support —the liberator—the father of the poor people! Ah! well, yes— you have to know me yet. Are you going?" added she to Comminges.

The latter smiled.

"Come, sir," said he, addressing Broussel, "silence that woman, and follow me."

"Silence me!—me! me!" said Nanette. "Ah! yet one wants

some beside you for that, my fine king's-bird. You shall see."
And Dame Nanette sprang to the window, threw it open, and in
such a piercing voice that it might have been heard in the square
of Nôtre Dame:

"Help!" she screamed, "my master is being arrested! the
Counsellor Broussel is arrested—help!"

"Sir," said Comminges, "declare yourself at once; will you
obey, or do you intend to rebel against the king?"

"I obey—I obey, sir," cried Broussel, trying to disengage himself from the grasp of his two daughters, and to restrain, by his
look, his son, always ready to escape from it.

"In that case," said Comminges, "silence that old woman."

"Ah! old woman!" screamed Nanette.

And she began to shriek loudly, clinging to the bars of the
window.

"Help! help! for Master Broussel, who is arrested because he
has defended the people—help!"

Comminges seized the servant round the waist, and would have
dragged her from her post; but at that instant a treble voice, proceeding from a kind of "entresol," was heard screeching:

"Murder! fire! assassins! Master Broussel is being killed—
Master Broussel is being strangled."

It was Friquet's voice; and Dame Nanette, feeling herself supported, recommenced with all her strength to make a chorus.

Many curious faces had already appeared at the windows, and
the people, attracted to the end of the street, began to run—first,
men, then groups, and then a crowd of people; hearing cries, and
seeing a chariot, they could not understand it; but Friquet sprang
from the entresol on to the top of the carriage.

"They want to arrest Master Broussel," he cried; "the guards
are in the carriage, and the officer is upstairs!"

The crowd began to murmur, and approached the houses. The
two guards who had remained in the lane mounted to the aid of
Comminges; those who were in the chariot opened the doors and
presented arms.

"Don't you see them?" cried Friquet, "don't you see?—there
they are!"

The coachman turned round, and gave Friquet a cut with his
whip, which made him scream with pain.

"Ah! devil's coachman!" cried Friquet, "you're meddling too;
—wait!"

And regaining his 'entresol,' he overwhelmed the coachman
with every projectile he could lay hands on.

The tumult now began to increase; the street was not able to contain the spectators, who assembled from every direction; the crowd invaded the space which the dreaded pikes of ·the guards kept clear, between them and the carriage. The soldiers, pushed back by these living walls, were about to be crushed against the nuts of the wheels and the panels of the carriage. The cries which the police-officer repeated twenty times, of "In the king's name," were powerless against the formidable multitude, and seemed on the contrary to exasperate it still more; when, at the cries, "In the name of the king," an officer ran up, and seeing the uniforms much ill-treated, he sprang into the scuffle, sword in hand, and brought unexpected help to the guards. This gentleman was a young man, scarcely sixteen years of age, perfectly pale with anger. He sprang on foot, as the other guards, placed his back against the shaft of the carriage, making a rampart of his horse, drew his pistols from their holsters, and fastened them to his belt, and began to fight with the back sword, like a man accustomed to the handling of his weapon.

During ten minutes he alone kept the crowd at bay; at last Comminges appeared, pushing Broussel before him.

"Let us break the carriage!" cried the people.

"In the king's name!" cried Comminges.

"The first who advances is a dead man!" cried Raoul, for it was in fact he, who, feeling himself pressed and almost crushed by a kind of giant, pricked him with the point of his sword, and sent him groaning back.

Comminges, so to speak, threw Broussel into the carriage, and sprang in after him. At this moment a shot was fired, and a ball passed through the hat of Comminges, and broke the arm of one of the guards. Comminges looked up, and saw among the smoke the threatening face of Louvières, appearing at the window of the second floor.

"Very well, sir," said Comminges, "you shall hear of me again."

"And you of me, too, sir," said Louvières; "and we shall see who can speak the loudest."

Friquet and Nanette continued to shout; the cries, the noise of the shot, and the intoxicating smell of powder, produced their effect.

"Down with the officer! down with him!" was the cry.

"One step nearer," said Comminges, putting down the sashes that the interior of the carriage might be well seen, and placing his sword on his prisoner's breast, "one step nearer, and I kill the prisoner; my orders were to bring him off alive or dead. I will take him dead, that's all."

A terrible cry was heard, and the wife and daughters of Broussel held up their hands in supplication to the people; the latter knew that this officer, who was so pale, but who appeared so determined, would keep his word; they continued to threaten, but they began to disperse.

"Drive to the palace," said Comminges to the coachman, more dead than alive.

The man whipped his animals, which cleared a way through the crowd; but on arriving on the Quai, they were obliged to stop; the carriage was upset, the horses were carried off, stifled, mangled by the crowd. Raoul, on foot, for he had not had time to mount his horse again, tired, like the guards, of distributing blows with the flat of his sword, had recourse to its point. But this last and dreaded resource served only to exasperate the multitude. From time to time a shot from a musket, or the blade of a rapier, flashed among the crowd; the projectiles continued to rain from the windows, and some shots were heard, the echo of which, though they were probably fired in the air, made all hearts vibrate. Voices, which are heard but on days of revolution, were distinguished; faces were seen that only appeared on days of bloodshed. Cries of "Death!—death to the guards!—to the Seine with the officer!" were heard above all the noise, deafening as it was. Raoul, his hat ground to powder, and his face bleeding, felt not only his strength, but also his reason going; a red mist covered his sight, and through this mist he saw a hundred threatening arms stretched over him, ready to seize upon him when he fell. The guards were unable to help any one—for each was occupied with his personal preservation. All was over; carriages, horses, guards, and perhaps even the prisoner, were about to be torn to shreds, when all at once a voice well known to Raoul was heard, and suddenly a large sword glistened in the air; at the same time the crowd opened —upset, trodden down—and an officer of the Musketeers, striking and cutting right and left, rushed up to Raoul, and took him in his arms, just as he was about to fall.

"God's-blood," cried the officer, "have they killed him? Woe to them if it be so."

And he turned round, so stern with anger, strength, and threat, that the most excited rebels hustled back against one another, in order to escape, and some of them even rolled into the Seine.

"Monsieur d'Artagnan!" murmured Raoul.

"Yes, s'death, in person, and fortunately it seems for you, my young friend. Come on — here—you others," he continued, rising in his stirrups and raising his sword, and addressing those

Musketeers who had not been able to follow his rapid pace, " come, sweep away all that for me—shoulder muskets—present arms—aim——"

At this command the mountains of populace thinned so suddenly that D'Artagnan could not repress a burst of Homeric laughter.

" Thank you, D'Artagnan," said Comminges, showing half of his body through the window of the broken vehicle, " thanks, my young friend ; your name?—that I may mention it to the queen."

Raoul was about to reply, when D'Artagnan bent down to his ear.

" Hold your tongue," said he, " and let me answer. Do not lose time, Comminges," he continued ; " get out of the carriage, if you can, and make another draw up ; be quick, or in five minutes all the mob will be back with swords and muskets, you will be killed, and your prisoner freed. Hold—there is a carriage coming down there."

Then, bending again to Raoul, he whispered, " Above all things, don't tell your name."

" That's right. I will go," said Comminges ; " and if they come back, fire !"

" Not at all—not at all," replied D'Artagnan ; " let no one move. On the contrary, one shot at this moment would be paid for dearly to-morrow."

Comminges took his four guards and as many Musketeers, and ran to the carriage, from which he made the people inside dismount, and brought them to the vehicle which had upset. But when it was necessary to convey the prisoner from one carriage to the other, the people, catching sight of him whom they called their liberator, uttered every imaginable cry, and knotted once more against the vehicle.

" Start off !" said D'Artagnan. " There are ten men to accompany you. I will keep twenty to hold in the mob ; go, and lose not a moment. Ten men for Monsieur de Comminges !"

As the carriage started off the cries were redoubled, and more than ten thousand were hurried on the Quai, and encumbered the Pont-Neuf and the adjacent streets. A few shots were fired, and a Musketeer wounded.

" Forward !" cried D'Artagnan, driven to extremities, biting his moustache ; and then he charged with his twenty men, and dispersed them in fear. One man alone remained in his place, gun in hand.

"Ah !" he exclaimed, "it is thou who wouldst have him assassinated?—wait an instant." And he pointed his gun at D'Artagnan, who was riding towards him at full speed. D'Artagnan bent down to his horse's neck, the young man fired, and the ball severed the feather from the hat. The horse, startled, brushed against the imprudent man, who thought by his strength alone to stay the tempest, and he fell against the wall. D'Artagnan pulled up his horse, and while his Musketeers continued to charge, he returned, and bent with drawn sword over the man whom he had knocked down.

"Oh, sir !" exclaimed Raoul, recognising the young man as having seen him in the Rue Cocatrix—"spare him—it is his son !"

D'Artagnan's arm dropped to his side. "Ah, you are his son !" he said—"that is a different thing."

"Sir, I surrender," said Louvières, presenting his unloaded gun to the officer.

"Eh, no; do not surrender, egad ! On the contrary, be off, and quickly. If I take you, you will be hung."

The young man waited not to be told twice; but, passing under the horse's head, disappeared at the corner of the Rue Guénégaud.

"I'faith !" said D'Artagnan to Raoul, "you were just in time to stay my hand. He was a dead man : and, by my faith, if I had discovered that it was his son, I should have regretted having killed him."

"Ah ! sir," said Raoul, "allow me, after thanking you for that poor fellow, to thank you on my own account. I too, sir, was almost dead when you arrived."

"Wait—wait, young man, and do not fatigue yourself with speaking. We can talk of it afterwards."

Then, seeing that the Musketeers had cleared the Quai from the Pont-Neuf to the Quai St. Michael, and that they were returned, he raised his sword for them to double their speed. The Musketeers trotted up, and at the same time the ten men whom D'Artagnan had given to Comminges appeared.

"Holloa !" cried D'Artagnan ; "has something fresh happened ?"

"Eh, sir !" replied the sergeant, "their vehicle has broken down a second time—it is really doomed."

"They are bad managers," said D'Artagnan, shrugging his shoulders. "When a carriage is chosen, it ought to be strong. The carriage in which a Broussel is to be arrested ought to be able to bear ten thousand men."

"What are your commands, my lieutenant?"

"Take the detachment, and conduct him to his place."

"But you will be left alone?"

"Certainly. Do you suppose I have need of an escort? Go."

The Musketeers set off, and D'Artagnan was left alone with Raoul.

"Now," he said, "are you in pain?"

"Yes, my head is heavy and burning."

"What's the matter with this head?" said D'Artagnan, raising the battered hat. "Ah! ah! a bruise."

"Yes, I think I received a flower-pot upon my head."

"Brutes!" said D'Artagnan. "But were you not on horseback? —you have spurs."

"Yes, but I got down to defend Monsieur de Comminges, and my horse was taken away. Here it is, I see."

At this very moment Friquet passed, mounted on Raoul's horse, waving his parti-coloured cap, and crying, "Broussel! Broussel!"

"Holloa! stop, rascal!" cried D'Artagnan. "Bring hither that horse."

Friquet heard perfectly, but he pretended not to do so, and tried to continue his road. D'Artagnan felt inclined for an instant to pursue Master Friquet, but not wishing to leave Raoul alone, he contented himself with taking a pistol from the holster, and cocking it.

Friquet had a quick eye and a fine ear. He saw D'Artagnan's movement; heard the sound of the click, and stopped at once.

"Ah! it is you, your honour," he said, advancing towards D'Artagnan; "and I am truly pleased to meet you."

D'Artagnan looked attentively at Friquet, and recognised the little boy of the Rue de la Calandre.

"Ah, 'tis thou, rascal!" said he, "come here. So thou hast changed thy trade; thou art no longer a choir-boy, or a tavern-boy; thou art then become a horse stealer?"

"Ah, your honour, how can you say so!" exclaimed Friquet. "I was seeking the gentleman to whom this horse belongs—an officer, brave and handsome as a Cæsar"—then, pretending to see Raoul for the first time,—

"Ah! but if I mistake not," continued he, "here he is; you won't forget the boy, sir?"

Raoul put his hand in his pocket.

"What are you about?" asked D'Artagnan.

"To give ten francs to this honest fellow," replied Raoul, taking a pistole from his pocket.

"Ten kicks on his back !" said D'Artagnan; "be off, you little rascal, and forget not that I have your address."

Friquet, who did not expect to be let off so cheaply, made but one bound to the Quai à la Rue Dauphine, and disappeared. Raoul mounted his horse, and both leisurely took their way to the Rue Tiquetonne.

D'Artagnan protected the youth as if he were his own son.

They arrived without accident at the Hôtel de la Chevrette.

The handsome Madeleine announced to D'Artagnan that Planchet had returned, bringing Mousqueton with him, who had heroically borne the extraction of the ball, and was as well as his state would permit.

D'Artagnan desired Planchet to he summoned, but he had disappeared.

"Then bring some wine," said D'Artagnan. "You are much pleased with yourself?" said he to Raoul, when they were alone, "are you not?"

"Well, yes," replied Raoul; "it seems to me that I did my duty. I defended the king."

"And who told you to defend the king?"

"The Count de la Fère himself !"

"Yes, the king; but to-day you have not fought for the king, you have fought for Mazarin; it is not the same thing."

"But you yourself?"

"Oh, for me; it is another matter. I obey my captain's orders. As for you, your captain is the prince. Understand that rightly; you have no other. But has one ever seen such a wild fellow," continued he, "making himself a Mazarinist, and helping to arrest Broussel ! Breathe not a word of that, or the Count de la Fère will be furious."

"You think that the count will be angry with me?"

"Do I think it?—I am sure of it; were it not for that, I should thank you, for you have worked for us. However, I scold you instead of him, and in his place; the storm will blow over more easily, believe me. And, moreover, my dear child," continued D'Artagnan, "I am making use of the privilege conceded to me by your guardian."

"I do not understand you, sir," said Raoul.

D'Artagnan rose, and taking a letter from his writing-desk, presented it to Raoul. The face of the latter became serious when he had cast his eyes on the paper.

"Oh, 'mon Dieu !'" he said, raising his fine eyes to D'Artagnan, moist with tears, "the count has then left Paris without seeing me ?"

" He left four days ago," said D'Artagnan.

" But his letter seems to intimate that he is about to incur danger, perhaps of death."

" He—he—incur danger of death !—no—be not anxious ; he is travelling on business, and will return ere long.   I hope you have no repugnance to accept me as a guardian in the interim ?"

" Oh, no, Monsieur D'Artagnan," said Raoul, "you are such a brave gentleman, and the Count de la Fère has so much affection for you !"

" Eh, egad ! love me too ; I will not torment you much, but only on condition that you become a Frondist, my young friend, and a hearty Frondist, too."

" Well, sir, I will obey you, although I do not understand you."

" It is unnecessary for you to understand ; hold," continued D'Artagnan, turning towards the door, which had just opened, " here is Monsieur de Valon, who comes with his coat torn."

" Yes, but in exchange," said Porthos, covered with perspiration, and soiled in dust—" in exchange, I have torn many skins. Those wretches wanted to take away my sword !   Deuce take 'em, what a popular commotion !" continued the giant, in his quiet manner ; "but I knocked down more than twenty with the hilt of Balizarde ;—a drop of wine, D'Artagnan."

" Oh, I'll answer for you," said the Gascon, filling Porthos' glass to the brim, "but, when you have drunk, give me your opinion."

" Upon what ?" asked Porthos.

" Look here," resumed D'Artagnan ; "here is Monsieur de Bragelonne, who determined, at all risks, to aid the arrest of Broussel, and whom I had great difficulty to prevent defending Monsieur de Comminges."

" The devil !" said Porthos ; "and the guardian, what would he have said to that ?"

" Do you hear ?" interrupted D'Artagnan ; "be a Frondist, my friend, belong to the Fronde, and remember that I fill the count's place in everything ;" and he jingled his money.

" Will you come ?" said he to Porthos.

" Where to ?" asked Porthos, filling a second glass of wine.

" To present our respects to the Cardinal."

Porthos swallowed the second glass with the same ease with which he had drunk the first, took his beaver, and followed D'Artagnan.   As for Raoul, he remained bewildered with what he had seen, having been forbidden by D'Artagnan to leave the room until the tumult was over.

CHAPTER XLIII.

THE BEGGAR OF ST. EUSTACHE.

D'ARTAGNAN had calculated that in not going at once to the Palais Royale he would give time to Comminges to arrive there before him, and consequently to make the Cardinal acquainted with the eminent services which he, D'Artagnan and his friend, had rendered to the queen's party in the morning.

They were indeed admirably received by Mazarin, who paid them numerous compliments, and announced that they were more than half on their way to obtain what they desired, namely, D'Artagnan his captaincy, and Porthos his barony.

Whilst the two friends were with the Cardinal, the queen sent for him. Mazarin, thinking that it would be the means of increasing the zeal of his two defenders if he procured them personal thanks from the queen, motioned to them to follow him. D'Artagnan and Porthos pointed to their dusty and torn dresses, but the Cardinal shook his head.

"Those costumes," he said, "are of more worth than most of those which you will see on the queen's courtiers; they are the costumes of battle."

D'Artagnan and Porthos obeyed. The court of Anne of Austria was full of gaiety and animation; for, after having gained a victory over the Spaniard, it had just gained another over the people. Broussel had been conducted out of Paris without resistance, and was at this time in the prison of St. Germain; and Blancmesnil, who was arrested at the same time, but whose arrest had been made without difficulty or noise, was safe in the Castle of Vincennes.

Comminges was near the queen, who was questioning him upon the details of his expedition, and everyone was listening to his account when D'Artagnan and Porthos were perceived at the door behind the Cardinal.

"Hey, madame," said Comminges, hastening to D'Artagnan, "here is one who can tell you better than myself, for he is my protector. Without him I should probably, at this moment, be caught in the nets at St. Cloud, for it was a question of nothing less than throwing me into the river. Speak, D'Artagnan, speak."

D'Artagnan had been a hundred times in the same room with the queen since he had become lieutenant of the Musketeers, but her majesty had never once spoken to him.

" Well, sir," at last said Anne of Austria, "you are silent, after rendering such a service ?"

" Madame," replied D'Artagnan, "I have nought to say, save that my life is ever at your majesty's service; and that I shall only be happy the day that I lose it for you."

" I know that, sir; I have known that," said the queen, "a long time; therefore I am delighted to be able thus publicly to mark my gratitude and my esteem."

" Permit me, madame," said D'Artagnan, "to reserve a portion for my friend; like myself "—(he laid an emphasis on these words) —"an ancient Musketeer of the company of Tréville, and he has done wonders."

" His name ?" asked the queen.

" In the regiment," said D'Artagnan, "he is called Porthos " (the queen started), "but his true name is the Chevalier de Valon."

" De Bracieux de Pierrefonds," added Porthos.

" These names are too numerous for me to remember them all, and I will content myself with the first," said the queen, graciously. Porthos bowed. At this moment the Coadjutor was announced; a cry of surprise ran through the royal assemblage. Although the Coadjutor had preached that same morning, it was well known that he leant much to the side of the Fronde; and Mazarin, in requesting the Archbishop of Paris to make his nephew preach, had evidently had the intention of administering to Monsieur de Retz one of those Italian kicks which he so much enjoyed giving.

The fact was, in leaving Nôtre Dame the Coadjutor had learnt the event of the day. Although almost engaged to the leaders of the Fronde, he had not gone so far but that retreat was possible, should the court offer him the advantages for which he was ambitious, and to which the Coadjutorship was but a stepping stone. Monsieur de Retz wished to be archbishop in his uncle's place, and cardinal, like Mazarin; and the popular party could with difficulty accord to him favours so entirely royal. He, therefore, hastened to the palace to congratulate the queen on the battle of Lens, determined beforehand to act with or against the court, according as his congratulations were well or ill received.

The Coadjutor had, perhaps, in his own person, as much wit as all those together who were assembled at the court to laugh at him. His speech, therefore, was so well turned, that in spite of the great wish felt by the courtiers to laugh, they could find no point upon which to vent their ridicule. He concluded by saying that he placed his feeble influence at her majesty's command.

During the whole time that he was speaking the queen appeared to be well pleased with the Coadjutor's harangue; but terminating as it did with such a phrase, the only one which could be caught at by the jokers, Anne turned round and directed a glance towards her favourites, which announced that she delivered up the Coadjutor to their tender mercies. Immediately the wits of the court plunged into satire. Nogent-Beautin, the fool of the court, exclaimed that "the queen was very happy to have the succour of religion at such a moment." This caused a universal burst of laughter. The Count de Villeroy said "that he did not know how any fear could be entertained for a moment when the court had, to defend itself against the parliament and the citizens of Paris, his holiness the Coadjutor, who by a signal could raise an army of curates, church porters and vergers;" and so on.

During this storm, Gondy, who had it in his power to make it fatal to the jesters, remained calm and stern. The queen at last asked him if he had anything to add to the fine discourse which he had just made to her.

"Yes, madame," replied the Coadjutor; "I have to beg you to reflect twice ere you cause a civil war in the kingdom."

The queen turned her back, and the laughs recommenced.

The Coadjutor bowed and left the palace, casting upon the Cardinal such a glance as is understood best between mortal foes.

"Oh!" muttered Gondy, as he left the threshold of the palace —"ungrateful court! faithless court! cowardly court! I will teach you how to laugh to-morrow—but in another manner."

But whilst they were indulging in extravagant joy at the Palais Royale, to increase the hilarity of the queen, Mazarin, a man of sense, and whose fear, moreover, gave him foresight, lost no time in making idle and dangerous jokes; he went out after the Coadjutor, settled his account, locked up his gold, and had confidential workmen to contrive hiding-places in his walls.

On his return home the Coadjutor was informed that a young man had come in after his departure, and was waiting for him; he started with delight when, on demanding the name of this young man, he learnt that it was Louvières.

He immediately went to his room, and advancing towards him, held out his hand. The young man gazed at him as if he would have read the secret of his heart.

"My dear Monsieur Louvières," said the Coadjutor, "believe how truly concerned I am for the misfortune which has happened to you."

"Is that true, and do you speak seriously?" asked Louvières.

"From the depth of my heart," said Gondy.

" In that case, my lord, the time for words has passed, and the hour for action is come. My lord, in three days, if you wish it, my father will be out of prison, and in six months you may be Cardinal."

The Coadjutor started.

" Oh! let us speak frankly," continued Louvières, "and act in a straightforward manner. Thirty thousand crowns in alms is not given—as you have done for the last six months—out of pure Christian charity; that would be too grand. You are ambitious, it is natural; you are a man of genius, and you know your worth. As for me, I hate the court, and have but one desire at this moment—it is for vengeance. Give us the clergy and the people, of whom you can dispose, and I will bring you the citizens and the parliament : with these four elements Paris is ours in a week ; and believe me, Monsieur Coadjutor, the court will give from fear what she will not give from good will."

It was now the Coadjutor's turn to fix his piercing glance on Louvières.

" But, Monsieur Louvières, are you aware that it is simply civil war that you propose to me ?"

" You have been preparing it long enough, my lord, for it to be welcome to you now."

" Never mind," said the Coadjutor ; " you must know that this requires reflection."

" And how many hours of reflection do you ask ?"

" Twelve hours, sir ; is it too long ?"

" It is now noon : at midnight I will be at your house."

" If I am not come in, wait for me."

" Good ! at midnight, my lord."

" At midnight, my dear Monsieur Louvières."

When once more alone, Gondy sent to summon all the curates with whom he had any connection, to his house. Two hours later, thirty officiating ministers from the most populous, and consequently the most disturbed, parishes of Paris, had assembled together there. Gondy related to them the insults he had received at the Palais Royal, and retailed the jests of Beautin, Count de Villeroy, and the Maréchal de la Meilleraie. The curates demanded what was to be done.

" Simply this," said the Coadjutor ; "you are the directors of consciences. Well, undermine in them the miserable prejudice of respect and fear of kings—teach to your flocks that the queen is a tyrant ; and repeat, often and loudly, so that all may know it, that the misfortunes of France are caused by Mazarin, her lover and her destroyer; begin this work to-day, this instant even, and in three days I shall expect the result. For the rest, if any one of you have good counsel to give me, I shall listen to him with pleasure."

Three curates remained : those of St. Merri, St. Sulpice, and St. Eustache.

"You think, then, that you can help me more efficaciously than your brothers ?" said Gondy.

"We hope so," answered the curates.

"Let us hear. Monsieur de St. Merri, you begin."

"My lord, I have in my parish a man who might be of the greatest use to you."

"What is this man ?"

"A shopkeeper in the Rue des Lombards, who has great influence upon the little commerce of his quarter."

"What is his name ?"

"He is named Planchet, who himself also caused an *émeute* about six weeks ago; but as he was searched for after this *émeute*, he disappeared."

"And could you find him ?"

"I hope so. I think he has not been arrested, and as I am his wife's confessor, if she knows where he is, I shall know it too."

"Very well, sir; find this man, and when you have found him, bring him to me."

"We will be with you at six o'clock, my lord."

"Go, my dear curate, and may God aid you !"

"And you, sir," continued Gondy, turning to the curate of St. Sulpice——"

"I, my lord," said the latter, "I know a man who has rendered great services to a very popular prince, and who would make an excellent leader of a revolt, and whom I can put at your disposal; it is Count de Rochefort."

"I know him also, but unfortunately he is not in Paris."

"My lord, he has been for three days at the Rue Cassette."

"And wherefore has he not been to see me ?"

"He was told—my lord will pardon me——?"

"Certainly; speak."

"That your lordship was about to treat with the court."

Gondy bit his lips.

"They are mistaken; bring him here at eight o'clock, sir, and may Heaven bless you as I bless you !"

"And now 'tis your turn," said the Coadjutor, turning to the last that remained, "have you anything so good to offer me as the two gentlemen who have left us ?"

" Better, my lord."

" *Diable !* think what a solemn engagement you are making there; one has offered a shopkeeper, the other a count; you are going, then, to offer a prince, are you ?"

" I offer you a beggar, my lord."

" Ah ! ah !" said Gondy, reflecting, " you are right, sir; some one who could raise the legion of paupers who choke up the crossings of Paris, some one who would know how to cry aloud to them, that all France might hear it, that it is Mazarin who has reduced them to the wallet——"

" Exactly your man."

" Bravo ! and what is the man ?"

" A simple beggar, as I have said, my lord, who asks for alms, as he gives holy water, a practice he has carried on for about six years on the steps of the Church of St. Eustache."

" And you say that he has a great influence over his compeers ?"

" Are you aware, my lord, that mendicity is an organised body, a kind of association of those who have not, against those who have—an association in which every one takes his share, and which elects a leader."

" Yes, I have heard that said," replied the Coadjutor.

" Well, the man whom I offer to you is a universal authority."

" And what do you know of this man ?"

" Nothing, my lord, except that he is tormented with remorse."

" What makes you think so ?"

" On the twenty-eighth of every month, he makes me say a mass for the repose of the soul of a person who died a violent death ; yesterday I said this mass again."

" And his name ?"

" Maillard ; but I do not think it is his true name."

" And think you that we should find him at this hour at his post ?"

" Certainly."

" Let us go and see your beggar, sir, and if he is such as you describe him, you are right—it will be you who have found the true treasure."

Gondy dressed himself as an officer, put on a felt cap with a red feather, hung on a long sword, buckled spurs to his boots, wrapped himself in an ample cloak, and followed the curate.

On arriving at the Rue des Prouvaires, the curate pointed towards the square before the church.

" Stop !" he said, " there he is at his post."

Gondy looked at the spot indicated, and perceived a beggar

seated in a chair, and leaning against one of the mouldings; a little basin was near him, and he held a holy-water brush in his hand.

"Is it by permission that he remains there?" asked Gondy.

"No, my lord; these places are bought; I think that this man paid his predecessor a hundred pistoles for his."

"The rascal is rich, then?".

"Some of these men sometimes die worth twenty thousand, and twenty-five, and thirty thousand francs, and sometimes more."

"Hum!" said Gondy, laughing; "I was not aware that my alms were so well invested."

In the meantime they were advancing towards the square, and the moment the Coadjutor and the curate put their feet on the first church step, the mendicant rose and proffered his brush.

He was a man between sixty-six and sixty-eight years of age, little, rather stout, with grey hair, and light eyes. His countenance denoted the struggle between two opposite principles—a wicked nature subdued by determination, perhaps by repentance.

He started on seeing the cavalier with the curate. The latter and the Coadjutor touched the brush with the tips of their fingers, made the sign of the cross; the Coadjutor threw a piece of money into the hat, wi. ` was on the ground.

"Maillard," began the curate, ' this gentleman and I have come to talk with you a little."

"With me!" said the mendicant; "it is a great honour for a poor giver of holy water."

There was an ironical tone in his voice, which he could not quite prevent, and which astonished the Coadjutor.

"Yes," continued the curate, apparently accustomed to his tone, "yes, we wish to know your opinion of the events of to-day, and what you have heard said by people going in and out of the church."

The mendicant shook his head.

"These are melancholy doings, your reverence, which always fall again upon the poor people. As to what is said, everybody is discontented—everybody complains—but——"

"Explain yourself, my good friend," said the Coadjutor.

"I mean that all these cries, all these complaints, these curses, produce nothing but storms and flashes, and that is all; but the lightning will not strike until there is a hand to guide it."

"My friend," said Gondy, "you seem to be a clever man; are you disposed to take a part in a little civil war, should we have one, and put at the command of the leader—should we find one

—your personal influence, and the influence you have acquired over your comrades."

"Yes, sir, provided this war was approved by the church, and would advance the end I wish to attain—I mean the remission of my sins."

"This war will not only be approved of, but directed by the church. As for the remission of your sins, we have the Archbishop of Paris, who has great power at the court of Rome, and even the Coadjutor, who possesses some particular indulgences—we will recommend you to him. And do you think your power as great with your fraternity as Monsieur le Curé told me it was just now?"

"I think they have some esteem for me," said the mendicant, with pride, "and not only they will obey me, but that, wherever I go, they will follow me."

"And could you count upon fifty resolute men, good, unemployed, but active souls, brawlers capable of bringing down the walls of the Palais Royal by crying 'Down with Mazarin,' as fell all those at Jericho?"

"I think," said the beggar, "that I can undertake things more difficult, and more important than that."

"Ah, ah," said Gondy, "you will undertake, then, some night, to throw up some ten barricades."

"I will undertake to throw up fifty, and when the day comes to defend them."

"I'faith!" exclaimed Gondy, "you speak with a certainty that gives me pleasure; and since Monsieur le Curé can answer for you——"

"I answer for him," said the curate.

"Here is a bag containing five hundred pistoles in gold—make all your arrangements, and tell me where I shall be able to find you this evening at ten o'clock."

"It must be on some elevated place, whence a given signal may be seen in every quarter of Paris."

"Shall I give you a line for the Vicar of St. Jaques-de-la Boucherie? he will let you into the rooms in his tower," said the curate.

"Capital," answered the mendicant.

"Then," said the Coadjutor, "this evening, at ten o'clock; and if I am pleased with you, another bag of five hundred pistoles will be at your disposal."

The eyes of the mendicant flashed with cupidity, but he suppressed this emotion.

"This evening, sir," he replied, "all will be ready."

CHAPTER XLIV.

THE TOWER OF ST. JAQUES-DE-LA-BOUCHERIE.

AT a quarter to six o'clock, Monsieur de Gondy, having finished all his business, returned to the archiepiscopal palace.

At six o'clock the Curate of St. Merri was announced.

The Coadjutor glanced rapidly behind, and saw that he was followed by another man. The curate then entered, followed by Planchet.

"Your holiness," said the curate, "here is the person of whom I had the honour to speak to you."

"And you are disposed to serve the cause of the people ?" asked Gondy.

"Most undoubtedly," said Planchet. "I am a Frondist from my heart. You see in me, such as I am, my lord, a person sentenced to be hung."

"And on what account ?"

"I rescued from the hands of Mazarin's police a noble lord, whom they were conducting again to the Bastille, where he had been for five years."

"Will you name him ?"

"Oh, you know him well, my lord :—it is Count de Rochefort."

"Ah ! really, yes," said the Coadjutor, "I have heard this affair mentioned. You raised the whole district, they told me ?"

"Very nearly," replied Planchet, with a self-satisfied air.

"And your business is——"

"That of a confectioner, in the Rue des Lombards."

"Explain to me how it happens that, following so peaceful a business, you had such warlike inclinations."

"Why does my lord, belonging to the church, now receive me in the dress of an officer with a sword at his side, and spurs to his boots ?"

"Not badly answered, i'faith," said Gondy, laughing; "but I have, you must know, always had, in spite of my bands, warlike inclinations."

"Well, my lord, before I became a confectioner, I myself was three years sergeant in the Piedmontese regiment, and before I became sergeant I was for eighteen months the servant of Monsieur D'Artagnan."

"The lieutenant of the Musketeers ?" asked Gondy.

"Himself, my lord."

" But he is said to be a furious Mazarinist."

" Hew !" said Planchet.

" What do you mean by that ?"

" Nothing, my lord; Monsieur D'Artagnan belongs to the service; Monsieur D'Artagnan makes it his business to defend the Cardinal, who pays him, as much as we make it ours—we citizens —to attack him, whom he robs."

" You are an intelligent fellow, my friend; can we count upon you ?"

" You may count upon me, my lord, provided you want to make a total overturning in the city."

" 'Tis that exactly. How many men, think you, you could collect together to-night ?"

" Two hundred muskets, and five hundred halberds."

" Let there be only one man in every district who can do as much, and by to-morrow we shall have a tolerably strong army. Are you disposed to obey Count de Rochefort ?"

" I would follow him to hell; and that is not saying a little, as I believe him quite capable of descending there."

" Bravo !"

" By what sign to-morrow shall we be able to distinguish friends from foes ?"

" Every Frondist must put a knot of straw in his hat."

" Good ! Give the watchword."

" Do you want money ?"

" Money never comes amiss at any time, my lord; if one has it not, one must do without it; with it matters go on much better, and more rapidly."

Gondy went to a box and drew forth a bag.

" Here are five hundred pistoles," he said; " and if the action goes off well you may reckon upon a similar sum to-morrow."

" I will give a faithful account of the sum to your lordship," said Planchet, putting the bag under his arm.

" That is right: I recommend the Cardinal to your attention."

" Make your mind easy, he is in good hands."

Planchet went out, and ten minutes later the curate of St. Sulpice was announced. As soon as the door of Gondy's study was opened, a man rushed in; it was Count de Rochefort.

" It is you, then, my dear count," cried Gondy, offering his hand.

" You are decided at last, my lord ?" said Rochefort.

" I have ever been so," said Gondy.

"Let us speak no more on that subject : you tell me so—I believe you. Well, we are going to give a ball to Mazarin."

"I hope so."

"And when will the dance begin ?"

"The invitations are given for this evening," said the Coadjutor, "but the violins will only begin to play to-morrow morning."

"You may reckon upon me, and upon fifty soldiers which the Chevalier d'Humières has promised to me, whenever I might need them."

"Upon fifty soldiers ?"

"Yes, he is making recruits, and he will lend them to me; if any are missing, when the fête is over, I shall replace them."

"Good, my dear Rochefort; but that is not all. What have you done with Monsieur de Beaufort ?"

"He is in Vendôme, where he waits until I write to him to return to Paris."

"Write to him—now's the time."

"You are sure of your enterprise ?"

"Yes, but he must hurry himself ;—for hardly shall the people of Paris have revolted, than we shall have ten princes to one, wishing to be at their head : if he defers, he will find the place taken."

"And you will leave all command to him ?"

"For the war, yes ; but in politics——"

"You know it is not his element."

"He must leave me to negotiate for my cardinal's hat in my own fashion."

"You care about it so much ?"

"Since they force me to wear a hat of a form which does not become me," said Gondy, "I wish at least that the hat should be red."

"One must not dispute taste and colours," said Rochefort, laughing. "I answer for his consent."

"How soon can he be here ?"

"In five days."

"Let him come, and he will find a change, I will answer for it. Therefore, go and collect your fifty men, and hold yourself in readiness."

"For what ?"

"For everything."

"Is there any signal for rallying ?"

"A knot of straw in the hat."

"Very good. Adieu, my lord."

"Adieu, my dear Rochefort."

"Ah! Monsieur Mazarin, Monsieur Mazarin," said Rochefort, leading off his curate, who had not found an opportunity of uttering a single word during the foregoing dialogue, "you will see whether I am too old to be a man of action."

It was half-past nine o'clock, and the Coadjutor required half an hour to go from the Archbishop's palace to the tower of St. Jaques-de-la-Boucherie. He remarked that a light burnt in one of the highest windows of the tower. "Good," said he, "our syndic is at his post."

He knocked, and the door was opened. The vicar himself awaited him, conducted him to the top of the tower, and when there pointed to a little door, placed the light which he had brought with him in a corner of the wall, that the Coadjutor might be able to find it on his return, and went down again. Although the key was in the door, the Coadjutor knocked.

"Come in," said a voice which he recognised as that of the mendicant, whom he found lying on a kind of truckle bed. He rose on the entrance of the Coadjutor, and at that moment ten o'clock struck.

"Well," said Gondy, "have you kept your word with me?"

"Not quite," replied the mendicant.

"How is that?"

"You asked me for five hundred men, did you not? Well, I shall have ten thousand for you."

"You are not boasting?"

"Do you wish for a proof?"

"Yes."

There were three candles alight—each of which burnt before a window—one looking upon the City, the other upon the Palais Royal, and a third upon the Rue St. Denis.

The man went silently to each of the candles, and blew them out one after the other.

"What are you doing?" asked the Coadjutor.

"I have given the signal."

"For what?"

"For the barricades. When you leave this, you will see my men at their work. Only take care not to break your legs in stumbling over some chain, nor to fall into some hole."

"Good! there is your money,—the same sum as that which you have received already. Now remember that you are a general, and do not go and drink."

"For twenty years I have tasted nothing but water."

The man took the bag from the hands of the Coadjutor, who heard the sound of his fingers counting and handling the gold pieces.

"Ah! ah!" said the Coadjutor, "you are avaricious, my good fellow."

The mendicant sighed, and threw down the bag.

"Must I always be the same," said he, "and shall I never succeed in overcoming the old leaven? Oh misery, oh vanity!"

"You take it, however."

"Yes, but I make a vow in your presence, to employ all that remains to me in pious works."

His face was pale and drawn, like that of a man who had just undergone an inward struggle.

"Singular man!" muttered Gondy, taking his hat to go away, when he saw the beggar between him and the door. His first idea was that this man intended to do him some harm—but on the contrary he soon fell on his knees before him, with his hands clasped.

"Your blessing, your holiness, before you go, I beseech you!" he cried.

"Your holiness!" said Gondy; "my friend, you take me for some one else."

"No, your holiness, I take you for what you are; that is to say, the Coadjutor—I recognised you at the first glance."

Gondy smiled—"And you want my blessing?" he said.

"Yes, I have need of it."

The mendicant uttered these words in a tone of such great humility, and such earnest repentance, that Gondy placed his hand upon him, and gave him his benediction with all the unction of which he was capable.

"Now," said the Coadjutor, "there is a communion between us. I have blessed you, and you are sacred to me. Come, have you committed some crime, pursued by human justice, from which I can protect you?"

The beggar shook his head.—"The crime which I have committed, my lord, has no call upon human justice, and you can only deliver me from it in blessing me frequently, as you have just done."

"Come, be candid," said the Coadjutor, "you have not all your life followed the trade which you do now?"

"No, my lord. I have pursued it for six years only."

"And, previously, where were you?"

"In the Bastille."

"And before you went to the Bastille?"

" I will tell you, my lord, on the day when you are willing to hear my confession."

" Good ! at whatever hour of the day, or of the night on which you present yourself, remember that I shall be ready to give you absolution."

" Thank you, my lord," said the mendicant in a hoarse voice. " But I am not yet ready to receive it."

" Very well.　Adieu."

" Adieu, your holiness," said the mendicant, opening the door, and bending low before the prelate.

CHAPTER XLV.

THE RIOT.

IT was about eleven o'clock at night.　Gondy had not walked a hundred steps ere he perceived the strange change which had been made in the streets of Paris.

The whole city seemed peopled with fantastic beings ; silent shadows were seen unpaving the streets, and others dragging and upsetting great waggons, whilst others again dug ditches large enough to engulph whole regiments of horsemen.　These active beings flitted here and there like so many demons completing some unknown labour—these were the beggars of the Court of Miracles—the agents of the giver of holy water in the square of St. Eustache—preparing the barricades for the morrow.

Gondy gazed on these men of darkness—these nocturnal labourers, with a kind of fear : he asked himself if, after having called forth these foul creatures from their dens, he should have the power of making them retire again.　He felt almost inclined to cross himself when one of these beings happened to approach him.　He reached the Rue St. Honore, and went up it towards the Rue de la Ferronière : there, the aspect changed ; here it was the tradesmen who were running from shop to shop : their doors seemed closed like their shutters ; but they were only pushed-to in such a manner as to open and allow the men, who seemed fearful of showing what they carried, to enter, closing immediately. These men were shopkeepers, who had arms to lend to those who had none.

One individual went from door to door, bending under the weight of swords, guns, muskets, and every kind of weapon, which he deposited as fast as he could. By the light of a lantern the Coadjutor recognised Planchet.

On reaching the Pont-Neuf, the Coadjutor found this bridge guarded, and a man approached him.

"Who are you?" asked the man; "I do not know you for one of us."

"Then it is because you do not know your friends, my dear Monsieur Louvières," said the Coadjutor, raising his hat.

Louvières recognised him and bowed.

Gondy continued his way, and went as far as the Tour de Nesle. There he saw a long line of people gliding under the walls. They might be said to be a procession of ghosts, for they were all wrapped in white cloaks. When they reached a certain spot, these men seemed to be annihilated one after the other, as if the earth had opened under their feet. Gondy edged into a corner, saw them vanish from the first until the last but one. The last raised his eyes, to ascertain doubtless that neither his companions nor himself had been watched, and in spite of the darkness he perceived Gondy. He walked straight up to him, and placed a pistol to his throat.

"Holloa, Monsieur de Rochefort," said Gondy, laughing, "do not let us play with fire-arms."

Rochefort recognised the voice.

"Ah, it is you, my lord," said he.

"Myself. What people are you leading thus into the bowels of the earth?"

"My fifty recruits from the Chevalier d'Humières, who are destined to enter the light cavalry, and who have only received for their equipment their white cloaks."

"And where are you going?"

"To one of my friends, a sculptor, only we descend by the trap through which he lets down his marble."

"Very good," said Gondy, shaking Rochefort by the hand, who descended in his turn, and closed the trap after him.

It was now one o'clock in the morning, and the Coadjutor returned home. He opened a window and leant out to listen. A strange, incomprehensible, unearthly sound seemed to pervade the whole city; one felt that something unusual and terrible was happening in all the streets, now dark as abysses.

The work of revolt continued the whole night thus. The next morning, on awaking, Paris seemed to be startled at her own appearance. It was like a besieged town. Armed men, shouldering muskets, watched over the barricades with menacing looks; words of command, patrols, arrests, executions, even, were encountered at every step. Those bearing plumed hats and gold swords were stopped and made to cry, "Long live Broussel!" "Down with Mazarin!" and whoever refused to comply with this ceremony was hooted at, spat upon, and even beaten. They had not yet begun to slay, but it was well felt that the inclination to do so was not wanting.

The barricades had been pushed as far as the Palais Royal, and the astonishment of Mazarin and of Anne of Austria was great when it was announced to them that the city, which the previous evening they had left tranquil, had awakened so feverish and in such commotion ; nor would either the one or the other believe the reports which were brought to them, and declared that they would rather rely on the evidence of their own eyes and ears. Then a window was opened, and when they saw and heard, they were convinced.

Mazarin shrugged his shoulders, and pretended to despise the populace much ; but he turned visibly pale, and ran to his closet trembling all over, locked up his gold and jewels in his caskets, and put his finest diamonds on his fingers. As for the queen, furious, and left to her own guidance, she sent for the Maréchal de la Meilleraie, and desired him to take as many men as he pleased, and to go and see what was the meaning of this pleasantry.

We have already said that Mazarin was in his closet, putting his little affairs into order. He called for D'Artagnan, but in the midst of such tumult he little expected to see him, D'Artagnan not being on service. In about ten minutes D'Artagnan appeared at the door, followed by his inseparable, Porthos.

"Ah, come—come in, Monsieur d'Artagnan," cried the Cardinal, "and be welcome, as well as your friend. But what is going on, then, in this cursed Paris?"

"What is going on, my lord? nothing good," replied D'Artagnan, shaking his head : "the town is in open revolt ; and just now, as I was crossing the Rue Montorgueil with Monsieur de Valon, who is here, and is your humble servant, they wanted, in spite of my uniform, or, perhaps, because of my uniform, to make us cry, 'Long live Broussel!' and must I tell you, my lord, what they wished us to cry as well?"

"Speak, speak."

"'Down with Mazarin!' I'faith, the big word is out now."

Mazarin smiled, but became very pale.

"And you did cry?" he asked.

"I'faith, no," said D'Artagnan, "I was not in voice ; Monsieur de Valon has a cold, and did not cry either. Then. my lord——"

"Then what?" asked Mazarin.

"Look at my hat and cloak."

And D'Artagnan displayed four gun-shot holes in his cloak and two in his beaver. As for Porthos' coat, a blow from a halberd had cut it open on the flank, and a pistol-shot had cut his feather in two.

"Diavolo!" said the Cardinal, pensively, gazing at the two friends with lively admiration; "I should have cried, I should."

At this moment the tumult was heard nearer.

Mazarin wiped his forehead and looked around him. He had a great desire to go to the window, but he dared not.

"See what is going on, Monsieur d'Artagnan," said he.

D'Artagnan went to the window, with his habitual composure.

"Oh, oh!" said he, "what is that? Maréchal de la Meilleraie returning without a hat—Fontrailles with his arm in a sling—— —wounded guards—horses bleeding—eh, then, what are the sentinels about? they are aiming—they are going to fire!"

"They have received orders to fire on the people, if the people approach the Palais Royal!" exclaimed Mazarin.

"But if they fire, all is lost!" cried D'Artagnan.

"We have the gates."

"The gates! to hold for five minutes—the gates, they will be torn down, bent, ground to powder! God's death, don't fire!" screamed D'Artagnan, throwing open the window.

In spite of this recommendation, which, owing to the noise, could not have been heard, two or three musket-shots resounded, which was succeeded by a terrible discharge. The balls might be heard peppering the façade of the Palais Royal, and one of them, passing under D'Artagnan's arm, entered and broke a mirror, in which Porthos was complacently admiring himself.

"Alack, alack," cried the Cardinal; "a Venetian glass!"

"Oh, my lord," said D'Artagnan, quietly shutting the window, "it is not worth while weeping yet, for probably an hour hence there will not be one of your mirrors remaining in the Palais Royal, whether they be Venetian or Parisian."

"But what do you advise, then?" asked Mazarin, trembling.

"Eh, egad, to give up Broussel, as they demand! What the devil do you want with a member of the parliament? He is of no use for anything."

"And you, Monsieur de Valon, is that your advice? What would you do?"

"I should give up Broussel."

"Come, come with me, gentlemen!" exclaimed Mazarin. "I

will go and discuss the matter with the queen."

He stopped at the end of the corridor, and said :

"I can count upon you, gentlemen, can I not ?"

"We do not give ourselves twice over," said D'Artagnan ; "we have given ourselves to you—command, we shall obey."

"Very well, then," said Mazarin ; "enter this closet and wait there."

And turning off, he entered the drawing-room by another door.

CHAPTER XLVI.

THE RIOT BECOMES A REVOLUTION.

THE closet into which D'Artagnan and Porthos had been ushered was separated from the drawing-room where the queen was by tapestried curtains only, and this thin partition enabled them to hear all that passed in the adjoining room, while the aperture between the two hangings, small as it was, permitted them to see.

The queen was standing in the room, pale with anger ; her self-control, however, was so great that it might have been supposed that she was calm. Comminges, Villequier, and Guitant were behind her, and the women again were behind the men. The Chancellor Séguier, who twenty years previously had persecuted her so violently, was before her, relating how his carriage had been broken, how he had been pursued, and had rushed into the Hôtel d'O——, that the hotel was immediately invested, pillaged, and devastated : happily, he had time to reach a closet hidden behind tapestry, in which he was secreted by an old woman, together with his brother, the Bishop of Meaux. Fortunately, however, he had not been taken ; the people, believing that he had escaped by some back entrance, had retired, and left him to retreat at liberty. Then, disguised in the clothes of the Marquis d'O—— he had left the hotel, stumbling over the bodies of an officer and those of two guards who were killed whilst defending the street door.

During the recital Mazarin entered and glided noiselessly up to the queen to listen.

"Well." said the queen, when the chancellor had finished speaking ; "what do you think of it all ?"

"I think that matters look very gloomy, madame."

"But what step would you propose to me ?"

"I could propose one to your majesty—but I dare not."

"You may, you may, sir," said the queen, with a bitter smile; "you were not so timid once."

The chancellor reddened, and stammered some words.

"It is not a question of the past, but of the present," said the queen; "you said you could give me advice—what is it?"

"Madame," said the chancellor, hesitating, "it would be to release Broussel."

The queen, although already pale, became visibly paler, and her face was contracted.

"Release Broussel!" she cried, "never!"

At this moment steps were heard in the ante-room, and, without any announcement, the Maréchal de la Meilleraie appeared at the door.

"Ah, there you are, maréchal," cried Anne of Austria, joyfully. "I trust you have brought this rabble to reason."

"Madame," replied the maréchal, "I have left three men on the Pont Neuf, four at the Halle, six at the corner of the Rue de l'Arbre-Sec, and two at the door of your palace—fifteen in all. I have brought away ten or twelve wounded. I know not where I have left my hat, and in all probability I should have been left with my hat, had the Coadjutor not arrived in time to rescue me."

"Ah, indeed!" said the queen, "it would have astonished me if that low cur, with his distorted legs, had not been mixed up with it."

"Madame," said La Meilleraie, "do not say too much against him before me, for the service he rendered me is still fresh."

"Very good," said the queen, "be as grateful as you like, it does not implicate me; you are here safe and sound, that is all I wished for, therefore you are not only welcome, but welcome back."

"Yes, madame; but I only came back on one condition—that I would transmit to your majesty the will of the people."

"The will!" exclaimed the queen, frowning. "Oh! oh! Monsieur Maréchal, you must indeed have found yourself in great peril to have undertaken so strange a commission!"

The irony with which these words were uttered did not escape the maréchal.

"Pardon, madame," he said, "I am not a lawyer, I am a mere soldier, and probably, therefore, I do not quite comprehend the value of certain words; I ought to have said the wishes, and not the will, of the people. As for what you do me the honour to say, I presume that you mean that I felt fear."

The queen smiled.

" Well, then, madame, yes I did feel fear; and though I have seen twelve pitched battles, and I know not how many fights and skirmishes, I own that, for the third time in my life, I was afraid. Yes; and I would rather face your Majesty, however threatening your smile, than face those hell-demons who accompanied me hither, and who spring from I know not where."

("Bravo," said D'Artagnan, in a whisper to Porthos; " well answered.")

":Well," said the queen, biting her lips, whilst her courtiers looked at each other with surprise, " what is the desire of my people?"

" That Broussel should be given up to them, madame."

" Never!" said the queen, "never!"

" Your majesty is mistress," said La Meilleraie, retreating a few steps.

" Where are you going, maréchal?" asked the queen.

" To give your majesty's reply to those who await it."

"Stay, maréchal; I will not appear to parley with the rebels."

" Madame, I have given my word; and unless you order me to be arrested, I shall be forced to return."

Anne of Austria's eyes shot glances of fire.

" Oh! that is no impediment, sir," said she; " I have had greater men than you arrested.—Guitant!"

Mazarin sprang forward.

" Madame," said he, " if I dared in my turn advise——"

"Would it be to give up Broussel, sir? If so, you can spare yourself the trouble."

" No," said Mazarin; " although, perhaps, that is as good a counsel as any other."

"Then what may it be?"

" To call for Monsieur le Coadjuteur."

" And hold, madame," suggested Comminges, who was near a window, out of which he could see; " hold, the moment is a happy one, for there he is now giving his blessing in the square of the Palais Royal."

The queen sprang to the window.

" It is true," she said; " the arch-hypocrite!—see!"

" I see," said Mazarin, " that everybody kneels before him, although he be but Coadjutor, whilst I—were I in his place— though I be Cardinal, should be torn to pieces. I persist, then, madame, in my wish" (he laid an emphasis on the word) " that your majesty should receive the Coadjutor."

" And wherefore say you not, like the rest, your will?" replied the queen, in a low voice.

Mazarin bowed.

"Monsieur le maréchal," said the queen, after a moment's reflection, "go and find the Coadjutor, and bring him to me."

"And what shall I say to the people?"

"That they must have patience," said Anne, "as I have."

The maréchal bowed and went out; and, during his absence, Anne of Austria approached Comminges, and conversed with him in a subdued tone, whilst Mazarin glanced uneasily at the corner occupied by D'Artagnan and Porthos. Ere long the door opened, and the maréchal entered, followed by the Coadjutor.

"There, madame," he said, "is Monsieur Gondy, who hastens to obey your majesty's summons."

The queen advanced a few steps to meet him, and then stopped, cold, severe, and unmoved, and her lower lip scornfully projected. Gondy bowed respectfully.

"Well, sir," said the queen, "what is your opinion of this riot?"

"That it is no longer a riot, madame," he replied, "but a revolt."

"The revolt is in those who think that my people can revolt," cried Anne, unable to dissimulate before the Coadjutor, whom she looked upon—and perhaps with reason—as the promoter of the tumult. "Revolt! thus is it called by those who have wished for this demonstration, and who are, perhaps, the cause of it; but wait, wait! the king's authority will put it all to rights."

"Was it to tell me that, madame," coldly replied Gondy, "that your majesty admitted me to the honour of entering your presence?"

"No, my dear Coadjutor," said Mazarin; "it was to ask your advice in the unhappy dilemma in which we find ourselves."

"Is it true?" asked Gondy, feigning astonishment, "that her majesty summoned me to ask for my opinion?"

"Yes," said the queen, "it was requested."

The Coadjutor bowed.

"Your majesty wishes then——"

"You to say what you would do in her place," Mazarin hastened to reply.

The Coadjutor looked at the queen, who replied by a sign in the affirmative.

"Were I in her majesty's place," said Gondy, coldly, "I should not hesitate, I should release Broussel."

"And if I do not give him up, what think you will be the result?" exclaimed the queen.

"I believe that not a stone in Paris will remain unturned," said the maréchal.

"It was not your opinion that I asked," said the queen, sharply, without even turning round.

"If it is I whom your majesty interrogates," replied the Coadjutor, in the same calm manner, "I reply that I hold Monsieur le Maréchal's opinion in every respect."

The colour mounted to the queen's face: her fine blue eyes seemed to start out of her head, and her carmine lips, compared by all the poets of the day to a pomegranate in flower, were white, and trembling with anger. Mazarin himself, who was well accustomed to the domestic outbreaks of this disturbed household, was alarmed.

"Give up Broussel!" she cried; "a good counsel, indeed. Upon my word! one can easily see that it comes from a priest."

Gondy remained firm; and the abuse of the day seemed to glide over his head as the sarcasms of the evening before had done; but hatred and revenge were accumulating in the depth of his heart, silently, and drop by drop.

"Madame," he said, "if the opinion I have submitted to you does not please you, it is doubtless because you have better counsels to follow. I know too well the wisdom of the queen, and that of her adviser, to suppose that they will leave the capital long in trouble that might lead to a revolution."

"Thus, then, it is your opinion," said Anne of Austria, with a sneer, and biting her lips with rage, "that yesterday's riot, which, as to-day, is already a rebellion, to morrow might become a revolution."

"Yes, madame," replied the Coadjutor, gravely.

"But, if I believe you, sir, the people seem to have thrown off all restraint."

"It is a bad year for kings," said Gondy, shaking his head; "look at England, madame."

"Yes; but fortunately we have no Oliver Cromwell in France," replied the queen.

"Who knows?" said Gondy; "these men are like thunderbolts —one recognises them only when they have struck."

Every one shuddered; and there was a moment of silence, during which the queen pressed her hand to her side, evidently to still the beatings of her heart. At last she made a sign for every one except Mazarin, to quit the room; and Gondy bowed, as if to leave with the rest.

"Stay, sir," said Anne to him.

"Good," thought Gondy, "she is going to yield."

("She is going to have him killed," said D'Artagnan to Porthos, "but, at all events, it shall not be by me. I swear to Heaven, on the contrary, that if they fall upon him, I will fall upon them."

"And I too," said Porthos.

"Good," muttered Mazarin, sitting down, " we shall see something fresh."

The queen's eyes followed the retreating figures, and, when the last had closed the door, she turned away. It was evident that she was making unnatural efforts to subdue her anger; she fanned herself, smelt at her vinaigrette, and walked up and down. Gondy, who began to feel uneasy, examined the tapestry with his eyes, touched the coat of mail which he wore under his long gown, and felt from time to time to see if the handle of a good Spanish dagger, which was hidden under his cloak, was well within reach of his hand.

"And now," at last said the queen, "now that we are alone, repeat your counsel, Monsieur le Coadjuteur."

"It is this, madame ; that you should appear to have reflected, and publicly acknowledge an error,—which constitutes the strength of a strong government,—release Broussel from prison, and give him back to the people."

"Oh !" cried Anne, " to humble myself thus ! Am I, or am I not, the queen ? This screaming mob, are they, or are they not, my subjects ? Have I friends? Have I guards? Ah ! by Nôtre Dame ! as Queen Catherine used to say," continued she, excited by her own words, "rather than give up this infamous Broussel to them, I will strangle him with my own hands."

And she sprang towards Gondy, whom assuredly at that moment she hated more than Broussel, with outstretched arms. The Coadjutor remained immovable, and not a muscle of his face was discomposed : only his glance flashed like a sword, in returning the furious looks of the queen.

(" He were a dead man," said the Gascon, "if there were still a Vitry at the court, and if Vitry entered at this moment : but for my part, before he could reach the good prelate, I would kill Vitry at once ; the Cardinal would be infinitely pleased with me."

"Hush !" said Porthos, "and listen.")

" Madame," cried the Cardinal, seizing hold of Anne, and drawing her back—"madame what are you about ?"

Then he added in Spanish, "Anne, are you mad? You a queen and quarrelling thus like a shopwoman ! And do you not perceive that in the person of this priest is represented the whole people of Paris, and that it is dangerous to insult him at this moment, and that if this priest wished it, in an hour you would be without a crown ? Come, then, on another occasion you can be firm and

18

strong ; but to-day is not the proper time ; to-day, you must flatter
and caress, or you will be but an ordinary person."

This rough appeal, marked by the eloquence which characterised
Mazarin when he spoke in Italian or Spanish, and which he lost
entirely in speaking French, was uttered with such impenetrable
expression that Gondy, clever physiognomist as he was, had no
suspicion of its being more than a simple warning to be more
subdued.

The queen, on her part, thus chided, softened immediately, and
sat down, and in an almost weeping voice, letting her arms fall by
her sides, said :

" Pardon me, sir, and attribute this violence to what I suffer. A
woman, and, consequently, subject to the weaknesses of my sex, I
am alarmed at the idea of civil war ; a queen—and accustomed to
be obeyed—I am excited at the first opposition."

" Madame," replied Gondy, bowing, "your majesty is mistaken
in qualifying my sincere advice as opposition.   Your majesty has
none but submissive and respectful subjects. It is not the queen
with whom the people are displeased ; they ask for Broussel, and
are only too happy, if you release him to them, to live under your
government."

Mazarin, who at the words "It is not the queen with whom
the people are displeased," had pricked up his ears, thought that
the Coadjutor was about to speak of the cries, "Down with
Mazarin !" and pleased with Gondy's suppression of this fact, he
said, with his sweetest voice, and his most gracious expression :

" Madame, believe the Coadjutor, who is one of the most able
politicians that we have ; the first vacant cardinal's hat seems to
belong to his noble head."

" Ah ! how much you have need of me, cunning rogue," thought
Gondy.

" And what will he promise us ?" said D'Artagnan.   "*Peste*, if
he is giving away hats like that, Porthos, let us look out, and each
ask a regiment to-morrow.   *Corbleu*, let the civil war last but one
year, and I will have a constable's sword gilt for me."

" And for me ?" said Porthos.

" For you ! I will give you the *baton* of the Maréchal de la
Meilleraie, who does not seem to be much in favour just now."

" And so, sir," said the queen, "you are seriously afraid of a
public tumult ?"

" Seriously," said Gondy, astonished at not having further advanced ; "I fear that when the torrent has broken down its em-
bankment it will cause fearful destruction."

" And I," said the queen, "think that in such a case new embankments must be raised to oppose it. Go—I will reflect."

Gondy looked at Mazarin, astonished, and Mazarin approached the queen to speak to her, but at this moment a frightful tumult arose from the square of the Palais Royal.

Gondy smiled, the queen's colour rose, and Mazarin became very pale.

" What is that again ?" he asked.

At this moment Comminges rushed into the room.

" Pardon, your majesty," he cried, " but the people have dashed the sentinels against the gates, and they are now forcing the doors ; what are your commands—for time presses."

" How many men have you about at the Palais Royal ?"

" Six hundred men."

" Place a hundred men round the king, and with the remainder sweep away this mob for me."

" Madame," cried Mazarin, " what are you about ?"

" Go," said the Queen.

At this moment a terrible crash was heard. One of the gates began to yield.

" Oh ! madame," cried Mazarin, " you have lost us all ; the king, yourself, and me."

At this cry from the soul of the frightened Cardinal, Anne became alarmed in her turn, and would have recalled Comminges.

" It is too late !" said Mazarin, tearing his hair, " too late !"

The gate had given way, and shouts were heard from the mob. D'Artagnan put his hand to his sword, motioning to Porthos to follow his example.

" Save the queen !" cried Mazarin to the Coadjutor.

Gondy sprang to the window and threw it open ; he recognised Louvières at the head of a troop of about three or four thousand men.

" Not a step further," he shouted, " the queen is signing !"

" What are you saying ?" asked the queen.

" The truth, madame," said Mazarin, placing a pen and a paper before her ; " you must ;" then he added, " Sign, Anne, I implore you—I command you."

The queen fell into a chair, took the pen and signed.

The people, kept back by Louvières, had not made another step forward ; but the awful murmuring, which indicates an angry people, continued.

The queen had written, " The keeper of the prison of St.

Germain will put Counsellor Broussel at liberty ;" and she had signed it.

The Coadjutor, whose eyes devoured her slightest movements, seized the paper immediately the signature had been affixed to it, returned to the window, and waved it in his hand.

" This is the order," he said.

All Paris seemed to shout with joy ; and then the air resounded with the cries of " Long live Broussel !" " Long live the Coadjutor !"

" Long live the queen !" cried De Gondy : but the cries which replied to his were poor and few ; and perhaps he had but uttered it to make Anne of Austria sensible of her weakness.

" And now that you have obtained what you want, go," said she, " Monsieur de Gondy."

" Whenever her majesty has need of me," replied the Coadjutor, bowing, " her majesty knows that I am at her command."

" Ah, cursed priest !" cried Anne, when he had retired, stretching out her arm to the scarcely closed door, " one day I will make you drink the remains of the gall which you have poured out on me to-day."

Mazarin wished to approach her. " Leave me !" she exclaimed ; " you are not a man !" and she went out of the room.

" It is you who are not a woman," muttered Mazarin.

Then, after a moment of reverie, he remembered where he had left D'Artagnan and Porthos, and that they must have overheard everything. He knit his brows, and went direct to the tapestry, which he pushed aside. The closet was empty.

At the queen's last word, D'Artagnan had dragged Porthos into the gallery. Thither Mazarin went in his turn, and found the two friends walking up and down.

" Why did you leave the closet, Monsieur d'Artagnan ?" asked the Cardinal.

" Because," replied D'Artagnan, " the queen desired every one to leave, and I thought that this command was intended for us as well as for the rest."

" And you have been here since——"

" About a quarter of an hour," said D'Artagnan, motioning to Porthos not to contradict him.

Mazarin saw the sign, and remained convinced that D'Artagnan had seen and heard everything ; but he was pleased with his falsehood.

" Decidedly, Monsieur d'Artagnan, you are the man I have been seeking—and you may reckon upon me, as may your friend, too."

Then, bowing to the two friends, with his most gracious smile, he re-entered his closet more calmly, for on the departure of De Gondy, the uproar had ceased as if by enchantment.

CHAPTER XLVII.

MISFORTUNE REFRESHES THE MEMORY.

ANNE OF AUSTRIA returned to her oratory furious.

"What!" she cried, wringing her beautiful hands, "what! the people have seen Monsieur de Condé, a prince of the blood royal, arrested by my mother-in-law, Maria de Medicis; they saw my mother-in-law, their former regent, expelled by the Cardinal; they saw Monsieur de Vendome, that is to say, the son of Henry IV., a prisoner at Vincennes; and whilst these great personages were imprisoned, insulted, and threatened, they said nothing; and now for a Broussel—good God—what then is become of royalty!"

The queen unconsciously touched here upon the exciting question. The people had made no demonstration for the princes, but they had risen for Broussel; they were taking the part of a plebeian, and in defending Broussel, they instinctively felt that they were defending themselves.

During this time Mazarin walked up and down his study, glancing from time to time at his beautiful Venetian mirror, starred all over. "Ah!" he said, "it is sad, I know well, to be forced to yield thus; but—pshaw—we shall have our revenge; what matters it about Broussel—it is a name, not a thing."

Mazarin, clever politician as he was, was for once mistaken; Broussel was a thing, not a name.

The next morning, therefore, when Broussel made his entrance into Paris in a large carriage, having his son Louvières at his side, and Friquet behind the vehicle, the people threw themselves in his way, and cries of "Long live Broussel!" "Long live our father!" resounded from all parts, and was death to Mazarin's ears; and the Cardinal's spies brought bad news from every direction, which greatly agitated the minister, but were calmly received by the queen. The latter seemed to be maturing in her mind some great stroke—a fact which increased the uneasiness of the Cardinal, who knew the proud princess, and who dreaded much the determination of Anne of Austria.

The Coadjutor returned to parliament more a monarch than the

King, Queen, and Cardinal were, all three together. By his advice, a decree from parliament had summoned the citizens to lay down their arms, and to demolish the barricades. They now knew that it required but one hour to take up arms again, and only one night to reconstruct the barricades.

D'Artagnan profited by a moment of calm to send away Raoul, whom he had had great difficulty in keeping shut up during the riot, and who wished positively to strike a blow for one party or the other. Raoul had offered some opposition at first; but D'Artagnan made use of Count de la Fère's name, and, after paying a visit to Madame de Chevreuse, Raoul started to rejoin the army.

Rochefort alone was dissatisfied with the termination of affairs. He had written to the Duc de Beaufort to come, and the duke was about to arrive, and he would find Paris tranquil. He went to the Coadjutor to consult with him whether it were not better to send word to the duke to stop on the road, but Gondy reflected for a moment, and then said:

"Let him continue his journey."

"But all is not then over?" asked Rochefort.

"Good, my dear count; we have only just begun."

"What induces you to think so?"

"The knowledge that I have of the queen's heart; she will not rest beaten."

"Come, let us see what you know."

"I know that she has written to the prince to return in haste from the army."

"Ah! ah!" said Rochefort, "you are right. We must let Monsieur de Beaufort come."

In fact, the evening after this conversation, the report was circulated that the Prince Condé had arrived. It was a very simple and natural circumstance, and yet it created a great sensation. It was said that Madame de Longueville, for whom the prince had more than a brother's affection, and in whom he had confided, had been indiscreet. His confidence had unveiled the sinister projects of the queen.

Even on the night of the prince's return, some citizens, more bold than the rest, such as the sheriffs, the captains, and the quartermaster, went from house to house among their friends, saying:

"Why do we not take the king, and place him in the Hôtel de Ville? It is a shame to leave him to be educated by our enemies, who will give him evil counsels; whereas, brought up by the Coadjutor, for instance, he would imbibe national principles, and love his people."

That night was secretly agitated, and on the morrow the grey and black cloaks, the patrols of armed shop-people, and the bands of mendicants had re-appeared.

The queen had passed the night in conference alone with the prince, who had entered her oratory at midnight, and did not leave till five o'clock in the morning.

At five o'clock Anne went to the Cardinal's room. If she had not yet taken any repose, he at least was already up. Six days had already passed out of the ten he had asked from Mordaunt; he was therefore occupied in correcting his reply to Cromwell, when some one knocked gently at the door of communication with the queen's apartments. Anne of Austria alone was permitted to enter by that door. The Cardinal therefore rose to open it.

The queen was in a morning gown, but it became her still; for, like Diana of Poictiers and Ninon, Anne of Austria enjoyed the privilege of remaining ever beautiful; nevertheless, this morning she looked handsomer than usual, for her eyes had all the sparkle which inward satisfaction added to their expression.

"What is the matter, madame?" said Mazarin uneasily. "You have quite a proud look."

"Yes, Giulio," she said, "proud and happy; for I have found the means of stifling this hydra."

"You are a great politician, my queen," said Mazarin; "let us see the means." And he hid what he had written by sliding the letter under a sheet of white paper.

"You know," said the queen, "that they want to take the king away from me."

"Alas! yes, and to hang me!"

"They shall not have the king."

"Nor hang me."

"Listen. I want to carry off my son from them—with yourself and myself. I wish that this event, which, on the day it is known, will completely change the aspect of affairs, should be accomplished without the knowledge of any others but yourself, myself, and a third person."

"And who is this third person?"

"Monsieur le Prince."

"And you have seen him?"

"He has just left me."

"And will he aid this project?"

"The plan is his own."

"And Paris?"

" He will starve it out and force it to surrender at discretion."

"The plan is wanting not in grandeur, but I only see one impediment to it."

" What is it ?"

" Impossibility."

" A senseless word ; nothing is impossible. Have we money ?"

" A little," said Mazarin, trembling lest Anne should ask to draw upon his purse.

" Have we troops ?"

" Five or six thousand men."

" Have we courage ?"

" Much."

" Then the thing is easy. Oh ! do think of it, Giulio ! Paris, this odious Paris, awaking one morning without queen or king, surrounded, besieged, famished—having, as an only resource, its stupid parliament, and their Coadjutor, with crooked limbs !"

"Charming ! charming !" said Mazarin. "I see the effect, but I do not see the way to obtain it."

" I will find it out myself."

" You are aware that it will be war—civil war—furious, burning, and implacable ?"

" Oh ! yes, yes. War," said Anne of Austria. "Yes, I will reduce this rebellious city to ashes. I will extinguish the fire by blood ! I will perpetuate the crime and the punishment by making a frightful example. Paris !—I hate it !—I detest it !"

"Very fine, Anne. You are now sanguinary ; but take care. We are not in the time of the Malattesta and the Castrucio Castracani. You will get yourself decapitated, my beautiful queen, and that would be a pity."

" You laugh."

" Faintly. It is dangerous to go to war with a whole nation Look at your brother monarch, Charles I. He is badly off—very badly."

" We are in France, and I am Spanish."

" So much the worse ; I would much rather you were French, and myself also—they would hate us both less."

" Nevertheless, you consent ?"

" Yes, if the thing be possible."

" It is ; it is I who tell you so ; make your preparations for departure."

" I ! I am always prepared to go, only you know I never do go and, perhaps, shall do so this time as little as before."

" In short, if I go, will you go too ?"

"I shall try."

"You torment me, Giulio, with your fears; and what are you afraid of, then?"

"Of many things."

"What are they?"

Mazarin's face, smiling as it was, became clouded.

"Anne," said he, "you are but a woman, and as a woman you may insult men at your ease, knowing that you can do it with impunity; you accuse me of fear; I have not so much as you have, since I do not fly as you do. Against whom do they cry out? is it against you, or against myself? Whom would they hang— yourself or me? Well, I can weather the storm;—I—whom, notwithstanding, you tax with fear—not with bravado, that is not my way, but I am firm. Imitate me; make less noise, and do more. You cry very loud, you end by doing nothing; you talk of flying——"

Mazarin shrugged his shoulders, and taking the queen's hand, led her to the window.

"Look!" he said.

"Well?" said the queen, blinded by her obstinacy.

"Well, what do you see from this window? If I am not mistaken, those are citizens, helmeted and mailed, armed with good muskets, as in the time of the League, and whose eyes are so intently fixed on this window, that they will see you if you raise that curtain much; and now come to the other side—what do you see? Creatures of the people, armed with the halberds, guarding your doors. You will see the same at every opening from this palace to which I should lead you. Your doors are guarded, the air-holes of your cellars are guarded, and I could say to you, as that good La Ramée said to me of the Duc de Beaufort, you must be either bird or mouse to get out."

"He did get out, however."

"Do you think of escaping in the same way?"

"I am a prisoner, then?"

"*Parbleu!*" said Mazarin, "I have been proving it to you this last hour."

And he quietly resumed his despatch at the place where he had been interrupted.

Anne, trembling with anger, and red with humiliation, left the room, shutting the door violently after her. Mazarin did not even turn round. When once more in her own apartment, Anne fell into a chair and wept; then, suddenly struck with an idea:

"I am saved!" she exclaimed, rising; "oh, yes! yes! I know

a man who will find the means of taking me from Paris; a man whom I have too long forgotten." Then, falling into a reverie, she added, however, with an expression of joy, "Ungrateful woman that I am, for twenty years I have forgotten this man, whom I ought to have made maréchal of France. My mother-in-law expended gold, caresses, and dignities on Concini, who ruined her; the king made Vitry maréchal of France for an assassination; while I have left in obscurity, in poverty, that noble D'Artagnan, who saved me!"

And running to a table, upon which were placed paper and ink, she began to write.

CHAPTER XLVIII.

THE INTERVIEW.

IT had been D'Artagnan's practice, ever since the riots, to sleep in the same room as Porthos, and on this eventful morning he was still there, sleeping, and dreaming that a large yellow cloud had overspread the sky, and was raining gold pieces into his hat, whilst he held it under a spout. As for Porthos, he dreamed that the panels of his carriage were not spacious enough to contain the armorial bearings which he had ordered to be painted upon them. They were both aroused at seven o'clock by the entrance of an un-liveried servant, who had brought a letter to D'Artagnan.

"From whom is it?" asked the Gascon.

"From the queen," replied the servant.

"Ho!" said Porthos, raising himself in his bed, "what does she say?"

D'Artagnan requested the servant to wait in the next room, and when the door was closed, he sprang up from his bed, and read rapidly, whilst Porthos looked at him with starting eyes, not daring to ask a single question.

"Friend Porthos," said D'Artagnan, handing the letter to him, "this time, at least, you are sure of your title of baron, and I of my captaincy. There, read and judge."

Porthos took the letter, and with a trembling voice read the following words:

"The queen wishes to speak to Monsieur d'Artagnan, who must follow the bearer."

"Well!" exclaimed Porthos, "I see nothing in that very extraordinary."

"But I see much that is extraordinary in it," replied D'Artagnan. "It is evident, by their sending for me, that matters are becoming complicated. Just reflect a little what an agitation the queen's mind must be in, for her to have remembered me after twenty years."

"It is true," said Porthos.

"Sharpen your sword, baron, load your pistols, and give some corn to the horses, for I will answer for it, something new will happen before to-morrow."

"But stop; do you think it can be a trap that they are laying for us?" suggested Porthos, incessantly thinking how his greatness must be irksome to other people.

"If it is a snare," replied D'Artagnan, "I shall scent it out, be assured. If Mazarin be an Italian, I am a Gascon."

And D'Artagnan dressed himself in an instant.

Whilst Porthos, still in bed, was hooking on his cloak for him, a second knock at the door was heard.

"Come in," cried D'Artagnan; and another servant entered.

"From his Eminence, Cardinal Mazarin," he said, presenting a letter.

D'Artagnan glanced at Porthos, and said:

"It is arranged capitally; his Eminence expects me in half an hour."

"Good."

"My friend," said D'Artagnan, turning to the servant, "tell his Eminence that in half an hour I shall be at his command."

"It is very fortunate," resumed the Gascon, when the valet had retired, "that he did not meet the other one."

"Do you not think that they have sent for you, both for the same thing?"

"I do not think it, I am certain of it."

"Quick, quick, D'Artagnan. Remember that the queen awaits you; and after the queen, the Cardinal; and after the Cardinal, myself."

D'Artagnan summoned Anne of Austria's servant, and answered that he was ready to follow him.

The servant conducted him by the Rue des Petits-Champs, and turning to the left, entered the little garden gate leading into the Rue Richelieu; then they gained the private staircase, and D'Artagnan was ushered into the oratory. A certain emotion, for which he could not account, made the lieutenant's heart beat: he had no longer the assurance of youth, and experience taught him all the importance of past events. Formerly, he would have approached the queen, as a young man, who bends before a woman; but now it was a different thing : he answered her summons as an humble soldier obeys an illustrious general.

The silence of the oratory was at last disturbed by a slight rustling sound, and D'Artagnan started when he perceived the tapestry raised by a white hand, which, by its form, its colour, and its beauty, he recognised as that royal hand, which had one day been presented to him to kiss. The queen entered.

"It is you, Monsieur d'Artagnan," she said, fixing a gaze full of melancholy interest on the countenance of the officer, "and I know you well. Look at me well in your turn. I am the queen ; do you recognise me ?"

"No, madame," replied D'Artagnan.

"But are you no longer aware," continued Anne, giving that sweet expression to her voice which she could do at will, "that in former days the queen had once need of a young, brave, and devoted cavalier ; that she found this cavalier ; and that although he might have thought that she had forgotten him, she had kept a place for him in the depths of her heart."

"No, madame, I was ignorant of that," said the Musketeer.

"So much the worse, sir," said Anne of Austria, "so much the worse, at least for the queen ; for to-day she has need of the same courage, and of that same devotion."

"What !" exclaimed D'Artagnan, "does the queen, surrounded as she is by such devoted servants, such wise counsellors, men, in short, so great by their merit or their position—does she deign to cast her eyes on an obscure soldier ?"

Anne understood this covert reproach, and was more moved than irritated by it. She had many a time felt humiliated by the self-sacrifice and disinterestedness shown by the Gascon gentleman, and she had allowed herself to be exceeded in generosity.

"All that you tell me of those by whom I am surrounded, Monsieur d'Artagnan, is doubtless true," said the queen, "but I have confidence in you alone. I know that you belong to the Cardinal—but belong to me as well—and I will take upon myself the making of your fortune. Come, will you do to-day what formerly the gentleman whom you do not know did for the queen ?"

"I will do everything which your majesty commands," replied D'Artagnan.

The queen reflected for a moment, and then, seeing the cautious demeanour of the Musketeer,—

"Perhaps you like repose ?" she said.

" I do not know, for I have never had it, madame."

" Have you any friends ?"

" I had three, two of whom have left Paris, to go I know not where. One alone is left to me, but he is one of those known, I believe, to the cavalier, of whom your majesty did me the honour to speak to me."

" Very good," said the queen, " you and your friend are worth an army."

" What am I to do, madame ?"

" Return at five o'clock, and I will tell you : but do not breathe to a living soul, sir, the rendezvous which I give you."

" No, madame."

" Swear it by Christ."

" Madame, I have never been false to my word—when I say no, it means no."

The queen, although astonished at this language, to which she was not accustomed from her courtiers, argued from it a happy omen of the zeal with which D'Artagnan would serve her in the accomplishment of her project. It was one of the Gascon's artifices to hide his deep cunning occasionally under an appearance of rough loyalty.

" Has the queen any further commands for me now?" asked D'Artagnan.

" No, sir," replied Anne of Austria, "and you may retire until the time that I mentioned to you."

D'Artagnan bowed and went out.

" Diable !" he exclaimed, when the door was shut, " they seem to have great need of me here."

Then, as the half hour had already glided by, he crossed the gallery, and knocked at the Cardinal's door.

" I come for your commands, my lord," he said.

And according to his custom, D'Artagnan glanced rapidly round him, and remarked that Mazarin had a sealed letter before him.

" You come from the queen?" said Mazarin, looking fixedly at D'Artagnan.

" I ! my lord, who told you that ?"

" Nobody, but I know it."

" I regret, infinitely, to tell you, my lord, that you are mistaken," replied the Gascon impudently, firm to the promise he had just made to Anne of Austria.

" I opened the door of the anteroom myself, and I saw you enter at the end of the corridor."

" Because I was shown up the private stairs."

"How so?"

"I know not, it must have been a mistake."

Mazarin was aware that it was not easy to make D'Artagnan reveal anything which he was desirous of hiding, so he therefore gave up, for the time, the discovery of the mystery which the Gascon made.

"Let us speak of my affairs," said Mazarin, "since you will tell me nought of yours. Are you fond of travelling?"

"My life has been passed on the high roads."

"Would anything retain you particularly in Paris?"

"Nothing but an order from a superior would retain me in Paris."

"Very well. Here is a letter which must be taken to its address."

"To its address, my lord? But it has none."

"I regret to say," resumed Mazarin, "that it is in a double envelope."

"I understand; and I am only to take off the first one when I have reached a certain place?"

"Just so—take it and go. You have a friend, Monsieur de Valon, whom I like much; let him accompany you."

"The devil!" said D'Artagnan to himself. "He knows that we overheard his conversation yesterday, and he wants to get us away from Paris."

"Do you hesitate?" asked Mazarin.

"No, my lord, and I will set out at once. There is one thing only which I must request."

"What is it? speak."

"That your Eminence will at once go to the queen."

"What for?"

"Merely to say these words: 'I am going to send Monsieur d'Artagnan away, and I wish him to set out directly.'"

"I told you," said Mazarin, "that you had seen the queen."

"I had the honour of saying to your Eminence that there had been some mistake."

"Very well; I will go. Wait here for me." And looking attentively around him, to see if he had forgotten any keys in his closets, Mazarin went out. Ten minutes elapsed ere he returned, pale, and evidently thoughtful. He seated himself at his desk, and D'Artagnan proceeded to examine his face, as he had just examined the letter he held; but the envelope which covered his countenance was almost as impenetrable as that which covered the letter.

"Eh ! eh !" thought the Gascon ; "he looks displeased. Can it be with me? He meditates. Is it about sending me to the Bastille? All very fine, my lord; but at the very first hint you give of such a thing, 'I will strangle you, and become Frondist.' I should be carried in triumph like Monsieur Broussel, and Athos would proclaim me the French Brutus. It would be droll."

The Gascon, with his vivid imagination, had already seen the advantage to be derived from his situation; Mazarin gave, however, no order of the kind, but, on the contrary, began to be insinuating.

"You were right," he said, "my dear Monsieur d'Artagnan, and you cannot set out yet. I beg you to return me that despatch."

D'Artagnan obeyed, and Mazarin ascertained that the seal was intact.

"I shall want you this evening," he said. "Return in two hours."

"My lord," said D'Artagnan, "I have an appointment in two hours, which I cannot miss."

"Do not be uneasy," said Mazarin; "it is the same."

"Good !" thought D'Artagnan ; "I fancied it was so."

"Return then at five o'clock, and bring that worthy Monsieur de Valon with you. Only, leave him in the anteroom, as I wish to speak to you alone."

D'Artagnan bowed, and thought—"Both at the same hour ; both commands alike—both at the Palais Royal. I guess. Ah ! Monsieur de Gondy would pay a hundred thousand francs for such a secret !"

"You are thoughtful," said Mazarin uneasily.

"Yes ; I was thinking whether we ought to come armed or not."

"Armed to the teeth !" replied Mazarin.

"Very well, my lord, it shall be so."

CHAPTER XLIX.

THE FLIGHT.

WHEN D'Artagnan returned to the Palais Royal at five o'clock, it presented, in spite of the excitement which reigned in the town, a spectacle of the greatest rejoicing. Nor was that surprising. The queen had restored Broussel and Blancmesnil to the people, and had therefore nothing to fear, since the people had nothing more to ask for. The return also of the conqueror of Lens was the pretext for giving a grand banquet. The princes and princesses were invited, and their carriages had crowded the court since noon; then after dinner the queen was to form her poole of quadrille. Anne of Austria had never appeared more brilliant than on that day—radiant with grace and wit. Mazarin disappeared as they rose from table. He found D'Artagnan waiting for him already at his post in the anteroom. The Cardinal advanced to him with a smile, and taking him by the hand, led him into his study.

"My dear *Monson* d'Artagnan," said the minister, sitting down, "I am about to give you the greatest proof of confidence that a minister can give to an officer."

"I hope," said D'Artagnan bowing, "that you give it, my lord, without hesitation, and with the conviction that I am worthy of it."

"More worthy than every one, my dear friend; therefore I apply to you. You are about to leave this evening," continued Mazarin. "My dear Monson d'Artagnan, the welfare of the state is reposed in your hand." He paused.

"Explain yourself, my lord; I am listening."

"The queen has resolved to make a little excursion with the king to St. Germain."

"Ah! ah!" said D'Artagnan, "that is to say, the queen wishes to leave Paris."

"A woman's caprice—you understand."

"Yes, I understand perfectly," said D'Artagnan.

"It was for this that she summoned you this morning, and that she told you to return at five o'clock."

"Was it worth while to wish me to swear this morning that I would mention the appointment to no one?" muttered D'Artagnan. "Oh, women! women! whether queens or not, they are always the same."

"Do you disapprove of this journey, my dear Monson d'Artagnan?" asked Mazarin, anxiously.

"I, my lord?" said D'Artagnan; "and why?"

"Because you shrug your shoulders."

"It is a way I have of speaking to myself. I neither approve nor disapprove, my lord; I merely await your commands."

"Good; it is you, therefore, that I have pitched upon to conduct the king and the queen to St. Germain."

"Liar!" said D'Artagnan to himself.

" You see, therefore," continued Mazarin, perceiving D'Artagnan's composure, " that, as I have told you, the welfare of the state is placed in your hands."

" Yes, my lord, and I feel the whole responsibility of such a charge."

" Do you think the thing possible ?"

" Everything is."

" Shall you be attacked on the road ?"

" Probably."

" And what would you do in that case ?"

" I shall pass through those who attack me."

" And suppose you cannot pass through them ?"

" So much the worse for them. I must pass over them."

" And you will place the king and queen safe also and at St. Germain ?"

" Yes."

" On your life."

" On my life."

" You are a hero, my friend," said Mazarin, gazing at the Musketeer with admiration.

D'Artagnan smiled.

" And I ?" asked Mazarin, after a moment's silence.

" How ?—and you, my lord ?"

" If I wish to leave ?"

" That would be more difficult."

" Why so ?"

" Your Eminence might be recognised."

" Even under this disguise ?" asked Mazarin, raising a cloak which covered an arm-chair, upon which lay a complete dress for an officer, of pearl-grey and red, entirely embroidered with silver.

" If your Eminence is disguised, it will be more easy."

" Ah !" said Mazarin, breathing more freely.

" But it will be necessary for your Eminence to do what the other day you declared you should have done in our place—cry, ' Down with Mazarin !' "

" I will cry it."

" In French—in good French, my lord—take care of your accent ; they killed six thousand Angerines in Sicily, because they pronounced Italian badly. Take care that the French do not take their revenge on you for the Sicilian vespers."

" I will do my best."

" The streets are full of armed men," continued D'Artagnan.

19

" Are you sure that no one is aware of the queen's project ?"
Mazarin reflected.

" This affair would give a fine opportunity for a traitor, my
lord ; the chance of being attacked would be an excuse for
everything."

Mazarin shuddered ; but he reflected that a man who had an
intention to betray would not warn first.

" And, therefore," added he quietly, " I have not confidence in
every one ; the proof of which is, that I have fixed upon you to
escort me."

" Shall you not go with the queen ?"

" No," replied Mazarin.

" Then you will start after the queen ?"

" No," said Mazarin again.

" Ah !" said D'Artagnan, who began to understand.

" Yes," continued the Cardinal.   " I have my plan :—with the
queen, I double her risk,—after the queen, her departure would
double mine—then, the court once safe, I might be forgotten ;
the great are often ungrateful."

" Very true," said D'Artagnan, fixing his eyes, in spite of himself, on the queen's diamond, which Mazarin wore on his finger.
Mazarin followed the direction of his eyes, and gently turned the
hoop of the ring inside.

" I wish," he said, with his cunning smile, " to prevent them
from being ungrateful to me."

" It is but Christian charity," replied D'Artagnan, " not to lead
one's neighbours into temptation."

" It is exactly for that reason," said Mazarin, " that I wish to
start before them."

D'Artagnan smiled—he was quite the man to understand the
astute Italian.   Mazarin saw the smile, and profited by the moment.

" You will begin, therefore, by taking me first out of Paris, will
you not, my dear Monson D'Artagnan ?"

" A difficult commission, my lord," replied d'Artagnan, resuming his serious manner.

" But," said Mazarin, " you did not make so many difficulties
with regard to the king and queen."

" The king and the queen are my king and queen, my lord,"
replied the Musketeer, " my life is theirs, and I ought to give it
for them.   They ask it ; and I have nothing to say."

" That is true," murmured Mazarin, in a low tone, " but as thy
life is not mine, I suppose I must buy it, must I not ?" and sighing
deeply, he began to turn the hoop of his ring outside again.

D'Artagnan smiled. These two men met at one point, and that was, cunning; had they been actuated alike by courage, the one would have done great things for the other.

"But also," said Mazarin, "you must understand that if I ask this service from you it is with the intention of being grateful."

"Is it still only in intention, my lord?" asked D'Artagnan.

"Stay," said Mazarin, drawing the ring from his finger, "my dear Monson d'Artagnan,—here is a diamond which belonged to you formerly, it is but just that it should return to you—take it, I pray."

D'Artagnan spared Mazarin the trouble of insisting, and after looking to see if the stone were the same, and assuring himself of the purity of its water, he took it, and passed it on to his finger with indescribable pleasure.

"I valued it much," said Mazarin, giving a last look at it; "nevertheless I give it to you with great pleasure."

"And I, my lord," said D'Artagnan, "accept it as it is given. Come, let us speak of your little affairs. You wish to leave before everybody, and at what hour?"

"At ten o'clock."

"And the queen, at what time does she wish to start?"

"At midnight."

"Then it is possible. I can get you out of Paris and leave you beyond the 'barrière,' and can return for her."

"Capital, but how will you get me out of Paris?"

"Oh! as to that, you must leave it to me."

"I give you full power, therefore take as large an escort as you like."

D'Artagnan shook his head.

"It seems to me, however," said Mazarin, "the safest method."

"Yes, for you, my lord, but not for the queen; you must leave it to me, and give me the entire direction of the undertaking."

"Nevertheless——"

"Or find some one else," continued D'Artagnan, turning his back.

"Oh!" muttered Mazarin; "I do believe he is going off with the diamond!"

"Monson d'Artagnan, my dear Monson d'Artagnan," he called out in a coaxing voice, "will you answer for everything?"

"I will answer for nothing, I will do my best."

"Well, then, let us go, I must trust to you."

"It is very fortunate," said D'Artagnan to himself.

"You will be here at half-past nine?"

" And I shall find your Eminence ready ?"

" Certainly, quite ready."

" Well, then, it is a settled thing ; and now, my lord, will you obtain for me an audience of the queen ?"

" For what purpose ?"

" I wish to receive her majesty's commands from her own lips."

" She desired me to give them to you."

" She may have forgotten something."

" You really wish to see her !"

" It is indispensable, my lord."

Mazarin hesitated for one instant, whilst D'Artagnan remained firm.

" Come, then," said the minister ; " I will conduct you to her —but, remember, not one word of our conversation."

" What has passed between us concerns us alone, my lord," replied D'Artagnan.

" Swear to be mute."

" I never swear, my lord, I say yes or no ; and, as I am a gentleman, I keep my word."

" Come, then, I see that I must trust unreservedly to you."

" Believe me, my lord, it will be your best plan."

" Come," said Mazarin, conducting D'Artagnan into the queen's oratory, and desiring him to wait there. He did not wait long, for in five minutes the queen entered in full gala costume. Thus dressed, she scarcely appeared thirty-five years of age, and was still handsome.

" It is you, Monsieur d'Artagnan," she said, smiling graciously, " I thank you for having insisted on seeing me."

" I ought to ask your majesty's pardon ; but I wished to receive your commands from your own mouth."

" Will you accept the commission which I have entrusted to you ?"

" With gratitude."

" Very well, be here at midnight."

" I will not fail."

" Monsieur d'Artagnan," continued the queen, " I know your disinterestedness too well to speak of my gratitude at this moment ; but I swear to you that I shall not forget this second service as I forgot the first."

" Your majesty is free to forget or to remember as it pleases you ; and I know not what you mean," said D'Artagnan, bowing.

" Go, sir," said the queen, with her most bewitching smile, "go and return at midnight."

And D'Artagnan retired, but as he passed out he glanced at the curtain through which the queen had entered, and at the bottom of the tapestry he remarked the tip of a velvet slipper.

"Good," thought he; "Mazarin has been listening to discover whether I had betrayed him. In truth, that Italian puppet does not deserve the services of an honest man."

D'Artagnan was not less exact to his appointment, and at half-past nine o'clock he entered the anteroom.

He found the Cardinal dressed as an officer, and he looked very well in that costume, which, as we have already said, he wore elegantly—only he was very pale, and trembled a little.

"Quite alone?" he asked.

"Yes, my lord."

"And that worthy Monsieur de Valon, are we to enjoy his society?"

"Certainly, my lord, he is waiting in his carriage at the gate of the garden of the Palais Royal."

"And we start in his carriage then."

"Yes, my lord."

"And with us no other escort but you two?"

"Is it not enough? One of us would suffice."

"Really, my dear Monsieur d'Artagnan," said the Cardinal, "your coolness startles me."

"I should have thought, on the contrary, that it ought to have inspired you with confidence."

"And Bernouin, do I not take him with me?"

"There is no room for him; he will rejoin your Eminence."

"Let us go," said Mazarin, "since everything must be ready—do you wish it?"

"My lord, there is time to draw back," said D'Artagnan, "and your Eminence is perfectly free."

"Not at all, not at all," said Mazarin; "let us be off."

And they both descended the private stair, Mazarin leaning on the arm of D'Artagnan, an arm which the Musketeer felt trembling upon his own. At last, after crossing the courts of the Palais Royal, where there still remained some of the conveyances of late guests, they entered the garden and reached the little gate. Mazarin attempted to open it by a key which he took from his pocket, but his hand trembled so much that he could not find the keyhole.

"Give it to me," said D'Artagnan, who, when the gate was opened, deposited the key in his pocket, reckoning upon returning by that means.

The steps were already down, and the door open. Mousqueton held open the door, and Porthos was inside the carriage.

" Mount, my lord," said D'Artagnan to Mazarin, who sprang into the carriage without waiting for a second bidding. D'Artagnan followed him ; and Mousqueton, having closed the door, mounted behind the carriage with many groans. He had made some difficulties about going, under pretext that he still suffered from his wound, but D'Artagnan had said to him :

" Remain· if you like, my dear Monsieur Mouston, but I warn you that Paris will be burnt down to-night ;" upon which Mousqueton had declared, without asking anything further, that he was ready to follow his master and Monsieur D'Artagnan to the end of the world.

The carriage started at a measured pace, without betraying in the least that it contained people in a hurry. The Cardinal wiped his forehead with his handkerchief, and looked around him. On his left was Porthos, whilst D'Artagnan was on his right ; each guarded a door, and served as a rampart to him on either side. Before him, on the front seat, lay two pairs of pistols—one before Porthos, and the other before D'Artagnan. About a hundred paces from the Palais Royal a patrol stopped the carriage.

" Who goes ?" asked the captain.

" Mazarin !" replied D'Artagnan, bursting into a laugh. The Cardinal's hair stood on end. But the joke appeared excellent to the citizens, who, seeing the conveyance without escort and un-armed, would never have believed in the reality of so great an imprudence.

" A good journey to ye !" they cried, allowing it to pass.

" Hem !" said D'Artagnan, " what does my lord think of that reply ?"

" Man of talent !" cried Mazarin.

" In truth," said Porthos, " I understand ; but now——"

About the middle of the Rue des Petits-Champs they were stopped by a second patrol.

" Who goes there ?" inquired the captain of the patrol.

" Keep back, my lord," said D'Artagnan. And Mazarin buried himself so far behind the two friends that he disappeared, com-pletely hidden between them.

" Who goes there ?" cried the same voice, impatiently, whilst D'Artagnan perceived that they had rushed to the horses' heads. But, putting his head half out of the carriage,—

" Eh ! Planchet," said he.

The chief approached, and it was indeed Planchet; D'Artagnan had recognised the voice of his old servant.

"How, sir!" said Planchet, "is it you?"

"Eh! mon Dieu! yes, my good friend, this worthy Porthos has just received a sword wound, and I am taking him to his country house at St. Cloud."

"Oh! really," said Planchet.

"Porthos," said D'Artagnan, "if you can still speak, say a word, my dear Porthos, to this good Planchet."

"Planchet, my friend," said Porthos, in a melancholy voice, "I am very ill; should you meet a doctor, you will do me a favour by sending him to me."

"Oh! good Heaven," said Planchet, "what a misfortune; and how did it happen?"

"I will tell you all about it," replied Mousqueton.

Porthos uttered a deep groan.

"Make way for us, Planchet," said D'Artagnan in a whisper to him, "or he will not arrive alive; the lungs are attacked, my friend."

Planchet shook his head with the air of a man who says: "In that case, things look ill." Then he exclaimed, turning to his men, "Let them pass, they are friends."

The carriage resumed its course, and Mazarin, who had held his breath, ventured to breathe again.

"*Bricconi!*" muttered he.

A few steps in advance of the gate of St. Honoré, they met a third troop; this latter party was composed of ill-looking fellows, who resembled bandits more than anything else; they were the men of the beggar of St. Eustache.

"Attention, Porthos!" cried D'Artagnan. Porthos placed his hand on the pistols.

"What is it?" asked Mazarin.

"My lord, I think we are in bad company."

A man advanced to the door with a kind of scythe in his hand.

"Eh, rascal!" said D'Artagnan, "do you not know his highness the prince's carriage?"

"Prince or not," said the man, "open; we are here to guard the gate, and no one whom we do not know shall pass."

"What is to be done?" said Porthos.

"*Pardieu!* to pass," replied D'Artagnan.

"But how pass?" asked Mazarin.

"Through or over; coachman, gallop on."

"Not a step further," said the man, who appeared to be the captain, "or I will hamstring your horses."

"*Peste !*" said Porthos, "it would be a pity; animals which cost me a hundred pistoles each."

"I will pay you two hundred for them," said Mazarin.

"Yes, but when once they are hamstrung, our necks will be strung next."

"If one of them comes to my side," asked Porthos, "must I kill him ?"

"Yes, by a blow of your fist, if you can; we will not fire but at the last extremity."

"I can do it," said Porthos.

"Come and open then," cried D'Artagnan to the man with the scythe, taking one of the pistols up by the muzzle, and preparing to strike with the handle.   And as the man approached, D'Artagnan, in order to have more freedom for his actions, leant half out of the door; his eyes were fixed upon those of the mendicant, which were lighted up by a lantern.   Doubtless he recognised D'Artagnan, for he became deadly pale; doubtless, the Musketeer knew him, for his hair stood up on his head.   .

"Monsieur d'Artagnan !" he cried, falling back a step, "Monsieur d'Artagnan ! let him pass."

D'Artagnan was, perhaps, about to reply, when a blow similar to that of a mallet falling on the head of an ox was heard; it was Porthos, who had just knocked down his man.

D'Artagnan turned round and saw the unfortunate man writhing about four steps off.

"'Sdeath !" cried he to the coachman.   "Spur your horses ! whip ! get on !"

The coachman bestowed a heavy blow of the whip upon his horses; the noble animals reared, then cries of men who were knocked down were heard; then a double concussion was felt, and two of the wheels had passed over a round and flexible body. There was a moment's silence; the carriage had cleared the gate.

"To Cours la Reine !" cried D'Artagnan to the coachman; then turning to Mazarin, he said, "Now, my lord, you can say five *paters* and five *aves*, to thank Heaven for your deliverance. You are safe, you are free."

Mazarin replied only by a groan; he could not believe in such a miracle.   Five minutes later the carriage stopped, having reached Cours la Reine.

"Is my lord pleased with his escort ?" asked D'Artagnan.

"Enchanted, *Monson*," said Mazarin, venturing his head out of one of the windows; "and now do as much for the queen."

"It will be less difficult," replied D'Artagnan, springing to the ground. " Monsieur de Valon, I commend his Eminence to your care."

" Be quite at ease," said Porthos, holding out his hand, which D'Artagnan took and shook in his.

"Oh !" said Porthos.

D'Artagnan looked with surprise at his friend.

" What is the matter, then ?" he asked.

" I think I have sprained the wrist," said Porthos.

" The devil ! why you strike like a blind or a deaf man."

" It was necessary—my man was going to fire a pistol at me ; but you—how did you get rid of yours ?"

" Oh ! mine," replied D'Artagnan, " was not a man."

" What was it, then?"

" It was an apparition."

" And——"

" I charmed it away."

Without further explanation, D'Artagnan took the pistols which were upon the front seat, and placed them in his belt, wrapped himself in his cloak, and, not wishing to enter by the same gate as that by which they had left, he took his way towards the Richelieu gate.

CHAPTER L.

THE CARRIAGE OF MONSIEUR LE COADJUTEUR.

INSTEAD of returning, then, by the St. Honoré gate, D'Artagnan,. who had time before him, walked round and re-entered by the Porte Richelieu. He was approached to be examined ; and when it was discovered by his plumed hat and his laced coat that he was an officer of the Musketeers, he was surrounded, with an intention to make him cry " Down with Mazarin !" Their first demonstration did not fail to make him uneasy at first ; but when he knew what it concerned, he shouted in such a fine voice that even the most exacting were satisfied. He walked down the Rue Richelieu, meditating how he should carry off the queen in her turn—for to take her in a carriage bearing the arms of France was not to be thought of—when he perceived an equipage standing at the door of the hotel belonging to Madame de Guéménée.

He was struck by a sudden idea.

" Ah, *pardieu !*" he exclaimed ; " that would be fair play."

And approaching the carriage, he examined the arms on the.

panels, and the livery of the coachman on his box. This scrutiny was so much the more easy, the coachman being asleep with the reins in his hands

"It is, in truth, Monsieur le Coadjuteur's carriage," said D'Artagnan ; "upon my honour I begin to think that Heaven is prospering us."

He mounted noiselessly into the chariot, and pulled the silk cord which was attached to the coachman's little finger.

"To the Palais Royal," he called out.

The coachman awoke with a start, and drove off in the direction he was desired, never doubting but that the order had come from his master. The porter at the palace was about to close the gates, but seeing such a handsome equipage, he fancied that it was some visit of importance, and the carriage was allowed to pass, and to stop under the porch. It was then only that the coachman perceived that the grooms were not behind the vehicle ; he fancied Monsieur le Coadjuteur had sent them back, and without leaving the reins he sprang from his box to open the door D'Artagnan sprang in his turn to the ground, and just at the moment when the coachman, alarmed at not seeing his master, fell back a step, he seized him by his collar with the left, whilst with the right he placed a pistol to his throat.

"Try to pronounce one single word," muttered D'Artagnan, "and you are a dead man."

The coachman perceived at once, by the expression in the countenance of the man who thus addressed him, that he had fallen into a trap, and he remained with his mouth wide open and his eyes immoderately starting.

Two Musketeers were pacing the court, to whom D'Artagnan called by their names.

"Monsieur Bellière," said he to one of them, "do me the favour to take the reins from the hands of this worthy man, to mount upon the box, and to drive to the door of the private stair, and to wait for me there ; it is on an affair of importance which is for the service of the king."

The Musketeer, who knew that his lieutenant was incapable of jesting with regard to the service, obeyed without saying a word, although he thought the order strange. Then turning toward the second Musketeer, D'Artagnan said :

"Monsieur de Verger, help me to place this man in a place of safety."

The Musketeer, thinking that his lieutenant had just arrested some prince in disguise, bowed, and drawing his sword, signified

that he was ready. D'Artagnan mounted the staircase, followed
by his prisoner, who in his turn was followed by the soldier, and
entered Mazarin's anteroom. Bernouin was waiting there, impatient for news of his master.

"Well, sir ?" he said.

"Everything goes on capitally, my dear Monsieur Bernouin, but
here is a man whom I must beg you to put in a safe place."

"Where then, sir ?"

"Where you like, provided that the place which you shall
choose has shutters secured by padlocks and a door which can be
locked."

"We have that, sir," replied Bernouin ; and the poor coachman
was conducted to a closet, the windows of which were barred, and
which looked very much like a prison.

"And now, my good friend," said D'Artagnan to him, "I must
invite you to deprive yourself, for my sake, of your hat and
cloak."

The coachman, as we can well understand, made no resistance ;
in fact, he was so astonished at what had happened to him that
he stammered and reeled like a drunken man. D'Artagnan deposited his clothes under the arm of one of the valets.

"And now, Monsieur Verger," he said, "shut yourself up with
this man until Monsieur Bernouin returns to open the door.
Your office will be tolerably long and not very amusing, I know ;
but," added he seriously, "you understand, it is on the king's
service."

"At your command, lieutenant," replied the Musketeer, who
saw that the business was a serious one.

"By-the-bye," continued D'Artagnan, "should this man attempt
to fly or to call out, pass your sword through his body."

The Musketeer signified by a nod that the commands should
be obeyed to the letter, and D'Artagnan went out, followed by
Bernouin : midnight struck.

"Lead me into the queen's oratory," said D'Artagnan, "announce to her I am there, and put this parcel, with a well-loaded
musket, under the seat of the carriage which is waiting at the foot
of the private stair."

Bernouin conducted D'Artagnan to the oratory, where he sat
down pensively. Everything had gone on as usual at the Palais
Royal. As we said before, at ten o'clock almost all the guests
were dispersed ; those who were to fly with the court had the
word of command, and they were each severally desired to be
from twelve o'clock to one at Cours la Reine.

At ten o'clock Anne of Austria had entered the king's room. *Monsieur* had just retired, and the youthful Louis remaining the last, was amusing himself by placing some lead soldiers in a line of battle, a game which delighted him much. Two royal pages were playing with him.

"Laporte," said the queen, "it is time for his majesty to go to bed."

The king asked to remain up, having, he said, no wish to sleep; but the queen was firm.

"Are you not going to-morrow morning at six o'clock, Louis, to bathe at Conflans? I think you asked to do so yourself."

"You are right, madame," said the king, "and I am ready to retire to my room when you have kissed me. Laporte, give the light to Monsieur the Chevalier de Coislin."

The queen touched with her lips the white, smooth brow which the royal child presented to her with the gravity which already partook of etiquette.

"Go to sleep soon, Louis," said the queen, "for you must be woke very early."

"I will do my best to obey you, madame," said the youthful king, "but I have no inclination to sleep."

"Laporte," said Anne of Austria, in an under tone, "find some very dull book to read to his Majesty, but do not undress yourself."

The king went out, accompanied by the Chevalier de Coislin bearing the candlestick, and then the queen returned to her own apartment. Her ladies—that is to say, Madame de Brey, Mademoiselle de Beaumont, Madame de Motteville, and Socraytine, her sister, so called on account of her sense, had just brought into her dressing-room the remains of the dinner, upon which, according to her usual custom, she supped. The queen then gave her orders, spoke of a banquet which the Marquis de Villequier was to give to her on the day after the morrow, indicated the persons whom she should admit to the honour of being at it, announced another visit on the following day to Val-de-Grace, where she intended to pay her devotions, and gave her commands to her senior valet to accompany her. When the ladies had finished their supper, the queen feigned extreme fatigue, and passed into her bedroom. Madame de Motteville, who was on especial duty that evening, followed to aid and undress her. The queen then began to read, and, after conversing with her affectionately for a few minutes, dismissed her.

It was at this moment that D'Artagnan entered with the Coadjutor's carriage into the courtyard of the palace, and a few seconds later the carriage of the ladies in waiting drove out, and the gates were shut after them.

A few minutes after twelve o'clock Bernouin knocked at the queen's bedroom door, having come by the Cardinal's secret corridor. Anne of Austria opened the door herself. She was undressed—that is to say, she had drawn on her stockings again, and was wrapped in a long dressing-gown.

"It is you, Bernouin," she said. "Is Monsieur d'Artagnan there?"

"Yes, madame, in your oratory; he is waiting till your majesty be ready."

"I am. Go and tell Laporte to wake and dress the king, and then pass on to the Maréchal de Villeroy and summon him to me."

Bernouin bowed and retired.

The queen entered her oratory, which was lighted by a single lamp of Venetian crystal. She saw D'Artagnan, who stood expecting her.

"Is it you?" she said.

"Yes, madame."

"Are you ready?"

"I am."

"And his Eminence, the Cardinal."

"Has got off without any accident. He is awaiting your majesty at Cours la Reine."

"But in what carriage do we start."

"I have provided for everything—a carriage is waiting below for your majesty."

"Let us go to the king."

D'Artagnan bowed, and followed the queen. The young Louis was already dressed, with the exception of his shoes and doublet; he had allowed himself to be dressed in great astonishment, overwhelming with questions Laporte, who replied only in these words: "Sire, it is by the queen's commands."

The bed was open, and the sheets were so worn that holes could be seen in some places—another evidence of the stinginess of Mazarin.

The queen entered, and D'Artagnan remained at the door. As soon as the child perceived the queen he escaped from Laporte, and ran to meet her. Anne then motioned to D'Artagnan to approach, and he obeyed.

"My son," said Anne of Austria, pointing to the Musketeer, calm, standing uncovered, "here is Monsieur d'Artagnan, who is

as brave as one of those ancient heroes of whom you like so much
to hear from my women. Remember his name well, and look at
him well, that his face may not be forgotten, for this evening he is
going to render us a great service."

The young king looked at the officer with his large-formed eye,
and repeated :

" Monsieur d'Artagnan."

" That is it, my son."

The young king slowly raised his little hand, and held it out
to the Musketeer; the latter bent on his knee, and kissed it.

" Monsieur d'Artagnan," repeated Louis ; " very well, madame."

At this moment they were startled by a noise as if a tumult
were approaching.

" What is that ?" exclaimed the queen.

" Oh, oh !" replied D'Artagnan, straining both at the same time
his quick ear, and his intelligent glance, " it is the sound of the
people revolting."

" We must fly," said the queen.

" Your majesty has given me the control of this business ; we
must wait and see what they want."

" Monsieur d'Artagnan !"

" I will answer for everything."

Nothing is so catching as confidence. The queen, full of
strength and courage, was quickly alive to these two virtues in
others.

" Do as you like," she said, " I rely upon you."

" Will your majesty permit me to give orders in your name in
this whole business."

" Command, sir."

" What do the people want again ?" asked the king.

" We are about to know, sire," replied D'Artagnan, as he rapidly
left the room.

The tumult continued to increase, and seemed to surround the
Palais Royal entirely. Cries were heard from the interior, of
which they could not comprehend the sense. It was evident that
there was clamour and sedition.

The king, half-dressed, the queen and Laporte remained each
in the same state, and almost in the same place, where they were
listening and waiting. Comminges, who was on guard that night
at the Palais Royal, ran in. He had about two hundred men in the
courtyards and stables, and he placed them at the queen's disposal.

" Well," asked Anne of Austria, when D'Artagnan reappeared,
" what is it ?"

" It is, madame, that the report has spread that the queen has left the Palais Royal, carrying off the king, and the people ask to have proof to the contrary, or threaten to demolish the Palais Royal."

" Oh, this time it is too much," exclaimed the queen, " and I will prove to them that I have not left."

D'Artagnan saw from the expression of the queen's face that she was about to issue some violent command. He approached her, and said, in a low voice :

" Has your majesty still confidence in me ?"

This voice startled her. " Yes, sir," she replied, " every confidence—speak."

" Will the queen deign to follow my advice ?"

" Speak."

" Let your majesty dismiss M. de Comminges, and desire him to shut himself up with his men, in the guard-house and in the stables."

Comminges glanced at D'Artagnan, with the envious look with which every courtier sees a new favourite spring up.

" You hear, Comminges ?" said the queen.

D'Artagnan went up to him ; with his usual quickness he had caught the anxious glance.

" Monsieur de Comminges," he said, " pardon me ; we are both the queen's servants, are we not ? it is my turn to be of use to her ; do not envy me this happiness."

Comminges bowed and left.

" Come," said D'Artagnan to himself, " that is one more enemy for me there."

" And now," said the queen, addressing D'Artagnan, " what is to be done ? for you hear that, instead of becoming calmer, the noise increases."

" Madame," said D'Artagnan, " the people want to see the king, and they must see him."

" How ! they must see him ! where, on the balcony ?"

" Not at all, madame, but here, sleeping in his bed."

" Oh, your majesty," exclaimed Laporte, " Monsieur d'Artagnan is right."

The queen became thoughtful, and smiled, like a woman to whom duplicity is no stranger.

" Without doubt," she murmured.

" Monsieur Laporte," said D'Artagnan, " go and announce to the people through the grating that they are going to be satisfied, and that in five minutes they shall not only see the king, but they shall see him in bed ; and that the king sleeps, and that the queen begs that they will keep silence, so as not to awaken him."

" But not every one ; a deputation of two or four people."

" Every one, madame."

" But reflect, they will keep us here till daybreak."

" It shall take but a quarter of an hour. I answer for everything, madame ; believe me, I know the people—they are like a great child, who only wants humouring. Before the sleeping king, they will be mute, gentle, and timid as lambs."

" Go, Laporte," said the queen.

The young king approached his mother and said : " Why do as these people ask ?"

" It must be so, my son," said Anne of Austria.

" But then, if they say ' it must be' to me, am I no longer king ?"

The queen remained silent.

" Sire," said D'Artagnan, " will your majesty permit me to ask you a question ?"

Louis XIV. turned round, astonished that any one should dare to address him. But the queen pressed the child's hand.

" Yes, sir," he said.

" Does your majesty remember when playing in the park of Fontainebleau, or in the palace-courts at Versailles, to have seen the sky suddenly become dark, and have heard the sound of thunder ?"

" Yes, certainly."

" Well, then, this noise of thunder, however much your majesty may have wished to play on, has said : ' Go in, sire.' You must do so."

" Certainly, sir ; but they tell me that the noise of thunder is the voice of God."

" Well, then, sire," continued D'Artagnan, " listen to the noise of the people, and you will see that it resembles that of thunder."

In truth, at that moment a terrible murmur was wafted to them by the night breeze ; then all at once it ceased.

" Hold, sire," said D'Artagnan, " they have just told the people that you are asleep; you see that you are still king."

The queen looked with surprise at this strange man, whose brilliant courage made him the equal of the bravest, and who was, by his fine and ready intelligence, the equal of all.

Laporte entered.

" Well, Laporte," asked the queen.

" Madame," he replied, " Monsieur d'Artagnan's prediction has been accomplished; they were calmed as if by enchantment. The doors are about to be opened, and in five minutes they will be here."

"Laporte," said the queen, "suppose you put one of your sons in the king's place; we might be off during the time."

"If your majesty desires it," said Laporte, "my sons, like myself, are at the queen's service."

"Not at all," said D'Artagnan; "for should one of them know his majesty, and find out the substitute, all would be lost."

"You are right, sir—always right," said Anne of Austria. "Laporte, place the king in bed."

Laporte placed the king, dressed as he was, in the bed, and then covered him as far as the shoulders with the sheet. The queen bent over him, and kissed his brow.

"Pretend to sleep, Louis," said she.

"Yes," said the king, "but I wish not to be touched by one of those men."

"Sire, I am here," said D'Artagnan, "and I give you my word that if a single man has the audacity, his life shall pay for it."

"And now what is to be done?" asked the queen, "for I hear them."

"Monsieur Laporte, go to them, and again recommend silence. Madame, wait at the door, whilst I shall be at the head of the king's bed, ready to die for him."

Laporte went out; the queen remained standing near the hangings, whilst D'Artagnan glided behind the curtains.

Then the heavy and collected steps of a multitude of men were heard, and the queen herself raised the tapestry hangings, and put her finger on her lips.

On seeing the queen, the men stopped short, respectfully.

"Enter, gentlemen; enter," said the queen.

There was then amongst that crowd a moment's hesitation, which looked like shame. They had expected resistance—they had expected to be thwarted—to have to force the gates, and to overturn the guards. The gates had opened of themselves; and the king, ostensibly at least, had no other guard at his bed-head, but his mother. The foremost of them stammered, and attempted to fall back.

"Enter then, gentlemen," said Laporte, "since the queen permits you to do so."

Then, one more bold than the rest, ventured to pass the door, and to advance on tip-toe. This example was imitated by the rest, until the room filled silently, as if these men had been the most humble and devoted courtiers. Far beyond the door, the heads of those who were not able to enter could be seen, all rising on the tips of their feet.

D'Artagnan saw it all through an opening that he had made in the curtain, and in the first man who had entered he had recognised Planchet.

"Sir," said the queen to him, thinking that he was the leader of the band, "you wished to see the king, and therefore I determined to show him to you myself. Approach, and look at him, and say if we have the appearance of people who wish to escape."

"No, certainly," replied Planchet, rather astonished at the un-expected honour conferred upon him.

"You will say, then, to my good and faithful Parisians," continued Anne, with a smile, the expression of which did not deceive D'Artagnan, "that you have seen the king in bed and asleep, and the queen also ready to retire."

"I shall tell them, madame, and those who accompany me will say the same thing, but——"

"But what?" asked Anne of Austria.

"May your majesty pardon me," said Planchet; "but is it really the king who is lying there?"

Anne of Austria started. "If," she said, "there is one among you who knows the king, let him approach, and say whether it is really his majesty lying there."

A man, wrapped in a cloak, in the folds of which his face was hidden, approached, and leant over the bed and looked.

For one second D'Artagnan thought the man had some evil design, and he put his hand to his sword; but in the movement made by the man in stooping, a portion of his face was uncovered, and D'Artagnan recognised the Coadjutor.

"It is certainly the king," said the man, rising again. "God bless his majesty!"

"Yes," repeated the leader in a whisper, "God bless his majesty!" and all these men who had entered furious, passed from anger to pity, and blessed the royal infant in their turn.

"Now," said Planchet, "let us thank the queen. My friends, retire."

They all bowed, and retired by degrees, as noiselessly as they had entered. Planchet, who had been the first to enter, was the last to leave. The queen stopped him.

"What is your name, my friend?" she said.

Planchet, much surprised at the inquiry, turned back.

"Yes," continued the queen, "I think myself as much honoured to have received you this evening as if you had been a prince, and I wish to know your name."

"Yes," thought Planchet, "to treat me as a prince. No, thank you."

D'Artagnan trembled lest Planchet, seduced like the crow in the fable, should say his name, and that the queen, knowing his name, would discover that Planchet had belonged to him.

"Madame," replied Planchet, respectfully, "I am called Dulaurier, at your service."

"Thank you, Monsieur Dulaurier," said the queen, "and what is your business?"

"Madame, I am a clothier in the Rue Bourdonnais."

"That is all that I wished to know," said the queen. "Much obliged to you, Monsieur Dulaurier. You will hear again from me."

"Come, come," thought D'Artagnan, emerging from behind the curtain; "decidedly Monsieur Planchet is no fool, and it is evident he has been brought up in a good school."

The different actors in this strange scene remained facing one another, without uttering a single word; the queen standing near the door—D'Artagnan half out of his hiding place—the king raised on his elbow, ready to fall down on his bed again, at the slightest sound which should indicate the return of the multitude; but instead of approaching, the noise became more and more distant, and finished by dying away entirely.

The queen breathed more freely. D'Artagnan wiped his damp forehead, and the king slid off his bed, saying,—"Let us go."

At this moment Laporte re-appeared.

"Well?" asked the queen.

"Well, madame!" replied the valet; "I followed them as far as the gates They announced to all their comrades that they had seen the king, and that the queen had spoken to them; and, in fact, they have gone off quite proud and happy."

"Oh, the miserable wretches!" murmured the queen, "they shall pay dearly for their boldness, and it is I who promise it to them."

Then turning to D'Artagnan, she said :

"Sir, you have given me this evening the best advice that I have ever received. Continue, and say what we must do now."

"Monsieur Laporte," said D'Artagnan, "finish dressing his majesty."

"We may go then?" asked the queen.

" When your majesty pleases. You have only to descend by the private stairs, and you will find me at the door."

" Go, sir," said the queen ; " I will follow you."

D'Artagnan went down, and found the carriage at its post, and the Musketeer on the box. D Artagnan took out the parcel, which he had desired Bernouin to place under the seat. It may be remembered that it was the hat and cloak belonging to Monsieur de Gondy's coachman.

He placed the cloak on his shoulders, and the hat on his head, whilst the Musketeer got off the box.

" Sir," said D'Artagnan, " you will go and release your companion, who is guarding the coachman. You must mount your horse, and proceed to Rue Tiquetonne, Hôtel de la Chevrette, whence you will take my horse, and that of Monsieur de Valon, which you must saddle and equip as if for war, and then you will leave Paris, bringing them with you to Cours la Reine. If, when you arrive at Cours la Reine, you find no one, you must go on to St. Germain. On the king's service."

The Musketeer touched his cap, and went away to execute the orders he had received.

D'Artagnan mounted on the box, having a pair of pistols in his belt, a musket under his feet, and a naked sword behind him.

The queen appeared, and was followed by the king and the Duke d'Anjou, his brother.

" Monsieur the Coadjutor's carriage !" she exclaimed, falling back.

" Yes, madame," said D'Artagnan ; " but get in fearlessly, for I drive you."

The queen uttered a cry of surprise, and entered the carriage, and the king and monsieur took their places at her side.

" Come, Laporte," said the queen.

" How, madame !" said the valet, " in the same carriage as your majesties !"

" It is not a matter of royal etiquette this evening, but of the king's safety. Get in, Laporte."

Laporte obeyed.

" Pull down the blinds," said D'Artagnan.

" But will that not excite suspicion, sir ?" asked the queen.

" Your majesty's mind may be quite at ease," replied the officer. " I have my answer ready."

The blinds were pulled down, and they started at a gallop by the Rue Richelieu. On reaching the gate, the captain of the post advanced at the head of some ten men, holding a lantern in his hand.

D'Artagnan signed to them to draw near.

" Do you recognise the carriage ?" he asked the sergeant.

" No," replied the latter.

" Look at the arms."

The sergeant put the lantern near the panel.

" They are those of Monsieur le Coadjuteur," he said.

" Hush ; he is enjoying a ride with Madame de Guéménée."

The sergeant began to laugh.

" Open the gate," he cried, " I know who it is !" Then putting his face to the lowered blinds, he said :

" I wish you joy, my lord !"

" Impudent fellow," cried D'Artagnan, " you will get me turned off."

The gate groaned on its hinges, and D'Artagnan, seeing the way cleared, whipped on his horses, who started at a canter, and five minutes later they had rejoined the Cardinal.

" Mousqueton !" exclaimed D'Artagnan, " draw up the blinds of his majesty's carriage."

" It is he !" cried Porthos.

" As a coachman !" exclaimed Mazarin.

" And with the Coadjutor's carriage !" said the queen.

" Corpo di Dio ! Monson d'Artagnan," said Mazarin, " you are worth your weight in gold."

CHAPTER LI.

HOW D'ARTAGNAN AND PORTHOS EARNED BY THE SALE OF STRAW, THE ONE TWO HUNDRED AND NINETEEN, AND THE OTHER TWO HUNDRED AND FIFTEEN, LOUIS D'OR.

MAZARIN was desirous of setting out instantly for St. Germain ; but the queen declared that she should wait for the people whom she had appointed to meet her. However, she offered the Cardinal, Laporte's place, which he accepted, and went from one carriage to the other.

It was not without foundation that a report of the king's intending to leave Paris by night had been circulated. Ten or twelve persons had been in the secret since six o'clock, and how great soever their prudence might be, they could not issue the necessary orders for the departure without the thing transpiring a little. Besides, each individual had some one or two others interested in him ; and as there could be no doubt but that the queen was leaving Paris full of terrible projects of vengeance, every one had warned parents and friends of what was going to happen ; so that the news of the approaching exit ran like a train of lighted gunpowder through the streets.

The first carriage which arrived after that of the queen was that of the Prince de Condé, who, with the princess and dowager princess, was in it. Both these ladies had been awakened in the middle of the night, and did not know what it was all about. The second contained the Duke and Duchess of Orleans, the tall young Mademoiselle, and the Abbé de la Rivière ; and the third, the Duke de Longueville and the Prince de Conti, brother and brother-in-law of Condé. They all alighted, and hastened to pay their respects to the king and queen in their coach. The queen fixed her eyes upon the carriage they had left, and seeing that it was empty, she said :

"But where is Madame de Longueville ?"

"Ah, yes, where is my sister?" asked the prince.

"Madame de Longueville is ill," said the duke, "and she desired me to excuse her to your majesty."

Anne gave a quick glance at Mazarin, who replied by an almost imperceptible shake of his head.

"What do you say of this ?" asked the queen.

"I say that she is an hostage for the Parisians," answered the Cardinal.

"Why is she not come?" asked the prince in a low voice, addressing his brother.

"Silence," whispered the duke ; "she has her reasons."

"She will ruin us !" returned the prince.

"She will save us," said Conti.

Carriages now arrived in crowds : those of the Maréchal de Villeroy, Guitant, Villequier, and Comminges came into the line. The two Musketeers arrived in their turn, holding the horses of D'Artagnan and Porthos in their hands, These two instantly mounted ; the coachman of the latter replacing D'Artagnan on the coach-box of the royal coach. Mousqueton took the place of the coachman, and drove standing—for reasons known to himself —like the Phaeton of antiquity.

The queen, though occupied by a thousand details, tried to catch the Gascon's eye ; but he, with his wonted prudence, had mingled with the crowd.

"Let us be the avant-guard," said he to Porthos, "and find out good quarters at St. Germain ; nobody will think of us, and for my part, I am much fatigued."

" As for me," replied Porthos, " I'm falling asleep, considering that we have not had any fighting ; truly, the Parisians are idiots."

" Or rather, we are very clever," said D'Artagnan.

" Perhaps."

" And your wrist—how is it ?"

" Better—but do you think that we've got them this time ?"

" Got what ?"

" You, your promotion—and I, my title."

" I'faith ! yes—I should expect so—besides, if they forget, I shall take the liberty of reminding them."

"The Queen's voice ! She is speaking," said Porthos ; " I think she wants to ride on horseback."

" Oh, she would like it—she would—but——"

"But what ?"

" The Cardinal won't allow it. Gentlemen," he said, addressing the two Musketeers, " accompany the royal carriage ; we are going on to seek for lodgings."

" Let us depart, gentlemen," said the queen.

And the royal carriage drove on, followed by the other coaches and about fifty horsemen.

They reached St. Germain without any accident : on descending the footstep, the queen found the prince awaiting her, bareheaded, to offer her his hand.

" What an alarum for the Parisians !" said the queen.

" It is war," were the emphatic words of the prince.

" Well, then, let it be war ! Have we not on our side the conqueror of Mocroy, of Nordlingen, of Lens ?"

The prince bowed low.

It was then nine o'clock in the morning. The queen walked first into the château ; everyone followed her. About two hundred persons had accompanied her in her flight.

" Gentlemen," said the queen, laughing, " pray take up your abode in the château ; it is large, and there will be no want of room for you all ; but, as we never thought of coming here, I am informed that there are, in all, only three beds here, one for the king, one for me——"

" And one for the Cardinal," muttered the prince.

" Am I—am I then to sleep on the floor ?" asked Gaston D'Orleans, with a forced smile.

" No, my prince," replied Mazarin, " for the third bed is intended for your highness."

" But your Eminence ?" replied the prince.

" I "—answered Mazarin—" I shall not sleep at all ; I shall have work to do."

Gaston desired that he should be shown into the room where he was to sleep, without in the least concerning himself as to where his wife and daughter were to repose.

" Well, for my part, I shall go to bed," said D'Artagnan ; " come, Porthos."

Porthos followed the lieutenant with that profound confidence which he had in the wisdom of his friend. They walked from one end of the château to the other, Porthos looking with wondering eyes at D'Artagnan, who was counting on his fingers.

" Four hundred, at a pistole each—four hundred pistoles."

" Yes," interposed Porthos, " four hundred pistoles ; but who is to make four hundred pistoles ?"

" A pistole is not enough," said D'Artagnan, " 'tis worth a louis."

" What is worth a louis ?"

" Four hundred, at a louis each, make four hundred louis."

" Four hundred !" exclaimed Porthos.

" Listen !" cried D'Artagnan.

But, as there were all descriptions of people about, who were in a state of wonderment at the arrival of the court, which they were watching, he whispered in his friend's ear.

" I understand," answered Porthos, " I understand you perfectly, on my honour : two hundred louis, each of us, would be making a pretty thing of it ; but what will people say ?"

" Let them say what they will ; besides, how will they know it's us."

" But who will distribute these things ?" asked Porthos.

" I, and Mousqueton there."

" But he wears my livery ; my livery will be known," replied Porthos.

" He can turn his coat inside out."

" You are always in the right, my dear friend," cried Porthos ; " but where the devil do you discover all the notions you put into practice ?"

D'Artagnan smiled. The two friends turned down the first street they came to. Porthos knocked at the door of a house to the right, whilst D'Artagnan knocked at the door of a house to the left.

" Some straw," they said.

" Sir, we don't keep any," was the reply of the people who opened the doors ; " but ask, please, at the hay-dealer's."

" Where is the hay-dealer's ?"

" At the last large door in the street."

" Are there any other people in Saint Germain who sell straw ?"

"Yes; there's the landlord of the Lamb, and Gros-Louis, the farmer—they live in the Rue des Ursulines."

"Very well."

D'Artagnan went instantly to the hay-dealer, and bargained with him for a hundred and fifty trusses of straw, which he had, at the rate of three pistoles each. He went afterwards to the innkeeper, and bought from him two hundred trusses at the same price. Finally, Farmer Louis sold them eighty trusses, making in all four hundred and thirty.

There was no more to be had in Saint Germain. This foraging did not occupy more than half an hour. Mousqueton, duly instructed, was put at the head of this sudden and new business. He was cautioned not to let a bit of straw out of his hands under a louis a truss, and they entrusted to him straw to the amount of four hundred and thirty louis. D'Artagnan, taking with him three trusses of straw, returned to the château, where everybody, freezing with cold, and falling asleep, envied the king, the queen, and the Duke of Orleans, on their camp-beds. The lieutenant's entrance produced a burst of laughter in the great drawing-room; but he did not appear to notice that he was the object of general attention, but began to arrange with so much cleverness, nicety, and gaiety, his straw bed, that the mouths of all these sleepy creatures, who could not go to sleep, began to water.

"Straw!" they all cried out, "straw! where is any to be found?"

"I can show you," answered the Gascon.

And he conducted them to Mousqueton, who distributed lavishly the trusses at a guinea a-piece. It was thought rather dear, but people wanted to go to sleep, and who would not give even two or three louis for some hours of sound sleep?

Mousqueton, who knew nothing of what was going on in the château, wondered that the idea had not occurred to him sooner. D'Artagnan put the gold in his hat, and, in going back to the château, settled the reckoning with Porthos; each of them had cleared two hundred and fifteen louis.

Porthos, however, found that he had no straw left for himself. He returned to Mousqueton, but the steward had sold the last wisp. He then repaired to D'Artagnan, who, thanks to his four trusses of straw, was in the act of making up and of tasting, by anticipation, the luxury of a bed so soft, so well stuffed at the head, so well covered at the foot, that it would have excited the envy of the king himself, if his majesty had not been fast asleep in his own. D'Artagnan could, on no account, consent to pull his bed to pieces again for Porthos, but for a consideration of four louis that the latter paid him for it, he consented that Porthos should share his couch with him. He laid his sword at the head, his pistols by his side, stretched his cloak over his feet, placed his felt hat on the top of his cloak, and extended himself luxuriously on the straw, which rustled under him. He was already enjoying the sweet dreams engendered by the possession of two hundred and nineteen louis, made in a quarter of an hour, when a voice was heard at the door of the hall, which made him stir.

" Monsieur D'Artagnan !" it cried.

" Here !" cried Porthos, " here !"

Porthos foresaw that if D'Artagnan was called away he should remain sole possessor of the bed. An officer approached.

" I am come to fetch you, Monsieur D'Artagnan."

" From whom ?"

" His Eminence sent me."

" Tell my lord that I'm going to sleep, and I advise him, as a friend, to do the same."

" His Eminence is not gone to bed, and will not go to bed, and wants you instantly."

" The devil take Mazarin, who does not know when to sleep at the proper time. What does he want with me ? Is it to make me a captain ? In that case I forgive him."

And the Musketeer rose, grumbling, took his sword, hat, pistols, and cloak, and followed the officer, whilst Porthos, alone, and sole possessor of the bed, endeavoured to follow the good example of falling asleep, which his predecessor had set him.

" Monsieur D'Artagnan," said the Cardinal, on perceiving him, " I have not forgotten with what zeal you have served me. I am going to prove to you that I have not."

" Good," thought the Gascon, " this begins well."

" Monsieur d'Artagnan," he resumed, " do you wish to become a captain ?"

" Yes, my lord.".

" And your friend still wishes to be made a baron ?"

" At this very moment, my lord, he's dreaming that he is one."

" Then," said Mazarin, taking from his portfolio the letter which he had already shown D'Artagnan, " take this despatch, and carry it to England."

D'Artagnan looked at the envelope, there was no address on it.

" Am I not to know to whom to present it ?"

" You will know when you reach London : at London you may tear off the outer envelope."

" And what are my instructions ?"

"'To obey, in every particular, him to whom this letter is addressed. You must set out for Boulogne. At the 'Royal Arms of England' you will find a young gentleman, named Mordaunt."

"Yes, my lord; and what am I to do with this young gentleman?"

"To follow wherever he leads you."

D'Artagnan looked at the Cardinal with a stupefied air.

"There are your instructions," said Mazarin; "go!"

"Go! 'tis easy to say so, but that requires money, and I haven't any."

"Ah!" replied Mazarin, "so you've no money?"

"None, my lord."

"But the diamond I gave you yesterday?"

"I wish to keep it in remembrance of your Eminence."

Mazarin sighed.

"'Tis very dear living in England, my lord, especially as envoy extraordinary."

"Zounds!" replied Mazarin, "the people there are very sedate, and their habits, since the revolution, simple; but no matter."

He opened a drawer, and took out a purse.

"What do you say to a thousand crowns?"

D'Artagnan pouted out his lower lip in a most extraordinary manner.

"I reply, my lord, 'tis but little, as certainly I shall not go alone."

"I suppose not. Monsieur de Valon, that worthy gentleman, for, with the exception of yourself, Monson d'Artagnan, there's not a man in France that I esteem and love so much as him——"

"Then, my lord," replied D'Artagnan, pointing to the purse which Mazarin still held, "if you love and esteem him so much, you—understand me?"

"Be it so! on his account I add two hundred crowns."

"Scoundrel!" muttered D'Artagnan—"but on our return," he said aloud, "may we, that is, my friend and I, depend on having, he his barony, and I my promotion?"

"On the honour of Mazarin."

"I should like another sort of oath better," said D'Artagnan to himself—then aloud, "May I not offer my duty to her majesty the queen?"

"Her majesty is asleep, and you must set off directly," replied Mazarin, "go, pray, sir——"

"One word more, my lord; if there's any fighting where I'm going, ought I to fight?"

" You are to obey the commands of the personage to whom I have addressed the enclosed letter."

" 'Tis well," said D'Artagnan, holding out his hand to receive the money. " I offer my best respects and services to you, my lord."

D'Artagnan then, returning to the officer, said,—

" Sir, have the kindness also to awaken Monsieur de Valon, and to say 'tis by his Eminence's orders, and that I shall wait for him at the stables."

The officer went off with an eagerness that showed the Gascon that he had some personal interest in the matter.

Porthos was snoring most musically, when some one touched him on the shoulder.

" I come from the Cardinal," said the officer.

" Heigho !" said Porthos, opening his large eyes ; "what do you say ?"

" I say that his eminence has ordered you to go to England, and that Monsieur D'Artagnan is waiting for you in the stables."

Porthos sighed heavily—arose, took his hat, his pistols, and his cloak, and departed, casting a look of regret on the bed where he had hoped to sleep so well.

Scarcely had he turned his back than the officer laid himself down in it, and he had not crossed the threshold of the door, before his successor, in his turn, snored immoderately. It was very natural, he being the only man in the whole assemblage of people, except the king, the queen, and the Duke of Orleans, who slept gratis.

CHAPTER LII.

IN WHICH WE HEAR TIDINGS OF ARAMIS.

D'ARTAGNAN went straight to the stables; day had just dawned. He found his horse and that of Porthos fastened to the manger, but to an empty manger. He took pity on these poor animals, and went to a corner of the stable, where he saw a little straw, but in doing so he struck his foot against a round body, which uttered a cry, and arose on its knees, rubbing its eyes. It was Mousqueton, who, having no straw to lie upon himself, had helped himself to that of the horses.

" Mousqueton," cried D'Artagnan, " let us be off ! Let us set off."

Mousqueton, recognising the voice of his master's friend, got up suddenly, and in doing so, let fall some louis which he had appropriated to himself illegally during the night.

"Ho! ho!" exclaimed D'Artagnan, picking up a louis and displaying it; "here's a louis that smells of straw a little."

Mousqueton blushed so confusedly that the Gascon began to laugh at him, and said:

"Porthos would be angry, my dear Monsieur Mouston, but I pardon you—only let us remember that this gold must serve us as a joke—so be gay—come along."

Mousqueton instantly assumed a most jovial countenance, saddled the horses quickly, and mounted his own without making faces over it.

Whilst this went on, Porthos arrived with a very cross look on his face, and was astonished to find the lieutenant resigned, and Mousqueton almost merry.

"Ah, that's it," he cried, "you have your promotion, and I my barony."

"We are going to fetch our brevets," said D'Artagnan, "and when we come back, master Mazarin will sign them."

"And where are we going?" asked Porthos.

"To Paris first—I have affairs to settle."

And they both set out for Paris.

On arriving at its gates they were astounded to see the threatening aspect of the capital. Around two broken-down carriages the people were uttering imprecations, whilst the persons who had attempted to escape were made prisoners—that is to say, an old man and two women. On the other hand, when the two friends wanted to enter, they showed them every kind of civility, thinking them deserters from the royal party, and wishing to bind them to their own.

"What's the king doing?" they asked.

"He is sleeping."

"And the Spanish woman?"

"She's dreaming."

"And the cursed Italian?"

"He is awake, so keep on the watch—as they are gone away, it's for some purpose, rely on it. But as you are the strongest, after all," continued D'Artagnan, "don't be furious with old men and women, and keep your wrath for good occasions."

The people listened to these words, and let go the ladies, who thanked D'Artagnan with an appealing look.

"Now! onward!" cried the Gascon.

And they continued their way, crossing the barricades, getting the chains about their legs, pushed about, questioning, and questioned.

In the place of the Palais Royal D'Artagnan saw a sergeant, who was drilling six or seven hundred citizens. It was Planchet, who brought into play profitably the recollections of the regiment de Piédmont. He recognised his old master, and, staring at him with wondering eyes, stood still. The first row, seeing their sergeant stop, stopped, and soon to the very last.

"These citizens are awfully ridiculous," observed D'Artagnan to Planchet, and went on his way.

Five minutes afterwards he entered the hotel of La Chevrette, where pretty Madeleine, the hostess, came to him.

"My dear Mistress Turquanie," said the Gascon, "if you happen to have any money, lock it up quickly. If you happen to have any jewels, hide them directly—if you happen to have any debtors, make them pay you, or have any creditors, don't pay them."

"Why, prythee?" asked Madeleine.

"Because Paris is going to be reduced to dust and ashes like Babylon, of which you have heard speak "

"And you are going to leave me at such a time?"

"This very instant."

"And where are you going?"

"Ah, if you could tell me that you'd be doing me a service."

"Ah, me! ah, me!"

"Have you any letters for me?" inquired D'Artagnan, wishing to signify to the hostess that her lamentations were superfluous, and that therefore she had better spare him the demonstrations of her grief.

"There's one just arrived."

"From Athos;" and he read as follows :

" ' DEAR D'ARTAGNAN, DEAR DE VALON—My good friends, perhaps this may be the last time that you will ever hear from me. Let God, our courage, and the remembrance of our friendship, support you, nevertheless. I entrust to you certain papers which are at Blois, and in two months and a half, if you do not hear of us, take possession of them.

" ' Embrace, with all your heart, the vicomte, for your devoted friend, " ' ATHOS.'

"I believe, by heaven," said D'Artagnan, "that I shall embrace him, since he's upon our road; and if he is so unfortunate as to lose our dear Athos, from this very day he becomes my son."

"And I," said Porthos, "shall make him my sole heir."

"Let us see, what more does Athos say?"

"'Should you meet on your journey a certain Monsieur Mordaunt, distrust him—in a letter I cannot say more.'

"Monsieur Mordaunt!" exclaimed the Gascon, surprised.

"Monsieur Mordaunt! 'tis well," said Porthos; "we shall remember that—but look, there's a postscript."

"'We conceal the place where we are, dear friend, knowing your brotherly affection, and that you would come and die with us were we to reveal it.'"

"Confound it," interrupted Porthos, with an explosion of passion which sent Mousqueton to the other end of the room; "are they in danger of dying?"

D'Artagnan continued,—

"'Athos bequeaths to you Raoul, and I bequeath to you my revenge. If by any good luck you lay your hand on a certain man, named Mordaunt, tell Porthos to take him into a corner, and to wring his neck. I dare not say more in a letter.'"

"If that is all, Aramis, it is easily done," said Porthos.

"On the contrary," observed D'Artagnan, with a vexed look; "it would be impossible."

"How so?"

"This is precisely this Monsieur Mordaunt, whom we are going to join at Boulogne, and with whom we cross to England."

"Well, suppose instead of joining this Monsieur Mordaunt, we were to go and join our friends?" said Porthos, with a gesture fit to frighten a whole army.

"I did think of it, but this letter has neither date nor postmark."

"True," said Porthos. And he began to wander about the room like a man beside himself, gesticulating, and half drawing his sword out of the scabbard.

As to D'Artagnan, he remained standing like a man in consternation, with the deepest affliction depicted on his face.

"Ah, 'tis not right; Athos insults us; he wishes to die alone—that's bad."

Mousqueton, witnessing this despair, melted into tears, in a corner of the room.

"Stop—an idea!" cried Porthos; "indeed, my dear D'Artagnan, I don't know how you manage, but you are always full of ideas; let us go and embrace Raoul."

"Woe to that man who should happen to contradict my master at this moment," said Mousqueton to himself, "I wouldn't give a farthing for his skin."

They set out. On arriving at St. Denis, the friends found a vast concourse of people. It was the Duc de Beaufort who was coming from the Vendômois, and whom the Coadjutor was showing to the Parisians, intoxicated with joy. With the duke's aid, they considered themselves already as invincible.

" Is it true," said the guard to the two cavaliers, " that the Duc de Beaufort has arrived in Paris ?"

" Nothing more certain ; and the best proof of it is," said D'Artagnan, " that he has despatched us to meet the Duc de Vendômee, his father, who is coming in his turn."

" Long live De Beaufort !" cried the guards, and they drew back respectfully to let the two friends pass. Once across the barriers, these two knew neither fatigue nor fear. Their horses flew, and they never ceased speaking of Athos and Aramis.

The camp had entered Saint Omer : the friends made a little round, and went to the camp, and gave the army an exact account of the flight of the king and queen. They found Raoul near his tent, reclined upon a truss of hay, of which his horse stole some mouthfuls ; the young man's eyes were red, and he seemed dejected. The Maréchal de Grammont and the Duc de Guiche had returned to Paris, and he was quite lonely. As soon as he saw the two cavaliers, he ran to them with open arms.

" Oh, is it you, dear friends ? Do you come here to fetch me ? Shall you take me away with you ? Do you bring me tidings of my guardian ?"

" Have you not received any ?" said D'Artagnan to the youth.

" Alas ! sir, no—and I do not know what has become of him— so that I am really so unhappy as to weep."

In fact, tears rolled down his cheeks.

Porthos turned aside, in order not to show on his good round face what was passing in his mind.

" Deuce take it," cried D'Artagnan, more moved than he had been for a long time—" don't despair, my friend, if you have not received any letters from the count, we have received—we— one."

" Oh, really !" cried Raoul.

" And a comforting one, too," added D'Artagnan, seeing the delight that his intelligence gave the young man.

" Have you got it ?" asked Raoul.

" Yes—that is, I had it," replied the Gascon, making believe to try and find it. " Wait, it ought to be there, in my pocket ; it speaks of his return, does it not, Porthos ?"

" Yes," replied Porthos, laughing.

"Eh! I read it a little while since. Can I have lost it? Ah! confound it! my pocket has a hole in it."

"Oh yes, Monsieur Raoul!" said Mousqueton; "the letter was very consoling. These gentlemen read it to me, and I wept for joy."

"But then, at any rate, you know where he is, Monsieur D'Artagnan?" asked Raoul, somewhat comforted.

"Ah! that's the thing!" replied the Gascon. "Undoubtedly I know it, but it is a mystery."

"Not to me, I hope?"

"No, not to you, so I am going to tell you where he is."

Porthos looked at D'Artagnan with his large wondering eyes.

"Where the devil shall I say that he is, so that he cannot try to rejoin him?" thought D'Artagnan.

"Well, where is he, sir?" asked Raoul, in a soft and coaxing voice.

"He is at Constantinople."

"Among the Turks!" exclaimed Raoul, alarmed. "Good heavens! how can you tell me that?"

"Does that alarm you?" cried D'Artagnan. "Pooh! what are the Turks to such a man as the Count de la Fère and the Abbé D'Herblay?"

"Ah, his friend is with him!" said Raoul; "that consoles me a little."

"Has he wit or not—this demon D'Artagnan?" said Porthos, astonished at his friend's deception.

"Now, sir," said D'Artagnan, wishing to change the conversation, "here are fifty pistoles that the count has sent you by the same courier. I suppose you have no more money, and that they will be welcome."

"I have still twenty pistoles, sir."

"Well, take them; that makes seventy."

"And if you wish for more," said Porthos, putting his hand to his pocket——

"Thank you, sir," replied Raoul, blushing; "thank you a thousand times."

At this moment Olivain appeared. "Apropos," said D'Artagnan, loud enough for the servant to hear him, "are you satisfied with Olivain?"

"Yes, in some respects, pretty well."

"What fault do you find with the fellow?"

"He is a glutton."

"Oh, sir," cried Olivain, reappearing at this accusation.

" And somewhat of a thief."

" Oh, sir ! oh !"

" And, more especially, a great coward."

" Oh, oh, sir ! you really villify me !" cried Olivain.

" The deuce !" cried D'Artagnan. " Pray learn, Monsieur Olivain, that people like us are not to be served by cowards. You rob your master—you eat his sweetmeats and drink his wine ; but, by Jove ! don't be a coward, or I shall cut off your ears. Look at Monsieur Mouston, see the honourable wounds he has received, and look how his habitual valour has given dignity to his countenance."

Mousqueton was in the third heavens, and would have embraced D'Artagnan had he dared ; meanwhile, he resolved to sacrifice his life for him on the next occasion that presented itself.

" Send away that fellow, Raoul," said the Gascon ; " for if he's a coward he will disgrace thee some day."

" Monsieur says I am a coward," cried Olivain, "because he wanted the other day to fight a cornet in Grammont's regiment, and I refused to accompany him."

" Monsieur Olivain, a lacquey ought never to disobey," said D'Artagnan, sternly; then, taking him aside, he whispered to him, " Thou hast done right; thy master was wrong; here's a crown for thee; but should he ever be insulted, and thou dost not let thyself be cut in quarters for him, I will cut out thy tongue. Remember that well."

Olivain bowed, and slipped the crown into his pocket.

" And now, Raoul," said the Gascon, " Monsieur de Valon and I are going away as ambassadors—where, I know not; but should you want anything, write to Madame Turquaine, at La Chevrette, Rue Tiquetonne, and draw upon her money as on a banker— with economy ; for it is not so well filled as that of Monsieur St. Emery."

And having, meantime, embraced his ward, he passed him into the robust arms of Porthos, who lifted him up from the ground and held him a moment suspended, near the noble heart of the formidable giant.

" Come," said D'Artagnan, " let us go."

And they set out for Boulogne, where, towards evening, they arrived, their horses covered with foam and heat.

At ten steps from the place where they halted was a young man in black, who seemed waiting for some one, and who, from the moment he saw them enter the town, never took his eyes off them.

D'Artagnan approached him, and seeing him stare so fixedly, said :

"Well, friend ! I don't like people to scan me !"

"Sir," said the young man, "do you not come from Paris, if you please ?"

D'Artagnan thought it was some gossip who wanted news from the capital.

" Yes, sir," he said in a softened tone.

" Are you not to lodge at the ' Arms of England ?' "

" Yes, sir."

" Are you not charged with a mission from his Eminence Cardinal Mazarin !"

" Yes, sir."

"In that case I am the man you have to do with. I am Mr. Mordaunt."

"Ah !" thought D'Artagnan, "the man I am warned against by Athos."

"Ah !" thought Porthos, "the man Aramis wants me to strangle."

"Well, gentlemen," resumed Mordaunt, "we must set off without delay; to-day is the last day granted me by the Cardinal. My ship is ready, and had you not come, I must have set off without you, for General Cromwell expects my return, impatiently."

"So !" thought the lieutenant, "'tis to General Cromwell that our despatches are addressed."

" Have you no letter to him ?" asked the young man.

"I have one, the seal of which I was not to break till I reached London ; but since you tell me to whom it is addressed, 'tis useless to wait till then."

D'Artagnan tore open the envelope of the letter. It was directed to " Mr. Oliver Cromwell, General of the army of the English nation."

"Ah !" said D'Artagnan, "a singular commission."

"Who is this Monsieur Oliver Cromwell ?" asked Porthos.

" Formerly a brewer," replied the Gascon.

" Perhaps Mazarin wishes to make a speculation in beer, as we have in straw," said Porthos.

"Come, come, gentlemen," said Mordaunt impatiently, "let us depart."

"What !" cried Porthos, " without supper ? Cannot Monsieur Cromwell wait a little ?"

"Yes, but I cannot," answered Mordaunt.

"Oh ! as to you, that is not my concern, and I shall sup either with or without your permission."

The young man's eyes kindled a little, but he restrained himself.

"Just as you please, gentlemen, provided we set sail," he said.

"The name of your ship ?" inquired D'Artagnan.

"The *Standard.*"

"Very well ; in half an hour we shall be on board." And the friends, spurring on their horses, rode to the hotel, the "Arms of England," where they supped with hearty appetite, and then at once proceeded to the port.

There they found a brig ready to set sail, upon the deck of which they recognised Mordaunt, walking up and down impatiently.

"It is singular," said D'Artagnan, whilst the boat was taking them to the *Standard,* "it is astonishing how that young man resembles some one whom I have known—but whom I cannot name."

A few minutes later they were on board ; but the embarkation of horses was a longer matter than that of the men, and it was eight o'clock before they raised the anchor.

CHAPTER LIII.

THE SCOTCHMAN.

AND now our readers must leave the *Standard* to sail peaceably, not towards London, where D'Artagnan and Porthos believed they were going, but to Durham, whither Mordaunt had been ordered to repair by the letter he had received during his sojurn at Boulogne, and accompany us to the Royalist camp, on this side of the Tyne, near Newcastle.

There, placed between two rivers on the borders of Scotland, but still on English soil, were the tents of a little army extended. It was midnight. Some Highlanders were carelessly keeping watch. The moon, which was partially obscured by two heavy clouds, now and then lit up the muskets of the sentinels, or silvered the walls, the roofs, and the spires of the town that Charles I. had just surrendered to the parliamentary troops, whilst Oxford and Newark still held out for him, in the hopes of coming to some arrangement.

At one of the extremities of the camp, near an immense tent, in which the Scottish officers were holding a kind of council, presided over by Lord Leven, lay their commander, a man attired as a cavalier, sleeping on the turf, his right hand extended over his sword.

About fifty paces off, another young man, also apparelled as a cavalier, was talking to a Scotch sentinel, and, though a foreigner, he seemed to understand, without much difficulty, the answers given him in broad Perthshire dialect.

As the town clock of Newcastle struck one the sleeper awoke, and, with all the gestures of a man rousing himself out of a deep sleep, he looked attentively about him. Perceiving that he was alone, he rose, and making a little circuit, passed close to the young man who was speaking to the sentinel. The former had, no doubt, finished his questions, for a moment after he said good-night, and carelessly followed the same path taken by the first cavalier.

In the shadow of a tent the former was awaiting him.

" Eh bien, mon cher ami," said he, in as pure French as has ever been uttered between Rouen and Tours. " Eh bien, mon ami; there is not a moment to lose; we must let the king know immediately."

" Why, what is the matter ?"

" It is too long to tell you; besides, you wish to hear it all directly, and the least word dropped here might ruin all. We must go and find Lord Winter."

They both set off to the other end of the camp, but as it did not cover more than a surface of five hundred feet, they quickly arrived at the tent they were looking for.

" Tony, is your master sleeping ?" said one of the two cavaliers to a servant who was lying in the outer compartment, which served as a kind of ante-room.

" No, Monsieur le Comte," answered the servant, " I think not; or at least, he has not long been so, for he was pacing up and down for more than two hours after he left the king, and the sound of his footsteps has only ceased during the last ten minutes; however, you may look and see," added the lacquey, raising the curtained entrance of the tent.

As he had said, Lord Winter was seated near an aperture, arranged as a window to let in the night air, his eyes mechanically following the course of the moon, hidden, as we before observed, by heavy black clouds. The two friends approached Winter, who, leaning his head on his hand, was gazing at the heavens : he did not hear them enter, and remained in the same attitude till he felt a hand placed on his shoulder.

He turned round, recognised Athos and Aramis, and held out his hand to them.

" Have you observed," said he to them, " what a blood-red colour the moon is to-night ?"

" No," replied Athos; " I thought she looked much the same as usual."

" Look again, chevalier," returned Lord Winter.

" I must own," said Aramis, " I am like the Count de la Fère, I cannot see anything remarkable about it."

" My lord," said Athos, " in a position so precarious as ours, we must examine the earth, and not the heavens. Have you studied our Scotch troops, and have you confidence in them ?"

" The Scotch ?" inquired Winter. " What Scotch ?"

" Ours ! Egad !" exclaimed Athos. " Those to whom the king has confided Lord Leven's Highlanders."

" No," said Winter, then he paused ; " but tell me, can you not perceive the roseate tint which covers the heavens ?"

" Not the least in the world," said Aramis and Athos at once.

" Tell me," continued Winter, always possessed by the same idea, " is there not a tradition in France that Henry IV., the evening before the day he was assassinated, when he was playing at chess with M. de Bassompierre, saw spots of blood on the chess-board."

" Yes," said Athos, " and the Maréchal has often told me so himself."

" Then it was so," murmured Winter, " and the next day Henry IV. was killed."

" But what has this vision of Henry IV. to do with you, my lord ?" inquired Aramis.

" Nothing ; and, indeed, I am mad to amuse you with such things, when your coming to my tent at such an hour announces that you are the bearers of important news."

" Yes, my lord," said Athos. " I wish to speak to the king."

" To the king ! but the king is asleep."

" I have something important to reveal to him."

" Cannot that be put off till to-morrow ?"

" He must know it this moment ; and, perhaps, it is already too late."

" Come, then," said Lord Winter.

Lord Winter's tent was pitched by the side of the royal one ; a kind of corridor communicating between the two. This corridor was guarded, not by a sentinel, but by a confidential servant, through whom in any case of urgency Charles could communicate instantly with his faithful subject.

" These gentlemen are with me," said Winter.

The lacquey bowed and let them pass. As he had said, on a camp-bed, dressed in his black doublet, booted, unbelted, with his felt hat beside him, lay the king, overcome by sleep and fatigue. They advanced, and Athos, who was first to enter, gazed a moment in silence on that pale and noble face, encircled by his long and matted dark hair, the blue veins showing through his transparent skin; his eyes seemingly swollen by tears.

Athos sighed deeply; the sigh awoke the king—so lightly did he sleep.

He opened his eyes.

" Ah!" said he, raising himself on his elbow, " is it you, Count de la Fère?"

" Yes, sire," replied Athos.

" You were watching me while I slept, and you come to bring me some news?"

" Alas! sire," answered Athos, " your majesty has guessed rightly."

" Then it is bad news?"

" Yes, sire."

" Never mind! the messenger is welcome, and you never come here without giving me pleasure. You, whose devotion recognises neither country nor misfortune—you, who are sent to me by Henrietta; whatever news you bring, speak out."

" Sire, Cromwell has arrived this night at Newcastle."

" Ah!" exclaimed the king, " to fight?"

" No, sire, but to purchase your majesty!"

" What did you say?"

" I said, sire, that he owes four hundred thousand pounds to the Scottish army."

" For unpaid wages—yes, I know it. For the last year my faithful Highlanders have fought for honour alone."

Athos smiled.

" Well, sire! although honour is a fine thing, they are tired of fighting for it, and to-night they have sold you for two hundred thousand pounds—that is to say, the half of what is owing to them."

" Impossible!" cried the king; " the Scotch sell their king for two hundred thousand pounds? and who is the Judas who has concluded this infamous bargain?"

" Lord Leven."

" Are you certain of it, sir?"

" I heard it with my own ears."

The king sighed deeply, as if his heart would break, and then buried his face in his hands.

"Oh! the Scotch," he exclaimed—"the Scotch that I called
'my faithful,' to whom I trusted myself, when I could have fled
to Oxford—the Scotch!—my countrymen—the Scotch! my
brothers! But are you well assured of it, sir?"

"Lying behind the tent of Lord Leven, I raised it, and saw all
—heard all!"

"And when is this to be consummated?"

"To-day, in the morning; so your majesty must perceive there
is no time to lose!"

"To do what? since you say I am sold."

"To cross the Tyne, reach Scotland, rejoin Lord Montrose, who
will not sell you."

"And what shall I do in Scotland? a war of partizans, unworthy
of a king."

"Robert Bruce's example will absolve you, sire."

"No! no, I have fought too long; they have sold me, they
shall give me up, and the eternal shame of their treason shall fall
on their heads."

"Sire," said Athos, "perhaps a king should act thus, but not a
husband and a father. I have come in the name of your wife and
daughter and two other children you have still in London, and I
say to you, 'Live, sire, God wills it!'"

The king raised himself, buckled on his belt, and passing his
handkerchief over his moist forehead, said,—

"Well, what is to be done?"

"Sire, you have in the army only one regiment on which you
may rely."

"Winter," said the king, "do you believe in the fidelity of
yours?"

"Sire, they are but men, and men are become both weak and
wicked. I will not answer for them. I would confide my life to
them, but I should hesitate ere I confided to them that of your
majesty."

"Well!" said Athos, "since you have not a regiment, we are
three devoted men, we are enough. Let your majesty mount on
horseback, and place yourself in the midst of us, and we will cross
the Tyne, reach Scotland, and you are saved."

"Is this your counsel also, Winter?" inquired the king.

"Yes, sire!"

"And yours, Monsieur d'Herblay?"

"Yes, sire!"

"As you wish, then. Winter, give all the necessary orders."

Winter left the tent; in the meantime the king finished his

toilette. The first rays of daybreak penetrated through the apertures of the tent as Winter re-entered it.

" All is ready, sire," said he.

" For us also?" enquired Athos.

" Grimaud and Blaisois are holding your horses, ready saddled."

" In that case," exclaimed Athos, " let us not lose an instant
in setting off."

" Come," added the king.

" Sire," said Aramis, " will not your majesty acquaint some of
your friends of this?"

" My friends!" answered Charles, sadly, "I have but three—one
of twenty years, who has never forgotten me, and two of a week's
standing, whom I shall never forget. Come, gentlemen, come."

The king quitted his tent, and found his horse ready waiting for
him. It was a chestnut that the king had ridden for three years,
and of which he was very fond.

The horse neighed with delight at seeing him.

" Ah!" said the king, "I was unjust, here is a creature that
loves me. You, at least, will be faithful to me, Arthur."

The horse, as if it had understood those words, bent its red
nostrils towards the king's face, and parting its lips, displayed all
its white teeth as if with pleasure.

" Yes, yes," said the king, caressing it with his hand, "yes, my
Arthur, thou art a good creature."

After this little scene, Charles threw himself into the saddle, and,
turning to Athos, Aramis, and Winter, said :

" Now, gentlemen, I am at your service."

But Athos was standing with his eyes fixed on a black line which
bordered the banks of the Tyne, and seemed to extend double the
length of the camp.

" What is that line?" cried Athos, whose vision was still rather
obscured by the uncertain light of daybreak. " What is that line?
I did not perceive it yesterday."

" It must be the fog rising from the river," said the king.

" Sire, it is something more opaque than the fog."

" Indeed," said Winter. " It appears to me like a bar of red
colour."

" It is the enemy, who have made a sortie from Newcastle, and
are surrounding us!" exclaimed Athos.

" The enemy!" cried the king.

" Yes, the enemy. It is too late. Stop a moment; does not
that sunbeam yonder, just by the side of the town, glitter on the
Ironsides?"

This is the name given to the cuirassiers whom Cromwell had made his body-guard.

" Ah !" said the king, " we shall soon prove whether my high-landers have betrayed me or not."

"What are you going to do?" exclaimed Athos.

" To give them the order to charge, and run down these miserable rebels."

And the king, putting spurs to his horse, set off to the tent of Lord Leven.

" Follow him," said Athos.

" Come !" exclaimed Aramis.

" Is the king wounded?" cried Lord Winter. " I see spots of blood on the ground,"—and he set off to follow the two friends.

He was stopped by Athos.

" Go and call out your regiment," said he, " I can foresee that we shall have need of it directly."

Winter turned his horse, and the two friends rode on. It had taken but two minutes for the king to reach the tent of the Scottish commander; he dismounted and entered.

" The king !" they exclaimed, as they all rose in bewilderment.

Charles was indeed in the midst of them ; his hat on his head, his brows bent, striking his boot with his riding-whip.

" Yes, gentlemen, the king in person, the king who has come to ask some account of all that has happened."

"What is it, sire ?" exclaimed Lord Leven.

" It is, sir," said the king angrily, " that General Cromwell has arrived at Newcastle; that you knew it, and I have not been informed of it; that the enemy have left the town, and are now closing the passages of the Tyne against us; that our sentinels have seen this movement, and I have been left unacquainted with it. It is that, by an infamous treaty, you have sold me for two hundred thousand pounds to the parliament. Of this treaty at least I have been warned. This is the matter, gentlemen; answer and exculpate yourselves, for I stand here to accuse you."

" Sire," said Lord Leven, with hesitation, " sire, your majesty has been deceived by a false report."

" My own eyes have seen the enemy extend itself between myself and Scotland. With my own ears I have heard the clauses of the treaty debated."

The Scotch chieftains looked at each other in their turn with frowning brows.

" Sire," murmured Lord Leven, crushed down by shame; "sire, we are ready to give you every proof of our fidelity."

" I ask but one," said the king ; "put the army in battle array and face the enemy."

" That cannot be, sire," said the earl.

" How—cannot be ? and what hinders it ?" exclaimed Charles.

" Your majesty is well aware that there is a truce between us and the English army."

" And if there is a truce, the English army has broken it in leaving the town, contrary to the agreement which kept it there. Now, I tell you, you must pass with me through this army across to Scotland, and if you refuse, you may choose between two names—which the contempt of all honest men will brand you with, you are either cowards or traitors !"

The eyes of the Scotch flashed fire ; and, as often happens on such occasions, from shame they passed to extreme effrontery, and two heads of clans advanced towards the king.

" Yes," said they, " we have promised to deliver Scotland and England from him who for the last five-and-twenty years has sucked the blood and gold of Scotland and England. We have promised, and we will keep our promise. Charles Stuart, you are our prisoner."

And both extended their hands as if to seize the king; but before they could touch him with the tips of their fingers both had fallen—one dead and the other stunned.

Aramis had passed his sword through the body of the first, and Athos had knocked down the other with the butt-end of his pistol.

Then, as Lord Leven and the other chieftains retired, alarmed at this unexpected succour, which seemed to fall from heaven for him whom they believed already their prisoner, Athos and Aramis dragged the king from the perjured assembly, into which he had so imprudently ventured, and throwing themselves on horseback, all three returned at full gallop to the royal tent.

On their road they perceived Lord Winter marching at the head of his regiment. The king motioned him to accompany them.

CHAPTER LIV.

THE AVENGER.

THEY all four entered the tent ; they had no plan ready—they must think of one.

The king threw himself into an arm-chair. " I am lost ;" said he.

" No, sire," replied Athos; "you are only betrayed."

The king sighed deeply.

" Betrayed ! yes—betrayed by the Scotch, amongst whom I was born ; whom I have always loved better than the English. Oh, traitors that ye are !"

" Sire," said Athos, "this is not a moment for recrimination, but a time to show yourself a king and a gentleman. Up, sire, up ! for you have here at least three men who will not betray you. Ah ! if we had been five !" murmured Athos, thinking of D'Artagnan and Porthos.

" What are you saying ?" inquired Charles, rising.

" I said, sire, there is more than one thing open. Lord Winter answers for his regiment, or at least very nearly so—we will not split straws about words—let him place himself at the head of his men, we will place ourselves at the side of your majesty, and let us cut through Cromwell's army, and reach Scotland."

" There is another method," said Aramis.   " Let one of us put on the dress, and mount the king's horse. Whilst they pursue him the king might escape."

" It is good advice," said Athos, "and if the king will do us the honour, we shall be truly grateful to him."

" What do you think of this counsel, Winter ?" asked the king, looking with admiration at these two men, whose chief idea seemed to be how they could take on their own shoulders all the dangers which threatened him.

" I think that the only chance of saving your majesty has just been proposed by Monsieur d'Herblay. I humbly entreat your majesty to choose quickly, for we have not a moment to lose."

" But if I accept, it is death, or at least imprisonment, for him who takes my place."

" It is the glory of having saved his king," cried Winter.

The king looked at his old friend with tears in his eyes, undid the order of the Saint-Esprit which he wore, to honour the two Frenchmen who were with him, and passed it round Winter's neck, who received, on his knees, this striking proof of his sovereign's confidence and friendship.

" It is right," said Athos; "he has served your majesty longer than we have."

The king overheard these words, and turned round, with tears in his eyes.

" Wait a moment, sirs," said he; "I have an order for each of you also."

He turned to a closet where his own orders were locked up, and took out two ribbons of the Order of the Garter.

"These cannot be for us?" said Athos.

"Why not, sir?" asked Charles.

"Such are for royalty, and we are simple commoners."

"Speak not of crowned heads. I shall not find amongst them such great hearts as yours. No, no—you do yourselves injustice; but I am here to do justice to you. On your knees, count."

Athos knelt down, and the king passed the ribbon from left to right as usual, and said : "I make you a knight. Be brave, faithful, and loyal. You are brave, faithful, and loyal. I knight you, Monsieur le Comte."

Then, turning to Aramis, he said :

"It is now your turn, Monsieur le Chevalier."

The same ceremony recommenced, with the same words, whilst Winter unlaced his leather cuirass, that he might disguise himself like the king. Charles, having ended with Aramis the same as Athos, embraced them both.

"Sire," said Winter, who in this trying emergency felt all his strength and energy fire up, "we are ready."

The king looked at the three gentlemen, "Then we must fly!" said he.

"Fly through an army, sire?" said Athos.

"Then I shall die sword in hand," said Charles. "Monsieur le Comte, Monsieur le Chevalier, if ever I am king——"

"Sire, you have already honoured us more than simple gentlemen could ever aspire to, therefore gratitude is on our side. But we must not lose time; we have already wasted too much."

The king again shook hands with all three, exchanged hats with Winter, and went out.

Winter's regiment was ranged on some high ground above the camp. The king, followed by the three friends, turned his steps that way. The Scotch camp seemed as if at last awakened; the soldiers had come out of their tents, and taken up their station in battle array.

"Do you see that?" said the king. "Perhaps they are penitent, and preparing to march."

"If they are penitent," said Athos, "let them follow us."

"Well!" said the king, "what shall we do?"

"Let us examine the enemy's army."

At the same instant the eyes of the little group were nxed on the same line which at daybreak they had mistaken for fog, and which the morning sun now plainly showed was an army in order of battle. The air was soft and clear, as it always is at this hour of the morning. The regiments, the standards, and even the colours of the horses and uniforms were now clearly distinct.

On the summit of a rising ground, a little in advance of the enemy, appeared a short and heavy-looking man; this man was surrounded by officers. He turned a spy-glass towards the little group amongst which the king stood.

"Does this man know your majesty personally?" inquired Aramis.

Charles smiled.

"That man is Cromwell!" said he.

"Ah!" said Athos, "how much time we have lost."

"Now," said the king, "give the word, and let us start."

"Will you not give it, sire?" asked Athos.

"No; I make you my lieutenant-general," said the king.

"Listen, then, Lord Winter. Proceed sire, I beg. What we are going to say does not concern your majesty."

The king, smiling, turned a few steps back.

"This is what I propose to do," said Athos. "We will divide our regiment into two squadrons. You will put yourself at the head of the first; we and his majesty at the head of the second. If no obstacle occurs, we will both charge together, force the enemy's line, and throw ourselves into the Tyne, which we must cross, either by fording or swimming; if, on the contrary, any repulse should take place, you and your men must fight to the last man, whilst we and the king proceed on our road. Once arrived at the brink of the river, should we even find them three ranks deep, as long as you and your regiment do your duty, we will look to the rest."

"To horse!" said Lord Winter.

"To horse!" re-echoed Athos; "all is arranged and decided."

"Now, gentlemen," cried the king, "forward! and rally to the old cry of France—Montjoy and St. Denis. The war-cry of England is too often in the mouths of those traitors."

The Scotch army stood motionless and silent with shame on viewing these preparations.

Some of the chieftains left the ranks, and broke their swords in two.

"There," said the king, "that consoles me; they are not all traitors."

At this moment Winter's voice was raised with the cry of "Forward!"

The first squadron moved off; the second followed it, and

descended from the platform. A regiment of cuirassiers, nearly equal as to numbers, issued from behind the hill, and came full gallop towards it.

The king pointed this out.

"Sire," said Athos, "we foresaw this, and if Lord Winter's men do their duty, we are saved instead of lost."

At this moment they heard, above all the galloping and neighing of the horses, Winter's voice crying out:

"Sword in hand."

At these words every sword was drawn, and glittered in the air like lightning.

"Now, gentlemen," said the king in his turn, excited by this sight, and the sound of it, "come, gentlemen, sword in hand."

But Aramis and Athos were the only ones to obey this command, and the king's example.

"We are betrayed," said the king, in a low voice.

"Wait a moment," said Athos, "perhaps they do not recognise your majesty's voice, and await the order of their captain."

"Have they not heard that of their colonel? But look! look!" cried the king, drawing up his horse with a sudden jerk, which threw it back on its haunches, and seizing the bridle of Athos' horse.

"Ah, cowards! ah, traitors!" cried out Lord Winter, whose voice they heard, whilst his men, quitting their ranks, dispersed all over the plain.

About fifteen men were ranged around him, and awaited the charge of Cromwell's cuirassiers.

"Let us go and die with them!" said the king.

"Let us go," said Athos and Aramis.

"All faithful hearts with me!" cried out Winter.

This voice was heard by the two friends, who set off at full gallop.

"No quarter," cried out a voice in French, answering to that of Winter, which made them tremble.

It was the voice of a cavalier mounted on a magnificent black horse, who was charging at the head of the English regiment, of which, in his ardour, he was ten steps in advance.

"'Tis him!" murmured Winter; his eyes glazed, and letting his sword fall to his side.

"The king! the king!" cried out several voices, deceived by the blue ribbon, and chestnut horse of Winter; "take him alive."

"No! it is not the king!" exclaimed the cavalier. "Lord Winter, you are not the king; you are my uncle."

At the same moment Mordaunt, for it was he, cocked his pistol at Winter, the fire flashed, and the ball entered the heart of the old cavalier, who, with one bound on his saddle, fell back into the arms of Athos, murmuring, " He is revenged."

" Think of my mother !" shouted Mordaunt, as his horse plunged and darted off at full gallop.

" Wretch !" exclaimed Aramis, raising his pistol, as he passed by him ; but the fire flashed in the pan, and did not go off.

At this moment the whole regiment came up, and they fell upon the few men who had held out, surrounding the two Frenchmen. Athos, after making sure that Lord Winter was really dead, let fall the corpse, and said :

" Come, Aramis, now for the honour of France," and the two Englishmen, who were nearest to them, fell mortally wounded.

At the same moment a fearful " hurrah !" rent the air, and thirty blades glittered above their heads.

Suddenly a man sprang out of the English ranks, fell upon Athos, entwined his muscular arms around him, and tearing his sword from him, said in his ear :

" Silence ! yield yourself—you yield to me ; do you not ?"

A giant had seized also Aramis' two wrists, who struggled in vain to release himself from this formidable grasp.

" D'Art . . . ." exclaimed Athos, whilst the Gascon covered his mouth with his hand.

" I yield myself prisoner, said Aramis," giving up his sword to Porthos.

" Fire, fire," cried out Mordaunt, returning to the group of friends.

" And wherefore fire ?" said the colonel ; " every one has yielded."

" It is the son of Milady," said Athos to D'Artagnan, " I recognised him."

" It is the monk," whispered Porthos to Aramis.

" I know it."

And now the ranks began to open. D'Artagnan held the bridle of Athos' horse, and Porthos that of Aramis. Both of them attempted to lead his prisoner off the battle-field.

This movement revealed the spot where Winter's body had fallen. Mordaunt had found it out, and was gazing at it with an expression of hatred.

Athos, though now quite cool and collected, put his hand to his belt, where his loaded pistols still remained.

" What are you about ?" said D'Artagnan.

" Let me kill him."

" We are all four lost, if, by the least gesture, you discover that you recognise him."

Then, turning to the young man, he exclaimed :

" A fine prize ! a fine prize, friend Mordaunt ; we have, both myself and Monsieur de Valon, taken two knights of the garter, nothing less."

" But," said Mordaunt, looking at Athos and Aramis with bloodshot eyes, " these are Frenchmen, I imagine."

"I'faith, I don't know. Are you French, sir ?" said he to Athos.

" I am," replied the latter gravely.

"Very well, my dear sir ! you are the prisoner of a fellow countryman."

" But the king—where is the king ?" exclaimed Athos anxiously.

" Ah ! we have got him."

" Yes," said Aramis, " through an infamous act of treason."

Porthos pressed his friend's hand, and said to him :

" Yes, sir, all is fair in war—stratagem as well as force. Look yonder !"

At this instant the squadron—that ought to have protected Charles's retreat—was advancing to meet the English regiments. The king, who was entirely surrounded, walked alone on foot. He appeared calm, but it was evidently not without a great effort. Drops of perspiration rolled down his face ; and from time to time he put a handkerchief to his mouth, to wipe off the blood that flowed from it.

" Behold Nebuchadnezzar !" exclaimed an old Puritan soldier, whose eyes flashed at the sight of one whom he called the tyrant.

" Do you call him Nebuchadnezzar ?" said Mordaunt, with a terrible smile ; " no, it is Charles the First, the king, the good king Charles, who despoils his subjects to enrich himself."

Charles glanced a moment at the insolent creature who uttered this, but he did not recognise him. Nevertheless, the calm and religious dignity of his countenance abashed Mordaunt.

" Bon jour, messieurs," said the king to the two gentlemen who were held by D'Artagnan and Porthos. " The day has been unfortunate, but it is not your fault, thank God ! But where is my old friend, Winter ?"

The two gentlemen turned away their heads in silence.

" Look for him with Strafford," said Mordaunt tauntingly.

Charles shuddered. The demon had known how to wound him. The remembrance of Strafford was a source of lasting remorse to him, the shadow that haunted him by day and night. The king looked around him. He saw a corpse at his feet : it was Winter's.

He uttered not a word nor shed a tear, but a deadly pallor spread over his face : he knelt down on the ground, raised Winter's head, and unfastening the order of the Saint-Esprit, placed it on his own breast.

"Lord Winter is killed, then ?" inquired D'Artagnan, fixing his eyes on the corpse.

"Yes," said Athos, "by his own nephew "

"Come, he was the first of us to go ; peace be to him ! he was an honest man," said D'Artagnan.

"Charles Stuart," said the colonel of the English regiment, approaching the king, who had just put on the insignia of royalty, "do you yield yourself a prisoner ?"

"Colonel Tomlinson," said Charles, "the king cannot yield ! the man alone submits to force."

"Your sword."

The king drew his sword and broke it on his knee.

At this moment a horse without a rider, covered with foam, his nostrils extended, and eyes all fire, galloped past, and recognising his master, stopped and neighed with pleasure ; it was Arthur.

The king smiled, patted it with his hand, and then jumped lightly into the saddle.

"Now, gentlemen," said he, "conduct me where you will."

Turning back again, he said, "I thought I saw Winter move ; if he still lives, by all you hold most sacred, do not abandon him."

"Never fear, King Charles," said Mordaunt, "the ball pierced his heart."

"Do not breathe a word, nor make the least sign to me or Porthos," said D'Artagnan to Athos and Aramis, "that you recognise this man, for Milady is not dead ; her soul lives in the body of this demon."

The detachment now moved towards the town with the royal captive ; but on the road an aide-de-camp from Cromwell sent orders that Colonel Tomlinson should conduct him to Holdenby Castle.

At the same time couriers started in every direction over England and Europe, to announce that Charles Stuart was now the prisoner of Oliver Cromwell.

CHAPTER LV.

OLIVER CROMWELL.

" HAVE you been to the general ?" said Mordaunt to D'Artagnan and Porthos ; "you know he sent for you after the action."

"We went first to put our prisoners in a place of safety,"replied D'Artagnan. " Do you know, sir, these gentlemen are each of them worth fifteen hundred pounds ?"

" Oh ! be assured," said Mordaunt, looking at them with an ex- pression he in vain endeavoured to soften, " my soldiers will guard them—and guard them well, I promise you."

"I shall take better care of them myself," answered D'Artagnan; " besides, all they require is a good room, with sentinels, from which their parole is enough that they will not attempt to escape. I will go and see about that, and then we shall have the honour of presenting ourselves to your general, and receiving his commands for his Eminence."

" You are thinking of starting soon, then ?" inquired Mordaunt.

" Our mission is ended, and there is nothing more to retain us now but the good pleasure of the great man to whom we have been sent."

The young man bit his lips, and whispering to his sergeant :

"You will follow these men, and not lose sight of them ; when you have discovered where they lodge, come and await me at the town gate."

The sergeant made a sign that he should be obeyed.

Instead of following the mass of prisoners that were being taken into the town, Mordaunt turned his steps towards the rising ground from whence Cromwell had witnessed the battle, and on which he had just had his tent pitched.

Cromwell had given orders that no one was to enter it ; but the sentinel, who knew that Mordaunt was one of the most confiden- tial friends of the general, thought the order did not extend to the young man. Mordaunt, therefore, raised the canvas, and saw Cromwell seated before a table, his head buried in his hands ; his back was turned to him.

Whether he heard Mordaunt or not as he entered, Cromwell did not move. Mordaunt remained standing near the door. At last, after a few moments, Cromwell raised his head, and, as if he divined that some one was there, he turned slowly round.

" I said I wished to be alone !" he exclaimed, on seeing the young man.

" They thought this order did not concern me, sir ; nevertheless, if you wish it, I am ready to go."

" Ah ! it is you, Mordaunt !" said Cromwell, the cloud passing away from over his face ; " since you are here, it is well, you may remain."

" I come to congratulate you."

" To congratulate me—what for ?"

" On the capture of Charles Stuart. You are now master of England."

" I was much more really so two hours ago."

" How so, general ?"

" Because England had need of me to take the tyrant, and now the tyrant is taken. Have you seen him ?"

" Yes, sir," said Mordaunt.

" What is his bearing ?"

Mordaunt hesitated ; but he seemed as if compelled to speak the truth.

" Calm and dignified," said he.

" What did he say ?"

" Some parting words to his friends."

" His friends !" murmured Cromwell. " Has he any friends ?" Then he added aloud, " Did he make any resistance ?"

" No, sir ; with the exception of two or three friends, every one deserted him ; he had no means of resistance."

" To whom did he give up his sword ?"

" He did not give it up—he broke it."

" He did well ; but, instead of breaking it, he might have used it to more advantage."

There was a momentary pause.

" I heard that the colonel of the regiment that escorted Charles was killed ?" said Cromwell, staring very fixedly at Mordaunt.

" Yes, sir."

" By whom ?" inquired Cromwell.

" By me."

" What was his name ?"

" Lord Winter."

" Your uncle ?" exclaimed Cromwell.

" My uncle ?" answered Mordaunt ; " but traitors to England are not of my family."

Cromwell observed the young man a moment in silence, and then added :

" Mordaunt, you are strong among the strong ones. And the Frenchmen, how did they behave ?"

" Most fearlessly."

" Yes, yes," murmured Cromwell; "the French fight well; and if my glass was good, and I mistake not, they were foremost in the fight."

" They were," replied Mordaunt.

" After you, however," said Cromwell.

" It was the fault of their horses, not theirs."

Another pause.

" And the Scotch?"

" They kept their word, and never stirred," said Mordaunt.

" Wretched men !"

" Their officers wish to see you, sir."

" I have no time for them. Have they been paid?"

" Yes, to-night."

" Let them set off and return to their mountains, and there hide their shame, if their mountains are high enough. I have nothing more to do with them, or they with me. And now, go, Mordaunt."

" Before I go," said Mordaunt, " I have some questions and a favour to ask you, sir."

" A favour from me ?"

Mordaunt bowed.

" I come to you, my leader, my head, my father, and I ask you, master, are you contented with me ?"

Cromwell looked at him with astonishment. The young man remained immovable.

" Yes," said Cromwell; " you have done, since I knew you, not only your duty, but more than your duty ; you have been a faithful friend, a clever negotiator, and a good soldier."

" Do you remember, sir, it was my idea, the Scotch treaty, for giving up the king?"

" Yes, the idea was yours. I had not such a contempt for men before that."

" Was I not a good ambassador in France ?"

" Yes, for Mazarin has granted what I desired."

" Have I not always fought for your glory and interests ?"

" Too ardently, perhaps ; it is what I have just reproached you for ; but what is the meaning of all these questions ?"

" To tell you, my lord, that the moment has now arrived when, with a single word, you may recompense all these services."

" Oh !" said Oliver, with a slight curl of his lip, " I forgot that every service merits some reward, and that up to this moment you have served me for nothing.

" Sir, you can give me in a moment all that I look for."

"What is it? Have they offered you money? Do you wish a step? or some place in the government?"

"Sir, will you grant me my request?"

"Let us hear what it is first."

"Sir, when you have told me to obey an order, have I ever inquired what it is first? I cannot tell you."

"But a request made so formally——"

"Ah! do not fear, sir," said Mordaunt, with apparent simplicity, "it will not ruin you."

"Well, then," said Cromwell, "I promise, as far as lies in my power, to grant your request. Proceed."

"Sir, two prisoners were taken this morning; will you let me have them?"

"For their ransom? Have they, then, offered a large one?" inquired Cromwell.

"On the contrary, I think they are poor, sir."

"They are friends of yours, then?"

"Yes, sir," exclaimed Mordaunt, "they are friends, dear friends of mine, and I would lay down my life for them."

"Very well, Mordaunt," said Cromwell, pleased at having his opinion of the young man raised once more, "I will give them to you; I will not even ask who they are—do as you like with them."

"Thank you, sir!" exclaimed Mordaunt, "thank you; my life is always at your service, and should I lose it, I should still owe you something; thank you—you have, indeed, repaid me munificently for my services."

And he threw himself at the feet of Cromwell; and in spite of the efforts of the Puritan general, who did not like this almost kingly homage, he took his hand and kissed it.

"What!" said Cromwell, arresting him for a moment as he rose, "is there nothing more you wish? neither gold nor rank?"

"You have given me all you can give me, and from to-day your debt is paid."

And Mordaunt darted out of the general's tent, his heart beating, and his eyes sparkling with joy

Cromwell gazed a moment after him.

"He has killed his uncle!" he murmured. "Alas! what are my servants? Perhaps those who ask nothing, or seem to ask nothing, have asked more in the eyes of heaven than those who tax the country, and steal the bread of the poor Nobody serves me for nothing! Charles, who is my prisoner, may still have friends; but I have none!"

And with a deep-sigh he again sank into the reverie which had been interrupted by Mordaunt.

CHAPTER LVI.

MAHOMET.

WHILST Mordaunt was making his way to Cromwell's tent, D'Artagnan and Porthos had brought their prisoners to the house which had been assigned to them as their dwelling at Newcastle.

The two friends made the prisoners enter the house first, whilst they stood at the door, desiring Mousqueton to take all the four horses to the stable.

" Why don't we go in with them ?" asked Porthos.

"We must first see what the sergeant wishes us to do," replied D'Artagnan ; and he then asked the sergeant his wishes.

"We have had orders," answered the man, "to help you in taking care of your prisoners."

There could be no fault found with this arrangement; on the contrary, it seemed to be a delicate attention to be received gratefully. D'Artagnan, therefore, thanked the man, and gave him a crown piece, to drink to General Cromwell's health.

The sergeant answered that Puritans never drank, and put the crown piece into his pocket.

" Ah !" said Porthos, "what a fearful day, my dear D'Artagnan."

"What ! a fearful day, when we have to-day found our friends."

" Yes ; but under what circumstances ?"

" 'Tis true that our position is an awkward one ; but let us go in and see more clearly what is to be done."

" Things look very bad," replied Porthos ; " I understand now why Aramis advised me to strangle that horrible Mordaunt."

"Silence !" cried the Gascon ; " do not utter that name."

" But," argued Porthos, " I speak French, and they are all English."

D'Artagnan looked at Porthos with that air of wonder which a sensible man cannot help feeling at stupidity in every degree.

But, as Porthos on his side could not comprehend his astonishment, he merely pushed him indoors, saying : " Let us go in."

They found Athos in a profound despondency. Aramis looked first at Porthos and then at D'Artagnan, without speaking ; but the latter understood his meaning look.

" You want to know how we came here; 'tis easily guessed.
Mazarin sent us with a letter to General Cromwell."

" But how came you to fall into company with Mordaunt, whom
I bade you distrust ?" asked Porthos.

" Mazarin again.   Cromwell had sent him to Mazarin.   Mazarin
sent us to Cromwell.   There has been a fate in it."

" Yes, you are right, D'Artagnan—a fate which will separate
and ruin us ; so, my dear Aramis, say no more about it, and let
us prepare to submit to our destiny "

" Zounds ! let us speak about things, on the contrary !—for we
always agreed to keep on the same side ; and here we are engaged
in conflicting parties."

" Yes," added Athos, " I now ask you, D'Artagnan, what side
you are on ?   Ah ! behold for what end the wretched Mazarin has
made use of you.   Do you know in what crime you are to-day concerned ?   In the capture of a king, in his degradation, in his death."

" Oh ! oh !" cried Porthos, " do you think so ?"

" You are exaggerating, Athos ; we are not so far gone as that,"
replied the lieutenant.

" Good heavens ! we are on the very eve of it.   I say why is the
king taken prisoner ?   Those who wish to respect him as a master,
would not buy him as a slave."

" I don't say to the contrary," said D'Artagnan.   " But what's
that to us? I am here, because I am a soldier, and have to obey orders;
I have taken an oath to obey, and I do obey ; but you, who have
taken no oath, why are you here, and what cause do you serve ?"

" That most sacred in the world," said Athos ; " the cause of
misfortune, of religion, of royalty.   A friend, a wife, a daughter,
have done us the honour to call us to their aid.   We have served
them to the best of our poor means, and God will recompense the
will, and forgive the want of power : you may see matters differently,
D'Artagnan, and think otherwise.   I do not attempt to argue with
you, but I blame you."

" Hey-day !" cried D'Artagnan : " what matters it to me, after
all, if Cromwell, who's an Englishman, revolts against his king, who
is a Scotchman ?   I am myself a Frenchman, I have nothing to do
with these things—why make me responsible for them ?"

" Why you ?   Because you, D'Artagnan, a man sprung from the
ancient nobility of France, bearing a good name, carrying a sword,
have helped to give up a king to beersellers, shopkeepers, and
wagoners—Ah ! D'Artagnan ! perhaps you have done your duty
as a soldier, but, as a gentleman, I say that you are very
culpable."

D'Artagnan was chewing the stalk of a flower, unable to reply, and very uncomfortable.

" And you, Porthos—you, a gentleman in manners—in tastes—in courage, are as much to blame as D'Artagnan."

Porthos coloured, and hanging his head, said :

" Yes, yes, my dear count, I feel that you are right."

Athos rose.

" Come," he said, stretching out his hand to D'Artagnan, "come, don't be sullen, my dear son, for I have said all this to you, if not in the tone, at least with the feelings of a father. It would have been easier to me merely to have thanked you for preserving my life, and not to have uttered a word of all this."

" Doubtless, doubtless, Athos. But this is it—you have sentiments, the devil knows what, such as every one can't have. Who could suppose that a sensible man could leave his house—France —his ward—a charming youth—for we saw him in the camp—to fly to the aid of a rotten, worm-eaten royalty, which is going to crumble one of these days like an old cask ? The sentiments you sport are certainly fine—so fine, that they are superhuman."

" However that may be, D'Artagnan," replied Athos, without falling into the snare which his Gascon friend had prepared for him by an appeal to his parental love, " whatsoever may be, you know, in the bottom of your heart, that it is true ; but I am coming to dispute with my superiors. D'Artagnan, I am your prisoner —treat me as such."

D'Artagnan said nothing ; but, after having gnawed the flower-stalk, he began to bite his nails. At last,—

" Do you imagine," he resumed, " that they mean to kill you ? And wherefore should they do so ? What interest have they in your death ? Moreover, you are *our* prisoners."

" Fool !" cried Aramis ; " knowest thou not, then, Mordaunt ? I have merely exchanged with him one look, but that look convinced me that we were doomed."

" The truth is, I'm very sorry that I did not strangle him as you advised me to do," said Porthos.

" Stop," cried Athos, extending his hand to one of the grated windows by which the room was lighted ; " you will soon know what to expect, for here he is."

In fact, looking at the place to which Athos pointed, D'Artagnan saw a cavalier coming towards the house full gallop.

It was Mordaunt.

D'Artagnan rushed out of the room.

Porthos wanted to follow him.

"Stay," said D'Artagnan, "and do not come till you hear me beat like a drum with my fingers upon the door."

When Mordaunt arrived opposite the house he saw D'Artagnan upon the threshold, and the soldiers lying on the grass, here and there, with their arms.

"Hallo!" he cried, "are the prisoners still there?"

"Yes, sir," answered the sergeant, uncovering his head.

"'Tis well: order four men to conduct them to my lodging."

Four men prepared to do so.

"What do you want, sir?" asked D'Artagnan.

"Sir," replied Mordaunt, "I have ordered the two prisoners that we made this morning to be conducted to my lodging."

"Wherefore, sir? Excuse curiosity, but I wish to be enlightened on the subject."

"Because these prisoners, sir, are at my disposal, and I choose to dispose of them as I like."

"Allow me—allow me, sir," said D'Artagnan, "to observe you are in error. The prisoners belong to those who took them, and not to those who only saw them taken. You might have taken Lord Winter—who, 'tis said, is your uncle—prisoner, but you preferred killing him; 'tis well—we, that is, Monsieur de Valon and I, could have killed our prisoners—we preferred taking them."

Mordaunt's very lips were white with rage.

D'Artagnan now saw that affairs were growing worse, and he beat the guard's march upon the door. At the first beat Porthos rushed out, and stood on the other side of the door.

This movement was observed by Mordaunt.

"Sir!" he thus addressed D'Artagnan, "your resistance is useless—these prisoners have just been given me by my illustrious patron, Oliver Cromwell."

These words struck D'Artagnan like a thunderbolt. The blood mounted to his temples, his eyes became dim; he saw from what source the ferocious hopes of the young man arose. He put his hand to the hilt of his sword.

As to Porthos, he looked inquiringly at D'Artagnan.

This look of Porthos's made the Gascon regret that he had summoned the brute force of his friend to aid him in an affair which seemed to require chiefly cunning.

"Violence," he said to himself, "would spoil all; D'Artagnan, my friend, prove to this young serpent that thou art not only stronger, but more subtle than he is."

"Ah!" he said, making a low bow, "why did you not begin by saying that, Monsieur Mordaunt? What! are you sent by General Oliver Cromwell, the most illustrious captain of his age?"

"I have this instant left him,' replied Mordaunt, alighting, in order to give his horse to a soldier to hold.

"Why did you not say so at once, my dear sir! all England is with Cromwell; and since you ask for my prisoners, I bend, sir, to your wishes. They are yours; take them."

Mordaunt, delighted, advanced—Porthos looking at D'Artagnan with open-mouthed astonishment. Then D'Artagnan trod on his foot, and Porthos began to understand that this was all acting.

Mordaunt put his foot on the first step of the door, and, with his hat in his hand, prepared to pass by the two friends, motioning to the four men to follow him.

"But pardon me," he said, stopping short, "since the illustrious general has given my prisoners into your hands, he has of course confirmed that act in writing."

Mordaunt stood still, then retreated—cast a terrible glance at D'Artagnan, which was answered by the most amicable and friendly mien that could be imagined.

"Speak out, sir," said Mordaunt.

"Monsieur de Valon, yonder, is rich, and has forty thousand francs yearly, so he does not care about money. I do not speak for him, but for myself."

"Well, sir? What more?"

"Well—I—I'm not rich. In Gascony 'tis no dishonour, sir, nobody is rich; and Henry IV., of glorious memory, who was the king of the Gascons, as his majesty Philip IV. is the king of the Spaniards, never had a penny in his pocket."

"Go on, sir. I see where you wish to come to; and if it is what I think that stops you, I can obviate that difficulty."

"Ah, I knew well," said the Gascon, "that you were a man of talent. Well, here's the case; here's where the saddle hurts me, as we French say. I am an officer of fortune, nothing else; I have nothing but what my sword brings me in—that is to say, more blows than bank notes. Now, on taking prisoners this morning two Frenchmen, who seemed to me of high birth—in short, two knights of the Garter—I said to myself, my fortune is made."

Mordaunt, completely deceived by the wordy civility of D'Artagnan, smiled like a man who understands perfectly the reasons given him, and said:

"I shall have the order signed directly, sir, and with it two thousand pistoles; meanwhile, let me take these men away."

"No," replied D'Artagnan; "what signifies a delay of half an hour? I am a man of order, sir; let us do things in order."

"Nevertheless," replied Mordaunt, "I could compel you; I command here."

"Ah, sir !" said D'Artagnan, "I see that although we have had the honour of travelling in your company, you do not know us. We are gentlemen ; we are, both of us, able to kill you and your eight men ; we two only. For heaven's sake don't be obstinate, for when others are obstinate, I am obstinate likewise, and then I become ferocious and headstrong ; and there's my friend, who is even more headstrong and ferocious than I am ; besides, we are sent here by Cardinal Mazarin, and at this moment represent both the king and the cardinal, and are therefore, as ambassadors, able to act with impunity, a thing that General Oliver Cromwell, who is assuredly as great a politician as he is a general, is quite a man to understand. Ask him then for the written order. What will that cost you, my dear Monsieur Mordaunt ?"

"Yes, the written order," said Porthos, who now began to comprehend what D'Artagnan was aiming at, "nothing but that will satisfy us."

However anxious Mordaunt was to have recourse to violence, he quite understood the reasons that D'Artagnan gave him ; and, besides, completely ignorant of the friendship which existed between the four Frenchmen, all his uneasiness disappeared when he heard of the plausible motive of the ransom. He decided, therefore, not only to fetch the order, but the two thousand pistoles at which he estimated the prisoners. He therefore mounted his horse, and disappeared.

"Good !" thought D'Artagnan ; "a quarter of an hour to go to the tent, a quarter of an hour to return ;" then turning, without the least change of countenance to Porthos, he said, looking him full in the face, " Friend Porthos, listen to this : first, not a syllable to either of our friends about the service we are going to render them."

"Very well ; I understand."

"Go to the stable ; you will find Mousqueton there. Saddle your horses, put your pistols in your saddle-bags, take out the horses, and lead them to the street below this, so that there will be nothing to do but to mount them ; all the rest is my business."

Porthos made no remark, but obeyed, with the sublime confidence that he had in his friend. He then proceeded, with his usual calm gait, to the stable, and went into the very midst of the soldiery, who, Frenchman as he was, could not help admiring his height and the strength of his powerful limbs.

At the corner of the street he met Mousqueton and took him with him.

D'Artagnan, meantime, went into the house, whistling a tune which he had begun before Porthos went away. "My dear Athos, I have reflected on your arguments, and am convinced. I am sorry to have had anything to do with this matter. As you say Mazarin is a knave. I have resolved to fly with you; not a word; be ready; your swords are in the corner; do not forget them, they are, in many circumstances, very useful; there's Porthos' purse, too."

He put it into his pocket. The two friends were perfectly stupefied.

"Well—pray is there anything to be so surprised at?" he said. "I was blind; Athos made me see clearly; that's all. Come here."

The two friends went near him.

"Do you see that street? There are the horses. Go out by the door, turn to the right, jump into your saddles, all will be right; don't be uneasy at anything except mistaking the signal. That will be the signal when I call out 'Mahomet!'"

"But give us your word that you will come too, D'Artagnan," said Athos

"I swear I will, by heaven!"

"'Tis settled," said Aramis; "at the cry 'Mahomet,' we go out, upset all that stands in our way, run to our horses, jump into our saddles, spur them—is that all?"

"Exactly."

"See, Aramis, as I have told you, D'Artagnan is the best of us all," said Athos.

"Very true," replied the Gascon, "but I always run away from compliments. Don't forget the signal—Mahomet!" and he went out as he came in, whistling the air that he had been whistling when he came in.

The soldiers were playing or sleeping; two of them were singing in a corner, out of tune, the psalm—"On the rivers of Babylon."

D'Artagnan called the sergeant. "My dear friend, General Cromwell has sent Monsieur Mordaunt to fetch me. Guard the prisoners well, I beg of you."

The sergeant made a sign, as much as to say he did not under-derstand French, and D'Artagnan tried to make him comprehend him by signs and gestures. Then he went into the stable; he found the five horses and his own, among others, saddled. He gave his instructions, and Porthos and Mousqueton went to their post according to his directions.

Then D'Artagnan, being alone, struck a light and lighted a small bit of the tinder, mounted his horse, and stopped at the door, in the midst of the soldiers　There, caressing, as he pretended, the animal with his hand, he put this bit of tinder, while burning, into his ear.

It was necessary to be as good a horseman as he was to risk such a scheme; for hardly had the animal felt the burning tinder than he uttered a cry of pain, and reared and jumped as if he had been mad.

The soldiers, whom he nearly trampled upon, ran away from him.

"Help! help!" cried D'Artagnan; "stop, my horse has the staggers."

In an instant blood came from his eyes, and he was white with foam.

"Help!" cried D'Artagnan.　"What! will you let me be killed? By Mahomet!"

Scarcely had he uttered this cry than the door opened, and Athos and Aramis rushed out.　The coast, owing to the Gascon's stratagem, was clear.

"The prisoners are escaping! the prisoners are escaping!" cried the sergeant.

"Stop! stop!" cried D'Artagnan, giving rein to his famous steed, who, darting forth, overturned several men.

"Stop! stop!" cried the soldiers, and ran for their arms.

But the prisoners were on their saddles, and lost no time, hastening to the nearest gate.

In the middle of the street they saw Grimaud and Blaisois, who were coming to find their masters.　With one wave of his hand, Athos made Grimaud, who followed the little troop, understand everything, and they passed on like a whirlwind, D'Artagnan still directing them from behind with his voice.

They passed through the gate like apparitions, without the guards thinking of detaining them, and reached the open country.

All this while the soldiers were calling out "Stop! stop!" and the sergeant, who began to see that he was the victim of an artifice, was almost in a frenzy of despair: whilst all this was going on, a cavalier in full gallop was seen approaching. It was Mordaunt with the order in his hand.

"The prisoners!" he exclaimed, jumping off his horse.

The sergeant had not the courage to reply; he showed him the open door and the empty room.　Mordaunt darted to the steps— understood all, uttered a cry as if his very heart were pierced, and fell fainting on the stone steps.

CHAPTER LVII.

IN WHICH IT IS SHOWN THAT UNDER THE MOST TRYING CIR-
CUMSTANCES NOBLE NATURES NEVER LOSE THEIR COURAGE,
NOR GOOD STOMACHS THEIR APPETITES.

THE little troop, without looking behind them, or exchanging a
single word, fled at a rapid gallop, crossing on foot a little stream,
of which none of them knew the name, and leaving on their left a
town, which Athos declared to be Durham. At last they came in
sight of a small wood, and spurring their horses afresh, they rode
in the direction of it.

As soon as they had disappeared behind a green curtain sufficiently thick to conceal them from the sight of any who might be
in pursuit of them, they drew up to hold a council together. The
two grooms held the horses, that they might take rest without
being unsaddled, and Grimaud was posted as sentinel.

"Come, first of all," said Athos to D'Artagnan, "my friend,
that I may shake hands with you—you, our rescuer; you, the true
hero among us all."

"Athos is right, and you have my admiration," said Aramis, in
his turn pressing his hand; "to what are you not equal? with
superior intelligence, and an infallible eye; an arm of iron, and
an enterprising mind!"

"Now," said the Gascon, "that is all well, I accept for Porthos
and myself everything—thanks and embracings—we have plenty
of time to lose."

The two friends, recalled by D'Artagnan to what was also due
to Porthos, pressed his hand in their turn.

"And now," said Athos, "it is not our plan to run anywhere,
and like madmen; but we must arrange some plan. What shall
we do?"

"What are we going to do, i'faith? It is not very difficult to
say!"

"Tell us then, D'Artagnan."

"We are going to reach the nearest sea-port, unite our little
resources, hire a vessel, and return to France. As for me, I will
give my last sou for it. Life is the greatest treasure, and speaking
candidly, ours is only held by a thread."

"What do you say to this, De Valon?"

"I," said Porthos—"I am entirely of D'Artagnan's opinion;
this is a beastly country—this England."

"You are quite decided then to leave it?" asked Athos of D'Artagnan

"Egad! I don't see what is to keep me here."

A glance was exchanged between Athos and Aramis.

"Go, then, my friends," said the former, sighing.

"How, go then?" exclaimed D'Artagnan. "Let us go, you mean!"

"No, my friend," said Athos, "you must leave us."

"Leave you!" cried D'Artagnan, quite bewildered at this unexpected announcement.

"Bah!" said Porthos, "why separate, since we are all together?"

"Because you can, and you ought, to return to France; your mission is accomplished, but ours is not."

"Your mission is not accomplished!" exclaimed D'Artagnan, looking in astonishment at Athos.

"No, my good fellow," replied Athos, in his gentle, but decided voice, "we came here to defend King Charles; we have but ill defended him, it remains for us to save him."

"To save the king?" said D'Artagnan, looking at Aramis as he had looked at Athos.

Aramis contented himself by making a sign with his head.

D'Artagnan's countenance took an expression of the deepest compassion; he began to think he had to do with two madmen.

"You cannot be speaking seriously, Athos?" said he; "the king is surrounded by an army, which is conducting him to London. This army is commanded by a butcher, or the son of a butcher—it matters little—Colonel Harrison. His Majesty, I can assure you, is about to be tried on his arrival in London; I have heard enough from the lips of Mr. Oliver Cromwell to know what to expect."

A second look was exchanged between Athos and Aramis.

"And when his trial is ended, there will be no delay in putting the sentence into execution," continued D'Artagnan.

"And to what penalty do you think the king will be condemned?" asked Athos.

"To the penalty of death, I much fear; they have gone too far for him to pardon them, and there is nothing left to them but one thing—and that is to kill him. Do you not know Oliver Cromwell's speech when he came to Paris, and when he was shown the dungeon at Vincennes where Monsieur de Vendôme was imprisoned?"

"What was the speech?" asked Porthos.

"Princes must be knocked on the head."

"I remember it," said Athos.

"And you fancy he will not put his maxim into execution, now that he has hold of the king?'

"On the contrary, I am certain he will do so; but then there is the more reason why we must not abandon the august head so threatened."

"Athos, you are becoming mad."

"Well, you know beforehand that you must perish!" said D'Artagnan.

"We fear so, and our only regret is, to die so far from you both."

"What will you do in a foreign land—an enemy's country?"

"I have travelled in England when young—I speak English like an Englishman—and Aramis, too, knows something of the language. Ah! if we had you, my friends! With you, D'Artagnan, with you, Porthos—all four, and reunited for the first time for twenty years—we would dare, not only England, but the three kingdoms together!"

"And did you promise the queen," resumed D'Artagnan, petulantly, "to storm the Tower of London with a hundred thousand soldiers, to fight victoriously against the wishes of a nation and the ambition of a man, and when that man is called Cromwell? Do not exaggerate your duty. In Heaven's name, my dear Athos, do not make a useless sacrifice. When I see you merely, you look like a reasonable being; when you speak, I seem to have to do with a madman. Come, Porthos, join me; say, frankly, what do you think of this business?"

"Nothing good," replied Porthos.

"Come," continued D'Artagnan, who, irritated, that instead of listening to him, Athos seemed to be attending to his own thoughts, "you have never found yourself the worse for my advice. Well, then, believe me, Athos, your mission is ended, and ended nobly—return to France with us."

"Friend," said Athos, "our resolution is unchangeable."

"Then you have some other motive unknown to us?"

Athos smiled, and D'Artagnan struck his heels in anger, and muttered the most convincing reasons that he could discover; but to all these reasons Athos contented himself by replying with a calm sweet smile, and Aramis by nodding his head.

"Very well," cried D'Artagnan at last, furious,—"very well—since you wish it, let us leave our bones in this beggarly land, where it is always cold—where the fine weather comes after a fog, and a fog after rain—and the rain after the deluge—where the sun represents the moon, and the moon a cream cheese;—in truth, whether we die here or elsewhere, matters little, since we must die."

" Only reflect, my good fellow," said Athos, "it is but dying rather sooner."

" Pooh ! a little sooner, or a little later, that isn't worth quar-relling about."

" But your future career, D'Artagnan ?—your ambition, Por-thos ?"

" Our future, our ambition !" replied D'Artagnan, with feverish volubility; "need we think of that since we are to save the king? The king saved—we shall assemble our friends together—we will head the Puritans — re-conquer England; we shall re-enter London—place him securely on his throne——"

" And he will make us dukes and peers," said Porthos, whose eyes sparkled with joy at this imaginary prospect.

" Or he will forget us," added D'Artagnan.

" Well ! then," said Athos, offering his hand to D'Artagnan.

" 'Tis settled," replied D'Artagnan. " I find England a charming country, and I stay—but only on one condition."

" What is it ?"

" That I am not forced to learn English !"

" Well then, now," said Athos, triumphantly, "I swear to you, my friend, by the God who hears us, I believe that there is a power watching over us, and I hope we shall all four meet in France."

" So be it !" said D'Artagnan, " but I—I confess I have quite a contrary conviction."

" Our good D'Artagnan," said Aramis, "represents among us the opposition in parliament, which says always *no*, and does always *aye*."

" But which in the meantime saves the country," added Athos.

" Well, now that everything is decided," cried Porthos, rubbing his hands, " suppose we think of dinner ! It seems to me that in the most critical positions of our lives we have always dined."

" Oh ! yes, speak of dinner in a country where for a feast they eat boiled mutton, and where as a treat they drink beer. What the devil did you come to such a country for, Athos ?"

" But, I forgot," added the Gascon, smiling, "pardon, I forgot you are no longer Athos ; but never mind, let us hear your plan for dinner, Porthos."

" My plan !"

" Yes ; have you a plan ?"

" No ! I am hungry, that is all."

" *Pardieu*, if that is all, I am hungry too ; but it is not every-thing to be hungry ; one must find something to eat, unless we browse on the grass, like our horses——"

"Ah !" exclaimed Aramis, who was not quite so indifferent to the good things of the earth as Athos, "do you remember, when we were at Gravesend, the beautiful oysters that we ate ?"

"And the legs of mutton of the salt marshes," said Porthos, smacking his lips.

"But," suggested D'Artagnan, "have we not our friend Mousqueton, he who managed for us so well at Chantilly, Porthos ?"

"By the bye," said Porthos, "have we Mousqueton, but since he has been steward, he has become very heavy ; never mind, let us call him : and to make sure that he will reply agreeably— Here ! Mouston," cried Porthos.

Mouston appeared, with a very piteous face.

"What is the matter, my dear Mr. Mouston?" asked D'Artagnan. "Are you ill ?"

"Sir, I am very hungry !" replied Mouston.

"Well, it is just for that reason that we have called you, my good Mr. Mouston. Could you not procure us a few of those nice little rabbits and some of those delicious partridges, of which you used to make fricassees at the hotel——? Faith, I do not remember the name of the hotel."

"At the hotel of——," said Porthos, "by my faith—nor do I remember it either."

"It does not matter ; and a few of those bottles of old Burgundy wine, which cured your master so quickly of his sprain !"

"Alas ! sir," said Mousqueton, "I much fear that what you ask for are very rare things in this frightful country, and I think we should do better to go and seek hospitality from the owner of a little house that we see at the extremity of the wood."

"How ! is there a house in the neighbourhood?" asked D'Artagnan.

"Yes, sir !" replied Mousqueton.

"Well, let us, as you say, go and ask a dinner from the master of that house. What is your opinion, gentlemen, and does not Mr. Mouston's suggestion appear to you full of sense ?"

"Oh ! oh !" said Aramis, "suppose the master is a Puritan ?"

"So much the better, *Mordioux !*" replied D'Artagnan ; "if he is a Puritan, we will inform him of the capture of the King, and in honour of the news he will kill for us his white hens."

"But if he should be a cavalier ?" said Porthos.

"In that case, we will put on an air of mourning, and we will pluck his black fowls."

"You are very happy," exclaimed Athos, laughing in spite of

himself, at the sally of the irresistible Gascon ; "for you see the bright side of everything."

"What would you have ?" said D'Artagnan. "I come from a land where there is not a cloud in the sky."

"It is not like this, then," said Porthos, stretching out his hand to assure himself whether a sensation of freshness which he had just felt on his cheek was not really caused by a drop of rain.

"Come, come," said D'Artagnan, "more reason why we should start on our journey—holloa, Grimaud !"

Grimaud appeared.

"Well, Grimaud, my friend, have you seen anything?" asked the Gascon.

"Nothing !" replied Grimaud.

"Those idiots !" cried Porthos. "they have not even pursued us. Oh ! if we had been in their place !"

"Yes, they are wrong," said D'Artagnan. "I would willingly have said two words to Mordaunt in this little Thebes. See what a nice place for bringing down a man properly"

"I think, decidedly," observed Aramis, "gentlemen, that the son is not so bad as his mother."

"What, my good fellow !" replied Athos; "wait awhile, we have scarcely left him two hours ago—he does not know yet in what direction we came, nor where we are. We may say that he is not equal to his mother when we put foot in France, if we are not poisoned nor killed before then."

"Meanwhile, let us dine," suggested Porthos.

"I' faith, yes !" said Athos, "for I am very hungry."

"Look out for the black fowls !" cried Aramis.

And the four friends, guided by Mousqueton, took up the way towards the house, already almost restored to their former gaiety; for they were now, as Athos had said, all four united and of one mind.

CHAPTER LVIII.

RESPECT TO FALLEN MAJESTY.

As our fugitives approached the house, they found the ground cut up, as if a considerable body of horsemen had preceded them. Before the door, the traces were yet more apparent ; these horsemen, whoever they might be, had halted there.

"Egad !" cried D'Artagnan, " it's quite clear that the king and his escort have been by here."

He pushed open the door, and found the first room empty and deserted.

" Well !" cried Porthos.

" I can see nobody," said D'Artagnan. " Aha !"

" What ?"

" Blood !"

At this word the three friends leapt from their horses, and entered. D'Artagnan had already opened the door, of the second room, and, from the expression of his face, it was clear that he there beheld some extraordinary object.

The three friends drew near, and discovered a young man stretched on the ground, and bathed in a pool of blood. It was evident that he had attempted to regain his bed, but had not had the strength to do so.

Athos, who imagined that he saw him move, was the first to go up to him.

" Well ?" inquired D'Artagnan.

" Well, if he is dead," said Athos, " he has not been so long, for he is still warm. But no, his heart is beating. Eh ! there, my friend."

The wounded man heaved a sigh. D'Artagnan took some water in the hollow of his hand, and threw it upon his face. The man opened his eyes, made an effort to raise his head, and fell back again. The wound was in the top of the skull, and the blood was flowing copiously.

Aramis dipped a cloth in some water, and applied it to the gash. Again the wounded man opened his eyes, and looked in astonishment at these strangers, who appeared to pity him.

" You are among friends," said Athos, in English; " so cheer up, and tell us, if you have the strength to do so, what has happened."

" The king," muttered the wounded man, " the king is a prisoner."

" Make your mind easy," resumed Athos, " we are all faithful servants of his majesty."

" Is what you tell me true ?" asked the wounded man.

" On our honour as gentlemen."

" Then I may tell you all. I am the brother of Parry, his majesty's lackey."

Athos and Aramis remembered that this was the name by which De Winter had called the man whom they had found in the passage of the king's tent.

" We know him," said Athos ; " he never left the king."

" Yes, that is he; well, he thought of me, when he saw that

the king was taken, and as they were passing before the house here, he begged in the king's name that they would stop, as the king was hungry. They brought him into this room, and placed sentinels at the doors and windows. Parry knew this room, as he had often been to see me when the king was at Newcastle. He knew that there was a trap-door communicating with a cellar, from which one could get into the orchard. He made me a sign, which I understood, but the king's guards must have noticed it, and put themselves on their guard. I went out, as if to fetch wood, passed through the subterranean passage into the cellar, and while Parry was gently bolting the door, pushed up the board, and beckoned to the king to follow me. Alas! he would not. But Parry clasped his hands and implored him, and at last he agreed. I went on first, quite delighted. The king was a few steps behind me, when suddenly I saw something rise up in front of me, like a huge shadow. I wanted to cry out to warn the king, but the same moment I felt a blow as if the house was falling on my head, and fell insensible. When I came to myself again, I was stretched in the same place. I dragged myself as far as the yard. The king and his escort were gone."

"And now what can we do for you?" asked Athos.

"Help me to get on to the bed; that will ease me."

They helped him on to the bed, and, calling Grimaud to dress his wound, returned to the outer room to consult.

"Now," said Aramis, "we know how the matter stands. The king and his escort have gone this way; we had better take the opposite direction, eh?"

"Yes," said Porthos; "if we follow the escort we shall find everything devoured, and die of hunger. What a confounded country this England is! This is the first time I shall have lost my dinner, and it's my best meal."

"What do you say about it, D'Artagnan," said Athos.

"Just the contrary to Aramis."

"What! follow the escort?" cried Porthos, quite alarmed.

"No, but join them. They will never look for us among the Puritans!"

"A good idea," said Athos, "they will think we want to leave England, and seek us in the ports. Meanwhile we shall reach London with the king, and, once there, it is not difficult to conceal one's self."

"But," said Aramis, "sha'n't we be suspected by Colonel Harrison?"

"Egad!" cried D'Artagnan, "he's just the man I count upon.

Colonel Harrison is one of our friends. We have met him twice at General Cromwell's. He knows that we were sent from France by Monsieur Mazarin; he will consider us as brothers. Besides, is he not a butcher's son! Well, then, Porthos will show him how to knock down an ox with a blow of the fist; and I, how to trip up a bull by taking him by the horns. That will ensure his confidence."

Athos smiled.

At this moment Grimaud came in. He had staunched the wound and the man was better.

The little troop recommenced their march, and, at the end of two hours, perceived a considerable body of horsemen about half a league ahead.

"My dear friends," said D'Artagnan, "give your swords to Monsieur Mouston, who will return them to you in proper time and place, and do not forget you are our prisoners."

It was not long ere they joined the escort. The king was in the front, surrounded by troopers, and when he saw Athos and Aramis a glow of pleasure lighted up his pale cheeks.

D'Artagnan passed to the head of the column, and, leaving his friends under the guard of Porthos, went straight to Harrison, who recognised him as having met him at Cromwell's, and received him as politely as a man of his breeding and disposition could. It turned out as D'Artagnan had foreseen. The colonel neither had nor could have any suspicion.

They halted for the king to dine. This time, however, due precautions were taken to prevent any attempt at escape. In the large room of the hotel a small table was placed for him, and a large one for the officers.

"Will you dine with me?" asked Harrison of D'Artagnan.

"'Gad, I should be very happy, but I have my companion, Monsieur de Valon, and the two prisoners, whom I cannot leave. Let us manage it better. Have a table set for us in a corner, and hand us whatever you like from yours."

"Good," answered Harrison.

The table at which the Puritan officers were seated was round, and whether by chance or a coarse intention, Harrison had his back turned to the king.

The king saw the four gentlemen come in, but appeared to take no notice of them.

They sat down in such a manner as to turn their backs upon nobody.

"I'faith, colonel," said D'Artagnan, "we are very grateful for your gracious invitation; for, without you, we ran the risk of going without dinner, as we have without breakfast. My friend here, Monsieur de Valon, shares my gratitude, for he was particularly hungry."

"And I am so still," said Porthos, bowing to Harrison.

"And how," said Harrison, laughing, "did this serious calamity of going without breakfast happen to you?"

"In a very simple manner, colonel," said D'Artagnan. "I was in a hurry to join you, and took the road you had already gone by. You can understand our disappointment when, arriving at a pretty little house on the skirts of a wood, which at a distance had quite a gay appearance with its red roof and green shutters, we found nothing but a poor wretch bathed——Ah! colonel, pay my respects to the officer of yours who struck that blow."

"Yes," said Harrison laughing, and looking over at one of the officers seated at his table. "When Groslow undertakes this kind of thing, there's no need to go over the ground after him."

"Ah! it's that gentleman?" said D'Artagnan, bowing to the officer. "I am sorry he does not speak French, that I might offer him my compliments."

"I am ready to receive and return them, sir," said the officer, in pretty good French. "For I resided three years in Paris."

"Then, sir, allow me to assure you that your blow was so well directed that you have nearly killed your man."

"Nearly? I thought it was quite," said Groslow.

"No. It was a very near thing, but he is not dead."

As he said this, D'Artagnan gave a glance at Parry, who was standing in front of the king, to show him that the news was meant for him.

The king, too, who had listened in the greatest agony, now breathed again.

"Hang it," said Groslow, "I thought I had succeeded better. If it were not so far from here to the house, I would return and finish him."

"And you would do well, if you are afraid of his recovering; for you know, if a wound in the head does not kill at once, it is cured in a week."

And D'Artagnan threw a second glance towards Parry, on whose face such an expression of joy was manifested that Charles stretched out his hand to him, smiling.

Parry bent over his master's hand, and kissed it respectfully.

"I have a great desire to drink the king's health," said Athos.

"Let me propose it, then," said D'Artagnan.

Porthos looked at D'Artagnan, quite amazed at the resources with which his companion's Gascon sharpness continually supplied him.

D'Artagnan took his tin cup, filled it, and rose.

"Gentlemen," said he, "let us drink to him who presides at our repast. Here's to our colonel, and let him know that we are always at his commands, as far as London, and further."

And as D'Artagnan, as he spoke, looked at Harrison, the colonel imagined the toast was for himself. He rose and bowed to the four friends, whose eyes were fixed on Charles, while Harrison emptied his glass without the slightest misgiving.

The king, in return, looked at the four gentlemen, and drank, with a smile full of nobleness and gratitude.

"Come, gentlemen," cried Harrison, quite regardless of his illustrious captive, "let us be off."

"Where do we sleep, colonel?"

"At Thirsk," replied Harrison.

"Parry," said the king, rising too, "my horse; I desire to go to Thirsk."

"Egad," said D'Artagnan to Athos; "your king has thoroughly taken me, and I am quite at his service."

"If what you say is sincere," replied Athos, "he will never reach London."

"How so?"

"Because, before then, we shall have carried him off."

"Well, this time, Athos," said D'Artagnan, "upon my word you are mad."

"Have you some plan in your head, then?" asked Aramis.

"Ay," said Porthos, "the thing would not be impossible with a good plan."

"I have none," said Athos, "but D'Artagnan will discover one."

D'Artagnan shrugged his shoulders and went on.

CHAPTER LIX.

D'ARTAGNAN HITS ON A PLAN.

As night closed in they arrived at Thirsk.

D'Artagnan was thoughtful, and seemed for the moment to have lost his usual loquacity. Porthos, who could never see anything that was not self-evident, talked to him as usual. He replied in monosyllables, and Athos and Aramis looked significantly at one another.

Next morning, D'Artagnan was the first to rise. He had gone down to the stables, had already had a look at the horses, and given all the necessary orders for the day, while Athos and Aramis were still in bed, and Porthos snoring.

At eight o'clock, the march was resumed in the same order as the night before, except that D'Artagnan left his friends and began to renew the acquaintance which he had already struck up with Monsieur Groslow.

"Really, sir," D'Artagnan said to him, "I am happy to find some one with whom to talk in my own poor tongue. My friend, Monsieur de Valon, is of a very melancholy disposition—so much so, that one can scarcely get three words a day out of him. As for our two prisoners, you can imagine that they are but little in the humour for conversation."

"They are hot Royalists," said Groslow.

"The more reason they should be sulky with us for having captured the Stuart, for whom, I hope, you are preparing a pretty trial."

"Why," said Groslow, "that's just what we are taking him to London for."

"And you don't lose sight of him, I presume?"

"I should think not, indeed. You see he has a truly royal escort."

"Aye, there's no fear in the daytime; but at night."

"We double our precautions."

"And what method of surveillance do you employ?"

"Eight men remain constantly in his room."

"The deuce, he is well guarded then. But, besides these eight men, you doubtless place some guard outside?"

"Oh, no! Just think. What would you have two men without arms do against eight armed men?"

"Two men—how do you mean?"

"Yes, the king and his lackey."

"Oh! then they allow the lackey to remain with him?"

"Yes; Stuart begged for this favour, and Harrison consented. Under pretence that he's a king, it appears he cannot dress or undress without assistance."

"Really, captain," said D'Artagnan, determined to continue on the laudatory tack on which he had commenced—"the more I listen to you, the more surprised I am at the easy and elegant manner in which you speak French. You have lived three years in Paris? May I ask what you were doing there?"

"My father, who is a merchant, placed me with his correspondent, who, in turn, sent his son to my father's."

"Were you pleased with Paris, sir?"

"Yes, but you are much in want of a revolution like ours; not against your king, who is merely a child, but against that lazar of an Italian, the queen's favourite."

"Ah! I am quite of your opinion, sir; and we should soon make an end of Mazarin, if we had only a dozen officers like yourself, without prejudices, vigilant, and incorruptible."

"But," said the officer, "I thought you were in his service, and that it was he who had sent you to General Cromwell?"

"That is to say I am in the king's service, and that knowing he wanted to send some one to England, I solicited the appointment, so great was my desire to know the man of genius who now governs the three kingdoms. So that when he proposed to us to draw our swords in honour of Old England, you see how we snatched at the proposition."

"Yes, I know that you charged by the side of Mordaunt."

"On his right and left, sir. Ah! that's another brave and excellent young man."

"Do you know him?" asked the officer.

"Yes, very well. Monsieur de Valon and myself came from France with him."

"It appears, too, you kept him waiting a long time at Boulogne."

"What would you have? I was like you, and had a king in keeping."

"Aha!" said Groslow; "what king?"

"Our own, to be sure—the little one. Louis XIV."

"And how long had you to take care of him?"

"Three nights; and, by my troth, I shall always remember those three nights with pleasure."——"How do you mean?"

"I mean that my friends, officers in the guards and 'Mousquetaires,' came to keep me company, and we passed the night in eating and play."

"Ah! true," said the Englishman, with a sigh, "you Frenchmen are jovial boon companions."

"And don't you play, too, when you are on guard?"

"Never," said the Englishman.

"In that case you must be horribly bored, and I pity you."

"The fact is, I look to my turn for keeping guard with horror. It's tiresome work to keep awake a whole night."

"Yes; but with a jovial partner, and the gold and dice rolling on the table, the night passes like a dream. You don't like playing, then?"

"On the contrary, I do."

"Lansquenet, for instance?"

"I'm devoted to it. I used to play almost every night in France."

"And since your return to England?"

"I have not handled a single card or dice-box."

"I sincerely pity you," said D'Artagnan, with an air of profound compassion.

"Look here!" said the Englishman.——"Well?"

"To-morrow I am on guard."

"In Stuart's room?"

"Yes; come and pass the night with me?"

"Impossible!"

"Impossible! why so?"

"I play with Monsieur de Valon every night. Sometimes we don't go to bed at all."

"Well, what of that?"

"Why, he would be annoyed if I did not play with him?"

"Does he play well?"

"I have seen him lose as much as two thousand pistoles— laughing all the while till the tears rolled down."

"Bring him with you, then."

"But how about our prisoners?"

"Let your servants guard them."

"Yes, and give them a chance of escaping," said D'Artagnan. "Why, one of them is a rich lord from Touraine, and the other a knight of Malta, of noble family. We have arranged the ransom of each of them—£2000 on arriving in France."

"Aha!" exclaimed Groslow. "But come," he continued, "are they dangerous men?"

"In what respect?"

"Are they capable of attempting violence?"

D'Artagnan burst out laughing at the idea.

"Well, then," said Groslow, "bring them with you."

"But really——" said D'Artagnan.

"I have eight men on guard, you know. Four of them can guard the king, and the other four your prisoners. I shall manage it somehow, you will see."

"But," said D'Artagnan, "now I think of it—what is to prevent our beginning to-night?"

" Nothing at all," said Groslow.

" Just so. Come to us this evening, and to-morrow we'll return your visit."

" Capital ! This evening with you, to-morrow at Stuart's, the next day with me."

" You see one can lead a merry life everywhere," said D'Artagnan.

" Yes, with Frenchmen, and Frenchmen like you."

" And Monsieur de Valon," added the other. " You will see what a fellow he is ; a man who nearly killed Mazarin between two doors. They employ him because they are afraid of him. Ah, there he is, calling me now. You'll excuse me, I know."

They exchanged bows, and D'Artagnan returned to his companions.

" What on earth can you have been saying to that bull-dog ?" exclaimed Porthos.

" My dear fellow, don't speak like that of Monsieur Groslow. He's one of my intimate friends."

" One of your friends !" cried Porthos; "this butcherer of peasants !"

" Hush ! my dear Porthos. Monsieur Groslow is perhaps rather quick, it's true, but at bottom I have discovered good qualities in him. He is conceited and stupid."

Porthos opened his eyes in amazement; Athos and Aramis looked at one another and smiled.

" But," continued D'Artagnan, " you shall judge of him for yourself. He is coming to play with us this evening."

" Oho !" said Porthos, his eyes glistening at the news. " Is he rich ?"

" He's the son of one of the wealthiest merchants in London."

" And knows lansquenet ?"

" He adores it."

" Basset ?"

" His mania."

" Biribi ?"

" He revels in it."

" Good," said Porthos ; " we shall pass an agreeable evening."

" The more so, as it will be the prelude to a better."

" How so ?"

" We invite him to play to-night ; he has invited us in return for to-morrow. But wait. To-night we stop at Derby ; and if there is a bottle of wine in the town, let Mousqueton buy it. It will be well too to prepare a light supper, of which you, Athos, and Aramis are not to partake. Athos, because I told him you had a fever ; Aramis, because you are a knight of Malta, and won't mix with fellows like us. Do you understand ?"

" Yes," said Porthos ; " but deuce take me if I understand at all."

" Porthos, my friend, you know that I am descended on the father's side from the Prophets, and on the mother's from the Sybils, and that I only speak in parables and riddles. That is all I can say for the present."

" The fact is," said Porthos, with an air of finesse, " I am rather incredulous."

D'Artagnan gave him a clap on the shoulder, and as they had reached the station where they were to breakfast, the conversation ended there.

At five in the evening they sent Mousqueton on before, as agreed upon.

In crossing the principal street in Derby, the four friends perceived their man standing in the doorway of a handsome house. It was there that their lodging was prepared for them.

At the hour agreed upon Groslow came. D'Artagnan received him as he would have done a friend of twenty years standing. Porthos scanned him from head to foot, and smiled when he discovered, that in spite of the blow he had administered to Parry's brother, he was not so strong as himself.

Athos and Aramis kept to the parts they had to play, and at midnight they retired to their room, leaving the door open. D'Artagnan accompanied them, and left Porthos to win fifty pistoles of Groslow, and to come to the conclusion when he left, that he was not such bad company as he had first imagined.

Groslow left with the determination of retrieving his losses the next night, and reminded the Gascon of the appointment.

The day passed as usual. In his ordinary relations D'Artagnan was the same as ever ; but with his friends, that is to say, Athos and Aramis, his gaiety was at fever-heat.

Arrived at Ryston, D'Artagnan assembled his friends. His face had lost the expression of careless gaiety which it had worn like a mask the whole day. Athos pinched Aramis's hand.

" The moment is at hand," he said.

" Yes," said D'Artagnan, who had overheard him, " to-night, gentlemen we rescue the king."

" D'Artagnan," said Athos, " this is not a joke, I trust ? It would quite cut me up."

" You are very odd, Athos," he replied, " to doubt me thus. Where and when have you seen me trifle with a friend's heart and a king's life ? I have told you, and I repeat it, that to-night we rescue Charles I. You left it to me to discover the means of doing so, and I have done so."

Porthos looked at D'Artagnan with an expression of profound admiration. Aramis smiled as one who hopes. Athos was pale, and trembled in every limb.

" Speak," said Athos.

".We are invited," replied D'Artagnan, "to pass the night with Mr. Groslow. But do you know where?"

" No."

" In the king's room."

" The king's room?" cried Athos.

" Yes, gentlemen, in the king's room. Groslow is on guard there this evening, and, to pass his time, has invited us to keep him company."

" Aha !" exclaimed Aramis.

" We are going, then—we two with our swords, you with daggers. We four are to make ourselves masters of these eight fools and their stupid captain. Monsieur Porthos, what do you say to it?"

" That it is easy enough," answered Porthos.

" We dress the king in Groslow's clothes. Mousqueton, Grimaud, and Blaisois have our horses saddled at the end of the first street. We mount them, and before daylight are twenty leagues distant."

Athos placed his two hands on D'Artagnan's shoulders, and gazed at him with his calm, mild smile.

" I declare, my friend," said he, "that there is not a creature under the sky who equals you in prowess and courage."

" And to think that I couldn't find that out," said Porthos, scratching his head; "it is so simple."

" But," said Aramis, "if I understand rightly, we are to kill them all, eh ?"

Athos shuddered and turned pale.

" Mordioux," answered D'Artagnan; "I believe we must. I confess I can discover no help for it."

" Let us see," said Aramis, "how are we to act ?"

" I have arranged two plans. Firstly, at a given signal, which shall be the words ' At last,' you each plunge a dagger into the heart of the soldier nearest to you. We, on our side, do the same. That will be four killed. We shall then be matched—four against the remaining five. If those five give themselves up we gag them, if they resist, we kill them."

" Very good," said Porthos; "it will be a nice little throat-cutting."

"Horrible, horrible," exclaimed Athos.

"Nonsense," said D'Artagnan; "you would do as much, Mr. Sensitive, in a battle. But, if you think the king's life is not worth what it must cost, there's an end of the matter, and I send to Groslow to say I am ill."

"No, you are right," said Athos.

At this moment a soldier entered to inform them that Groslow was waiting for them.

"Where?" asked D'Artagnan.

"In the room of the English Nebuchadnezzar," replied the staunch Puritan.

"Good," replied Athos, whose blood mounted to his face at the insult offered to royalty; "tell the captain we are coming."

"Faith," said Groslow, as the four friends entered, "I had almost given you up."

D'Artagnan went up to him, and whispered in his ear:

"The fact is we, that is, Monsieur de Valon and I, hesitated a little."

"And why?"

D'Artagnan looked significantly towards Athos and Aramis.

"Aha," said Groslow, "on account of opinions? No matter. On the contrary," he added, laughing, "if they want to see their Stuart they shall see him."

"Are we to pass the night in the king's room?" asked D'Artagnan.

"No, but in the one next to it; and as the door will remain open, it's the same thing. Have you provided yourself with money? I assure you I intend to play the devil's game to-night."

D'Artagnan rattled the gold in his pockets.

"Very good," said Groslow, and opened the door of the room.

"I will show you the way," and he went in first.

D'Artagnan turned to look at his friends. Porthos was perfectly indifferent; Athos pale, but resolute. Aramis was wiping a slight moisture from his brow.

The eight guards were at their posts—four in the king's room, two at the door between the rooms, and two at that by which the friends had entered. Athos smiled when he saw their bare swords; he felt it was no longer to be a butchery but a fight, and his usual good humour returned to him.

Charles was perceived through the door, lying dressed upon his bed, at the head of which Parry was seated, reading, in a low voice, a chapter from the Bible.

A candle of coarse tallow on a black table lit up the resigned face of the king, and that of his faithful retainer, far less calm.

From time to time Parry stopped, thinking the king, whose eyes were closed, was really asleep, but Charles would open his eyes, and say with a smile :

"Go on, my good Parry, I am listening."

Groslow advanced to the door of the king's room, replaced on his head the hat which he had taken off to receive his guests, looked for a moment contemptuously at this simple and touching scene, and, turning again to D'Artagnan, assumed an air of triumph at what he had achieved.

"Capital," cried the Gascon, "you would make a distinguished general."

"And do you think," asked Groslow, "that the Stuart will ever escape while I am guard?"

"No, to be sure," replied D'Artagnan ; "unless, forsooth, the sky rains friends upon him."

Groslow's face brightened.

It is impossible to say whether Charles, who kept his eyes constantly closed, had noticed the insolence of the Puritan captain, but the moment he heard the clear tone of D'Artagnan's voice, his eyelids rose in spite of himself.

Parry, too, started and stopped reading.

"What are you thinking about?" said the king ; "go on, my good Parry, unless, at least, you are tired."

Parry resumed his reading.

On a table in the next room were lighted candles, cards, two dice-boxes and dice.

"That's it," said D'Artagnan; "you Monsieur le Comte de la Fère to the right of Monsieur Groslow. You, Chevalier d'Herblay to his left. De Valon next me. You'll bet for me, and those gentlemen for Monsieur Groslow."

By this arrangement, D'Artagnan could nudge Porthos with his knee, and make signs with the eyes to Athos and Aramis.

At the names of Comte de la Fère and Chevalier d'Herblay, Charles opened his eyes, and raising his noble head in spite of himself, threw a glance at all the actors in the scene.

"You asked me just now if I was in funds," said D'Artagnan, placing some twenty pistoles upon the table ; "well, in my turn I advise you to keep a sharp look out on your TREASURE, my dear Monsieur Groslow, for I can tell you we shall not leave this without robbing you of it."

"Not without my defending it," said Groslow.

"So much the better," said D'Artagnan. "Fight, my dear

captain, fight. You know, or you don't know, that that is what we ask of you."

"Oh! yes," said Groslow, bursting with his usual hoarse laugh, "I know you Frenchmen want nothing but cuts and bruises."

Charles had heard and understood it all. A slight colour mounted to his cheeks. The soldiers then saw him stretch his limbs little by little, and under the pretence of much heat, throw off the Scotch plaid which covered him.

Athos and Aramis started with delight to find that the king was lying with his clothes on.

The game began. The luck had turned, and Groslow having won some hundred pistoles, was in the merriest possible humour.

Porthos, who had lost the fifty pistoles he had won the night before, and thirty more besides, was very cross, and questioned D'Artagnan with a nudge of the knee, as to whether it would not soon be time to change the game. But D'Artagnan remained impassible.

It struck ten. They heard the guard going its rounds.

"How many rounds do they make a night?" asked D'Artagnan, drawing more pistoles from his pocket.

"Five," answered Groslow, "one every two hours."

D'Artagnan glanced at Athos and Aramis, and for the first time replied to Porthos's nudge of the knee by a nudge responsive. Meanwhile the soldiers, whose duty it was to remain in the king's room, attracted by that love of play so powerful in all men, had stolen little by little towards the table, and standing on tip-toe, were watching the game over the shoulders of D'Artagnan and Porthos. Those on the other side had followed their example, thus favouring the views of the four friends.

D'Artagnan turned, mechanically looking behind him, and between the figures of two soldiers he could see Parry standing up, and Charles leaning on his elbow, with his hands clasped, and apparently offering a fervent prayer to God.

D'Artagnan saw that the moment was come. He darted a preparatory glance at Athos and Aramis, who gently pushed back their chairs a little so as to leave themselves space for action. He gave Porthos a second nudge of the knee; and Porthos got up as if to stretch his legs, and took care at the same time to ascertain that his sword could be drawn glibly from the scabbard.

"Hang it," cried D'Artagnan; "another twenty pistoles lost. Really, Captain Groslow, you are too much in luck's way. This can't last;" and he drew another twenty from his pocket. "One more turn, captain, twenty pistoles on one throw—only one, the last."

" Done for twenty," replied Groslow.

And he turned up two cards as usual, a king for D'Artagnan, and an ace for himself.

" A king," said D'Artagnan; "it's a good omen, Master Groslow, look out for the king."

And in spite of his power over himself, there was a strange vibration in the Gascon's voice, which made his partner start.

Groslow began turning the cards one after another. If he turned up an ace first he won; if a king he lost.

He turned up a king.

" At last !" cried D'Artagnan.

At this word Athos and Aramis jumped up. Porthos drew back a step. Daggers and swords were just about to shine, when suddenly the door was thrown open, and Harrison appeared on the doorway, accompanied by a man enveloped in a large cloak. Behind this man could be seen the glistening muskets of five or six soldiers.

Groslow jumped up, ashamed at being surprised in the midst of wine, cards, and dice. But Harrison paid no attention to him, and entering the king's room, followed by his companion,—

" Charles Stuart," said he, " an order has come to conduct you to London without stopping day or night. Prepare yourself, then to start at once."

" And by whom is this order given ?" asked the king.

" By General Oliver Cromwell. And here is Mr. Mordaunt, who has brought it, and is charged with its execution."

" Mordaunt !" muttered the four friends, exchanging looks.

D'Artagnan swept up the money that he and Porthos had lost, and buried it in his huge pocket. Athos and Aramis placed themselves behind him. At this movement Mordaunt turned round, recognised them, and uttered an exclamation of savage delight.

" I'm afraid we are taken," whispered D'Artagnan to his friend.

" Not yet," replied Porthos.

" Colonel, colonel," cried Mordaunt, " you are betrayed. These four Frenchmen have escaped from Newcastle, and no doubt want to carry off the king. Arrest them."

" Ah ! my young man," said D'Artagnan, drawing his sword, " that is an order sooner given than executed. Fly, friends, fly," he added, whirling his sword around him.

The next moment he darted to the door and knocked down two of the soldiers who guarded it, before they had time to cock their muskets. Athos and Aramis followed him, Porthos brought up

the rear, and before soldiers, officers, or colonel had time to recover their surprise, all four were in the street.

" Fire !" cried Mordaunt ; " fire upon them."

Three or four shots were fired, but with no other result than
to show the four fugitives turning the corner of the street safe and
sound.

The horses were at the place fixed upon, and they leapt lightly
into their saddles.

" Forward !" cried D'Artagnan, "and put the spur in."

They galloped away, and took the road they had come by in the
morning, namely, in the direction towards Scotland. A few yards
beyond the town D'Artagnan drew rein.

" Halt !" he cried ; " this time we shall be pursued. We must
let them leave the village and ride after us on the northern road,
and when they are passed we will take the opposite direction."

There was a stream close by, and a bridge across it. D'Artagnan
led his horse under the arch of the bridge. The others followed.
Ten minutes later they heard the rapid gallop of a troop of horsemen. A few minutes more, and the troop passed over their heads.

CHAPTER LX.

LONDON.

As soon as the noise of the hoofs was lost in the distance,
D'Artagnan remounted the bank of the stream and scoured the
plain, followed by his three friends, directing himself as much as
possible towards London.

" This time," said D'Artagnan, when they were sufficiently
distant to proceed at a trot, " I think all is lost, and we have
nothing better to do than to reach France. What do you think, Athos?"

" True," said Athos ; " but we ought, I think, to see this great
tragedy played out. Do not let us leave England before the crisis.
Don't you agree with me, Aramis ?"

" Entirely, my dear count. Then, too, I confess I should not
be sorry to come across Mordaunt again. It appears to me that
we have an account to settle with him, and that it is not our
custom to leave a place without paying our debts, of this kind at least."

" Ah ! that's another thing," said D'Artagnan ; " and I should
not mind waiting in London a whole year for a chance of meeting
this Mordaunt in question. Only let us lodge with some one
on whom we can count ; for I imagine that, just now, Mr. Cromwell would not be inclined to trifle with us. Athos, do you know

any inn in the whole town where one can find white sheets, roast beef reasonably cooked, and wine which is not made of hops or gin ?"

"I think I know what you want," replied Athos. "De Winter took us to the house of a Spaniard, who, he said, had been naturalised in England by his new fellow-countrymen's guineas."

"Well, we must take every precaution."

"Yes, and among others, that of changing our clothes."

"Changing our clothes !" exclaimed Porthos. "I don't see why ; we are very comfortable in those we have on."

"To prevent recognition," said D'Artagnan. "Our clothes have a cut which would denounce the Frenchman at first sight. Now, I don't care sufficiently about the cut of my jerkin to risk being hung at Tyburn, or sent for change of scene to the Indies. I shall buy a chestnut-coloured suit. I've remarked that your Puritans revel in that colour."

"But can you find your man ?" said Aramis to Athos.

"Oh ! to be sure, yes. He lives at the Bedford Tavern, Green Hall Street. Besides, I can find my way about the city with my eyes shut."

Athos was right. He went direct to the Bedford Tavern, and the host, who recognised him, was delighted to see him again with such worthy and numerous company.

Though it was scarcely daylight, our four travellers found the town in a great bustle, owing to the reported approach of Harrison and the king.

The plan of changing their clothes was unanimously adopted. The landlord sent out for every description of garment, as if he wanted to fit up his wardrobe. Athos chose a black coat, which gave him the appearance of a respectable citizen. Aramis, not wishing to part with his sword, selected a dark one of a military cut. Porthos was seduced by a red doublet with green pockets. D'Artagnan, who had fixed on his colour beforehand, had only to select the shade, and looked in his chestnut suit exactly like a retired sugar-dealer.

"Now," said D'Artagnan, "for the actual man. We must cut off our hair, that the populace may not insult us. As we no longer wear the sword of the gentleman, we may as well have the head of the Puritan. This, as you know, is the important point of distinction between the Covenanter and the Cavalier."

"We look hideous," said Athos.

"And smack of the Puritan to a frightful extent," said Aramis.

"My head feels quite cold," said Porthos.

"And as for me, I feel anxious to preach a sermon," said D'Artagnan.

"Now," said Athos, "that we cannot even recognise one another, and have, therefore, no fear of others recognising us, let us go and see the king's entrance."

They had not been long in the crowd before loud cries announced the king's arrival. A carriage had been sent to meet him; and the gigantic Porthos, who stood a head above all the other heads, soon announced that he saw the royal equipage approaching. D'Artagnan raised himself on tip-toe, and as the carriage passed, saw Harrison at one window and Mordaunt at the other.

The next day, Athos leaning out of his window, which looked upon the most populous part of the city, heard the Act of Parliament, which summoned the ex-king, Charles I., to the bar, publicly cried.

"The parliament, indeed!" cried Athos. "Parliament can never have passed such an act as that."

At this moment the landlord came in.

"Did parliament pass this act?" Athos asked of him in English.

"Yes, my lord, the pure parliament."

"Come," said D'Artagnan, "as I don't understand English, suppose you speak to us in Spanish, which we all do understand."

"Do you mean to say, then," resumed Athos, "that there are two parliaments, one pure, and the other impure?"

"When I speak of the pure parliament," resumed the host, "I mean the one which Colonel Bridge has weeded."

"Ah! really," said D'Artagnan, "these people are very ingenious. When I go back to France I must suggest that to Cardinal Mazarin. One shall weed the parliament in the name of the court, and the other in the name of the people; so that there won't be any parliament left at all."

"And who is this Colonel Bridge?" asked Aramis.

"Colonel Bridge," replied the Spaniard, "is a retired waggoner, a man of much sense, who made one observation in driving his team, namely, that where there happened to be a stone on the road, it was much easier to remove the stone, than to try and make the wheel pass over it. Now, of 251 members who composed the parliament, there were 191 who were in his way, and might have upset his political waggon. He took them up, just as he formerly used to take up the stones from the road, and threw them out of the house."

" Neat," remarked D'Artagnan. " Very !"

" And all these 191 were Stuartists ?" asked Athos.

" Without doubt, señor; and, you understand, that they would have saved the king."

" To be sure," said Porthos, majestically, " they were in the majority."

" And you think," said Aramis, " he will consent to appear before such a tribunal ?"

" He will be forced to do so," answered the Spaniard.

" Now, Athos !" said D'Artagnan, " do you begin to believe that it's a ruined cause ? and that what with your Harrisons, Joyces, Bridges, and Cromwells, we shall never get the upper hand ?"

" But," said Aramis, " if they dare to condemn their king, it can only be to exile or imprisonment."

D'Artagnan whistled a little air of incredulity.

" We shall see," said Athos, " for we shall go to the sittings, I presume."

" You will not have long to wait," said the landlord; " they begin to-morrow."

" So, then, they drew up the indictment before the king was taken ?"

" Of course," said D'Artagnan ; " they began the day he was sold."

" And you know," said Aramis, " that it was our friend Mordaunt who made, if not the bargain, at least the first overtures."

" And you know," added D'Artagnan, " that whenever I catch him, I kill him, this Mr. Mordaunt."

" And I, too," exclaimed Porthos.

" And I, too," added Aramis.

" Touching unanimity !" cried D'Artagnan, " which well becomes good citizens like us. Let us take a turn round the town, and imbibe a little fog."

" Yes," said Porthos. " It will be a change from the beer."

<hr />

CHAPTER LXI.

THE TRIAL.

THE next morning King Charles I. was brought by a strong guard before the high court which was to judge him. All London was crowding to the doors of the house. The throng was terrific; and it was not till after much pushing and some fighting that our four friends reached their destination. When they did so, they found the three lower rows of benches already occupied; but, as they were not anxious to be too conspicuous, all, with the exception of Porthos, who was anxious to display his red doublet, were quite satisfied with their places, the more so as chance had brought them to the centre of their row, so that they were exactly opposite the arm-chair prepared for the royal prisoner.

Towards eleven o'clock the king entered the hall, surrounded by guards, but wearing his head covered, and with a calm expression turned to every side with a look of complete assurance, as if he were there to preside at an assembly of submissive subjects, rather than to reply to the accusations of a rebel court.

The judges, proud of having a monarch to humble, evidently prepared to employ the right they had arrogated to themselves, and sent an officer to inform the king that it was customary for the accused to uncover his head.

Charles, without replying a single word, turned his head in another direction, and pulled his felt hat over it. Then, when the officer was gone, he sat down in the arm-chair opposite the president, and struck his boot with a little cane which he carried in his hand. Parry, who accompanied him, stood behind him.

D'Artagnan was looking at Athos, whose face betrayed all those emotions which the king, possessing more power over himself, had chased from his own. This agitation, in one so cool and calm as Athos, frightened him.

"I hope," he whispered to him, "that you will follow his majesty's example, and not get killed for your folly in this den."

"Set your mind at rest," replied Athos.

"Aha!" continued D'Artagnan, "it is clear that they are afraid of something or other; for, look, the sentinels are being reinforced. They had only halberds before, and now they have muskets. The halberds were for the audience in the area. The muskets are for us."

"Thirty, forty, fifty, sixty-five men," said Porthos, counting the reinforcements.

"Ah!" said Aramis. "But you forget the officer."

D'Artagnan grew pale with rage. He had recognised Mordaunt, who, with bare sword, was marshalling the musketeers before the king, and opposite the benches.

"Do you think they have recognised us?" said D'Artagnan. "In that case I should beat a retreat. I don't care to be shot in a box."

"No," said Aramis, "he has not seen us. He sees no one but the king. 'Mon Dieu!' how he stares at him, the insolent dog! Does he hate his majesty as much as he does us?"

"Pardi," answered Athos, "we only carried off his mother, and the king has spoiled him of his name and property."

"True," said Aramis; "but silence! the president is speaking to the king."

"Stuart," Bradshaw was saying, "listen to the roll-call of your judges, and address to the court any observations you may have to make."

The king turned his head away, as if these words had not been intended for him. Bradshaw waited, and, as there was no reply, there was a moment of silence.

Out of the hundred and sixty-three members designated, there were only seventy-three present, for the rest, fearful of taking part in such an act, had remained away.

When the name of Colonel Fairfax was called, one of those brief but solemn silences ensued, which announced the absence of the members who had no wish to take a personal part in the trial.

"Colonel Fairfax," repeated Bradshaw.

"Fairfax?" answered a laughing voice, the silvery tone of which betrayed it as that of a woman, "he is not such a fool as to be here."

A loud laugh followed these words, pronounced with that boldness which women draw from their own weakness—a weakness which removes them beyond the power of vengeance.

"It is a woman's voice," cried Aramis; "faith, I would give a good deal for her to be young and pretty." And he mounted on the bench to try and get a sight of her.

"By my soul," said Aramis, "she is charming. Look, D'Artagnan; everybody is looking at her; and in spite of Bradshaw's gaze, she has not turned pale."

"It is Lady Fairfax herself," said D'Artagnan, "don't you remember, Porthos, we saw her at General Cromwell's?"

The roll-call continued.

"These rascals will adjourn when they find that they are not in sufficient force," said the Comte de la Fère.

"You don't know them, Athos; look at Mordaunt's smile. Is that the look of a man whose victim is likely to escape him. Ah, cursed basilisk, it will be a happy day for me when I can cross something more than a look with you."

"The king is really very handsome," said Porthos; "and look, too, though he is a prisoner, how carefully he is dressed. The feather in his hat is worth at least fifty pistoles. Look at it, Aramis."

The roll-call finished, the president ordered them to read the act of accusation. Athos turned pale. A second time he was disappointed in his expectation.

"I told you so, Athos," said D'Artagnan, shrugging his shoulders. "Now take your courage in both hands, and hear what this gentleman in black is going to say about his sovereign, with full licence and privilege."

Never till then had a more brutal accusation or meaner insults tarnished the kingly majesty.

Charles listened with marked attention, passing over the insults, noting the grievances, and, when hatred overflowed all bounds, and the accuser turned executioner beforehand, replying with a smile of contempt.

"The fact is," said D'Artagnan, "if men are punished for imprudence and triviality, this poor king deserves punishment. But it seems to me that that which he is just now undergoing is hard enough."

At this moment the accuser concluded with these words :— "The present accusation is preferred by us in the name of the English people."

At these words there was a murmur along the benches, and a second voice, not that of a woman, but a man's, stout and furious, thundered behind D'Artagnan :

"You lie," it cried, "and nine-tenths of the English people shudder at what you say."

This voice was that of Athos, who, standing up with outstretched arm, and quite out of his mind, thus assailed the public accuser.

King, judges, spectators, all turned their eyes to the bench where the four friends were seated. Mordaunt did the same, and recognised the gentleman, around whom the three other Frenchmen were standing, pale and menacing. His eyes glittered with delight. He had discovered those to whose death he had devoted his life. A movement of fury called to his side some twenty of his musketeers, and, pointing to the bench where his enemies were, —"Fire on that bench," he cried.

But, rapid as thought, D'Artagnan seized Athos by the middle of the body, and, followed by Porthos with Aramis, leapt down from the benches, rushed into the passages, and, flying down the staircase, was lost in the crowd without, while the muskets within were pointed on some three thousand spectators, whose piteous cries and noisy alarms stopped the impulse already given to bloodshed.

Mordaunt, pale and trembling with anger, rushed from the hall, sword in hand, followed by six pikemen, pushing, inquiring, and panting in the crowd ; and then, having found nothing, returned.

Quiet was at length restored.

"What have you to say in your defence ?" asked Bradshaw of the king.

Then, rising with his head still covered, in the tone of a judge rather than a prisoner, Charles began.

"Before questioning me," he said, "reply to my question. I was free at Newcastle, and had there concluded a treaty with both houses. Instead of performing your part of this contract, as I performed mine, you bought me from the Scotch—not dear, I know, and that does honour to the economy of your government. But because you have paid the price of a slave, do you expect that I have ceased to be your king ? No. To answer you would be to forget it. I shall only reply to you when you have satisfied me of your right to question me. To answer you would be to acknowledge you as my judges, and I only acknowledge you as my executioners." And in the midst of a death-like silence, Charles, calm, lofty, and with his head still covered, sat down again in his arm-chair.

"Why are not my Frenchmen here ?" he murmured proudly, and turning his eyes to the benches where they had appeared for a moment ; "they would have seen that their friend was worthy of their defence, while alive ; and of their tears, when dead."

"Well," said the president—seeing that Charles was determined to remain silent—"so be it. We will judge you in spite of your silence. You are accused of treason, of abuse of power, and murder. The evidence will support it. Go, and another sitting will accomplish what you have refused to do in this."

Charles rose, and turned towards Parry, whom he found pallid, and with his temples covered with moisture.

"Well, my dear Parry," said he, "what is the matter ? and what can affect you in this manner ?"

"Oh, my king," said Parry, with tears in his eyes, and in a tone of supplication, "do not look to the left as we leave the hall."

"And why, Parry?"

"Do not look, I implore you, my king."

"But what is the matter ? speak," said Charles, attempting to look across the hedge of guards which surrounded him.

"It is—but you will not look, will you?—it is, because they have had the axe, with which criminals are executed, brought and placed there on a table. The sight is hideous."

"Fools," said Charles, "do they take me for a coward like themselves? You have done well to warn me. Thank you, Parry."

When the moment arrived, the king followed his guards out of the hall. As he passed the table on which the axe was laid, he stopped, and turning with a smile, said:

"Ah! the axe, an ingenious device, and well worthy of those who know not what a gentleman is. You frighten me not, executioner's axe," added he, touching it with the cane which he held in his hand, "and I strike you now, waiting patiently and christianly for you to return the blow."

And, shrugging his shoulders with real contempt, he passed on. When he reached the door, a long stream of people, who had been disappointed in not being able to get into the house, and to make amends had collected to see him come out, stood on each side as he passed, many among them glaring on him with threatening looks.

"How many people," thought he, "and not one true friend." And as he uttered these words of doubt and depression within his mind, a voice near him said:

"Respect to fallen majesty."

The king turned quickly round, with tears in his eyes and heart. It was an old soldier of the guards, who could not see his king pass captive before him without rendering him this last homage. But the next moment the unfortunate man was nearly stunned with blows from the hilts of swords; and among those who set upon him the king recognised Captain Groslow.

"Alas!" said Charles, "that is a severe chastisement for a very slight fault."

He continued his way; but he had scarcely gone a hundred paces, when a furious fellow, leaning between two soldiers, spit in the king's face. Loud roars of laughter and sullen murmurs rose together. The crowd opened and closed again, undulating like a stormy sea; and the king imagined that he saw shining in the midst of this living wave the bright eyes of Athos.

Charles wiped his face, and said, with a sad smile, "Poor wretch, for half-a-crown he would do as much to his own father."

The king was not wrong. Athos and his friends, again mingling with the throng, were taking a last look at the martyr king.

When the cowardly insulter had spat in the face of the captive monarch, Athos had grasped his dagger. But D'Artagnan stopped his hand, and in a hoarse voice cried, "Wait !"

Athos stopped. D'Artagnan leaning on Athos, made a sign to Porthos and Aramis to keep near them, and then placed himself behind the man with the bare arms, who was still laughing at his own vile pleasantry, and receiving the congratulations of several others.

The man took his way towards the city. The four friends followed him. The man, who had the appearance of being a butcher, descended a little steep and isolated street, looking on to the river, with two of his friends. Arrived at the bank of the river, the three men perceived that they were followed, turned round, and looked insolently at the Frenchmen.

"Athos," said D'Artagnan, "will you interpret for me ?"

At this, D'Artagnan walked straight up to the butcher, and touching him on the chest with the tip of his finger, said to Athos :

"Say this to him in English, 'You are a coward. You have insulted a defenceless man. You have befouled the face of your king. You must die.' "

Athos, pale as a ghost, repeated these words to the man, who, seeing the unpleasant preparations that were making, put himself in an attitude of defence. Aramis, at this movement, drew his sword.

"No," cried D'Artagnan, "no steel. Steel is for gentlemen."

And seizing the butcher by the throat,—

"Porthos," said he, "knock this fellow down for me with a single blow."

Porthos raised his terrible arm, which whistled through the air like a sling, and the heavy mass fell with a dull noise on the skull of the coward, and broke it. The man fell like an ox under the mallet. His companions, horrorstruck, could neither move nor cry out.

"Tell them this, Athos," resumed D'Artagnan ; "'thus shall all die who forget that a fettered man wears a sacred head."

The two men looked at the body of their companion, swimming in black blood ; and then, recovering voice and legs together, ran shouting away.

"Justice is done," said Porthos, wiping his forehead.

"And now," said D'Artagnan to Athos, "do not have any doubts about me ; I undertake everything that concerns the king."

CHAPTER LXII.

WHITEHALL.

IT was easy to foresee that the Parliament would condemn Charles to death. Political judgments are generally merely vain formalities, for the same passions which give rise to the accusation give rise also to the condemnation. Such is the terrible logic of revo lutions.

Meanwhile, before our four friends could mature their plans, they determined to put every possible obstacle in the way of the execution of the sentence. To this end they resolved to get rid of the London executioner; for though, of course, another could be sent for from the nearest town, there would be still a delay of a day or two gained. D'Artagnan undertook this more than diffi- cult task. The next thing was to warn Charles of the attempt about to be made to save him. Aramis undertook the perilous office. Bishop Juxon had received permission to visit Charles in his prison at Whitehall; Aramis resolved to persuade the bishop to let him enter with him. Lastly, Athos was to prepare, in every emergency, the means of leaving England.

The palace of Whitehall was guarded by three regiments of cavalry, and still more by the anxiety of Cromwell, who came and went, or sent his generals or his agents continually. Alone, in his usual room, lighted by two candles, the condemned monarch gazed sadly on the luxury of his past greatness, just as, at the last hour, one sees the image of life, milder and more brilliant than ever.

Parry had not quitted his master, and, since his condemnation, had not ceased to weep. Charles, leaning on a table, was gazing at a medallion of his wife and daughter; he was waiting first for Juxon, next for martyrdom.

"Alas!" he said to himself, "if I only had for a confessor one of those lights of the Church, whose soul has sounded all the mysteries of life, all the littlenesses of greatness, perhaps his voice would choke the voice that wails within my soul. But I shall have a priest of vulgar mind, whose career and fortune I have ruined by my misfortune. He will speak to me of God and of death, as he has spoken to many another dying man, not under- standing that this one leaves his throne to a usurper and his children to starve."

And he raised the medallion to his lips.

It was a dull, foggy night. A neighbouring church clock slowly struck the hour. The pale light of the two candles raised flickering phantoms in the lofty room. These phantoms were the ancestors of King Charles, standing out from their gilt frames. A profound melancholy had possessed itself of Charles. He buried his brow in his hands, and thought of all that was so dear to him, now to be left for ever. He drew from his bosom the diamond cross which La Garretière had sent him by the hands of those generous Frenchmen, and kissed it, and remembered that she would not see it again till he was lying cold and mutilated in the tomb.

Suddenly the door opened, and an ecclesiastic, in episcopal robes, entered, followed by two guards, to whom the king waved an imperious gesture. The guards retired. The room resumed its obscurity.

"Juxon!" cried Charles, "Juxon, thank you, my last friend, you are come at a fitting moment."

The bishop looked anxiously at the man sobbing in the inglenook.

"Come, Parry," said the king, "cease your tears."

"If it's Parry," said the bishop, "I have nothing to fear; so allow me to salute your majesty, and to tell him who I am, and for what I am come."

At this sight, and this voice, Charles was about to cry out, when Aramis placed his finger on his lips, and bowed low to the King of England.

"The knight!" murmured Charles.

"Yes, sire," interrupted Aramis, raising his voice, "the bishop Juxon, faithful knight of Christ, and obedient to your majesty's wishes."

Charles clasped his hands, amazed and stupefied to find that these foreigners, without other motive than that which their conscience imposed on them, thus combated the will of a people, and the destiny of a king.

"You!" he said, "you! how did you penetrate hither? If they recognise you, you are lost."

"Care not for me, sire; think only of yourself. You see, your friends are wakeful. I know not what we shall do yet, but four determined men can do much. Meanwhile, do not be surprised at anything that happens; prepare yourself for every emergency."

Charles shook his head.

"Do you know that I die to-morrow, at ten o'clock?

"Something, your majesty, will happen, between now and then, to make the execution impossible."

At this moment, a strange noise, like the unloading of a cart, and followed by a cry of pain, was heard beneath the window.

"What is this noise and this cry?" said Aramis, perplexed.

"I know not who can have uttered that cry," said the king, "but the noise is easily understood. Do you know that I am to be beheaded outside this window? Well, this wood, that you hear fall, is the posts and planks to build my scaffold. Some workmen must have been hurt in unloading them."

Aramis shuddered, in spite of himself.

"You see," said the king, "that it is useless for you to resist. I am condemned; leave me to my death."

"My king," said Aramis, "they may well raise a scaffold, but they cannot make an executioner."

"What do you mean?" asked the king.

"I mean that, at this hour, the headsman is removed by force or persuasion. The scaffold will be ready by to-morrow, but the headsman will be wanting, and they will put it off till the day after to-morrow."

"What then?" said the king.

"To-morrow night we shall rescue you."

"Oh! sir," cried Parry, "may you and yours be blessed!"

"I know nothing about it," continued Aramis, "but the cleverest, the bravest, the most devoted of us four, said to me, when I left him, 'Knight, tell the king, that to-morrow, at ten o'clock at night, we shall carry him off. He has said it, and will do it."

"You are really wonderful men," said the king; "take my hand, knight, it is that of a friend, who will love you to the last."

Aramis stooped to kiss the king's hand, but Charles clasped his and pressed it to his heart.

At this moment a man entered, without even knocking at the door. Aramis tried to withdraw his hand, but the king still held it. The man was one of those Puritans, half preacher and half soldier, who swarmed around Cromwell.

"What do you want, sir?" said the king.

"I desire to know if the confession of Charles Stuart is at an end?" said the stranger.

"And what is it to you?" replied the king; "we are not of the same religion."

"All men are brothers," said the Puritan. "One of my brothers is about to die, and I come to prepare him."

"Bear with him," whispered Aramis; "it is doubtless some spy."

"After my reverend Lord Bishop," said the king, to the man, "I shall hear you with pleasure, sir."

The man retired, but not before examining the supposed Juxon with an attention which did not escape the king.

"Knight," said the king, when the door was closed, "I believe you are right, and that this man only came here with evil intentions. Take care that no misfortune befalls you when you leave."

"I thank your majesty," said Aramis, "but, under these robes, I have a coat of mail and a dagger."

"Go, then, sir, and God keep you!"

The king accompanied him to the door, where Aramis pronounced his benediction upon him, and, passing through the anterooms, filled with soldiers, jumped into his carriage, and drove to the bishop's palace. Juxon was waiting for him impatiently.

Aramis resumed his own attire, and left Juxon with the assurance that he might again have recourse to him.

He had scarcely gone ten yards in the street, when he perceived that he was followed by a man, wrapped in a large cloak. He placed his hand on his dagger, and stopped. The man came straight towards him. It was Porthos.

"My dear friend," cried Aramis.

"You see, we had each our mission," said Porthos; "mine was to guard you, and I was doing so. Have you seen the king?"

"Yes, and all goes well."

"We are to meet our friends at the hotel, at eleven."

It was then striking half-past ten by St. Paul's.

Arrived at the hotel, it was not long before Athos entered.

"All's well," he cried, as he entered; "I have hired a little skiff, as narrow as a canoe, and as light as a swallow. It is waiting for us at Greenwich, opposite the Isle of Dogs, manned by a captain and four men, who, for the sum of fifty pounds sterling, will keep themselves at our disposition three successive nights. Once on board, we drop down the Thames, and, in two hours, are in the open sea. In case I am killed, the captain's name is Roger, and the skiff is called the 'Lightning.' A handkerchief, tied at the four corners, is to be the signal."

Next moment, D'Artagnan entered.

"Empty your pockets," said he, "I want a hundred pounds, and as for my own——" and he emptied them inside out.

The sum was collected in a minute. D'Artagnan ran out, and returned directly after.

"There," said he, "it's done. Ough! and not without a deal of trouble too."

"Has the executioner left London?" said Aramis.

"No, he is in the cellar."

"The cellar—what cellar?"

"Our landlord's, to be sure. Mousqueton is sitting on the door, and here's the key."

"Bravo !" said Aramis ; "but how did you manage it ?"

"Like everything else—with money ; it cost me dear."

"How much ?" asked Athos.

"Five hundred pounds."

"And where did you get all that from ?" said Athos.

"The queen's famous diamond," answered D'Artagnan with a sigh.

"Ah ! true," said Aramis, "I recognised it on your finger."

"You bought it back, then from Monsieur des Essarts ?" asked Porthos.

"Yes, but it was fated that I should not keep it."

"Well, so much for the executioner," said Athos ; "but unfortunately, every executioner has his assistant, his man, or whatever you call him."

"And this one had his," said D'Artagnan ; "but, as good luck would have it, just as I thought I should have two affairs to manage, my friend was brought home with a broken leg. In the excess of his zeal, he had accompanied the cart containing the scaffolding as far as the king's window, and one of the planks fell on his leg and broke it."

"Ah !" cried Aramis "that accounts for the cry that I heard."

"Probably," said D'Artagnan ; "but as he is a thoughtful young man, he promised to send four expert workmen in his place to help those already at the scaffold, and wrote, the moment he was brought home, to Master Tom Lowe, an assistant carpenter and friend of his, to go down to Whitehall, with three of his friends. Here's the letter he sent by a messenger for sixpence, who sold it to me for a guinea."

"And what on earth are you going to do with it ?" asked Athos.

"Can't you guess, my dear Athos ? You, who speak English like John Bull himself, are Master Tom Lowe, we, your three companions Do you understand now ?"

CHAPTER LXIII.

THE WORKMEN.

TOWARDS midnight Charles heard a great noise beneath his window. It arose from blows of the hammer and hatchet, clinking of pincers and crinching of saws.

Lying dressed upon his bed, this noise awoke him with a start, and found a gloomy echo in his heart. He could not endure it, and sent Parry to ask the sentinel to beg the workmen to strike more gently, and not disturb the last slumber of one who had been their king. The sentinel was unwilling to leave his post, but allowed Parry to pass.

Arriving at the window, Parry ound an unfinished scaffold, over which they were nailing a covering of black serge. Raised to the height of twenty feet, so as to be on a level with the window, it had two lower stories. Parry, odious as was this sight to him, sought for those among some eight or ten workmen, who were making the most noise; and fixed on two men, who were loosening the last hooks of the iron balcony.

"My friends," said Parry, when he had mounted the scaffold and stood beside them, "would you work a little more quietly? The king wishes to get a sleep." One of the two, who was standing up, was of gigantic size, and was driving a pick with all his might into the wall, while the other kneeling beside him was collecting the pieces of stone. The face of the first was lost to Parry in the darkness, but as the second turned round and placed his finger on his lips, Parry started back in amazement.

"Very well, very well," said the workman aloud in excellent English. "Tell the king that if he sleeps badly to-night, he will sleep better to-morrow."

These blunt words, so terrible if taken literally, were received by the other workmen with a roar of laughter. But Parry withdrew, thinking he was dreaming.

"Sire," said he to the king, when he had returned, "do you know who these workmen are who are making so much noise?"

"I! no, how would you have me know?"

Parry bent his head and whispered the king, "It is the Count de la Fère and his friend."

"Raising my scaffold," cried the king, astonished.

"Yes, and at the same time making a hole in the wall."

The king clasped his hands, and raised his eyes to heaven; then, leaping down from his bed, he went to the window, and pulling aside the curtain, tried to distinguish the figures outside, but in vain.

Parry was not wrong. It was Athos whom he had recognised, and it was Porthos who was boring a hole through the wall.

This hole communicated with a kind of low loft—the space between the floor of the king's room and the ceiling of the one below it. Their plan was to pass through the hole they were making into this loft, and cut out from below a piece of the flooring of the king's room, so as to form a kind of trap-door.

Through this the king was to escape the next night, and, hidden by the black covering of the scaffold, was to change his dress for that of a workman, slip out with his deliverers, pass the sentinels, who would suspect nothing, and so reach the skiff that was waiting for him at Greenwich.

Day gilded the tops of the houses. The hole was finished, and Athos passed through it, carrying the clothes destined for the king, wrapped in a piece of black cloth, and the tools with which he was to open a communication with the king's room.

D'Artagnan returned to change his workman's clothes for his chestnut-coloured suit, and Porthos to put on his red doublet. As for Aramis, he went off to the bishop's palace to see if he could possibly pass in with Juxon to the king's presence. All three agreed to meet at noon in Whitehall-place to see how things went on.

Aramis found his two friends engaged with a bottle of port and a cold chicken, and explained the arrangement to them.

"Bravo!" said Porthos, "besides, we shall be there at the time of the flight. What with D'Artagnan, Grimaud, and Mousqueton, we can manage to despatch eight of them. I say nothing about Blaisois, for he is only fit to hold the horses. Two minutes a man makes four minutes. Mousqueton will lose another, that's five; and in five minutes they can have galloped a quarter of a league."

Aramis swallowed a hasty mouthful, drank off a glass of wine, and changed his clothes.

"Now," said he, "I'm off to the bishop's. Take care of the executioner, D'Artagnan."

"All right. Grimaud has relieved Mousqueton, and has his foot on the cellar-door."

"Well, don't be inactive."

"Inactive, my dear fellow! Ask Porthos. I pass my life upon my legs, like a ballet-dancer."

Aramis again presented himself at the bishop's. Juxon consented the more readily to take him with him, as he would require an assistant priest, in case the king should wish to communicate. Dressed as Aramis had been the night before, the bishop got into his carriage, and the former, more disguised by his pallor and sad countenance than his deacon's dress, got in by his side. The carriage stopped at the door of the palace.

It was about nine o'clock in the morning.

Nothing was changed. The ante-rooms were still full of soldiers, the passages still lined by guards. The king was already sanguine, but when he perceived Aramis his hope turned to joy.

"Sire," said Aramis, the moment they were alone, "you are saved, the London executioner has vanished. His assistant broke his leg last night, beneath your majesty's window—the cry we heard was his—and there is no executioner nearer at hand than Bristol."

"But the Comte de la Fère?" asked the king.

"Two feet below you; take the poker from the fire-place, and strike three times on the floor. He will answer you."

The king did so, and the moment after, three dull knocks, answering the given signal, sounded beneath the floor.

"So," said Charles, "he who knocks down there——"

"Is the Comte de la Fère, sire," said Aramis. "He is preparing a path for your majesty to escape by. Parry, for his part, will raise this slab of marble, and a passage will be opened."

"Oh! Juxon," said the king, seizing the bishop's two hands in his own, "promise that you will pray all your life for this gentleman, and for the other that you hear beneath your feet, and for two others again, who, wherever they may be, are vigilant, I am sure, for my safety."

"Sire," replied Juxon, "you shall be obeyed."

Meanwhile, the miner underneath was heard working away incessantly, when suddenly an unexpected noise resounded in the passage. Aramis seized the poker, and gave the signal to stop; the noise came nearer and nearer. It was that of a number of men steadily approaching. The four men stood motionless. All eyes were fixed on the door, which opened slowly, and with a kind of solemnity.

A parliamentary officer, clothed in black, and with a gravity that augured ill, entered, bowed to the king, and, unfolding a parchment, read him the arrest which is usually made to criminals before their execution.

"What is this?" said Aramis to Juxon.

Juxon replied with a sign which meant that he knew as little as Aramis about it.

"Then it is for to-day?" asked the king.

"Was not your majesty warned that it was to take place this morning?"

"Then I must die like a common criminal by the hand of the London executioner?"

"The London executioner has disappeared, your majesty, but a man has offered his services instead. The execution will therefore only be delayed long enough for you to arrange your spiritual and temporal affairs."

A slight moisture on his brow was the only trace of emotion that Charles evinced, as he learnt these tidings. But Aramis was livid. His heart ceased beating, he closed his eyes, and leant upon the table. Charles perceived it, and took his hand.

"Come, my friend," said he, "courage." Then he turned to the officer. "Sir, I am ready. I have little to delay you. Firstly, I wish to communicate; secondly, to embrace my children, and bid them farewell for the last time. Will this be permitted me?"

"Certainly," replied the officer, and left the room.

Aramis dug his nails into his flesh and groaned aloud.

"Oh, my Lord Bishop!" he cried, seizing Juxon's hands, "where is God? where is God?"

"My son," replied the bishop with firmness, "you see him not, because the passions of the world conceal him."

"Be seated, Juxon," said the king, falling upon his knees. "I have now to confess to you. Remain, sir," he added to Aramis, who had moved to leave the room. "Remain, Parry. I have nothing to say that cannot be said before all."

Juxon sat down, and the king, kneeling humbly before him, began his confession.

CHAPTER LXIV.

REMEMBER!

The populace was already assembled when the confession terminated. The king's children then arrived—first, the Princess Elizabeth, a beautiful fair-haired child, with tears in her eyes, and then the Duke of Gloucester, a boy eight or nine years old, whose tearless eyes and curling lip revealed a growing pride. He had wept all night long, but would not show his grief to the people.

Charles's heart melted within him. He turned to brush away a tear, and then, summoning up all his firmness, drew his daughter towards him, recommending her to be pious and resigned. Then he took the boy upon his knee.

"My son," he said to him, "you saw a great number of people in the streets as you came here. These men are going to behead your father. Do not forget that. Perhaps some day they will want to make you king, instead of the Prince of Wales, or the Duke of York, your elder brothers. But you are not the king, my son, and can never be so while they are alive. Swear to me, then, never to let them put the crown on your head. For one day—listen, my son—one day, if you do so, they will throw it all down, head and crown too, and then you will not be able to die calm and remorseless, as I die. Swear, my son."

The child stretched out his little hand towards that of his father, and said, "I swear to your majesty."

"Henry," said Charles, "call me your father."

"Father," replied the child, "I swear to you, that they shall kill me sooner than make me king."

"Good, my child. Now kiss me, and you too, Elizabeth—never forget me."

"Oh, never! never!" cried both the children, throwing their arms round their father's neck.

"Farewell," said Charles, "farewell, my children. Take them away, Juxon; their tears will deprive me of the courage to die."

Juxon led them away, and this time the doors were left open.

Meanwhile, Athos, in his concealment, waited in vain the signal to recommence his work. Two long hours he waited in terrible inaction. A death-like silence reigned in the room above. At last he determined to discover the cause of this stillness. He crept from his hole, and stood, hidden by the black drapery, beneath the scaffold. Peeping out from the drapery, he could see the rows of halberdiers and musketeers round the scaffold, and the first ranks of the populace, swaying and groaning like the sea.

"What is the matter, then?" he asked himself, trembling more than the cloth he was holding back. "The people are hurrying on, the soldiers under arms, and among the spectators I see D'Artagnan. What is he waiting for? What is he looking at? Good God! have they let the headsman escape?"

Suddenly the dull beating of muffled drums filled the square. The sound of heavy steps was heard above his head. The next moment the very planks of the scaffold creaked with the weight of an advancing procession, and the eager faces of the spectators confirmed what a last hope at the bottom of his heart had prevented him believing till then. At the same moment a well-known voice above him pronounced these words:

"Colonel, I wish to speak to the people."

Athos shuddered from head to foot. It was the king speaking on the scaffold. By his side stood a man wearing a mask, and carrying an axe in his hand, which he afterwards laid upon the block.

The sight of the mask excited a great amount of curiosity in the people, the foremost of whom strained their eyes to discover who it could be. But they could discern nothing but a man of middle height, dressed in black, apparently of a certain age, for the end of a grey beard peeped out from the bottom of the mask which concealed his features.

The king's request had undoubtedly been acceded to by an affirmative sign, for, in firm, sonorous accents, which vibrated in the depths of Athos' heart, the king began his speech, explaining his conduct, and counselling them for the welfare of England.

He was interrupted by the noise of the axe grating on the block.

"Do not touch the axe," said the king, and resumed his speech.

At the end of his speech, the king looked tenderly round upon the people. Then, unfastening the diamond ornament which the queen had sent him, he placed it in the hands of the priest who accompanied Juxon. Then he drew from his breast a little cross set in diamonds, which, like the order, had been the gift of Henrietta Maria.

"Sir," said he to the priest, "I shall keep this cross in my hand till the last moment. You will take it from me when I am dead."

He then took his hat from his head, and threw it on the ground. One by one, he undid the buttons of his doublet, took it off, and deposited it by the side of his hat. Then, as it was cold, he asked for his gown, which was brought to him.

All the preparations were made with a frightful calmness. One would have thought the king was going to bed, and not to his coffin.

"Will these be in your way?" he said to the executioner, raising his long locks; "if so they can be tied up."

Charles accompanied these words with a look designed to penetrate the mask of the unknown headsman. His calm, noble gaze forced the man to turn away his head, and the king repeated his question.

"It will do," replied the man in a deep voice, "if you separate them across the neck."

"This block is very low; is there no other to be had?"

"It is the usual block," answered the man in the mask.

"Do you think you can behead me with a single blow?" asked the king.

"I hope so," was the reply. There was something so strange in these three words that everybody except the king, shuddered.

" I do not wish to be taken by surprise," added the king. "I shall kneel down to pray, do not strike then."

" When shall I strike ?"

" When I shall lay my head on the block, and say '*Remember !*' —then strike boldly."

" Gentlemen," said the king to those around him, " I leave you to brave the tempest, and go before you to a kingdom which knows no storms. Farewell."

Then he knelt down, made the sign of the cross, and lowering his face to the planks, as if he would have kissed them, said in a low tone, in French, " Comte de la Fère, are you there ?"

" Yes, your majesty," he answered, trembling.

" Faithful friend, noble heart !" said the king, " I should not have been rescued. I have addressed my people, and I have spoken to God ; last of all I speak to you. To maintain a cause which I believe sacred, I have lost the throne, and my children their inheritance. A million in gold remains : I buried it in the cellars of Newcastle Keep. You only know that this money exists. Make use of it, then, whenever you think it will be most useful, for my eldest son's welfare. And now, farewell."

" Farewell, saintly, martyred majesty," lisped Athos, chilled with terror.

A moment's silence ensued, and then, in a full, sonorous voice, the king said, " *Remember !*"

He had scarcely uttered the word when a heavy blow shook the scaffold, and where Athos stood immovable a warm drop fell upon his brow. He reeled back with a shudder, and the same moment the drops became a black torrent.

Athos fell on his knees, and remained some moments, as if bewildered or stunned. At last he rose, and taking his handkerchief, steeped it in the blood of the martyred king. Then, as the crowd gradually dispersed, he leapt down, crept from behind the drapery, gliding between two horses, mingled with the crowd, and was the first to arrive at the inn.

Having gained his room, he raised his hand to his forehead, and finding his fingers covered with the king's blood, fell down insensible.

CHAPTER LXV.

THE MAN IN THE MASK.

THE snow was falling thick, and frozen. Aramis was the next to come in, and to discover Athos almost insensible. But at the first words he uttered, the Count roused from the kind of lethargy in which he had sunk.

"Are you wounded?" cried Aramis.

"No, this is his blood."

"Where were you, then?"

"Where you left me, under the scaffold."

"Did you see it all?"

"No, but I heard all. God preserve me from another such hour as I have just passed."

"Here is the order he gave me, and the cross I took from his hand; he desired they should be returned to the queen."

"Then here's a handkerchief to wrap them in," replied Athos, drawing from his pocket the one he had steeped in the king's blood.

"And what," he continued, "has been done with the wretched body?"

"By order of Cromwell, royal honours will be accorded to it. The doctors are busied embalming the corpse, and when ready it will be placed in a lighted chapel."

"Mockery," muttered Athos, savagely; "royal honours to one whom they have murdered!"

"Well, cheer up," said a loud voice from the staircase, which Porthos had just mounted. "We are all mortal, my poor friends."

"You are late, my dear Porthos."

"Yes, there were some people on the way who delayed me. The wretches were dancing. I took one of them by the throat, and think I throttled him a little. Just then a patrol rode up. Luckily the man I had had most to do with was some minutes before he could speak, so I took advantage of his silence to walk off."

"Have you seen D'Artagnan?"

"We got separated in the crowd, and I could not find him again."

"Oh!" said Athos, satirically, "I saw him. He was in the front row of the crowd, admirably placed for seeing; and, as on the whole, the sight was curious, he probably wished to stay to the end."

"Ah! Count de la Fère," said a calm voice, though hoarse with running, "is it you who calumniate the absent?"

This reproof stung Athos to the heart, but as the impression produced by seeing D'Artagnan foremost in a coarse, ferocious crowd had been very strong, he contented himself with replying:

"I do not calumniate you, my friend. They were anxious about you here, and I told them where you were."

So saying, he stretched out his hand, but the other pretended not to see it, and he let it drop again slowly by his side.

"Ugh! I am tired," cried D'Artagnan, sitting down.

"Drink a glass of port," said Aramis; "it will refresh you."

"Yes, let us drink," said Athos, anxious to make it up by hob-nobbing glasses with D'Artagnan, "let us drink, and get away from this hateful country."

"You are in a hurry, sir count," said D'Artagnan.

"But what would you have us do here, now that the king is dead?"

"Go, sir count," replied D'Artagnan, carelessly; "you see nothing to keep you a little longer in England? Well, for my part, I, a bloodthirsty ruffian, who can go and stand close to a scaffold, in order to have a better view of the king's execution—I remain."

Athos turned pale. Every reproach his friend made struck deeply into his heart.

"Hang it!" said Porthos, a little perplexed between the two, "I suppose, as I came with you, I must leave with you. I can't leave you alone in this abominable country."

"Thanks, my worthy friend. So then I have a little adventure to propose to you when the count is gone. I want to find out who was the man in the mask, who so obligingly offered to cut the king's throat."

"A man in a mask?" cried Athos. "You did not let the executioner escape, then?"

"The executioner is still in the cellar, where, I presume, he has had a few words' conversation with mine host's bottles. But you remind me. Mousqueton!"

"Sir," answered a voice from the depths of the earth.

"Let out your prisoner. All is over."

"But," said Athos, "who is the wretch who has dared to raise his hand against his king?"

"An amateur headsman," replied Aramis, "who, however, does not handle the axe amiss."

" Did you not see his face ?" asked Athos.

" He wore a mask."

" But you, Aramis, who were close to him ?"

" I could see nothing but a grey beard under the bottom of the mask."

" Then it must be a man of a certain age."

" Oh !" said D'Artagnan, " that matters little. When one puts on a mask, it is not difficult to wear a beard under it."

" I am sorry I did not follow him," said Porthos.

" Well, my dear Porthos," said D'Artagnan, " that's the very thing which it came into my head to do."

Athos understood it all now.

" Forgive me, my friend," he said, offering his hand to D'Artagnan.

" Well," said D'Artagnan, " while I was looking on, the fancy took me to discover who this masked individual might be. Well, I looked about for Porthos, and as I did so, I saw near me a head which had been broken, but which, for better or worse, had been mended with black silk. Humph !" thought I, " that looks like my cut ; I fancy I must have mended that skull somewhere or other. And in fact, it was that unfortunate Scotchman, Parry's brother, you know, on whom Groslow amused himself by trying his strength. Well, this man was making signs to another at my left, and turning round, I recognised the honest Grimaud. 'Oh !' said I to him. Grimaud turned round with a jerk, recognised me, and pointed to the man in the mask. 'Eh ?' said he, which meant, 'Do you see him ?' 'Parbleu !' I answered, and we perfectly understood one another. Well, everything finished you know how. The mob dispersed. I made a sign to Grimaud and the Scotchman, and we all three retired into a corner of the square. I saw the executioner return into the king's room, change his clothes, put on a black hat and a large cloak, and disappear. Five minutes later he came down the grand staircase."

" You followed him ?" cried Athos.

" I should think so, but not without difficulty. Every minute he turned round, and thus obliged us to conceal ourselves. I might have gone up to him and killed him. But I am not selfish ; and I thought it might console you all a little to have a share in the matter. So we followed him through the lowest streets in the city, and, in half an hour's time, he stopped before a small isolated house. Grimaud drew out a pistol. 'Eh ?' said he, showing it. I held back his arm. The man in the mask stopped before a low door, and drew out a key ; but before he placed it in the lock, he turned round to see if he was not followed. Grimaud and I had got behind a tree, and the Scotchman having nowhere to hide himself, threw himself on his face in the road. Next moment the door opened, and the man disappeared. I placed the Scotchman at the door by which he entered, making a sign to him to follow the man wherever he might go, if he came out again. Then going round the house, I placed Grimaud at the other exit, and here I am. Our game is beaten up. Now for the tally-ho !"

Athos threw himself into D'Artagnan's arms.

"Humph !" said Porthos. "Don't you think the executioner might be Master Cromwell himself, who, to make sure of his affair, undertook it himself ?"

"Ah ! just so. Cromwell is stout and short, and this man thin and lank, and rather tall than otherwise."

"Some condemned soldier, perhaps," suggested Athos, "whom they have pardoned at the price of this deed."

"No, no," continued D'Artagnan. "It was not the measured step of a foot-soldier, nor the easy gait of a horseman. If I am not mistaken, it was a gentleman's walk."

"A gentleman !" exclaimed Athos. "Impossible ! It would be a disgrace to his whole family."

"Fine sport, by Jove !" cried Porthos, with a laugh that shook the windows. "Fine sport !"

"Swords !" cried Aramis, "swords ! and let us not lose a moment."

The four friends resumed their own clothes, girt on their swords, ordered Mousqueton and Blaisois to pay the bill, and to arrange everything for immediate departure, and, wrapped in their large cloaks, left in search of their game.

The night was dark, the snow still falling, and the streets deserted. D'Artagnan led the way through the intricate windings and narrow alleys of the city, and ere long they had reached the house in question. For a moment D'Artagnan thought that Parry's brother had disappeared; but he was mistaken. The robust Scotchman, accustomed to the snows of his native hills, had stretched himself against a post, and like a fallen statue, insensible to the inclemencies of the weather, had allowed the snow to cover him. He rose, however, as they approached.

"Come," said Athos, "here's another good servant. Really, honest men are not so scarce as I thought."

"Don't be in a hurry to weave crowns for our Scotchman. I elieve the fellow is here on his own account; for I have heard that these gentlemen born beyond the Tweed are very vindictive. I should not like to be Groslow, if he meets him."

"Well ?" said Athos to the man in English.

"No one has come out," he replied.

"Then Porthos and Aramis, will you remain with this man, while we go round to Grimaud ?"

Grimaud had made himself a kind of sentry-box out of a hollow willow, and as they drew near, he put his head out and gave a low whistle.

"Oh !" said Athos.

"Yes," replied Grimaud.

"Well, has anybody come out ?"

"No, but somebody has gone in."

"A man or a woman ?"

"A man." At the same time he pointed to a window, through the shutters of which a faint light streamed.

They returned round the house to fetch Porthos and Aramis.

"Have you seen anything ?" they asked.

"No, but we are going to," replied D'Artagnan, pointing to Grimaud, who had already climbed some five or six feet from the ground.

All four came up together. Grimaud continued to climb like a cat, and succeeded at last in catching hold of a hook which served to keep one of the shutters back when opened. Then resting his foot on a small ledge, he made a sign to show that he was all right.

"Well ?" asked D'Artagnan.

Grimaud showed his closed hand, with two fingers spread out.

"Speak," said Athos ; "we cannot see your signs. How many are they ?"

"Two. One opposite to me, the other with his back to me."

"Good. And the man opposite to you is——?"

"The man I saw go in."

"Do you know him ?"

"I thought I recognised him, and was not mistaken. Short and stout."

"Who is it ?" they all asked together in a low tone.

"General Oliver Cromwell."

The four friends looked at one another.

"And the other ?" asked Athos.

"Thin and lank."

"The executioner," said D'Artagnan and Aramis at the same time.

"I can see nothing but his back," resumed Grimaud. "But wait. He is moving ; and if he has taken off his mask I shall be able to see. Ah !——"

And, as if struck in the heart, he let go the hook, and dropped with a groan.

"Did you see him?" they all asked.

"Yes," said Grimaud, with his hair standing on end.

"The thin and spare man?"

"Yes."

"The executioner, in short?" asked Aramis.

"Yes."

"And who is it?" said Porthos.

"He—he—" murmured Grimaud, pale as death, and seizing his master's hand.

"Who? He?" asked Athos.

"Mordaunt!" replied Grimaud.

D'Artagnan, Porthos, and Aramis uttered a cry of joy.

Athos stepped back, and passed his hand over his brow.

"Fatality!" he muttered.

CHAPTER LXVI.

CROMWELL'S HOUSE.

It was, in fact, Mordaunt, whom D'Artagnan had followed, without knowing it. On entering the house he had taken off his mask and the false beard, and mounting a staircase, had opened a door, and in a room lighted by a single lamp, found himself face to face with a man seated behind a desk.

This man was Cromwell.

Cromwell had two or three of these retreats in London, unknown except to the most intimate of his friends. Now Mordaunt was among these.

"It is you, Mordaunt," he said. "You are late."

"General, I wished to see the ceremony to the end, which delayed me."

"Ah! I scarcely thought you were so curious as that."

"I am always curious to see the downfall of your honour's enemies, and that one was not among the least of them. But you, general, were you not at Whitehall?"

"No," said Cromwell.

There was a moment's silence.

"Have you had any account of it?"

"None. I have been here since the morning. I only know that there was a conspiracy to rescue the king."

" Ah, you knew that," said Mordaunt.

" It matters little.   Four men, disguised as workmen, were to get the king out of prison, and take him to Greenwich, where a skiff was waiting."

" And, knowing all that, your honour remained here, far from the city, calm and inactive ?"

" Calm ? yes," replied Cromwell.   " But who told you I was inactive ?"

" But—if the plot had succeeded ?"

" I wished it to do so."

" I thought your excellence considered the death of Charles I. as a misfortune necessary to the welfare of England ?"

" Yes, his death ; but it would have been better not on the scaffold."

" Why so ?" asked Mordaunt.

Cromwell smiled.   " Because it could have been said that I had had him condemned for the sake of justice, and had let him escape out of pity."

" But if he had escaped ?"

" Impossible ; my precautions were taken."

" And does your honour know the four men who undertook to rescue him ?"

" The four Frenchmen, of whom two were sent by the queen to her husband, and two by Mazarin to me."

" And do you think Mazarin commissioned them to act as they have done ?"

" It is possible.   But he will not avow it."

" How so ?"

" Because they failed."

" Your honour gave me two of these Frenchmen when they were only fighting for Charles I.   Now that they are guilty of a conspiracy against England, will your honour give me all four of them ?"

" Take them," said Cromwell.

Mordaunt bowed with a smile of triumphant ferocity.

" Did the people shout at all ?" Cromwell asked.

" Very little, except ' Long live Cromwell ! ' "

" Where were you placed ?"

Mordaunt tried for a moment to read in the general's face if this was simply a useless question, or whether he knew everything. But his piercing eye could not penetrate the sombre depths of Cromwell's.

" I was placed so as to hear and see everything," he answered.

It was now Cromwell's turn to look fixedly at Mordaunt, and Mordaunt's to make himself impenetrable.

"It appears," said Cromwell, "that this improvised executioner did his duty very well. The blow, so they told me at least, was struck with a master's hand."

Mordaunt remembered that Cromwell had told him he had had no detailed account, and he was now quite convinced that the general had been present at the execution, hidden behind some curtain or blind.

"Perhaps it was some one in the trade?" said Cromwell.

"Do you think so, sir? He did not look like an executioner."

"And who else than an executioner would have wished to fill that horrible office?"

"But," said Mordaunt, "it might have been some personal enemy of the king, who may have made a vow of vengeance, and accomplished it in this manner."

"Possibly."

"And if that were the case, would your honour condemn his action?"

"It is not for me to judge. It rests between him and God."

"But if your honour knew this man?"

"I neither know, nor wish to know him. Provided Charles is dead, it is the axe, not the man, we must thank."

"And yet, without the man, the king would have been rescued."

Cromwell smiled.

"They would have carried him to Greenwich," he said, "and put him on board a skiff, with five barrels of powder in the hold. Once out at sea, you are too good a politician not to understand the rest, Mordaunt."

"Yes, they would all have been blown up."

"Just so. The explosion would have done what the axe had failed to do. They would have said that the king had escaped human justice, and been overtaken by God's arm. You see now why I did not care to know your gentleman in a mask."

Mordaunt bowed humbly. "Sir," he said, "you are a profound thinker, and your plan was sublime."

"Say absurd, since it is become useless. The only sublime ideas in politics are those which bear fruit. So, to-night, Mordaunt, go to Greenwich, and ask for the captain of the skiff 'Lightning.' Show him a white handkerchief knotted at the four corners, and tell the crew to disembark, and carry the powder back to the Arsenal, unless indeed——"

"Unless?"

"This skiff might be of use to you for your personal projects."

"Oh my lord, my lord!"

"That title," said Cromwell, laughing, "is all very well here, but take care a word like that does not escape in public."

"But your honour will soon be called so generally."

"I hope so, at least," said Cromwell, rising and putting on his cloak.

"Then," said Mordaunt, "your honour gives me full power?"

"Certainly."

"Thank you, thank you."

Cromwell turned as he was going.

"Are you armed?" he asked.

"I have my sword."

"And no one waiting for you outside?"

"No."

"Then you had better come with me."

"Thank you, sir, but the way by the subterranean passage would take me too much time, and I have none to lose."

Cromwell placed his hand on a hidden handle, and opened a door so well concealed by the tapestry, that the most practised eye could not have discovered it, and which closed after him with a spring. This door communicated with a subterranean passage, leading under the street to a grotto in the garden of a house about a hundred yards from that of the future Protector.

It was just before this that Grimaud had perceived the two men seated together.

D'Artagnan was the first to recover from his surprise.

"Mordaunt," he cried, "thank heaven!"

"Yes," said Porthos, "let us knock the door in, and fall upon him."

"No," replied D'Artagnan, "no noise. Now, Grimaud, you come here, climb up to the window again, and tell us if Mordaunt is alone, and whether he is preparing to go out or to go to bed. If he comes out, we shall catch him. If he stays in, we will break in the window. It is easier and less noisy than the door."

Grimaud began to scale the wall again.

"Keep guard at the other door, Athos and Aramis. Porthos and I will stay here."

The friends obeyed.

"He is alone," said Grimaud.

"We did not see his companion come out."

"He may have gone by the other door."

"What is he doing?"

"Putting on his cloak and gloves."

"He is ours," muttered D'Artagnan.

Porthos mechanically drew his dagger from the scabbard.

"Put it up again, my friend," said D'Artagnan. "We must proceed in an orderly manner."

"Hush!" said Grimaud, "he is coming out. He has put out the lamp. I can see nothing now."

"Get down then, get down."

Grimaud leapt down, and the snow deadened the noise of his fall.

"Now, go and tell Athos and Aramis to stand on each side of their door, and clap their hands if they catch him. We will do the same."

The next moment the door opened, and Mordaunt appeared on the threshold, face to face with D'Artagnan. Porthos clapped his hands, and the other two came running round. Mordaunt was livid, but he uttered no cry, nor called for assistance. D'Artagnan quietly pushed him in again, and by the light of a lamp on the staircase, made him ascend the steps backward one by one, keeping his eyes all the time on Mordaunt's hands, who, however, knowing that it was useless, attempted no resistance. At last they stood face to face in the very room where ten minutes before Mordaunt had been talking to Cromwell.

Porthos came up behind, and unhooking the lamp on the staircase re-lit that in the room. Athos and Aramis entered last and locked the door after them.

"Oblige me by taking a seat," said D'Artagnan, pushing a chair towards Mordaunt, who sat down, pale but calm. Aramis, Porthos, and D'Artagnan drew their chairs near him. Athos alone kept away, and sat in the furthest corner of the room, as if determined to be merely a spectator of the proceedings. He seemed to be quite overcome. Porthos rubbed his hands in feverish impatience. Aramis bit his lips till the blood came.

D'Artagnan alone was calm, at least in appearance.

"Monsieur Mordaunt," he said, "since, after running after one another so long, chance has at last brought us together, let us have a little conversation, if you please."

CHAPTER LXVII.

CONVERSATIONAL.

THOUGH Mordaunt had been so completely taken by surprise, and had mounted the stairs under the impression of utter confusion, when once seated he recovered himself, as it were, and prepared to seize any possible opportunity of escaping. His eye wandered to a long stout sword on his flank, and he instinctively slipped it round within reach of his right hand.

D'Artagnan was waiting for a reply to his remark, and said nothing. Aramis muttered to himself, "We shall hear nothing but the usual commonplace things."

Porthos sucked his moustache, muttering, "A good deal of ceremony here about crushing an adder." Athos shrunk into his corner, pale and motionless as a bas-relief.

The silence, however, could not last for ever. So D'Artagnan began :

"Sir," he said, with desperate politeness, "it seems to me that you change your costume almost as rapidly as I have seen the Italian mummers do, whom the Cardinal Mazarin brought over from Bergamo, and whom he doubtless took you to see, during your travels in France."

Mordaunt did not reply.

"Just now," D'Artagnan continued, "you were disguised—I mean to say, attired—as a murderer, and now——"

"And now I look very much like a man who is going to be murdered."

"Oh! sir," answered D'Artagnan, "how can you talk like that, when you are in the company of gentlemen, and have such an excellent sword at your side."

"No sword is good enough to be of any use against four swords and four daggers."

"Well, that is scarcely the question. I had the honour of asking you why you altered your costume. Surely the mask and beard suited you very well, and as to the axe, I do not think it would be out of keeping even at this moment."

"Because, remembering the scene at Armentières, I thought I should find four axes for one, as I was to meet four executioners."

"Sir," replied D'Artagnan, in the calmest manner possible "you are very young; I shall therefore overlook your frivolous remarks. What took place at Armentières has no connection whatever with the present occasion. We could scarcely have requested your mother to take a sword and fight with us."

"Aha! It's a duel then?" cried Mordaunt, as if disposed to reply at once to the provocation.

Porthos rose, always ready for this kind of adventure.

" Pardon me," said D'Artagnan. " Do not let us be in a hurry. We will arrange the matter rather better. Confess, Monsieur Mordaunt, that you are anxious to kill some of us."

" All," replied Mordaunt.

"Then, my dear sir, I am convinced that these gentlemen return your kind wishes, and will be delighted to kill you also. Of course they will do so as honourable gentlemen, and the best proof I can furnish is this——"

So saying, he threw his hat on the ground, pushed back his chair to the wall, and bowed to Mordaunt with true French grace.

"At your service, sir," he continued. " My sword is shorter than yours, it's true, but bah ! I hope the arm will make up for the sword."

"Halt !" cried Porthos, coming forward. " I begin, and that's logic."

" Allow me, Porthos," said Aramis.

Athos did not move. You might have taken him for a statue.

"Gentlemen," said D'Artagnan, "you shall have your turn. Monsieur Mordaunt dislikes you sufficiently not to refuse you afterwards. You can see it in his eye. So pray keep your places. like Athos, whose calmness is most laudable. Besides, we will have no words about it. I have a particular business to settle with this gentleman, and I shall and will begin."

Porthos and Aramis drew back disappointed ; and, drawing his sword, D'Artagnan turned to his adversary.

" Sir, I am waiting for you."

" And for my part, gentlemen, I admire you. You are disputing which shall fight me first, and you do not consult me, who am most concerned in the matter. I hate you all, but not equally. I claim the right to choose my opponent. If you refuse this right, you may kill me, for I shall not fight."

" It is but fair," said Porthos and Aramis, hoping he would choose one of them.

"Well, then," said Mordaunt, "I choose for my adversary the man who, not thinking himself worthy to be called Comte de la Fère, calls himself Athos."

Athos sprang up, but after an instant of motionless silence, he said, to the astonishment of his friends, "Monsieur Mordaunt, a duel between us is impossible. Give this honour to somebody else." And he sat down.

"Ah!" said Mordaunt with a sneer, "there's one who is afraid."

"Zounds!" cried D'Artagnan, bounding towards him, "who says that Athos is afraid?"

"Let him go on, D'Artagnan," said Athos, with a smile of sadness and contempt.

"Is it your decision, Athos?" resumed the Gascon.

"Yes, irrevocably."

"You hear, sir," said D'Artagnan, turning to Mordaunt, "choose one of us to replace the Comte de la Fère."

"As long as I don't fight with him, it is the same to me with whom I fight. Put your names into a hat, and draw lots."

"At least that will conciliate us all," said Aramis.

"I should never have thought of that," said Porthos, "and yet it's a very simple plan."

Aramis went to Cromwell's desk, and wrote the three names on slips of paper, which he threw into a hat.

Mordaunt drew one and threw it on the table.

"Ah! serpent," muttered D'Artagnan; "I would give my chance of a captaincy in the '*Mousquetaires*' for that to be my name."

Aramis opened the paper, and in a voice trembling with hate and vengeance, read, "D'Artagnan."

The Gascon uttered a cry of joy, and turning to Mordaunt,—

"I hope, sir," said he, "you have no objection to make."

"None whatever," replied the other, drawing his sword and resting the point on his boot."

The moment that D'Artagnan saw that his wish was accomplished, and his man would not escape him, he recovered his usual tranquillity. He turned up his cuffs neatly, and rubbed the sole of his right boot on the floor, but did not fail, however, to remark that Mordaunt was looking about him in a singular manner.

"Are you ready, sir?" he said at last.

"I was waiting for you, sir," said Mordaunt, raising his head and casting at his opponent a look which it would be impossible to describe.

"Well, then," said the Gascon, "take care of yourself, for I am not a bad hand at the rapier."

"Nor I either."

"So much the better. That sets my mind at rest. Defend yourself!"

"One minute," said the young man; "give me your word, gentlemen, that you will not attack me otherwise than one after the other."

"Is it to have the pleasure of insulting us that you say that, little serpent?"

"No, but to set my mind at rest, as you said just now."

"It is for something else than that, I imagine," muttered D'Artagnan, shaking his head doubtfully.

"On the honour of gentlemen," said Aramis and Porthos.

"In that case, gentlemen, have the kindness to retire into the corners, and leave us room. We shall want it."

"Yes, gentlemen," said D'Artagnan, "we must not leave this person the slightest pretext for behaving badly, which, with all due respect, I fancy he is anxious to do."

This new attack made no impression on Mordaunt. The space was cleared, the two lamps placed on Cromwell's desk, in order that the combatants might have as much light as possible; and the swords crossed.

D'Artagnan was too good a swordsman to trifle with his opponent. He made a rapid and brilliant feint, which Mordaunt parried.

"Aha!" he cried, with a smile of satisfaction.

And without losing a minute, thinking he saw an opening, he thrust right in, and forced Mordaunt to parry a counterquart so fine that the point of the weapon might have turned within a wedding ring.

This time it was Mordaunt who smiled.

"Ah, sir," said D'Artagnan, "you have a wicked smile. It must have been the devil who taught it you, was it not?"

Mordaunt replied by trying his opponent's weapon with an amount of strength which the Gascon was astonished to find in a form apparently so weak; but, thanks to a parry no less clever than that which Mordaunt had just achieved, he succeeded in meeting his sword, which slid along his own without touching his chest.

Mordaunt rapidly sprang back a step.

"Ah, you lose ground, you are turning? Well, as you please. I even gain something by it, for I no longer see that wicked smile of yours. You have no idea what a false look you have, particularly when you are afraid. Look at my eyes, and you will see what your looking-glass never showed you—a frank and honourable countenance."

To this flow of words, not perhaps in the best taste, but characteristic of D'Artagnan, whose principal object was to divert his opponent's attention, Mordaunt did not reply, but, continuing to turn round, he succeeded in changing places with D'Artagnan.

He smiled more and more, and his smile began to make the Gascon anxious.

"Come, come," said D'Artagnan, "we must finish 'with this," and in his turn he pressed Mordaunt hard, who continued to lose ground, but evidently on purpose, and without letting his sword leave the line for a moment. However, as they were fighting in a room, and had not space to go on like that for ever, Mordaunt's foot at last touched the wall, against which he rested his left hand.

"Ah, this time you cannot lose ground, my fine friend," exclaimed D'Artagnan. "Gentlemen, did you ever see a scorpion pinned to a wall? No. Well, then, you shall see it now."

In a second D'Artagnan had made three terrible thrusts at Mordaunt, all of which touched but only pricked him. The three friends looked on panting and astonished. At last D'Artagnan, having got up too close, stepped back to prepare a fourth thrust, but the moment when, after a fine, quick feint, he was attacking as sharply as lightning, the wall seemed to give way, Mordaunt disappeared through the opening, and D'Artagnan's sword, caught between the panels, shivered like glass. D'Artagnan sprang back; the wall had closed again.

Mordaunt, in fact, while defending himself, had manœuvred so as to reach the secret door by which Cromwell had left, had felt for the handle with his left hand, turned it, and disappeared.

The Gascon uttered a furious imprecation, which was answered by a wild laugh on the other side of the iron panel.

"Help me, gentlemen," cried D'Artagnan, "We must break in this door."

"He escapes us," growled Porthos, pushing his huge shoulder against the hinges, but in vain. "'Sblood, he escapes us."

"So much the better," muttered Athos.

"I thought as much," said D'Artagnan, wasting his strength in useless efforts. "Zounds, I thought as much, when the wretch kept moving round the room. I thought he was up to something!"

"It's a misfortune which his friend, the devil, sends us," said Aramis.

"It's a piece of good fortune sent from heaven," said Athos, evidently pleased.

"Really!" said D'Artagnan, abandoning the attempt to burst open the panel after several ineffectual attempts, "Athos, I cannot imagine how you can talk to us in that way. You cannot understand the position we are in. In this kind of game, not to kill, is to let one's self be killed. This wretched fellow will be sending us a hundred Iron-sided beasts who will pick us off like berries in this place. Come, come, we must be off. If we stay here five minutes more, there's an end of us."

"Yes, you are right."

"But where shall we go to?" asked Porthos.

"To the hotel, to be sure, to get our baggage and horses; and from there, if it please God, to France, where, at least, I understand the architecture of the houses."

So, suiting the action to the word, D'Artagnan thrust the remains of his sword into its scabbard, picked up his hat, and ran down the stairs followed by the others.

CHAPTER LXVIII.

THE SKIFF "LIGHTNING."

MORDAUNT glided through the subterranean passage, and, gaining the neighbouring house, stopped to take breath.

"Good," said he, "a mere nothing. Scratches, that is all. Now to my work."

He walked on at a quick pace, till he reached a neighbouring cavalry-barrack, where he happened to be known. Here he borrowed a horse, the best in the stables, and in a quarter of an hour was at Greenwich.

"'Tis well," said he, as he reached the river bank. "I am half an hour before them. Now," he added, rising in the stirrup, and looking about him, "which, I wonder, is the 'Lightning?'"

At this moment, as if to reply to his words, a man lying on a heap of cables rose and advanced a few steps towards him. Mordaunt drew a handkerchief from his pocket, and tying a knot at each corner—the signal agreed upon—waved it in the air, and the man came up to him. He was wrapped in a large rough cape, which concealed his form and partly his face.

"Do you wish to go on the water, sir?" said the sailor.

"Yes, just so. Along the Isle of Dogs."

"And perhaps you have a preference for one boat more than another. You would like one that sails as rapidly——"

"As lightning," interrupted Mordaunt.

"Then mine is the boat you want, sir. I'm your man."

"I begin to think so, particularly if you have not forgotten a certain signal."

"Here it is, sir," and the sailor took from his coat a handkerchief, tied at each corner.

"Good; quite right!" cried Mordaunt, springing off his horse. "There is no time to lose; now take my horse to the nearest inn, and conduct me to your vessel."

"But," asked the sailor, "where are your companions? I thought there were four of you."

"Listen to me, sir; I'm not the man you take me for; you are in Captain Rogers's post, are you not? under orders from General Cromwell? Mine, also, are from him!"

"Indeed, sir, I recognise you; you are Captain Mordaunt. Don't be afraid, you are with a friend. I am Captain Groslow. The general remembered that I had formerly been a naval officer, and he gave me the command of this expedition; has anything new occurred?"

"Nothing."

"I thought, perhaps, that the king's death——"

"It has only hastened their flight; in ten minutes they will, perhaps, be here. I am going to embark with you. I wish to aid in the deed of vengeance. All is ready, I suppose?"

"Yes."

"The cargo on board?"

"Yes—and we are sailing from Oporto to Antwerp, remember."

"'Tis well."

They then went down to the Thames. A boat was fastened to the shore by a chain fixed to a stake. Groslow jumped in, followed by Mordaunt, and in five minutes they were quite away from that world of houses which then crowded the outskirts of London; and Mordaunt could discern the little vessel riding at anchor near the Isle of Dogs. When they reached the side of this felucca, Mordaunt, dexterous in his eager desire for vengeance, seized a rope, and climbed up the sides of the vessel with a coolness and agility very rare among landsmen. He went with Groslow to the captain's berth—a sort of temporary cabin of planks—for the chief apartment had been given up by Captain Rogers to the passengers, who were to be accommodated at the other extremity of the boat.

"They will have nothing to do with this side of the ship, then," said Mordaunt.

"Nothing at all."

"That's a capital arrangement. Return to Greenwich, and

bring them here. I shall hide myself in your cabin. You have a long boat?"

"That in which we came."

"It appeared light, and well-constructed."

"Quite a canoe."

"Fasten it to the poop with ropes—put the oars into it, so that it may follow in the track, and that there will be nothing to do except to cut the cord away. Put a good supply of rum and biscuit in it for the seamen; should the night happen to be stormy, they will not be sorry to find something to console themselves with."

"All shall be done. Do you wish to see the powder-room?"

"No; when you return, I will put the match myself; but be careful to conceal your face, so that you cannot be recognised by them."

"Never fear."

"There's ten o'clock striking, at Greenwich."

Groslow, then, having given the sailor on duty an order to be on the watch with more than usual attention, went down into the long boat, and soon reached Greenwich. The wind was chilly, and the jetty was deserted as he approached it; but he had no sooner landed, than he heard a noise of horses galloping upon the paved road.

These horsemen were our friends, or rather, an avant-garde, composed of D'Artagnan and Athos. As soon as they arrived at the spot where Groslow stood, they stopped, as if guessing that he was the man they wanted. Athos alighted, and calmly opened the handkerchief tied at each corner, and unfolded it; whilst D'Artagnan, ever cautious, remained on horseback, one hand upon his arms, leaning anxiously forward.

On seeing the appointed signal, Groslow, who had, at first, crept behind one of the cannon planted on that spot, walked straight up to the gentlemen. He was so well wrapt up in his cloak that it would have been impossible to have seen his face even if the night had not been so dark as to render any precaution superfluous; nevertheless, the keen glance of Athos perceived that it was not Rogers who stood before them.

"What do you want with us?" he asked of Groslow.

"I wish to inform you, my lord," replied Groslow, with an Irish accent, feigned of course, "that if you are looking for Captain Rogers you will not find him. He fell down this morning and broke his leg; but I'm his cousin; he told me everything, and desired me to look out for, and to conduct you to any place named by the four gentlemen who should bring me a handkerchief tied at each corner, like that one which you hold, and one which I have in my pocket."

And he drew out the handkerchief.

" Was that all he said ?" inquired Athos.

" No, my lord ; he said you had engaged to pay seventy pounds if I landed you safe and sound at Boulogne, or any other port you chose, in France."

" What do you think of all this ?" said Athos, in a low tone to D'Artagnan, after explaining to him in French what the sailor had said in English.

" It seems a likely story to me."

" And to me, too."

" Besides, we can but blow out his brains if he proves false," said the Gascon ; " and you, Athos, you know something of everything, and can be our captain. I dare say you know how to navigate, should he fail us."

" My dear friend, you guess well ; my father destined me for the navy, and I have some vague notions about navigation."

" You see !" cried D'Artagnan.

They then summoned their friends, who, with Blaisois, Mousqueton, and Grimaud, promptly joined them—leaving behind them Parry, who was to take their horses back to London ; and they all proceeded instantly to the shore, and placed themselves in the boat, which, rowed by Groslow, began rapidly to clear the coast.

" At last," exclaimed Porthos, " we are afloat."

" Alas !" said Athos, " we depart alone."

" Yes ; but all four together, and without a scratch ; which is a consolation."

" We are not yet arrived at our destination," observed the prudent D'Artagnan ; " beware of rencontres."

" Ah ! my friend !" cried Porthos ; " like the crows, you always bring bad omens. Who could intercept us in such a night as this —pitch dark—when one does not see more than twenty yards before one ?"

" Yes—but to-morrow morning——"

" To-morrow we shall be at Boulogne ; however, I like to hear Monsieur d'Artagnan confess that he's afraid."

" I not only confess it, but am proud of it," returned the Gascon ; " I'm not such a rhinoceros as you are. Oho ! what's that ?"

" The ' Lightning,' " answered the captain, " our felucca."

" We are then arrived ?" said Athos.

They went on board, and the captain instantly conducted them to the berth destined for them—a cabin which was to serve for all purposes, and for the whole party; he then tried to slip away under pretext of giving orders to some one."

"Stop a moment," cried D'Artagnan; "pray how many men have you on board, captain?"

"I don't understand," was the reply.

"Explain it, Athos."

Groslow, on the question being interpreted, answered:

"Three, without counting myself."

"Oh!" exclaimed D'Artagnan. "I begin to be more at my ease; however, whilst you settle yourselves, I shall make the round of the boat."

"As for me," said Porthos, "I will see to the supper."

"A very good deed, Porthos," said the Gascon. "Athos, lend me Grimaud, who in the society of his friend Parry, has, perhaps, picked up a little English, and can act as my interpreter."

"Go, Grimaud," said Athos.

D'Artagnan, finding a lanthorn on the deck, took it up, and with a pistol in his hand, he said to the captain, in English, "Come" (being, with the usual English oath, the only English words he knew), and so saying, he descended to the lower deck.

This was divided into three compartments; one which was covered by the floor of that room in which Athos, Porthos, and Aramis were to pass the night; the second was to serve as the sleeping room for the servants; the third, under the prow of the ship, was underneath the temporary cabin in which Mordaunt was concealed.

"Oho!" cried D'Artagnan, as he went down the steps of the hatchway, preceded by the lanthorn; "what a number of barrels! one would think one was in the cave of Ali Baba. What is there in them?" he added, putting his lanthorn on one of the bins.

The captain seemed inclined to go upon deck again, but, controlling himself, he answered:

"Port wine."

"Ah! port wine! 'tis a comfort," said the Gascon, "that we shall not die of thirst; are they all full?"

Grimaud translated the question, and Groslow, who was wiping the perspiration from off his forehead, answered:

"Some full, others empty."

D'Artagnan struck the barrels with his hand, and having ascertained that he spoke the truth, pushed his lanthorn, greatly to the captain's alarm, into the interstices between the barrels, and finding that there was nothing concealed in them,—

" Come along," he said ; and he went towards the door of the second compartment.

" Stop !" said the Englishman. " I have the key of that door;" and he opened the door with a trembling hand, into the second compartment, where Mousqueton and Blaisois were just going to supper.

Here there was evidently nothing to seek, or to reprehend, and they passed rapidly to examine the third compartment.

This was the room appropriated to the sailors. Two or three hammocks hung up on the ceiling, a table and two benches, composed all the furniture. D'Artagnan picked up two or three old sails, hung on the walls, and seeing nothing to suspect, regained, by the hatchway, the deck of the vessel.

" And this room ?" he asked, pointing to the captain's cabin.

" That's my room," replied Groslow.

" Open the door."

The captain obeyed. D'Artagnan stretched out his arm, in which he held the lanthorn, put his head in at the half-opened door, and seeing that the cabin was nothing better than a shed,—

" Good !" he said. " If there is an army on board, it is not here that it is hidden. Let us see what Porthos has found for supper." And thanking the captain, he regained the state cabin, where his friends were.

Porthos had found nothing ; and fatigue had prevailed over hunger. He had fallen asleep, and was in a profound slumber when D'Artagnan returned. Athos and Aramis were beginning to close their eyes, which they half opened when their companion came in again.

" Well ?" said Aramis.

" All is well ; we may sleep tranquilly."

On this assurance the two friends fell asleep ; and D'Artagnan, who was very weary, bade good night to Grimaud, and laid himself down in his cloak, with a naked sword at his side, in such a manner that his body might barricade the passage, and that it should be impossible to enter the room without overturning him.

CHAPTER LXIX.

PORT WINE.

In ten minutes the masters slept; not so the servants—hungry and uncomfortable.

" Grimaud," said Mousqueton to his companion, who had just come in after his round with D'Artagnan, " art thou thirsty ?"

" As thirsty as a Scotchman !" was Grimaud's laconic reply.

And he sat down and began to cast up the accounts of his party, whose money he managed.

"Oh law ! lackadaisy ! I'm beginning to feel queer !" cried Blaisois.

" If that's the case," said Mousqueton, with a learned air, "take some nourishment."

" Do you call that nourishment ?" asked Blaisois, pointing to the barley bread and the pot of beer.

" Blaisois," replied Mousqueton, "remember that bread is the true nourishment of a Frenchman, who is not always able to get bread : ask Grimaud."

" Yes, but beer ?" asked Blaisois, sharply ; " is that their true drink ?"

" As to that," answered Mousqueton, puzzled how to get out of the difficulty, " I must confess, that to me, beer is as disagreeable as wine to the English."

" How ? Monsieur Mousqueton ! How—the English—do they dislike wine ?"

" They hate it."

" But I have seen them drink it."

"—As a punishment ; for example, an English prince died one day because he was put into a butt of Malmsey. I heard the Chevalier d'Herblay say so."

" The fool !" cried Blaisois ; " I wish I had been in his place."

" Thou canst be," said Grimaud, writing down his figures.

" How ?" asked Blaisois ; " I can ? Explain yourself."

Grimaud went on with his sum, and cast up the whole.

" Port !" he said, extending his hand in the direction of the first compartment examined by D'Artagnan and himself.

" How—those barrels I saw through the door ?"

" Port !" replied Grimaud, who began a fresh sum.

" I have heard," said Blaisois, "that port is a very good wine."

" Excellent !" cried Mousqueton, smacking his lips.

" Excellent !"

" Supposing these Englishmen would sell us a bottle," said the honest Blaisois.

" Sell !" cried Mousqueton, about whom there was a remnant of his ancient marauding character left. " One may well perceive, young man, that you are still inexperienced. Why buy when one can take ?"

" To take ?" answered Blaisois. " To covet one's neighbour's goods is forbidden, I believe."

"What a childish reason!" said Mousqueton, condescendingly; "yes, childish; I repeat the word. Where did you learn, pray, to consider the English as your neighbours?"

"The saying's true, dear Mouston; but I don't remember where."

"Childish—still more childish," replied Mousqueton. "Hadst thou been ten years engaged in war, as Grimaud and I have been, my dear Blaisois, you would know the difference that there is between the goods of others and the goods of your enemies. Now an Englishman is an enemy; as this port wine belongs to the English, therefore it belongs to us."

"And our masters?" asked Blaisois, stupefied by this harangue, delivered with an air of profound sagacity, "will they be of your opinion?"

Mousqueton smiled disdainfully.

"I suppose you think it necessary that I should disturb the repose of these illustrious lords to say, 'Gentlemen, your servant, Mousqueton, is thirsty.' What does Monsieur de Bracieux care, think you, whether I am thirsty or not?"

"'Tis a very expensive wine," said Blaisois, shaking his head.

"Were it gold, Monsieur Blaisois, our masters would not deny themselves this wine. Know that Monsieur de Bracieux is rich enough to drink a tun of port wine, even if obliged to pay a pistole for every drop." His manner became more and more lofty every instant: then he arose, and after finishing off the beer at one draught, he advanced majestically to the door of the compartment where the wine was. "Ah! locked!" he exclaimed; "these devils of English, how suspicious they are!"

"Shut!" cried Blaisois; "ah, the deuce it is; unlucky, for I feel the sickness coming on more and more."

"Shut!" repeated Mousqueton.

"But," Blaisois ventured to say, "I have heard you relate, Monsieur Mousqueton, that once on a time, at Chantilly, you fed your master and yourself with partridges which were snared, carps caught by a line, and wine drawn with a corkscrew."

"Perfectly true; but there was an air-hole in the cellar, and the wine was in bottles. I cannot throw the loop through this partition, nor move with a pack-thread a cask of wine which may, perhaps, weigh two hogsheads."

"No, but you can take out two or three boards of the partition," answered Blaisois, "and make a hole in the cask with a gimlet."

Mousqueton opened his great round eyes to the utmost, astonished to find in Blaisois qualities for which he did not give him credit.

" 'Tis true," he said, " but where can I get a chisel to take the planks out—a gimlet to pierce the cask ?"

" The trousers !" said Grimaud, still balancing his accounts.

" Ah, yes !" said Mousqueton.

Grimaud, in fact, was not only the accountant, but the armourer of the party ; and as he was a man full of forethought, these trousers, carefully rolled up in his valise, contained every sort of tool for immediate use.

Mousqueton, therefore, was soon provided with tools, and he began his task. In a few minutes he had got out three pieces of board. He tried to pass his body through the aperture ; but, not being like the frog in the fable, who thought he was larger than he really was, he found he must take out three or four more pieces of wood before he could get through.

He sighed, and began to work again.

Grimaud had now finished his accounts. He arose, and stood near Mousqueton.

" I——" he said.

" What ?" said Mousqueton.

" I can pass——"

" True—you—" answered Mousqueton, casting a glance at the long thin form of his friend ; " you can pass, and easily—go in then."

" Rinse the glasses," said Grimaud.

" Now," said Mousqueton, addressing Blaisois, " now you will see how we old soldiers drink when we are thirsty."

" My cloak," said Grimaud, from the bottom of the cellar.

" What do you want ?" asked Blaisois.

" My cloak—stop up the aperture with it."

" Why ?" asked Blaisois.

" Simpleton !" exclaimed Mousqueton ; " suppose any one came into the room."

" Ah, true !" cried Blaisois, with evident admiration ; " but it will be dark in the cellar."

" Grimaud always sees, dark or light—night as well as day," answered Mousqueton.

" Silence !" cried Grimaud, " some one is coming."

In fact, the door of their cabin was opened. Two men, wrapped in their cloaks, appeared.

" Oh, ho !" said they, " not in bed at a quarter past eleven.

That's against all rules.   In a quarter of an hour let every one be in bed, and snoring."

These two men then went towards the compartment in which Grimaud was secreted; opened the door, entered, and shut it after them.

"Ah!" cried Blaisois; "he's lost!"

"Grimaud's a cunning fox," murmured Mousqueton.

They waited for ten minutes, during which time no noise was heard which might indicate that Grimaud was discovered; and at the expiration of that anxious interval the two men returned, closed the door after them, and repeating their orders that the servants should go to bed, and extinguish their lights, disappeared.

At that very moment Grimaud drew back the cloak which hid the aperture, and came in with his face livid, his eyes staring wide open with terror, so that the pupil was contracted almost to nothing, with a large circle of white around it.   He held in his hand a tankard full of some substance or another; and approaching the gleam of light shed by the lamp he uttered this single monosyllable—"Oh!" with such an expression of extreme terror that Mousqueton started, alarmed, and Blaisois was near fainting from fright.

Both, however, cast an inquisitive glance into the tankard—it was full of powder.

Convinced that the ship was full of powder instead of having a cargo of wine, Grimaud hastened to awake D'Artagnan, who had no sooner beheld him than he perceived that something extraordinary had taken place.   Imposing silence, Grimaud put out the little night lamp, then knelt down, and poured into the lieutenant's ear a recital melodramatic enough not to require play of feature to give it force.

This was the pith of his story.

The first barrel that Grimaud had found on passing into the cellar, he struck—it was empty.   He passed on to another—it was also empty; but the third which he tried was, from the dull sound that it gave out, evidently full.   At this point, Grimaud stopped, and was preparing to make a hole with his gimlet, when he found a spigot: he therefore placed his tankard under it, and turned the spout; something, whatever it was that the cask contained, fell into the tankard.

Whilst he was thinking that he should first taste the liquor which the tankard contained, before taking it to his companions, the door of the cellar opened, and a man with a lanthorn in his hands, and enveloped in a cloak, came and stood just before the barrel, behind which Grimaud, on hearing him come in, instantly crept. This was Groslow. He was accompanied by another man who carried in his hand something long and flexible, rolled up, resembling a washing line.

" Have you the wick ?" asked the one who carried the lanthorn.

" Here it is," answered the other.

At the voice of this last speaker, Grimaud started, and felt a shudder creeping through his very bones. He rose gently, so that his head was just above the round of the barrel; and, under the large hat, he recognised the pale face of Mordaunt.

" How long will this match burn ?" asked this person.

" Nearly five minutes," replied the captain.

" Then tell the men to be in readiness—don't tell them why now; when the clock strikes a quarter after midnight collect your men. Get down into the long-boat."

" That is, when I have lighted the match ?"

" I shall undertake that. I wish to be sure of my revenge—are the oars in the canoe ?"

" Everything is ready."

" 'Tis well."

Mordaunt knelt down and fastened one end of the train to the spigot, in order that he might have nothing to do but to set it on fire at the opposite end with the match.

He then arose.

" You heard me—at a quarter past midnight—in fact, in twenty minutes."

" I understand it all perfectly, sir," replied Groslow; " but allow me to say, there is great danger in what you undertake— would it not be better to entrust one of the men to set fire to the train ?"

" My dear Groslow," answered Mordaunt, " you know the French proverb, ' Nothing that one does not do one's self is ever well done.' I shall abide by that rule."

Grimaud had heard all this—had seen the two mortal enemies of the Musketeers—had seen Mordaunt lay the train : then he felt, and felt again, the contents of the tankard that he held in his hand ; and, instead of the liquid expected by Blaisois and Mousqueton, he found beneath his fingers the grains of some coarse powder.

Mordaunt went away with the captain. At the door he stopped to listen.

" Do you hear how they sleep ?" he said.

In fact, Porthos could be heard snoring through the partition.

" 'Tis God who gives them into our hands," answered Groslow.

"This time the devil himself shall not save them," rejoined Mordaunt.

And they went out together.

CHAPTER LXX.

END OF THE PORT-WINE MYSTERY.

D'ARTAGNAN, as one may suppose, listened to all these details with a growing interest.   He awoke Aramis, Athos, and Porthos; and then, stretching out his arms, and closing them again, the Gascon collected in one small circle the three heads of his friends, so near as almost to touch each other.

He then told them under whose command the vessel was in which they were sailing that night; that they had Groslow for their captain, and Mordaunt acting under him as his lieutenant. Something more deathlike than a shudder, at this moment, shook the brave Musketeers. The name of Mordaunt seemed to exercise over them a mysterious and fatal influence to bring terror even at the very sound.

" What is to be done ?" asked Athos.

" You have some plan ?"

D'Artagnan replied by going towards a very small, low window, just large enough to let a man through. He turned it gently on its hinges.

" There," he said, " is our road."

" The deuce—'tis very cold, my dear friend," said Aramis.

" Stay here, if you like, but I warn you, 'twill be rather too warm presently."

" But we cannot swim to the shore."

" The long boat is yonder, lashed to the felucca; we can take possession of it, and cut the cable.   Come, my friends."

" A moment's delay," said Athos ; " our servants ?"

" Here we are," they cried.

Meantime the three friends were standing motionless before the awful sight which D'Artagnan, in raising the shutters, had disclosed to them through the narrow opening of the window.

Those who have once beheld such a spectacle know that there is nothing more solemn, more striking than the raging sea, rolling, with its deafening roar, its dark billows, beneath the pale light of a wintry moon.

"Gracious heaven! we are hesitating," cried D'Artagnan; "if we hesitate, what will the servants do?"

"I do not hesitate, you know," said Grimaud.

"Sir," interposed Blaisois, "I warn you that I cannot swim except in rivers."——"And I not at all," said Mousqueton.

But D'Artagnan had now slipped through the window.

"You have then decided, my friend?" said Athos.

"Yes," the Gascon answered; "Athos! you, who are a perfect being, bid the spirit to triumph over the body."

"Do you, Aramis, order the servants—Porthos kill every one who stands in your way."

And, after pressing the hand of Athos, D'Artagnan chose a moment when the ship rolled backwards, so that he had only to plunge into the water up to his waist.

Athos followed him before the felucca rose again on the waves: the cable which tied the boat to the vessel was then seen plainly rising out of the sea.

D'Artagnan swam to it, and held it, suspending himself by this rope, his head alone out of the water.

In one second Athos joined him.

They then saw, as the felucca turned, two other heads peeping—those of Aramis and Grimaud.

"I am uneasy about Blaisois," said Athos; "he can, he says, only swim in rivers."

"When people can swim at all they can swim everywhere. To the bark! to the bark!"

"But Porthos, I do not see him."

"Porthos is coming—he swims like Leviathan."

Porthos, in fact, did not appear. Mousqueton and Blaisois had been appalled by the sight of the black gulf below them, and had shrunk back.

"Come along! I shall strangle you both if you don't get out," said Porthos, at last seizing Mousqueton by the throat.

"Forward! Blaisois."

A groan, stifled by the grasp of Porthos, was all the reply of poor Blaisois, for the giant, taking him neck and heels, plunged him into the water head foremost, pushing him out by the window as if he had been a plank.

"Now, Mouston," he said, "I hope you don't mean to desert your master?"

"Ah, sir," replied Mousqueton, his eyes filling with tears, "why did you re-enter the army? We were so happy in the Château de Pierrefonds!"

And, without any other complaint, passive and obedient, either from true devotion to his master, or from the example set by Blaisois, Mousqueton went into the sea head foremost. A sublime action, at all events, for Mousqueton looked upon himself as dead. But Porthos was not a man to abandon an old servant; and when Mousqueton rose above the water, blinded, he found that he was supported by the large hand of Porthos, and that he could, without having occasion even to move, advance towards the cable with the dignity of a sea-god.

In a few minutes, Porthos had rejoined his companions, who were already in the canoe ; but when, after they had all got in, it came to his turn, there was great danger that in putting his huge leg over the edge of the boat he would have upset the little vessel. Athos was the last to enter.

" Are you all here ?" he asked.

" Ah ! have you your sword, Athos ?" cried D'Artagnan.

" Yes."

" Cut the cable, then."

Athos drew a sharp poignard from his belt, and cut the cord. The felucca went on ; the bark continued stationary, only moved by the waves.

"Come, Athos!" said D'Artagnan, giving his hand to the count; " you are going to see something curious," added the Gascon.

CHAPTER LXXI.

FATALITY.

Scarcely had D'Artagnan uttered these words than a ringing and sudden noise was heard resounding through the felucca, which now became dim in the obscurity of the night.

" That, you may be sure," said the Gascon, "means something."

They then, at the same instant, perceived a large lanthorn carried on a pole appear on the deck, defining the forms of shadows behind it.

Suddenly a terrible cry, a cry of despair, was wafted through the space, and, as if the shrieks of anguish had driven away the clouds, the veil which hid the moon was cleared away, and the gray sails and dark shrouds of the felucca were seen beneath the silvery night of the skies.

Shadows ran, as if bewildered, to and fro, on the vessel, and mournful cries accompanied these delirious walkers. In the midst of these screams they saw, standing on the top of the poop, Mordaunt, with a torch in his hand.

The figures, apparently excited with terror, were Groslow, who, at the hour fixed by Mordaunt, had collected his men and the sailors. Groslow, after having listened at the door of the cabin to hear if the Musketeers were still asleep, had gone down into the cellar, convinced by their silence that they were all in a deep slumber. Then Mordaunt had opened the door, and run to the train—impetuous as a man who is excited by revenge and full of confidence—as are those whom God blinds—he had set fire to the sulphur !

All this while, Groslow and his men were assembled on deck.

"Haul up the cable, and draw the boat to us," said Groslow.

One of the sailors got down the side of the ship, seized the cable, and drew it—it came without any resistance.

"The cable is cut !" he cried, "no canoe !"

"How ! no canoe !" exclaimed Groslow; "'tis impossible."

"'Tis true, however," answered the sailors; "there's nothing in the wake of the ship, besides, here's the end of the cable."

"What's the matter ?" cried Mordaunt, who, coming up out of the hatchway, rushed to the stern, his torch in his hand.

"Only that our enemies have escaped—they have cut the cord, and gone off wit' the canoe."

Mordaunt bounded with one step to the cabin and kicked open the door.

"Empty !" he exclaimed; "the demons !"

"We must pursue them," said Groslow; "they can't be gone far, and we shall sink them, passing over them."

"Yes, but the fire," ejaculated Mordaunt; "I have lighted it."

"A thousand devils !" cried Groslow, rushing to the hatchway; "perhaps there is still time to save us."

Mordaunt answered only by a terrible laugh, threw his torch into the sea, and then plunged himself into it. The instant that Groslow put his foot upon the steps of the hatchway the ship opened like the crater of a volcano,—a burst of flame arose towards the skies with an explosion like that of a thousand cannon; the air burned, ignited by embers in flames—then the frightful lightning disappeared, the embers sank down, one after another, into the abyss, where they were extinguished; and, except a slight vibration in the air, after a few minutes had elapsed, one would have thought that nothing had happened.

Only—the felucca had disappeared from the surface of the sea—and Groslow and his three sailors were consumed.

The four friends saw all this—not a single detail of this fearful scene escaped them : at one moment, bathed as they were in a flood of brilliant light, which illumined the sea for the space of a league, they might each be seen—each in his own peculiar attitude and manner, expressing the awe, which, even in their hearts of bronze, they could not help feeling. Soon the torrent of flame fell all around them—then, at last, the volcano was extinguished —all was dark—the floating bark and the heaving ocean.

They were all silent and dejected.

" By heaven !" at last said Athos, the first to speak, " by this time, I think, all must be over."

" Here ! my lords ! save me ! help !" cried a voice, whose mournful accents reaching the four friends, seemed to proceed from some phantom of the ocean.

All looked around—Athos himself started.

" 'Tis he ! 'tis his voice !" he said.

All still remained silent—the eyes of all were still turned in the direction where the vessel had disappeared — endeavouring in vain to penetrate the darkness. After a minute or two they were able to distinguish a man, who approached them, swimming vigorously.

Athos extended his arm towards him—" Yes, yes, I know him well," he said.

" He—again !" cried Porthos, who was breathing like a blacksmith's bellows, " why, he's made of iron."

" Oh my God !" muttered Athos.

Aramis and D'Artagnan whispered to each other.

Mordaunt made several strokes more, and raising his arm in sign of distress above the waves—" Pity, pity on me ! gentlemen—in Heaven's name—I feel my strength failing me ; I am dying."

The voice that implored aid was so piteous, that it awakened pity in the heart of Athos.

" Miserable wretch !" he exclaimed.

" Indeed !" said D'Artagnan, " people have only to complain to you. I believe he's swimming towards us. Does he think we are going to take him in ? Row, Porthos, row."—And setting the example, he ploughed his oar into the sea—two strokes took the bark on twenty fathoms further.

" Ah ! ah !" said Porthos to Mordaunt, " I think we have you here, my hero !"

" Oh ! Porthos !" murmured the Comte de la Fère.

" Oh, pray ! for mercy's sake don't fly from me. For pity's sake !" cried the young man, whose agonised breathing at times, when his head was under the wave, made the icy waters bubble.

D'Artagnan, however, who had consulted with Aramis, spoke to the poor wretch. " Go away," he said, " your repentance is too recent to inspire confidence. See ! the vessel in which you wished to fry us is still smoking ; and the situation in which you are is . a bed of roses compared to that in which you wished to place us, and in which you have placed Monsieur Groslow and his companions."

" Sir !" replied Mordaunt, in a tone of deep despair, " my penitence is sincere. Gentlemen, I am young, scarcely twenty-three years old. I was drawn on by a very natural resentment to avenge my mother. You would have done what I did."

Mordaunt wanted now only two or three fathoms to reach the boat—for the approach of death seemed to give him supernatural strength.

" Alas !" he said, " I am then to die ! you are going to kill the son, as you killed the mother ! Surely, if I am culpable, and if I ask for pardon, I ought to be forgiven."

Then—as if his strength failed him—he seemed unable to sustain himself above the water, and a wave passed over his head, which drowned his voice.

" Oh! that agonises me !" cried Athos.——Mordaunt reappeared.

" For my part," said D'Artagnan, " I say, this must come to an end :—a murderer as you were of your uncle ; executioner, as you were of King Charles ! Incendiary ! I recommend you to sink forthwith to the bottom of the sea ; and if you come another fathom nearer, I'll break your head with my oar."

" D'Artagnan ! D'Artagnan !" cried Athos, " my son ! I entreat you : the wretch is dying ; and it is horrible to let a man die without extending a hand to save him. I cannot resist doing so— he must live."

" Zounds !" replied D'Artagnan, " why don't you give yourself up directly, feet and hands bound, to that wretch ? Ah ! Comte de la Fère, you wish to perish by his hands ? I, your son, as you call me ; I will not !"

'Twas the first time that D'Artagnan had ever refused a request of Athos.

Aramis calmly drew his sword, which he had carried between his teeth as he swam.

" If he lays his hand on the boat's edge, I will cut it off—regicide as he is."

"And I," said Porthos.   "Wait."

"What are you going to do?" asked Aramis.

"To throw myself in the water and strangle him."

"Oh, gentlemen!" cried Athos; "be men! be Christians! See! death is depicted on his face! Ah! do not bring on me the horrors of remorse! Grant me this poor wretch's life. I will bless you. I——"

"I am dying!" cried Mordaunt, "come to me! come to me!"

D'Artagnan began to be touched. The boat at this moment turned round, and the dying man was by that turn brought nearer to Athos.

"Monsieur the Comte de la Fère!" he cried; "I supplicate you!—pity me! I call on you! where are you? I see you no longer—I am dying—help me!—help me!"

"Here I am, sir!" said Athos, leaning, and stretching out his arm to Mordaunt with that air of dignity and nobleness of soul habitual to him; "here I am; take my hand, and jump into our boat."

Mordaunt made a last effort—rose, seized the hand thus extended to him, and grasped it with the vehemence of despair.

"That's right," said Athos, "put your other hand here."

And he offered him his shoulders as another stay and support, so that his head almost touched that of Mordaunt; and these two mortal enemies were in as close an embrace as if they had been brothers.

"Now, sir," said the count, "you are safe—calm yourself!"

"Ah! my mother!" cried Mordaunt, with an eye of fire and a look of hatred impossible to describe, "I can only offer thee one victim, but it shall, at any rate, be the one whom thou wouldst have chosen!"

And whilst D'Artagnan uttered a cry, whilst Porthos raised the oar, and Aramis sought a place to strike, a frightful shake given to the boat precipitated Athos into the sea; whilst Mordaunt, with a shout of triumph, grasped the neck of his victim, and, in order to paralyse his movements, intertwined his legs with his—as a serpent might have done around some object. In an instant, without uttering an exclamation, without a cry for help, Athos tried to sustain himself on the surface of the waters; but the weight dragged him down: he disappeared by degrees; soon nothing was to be seen except his long floating hair; then everything disappeared, and the bubbling of the water, which, in its turn, was effaced, alone indicated the spot where these two men had sunk.

Mute with horror, the three friends had remained open-mouthed, their eyes dilated, their arms extended like statues, and motionless as they were, the beating of their hearts was audible. Porthos was the first who came to himself—he tore his hair.

"Oh !" he cried, "Athos ! Athos ! thou man of noble heart ! Woe is me ! I have let thee perish !"

At this instant, in the midst of a vast circle, illumined by the light of the moon, the same whirlpool which had been made by the sinking men was again obvious ; and first were seen, rising above the waves, locks of hair—then a face, pale—with open eyes, yet, nevertheless, those of death ; then a body which, after having raised itself even to the waist above the sea, turned gently on its back, according to the caprice of the waves, and floated.

In the bosom of this corpse was plunged a poniard, the gold hilt of which shone in the moonbeams.

"Mordaunt ! Mordaunt !" cried the three friends ; "'tis Mordaunt !"

"But Athos !" exclaimed D'Artagnan.

Suddenly the boat leaned on one side, beneath a new and unexpected weight, and Grimaud uttered a shout of joy ; everyone turned round, and beheld Athos, livid, his eyes dim, and his hands trembling, supporting himself on the edge of the boat. Eight vigorous arms bore him up immediately, and laid him in the bark, where, directly, Athos was warmed, reanimated, reviving with the caresses and cares of his friends, who were intoxicated with joy.

"You are not hurt ?" asked D'Artagnan.

"No," replied Athos, "and he——"

"Oh, he ! Now we may say, thank God ! he is really dead. Look !"—and D'Artagnan, obliging Athos to look in the direction that he pointed, showed him the body of Mordaunt floating on its back, and which, sometimes submerged, sometimes rising, seemed still to pursue the four friends with a look full of insult and mortal hatred.

At last he sank. Athos had followed him with a glance in which the deepest melancholy and pity were expressed.

"Bravo, Athos !" cried Aramis, with an emotion very rare in him.

"A capital blow you gave !" cried Porthos.

"I have a son," said Athos ; "I wished to live."

"In short," said D'Artagnan, "this has been the will of God."

"It is not I who killed him," added Athos, in a soft, low tone : "it is destiny."

CHAPTER LXXII.

HOW MOUSQUETON, AFTER BEING VERY NEARLY ROASTED, HAD A NARROW ESCAPE OF BEING EATEN.

A DEEP silence reigned for a long time in the canoe after the fearful scene just described.

The moon, which had shone for a short time, disappeared behind the clouds : every object was again plunged in that obscurity so awful in deserts, and still more so in that liquid desert, the ocean, and nothing was heard, save the whistling of the west wind driving along the tops of the crested billows.

Porthos was the first to speak.

"I have seen," he said, "many things, but nothing that ever agitated me so much as what I have just witnessed. Nevertheless, even in my present state of perturbation, I protest I feel happy. I have a hundred pounds' weight less upon my chest. I breathe more freely." In fact, Porthos breathed so loud as to do credit to the powerful play of his lungs.

"For my part," observed Aramis, "I cannot say the same as you do, Porthos. I am still terrified to such a degree that I scarcely believe my eyes. I look around the canoe, expecting, every moment, to see that poor wretch holding in his hands the poniard which was plunged into his heart."

"Oh, I am quite easy," replied Porthos. "The sword was pointed at the sixth rib, and buried up to the hilt in his body. I do not reproach you, Athos, for what you have done ; quite the contrary ; when one aims a blow, that is the way to strike. So now, I breathe again, I am happy !"

"Don't be in haste to celebrate a victory, Porthos," interposed D'Artagnan ; "never have we incurred a greater danger than we are now encountering. A man may subdue a man—he can't conquer an element. We are now on the sea, at night, without any pilot, in a frail bark ; should a blast of wind upset the canoe, we are lost."

Mousqueton heaved a deep sigh.

"You are ungrateful, D'Artagnan," said Athos ; "yes, ungrateful to Providence—to whom we owe our safety in a miraculous manner. Let us sail before the wind, and, unless it changes, we shall be drifted either to Calais or Boulogne. Should our bark be upset, we are five of us good swimmers, and able enough to turn it over again ; or, if not, to hold on by it. Now we are on the very road which all the vessels between Dover and Calais take, 'tis impossible but that we should meet with a fisherman who will pick us up."

"But should we not find any fisherman, and should the wind shift to the north?"

"Then," said Athos, "it would be quite another thing; and we should never see land until we were on the other side of the Atlantic."

"Which implies that we may die of hunger," said Aramis.

"'Tis more than probable," answered the Comte de la Fère.

Mousqueton sighed again, more deeply than before.

"What is the matter? what ails you?" asked Porthos.

"I am cold, sir," said Mousqueton.

"Impossible! your body is covered with a coating of fat, which preserves it from the cold air."

"Ah! sir, 'tis that very coating of fat which alarms me."

"How is that, Mousqueton?"

"Alas! your honour! in the library of the Château of Bracieux there's a number of books of travels."

"What then?"

"Amongst them the voyages of Jean Mocquet in the time of Henry IV."

"Well?"

"In these books, your honour, 'tis told how hungry voyagers, drifted out to sea, have a bad habit of eating each other, and beginning by——"

"By the fattest among them!" cried D'Artagnan, unable, in spite of the gravity of the occasion, to help laughing.

"Yes, sir," answered Mousqueton; "but permit me to say, I see nothing laughable in it. However," he added, turning to Porthos, "I should not regret dying, sir, were I sure that by doing so I might still be useful to you."

"Mouston," replied Porthos, much affected, "should we ever see my castle of Pierrefonds again, you shall have as your own, and for your descendants, the vineyard which surrounds the farm."

"And you shall call it,—Mouston," added Aramis, "the vineyard of self-sacrifice, to transmit to latest ages the recollection of your devotion to your master."

One may readily conceive that during these jokes, which were intended chiefly to divert Athos from the scene which had just taken place, the servants, with the exception of Grimaud, were not silent. Suddenly Mousqueton utttered a cry of delight, in taking from beneath one of the benches a bottle of wine; and, on looking more closely still in the same place, he discovered dozen of similar bottles, some bread, and a piece of salted beef.

"Oh, sir!" he cried, passing the bottle to Porthos, "we are saved—the bark is supplied with provisions."

This intelligence restored every one, save Athos, to gaiety.

"Zounds!" exclaimed Porthos, "'tis astonishing how empty violent agitation makes the stomach."

And he drank off one bottle at a draught, and ate a good third of the bread and salted meat.

"Now," said Athos, "sleep, or try to sleep, my friends, I will watch."

In a few moments, notwithstanding their wet clothes, the icy blast that blew, and the previous scene, these hardy adventurers, with their iron frames, fitted for every hardship, threw themselves down, intending to profit by the advice of Athos, who sat at the helm, pensive and wakeful, guiding the little barque in the way it was to go, his eyes fixed on the heavens, as if he sought to discern, not only the road to France, but the benign aspect of protecting Providence. After some hours of repose, the sleepers were aroused by Athos.

Dawn had shed its light upon the blue ocean, and the distance of a musket's shot from them was seen a dark mass, above which was displayed a triangular sail; then masters and servants joined in a fervent cry to the crew of that vessel, to hear them, and to save.

"A barque!" all cried together.

It was, in fact, a small craft from Dunkirk, which was sailing towards Boulogne.

A quarter of an hour afterwards, the boat of this craft took them on board the little vessel. Grimaud offered twenty guineas to the captain from his master, and, at nine o'clock in the morning, having a fair wind, our Frenchmen set foot on their native land.

"Egad! how strong one feels here!" said Porthos, almost burying his large feet in the sands. "Zounds! I could now defy a whole nation!"

"Be quiet, Porthos," said D'Artagnan, "we are observed."

"We are admired, i'faith," answered Porthos.

"These people who are looking at us, are only merchants," said Athos, "and are looking more at the cargo than at us."

"I shall not trust to that," said the lieutenant, "and I shall make for the Dunes* as soon as possible."

* Sandy hills about Dunkirk, from which it derives its name.

The party followed him, and soon disappeared with him behind the hillocks of sand unobserved. Here, after a short conference, they proposed to separate.

"And why separate?" asked Athos.

"Because," answered the Gascon, "we were sent by Cardinal Mazarin to fight for Cromwell; instead of fighting for Cromwell, we have served Charles I., not the same thing at all. In returning with the Comte de la Fère and Monsieur d'Herblay, our crime would be confirmed. We have escaped Cromwell, Mordaunt, and the sea, but we should not escape from Mazarin."

"You forget," replied Athos, "that we consider ourselves as your prisoners, and not free from the engagement we entered into."

"Truly, Athos," interrupted D'Artagnan, "I am vexed that such a man as you are should talk nonsense which schoolboys would be ashamed of. Chevalier," he continued, addressing Aramis, who, leaning proudly on his sword, seemed to agree with his companion, "Chevalier, Porthos and I run no risk; besides, should any ill-luck happen to two of us, will it not be much better that the other two should be spared to assist those who may be apprehended? Besides, who knows whether, divided, we might not obtain a pardon—you from the queen, we from Mazarin—which, were we all four together, would never be granted. Come, Athos and Aramis, go to the right; Porthos, come with me to the left; these gentlemen should file off towards Normandy, we will, by the nearest road, reach Paris."

He then gave his friends minute directions as to their route.

"Ah! my dear friend," cried Athos, "how I should admire the resources of your mind, did I not stop to adore those of your heart."

And he gave him his hand.

"Is the fox a genius, Athos?" asked the Gascon. "No! he knows how to crunch fowls, to dodge the huntsman, and to find his way home by day or by night, that's all. Well, is all said?"

"All."

"Then let's count our money, and divide it. Ah! hurrah! there's the sun! Good morrow, my friend, the sun! 'tis a long time since I saw you!"

"Come, come, D'Artagnan," said Athos, "do not affect to be strong-minded: there are tears in your eyes; let us always be open to each other, and sincere."

"What!" cried the Gascon, "do you think, Athos, we can take leave, calmly, of two friends, at a time not free from danger to you and Aramis?"

"No," answered Athos; "embrace me, my son."

"Zounds!" said Porthos, sobbing, "I believe I'm crying; but how foolish it is!"

They then embraced. At that moment, their fraternal bond of union was closer than ever, and, when they parted, each to take the route agreed on, they turned back, to utter to each other affectionate expressions, which the echoes of the Dunes repeated. At last they lost sight of each other; Porthos and D'Artagnan taking the road to Paris, followed by Mousqueton, who, after having been too cold all night, found himself, at the end of half an hour, far too warm.

CHAPTER LXXIII.

THE RETURN.

DURING the six months that Athos and Aramis had been absent from France, the Parisians, finding themselves, one morning, without either a queen or a king, were greatly annoyed at being thus deserted, and the absence of Mazarin, so much desired, did not compensate for that of the two august fugitives.

The first feeling which pervaded Paris on hearing of the flight to Saint Germain, was that sort of affright which seizes children when they awake in the night, and find themselves alone. A deputation was therefore sent to the queen, to entreat her to return soon to Paris; but she not only declined to receive the deputies, but sent an intimation by Chancellor Sequier, implying that if the parliament did not humble itself before her majesty, by negativing all the questions that had been the cause of the quarrel, Paris would be besieged the next day.

This threatening answer, unluckily for the court produced quite a different effect to that which was intended. It wounded the pride of the parliament, which, supported by the citizens, replied by declaring that Cardinal Mazarin was the cause of all the discontents; denounced him as the enemy both to the king and the state; and ordered him to retire from the court that very day, and from France within a week afterwards; and enjoining, in case of disobedience on his part, all the subjects of the king to pursue and take him.

Mazarin being thus put out of the protection of the law, preparations on both sides were commenced: the queen, to attack Paris—the citizens, to defend it. The latter were occupied in breaking up the pavement, and stretching chains across the street, when, headed by the Coadjutor, appeared the Prince de Conti (the brother of the Prince de Condé) and the Duc de Longueville, his brother-in-law. This unexpected band of auxiliaries arrived in Paris on the tenth of January, and the Prince of Conti was named, but not until after a stormy discussion, generalissimo of the army of the king, out of Paris.

As for the Duc de Beaufort, he arrived from Vendôme, according to the annals of the day, bringing with him his high bearing, and his long and beautiful hair, qualifications which ensured him the sovereignty of the market-places and their occupants.

It was just at this epoch that the four friends had landed at Dunkirk, and begun their route towards Paris. On reaching that capital, Athos and Aramis found it in arms. The sentinel at the gate refused even to let them pass, and called his sergeant.

The sergeant, with that air of importance which such people assume when they are clad with military dignity, said :

" Who are you, gentlemen ?"

" Two gentlemen."

" And where do you come from ?"

" From London."

" And what are you going to do in Paris ?"

" We are going with a mission to her Majesty the Queen of England."

" Where are your orders ?"

" We have none : we left England, ignorant of the state of politics here, having left Paris before the departure of the king."

" Ah !" said the sergeant, with a cunning smile, " you are Mazarinists, who are sent as spies."

" My dear friend," here Athos spoke, " be assured, if we were Mazarinists, we should have all sorts of passports. In your situation, distrust those who are well provided with every formality."

" Enter into the guard-room," said the sergeant; " we will lay your case before the commandant of the post."

The guard-room was filled with citizens and common people, some playing, some drinking, some talking. In a corner, almost hidden from view, were three gentlemen, who had preceded Athos and Aramis, and an officer was examining their passports. The first impulse of these three gentlemen, and of those who last entered, was to cast an inquiring glance to each other. Those first arrived wore long cloaks, in the drapery of which they were carefully enveloped; one of them, shorter than the rest, remained pertinaciously in the background.

When the sergeant, on entering the room, announced that, in all probability, he was bringing in two Mazarinists, it appeared to be the unanimous opinion of the officers on guard that they ought not to pass.

"Be it so," said Athos; "yet it is probable, on the contrary, that we shall enter, because we seem to have to do with sensible people. There seems to be only one thing to do, which is, to send our names to her Majesty the Queen of England, and, if she engages to answer for us, I presume we shall be allowed to enter."

On hearing these words, the shortest of the other three men seemed more attentive than ever to what was going on, and he wrapped his cloak around him more carefully than before.

"Merciful goodness!" whispered Aramis to Athos, "did you see?"

"What?" asked Athos.

"The face of the shortest of those three gentlemen?"

"No."

"He seemed to me—but 'tis impossible."

At this instant the sergeant, who had been for his orders, returned, and, pointing to the three gentlemen in cloaks, said:

"The passports are right; let these three gentlemen pass."

The three gentlemen bowed, and hastened to take advantage of this permission.

Aramis looked after them, and, as the least of them passed close to him, he pressed the hand of Athos.

"What is the matter with you, my friend?" asked the latter.

"I have—doubtless I am dreaming: tell me, sir," he said to the sergeant, "do you know those three gentlemen who are just gone out?"

"Only by their passports: they are three Frondists, who are gone to rejoin the Duc de Longueville."

"'Tis strange," said Aramis, almost involuntarily; "I fancied that I recognized Mazarin himself."

The sergeant burst out into a fit of laughter.

"He!" he cried; "he venture himself amongst us to be hung! Not so foolish as all that."

"Ah!" muttered Athos, "I may be mistaken; I haven't the unerring eye of D'Artagnan."

"Who is speaking of D'Artagnan?" asked an officer, who appeared at that moment upon the threshold of the room.

"What !" cried Aramis and Athos, "what ! Planchet !"

"Planchet," added Grimaud, "Planchet, with a gorget, indeed !"

"Ah, gentlemen !" cried Planchet, "so you are back again in Paris. Oh, how happy you make us ! no doubt you are come to join the princes !"

"As thou seest, Planchet," said Aramis, whilst Athos smiled at the importance now assumed by the old comrade of Mousqueton in his new rank in the City Militia.

"Ah ! so !" said Aramis; "allow me to congratulate you, Monsieur Planchet."

"Ah, the chevalier !" returned Planchet, bowing.

"Lieutenant ?" asked Aramis.

"Lieutenant, with a promise of becoming a captain."

"'Tis capital : and pray how did you acquire all these honours ?"

"In the first place, gentlemen, you know that I was the means of Monsieur de Rochefort's escape ; well, I was very near being hung by Mazarin, and that made me more popular than ever."

"So, owing to your popularity——"

"No : thanks to something better. You know, gentlemen, that I served in Piedmont's regiment, and had the honour of being a sergeant ?"

"Yes."

"Well, one day when no one could drill a mob of citizens, who began to march, some with the right foot, others with the left, I succeeded, I did, in making them all begin with the same foot, and I was made a lieutenant on the field."

"So, I presume," said Athos, "that you have a large number of the nobles with you ?"

"Certainly. There are the Prince de Conti, the Duc de Longueville, the Duc de Beaufort, the Duc de Bouillon, the Maréchal de la Mothe, the Marquis de Sevigné, and I don't know who, for my part."

"And the Vicomte Raoul de Bragelonne ?" inquired Athos, in a tremulous voice; "D'Artagnan told me that he had recommended him to your care, in parting."

"Yes, count; nor have I lost sight of him for an instant since."

"Then," said Athos, in a tone of delight, "he is well? no accident has happened to him ?"

"None, sir."

"And he lives ?"

"Still—at the hotel of the Great Charlemagne."

" And passes his time ?"

"Sometimes with the Queen of England,—sometimes with Madame de Chevreuse. He and the Count de Guiche are never asunder."

" Thanks,—Planchet—thanks," cried Athos, extending his hand to the lieutenant.

" Oh, sir !" Planchet only touched the tips of the count's fingers. "Oh, sir !—and now, gentlemen, what do you intend to do ?"

" To re-enter Paris, if you will let us, my good Planchet."

" Let you, sir ?—I am nothing but your servant !" Then, turning to his men,—

" Allow these gentlemen to pass," he said ; "they are friends of the Duc de Beaufort."

" Long live the Duc de Beaufort !" cried all the sentinels.

" Farewell till we meet again," said Aramis, as they took leave of Planchet ; "if anything happens to us, we shall blame you for it."

" Sir," answered Planchet, " I am in all things yours to command."

" That fellow is no fool," said Aramis, as he got on his horse.

" How should he be ?" replied Athos, whilst mounting also, " seeing that he has been so long used to brush his master's hats ?"

CHAPTER LXXIV.

THE AMBASSADORS.

THE two friends rode rapidly down the declivity of the Faubourg, but on arriving at the bottom were surprised to find that the streets of Paris had become rivers, and the open places lakes ; after the great rains which fell in the month of January, the Seine had overflowed its banks, and the river had inundated half the capital. The two gentlemen were obliged, therefore, to get off their horses and take a boat, and in that manner they approached the Louvre.

Night had closed in, and Paris, seen thus, by the light of some lanthorns, flickering on the pools of water, with boats laden with patrols with glittering arms, the watchword passing from post to post, Paris presented such an aspect as to seize strongly on the senses of Aramis—a man most susceptible of warlike impressions.

They reached the queen's apartments, and were instantly admitted to the presence of Henrietta Maria, who uttered a cry of joy on hearing of their arrival.

"Let them come in! let them come in!" exclaimed the poor queen.

"Let them come in!" reiterated the young princess, who had never left her mother's side, but essayed in vain to make her forget, by her filial affection, the absence of her two sons and her other daughter.

"Come in, gentlemen," repeated the princess, opening the door herself.

The queen was seated in a fauteuil, and before her were standing two or three gentlemen, and, among them, the Duc de Châtillon, the brother of the nobleman who was killed eight or nine years previously in a duel, on account of Madame de Longueville, on the Place Royale. All these gentlemen had been noticed by Athos and Aramis in the guard-house; and, when the two friends were announced, they started, and exchanged some words in a low tone.

"Well, sirs!" cried the queen, on perceiving the two friends; "you are come, faithful friends!—but the royal couriers have been more expeditious than you; and here are Monsieur de Flamareus and Monsieur de Châtillon, who bring me, from Her Majesty the Queen Anne, of Austria, the most recent intelligence."

Aramis and Athos were astonished by the calmness, even the gaiety, of the queen's manner.

"Go on with your recital, sirs," said the queen, turning to the Duc de Châtillon. "You said that his Majesty King Charles, my august consort, had been condemned to death by a majority of his subjects!"

"Yes, madame," Châtillon stammered out.

Athos and Aramis seemed more and more astonished.

"And that, being conducted to the scaffold," resumed the queen, "—oh, my God! oh, my king!—and that, being led to the scaffold, he had been saved by an indignant people?"

"Just so, madame," replied Châtillon, in so low a voice that, though the two friends were listening eagerly, they could hardly hear this affirmation.

The queen clapped her hands in enthusiastic gratitude, whilst her daughter threw her arms round her mother's neck, and kissed her, her own eyes streaming with tears.

"Now, madame, nothing remains to me except to proffer my respectful homage," said Châtillon, who felt confused and ashamed beneath the stern gaze of Athos.

"One moment, yes," answered the queen. "One moment, I beg, for here are the Chevalier d'Herblay and the Comte de la Fère—just arrived from London—and they can give you, as eye-witnesses, such details as you can convey to the queen, my royal sister. Speak, gentlemen, speak—I am listening—conceal nothing —gloss over nothing. Since his majesty still lives—since the honour of the throne is in safety, everything else is a matter of in-difference to me."

Athos turned pale, and laid his hand on his heart.

"Well!" exclaimed the queen, who remarked this movement and this paleness. "Speak, sir!—I beg you to do so."

"I beg you to excuse me, madame,—I wish to add nothing to the recital of these gentlemen until they perceive themselves that they have, perhaps, been mistaken."

"Mistaken!" cried the queen, almost suffocated by emotion; "mistaken! What has happened, then!"

"Sir," interposed Monsieur de Flamareus to Athos, "if we are mistaken, the error has originated with the queen. I do not suppose you will have the presumption to set it to rights,—that would be to accuse her Majesty, Queen Anne, of falsehood."

Athos sighed deeply.

"Or rather, sir," said Aramis, with his irritating politeness, "the error of that person who was with you when we met you in the guard-room, for if the Comte de la Fère and I are not mistaken, when we saw you there you had with you a third gentleman."

Châtillon and Flamareus started.

"Explain yourself, count!" cried the queen, whose anguish became greater every moment. "On your brow I read despair— your lips falter, ere you announce some terrible tidings—your hands tremble. Oh, my God! my God! what has happened!"

"Lord!" ejaculated the young princess, falling on her knees, "have mercy on us!"

A short altercation ensued in a low tone between the Duc de Châtillon and Aramis, during which Athos, his hands on his heart, his head bent low, approached the queen, and in a voice of deep sorrow, said:

"Madame! princes—who by nature are above other men— receive from heaven courage to support greater misfortunes than those of lower rank, for their hearts are elevated as their fortunes. We ought not, therefore, I think, to act towards a queen so illus-trious as your majesty, as we should do towards a woman of our lowlier condition. Queen—destined as you are to endure every sorrow on this earth, hear the result of our mission."

Athos, kneeling down before the queen, trembling and very cold, drew from his bosom, inclosed in the same case, the order set in diamonds, which the queen had given to Lord de Winter, and the wedding-ring which Charles I. before his death had placed in the hands of Aramis. Since the moment that he had first received these two things, Athos had never parted with them.

He opened the case, and offered them to the queen, with silent and deep anguish.

The queen stretched out her hand—seized the ring—pressed it convulsively to her lips—and without being able to breathe a sigh, to give vent to a sob, she extended her arms, became deadly pale, and fell senseless in the arms of her attendants and her daughter.

Athos kissed the hem of the robe of the widowed queen, and rising, with a dignity that made a deep impression on those around :

"I, the Comte de la Fère, a gentleman who has never deceived any human being, swear before God, and before this unhappy queen, that all that was possible to save the king of England was done whilst we were on English ground. Now, chevalier," he added, turning to Aramis, "let us go. Our duty is fulfilled."

"Not yet," said Aramis. "We have still a word to say to these gentlemen."

And turning to Châtillon, he said,—"Sir, be so good as not to go away without hearing something that I cannot say before the queen."

Châtillon bowed in token of assent, and they all went out, stopping at the window of a gallery on the ground floor.

"Sir !" said Aramis, "you allowed yourself just now to treat us in a most extraordinary manner."

"Sir !" cried De Châtillon.

"What have you done with Monsieur de Bruy ? Has he, perchance, gone to change his face, which was too like that of Monsieur de Mazarin ? There are abundance of Italian masks at the Palais Royal : from harlequin even to pantaloon."

"Chevalier ! chevalier !" said Athos.

"Leave me alone," replied Aramis, impatiently. "I don't like things that stop half way."

"Finish then, sir," answered De Châtillon, with as much hauteur as Aramis.

"Gentlemen," resumed Aramis, "any one but the Comte de la Fère and myself would have had you arrested — for we have friends in Paris—but we are contented with another course.

Come and talk with us for five minutes—sword in hand—upon
this deserted terrace."

"Willingly," replied De Châtillon.

"Duke," said Flamareus, "you forget that to-morrow you are
to command an expedition of the greatest importance, projected
by the prince, assented to by the queen. Until to-morrow evening
you are not at your own disposal."

"Let it be then, the day after to-morrow," said Aramis.

"To-morrow, rather," said De Châtillon, "and if you will take
the trouble of coming so far as the gates of Charenton."

"Well, then, to-morrow. Pray, are you going to rejoin your
Cardinal? Swear first, on your honour, not to inform him of our
return."

De Châtillon looked at him. There was so much of irony in
his speech, that the duke had great difficulty in bridling his anger;
but, at a word from Flamareus, he restrained himself, and contented himself with saying :

"You promise me, sir—that's agreed—that I shall find you to-
morrow at Charenton?"

"Oh, sir, don't be afraid!" replied Aramis; and the two gentlemen shortly afterwards left the Louvre.

"For what reason is all this fume and fury?" asked Athos.
"What have they done to you?"

"They did—did you not see them?"

"No."

"They laughed when we swore that we had done our duty in
England. Now, if they believed us, they laughed in order to
insult us; if they did not believe it, they insulted us still more.
However, I'm glad not to fight them until to-morrow. I hope to
have something better to do to-night than to draw my sword."

"What have you to do?"

"Egad! to take Mazarin."

Athos curled his lip with disdain.

"These undertakings do not suit me, as you know, Aramis."

"Why?"

"Because they are taking people unawares."

"Really, Athos, you would make a singular general. You
would fight only by broad daylight. Warn your foe before an
attack; and never attempt anything by night, lest you should be
accused of taking advantage of the darkness."

Athos smiled.

"Say, at once, you disapprove of my proposal."

"I think you ought to do nothing, since you exacted a promise from these gentlemen not to let Mazarin know that we were in France."

" I have entered into no engagement, and consider myself quite free. Come, come."

" Where ?"

" Either to seek the Duc de Beaufort, or the Duc de Bouillon, and to tell them about this."

" Yes, but on one condition—that we begin by the Coadjutor. He is a priest, learned in cases of conscience, and we will tell him ours."

It was then agreed that they were to go first to Monsieur de Bouillon, as his house came first; but first of all Athos begged that he might go to the Hôtel du Grand Charlemagne, to see Raoul.

They re-entered the boat which had brought them to the Louvre, and went thence to the Halles; and finding there Grimaud and Blaisois, they proceeded to the Rue Guénégand.

But Raoul was not at the Hôtel du Grand Charlemagne. He had received a message from the prince, to whom he had hastened with Olivain the instant he had received it.

CHAPTER LXXV.

THE THREE LIEUTENANTS OF THE GENERALISSIMO.

THE night was dark; and the town still resounded with all those noises which disclose a city in a state of siege. Athos and Aramis did not proceed a hundred steps without being stopped by sentinels placed before the barricades, who asked them the word; and on their saying that they were going to Monsieur de Bouillon on a mission of importance, a guide was given them under pretext of conducting them, but, in fact, as a watch over their movements.

On arriving at the Hôtel de Bouillon, they came across a little troop of three cavaliers, who seemed to know every possible watchword; for they walked without either guide or escort, and on arriving at the barricades had nothing to do but to speak to those who guarded them, and who let them pass with all the deference due probably to their birth.

On seeing them, Athos and Aramis stood still.

" Oh !" cried Aramis, " do you see, count ?"

" Yes," said Athos.

"Who do these three cavaliers appear to you to be? These are our men."

"You are not mistaken; I recognize Monsieur de Flamareus."

"And Monsieur de Châtillon."

"As to the cavalier in the brown cloak——"

"It is the Cardinal."

"How the devil do they venture so near the Hôtel de Bouillon?"

Athos smiled, but did not reply. Five minutes afterwards they knocked at the prince's door.

This door was guarded by a sentinel, and there was also a guard placed in the courtyard, ready to obey the orders of the lieutenant of the Prince de Conti.

Monsieur de Bouillon had the gout, and was in bed; but notwithstanding his illness, which had prevented his mounting on horseback for the last month—that is, since Paris had been besieged—he was ready to receive the Comte de la Fère and the Chevalier d'Herblay.

He was in bed, but surrounded with all the paraphernalia of war. Everywhere were swords, pistols, cuirasses, and arbuses, and it was plain that as soon as his gout was cured, Monsieur de Bouillon would give a pretty skein of silk to the enemies of the parliament to unravel. Meanwhile, to his great regret, as he said, he was obliged to keep his bed.

"Ah! gentlemen," he cried, as the two friends entered, "you are very happy! you can ride. Come, go fight for the cause of the people. But I, as you see, am nailed to my bed—ah! this demon, the gout—this demon, the gout!"

"My lord," said Athos, "we are just arrived from England, and our first concern is to inquire after your health."

"Thanks, gentlemen! thanks! As you see, my health is bad, but you come from England. And King Charles is well, as I have just heard?"

"He is dead! my lord," said Aramis.

"Pooh!" said the duke, astonished.

"Dead on the scaffold; condemned by the parliament."

"Impossible!"

"And executed in our presence."

"What then has Monsieur de Flamareus been saying to me?"

"Monsieur de Flamareus?"

"Yes, he has just gone out. Deuce take it! this gout!" said the duke.

. "My lord," said Athos, "we admire your devotion to the cause you have espoused, in remaining at the head of the army whilst so ill, in so much pain."

"One must," replied Monsieur de Bouillon, "sacrifice one's self to the public good; but, I confess to you, I am now almost exhausted. My spirit is willing, my head is clear, but this demon, the gout, galls me ! I confess, if the court would do justice to my claims, and give to the head of my house the title of prince, and if my brother De Turenne were reinstated in his command, I would return to my estates and leave the court and the parliament to settle things between themselves as they could."

"You are perfectly right, my lord."

"You think so ? At this very moment the court is making overtures to me : hitherto I repulsed them; but since such men as you assure me that I am wrong in doing so, I've a good mind to follow your advice, and to accept a proposition made to me by the Duc de Châtillon, just now."

"Accept it, my lord, accept it," said Aramis.

He and Athos then took their departure.

"And what think you of the Duc de Bouillon ?" asked Aramis of his friend.

"I think," answered Athos, "that we have acted wisely in not breathing a syllable of the reason for our visit; and now let us proceed forthwith to the Hôtel de Vendôme." It was ten o'clock when they reached it, and they found it as closely guarded as that of the Duc de Bouillon. As they entered the courtyard, two cavaliers were coming out, and Athos and Aramis recognised the Duc de Châtillon and Monsieur de Flamareus, who had evidently been paying their respects to the Duc de Beaufort.

Scarcely had the two friends dismounted when a man approached them, and after looking at them for an instant by the doubtful light of the lanthorn, hung in the centre of the courtyard, he uttered an exclamation of joy, and ran to embrace them.

"Rochefort !" cried the two friends.

"Yes ! We arrived four or five days ago from the Vendômois, as you know, and we are going to give Mazarin something to do. You are still with us, I presume ?"

"More than ever. And the duke ?"

"Furious against the Cardinal. You know his success—our dear duke ? He's really the king of Paris; he can't go out without being almost stifled."

"Ah ! so much the better ! Can we have the honour of seeing his highness ?"

"I shall be proud to present you ; " and Rochefort walked on;

every door was opened to him. Monsieur de Beaufort was at supper, but he rose quickly on hearing the two friends announced.

"Ah!" he cried, "by Jove! you're welcome, sirs. You are coming to sup with me, are you not? Boisgoli, tell Noirmont that I have two guests. You know Noirmont, do you not? The successor of Father Marteau, who makes the excellent pies you know about. Boisgoli, let him send one of his best, but not such an one as he made for La Ramée. Thank God! we don't want either ropes, ladders, or pears of anguish."

"My lord," said Athos, "do not let us disturb you. We came merely to inquire after your health and to take your orders."

"As to my health, since it has stood five years of prison, with Monsieur de Chevigny to boot, 'tis excellent! As to my orders, since every one gives his own commands in our party, I shall end, if this goes on, in giving none at all."

"In short, my lord," said Athos, glancing at Aramis, "your highness is dicontented with your party?"

"Discontented, sir; say that my highness is furious! To such a degree, I assure you, though I would not say so to others, that if the queen, acknowledging the injuries she has done me, would recall my mother, and give me the reversion of the Admiralty, which belonged to my father, and was promised to me at his death —well! I should not be long before I could train dogs to say, 'that there were greater traitors in France than the Cardinal Mazarin.'"

At this Athos and Aramis could not help exchanging not only a look but a smile; and, had they not known it for a fact, they could have been sure that De Châtillon and De Flamareus had been there before them.

"My lord!" said Athos, "we are satisfied; we came here only to express our loyalty, and to say that we are at your lordship's service, and his most faithful servants," and, bowing low, they went out.

"My dear Athos," cried Aramis; "I think you consented to accompany me only to give me a lesson—God forgive me!"

"Wait a little, Aramis; it will be time for us to perceive my motive when we have paid our visit to the Coadjutor."

"Let us, then, go to the Archiepiscopal palace," said Aramis.

They directed their horses to the city. On arriving at the cradle from which Paris sprang, they found it inundated with water; and it was again necessary to take a boat. The palace rose from the bosom of the water, and, to see the number of boats around it, one would have fancied one's self not in Paris, but in Venice. Some of these boats were dark and mysterious, others noisy, and lighted up with torches. The friends glided in between this confusion of embarkations, and landed in their turn. All the palace was under water, but a kind of staircase had been fixed to the lower walls ; and the only difference was that, instead of entering by the doors, people entered by the windows.

Thus did Athos and Aramis make their appearance in the ante-chamber, where about a dozen noblemen were collected and waiting.

" Good heavens !" said Aramis to Athos ; " does the Coadjutor intend to indulge himself in the pleasure of making us wait in his antechamber ?"

" My dear friend, we must take people as we find them. The Coadjutor is at this moment one of the seven kings of Paris, and has a court. Let us send in our names, and if he does not send us a suitable message, we will leave him to his own affairs, or to those of France. Let us call one of these lacqueys, with a demi-pistol in one hand. Exactly so—ah ! if I'm not mistaken, here's Bazin. Come here, fellow !"

Bazin, who was crossing the antechamber majestically in his clerical dress, turned round to see who the impertinent gentleman was who thus addressed him ; but seeing the friends, he went up to them quickly, and expressed great delight on seeing them.

" A truce to compliments," said Aramis ; " we want to see the Coadjutor, and instantly, as we are in haste."

"Certainly, sir,—it is not such lords as you are who are allowed to wait in the antechamber, only just now he has a secret confer-ence with Monsieur de Bruy."

" De Bruy !" cried the friends ; " 'tis then useless our seeing Monsieur the Coadjutor this evening," said Aramis, " so we give it up."

And they hastened to quit the palace, followed by Bazin, who was lavish of his bows and compliments.

At ten. o'clock the next day the friends met again.

There were still no tidings of D'Artagnan or Porthos, whom they had expected. Raoul was gone to Saint Cloud, in conse-quence of a message from the Prince de Condé, and had not returned ; and Aramis had not been able to see Madame de Longueville, who was installed at the Hôtel de Ville, where she played the part of queen, not having quite courage enough, as Aramis remarked, to take up her abode at the Palais Royal or the Tuileries.

" Well, then," said Athos, " now, then, what shall we do this evening ?"

"You forget, my friend, that we have work cut out for us in the direction of Charenton; I hope to see Monsieur de Châtillon, whom I've hated a long time, there."

"Why have you hated him?"

"Because he is the brother of Coligny."

"Ah, true! he who presumed to be a rival of yours, for which he was severely punished—that ought to satisfy you."

"Yes, but it does not; I am rancorous, the only point which shows me to be a churchman. Do you understand? Let us go, then, Aramis."

"If we go, there is no time to lose; the drum has beat; I saw cannon on the road; I saw the citizens in order of battle on the Place of the Hôtel de Ville; certainly the fight will be in the direction of Charenton, as the Duc de Châtillon said."

"Poor creatures!" said Athos, "who are going to be killed, in order that Monsieur de Bouillon should have his estate at Sedan restored to him, that the reversion of the Admiralty should be given to the Duc de Beaufort, and that the Coadjutor should be made a Cardinal."

"Come! come, dear Athos, you will not be so philosophical if your Raoul should happen to be in all this confusion."

"Perhaps you speak the truth, Aramis."

"Well, let us go, then, where the fighting is, for that is the most likely place to meet with D'Artagnan, Porthos, and Raoul. Stop, there are a fine body of citizens passing; quite attractive, by Jupiter! and their captain! see! in the true military style."

"What ho!" said Grimaud.

"What?" asked Athos.

"Planchet, sir."

"Lieutenant yesterday," said Aramis, "a captain to-day, a colonel, doubtless, to-morrow: in a week the fellow will be a field-marshal of France."

"Ask him some questions about the fight," said Athos.

Planchet, prouder than ever of his new duties, deigned to explain to the two gentlemen that he was ordered to take up his position on the Place Royale, where two hundred men formed the rear of the army of Paris, and to march towards Charenton, when necessary.

"The day will be warm," said Planchet, in a warlike tone.

But the friends, not caring to mix themselves up with the citizens, set off towards Charenton, and passed the valley of Fecamp, darkened by the presence of armed troops.

CHAPTER LXXVI.

THE BATTLE OF CHARENTON.

As Athos and Aramis proceeded, and passed different companies on the road, they became aware that they were arriving near the field of battle.

"Ah! my friend cried Athos, suddenly, "where have you brought us? I fancy I perceive around us faces of different officers in the royal army: is it not the Duc de Châtillon himself who is coming towards us with his brigadiers?"

"Good day, sirs," said the duke, advancing; "you are puzzled by what you see here, but one word will explain everything. There is now a truce, and a conference. The prince, Monsieur de Retz, the Duc de Beaufort, the Duc de Bouillon, are talking over public affairs. Now, one of two things must happen; either matters will be arranged, or they will not be arranged, in which last case I shall be relieved of my command, and we shall still meet again."

"This conference has not then been preconcerted?"

"No; 'tis the result of certain propositions made yesterday by Cardinal Mazarin to the Parisians."

"Where, then, are the plenipotentiaries?" asked Athos.

"At the house of Monsieur de Chauleu, who commands your troops at Charenton. I say your troops, for I presume that you gentlemen are Frondeurs?"

"Yes—almost," said Aramis.

"We are for the king, and the princes," added Athos.

"We must understand each other," said the duke; "the king is with us, and his generals are, the Duke of Orleans and the Prince de Conti, although, I must add, 'tis almost impossible now to know what party one is on."

"Yes," answered Athos, "but his right place is in our ranks, with the Prince de Conti, De Beaufort, D'Elbeuf, and De Bouillon; but, my lord, supposing that the conferences are broken off, are you going to try to take Charenton?"

"Such are my orders."

"My lord, since you command the cavalry——"

"Pardon me, I am commander-in-chief."

"So much the better. There is a youth, of fifteen years of age, the Vicomte de Bragelonne, attached to the Prince de Conti:— has he the honour of being known to you?" inquired Athos, diffident in allowing the sceptical Aramis to perceive how strong were his paternal feelings.

"Yes, surely, he came with the prince; a charming young man; he is one of your friends, then, Monsieur le Comte?"

"Yes, sir," answered Athos, slightly agitated; "so much so, that I wish to see him, if possible."

"Quite possible, sir; do me the favour to accompany me, and I will conduct you to head-quarters."

"Hallo, there!" cried Aramis, turning round, "what a noise behind us."

"A stout cavalier coming towards us," said Châtillon: "I recognise the Coadjutor, by his Frondist hat."

"And I, the Duc de Beaufort, by his plume of white feathers."

"They are coming full gallop; the prince is with them: ah! he is leaving them."

"They are beating the rappel!" cried Châtillon; "we must find out what's going on."

In fact, they saw the soldiers running to their arms; the trumpets sounded; the drum beat; the Duc de Beaufort drew his sword. On his side, the prince sounded a rappel, and all the officers of the royalist army, mingled momentarily with the Parisian troops, ran to him.

"Gentlemen," cried Châtillon, "the truce is broken, that's evident; they are going to fight; go, then, into Charenton, for I shall begin in a short time—hark! there's a signal from the prince!"

The cornet of the troop had, in fact, just raised the standard of the prince.——"Farewell, till the next time!" cried Châtillon, and he set off, full gallop.

Aramis and Athos turned also, and went to salute the Coadjutor, and the Duc de Beaufort. As to the Duc de Bouillon, he had such a fit of gout as obliged him to return to Paris in a litter; but his place was supplied by the Duc d'Elbeuf and his four sons, ranged around him like a staff. Meantime, between Charenton and the royal army, was left a long space, which seemed prepared to serve as a last resting-place for the dead.

"Gentlemen," cried the Coadjutor, tightening his sash, which he wore after the fashion of the ancient military prelates, over his Archiepiscopal simar, "there's the enemy approaching us; we shall, I hope, save them the half of their journey."

And, without caring whether he were followed or not, he set off: his regiment, which bore the name of the regiment of Corinth, from the name of his Archbishopric, darted after him, and began the fight. Monsieur de Beaufort sent his cavalry towards

Etampes, and Monsieur de Chauleu, who defended the place, was ready to resist an assault, or, if the enemy were repulsed, to attempt a sortie.

The battle soon became general, and the Coadjutor performed miracles of valour. His proper vocation had always been the sword, and he was delighted whenever he could draw it from the scabbard, no matter for whom, or against whom.

Chauleu, whose fire at one time repulsed the royal regiments, thought that the moment was come to pursue it; but it was re-formed, and led again to the charge, by the Duc de Châtillon, in person. This charge was so fierce, so skilfully conducted, that Chauleu was almost surrounded. He commanded a retreat, which began, step by step, foot by foot—unhappily, in an instant, he fell, mortally wounded. De Châtillon saw him fall, and announced it, in a loud voice, to his men, which raised their spirits, and completely disheartened their enemies, so that every man thought only of his personal safety, and tried to regain the trenches, where the Coadjutor was trying to reform his disorganised regiment.

Suddenly, a squadron of cavalry came to an encounter with the royal troops who were entering, *pêle mêle*, into the entrenchments with the fugitives. Athos and Aramis charged at the head of their squadron; Aramis with his sword and pistol in his hands; Athos, with his sword in the scabbard, his pistol in his saddle bags; calm and cool as if on the parade, except that his noble and beautiful countenance became sad as he saw slaughtered, so many men who were sacrificed on the one side to the obstinacy of royalty, on the other to the rancorous party feeling of the princes; Aramis, on the contrary, struck right and left, and was almost delirious with excitement. His bright eyes kindled, and his mouth, so finely formed, assumed a dark smile; every blow he aimed was sure, and his pistol finished the deed—and annihilated the wounded wretch who tried to rise again.

On the opposite side, two cavaliers, one covered with a gilt cuirass, the other wearing simply a buff doublet, from which fell the sleeves of a vest of blue velvet, charged in front. The cavalier in the gilt cuirass fell upon Aramis and hit him a blow that Aramis parried with his wonted skill.

"Ah! 'tis you, Monsieur de Châtillon," cried the chevalier, "welcome to you—I await you."

"I hope I have not made you wait too long, sir," said the duke; "at all events, here I am."

"Monsieur de Châtillon," cried Aramis, taking from his saddle bags a second pistol, "I think if your pistols have been discharged, you are a dead man."

"Thank God, sir, they are not!"

And the duke, pointing his pistol at Aramis, fired. But Aramis instantly bent his head, and the ball passed without touching him

"Oh! you've missed me," cried Aramis; "but I swear to Heaven, I will not miss you."

"If I give you time!" cried the duke, spurring on his horse, and rushing upon him with his drawn sword.

Aramis awaited him with that terrible smile which was peculiar to him on such occasions; and Athos, who saw the duke advancing towards Aramis with the rapidity of lightning, was just going to cry out "fire! fire then!" when the shot was fired, De Châtillon opened his arms and fell back on the cruppers of his horse.

The ball had penetrated into his chest through the crank of his cuirass.

"I am a dead man," he said, and he fell from his horse to the ground.

"I told you this; I am now grieved I have kept my word; can I be of any use to you!"

Châtillon made a sign with his hand, and Aramis was about to dismount, when he received a violent shock in the side, 'twas a thrust from a sword, but his cuirass turned aside the blow.

He turned round and seized his new antagonist by the wrist, when he started back, exclaiming, "Raoul!"

"Raoul?" cried Athos.

The young man recognised at the same time the voice of his father and that of the Chevalier d'Herblay; several chevaliers in the Parisian forces rushed at that instant on Raoul, but Aramis protected him with his sword.

"My prisoner!" he cried.

At this crisis of the battle, the Prince, who had seconded De Châtillon in the second line, appeared in the midst of the fight; his eagle eye made him known, and his blows proclaimed the hero.

On seeing him the regiment of Corinth, which the Coadjutor had not been able to reorganise in spite of his efforts, threw itself into the midst of the Parisian forces, put them into confusion, and re-entered Charenton flying. The Coadjutor, dragged along with his fugitive forces, passed near the group formed by Athos, Raoul, and Aramis. Aramis could not in his jealousy avoid being pleased at the Coadjutor's misfortune, and was about to make some bon-mot, more witty than correct, when Athos stopped him.

"On, on!" he cried, "this is no moment for compliments; or rather back, for the battle seems to be lost by the Frondeurs."

"That's a matter of indifference to me," said Aramis, "I came here only to meet De Châtillon; I have met him, I am contented; 'tis something to have met De Châtillon in a duel!"

The three cavaliers continued their road on a full gallop.

"What were you doing in the battle, my friend?" inquired Athos of the youth; "'twas not your right place, I think, as you were not equipped for an engagement!"

"I had no intention of fighting to-day, sir; I was charged, indeed, with a mission for the Cardinal, and had set out for Rueil, when seeing Monsieur de Châtillon charge, a wish possessed me to charge at his side. Two cavaliers from the Parisian troops told me that you were there."

"What! you knew we were there, and yet wished to kill your friend and the chevalier?"

"I did not recognise the chevalier in his armour, sir!" said Raoul, blushing; "though I might have known him by his skill and coolness in danger."

"Thank you for the compliment, my young friend," replied Aramis, "we can see from whom you learnt lessons of courtesy; you were going, then, to Rueil?"

"Yes! I have a despatch from the Prince to his Eminence."

"You must still deliver it," said Athos.

"No false generosity, count! the fate of our friends—to say nothing of our own—is, perhaps, in that very despatch."

"This young man must not, however, fail in his duty," said Athos.

" In the first place, count, this youth is our prisoner; you seem to forget that. What I propose to do is fair in war, and the conquered must not be dainty in the true choice of means."

"Give him the despatch, Raoul! you are the chevalier's prisoner."

Raoul gave it up reluctantly; Aramis instantly seized and read it.

"You," he said, "you, who are so trusting, read and reflect that there is something in this letter important for us to see."

Athos took the letter, frowning, but an idea that he should hear something in this letter about D'Artagnan conquered his unwillingness to finish it.

"My lord I shall send this evening to your Eminence in order to reinforce the troop of Monsieur de Comminges, the ten men whom you demand. They are good soldiers, fit to support the two violent adversaries whose address and resolution your Eminence is fearful of."

" Oh !" cried Athos.

" Well," said Aramis, " why think you about these two enemies, when it requires, besides Comminges' troop, ten good soldiers to guard; are they not as like as two drops of water to D'Artagnan and Porthos ?"

" We'll search Paris all to-day," said Athos, " and if we have no news this evening, we will return to the road to Picardy ; and I feel no doubt that, thanks to D'Artagnan's ready invention, we shall then find some clue which will solve our doubts."

It was, then, with a sentiment of uneasiness whether Planchet, who alone could give them information, was alive or not, that the friends returned to the Palais Royal ; to their great surprise they found all the citizens still encamped there, drinking and bantering each other ; although, doubtless, mourned by their families, who thought they were at Charenton, in the thick of the firing.

Athos and Aramis again questioned Planchet, but he had seen nothing of D'Artagnan ; they wished to take Planchet with them, but he could not leave his troop ; who, at five o'clock returned home, saying that they were returning from the battle, whereas they had never lost sight of the equestrian statue in bronze of Louis XIII.

CHAPTER LXXVII.

THE ROAD TO PICARDY.

In leaving Paris, Athos and Aramis well knew that tney would be encountering great danger ; but one can imagine how such men look at a question of personal risk. Paris, however, itself was not tranquil ; food began to be scarce ; and wheresoever any of the Prince de Conti's generals wanted to succeed him in his command, some little *émeute*, which he always put a stop to instantly, took place.

In one of these risings, the Duc de Beaufort pillaged the house and library of Mazarin, in order to give the populace, as he said, something to gnaw at. Athos and Aramis left Paris after this *coup d'état*, which took place on the very evening of the day in which the Parisians had been beaten at Charenton.

They quitted Paris, beholding it abandoned to extreme want bordering on famine : agitated by fear, torn by faction. Parisians and Frondeurs as they were, the two friends expected to find the same misery, the same fears, the same intrigues in the enemy's camp; but what was their surprise, after passing St. Denis, to hear that, at St. Germains, people were singing and laughing, and leading a cheerful life. The two gentlemen travelled by by-ways, in order not to encounter Mazarinists, who were scattered about the Isle of France, and also to escape the Frondeurs, who were in possession of Normandy, and who would not have failed to conduct them to the Duc de Longueville, in order that he might know whether they were friends or enemies. Having escaped these dangers, they returned by the main road to Boulogne, at Abbeville, and followed it step by step, examining every track.

Nevertheless, they were still in a state of uncertainty. Several inns were visited by them, several innkeepers questioned, without a single clue being given to guide their inquiries. When at Montreuil Athos felt, upon the table, that something rough was touching his delicate fingers. He turned up the cloth, and found these hieroglyphics carved upon the wood with a knife :—

"Port . . . . D'Art . . . . 2nd February."

"This is capital," said Athos to Aramis; "we were to have slept here, but we cannot, we must push on." They rode forward, and reached Abbeville. There the great number of inns puzzled them; they could not go to all; how could they guess in which he whom they were seeking had stayed.

"Trust me," said Aramis; "do not expect to find anything in Abbeville. If we had only been looking for Porthos, Porthos would have fixed himself in one of the finest of the hotels, and we could easily have traced him. Dut D'Artagnan is devoid of such weaknesses. Porthos would have found it very difficult even to make him see that he was dying of hunger; he has gone on his road as inexorable as fate, and we must seek him somewhere else."

They continued their route; it had now become a weary and almost hopeless task; and had it not been for the threefold motives of honour, friendship, and gratitude, implanted in their hearts, these two travellers would have given up, many a time, their rides over the sand, their interrogatories of the peasantry, and their close inspection of faces.

They proceeded to Compiègne.

Athos began to despair. His noble nature felt that their ignorance was a sort of reflection upon them. They had not looked well enough for their lost friends. They had not shown sufficient pertinacity in their inquiries. They were willing and ready to retrace their steps, when, in crossing the suburb which leads to

the gates of the town, upon a white wall which was at the corner
of a street turning round the rampart, Athos cast his eyes upon
a drawing in black chalk, which represented, with the awkwardness of a first attempt, two cavaliers riding furiously, and carrying
a roll of paper, on which were written these words,—"They are
following us."

"Oh !" exclaimed Athos ; " here it is as clear as day.   Pursued
as he was, D'Artagnan would not have tarried here five minutes
had he been pressed very closely, which gives us hopes that he
may have succeeded in escaping."

Athos shook his head.

"Had he escaped we should either have seen him or have heard
him spoken of."

"You are right, Aramis ; let us travel on."

To describe the impatience and uneasiness of these two gentlemen would be impossible.   Anxiety took possession of the tender
and constant heart of Athos ; and impatience was the torment of
the impulsive Aramis.   They galloped on for two or three hours
with the frenzy of two knights in pursuit.   All at once, in a narrow
pass, they perceived that the road was partially barricaded by an
enormous stone.   It had evidently been rolled across the path by
some arm of gigantic power.

Aramis stopped.

"Oh !" he said, looking at the stone, "this is the work either of
Ajax, or of Briareus, or of Porthos.   Let us get down, count, and
examine this rock."

They both alighted.   The stone had been brought with the
evident intention of barricading the road ; but some one, having
perceived the obstacle, had partially turned it aside.

With the assistance of Blaisois and Grimaud, the friends succeeded in turning the stone over.   Upon the side next the ground
was written :

"Eight of the Light Dragoons are pursuing us.   If we reach
Compiègne, we shall stop at the Peacock.   It is kept by a friend
of ours."

"This is something positive," said Athos, "let us go to the
Peacock."

"Yes," answered Aramis, "but if we are to get there, we must
rest our horses, for they are almost broken-winded."

Aramis was right ; they stopped at the first tavern, and made
each horse swallow a double quantity of corn steeped in wine ;
they gave them three hours' rest, and then set off again.   The
men themselves were almost killed with fatigue, but hope supported
them.

In six hours they reached Compiègne, and alighted at the Peacock. The host proved to be a worthy man, as bald as a Chinaman. They asked him if some time ago he had not received in his house two gentlemen who were pursued by Dragoons: without answering, he went out and brought in the blade of a rapier.

" Do you know that ?" he asked.

Athos merely glanced at it.

" 'Tis D'Artagnan's sword," he said

" Does it belong to the smaller, or to the larger of the two ?" asked the host.

" To the smaller."

" I see that you are the friends of these gentlemen."

" Well, what has happened to them?"

" They were pursued by eight of the Light Dragoons, who rode into the court yard, before they had time to close the gate ; but these men would not have succeeded in taking them prisoners, had they not been assisted by twenty soldiers of the regiment of Italians in the king's service, who are in garrison in this town— so that your friends were overpowered by numbers."

" Arrested, were they ?" asked Athos ; " is it known why ?"

" No, sir, they were carried off directly, and had not time to tell me why ; but, as soon as they were gone, I found this broken blade of a sword—as I was helping in raising up two dead men, and five or six wounded ones."

" 'Tis still a consolation that they were not wounded," said Aramis.

" Where were they taken ?" asked Athos.

" Towards the town of Louvres," was the reply.

The two friends, having agreed to leave Blaisois and Grimaud at Compiègne with the horses, resolved to take post horses ; and having snatched a hasty dinner, they continued their journey to Louvres.

Here they found only one inn, in which was drunk a liquor which still preserves its reputation in our own time, and which is still made in that town.

" Let us alight here," said Athos, " D'Artagnan will not have let slip an opportunity of drinking a glass of this liquor, and, at the same time, leaving some trace of himself."

They went into the town, and asked for two glasses of liquor, at the counter—as their friends must have done before them. The counter was covered generally with a plate of pewter ; upon this plate was written with the point of a large pin,— " Rueil . . . . D . . . ."

"They went to Rueil," cried Aramis.

"Let us go to Rueil," said Athos. "Had I been as great a friend of Jonah's as I am of D'Artagnan, I should have followed him even into the whale itself; and you would have done the same," observed Athos.

"Certainly—but you make me better than I am, dear count. Had I been alone, I should scarcely have gone to Rueil without great caution."

They then set off for Rueil. Here the deputies of the Parliament had just arrived, in order to enter upon those famous conferences which were to last three weeks, and produced, eventually, that shameful peace, at the end of which the prince was arrested. Rueil was crowded with advocates, presidents, and counsellors, who came from the Parisians; and, on the side of the court, with officers and guards; it was, therefore, easy, in the midst of this confusion, to remain as much unobserved as might be wished; besides, the conferences implied a truce, and to arrest two gentlemen, even *Frondeurs*, at this time, would have been an attack on the rights of the people.

The two friends mingled in the crowd, and fancied that every one was occupied with the same thought that tormented them.

But every one was engrossed by articles and reforms. It was the advice of Athos to go straight to the ministers.

"My friend," said Aramis, "take care; our safety proceeds from our obscurity. If we were to make ourselves known, we should be sent to rejoin our friends in some deep ditch, from which the devil himself cannot take us out. Let us try not to find them out by accident, but from our own notions. Arrested at Compiègne, they have been carried to Rueil; at Rueil they have been questioned by the Cardinal, who has either kept them near him, or sent them to St. Germains. As to the Bastille, they are not there, though the Bastille is especially for the 'Frondeurs.' They are not dead, for the death of D'Artagnan would make a sensation. Do not let us despond—but wait at Rueil, for my conviction is that they are at Rueil. But what ails you? you are pale."

"It is this," answered Athos, with a trembling voice, "I remember that, at the Castle of Rueil, the Cardinal Richelieu has some horrible 'oubliettes' constructed."

"Oh! never fear," said Aramis. "Richelieu was a gentleman, our equal in birth, our superior in position. He could, like the king, touch the greatest of us on the head, and in touching them, make the head shake on the shoulders. But Mazarin is a low-born rogue, who could only take us by the neck, like an archer. Be calm—for I am sure that D'Artagnan and Porthos are alive and well."

"Well," resumed Athos, "I recur to my first proposal. I know no better means than to act with candour. I shall seek not Mazarin, but the queen—and say to her, 'Madame, restore to us our two servants and our two friends.'"

Aramis shook his head.

"'Tis a last resource; but let us not employ it till it is imperatively necessary; let us rather continue our researches."

They continued their inquiries, and at last met with a Light Dragoon, who had formed one of the guard which had escorted D'Artagnan to Rueil, by which they knew that they had entered that house.

Athos, therefore, perpetually recurred to his proposed interview with the queen.

"I shall go," he said, "to the queen."

"Well, then," answered Aramis, "Pray tell me a day or two beforehand, that I may take that opportunity of going to Paris."

"To whom?"

"Zounds! how do I know? perhaps to Madame de Longueville. She is all powerful yonder; she will help me. But send me word should you be arrested, for then I will return directly."

"Why do you not take your chance, and be arrested with me?"

"No, I thank you."

"Should we, by being arrested, be all four together again, we should not, I am sure, be twenty-four hours in prison without getting free."

"My friend, since I killed Châtillon, the adored of the ladies of St. Germains, I have too great a celebrity not to fear a prison doubly. The queen is likely to follow Mazarin's counsels, and to have me tried. Do you think that she loves this Italian so much as they say she does?"

"She loved an Englishman passionately."

"Well, my friend, she is a woman."

"No, no, you are deceived—she is a queen."

"Dear friend, I shall sacrifice myself, and go and see Anne of Austria."

"Adieu, Athos, I am going to raise an army."

"For what purpose?"

"To come back, and besiege Rueil."

"Where shall we meet again?"

"At the foot of the Cardinal's gallows."

The two friends parted — Aramis to return to Paris, Athos to take some measures preparatory to an interview with the queen.

CHAPTER LXXVIII.

THE GRATITUDE OF ANNE OF AUSTRIA.

ATHOS found much less difficulty than he had expected in obtaining an audience of Anne of Austria; it was granted, and was to take place, after her morning's 'levée,' at which, in accordance with the rights he derived from his birth, he was entitled to be present. A vast crowd filled the apartments of St. Germains; Anne had never, at the Louvre, had so large a court; but this crowd represented chiefly the second class of nobility, which the Prince de Conti, the Duc de Beaufort, and the Coadjutor assembled around them,—the first men in France.

The greatest possible gaiety prevailed at the court. The particular characteristic of this was, that more songs were made than cannon fired during its continuance. La Court made songs on the Parisians, and the Parisians on the court; and the wounds, though not mortal, were painful, as they were made by the arms of ridicule.

In the midst of this seeming hilarity, nevertheless, people's minds were uneasy. Was Mazarin to remain the favourite and minister of the queen? was he to be carried back by the wind which had blown him there? Every one hoped so, so that the minister felt that all around him, beneath the homage of the courtiers, lay a fund of hatred, ill disguised by fear and interest. He was ill at ease, and at a loss what to do.

Condé, himself, while fighting for him, lost no opportunity of ridiculing, or of humbling him. The queen, on whom he threw himself, as his sole support, seemed to him, now, very little to be relied upon.

When the hour appointed for the audience arrived, Athos was obliged to stay until the queen, who was waited upon by a new deputation from Paris, had consulted with her minister as to the propriety and manner of receiving them. All were fully engrossed with the affairs of the day, and there could be few opportunities less favourable to make an appeal upon; but Athos was a man of inflexible temper, and insisted on his right of being admitted into the queen's presence. Accordingly, at the close of the audience, she sent for him to her room.

The name of the Count de la Fère was then announced to Anne. Often must she have heard that name, and felt that it had made her heart beat; nevertheless, she remained unmoved, and was contented to look steadfastly at this gentleman, with that set stare which can alone be permitted to a queen.

"Do you come, then, to offer me your services?" she asked, after some moments' silence.

"Yes, madame," replied Athos, shocked at her not recognising him. Athos had a noble heart, and made, therefore, but a poor courtier.

Anne frowned. Mazarin, who was sitting at a table, folding up papers, as if he had only been a secretary of state, looked up.

"Speak," said the queen.

Mazarin turned again to his papers.

"Madame," resumed Athos, "two of my friends, named D'Artagnan and Porthos, sent to England by the Cardinal, have suddenly disappeared ever since they set foot on the shores of France; no one knows what has become of them."

"Well?" said the queen.

"I address myself, therefore, first to the benevolence of your majesty, that I may know what has become of my friends, reserving to myself, if necessary, the right of appealing afterwards to your justice."

"Sir," replied Anne, with a degree of haughtiness, which, to certain persons, became impertinence, "this is the reason that you trouble me in the midst of so many absorbing concerns! An affair for the police! Well, sir, you ought to know that since we left Paris there no longer exists a police."

"I think that your majesty will have no need to apply to the police to know where my friends are, but that if you will deign to interrogate the Cardinal, he can reply without any further inquiry than into his own recollections."

"But, God forgive me!" cried Anne, with that disdainful curl of the lip peculiar to her, "I think you can inquire yourself."

"Yes, madame, here I have a right to do so, for it concerns Monsieur D'Artagnan—D'Artagnan," he repeated, in such a manner as to bow down the regal brow beneath the recollections of the weak and erring woman.

The Cardinal saw that it was now high time to come to the assistance of Anne.

" Sir," he said, " I can tell what is at present unknown to her majesty. These individuals are under arrest; they disobeyed orders."

" I beg of your majesty, then," said Athos, calm, and not replying to Mazarin, " to take off these arrests from Monsieur d'Artagnan and De Valon."

" What you ask is an affair of discipline and police," said the queen.

" Monsieur d'Artagnan never made such an answer as that when the service of your majesty was concerned," said Athos, bowing with great dignity. He was going towards the door, when Mazarin stopped him.

" You have also been in England, sir ?" he said, making a sign to the queen, who was evidently going to issue a severe order.

" I was present at the last hours of Charles I. Poor king ! Culpable, at the most, of weakness, how cruelly punished by his subjects ! Thrones are at this time shaken, and it is to little purpose for devoted hearts to serve the interests of princes. This is the second time that Monsieur D'Artagnan has been in England. He went the first time to save the honour of a great queen ; the second, to avert the death of a great king."

" Sir," said Anne to Mazarin, with an accent from which daily habits of dissimulation could not entirely chase the real expression, " see, if we cannot do something for these gentlemen."

" I wish to do, madame, all that your majesty pleases."

" Do what Monsieur de la Fère requests ; that is your name, is it not, sir ?"

" I have another name, madame—I am called Athos."

" Madame," said Mazarin, with a smile, " you may be easy—your wishes shall be fulfilled."

" You hear, sir ?" said the queen.

" Yes, madame ; I expected nothing less from the justice of your majesty. May I not, then, go and see my friends ?"

" Yes, sir, you shall see them. But, *à propos*, you belong to the Fronde, do you not ?"

" Madame, I serve the king."

" Yes, in your own way."

" My way is the way of all gentlemen ; and I know only one way," answered Athos, haughtily.

" Go, sir, then," said the queen; " you have obtained what you wish, and we know all we wish to know."

Scarcely, however, had the tapestry closed behind Athos than she said to Mazarin :

"Cardinal, desire them to arrest that insolent fellow before he leaves the Court."

"Your majesty," answered Mazarin, "desires me to do only what I was going to ask you to let me do. These bravos, who bring back to our epoch the traditions of the other reign, are troublesome; since there are two of them already there, let us add a third."

Athos was not completely the queen's dupe, but he was not a man to run away merely on suspicion—above all, when distinctly told that he should see his friends again. He waited, then, in the antechamber with impatience, till he should be conducted to them.

He walked to the window and looked into the court. He saw the deputation from the Parisians enter it: they were coming to sign the definitive place for the conference, and to make their bow to the queen. A very imposing escort awaited them without the gates.

Athos was looking on attentively when some one touched him softly on the shoulder.

"Ah! Monsieur de Comminges," he said.

"Yes, count, and charged with a commission for which I beg of you to accept my excuses."

"What is it?"

"Be so good as to give me up your sword, count."

Athos smiled and opened the window.

"Aramis!" he cried.

A gentleman turned round. Athos fancied he had seen him among the crowd. It was Aramis. He bowed with great friendship to the count.

"Aramis!" cried Athos; "I am arrested."

"Good," replied Aramis calmly.

"Sir," said Athos, turning to Comminges, and giving him politely his sword by the hilt—"there is my sword—have the kindness to keep it for me until I shall quit my prison. I prize it—it was given to my ancestors by King Francis I. In his time they armed gentlemen, they did not disarm them. Now, whither do you conduct me?"

"Into my room at first," replied Comminges, "the queen will ultimately decide on the place of your domicile."

Athos followed Comminges without saying a single word.

CHAPTER LXXIX.

THE ROYALTY OF CARDINAL MAZARIN.

THE arrests produced no sensation, and were almost unknown, and scarcely interrupted the course of events. To the deputation it was formally announced that the queen would receive it.

Accordingly it was admitted to the presence of Anne, who, silent and lofty as ever, listened to the speeches and complaints of the deputies; but when they had finished their harangues, not one of them could say, so calm had been her face, whether she had heard them or not. Whilst thus she was silent, Mazarin, who was present, and knew what the deputies asked, answered in these terms :

" Gentlemen," he said, " I shall join with you in supplicating the queen to put an end to the miseries of her subjects. I have done all in my power to ameliorate them, and yet the belief of the public, you say, is that they proceed from me, an unhappy foreigner who has been unable to please the French. Alas ! I have never been understood, and no wonder. I succeeded a man of the most sublime genius that ever upheld the sceptre of France. The memory of Richelieu annihilates me. In vain—were I an ambitious man—should I struggle against such a remembrance as he has left ; but that I am not ambitious I am going to prove to you. I own myself conquered. I shall obey the wishes of the people. If Paris has injuries to complain of, who has not some wrongs to be redressed ? Paris has been sufficiently punished— enough blood has flowed—enough misery has humbled a town deprived of its king, and of its justice. 'Tis not for me, a private individual, to disunite a queen from her kingdom. Since you require my resignation, I shall retire."

" Then," said Aramis, in his neighbour's ears, " the conferences are over. There is nothing to do but to send Monsieur Mazarin to the most distant frontier, and to take care that he does not return even by that, nor any other entrance, into France."

" One instant, sir," said the man in a gown, whom he addressed ; " a plague on't ! how fast you go ! one may soon see that you're a soldier. There's the article of remunerations and indemnifications to be discussed and set to rights."

" Chancellor," said the queen, turning to this same man, " do you, our old acquaintance, open the conferences. They can take place at Rueil. The Cardinal has said several things which have agitated me, therefore I do not speak more fully now. As to his going or staying, I feel too much gratitude to the Cardinal not to leave him free in all his actions; he shall do what he wishes to do."

A transient pallor overspread the speaking countenance of the prime minister—he looked at the queen with anxiety. Her face was so passionless, that he was, as every one else was, incapable of reading her thoughts.

"But," added the queen, "in awaiting the Cardinal's decisions, let there be, if you please, a reference to the king only."

The deputies bowed, and left the room.

"What!" exclaimed the queen, when the last of them had quitted the apartment, "you would yield to these limbs of the law—those advocates?"

"To promote your majesty's welfare, madame," replied Mazarin, fixing his penetrating eye on the queen; "there's no sacrifice that I would not make."

Anne dropped her head and fell into one of those reveries so habitual with her. Her recollection of Athos came into her mind. His fearless deportment—his words, so firm yet so dignified, the shades which by one word he had evoked, recalled to her the past in all its intoxication of poetry and romance, youth, beauty, the éclat of love at twenty years of age, the bloody death of Buckingham, the only man whom she ever really loved, and the heroism of those obscure champions who had saved her from the double hatred of Richelieu and of the king.

Mazarin looked at her, and whilst she deemed herself alone and freed from that world of enemies who sought to spy into her secret thoughts, he read her thoughts in her countenance, as one sees in a transparent lake clouds pass—reflections, like thoughts, of the heavens.

"Must we, then," asked Anne of Austria, "yield to the storm, purchase a peace, and await patiently and piously for better times?"

Mazarin smiled sarcastically at this speech, which showed that she had taken the minister's proposal seriously.

Anne's head was bent down, and she did not see this smile; but finding that her question elicited no reply, she looked up.

"Well, you do not answer, Cardinal; what do you think about it?"

"I am thinking, madame, of the allusion made by that insolent gentleman, whom you have caused to be arrested, to the Duke of Buckingham—to him whom you suffered to be assassinated—to the Duchesse de Chevreuse, whom you suffered to be exiled—to the Duc de Beaufort, whom you exiled; but he made no allusion to me, because he is ignorant of the relation in which I stand to you."

Anne drew up, as she always did, when anything touched her pride. She blushed, and that she might not answer, clasped her beautiful hands till her sharp nails almost pierced them.

"That man has sagacity, honour, and wit, not to mention likewise that he is a man of undoubted resolution. You know something about him, do you not, madame? I shall tell him, therefore, and in doing so I shall confer a personal favour on him, how he is mistaken in regard to me. What is proposed to me would be, in fact almost an abdication, and an abdication requires reflection."

"An abdication?" repeated Anne; "I thought, sir, that it was only kings who abdicated?"

"Well," replied Mazarin, "and am I not almost a king—king, indeed, of France? Thrown over the foot of the royal bed, my simar, madam, is not unlike the mantle worn by a king."

This is one of the humiliations which Mazarin made Anne undergo more frequently than any other, and which bowed her head with shame. Queen Elizabeth and Catherine II. of Russia are the only two monarchs on record who were at once sovereigns and lovers. Anne of Austria looked with a sort of terror at the threatening aspect of the Cardinal—his physiognomy in such moments was not destitute of a certain grandeur.

"Sir," she replied, "did I not say, and did you not hear me say to those people, that you should do as you pleased?"

"In that case," said Mazarin, "I think it must please me best to remain: not only on account of my own interest, but for your safety."

"Remain, then, sir; nothing can be more agreeable to me; only do not allow me to be insulted."

"You are referring to the demands of the rebels, and to the tone in which they stated them? Patience! They have selected a field of battle on which I am an abler general than they are—that of a conference. No, we shall beat them by merely temporising. They want food already. They will be ten times worse off in a week."

"Ah, yes! Good heavens! I know it will end in that way; but it is not they who taunt me with the most wounding reproaches—but——"

"I understand; you mean to allude to the recollections perpetually revived by these three gentlemen. However, we have them safe in prison : and they are just sufficiently culpable for us to keep them in prison as long as is convenient to us. One, only,. is still not in our power, and braves us. But, devil take him ! we shall soon succeed in sending him to rejoin his companions. We have accomplished more difficult things than that. In the first place, I have, as a precaution, shut up, at Rueil, near me, under my own eyes, within reach of my hand, the two most intractable ones. To-day the third will be there also."

" As long as they are in prison, all will be well," said Anne ;. " but one of these days they will get out."

" Yes ; if your majesty releases them."

" Ah !" exclaimed Anne, following the train of her own thoughts. on such occasions ; " one regrets Paris !"

" Why so ?"

" On account of the Bastille, sir ; which is so strong and so secure."

" Madame, these conferences will bring us peace ; when we have peace we shall regain Paris ; with Paris, the Bastille, and our three bullies shall rot therein."

Anne frowned slightly, when Mazarin, in taking leave, kissed her hand.

Mazarin, after this half humble, half gallant attention, went away. Anne followed him with her eyes, and as he withdrew, at every step he took, a disdainful smile was seen playing, then gradually burst upon her lips.

" I once," she said, " despised the love of a Cardinal who never said 'I shall do,' but 'I have done.' That man knew of retreats more secure than Rueil—darker, and more silent even than the Bastille. Oh, the degenerate world !"

CHAPTER LXXX.

PRECAUTIONS.

AFTER quitting Anne, Mazarin took the road to Rueil, where he usually resided ; in those times of disturbance he went about with numerous followers, and often disguised himself. In the military dress he was indeed, as we have before stated, a very handsome man.

In the court of the old château of St. Germains, he entered his coach, and reached the Seine at Chalon. The prince had supplied him with fifty light horse, not so much by way of a guard, as to show the deputies how readily the queen's generals dispersed their troops, and to prove that they might be scattered about at pleasure. Athos, on horseback, without his sword, and kept in sight by Comminges, followed the Cardinal in silence. Grimaud, finding that his master had been arrested, fell back into the ranks, near Aramis, without saying a word, and as if nothing had happened.

Grimaud had, indeed, during twenty-two years of service, seen his master extricate himself from so many difficulties, that nothing made him uneasy.

At the branching off of the road towards Paris, Aramis, who had followed in the Cardinal's suite, turned back. Mazarin went to the right hand, and Aramis could see the prisoner disappear at the turning of the avenue. Athos, at the same moment, moved by a similar impulse, looked back also. The two friends exchanged a simple inclination of the head, and Aramis put his finger to his hat, as if to bow ; Athos, alone, comprehending by that signal that he had some project in his head.

Ten minutes afterwards, Mazarin entered the court of that château which his predecessor had built for him, at Rueil ; as he alighted, Comminges approached him.

" My lord," he asked, " where does your eminence wish Monsieur Comte de la Fère to be lodged ?"

"Certainly in the pavilion of the orangery—in front of the pavilion where the guard is. I wish every respect shown to the count, although he is the prisoner of her majesty the queen."

" My lord," answered Comminges, " he begs to be taken into the place where Monsieur d'Artagnan is confined—that is, in the hunting lodge opposite the orangery."

Mazarin thought for an instant.

Comminges saw that he was undecided.

" 'Tis a very strong post," he resumed ; " and forty good men, tried soldiers, and consequently having nothing to do with Fron deurs, nor any interest in the Fronde."

" If we put these three men together, Monsieur Comminges," said Mazarin, " we must double the guard, and we are not rich enough in defenders to commit such acts of prodigality."

Comminges smiled ; Mazarin read, and construed that smile.

"You do not know these men, *Monson* Comminges, but I know them—first, personally ; also, by hearsay. I sent them to carry aid to King Charles, and they performed prodigies to save him :

had it not been for an adverse destiny, that beloved monarch would, this day, have been among us."

" But, since they served your Éminence so well, why are they, my lord Cardinal, in prison ?"

" In prison ?" asked Mazarin; "and when has Rueil been a prison ?"

" Ever since there were prisoners in it," answered Comminges.

" These gentlemen, Comminges, are not prisoners," returned Mazarin, with his ironical smile, "but guests; and guests so precious, that I have put a grating before each of their windows, and bolts to their doors, that they may not be weary of being my visitors. So much do I esteem them, that I am going to make the Count de la Fère a visit, that I may converse with him tête-a-tête ; and that we may not be disturbed at our interview, you must conduct him, as I said before, into the pavilion of the orangery; that, you know, is my daily promenade."

Comminges bowed, and returned to impart to Athos the result of his request. Athos, who had been awaiting the Cardinal's decision with outward composure, but secret uneasiness, then entreated that Comminges would do him one favour, which was to intimate to D'Artagnan that he was placed in the pavilion of the orangery for the purpose of receiving a visit from the Cardinal, and that he should profit by the opportunity, in order to ask for some mitigation of their close imprisonment.

" Which cannot last," interrupted Comminges, "the Cardinal said so ; there is no prison here."

" But there are oubliettes !" replied Athos, smiling.

" Oh ! that's a different thing; yes—I know there are traditions of that sort," said Comminges : it was in the time of the other Cardinal, who was a great nobleman; but our Mazarin—impossible ! an Italian adventurer could not go to such lengths towards such men as ourselves. Oubliettes are employed as a means of kingly vengeance, and a low-born fellow such as he is dare not have recourse to them. No, no, be easy on that score. I shall, however, inform Monsieur d'Artagnan of your arrival here."

Comminges then led the count to a room on the ground floor of a pavilion, at the end of the orangery. They passed through a court-yard, as they went, full of soldiers and courtiers. In the centre of this court, in the form of a horse-shoe, were the buildings occupied by Mazarin, and at each wing the pavilion (or smaller building) where D'Artagnan was, and that, level with the orangery, where Athos was to be. Behind each end of these two wings extended the park.

Athos, when he reached his appointed room, observed, through the gratings of his window, walls, and roofs; and was told, on inquiry, by Comminges, that he was looking on the back of the pavilion where D'Artagnan was confined.

"Yes, 'tis too true," said Comminges, "'tis almost a prison; but what a singular fancy this is of yours, count—you, who are the very flower of our nobility—to go and spend your valour and your loyalty amongst these upstarts, the Frondists! Really and truly, if ever I thought that I had a friend in the ranks of the royal army, it was you. A Frondeur! you, the Comte de la Fère, on the side of Broussel, Blancmesnil, and Viole! For shame! you, a Frondeur!"

"On my word of honour," said Athos, "one must be either a Mazarinist or a Frondeur. For a long time I had these words whispered in my ears, and I chose the last; at any rate, it is a French word. And now, I am a Frondeur—not of Broussel's party, nor of Blancmesnil's, nor am I with Viole—but with the Duc de Beaufort, the Ducs de Bouillon and D'Elbeuf; with princes, not with presidents, councillors, and low-born lawyers. Besides, what a charming thing it would have been to serve the Cardinal! Look at that wall—without a single window—which tells you fine things about Mazarin's gratitude!"

"Yes," replied De Comminges, "more especially if that could reveal how Monsieur d'Artagnan for this last week has been swearing at him."

"Poor D'Artagnan," said Athos, with that charming melancholy which was one of the external traits of his character, "so brave, so good, so terrible to the enemies of those whom he loves; you have two unruly prisoners there, sir."

"Unruly," Comminges smiled, "you wish to make me afraid, I suppose. When he came here, Monsieur d'Artagnan provoked and braved all the soldiers and inferior officers, in order, I suppose, to have his sword back—that mood lasted some time—but now, he's as gentle as a lamb, and sings Gascon songs which make one die with laughing."

"And De Valon?" asked Athos.

"Ah, he's quite another sort of person—a formidable gentleman, indeed. The first day he broke all the doors in with a single push of his shoulder; and I expected to see him leave Rueil in the same way as Samson left Gaza. But his temper cooled down like his friend's—he not only gets used to his captivity, but jokes about it."

"So much the better," said Athos; and, on reflection, he

felt convinced that this improvement in the spirits of the two captives proceeded from some plan formed by D'Artagnan for their escape.

CHAPTER LXXXI.

STRENGTH AND SAGACITY.

Now let us pass the orangery, to the hunting lodge. At the extremity of the court-yard, where, close to a portico formed of Ionic columns, there were dog-kennels, rose an oblong building, the pavilion of the orangery, a half-circle, enclosing the court of honours. It was in this pavilion, on the ground floor, that D'Artagnan and Porthos were confined, suffering the hours of a long imprisonment in a manner suitable to each different temperament.

D'Artagnan was walking about like a tiger, his eye fixed, growling as he paced along by the bars of a window looking upon the yard of servant's offices.

Porthos was ruminating over an excellent dinner which had been served up to him.

The one seemed to be deprived of reason, yet he was meditating. The other seemed to meditate, yet he was sleeping. But his sleep was a nightmare, which might be guessed by the incoherent manner in which he snored.

"Look," said D'Artagnan, "day is declining. It must be nearly four o'clock. We have been in this place nearly eighty-three hours."

"Hem!" muttered Porthos, with a kind of pretence of answering.

"Did you hear, eternal sleeper?" cried D'Artagnan, irritated that any one could doze during the day, when he had the greatest difficulty in sleeping during the night.

"What?" said Porthos.

"I say we have been here eighty-three hours."

"'Tis your fault," answered Porthos.

"How, my fault?"

"Yes, I offered to you to escape."

"By tearing down an iron bar and pushing in a door, Porthos. People like us cannot just go out as they like; besides, going out of this room is not everything."

"Well, then, let us kill the sentinel, and then we shall have arms."

"Yes; but before we can kill him—and he is hard to kill, that Swiss—he will shriek out, and the whole piquet will come, and we shall be taken like foxes—we, who are lions—and thrown into some dungeon, where we shall not even have the consolation of seeing this frightful grey sky of Rueil, which is no more like the sky of Tarbes than the moon to the sun. Lack-a-day! if we only had some one to instruct us about the physical and moral topography of this castle. Ah! when one thinks that for twenty years —during which time I did not know what to do with myself—it never occurred to me to come to study Rueil. And after all, 'tis impossible but that Master Aramis, that Athos, that wise gentleman, should not discover our retreat; then, faith, it will be time to act."

"Yes, more especially as it is not very disagreeable here, with one exception."

"What?"

"Did you observe, D'Artagnan, that three days running they have brought us brased mutton?"

"No; but if that occurs a fourth time I shall complain of it, so never mind."

"And then I feel the loss of my house; 'tis a long time since I visited my castles."

"Forget them for a time; we shall return to them, unless Mazarin razes them to the ground."

"Do you think that likely?"

"No—the other Cardinal would have done so: but this one is too low a fellow to risk it."

"You console me, D'Artagnan."

The two prisoners were at this point of their conversation when Comminges entered, preceded by a sergeant and by two men, who brought supper in a basket with two handles, filled with basons and plates.

"What!" exclaimed Porthos, "mutton again?"

"My dear Monsieur de Comminges," said D'Artagnan, "you will find my friend, De Valon, will go to the most fatal lengths if Monsieur Mazarin continues to provide us with this sort of meat; mutton every day."

"I declare," said Porthos, "I shall eat nothing if they do not take it away."

"Take away the mutton," said Comminges; "I wish Monsieur de Valon to sup well, more especially as I have news to give him which will improve his appetite."

"Is Mazarin put to death?" asked Porthos.

"No; I am sorry to tell you he is perfectly well."

"So much the worse," said Porthos.

"Should you be very glad to hear that the Count de la Fère was well?" asked De Comminges.

D'Artagnan's small eyes were opened to the utmost.

"Glad!" he cried; "I should be more than glad! Happy!—beyond measure!"

"Well, I am desired by him to give you his compliments, and to say that he is in good health."

"Then you have seen him?"

"Certainly, I have."

"Where—if it is not impertinent."

"Near here," replied De Comminges, smiling; "so near that if the windows which look on the orangery were not stopped up you might see the place where he is."

"He is wandering about the environs of the castle," thought D'Artagnan. Then he said aloud:

"You met him, I dare say, in the park—hunting, perhaps?"

"No; nearer, nearer still. Look behind this wall," said De Comminges, knocking against the wall.

"Behind this wall? What is there, then, behind this wall? I was brought here by night, so devil take me if I know where I am. The count is then in the château!"

"Yes?"

"For what reason?"

"The same as yourself."

"Athos is, then, a prisoner?"

"You know well," replied De Comminges, "that there are no prisoners at Rueil, because there is no prison."

"Don't let us play upon words, sir. Athos has been arrested?"

"Yesterday, at Saint Germains, as he came out from the presence of the queen."

The arms of D'Artagnan fell powerless by his side. One might have supposed him thunderstruck; a paleness ran like a cloud over his dark skin, but disappeared immediately.

"A prisoner?" he reiterated.

"A prisoner," repeated Porthos, quite dejected.

Suddenly D'Artagnan looked up, and in his eyes there was a gleam which scarcely even Porthos observed; but it died away, and he remained more sorrowful than before.

"Come, come," said Comminges, who, since D'Artagnan, on the day of Broussel's arrest, had saved him from the hands of the Parisians, had entertained a real affection for him; "don't be unhappy, I never thought of bringing you bad news. Laugh at the mischance which has befallen your friend and Monsieur de Valon, instead of being in the depths of despair about it."

But D'Artagnan was still in a desponding mood.

"And how did he look?" asked Porthos, who, perceiving that D'Artagnan had allowed the conversation to drop, profited by it to put in his word.

"Very well, indeed, sir," replied Comminges; "at first, like you, he seemed distressed; but when he heard that the Cardinal was going to pay him a visit this very evening——"

"Ah!" cried D'Artagnan; "the Cardinal going to visit the Count de la Fère?"

"Yes; and the count desired me to tell you that he should take advantage of this visit to plead for you and for himself."

"Ah! the dear count!" said D'Artagnan.

"A fine thing, indeed!" grunted Porthos. "A great favour! Zounds! Monsieur the Count de la Fère, whose family is allied to the Montmorency and the Rohan, is well worthy of Monsieur Mazarin's civilities."

"Never mind!" said D'Artagnan, in his calmest tone, and looking, but in vain, at Porthos, to see if he comprehended all the importance of this visit. "'Tis then Monsieur Mazarin's custom to walk in his orangery?" he added.

"He shuts himself up there every evening, and there, 'tis said, ponders over state affairs."

"Let the Cardinal take care of going alone to visit the Count de la Fère," said D'Artagnan; "for the count must be furious."

Comminges began to laugh. "Really, to hear you talk, one would suppose you were cannibals. The count is an affable man; besides, he is unarmed; at the first word from his Eminence the two soldiers about him would run to him."

"Now," said D'Artagnan; "I've one last favour to ask of you, Monsieur de Comminges."

"At your service, sir."

"You will see the count again?"

"To-morrow morning."

"Will you remember us to him, and ask him to solicit one favour for me—that his Eminence should do me the honour to give me a hearing: that is all I want."

"Oh!" muttered Porthos, shaking his head; "never should I have thought this of *him!* How misfortune humbles a man!"

"That shall be done," answered De Comminges.

"Tell the count that I am well; that you found me sad, but resigned."

" I am pleased, sir, to hear that."

" And the same, also, for Monsieur de Valon——"

" Not for me !" cried Pathos ; " I am not at all resigned."

" He will be so, monsieur ; I know him better than he knows himself. Be silent, dear De Valon, and resign yourself."

" Adieu, gentlemen," said De Comminges ; " sleep well !"

" We will try."

De Comminges went away, D'Artagnan remaining apparently in the same attitude of humble resignation ; but scarcely had he departed than he turned, and clasped Porthos in his arms, with an expression not to be doubted.

" Oh !" cried Porthos ; " what's the matter now ? Are you mad, my dear friend ?"

" What's the matter ?" returned D'Artagnan ; " we are saved !"

" I don't see that at all," answered Porthos. " I think we are all taken prisoners, except Aramis, and that our chances of going out are lessened since we were entangled in Mazarin's witchcraft."

" Which is far too strong for two of us, but not strong enough for three of us," returned D'Artagnan.

" I don't understand," said Porthos.

" Never mind ; let's sit down to table, and take something to strengthen us for the night."

" What are we to do, then, to-night ?"

" To travel—perhaps."

" But——"

" Sit down, dear friend, to table. Whilst we are eating, ideas flow easily. After supper, when they are perfected, I will communicate my plans to you."

So Porthos sat down to table without another word, and ate with an appetite that did honour to the confidence which D'Artagnan's imagination had inspired him with.

CHAPTER LXXXII.

STRENGTH AND SAGACITY—CONTINUED.

SUPPER was eaten in silence, but not in sadness ; for from time to time one of those sweet smiles which were habitual to him in his moments of good-humour illumined the face of D'Artagnan. Not one of these smiles was lost on Porthos ; and at every one he uttered an exclamation which betrayed to his friend that he had not lost sight of the idea which possessed his brain.

At dessert D'Artagnan reposed in his chair, crossed one leg over another, and lounged about like a man perfectly at his ease.

" Well ?" he said, at làst.

" Well," repeated Porthos.

" You were saying, my dear friend——"

" No ; I said nothing."

" Well, you were saying you wished to leave this place."

" Ah, indeed ! will is not wanting."

" To go away hence you would not mind, you added, knocking down a door or a wall."

" 'Tis true, I said so, and I say it again."

" At what o'clock did we see, pray, the two Swiss guards walk last night ?"

" An hour after sunset."

" If they go out to-day, as they did yesterday, we shall have the honour, then, of seeing them in half-an-hour ?"

" In a quarter of an hour, at most."

" Your arm is still strong enough, is it not, Porthos ?"

Porthos unbuttoned his sleeve, raised his shirt, and looked complacently on his strong arm, as large as the leg of any ordinary man.

" Yes, indeed," he said ; " pretty good."

" So that you could, without trouble, convert these tongs into a hoop, and the shovel into a corkscrew ?"

" Certainly." And the giant took up these two articles, and, without any apparent effort, produced in them the metamorphosis requested by his companion.

" There !" he cried.

" Capital !" exclaimed the Gascon. " Really, Porthos, you are a gifted individual !"

" I have heard speak," said Porthos, " of a certain Milo of Crete, who performed wonderful feats, such as binding his forehead with a cord and bursting it—of killing an ox with a blow of his fist, and carrying it home on his shoulders, etc. I used to learn all these feats by heart yonder, down at Pierrefonds, and I have done all that he did except breaking a cord by the swelling of my temples."

" Because your strength is not in your head, Porthos," said his friend.

" No ; it is in my arms and shoulders," answered Porthos, with *naïveté.*

" Well, my dear friend, let us go near the window, and try your strength in severing an iron bar."

Porthos approached the window, took a bar in his hands, clung to it, and bent it like a bow; so that the two ends came out of the socket of stone in which for thirty years they had been fixed.

"Well, friend—the Cardinal, although such a genius, could never have done that."

"Shall I take out any more of them?" asked Porthos.

"No; that is sufficient; a man can pass through that."

Porthos tried, and passed the trunk of his body through.

"Yes," he said.

"Now pass your arm through this opening."

"Why?"

"You will know presently—pass it."

"I wish to know, however, that I may understand," said Porthos.

"You will know directly; see, the door of the guard-room opens. They are going to send into the court the two guards who accompany Monsieur Mazarin when he crosses into the orangery. See, they are coming out, and have closed the door of the guard-room after them."

In fact, the two soldiers advanced on the side where the window was, rubbing their hands, for it was cold, it being the month of February.

At this moment the door of the guard-house was opened, and one of the soldiers was summoned away.

"Now," said D'Artagnan, "I am going to call this soldier and talk to him. Don't lose a word of what I am going to say to you, Porthos. Everything is in the execution."

"Good; the execution of a plot is my forte."

"I know it well. I depend on you. Look, I shall turn to the left; so that the soldier will be at your right, as soon as he mounts on the bench to talk to us."

"But supposing he doesn't mount?"

"He will; rely on it. As soon as you see him get up, stretch out your arm and seize him by his neck. Then, raising him up as Tobit raised the fish by the gills, you must pull him into your room, taking care to squeeze so tight that he can't cry out."

"Oh!" said Porthos. "Suppose I were to strangle him?"

"To be sure there would only be a Swiss the less in the world; but you will not do so, I hope. Lay him down here; we'll gag him, and tie him—no matter where—somewhere. So we shall get from him one uniform and a sword."

"Marvellous!" exclaimed Porthos; looking at the Gascon with the most profound admiration.

"Pooh!" replied D'Artagnan.

"Yes," said Porthos, recollecting himself, "but one uniform and one sword are not enough for two."

"Well; but there's his comrade?"

"True," said Porthos.

"Therefore, when I cough, stretch out your arm."

"Good!"

The two friends then placed themselves as they had agreed; Porthos being completely hidden in an angle of the window.

"Good evening, comrade," said D'Artagnan, in his most fascinating voice and manner.

"Good evening, sir," answered the soldier, in a strong provincial accent.

"'Tis not too warm to walk," resumed D'Artagnan.

"No, sir."

"And I think a glass of wine will not be disagreeable to you?"

"A glass of wine will be very welcome."

"The fish bites! the fish bites!" whispered the Gascon to Porthos.

"I understand," said Porthos.

"A bottle, perhaps?"

"A whole bottle? Yes, sir."

"A whole bottle, if you will drink to my health."

"Willingly," answered the soldier.

"Come then and take it, friend," said the Gascon.

"With all my heart. How convenient that there's a bench here. Egad! one would think it had been placed here on purpose."

"Get on it; that's it, friend."

And D'Artagnan coughed.

That instant the arm of Porthos fell. His hand of iron grasped, quick as lightning, and firm as a pair of pincers, the soldier's throat. He raised him, almost stifling him as he drew him through the aperture at the risk of flaying him as he pulled him through. He then laid him down on the floor, where D'Artagnan, after giving him just time enough to draw his breath, gagged him with his scarf; and the moment he had done so, began to undress him with the promptitude and dexterity of a man who learned his business on the field of battle. Then the soldier, gagged and bound, was carried inside the hearth, the fire of which had been previously extinguished by the two friends.

"Here's a sword and a dress," said Porthos.

"I take them," said D'Artagnan, "for myself. If you want

another uniform and sword, you must play the same trick over again. Stop! I see the other soldier issue from the guard-room, and come towards us."

" I think," replied Porthos, "it would be imprudent to attempt the same manœuvre again; a failure would be ruinous. No: I will go down, seize the man unawares, and bring him to you ready gagged."

He did as he said. Porthos seized his opportunity—caught the next soldier by his neck, gagged him, and pushed him like a mummy through the bars into the room, and entered after him. Then they undressed him as they had done the first; laid him on their bed, and bound him with the straps which composed the bed—the bedstead being of oak. This operation proved as successful as the first.

" There," said D'Artagnan, " 'tis capital! Now let me try on the dress of yonder chap. Porthos, I doubt if you can wear it; but should it be too tight, never mind, you can wear the breastplate, and the hat with the red feathers."

It happened, however, that the second soldier was a Swiss of gigantic proportions, so, except that some of the seams split, his dress fitted Porthos perfectly.

They then dressed themselves.

" 'Tis done !" they both exclaimed at once. " As to you, comrades," they said to the men, " nothing will happen to you if you are discreet; but if you stir, you are dead men."

The soldiers were complaisant; they had found the grasp of Porthos rather powerful, and that it was no joke to contend against it.

D'Artagnan then made Porthos aware of his plan of action, which Porthos then only partially comprehended.

"What is to happen ?" he asked.

" Follow me," replied D'Artagnan. "The man who lives to see, shall see."

And, slipping through the aperture, he alighted in the court.

Scarcely had the two Frenchmen touched the ground than a door opened, and the voice of the valet-de-chambre called out, " Make ready !"

At the same moment the guard-house was opened, and a voice called out :

"La Bruyère and Du Barthois ! March !"

" It seems that I am named La Bruyère," said D'Artagnan.

"And I, Du Barthois," added Porthos.

"Where are you !" asked the valet-de-chambre, whose eyes,

dazzled by the light, could not clearly distinguish cur heroes in the gloom.

"Here we are," said the Gascon.

"What say you to that, Monsieur de Valon?" he added, in a low tone, to Porthos.

"If it lasts, it is capital," answered Porthos.

These two newly-enlisted soldiers marched gravely after the valet-de-chambre, who opened the door of the vestibule; then another, which seemed to be that of a waiting-room, and showing them two stools,—

"Your orders are very simple," he said; "don't allow anybody, except one person, to enter here. Do you hear?—not a single creature! Obey that person completely. On your return you cannot make a mistake. You have only to wait here till I release you."

D'Artagnan was known to this valet-de-chambre, who was no other than Bernouin, and he had, during the last six or eight months, introduced the Gascon a dozen times to the Cardinal. The Gascon, therefore, instead of answering, growled out "Ja! Ja!" in the most German and the least Gascon accent possible.

As to Porthos, with whom D'Artagnan had insisted on a perfect silence, and who did not even now begin to comprehend the scheme of his friend, which was to follow Mazarin in his visit to Athos, he was mute. All that he was allowed to say, in case of emergencies, being the proverbial and solemn *Der Tœffel!*

Bernouin went away and shut the door. When Porthos heard the key of the lock turn, he began to be alarmed, lest they should only have exchanged one prison for another.

"Porthos, my friend," said D'Artagnan, "don't distrust Providence! Let me meditate and consider."

"Meditate and consider as much as you like," replied Porthos, who was now quite out of humour at seeing things take this turn.

"We have walked eight paces," whispered D'Artagnan, "and gone up six steps, so hereabouts is the pavilion, called the Pavilion of the Orangery. The Comte de la Fère cannot be far off, only the doors are locked."

"A grand difficulty!" cried Porthos.

"Hush!" said D'Artagnan.

The sound of a light step was heard in the vestibule. The hinges of the door creaked, and a man appeared in the dress of a cavalier, wrapped in a brown cloak, with a lanthorn in his hand, and a large beaver hat pulled down over his eyes.

Porthos stood with his face against the wall, but he could not render himself invisible ; and the man in the clóak said to him, giving him his lanthorn :

" Light the lamp which hangs from the ceiling."

Then, addressing D'Artagnan,—

" You know the watchword ?" he said.

" Ja !" replied the Gascon, determined to confine himself to this specimen of the German tongue.

" *Tedesco !* answered the cavalier ; " *va bene.*"

And advancing towards the door opposite to that by which he came in, he opened it and disappeared behind it, shutting it as he went.

" Now," asked Porthos, " what are we to do ?"

" Now we shall make use of your shoulder, friend Porthos, if this door should be locked. Everything in its proper time, and all comes right to those who know how to wait patiently. But first barricade the first door well, and then we will follow yonder cavalier."

The two friends set to work and crowded the space before the door with all the furniture in the room, so as not only to make the passage impassable, but that the door could not open inwards.

" There !" said D'Artagnan, " we can't be overtaken. Come ! forwards !"

CHAPTER LXXXIII.

THE OUBLIETTES OF CARDINAL MAZARIN.

At first, on arriving at the door through which Mazarin had passed, D'Artagnan tried in vain to open it ; but on the powerful shoulder of Porthos being applied to one of the panels, which gave way, D'Artagnan introduced the point of his sword between the bolt and the staple of the lock. The bolt gave way and the door opened.

" As I told you, everything can be got, Porthos, by means of women and doors."

" You're a great moralist, and that's the fact," said Porthos.

They entered : behind a glass window, by the light of the Cardinal's lanthorn, which had been placed on the floor in the midst of the gallery, they saw the orange and pomegranate trees of the castle of Rueil, in long lines, forming one great alley and two smaller side alleys.

"No Cardinal!" said D'Artagnan, "but only his man; where the devil is he then?"

Exploring, however, one of the side wings of the gallery, he saw all at once, at his left, a tub containing an orange tree, which had been pushed out of its place, and in its place an open aperture. He also perceived in this hold the steps of a winding staircase.

He called Porthos to look at it.

"Had our object been money only," he said, "we should be rich directly."

"How's that?"

"Don't you understand, Porthos? At the bottom of that staircase is, probably, the Cardinal's treasury, of which every one speaks so much; and we should only have to descend—empty a chest —shut the Cardinal up in it—double-lock it—go away, carrying off as much gold as we could—put this orange-tree over the place, and no one would ever ask us where our fortune came from—not even the Cardinal."

"It would be a happy hit for clowns to make, but as it seems to be unworthy of two gentlemen," said Porthos.

"So I think; and we don't want gold—we want other things," replied the Gascon.

At the same moment, whilst D'Artagnan was leaning over the aperture to listen, a metallic sound, as if some one was moving a bag of gold, struck on his ear; he started; instantly afterwards a door opened, and a light played upon the staircase.

Mazarin had left his lamp in the gallery to make people believe that he was walking about, but he had with him a wax-light to explore with its aid his mysterious strong box.

"'Faith!" he said, in Italian, as he was reascending the steps, and looking at a bag of reals, "'faith, there's enough to pay five councillors of the Parliament, and two generals in Paris. I am a great captain—that I am! but I make war in my own way."

The two friends were crouching down, meantime, behind a tub in the side alley.

Mazarin came within three steps of D'Artagnan, and pushing a spring in the wall, the slab on which the orange-tree was, turned, and the orange-tree resumed its place.

Then the Cardinal put out the wax-light, slipped it into his pocket, and taking up the lanthorn—"Now," he said, "for Monsieur de la Fère."

"Very good," thought D'Artagnan, "'tis our road likewise; we can go together."

All three set off on their walk, Mazarin taking the middle alley and the friends the side one.

The Cardinal reached a second door without perceiving that he was followed; the sand by which the alley was covered deadened the sound of footsteps.

He then turned to the left, down a corridor which had escaped the attention of the two friends; but as he opened the door, he stopped, as if in thought.

"Ah! Diavolo!" he exclaimed, "I forgot the recommendation of De Comminges, who advised me to take a guard and place it at this door, in order not to put myself at the mercy of that four-headed devil." And, with a movement of impatience, he turned to retrace his steps.

"Do not give yourself the trouble, my lord," said D'Artagnan, with his right foot forward, his beaver in his hand, a smile on his face; "we have followed your Eminence step by step, and here we are."

"Yes—here we are," said Porthos.

And he made the same friendly salute as D'Artagnan.

Mazarin gazed at each of them with an affrighted stare, recognised them, and let drop his lanthorn, uttering a cry of terror.

D'Artagnan picked it up; by good luck it had not been extinguished by the fall.

"Oh! what imprudence, my lord," said D'Artagnan; "'tis not good to go about here without a light. Your Eminence might knock against something or fall into some hole."

"Monsieur D'Artagnan!" muttered Mazarin, not able to recover from his astonishment.

"Yes, my lord, it is I—I've the honour of presenting you Monsieur de Valon, that excellent friend of mine, in whom your Eminence had the kindness to interest yourself formerly."

And D'Artagnan held the lamp before the merry face of Porthos, who now began to comprehend the affair, and be very proud of the whole undertaking.

"You were going to visit Monsieur de la Fère?" said D'Artagnan. "Don't let us disarrange your Eminence. Be so good as to show us the way, and we will follow you."

Mazarin was by degrees recovering his senses.

"Have you been long in the orangery?" he asked in a trembling voice, remembering the visit he had been paying to his treasury.

"We are just come, my lord."

Mazarin breathed again. His fears were now no longer for his hoards, but for himself. A sort of smile played on his lips.

"Come," he said, "you have taken me in a snare, gentlemen. I confess myself conquered. You wish to ask for your liberty, and I give it you."

"Oh, my lord!" answered D'Artagnan, "you are very good; as to our liberty, we have that; we want to ask something else of you."

"You have your liberty?" repeated Mazarin, in terror.

"Certainly; and on the other hand, my lord, you have lost it; and now 'tis the law of war, sir, you must buy it back again."

Mazarin felt a shiver all over him, a chill even to his heart's core. His piercing look was fixed in vain on the satirical face of the Gascon and on the unchanging countenance of Porthos. Both were in shadow, and even a sybil could not have read them.

"To purchase back my liberty?" said the Cardinal.

"Yes, my lord."

"And how much will that cost me, Monsieur D'Artagnan?"

"Zounds, my lord, I don't know yet. We must ask the Count de la Fère the question. Will your Eminence deign to open the door which leads to the count's room, and in ten minutes it will be settled."

Mazarin started.

"My lord," said D'Artagnan, "your Eminence sees that we wish to act with all due forms of respect; but I must warn you that we have no time to lose; open the door then, my lord, and be so good as to remember, once for all, that on the slightest attempt to escape or the least cry for help, our position being a very critical one, you must not be angry with us if we go to extremities."

"Be assured," answered Mazarin, "that I shall attempt nothing; I give you my word of honour."

D'Artagnan made a sign to Porthos to redouble his watchfulness; then turning to Mazarin:

"Now, my lord, let us enter, if you please."

CHAPTER LXXXIV.

CONFERENCES.

MAZARIN turned the lock of a double door, on the threshold of which they found Athos ready to receive his illustrious guest ; on seeing his friends he started with surprise.

"D'Artagnan ! Porthos !" he exclaimed.

"My very self, dear friend."

"Me also," repeated Porthos.

"What means this ?" asked the Count.

"It means," replied Mazarin, trying to smile, and biting his lips in smiling, "that our parts are changed, and that instead of these gentlemen being my prisoners, I am theirs ; but, gentlemen, I warn ye, unless you kill me, your victory will be of short duration —people will come to the rescue."

"Ah ! my lord," cried the Gascon, "don't threaten ! 'tis a bad example. We are so good and gentle to your Eminence. Come, let us put aside all rancour and talk pleasantly."

"There's nothing I wish more," replied Mazarin. "But don't think yourselves in a better position than you are. In ensnaring me you have fallen into the trap yourselves. How are you to get away from here ? remember the soldiers and sentinels who guard these doors. Now I am going to show to you how sincere I am."

"Good," thought D'Artagnan, "we must look about us; he's going to play us a trick."

"I offered you your liberty," continued the minister ; "will you take it ? Before an hour will have passed you will be discovered, arrested, obliged to kill me, which would be a crime unworthy of loyal gentlemen like you."

"He is right," thought Athos.

And, like every other reflection passing in a mind that entertained none but noble thoughts, this feeling was expressed in his eyes.

"We shall not," answered D'Artagnan, "have recourse to violence, except in the last extremity" (for he saw that Athos seemed to lean towards Mazarin).

"If, on the contrary," resumed Mazarin, "you accept your liberty——"

"Why you, my lord, might take it away from us five minutes

afterwards; and from my knowledge of you, I believe you will take it away from us."

"No—on the faith of a Cardinal. You do not believe me?"

"My lord, I never believe Cardinals who are not priests."

"Well, on the faith of a minister."

"You are no longer a minister, my lord; you are a prisoner."

"Then, on the honour of a Mazarin, as I am, and ever shall be, I hope," said the Cardinal.

"Hem!" replied D'Artagnan. "I have heard speak of a Mazarin who had little religion when his oaths were in question. I fear he may have been an ancestor of your Eminence."

"Monsieur D'Artagnan, you are a great wit, and I'm quite sorry to be on bad terms with you."

"My lord, let us make it up; one resource always remains to us."

"What?"

"That of dying together."

Mazarin shuddered.

"Listen," he said; "at the end of yonder corridor is a door, of which I have the key; it leads into the park. Go, and take this key with you; you are active, vigorous, and you have arms. At a hundred steps, to the left, you will find the wall of the park; get over it, and in three jumps you will be on the road, and free."

"Ah! by Jove, my lord," said D'Artagnan, "you have well said, but these are only words. Where is the key you spoke of?"

"Here it is."

"Ah, my lord! You will conduct us yourself, then, to that door?"

"Very willingly, if it be necessary to reassure you," answered the minister; and Mazarin, who was delighted to get off so cheaply, led the way, in high spirits, to the corridor, and opened the door.

It led into the park, as the three fugitives perceived by the night breeze which rushed into the corridor, and blew the wind into their faces.

"The devil!" exclaimed the Gascon. "'Tis a dreadful night, my lord. We don't know the localities, and shall never find the wall. Since your Eminence has come so far, a few steps farther conduct us, my lord, to the wall."

"Be it so," replied the Cardinal; and walking at a staight line he walked to the wall, at the foot of which they all four arrived at the same instant.

"Are you satisfied, gentlemen?" asked Mazarin.

" I think so, indeed; we should be hard to please if we were not. Deuce take it! three poor gentlemen escorted by a prince of the Church! Ah! apropos, my lord! you remarked that we were all vigorous, active, and armed."

" Yes."

" You are mistaken. Monsieur de Valon and I are the only two who are armed. The count is not; and should we meet with any patrol, we must defend ourselves."

" 'Tis true."

" Where can we find a sword?" asked Porthos.

" My lord," said D'Artagnan, "will lend his—which is no use to him—to the Count de la Fère."

" Willingly," said the Cardinal; "I will even ask the Count to keep it for my sake."

" I promise you, my lord, never to part with it," replied Athos.

" Well," remarked D'Artagnan, "this change of measures, how touching it is! have you not tears in your eyes, Porthos?"

" Yes," said Porthos; "but I do not know if it is that or the wind that makes me weep; I think it is the wind."

" Now climb up, Athos, quickly," said D'Artagnan. Athos, assisted by Porthos, who lifted him up like a feather, arrived at the top.

" Now jump down, Athos."

Athos jumped, and disappeared on the other side of the wall.

" Porthos, whilst I get up, watch the Cardinal. No, I don't want your help. Watch the Cardinal. Lend me your back—but don't let the Cardinal go."

Porthos lent him his back, and D'Artagnan was soon on the summit of the wall, where he seated himself.

" Now, what?" asked Porthos.

" Now give me the Cardinal up here; if he makes any noise, stifle him."

Mazarin wished to call out, but Porthos held him tight, and passed him to D'Artagnan, who seized him by the neck and made him sit down by him: then, in a menacing tone, he said:

" Sir! jump directly down, close to Monsieur de la Fère, or, on the honour of a gentleman, I'll kill you!"

" *Monson, Monson,*" cried Mazarin, "you are breaking your word to me!"

" I—did I promise you anything, my lord?"

Mazarin groaned.

" You are free," he said, "through me; your liberty was my ransom."

"Agreed; but the ransom of that immense treasure buried under the gallery—must not one speak of that a little, my lord?"

"Diavolo!" cried Mazarin, almost choked, and clasping his hands; "I am a ruined man!"

But, without listening to his grief, D'Artagnan slipped him gently down into the arms of Athos, who stood immovable at the bottom of the wall.

Porthos next made an effort, which shook the wall; and by the aid of his friend's hand, gained the summit.

"I did not understand at all," he said, "but I understand now; how droll it is!"

"You think so? so much the better; but, that it may be droll even to the end, let us not lose time." And he jumped off the wall.

Porthos did the same.

The Gascon then drew his sword, and marched as an avant-guard.

"My lord, which way do we go? think well of your reply; for should your Eminence be mistaken, there might be very grave results for all of us."

"Along the wall, sir," said Mazarin, "there will be no danger of losing yourselves."

The three friends hastened on, but in a short time were obliged to slacken their pace. The Cardinal could not keep up with them, though with every wish to do so.

Suddenly D'Artagnan touched something warm, and which moved.

"Stop! A horse!" he cried; "I have found a horse!"

"And I likewise," said Athos.

"I, too," said Porthos, who, faithful to the instructions, still held the Cardinal's arm.

"There's luck, my lord! just as you were complaining of being tired, and obliged to walk."

But, as he spoke, a pistol ball fell near his feet, and these words were pronounced:

"Touch it not!"

"Grimaud!" he cried, "Grimaud! what art thou about! wert thou sent by heaven?"

"No, sir," said the honest servant; "it was Monsieur Aramis who told me to take care of the horses."

"Is Aramis here?"

"Yes, sir; he has been here since yesterday."

"What are you doing?"

" On the watch——

" What ! Aramis here ?" cried Athos.

" At the lesser gate of the castle ; he's posted there."

" Are you a large party ?"

" Sixty."

" Let him know."

" This moment, sir."

And, believing that no one could execute the commission better than he could, Grimaud set forth at full speed ; whilst, enchanted at being all together again, the three friends awaited his return.

There was no one in the whole group in ill humour except Cardinal Mazarin.

CHAPTER LXXXV.

IN WHICH WE BEGIN TO THINK THAT PORTHOS WILL BE AT LAST A BARON, AND D'ARTAGNAN A CAPTAIN.

AT the expiration of ten minutes Aramis arrived, accompanied by Grimaud, and eight or ten followers. He was much delighted, and threw himself into his friends' arms.

" You are then free, brothers ! free without my aid !"

" Do not be unhappy, dear friend, on that account ; if you have done nothing as yet, you will do something," replied Athos.

" I had well concerted my plans," pursued Aramis ; " the Coadjutor gave me sixty men ; twenty guard the walls of the park, twenty the road from Rueil to Saint Germains, twenty are dispersed in the woods. I lay in ambuscade with my sixty men ; I encircled the castle ; the riding horses I entrusted to Grimaud, and I awaited your coming out, which I did not expect till to-morrow, and I hoped to free you without a skirmish. You are free to-night, without fighting : so much the better ! how could you escape that scoundrel, Mazarin ?"

" 'Tis thanks to him," said D'Artagnan. " that we made our escape, and——"

" Impossible !"

" Yes, indeed, 'tis owing to him that we are at liberty."

" Well !" exclaimed Aramis, " this will reconcile me to him ; but I wish he were here that I might tell him that I did not believe him to be capable of so noble an act."

" My lord," said D'Artagnan, no longer able to contain himself, " allow me to introduce to you the Chevalier d'Herblay, who wishes—as you may have heard—to offer his congratulations to your Eminence."

And he retired, discovering Mazarin—who was in great confusion—to the astonished gaze of Aramis.

"Ho! ho!" exclaimed the latter, "the Cardinal! a fine prize! halloo! halloo! friends! to horse! to horse!"

Several horsemen quickly ran to him.

"Zounds!" cried Aramis, "I may have done some good, then; my lord, deign to receive my most respectful homage! I will lay a wager that 'tis that Saint Christopher, Porthos, who performed this feat! Apropos! I forgot——" and he gave some orders in a low voice to one of the horsemen.

"I think it will be wise to set off," said D'Artagnan.

"Yes; but I am expecting some one—a friend of Athos."

"A friend!" exclaimed the count.

"And here he is, galloping away through the bushes."

"The count! the count!" cried a young voice, which made Athos start.

"Raoul! Raoul!" he ejaculated.

For one moment the young man forgot his habitual respect—he threw himself on his father's neck.

"Look, my Lord Cardinal," said Aramis, "would it not have been a pity to have separated those who love each other as we love? Gentlemen," he continued, addressing the cavaliers, who became more and more numerous every instant, "gentlemen, encircle his Eminence, that you may show him the greater honour. He will, indeed, give us the favour of his company; you will, I hope, be grateful for it. Porthos, do not lose sight of his Eminence."

Aramis then joined Athos and D'Artagnan, who were consulting together.

"Come," said D'Artagnan, after a conference of five minutes' duration, "let us begin our journey."

"Where are we to go?" asked Porthos.

"To your house, dear Porthos, at Pierrefonds; your fine château is worthy of affording a princely hospitality to his Eminence; it is also well situated; neither too near Paris, nor too far from it. We can establish a communication between it and the capital with great facility. Come, my lord, you shall there be treated like a prince, as you are."

"A fallen prince!" exclaimed Mazarin, piteously.

"The chances of war," said Athos, "are many; but be assured we shall not take an improper advantage of them."

"No; but we shall make use of them," interposed D'Artagnan.

The rest of the night was employed by these cavaliers in travelling, with the wonderful rapidity of former days. Mazarin, continuing sombre and pensive, permitted himself to be dragged along in this way, which was like a race of phantoms. At dawn twelve leagues had been passed, without stopping; half the escort were exhausted, and several horses fell down.

"Horses now-a-days are not what they were formerly," observed Porthos; "everything degenerates."

In about ten minutes the escort stopped at Ermenonville, but the four friends went on with fresh ardour, guarding Mazarin carefully. At noon they rode into the avenue of Pierrefonds.

"We are four of us," said D'Artagnan; "we must relieve each other in mounting guard over my lord, and each of us must watch for three hours at a time. Athos is going to examine the castle, which it will be necessary to render impregnable in case of a siege; Porthos will see to the provisions, and Aramis to the troops of the garrison. That is to say, Athos will be chief engineer, Porthos purveyor in general, and Aramis governor of the fortress."

Meanwhile they gave up to Mazarin the handsomest room in the château.

"Gentlemen," he said, when he was in his room, "you do not expect, I presume, to keep me here a long time incognito?"

"No, my lord," replied the Gascon; "on the contrary, we think of announcing very soon that we have you here."

"Then you will be besieged."

"We expect it."

"And what shall you do?"

"Defend ourselves. Were the late Cardinal Richelieu alive, he would tell you a certain story of the Bastion Saint Gervaise, which we four, with our four lacqueys and twelve dead men, held out against a whole army."

"Such feats, sir, are done once, and are never repeated."

"However, now-a-days there's not need of so much heroism. To-morrow the army of Paris will be summoned—the day after it will be here! The field of battle, instead, therefore, of being at St. Denis, or at Charenton, will be near Compiègne, or Villars-Cotterets."

"The prince will beat you, as he has always done."

"'Tis possible, my lord; but before an engagement we shall move away your Eminence to another castle belonging to our friend De Valon, who has three. We will not expose your Eminence to the chances of war."

"Como," answered Mazarin. "I see it will be necessary for you to capitulate."

"Before a siege?"

"Yes; the conditions will be better than afterwards."

"Ah, my lord! as to conditions, you would soon see how moderate and reasonable we are!"

"Come, now, pray what are your conditions? I wish to know whether I am among enemies or friends."

"Friends, my lord! friends!"

"Well, then, tell me at once what you want, that I may see if an arrangement be possible. Speak, Count de la Fère!"

"My lord," replied Athos, "for myself I have nothing to ask; for France, were I to specify, I should have too much. I beg you excuse me, and propose to the chevalier."

And Athos, bowing retired, and remained leaning against the mantelpiece, merely as a spectator of the scene.

"Speak, then, chevalier!" said the Cardinal. What do you want? Nothing ambiguous, if you please. Be clear, short, and precise."

"As for me," replied Aramis, "I have in my pocket that programme of the conditions which the deputation—of which I formed one—went yesterday to St. Germains to impose on you. Let us consider the debts and claims the first. The demands in that programme must be granted."

"We were almost agreed as to those," replied Mazarin; "let us pass on to private and personal stipulations."

"You suppose, then, that there will be some?" asked Aramis, smiling.

"I do not suppose that you will all be so disinterested as Monsieur de la Fère," replied the Cardinal, bowing to Athos.

"My lord! you are right! The count has a mind far above vulgar desires and human passions! He is a proud soul—he is a man by himself! You are right—he is worth us all—and we avow it to you!"

"Aramis!" said Athos, "are you jesting?"

"No, no, dear friend; I state only what we all know. You are right; it is not you alone this matter concerns, but my lord, and his unworthy servant, myself."

"Well, then, what do you require besides the general conditions before recited?"

"I require, my lord, that Normandy should be given to Madame de Longueville, with five hundred thousand francs, and full absolution. I require that his Majesty should deign to be godfather to the child she has just borne; and that my lord, after having been present at the christening, should go to proffer his homage to our Holy Father the Pope."

" That is, that you wish me to lay aside my ministerial functions, to quit France, and be an exile."

" I wish his Eminence to become Pope on the first opportunity, allowing me then the right of demanding full indulgences for my-self and my friends."

Mazarin made a grimace which was quite indescribable, and turned to D'Artagnan,—

" And you, sir ?" he said.

" I, my lord," answered the Gascon, " I differ from Monsieur D'Herblay totally in the last point, though I agree with him in the first.   Far from wishing my lord to quit Paris, I hope he will stay there and continue to be Prime Minister, as he is a great states-man.   I shall try, also, to help him to put down the Fronde ; but on one condition—that he sometimes remembers the king's faith-ful servants, and gives the first vacant company of Musketeers to some one I can mention to him.   And you, Monsieur de Valon——"

" Yes, you, sir !   Speak, if you please," said Mazarin.

" As to me," answered Porthos, " I wish my lord Cardinal—to do honour to my house, which has given him an asylum—would, in remembrance of this adventure, erect my estate into a barony, with a promise to confer that order on one of my friends, when-ever his majesty next creates peers."

Mazarin bit his lip.

" All that," he said, " appears to me to be ill-connected, gentle-men ; for if I satisfy some I shall displease others.   If I stay in Paris, I cannot go to Rome ; and if I become Pope I could not continue to be Prime Minister ; and it is only by continuing Prime Minister that I can make Monsieur D'Artagnan a captain, and Monsieur de Valon a baron."

" True," said Aramis, " so, as I am in my minority, I give up my proposal."

" Well, then, gentlemen, take care of your own concerns, and let France settle matters as she will with me," resumed Mazarin.

" Ho ! ho !" replied Aramis.   " The Frondeurs will have a treaty, and your Eminence must sign it before us, promising, at the same time, to obtain the queen's consent to it—here is the treaty,—may it please your Eminence, read and sign it."

" I know it," answered Mazarin.

" Then sign it."

" But, suppose I refuse ?"

"Then," said D'Artagnan, "your Eminence must expect the consequences of a refusal."

"Would you dare to touch a Cardinal?"

"You have dared, my lord, to imprison her Majesty's Musketeers."

"The queen will revenge me, gentlemen."

"I do not think so, although inclination might lead her to do so, but we shall take your Eminence to Paris—and the Parisians will defend us; therefore, sign this treaty, I beg of you."

"Suppose the queen should refuse to ratify it?"

"Ah! nonsense!" cried D'Artagnan, "I can manage so that her Majesty will receive me well; I know one method."

"What?"

"I shall take her Majesty the letter in which you tell her that the finances are exhausted."

"And then?" asked Mazarin, turning pale.

"When I see her Majesty embarrassed, I shall conduct her to Rueil, make her enter the orangery, and show her a certain spring which turns a box."

"Enough, sir," muttered the Cardinal, "you have said enough —where is the treaty?"

"Here it is," replied Aramis. "Sign, my lord," and he gave him a pen.

Mazarin arose—walked some moments, thoughtful, but not dejected.

"And when I have signed," he said, "what is to be my guarantee?"

"My word of honour, sir," said Athos.

Mazarin started—turned towards the Count de la Fère—and, looking for an instant at his noble and honest countenance, took the pen.

"It is sufficient, count," he said, and he signed the treaty.

"And now, Monsieur d'Artagnan," he said, "prepare to set off for Saint Germains, and to leave a letter from me to the queen."

CHAPTER LXXXVI.

SHOWS HOW WITH A THREAT AND A PEN MORE IS EFFECTED THAN BY THE SWORD.

D'ARTAGNAN knew his part well; he was aware that opportunity has a forelock only for him who will take it, and he was not a man to let it go by him without seizing it. He soon arranged a prompt and certain manner of travelling, by sending relays of horses to Chantilly, so that he could be in Paris in five or six hours.

Nothing was known at St. Germains about Mazarin's disappearance, except by the queen, who concealed, to her friends even, her uneasiness. She had heard all about the two soldiers who were found, bound and gagged. Bernouin, who knew more about the affair than anybody, had, in fact, gone to acquaint the queen of the circumstances which had occurred. Anne had enforced the utmost secrecy, and had disclosed the event to no one except the Prince de Condé, who had sent five or six horsemen into the environs of St. Germains, with orders to bring any suspicious person who was going away from Rueil, in whatsoever direction it might be.

On entering the court of the palace, D'Artagnan encountered Bernouin, to whose instrumentality he owed a prompt introduction to the queen's presence. He approached the sovereign with every mark of profound respect, and having fallen on his knees, presented to her the Cardinal's letter.

It was, however, merely a letter of introduction. The queen read it, recognised the writing, and, since there were no details in it of what had occurred, asked for particulars. D'Artagnan related everything, with that simple and ingenuous air which he knew how to assume on some occasions. The queen, as he went on, looked at him with increasing astonishment. She could not comprehend how a man could conceive such an enterprise, and still less how he could have the audacity to disclose it to her whose interest, and almost duty, it was to punish him.

"How, sir!" she cried, as D'Artagnan finished, "you dare to tell me the details of your crime—to give me an account of your treason!"

"Your majesty, on your side," said D'Artagnan, "is as much mistaken as to our intentions as the Cardinal Mazarin has always been."

"You are in error, sir," answered the queen. "I am so little mistaken, that in ten minutes you shall be arrested, and in an hour I shall set off to release my minister."

"I am sure your majesty will not commit such an act of imprudence; first, because it would be useless, and would produce the most serious results. Before he could be set free, the Cardinal would be dead; and, indeed, so convinced is he of this, that he entreated me, should I find your majesty disposed 'to act in this way, to do all I could to induce you to change your intentions."

"Well, then! I shall be content with only arresting you!"

"Madame, the possibility of my arrest has been foreseen, and should I not have returned to-morrow, at a certain hour the next day, the Cardinal will be brought to Paris, and delivered up to the Parliament."

"I think," returned Anne of Austria, fixing upon him a glance which, in any woman's face, would have expressed disdain, but in a queen's, spread terror to those she looked upon—"I perceive that you dare to threaten the mother of your sovereign."

"Madame," replied D'Artagnan, "I threaten only because I am forced to do so. Believe me, madam, as true a thing as it is that a heart beats in this bosom—a heart devoted to you—believe that you have been the idol of our lives; that we have—as you well know—good Heaven!—risked our lives twenty times for your majesty. Have you then, madame, no compassion on your people, who love you, and yet who suffer—who love you, and who are yet famished—who have no other wish than to bless you, and who, nevertheless——no, I am wrong, your subjects, madam, will never curse you! Say one word to them! and all will be ended; peace succeeds to war, joy to tears, happiness to misfortune!"

Anne of Austria looked with wonderment on the warlike countenance of D'Artagnan, which betrayed a singular expression of deep feeling.

"Why did you not say all this before you acted?" she said.

"Because, madame, it was necessary to prove to your majesty one thing of which you doubted, that is, that we still possess amongst us some valour, and are worthy of some consideration at your hands."

"Then, in case of my refusal, this valour, should a struggle occur, will go even to the length of carrying me off in the midst of my court, to deliver me into the hands of the Fronde, as you have done my minister?"

"We have not thought about it, madame," answered D'Artagnan, with that Gasgon effrontery which had in him the appearance of "naïveté;" "but if we four had so settled it, we should certainly have done so."

"I ought," muttered Anne to herself, "by this time to remember that these are men of iron mould."

"Alas! madame!" exclaimed D'Artagnan, "this proves to me that it is only since yesterday that your majesty has imbibed a true opinion of us. Your majesty will do us justice. In doing us justice you will no longer treat us as men of ordinary stamp. You will see in me an ambassador worthy of the high interests which he is authorised to discuss with his sovereign."

"Where is the treaty?"

" Here it is."

Anne of Austria cast ner eyes upon the treaty that D'Artagnan presented to her.

" I do not see here," she said, " anything but general conditions; the interests of the Prince de Conti, or of the Ducs de Beaufort, de Bouillon, and d'Elbeuf, and of the Coadjutor, are herein consulted; but with regard to yours?"

" We do ourselves justice, madame, even in assuming the high position that we have. We do not think ourselves worthy to stand near such great names."

" But you, I presume, have decided to assert your pretensions, ' viva vôce ?' "

" I believe you, madame, to be a great and powerful queen, and that it will be unworthy of your power and greatness if you do not recompense the arm which will bring back his Eminence to St. Germains."

" It is my intention so to do ; come—let us hear—speak."

" He who has negotiated these matters (forgive me if I begin by speaking of myself, but I must take that importance to myself which has been given to me, not assumed ' by me), he who has arranged matters for the return of the Cardinal, ought, it appears to me, in order that his reward may not be unworthy of your Majesty, to be made commandant of the Guards—an appointment something like that of captain of the Musketeers."

" 'Tis the appointment that Monsieur de Treville had, that you ask of me."

" The place, madame, is vacant ; and although 'tis a year since Monsieur de Treville has left it, is not yet filled up."

" But it is one of the principal military appointments in the king's household."

" Monsieur de Treville was merely a younger son of a Gascon family, like me, madame ; he occupied that post for twenty years."

" You have an answer ready for everything," replied the queen, and she took a document, which she filled up and signed, from her bureau.

" Undoubtedly, madame," said D'Artagnan, taking the document and bowing, " this is a noble reward; but everything in this world is unstable; and any man who happened to fall into disgrace with your majesty would lose everything."

" What then do you want ?" asked the queen, colouring, as she found that she had to deal with a mind as subtle as her own.

" A hundred thousand francs for this poor captain of Musketeers, to be paid whenever his services should no longer be acceptable to your majesty."

Anne hesitated.

"To think of the Parisians," resumed D'Artagnan, "offering the other day, by an edict of the parliament, six hundred thousand francs to any man soever who would deliver up the Cardinal to them, dead or alive—if alive, in order to hang him : if dead, to deny him the rights of Christian burial !—"

"Come," said Anne, " 'tis reasonable,—since you only ask from a queen the sixth of what the parliament has proposed "—and she signed an order for a hundred thousand francs.

"Now then ?" she said, "what next ?"

"Madame, my friend De Valon is rich : and has therefore nothing in the way of fortune to desire : but I think I remember that there was a dispute between him and Monsieur Mazarin as to making his estate a barony or not. 'Twas even a promise."

"A country clown," said Anne of Austria ; "people will laugh."

"Let them !" answered D'Artagnan ; "but I am sure of one thing—that those who laugh at him in his presence will never laugh a second time."

"Here goes the barony," said the queen, and she signed a patent.

"Now there remains the chevalier, or the Abbé d'Herblay, as your majesty pleases."

"Does he wish to be a bishop ?"

"No, madame, something easier to grant."

"What ?"

"It is that the king should deign to stand godfather to the son of Madame de Longueville."

The queen smiled.

"Nothing more ?" she asked.

"No, madame, for I presume that the king, standing godfather to him, could do no less than present him with five hundred thousand francs, giving his father, also, the government of Normandy."

"As to the government of Normandy," replied the queen, "I think I can promise ; but, with regard to the present, the Cardinal is always telling me there is no more money in the royal coffers."

"We shall search for some, madame, and I think we can find some, and if your majesty permits, we will seek for some together."

"What next ?"

"Madame, the Count de la Fère."

"What does he ask ?"

"Nothing."

"There is in the world, then, one man who, having the power to ask—asks for nothing."

"The Count de la Fère, madam, is more than a man; he is a demi-god."

"Are you satisfied, sir?"

"There is one thing which the queen has not signed—her consent to the treaty."

"Of what use to-day? I will sign to-morrow."

"I can assure her majesty that if she does not sign to-day, she will not have time to sign to-morrow. Consent, then, I beg you, madame, to write at the bottom of this schedule, which has been drawn up by Mazarin, as you see."

"I consent to ratify the treaty proposed by the Parisians."

Anne was ensnared: she could not draw back—she signed; but scarcely had she done so, when pride burst forth in her like a tempest, and she began to weep.

D'Artagnan started on seeing these tears: since that time queens have shed tears like other women.

The Gascon shook his head: these tears from royalty melted his heart.

"Madame,' he said, kneeling, "look upon the unhappy man at your feet. Behold, madame! here are the august signatures of your majesty's hand: if you think you are right in giving them to me, you shall do so :—but, from this very moment, you are free from any obligation to keep them."

And D'Artagnan, full of honest pride and of manly intrepidity, placed in Anne's hands, in a bundle, the papers that he had, one by one, won from her with so much difficulty.

There are moments—for if everything is not good, everything in this world is not bad—in which the most rigid and the coldest hearts are softened by the tears of strong emotion—of a generous sentiment; one of these momentary impulses actuated Anne. D'Artagnan, when he gave way to his own feelings—which were in accordance with those of the queen—had accomplished all that the most skilful diplomacy could have done. He was, therefore, instantly recompensed, either for his address, or for his sensibility, whichever it might be termed.

"You were right, sir," said Anne. "I misunderstood you. There are the acts signed: I deliver them to you without compulsion: go and bring me back the Cardinal as soon as possible."

"Madame," faltered D'Artagnan, "it is twenty years ago—I have a good memory—since I had the honour, behind a piece of tapestry in the Hôtel de Ville, to kiss one of those beautiful hands."

" There is the other," replied the queen ; and that the left hand should not be less liberal than the right, she drew from her fingers a diamond—nearly similar to the one formerly given to him—" take and keep this ring in remembrance of me."

"Madam," said D'Artagnan, rising, "I have only one thing more to wish, which is, that the next thing you ask from me, should be my life."

And with this way of concluding—a way peculiar to himself— he arose and left the room.

"I have never rightly understood these men," said the queen, as she watched him retiring from her presence ; "and it is now too late—for in a year the king will be of age."

In twenty-four hours D'Artagnan and Porthos conducted Mazarin to the queen ; and the one received his commission, the other his patent of nobility.

On the same day the Treaty of Paris was signed ; and it was everywhere announced that the Cardinal had shut himself up for three days, in order to draw it out with the greatest care.

CHAPTER LXXXVII,

IN WHICH IT IS SHOWN THAT IT IS SOMETIMES MORE DIFFICULT FOR KINGS TO RETURN TO THE CAPITALS OF THEIR KINGDOMS, THAN TO GO OUT OF THEM.

WHILST D'Artagnan and Porthos were engaged in conducting the Cardinal to St. Germains, Athos and Aramis returned to Paris.

Each had his own particular visit to make.

Aramis rushed to the Hôtel de Ville, where Madame de Longue-ville was sojourning. The duchess had loudly lamented the an-nouncement of peace. War had made her a queen ; peace-brought her abdication. She declared that she had never expected the treaty, and that she wished for eternal war.

But Aramis consoled her, and pointed out the solid advantages that were the result of peace—the precarious tenure of all she had prized during war.

" Now," said Aramis to her, " detach your brother, the Prince of Condé, from the queen, whom he does not like—from Mazarin, whom he despises. The Fronde is a comedy, of which the first act only is played. Let us wait for a denouement—for the day when the Prince, thanks to you, shall have turned against the court."

Madame de Longueville was persuaded of the influence of her fine eyes, and was appeased; but Madame de Chevreuse frowned, and, in spite of all the logic of Athos to show her that a prolonged war would have been impracticable, contended in favour of hostilities.

"My fair friend," said Athos, "allow me to tell you that everybody is tired of war. You will get yourself exiled, as you did in the time of Louis XIII. Believe me, we have passed the time of success in intrigue, and your beautiful eyes are not destined to be blinded by regretting Paris, where there will always be two queens as long as you are there."

"Oh," cried the duchess, "I cannot make war alone, but I can avenge myself on that ungrateful queen and ambitious favourite—on the honour of a duchess, I will avenge myself."

"Madame," replied Athos, "do not injure the Vicomte de Bragelonne—do not ruin his prospects. Alas! excuse my weakness! There are moments when a man grows young again in his children."

The duchess smiled; half tenderly, half ironically.

"Count," she said, "you are, I fear, gained over to the court. I suppose you have a blue ribbon in your pocket?"

"Yes, madame; I have that of the Garter, which King Charles I. gave me some days before he died."

"Come! one must grow into an old woman," said the duchess, pensively.

Athos took her hand, and kissed it. She sighed, as she looked at him.

"Count," she said, "Bragelonne must he a charming place. You are a man of taste. You have water—woods—flowers—there?"

She sighed again, and leaned her charming head, gracefully reclined, on her hand—still beautiful in form and colour.

"Madame!" exclaimed Athos, "what were you saying just now about growing old? Never have I seen you look so young—never more beautiful!"

The duchess shook her head.

"Does Monsieur de Bragelonne remain in Paris?" she inquired.

"What think you of it?" answered Athos.

" Leave it to me," replied the duchess ; " really, sir, you are delightful, and I should like to spend a month at Bragelonne."

" Are you not afraid of making people envious, duchess ?" replied Athos.

" No, I shall go incognito, count, under the name of Marie Michou. But do not keep Raoul with you."

" Why not ?"

" Because he is in love."

" He—he is quite a child."

" And it is a child whom he loves."

Athos became thoughtful.

" You are right, duchess. This singular passion for a child of seven years old may some day make him very unhappy. There is to be war in Flanders. He shall go thither."

" And at his return you will send him to me. I will arm him against love."

" Alas, madame !" exclaimed Athos, " to-day love is like war, and the breastplate is become useless."

Raoul entered at this moment ; he came to announce that the solemn entrance of the king, the queen, and her ministers was to take place on the ensuing day.

On the next day, in fact, at daybreak, the court made preparations to quit St. Germains.

Meanwhile, the queen every hour had been sending for D'Artagnan.

" I hear," she said, " that Paris is not quiet. I am afraid for the king's safety; place yourself close to the coach-door on the right."

" Be assured, madame ; I will answer for the king's safety."

As he left the queen's presence, Bernouin summoned him to the Cardinal.

" Sir," said Mazarin to him, " an ' émeute ' is spoken of in Paris. I shall be on the king's left, and as I am the chief person threatened, remain at the coach-door to the left."

" Your Eminence may be perfectly easy," replied D'Artagnan ; "they will not touch a hair of your head."

" Deuce take it," he thought to himself, " how can I take care of both ? Ah ! plague on't, I shall guard the king, and Porthos the Cardinal."

This arrangement pleased everyone. The queen had confidence in the courage of D'Artagnan, and the Cardinal in the strength of Porthos.

The royal procession set out for Paris. Guitant and Comminges, at the head of the Guards, marched first; then came the royal carriage, with D'Artagnan on one side, Porthos on the other; then the Musketeers, for twenty-two years the old friends of D'Artagnan. During twenty he had been their lieutenant, their captain since the night before.

The cortège proceeded to Nôtre Dame, where a *Te Deum* was chaunted. All the people of Paris were in the streets. The Swiss were drawn up along the road, but as the road was long, they were placed at six or eight feet distance from each other, and one man deep only. This force was, therefore, wholly insufficient, and from time to time the line was broken through by the people, and was formed again with difficulty. Whenever this occurred, although it proceeded only from goodwill and a desire to see the king and queen, Anne looked at D'Artagnan anxiously.

Mazarin, who had dispensed a thousand louis to make the people cry "Long live Mazarin," and who had, therefore, no confidence in acclamations bought at twenty pistoles each, looked also at Porthos; but the gigantic body-guard replied to that look with his fine bass voice, "Be tranquil, my lord;" and Mazarin became more and more composed.

At the Palais Royal the crowd, which had forced in from the adjacent streets, was still greater; like a large impetuous crowd, a wave of human beings came to meet the carriage, and rolled tumultuously into the Rue St. Honoré.

When the procession reached the palace, loud cries of "Long live their Majesties!" resounded. Mazarin leaned out of the window. One or two shouts of "Long live the Cardinal!" saluted his shadow, but instantly hisses and yells stifled them remorselessly. Mazarin turned pale, and sank back in his coach.

"Low-born fellows!" ejaculated Porthos.

D'Artagnan said nothing, but twirled his moustache with a peculiar gesture which showed that his fine Gascon humour was kindled.

Anne of Austria bent down and whispered in the young king's ear:

"Say something gracious to Monsieur D'Artagnan, my lord."

The young king leaned towards the door.

"I have not said good morning to you, Monsieur D'Artagnan," he said; "nevertheless, I have remarked you. It was you who were behind my bed-curtains that night when the Parisians wished to see me asleep."

"And if the king permits me," returned the Gascon, "I shall be near him whenever there is danger to be encountered."

"Sir," said Mazarin to Porthos, "what would you do if the crowd fell upon us?"

"Kill as many as I could, my lord."

"Hem! Brave as you are, and strong as you are, you could not kill all."

"'Tis true," answered Porthos, rising in his saddle, in order that he might see the immense crowd—"there are many of them."

"I think I should like the other man better than this one," said Mazarin to himself, and he threw himself back in his carriage.

The queen and her minister, more especially the latter, had reason to feel anxious. The crowd, whilst preserving an appearance of respect, and even of affection, for the king and queen-regent, began to be tumultuous. Reports were whispered about, like certain sounds which announce, as they are echoed from wave to wave, the coming storm—and when they pass through a multitude, presage an *émeute*.

D'Artagnan turned towards the Musketeers, and made a sign imperceptible to the crowd, but very easily understood by that chosen regiment, the flower of the army.

The ranks were closed, and a kind of shudder ran from man to man.

At the Barrière des Sergents the procession was obliged to stop. Comminges left the head of the escort, and went to the queen's carriage. Anne questioned D'Artagnan by a look. He answered in the same language.

"Proceed," she said.

Comminges returned to his post. An effort was made, and the living barrier was violently broken through.

Some complaints arose from the crowd, and were addressed this time to the king, as well as the Minister.

"Onwards!" cried D'Artagnan, with a loud voice.

"Onwards!" cried Porthos.

But, as if the multitude had waited only for this demonstration to burst out, all the sentiments of hostility that possessed it broke out at once. Cries of "Down with Mazarin!" "Death to the Cardinal!" resounded on all sides.

At the same time, through the streets of Grenelle, Saint Honoré, and Du Coq, a double stream of people broke the feeble hedge of Swiss Guards, and came, like a whirlwind, even to the very legs of Porthos' horse and that of D'Artagnan.

This new eruption was more dangerous than the others, being

composed of armed men. It was plain that it was not the chance combination of those who had collected a number of the mal-contents at the same spot, but the concerted attack organised by an hostile spirit.

Each of these two mobs was led on by a chief, one of whom appeared to belong, not to the people, but to the honourable cor-poration of mendicants, and the other, who, notwithstanding his affected imitation of the people, might easily be discovered to be a gentleman. Both were evidently stimulated by the same impulse.

There was a shock which was perceived even in the royal carriage. Then, millions of cries, forming one vast uproar, were heard, mingled with guns firing.

"The Musketeers! here!" cried D'Artagnan.

The escort divided into two files. One of them passed round to the right of the carriage; the other to the left. One went to support D'Artagnan, the other Porthos. Then came a skirmish, the more terrible, because it had no definite object; the more melancholy, because those engaged in it knew not for whom they were fighting. Like all popular movements, the shock given by the rush of this mob was formidable. The Musketeers, few in number, not being able, in the midst of this crowd, to make their horses wheel round, began to give way. D'Artagnan offered to lower the blinds of the royal carriage, but the young king stretched out his arm, saying:

"No, sir! I wish to see everything."

"If your majesty wishes to look out—well, then, look!" replied D'Artagnan. And turning with that fury which made him so formidable, he rushed towards the chief of the insurgents, a man who, with a large sword in his hand, tried to clear out a passage to the coach door, by a combat with two Musketeers.

"Make room!" cried D'Artagnan. "Zounds! give way!"

At these words, the man with a pistol and sword raised his head; but it was too late. The blow was sped by D'Artagnan; the rapier had pierced his bosom.

"Ah! confound it!" cried the Gascon, trying in vain, too late, to retract the thrust. "What the devil are you doing here, count?"

"Accomplishing my destiny," replied Rochefort, falling on one knee. "I have already got up again after three stabs from you; but I shall not rise after a fourth."

"Count!" said D'Artagnan, with some degree of emotion, "I struck without knowing that it was you. I am sorry, if you die, that you should die with sentiments of hatred towards me."

Rochefort extended his hand to D'Artagnan, who took it. The count wished to speak, but a gush of blood stifled him. He stiffened in the last convulsions of death, and expired!

"Back, people!" cried D'Artagnan; "your leader is dead, and you have no longer anything to do here."

"Indeed, as if De Rochefort had been the soul of the attack, all the crowd who had followed and obeyed him took flight on seeing him fall. D'Artagnan charged with a party of Musketeers in the Rue de Coq, and that portion of the mob whom he assailed disappeared like smoke, dispersing near the Place St. Germains L'Auxerrois, and taking the direction of the quays.

D'Artagnan returned to help Porthos, if Porthos needed it; but Porthos, on his side, had done his work as conscientiously as D'Artagnan. The left of the carriage was as well cleared as the right; and they drew up the blind of the window, which Mazarin, less heroic than the king, had taken the precaution to lower.

Porthos looked very melancholy.

"What a devil of a face you have Porthos! and what a strange air for a victorious man!"

"But you," answered Porthos, "seem to me agitated."

"There's a reason! Zounds! I have just killed an old friend."

"Indeed!" replied Porthos; "who?"

"That poor Count de Rochefort."

"Well! exactly like me! I have just killed a man whose face is not unknown to me. Unluckily, I hit him on the head, and immediately his face was covered with blood."

"And he said nothing as he died?"

"Yes; he said 'Oh!'"

"I suppose," answered D'Artagnan, laughing, "if he only said that it did not enlighten you much."

"Well, sir!" cried the queen.

"Madame, the passage is quite clear, and your Majesty can continue your road."

In fact, the procession arrived in safety at Nôtre Dame, at the front gate of which all the clergy, with the Coadjutor at their head, awaited the king, the queen and the minister, for whose happy return they chanted a *Te Deum*.

CONCLUSION.

On going home, the two friends found a letter from Athos, who desired them to meet him at the Grand Charlemagne on the following day.

Both of the friends went to bed early, but neither of them slept. When we arrive at the summit of one's wishes, success has usually the power of driving away sleep on the first night after the fulfilment of long-cherished hopes.

The next night, at the appointed hour, they went to see Athos, and found him and Aramis in travelling costume.

"What!" cried Porthos, "are we all going away then? I have also made my preparations this morning."

"Oh, heavens! yes," said Aramis. "There's nothing to do in Paris now there's no Fronde. The Duchesse de Longueville has invited me to pass some days in Normandy, and has deputed me, while her son is being baptised, to go and prepare her residence at Rouen; after which, if nothing new occurs, I shall go and bury myself in my convent at Noisy-le-Lec."

"And I," said Athos, "am returning to Bragelonne. You know, dear D'Artagnan, I am nothing more than a good honest country gentleman. Raoul has no other fortune but what I possess, poor child! and I must take care of it for him, since I only lend him my name."

"And Raoul—what shall you do with him?"

"I leave him with you, my friend. War in Flanders has broken out; you shall take him with you there. I am afraid that remaining at Blois would be dangerous to his youthful mind. Take him, and teach him to be as brave and loyal as you are yourself."

"Then," replied D'Artagnan, "though I shall not have you, Athos, at all events, I shall have that dear fair-haired head by me; and though he is but a boy, yet, since your soul lives again in him, dear Athos, so I shall always fancy that you are near me, sustaining and encouraging me."

The four friends embraced, with tears in their eyes.

Then they departed, without knowing whether they should ever see each other again.

D'Artagnan returned to the Rue Tiquetonne with Porthos, still possessed by the wish to find out who the man was whom he had killed. On arriving at the Hotel de la Chevrette they found the Baron's equipages all ready, and Mousqueton on his saddle.

"Come, D'Artagnan," said Porthos, "bid adieu to your sword, and go with me to Pierrefonds, to Bracieux, or to De Valon. We will grow old together, and talk of our companions."

"No!" replied D'Artagnan, "deuce take it, the campaign is going to begin; I wish to be there, I expect to get something by it."

"What do you expect to get?"

"Why, I expect to be a Maréchal of France!"

"Ha, ha!" cried Porthos, who was not completely taken in by D'Artagnan's gasconades.

"Ha!"

"Come, my brother, go with me," added D'Artagnan, "and I will make you a duke!"

"No," answered Porthos, "Mouston has no desire to fight—besides, they have made a triumphal entrance for me into my barony, which will kill my neighbours with envy."

"To that I can say nothing," returned D'Artagnan, who knew the vanity of the new baron. "Here, then, to our next merry meeting."

"Adieu, dear Captain," said Porthos, "I shall always be happy to welcome you to my barony."

"True,—when the campaign is over," replied the Gascon.

"The equipage of his honour is waiting," said Mousqueton.

The two friends, after a cordial pressure of the hand, thereupon separated. D'Artagnan was standing at the door, looking after Porthos with a mournful gaze, when the baron, after walking scarcely more than twenty paces, returned—stood still—struck his forehead with his finger, and exclaimed:

"I recollect!"

"What?" inquired D'Artagnan.

"Who the beggar that I killed was."

"Ah! indeed! and who was he?"

"'Twas that low fellow, Bonacieux."

And Porthos, enchanted at having relieved his mind, rejoined Mousqueton, and they disappeared round an angle of the street; D'Artagnan stood for an instant, mute, pensive, and motionless; then, as he went in, he saw the fair Madeleine, his hostess, standing on the threshold.

"Madeleine," said the Gascon, "give me your apartment on the first floor; now that I am a captain in the Royal Musketeers, I must make an appearance: nevertheless, still keep my room on the fifth story for me; one never knows what may happen."

If you enjoyed this quality
edition you can add the
following titles to your Classic Collection:

THE COMPLETE WORKS OF WILLIAM SHAKESPEARE

THE WORKS OF THOMAS HARDY

THE TALES OF EDGAR ALLAN POE

THE WORKS OF CHARLES DICKENS

THE WORKS OF CHARLOTTE AND EMILY BRONTË

CLASSICS OF HORROR— FRANKENSTEIN/DRACULA

THE WORKS OF VICTOR HUGO

THE WORKS OF MARK TWAIN

THE CLASSIC MYSTERIES OF SHERLOCK HOLMES

THE ILIAD AND THE ODYSSEY

THE WORKS OF JAMES FENIMORE COOPER

THE WORKS OF JULES VERNE

THE WORKS OF HERMAN MELVILLE

THE WORKS OF ALEXANDRE DUMAS

Ordering is easy and convenient. Order by phone
with Visa, MasterCard, American Express or Discover:

1-800-322-2000, Dept. 708